Charles Hole, William Adolphus Wheeler

A Brief Biographical Dictionary

Charles Hole, William Adolphus Wheeler

A Brief Biographical Dictionary

ISBN/EAN: 9783337030162

Printed in Europe, USA, Canada, Australia, Japan

Cover: Foto ©Raphael Reischuk / pixelio.de

More available books at **www.hansebooks.com**

A BRIEF

BIOGRAPHICAL DICTIONARY.

COMPILED AND ARRANGED BY

THE REV. CHARLES HOLE, B. A.,

TRINITY COLLEGE, CAMBRIDGE;

WITH ADDITIONS AND CORRECTIONS

BY

WILLIAM A. WHEELER, M. A.,

ASSISTANT EDITOR OF WEBSTER'S DICTIONARIES, AND AUTHOR OF "A DICTIONARY
OF THE NOTED NAMES OF FICTION," ETC.

NEW YORK:
PUBLISHED BY HURD AND HOUGHTON.
1866.

INTRODUCTORY NOTE BY THE AMERICAN EDITOR.

THE serviceable little Dictionary of the Rev. Mr. Hole — reprinted by arrangement with the English publishers — was placed in my hands with the request that I would make such additions of American names as would fit it for use and acceptance in this country. Supposing that the labor involved would be but slight, I readily undertook the task. An examination of the work, however, soon satisfied me that extensive additions and alterations were needed; for, while it was apparent that the compiler was justly entitled to the praise of having produced a manual embodying in a condensed form a large amount of biographical memoranda, and of having taken especial pains to secure correctness in the important matter of dates, it was equally evident that much which the users of the book might reasonably look for with the expectation of finding, had been omitted.

To point out the defects of a book which, after all, shows great industry, conscientious research, and general accuracy, is an ungrateful duty; but justice to the public and myself, as well as to the English editor, requires that I should state the limits of my own revisionary labor and responsibility, and, in doing this, I shall necessarily indicate some of the deficiencies and imperfections of the original work.

My attention was directed, in the first place, to the collection and insertion of American names, of which only a very meager list is given in the English publication. The additions which I have made amount to many hundreds, and include such names as Arnold, Burr, Choate, Douglas, Foote, Gallatin, Hancock, Marion, Otis, Paulding, Percival,

Pocahontas, Randolph, Standish,. Sumter, Taney, Wirt, and many others. There are some, it is true, of much less note than these, yet they are important in a work designed for circulation in America.

To carry out more fully the plan of the book, and make it still more useful and acceptable, I have added a large number of European names of undoubted importance which the English editor had omitted, and which one would naturally expect to find in a work of this sort; as, for example, Abraham-a-Sancta Clara, Banim, Chlopicki, De Wette, Immermann, Miaulis, Passow, Töpffer, Torquemada, &c.

In not a few instances, I have been able to supply missing dates; while of dates erroneously given or marked as doubtful, I have corrected or verified a still larger number.

The orthography of the names has received much of my attention. Besides rectifying some grave mistakes, and some hardly less grievous inconsistencies, I have been at a good deal of pains to supply accents in the French, German, and other Continental names, which are for the most part printed without them in the English book, and have in consequence a very awkward and unfamiliar look. It is not always easy, however, to determine what accent a particular letter should have, or whether it should have any, as authorities are sometimes at variance. A notable example of this is *Fénelon*, which in some standard works of reference is printed, though incorrectly, *Fénélon*.

The English edition of this Dictionary gives the month and day as well as the year of death, but not the month and day of birth, though by most persons the latter would be considered no less important than the former. For this and for other reasons, it has been thought advisable to give, in this reprint, nothing more than the years of birth and death, which are all, probably, that the consulter of the book will generally require.

Some minor changes, deemed to be improvements, are perhaps scarcely worth mentioning: such as the substitution of the customary and legitimate abbreviations of common Christian names, or their full forms, for the uncouth and arbitrary contractions adopted by the English editor, — Fces.

for Frances, Hy. for Henry, Jam. for James, Jph. for Joseph, and the like; the re-arrangement of individuals of the same surname according to the alphabetical order of their Christian names, — the usual method in Biographical Dictionaries, — and not according to the order of their deaths; and the frequent amendment or modification of the compendious biographical information attached to the names for the purpose of identifying the individuals who bore them. In general, however, the intention has been to adhere to the plan of the English work; and hence the editor's rule of substituting the English equivalents of foreign Christian names for the vernacular forms has been almost uniformly followed, though not without much misgiving and dissatisfaction.

After the stereotyping had proceeded as far as the middle of the letter E, there came into my hands a copy of the second London edition, containing a list of some hundreds of omitted names. From this point onward, I incorporated into the body of the work such of these names as I had not already inserted; the remainder, together with some other names which had either been overlooked, or which belonged to persons very recently deceased, are given in an appendix. (See p. 442.)

It is in contemplation to follow this work with a companion volume, on the same general plan, devoted to distinguished living characters.

Having long felt the want of a comprehensive and thoroughly trustworthy biographical index, such as the present compilation aspires to be, and knowing well the great liability to error in any work containing so many thousands of names and dates, I shall thankfully avail myself not only of public criticism, but of any corrections or suggestions that may be privately communicated to me.

WM. A. WHEELER.

ROXBURY, *Massachusetts*, March, 1866.

PREFACE.

———◆———

THE principal object of this work is to afford ready information of the births and deaths of deceased persons, more or less noteworthy, of all countries and periods. Biographical dictionaries on the ordinary plan, besides being more and more voluminous in proportion to their value, and consequently more cumbrous to consult for a passing occasion, fall necessarily and rapidly into chronological arrears; while a less pretending book, like the present, by allowing usually no more than a line to a single name, containing, therefore, many more entries than even some bulky quartos of biographical matter, and so being for the mere purpose of the above-named dates more serviceable than they, stands also from its size a greater chance of frequent reprints, and keeping its information level with the times. This is the claim it ventures to put forth to the notice and favor of the public. It hopes to lie upon the desk, an unobtrusive companion of other books of many sorts, to give a reader its rapid answer whenever he is tempted to pause at a name, and ask no more than — " When did he live ? "

In explanation of the contents, it will be necessary to preface a few brief remarks. The additions, for instance, that will be found attached to the names, are not to be understood as intended vainly to furnish any condensed biographical information, nor always to indicate the person's title to a place in a biographical list, but chiefly for identifying the individual; which will be felt a matter of some utility when it is remembered how frequently talents of the same description run in families, and how successive generations of the same name — on the Continent especially — appear as paint-

ers, engravers, printers, and scholars. Again, to avoid con-
fusion, and secure a more complete distinction of the greater
personages, others bearing the same surnames are frequently
added, and this is the apology for the appearance of some
that might be considered in themselves too obscure to deserve
insertion. The Italics within brackets in all cases indicate
some production of the pen, or some work of art; and these,
too, are for assisting in the identification, rather than for
marking the special claim to distinction; for in innumerable
instances of prolific genius it would be quite impossible to
select any single production as a *chef-d'œuvre*, though frequently it will be found that the work quoted is one upon
which a reputation rests. The Italics without brackets are
confined to a second, or an assumed, or an original name, or
perhaps a *sobriquet* by which, in occasional instances, a person is best known. A figure that is not of established certainty is marked by an asterisk [interrogation point]. In
cases where an individual has had a separate biographer, this
is indicated by the letter L., or the word Life.

At the close of his undertaking, the compiler has become
abundantly aware, from experience, of the truth of a common remark, that there is nothing so liable to error and corruption as that most happy invention of figures; and he be-
lieves it will not prove unsuitable or useless to make a few
observations on this subject.

A general reader, wishing to know the time of a birth or
a death, can turn, say, to the biographical compendiums —
small, compact, single volumes, extending to a very recent
period — which an ordinary household may probably be sup-
plied with, or to a cyclopædia of many quartos or large oc-
tavos on the shelves of a more ambitious library, and if he
finds his date in any one of these he is probably content, and
asks no further. But if, requiring greater exactness, or being
suspicious and desirous of corroboration, he should take an
opportunity of consulting several, he is then but too likely to
become aware of unwelcome discrepancies. The professional
man of letters, who has access to the largest and best works
of the class, such as the *Biographie Universelle*, the *Nouvelle
Biographie Générale*, or the *Biographia Britannica*, is of

course better off, but even he does not escape his disappointments so often as might be imagined. And what is the more perplexing, and, in truth, not a little irritating, the dates are given with all the air of absolute certainty, so far as silence conveys this; only the very first-class books — and not always these — informing the reader that there are other dates assigned, or that some current figures have been proved wrong, and giving any hint that pains have been taken to sift discrepancies.

The plan of this volume does not admit of a variation of dates being discussed or even stated, and only allows an established uncertainty to be intimated by an asterisk [mark of interrogation]. But the author is reluctantly obliged to admit, that, if any one of the following pages were taken at random and examined with half a dozen of the usually accredited authorities, discrepant figures would be found amongst them, for, perhaps, on an average, every fourth or fifth name; while even when no absolute conflict presents itself, one of the dates, the birth for instance or the death, is entirely omitted, and some works, not even professing to give any nearer information than the year, seldom mentioning the day. This estimate of the degree of faultiness in our current information is certainly within the mark, as the compiler's memoranda of the variations he has observed, in figures alone, to say nothing of errors in spelling, too amply testify, and it is a discovery not a little disheartening to those who have ever made it, whose studies lead them to take an interest in this class of dates.

Happily, however, the uncertainty in nativities and obituaries here implied need not be acquiesced in as a finality in every instance. Things are not so bad as they look. A very brief practical acquaintance with the current statements shows us that a large crop of errors is due to the culpability of the more recent copyists and editors, and that, with patience and sufficient comparison, the true figures are, in a considerable number of instances, not beyond recovery. By paying attention to the various errors corrected in carrying a work like the present through the press, one has an opportunity of becoming aware of the kinds of mistakes which compositors on the one hand are more particularly liable to, as well as those for which an editor on the other hand has himself solely to blame ; and, as this may sometimes aid in accounting for discrepancies, a few illustrations will perhaps be acceptable.

For instance, the figures 8, 3, 5, frequently get put in each other's places, owing probably to a rough resemblance among them, especially in indistinct manuscript ; and not only in manuscript, for any one who has to consult the new edition of the *Biographie Universelle* must often have regretted that the type there used makes the 5 and 3 so nearly alike as to require a close scrutiny to detect the difference. Examples occurring in the preparation of the present work of 6 in the copy appearing as 9 in the proof, and instances in other works of these two figures being interchanged, make it tolerably evident that they sometimes get inverted by the printer, either in sorting the types or in the act of composition. Imperfect formations in the copy have also, it would appear, caused 6 and 9 both to be replaced by 0. Cases of 6 for 0 have been remarked in correcting these sheets, and in the *Biographie Universelle*, John Hübner appears as born in 1608 for 1668. The figures 1 and 7 [1 and 9, 7 and 9] have also been interchanged.

A very common error is when a date contains the same figure repeated consecutively, and the wrong duplicate gets into the copy by a natural trick of the eye of a rapid worker, especially when the difference in the value of the two figures exchanged is not so glaringly large ; thus, 1779 becoming 1799, and *vice versâ*, 1669 for 1699, 1445 for 1455. In the proof-sheets of this work, 1755 of the copy once became 1775. But 1449 for 1499, or 1228 for 1288, would be more seldom found, though the *Biographie Universelle* has it that St. Oswald died 922 instead of 992. The culprit years, however, which most frequently sin in this way are 1668 and 1688. Perhaps the similarity of sound may have produced some errors, as for instance, when Gaspar Bartholin was born July 13, according to one, and July 30, according to another. Two certain instances of this mistake, and both with the same pair of numbers, have been noticed in these proofs, where

Oct. 13 appeared instead of Oct. 30, and 1530 * ['] for 1513 * [']. In the days of the month, one of the figures is occasionally omitted, as when 2 stands for 12 and 3 for 30. The days of the month also get inverted, as when the death of Eller de Brockhusen appears in the *Biographie Universelle* to have occurred Sept. 31, and in the *Nouvelle Biographie Générale*, Sept. 13. One frequently finds the months Jan. and June put for each other, and in the French dictionaries, March and May (Mars and Mai), as also April and August (Avril and Août). Thus, Louis Anthony de Bougainville is said, in the *Nouvelle Biographie Générale*, to have died April 31, an error which betrays itself, and we expect to find other authorities giving Aug. 31, which in fact they do.

But the editor cannot forbear remarking more at length upon an error arising not so much from accident and inadvertence as from a want of thought, and a false principle of calculation that is likely enough to become a fixed habit in the mind. Thus a composer of a biographical notice, finding it announced that a person died in 1850, aged 50, and wishing to put the fact in another shape, states that he was " born in 1800, and died in 1850 ; " whereas, from the loose way in which that phrase " aged so and so " often occurs, this 1800 is not at all certain, To give actual instances. The *Annual Register* records that Richard Ford was born 1796, and died Sept. 1, 1858, aged 61 ; but had we calculated the birth from the death and age, by subtracting 61 from 1858, we should have fixed on 1797, which would have been wrong. The same work says of the Earl of Ripon, born in 1782, died Jan. 28, 1859, aged 76 ; but 1859 minus 76 is 1783. Even if the " years " of a person's age always meant completed years, this method of arriving at the birth would be uncertain ; for a person born either in Dec. 1799 or Jan. 1800, and dying in Feb. 1850, would just the same be said to be " aged 50." But sometimes it is stated that a person is " aged 50," when he is more properly within a month or so of reaching that number of years. Thus the Obituary of the *London Almanac* says that Walter Savage Landor " died Sept. 17, 1864, aged 90 ; " but if we were to infer his birth to have been in 1864 — 90, or 1774, we should err, as he was actually born in Jan.

1775, and wanted as much as three or four months of being
" aged 90." In fact, a person who " died in 1850, aged 50,"
and no month stated, may have been born in 1799, 1800, or
1801. When, therefore, the *Biographia Britannica* states that
Henry Burton " was 67 years of age in 1646, consequently he
must have been born in 1579," the inference is not to be
trusted ; and similarly, when the Biographical Dictionary of
the *English Cyclopædia* makes a like calculation of the births
of Melchizedec Thévenot and Spinello Aretino. It may also
be remarked that from this·process of backward reckoning we
may suspect to have arisen a frequent discrepancy of 10 years
in the birth, as though there had been an error of 1 in per-
forming the subtraction sum.

Other discrepancies arise from causes less culpable ; as when
a person dies in the night, the hour not being stated, or is
found dead in the morning, the hour of decease not being
known, and one account makes the occurrence to have hap-
pened the day before and another the day after. Thus, *L'Art
de Vérifier les Dates* states the Emperor Lothaire II. to have
died in the night between Dec. 3 and 4, explaining why in
the two great French dictionaries we find Dec. 3 and Dec. 4
respectively. When a person dies abroad, especially in circum-
stances of turmoil and excitement, reports of the event are
likely enough to vary. This may possibly explain how it occurs
that no less than four dates are assigned for the death of so
eminent and so recent a man as Sir Henry Havelock ; Maunder giving Nov. 21, the *Book of Dates* and the *Nouvelle Biographie Générale*, Nov. 25, the *London Almanac*, Nov. 27,
while the *Life* of the hero, by Marshman, his brother-in-law,
as well as the *Annual Register*, gives Nov. 24, which may be
presumed to be the correct day. One would have thought
that the very hour and day of the execution of Robespierre
would have been well remarked ; nevertheless, we find in
Chalmers that he died July 10 ; *Rees's Cyclopædia* gives July
28 ; Lemprière and Rose, July 28, 4 P. M. ; and Alison in
his *History*, July 29, 4 A. M.

Discrepancies are also due to the change of the style, an
innovation not effected without some unnecessary complica-
tion. For when in 1582 the 10 superfluous days were pro-

posed by the Pope to be omitted from the Calendar, the various countries unfortunately were not unanimous in adopting the improvement : Spain, Portugal, and a part of Italy accepting the alteration on the same day ; France following the example two months later ; but England holding out for no less than 170 years, when in 1752 she omitted 11 days (as the 10 had become since 1700), and reckoned Sept. 3 as Sept. 14 ; during which period, therefore, our chronology and that of other countries differ by 10 or 11 days, and historians, having to express the date of any transaction affecting ourselves and them, have to mention two days at once, as Nov. $\frac{5}{16}$, 1688, or Sept. $\frac{1}{12}$, 1715. One important country, Russia, to this day retains the old style, which is no longer 10 days, or 11, but 12 in advance. Russian dates, consequently, will often differ by 12 days, and other continental dates by 10 or 11, from those accepted by us ; the ambiguity not being always apparent, owing to their having been recorded originally, not with the double notation for historical purposes, but in the current style of the country as referring to purely domestic and internal events.

But the change of style, as far as England was concerned, embraced yet another peculiarity which has to be observed. For whereas up to the period of that change the civil year began on March 25, and the period between Jan. 1 and March 25 was reckoned to the old year, it was then ordered by Act of Parliament that this practice should be discontinued, and the year in all cases commence with Jan. 1. But according to the old practice, the dates within that interval of Jan. 1 and March 25 would express both years, and thus what we now write Feb. 4, 1726, used inconveniently to be written Feb. 4, 1725–6 ; for want of attention to which fact the year would be copied as 1725 by one, and as 1726 by another. Hence it happens that while the change of style may be the parent of an error of 10 or 11 days, or 12, between England and a foreign country, it may also occasionally have produced an error of one year in purely domestic dates, which is to be suspected when the day belongs to the interval between Jan. 1 and March 25. In this volume, the new style is always used.

An error in the letters of a word is generally obvious, and

can be rectified by any one, while an error in the figure of
a date is far otherwise, and even when obvious seldom pro-
nounces or suggests its own correction.   Hence so many vex-
atious discrepancies, and we are startled at finding the most
notorious events of but yesterday wrongly dated.   It is only
a matter of industry and conscientious care to weed out errors
of no longer standing than this ; but dates of early and me-
diæval times, that come down to us with discrepancies all the
way, must stand far less chance, and here we must often rest
satisfied with approximations.   But even in some of these an
additional light has occasionally been discovered, as in the
case of Holbein's death, which within the last few years has
been proved in the *Archæologia* to have occurred in 1543, instead of the currently adopted 1554.

It might, perhaps, have been expected, that, in the case of
historical personages, and especially in the case of reigning
sovereigns, fewer discrepancies than usual would be met with ;
and yet this is by no means the fact.   As to the former, we
should not have thought that such an authority as the *Historic
Peerage* (formerly the *Synopsis of the Peerage* of Sir Harris
Nicolas) would give a wrong date for the famous assassination
of the Duke of Buckingham.   It gives 1629, and all other
authorities 1628 ; and for the day, the *English Cyclopædia*
says Aug. 24, against Aug. 23 of every one else.   And then,
in regard to reigning sovereigns, that the year of their accession should be variously stated need excite no surprise ; for,
what with disputed successions, the *de jure* and *de facto*, and
minorities, in troublous times and in heterogeneous domin-
ions, an actual accession may be variously estimated, as also
may depositions ; and this is the reason why in this work
the years of a reign are in so many instances omitted entirely.   Nor, again, may the birth be always ascertainable,
especially in the cases where this occurred during the obscu-
rity of the family ; but one does look for more certainty and
accuracy in the record of a sovereign's death than it is always
our good fortune to find.   As regards our own kings, writers
are not in every instance at one in the year of the birth or
the day of the death, even for the times after the Conquest.
. . . . To prevent incessant cross references and disap-

pointments in foreign names beginning with La, Le, De, Van, &c., the names are, in frequent instances, repeated under those prefixes.

A work of this kind, consisting of some 18,000 entries, must necessarily have been in the first instance compiled from the leading biographical dictionaries, among which it is needless to particularize the *Biographie Universelle*, the *Nouvelle Biographie Générale*, the *Biographia Britannica*, and the works of Chalmers, Rose, Aikin, Gorton, and others. The dates that seemed undisputed were adopted without going further; but in all cases of discrepancy, biographical collections for particular series or special professions were resorted to, as Wood's *Athenæ Oxonienses*, Cooper's *Athenæ Cantabrigienses*, Fetis's *Musicians*, Strutt's *Engravers*, Pilkington's *Painters*, the *Historic Peerage*; such contemporary records as the *Annual Obituary*, the *Annual Register*; *L'Art de Vérifier les Dates*, the early Chronicles, Smith's *Dictionary of Greek and Roman Biography*, and Clinton's *Fasti*, for historical names; besides many single biographies and other primary authorities.

The editor, however, is well enough aware, that, with all the pains he has taken to avoid them, his own volume cannot have altogether escaped the errors he has been adverting to in other works; and he has seen too much of the difficulty of perfect accuracy, not to be prompted by entire sincerity in asking the indulgence of his readers. He will spare no pains in revising each successive edition that may be called for; and if those who feel the convenience of consulting an accurate work of this nature will kindly communicate any errors they may discover, with authorities for their correction, the compilation must needs win increasing confidence at every re-issue.

The editor apologizes for leaving in his pages a very few names whose dates he was unable to ascertain at the moment of going to press.

SHANKLIN, I. W.
July 27th, 1865.

A LIST OF THE PRINCIPAL ABBREVIATIONS USED IN THIS BOOK.

ab.,.................... about.
Abp., Archbp.,...... Archbishop.
aft.,..................... after.
Amer.,............... American.
Antiq.,... Antiquary, Antiquities.

bef.,.................. before.
beh.................... beheaded.
Bibliog.,......... Bibliographer.
Biog.,............. Biographer.
Bn.,................... Baron.
Bot.,................ Botanist.
Bp.,.................. Bishop.
br.,.................. brother.

c.,.................... century.
Chem.,............... Chemist.
cr.,................... created.
Ct.,.................. Count.
Ctss., or Css.,......... Countess.

Diplom.,........... Diplomatist.
Div.,................ Divine.
Dk.,.................. Duke.
Dram.,............. Dramatist.

E.,.................. Earl.
Eng.,........ England, English.

fl.,................. flourished.
Fr.,............. France, French.

Geog.,............ Geographer.
Geol.,.............. Geologist.
Ger.,........ German, Germany.
Gr.,.................. Greek.

Hist.,...... Historian, Historical.

Ital.,................ Italian.

K.,.................... King.

L.,..................... Life.
Ld.,.................. Lord.

Math., Mathem., . Mathematician.
Med.,................ Medical.
Misc., Miscel.,.... Miscellaneous.
Miss.,.............. Missionary.
mo.,................. mother.
Mqs.,..... Marquis, or Marquess.
Mus.,......... Musical, Musician.

Nat.,........ Natural, Naturalist.
neph.,................ nephew.

Orient.,............ Orientalist.

Pa., Paint.,............. Painter.
Philol.,............. Philologist.
Philos.,............ Philosopher.
Phys.,.............. Physician.
Po.,................. Poet.
Polit.,...... Political, Politician.
Port.,............. Portuguese.
Prof.,.............. Professor.
Prot.,.............. Protestant.

Q., or Qu.,............. Queen.

R., or Rom.,Cath., Roman Catholic.
Russ.,............... Russian.

Sch., Schol.,........... Scholar.
Scot.,................ Scottish.
Sp., Span.,........... Spanish.
Statesm.,............ Statesman.
Swed.,............... Swedish.

Theol.,.. Theological, Theologian.
ti.,................... time.
tr.,.................. translated.
Transl.,............. Translator.
Trav.,............... Traveler.

U. S.,........... United States.

Vsct., Visct.,......... Viscount.

Wr., Wri., Writ.,........ Writer.

? indicates an approximate or doubtful date.

A BRIEF

BIOGRAPHICAL DICTIONARY.

——◆——

	BORN.	DIED.
Aa, Christian Charles Henry van der. Dutch Scholar....	1718	1792
Aa, Pet. van der. Bookseller of Leyden. (*Galerie du Monde*)	—	1730?
Aagard, Christian. Danish Poet......................	1616	1664
Aagard, Nicholas, brother. Philosopher	1612	1657
Aagesen, Svend. Earliest Danish Historian...........		
Aal, Jacob. Norwegian Metallurgist..................	1773	1844
Aalst, Everard. Dutch Painter	1602	1658
Aalst, William, nephew. Dutch Painter..............	1620	1679
Aaron, St. British Martyr...........................	—	303
Aaron-Acharon. Caraite Rabbi. (*Garden of Eden*)....	fl.	1346
Aarsens, or Aertsen, Peter. *Lange Peter.* Dutch Painter.	1519	1575?
Aarsens, Francis van. Dutch Diplom. L. by Du Maurier	1572	1641
Aarssens, Cornelius van. Dutch Statesman	1543	1624
Aartgens. Dutch Painter............................	1498	1564
Aartsen, or Aarsens, *q. v.* Dutch Painter.............	1519	1575?
Aba, Samuel. Third Christian King of Hungary	—	1044
Abaka Khan. Second Mongol Emperor of Persia	—	1282
Abancourt, Chas. Xavier Jos. d'. Min. of Louis XVI....	1758	1792
Abancourt, Charles Frerot d'. French Engineer........	—	1801
Abano, or Apono, Peter of. Astrologer and Physician ..	1250	1315
Abarbanel, Isaac Darbanella. Learned Spanish Jew....	1437	1508
Abarca, Joachim. Spanish Prelate...................	—	1844
Abascal, Joseph Ferd. Span. Viceroy of Peru (1804–16)	1743	1821
Abasola, Mariano. Mexican Revolutionist.............	—	1811
Abate, Andrew. Italian Painter of Natural History.....	—	1732
Abati, Antonio. Italian Poet	—	1667
Abati, or Abbat, Nicholas. *Dell' Abate.* Painter in Fresco	1512	1571
Abatin, Guido Ubaldo. Painter in Fresco	1600	1656
Abauzit, Firmin. French Writer.....................	1679	1767
Abbadie, James. Dean of Killaloe. Theologian.......	1658	1727
Abbas. Uncle of Mahomet...........................	—	652?
Abbas I. Schah of Persia (1585–1628.) *The Great*.....	1557	1628
Abbas II. (1642–66)	1629	1666
Abbas III. (1731–36)	1732	1736
Abbas Mirza. Persian Prince........................	1783	1833
Abbatissa, or Badessa, Paul. Sicilian Poet	fl.	1560
Abbatucci, Charles. French General..................	1771	1796

	BORN.	DIED.
Abbatucci, James Peter. French General	1726	1812
Abbatucci, John Charles. French Diplomatist	1791	1857
Abbiati, Philip. Historical Painter	1640	1715
Abbo Floriacensis. Abbot of Fleury. Life by Aimoin	945	1004
Abbot, Abiel. American Divine	1770	1828
Abbot, Benjamin. American Educator	—	1849
Abbot, Charles, First Lord Colchester. Speaker	1757	1829
Abbot, Geo. Abp. Cant. (1611–33). L. by W. Russell, 1777	1562	1633
Abbot, George. Parliamentarian. (*Paraphrase on Job*)	1600	1648
Abbot, Lemuel. Portrait-Painter	1762?	1803
Abbot, Robert. Bp. of Salisbury. Divine. Life by Featley	1560	1618
Abbott, Charles, 1st Ld. Tenterden. Lord Chief Justice.	1762	1832
Abbt, Thomas. German Writer	1738	1766
Abdallah Ben Abd el Mottallib. Father of Mohammed	545	570
Abdallah Ben Yassim. Founder of Almoravides	fl. ab. 1050	
Abdallah Ben Zobair. Sultan of Mecca	—	692
Abdallatif. Arabian Philos. (*Historiæ Ægypti Compend.*)	1162	1231
Abdalmalek. Ommiad Caliph of Damascus (685–705)	—	705
Abd el Mottallib. Grandfather of Mohammed	497	579
Abd el Mumen. First Caliph of the Almohades	—	1163
Abd el Wahab. Founder of the Wahabees	1692	1787
Abderahman I. *The Wise.* Founder of Cordova Caliphate	731	787
Abderahman III. *The Great.* Moorish Sovereign	—	961
Abdul-Hamet. Sultan of Turkey (1774–1789)	—	1789
Abdul-Medjid. Sultan of Turkey (1839–1861)	1823	1861
A'Becket. *See* Becket.		
A'Beckett, Gilbert Abbot. (*Comic History of England*).	1810	1856
Abeel, David. American Missionary	1804	1846
Abegg, Bruno Erhard. German Lawyer and Politician	1803	1848
Abeille, Gaspar. French Poet and Dramatist	1648	1718
Abeille, John Christian Louis. Ger. Musician and Comp.	1761	1832
Abeille, Scipio, brother. (*History of the Bones*)	—	1697
Abeken, William Louis Albert Rudolph	1813	1843
Abel, Charles Frederick. German Musical Composer	1725	1787
Abel, Dr. Clarke. Historian of Chinese Embassy	—	1826
Abel, Gaspar. Historian of Germany	1676	1763
Abel, Jacob Frederick von. German Philosopher	1751	1829
Abel, Joseph. German Painter	1768	1818
Abel, Nicholas Henry. Swedish Mathematician	1802	1829
Abela, John Francis. (*Malta Illustrata*)	1582	1655
Abelard, Peter. Schoolman. L. by F. A. Gervaise, 1720; J. Hughes, 1751; Muechler, 1755; J. Berington, 1784; A. Metrà, 1794; H. Mills, 1807; Fessler, 1807; Schlosser, 1807; Follin, 1809; Turlot, 1822; Feuerbach, 1833; Villenave, 1834; Cousin, 1836; Guizot, 1839; Weyland, 1840; Remusat, 1845; Jacobi, 1850; Tosti, 1851	1079	1142
Abell, John. English Singer and Musician	fl. ab. 1701	
Abelli, Louis. Bishop of Rhodes. (*Medulla Theologica*)	1603	1691
Abendana, Jacob. Spanish Jew. Commentator	—	1685
Abendroth, Amadeus August. Ger. Lawyer and Patriot.	1767	1842
Abenezra, Abraham. Jewish Writer	1119?	1174?
Abercrombie, James. American Divine	1758	1841
Abercrombie, James. British General		
Abercrombie, John. Horticulturist	1726	1806

BORN. DIED.

Abercrombie, John, M. D. (*Intellectual Powers*)....... 1781..1844
Abercromby, Alex., Lord. Scotch Judge and Writer .. 1745..1796
Abercromby, Patrick, M. D. (*Martial Achievements*)... 1656..1716?
Abercromby, Gen. Sir Ralph. L. by Ld. Dumferline, 1861 1738?.1801
Aberdeen, Geo. Hamilton Gordon, Earl of. Statesman.. 1784..1860
Aberli, John Louis. Swiss Landscape-Painter.......... 1723..1786
Abernethy, John. Irish Presbyterian. (*Divine Attributes*) 1680..1740
Abernethy, John. Surgeon. Life by Macilwain, 1853. 1764..1831
Abildgaard, Nicholas Abraham. Danish Hist. Painter. 1744..1809
Abinger, James Scarlett, First Lord. Judge........... 1769..1844
Abington, Frances. Comic Actress................. 1731or8.1815
Abisbal, Henry O'Donnell. Spanish General........... 1770..1734
Ablancourt, Nicholas Perrot d'. French Writer .... 1606..1664
Abney, Sir Thomas, M. P. Lord Mayor .... 1639..1722
Abrabanel, Isaac. Commentator. Life by Mai, 1708... 1437..1508
Abraham-a-Sancta Clara. Celeb. German Preacher ... 1642..1709
Abraham-ben-Chaila. Span. Rabbi and Astrologer.... — ..1303
Abrahamson, Abraham. German Jew. Medalist...... 1754..1811
Abrahamson, Werner John Fred. Ger. Crit. and Antiq. 1744..1812
Abrantès, Andoche Junot, Duc d'. French General..... 1771..1813
Abrantès, Joseph, Marquess d'. Portuguese Statesman. 1784..1827
Abrantès, Laurette Junot, Duchess d'. (*Memoires sur
  Napoleon.*) Life by Cantu, 1837 .... 1784..1838
Abresch, Frederick Louis. Dutch Critic and Scholar... 1699..1782
Abrial, Andrew Joseph. French Statesman............•1750..1828
Abruzzo, Balthasar. Sicilian Philosopher and Civilian. 1601?.1665
Abubeker. First Caliph (632–4)..................... 571.. 634
Abulfaragius, Gregory. Armenian Bp., Phys., and Hist. 1226..1286
Abulfazel. Vizier of Akbar. (*Ayeen Akberry*)........ — ..1604
Abulfeda, Ismael. Soldier and Writer............... 1273..1331
Abulgasi-Bayatur. Khan of Tartary. (*Hist. of Tartars*) 1605..1663
Abulola. Arabian Poet.............................. 973..1057
Abumansur, or Albumanzar. Arabian Astron. and Biogr. 885.. —
Abunowas. Arabian Poet............................ 762.. 810
Abu-Obeidah. Mahometan Conqueror............... 581.. 639
Abu-Rihan. *Al Mohakabad.* Geograph. and Astrologer. fl. 11th c.
Abu-Said. *Bahadur Khan.* Persian King (1317–35)... 1305?.1335
Abu-Said-Mirza. Sovereign of the Moguls........... 1427..1469
Abu-Teman. Arabian Poet .... — .. 845?
Acca. Bishop of Hexham............................ — .. 740
Acciaioli, Donatus. Florentine Scholar and Statesman.. 1428..1478
Acciaioli, Zenobio. Italian Scholar .... 1461..1519
Acciaioli Salvetti, Magdalen. Florentine Poetess...... — ..1610
Accolti, Benedict. Florentine Lawyer and Historian.... 1415..1466
Accolti, Benedict, grandson. *Cardinal of Ancona.* Latinist. 1497..1549
Accolti, Francis. *Francis of Arezzo,* or *Aretino.* Jurist. 1418?.1485?
Accords, Stephen Tabourot, Seigneur des. French Poet. 1516?.1561
Accorso, Mariangelo. Collector of MSS. (*Diatribæ*)... 1490?. —
Accorso, or Accursius, Francis. Ital. Lawyer. (*Great Gloss*) 1182?.1260
Ach, or Achen, John van. Historical and Portrait Painter. 1556..1621
Achard, Francis Charles. Experimental Philosopher.... 1753..1821
Achards, Eleazar Francis des. Missionary to Cochin.... 1679..1741
Achery, Luke d'. *See D'Achery.*................. 1609..1685
Achilles Tatius. Alexandrian Rhetorician and Bishop. fl.ab.500A.D.

BORN.   DIED.

Achillini, Alex. Philosopher and Physician of Bologna. 1463..1512
Achillini, John Philotheus, brother. Poet. (*Viridario*).. 1466..1538
Achillini, Claude. Italian Savant .... 1574..1640
Achmet I. Sultan of Turks (1603–17)................. 1590..1617
Achmet II. (1691–95).............................. 1643..1695
Achmet III. (1703–30)............................. 1673..1739
Achtschelling, Lucas, of Brussels. Landscape Painter . fl. 1600?
Acidalius, Valens. German Critic and Philologist...... 1567..1605
Ackermann, Conrad. German Comedian .... 1710..1771
Ackermann, John Christian Theoph. Ger. Med. Writer. 1756..1801
Ackermann, Rudolph. Publisher; introd. of lithography
  into England .... 1764..1834
Ackmar, William. Scottish Portrait Painter........... 18th cen.
Acland, Rev. Charles. Writer on India .... 1814..1845
Acontius, or Aconcio, James. Philosopher ; Divine;
  Civilian. (*De Stratagematibus Satanæ*) .... 1492..1566
Acosta, Gabriel, of Coimbra. Commentator on O. T..... — ..1616
Acosta, Joseph d'. Jesuit Missionary in Peru. (*Hist.
  of West Indies*)...................................... 1539?.1600
Acosta, Uriel, of Oporto. Convert to Judaism......... — ..1647
Acquaviva, Andrew Matt. Originator of Cyclopedias ... 1456..1528
Acrel, Olof. Swedish Medical Writer.................. 1717..1807
Acropolita, George. Byzantine Historian .... 1220..1282
Acton, Joseph. Neapolitan Prime Minister .... 1737..1811
Acuna, Christopher d'. Span. Jesuit Miss. in America.. 1597..1676?
Acuna, Ferdinand d'. Spanish Poet and Soldier .... — ..1580
Adair, James. Trader. (*Hist. of the American Indians*).fl.1735–1775
Adair, James. Sergeant-at-Law....................... — ..1798
Adair, James Makittrick. Scottish Medical Writer......1728..1802
Adair, Sir Robert, G.C.B. Diplomatist................. 1763..1855
Adalard, or Alelard, *which see.* Cousin of Charlemagne.. 753?. 826
Adalberon. Archbishop of Reims (969–88) .... — .. 988
Adalberon, Ascelinus. Bishop of Laon (977–1030) ..... 950?.1030
Adalbert, Bp. of Magdeburg; Miss. to the Sclavonians .. — .. 981
Adalbert, St. Archbishop of Prague.................. 939.. 997
Adalbert. *See* Adelbert. Archbishop of Bremen....... — ..1072
Adam, Albert. German Artist....................... 1786?.1862
Adam, Alex., LL.D., of Edinburgh. (*Roman Antiquities*). 1741..1809
Adam, Billaut. *Master Adam.* Joiner and Poet of Nevers. — ..1662
Adam, Francis Gaspard. French Sculptor............. 1710..1759
Adam, Lambert Sigisbert. French Sculptor........... 1700..1759
Adam, Melchior. German Divine and Biographer ...... — ..1622
Adam, Nicholas. French Grammarian .... 1716..1792
Adam, Nich. Sebast. French Sculpt. (*Prometheus Chained*) 1705..1778
Adam, Robert. Architect............................ 1728..1792
Adam, Rev. Robert. (*Religious World Displayed.*)..... 1770..1826
Adam, Thomas. Divine .... 1701..1784
Adam, Right Hon. William. Lawyer and Politician .... 1751..1839
Adam de Marisco. Scholar .... fl. 1250
Adam of Bremen. Eccles. Historian and Missionary .... fl. 1067
Adam of Orleton. Bishop of Winchester .... 1285..1375
Adam of Murimuth. Chronicler ....Ed.III&Rd II
Adam Scotus. Doctor of the Sorbonne. Biographer... — ..1180
Adamanteo. Italian Mathematician and Orientalist. ... — ..1581

BORN. DIED.

Adamantius. Greek Physician...................... fl. A.D. 415?
Adami, Leonard. Italian Scholar.................... 1690..1719
Adami, Tobias. Ger. Scholastic. (*Prodromus Philosophiæ*) 1581..1643
Adams, Abigail. Wife of President John Adams. (*Letters*) 1744..1818
Adams, Charles Baker. American Chemist and Zoölogist 1814..1853
Adams, Francis, M.D. Medical Translator .... 1797..1861
Adams, Geo. Instrument Maker. (*Micrographia Illustrata*) — ..1786
Adams, Geo., son. Instrument Maker. (*Essay on Vision*) 1750..1795
Adams, Hannah. American Authoress. (*Hist. of the Jews*) 1756..1832
Adams, Jasper. American Divine and Educator........ 1793..1841
Adams, John. Second President of United States (1797–
    1802). Life by G. Gibbs, 1848; C. F. Adams, 1851 .. 1735..1826
Adams, John. Colonizer of Pitcairn's Island........... 1764..1829
Adams, John Quincy. Sixth President of United States
    (1825–29). Life by W. H. Seward, 1849; Josiah Quincy 1767..1848
Adams, Joseph, M.D. Medical Writer .... 1756..1818
Adams, Richard. Ejected Nonconformist. Ed. of Charnock 1630..1698
Adams, Samuel. American Statesman .... 1722..1803
Adams, Thos. Ejected Nonconformist. (*Protestant Union*) — ..1670
Adams, Sir Thomas. Lord Mayor; Loyalist; Benefactor. 1586..1667
Adams, Rev. William, D.D. Writer against Hume...... 1707..1789
Adamson, Patrick. Archbishop of St. Andrews........ 1536..1592
Adanson, Michael. French Naturalist...... .... 1727..1806
Addington, Henry, First Viscount Sidmouth. Statesman.
    Life by Pellew, 1847 .... 1755..1844
Addison, Joseph. (*Spectator.*) Life by Richard Steele,
    1724; Sprengel, 1810; Lucy Aikin, 1843; Macaulay,
    1843; Elwin, 1857 .... 1672..1719
Addison, Launcelot. Dean of Lichfield................ 1632..1703
Adelaar, Cord Sivertsen. Naval Commander.......... 1622..1675
Adelaide, Madame. Aunt of Louis XVI................ 1732..1800
Adelaide. Princess of Orleans; sister of Louis Philippe.. 1777..1847
Adelaide. Q. of Eng. Consort of Wm. IV. Life by Doran 1792..1849
Adelard. Cousin of Charlemagne. Founder of New Corbie
    Abbey.. 753?. 826
Adelard. Monk of Bath. Translator and Writer ...... fl. 1130
Adelbert, Abp. of Bremen and Hamburg. Regent...... — ..1072
Adelbold. Bishop of Utrecht. (*Life of Emp. Henry II.*) 960?.1027
Adeler, or Adelaar. *Cord Sivertsen.* Naval Commander 1622..1675
Adelgrief, John Albert. German Religious Enthusiast.. — ..1636
Adelm, or Aldhelm, *which see....*................... 656.. 709
Adelung, John Christopher. German Philologist....... 1732..1806
Ademar, or Aymar. Monk and Chronicler of St. Martial.
    Life by Castaigne, 1850 .... 998?.1030?
Adeodatus I., or Dieudonné. Bishop of Rome (615-18). — .. 618
Adeodatus II., or Dieudonné. (672-76)............. — .. 676
Ader, Wm. Phys. of Toulouse. (*De Ægrotis Evangelicis*) fl. 1621
Adet, Peter Aug. French Envoy and Chemical Writer.. 1763..1832?
Adhad-Eddoulat. Emperor of Persia. Friend of learning 936.. 983
Adhelm, St. *See* Aldhelm............................ 656.. 709
Adhemar, William. Provençal Poet................... — ..1190?
Adimari, Alexander, of Florence. Scholar and Poet..... 1579..1649
Adimari, Louis, of Florence. Satirist................. 1644..1708
Adler, Philip. *Patricius,* or *Paticina.* German Engraver 1484..1530?

BORN. DIED.

Adler, James George Christian. Danish Orientalist.
(*Museum Cuficum*).............................. 1755..1805
Adler Salvius, John. Swedish Statesman............. 1590..1652
Adlerbeth, Gudmund Jöran. Swedish Author......... 1751..1818
Adlerfeldt, Gustavus. Swedish Historian.............. 1671..1709
Adlzreitter, John. (*Annals of Bavaria*)............... 1596..1662
Ado. Abp. of Vienna (860–75). Historian......... 800?. 875
Adolphus of Nassau. German Emperor. Life by Wag-
   ner, 1775; Leuchs, 1798; Spandau, 1827 .... 1252?.1298
Adolphus Frederick II. King of Sweden (1751–71)... 1710..1771
Adolphus, John. Historical Writer. (*Life of Geo. III.*) 1766..1845
Adorni, Catherine Fieschi. Italian Religious Writer .... 1447?.1510
Adrain, Robert. Irish-American Educator........... 1775..1843
Adrets, Frs. de Beaumont, Baron des. Huguenot Leader 1513..1587
Adriam, Marie, of Lyons. Female Patriot .... 1777..1793
Adrian. Emperor of Rome (117–138). Life by Flemmer,
   1836; Gregorovius, 1851.............................. 76.. 138
Adrian. Greek Writer on the Scriptures .... fl 5th. c.
Adrian I. Pope (772–95)............................. — .. 795
Adrian II. (867–72.)................................. — .. 872
Adrian III. (884–85.) *Agapit*....................... — .. 885
Adrian IV. (1154–59.) *Nich. Breakspear.* Life by Raby, 1849 1100?.1159
Adrian V. (1276.) *Ottoboni Fieschi* .... — ..1276
Adrian VI. (1522–3.) L. by Moring, 1536; Burmann, 1727 1459..1523
Adrian de Castello. Cardinal. Bp. Bath & W. (1504–18) 1450?.1518
Adriani, John Baptist. (*History of his Own Times*) ..... 1513..1579
Adriani, Marcel. Florentine Writer.................. 1533..1604
Adriani, Marcel Virgil. Florentine Scholar............. 1464..1521
Adriano. Spanish Painter .... — ..1630
Adriansen, Alexander. Flemish Artist................ 1625?. —
Adrichomius, Christian. Dutch Writer on Holy Land.. 1533..1585
Adry, John Felicissime. French Writer................ 1749..1818
Ægidius de Columna. *Most Profound Doctor.* Schoolman — ..1316
Ægidius, Peter, of Antwerp. Scholar; friend of Sir T. More 1486..1533
Ægidius, Peter, of Antwerp. Oriental Traveler ...….... 1490..1555
Ægineta, Pancus, of Ægina. Medical Writer.......... • — .. 630?
Æginhard, or Eginhard. (*Life of Charlemagne*)........ 771?. 839
Ælfric. See Alfric.
Ælian, Claudius. Historian and Rhetorician...........fl.ab.250A.D.
Ælius Donatus. Grammarian at Rome................ fl. 356
Ælius Spartianus. · Biographer of Roman Emperors ... fl. 300?
Ælred. *See* Ailred. Historian..................... 1109..1166
Ælst, Everhard van. Dutch Painter .... 1602..1658
Ælst, William van, nephew. Dutch Painter. .... 1620..1679
Æmilianus, C. Julius. Emperor (253)................ 208?. 253
Æmilius, Paulus. *Macedonicus.* Captor of Perseus ....230?B.C.160
Æmilius, Paulus. French Historian .... — ..1529
Æneas, or Ængus. Irish Bishop and Hagiographer..... — .. 820
Æneas Gazæus. Christian Writer. (*Theophrastus*).... fl. 487
Æneas Sylvius. Pope Pius II. Life by himself........ 1405..1464
Ænæas Tacticus. Greek Military Writer............. fl. D.C. 362?
Æpinus, Francis Maria Ulric Theodore. Electrician..... 1724..1802
Æpinus, John. German Reformer .... 1499..1553
Ærsens, or Ærtsen, Peter. *Lange Peter.* Dutch Painter 1519..1575?

BORN. DIED.

Aerts, Richard. Dutch Painter .... 1482..1577
Æschines. Athenian Orator. Life by Wolf, 1572;
· Matthæi, 1770; Norberg, 1792; Stechow, 1841 .... 389B.C.314
Æschylus. Greek Tragedian 525B.C.456
Æsop. Fabulist. Life by Planudes, 14th cent.; Meziriac,
1632, tr. by Toland; Westermann, 1845 .... fl.570? B.C.
Æthicus, or Ethicus. Latin Writer of Istria. (*Cosmogra-
phia*)... fl. 4th c.
Aetion. Greek Painter. (*Alexander's Nuptials*) .... fl. ti. Had'n
Aetius. Greek Medical Writer of Mesopotamia........ fl.A.D.500?
Aetius. Roman Commander in Chief of the West ...... —'A.D.454
Afer, Domitius, of Nismes. Roman Orator. .... — .. 60
Afflitto, Matthew. Italian Law-Writer .... 1448..1524
Affo, Irenæus. Italian Historian. (*History of Parma*) .. 1742..1800?
Affre, Denis Augustus. Archbishop of Paris ....·..... 1793..1848
Affry, Louis Augustine Philip, Ct. d'. Swiss Statesman. 1743..1810
Afranius, Lucius. Roman Comic Poet................. fl. B.C. 100?
Africanus, John Leo. Traveler and Geographer........ 1483?.1552
Africanus, Sextus Cæcilius. Roman Jurisconsult ...... fl. 138–160
Africanus, Sextus Julius. Christian Historian........ fl. 220?
Afzelius, Adam. Swedish Naturalist................. 1750..1837
Afzelius, John. Swedish Chemist .... 1753..1837
Aganduru, Roderick Maurice. Spanish Miss. to the East fl. 1640?
Agapetus I. Pope (535–536)........................ — .. 536
Agapetus II. (946–950)............................ — .. 956
Agar, James d'. French Portrait Painter .... 1640..1716
Agar, John Anthony Michael. French Financier........ 1771..1844
Agard, Arthur. Antiquary.......................... 1540..1615
Agas, or Aggas, Ralph. Engraver and Surveyor........ —aft.1596
Agasias, of Ephesus. Sculptor. (*Borghese Gladiator*).... fl.4th c.B.C.?
Agathangelus. Armenian Historian.................. fl. 11th c.?
Agathemerus. Greek Geographer.................... fl.200? A.D.
Agathias. *The Scholar.* Byzantine Historian .... 536?A.D.582?
Agatho. Pope (679–682) .... — .. 682
Agathocles. K. of Sicily. Life by R. Perrinchiefe, 1676 360?B.C.289
Agathodæmon, of Alexandria. Geographer........... fl. 200? A.D.
Agelnoth, or Ethelnoth. Abp. of Canterbury (1020–38).. — ..1038
Agesander, of Rhodes. Sculptor. (*Laocoön*) .... fl. ti. Titus
Agesilaus II. King of Sparta (338–361) and General... 444B.C.360?
Aggas, Ralph. Engraver and Surveyor................ —aft.1596
Aggas, or Augus, Robert. Landscape-Painter........... 1619?.1679
Aggrippa, M. Vipsanius. Statesm. Life by Gebauer, 1717;
Frandsen, 1836; Laukeren Mathes, 1841; Eck, 1842... 63 B.C. 12
Agilulph. King of the Lombards (591–619)............ — .. 619?
Agis II. King of Sparta (427–398) .... —B.C. 398
Agis III. (338–330)................................ —B.C. 330
Agis IV. (244–240) .... —B.C. 240
Aglionby, Edward. Poet .... fl. ti. Eliz.
Aglionby, John, D.D. Chaplain to Eliz. and James. Divine 1567..1610
Agnesi, Maria Gaetana. Mathematician. Life by Frisi,
1807; Milesi-Mojon, 1836 .... 1718..1799
Agnesi, Maria Theresa, sister. Musical Composer ...... 1724?. —
Agnew, Sir Andrew. Scottish Publicist.............. 1793..1849
Agnolo, Baccio d'. Florentine Engraver and Architect.. 1460..1543

BORN. DIED.

Agobard. Abp. of Lyons (816–40). Life by Hundes-
hagen, 1831; Macé, 1846 .... 779.. 840
Agostini, Leonard. Italian Antiquary .... — ..1686?
Agostino, Paul, of Valerano. Musical Composer........ 1593..1629
Agoult, William d'. Provençal Poet .... — ..1181
Agreda, Mary of. Spanish Abbess. (*Life of Virgin Mary*) 1602..1665
Agresti, Livio. Historical Painter .... — ..1580
Agricola, Christopher Louis. Painter and Engraver .... 1667..1719
Agricola, Cn. Julius. Roman General. Life by Tacitus. 37.. 93
Agricola, George, of Saxony. Metallurgist .... 1494..1555
Agricola, Geo. And. German Phys. and Arboriculturist . 1672..1738
Agricola, John. Antinomian Divine of Saxony. Life by
Unger, 1732; Kordes, 1817 .... 1492..1566
Agricola, John Frederick. Ger. Musician and Composer 1720..1774
Agricola, Martin, of Magdeburg. (*Musica Instrumentalis*) 1486..1556
Agricola, Michael. Finnish Translator of Bible .... — ..1557
Agricola, Rudolph. Scholar. Life by Tresling, 1830.... 1443..1485
Agrippa, Camillus. Milanese Architect............... fl. 1583
Agrippa, Henry Cornelius. Soldier, Writer, &c. (*Occult
Philosophy.*) Life by H..Morley .... 1486..1535
Agrippa I., Herod. King of the Jews. Acts xii. ...... 9B.C.44A.D.
Agrippa II., Herod. Son of Agrippa I. Acts xxvi..... 31.. 100
Agrippa, Postumus, son; grandson of Augustus......... 12B.C.14A.D.
Agrippina I. *The Elder.* Wife of Germanicus. Life by
Eliz. Hamilton, 1800; Burkhardt, 1846.............. 12?BC.33A.D
Agrippina II. *The Younger.* Daughter of Germanicus;
mother of Nero .... 15?. 60
Aguado, Alexander Maria. French Financier .... 1784..1842
Aguesseau, H. F. d'. Chancellor of Fr. *See* D'Aguesseau 1668..1751
Aguilar, Grace. Writer. (*Home Influence*) .... 1816..1847
Aguillon, Francis. Flemish Mathematician............. 1566..1617
Aguirre, Joseph Saenz de. Cardinal. Writer and Com-
piler.. 1630..1699
Agujari, Lucretia. Italian Vocalist.................... — ..1783
Agustina, of Saragossa. Spanish Patriot............. —..1857
Agylæus, Henry. Lawyer and Scholar............... 1533?.1595
Ahlwardt, Peter. German Metaphysician............. 1710..1791
Ahmed. Ottoman Emperors. *See* Achmet.
Ahmed-ben-Fares, or El Razi. Ar. Lawyer and Lex. — .. 990
Ahmed Khan. Mogul King of Persia (1282–84)....... — ..1284
Ahmed Shah el Abdaly. 1st K. of Candahar & Cabul.. 1723..1773
Ahrendt, or Arents, Martin Frederick. Antiquary...... 1769..1824
Aidan. King of Scotland (578–606).................. 528.. 606
Aidan, St. Bishop of Lindisfarne.................... — .. 651
Aignan, Stephen. French Republican and Writer....... 1773..1824
Aikin, Arthur. Scientific Writer...................... 1784..1854
Aikin, John, M. D. Biog. Life by Lucy Aikin, 1823 ..... 1747..1822
Aikin, Miss Lucy. Writer. Life by Le Breton......... 1781..1864
Aikman, William. Scottish Portrait-Painter........... 1682..1731
Ailly, Peter d'. Cardinal. *L'Aigle des Docteurs de France.*. 1350..1425?
Ailred. Abbot of Revesby. Historical Writer......... 1109..1166
Aimé-Martin, Louis. French Writer. (*Éducation des
mères de famille*).................................... — ..1846
Aimoin, of Aquitaine. (*History of France*)............ — ..1008

BORN. DIED.

Ainsworth, Henry. Nonconf. Divine and Commentator — ..1622?
Ainsworth, Robert. (*Latin Dictionary*)............... 1660..1743
Airault, Peter. Advocate of Paris.................... 1536..1601
Airay, Rev. Christopher. Writer on Logic............ 1609?.1670
Airay, Henry, of Oxford. Calvinistic Divine.......... 1560..1616
Aistulph. King of the Lombards; defeated by Pepin.. — .. 756
Aiton, William. Botanist. (*Hortus Kewensis*)......... 1731..1793
Aitzema, Leo van. (*History of United Provinces*)...... 1600..1669
Ajala, Martin Perez d'. Abp. of Valencia. (*Apostolic
  Tradition*)'.. 1504..1566
Akakia, Martin. Medical Writer at Paris............. 1539..1588
Akbar, Emp. of Hindostan (1556-1605). L. by Aboul-Fazl 1542..1605
Akenside, Mark, M. D. Poet. L. by Bucke, 1832; Dyce 1721..1770
Akerblad, John David. Swed. Orientalist and Antiq... 1760?.1819
Akers, Benjamin Paul. American Sculptor............. 1825..1862
Akiba-ben-Joseph. Jewish Rabbi and Cabalist....... — .. 135
Alabaster, William. (*Lexicon Pentaglotton: Roxana*)... 1567?.1640
Alain Chartier. (*Chronicle of Charles VII.*).......... 1386..1458
Alain de Lille. *Universal Doctor*..................... 1114..1203?
Alain, John. Danish Writer. (*Origin of the Cimbri*).... 1569..1630
Alaman, Lucas. Mexican Statesman................. — ..1853
Alamandus, Louis. *Aleman*. French Cardinal........ 1390..1450
Alamanni, Louis. Florentine Statesman and Poet...... 1495..1556
Alan. Abbot of Tewkesbury. (*Life of Thomas à Becket*) 1171?.1201
Alan, of Lynn. Theologian. (*Moralia Bibliorum*)....... — ..1420
Alan, Cardinal. *See* Allen.......................... 1532..1594
Aland, Sir John Fortescue, Baron Fortescue. Judge.
  (*Stradling versus Styles*)....................... 1670..1746
Alarcon y Mendoza, Juan Ruiz de. Span. Dramatist.. —aft.1634
Alard, Lambert. Theologian and Lexicographer........ 1602..1672
Alard, Maria Jos. Louis. French Physician............ 1779..1850
Alaric I. King of Visigoths. Conqueror of Rome, 410.. — .. 410
Alaric II. (484-507.) Defeated by Clovis, 507....:..... — .. 507
Alasco, John. Reformer of Poland.................... 1499..1560
Alava, Miguel Ricardo d'. Spanish Statesman......... 1771..1843
Alava Esquviel, Diego d'. Bishop of Cordova. (*Gen.
  Councils*)... — ..1562
Alban, St. British Protomartyr....................... — .. 285?
Albanese. Italian Musician......................... 1729?.1800
Albani, Alexander. Cardinal. Virtuoso and Historical
  Writer. Life by Strocchi, 1790.................... 1692..1779
Albani, or Albano, Francis. Painter of Females......... 1578..1660
Albani, John Francis. Cardinal. Roman Statesman.... 1720..1809
Albani, John Jerome. Cardinal. Civilian........... 1504..1591
Albano, John Baptist. Historical and Landscape Painter. — ..1668
Albany, Louisa, Countess of. Wife of Young Pretender.. 1753..1824
Albaten, or Albategni. Arabian Geometer and Astron-
  omer. Inventor of Sines.......................... — .. 929
Albenas, John J., Viscount of. French Politician ...... 1760..1824
Albergati Capacelli, Francis, Marquis d'. Dramatist... 1729..1804
Albergotti. Francis. Civilian at Florence. (*On the
  Digest*)... — ..1376
Alberic of Trois-Fontaines. Chronicler............. fl.ab. 1241
Alberici, Henry. Italian Historical and Religious Painter. 1714..1775

BORN. DIED.

Albericus, John. Antiquary. *See* Aubrey............ 1626..1697?
Alberoni, Julius. Cardinal. Spanish Minister. Life by
   Rousset de Missy, 1719; G. Moore, 1806............ 1664..1752
Albert I. Emperor. Duke of Austria I............ 1248..1308
Albert II. Duke of Austria V. Life by Wenck, 1770.. 1398..1439
Albert I. Duke of Austria. Emperor I............ 1248..1308
Albert II. *The Lame* and *The Wise*............ 1289..1358
Albert III............ 1348..1395
Albert IV. *The Patient.*............ 1377..1404
Albert V. *The Illustrious.* Emperor II............ 1398..1439
Albert VI. *The Prodigal*............ 1418..1463
Albert. Archduke of Austria. Gov. of Netherlands.
   Life by Lemire, 1622; Montgalllard, 1622; Brusle de
   Montplainchamp, 1683; Charles Dubois, 1847........ 1559..1621
Albert I. Margrave of Brandenburg. *The Bear* and *The
   Fair*............ 1106..1170
Albert II............ — ..1221
Albert III. *The Achilles* and *The Ulysses.*............ 1414..1486
Albert. First Duke of Prussia............ 1490..1568
Albert. Margrave of Baireuth. *Alcibiades of Germany*.. 1522..1555
Albert. Prince Consort of England............ 1819..1861
Albert. Abp. of Mentz. Conspirator against Henry VII. — ..1137
Albert. *The Great. See* Albertus Magnus............ 1193..1280
Albert. Cardinal. Archbishop of Magdeburg......... 1489..1545
Albert of Aix, or Albertus Aquensis. Historian........ 1060?.1120
Albert, of Mecklenburg. King of Sweden............ — ..1412
Albert of Stade. Chronicler (from Creation to 1256).
   Life by Eckhard, 1726............ —aft.1260
Albert of Strasburg. Chronicler (from 1270 to 1378).. fl. 14th c.
Albert, Charles d'. Duke of Luynes. Constable of Fr.. 1578..1621
Albert, Erasmus. German Divine. (*Koran of the Cor-
   deliers*)............ — ..1551
Albert, Krantz. (*History of Saxony and the Vandals*).... — ..1517
Alberti, Aristotile. Italian Engineer............ fl. 16th c.
Alberti, Cherubino. Florentine Painter............ 1552..1615
Alberti, Dominic. Venetian Musician............ fl. 18th c.
Alberti, Durante. Painter in Oil and Fresco............ 1538..1613
Alberti, Joh. German Orientalist. (*Observat. Philolog. in
   N. T.*)............ — ..1559
Alberti, John. Painter of Perspective and History...... 1558..1601
Alberti, John Charles. Fresco Painter............ 1680..1740
Alberti, Leander. Dominican Writer............ 1479..1552?
Alberti, Leon Baptist. Poet, Architect, Painter, Sculptor. 1404..1472
Alberti, Louis Joseph d'. Prince of Grimberghen. Field
   Marshal and Ambassador of Emperor Charles VII.... 1672..1758
Alberti, Michael. Medical Writer at Hall............ 1682..1757
Alberti, Solomon. Anatomist............ 1549..1600
Alberti di Villanova, Francis. Italian Lexicographer.. 1731..1800?
Albertinelli, Mariotto di Bagio. Florentine Painter.... 1475?.1520?
Albertini, Francis. Florentine Antiquary............ fl. 16th c.
Albertini, Francis. Calabrian Jesuit. (*De Angelo
   Custode*)............ — ..1619
Albertini, Paul. Venetian Priest, Author and Politician. 1430?.1475
Albertrandy, John Christian. Polish Numismatist..... 1731..1808

BORN. DIED.

Albertus Magnus. Schoolman. Life by Flaminio.... 1193?.1280
Albertus, H. C. German Painter and Engraver........ — ..1680?
Albezi, Bartholomew. Franciscan Monk.............. — ..1401
Albi, Henry. Jesuit Writer. (*History of Illustrious Car-*
    dinals)... 1519..1659
Albignac, Maurice. French Soldier................... 1775..1824
Albini, Alexander. Italian Painter.................. 1568?.1646
Albini, Francis Joseph. German Diplomatist........... 1748..1816
Albinus, Bernard. *Weiss.* Medical Writer........... 1653..1721
Albinus, Bernard Siegfried, son. German Anatomist.... 1696..1770
Albinus, Christian Bernard, brother. Anatomical Writer. — ..1752
Albinus, Decimus Clodius. Rival of Septimus Severus. — .. 197
Albinus, L. Postumius. Consul; slain by the Boii...... —B.C.216
Albis, or White, Thomas. Philosopher. Friend of Hobbes. 1582..1676
Albisson, John. French Lawyer and Author........... 1732..1810
Albitte, Anthony Louis. French Jacobin............. — ..1812
Albizzi, Bartholomew. Tuscan Cordelier: Writer....... — ..1401
Albo, Joseph. Spanish Rabbi. (*Sepher Hikkarim*)...... — ..1428
Alboin. King of the Lombards...................... — .. 573
Albon, James d', Marquis of Fronsac. French General.. — ..1562
Alboresi, James, of Bologna. Landscape and Architect-
    ural Painter...................................... 1632..1677
Albornoz, Giles Alvarez Carillo. Abp. of Toledo: Card.. — ..1367
Albrecht, William. German Agriculturist............. 1786..1848
Albrechtsberger, John George. German Composer.... 1736..1809
Albret, Jeanne d'. ·Queen of Navarre. *See D'Albret...* 1528..1572
Albucasis. Arabian Physician...................... — ..1106?
Albumazar. Arabian Astronomer.................... 776?. 885
Albuquerque, Alphonso d'. Portuguese Conqueror in
    India. Life by his son, 1557..................... 1453..1515
Albuquerque, Matthias. Portuguese General......... — ..1646
Albuquerque Coelho, Edward d'. Soldier. (*Wars of*
    Brazil)....................................... — ..1658
Alcæus. Lyric Poet of Lesbos..................fl.ab.611B.C.
Alcamenes. Athenian Sculptor...................fl.444B.C.400
Alcasar, Louis de. Span. Jesuit. Writer on Apocalypse. 1554..1613
Alciati, Andrew. Civilian; Restorer of Roman Law.... 1492..1550
Alciati, John Paul, of Milan. Socinian Writer......... fl. 16th c.
Alcibiades. Athenian General and Statesman......... 450?B.C.404
Alcinous. Platonic Phil. (*Doctrines of Plato*)...fl.1st or 2d c.A.D.
Alciphon. Greek Writer..........................fl.ab.A.D.170
Alcman. Lyric Poet of Sardis..................... fl.B.C.670?
Alcock, John. Bp. of Ely. Founder of Jesus Coll. Camb. — ..1500
Alcock, John. Musical Composer................... 1715..1806
Alcred. King of Northumbria (765–774)............. 740?. 789
Alcuin. *Flacius Albinus.* Theologian. Life by Lorenz,
    1829, translated by Slee, 1837................... 725?. 804
Alcyonius, Peter. Italian Writer................... 1487..1527?
Alday, John. Translator of *Theatrum Mundi*.......... fl. 16th c.
Aldegrever, or Oldegræf, Henry. Paint. and Engr... 1502..1563
Alden, John. Early Settler in Plymouth, New England. — ..1687
Alderete, Diego Gratian. Spanish Writer..........—d.ti.Phil.II.
Alderoti, Thaddeus. Florentine Phys. L. by Villani.. 1215..1295
Aldhelm, St. Bishop of Sherborne. Life by Faricius.. 656.. 709

BORN. DIED.

Aldhun. First Bishop of Durham...................... — ..1018
Aldred. Archbishop of York.......................... — ..1069
Aldrich, Henry. Dean. Theol., Logician, Composer .. 1647..1710
Aldrich, Robert. Bishop of Carlisle .... —..1556
Aldrovandini, Thomas, of Bologna. Painter.......... 1653..1736
Aldrovandus, Ulysses. Naturalist.................. 1522..1607
Aldus. *See* Manutius................................ 1449..1515
Aleander, Jerome. Cardinal. Opponent of Luther.... 1480..1542
Aleander, Jerome, nephew. *The Younger.* Scholar and
    Antiquary....................................... 1574..1629
Alegambe, Philip. Jesuit. (*Bibl. Scriptorum Soc. Jesu*) 1592..1652
Aleman, Louis. Cardinal. Abp. of Arles. Statesman... 1390..1450
Aleman, Matthew. Span. Writ. (*Guzman d'Alfarache*). fl. 16th c.
Alemand, Lewis Aug., of Grenoble. Advocate and Writ. 1653..1728
Alembert d'. *See* D'Alembert. Mathematician........ 1717..1783
Alen, or Olen, John van. Dutch Painter.............. 1651..1698
Alençon, Charles de Valois, Count of; fell at Crecy ..... — ..1346
Alençon, Charles, Duke of, and of Anjou. Suitor of Eliz.. 1489..1584
Alençon, John de Valois, First Duke of; fell at Agincourt 1385..1415
Aleni, Thomas. Italian Painter.................... 1500..1560
Alenio, Julius. Jesuit Missionary to China .... 1582..1649
Aleotti, John Baptist. Italian Architect................ 1546..1636
Aler, Paul. Jesuit. (*Gradus ad Parnassum*) .... 1656..1727
Ales, or Alesius, Alexander. Scottish Protestant Divine. 1500..1565
Alesio, Matthew Peter d'. Roman Painter and Engraver — ..1600
Alessi, Galeas. Architect........................ 1500..1572
Aletino, Benedict. Anti-Cartesian Philosopher......... — ..1719
Alexander. Tyrant of Pheræ .... — B.C.359
Alexander the Great. K. Maced. (336–23). Life by Q.
    Curtius; Jul. Valerius, 1589; Lesfargues, 1639; Gau-
    denzio, 1645; Lehmann, 1667; Fessler, 1797; Müller,
    1830; Archd. John Williams, 1830; Droysen, 1833;
    Pfizer, 1845..................................... 356B.C.323
Alexander Balas. King of Syria (150–146)........... — B.C.146
Alexander Jannæus. King of the Jews (104–77) ...... — B.C. 77
Alexander. King of the Jews; son of Aristobulus II..... — B.C. 49
Alexander Severus. Emperor of Rome (222–235) ..... 205.. 235
Alexander I. Pope (109–119)....................... — .. 119
Alexander II. (1061–73.) *Anselm de Badage* .... — ..1073
Alexander III. (1159–81.)......................... — ..1181
Alexander IV. (1254–61.) *Raynald,* or *Roland*........ — ..1261
Alexander V. (1409–10.) *Peter Filargo* .... 1339?.1410
Alexander VI. (1492–1503.) *Borgia.* Life by J. Burchard,
    1697; Alex. Gordon, 1729; Masse, 1830; Delafontaine,
    1844..1430–1..1503
Alexander VII. (1655–67.) Life by Pallavicino, 1840. 1599..1667
Alexander VIII. (1689–91.) *Peter Ottobon* .... 1610..1691
Alexander I. King of Scotland (1107–24.) *The Fierce.* — ..1124
Alexander II. (1214–1249.) .... 1198..1249
Alexander III. (1249–85.) .... 1241..1285
Alexander Jagellon. King of Poland (1501–6) .... 1461..1506
Alexander Nevskoi, St. Grand Duke of Russia....... 1218?.1263
Alexander I. Emp. Russia (1801–25). Life by Rumpf,
    1814; Cousin d'Avallon, 1826 ; Leidenfrost, 1826 ;

BORN. DIED.

. Egron, 1826; Rabbe, 1826; Henry Evans Lloyd, 1826;
Morgenstern, 1827; Broecker, 1827; Choiseul-Gouffier,
1829; Voigt, 1830; Schischkoff, 1832................. 1777..1825
Alexander. Bishop of Jerusalem (211?–251)........... — .. 251
Alexander. Bp. of Alexandria (312?–25?); Opp. of Arius — .. 326
Alexander. Bishop of Lincoln (1123–47)............. — ..1147
Alexander, of Paris. Poet. Inventor of "Alexandriue"
Measure. (*Alexander the Great*)................... fl. 12th c.
Alexander. English Abbot, Envoy, and Writer........ — ..1217?
Alexander, Archibald. American Divine.............: 1772..1851
Alexander, Benedictus, of Verona. Anatomist......... fl. 1503
Alexander, Massarias, of Vicenza. Medical Writer..... — ..1598
Alexander, Nich., of St. Maur. Med. and Bot. Writer... 1654..1728
Alexander, Noel, or Natalis. Dominican Church Hist... 1639..1724
Alexander, Thomas. Earl of Selkirk. Political Writer. — ..1820
Alexander, Wm., Earl *of Stirling*. Officer and Astron. 1726..1783
Alexander, Sir Wm. E., of Stirling. Statesman and Poet 1580?.1640
Alexander, ab Alexandro. Lawyer. (*Genial. Dierum*) 1461..1523
Alexander of Hales. *Irrefragable Doctor* .... — ..1245
Alexander Neckam, or Nequam. Abbot of Exeter..... — ..1227
Alexander Trallianus. Greek Physician .... fl. 6th c.
Alexandrini de Neustain, Julius. Medical Writer .... 1506..1590
Alexis. Piedmontese Traveler. (*De Secretis*) .... — ..1465?
Alexis. *Michaelovitch*. Czar of Russia (1645–76)....... 1630..1676
Alexis. *Petrovitch*. Czar of Russia .... 1690..1718
Alexis del Arco. Spanish Portrait-Painter .... 1625..1700
Alexius I., Comnenus. Emperor. Life by A. Comnena. 1048..1118
Alexius II., Comnenus. *Porphyrogenitus*. Eastern Em-
peror (1180–83)................................... 1167..1183
Alexius III., Angelus Comnenus. (1195–1203) .... —aft.1210
Alexius IV., Angelus .... 1190?.1204
Alexius V., Ducas. *Murtzuffle*. (1204)............... — ..1204
Aleyn, Charles. Historical Poet .... — ..1640?
Alfani, Horatius. Italian Painter.............#........ 1530?.1583
Alfarabius. Arabian Philosopher .... —.. 950
Alfaroy Gamon, John de. Spanish Painter .... 1640..1680
Alfieri, Victor. Italian Poet. Life by himself; Zezou, 1835 1749..1803
Alfonso. *See* Alphonso'.
Alford, Michael. *Griffith*. Jesuit Missionary in England.
(*Britannia Illustrata*)........................... 1587..1652
Alfragan. *The Calculator*. Arabian Astronomer....... — .. 820
Alfrago, Andrew. Italian Physician .... — ..1520
Alfred. King of Northumbria (686–705).............. — .. 705
Alfred the Great. Life by Asser; Robert Powell, 1634;
Spelman, 1678; A. Bicknell, 1777; Stolberg, 1815; Dr.
Pauli; Giles (*Harmony of the Chroniclers of Alfred*) .. 849.. 901
Alfred. Monk of Malmesbury; Bp. of Crediton. Writer fl. 10th c.
Alfred, or Alured, of Beverley. Historian .... — ..1126?
Alfred, or Alured. *Anglicus* and *The Philosopher*........ — ..1270
Alfric. Abp. of Cant. (994–1006). *Abbas* or *Grammaticus*) — ..1006
Alfric. Archbishop of York (1023–51). Writer........ — ..1051
Algardi, Alexander. Sculptor and Architect .... 1598?.1654
Algarotti, Francis. Ital. Critic and Philosophical Writer 1712..1764
Alghalib-Billah. First Moorish King of Granada ...... 1195..1273

BORN. DIED.

Alghazzal. Arabian Philosopher .... 1058..1111
Alghisi, Francis, of Brescia. Musical Composer......... 1666..1733
Alghisi, Thomas. Italian Lithotomist .... 1669..1713
Alhazel, or **Alhazen.** Arabian Astronomer and Optician — ..1038
Ali. Son-in-law of Mahomet. Fourth Caliph (1655-61).. 602?. 661
Ali-bassa. Ottoman General .... 1594?.1663
Alibaud, Louis. Fr. Fanatic who attempt. life of L. Philippe 1810..1836
Ali Beg, or **Beigh.** Dragoman and Translator of Bible.. — ..1675
Ali Bey. Adventurer. Ruler of Egypt (1766-73) ...... 1728..1773
Ali Bey. *See* Badia. Spanish Traveler and Projector .. 1766..1818
Ali Pasha. Viziir of Janina. Life by Pouqueville, 1820;
    Beauchamps, 1822; Alcaini, 1823; Davenport, 1837 ... 1741?.1822
Alibrandi, Jerome. Sicilian Painter .;.............. 1470..1524
Alison, Rev. Archibald. (*Essays on Taste*)............. 1757..1839
Alison, Wm. Pulteney, M.D., of Edinb. Medical Writer. 1770..1859
Allainval, Leonor Soulas d'. French Dramatic Poet.... — ..1753
Allam, Andrew, of Oxford. Writer .... 1655..1685
Allamand, John Nich. Sebastian. French Naturalist.... 1713..1787
Allan, David. Portrait and Historical Painter .... 1744..1796
Allan, George. Antiquary .... — ..1800
Allan, Thomas. Mathematician and Antiquary......... 1542..1632
Allan, Sir William. Historical Painter .... 1782..1850
Allard, Guy. French Writer .... 1645..1716
Allard, John Francis. French General................. 1785..1839?
Allard, Peter Gilbert Leroi Baron d'. Fr. Political Econ. 1749..1809
Allardice, Robert Barclay. Scottish Pedestrian .... 1779..1854
Allart, Mary Gay. French Authoress................. 1750..1821
Allatius, or **Allacci, Leo.** Wr. at Rome. (*Apes Urbanæ*). 1586..1669
Allegrain, Christopher Gabriel. French Sculptor....... 1711..1795
Allegri, Antonio. *Correggio.* Italian Painter......... 1494..1534
Allegri, Gregory. Musical Composer. (*Miserere*)....... 1580?.1652
Allein, Joseph. (*Alarm.*) Life by Stanford; Baxter..... 1633..1668
Allein, Richard. Ejected Nonconf. Div. (*Vindiciæ Pietatis*) 1611..1681
Allein, Wm., son. Ejected Nonconformist. (*Millennium*) 1623..1677
Allemand, Zachary Jas. Thos. French Vice-Admiral ... 1762..1826
Allen, Alexander. Philologist .... 1814..1842
Allen, Benjamin, M.D. Writer on Medicinal Waters.... fl. 1700
Allen, Ethan. American Colonel ....‹.......... 1737..1789
Allen, Henry. American Religious Enthusiast .... 1748..1784
Allen, John. Archbishop of Dublin. Canonist; murdered 1476?.1534
Allen, John, M.D. (*Synopsis Medicinæ Practicæ*)........ — ..1741
Allen, John. Dissenting Theologian .... 1771..1839
Allen, John, M.D. Historical Writer. (*Royal Prerogative*) 1771..1843
Allen, Joseph W. Landscape-Painter.................. 1803..1852
Allen, Paul. American Journalist and Author .... 1775..1826
Allen, Richard. Theologian. (*Biographia Ecclesiastica*) — ..1717
Allen, Solomon. American Revolutionary Patriot ...... 1751..1821
Allen, or **Allan, Thomas.** Mathematician and Antiquary 1542..1632
Allen, Thomas. Fellow of Eton; Theological Critic...... 1573..1636
Allen, Sir Thomas. Admiral fl.1648-78
Allen, Thomas. Theologian. (*Practice of a Holy Life*) 1682..1755
Allen, Thomas. Antiquary. (*Antiquities of London*) ... 1803..1833
Allen, or **Alanus, Wm.** Cardinal. Archbishop of Mechlin.
    Life by Fitz-Herbert, 1608; London, 3 vols. 8vo, 1846 . 1532..1594

BORN. DIED.

Allen, William. Chemical Philosopher and Philanthropist 1770..1843
Allen, William Henry. American Naval Officer........ 1784..1813
Allent, Peter Alexander Joseph. French General....... 1772..1837
Allerstain, Aug. German Jesuit Missionary to China.. 1700?.1777?
Allestry, or Allestree, Rd. Royalist, Soldier, and Divine. 1619..1681
Allestry, Jacob. English Poet....................... — ..1686
Alletz, Peter Edw. French Writer.................... 1798..1850
Alletz, Pons Augustin. French Writer............... 1703?.1785
Alley, Wm. Bp. of Exeter; Divine and Transl. of Bible.. — ..1570
Alleyn, Edw. Founder of Dulwich Coll. Life by Collier 1566..1626
Allgaier, John. Chess-Player and Writer............. — ..1826
Allingham, John Till. Dramatist.................... fl. 1800?
Allioni, Charles. Italian Physician and Medical Writer . 1725..1804
Allix, Peter, D.D. Divine........................... 1641..1717
Alloisi, Balthasar, of Bologna. Galanino. Painter ..... 1578..1638
Allori, Alexander. Bronzino. Florentine Painter....... 1535..1607
Allori, Christopher, son. Bronzino. Painter........... 1577..1619
Allston, Washington. American Painter and Poet...... 1779..1843
Almagro, Diego de. Companion of Pizarro in Peru .... 1463..1536
Almain, James. French Scholastic Divine .... — ..1515
Almamoun. Caliph of Bagdad (814–33). Philos. & Astron. 786.. 833
Almansor, Abu Amer. Caliph of Cordova (976–1002)... 939..1002
Almansor, Abu Jafar. Sec. Abbaside Caliph (754–75).. 712?. 775
Almeida, Apollinarius d'. Port. Missionary to Ethiopia.. 1587..1638
Almeida, Francis. First Portuguese Viceroy in India ... — ..1510
Almeida, Lawrence, son. Navigator.................. — ..1508
Almeida, Manuel d'. Portuguese Missionary to Indies .. 1580..1646
Almeloveen, Theodore Janssen van. Medical Writer... 1657..1712
Almendingen, Ludwig Harscher von. German Jurist.. 1766..1827
Alméras, Louis. French General..................... 1768..1828
Almici, Peter Camillus. Italian Classical Scholar ...... 1714..1779
Almon, John. Political Writer .... 1738?.1805
Aloaddin. Old Man of the Mountains. Chief of the Assass. 1211.. —
Alpago, Andrew. Italian Physician.................. — ..1555
Alphen, Jerome van. Dutch Poet, Theol., Jurist, and Hist.1746..1803
Alp Arslan. Second Sultan of the Seljuk Turks .... 1030?.1072
Alphanus, Benedict. Abp. of Palermo. Phys. and Poet. — ..1086
Alphege, or Elphege, St. Archbishop of Canterbury.... 954?.1012
Alphonso I. King of Asturias (739–57). The Catholic. 693.. 757
Alphonso II. of Astur. and Leon (791–842). The Chaste 758.. 842
Alphonso III. of Astur. and Leon (866–912). The Great 848.. 912
Alphonso IV. of Leon (924–927.) The Monk .... — .. 932
Alphonso V. of Leon (999–1028)..................... 994..1028
Alphonso VI.of Leon (1066–1109); I. of Castile. The Brave 1030..1109
Alphonso VII. (consort of Queen Urraque); not gen-
    erally reckoned................................ — ..1134
Alphonso VII. (or VIII.) of Leon (1126–57); II. of
    Castile. Raymond............................... 1106..1157
Alphonso VIII. (or IX.) of Leon (1158–1214); III. of
    Castile. The Noble and The Good................. 1155..1214
Alphonso X. (or IX.) of Leon (1252–85); IV. of Castile.
    The Wise and The Astronomer.................... 1203..1284
Alphonso XI. of Leon (1327–50); V. of Castile. The
    Avenger .... 1310..1350

BORN. DIED.

Alphonso I. of Aragon (1104–34). *The Battler*....... — ..1134
Alphonso II. of Aragon (1162–96)................... 1152..1196
Alphonso III. of Aragon (1285–91)................... 1265..1291
Alphonso IV. of Aragon (1327–36) .... 1299..1336
Alphonso V. of Aragon (1416–58); I. of Naples. *The*
    Magnanimous. Life by Becatelli, 1455. .... 1385..1458
Alphonso I. of Portugal (1137–85). *Henriquez*......... 1094..1185
Alphonso II. (1212–23.) *The Fat*.................... 1185..1223
Alphonso III. (1248–79.)........................... 1210..1279
Alphonso IV. (1324–57.) *The Brave*............... 1290..1357
Alphonso V. (1438–81.) *The African*............. 1432..1481
Alphonso VI. (1656–83)........................... 1643..1683
Alphonso I. of Naples (1416–58); V. of Aragon......... 1385..1458
Alphonso II. of Naples (1494–95)................... 1448..1495
Alphonsus, Tostatus. Spanish Bishop and Theologian. 1420..1445
Alpini, Prosper. Venetian Phys. (*De Plantis Exoticis*).. 1553?.1617
Alsop, Anthony. Poet and Miscellaneous Writer....... — ..1727
Alsop, Richard. American Writer................... 1761..1815
Alsop, Vincent. Ejected Nonconformist. (*Anti Sozzo*).. — ..1703
Alsted, John Henry. Ger. Protestant Div. and Philos.. 1588..1638
Alston, Chas., M.D. Scottish Writ. on Bot. and Medicine. 1683..1760
Alstroemer, Jonas. Swedish Public Benefactor....... 1685..1761
Altdorfer, or Altorf, Albert. Ger. Engrav. and Painter. 1488..1538
Alten, Charles Augustus, Count. Hanoverian General... 1764..1840
Alter, Francis Charles. German Jesuit and Critic..... 1749..1804
Althamerus, Andr., of Nuremberg. Reform. in Switz.. 1498..1540?
Althorp, John Chas., Visct., and Earl Spencer. Statesm. 1782..1845
Althusen, John. German Civilian. (*Politics*)......... 1557..1638
Altilio, Gabriel. Neapolitan Latin Poet............. 1440?.1501?
Alting, Henry. German Protestant Divine........... 1583..1644
Alting, James, son. Professor at Groningen........... 1618..1679
Alting, Menson. (*Description of the Low Countries*).... 1637..1713
Alton, Jos. Wm. Edw. d'. Ger. Archæol. and Nat...... 1772..1840
Altorf, Albert. Painter and Engraver................. 1488..1538
Altovitis, Marseille d'. Florentine Poetess at Marseilles. 1550..1606
Alunno, Nich. Italian Painter. (fl. 15th c.)............ —aft.1500
Alured, or Alred, of Beverly. Historian.......... — ..1126?
Alva, Duke of. *See* Alvarez. L. by De Rustant, 1750.. 1508..1582
Alvarado, Pet. de. Sp. Adventurer; Companion of Cortès — ..1541
Alvarez de Luna. Castilian Statesman; beheaded.... 1388?.1453
Alvarez, Diego. Spanish Dominican; Polemical Divine. — ..1635
Alvarez, Emanuel. Port. Jesuit (*De Institut. Grammat.*) 1526..1582
Alvarez, Ferd., Duke of Alva, *q. v.* Sp. Gen. in Netherl. 1505..1582
Alvarez, Francis. Portuguese Writer on Abyssinia..... 1515..1540?
Alvarez, Gomez. Spanish Poet...................... 1488..1538
Alvarez, Joseph. Spanish Sculptor.................. 1768..1830
Alvarez, Manuel. *El Griego.* Spanish Sculptor....... 1727..1797
Alvarotto, James of Padua. (*In Libros Feudorum*).... 1385..1453
Alvay Astorga, Peter d'. Span. Franciscan; Traveler. — ..1667
Alvensleben, Philip Chas., Count of. Diplom. and Hist. 1745..1802
Alviano, Bartholomew. Venetian General .... 1455..1515
Alypius, of Alexandria. (*Introduction to Music*)........ fl. ti. Julian
Amadeus V. Count of Savoy (1285–1323). *The Great.* 1249..1323
Amadeus VI. (1343–83)............................. 1334..1383

| | BORN. | DIED. |

Amadeus VII. (1383–91.) *The Red* .... 1360..1391
Amadeus VIII. (1391–1449.) *The Pacific* .... 1383..1451
Amadeus IX. Count or Duke of Savoy (1465–72)...... 1435..1472
Amaja, or Amaya, Francis. Spanish Civilian......... — ..1640?
Amalaric. King of the Visigoths (526–31)............ 502.. 531
Amalarius Symphosius, of Metz. Eccles. Antiquary.. —.. 837
Amalasontha. Queen of the Goths in Italy........... 498?. 535
Amalie. *See* Amelia.
Amalric, Arnold. Abp. of Narbonne. Albigens. Crusader — ..1225
Amalteo, Cornelius. Physician and Poet............. 1530?.1603
Amalteo, Jerome, br. Italian Physician and Poet....... 1506..1574
Amalteo, J. Bapt., br. Papal Secretary and Poet....... 1525..1573
Amalteo, Pomponio. Venetian Painter................. 1505.. —
Amama, Sixtinus. Dutch Orientalist.................... 1593..1629
Aman, John. German Architect........................ 1765..1834
Amand, St. Bp. of Maestricht; Apostle of the Netherl.. 589.. 679
Amand, Mark Anthony Gerard, St. *See* St. Amand.... 1594..1661
Amaseo, Romulus. Italian Scholar.................... 1489..1552
Amati, Pasquaile. Italian Antiquary .... 1716..1796
Amato, John Anthony d'. Neapolitan Painter....... 1475..1555
Amato, John Anth. d', neph. *The Younger.* Neapol. Pa. 1535..1598
Amaury I. King of Jerusalem (1162–73)............. 1136?.1173
Amaury II. King of Jerusalem and Cyprus (1194–1205). — ..1205
Amaya, Francis. Spanish Civilian.................... — ..1640?
Amberger, Christopher, of Nuremb. Pa. and Engraver. 1490..1569?
Amboise, Francis d'. French Lawyer and Poet; Writer.. 1550..1620
Amboise, George d'. Cardinal. *See* D'Amboise...... 1460..1510
Ambrogi, Dominic. *Menechino del Brizio.* Painter..... — ..1660?
Ambrogio, Theseus. Italian Orientalist.............. 1469..1540
Ambrose, Isaac. Nonconf. Divine. (*Looking unto Jesus*). — ..1664
Ambrose, St. Bp. Milan (374–97). Life by Garcæus,
   1571; Godfrey Hermant; Silbert, 1841............. 340?. 397
Ambrose de Lombez. (*Lettres Spirituelles*) .... 1708..1778
Ambrosini, Bartholomew, of Bologna. Phys. and Bot.. — ..1657
Ambrosius, Aurelianus. British King .... — .. 508?
Ambrosius, Catharinus Politus. Neapolitan Divine..... — ..1552
Ameilhon, Hubert Pascal. (*Commerce of the Egyptians*). 1730..1811
Amelia, Anna. Princess of Prussia. Musical Composer. 1723..1787
Amelia. Duchess of Saxe-Weimar. Patroness of Letters. 1739..1807
Amelia. Princess, daughter of George III............ 1783..1810
Amelot de la Houssaye, Abrah. Nich. Writer....... 1634..1706
Amelotte, Denis. Fr. Biblical Translator and Comment. 1606..1678
Amelunghi, Jerome. *Il Gobbo di Pisa.* (*La Gigantea*).. fl. 547
Amerbach, John. Learned Printer at Basle........... — ..1515
Amerbach, Vitus. Classical Scholar at Ingoldstadt.... 1487..1557?
Americus Vespucius. Navigator. Life by Bandini,
   1745; Lester and Foster, 1846...... .... 1451..1516
Ames, Fisher. American Politician .... 1758..1808
Ames, Joseph. (*Typographical Antiquities*).......... 1689..1759
Ames, William. Polem. Divine. (*Medulla Theologica*). 1576..1633
Amherst, Jeffery, Lord. Field-Marshal.............. 1717..1797
Amherst, William Pitt, Second Lord, First Earl, nephew.
   Governor-General of India (1823–27)............. 1773..1857
Amhurst, Nich. Poet and Polit. Writer. (*Craftsman*). 1706?.1742

BORN. DIED.

Amici, John Baptist. Italian Astronomer.............. 1784..1863
Amico, Antonine, of Palermo. (*Siciliæ Regum Annales*). — ..1641
Amiconi, or Amigoni, James. Venetian Painter....... 1675..1752
Amidano, Pomponio. Historical Painter............ —aft.1595
Amiot, Joseph. French Jesuit Missionary to China..... 1718..1794
Amling, Charles Gustavus. German Pa. and Engraver. 1651..1701
Amman, John Conrad. Physician for Deaf and Dumb.. 1669..1730?
Amman, John, son. Physician and Botanist........... 1707..1741
Amman, Justus, of Zurich. Engraver and Painter...... 1539..1591
Amman, Paul, of Leipsic. Medical and Botanical Writer. 1634..1691
Ammanate, Barthol. of Florence. Architect and Sculp.. 1511..1592?
Ammanate, Laura Battiferri, wife. Poetess............ 1513..1589
Ammianus Marcellinus. Soldier and Historian...... — .. 390?
Ammirato, Scipio. (*History of Florence*).......... 1531..1601
Ammon, Andrew. Ital. Latin Poet. Sec. to Henry VIII.. 1477..1517
Ammon, Christopher Frederick. German Theologian.. 1766..1820
Ammonius Saccas. Platonist of Alexandria. Life
  by Debaut, 1836................................... 160?. 243
Amontons, William. French Math. and Inventor...... 1663..1705
Amort, Eusebius. Bavarian Theologian.............. 1692..1775
Amory, Thos., D.D. Dissenting Divine and Biographer. 1701..1774
Amory, Thomas. Humorous Writer. (*John Buncle*)... 1619 ..1788
Ampère, Andrew Mary. Scientific Writer............. 1775..1836
Ampère, John James Anthony. Writer.............. 1800?.1864
Amrou. Saracen Conqueror of Egypt................. 600?.. 663
Amsdorf, Nicholas. Lutheran Divine............... 1483..1565
Amsler, Samuel. German Engraver................... 1791..1849
Amurath, or Morad, or Murad, I. Turk. Sultan (1360–89). 1319..1389
Amurath II. (1422–51)............................. 1404..1451
Amurath III. (1574–95)............................ 1544..1595
Amurath IV. (1023–40)............................. 1610?.1640
Amyn Ahmed. *El Razy.* Per.Wri.(*The Seven Climates*) fl. 17th c.
Amyot, James. Bishop of Auxerre. Savant.......... 1513..1593
Amyot, or Amiot, Joseph. French Jesuit Missionary.... 1718..1794
Amyraut, Moses. French Protestant Theologian........ 1596..1664
Anacharsis. Scythian Traveler and Philosopher........ fl. 594 B.C.
Anacletus. Bishop of Rome (78–91)................ — .. 91
Anacletus. Antipope (1130). *Peter de Léon*........... — ..1138
Anacreon. Greek Lyric Poet. Life by Joshua Barnes,
  1721; Axelson, 1755............................ 563?B.C.478?
Anastasius I. East. Emp. (491–518). *Silentiarius*..... 430 .. 518
Anastasius II. (713–19)............................ — .. 721
Anastasius I. Pope (398–401)....................... — .. 401
Anastasius II. (496–98)............................ — .. 498
Anastasius III. (911–13)........................... — .. 913
Anastasius IV. (1153–54.) *Conrad* .... — ..1154
Anastasius. Patriarch of Constantinople .... — .. 753
Anastasius, St. *Astric.* Apostle of the Hungarians.... 954..1044
Anaxagoras. Greek Philosopher...................... 500 B.C.428
Anaximander, of Miletus. Greek Philosopher......... 610 B.C.547
Ancharano, Peter. Civilian and Canonist.............. 1350?.1417?
Anchieta, Jos. Portug. Jesuit. *Apostle of N. World.*
  L. by Berettari, 1617; Vasconcellos, 1672; Oddi, 1824.. 1533..1597
Ancillon, Charles. Protestant Writer .... 1659..1715

BORN. DIED.

Ancillon, David. French Theologian................... 1617..1692
Ancillon, John Peter Fred. Pruss. Statesman and Hist.. 1766..1837
Ancourt, Florence Carton d'. Fr. Comic Actor & Writer. 1661..1726
Ancre, Concino Concini, Marshal d'.................... — ..1617
Ancus Marcius. Fourth king of Rome................ —B.C.614
Anderson, Adam. Writer on Trade .... 1692..1765
Anderson, Alexander. Scottish Mathematician .... 1582?. —
Anderson, Alexander. Naturalist.................... — ..1813
•Anderson, Sir Edmund. Lord Chief Justice. (*Reports*).. 1531?.1605
Anderson, George. Oriental Traveler.............. 1600?.1675?
Anderson, George. Writer on India................. 1760..1796
Anderson, George. Mathematician.................. 1760..1806
Anderson, James. Scotch Antiquary and Historian.... 1662..1728
Anderson, James, L.L.D. Agricultural Writer .... 1739..1808
Anderson, James, M.D. Naturalist. (*Cochineal*)....... — ..1809?
Anderson, John, of Hamburg. (*Nat. Hist. of Greenland*) 1674..1743
Anderson, John. Scottish Presbyterian Writer .... 1678?.1720
Anderson, John. ⋅ Prof. at Glasgow. Found. of Institut. 1726..1796
Anderson, John. Scottish Surgeon. (*House of Hamilton*) 1786..1832
Anderson, Lawrence. Swedish Reformer .... — ..1552
Anderson, Robert, M.D. Critic and Biographical Writer 1750..1830
Anderson, Robert. The Cumbrian Poet.............. 1770..1833
Anderson, Walter. Scottish Writer. (*Hist. of France*) 1720?.1800
Andersson, Charles John. Swedish African Explorer .. — ..1856
Anderton, Henry. English Hist. and Portrait Painter .. — ..1665?
Andier des Rochers, John. French Engraver .... — ..1741
Andrada. *See* D'Andrada, Anthony .... 1580?.1634
André. *See* Andrea, Andreæ, Andreas, Andrew.
André, Major John. Executed in American War....... 1751..1780
André, John. German Musical Composer ....'.. 1741..1799
André, Yves Mary. Fr. Jesuit. (*Essay on the Beautiful*) 1675..1764
Andrea. *See* André, Andreæ, Andreas, Andrew.
Andrea, Caval Canti. Italian Writer.................. — ..1672
Andrea di Luigi, of Aloisi. *L'Ingegno*............... 1450?.1520
Andrea da Pisa. Sculptor and Architect .... 1270..1345
Andrea del Sarto. Painter......................... 1488..1530
Andreæ. *See* André, Andrea, Andreas, Andrew.
Andreæ, John Gerhard Reinhard, of Hanover. Naturalist 1724..1793
Andreæ, John Valentine.. (*Mythologiæ Christianæ*).... 1586..1664
Andreæ, Tobias, of Groningen. Cartesian Philosopher.. 1604..1676
Andreæ, Tobias. Cartesian Philosopher.............. 1633..1685
Andreani, Andrew, of Mantua. Engraver .... 1540..1623
Andreas, *See* André, Andrea, Andreæ, Andrew.
Andreas, Jas. German Reformer. Life by J. V. Andreas 1528..1590
Andreas, John. Canonist at Bologna................. 1275?.1348
Andreas, Valerius. *Desselius*. Scholar of Brabant..... 1588..1656
Andreini, Francis, of Pistoia. Comic Writer .... — ..1616
Andreini, Isabella, wife. Comic Writer and Improvisatore 1562..1604
Andreini, J. Baptista. Poet and Dramatist. (*L'Adamo*) 1578?.1652?
Andrelinus, Publius Faustus. Latin Poet .... — ..1518
Andréossi, Anthony Francis, Ct. Fr. Officer and Diplom. 1761..1828
Andrew. *See* André, Andrea, Andreæ, Andreas.
Andrew I. King of Hungary (1047–61)............... — ..1061
Andrew II. (1204–35.) *Hierosolymitan* .... 1175?.1235

BORN. DIED.

Andrew III. (1290–1301.) *Venetian*.............. — ..1301
Andrew, of Pisa. Sculptor and Architect............ 1270..1345
Andrew, John, of Ratisbon. *Andreas Magister.* Hist.. fl. 1410
Andrews, James Pettit. Miscellaneous Writer........ 1737..1797
Andrews, Lancelot. Bishop of Winchester. Life by
    Isaacson; A. T. Russell.......................... 1555..1626
Andrews, Miles Peter. Dramatic Writer.............. — ..1814
Andrieu, Bertrand. French Medallic Engraver .... 1761..1822
Andrieux, Francis Wm. John Stanislaus. French Author 1759..1833
Andronicus, Livius. Latin Dramatic Poet............. —B.C.221?
Andronicus I. Comnenus. East. Emp. (1163–1185) . 1110..1185
Andronicus II. Palæologus. (1282–1328.) *Elder* ... 1260..1332
Andronicus III. Palæologus. (1328–41.) *Younger* .1296..1341
Andros, Sir Edmund. Colonial Governor of New York,
    New England, and Virginia........................ 1637..1714
Androuet du Cerceau, James. French Architect ..... — ..1592
Andry, Nicholas. (*Bois-Regard.*) French Medical Writer 1658..1742
Anel, Dominic, of Savoy. Medical Writer.......·..... 1679?.1730?
Anesi, Paul. Florentine Painter.................... — ..1750?
Aneurin, British Poet and Chieftain. (*Odes of the Months*) .. 570?
Angarville, Richard. *De Bury.* Bishop of Durham;
    Lord Chancellor. Life by S. Gibson .... 1287?.1345
Ange de St. Joseph. *Joseph Labrosse.* Mission. to Persia 1636..1697
Ange de St. Rosalie. Fr. Hist. (*L'État de la France*) 1655..1726
Angeli, Bonaventura, of Parma. Historian........... 1525?.1576
Angeli, or Angelio, Peter. Latin Poet............... 1517..1596
Angeli, Philip d'. *Napoletano.* Artist .... 1600..1640
Angelico. *See* Fiesole. Painter.................... 1387..1455
Angelis, Dominic de............................... 1675..1719
Angelis, Peter. Artist.............................. 1685..1734
Angelo, Fioriozzola. Florentine Poet .... — ..1548
Angelo. *See* Michael Angelo...................... 1474..1564
Angelo, Policiano. Italian Writer. (*Rusticus*).......... 1454.. —
Angeloni, Francis. (*Augustan History by Medals*) ...... — ..1652
Angeloni, Louis. Italian Politician and Writer .... 1758?.1842
Angelus, Christopher. Greek Refugee in Eng. Scholar. — ..1638
Angennes, Julia d', of Paris. *Artenice* .... 1607?.1671
Angerstein, John Julius. Collector of Paintings........ 1735..1822
Angier, Sam. Ejected Nonconf. Div. (*Help to Better Hearts*) 1605?.1677
Angilbert, or Engilbert, St. Statesman and Poet....... — .. 814
Angiolotto, or Giotto. Painter...................... 1276..1336
Anglesey, Arth. Annesley, Earl of. (*Troubles of Ireland*) 1614..1686
Anglesey, H. W. Paget, Marquess of. Field Marshal... 1768..1854
Anglus, Thomas. *Albius,* or *White.* R. Cath. Divine ... 1582..1676
Angoulême, Charles de Valois, Duke d', son of Charles
    IX. Commander.................................. 1573..1650
Angoulême, Maria Theresa Charlotte, Duchess d'.
    Madame Royale, dau. of Louis XVI. L. by Mrs.Romer 1778..1851
Anguier, Francis. French Sculptor ...., 1604..1669
Anguier, Michael, brother. Sculptor .... 1612..1686
Anguillara, John Andrew dell'. Italian Poet ....1517?aft.1564
Anguillara, Louis. Italian Botanist.................. — ..1570
Anguisciola, Sophonisba, of Cremona. Painter........ 1533?.1620?
Anicetus. Bishop of Rome (157?–161)................ — .. 161

BORN. DIED.

Anich, Peter, of Inspruck. Astronomer and Mechan..... 1723..1766
Aniello. *See* Masaniello................................. 1623..1646
Ankarström, J. Jacob. Assass. of Gustavus III. of Swed. 1761..1792
Anna Comnena. Byzantine Historian. (*Alexiad*) .... 1083..1148
Anna Ivanowna. Empress of Russia................. 1693..1740
Annand, William. Scottish Episcopal Divine.......... 1633..1689
Annat, Francis. French Jesuit; Anti-Jansenist......... 1590..1670
Anne, of Cyprus. Duchess of Savoy.................. — ..1462
Anne, of Brittany. Q. of France. Life by Costello, 1855 1476..1514
Anne, of Beaujeu, daughter of Louis XI............... 1462?.1522
Anne, of Hungary. Wife of Ferdinand of Austria....... 1503..1547
Anne, of Cleves. Queen of Henry VIII............... 1516..1557
Anne, of Denmark. Queen of James I............... 1574..1619
Anne, of Austria, wife of Louis XIII. of France. Life by
   Motteville; P. Pelisson-Fontanier................ 1602..1666
Anne, Queen of England. Life by Oldmixon, 1721;
   Boyer, 1722; Chamberlen, 1738.................... 1664..1714
Annebaut, Claude d'. *Marshal and Admiral of France.. — ..1552
Annesley, Arthur. E. of Anglesey. Statesm. and Writer 1614..1686
Annesley, Samuel. Ejected Nonconformist Divine...... 1620?.1696
Annett, Peter. Deistical Writer. (*Free Enquirer*)..... — ..1778
Annius, or John Nanni, of Viterbo. Literary Impostor.. 1432?.1502
Anquetil Duperron, Louis Peter. Historian.......... 1723..1808
Anquetil Duperron, Abr. Hyacinthe. Orientalist..... 1731..1805
Ansaldi, Casto Innocent. Italian Theologian.......... 1710..1779
Ansaloni, Giordano. Dominican Missionary in Japan ... — ..1634
Anscarius, or Ansgar. Bishop of Hamburg. Missionary
   to Scandinavia .... 801.. 864
Anselm, St. Bishop of Lucca. (*Contra Guibertum*)...... 1036..1086
Anselm, Apb. Canterb. (1093–1109). Life by Eadmer;
   F. R. Hasse, tr. by Turner, 1850; Möhler, tr. by Cox;
   Chas. de Remusat; W. and M. Wilks, 1862.......... 1033..1109
Anselm, of Laon. *Doctor Scholasticus.* Commentator... 1050?.1117
Anselme, Father. Hist. (*Geneal. of House of France*)... 1625..1694
Anselme, Anthony. French Preacher and Poet........ 1652..1737
Anselmi, Michael Angelo. Painter .... 1491..1554
Anson, Geo., Lord. Commodore. L. by Sir J. Barrow, 1838 1697..1762
Anspach, Elizb., Lady Craven, Margravine of. L. by self. 1750..1828
Anstey, Christopher. Poet. (*New Bath Guide*.) Life by
   J. Anstey, 1808................................... 1724..1805
Anstis, John, M.P. Garter King-at-Arms.............. 1669..1744
Anstis, John, son. Garter King-at-Arms .... 1708?.1754
Anstruther, Sir John. Chief Justice of Bengal .... 1753..1811
Antar. Arabian Chief and Poet....................... fl. 500?
Antelmi, Joseph. Fr. Antiq. and Writer on Church His. 1648..1697
Antesignanus, Peter. Fr. Class. Schol. and Grammarian fl. 1556
Anthemius. Roman Emperor of the West (467–72) .... — .. 472
Anthemius. Architect and Philos. at Constantinople ... — .. 534
Anthon, John. American Jurist....................... 1784..1863
Anthony, St., the Great. Founder of Monachism .... 251.. 356
Anthony, of Padua. Theologian and Preacher........ 1195..1231
Anthony, of Palermo. *Panormita. See* Beccadelli...... 1394..1471
Anthony, or Antonello, of Messina. Italian Painter..... 1447..1496
Anthony, of Lebrixa. *Antonius Nebrissensis.* Span. Writ. 1444..1522

BORN. DIED.

Anthony, Francis. London Apothecary. (*Aurum Potabile*) 1550..1623
Anthony, Marc. Engraver. *See* Raimondi............ 1475?.1534
Anthony, Nicholas. Spanish Hist. (*Bibliotheca Nova*) 1617..1684
Anthony, Paul Gabriel. French Jesuit. (*Theol. Dogmatica*) 1679..1743
Anthony de Bourbon. Titular King of Navarre...... 1518..1562
Antigonus. General of Alexander; fell at Ipsus........ 381 B.C.301
Antigonus Doson. King of Macedonia.............. — B.C. 220
Antigonus Gonatas. King of Macedonia (283–239).... 319 B.C.239
Antimaco, Mark Anthony. Greek Teacher in Italy..... 1473?.1552
Antine, Maur Francis d'. Benedictine. (*L'Art de Vérifier*) 1688..1746
Antiochus Epiphanes. King of Syria............... — B.C.164
Antiochus the Great. King of Syria................ 237 B.C.187
Antiochus Grypus. King of Syria 141 B.C.96
Antiochus Sidetes: King of Syria................. — B.C.126
Antiochus Soter. King of Syria (280–261)..... 323?B.C.261
Antiochus Theus. King of Syria (261–246)........... 286?B.C.246
Antipater. Regent of Macedonia................... — B.C. 319
Antiquus, John. Historical Painter............... 1702..1750
Antoinette, Marie. Queen of Louis XVI............ 1755..1793
Antommarchi, Francis. Physician and Author. (*Les Derniers Moments de Napoléon*) .... — ..1838
Anton Ulrich. Prince Regent in Russia............. 1714..1780?
Antonello, or Antonio, of Messina. Hist. and Portr. Pa... 1447..1496
Antoniano, Silvius. Roman Cardinal; Scholar........ 1540..1603
Antonides, John van der Goes. Dutch Poet.......... 1647..1684
Antoninus, M. Aurelius. *Philosopher.* Roman Emperor (161–80). Life by Guevara...................... 121.. 180
Antoninus Pius. Roman Emperor (138–61).......... 86.. 161
Antonio. *See* Anthony and Antonello.
Antonisze, Cornelius. Dutch Painter and Engraver.... 1500..1536
Antonius. *See* Anthony.
Antonius, Marcus, or Mark Antony. Triumvir........ 83? B.C. 30
Antraigues, Emanuel L. H. Delaunay, Ct. of. Fr. Polit. 1765..1812
Anville, John Baptist Bourguignon d'. Geographer.... 1697..1782
Anwari. *King of Khorassan.* Persian Poet........... — ..1200
Apafi, Michael I. Prince of Transylvania............. 1632..1713
Apelles. Greek Painter. Life by Carlo Dati.......... fl. B.C. 332
Apian, Peter. German Mathematician and Astronomer.. 1495..1552
Apollinaris, C. S. Sidonius. Rom. Patrician and Poet. 431?..484?
Apollinarius, Claudius. Bp. of Hierapolis. Apologist.. fl. ab. 177
Apollinarius or -ris, *the Elder.* Gramm. and Divine..... fl. 362
Apollinarius or -ris, *the Younger,* son. Bishop of Laodicea. Commentator............................ —.. 382?
Apollodorus. Grammarian of Athens .... fl.ab.140 B.C
Apollonio, Jacopo, of Bassano. Painter............. 1584..1654
Apollonius, of Alexandria. *Dyscolos.* Greek Gram..... fl. 2d c.
Apollonius, of Perga. Mathematician. (*Conic Sections*).. fl.240 B.C.
Apollonius Rhodius. Poet and Grammarian....... fl.222–188B.C.
Apollonius of Tyana. Philosopher. Life by Philostratus, tr. by Blount, 1680, and Berwick, 1809; Le Nain du Tillemont, tr. by Jenkin, 1703 .... 3?B.C.98?A.D.
Apono, or Abano, Peter of. Astrologer and Physician... 1250..1315
Appel, Jacob. Dutch Painter....................... 1680..1751
Appelman, Barent. Dutch Painter................... 1640..1686

BORN. DIED.

Apperley, Charles James. Eng. Sportsman and Writer. 1777 –1843
Appian. Roman Historian..................... fl.98?- 161?
Appiani, Andrew. Fresco Painter.................. 1754..1818
Appiani, Francis. Fresco Painter.................. 1702..1792
Appius Claudius. Roman Decemvir.................. — B.C.449
Appleton, Jesse. American Divine and Educator...... 1772..1819
Appuleius, Lucius. Platonic Philos. (*The Golden Ass*). 130?aft.173
Apreece, or Rhese, John. (*Fides Historiæ Britanniæ*)... — ..1555?
Aprosio, Angelico. Ital. Writer. (*Bibliotheca Aprosiana*) 1607..1681
Aproxin, Theo. Matvayevitch. Russian Admiral....... 1671..1728
Apthorp, East. English Divine and Author........... 1733..1816
Aquapendente. Italian Physician. *See* Fabricius..... 1537..1619
Aquaviva, Andrew Matthew. Neapol. Noble and Writ. 1457?.1528
Aquaviva, Claude. General of the Jesuits. Writer.... 1542..1615
Aquaviva, Octavius. Card. Abp. Naples; Patr. of Learn. 1560?.1612
Aquila, Pompeio del. Painter...................... fl. 1580?
Aquila, Ponticus. Trans. of the Old Test. into Greek... fl. ab. 130
Aquilano, Serafino. Italian Poet and Improvvisatore... 1466..1500
Aquinas, Thomas, St. *Angelic Doctor.* Life by Echard,
    Dr. Hampden..................... 1224?.1274
Aquino, Philip, of Carpentras. Converted Jew; Hebraist —..1650
Arabella Stuart. *See* Stuart..................... 1577?.1615
Arabschah, of Damascus. Historian.................. —..1450
Arago, Francis John Dominic. Fr. Astron. L. by self.. 1786..1853
Araldi, Alexander. Painter........................ —..1528
Aram, Eugene. Scholar; executed for murder.......... 1704..1759
Aranda, Peter P. A. de Bolea, Ct. of. Sp. Statesman... 1718..1799
Arantius, Julius Cæs., of Bologna. Anat. and Physiol.. 1530..1589
Aratus, of Sicyon. Achæan General and Historian...... 271B.C.213
Aratus. Astronomical Poet of Cilicia. (*Phænomena*)... fl. B.C. 272
Araujo, D'Azevedo Antonio. Portuguese Scientist...... 1754..1817
Arblay, Madame Frances d'. See D'Arblay.
Arbogast, Louis Francis Anth. (*Calcul des Dérivations*).. 1759..1803
Arbrissel, Robert d'. Founder of Fontevrault Abbey... 1047?.1117
Arbuckle, James. Scotch Poet...................... 1700?.1734?
Arbuthnot, Alexander. Scotch Reformer............. 1538..1583
Arbuthnot, John, M. D. (*Coins: Martinus Scriblerus*).. 1675..1735
Arc, Joan of. *See* Darc............................. 1412?.1431
Arcadius. Roman Emperor of the East (395–408)...... 383.. 408
Arcère, Anthony, of Marseilles. Orient.; Coll. of MSS. — ..1699
Arcère, Louis Stephen, of Marseilles. Poet and Topog.. 1598..1782
Arcesilaus. Athen. Philos. Found. of Middle Academy 316?B.C.241
Arcet, John d'. French Natural Philosopher.......... 1725..1801
Archdall, Mervyn. Irish Antiq. (*Monasticon Hibernicon*) 1723..1791
Archdekin, Richard. Irish Jesuit. (*Essay on Miracles*). 1619..1693
Archenholz, John Wm. von. Ger. Wr. (*Seven Yrs' War*) 1745..1812
Archer, John Wykeham. Painter and Antiquary....... 1809?.1864
Archer, Sir Simon. Warwickshire Antiquary......... 1581.. —
Archilocus, of Paros. Greek Lyric Poet............. 714?B.C.676
Archimedes. Mathematician. L. by Mazzuchelli, 1737 287?B.C.212
Archytas. Philosopher, of Tarentum................. fl. B.C. 400?
Arco, Alonzo del. Deaf and Dumb Spanish Painter..... 1625..1700
Arco, Nicholas, Count of. Italian Latin Poet.......... 1479..1546
Arçon, John Claude d'. French Engineer............. 1733..1800

BORN.   DIED.

Arcq, Philip Augustus de St. Foix d'. Fr. Hist. Writer. — ..1779
Arcudi, Alexander Thomas. Venetian Hist. and Biogr.. 1655..1720?
Arcudio, Peter. Italian Theologian.................. 1570?.1635?
Arculphus. French Bishop. Writer on the Holy Land. fl. 690?
Arden, Edward. Gentleman; executed for treason...... 1531..1583
Arden, Richard Pepper. First Lord Alvanley. Judge.. 1745..1804
Ardern, John. English Surgeon.................... fl. 1370
Ardicini, Louis. Italian Writer on Agriculture........ 1739..1833
Arena, Anthony d'. French Jurist and Macaronic Poet.. — ..1544
Arendt, Martin Frederick. Traveler................. 1769..1824
Aresi, Paul. Italian Theologian..................... 1574?.1644
Aretæus, of Cappadocia. Greek Physician............ fl. 70?
Aretin, John Christoph. Ant. Maria, Baron von. Writer.. 1773..1824
Aretino, Francis. Italian Scholar. *See* Accolti........ 1418?.1485?
Aretino, Leonard. *Bruni.* Italian Historian......... 1369..1444
Aretino, Peter. Ital. Satirist. Life by Berni, 1537; Dujardin, 1750; Mazzuchelli, 1763; Dubois Fontanelle, 1768................................... 1492..1557
Aretino, Spinello. Italian Painter.................. 1308?.1400?
Argall, Rev. John. Scholar. M. A. 1566............. — ..1606
Argall, Richard. English Poet...................... fl. 1621
Argall, Sir Samuel. English Adventurer in America.... fl 17th c.
Argand, Aimé. Inventor of Argand Lamp............. — ..1803
Argellati, Philip. Italian Writer. (*Milanese Writers*).. 1685..1755
Argens, J. Bapt. de Boyer, Marquis of. Fr. Soldier & Wr. 1704..1771
Argensola, Barthol. Leonard de. Hist., Poet, Theol..... 1566..1631
Argensola, Lupercio Leonard de, br. Span. Poet and Hist. 1565?.1613
Argenson, Mark Peter, Comte de. French Statesman... 1696..1764
Argentier, John, of Turin. Physician................. 1513..1572
Argentré, Bertrand d'. (*History of Brittany*).......... 1519..1590
Argentré, Chas. Duplessis d'. (*Collectio Judiciorum*)... 1673..1740
Argenville, Anthony Jos. Dezallier d'. (*L. of Painters*). 1680..1765?
Argoli, Andrew. Italian Mathematician.............. 1570..1653?
Argoli, John. Italian Poet and Archæologist.......... 1609?.1660?
Argonne, Noel Bonaventure d'. *Vigneul de Marville*.. 1640?.1704
Arguelles, Augustin. Spanish Politician.............. — ..1844
Argues, Gerard des. French Georneter............... 1593..1662
Argyle, Archibald Campbell, 8th Earl and 1st Marquess of. Covenanter. Beheaded.................... 1598..1661
Argyle, Archibald Campbell, 9th Earl of, son. *McCallum More.* Confederate of Monmouth. Beheaded...... — ..1685
Argyle and Greenwich, John Campbell, 2d Duke of. Commander. Life by Robert Campbell, 1745........ 1678..1743
Argyropulus, John. Reviver of Greek Learning in Italy.. —aft.1478
Arialdus, St...................................... — ..1066
Arias Montanus, Benedict. Cath. Divine and Linguist. 1527..1598
Ariosto, Gabriel. Poet............................. — ..1552
Ariosto, Louis, brother. Italian Poet. (*Orlando Furioso.*) Life by Pigna, 1554; Garofelo, 1554; Harrington, 1634; Hoole; A. Fabroni, 1800; Baruffaldi, 1807; Fernow, 1809; Panizzi.................................. 1474..1533
Arisi, Francis, of Cremona. Writer. (*Cremona Literata*) 1657..1743
Arista, Mariano. Mexican General and President....... 1802..1855
Aristarchus, of Samos. Greek Astron. and Philosopher. fl. B.C. 280?

BORN. DIED.

Aristarchus, of Samothrace. Greek Grammarian....... fl. B.C.150?
Aristides. Athenian Statesman..................... —B.C.468?
Aristippus. Founder of the Cyrenaic School of Phil.... fl.5thc.B.C.
Aristobulus I. High-Priest and King of the Jews..... —B.C.106
Asistobulus II. Deposed by Pompey................. —B.C.492
Aristophanes. Greek Comedian..................... 444?B.C.380?
Aristotle. Greek Philosopher. Life by Beurer, 1587;
   Schott, 1603; Blakesley, 1839...................... 384B.C.322
Arius. Founder of Arianism. Life by Travasa, 1746.... — .. 336
Arkel, Cornelius van, of Amsterdam. Arminian Divine
   and Preacher..................................... 1670..1724
Arkenholz, John. Swedish Writ. (*Mems. of Christina*) 1695..1777
Arkwright, Sir Richard. Inventor of Spinning-Jenny.. 1732..1792
Arland, James Anthony. Swiss Painter.............. 1668..1743
Arlington, Henry Bennet, 1st Earl of. Statesman...... 1618..1685
Arlotto. *Il Piovano,* or *The Dean.* Italian Humorist...1395..1483
Armfelt, Gustavus Maurice. Swedish Politician........ 1757..1814
Arminius. Cheruscan Chief...................... 18B.C.19A.D
Arminius, James. Dutch Theologian. Life by Petrus
   Bertius; Brandt, 1724............................ 1560..1609
Armstrong, John, M. D. Poet...................... 1709..1779
Armstrong, John, M. D. Med. Writ. L. by Boott, 1832. 1784..1829
Armstrong, John. Bp. of Grahamstown. L. by Carter. 1813..1856
Armstrong, Sir Thos. Royalist; partisan of Monmouth. — ..1684
Armyne, Mary, Lady. Benefactress................. — ..1675
Arnald, Richard. (*Commentary on the Apocrypha*)...... 1696..1756
Arnall, William. Political Writer. (*Free Briton*)...... 1715..1741
Arnau, John. Spanish Historical Painter............. 1595..1693
Arnaud, Francis. Abbot of Grand Champs. Writer.... 1721..1784
Arnaud, Francis Thos. Marie Baculard d'. French Writer 1718..1805
Arnaud, George d'. French Jurist................. 1711..1740
Arnaud, Henry. Vaudois Pastor and Leader.......... 1641..1721
Arnaud de Méreuil, Daniel. Troubadour Poet........ — ..1189?
Arnaud de Ronsil, George. French Surgeon in London. 1697..1774
Arnaud de Villa Nova, or Arnoldus, *which see*......... 1235?.1314
Arnauld, Anthony. *The Advocate.* Lawyer of Paris.. 1560..1619
Arnauld, Anthony. *The Great Arnauld;* of Port Royal. 1612..1694
Arnauld d'Andilly, Robert. Apologist for Port Royal.
   Life by himself................................... 1589..1674
Arnauld, Henry. Bishop of Angers. (*Negotiations*)... 1597..1692
Arnauld, Marie Angélique. Abbess of Port Royal...... 1591..1671
Arnauld, Marie Angélique, niece. Abbess of Pt. Royal. 1624..1684
Arnault, Anthony Vincent. French Author........... 1766..1834
Arnd, John, of Anhault. Lutheran. (*True Christianity*). 1555..1621
Arndt, C. Gottlieb von. (*Origin of European Dialects*).. — ..1829
Arndt, Ernest Maurice. German Political Writer........ 1769...—
Arndt, Joshua. (*Dictionary of Ecclesiastical Antiquities*). 1626..1685
Arne, Dr. Thomas Augustine. Musical Composer....... 1710..1778
Arnim, Louis Achim von. Ger. Poet and Romance Writ.. 1781..1831
Arnisæus, Heningus. Phys. and Polit. Wr. at Helmstadt. 1580?.1636
Arnobius. Christian Writer of Africa. (*Contra Gentes*). fl. 296
Arnold, Benedict. American General and Traitor....... 1740..1801
Arnold, Christoph. Prof. at Altorf. (*Testimon. Flavianum*) 1527..1685
Arnold, Godfrey. Ger. Mystic Div. and Eccles. Hist... 1666..1714

BORN.   DIED.

Arnold, John.   Cornish Watchmaker and Inventor ..... 1744..1799
Arnold, Dr. Samuel.   Musical Composer............. 1739?.1802
Arnold, Strutthan von Winckelried.   Swiss Patriot..... 1300..1386
Arnold, Thomas, M. D.   Physician for Insanity........ 1742..1816
Arnold, Rev. Thos., D. D., of Rugby.   L. by A. P. Stanley 1795..1842
Arnold, Rev. T. Kerchever.   Editor of School Classics.. 1800..1853
Arnold of Brescia.   Reformer.   Life by Koeler, 1742;
   Guadagnini, 1790; Francke, 1825; Niccolini......... — ..1155
Arnolde, Richard.   Chronicler...................... 1451?.1521?
Arnoldi, Bartholomew.   Anti-Lutheran Writer......... — ..1532
Arnoldi, John.   Dutch Diplomatist and Statesman...... 1751..1827
Arnoldus de Villa Nova.   French Physician, Theologian,
   Astrologer, Alchemist............................ 1235?.1314
Arnolfe di Lapo.   Italian Architect and Sculptor....... 1232..1300
Arnot, Hugo.   Scottish Writer. (History of Edinburgh).. 1749..1786
Arnoul.   Bishop of Lisieux.   Writer................... — ..1184
Arnould, Sophie.   French Actress................... 1740..1803
Arnoult, John Baptist.   Jesuit Author. (Le Précepteur). 1689..1753
Arntzenius, John Henry.   Jurist and Writer at Utrecht . 1734..1797
Arnu, Nicholas.   French Theologian and Philosopher.... 1629?.1692
Arnulph.   Emperor of Germany (896–99).............. — .. 899
Arnulph, or Ernulph.   Bp. of Rochest. (Textus Roffensis) 1040?.1124
Aromatari, Joseph of.   Italian Physician and Naturalist. 1586?.1660
Arouet, Francis Mary.   See Voltaire................. 1694..1778
Arpad.   Founder of the Hungarian Monarchy.......... 869.. 907
Arpino, Joseph Cæsar, or Josephin de.   Italian Painter.. 1560..1640
Arreboe, Anders.   Danish Bishop and Poet........... 1587..1637
Arredondo, Isidore.   Spanish Painter .... 1654..1702
Arriaga, Roderick de.   Spanish Jesuit; Philosopher..... 1592..1667
Arrian.   Greek Historian. (Expedition of Alexander)... 90?. 170?
Arriaza, John Baptist.   Spanish Poet................. 1770..1837
Arrivabene, John Peter.   Ital. Schol. & Poet. (Gonzagidos) 1441..1504
Arrowsmith, Aaron.   Geographer .... 1750..1823
Arrowsmith, John, D. D.   Puritan Divine............. 1602..1659
Arsaces I.   Founder of the Parthian Monarchy .... fl.3d c.B.C.
Arsaces VI. (or Mithridates I.)...................... fl.2d c.B.C.
Arsinoe.   Egyptian Princess........................ fl.4th c.B.C.
Artale, Joseph.   Sicilian Soldier and Poet............. 1628..1679
Artaxerxes I.   Longimanus.   King of Persia (465–25).. —B.C.425
Artaxerxes II.   Mnemon.   (405–362); brother of Cyrus. 453?B.C.362
Artaxerxes III.   Ochus.   (362–39) .... —B.C.339
Arteaga, Stephen.   Spanish Jesuit; Writer in Italian.... 1745?.1799
Artedi, Peter.   Swedish Naturalist; friend of Linnæus... 1705..1735
Artemisia, Queen of Caria; wife of Mausolus .... —B.C.350
Arteveld, James van.   Brewer of Ghent .... — ..1345
Arteveld, Philip van, son.   Killed at Rosbecq.......... — ..1382
Arthur.   British Prince .... — .. 542?
Arthur, Duke of Brittany, nephew of King John........ 1187?.1203
Arthur, Prince of Wales, son of Henry VII. .... 1486..1502
Artigas, Ferdinand Joseph.   South American Patriot ... 1746..1826
Artigni,, Anthony Gachet d'.   Writer of Vienna .... 1706..1778
Artois, James John van.   Flemish Landscape Painter... 1613..1665
Arundel, Blanche, Lady.   Defender of Wardour Castle . 1583..1649
Arundel, Mary, Countess of.   Writer .... fl. 1550?

BORN. DIED.

Arundel, Philip Howard, Earl of. Life edited by the
Duke of Norfolk, 1857 .... 1557..1595
Arundel, Thos. Archbishop of Canterbury (1396-1413) . 1353..1413
Arundel, Thos. Howard, Earl of. Collector of Marbles, &c. 1580?.1646
Arvieux, Lawrence d'. French Orientalist.............. 1635..1702
Asbury, Francis. American Divine.................... 1745..1816
Ascensius. Printer. *See* Badius.................... 1462..1535
Ascham, Roger. Instructor of Queen Elizabeth .... 1515..1568
Ascoli, Cecco di. *Francis de Stabili.* Poet and Mathemat. 1258?.1328
Ascough, Anne. *See* Askew........................ 1529..1546
Aselli, Gaspar. Italian Anatomist. (*De Lacteis Venis*) . 1581?.1626
Asfeld, James Vincent Bidal d'. Jansenist Theologian.. 1664..1745
Asgill, John. Political Writer .... 1650?.1738
Ash, John, LL.D. Anabaptist Divine. (*English Dict.*) .. 1724..1779
Ash, John, M.D. Analyst of Mineral Waters .... 1723..1798
Ashburnham, John. Royalist......................... 1604..1671
Ashburton, Alexander Baring, Lord. Statesman....·... 1774..1848
Ashburton, John Dunning, First Lord. Lawyer .... 1731..1783
Ashbury, Joseph. Comedian......................... 1638..1720
Ashby, Sir John. British Admiral .... — ..1693
Ashe, Andrew. Irish Flute-player.................... 1759..1838
Ashe, Simeon. Nonconformist Minister in Staffordshire . — ..1662
Ashley, Robert. Poet and Miscellaneous Writer .... 1565..1641
Ashley, Lord. Member of the "Cabal." *See* Cooper .. 1621..1683
Ashmole, Elias. Antiquary. Founder of Museum. Life
by self, edited by Burman, 1717 .... 1617..1692
Ashmun, Jehudi. American Philanthropist............. 1794..1828
Ashton, Charles. Master of Jesus College; Critic....... 1665..1752
Ashton, Thomas, D.D. Fellow of Eton Coll. Preacher.. 1717..1775
Ashwell, George. Divine. Writer on the Three Creeds. 1612..1693
Ashworth, Caleb, D.D. Baptist Divine............... 1722..1775
Askew, Anne. Martyr.............................. 1529..1546
Askew, Anthony, M.D. Book Collector............... 1722..1774
Asper, John, or Hans. Swiss Artist.................. 1499..1571
Aspertino, Guido, of Bologna. Historical Painter ...... 1460?.1500?
Aspinwall, William. American Physician............. 1743..1823
Asselin, Giles Thomas. French Poet................. 1682:.1767
Asselyn, John. Dutch Landscape Painter .... 1610..1660
Assemani, Joseph Louis. Orientalist at Rome......... 1710?.1782
Assemani, Joseph Simon. Syrian Orientalist in Italy .. 1687..1768
Assemani, Simon. Abbé. Orientalist at Padua........ 1752..1821
Assemani, Stephen Evode. Orientalist and Missionary.. 1707..1782
Asser, John, or Asserius Menevensis. Biog. of King Alfred — .. 909
Assereto, Joachim, of Genoa. Painter................ 1600..1649
Assheton, William, D.D. Divine. Life by Watts ...... 1641..1711
Assouci, Chas. Coypeau, Sieur d'. *Ape of Scarron.* Poet 1604?.1679?
Ast, George Anthony Fred. Ger. Philol. and Philos..... 1778..1841
Asta, Andrew dell', of Naples. Painter .... 1683..1721
Astbury, J., of Shelton. Potter .... 1680?.1743
Astell, Mary. Polemical Writer..................... 1668?.1731
Astle, Thomas. Archæologist. (*Origin of Writing*).... 1735..1803
Astley, John. Portrait-Painter...................... — ..1787
Astley, Philip. Founder of Amphitheatre .... 1742..1814
Aston, Sir Arthur. Royalist; Governor of Drogheda.... — ..1649

BORN. DIED.

Aston, Sir Thomas. Royalist; High Sheriff of Cheshire.. — ..1645
Astor, John Jacob. American Merchant............... 1763..1848
Astorga, Emanuel d'. Italian Musician. (*Stabat Mater*) 1680..1701
Astruc, John. French Medical Writer................ 1684..1766
Astulphus, or Aistulph. King of the Lombards (749–56) — .. 756
Astyages. Last King of Media (594–59)............. aft.B.C.559
Atahualpa. Last Inca of Peru....................... — ..1533
Atha Melik. Persian Statesman and Historian........ 1226?.1283
Athanaric. King of the Western Goths .... — .. 381
Athanasio, Peter. Spanish Historical Painter......... 1638..1688
Athanasius, St. Bishop of Alexandria (326–73). Life by
  Hermant, 1671; E. Renaudot...................... 296?. 373
Athelm. Archbishop of Canterbury (914–23).......... — .. 923
Athelstan. King of England .... 895?.941
Athenæus. Grammarian. (*Banquet of the Learned*).... fl. ab. 200
Athenagoras. An early Christian Philosopher.......... fl. 2d c.
Athenais. Wife of Theodosius II. Poetess .... — .. 460
Athias, Eman.-ben-Joseph. Learned Printer of Amsterdam — ..1700
Athlone, W. de R. de Ginkell, E. of. Officer of Wm. III. 1640..1702
Atkinson, Thomas. Miscellaneous Writer .... 1801..1833
Atkinson, Thomas Witlam. Architect and Traveler .... 1799..1861
Atkyns, Richard. (*Origin and Growth of Printing*).... 1615..1677
Atkyns, Sir Robert. Baron of the Exchequer and Speaker
  of the House of Commons .... 1621..1709
Atkyns, Sir Robert. Writer. (*Gloucester*) .... 1646..1711
Atratus, or Black Hugh. English Cardinal. Writer.... fl. 1281?
Attar, Ferideddin. Persian Poet and Historian .... 1119..1221
Atterbury, Francis. Bishop Roch. L. by Stackhouse, 1727 1662..1732
Atterbury, Lewis, brother. Divine .... 1657?.1731
Atticus, T. Pomponius. Roman Knight 109 B.C.32
Attila. King of the Huns. *Scourge of God*. Life by
  Callimachus, 1491; Calanus, 1502; Buonaccorsi...... — .. 453
Attiret, John Denis. *Frère Attiret*. French Painter .... 1702..1768
Atwell, Hugh. Actor.............................. — ..1621
Atwood, George. Mathematician. (*Arches*)........... 1745..1807
Atwood, Thomas. Musical Composer................. 1767..1838
Aubertin, Edmund. (*L'Eucharistie de l'Ancienne Église*) 1595..1652
Aubery, Anthony. French Hist. (*Hist. of the Cardinals*) 1616..1695
Aubery, Louis. *Sieur de Maurier*. (*Hist. of Holland*).. — ..1687
Aubespine, Gabriel de l'. Fr. Ambass. in Engl.; Writer 1579..1630
Aubespine, Magdalen de l'. Fr. Wit and Beauty; Poet 1546..1596
Aubigné, Theodore Agrippa d'. (*Histoire Universelle*).. 1550..1630
Aublet, J. Baptist Christopher Fusée. French Botanist.. 1720..1728
Aubrey, John. Topog. and Antiq. Life by Britton, 1843 1626..1697?
Aubriet, Claude. French Painter...................... 1651..1740
Aubry de Gouges, Marie Olympie. Republican .... 1755..1793
Aubusson, Peter d'. Cardinal; Warrior and Statesman 1423..1503
Auchmuty, Sir Samuel. General...................... 1756..1822
Auckland, George Eden, 2nd Baron, 1st Earl. Governor-
  General of India (1835–42).......................... 1784..1849
Auckland, William Eden, 1st Baron. Ambass. and Writer 1744..1814
Aude, Joseph. Kt. of Malta. Dramatist. (*Life of Buffon*) 1755..1841
Audebert, Germain. French Poet .... 1518..1598
Audebert, J. Baptist. French Naturalist and Engraver. 1759..1800
Audenaerd, or Gudenaerd, Rob. van. Pa. and Engraver 1663..1743

BORN. DIED.

Audifredi, J. Baptist. Italian Astronomer............ 1714..1794
Audifret, J. Baptist. French Geographer............. 1657..1733
Audiguier, Vital d'. French Adventurer and Romancist. 1569?.1624
Audley, James, Lord, K. G. English Warrior in France.. 1312?.1386
Audley, Thomas, Lord. Chancellor of England........ 1488..1544
Audouin, John Victor. French Entomologist.......... 1797..1841
Audouin, Peter. French Engraver.................... 1768..1822
Audran, Benoit. Engraver........................... 1661..1721
Audran, Charles. French Painter.................... 1594..1674
Audran, Claude, brother or cousin. French Engraver... 1592..1677
Audran, Claude. French Painter .... 1639..1684
Audran, Claude. Ornamental Designer .... 1685..1734
Audran, Gerard. French Painter and Engraver........ 1640..1703
Audran, Germain. Engraver.......................... 1631..1710
Audran, John. French Painter....................... 1667..1756
Audran, Louis. Engraver............................ 1670..1712
Audubon, John James. Naturalist. (*Birds of America*) 1782..1851
Augenio, Horace, de Monte Santo. Medical Writer..... 1527..1603
Auger, Athanasius. Abbé. Polit. and Classical Writer. 1734..1792
Auger, Edmund. French Jesuit....................... 1530..1591
Auger, Louis Simon. French Critic and Journalist..... 1772..1829
Augereau, Peter Francis Charles. Marshal of France... 1757..1816
Augurello, John Aurelius. Italian Poet.............. 1441?.1524
Augusta, Princess. Daughter of George III........... 1768..1840
Augustine, St. Missionary. Archbishop of Canterbury. — .. 607?
Augustine, St. Bishop of Hippo (395–430). Life by
 self (*Confessions*) ; Lancilottus, 1616 ; Mair, 1631;
 Rivius, 1646; Godeau, 1646; Friche; Mann, 1809;
 Kloth, 1840; Sintzel, 1845; Braune, 1846............ 354.. 430
Augustinus, Anthony. Sp. Writer on Law and Medals... 1517..1586
Augustulus, Romulus. Last Emp. of Western Rom. Empire fl. 5th c.
Augustus. Emperor of Rome (B.C. 31–A.D. 14). Life by
 Graeff, 1666; Dieterich, 1666; Larrey, 1690; Lefebvre,
 1760; Rolland, 1825............................... 63 B.C.14 A.D
Augustus I. Elector of Saxony....................... 1526..1586
Augustus Fred. II. King of Pol. and Elect. of Sax.... 1670..1733
Augustus Frederick III. King of Pol.; Elect. of Sax.. 1696..1763
Augustus Frederick, Duke of Sussex, son of Geo. III. 1773..1843
Aulisio, Dominic. Neapolitan Linguist and Writer.... 1639..1717
Aulus Gellius. Lat. Grammarian. (*Noctes Atticæ*).... fl.117?.180?
Aumale, Chas. de Lorr., Duke d'. Partis. of the League.. 1554..1631
Aumont, Anthony d'. Marshal of France............. 1601..1669
Aumont, John d', Ct. of Châteauroux. Marsh. of France 1522..1595
Aungerville, Richard. (*Philobiblion.*) See Angarville.. 1287?.1345
Aunoy, or Aulnoy, Mary Cath., Countess of. (*Fairy Tales*) 1650..1705
Aurelian. Roman Emperor (A.D. 270–75)............. 213?. 275
Aurelius, Marcus. See Antoninus.................... 121..180
Aurelius Victor. Latin Historian and Biographer..... fl.ab.350
Aurelli, Aurelio, or Arelli, John Mutio. Ital. Latin Poet. fl. 1520
Auria, Vincent. (*History of Eminent Sicilians*)........ 1625..1710
Aurispa, John, of Sicily. Collector of MSS............ 1369..1460
Aurogallus, Matthew. Philologist at Wittemberg...... 1480..1543
Aurungzebe. Emperor of Hindostan.................. 1618..1707
Ausonius, Decimus Magnus. Roman Poet............. 310?. 390?
Austen, Jane. Novelist............................. 1775..1817

BORN.   DIED,

Austen, William. Metal Founder.................... fl. 15th c.
Austin, John. R. Cath. Divine. (*Christian Moderator*). 1613..1669
Autelz, Wm. des. French Poet...................... 1529?.1576?
Auteroche, John Chappe d'. French Astronomer...... 1722..1769
Automne, Bernard, of Bourdeaux. Jurist............ 1587..1666
Auton, John d'. Abbé. Historiographer. (*Hist. of France*) 1466?.1527
Autreau, James d'. French Poet and Painter........ 1656..1745
Auvergne, Anthony d'. French Musical Composer. ... 1713..1797
Auvergne, Latour d'. Soldier and Sch. *See* Latour.. 1743..1800
Auvigny, J. du Castre d'. (*Lives of Ill. Men of France*) 1712..1743
Auxentius, Bishop of Milan. Arian Divine.......... 310?. 374
Auzout, Adrian. French Mathematician.............. — 1691 or 3
Avalos, Ferd. Francis d'. Neapolitan Soldier. (*Dialogue on
    Love*)... 1489..1525
Avantio, John Marion. Civilian and Writer at Padua.. 1564..1622
Avaux, Claude de Mesmes, Ct. d'. Diplom. and Scholar 1595..1650
Aved, James Andrew Joseph. French Portrait-Painter.. 1702..1766
Avellino, Julius. Italian Landscape-Painter........... 1645?.1700
Aventine, John Thürmayer. (*Annales Boiorum*)....... 1466..1534
Averani, Benedict. Florentine Writer and Poet....... 1645..1707
Averani, Jos. Mathematician and Natural Philosopher.. 1662..1738
Averdy, Clement Chas. de l'. Fr. Statesm. and Writer.. 1723?.1793
Averroes, or Ibn Roschid. Arabian Philos. and Phys... 1149?.1198
Avesbury, Robert of. Historian..................... — ..1356?
Avicenna. Mahometan Physician and Philosopher..... 980..1037
Avienus, Rufus Festus. Latin Poet.................. fl. 370?
Avila, Giles Gonzales. Spanish Divine and Historian... 1577?.1658
Aviler, Augustine Charles d'. French Architect........ 1653..1700
Avison, Chas., of Newcastle. Mus. Composer and Writer 1710?.1770
Avitus. Roman Emperor of the West (455–56)........ — .. 456
Avogadro, Peter, of Brescia. Historical Painter...... fl. 1730?
Avrigny, Chas. Joseph Læillard d'. French Poet........ 1670..1823
Avrigny, Hyacinth Robillard d'. French Historian..... 1675..1719
Axel. Abp. of Lund. Danish Minister and General.... 1128..1201
Axtel, Daniel. Parliamentarian Colonel. Executed.... — ..1660
Ayala, Balth. Flem. Lawyer. (*De Jure et Officiis Bellicis*) 1548?.1584
Ayala, Peter Lopez d'. Spanish Chronicler............ 1332..1407
Ayesha. Wife of Mahomet 611.677–8
Aylesbury, Sir Thos. Math. and Patron of Learning... 1576..1657
Aylmer, John. Bp. of London. Life by Strype, 1704... 1521..1594
Ayloffe, Sir Joseph. Antiquary...................... 1708?.1781
Aylward, Theodore. Musical Composer............... — ..1801
Aymar, James. French Professor of Divination........ — ..1662
Ayrer, Jacob. German Dramatic Writer............... — ..1605
Ayres, John. English Penman....................... — ..1705?
Ayrton, Edmund. Composer of Cathedral Music....... 1734..1808
Ayscough, Geo. Edw. Trav. and Dramatist. (*Semiramis*) — ..1779
Ayscough, Rev. Sam. Writer. (*Index to Shakespeare*). 1745..1804
Ayscue, or Ayscough, Sir George. Admiral.......... — aft.1672
Ayton, or Aytoun, Sir Robert. Scottish Poet.......... 1570..1638
Aytoun, Wm. E. Scottish Professor, Essayist, and Poet 1813..1865
Azara, Felix d'. Spanish Naturalist and Traveler ...... 1746..1811
Azara, Joseph Nicholas d'. Spanish Statesm. and Writ. 1731..1804
Azevedo, Ignatius. Portug. Missionary to West Indies. 1527..1570
Azorius, John. Spanish Jesuit. (*Institut. Moralium*)... 1533..1603

	BORN.	DIED.

Azpilcueta, Martin. *Navarre.* Spanish Lawyer....... 1494..1586
Azuni, Dominic Albert. (*Droit Maritime de l'Europe*).. 1749..1827
Azzi ne' Forti, Faustina. *Eurinomia.* Italian Poetess.. 1650..1724
Azzo, or Azo, Portius. Italian Lawyer................ — ..1200
Azzoguidi, Valerius Felix. Antiquary, of Bologna..... 1651..1728
Azzolini, Decius. Cardinal. (*Political Aphorisms*)..... 1623..1689
Azzolini, Lawrence. Bishop of Narni. Satirist........ — ..1632

B.

	BORN.	DIED.

Baader, Ferdinand Mary. Medical Writer............ 1747..1797
Baan, James de. Portrait-Painter.... .... 1673..1700
Baan, John de. Dutch Portrait-Painter .... 1633..1702
Baarsdorp, Cornelius. (*Methodus Universæ Artis Medicæ*) — ..1565
Baba, Ali. Founder of Algerine Independence......... — ..1718
Baber, or Babur. Emperor of Hindostan. Life by self, tr.
    by Leyden and Erskine, 1826; R. M. Caldecott, 1845 1483..1530
Babeuf, Francis. Noel Revolutionist. (*Tribune of People*) 1764..1797
Babin, Francis. French Theologian and Canonist ...... 1651..1734
Babington, Anthony. Conspirator..................... — ..1586
Babington, Gervase. Bishop of Worcester............. 1550?.1610
Babington, Wm., M.D. Philos. Life by Rd. Bright, M.D. 1756..1833
Babini, Matthew. Italian Vocalist................. 1754..1816
Babo, Joseph Maria. German Professor and Dramatist . 1756..1822
Babylas. Bishop of Antioch (238–51). Martyr........ — .. 251
Bacai, Ibrahim Ben-omar. Mussulman Writer .... — ..1480
Baccalar y Sanna, Vincent, Marquis of St. Philip. Soldier
    and Statesman.. 1660?.1726
Bacchanelli, John. Medical Writer of Rheggio .... fl. 1560?
Bacchini, Benedict, of Modena. Universal Scholar .... 1651..1721
Bacciochi, Madame, Princess Piombino. *See* Bonaparte 1777..1820
Baccio d'Agnolo. Florentine Architect............... 1460..1543
Baccio della Porta. *Fra Bartolomeo.* Italian Painter. 1469..1517
Baccius, Andrew. Italian Medical Writer fl.1567–1600
Bach, Charles Philip Emanuel. Life by self......... 1714..1788
Bach, John Sebastian. Musician. Life by Forkel, 1802;
    Grosser, 1829; Helgenfeldt, 1850 .... 1685..1750
Bachaumont, Francis le Coigneux de. Fr. Lawyer and Po. 1624..1702
Bachaumont, Louis Petit de. Fr. Writ. (*Mémoires Secrets*) — ..1771
Bachelier, John James. French Painter.............. 1724..1805
Bachelier, Nicholas, of Toulouse. Sculptor........... —aft.1553
Bachmeister, H. L. C. Miscellaneous Writer .... 1736..1806
Bachovius, Reinier. German Protestant Civilian ...... 1544..1614
Baciccio, J. Baptist Gauli. Italian Painter .... 1639..1709
Backer, or Bakkar, James. Dutch Historical Painter.. 1530..1560
Backer, James. Dutch Portrait and Historical Painter.. 1609..1641
Backhouse, William. Astrologer and Alchemist....... 1593..1662
Backhuysen, Ludolph. Dutch Painter................. 1631..1709
Bacon, Anne, Lady. Scholar and Writer............. 1528..1600
Bacon, Francis, Viscount St. Alban's. Life by Rawley;
    David Mallet, 1740; Basil Montagu, 1834; Lord
    Campbell; J. Sortain; Macaulay; W. H. Dixon; Mac-
    vey Napier, 1853; Ellis, &c., 1861 .... 1561..1626
Bacon, or Baconthorpe, John. *The Resolute Doctor* .... — ..1346
Bacon, John. Sculptor. Life by Rev. Richard Cecil.... 1740..1799
Bacon, Sir Nathaniel. Landscape-Painter .... — ..1615
Bacon, Sir Nicholas. Lord Keeper................... 1510..1579
Bacon, Phanuel. D.D. Divine and Poet. (*Artificial Kite*) — ..1783
Bacon, Robert. Divine. (*Life of Archbishop St. Edmund*) 1168?.1248
Bacon, Roger. Friar. (*Opus Majus*)................ 1214..1292?

BORN. DIED.

Bacsanyi, Janos. Hungarian Poet and Writer......... 1763..1845
Badalocchio, Sisto-Rosa. Italian Painter and Engraver 1581..1647
Badcock, Samuel. Polemical Writer.................. 1747..1788
Baddeley, Robert. Comedian....................... — ..1794
Baddeley, Sophia. Actress .... 1745..1801
Baden, or Badens, Francis. Dutch Hist. and Portr. Painter 1571..1603
Badia, Thomas. Cardinal........................... 1433..1547
Badia y Leblich, Domingo. *Ali Bey.* Traveler and
    Projector. *See* Ali Bey...................... 1766..1818
Badile, John Anthony. Italian Portrait-Painter........ 1480..1560·
Badius, Conrad. Scholar and Printer.................. 1510..1568?
Badius, Josse. *Ascensius.* Scholar and Printer........ 1462..1535
Badoara, Daniel, of Venice. Senator.................. — ..1584
Badoara, Frederick, of Venice. Statesman .... 1518..1595
Badoara, Lauro, of Venice. Poet.................... 1546..1593
Badoara, Peter, of Venice. Advocate................. — ..1591
Baduel, Claude. French Protestant Divine .... — ..1561
Baeli, Francis. Sicilian Mathematician and Poet .... 1639..1710?
Baerstraet, —. Dutch Painter...................... — ..1687
Baert, A. B. F. de Paul, Baron de. Fr. Senator and Author 1750..1825
Baffin, William. Navigator .... 1584?.1622
Bagard, Charles. French Medical Writer.............. 1696..1772
Bage, Robert. Novelist............................ 1728..1801
Bagford, John. Antiquary and Book Collector......... 1675..1716
Bagger, John. Bishop of Copenhagen. Danish Writer. 1646..1693
Baggesen, Jens, or Immanuel. Danish Poet........... 1764..1826
Bagieu, James. French Army Surgeon................ fl. 1750?
Baglione, John. Italian Painter. (*Lives of Painters*) .. 1573?.1644?
Baglivi, George. Italian Physician. (*Praxis Modica*).. 1669..1707
Bagnioli, Julius Cæsar. Ital. Poet. (*Judgment of Paris*) — ..1630?
Bagot, Louis. Bp. St. Asaph. (*Sermons on the Prophecies*) 1740..1802
Bagration, Peter Ivanoyitch, Prince. Russian General.. 1765..1812
Bagshaw, Edward. Civilian and Political Writer ...... — ..1662
Bagshaw, Wm. Ejected Nonconf. Life by Ashe, 1704. 1628..1702
Bahrdt, Charles Fred. Theologian and Satiric Writer .. 1741..1792
Baian, or Baion, Andrew. Indo-Portuguese Poet....... fl. 17th c.
Baier, John James. German Physician and Botanist ... 1677..1735
Baier, John Wm. *The Old.* Ger. Div. (*Compend. of Theol.*) 1647..1694
Baif, Lazarus de. French Poet and Scholar............ — ..1547
Baikie, Dr. African Explorer...................... — ..1864
Bail, Lewis. French Divine. (*Sapientia foris prædicans*). — ..1669
Bailey, Nathaniel. (*English Dictionary*) .... — ..1742
Bailey, Peter. Humorous Poet .... — ..1823
Bailey, or Baley, Walter. Medical Writer .... 1529..1592
Baillet, Adrian. French Critic. (*Jugemens des Savants*). 1649..1706
Baillie, George, of Jerviswood .... — ..1738
Baillie, Miss Joanna. Dramatic Writer............... 1762..1831
Baillie, John, M. P., Colonel. Indian Administrator and
    Persian Scholar .... 1772..1833
Baillie, Matthew, M. D. Anatomist and Physiologist.... 1761..1823
Baillie, Robert. Principal, of Glasgow. Covenanter.
    (*Letters and Journals.*) Life by D. Laing, 1841...... 1599..1662
Baillie, Robert, of Jerviswood....................... — ..1684
Baillie, Roche le. *La Rivière.* Fr. Phys. and Astrologer — ..1605

3

BORN. DIED.

Baillou, William de. French Medical Writer .... 1538..1616
Bailly, David. Dutch Painter .... 1584..1638
Bailly, Edmund Louis Barthélemy. French Politician.. 1760..1819
Bailly, James. French Painter...................... 1629..1679
Bailly, John Sylvanus. Astronomer. Mayor of Paris;
    guillotined .... 1736..1793
Baily, Francis. Eng. Astron. Disc. of *Baily's Beads*.. 1774..1844
Bainbridge, John, M. D. Astronomer .... 1582..1643
Bainbridge, William. American Commodore.......... 1774..1833
Bainbrigge, Christopher. Cardinal. Abp. York. Envoy — ..1514
Baines, Edward. Historical Writer. (*Leeds Mercury.*)
    Life by E. Baines, 1851.......................... 1774..1848
Baini, Joseph. Italian Musician .... 1775..1844
Baird, General Sir David. Life by T. Hook.. ...... 1757..1829
Baird, Robert. American Divine and Author .... 1798..1863
Bairuth, Margravine of. *See* Bareith. (*Memoirs*)...... 1709..1758
Baius, or De Bay, Michael, of Louvain. Theologian .... 1513..1589
Bajazet I. Sultan of the Turks (1389-1403)............ 1347..1403
Bajazet II. Sultan of Turks (1481-1512) .... 1447..1512
Baker, David. English Benedictine.................. 1575..1641 ·
Baker, David Erskine. (*Biographia Dramatica*) .... — ..1770'
Baker, Edward D. American Soldier and Statesman ... 1811..1861
Baker, Sir George, M. D. Antiquary .... 1722..1809
Baker, Henry. Naturalist. Founder of Bakerian Oration 1698..1774
Baker, John. Admiral .... — ..1716
Baker, Sir Richard. Historian...................... 1568?.1645
Baker, Thomas. Mathem. and Divine. (*Geometrical Key*) 1625..1690
Baker, Rev. Thos. Divine and Antiq. L. by Hor. Walpole 1656..1740
Bakewell, Robert. Agriculturist and Cattle-Breeder.... 1726..1795
Bakhuysen, Ludolph. Painter and Engrav. of Embden. 1631..1709
Baki, or Abd-al-Baki. Ottoman Lyric Poet............ — ..1600
Bakker, Peter Huysinga. Dutch Poet................. 1715..1801
Balassi, Mario. Florentine Painter.................. 1604..1667
Balbi, Adrian. Venetian Geographer................. 1782..1848
Balbi, Gaspar. Oriental Traveler fl.1579–88
Balbi, John. Genoese Dominican. (*Catholicon*) .... fl.13th c.
Balbinus. Roman Emperor (238)... .... — .. 238
Balbis, John Baptist. Italian Botanist............... 1765..1831
Balbo, Cæsar. Italian Statesman and Author .... 1789..1853
Balbo, Jerome. Bishop of Göritz. (*De Rebus Turcicis*). — ..1535
Balboa, Vasco Nuñez de. Spanish Adventurer......... 1475..1517
Balbuena, Bernardo de. Spanish Poet .... 1568..1627
Balcanqual, Walter. Scottish Divine................ — ..1642
Balcarres, Colin. Earl of. (*Historical Memoirs*)....... 1649..1722
Balchen, John. English Admiral..................... 1660..1744
Balde, James. German Latin Poet. (*Sylvæ*) .... 1603..1668
Balde de Ubaldis, Peter. Italian Lawyer and Writer.. 1324..1400
Balderic. Bp. of Noyon. Le Rouge. (*Chron. de Cambray*) — ..1097
Balderic, or Baudry. Bp. of Dol. Historian of Crusades — ..1130
Baldi, Bernardine. Italian Mathematician, Poet, and Phi-
    lologist. (*Lives of Mathematicians; La Nautica*).... 1553..1617
Baldi, Lazarus. Tuscan Historical Painter...........1623-4..1703
Baldinger, Ernest Godfrey. German Medical Writer ... 1738..1804
Baldini, Baccio. Florentine Engraver .... fl. 15th c.

BORN. DIED.

Baldini, John Anthony. Italian Statesman............ 1654..1725
Baldinucci, Philip. Florentine Artist................. 1624..1696
Baldock, Ralph de. Bp. London. (*Hist. British Affairs*) — ..1313
Baldovini, Francis. Italian Poet.................... 1635..1716
Balducci, Francis. Italian Anacreontic Poet.......... — ..1642
Balduccio, John. *Cosci*. Florentine Painter.......... — ..1600
Baldung, John. *Hans Grün*. Ger. Painter and Engraver 1470..1545?
Baldwin, Archbishop of Canterbury (1184–90)......... — ..1190
Baldwin I. Emperor of East. Count of Flanders...... 1171..1206
Baldwin II. Emperor of East (1228–61) .... 1217..1273
Baldwin I. King of Jerusalem (1100–18)............. — ..1118
Baldwin II. (1118–31) .... — ..1131
Baldwin III. (1143–63)............................... 1130..1163
Baldwin IV. (1174)................................ 1160..1186
Baldwin, Roger S. American Jurist and Statesman.... 1793..1863
Baldwin, Wm. Schoolm. and Div. (*Mirror for Mag.*) — ..1564?
Bale, John, Bishop of Ossory. (*Writers of Great Britain*). 1495..1563
Bale, Robt. Carmelite at Norw. (*Annales Ordinis Carmelit.*) — ..1503
Baléchou, John James. French Engraver............. 1715..1765
Balen, Henry van. Dutch Historical and Portrait Painter 1560..1632
Balen, John van, son. Painter...................... 1611.. —
Bales, Peter. Penman.............................. 1547..1610?
Balestra, Anthony. Historical Painter................ 1666..1720?
Baley, Walter. Medical Writer...................... 1529..1592
Balfour, Alex. Novelist and Misc. Writ. (*Highland Mary*) 1767..1829
Balfour, Sir James. Scottish Judge.................. — ..1583
Balfour, Sir James. Antiquary. Life by Haig, 1825.... — ..1657
Balfour, James, of Pilrig. Advocate................. 1703..1795
Balguy, Rev. John. Bangorian Controversialist........ 1686..1748
Balguy, Thos., son. Archdeacon. (*Divine Benevolence*) 1716..1795
Baliol, Edward.................................... — ..1363
Baliol, Sir John de. Founder of Baliol College, Oxford. — ..1269
Baliol, John, son. King of Scotland................. 1259?.1314
Ball, Sir Alexander. Rear-Admiral.................. — ..1659
Ball, John. Puritan Divine. (*Treatise on Faith*)....... 1585..1640
Ball, Thomas. Puritan Divine...................... — ..1659
Ballantyne, James, of Edinburgh. Printer and Journalist — ..1833
Ballantyne, John, brother. Printer.................. 1776?.1821
Ballantyne, Dr. J. R., of Benares. Orientalist......... — ..1864
Ballard, George. Biographer and Antiquary.......... — ..1755
Ballard, Samuel James. Admiral.................... — ..1829
Ballard, Volant Vashon. Admiral .... 1774..1832
Ballenden, or Bellenden, Sir John. Scot. Poet and Hist.. — ..1550
Ballexserd, James. Medical Writer at Geneva........ 1726..1774
Ballin, Claude. French Goldsmith.................. 1615..1678
Ballois, Louis Joseph Philip. Statistical Writer....... 1778..1803
Ballou, Hosea. Amer. Univers. Clergyman and Author. 1771..1852
Balmerino, Arthur Elphinstone, Lord. Beheaded....... 1688..1746
Balmez, James Lucia. Spanish Polit., Theol., Philos.... 1810..1848
Balnaves, Henry. Scottish Poet and Calvinistic Divine. 1520..1579
Balsham, Hugh de. Bp. Ely. Found. Pet. Coll. Camb. — ..1286
Balthasar, Christopher. French Protestant Theologian.. 1588..1670?
Baltimore, Geo. Calvert, 1st Ld. Founder of Maryland. 1582..1632
Baltus, John Francis. Jesuit of Metz. Writer........ 1667..1743

BORN. DIED.

Baltzar, Thomas, of Lubeck. Violinist in England..... — ..1663
Balue, John. Cardinal. Intriguer.................... 1420?.1491
Baluze, Stephen. Historical Writer.................. 1630..1718
Balzac, Honoré de. Novelist........................ 1799..1850
Balzac, John Louis Guez de. Writer. (*Letters*)........ 1594..1654
Bambocci, Anthony. Pa., Archit., Sculpt., Brass-founder 1368?.1435
Bamboccio, or Bamboche. *See* Peter van Laer......1613.1673 or 5
Bambridge, or Bainbrigge, Christoph. Cardl. Abp. Yk.. — ..1514
Bamfield, Francis. Ejected Nonconf. (*House of Wisdom*) — ..1684
Bampton, Rev. J. Founder of the Bampton Lecture.
Bancal des Issarts, John Henry. French Revolutionist. 1750..1826
Banck, Laurence. Swedish Civilian.................... — ..1662
Banck, Peter van der. Engraver in England........... 1649..1697
Bancroft, John. Master of Univ. College ; Bp. Oxford.. 1574..1640
Bancroft, Richard. Archbp. of Canterbury (1604–10)..._ 1544..1610
Bandarra, Gonzales. Portuguese Poet................. — ..1556
Bandello, Matthew. Italian Novelist and Poet........ 1480..1562
Bandiera, Attilio and Emilio. Venetian Revolutionists 1817&19..1844
Bandinelli, Baccio. Sculptor. Life by Vasari........ 1487..1559
Bandini, Angelo Maria. Antiquary and Bibliographer.. 1726..1800
Banduri, Anselm. (*Antiquities of Constantinople*) ...... 1671..1743
Bane, or Benn, Jas. Bp. of St. Andrews. Ld. Chamberlain — ..1332
Baner, Banier, or Bannier, John von. Swedish General. 1595..1641
Banes, Dominic. *See* Bannes........................ 1527..1604
Bangius, Peter. Swedish Div. (*Eccles. Hist. of Sweden*). 1633..1696
Bangius, Thomas. Danish Divine. (*Hebrew Lexicon*).. 1600..1661
Banier, Anthony. French Writer.................... 1673..1741
Banim, John. Irish Novelist.......................... 1800..1842
Banister, John. Physician and Surgical Writer........ 1553?.1630?
Banister, John. Violinist............................. 1630?.1676
Banister, John. Botanist............................. — ..1689
Bankert, Adrian. Dutch Admiral..................... — ..1684
Bankert, Joseph van Trappen. Dutch Admiral........ — ..1646?
Bankes, Henry, M. P. (*Constitutional History of Greece*).. 1757..1834
Bankes, Sir John. Lord Chief Justice................. 1589..1644
Banks, John. Dramatist. (*The Unhappy Favorite*).... fl. 1700?
Banks, John. Bookseller. (*Crit. Rev. of L. of Cromwell*). 1709..1751
Banks, Sir Joseph. Naturalist. Pres. Royal Society... 1743..1820
Banks, Thomas. Sculptor............................ 1735..1805
Banks, Thomas Christopher. Genealogist............. 1764..1854
Bannatyne, George. Antiquary....................1545 bef.1608
Bannatyne, Sir William. Scottish Judge and Writer... 1743..1834
Bannes, Dominic. Span.Writ. on Arist. and the Fathers. 1527..1604
Bannier, or Banier, John. Gen. under Gustav. Adolph.. 1595..1641
Bannister, John. Comedian. L. by J. Adolphus, 1839. 1760..1836
Banti, Brigida Georgi. Italian Singer................. 1757..1806
Baptist, John Bapt. *Monnoyer.* Pa. of Fruit and Flowers. 1635..1699
Baptist, John Gaspar. Pa. of Drapery and Background. — ..1691
Baptistin, John Bapt. Stuck. Ital. Musical Composer... 1677?.1755
Baradæus. *Jacob Zanzalus.* Bp. of Edessa. *See* Jacob. — .. 578
Baraguay d'Hilliers, Louis. French General.......... 1764..1812
Baranzano, Redemptus. Mathematician. (*Uranoscopia*). 1590..1622
Baratier, John Philip. Ger. Scholar. Life by Formey . 1721..1740
Barba, Alvarez Alonzo. (*Treatise on Metallurgy*)....... fl. 1620

BORN. DIED.

Barbacena, F. C. Braut, Mqs. of. Brazilian Soldier and
    Statesm. . . . . 1772. .1842
Barbadillo, Alphonso Jerome de Salas. Span. Dramat. . 1580?.1630
Barbarelli. *See* Giorgione. Venetian Painter. . . . . 1477. .1511
Barbarini, Francis. Italian Poet. (*Precepts of Love*). . . 1264. .1348
Barbaro, Dan. Coadj. Patr. of Aquileia. (*On Eloquence*) 1513. .1570
Barbaro, Francis. Venetian Orator. (*De Re Uxoria*). 1398. .1454
Barbaro, Hermolaos. Bp. of Verona. Schol.; tr. of Æsop 1410?.1471
Barbaro, Hermolaos, of Venice. Patriarch of Aquileia.
    Scholar; translator of Aristotle. . . . . 1454. .1495
Barbarossa. *See* Frederick I, Emperor. . . . . 1121. .1190
Barbarossa, Heyradin. Corsair King of Algiers. . . . . . . 1467?.1547
Barbarossa, Horuch. Corsair King of Algiers. . . . . 1475?.1518
Barbaroux, Chas. Fr. Scientific Writer and Politician. . 1767. .1794
Barbatelli, Bernardino. *Poccetti.* Italian Painter. . . . . . 1542. .1612
Barbauld, Mrs. Anna Lætit. Writ. L. by Lucy Aikin, 1825 1743. .1825
Barbazan, Armand William. *Le Chevalier sans Reproche* — . .1432
Barbazan, Stephen. Fr. Writer. (*A Father's Instructions*) 1696. .1770
Barbe. Queen of Poland. *Esther* . . . . — . .1525
Barbé-Marbois, Francis de, Ct. and Mqs. Fr. Statesm. 1745. .1837
Barbe Radziwil. Qu. of Poland, wife of Sigism. August. — . .1551
Barbeau de la Bruyère, John Louis. (*Hist. Map*). . . . . 1710. .1781
Barber du Bourg, James. Fr. Physician and Botanist. . 1709. .1779
Barber, John. Civilian; friend of Cranmer. . . . . — . .1549
Barberini, Anthony. Cardinal, Archbishop of Reims.
    Negotiator and Ambassador. 1608. .1671
Barberini, or Barbarini, Francis. Italian Poet. . . . . 1264. .1348
Barberini. *See* Urban VIII. . . . . 1568. .1644
Barbeyrac, Charles. Fr. Phys. (*Quæstiones Medicæ*). . . 1629. .1699
Barbeyrac, John. Fr. Historical and Juridical Writer. . 1674. .1744
Barbié d'Aucourt, John. Anti-Jesuit Writer. . . . . 1641. .1694
Barbié du Bocage, Alex. Francis. (*Dict. of Bibl. Geog.*) 1798. .1835
Barbié du Bocage, John Deuis. French Geographer. . . 1760. .1825
Barbier, Anthony Alexander. French Writer. (*Diction-*
    ary of Anonymous and Pseudonymous Works) . . . . 1765. .1825
Barbier, Charles. French Philanthropist. . . . . —ab.1830
Barbieri, Gianfrancesco. *Guercino da Cento.* Painter. . . 1590. .1666
Barbieri, Paul Anthony, brother. Painter of Still Life. . 1596. .1640
Barbosa, Arias, or Ayres. Port. Schol.; Reviver of Learn. — . .1530
Barbosa, Augustine. Canonist. 1590. .1638
Barbosa, Emanuel. Portuguese Lawyer. . . . . 1548?.1649
Barbosa, Peter. Portuguese Lawyer. . . . . — . .1606
Barbou, John Joseph. Printer at Paris. . . . . — . .1752
Barbou, Joseph, brother. Printer at Paris. . . . . — . .1737
Barbou, Joseph Gerard, neph. Classical Printer at Paris. 1715. .1813
Barbour, James. American Statesman. . . . . 1775. .1825
Barbour, John. Scottish Poet and Historian. . . . . 1316?.1395?
Barchusen, or Barkhausen, John Conrad. Phys. & Chem. 1666. .1723
Barclay, Alexander. Writer; translator of *Ship of Fools*. — . .1552
Barclay de Tolly, Michael. Russian General . . . . 1755. .1818
Barclay, John. Writer. (*Argenis.*) L. by Ld. Hailes, 1786 1582. .1621
Barclay, John. Scot. Div. (*Descrip. of the R. C. Church*) 1645. .1710
Barclay, John. Scot. Div. Found. of *Bereans*, or *Barclayans* 1734. .1798
Barclay, Robert. Quaker Writer. (*Apology*). . . . . 1648. .1690

BORN. DIED.

Barclay, Wm.   Scottish Civilian in France.   (*De Regno*) 1546..1605
Bar-Cokeba.   Jewish Impostor........................ — .. 134
Barcos, Martin de.   Writer in the Jansenist Controversy. 1600..1678
Bardesanos, of Edessa.   Heresiarch.................. fl. 172?
Bardet, Peter.   French Advocate.   (*Recueil d'Arrêts*).. 1591..1685
Bardin, Peter.   (*Le Grand Chambellan de France*)....... 1590..1637
Bardney, Rd.   English Benedictine. (*Life of Grosteste*).. — ..1504
Barebone, Praise-God............................... — ..1680
Bareith, Frederica Sophia Wilhelmina, Margravine of... 1709..1758
Barents, Dietrich.   Dutch Hist. and Portrait Painter.... 1534..1582
Barentz, William.   Dutch Navigator................. fl. 16th c.
Barère de Vieuzac, Bertrand.   Revolutionist.   Life by
   Carot and David, 1842........................... 1755..1841
Baretti, Joseph.   Italian Writer.   (*Ital. and Eng. Dict.*). 1716..1789
Bargagli, Scipione.   Tuscan Writer................... ..1612
Bargrave, Isaac.   Dean of Canterbury; Royal Chaplain. 1586..1643
Barham, Rev. Richard Harris.   (*Ingoldsby Legends*)..... 1788..1845
Barillon, Hen. de.   Bp. Luçon.   L. by C. F. Dubos, 1700 1639..1699
Barker, Benjamin, of Bath.   Painter................ 1776?.1838
Barker, Edmund Henry.   Philologist................. 1788..1839
Barker, George, of Birmingham.   Projector......... 1776?.1845
Barker, John.   Consul-General in Egypt.   Pomologist... — ..1850
Barker, Matthew Henry.   *The Old Sailor*.   Naval Novelist 1790..1846
Barker, Robert.   Painter and Panoramist............. 1739..1806
Barker, Thomas, of Bath.   Artist.   (*Woodman*)........ 1769..1847
Barkham, or Barcham, John.   Divine and Antiquary.... 1572?.1642
Barksdale, Rev. Clem.   Biographer. (*Monum. Literaria*) 1609..1688
Barlaam.   Italian Ecclesiastic and Greek Scholar....... — ..1348?
Barlæus, Gaspar.   Dutch Latin Poet.   (*Paradisius*)..... 1584..1648
Barlæus, Lambert.   Scholar and Annotator at Leyden... 1595..1655
Barland, Adrian.   Dutch Critic and Historical Writer... 1488?.1542
Barletta, Gabriel.   Dominican Preacher.............. 1400?. —
Barlow, Francis.   Painter of Animals................ 1626..1702
Barlow, Joel.   Amer. Statesm. & Poet.   L. by Oelsner, 1813 1755?.1812
Barlow, Peter, of Woolwich.   Mathematician.......... 1776..1862
Barlow, Thomas.   Bishop of Lincoln................. 1607..1691
Barlowe, Wm.   Bp. of Chichester.   Protestant Exile... — ..1569
Barlowe, William.   Archdeacon.   Nat. Philosopher .... — ..1625
Barnard, Sir Andrew Francis.   British General ....1773..1855
Barnard, Anne, Lady.   Ballad Poet.   (*Auld Robin Gray*) 1705..1825
Barnard, John, D. D.   Divine.   (*Life of Heylin*) .... — ..1683
Barnard, Sir John, M. P.   Lord Mayor and Statesman... 1685..1764
Barnaud, Nicholas.   French Alchemist............... fl. 16th c.
Barnave, Anthony Peter Joseph.   French Statesman.... 1761..1793
Barner, James.   Chemical Philos.   (*Chymia Philosophica*) 1641..1686
Barnes, Barnaby.   Poet .... 1569? aft.1607
Barnes, Daniel II.   American Conchologist............. — ..1818
Barnes, Joshua.   Critic and Historian.   (*Edward III.*).. 1654..1712
Barnes, or Berners, Juliana.   Prioress of Sopewell.   Writer —aft.1485
Barnes, Robert.   Chapl. to Henry VIII.   Protest. Martyr. — ..1540
Barnes, Thomas.   Editor of *Times* .... 1786..1841
Barnet, Curtis.   Commodore...................... — ..1746
Barneveldt, Jon van Olden.   Dutch Statesman .... 1547?.1619
Barney, Joshua.   American Naval Commander........1759..1818

BORN. DIED.

Baro, or Baron, Peter. Fr. Prot. Prof. of Div. at Cambridge 1534?.1599
Baroccio, Baroche, or Barroccio, Fred. Italian Painter.. 1528..1612
Baroccio, or Barozzi, da Vignola, James. Ital. Architect 1507..1573
Baron, Bonaventure. Irish Franciscan Writ. (*Theologia*) — ..1696
Baron, Michael. French Actor....................... 1653..1729
Baroni, Leonora. Italian Singer and Poet .... fl. 17th c.
Baronius, Cæsar. Cardinal. (*Ecclesiastical Annals.*) Life
    by Barnabæus, 1651 .... 1538..1607
Barozzi, James. *See* Baroccio. Architect............ 1507..1573
Barraband, Peter Paul. French Painter of Birds....... 1767..1809
Barral, Peter. French Abbé. (*Dict. des Hommes Célèbres*) — ..1772
Barras, Paul John Francis Nicholas. Fr. Revolutionist. 1755..1829
Barré, Col. Isaac. Life by Britton, in *Authorship of Junius* 1726..1802
Barré, Joseph, of Paris. (*History of Germany*)......... 1692?.1764
Barré, Louis Francis Joseph de la. Fr. Historical Writer 1688..1738
Barré, Madame du. *See* Dubarry........................1746..1793
Barré, Wm. Vincent. Fr. Writer. (*Hist. of First Consulate*) — ..1829
Barrelier, James. French Botanist .... 1606..1673
Barrère de Vieuzac. *See* Barère de Vieuzac.......... 1755..1841
Barrère, Peter. French Physician and Naturalist ...... 1690?.1755
Barrett, George. Landscape Painter .... 1732?.1784
Barrett, John, D. D. Orient. (*Origin of Constellations*).. — ..1821
Barrett, Wm., of Bristol. Frd. of Chatterton. (*Hist. of Bristol*) — ..1789
Barrington, Hon. Daines. Writer. (*Miscellanies*) ..... 1727..1800
Barrington, John Shute, First Viscount. Writer. (*Mis-
    cellanea Sacra.*) Life by Shute Barrington.......... 1678..1734
Barrington, Samuel. Admiral .... 1729..1800
Barrington, Hon. Shute. Bishop of Durham (1791–1826) 1734..1826
Barrington, William Wildman, Viscount. Statesman.. 1710..1793
Barroccio, or Baroccio, Frederick. Italian Painter...... 1528..1612
Barros, John de. *The Portuguese Livy.* Historian. (*Asia*) 1496..1570
Barrow, Isaac, D. D. Theologian and Mathematician.... 1630..1677
Barrow, Sir John. Biographer. Life by himself....... 1764..1848
Barruel Beauvert, Anthony Joseph, Ct. de. Fr. Writer 1756..1817
Barruel, Augustine. French Writer .... 1741..1820
Barry, Sir Charles. Architect of Houses of Parliament.. 1795..1860
Barry, Countess du. *See* Dubarry .... 1746..1793
Barry, Sir David. Physician and Physiologist .... 1780..1835
Barry, Elizabeth. Actress........................... 1658..1713
Barry, George, D. D. Scot. Div. (*History of the Orkneys*) 1748?.1805
Barry, Girald. *Giraldus Cambrensis.* Historian....... 1147..1222?
Barry, James, Lord Santry. Irish Judge. (*Tenures*)... 1598..1673
Barry, James. Painter. L. Pref. to Works, 4to, 2 vols. 1809 1741..1806
Barry, John. American Naval Commander........... 1745..1803
Barry, Martin. Physiologist........................ 1802..1855
Barry, Spranger. Actor............................ 1719..1777
Bartas, William Sallust du. French Poet.............. 1544..1590
Barth, or Bart, John. French Commodore............ 1651..1702
Barthe, Nicholas Thomas. French Writer............. 1737..1785
Barthelemon, Francis Hippolite. Composer and Violinist 1731..1808
Barthélemy, John James. (*Young Anacharsis.*) Life by
    Mancini-Nivernois, 1795 ....1716..1795
Barthez, Paul Joseph. French Medical Writer......... 1734..1806
Barthius, Gaspar. German Scholar. (*Soliluqua*)....... 1587..1658

BORN. DIED.

Bartholdy, Jacob Solomon. Prussian Diplomatist...... 1779..1825
Bartholine, Erasmus. Physician. (*De Cometis*) .... 1625..1698
Bartholine, Gaspar. Danish Medical Writer.......... 1585..1629
Bartholine, Gaspar. Phys. and Anat. (*De Tibiis Veterum*) 1650?.1705?
Bartholine, Thomas. Danish Medical Writer .... 1616..1680
Bartholine, Thomas. (*Antiquitates Danicæ*)........... 1659..1690
Bartholomew. *Anglius.* English Franciscan.......... fl. 1350?
Bartleman. *See* Barthelemon...................... 1731..1808
Bartlett, Josiah. American Physician and Politician.... 1759..1820
Bartlett, William Henry. Artist and Author.......... 1809..1854
Bartoli. Italian Civilian...................... 1312..1356
Bartoli, Cosmo. (*Life of Frederick Barbarossa*)........ fl. 1570
Bartoli, Daniel. Jesuit Writer. (*History of the Jesuits*).. 1608..1685
Bartoli, Peter Santo. *Perugino.* Italian Painter .... 1635?.1700
Bartolini, Lorenzo. Italian Sculptor................. 1777..1850
Bartolocci, Julius. Hebraist. (*Bibliotheca Rabbinica*).. 1613..1687
Bartolomeo, Andrew de. *Andrea Siculo.* Italian Jurist 1400..1479
Bartolomeo, Dionysius di. Neapolitan Architect....... fl. 16th c.
Bartolomeo, Fra. *See* Baccio della Porta .... 1469..1517
Bartolomeo, Leonardo di. Sicilian Statesman.......... — ..1450
Bartolozzi, Francis. Engraver.................... 1725?.1813?
Barton, Benjamin Smith, M. D. American Naturalist ... 1766..1815
Barton, Bernard. Quaker Poet.................... 1784..1849
Barton, Elizabeth. *Holy Maid of Kent.*.............. — ..1534
Bartram, John. American Botanist................. 1701..1777
Bartram, Wm. Amer. Naturalist. (*Amer. Ornithology*) 1739..1823
Bartsch, Adam von. Ger. Engrav. (*Le Peintre graveur*) 1757..1820
Baruffaldi. Jesuit Writer. (*Life of Ariosto*)........... 1740..1817
Barwick, John, D. D. Dean of St. Paul's. Life by Dr.
  Peter Barwick, 1721, tr. by Hilkiah Bedford ....1612..1664
Barwick, Peter, brother. Med. Writ. (*Defence of Harvey*) 1619..1705
Barziza, Gasparino. ·Reviver of Learning .... 1370?.1432
Bas, James Philip le. French Engraver .... 1707..1783
Bas, John le. French Surgeon and Accoucheur......... fl. 1756-65
Basaiti, Mark, of Friuli. Italian Painter............... fl. 1510-30
Basan, Peter Francis. Engraver and Print-seller .... 1723..1797
Baschenis, Evarista. Ital. Pa. of Musical Instruments. 1617..1677
Baschi, Matthew. Founder of Capuchin Friars........ 1500?.1552
Basedow, John Bernard. Ger. Philos. and Educationist 1723..1790
Baseilhac, John. French Lithotomist................. 1703..1781
Basevi, George. Architect...................... 1795..1845
Bashuysen, Hen. Jas. van. Hebrew Scholar and Printer 1679..1758
Basil, St. *The Great.* Bishop of Cæsarea (371-79). Life
  by Godf. Hermant (Dr. Menart), 1674; Agresta, 1681 329.. 379
Basiliscus. Emperor of East (475-77)............... —477 or 8
Basilius I. Emperor of East (867-86). *The Macedonian* 826?. 886
Basilius II. Emperor of East (976-1025).............. 958..1025
Basilovitch, John, or Ivan. Emperor of Russia........ 1529..1584
Basin, or Bazin, Thomas. Bishop. Historian.......... 1402..1491
Basingstoke, or Basinge, John. Archd. Greek Scholar — ..1252
Basire, or Basier, Isaac. Divine and Traveler.......... 1607..1676
Basire, James. Engraver......................... 1730..1802
Baskerville, Hannibal. Antiquary .... — ..1688
Baskerville, John. Printer .... 1706..1775

BORN. DIED.

Baskerville, Sir Simon. Physician .... 1573?.1641
Basnage, Benjamin. Fr. Protest. (*Treatise on the Church*) 1580..1652
Basnage du Franquenay, Henry. French Lawyer.
  Editor of *Coutume de Normandie* .... 1615..1695
Basnage de Beauval, Henry. (*Ouvrage des Savans*)... 1656..1710
Basnage de Beauval, James. Eccles. Writ. and Hist... 1653..1723
Basnage de Flottemanville, Samuel. (*Annales Politico-*
  Ecclesiasticæ) .... 1638..1721
Bass, George. Surgeon, R. N. Discov. *Bass's Straits*... —aft.1798
Bass, or Bassius, Henry. German Surgeon............. 1690..1754
Bassandyne, Thomas. Scottish Printer and Reformer.. — ..1591
Bassani, James Anthony. Jesuit of Vicenza. Preacher 1686..1747
Bassani, John Baptist. Musical Composer............. 1657?. —
Bassano. *James da Ponte*. Italian Painter........... 1510..1592
Bassano, Francis da Ponte. Painter .... 1548..1591
Bassano, Hugues Bernard Maret, Duc de. Fr. Statesman 1763..1839
Bassano, Jerome. Painter............................ 1560..1622
Bassano, John Baptist. Painter...................... 1553..1613
Bassano, Leander. Painter at Venice .... 1558..1623
Bassantin, or Bassantoun, James. Scottish Astrologer.. 1504?.1568
Basselm, Oliver. French Poet........................ —ab.1418
Bassi, Laura Maria Catherine. Italian Philosopher ..... 1711..1778
Bassiano, Laudi. Italian Medical Writer............. — ..1562
Bassius, or Bass, Henry. Medical Writer at Halle...... 1690..1754
Bassompierre, Francis de. Marsh. of France. Life by self 1579..1646
Basson, Sebastian. (*Philosoph. Natural. adversus Aristot.*)
Bassuel, Peter. French Surgical Writer.............. 1706..1757
Bassville, Nicholas John Hugo de. Fr. Envoy and Writer — ..1793
Bast, Frederick James. German Scholar............... 1772..1811
Basta, George. French Military Writer .... — ..1607
Bastard, Thomas. Clergyman and Poet .... — ..1618
Bastiat, Frederick. French Political Economist .... 1801..1850
Bastide, John Francis de la. Fr. Miscellaneous Writer . 1724..1798
Baston, Robert. Poet Laureate and Pub. Orator at Oxf. — ..1310?
Bastwick, John, M. D. Polemical Writer.........1593 aft.1648
Bate, George. Physician and Historical Writer........ 1608..1668
Bate, John, D. D. Prior of the Carmelites of York ...... — ..1429
Bate, Julius. Hutchinsonian Divine................... 1711..1771
Bateman, Chas. Philip Boteler. British Admiral....... 1775..1857
Bateman, Thomas. Physician .... — ..1821
Bateman, William. Bishop of Norwich (1344–55)...... — ..1355
Bates, John. Musical Composer .... 1740..1799
Bates, Joshua. Amer. Merch. in London; Philanthropist 1788..1864
Bates, William. Nonconf. Divine and Biographer...... 1625..1699
Bath, William Pulteney, Earl of. Statesman........... 1682..1764
Bathalmiusi. Mahometan Genealogical Writer....... — ..1030
Bathe, William. Irish Jesuit at Salamanca. Writer.
  (*Janua Linguarum*). .... 1564..1614
Bathori, Elizabeth. Niece of Stephen Bathori; Murderess — ..1614
Bathori, Stephen. King of Poland (1576–86)......... 1533..1586
Bathurst, Allen. First Earl. Statesman.............. 1684..1775
Bathurst, Hen. 2d E. L. Chanc. (*Theory of Evidence*) 1714..1794
Bathurst, Henry. Third Earl .... 1762..1834
Bathurst, Henry. Bp. Norwich. L. by Archd. H. Bathurst 1744 .1837

BORN. DIED.

Bathurst, Ralph, M. D.   Dean of Wells.   Philosopher, Wit, and Latin Poet.   Life by T. Warton, 1761 . . . . . 1620 . . 1704
Bathyllus.   Pantomime. . . . .   fl. 30? B.C.
Batman, or Bateman, Stephen, D. D.   Poet . . . .   — . . 1587
Batoni, Pompeo Jerome.   Italian Painter. . . . . 1708 . . 1787
Batou Khan.   Emperor of the Moguls . . . .   — . . 1255
Batsch, August.   John George Chas.   German Naturalist 1761 . . 1802
Battaglini, Mark.   Bishop of Cesena.   (*Hist. of Councils*) 1645 . . 1717
Battely, Dr. John.   Antiquary.   (*Antiquitates Rutupinæ*) 1647 . . 1708
Batteux, Charles.   French Critic. 1713 . . 1780
Batthyanyi, Count Louis.   Hungarian Statesman . . . . . . 1809 . . 1849
Battie, William, M. D.   (*Treatise on Mental Madness*) . . . 1704 . . 1776
Battishill, Jonathan.   Musical Composer . . . . 1738 . . 1801
Baudelocque, John Louis.   French Accoucheur. . . . . 1746 . . 1810
Baudelot de Dairval, Chas. Cæsar.   Medalist and Antiq. 1648 . . 1722
Bauderon, Brice.   Medical Writer. 1540 . . 1623
Baudet, Stephen.   French Engraver . . . . 1643 . . 1716
Baudier, Michael.   French Historical Writer . . . . fl. ti. Lou. XIII.
Baudin, Peter Charles Louis.   French Political Writer. . 1748 . . 1799
Baudius, Dominic, of Leyden.   Historiog. and Latin Poet 1561 . . 1613
Baudot de Juilli, Nicholas.   Historical Writer . . . . 1678 . . 1759
Baudouin, Frs. *Baldwinus*.   French Civilian and Scholar 1520 . . 1573
Baudouin, or Baudoin, John.   French Class. Translator. 1584? . 1650
Baudrand, Michael Anthony.   French Geographer . . . . . 1633 . . 1700
Bauer, Ferdinand.   Botanical Painter. . . . . 1744 . . 1826
Bauhin, Gaspar.   French Bot. (*Pinax Theatri Botanici*) 1560 . . 1624
Bauhin, John.   French Protestant Physician. . . . . 1511 . . 1582
Bauhin, John.   French Botanist.   (*Historia Plantarum*). 1541 . . 1613
Bauhin, John Gaspar.   Physician and Botanist . . . . 1606? . 1685
Bauldri, Paul.   Fr. Chron. and Hist. Writer at Utrecht 1639 . . 1706
Baulot, or Beaulieu, Jas. *Friar James*.   Fr. Surg. Operator 1651 . . 1720
Baumé, Anthony.   French Chemist . . . . 1728 . . 1804
Baume des Dossat, Jas. Francis de la.   Poet. (*Christiade*) 1705 . . 1756
Baume, Nicholas Augustus de la.   Marshal of France. . . 1636 . . 1716
Baumer, John Wm.   (*Nat. Hist. of Mineral Kingdom*). . 1719 . . 1788
Baumgarten, Alex. Theophilus.   German Philosopher . . 1714 . . 1762
Baumgarten, Sigismund Jacob.   Theologian . . . . 1706 . . 1775
Baune, Jas. de la.   Jesuit of Paris.   Latin Poet and Writer 1649? . 1725
Baur, Ferdinand Christian.   German Theologian . . . . 1792 . . 1861
Baur, Frederick William von.   Russian Military Engineer 1731 . . 1783
Baur, John William, of Strasburg.   *Wirlembaur*.   Architect, Painter, and Engraver. 1600 . . 1640
Bausch, John Lawrence.   Medical Writer . . . . 1605 . . 1665
Bautru, William.   French Wit . . . . 1588 . . 1665
Bavay, Paul Ignatius de, of Brussels.   Medical Writer . . 1704 . . 1768
Bawdween, William.   Divine and Antiquary. . . . . 1762? . 1816
Baxter, Andrew.   Metaphysician and Natural Philosopher 1686? . 1750
Baxter, Richard.   Nonconformist Divine.   Life by himself and Sylvester, 1696; Dr. E. Calamy, 1713; Orme . . . . 1615 . . 1691
Baxter, William.   Grammarian and Critic . . . . 1650 . . 1723
Bayard, James A.   American Statesman. . . . . 1767 . . 1815
Bayard, Peter du Terrail, Chevalier de.   *Le Chevalier sans Peur et sans Reproche*, &c.   Life by Champier, 4to, 1625; *Le Loyal Serviteur*, 1619; Lazare Bocquillot,

BORN. DIED.

Prior of Louval, 12mo, 1702; Guyard de Berville, 12mo,
1760; Dutems, 1770; Rev. Joseph Sterling, 1781;
Dochier, 1789; Bucholz, 1801; Pillot, 1816; Cohen, 1821;
The Loyal Servant, tr. by Croker, 1825; Lotz, 1826;
Terrebasse, 1828; Delandine de St. Esprit, 1842 ..... 1476..1524
Bayen, Peter. French Chemist .... 1725..1798
Bayer, John. German Astronomer. (*Cœlum Stellatum*) — ..1660
Bayer, Theoph. Siegfried, grandson. (*Museum Sinicum*). 1694..1738
Bayf, or Baif, Lazarus de. French Poet and Scholar.... — ..1547
Bayle, Francis. Medical Writer .... 1622..1709
Bayle, Moses. French Revolutionist .... 1760?.1815?
Bayle, Peter. (*Biographical and Historical Dictionary.*)
Life by Des Maizeaux, 1712; Durevost, 1716......... 1647..1706
Bayley, Anselm, of London. Divine .... — ..1794
Bayley, Sir John. Judge. (*Bills of Exchange*) .... 1763..1841
Bayley, Richard. American Medical Writer .... 1745..1801
Bayly, Lewis. Bishop of Bangor. (*Practice of Piety*) .. 1565?.1631
Bayly, Dr. Thomas. English Publicist................ — ..1659?
Bayly, Thomas Haynes. Lyric Poet .... 1797..1839
Bayly, William. Astronomer; companion of Capt. Cook — ..1810
Bayne, Alexander. Scottish Jurist................... — ..1737
Baynes, John. Political Writer...................... 1758..1787
Bayntun, Sir William Henry. Admiral.............. 1765?.1840
Bazard, Amand. Founder of Fr. Carbonarism; Socialist 1791..1832
Bazhenov, Basil Ivanovitch. Russian Architect .... 1737..1799
Bazin, Giles Augustine. French Physician and Naturalist — ..1754
Bazin, or Basin, Thomas. Bishop. Historian.......... 1402..1491
Bazire, or Basire, Claude. French Revolutionist ...... 1764..1794
Bé, William le. Printer and Type Founder at Troyes... 1525..1598
Beale, Mary. Portrait Painter...................... 1632..1697
Beard, John. Actor .... 1716?.1791
Beaton, or Bethune, David. Card.; Abp. of St. Andrew's 1494..1546
Beaton, James. Scottish Divine and Statesman....... — ..1539
Beaton, James. Bp. of Glasgow. (*History of Scotland*) 1530..1603
Beatson, Robert, L.L. D. (*Political Index, &c.*)......... 1742..1818
Beattie, James, L.L. D. Poet. Life by A. Bower, 1804;
Sir Wm. Forbes, 1806; Mudford, 1809; Dyce, 1831... 1735..1803
Beattie, James Hay. (*Essays and Fragments.*) Life by
his father, James Beattie, foregoing................. 1768..1790
Beattie, Sir William, M. D. Physician to the Fleet..... 1770..1842
Beatus Rhenanus. German Scholar and Historian..... 1485..1547
Beau, Charles le. (*Histoire du Bas Empire*)........... 1701..1778
Beau, John Louis le, brother, of Paris. Classical Editor. 1721..1766
Beaucaire de Beguillon, Francis. Archbishop of Mentz.
(*Rerum Gallicarum Commentaria*).................. 1514..1591
Beauchamp, Alphonse de. French Hist. and Publicist. 1767..1832
Beauchamp, Richard, Earl of Warwick. General in
France; died at Rouen.......................... — ..1439
Beauchamp, Richard. Bishop. Architect............. — ..1481
Beauchamps, Peter Francis Godard de. (*Théâtres de
France*) .... 1689..1761
Beauchateau, Francis Matthew Chatelet de. Fr. Poet. 1645.. —
Beauclerk, Topham. Scholar. Friend of Dr. Johnson. 1739..1780
Beaufils, Wm. Jesuit of Auvergne. Preacher and Writer 1674..1757

BORN. DIED.

Beaufort, Henry. Cardinal. Bishop of Winchester, 1405–47. Life by Gough in *Vetust. Monumenta* ...... 1370?..1447
Beaufort, Louis de. Historical Writer................. — ..1795
Beaufort, Margaret, mother of Henry VII. Life by Halsted, 1839.. 1441..1509
Beauharnais, Alexander, Viscount de. Fr. Revolutionary Statesman; First Husband of the Empress Josephine 1760..1794
Beauharnais, Eugene de. Viceroy of Italy. Life by Gallois, 1821; Aubriet, 1824; Schoenberg, 1825; Vau-, doncourt, 1825; Seel, 1827; D'Arnay, 1830; Armandi, 1838; Saint-You, 1838............................. 1781..1824
Beauharnais, Hortense Eugénie. Queen of Holland.... 1783..1837
Beaulieu, James. French Surgical Operator. *See* Baulot 1651..1720
Beaulieu, Sebastian de Pontault, Sieur de. (*Battles of Louis XIV.*)....................................... — ..1674
Beaumanoir, Philip de. (*Coûtumes de Beauvoisis*)...... — ..1296
Beaumarchais, Peter Augustin Caron de. Dramatic Writer, &c. Life by Cousin d'Avallon, 1802........ 1732..1799
Beaumelle, Laurence. French Wr. (*Letters to Voltaire*) 1727..1773
Beaumont, Elias de. *See* Élie de Beaumont........... 1732..1786
Beaumont, Frs. Poet; colleague of Fletcher. L. by Dyce 1586..1616
Beaumont, Sir George Howland. Artist............... 1753..1827
Beaumont de Perefixe, Hardouin. Archbishop of Paris. *See* Perefixe .... 1605..1670
Beaumont, Jane le Prince de. Writer for the Young... 1711..1780
Beaumont, Sir John. Poet. (*Bosworth Field*)........ 1582..1628
Beaumont, John Louis Moreau de. French Polit. Writer. 1715..1785
Beaumont, Joseph, D. D. Master of Peterhouse. Poet. (*Psyche*) Life by son, Charles Beaumont, 1749..... 1615..1699
Beaumont, Wm. American Surgeon............... 1796..1853
Beaune, Florimond de. French Mathematician......... 1601..1652
Beaurain, John de. Geogr. (*Campaigns of Luxemburg*) 1696..1771
Beaurieu, Gaspard Guillard de. (*L'Élève de la Nature*). 1728..1795
Beausobre, Isaac de. (*History of Reformation*)........ 1659..1738
Beausobre, Louis de, son. Writer at Berlin .... 1730..1783
Beauvais, Charles Nicholas. Fr. Phys., Polit., & Writer. — ..1704
Beauvais, John Bapt. Charles Mary de. Fr. Preacher... 1731..1790
Beauvais, Wm. Medalist. (*Medallic Hist. of Rom. Emp.*) 1698..1773
Beauvilliers, Frs. Honorat de. Soldier; Courtier; Poet. 1607..1687
Beauvilliers, Paul Hippolytus. Fr. Soldier and Negotiat. 1684..1776
Beauvois, Ambrose M. F. J. P. de. Fr. Nat. and Trav. 1752..1820
Beauzée, Nicholas. French Critic and Grammarian.... 1717..1789
Beaver, Capt. Phil., R. N. L. by Capt. W. H. Smyth, 1829 1766..1813
Beazley, Samuel. Architect and Play Writer.......... 1786..1851
Bebele, Henry. Lat. Schol. & Poet Laureate at Tübingen   fl. 1501
Beccadelli, Anthony. *Panormita*. (*Alphonso of Aragon*) 1394..1471
Beccadelli, Louis. (*Lives of Pole and Bembo*)......... 1502..1572
Beccafumi, Dominic. *Mecherino*. Italian Painter..... 1484..1549
Beccari, Augustine, of Ferrara. Pastoral Poet........ 1510?.1590
Beccari, James Bartholomew. (*Motion of Fluids*)...... 1682..1766
Beccaria, Cæs. Bonesana, Mqs. di. (*Crimes & Punishm.*) 1738..1794
Beccaria, John Baptist. Natural Philosopher.......... 1716..1781
Beccuti, Francis. *Il Copetta*. Italian Poet............ 1509..1553
Becerra, Gaspard. Spanish Painter and Sculptor....... 1520?.1570

BORN. DIED.

Becher, John Joachim. German Chemist............ . 1625..1685
Bechstein, John Matthias. German Ornithologist...... 1757..1822
Beck, Bek, or Beek, David. Dutch Portrait Painter.... 1621..1656
Becker, or Bekker, Balthasar. Dutch Divine......... 1634..1698
Becker, Chas. Ferd. Ger. Philol. (*Deutsche Grammnatik*) 1775..1849
Becker, Daniel. German Phys. (*De Cultivoro Prussiaco*) 1594..1655
Becker, Ferdinand Wm. German Natural Philosopher. 1805..1834
Becker, Gottfried Wm. Ger. Hist., Med., and Misc. Wr. 1778..1801
Becker, Wm. Adol. Ger. Author. (*Roman Antiquities*).. 1796..1846
Becket, Isaac. English Mezzotinto Engraver.......... 1653.. —
Becket, Thomas à. Edw. Grim; Roger de Pontigny;
Wm. Fitzstephen; John of Salisbury, d. 1180; Barthol-
omew, Bishop of Exeter, d. 1186; Herbert of Bosham,
fl. 1188; Anon. of Lambeth; Robert of Gloucester;
Edward, a Monk of Canterbury; E. a Monk of Eves-
ham; Benedict, Abbot of Peterborough, d. 1193;
Roger of Croyland, tem. John; Alan of Tewksbury,
d. 1202; Wm. of Canterbury; Stephen Langton, d.
1228; Alexander de Hales; John Grandison or Graun-
son, d. 1369; Thos. Stapleton, 1588; Laurence Vade or
Wade; *Quadrilogus* or *Quadripartita Historia*, pub.
1495; C. du Canda, 1615; Cambdoust de Pontchasteau,
1674; Richard James; Garnier of Port St. Maxence;
Christopher Wolf; Imman. Bekker, 1838; Charles
Bataille, 1843; Robert, 1844; J. A. Glles, 1846; Prof.
Stanley in *Canterbury Memorials; National Review*,
No. XX.; J. Morris, 1859; Hippeau, 1859; J. C.
Robertson, 1859; W. and M. Wilks, 1862........... 1119?.1170
Becket, William. Medical Writer.................... 1684..1738
Beckford, Wm. Poet. (*Vathek*.) L. by Cyrus Redding 1760..1844
Beckingham, Chas. Dram. and Poet. (*Scipio Africanus*) 1699..1730
Beckington, Thomas. Bp. of Bath and Wells. Privy
Seal. Life by Sir H. Nicholas................•. 1385?.1465
Beckmann, John Anthony. (*History of Inventions*)..... 1739..1811
Beckwith, Sir George. Governor of Bermuda......... 1753..1823
Beckwith, Thomas. Artist and Antiquary............ —..1786
Béclard, Peter Augustine. French Anatomist......... 1788..1825
Becman, John Christopher. Historian and Geographer. 1641..1717
Becon, Thomas. Reformer......................... 1511?.1570
Becquerel, Anthony Cæsar. French Electrician....... 1788.. —
Becquet, Anthony. Celestine Monk; Hist. of his Order. 1654..1730
Bectoz, Claudine de. French Abbess and Letter Writer. 1480?.1547
Beda, Noel. Doctor of the Sorbonne; Persecutor...... —..1537
Beddoes, Lovell Thos. English Poet. (*Bride's Tragedy*) 1803..1849
Beddoes, Thomas, M. D. Writer. Life by Stock, 1811. 1760..1808
Bede. *The Venerable*. Ecclesiastical Historian.......672 or 3 . 735
Bedell, Gregory T., D. D. American Divine........... 1793..1834
Bedell, William. Bp. of Kilmore. Life by Bp. Burnet,
1685; J. Monck Mason, 1840; Rev. Alex. Clogy, 1863 1570..1642
Bederic, Henry. English Monk and Theologian....... fl. 1380?
Bedford, Arthur. Divine. Writer against the Stage... 1668..1745
Bedford, Hilkiah. (*Hereditary Right of Crown*)........ 1663..1724
Bedford, John, Duke of. Regent of France............ 1389..1435
Bedford, John Russell, Fourth Duke of, K. G........... —..1771

BORN. DIED.

Bedford, John Russell, Sixth Duke of, K. G............ 1766..1839
Bedloe, Capt. Wm. Informer. Life, 8vo, London, 1861 — ..1680
Bedmar, Alphonso de Cueva, Mqs. of. Sp. Ambassador.. 1572..1655
Bedos de Celles, Frs. Bened. of St. Maur. (*On Dialing*) 1706..1779
Bedwell, William. Divine and Topographer.......... 1562?.1623
Beecher, Lyman. American Theologian. Life by self
    and Charles Beecher, his son, 1863............... 1813..1863
Beechey, Fred. William. Admiral. Arctic Navigator.. 1796..1856
Beechey, Sir William, R. A. Painter............... 1753..1839
Beek, or Beck, David. Dutch Portrait Painter........ 1621..1656
Beer, J. Meyer. See Meyerbeer..................... 1791..1864
Beer, Michael. German Musical Composer.......... 1800..1833
Beering, Behring, or Bhering, Vitus. Danish Navigator 1680?.1741
Beethoven, Louis van. Musical Composer. Life by
    Schlosser, 1828; Wegeler and Ries, 1838; A. Schindler
    and J. Moscheles, 1840........................... 1770..1827
Bega, Cornelius. Dutch Painter................... 1600..1664
Begarelli, Anthony. Modeler in Clay............... 1498..1565
Begas, Charles. German Painter................... 1794..1854
Beger, Laurence. German Antiquary............... 1653..1705
Begeyn, Abraham. Dutch Painter.................. 1650..1710?
Bégon, Michael. Fr. Collector of Books and Antiquities. 1638..1710
Beguillet, Edm. Writ. on Agricult. and Domestic Econ. — ..1786
Beham, Bartholomew. Painter.................... 1496?.1540?
Beham, John Sebald. Painter and Engraver at Rome.. 1500..1650?
Behem, or Behaim, Martin. Geogr. and Navigator..... 1430?.1506
Behmen, or Boehm, Jacob. German Theosophist....... 1575..1624
Behn, Mrs. Aphra. Dramatist; Poet; Novelist........ 1642..1689
Behnes, William. Sculptor...................... 1801?.1864
Behrens, Conrad Berthold....................... 1660..1738
Behring, Beering, or Bhering, Vitus. Danish Navigator 1680?.1741
Beich, or Beisch, Joachim Francis. Ger. Pa. & Engrav.. 1665..1748
Beinaschi, or Benaschi, J. Bapt. Italian Hist. Painter.. 1634..1688
Beithar. African Botanist and Physician............. — ..1248
Bek, or Beke, Anthony. Bishop of Durham (1283–1311) — ..1311
Bek, Beck, or Beek, David. Dutch Painter.......... 1621..1656
Bekker, Balthasar, of Amsterdam. (*World Bewitched*).. 1634..1698
Bekker, Elizabeth. Dutch Writer of Fiction.......... 1733..1804
Bel, Chas. Andrew, of Leipsic. Philosopher and Poet... 1717..1782
Bel, John James, of Bourdeaux. (*Dictionnaire Néologique*) 1693..1738
Bel, Matthias. Hungarian Divine and Historian........ 1684..1749
Belcamp, John van. Dutch Painter................. — ..1653
Belcher, Jonathan. Colonial Governor of Massachusetts,
    New Hampshire, and New Jersey................. 1681..1757
Belchier, John. Surgeon to Guy's Hospital.......... 1706..1785
Belgrado, James. Italian Jesuit; Math.; Antiq.; Poet. 1704..1789
Belidor, Bernard Forest de. Fr. Engineer and Math.... 1693..1761
Beling, Rd. Irish Rebel. (*Vindiciarum Catholic. Hiberniæ*) 1613..1677
Belisarius. Roman General. L. by Lord Mahon, 1829. 505?. 565
Belknap, Jeremy. American Historian and Biographer. 1744..1798
Bell, Andrew, D. D. Educationist.................. 1753..1832
Bell, Beaupré. Antiquary....................... — ..1745
Bell, Benjamin. Surgeon. (*Treatise on Ulcers*)....... 1749..1806
Bell, Sir Chas. Anatomist. (*Hand.*) L. by Pichot, 1860 1774..1842

BORN.   DIED.

Bell, George Joseph. Scottish Jurist.................. 1770..1843
Bell, Henry. Originator of Steam Navigation in England 1767..1830
Bell, James. Geographical Writer.................... 1769..1833
Bell, John, of Antermony. Traveler................... 1691..1780
Bell, John, of Edinburgh. Surgical Writer............ 1762..1820
Bell, John. Publisher. (*Weekly Messenger; Poets*).... 1746..1831
Bell, Luther V. American Physician.................. 1806.. —
Bell, Dr. William. Divine. Founder of Scholarship.... 1731..1816
Bella, Stephen della. Italian Etcher in Copper......... 1610..1664
Bellamy, Mrs. George Ann. Actress. Life by self..... 1733..1786
Bellamy, Jacob. Dutch Poet......................... 1757..1786
Bellamy, Joseph, D.D. American Divine and Writer... 1719..1790
Bellamy, Samuel. Pirate......:..................... — ..1717
Bellarmin, Robert. Cardinal. Life by James Fuligati,
    1624; Bartoli, 1678; Marazza, 1682; Frizon, 1708.... 1542..1621
Bellay, Joachim du. *The French Ovid*............... 1524?.1560
Bellay, John du. Cardinal; Statesman; Scholar; Poet. 1492..1560
Bellay, Martin du. Negotiator. (*Historical Memoirs*)... — ..1559
Bellay, Wm. du. French General. (*Hist. of Own Times*) 1491..1543
Belle, Alexis Simon. French Portrait Painter......... 1674..1734
Belle, Stephen de la. *See* Bella. Engraver........... 1610..1664
Belleau, Remy. French Pastoral Poet................. 1528..1577
Bellecour, Colson de. French Comic Actor............ 1725..1778
Belleforest, Francis de. French Historical Writer. .... 1530..1583
Bellegarde, Gabriel du Pac. French Critic and Historian 1717..1789
Bellegarde, J. Baptist Morvan de. Ex-Jesuit. Cartesian 1648..1734
Belleisle, Chas. Lou. Aug. Fouquet, Duke de. Fr. Marshal 1684..1761
Bellenden, or Ballenden, Sir or Dr. John. (*Hist. of Scot.*) — ..1550
Bellenden, Wm. Scottish Ciceronian Schol. (*De Statu*) fl. 1616
Bellenger, Francis. Dr. of Sorbonne; Classical Translator 1688..1749
Bellet, Charles. French Religious Writer............. 1702..1771
Bellevois. Marine Painter........................... — ..1684
Belliard, Augustine Dan., Count de. Fr. Gen. and Diplom. 1769..1832
Bellièvre, Pomponius. French Statesman............. 1529..1607
Bellingham, Richard. Colonial Gov. of Massachusetts. — ..1672
Bellini, Gentine. Venetian Historian and Portrait Painter 1421..1501
Bellini, James, of Venice. Painter.................... — ..1470
Bellini, James Nicholas. French Marine Geographer ... 1703..1772
Bellini, John. Venetian Painter...................... 1426..1516
Bellini, Laurence. Italian Medical Writer..........: 1643..1704
Bellini, Vincent. Musical Composer. Life by Gerardi,
    1835; Ventimiglia, 1835 .... 1802..1835
Bellius, Martin. (*De Hereticis.*) *See* Castalio.........1515..1563
Bellmann, Charles Michael. Swedish Poet............ 1741..1796
Bello, Francis. *Il Cieco*...............................
Bellocq, Peter. French Satirist...................... 1645..1704
Belloni, Jerome. Roman Banker. (*Essay on Commerce*) — ..1761
Bellori, John Peter. Antiquary and Biographer........ 1616?.1696
Belloste, Augustin. Fr. Surg. (*Chirurgeon de l'Hospital*) 1654..1730
Bellot, Joseph René. Lieutenant. Life by Lemer...... 1826..1853
Bellotti, Peter. Italian Portrait Painter and Caricaturist. 1625..1700
Belloy, Peter Laurence Buyrette du. French Dramatist. 1727..1775
Bellucci, Anthony. Historical and Portrait Painter ..... 1654..1726
Beloe, William. Scholar and Critic.................. 1756..1817

BORN. DIED.

Belon, Peter. French Naturalist and Traveler .... 1517..1564
Belsham, Thos. Unitarian. Life by Rev. J. Williams, 1836 1750..1829
Belsham, William. Essayist and Historian............ 1753..1827
Belsunce, Hen. Francis Xavier de. Bishop of Marseilles 1671..1755
Beltraffio, John Anthony. Italian Painter............ 1467..1516
Belzoni, John Baptist. Traveler..................... 1778?.1823
Bem, Joseph. Polish General and Turkish Pasha ...... 1795..1850
Bembo, Peter. Cardinal. Historian and Poet. Life by
    Beccadelli; La Casas.............................. 1470..1547
Bemmel, William van. Dutch Landscape Painter...... 1630..1708
Benaschi, or Beinaschi, J. Bapt. Ital. Painter and Engrav. 1634..1688
Benavidio, Mark. *Marco Mantuano.* Italian Civilian . 1489..1582
Benbow, John. Admiral ....;......... 1650?.1702
Benci, or Bencio, Francis. Italian Jesuit and Poet ......1542..1594
Bendish, Bridget, grand-daughter of Cromwell......... — ..1727
Bendlowes, Edward. Patron of Learning.............. 1613..1686
Benedetti, or Benedict, Alexander. Italian Anatomist.. — ..1511?
Benedetto da Majano. Flor. Sculptor and Architect .. 1444..1498
Benedetto, Le. *See* Castiglfone. Italian Painter...... 1616..1670
Benedict, St., of Nursia. Founder of Benedictine Order.
    Life by Gregory the Great; Castañiza, 1583; Butteau,
    1684; Mége, 1690; Chladenius, 1707; Waitzmann, 1825;
    Maetzler, 1831; Zoncada, 1843; Formby, 1858 .... 480?. 542?
Benedict Biscop. Abbot of Wearmouth.............. 629?. 690
Benedict of Aiane................................... 751.. 821
Benedict I. Pope (574–78). *Bonosus*................. — .. 578
Benedict II. (684–85)............................... — .. 685
Benedict III. (855–58)............................. — .. 858
Benedict IV. (900–3)............................... — .. 903
Benedict V. (964–65) .... — .. 965
Benedict VI. (972–74)............................. — .. 974
Benedict VII. (975–84)............................. — .. 984
Benedict VIII. (1012–24.) *John of Tusculum.*........ — ..1024
Benedict IX. (1033–54.) *Theophylact of Tusculum....* — ..1054
Benedict X. (1058–59.) Antipope .... — ..1059
Benedict XI. (1303–4.) *Nich. Boccasini.* L. by Cam-
    pana, 1736 .... 1240..1304
Benedict XII. (1334–42.) *James de Nouvellis.*........ — ..1342
Benedict XIII. (1724–30.) *Peter Francis Orsini.* Life
    by Borgia, 1741; Ranft, 1743...................... 1649..1730
Benedict XIV. (1740–58.) *Prosper Lambertini.*....... 1675..1758
Benedict, Abbot of Peterborough. Historian .... — ..1193
Benedict, Alexander. Italian Anatomist.............. — ..1511
Benefield, Sebastian. Calvinist Theologian at Oxford . 1559..1630
Beneke, Frederick Edward. German Philosopher...... 1798..1854
Benevoli, Horace. Composer of Church Music......... 1602..1672
Benezet, Anthony. American Philanthropist.......... 1713..1784
Benezra, or Abenezra, Abraham. Rabbi .... 1119?.1174?
Bengel, John Albert. (*Gnomon.*) Life by Nast, 1753;
    Fresenius, 1756; Burk, 1831, tr. by R. F. Walker, 1837 1687..1752
Benger, Miss Elizabeth Ogilvy. Biographer.......... 1778..1827
Beni, Paul. Italian Philologist...................... 1552?.1625
Benini, Vincent. Italian Physician. (*Notes on Celsus*). 1713..1764
Beniowsky, Moritz August von. Adventurous Hungarian 1741..1786

BORN. DIED.

Benivieni, Jerome. Florentine Poet .... 1453?.1542
Benizzi, Philip, Saint. Life by Francis Malaval, 1672.. 1233.. —
Benjamin of Tudela. Jewish Rabbi & Trav. (*Itinerary*) — ..1173
Bennet, Benjamin. Dissent. Divine. (*Christian Oratory*) 1674..1726
Bennet, Christopher. Physician. (*Tabulorum Theatrum*) 1617..1655
Bennet, Henry, First Earl Arlington. Statesman....... 1618..1685
Bennet, Robert. Ejected Nonconformist. (*Concordance of Scripture Synonyms*)............................ — ..1687
Bennet, Thomas, D. D. Divine and Hebraist........... 1673..1728
Bennett, James, D. D. Dissent. Div. (*Hist. of Dissenters*) 1774..1862
Bennigsen, Levin Aug. Theoph., Count. Russian General 1745..1826
Benoît, Father. Maronite Jesuit Scholar .... 1663..1742
Benoît, Elias. (*Histoire de l'Édit de Nantes*)........... 1640..1728
Benoît, René. French Theologian .... 1521..1608
Benserade, Isaac de. French Court Poet............. 1612..1691
Benson, Edward. Artist............................. 1808?.1863
Benson, Dr. George. Dissenting Divine............... 1699..1762
Bent, John van der. Dutch Landscape Painter......... 1650..1690
Bentham, Edward, D. D. Divinity Professor.......... 1707..1776
Bentham, James. Prebendary of Ely. (*History of Ely*) 1708..1794
Bentham, Jeremy. Polit. Writer. Life by Bowring, 1838 1748..1832
Bentham, Sir Samuel. Brig.-Gen. L. by S. M. Bentham 1757..1831
Bentham, Thomas. Bishop of Lichfield and Coventry.. 1513?.1579
Bentinck, Lord George. Statesman. Life by Disraeli. 1802..1848
Bentinck, W. H. Cavendish, 3d Dk. Portland. Prem. 1807 1738..1809
Bentinck, William. First Earl of Portland .... 1649..1709
Bentinck, Lord William. Governor-General of India... 1774..1839
Bentivoglio, Cornelius. Cardinal. Poet and Art-Patron 1668..1732
Bentivoglio, Guy. Cardinal. (*Civil Wars of Flanders*) 1579..1644
Bentivoglio, Hercules. Poet and Satirist .... 1506..1573
Bentivoglio, John II., Lord of, and adorner of, Bologna 1439?.1508
Bentley, Sir John. Admiral .... — ..1772?
Bentley, Richard, D. D. Critic. Life by Bishop Monk, 1823 1662..1742
Bentley, Thomas. Partner of Wedgwood. Writer..... 1730..1780
Benvenuti, Charles. Italian Jesuit; Math. and Philos. 1716..1789
Benvenuto Cellini. Florentine Artist. *See* Cellini.... 1500..1570
Benwell, William, of Caversham. Divine and Scholar.. 1765..1796
Benyowsky, Maurice Augustus, Count de. Hungarian Adventurer. Life by self, 2 vols. 4to, 1790 .... 1741..1786
Benzelius, Eric. Swedish Divine..................... 1642..1709
Benzelius, Eric, son. (*Acta Literaria Sueciæ*)........ 1675..1743
Benzio, Trifone. Italian Poet........................ — ..1570?
Benzoni, Jerome. Italian Voyager.................... 1519?. —
Beoer, or Beyer, Augustus. German Historian and Critic 1707..1741
Beolco, Angelo. *Ruzzante*. Italian Poet .... 1502..1542
Beranger, John Peter de. Lyric Poet. Life by himself 1780..1857
Berault, Nicholas. *Beraldus Aurelius*. French Scholar 1473..1550
Berchem, or Berghem, Nicholas. Dutch Painter....... 1624..1683
Berchett, Peter. French Historian, Painter, and Engraver 1659..1720
Bercheur, P. *Berchorius*. Fr. Div. (*Reductorium Morale*) — ..1362
Berchtold, Leopold, Count. Philanthropist............ 1758..1809
Berengaria, of Navarre. Queen of Richard I.......... — ..1230
Berengarius, of Tours. Theologian. Life by Roye, 1656 1000?.1088
Berenger I. King of Italy (888–922) .... — .. 924

4

BORN. DIED.

Berenger II.   King of Italy (950–961)............... — .. 966
Berenger, James, of Carpi.   Anatomist and Physician .. — ..1550
Berenger, Laurence Peter.   (*Les Soirées Provençales*)... 1749..1822
Berenice, or Bernice.   Jewish Queen; Favorite of Titus.   28? aft.70
Beresford, Rev. James.   (*Miseries of Human Life*)..... 1764..1840
Beresford, William Carr, Viscount.   General .... 1768..1854
Beretini, or Berretini, Peter, of Cortona.   Painter ...... 1596..1669
Berettini, Nicholas.   Historical Painter................. 1617..1682
Berettini, Peter.   *Pietro da Cortona.*   Painter......... 1596..1669
Berg, Matthias van den.   Flemish Painter .... 1615..1647
Bergamo, James Philip de.   *Foresti.*   Italian Chronicler 1434..1520
Bergen, Charles Augustus de.   Anatomist and Botanist. 1704..1760
Bergen, Dirk van den.   Painter...................... 1640?.1689
Bergerac, Cyrano de.   French Dramatist and Romancist 1620?.1655
Berghem, Nicholas.   Dutch Painter................. 1624..1683
Bergier, Nich.   Fr. Historian. (*Roads of Roman Empire*) 1567..1623
Bergier, Nicholas Sylvester.   French Divine at Besançon 1718..1790
Bergler, Joseph.   German Historical Painter........... 1753..1829
Bergman, Torbern Olof.   Swedish Chemist............ 1735..1784
Berhtwald.   Archbishop of Canterbury (692–731)....... — .. 731
Berigard, Claude.   Fr. Philos. in Italy. (*Circuli Pisani*) 1578..1663
Bering, Vitus.   Latin Poet at Copenhagen............ 1617..1675
Bering, or Behring, Vitus.   Danish Navigator.......... 1680?.1741
Berington, Joseph.   Roman Catholic Historical Writer. 1744..1827
Berkeley, George, First Earl of. (*Historical Applications*) 1627?.1698
Berkeley, George.   Bishop of Cloyne.   Metaphysician.
    Life, 8vo, 1784; Wright, 1843................... 1684..1753
Berkeley, Sir William.   Governor of Virginia.   Writer.. — ..1677
Berkenhout, Dr. John.   Biographer................. 1730?.1791
Berkheyden, or Breckberg, Gerard.   Architectural Pa... 1645..1693
Berkheyden, or Breckberg, Job, brother.   Dutch Painter 1628..1698
Berkley, John le Francq van.   Dutch Phys., Nat., Poet... 1729..1812
Berlichingen, Goetz von.   *Iron-handed.*   German Knight fl. 1513
Bernabei, Jos. Anth.   Comp. of Church Music at Munich 1659..1732
Bernabei, Jos. Herc.   Comp. of Church Music at Munich 1620?.1690
Bernadotte.   French General and King of Sweden.   Life
    by Nicolai, 1821; Meredith, 1829; Touchard-Lafosse,
    1838; Strombeck, 1841; Runkel, 1841; Grosse, 1844;
    Geijer, 1844; Héricourt, 1844; Sarrans, 1845........∴ 1764..1844
Bernaert, Nicasius.   Dutch Painter.................... 1593?.1663
Bernard, St., of Clairvaux.   Life by Alain de Lisle; A.
    Neander, tr. by Wrench, 1843; Antoine le Maistre;
    Villefore; Abbé Ratisbonne, tr. by Manning; J. Cot-
    ter Morison, 1863................................. 1091..1153
Bernard, St., of Menthon.   Founder of Hospice........ 923..1008
Bernard, of Brussels.   Pa. of Animals and Hunting-pieces — ..1540
Bernard, Duke of Weimar.   Protestant General .... 1604..1639
Bernard, Andrew.   Poet Laureate to Hen. VII. and VIII.   —aft.1522
Bernard, Catherine.   French Poetess.............. 1662..1712
Bernard, Chas.   French Hist. (*Wars of Louis XIII.*).. 1571..1640
Bernard, Claude, of Dijon.   *Poor Bernard.*   Philanthr. 1588..1641
Bernard, Edw.   Crit. & Astron. L. by Dr. T. Smith, 1704 1638..1697
Bernard, Sir Francis.   Governor.   Editor of *Alsop's Odes* — ..1779
Bernard, Dr. Hermann Hedwig, of Cambridge.   Hebraist 1785..1857

BORN. DIED.

Bernard, James. Fr. Prot. Div. (*Account of Europe*)... 1658..1718
Bernard, John, D. D. Divine. (*Theologo-Historicus*)... — ..1683
Bernard, John. Actor. (*Retrospections of the Stage*)... 1756..1828
Bernard, John Fred., of Amsterdam. Bookseller & Writer — ..1752
Bernard, John Stephen. German Medical Writer...... 1718..1793
Bernard, Nicholas, D. D. Friend & Biographer of Ussher — ..1661
Bernard, Peter Joseph. *Le Gentil Bernard*. French Poet 1710..1775
Bernard, Rd. Puritan Div. & Sch. (*Thesaurus Biblicus*) 1566..1641
Bernard, Samuel. French Painter and Engraver....... 1615..1687
Bernard, Samuel, son. *Lucullus*. Capitalist.......... 1651?.1739
Bernard, Simon. French General. Engineer.......... 1779..1839
Bernard, Solomon. *Petit Bernard*. Engraver at Lyons. fl. 1550–80
Bernard, Sir Thos. Philanthr. L. by Jas. Baker, 1819. 1750..1818
Bernardez, Diego. Portuguese Idyllic Poet........... 1540?.1596
Bernardi, Augustus Frederick. German Philologist.... 1761..1820
Bernardi, John. Italian Crystal Engraver............ 1495?.1555
Bernardi, Major John. Politician; died in Newgate... — ..1736
Bernardi, Stephen. Ital. Musical Writer and Comp..... fl. 1611–34?
Bernardín de St. Pierre. *See St. Pierre*............ 1737..1814
Bernardine, St., of Sienna.......................... 1380..1444
Bernazzano. Italian Painter .... fl. 1536
Berners, John Bourchier, Lord. Translator of Froissart. 1474?.1532
Berners, or Barnes, Juliana. Prioress of Sopewell. Writ. —aft.1485
Berni, or Bernia, Francis. Ital. Poet. (*Rime Burlesche*) 1490?.1536
Bernice, or Berenice. Jewish Queen; Favorite of Titus. 28? aft.70
Bernier, Francis. *Mogul*. Philosopher and Traveler... 1630?.1688
Bernier, John. Fr. Medical Writer. (*Histoire de Blois*) 1622..1698
Bernier, Nicholas. French Musical Composer.......... 1664..1734
Bernini, John Lawrence. Ital. Pa., Sculp., Arch., Mech.. 1598..1680
Bernis, Frs. Joach. de Pierre de. Cardinal. Fr. Poet.. 1715..1794
Berno. Abbot of Richenau. Poet, Musician, Philosopher — ..1045
Bernouilli, Daniel, M. D. Natural Philosopher........ 1700..1782
Bernouilli, James. Mathematician at Petersburg....... 1759..1789
Bernouilli, James. Mathemat. L. by J. J. Battier, 1705 1654..1705
Bernouilli, John, brother. Mathematician........... 1667..1748
Bernstorf, Andrew Peter, Ct. von. Danish Statesman.. 1735..1797
Bernstorf, John Hartwig Ern., Ct. von. Danish Statesm. 1712..1772
Beroald, Matthew, of Paris. Chronologist............ — ..1576?
Beroald de Verville, Francis, son. (*Moyen de parvenir*) 1558..1612
Beroaldo, Philip, *The Elder*, of Bologna. Scholar...... 1453..1505
Beroaldo, Philip, *The Younger*, nephew. Latin Poet... 1472..1518
Berosus. Priest of Belus at Babylon. Historian......fl. ab.250B.C.
Berquin, Arnauld. (*L'Ami des Enfans*).............. 1749..1791
Berquin, Louis de. French Protestant Martyr......... 1489?.1529
Berr, Frederick. French Musical Composer............ 1794..1838
Berretini, Nicholas. Italian Historical Painter......... 1627..1682
Berretini, Peter. *Pietro da Cortona*. Painter......... 1596..1669
Berridge, Rev. John. Divine........................ — ..1793
Berriman, William. Theologian .... 1683..1750
Berruyer, Jos. Isaac. Fr. Jesuit. (*Hist. of People of God*) 1681..1758
Berry, Charles Ferdinand. Duke de. Assassinated.... 1778..1820
Berry, Sir Edward. Rear-Admiral.................... 1768..1831
Berry, Hiram George. American General............. 1824..1863
Berry, John, Duke of, son of John II. of France........ 1340..1416

BORN. DIED.

Berry, Sir John. Naval Commander................. 1635..1691
Bersmann, George. German Scholar................. 1536..1611
Bertaut, John. Bishop of Séez. Poet............. 1552..1611
Bertheau, Charles. French Protestant Divine........ 1660..1732
Berthet, John. Jesuit of Terascon. Poet and Writer.. 1622..1692
Berthier, Alexander. French Marshal.............. 1753..1815
Berthier, Wm. Frs. Fr. Critic; Trans. of the Psalms... 1704..1782
Bertholet-Flemael, Bartholomew. Painter of Liege... 1614..1675
Bertholiet, Claude Louis, Count. Chemist........... 1748..1822
Bertholon, Nich. de St. Lazare. Fr. Chem. Philosopher — ..1799
Berthoud, Ferdinand. Swiss Chronometer-maker...... 1727..1807
Berti, Alexander Pompey. (*La Caduta de' Decemviri*).. 1686..1752
Berti, John Lawrence. (*De Disciplinis Theologicis*)..... 1696..1766
Bertie, Willoughby, Earl of Abingdon. Polit. and Satirist 1740..1799
Bertier, Joseph Stephen, of Aix. (*Physique des Comètes*) 1710..1783
Bertier, Louis Alexander. Marshal of France......... 1753..1815
Bertin, Anth. Fr. Officer & Poet. (*Collection of Elegiacs*) 1752..1790
Bertin, Exupère Jos. Fr. Phys. and Anat. (*Osteology*).. 1712..1781
Bertin, Louis Francis. French Journalist.............. 1766..1841
Bertin, Louis Mary Armand, son. Journalist........... 1801..1854
Bertin, Nicholas. French Historical Painter........... 1667..1736
Bertinazzi, Charles Anthony. *Carlin.* Comedian ..... 1713..1783
Bertius, Peter. Dutch Geographer................... 1565..1629
Bertoli, John Dominic, of Aquileia. Antiquary........1676 aft.1750
Bertram. (*De Corp. et Sang. Domini.*) See Ratramnus. —aft.868
Bertram, Cornelius Bonaventure. Swiss Orientalist..... 1531..1594
Bertrand, Henry Gratien, Ct. French General; Friend
     of Napoleon .... 1773..1844
Bertrand, J. Bapt., of Marseilles. Medical Writer..... 1670..1752
Bertrandi, John Ambrose Maria. Ital. Surgical Writer. 1723..1765
Berulle, Peter de. Cardinal. Founder of the Oratory.
     Life by G. Habert; Doni d'Attichi .... 1575..1629
Bervic, Charles Clement Balvay. French Engraver .... 1756..1822
Berwick, Jas. Fitzjames, Duke of. Marshal of France.
     Life by self; Margon........................... 1670..1734
Beryllus. Bishop of Bozra; refuted by Origen........ fl. 230?
Berzelius, James, Baron. Swedish Chemist........... 1779..1848
Besler, Basil. German Naturalist. (*Hort. Eystettensis*). 1561..1629
Besler, Michael Robert. Med. Writer. (*Gazophulacium*) 1607..1661
Besly, John, of Poictiers. (*Hist. of the Bps. of Poictiers*) 1572..1644
Besoigne, Jerome. Dr. of the Sorbonne. (*Port-Royal*). 1686..1763
Besolde, Christopher, of Vienna. (*Ottoman Empire*).... 1572..1638
Besplas, Joseph Mary Anne Gros de. French Preacher. 1734..1783
Bessarion, John, Cardinal. Life by Bandini, 1777...... 1395..1472
Bessé, John de. French Medical Writer .... fl. 1702-23
Bessel, Dr. Frederick William. Prussian Astronomer... 1784..1846
Besset, or Bessé, Henry de. (*Campaigns of Rocroi*)..... — ..1693
Bessières, John Baptist. Marshal of France........... 1768..1813
Bestuschew, Alexander. Russian Novelist........... 1795?..1837
Betanos, Dominic. Spanish Missionary to S. America.. — ..1549
Betham, Sir William. Antiquary and Genealogist..... 1779..1853
Bethencourt, James de. Physician at Rouen. (*Nova
     Penitentialis Quadrigesima*)........................ fl. 1527
Bethencourt, John de. Conqueror of Canary Islands.. + ..1425

BORN. DIED.

Bethlen, Gabriel. Prince of Transylvania (K. of Hung.) 1580..1629
Bethune, Alexander. (*Tales of the Scottish Peasantry*). 1804..1841
Bethune, George W. American Clergyman........... 1805..1862
Bethune, John, brother and colleague of Alexander..... 1810..1839
Bethune, John Elliot Drinkwater, afterwd. (*L. of Galileo*) 1801..1851
Bethune, John Drinkwater, afterward. Colonel. (*Siege
of Gibraltar*)...................................... 1762?.1844
Bethune, Philip de. French Ambassador............. 1561?.1649
Betterton, Thomas. Shakespearian Actor............. 1635..1710
Bettinelli, Xavier, of Mantua. Jesuit; Writer......... 1718..1808
Bettini, Dominic. Italian Painter.................... 1644..1705
Betuleius, Sixtus. Grammarian, Latin Poet, and Philos. 1500..1554
Betussi, Joseph. Italian Poet of Bassano............. —aft.1565
Beuf, John Le. French Antiquary. (*History of Paris*).. 1687..1760
Beurmann, Maurice von. African Explorer........... — ..1863
Beurs, William. Dutch Painter...................... 1656..1690?
Bever, Dr. Thos. Civilian. (*Legal Polity of the Romans*) 1725..1791
Beveridge, William. Bishop of St. Asaph (1704-8). .
Life by Isaac Kimber .... 1638..1708
Beverland, Adrian. Dutch Philologist............... 1653?.1712
Beverley, John of. Archbishop of York (688–722)...... — .. 722
Beverly, Robert. American Author................... — ..1716
Beverninck, Jerome van. Dutch Statesman.......... 1614..1690
Beverwick, John van. *Beverovicius*. Dutch Med. Writer 1594..1647
Bevin, Elway. Musical Composer.................... —aft.1636
Bewick, John. Artist. (*History of Quadrupeds*)....... 1760..1795
Bewick, Thos., brother. Naturalist. (*Fishes*) L. by self 1753..1828
Bewly, William. Chemist and Natural Philosopher..... — ..1783
Bexley, Nicholas Vansittart, Lord. Statesman........ 1766..1851
Bexon, Gabr. Leop. Chas. Aimé. French Naturalist.... 1748..1784
Bexon, Scipio Jerome. French Jurist................. 1753..1825
Beyer, or Beoer, Augustus. German Historian and Critic 1707..1741
Beyle, Mary Henry. French Novelist, Poet, Politician.. 1783..1842
Beys, Charles de. French Poet...................... 1610..1659
Beysser, John Michael. French Gen. at the Revolution. 1734..1794
Beza, Theodore. Reformer. L. by Noel Taillepied, 1577;
Bolsec, 1582; Laingé; La Faye, 1606; Solomeau,
1610; Vega, 1646; Ziegenbein, 1789; Schlosser, 1809;
Baum, 1843.. 1519..1605
Beziers, Michael. Historical and Antiquarian Writer... 1719..1782
Bezout, Stephen. French Mathematician............. 1730..1783
Bhering, Vitus. Danish Navigator................... 1680?.1741
Biancani, Joseph. Jesuit and Mathemat. of Bologna.... 1566..1624
Bianchi, Francis. *Il Frari*. Historical Painter........ 1447..1510
Bianchi, John. *Janus Blancus*. Phys., Anat., and Nat. 1693..1775
Bianchi, J. Bapt. Ital. Med. Writer. (*Hist. Hepatica*).. 1681..1761
Bianchi, Peter. Painter............................. 1694..1740?
Bianchini, Francis, of Verona. Philosoph. and Math... 1662..1729
Bianchini, John Fortunatus. Med. Writer at Padua... 1720..1779
Biancolelli, Peter Francis. *Dominique*. Fr. Dramatist. 1681..1734
Biard, Peter. French Sculptor and Architect.......... 1559..1609
Bibbiena, Bernard da. Cardinal. (*La Calandra*)...... 1470..1520
Bibiena, Ferdinand Galli. Painter and Architect ....1657.1741 or 3
Bibliander, Theodore. Protestant Divine............. 1504..1564

BORN. DIED.

Bichat, Mary Francis Xavier. French Medical Writer.. 1771..1802
Bickerstaff, Isaac. Dramatist ....1735?aft.1787
Bickersteth, Rev. Edw., of Watton. L. by Birks, 1851. 1786..1850
Bickersteth, Henry, Lord Langdale. Master of the
  Rolls. Life by T. D. Hardy..................... 1783..1851
Bicknell, Elhanan. Art Collector.................. — ..1861
Biddle, James. American Naval Commander.......... 1783..1848
Biddle, John. Socinian Writer. Life by John Farring-
  ton, 1682; Joshua Toulmin, 1815 .... 1615..1662
Biddle, Nicholas. American Naval Commander .... 1750..1778
Biddle, Nicholas. American Financier .... 1786..1844
Biddulph, Rev. Thomas Tregenna, of Bristol. Divine.. 1763..1838
Bidlake, Dr. John. Divine and Poet.................. 1755..1814
Bidloo, Godfrey. Dutch Anatomist................... 1649..1713
Bie, Adrian de. Flemish Artist...................... 1594..1640
Biel, John Christian, of Brunswick. (*Lexicon to the LXX.*) 1687..1745
Biela, William, Baron von. Astronomer............... 1782..1856
Bielefield, C. F. Modeler in Papier-mâché .... 1803?.1864
Bielfield, James Frederick, Baron de. (*Political Institut.*) 1717..1770
Bienaise, John. French Surgical Operator .... 1601..1681
Biesius, Nicholas. Flemish Medical Writer........... 1516..1572
Biezelingen, Christian John van. Dutch Portrait Painter 1558..1600
Bifield, Nicholas, of Chester and Isleworth. Divine..... 1578?.1622
Bigland, John. Writer............................. 1750..1832
Bigne, or Vigne, Gaces de la. (*Roman des Oiseaux*)..... 1428?.1472?
Bigne, Marguerin de la. (*Bibliotheca Patrum*) ..... 1546?.1591?
Bignicourt, Simon de. (*Pensées et Réflections*)......... 1709..1775
Bignon, Jerome. Fr. Schol. & Writ. L. by Perrault, 1757 1590..1656
Bignon, Louis Peter Edw. Fr. Statesman and Diplom... 1771..1841
Bigot, Emery. French Scholar; Promoter of Learning.. 1626..1689
Bilderdijk, or Bilderdyk, Wm. Dutch Writer and Trans. 1756..1831
Bilfinger, George Bernard. (*Dilucidationes Philosoph.*). 1693..1750
Bilguer, John Ulric. Swiss Surgical Writer........... 1720..1796
Billaud-Varenne, John Nicholas. French Revolutionist 1756..1819
Billaut, Adam. *Maître Adam.* French Poet.......... 1602..1662
Billaut, Augustus Adolphus Mary. French Statesman .. 1805..1863
Billi, James de. Trans. of Fathers. L. by Chatard, 1582 1535..1581
Billi, James de, of Compiègne. (*Opus Astronomicon*).... 1602..1679
Billing, Sigismond. French Politician.................. 1773..1832
Billingsley, Sir Henry. Lord Mayor; Mathematician .. — ..1606
Billington, Elizabeth. Vocalist...................... 1770..1818
Bilson, Thomas. Bishop of Winchester................ 1536..1616
Bingham, Rev. Joseph. (*Origines Ecclesiasticæ*)....... 1668..1723
Bingham, Peregrine. Legal Writer................... 1788?.1864
Bingley. Dutch Actor .... 1755..1818
Bingley, Rev. William C. Naturalist. (*Animal Biography*) — ..1823
Bink, or Binck, Jacob. German Engraver and Painter.. 1500?.1560?
Binney, Amos. American Patron of Art and Science ... 1803..1847
Bioernstahl, or Biörnstahl, James Jonas. Swedish Trav. 1731..1779
Bion, of Smyrna. Greek Bucolic Poet................ fl. 280B.C.
Bion, Nicholas. Fr. Mathematician. (*Use of the Globes*) 1652..1733
Biondi, John Francis. (*Civil Wars of York & Lancaster*) 1572..1644
Biondo, or Blondus, Michael Angelo. Ital. Med. Writer.. 1497..1560?
Biondo, or Blondus, Flavius. Italian Antiq. and Historian 1388..1463

BORN. DIED.

Biörnstahl, James Jonas. Swedish Traveler .... 1731..1779
Biot, Edward Constant. French Chinese Scholar .... 1803..1850
Biot, J. Bapt. French Mathemat. and Nat. Philosopher. 1774..1862
Birague, Clement. Spanish Engraver on Gems .... fl. 1550?
Birague, René de. Cardinal. French Politician........ 1507..1583
Birch, Rev. Thomas, D. D. Hist. and Biograph. Writer. 1705..1766
Bird, Edward, R. A. Painter........................... 1772..1819
Bird, Golding. Surgeon .... 1815..1854
Bird, John. Mathematical Instrument Maker .... 1709..1776
Bird, William. Sacred Composer .... 1540?.1623
Biren, or Biron, John Ernest de, Duke of Courland.
  Russian Statesman................................. 1690..1772
Biringuccio, Vannucci. Ital. Mathemat. (*Pirotecnia*) fl. 1530?
Birinus. Bishop of Dorchester....................... — .. 648
Birkbeck, George, M. D. Promoter of Mechanics' Instit. 1776..1841
Birkenhead, Sir John. Royalist Political Writer....... 1615..1679
Birney, James G. American Politician.............. 1792..1857
Biron, A. L. de Gonteau, Duc de Lauzun. Fr. Politician 1747..1793
Biron, Armand de Gontaut, Baron de. Marsh. of France 1524?.1592
Biron, Chas. de Gontaut, Duc de. Ambass., Adm., Marsh. 1562..1602
Biron, or Biren, John Ernest de. *See* Biren............ 1690..1772
Biscaino, Dominic. Italian Painter and Engraver...... 1632..1657
Bischop, or Biskop, Cornelius van. Painter 1630.1674
Bischop, or Biskop, John van. Designer and Engraver 1646..1686
Biscoe, Richard. Divine.............................. — ..1743
Biscop, Benedict. Abbot of Wearmouth .... 629?. 690
Biset, Chas. Emanuel. Paint. of Hist. and Conversations 1633 —
Bishop, George. Astronomer. .... — ..1861
Bishop, Sir Henry Rowley. Musical Composer .... 1780..1855
Bishop, Samuel. Poet................................ 1731..1795
Bisi, Bonaventure. Miniature Painter and Engraver.... 1612..1662
Bisset, Charles, M. D. Phys. and Writ. on Fortification . 1716..1791
Bisset, James. Artist and Humorist .... 1752..1832
Bisset, Robt., LL. D., of Chelsea. Hist. Writ. (*L. of Burke*) 1759?.1805
Bitaubé, Paul Jeremiah. French Writer .... 1732..1808
Bitzius, Albert. Swiss Author........................ 1797..1854
Bivar, Don Rodrigo Dias de. Spanish Hero. *The Cid*.. 1040?.1099
Bizot, Peter. Numismatist. (*Hist. Medal. de l'Hollande*) 1630..1696
Bizzari, Peter. Italian Poet and Historian............. fl. 1560
Bizzelli, John. Historical and Portrait Painter .... 1556?.1612
Björnstjerna, Magnus Fred. Ferdinand, Count. Swedish
  Statesman and Author .... 1779..1847
Black, John. English Journalist and Classical Scholar .. 1783..1855
Black, Joseph. Chemical Philosopher. (*Latent Heat*) .. 1728..1799
Blackall, Offspring. Bishop of Exeter. Controversialist 1654..1716
Blackburn, William. Architect...................... 1750..1790
Blackburne, Francis. Archdeacon. (*Confessional*).... 1705..1787
Black-Hawk. Celebrated Indian Chief .... 1768?.1838
Blacklock, Thos., D. D. Poet. L. by Spence; H. Mackenzie 1721..1791
Blackmore, Sir Richard, M. D. Physician and Poet .... 1650?.1729
Blackstone, John. Apothecary. (*Specimen Botanicon*) — ..1753
Blackstone, Sir William. Judge. (*Commentaries*) Life
  by James Clitherow, 1780 .... 1723..1780
Blackwall, Rev. Anthony. (*Sacred Classics Defended*).. — ..1730

BORN. DIED.

Blackwell, Alexander. English Physician . . . .   — ..1748
Blackwell, Mrs. Elizabeth. (*Herbal*). . . . .   fl. 1737
Blackwell, Thomas. Classical Writer. . . . .   1701..1757
Blackwood, Adam. (*Martyre de Marie Stuart*). . . . .   1539..1613
Blackwood, Sir Henry. Admiral . . . .   1770..1832
Blackwood, Wm. Scot. Publisher. (*Blackwood's Mag.*)   1776..1834
Bladen, Martin. Lieut.-Colonel. Translator of Cæsar. .   — ..1746
Blaeuw, John. Geographer and Printer. . . . .   — ..1680
Blaeuw, Wm. Dutch Geog. & Print. (*Theatrum Mundi*) 1571..1638
Blagden, Sir Charles. Experimental Philosopher . . . . . .   1748..1820
Blagrave, John, of Reading. Mathemat. and Benefactor   — ..1611
Blagrave, Joseph, of Reading. Astrologer. . . . .   1610..1679
Blainville, Henry Mary Ducrotay de. French Zoölogist 1777..1850
Blair, Hugh, D. D., of Edinb. Scot. Div. and Prof. of Rhet.
   (*Sermons ; Lectures.*) Life by Dr. Jas. Finlayson, 1801 1718..1800
Blair, James. Missionary to Virginia. . . . .   — ..1743
Blair, John. Prebendary of Westminster. (*Chronology*)   — ..1782
Blair, Patrick. Scottish Surgeon. (*Anat. of the Elephant*)   — ..1728?
Blair, Robert. Poet. (*The Grave*). . . . .   1699..1747
Blake, John Bradley. Botanist and Naturalist in China. 1745..1773
Blake, Robert. Admiral. Life by W. H. Dixon . . . .   1599..1657
Blake, Wm. Artist & Writ. L. by Alex. Gilchrist, 1863 1757..1827
Blakeway, Rev. John Brickdale. (*Hist. of Shrewsbury*). . 1766?.1826
Blampini, Thomas. Editor of St. Augustine. . . . .   1640..1710
Blanc de Guillet, Anthony le. French Writer . . . .   1730..1799
Blanc, Francis le. French Medalist. . . . .   — ..1698
Blanc, John Bernard le. (*Letters on the English Nation*) 1707..1781
Blanc, Louis le. Sieur de Beaulieu. (*Theses Theologicæ*) 1615..1675
Blanc, Louis le. Surgeon and Lithotomist at Orleans. . .   fl. 1770
Blanc, Thomas le. French Jesuit. (*Analysis Psalmorum*) 1599..1669
Blanc. *See* Le Blanc.
Blancard, Stephen. Dutch Med. Writer. (*Lexic. Medic.*)   fl. 1688
Blanchard, Elias. Writer in *Mém. de l'Acad. des Inscr.* 1672..1755
Blanchard, Francis. Fr. Jurist. (*Éloges des Présidents*)   — ..1650
Blanchard, Francis. French Aëronaut . . . .   1738..1809
Blanchard, Madame, wife. Aëronaut. . . . .   — ..1819
Blanchard, James. *French Titian.* Painter. . . . .   1600..1638
Blanchard, J. Bapt. Fr. Writer. (*Temple of the Muses*) 1731..1797
Blanchard, Laman. Period. Writ. L. by Sir B. Lytton, 1845 1803..1845
Blanchard, Wm. Fr. Advocate. (*Chron. Compilation*). .   — ..1724
Blanchard, William. Comedian. . . . .   1770?.1835
Blanche de Bourbon. Wife of Peter the Cruel, of Cast. 1338..1361
Blanche of Castile. Queen of Louis VIII. of France. . .   1197..1252
Blanchet, Francis. Abbé. Fr. Writer. (*Variétés Morales*) 1707..1784
Blanchet, Thomas. Historical and Portrait Painter . . . .   1617..1689
Bland, Elizabeth. Hebraist . . . .   — ..1720
Bland, Rev. Robert. Poet & Class. Edit. (*Lat. Verses*) 1779..1825
Blandrata, George. Italian Physician and Arian Writer   — ..1590?
Blane, Sir Gilbert, M. D. (*Elements of Medical Logic*) . 1749..1834
Blanken, John. Dutch Engineer . . . .   1755.. —
Blankoff, John Teunisz. *Jan Maat.* Flem. Marine Paint. 1628..1670
Blanqui, Jerome Adolphe. French Political Economist. 1798..1854
Blase. Saint and Martyr. . . . .   — .. 316?
Blaurer, Ambrose. Lutheran Div. in France and Germ. 1492..1568

BORN. DIED.

Blayney, Benjamin, D. D. Hebrew Critic.............. — ..1801
Bledri. Bp. of Llandaff; Schol. and Patron of Learning — ..1023
Bleeck, Peter van. Dutch Painter.................... 1700?.1764
Bleeker, Ann Eliza. American Author.............. 1752..1783
Bleeker, Anthony. American Miscellaneous Writer..... — ..1827
Blegny, Nicholas. French Medical Writer............. 1652..1722
Bleiswick, Peter van. Gd. Pensionary. (De Aggeribus) 1724..1790
Bless, Henry. Painter................................ 1480..1550
Blessington, Marg. Power, Css. of. L. by Dr. Madden, 1853 1789..1849
Bletterie, John Philip René de la. Abbé. Hist. Writer — ..1772
Bligh, William. Admiral. Captain of the " Bounty " .. 1753..1817
Blizard, Sir William. Surgeon and Anatomist......... 1743..1835
Bloch, Marcus Eliezer. Phys. and Natural. (Ichthyology) 1723..1799
Block, Benjamin. Portrait Painter.................... 1631.. —
Block, Daniel. Pomeranian Portrait Painter........... 1580..1661
Block, Joanna Koerten. Dutch Artist................. 1650..1715
Blockland, Anthony de Montfort. Painter............. 1532..1583
Bloemaert, Abraham. Dutch Painter.................. 1567..1647
Bloemaert, Cornelius, son. Engraver................. 1603..1680
Bloemen, John Francis van. Painter................. 1656..1740
Bloemen, Norbert van. Painter...................... 1672.. —
Bloemen, Peter van. Painter .... fl. 1699
Blois, Peter of. Petrus Blesensis. Writer .... 1120?.1200?
Blomefield, Rev. Francis. Topographer .... 1705..1751
Blomfield, Chas. Jas. Bp. Lond. L. by A. Blomfield, 1863 1786..1857
Blomfield, Edward Valentine. Grammarian........... 1788..1816
Blond, James Christopher le. Miniature Painter........ 1670..1741
Blondel, David. French Protestant. (On the Eucharist) 1591..1655
Blondel, Francis. Fr. Diplomatist and Military Engineer 1617..1686
Blondel, Francis. French Medical Writer at Paris...... 1613..1682
Blondel, Jas. Francis. Fr. Architect. (Civil Architecture) 1705..1774
Blondel, Peter James. Fr. Divine. (Truth of Christianity) 1674..1730
Blondin, Peter. French Botanist..................... 1682..1713
Blondus, or Biondo, Flavius. Antiq. (Roma Instaurata) 1388..1463
Blondus, or Biondo, Michael Angelo. Medical Writer... 1497..1560?
Blood, Thomas. Colonel. Adventurer............... 1628?.1680
Bloomfield, Robert. Pastoral Poet. (Farmer's Boy)... 1766..1823
Bloot, Peter. Flemish Painter....................... — ..1667
Blosius, or De Blois, Francis Louis. (Speculum Religo-
  sorum) .... 1506.1563 or 6
Blount, Charles, Earl of Devon........................ 1563..1606
Blount, Charles. Deistical Writer.................... 1654..1693
Blount, Sir Henry. Traveler and Writer.............. 1602..1682
Blount, Thomas. Miscellaneous Writer. (Boscobel).... 1618..1679
Blount, Sir Thos. Pope. (Censura Celebrium Auctorum) 1649..1697
Blow, Dr. John. Musical Composer.................... 1648..1708
Blücher, Marshal. Life by Foerster, 1821; Varnhagen,
  1827; Wallenrodt, 1832; Rauschniek, 1835; Burck-
  hardt, 1835; Kossarski, 1842; Pischou, 1842......... 1742..1819
Blum, Joachim Christian. German Poet.............. 1739..1790
Blum, Robert. German Publicist..................... 1807..1848
Blumauer, Louis. Ger. Poet. (Travesty of the Æneid) 1755..1798
Blumenbach, John Frederick. Naturalist............. 1752..1840
Blundeville, Thomas. Mathematician................. fl. 1594

BORN. DIED:

Blunt, Rev. Henry, of Chelsea. (*Sermons*)............ 1794..1843
Blunt, Prof. J. J., of Cambridge. L. in *Qu. Rev.* No. 207 — ..1855
Bluteau, Raphael. Fr. Div. in Port. (*Port. & Lat. Dict.*) 1638..1734
Boaden, James. Dramatist and Critic................ 1762..1839
Boadicea. British Queen............................ — .. 62
Boardman, George D. American Missionary........... 1801..1831
Bobart, James. German Botanist at Oxford........... 1598?.1679
Bobart, James, son. Botanist at Oxford.............. —aft.1713
Bobrov, Semen Sergæevitch. Russian Poet............ — ..1810
Boccaccino, Camillus. Italian Painter................ 1511..1546
Boccaccio, John. Italian Poet. Life by Betussi ; G. B.
    Baldelli, 1806...................................... 1313..1375
Boccage, Maria Anne le Page du. French Poetess...... 1710..1802
Boccalini, Trajan. Ital. Satirist. (*Ragguagli di Parnaso*) 1556..1613
Boccamazza, Angelus. Bp. of Catania. (*Brevis Chronica*) — ..1296
Boccherini, Louis. Composer of Instrumental Music... 1740..1805
Bocciardo, Clement. *Clementone.* Painter........... 1620..1658
Boccold, or Bockholdt, or Beukels. *See* John of Leyden 1510?.1536
Boccone, Paul. Italian Naturalist................... 1633..1704
Boch, or Bochius, John. *The Belgic Virgil.*......... 1555..1609
Bochart, Samuel. Orientalist. (*Geographia Sacra*).... 1599..1667
Bochel, or Bouchel, Lawrence. Fr. Writ. in Law & Hist. 1559..1629
Bock, or Le Boucq, Jerome. German Naturalist........ 1498..1553
Bockhorst, John van. Flemish Painter. *Langhen Jan.* 1610?. —
Bockhorst, John van. Dutch Painter in London....... 1661..1724
Bocquillot, Lazarus Andrew. French Divine.......... 1649..1728
Bocska, Robt. Nich. Chas. Fr. Harpist and Composer .. 1789..1856
Bode, Christopher Augustus. German Orientalist...... 1722..1796
Bode, John Ehlert. Astronomer..................... 1747..1826
Bodekker, John Francis. Dutch Portrait Painter....... 1660..1727
Bodenstein, Adam. German Medical Writer.......... 1528..1577
Bodin, John. French Political Writer. (*De Republica*). 1530..1596
Bodley, Sir Thos. Found. of Library. L. by Hearne, 1703 1544..1612
Bodmer, John Jacob. German Poet................. 1698..1783
Bodoni, John Baptist. Italian Printer.............. 1740..1813
Bodson, Joseph. French Engraver................... 1768.. —
Boece, or Boethius, Hector. Scottish Historian........ 1470?.1536
Boeckel, or Bockelius, John. Med. Writer at Hamburg. 1535..1605
Boecler, John Henry. German Philologist............ 1611..1692
Boehm, or Boehme, Jacob, of Görlitz. Visionary. (*Au-*
    rora.) Life by Frankenberg, 1651, tr. by Okely, 1780 1575..1624
Boehmer, John Frederick. German Historian......... 1795..1863
Boehmer, Philip Adolphus. German Anatomist....... 1717..1789
Boel, Peter. Dutch Painter........................ 1625..1680
Boerhaave, Abraham Kaan. Dut. Med. Writ. at Petersbg. 1715..1753
Boerhaave, Herman. Physician. Life by Dr. William
    Burton, 1746; Dr. Johnson........................ 1668..1732
Boerne, or Börne, Louis. Ger. Polit. Writ. L. by Gutzkow 1786..1837
Boethius. Roman Senator. (*De Consolatione.*) Life by
    N. Gervaise.. 470?. 524
Boethius, or Boece, Hector. Scottish Historian........ 1470?.1536
Boetie, Stephen de la. Fr. Repub. Writ. (*Le Contr' Un*) 1530..1563
Boetius, or Boot, Gerard. Dut. Phys. (*Philos. Naturalis*) 1604..1653
Boëttcher, John Fred. Alchemist and Porcelain-maker. 1681..1719

BORN. DIED.

Boettiger, Charles Augustus. German Archæologist.... 1760..1835
Boffrand, Germain. French Architect................. 1667..1754
Bogaert, Martin van den. *Desjardins.* Dutch Sculptor 1640..1694
Bogan, Zachary. Divine and Antiquary. (*Help to Prayer*) 1625..1659
Bogatzky, Chas. Henry. Ger. Theol. (*Golden Treasury*) 1690?.1774
Bogdanovitch, Hippolytus. Russian Scholar & Diplom. 1743..1803
Bogermann, John. Dutch Contra-Remonstrant Divine. 1576..1637
Bogue, David, of Gosport. Dissenting Divine. Life by
   Dr. James Bennett.................................. 1750..1825
Bohadin. Arabian Writer. (*Life of Saladin*)......... 1145..1235
Bohemond, Mark, Prince of Antioch. Crusader....... — ..1111
Bohlen, Peter von. Orientalist. (*Das Alte Indien.*)
   Life by self...................................... 1796..1840
Böhmer, John Frederick, of Frankfort. Historian...... 1795..1863
Bohn, John, of Leipsic. Physician and Chemist. (*De
   Officio Medici*) .... 1640..1718
Bohun, Edmund. Miscellaneous Writer............... —aft.1700
Boiardo, Matthew Maria. Italian Poet. *See* Bojardo... 1434?.1494
Boichot, William. French Sculptor.................. 1738..1814
Boieldieu, Adrian Francis. French Musical Composer.. 1775..1834
Boigne, Bened. le Borgne, Count de. Soldier of fortune 1741..1830
Boileau, Charles. Abbé of Beaulieu. Court Preacher.. — ..1704
Boileau, James. Ecclesiastical Historian............. 1635..1716
Boileau, John James. (*Letters on Morality and Devotion*) 1649..1735
Boileau-Despréaux, Nicholas. Poet, Satirist, Critic.
   Life by Desmaizeaux, 1712........................ 1636..1711
Boilly, Louis Leopold. French Painter............... 1761..1830?
Boindin, Nicholas. French Atheist and Writer....:.... 1676..1751
Bois, Gerard du. Fr. Writ. (*Hist. of the Church of Paris*) 1629..1696
Bois, John du. French Monk, Soldier, and Preacher... — ..1626
Bois, Boys, or Boyse, John. Translator of Bible........ 1560..1643
Bois de la Pierre, Louisa Mary du. Poet. & Hist.Writer 1663?.1730
Bois, Du. *See* Dubois.
Boismont. French Preacher......................... 1715..1786
Boismorand, Claude Joseph Cheron de. French Writer 1680?.1740
Boisrobert, Francis le Metel de. Writer and Wit...... 1592..1662
Boissard, John James. French Antiquary. (*Icones*).... 1528..1602
Boisserée, Sulpicius. German Collector of Paintings... 1783..1854
Boissière, Jos. de la Fontaine de la, of Dieppe. (*Sermons*) — ..1732
Boissieu, Barthol. Camillus de. Fr. Medical Writer... 1734..1770
Boissy d'Anglas, Frs. Anthony, Ct. de. Polit. and Writ. 1756..1826
Boissy, Louis de. French Dramatic Writer........... 1694..1758
Boiste, Peter Claude Victoire. (*Dict. de Géographie*)... 1765..1824
Boivin, Francis de, Baron de Villars. (*Wars of Piedmont*) — ..1618
Boivin de Villeneuve, John. Greek Scholar and Poet 1663..1726
Boivin, Louis. French Scholar...................... 1649..1724
Boizot, Louis Simon. French Sculptor............... 1743..1809
Bojardo, Matthew Maria. (*Orlando Innamorato*)........ 1434?.1494
Bol, Ferdinand. Dutch Painter..................... 1611.1681 or 6
Bol, John. Dutch Painter.......................... 1534..1583
Bolanger, John. Historical Painter................. 1606..1660
Bold, Samuel. (*Plea for Moderation towards Dissenters*). — ..1737
Boleslaus I. 1st King of Poland (992-1025). *The Great* — ..1025?
Boleslaus II. (1058-81.)* *The Bold*................. 1042..1090?

BORN. DIED.

Boleyn, Anne. Queen of Henry VIII. Life by George
Wayt, 1818; Miss Benger, 1821 .... 1507 or 1.1536
Boleyn, George, Lord Rochfort, brother. Poetical Writer — ..1536
Bolingbroke, Henry St. John, First Visct. Statesman
and Political Writer. L. by Mallet, 1754; St. Lambert,
1796; G. H. Cooke, 1835; Thomas Macknight, 1863. 1678..1751
Bolivar, Simon. Liberator of Spanish Colonies of South
America.. 1783..1830
Bollan, William. American Political Writer and Agent. — ..1776
Bollandus, John. Jesuit. (*Lives of the Saints*)........ 1596..1665
Bologna, John of. Flem. Sculpt. and Architect in Italy. 1524..1608
Bolognese. Painter. *See* Grimaldi.................. 1606..1680
Bolsec, Jerome Hermes. Anti-Protestant Writer....... — ..1585
Bolswert, Boëtius Adam. Flemish Engraver.......... fl. ab. 1620
Bolswert, Scheldt, brother. Flemish Engraver........ 1586.. —
Bolton, Edmund. Antiquary. (*Life of Henry II.*).... fl. 1624
Bolton, Robert. Puritan Divine. (*Four Last Things.*)
Life by Edward Bagshaw, 1633..................... 1572..1631
Bolton, Robert. Dean of Carlisle. Divine........... 1697..1763
Bolts, William. Merchant, East I. Co. Writer on India 1740..1808
Bolzani, Urbano Valeriano. Greek Scholar in Italy.... 1440..1524
Bombelli, Raphael. Algebraist...................... fl. 1572?
Bombelli, Sebastian, of Bologna. Hist. & Portr. Paint. 1635..1685
Bomberg, Daniel. Dutch Printer..................... — ..1549
Bon, John le. Fr. Med. Writer. (*Therapeia Puerorum*) fl. 1571
Bona, John. Cardinal. Devotional Writer........... 1609..1674
Bona, John de. Medical Writer at Padua .... 1712.. —
Bonac, John Louis d'Usson, Marquis de. Diplomatist.. 1672..1738
Bonacciolus, Louis. Med. Writer. (*Enneas Muliebris*) fl. 1503
Bonacossus, Hercules, of Ferrara. Medical Writer..... — ..1578
Bonamy, Peter Nich. Writ. in *Mém. de l'Acad. des Inscr.* 1694..1770
Bonanni, James. Syracusan Noble. (*Syracusa Illustrata*) — ..1636
Bonanni, Philip, of Rome. Hist. (*Medals of the Popes*) 1638..1725
Bonaparte, Caroline Maria Annunciata, wife of Murat,
sister of Napoleon I................................ 1782..1839
Bonaparte, Charles, of Corsica, father of Napoleon I.... 1744..1785
Bonaparte, Charles Lucien, Prince of Canino. Writer on
Natural Philosophy, &c............................. 1803..1857
Bonaparte, Jerome. King of Westphalia (1807–13) .... 1784..1860
Bonaparte, Joseph, King of Naples and Spain......... 1768..1844
Bonaparte, Louis Napoleon, King of Holland.......... 1778..1846
Bonaparte, Lucien, Prince of Canino. Poetical Writer.
(*Charlemagne.*) Life by self, 1836................. 1775..1840
Bonaparte, Maria Anne Eliza, sister of Napoleon I., wife
of Felix Bacciochi, Princess Piombino............... 1777..1820
Bonaparte, Maria Letitia. Mother of Napoleon I...... 1750..1836
Bonaparte, Maria Pauline, Prss. Borghese, sist. of Nap.. 1780..1825
Bonaparte, Napoleon I. Emperor. L. by Bourrienne;
Constant; Fleury de Chaboulon; Norvius; St. Hilaire;
Vieusieux; Savary, Duc de Rovigo; Ségur, 1812;
Wm. Burdon; Sir W. Scott; J. G. Lockhart, 1829;
W. Hazlitt, 1836; Michaud, 1844; Corresp. with Jos.
Bonaparte, 1855, 8vo; Correspondance, publiée par
ord. de Nap. III. 1858, &c.; J. S. C. Abbott, 1864... 1769..1821

BORN. DIED.

Bonaparte, Nap. Francis Chas. Jos., Duke of Reichstadt.
King of Rome; Napoleon II. Son of Napoleon I.... 1811..1832
Bonardi, J. Bapt. (*Dict. of Anon. and Pseudon. Writers*) — ..1756
Bonarelli, Guy Ubaldo. Italian Poet. (*Filli di Sciro*).. 1563..1608
Bonasoni, Julius. Bolognese Painter and Engraver .. 1498¹aft.1571
Bonaventure, St. Card. L. by Boule, 1747; Fessler, 1807 1221..1274
Bonaventure, of Padua. Cardinal; Friend of Petrarch . 1332..1388
Bonchamp, Chas. Melch. Arthur de. Vendean Royalist. 1759..1793
Bond, George Phillips. American Astronomer .... 1825..1865
Bond, John, of Taunton. Phys. and Classical Annotator 1550..1612
Bond, Oliver. Irish Rebel of 1797-98................. 1720..1798
Bond, William Cranch. American Astronomer......... 1789..1859
Bondi, Clement. Italian Poet..................... 1742..1821
Bone, Henry, R. A. Painter in Enamel .... 1755..1834
Bonecueil, Joseph Duranti de. Translator of the Fathers 1663?.1756
Boner, Ulrich. German Fabulist. (*Der Edelstein*)...... fl. 14th c.
Bonet, or Bonnet, Theophilus. Medical Writer......... 1620..1689
Bonfadio, James. Italian Letter Writer and Poet. (*An-* ,
nals of Genoa)................................... — ..1550
Bonfini, Anthony. (*History of Hungary*)............. 1427..1502
Bongars, James. French Scholar and Negotiator...... 1546..1612
Bonichon, Francis, of Angers. (*Pompa Episcopalis*).... — ..1662
Boniface, Hyacinthe, of Aix. Compiler of Decrees of
Parliament of Provence.......................... 1612..1695
Boniface, St. *Winifrid.* Apostle of Germany. Life by
Willibald; Geissler, 1796; Loeffler, 1812; Schmerbauch,
1827; Pfaff, 1835; Waitzmann, 1840; Seiters, 1845... 680?. 755
Boniface I. Pope (418–22). *Saint*.................... — .. 422
Boniface II. (530–32)............................. — .. 532
Boniface III. (606) .... — .. 606
Boniface IV. (607–15.) *Saint*..................... — .. 615
Boniface V. (617–25)............................. — .. 625
Boniface VI. (896)............................... — .. 896
Boniface VII. Anti-Pope (984–85). *Francon*......... — .. 985
Boniface VIII. Pope (1294–1303). *Benedict Cajetan.*
Life by Rubeis, 1651; Luigi Tosti, 1846 .... 1228..1303
Boniface IX. (1389–1404.) *Peter Thomacelli*........ — ..1404
Bonifacio, Balthasar. Venetian Historical Writer ...... 1584?.1659
Bonafacio, Venetiano. Italian Painter .... 1491..1553
Bonifacius. Roman General. Governor of Africa...... — .. 432
Bonifonius, or Bonnefons, John. French Latin Poet ... 1554..1614
Bonington, Richard Parkes. Artist.................. 1801..1828
Bonjour, Wm. Fr. Missionary to China and Bibl. Writ. 1670..1714
Bonnecorse. French Consul in Egypt. Poetical Writer — ..1706
Bonnefons, John. French Latin Poet................. 1554..1614
Bonnefoy, or Bonfidius, Edm. Writer on Oriental Law 1536..1574
Bonnell, James. Accountant-General of Ireland. Life
by Hamilton, 1707................................ 1653..1699
Bonner, Edmund. Bp. of London (1540–69). Persecutor 1500?.1569
Bonnet, Charles. Naturalist of Geneva................ 1720..1793
Bonnet, or Bonet, Theophilus, of Geneva. Med. Writer. 1620..1689
Bonneval, Claude Alexander, Count de. *Achmet Pasha.*
French Military Adventurer. Life by self (spurious),
1755; De Ligne, 1817............................. 1675..1747

BORN. DIED.

Bonneville, Nich. de. Fr. Polit. (*Poésies Républicaines*) 1760.. —
Bonnivard, Francis de. *Prisoner of Chillon* .... 1496..1570
Bonnycastle, John. Mathematician .... — ..1821
Bonomi, Joseph. Italian Architect in England .... 1739..1808
Bononcini, John. Opera Composer. Rival of Handel 1672 aft.1748
Bonpland, Aimé. French Botanist .... 1773..1858
Bonstettin, Charles Victor de. Swiss Author.......... 1745..1832
Bontempi, Geo. Andr. Angelini, of Perugia. (*Hist. Musica*) 1630?.1700?
Bontems, Mary Jane. Translator of *Thomson's Seasons* . 1718..1768
Bontius, Gerard. Phys. at Leyden. Inv. of *Pillulæ Tartaræ* 1536?.1599
Bontius, Jas. Dut. Phys. in East. (*De Medicinâ Indorum*) — ..1623
Bonvicino, Alex. *Il Moretto*. Hist. and Portrait Painter 1514..1564
Boodt, Anselm Boece von. Writer on Gems............ — ..1634?
Booker, John. Astrologer............................ 1601..1667
Booker, Rev. Luke, LL. D. Writer................... 1762..1835
Boone, Daniel. Dutch Painter....................... — ..1698
Boone, Daniel. American Explorer and Colonizer...... 1735..1820
Boonen, Arnold. Dutch Portrait Painter............. 1669..1729
Boos, Martin. Ger. Theologian. Life by C. Bridges, 1836 1762..1825
Boot, Arnold. Dutch Physician and Biblical Writer.... 1606..1653
Booth, Barton. Tragic Actor........................ 1681..1733
Booth, Sir Felix. Promoter of Arctic Discovery .... 1775..1850
Booth, Henry, Earl of Warrington. Statesman.......... 1651..1694
Booth, John Wilkes. Assassin of Abraham Lincoln .... — ..1865
Booth, Junius Brutus. Tragedian..................... 1796..1852
Bora, Katharina von. Wife of Luther................ 1499..1552
Borbonius, or Bourbon, Nich. Fr. Latin Poet. (*Nugæ*) 1503..1550
Borda, John Charles. French Mathemat. and Astronomer 1733..1799
Borde, Andrew. (*Madmen of Gotham*) .... 1500?.1549
Borde, John Benjamin de la. French Historian .... 1734..1794
Bordelon, Laurence. French Writer.................. 1653..1730
Bordenave, Toussaint. French Physiologist........... 1728..1782
Bordeu, Anthony de. French Physician.............. 1696.. —
Bordeu, Francis de, son. Medical Writer .... 1734.. —
Bordeu, Theophilus de, brother. Medical Writer....... 1722..1776
Bordley, John Beale. American Agriculturist .... 1728..1824
Bordone, Paris. Italian Painter..................... 1513..1588
Borel, Peter. French Medical Writer................. 1620?.1689
Borelli, John Alphonso. Italian Philosopher and Mathe-
    matician. (*De Motu Animalium*).................... 1608..1679
Borgarucci, Prosper. Italian Medical Writer.......... fl. 1567
Borghese, Maria Pauline Bonaparte, Princess .... 1780..1825
Borghesi, Paul Guidotto. Italian Painter and Poet.
    (*Jerusalem Ruined*)................................ 1566?.1626
Borghini, Raffaelle. *Il Riposo*. Florentine Poet .... — ..1584
Borghini, Vincent. Italian Scholar. (*Discorsi*) .... 1515..1580
Borgia, Cæsar. Life by Tomasi, 1655; Alex. Gordon, 1729 — ..1507
Borgia, Francis. Gen. of the Jesuits. Life by Schott, 1596 1510..1572
Borgia, Lucrezia. Duchess of Ferrara .... — ..1523
Borgia, Stephen. Cardinal. Virtuoso .... 1731..1804
Borgiani, Horace. Roman Painter and Engraver ...... 1630..1681
Borgo, Luca di. *Pacioli*. Italian Geometer .... —aft.1509
Borgognone, James Cortesi. Italian Painter.......... 1621..1676
Borie Cambort, John. French Revolutionist .... 1770?.1805

BORN. DIED.

Borlace, Edmund, M.D. Writ. on Hist. & Antiq. of Ireland — ..1682
Borlase, Rev. Henry. Founder of *Plymouth Brethren*.. — ..1835
Borlase, Rev. William. Antiquary.................. 1696..1772
Born, Ignatius. Hungarian Mineralogist and Philologist 1742..1791
Börne, or Boerne, Louis. Ger. Polit. Writ. L. by Gutzkow 1786..1837
Bornier, Philip de, of Montpellier. Writer on Law...... 1634..1711
Borowlaski, Count. Polish Dwarf................... 1739?.1837
Borrel, John. Writer on Geometry................. — ..1572
Borri, Jos. Francis. *Burrhus*. Ital. Impostor and Empiric 1627..1695
Borrichius, or Borch, Olaus. Danish Medical Writer... 1626..1690
Borromeo, Charles, St. Cardinal. Abp. of Milan. L. by
    Bimius, 1585; Magnago, 1587; Austin Valerio, 1588;
    Possevino, 1591; Boscape; Giussano, 1610; Withius,
    1611; Muñoz, 1624; Godeau, 1648; Touron, 1761;
    Stolz, 1781; Olcese, 1817; Alb. Butler, 1835; Chene-
    vières, 1840; Dragoni, 1844; Dieringer, 1846; Alex.
    Martin, 1847.................................... 1538..1584
Borromeo, Frederic. Cardinal. Archbishop of Milan.. 1564..1631
Borromini, Francis. Italian Architect.............. 1599..1667
Borroni, Paul Michael Benedict. Italian Painter....... — ..1819
Borthwick, David, of Lochhill. Lord Advocate........ — ..1581
Bory de St. Vincent, J. Bapt. George Mary. Naturalist 1780..1846
Borzoni, Francis Mary. Marine Painter............. 1625..1679
Borzoni, Lucian. Italian Historical and Portrait Painter 1590..1645
Bos, Charles Francis du. Theologian. (*Life of Barillon*) 1661..1724
Bos, or Bosche, Jerome. Dutch Painter and Engraver .. 1450?.1500
Bos, John Baptist du. French Critical and Hist. Writer. 1670..1742
Bos, Lambert. Philologist............................ 1670..1717
Bos, Louis Janssen, or John Louis, de. Painter........ — ..1507
Bosc, Claude du. French Engraver in England........ fl. 1714
Bosc, Louis Augustus William. French Naturalist ..... 1759..1828
Bosc, Peter du. French Protestant Preacher........... 1623..1692
Boscager, John. French Jurist...................... 1601..1687
Boscan Almogaver, John. Reformer of Spanish Poetry 1500?.1544
Boscawen, Right Hon. Edward. Admiral............ 1711..1761
Boscawen, William. Writer and Poet .... 1752..1811
Bosch, Balthasar van den. Pa. of Portr. & Conversations 1675..1715
Bosch, Jacob van den. Dutch Painter of Still Life...... 1636..1676
Bosch, Jerome. Dutch Book Collector .... 1740..1811
Boscoli, Andrew. Italian Historical Painter.......... 1553..1606
Boscovich, Roger Joseph. Mathematician .... 1711..1787
Bosio, Anthony. (*Roma Sotteranea*)................... — ..1629
Bosio, Francis Joseph. French Sculptor.............. 1769..1845
Bosio, James. (*Hist. of the Order of St. John of Jerusalem*) fl. 1600?
Bosquet, Frs. Bp. of Montpellier. (*Hist. of Gallican Ch.*) 1605..1676
Bosschaert, Thos. Willebrord. Dutch Hist. & Portr. Pa. 1631..1656
Bosse, Abraham. French Engraver and Architect...... — ..1678
Bossi, Joseph. Italian Painter and Poet .... 1777..1815
Bossi, Joseph Charles Aurelius, Baron de. Italian Poet
    and Diplomatist. (*Oromasia*)...................... 1758..1823
Bosso, Matthew. Italian Divine.................... 1428..1502
Bossu, René le. Fr. Scholar and Critic. (*On Epic Poetry*) 1631..1680
Bossuet, James Benignus le. Bp. of Meaux. Life by
    Levesque de Burigny, 1761; Talbert, 1772; Charles

BORN. DIED.

Butler, 1812; Card. de Bausset, 1814; St: Prosper,
  1822; Caillot, 1825; Roy, 1840; Abbé Guettée, 1856.. 1627..1704
Bossut, Charles. Mathematician .... 1730..1814
Boston, Thomas. Scottish Divine. (*Fourfold State*) ... 1676..1732
Boswell, Sir Alexander. Antiquarian and Song Writer . 1775..1822
Boswell, James. Biographer of Dr. Johnson........... 1740..1795
Boswell, James. Editor of Shakespeare .... 1779..1822
Botal, Leonard, of Asti. *Botallus*. Medical Writer ..... fl. 1550?
Botelho, Nuno Alvarez de. Portuguese Viceroy in India — ..1629
Botero, John. Jesuit Polit. Writer. (*Ragione di Stato*).. 1540..1617
Botfield, Beriah. Antiquary .... 1807?.1863
Both, Andrew. Painter........................... — ..1656
Both, John, brother. Dutch Landscape Painter......... 1610..1650
Bothwell, James Hepburn, Earl of. Husband of Mary
  of Scotland. Life by Lobanov Rostofsky, 1856...... — ..1576
Bott, John de. French Architect................... 1670..1745
Botta, Charles Joseph William. Italian Historian,...... 1766..1837
Bottari, John Gaetano. Florentine Scholar .... 1689..1775
Böttcher, or Böttger, or Böttiger. *See* Boettcher....... 1681..1719
Botticelli, Alexander. Painter of Florence .... 1437..1515
Böttiger, Charles Augustus. *See* Boettiger........... 1760..1835
Bottoni, Albertus. Medical Writer................... — ..1596
Bouchard, David. Governor of Perigord .... — ..1598
Bouchardon, Edm. Fr. Sculpt. Life by Count de Caylus 1698..1762
Bouchaud, Matthew Anthony. French Writer on Law. 1719..1804
Bouche, Honorius. (*History of Provence*)............. 1598..1671
Bouche, Martin. Engraver of Portraits.............. fl. 1680
Bouchel, Lawrence. *Bochelius*. Fr. Jurist and Historian 1559..1629
Boucher d'Argis, Anthony Gaspard. Fr. Writer on Law 1708..1791
Boucher, Francis. French Painter................... 1704..1770
Boucher, John. Doctor of the Sorbonne. Fanatic ... 1548?.1644
Boucher, Rev. Jonathan. Political Writer and Philologist 1738..1804
Bouchet, John, of Poictiers. (*Annals of Aquitaine*)...... 1476..1550
Bouchet, John du. French Genealogist.............. 1599..1684
Bouchet, William. Judge, of Poitiers. (*Sérées*) .... 1526..1606?
Boucheul, John Joseph, of Dorat. Law Writer .... — ..1706
Boucicault, Marshal. Life published by Theodore Gode-
  froy, 1820; De Pilham, 1697 .... 1364..1421
Boudewyns, Michael. Phys. of Antwerp. (*Ventilabrum*) — ..1681
Boudier, René. French Scholar. (*Roman History*)..... 1634..1723
Boudinot, Elias. American Lawyer and Philanthropist. 1740..1821
Boudon, Henry Mary, of Evreux. Devotional Writer... 1624..1702
Boudot, John, of Paris. (*Latin Dictionary*) .... 1685..1754
Boufflers, Louis Francis, Duc de. Marshal of France ... 1644..1711
Boufflers, Stanislaus, Chevalier de. French Emigrant .. 1737..1815
Bougainville, John Peter de. French Writer.......... 1722..1763
Bougainville, Louis Anthony de. Geograph. Discoverer 1729..1811
Bougainville, M. D. F. French Navigator and Discoverer — ..1792
Bougeant, Wm. Hyacinth. (*Hist. of Treaty of Westphalia*) 1690..1743
Bougerel, Jos. (*Mém. pour l'Histoire des Hommes Illustr.*) 1680..1753
Bouguer, Peter. French Mathematician .... 1698..1758
Bouhier, John. French Jurisconsult and Writer .... 1673..1746
Bouhours, Dominic. French Jesuit and Critic .... 1628..1702
Bouillard, James. French Engraver.................. 1744..1806

BORN. DIED.

Bouillart, Jas. Fr. Historian. (*Hist. of S.-Germ.-des-Prés.*) 1649..1726
Bouillaud, or Boulliaud, Ismael. Astronomer .... 1605..1694
Bouillé, Frs. Claude Amour, Mqs. de. (*Memoirs of Fr. Rev.*) 1759..1800
Bouillet, John, of Montpellier. Medical Writer .... 1690..1777
Bouillon, Emanuel Theodosius........................ 1644..1715
Bouillon, Godfrey de, Duke of Lorraine. First Christian K.
   of Jerusalem. Life by Prévault, 1833; Exenvillez, 1842 1058?.1100
Bouilly, John Nicholas. French Dramatic Author...... 1763..1842
Boulainvilliers, Henry de, Ct. de St. Saire. Historian.. 1658..1722
Boulanger, Andrew. *Petit Père André.* August. Preacher 1578?.1657
Boulanger, or Boullenger, Claude Frs. Felix. Fr. Scholar 1725..1758
Boulanger, John. French Engraver................... 1607.:1680
Boulanger, Nicholas Anthony. Fr. Math. and Engineer 1722..1759
Boulard, Anthony Mary Henry. French Savant .... 1754..1825
Boulay de lay Meurthe, A. J. C. Fr. Orator and Writer 1761..1840
Boulay, Cæsar Egasse du. (*Hist. of the University of Paris*) — ..1678
Boulaye, Francis le Gouz de la. French Traveler ...... 1610?.1669
Boulduc, Giles Francis, son. Chemist................ 1675..1742
Boulduc, Simon. French Chemist................... — ..1729
Boullenois, Louis. French Law Writer.............. 1680..1762
Boullier, David Renaud. Dutch Theologian......... 1699..1759
Boullongne, Bon de. Painter........................ 1649..1717
Boullongne, Louis de. *The Elder.* French Painter.... 1609..1674
Boullongne, Louis de. *The Younger*, son. Painter..... 1654..1733
Boulter, Hugh. Archbishop of Armagh.............. 1671..1742
Boulton, Matthew. Engineer. Life, Birmingham, 1809 1728..1809
Bouquet, Martin. (*Recueil des Historiens des Gaules*) ... 1685..1754
Bourbon, Charles I., Fifth Duke of................... 1401..1456
Bourbon, Charles, Duke of. Constable of France. Life
   by Baudot de Juilly, 1696........................ 1489..1527
Bourbon, Chas. de. Card. Abp. of Rouen. L. by Du Breul 1520..1590
Bourbon, John I., Fourth Duke of................... 1381..1434
Bourbon, John II., Sixth Duke of................... 1426?.1488
Bourbon, Louis I., Count de Clermont and First Duke of 1279..1341
Bourbon, Louis II., Third Duke of................... 1373..1410
Bourbon, Nicholas. Gr. Scholar and Latin Poet. (*Nugæ*) 1503..1550
Bourbon, Nicholas. Nephew. Latin and Greek Poet.. 1574..1644
Bourchenu, John Peter Moret de. (*Hist. of Dauphiné*).. 1651..1730
Bourchier, John, Lord Berners. Translator......... 1467?.1532
Bourchier, Thomas. Archbp. of Canterbury (1454–86). — ..1486
Bourdaloue, Louis. Jesuit Preacher. Life by Mad. de
   Prigny, 1705; Villenave, 1812; Labouderie, 1825; St.
   Amand, 1842 .... 1632..1704
Bourdeille, Claude de, Count de Montrésor. (*Memoirs*). 1608?.1663
Bourdeilles, Peter de. Abbot of Brantôme. (*Memoirs*). 1527?.1614
Bourdelot, John. French Critic.................... — ..1638
Bourdelot, Peter Michon, Abbé. Med. Writer at Paris. 1610..1685
Bourdigné, Charles, of Angers. Poet. (*Légende de Pi-*
   erre Faifeu) .... — ..1545
Bourdon, Aimé. French Anatomist .... 1638..1706
Bourdon de l'Oise, Francis Louis. French Revolutionist — ..1797
Bourdon, Sebastian. French Painter.............. 1616..1671
Bourdot, Chas. Anthony. Advocate. (*Coutumier Général*) 1685..1735
Bourgelat, Claude, of Berlin. Veterinarian Writer...... 1712?.1779

BORN. DIED.
Bourgeoise, Sir Francis. Painter .... 1756.. 1811
Bourgeoise, Louisa. *Boursier*. Fr. Writer on Midwifery   fl. 1600?
Bourges, Clémence de, of Lyons. Writer and Poetess...   — ..1562
Bourget, John. Benedictine. Hist. of Caen & Bec Abbeys 1724..1776
Bourgoing, John Francis, Baron de. Fr. Diplom. & Writ. 1748..1811
Bourguet, Louis. Fr. Prot. Refugee in Switzerland. Writer 1678..1742
Bourgueville, Charles de, of Caen. (*History of Caen*) .. 1504..1593
Bourguignon. French Painter. *See* Courtois .... 1621..1676
Bourignon, Antoinette de la Porte. Mystic. L. by Poiret 1616..1680
Bourlet de Vauxcelles, Simon Jerome. French Writer 1734?.1799
Bourmont, Louis A. V. de Ghaisne de. Marshal of France 1773..1846
Bourne, Hugh. Founder of Primitive Methodists ...... 1772..1852
Bourne, Vincent. Latin Poet .... 1697?.1747
Bourrienne, Louis Ant. Fauvelet de. (*Life of Napoleon*) 1769..1834
Boursault, Edmund. Fr. Dram. and Romance Writer .. 1638..1701
Boursier, Lawrence Francis. Fr. Theolog. and Metaphys. 1679..1749
Bourvalais, Paul Poisson. French Financier .... — ..1719
Bousseau, James. Sculptor.......................... 1681..1740
Bousset, René Drouard de, of Paris. Musical Composer.. 1703..1760
Boutaric, Francis de, of Toulouse. Law Writer .... 1672..1733
Boutauld, Michael.• Jesuit of Paris; Theologian........ 1607..1688
Bouteroue, Claude. Antiquary of Paris................ — ..1680?
Bouterwek, Frederick. (*History of Spanish Literature*)..1766..1828
Bouthrais, Raoul, of Châteaudun. Law Writer .... 1552?.1630
Bouvart, Michael Philip............................. 1717..1787
Bouvet, Joachim. French Jesuit and Missionary ...... — ..1732
Boverius, Zacharias. (*History of the Capuchins*) .... 1568..1638
Bovette de Blemur, Jacqueline. Theological Writer.. 1618..1696
Bovey, Mrs. Catherine. Extolled by Steele............ 1669?.1726
Bovillus, Charles. Mathematician.................... fl. 1510–33
Bovius, Thos. *Zephirielem*. Italian Empiric and Alchem. fl. 1590
Bowdich, Thomas Edward. African Traveler .... 1790..1824
Bowditch, Nathaniel. Amer. Writ. on Navig. and Math. 1793..1838
Bowdler, Miss Hannah. Poet and Writer .... 1754?.1830
Bowdler, Thomas, M. D. (*Family Shakespeare*) .... 1754..1825
Bowdoin, James. American Statesman .... 1727..1790
Bowen, John. Bishop of Sierra Leone .... 1815..1859
Bower, Archibald. Ex-Jesuit. (*Lives of Popes*) .... 1686..1766
Bowle, Rev. John. Writer on Span. Lit. Ed. of Cervantes 1725..1788
Bowles, Caroline. *See* Mrs. Southey................. 1787..1854
Bowles, William Lisle. Canon. Poet. (*Sonnets*)...... 1762..1850
Bowyer, William. Printer. Life by Nichols, 1782 ..... 1699..1777
Boxhorn, Mark Zuerius. Philologist, Historian, Antiq... 1612..1653
Boyce, Dr. William. Musical Composer............... 1710..1779
Boyd, Henry. Poet. Translator of Dante .... — ..1832
Boyd, Hugh Stuart. Greek Scholar.................. — ..1848
Boyd, Mark Alex. Scot. Writer. L. by Ld. Hailes, 1733 1562..1601
Boyd, Robert, Lord. Regent of Scotland.............. — ..1470
Boyd, Robert. Scottish Divine .... 1578..1627
Boyd, Wm., Fourth E. of Kilmarnock. Jacobite. Beheaded 1704..1746
Boyd, Zachary. Scottish Divine. (*Zion's Flowers*)..... — ..1653
Boydell, John. Lord Mayor. Art Publisher .... 1719..1804
Boyer, Abel. Lexicographer and Miscellaneous Writer.. 1664..1729
Boyer, Alexis, Baron de. French Surgeon......... 1757 or 60.1833

BORN. DIED.
Boyer, J. Bapt. Nich. Fr. Medical Writer on Contagion 1693..1768
Boyer, John Peter. President of Hayti...............1776..1850
Boyle, Charles, Fourth Earl of Orrery. (*Epistles of Pha-
  laris.*) (The *Orrery* called after him) .... 1676..1731
Boyle, John, Earl of Cork and Orrery. Writer on Swift;
  Translator of Pliny............................... 1707..1762
Boyle, Richard. First and Great Earl of Cork. Statesman 1566..1643
Boyle, Richard. Third Earl of Burlington, Fourth Earl of
  Cork. Pope's Epistle IV. dedicated to him .... 1695..1753
Boyle, Hon. Robert. Philosopher. Founder of Lecture.
  Life by Thomas Birch, 1744 .... 1627..1691
Boyle, Roger, First Earl of Orrery. Royalist General,
  Statesman, Writer............................... 1621..1679
Boylston, Zabdiel. American Physician............. 1684..1766
Boys, John, D. D. Dean of Canterbury. Divine. (*Postils*) 1571..1625
Boys, Boyse, or Bois, John. Translator of the Bible..... 1560..1643
Boys, William. Antiquarian and Topographer......... 1735..1803
Boyse, Joseph. Dissenting Divine................... 1660..1728?
Boyse, Samuel. Poet. (*The Deity*)................ 1708..1749
Boze, Claude Gros de. French Antiquary. (*Medallic
  History of Louis XIV.*)........................... 1680..1753
Bozzaris, Mark. Greek Patriot...................... 1789..1823
Bozzasotra, Anthony. Medical Writer at Naples ...... — ..1557
Braccio di Montone. Italian Soldier .... 1368..1424
Bracciolini dell' Api, Francis. Italian Poet .... 1566..1645
Bracciolini, Poggio. Reviver of Learning. Life by W.
  Shepherd, 1802................................... 1380..1459
Brackenridge, Hugh Henry. Amer. Miscellaneous Writ. 1748..1816
Bracton, Henry de. Law Writer...................ti. Hen. III.
Bradbury, Thomas, of Wakefield. Dissenting Preacher . 1677..1759
Braddock, Edward. British General in America .... 1715?.1755
Bradford, Alden. American Writer................... 1765..1843
Bradford, John. Protestant Martyr.................. — ..1555
Bradford, John. Welsh Poet........................ — ..1780
Bradford, William. Second Governor of Plymouth Colony 1589..1657
Bradford, William. American Jurist and Writer...... 1755..1795
Bradick, Walter. Merchant of Lisbon. Poet. (*Coheleth*) — ..1794
Bradley, James, D. D. Astronomer.................. 1692..1762
Bradley, Richard, of Cambridge. Writer on Botany.... — ..1732
Bradshaw, George. (*Railway Guide*) .... — ..1853
Bradshaw, Henry. Poet............................ 1450?.1508?
Bradshaw, John. Regicide ....'............... 1586..1659
Bradshaw, William. Puritan Divine................. 1571..1618
Bradstreet, Anne. New England Poetess .... 1612..1672
Bradstreet, John. English General in America....... — ..1774
Bradstreet, Simon. Colonial Gov. of Massachusetts ... 1603..1697
Bradwardine, Thos. Abp. of Canterbury. (*De Causâ Dei*) — ..1349
Brady, Nicholas, D. D. Versifier of the Psalms........ 1659..1726
Brady, Robert. Physician and Historian ....'... — ..1700
Braham, John. Singer. (*Death of Nelson*)........... 1774..1831
Brahé, Tycho. Astronomer Life by Gassendi, 1654;
  Weistritz, 1756; Helfrecht, 1798; Sir D. Brewster, 1841 1546..1601
Braidwood, Thomas. Teacher of Deaf and Dumb...... — ..1806
Brainard, John G. C. American Poet................. 1796..1828

BORN. DIED.

Brainerd, David. Missionary to American Indians. Life
  by Jonathan Edwards, 1765; Josiah Pratt, 1846...... 1718..1747
Braithwaite, John. Mechanic.......................... — ..1818
Brakenburg, Reinier. Dutch Painter.................. 1649.. —
Bramah, Joseph. Inventor of Bramah Press........... 1749..1814
Bramante d'Urbino. *Donato Lazzari.* Architect, Painter,
  Poet, Musician.................................. 1444..1514
Bramantino, Augustin da Milanese. Painter.......... fl. 1525
Bramer, Leonard. Flemish Historical Painter......... 1596.. —
Bramhall, John. Archbishop of Armagh. L. by Vesey. 1593?.1663
Bramston, Rev. James. Satirist...................... — ..1744
Bramston, Sir John. Lord Chief Justice. — ..1646
Brancas Villeneuve, Andrew Francis. Cosmographer. — ..1748
Brancas, Louis L. F., Duc de. Gt. de Lauraguais.. Savant 1733..1824
Brand, Rev. John. Antiquary. (*History of Newcastle*). 1743?.1806
Brand, Rev. John. Political Writer................... — ..1808
Brandel, Peter, of Prague. Portrait and Hist. Painter.. 1660..1739
Brander, Gustavus. Antiquary and Naturalist......... 1720?.1787
Brandi, Hyacinth. Italian Historical Painter.......... 1623..1691
Brandmüller, Gregory. German Painter.............. 1661..1691
Brandmüller, Jas. Biblical Writer. (*Analysis Typica*) 1565..1629
Brandmüller, John. Hebrew Professor at Basel....... 1533..1596
Brandolini, Aurelius. *Il Lippo.* Ital. Poet and Divine. 1440?.1497
Brandon, Charles, Duke of Suffolk. Fav. of Hen. VIII. — ..1545
Brandt, George. Swedish Natural Philosopher......... 1694..1768
Brandt, Gerard. Eccles. Historian. Life by Haes, 1740. 1626..1685
Brandt, Nich., or Sebastian. Discoverer of Phosphorus. — ..1692?
Brandt, Sebastian. *Titio.* Dutch Poet. (*Navis Stultifera*) 1458..1520
Branker, or Brancker, Thomas. English Mathematician 1636..1676
Brant, Brandt, or Brantz, John, of Antwerp. Philologist. 1559..1639
Brant, Joseph. *Thayendanega.* Mohawk Chief........ 1742?.1807
Brantôme. Chronicler. *See* Bourdeilles .... 1527?.1614
Branwhite, Peregrine. Poet............................ 1745..1794
Brarens, Henry. Danish Writer on Navigation........ 1751..1826
Brasbridge, Thomas. Divine and Medical Writer...... 1537..1593
Brasidas. Spartan General .... —B.C.422
Brassavola, Antonius Musa. Italian Medical Writer... 1500..1555
Brathwaite, Richard. Poet............................ 1588..1673
Braun, August Emil. German Archæologist .... 1809..1856
Brauwer, or Brouwer, Adrian. Flemish Painter........ 1608..1640
Bray, Jacob de. Historical Painter.................... 1604..1664
Bray, Sir Reginald. Statesman and Architect.......... — ..1503
Bray, Solomon de. Dutch Portrait Painter........... 1597?.1664
Bray, Rev. Thomas, D. D. Propagator of Christianity.. 1656..1730
Bray, William. Antiquary. Editor of Evelyn......... 1736..1832
Braybrooke, Rd. Cornwallis Neville, Lord. Antiquary. 1820..1861
Brayley, Edward Wedlake. Antiquary and Topographer.
  (*Westminster Abbey*) .... 1773..1854
Brébeuf, Geo.de. Fr. Poet. Trans. of Lucan's *Pharsalia* 1618..1661
Brébeuf, John de. French Jesuit Missionary to Canada. 1593..1649
Brebiette, Peter. French Painter and Engraver........ 1596.. —
Breckberg, or Berkheyden, Gerard. Painter.......... 1645..1693
Breckberg, or Berkheyden, Job, brother. Dutch Painter 1628..1698
Brecourt, William Marcoureau de. Fr. Poet and Actor. — ..1685

BORN. DIED.

Breda, John van. Dutch Painter..................... 1683..1750
Breda, Peter van. Landscape Painter of Antwerp...... 1630..1681
Brederode, Henry, Count. Dutch Patriot .... — ..1568
Bredow, Gabriel Godfrey. German Historian.......... 1773..1814
Bree, Matthew Ignatius van. Flemish Painter......... 1773..1839
Breenberg, Bartholomew. Dutch Landscape Painter... 1620..1660
Breguet, Abraham Louis, ot Paris. Swiss Watch-maker 1747..1823
Bregwin. Abp. Cant. (759–65). L. by Eadmer; Osbern — .. 765
Bregy, Charlotte Chaumaise de Chazan, Countess de.
    Beauty and Wit.................................... 1619..1693
Breislak, Scipio. Italian Geologist................... 1748..1826
Breitkopf, John Gottlob Immanuel. German Printer... 1719..1794
Bremer, Sir James John Gordon. Admiral............. 1786..1850
Bremont, Francis de. Writer of Paris................. 1713..1742
Brenner, Henry, of Stockholm. Orientalist........... 1669..1732
Brennus. Gallic Chief. Invader of Italy............. fl. 390 B. C.
Brennus. Gallic Chief. Invader of Greece........... fl. 280 B. C.
Brent, Sir Nathaniel. Warden of Merton Coll. Writer. 1573..1652
Brentano, Clemens. Ger. Novelist and Dramatic Poet.. 1777..1842
Brentius, or Brentzen, John. Lutheran Divine). 1499..1570
Brenton, Capt. Edward Pelham, R. N. (Naval History). 1774..1839
Brenton, Sir Jahleel, Admiral. Life by Raikes, 1846 ... 1770..1844
Brequigny, Louis Geo. (Histoire des Révolutions de Gênes) 1716..1795
Brereton, Jane. Poet................................ 1685..1740
Brerewood, Edward. Antiquary and Mathematician ... 1565..1613
Bresmal, John Francis. Medical Writer at Liege....... 1670?. —
Bret, Anthony. Fr. Writer and Poet. (Quatre Saisons) 1717..1792
Breteuil, Louis Auguste le Tonnelier. Fr. Diplomatist.. 1733..1807
Breton, Nicholas. Poet.............................. ti. Eliz.
Breton, Raymond. French Missionary to West Indies.. 1609..1679
Bretonneau, Francis. Jesuit of Tours. (Life of Jas. II.) 1660..1741
Bretschneider, Charles Theophilus. Ger. Theologian.. 1776..1848
Bretschneider, Henry Godfrey von. Hungarian Writer 1739..1810
Brett, Rev. Thomas, LL. D. Nonjuring Divine........ 1667..1743
Brettinger, John James, of Zurich. Hebraist and Writ. 1701?.1776
Breudel, Adam. Anat. and Botanist at Wittemberg.... fl. 1700
Breudel, John Godfrey, nephew. Anatomist at Göttingen 1711?.1758
Breughel, John. Velvet Breughel. Landscape Painter.. 1569..1625
Breughel, Peter. Old Breughel. Dutch Painter....... 1530..1590
Breughel, Peter, son. Hellish. Painter............... — ..1642
Breul, James du. French Benedictine. (Antiq. of Paris) 1528..1614
Breval, John Durant de. Eng. Officer. (House of Nassau) — ..1739
Brevint, Daniel, Dean of Lincoln. Divine............. 1616..1695
Brewer, Anthony. Poet and Dramatist................ ti. Chas. I.
Brewster, William. Elder of the Plymouth Pilgrims... 1560..1644
Breydel, Charles. Cavalier. Flem. Landscape Painter. 1677..1744
Breydel, Francis, brother. Painter................... 1679..1750
Breynius, James, of Dantzic. Botanist............... 1637..1697
Brian, Boru. Native Irish King..................... 927?.1014
Briconnet, William. Bishop of Meaux................ — ..1533
Bridaine, James. French Itinerant. (Spiritual Songs). 1701..1767
Bridault, John Peter. French Writer................. — ..1761
Bridge, William. Nonconformist Divine............. 1600..1670
Bridges, John. Antiquary and Topographer........... 1666?.1724

BORN. DIED.

Bridgewater, Francis Egerton, Sixth Earl and Third Duke of. Promoter of Canals .... 1729..1803
Bridgewater, Rev. Francis Henry Egerton, Eighth Earl of. Originator of the Bridgewater Treatises .... 1758..1829
Bridport, Alexander Hood, Lord. Admiral............ — ..1814
Brienne, John de. K. of Jerus. and Emp. of Constantinop. — ..1237
Brienne, Walter de, Duke of Athens. Constable....... — ..1356
Briet, or Brietius, Philip. French Historical and Geographical Writer. (*Parallela*)..................... 1601..1668
Briggs, George N. Amer. Statesman and Philanthropist 1796..1861
Briggs, Henry. (*Logarithmic Tables*)................. 1556..1630
Briggs, Henry Perronet. Historical and Portrait Painter 1793..1844
Briggs, William. Oculist. (*Ophthalmographia*)....... 1641..1704
Brigham, Nicholas. Writer and Poet. (*Memoirs of Eminent Persons*) .... — ..1559
Bright, Rev. Tim., M. D. Phys. (*Treatise on Melancholy*) — ..1615
Brightman, Rev. Thomas. Biblical Commentator...... 1557..1607
Brihtwald. Archbishop of Canterbury (693–731)....... 650?. 731
Bril, Matthew. Landscape Painter................. 1550..1584
Bril, Paul, brother. Landscape Painter...•........... 1556..1626
Brillat-Savarin, Anthelme. (*Physiologie du Goût*) ..... 1755..1826
Brindley, James. Mechanician and Canal Engineer.... 1716..1772
Brinkley, John. Bp. of Cloyne. Div. and Astronomer. 1763..1835
Brinvilliers, Marg. d'Aubrai, Marchioness of. Poisoner. — ..1676
Brisbane, Sir Charles. Admiral................... — ..1829
Brisbane, Sir Thos. Makdougal. Soldier and Astronomer 1773..1860
Brisseau, Peter. Fr. Med. Writer. (*Sur la Cataracte*). 1631..1717
Brisson, Barnabas. French Lawyer and Philologist.... 1531..1591
Brisson, Mathurin James. Fr. Chemist and Naturalist. 1723..1806
Brissot, John Peter. French Revolutionist............ 1754..1793
Brissot, Peter. French Physician..................... 1478..1522
Britannico, John. Italian Grammarian............... —aft.1518
Britannicus. Son of Emperor Claudius .... 42.. 55
Brito, Bernard de. Portuguese Historian............. 1569..1617
Brito, Gulielmus. *Brito Armoricus.* Historian and Poet 1150? 1226
Britton, John. Topog. and Archit. Writer. (*Cathedrals*) 1771..1857
Britton, Thomas. *Musical Small-coal Man.* .... 1654..1714
Brizard, or Britard, John Baptist. French Actor....... 1721..1791
Brizzio, or Briccio, Francis. Landsc. Painter of Bologna 1574..1623
Brocchi, John Baptist. Italian Mineralogist........... 1772..1826
Brockhaus, Frederick Arnold. German Publisher...... 1772..1823
Brocklesby, Richard. Physician and Writer.......... 1722..1797
Brodeau, John. *Brodæus.* French Critic............. 1500..1563
Broderip, William John. Naturalist and Shell Collector — ..1859
Brodie, Sir Benjamin Collins. Surgeon. (*Autobiography*) 1783..1862
Broeck, Crispin van den. Dutch Painter and Engraver. 1530..1601?
Broeck, Elias van den. Flemish Painter.............. 1657..1711
Broeckhuyse, John. *Broukhusius*................... 1649..1707
Broglie, Claude Victor, Prince de. Marshal of Fr.; guillot. 1757..1794
Broglie, Francis Mary, Duke de. Marshal of France.... 1671..1745
Broglie, Victor Francis, Duke de. French General ..... 1718..1804
Broglie, Victor·Maurice, Count de. Marshal of France.. 1647?.1727
Brogni, John de. Cardinal........................... 1342..1426
Broke, Sir Philip Bowes Vere. Rear-Admiral......... 1776..1841

BORN. DIED.

Brokesby, Rev. Francis. Relig. Writer. (*Life of Dodwell*) 1637..1718?
Brome, Adam de. Fav. of Edw. II.; Found. of Oriel Coll. — ..1332
Brome, Alexander. Satiric Anti-Puritan Poet......... 1620..1666
Brome, Richard. Dramatist.................... — ..1652
Bromfield, Sir Wm. Surgeon; Founder of Lock Hospital 1712..1792
Bromley, John. Mezzotint Engraver................ 1795..1839
Bromley, William. Line Engraver................. 1769..1842
Bromton, John. Historian..................... fl. 1193
Bronchorst, John, of Leyden. Animal Painter in Water
   Colors... 1648..1723
Bronchorst, Peter, of Delft. Historical Painter........ 1588..1661
Bröndsted, Peter Oluf. Danish Archæologist.......... 1781..1842
Brongniart, Alexander. Fr. Chemist and Mineralogist. 1770..1847
Brongniart, Anthony Louis. French Chemist......... — ..1804
Brontè, Anne. *Acton Bell.* Novelist................. 1820?.1849
Brontè, Charlotte. *Currer Bell.* L. by Mrs. Gaskell, 1857 1816..1855
Brontè, Emily Jane. *Ellis Bell.* Novelist............. 1818?.1848
Bronzino. *Alexander Allori.* Italian Painter.......... 1535..1607
Bronzino, Angelo. Historical and Portrait Painter..... 1511..1570
Bronzino. *Christopher Allori,* son of Alexander. Painter 1577..1619
Brook, Benjamin. (*Lives of the Puritans*).............. 1775..1848
Brooke, Charlotte. (*Irish Poetry.*) Life by Seymour, 1816 — ..1793
Brooke, Mrs. Frances. Novelist and Dramatic Writer .. — ..1789
Brooke, Sir Fulk Greville, Lord. Poet and Philosopher. 1554..1628
Brooke, Henry. Writer. (*The Fool of Quality*)........ 1706..1783
Brooke, John Charles. Somerset Herald; Topographer. 1748..1794
Brooke, Ralph. York Herald.................... 1550?.1625
Brooke, Sir Robert. Judge and Law Writer........... — ..1558
Brookes, Joshua. Anatomist..................... 1761..1833
Brooks, Maria. American Poetess .... 1795?.1845
Broome, William, LL. D. Poet; Translator of Anacreon.. — ..1745
Broschi, Charles. *Farinelli.* Italian Singer.......... 1705..1782
Brossard, Sebast. de. Fr. Musician. (*Prodromus Musicalis*) 1660..1730
Brosse, Guy de la. French Botanist................. — ..1641
Brosses, Charles de. French Writer............... 1709..1777
Brossette, Claude de, of Lyons. Writer. (*Hist. of Lyons*) 1671..1743
Brotero, Felix de Avellar. Portuguese Botanist........ 1744..1828
Brothers, Richard. Visionary...................... 1760?.1824
Brotier, Andrew Charles. Botanist.................. 1751..1798
Brotier, Gabriel, Abbé. Scholar.................. 1723..1789
Broughton, Hugh. Hebrew Scholar and Polem. Divine 1549..1612
Broughton, Thomas. Prebendary of Salisbury. Divine 1704..1774
Brouncker, or Brounker, Wm. Visct. Pres. of Royal Soc. 1620..1684
Brousson, Claude. French Protestant Martyr.......... 1647..1698
Brouwer, or Brauwer, Adrian. Flemish Painter .... 1608..1640
Browallius, John. Bishop of Abo. Naturalist........ 1707..1755
Brown, Charles Brockden. American Novelist. (*Wieland*) 1771..1810
Brown, Rev. David. Missionary in India.............. — ..1812
Brown, James. Traveler and Scholar. (*The Directory*) 1709..1788
Brown, Rev. John, D. D. (*Rise and Progress of Poetry*) 1715..1766
Brown, John. Scotch Divine. (*Self-Interpreting Bible*) 1722..1787
Brown, John. Scotch Painter. (*Letters on Italian Opera*) 1752..1787
Brown, John. Scot. Phys. Inventor of *Brunonian System*
   of Medicine. Life by Beddoes, 1801; W. C. Brown, 1804 1735..1788

BORN. DIED.

Brown, Capt. John. Amer. Abolitionist. L. by R. D. Webb 1800..1859
Brown, Launcelot. *Capability.* Landscape Gardener... 1715..1783
Brown, Matthew. Painter.............................. 1760?.1831
Brown, Moses. Vicar of Olney. Poet. Writer. *See* Browne 1703..1787
Brown, Robert. Founder of the *Brownists*............. 1550?.1630
Brown, Robert. Scottish Agricultural Writer........... 1770?.1831
Brown, Robert. President Linnæan Soc. Botan. Writer 1773..1858
Brown, Sir Samuel. Captain R. N. Civil Engineer..... 1776..1852
Brown, Thomas. Theologian; Translator of Camden... 1604..1673
Brown, Thomas. Satirical Writer and Poet............. 1663..1704
Brown, Dr. Thomas, of Edinburgh. Professor of Moral
   Philosophy. (*Philosophy of Human Mind.*) L. by Welsh 1778..1820
Brown, Ulysses Maximilian de. Imperial General........ 1705..1757
Brown, William. Botanist. (*Catalogus Horti Oxoniensis*) 1628..1678
Brown, Sir Wm., M. D. Phys. and Humorist. *See* Browne 1692..1774
Brown, Wm. Lawrence. Theol. at Utrecht and Aberdeen 1755..1830
Brown. *See* Browne.
Browne, Sir Anthony. Judge; Supporter of Mary Q. Scots — ..1567
Browne, Edward. Physician to Charles II., and Traveler 1642..1708
Browne, George. Abp. of Dublin. Protestant Reformer — ..1556?
Browne, Isaac Hawkins. Poet. (*Design and Beauty;*
   Immortality of the Soul)........................... 1706..1760
Browne, John. Surgeon. (*Myography*).............. 1642..1700?
Browne, Jos. Writ. agt. Circulat. of Blood. (*Antidotaria*) fl.1698–1721
Browne, Joseph, D. D. Provost of Queen's Coll. Scholar 1700..1767
Browne, Rev. Moses. Poet. (*Piscatory Eclogue*)...... 1703..1787
Browne, Patrick, M. D. Naturalist. (*History of Jamaica*) 1720..1790
Browne, Peter. Bishop of Cork. Writer against Toland — ..1735
Browne, Simon. Dissenting Divine................... 1680?.1732
Browne, Sir Thomas. (*Religio Medici.*) L. by Dr. Johnson 1605..1682
Browne, William. Poet. (*Britannia's Pastorals*)..... 1590..1645?
Browne, Sir Wm. Physician. Founder of Class. Medal. 1692..1774
Browne, William George. Oriental Traveler.......... 1768..1814
Browne. *See* Brown.
Browning, Mrs. Elizabeth Barrett. Poetess............ 1809..1861
Brownrig, Ralph. Bishop of Exeter .... 1592..1659
Brownrigg, William. Physician and Natural Philosopher 1711..1800
Brucæus, Henry, of Alost. Medical Writer............ 1531..1593
Bruce, Edward. Scottish Judge .... 1549?.1611
Bruce, James. African Traveler. Life by Alexander
   Murray, 1804; Sir F. B. Head, 1830................. 1730..1794
Bruce, James, Earl of Elgin. *See* Elgin .... 1811..1863
Bruce, John. Political Writer....................... 1744..1826
Bruce, Michael. Poet .... 1746..1767
Bruce, Peter Henry. German Officer and Diplomatist .. — ..1757
Bruce, Robert. King of Scotland .... 1274..1329
Bruce, Thomas, Earl of Elgin. *See* Elgin............. 1766..1841
Brucioli, Anthony. Florent. Transl. of Bible and Classics —aft.1554
Brucker, John James. (*Historia Critica Philosophiæ*)... 1696..1770
Bruckman, Francis Ernest. Ger. Physician & Naturalist 1697..1753
Bruère, Charles Anthony Leclerc de la. French Dramatist 1715?.1754
Brueys, David Augustine. Fr. Prot. Theol. and Dramatist 1640..1723
Brueys d'Aigalliers, Francis Paul. French Admiral ... 1753..1798
Bruges, John of, or John van Eyck. Painter.......... 1370..1441

BORN. DIED.

Brugmans, Sebald Justin. Dutch Military Physician.... 1763..1819
Bruguières, John Wm. French Naturalist and Physician 1749..1799
Bruhier d'Ablaincourt, John James. Fr. Med. Writer. — ..1756
Brühl, Henry, Count von. Polish Minister............ 1700..1764
Bruin, or Bruyn, John de. Experimen. Philos. at Utrecht 1620..1675
Bruix, Chevalier de. Fr. Writer. (*Réflexions Diverses*). 1728..1780
Brulart, Nicholas. Chancellor of France.............. 1544?.1624
Brulart, Peter. Ambassador and Secretary of State..... 1583?.1640
Brulliot, Francis. (*Dictionary of Monograms*)......... 1780..1836
Brummel, Geo. Bryan. *Beau.* Life by Capt. Jesse, 1844 1778..1840
Brumoy, Peter. French Writer. (*Théâtre des Grecs*) .. 1688..1742
Brun, Anthony, of Dole. Ambass. and Poetical Writer... 1600..1654
Brun, Anthony Louis. French Poet.................... 1680..1743
Brun, Charles le. French Painter and Writer.......... 1619..1690
Brun, J. Baptist le. *Desmarettes.* French Eccles. Writer — ..1731
Brun, Lawrence de, of Nantes. (*Virgilius Christianus*).. 1607..1663
Brun, Peter le. French Ecclesiastical Writer.......... 1661..1729
Brun, Wm. le. Jesuit. (*Latin and French Dictionary*). 1674?.1758
Brunck, Richard Francis Philip. Critic............... 1729..1803
Brune, William Mary Anne. Marshal of France........ 1763..1815
Brunehaut. Queen of Austrasia................... — :. 613
Brunel, Isambard Kingdom. Engineer of " Gt. Eastern " 1806..1859
Brunel, Sir Mark Isambard. Engineer of Thames Tunnel.
    Life by R. Beamish .... 1769..1849
Brunelleschi, Philip. Florentine Architect........... 1377..1444
Brunet, John Louis, of Arles. Ecclesiastical Writer..... 1688..1747
Brunetto Latini. Grammarian, of Florence. (*Il Tesoro*) 1230..1294
Brunfels, Otho. Physician and Botanist at Berlin...... 1464?.1534
Bruni, Anthony. Italian Poet..................... — ..1635
Bruni, Leonard. *Aretino.* Historian................. 1369..1444
Brunings, Christian. Writer on Greek and Jewish Antiq. 1702..1763
Brunings, Christian. Dutch Hydraulic Engineer....... 1736..1805
Brunn, John James, of Basel. (*Systema Materiæ Medicæ*) 1591..1660
Brunner, Balthazar. German Physician............. 1533..1604
Brunner, or Brunn, John Conrad. Swiss Phys. and Anat. 1653..1727
Bruno the Great. Archbishop of Cologne............ — .. 965
Bruno, St. Founder of Carthusians. Life by Madariaga,
    1596; Faria, 1649; Tromby, 1773; Tracy, 1786; Villerey,
    1808; Ducreux, 1808................... 1030?.1101
Bruno, James Pancrace. Swiss Physician............ 1629..1709
Bruno, Jordan. Italian Anti-Christian Writer. Life by
    Murr, 1805; Rixner, 1824; Debs, 1844; C. Bartholomew 1550..1600
Brunswick-Lunenburg, Charles William Ferd., Duke
    of. Prussian General against the French Republicans 1735..1806
Brunswick-Oels, Frederick Augustus, Duke of, brother.
    Prussian Gen. and Writer. (*On Alexander the Great*). 1740..1805
Brunswick, Frederick William, Duke of. Served in the
    English Army against France.................... 1771..1815
Brunswick, Maximil. Jul. Leop., Duke of. Pruss. General 1752..1785
Brunton, Mrs. Mary. Novelist.................... 1778..1818
Bruschius, Gaspar. Latin Historian and Poet of Bohemia 1518..1559
Brusoni, Jerome. Venetian Writer. (*History of Italy*).. 1610..1680?
Brusoni, Lucius Domitius. Facetious Writer. (*Speculum
    Mundi*).................................... fl. 16th c.

BORN. DIED.

Bruto, John Michael. Trav. and Writer. (*Hist. of Hungary*) 1518?.1594
Brutus, John. Ecclesiastic of Paris. Writer............ 1678?.1762
Brutus, Lucius Junius. Estab. Repub. Governmt. at Rome fl. 500 B.C.
Brutus, Marcus Junius. Murderer of Cæsar.......... B.C.85 B.C.42
Bruyère, John de la. French Writer. (*Caractères*).... 1644?.1696
Bruyn, Cornelius le. Traveler and Painter............ 1652..——
Bruyn, or Bruin, John de. Experimen. Philos. at Utrecht 1620..1675
Bruys, Francis. French Critic. (*History of the Popes*).. 1703..1738
Bruys, Peter de, of Languedoc. Found. of *Petro-Brussians* ——..1130
Bruzen de la Martinière. *See* Martinière............ 1666..1740
Bry, Theodore de. (*Collectiones Peregrinationum*)....... 1528..1598
Bryan, or Bryant, Sir Francis. Soldier, Statesman, Poet ——..1550?
Bryan, Michael. (*Dictionary of Painters*)............... 1757..1821
Bryant, Jacob. Antiquary and Philologist........... 1715..1804
Brydges, Sir Sam. Egerton. Miscel. Writ. L. by self, 1834 1762..1837
Brydone, Patrick. (*Travels in Sicily and Malta*)........ 1741?.1818
Bryennius, Nicephorus. Byzantine Historian......... ——..1137
Buache, Philip. French Hydrographer........... 1700..1773
Buat Nancay, Louis Gabr., Ct. du. Fr. Diplom. & Writer 1732..1787
Bucer, Martin. Reformer. Life by Conrad Huber, 1537 1491..1551
Buch, Baron Leopold von. Scientific Writer........... 1774..1853
Buchan, Mrs. Elspeth, or Elizabeth. Scottish Fanatic... 1738..1791
Buchan, Stuart Erskine, Earl of. Scientific Writer..... 1742..1829
Buchan, William, M. D. (*Domestic Medicine*).......... 1729..1805
Buchanan, Claudius, D. D. Bengal Chaplain. (*Christian
    Researches.*) Life by H. Pearson, 1819........... 1766..1815
Buchanan, George. Scotch Historian and Poet. (*History
    of Scotland.*) Life by Dr. David Irving, 1807........ 1506..1582
Buchanan, Walter. Writer on Art................ 1777?.1864
Buchner, Augustus. Professor at Wittenberg.......... 1591..1661
Buchner, John Andrew Elias. German Medical Writer 1701..1769
Bucholtzer, Abraham. Ger. Divine. (*Index Chronolog.*) 1529..1584
Buchon, John Alexander. Historical Writer........... 1791..1846
Buchoz, Peter Joseph, of Metz. Naturalist............ 1731..1807
Buck, Sir George. Antiquary. (*Life of Richard III.*). ——..1622?
Buckeridge, John. Bp. of Ely. (*De Potestate Papæ*). ——..1631
Buckhurst, Thos. Sackville, Lord. Statesm. and Poet. 1527..1608
Buckingham, Geo. Villiers, First Duke of. Lord High
    Admiral. Assassinated. L. by Sir H. Wotton, 1642. 1592..1628
Buckingham, Geo. Villiers, son, 2d Duke of. Courtier.. 1627..1688
Buckingham, James Silk. Traveler. Life by self..... 1786..1855
Buckingham and Chandos, Richard, First Duke of.... 1776..1839
Buckingham and Chandos, Richard, Second Duke of.. ——..1861
Buckinghamshire, John Sheffield, Duke of. Poet...... 1649..1720
Buckink, Arnold. German Engraver................ fl. 1450?
Buckland, William, D. D. Dean of Westm. Geologist.. 1784..1856
Buckle, Henry Thomas. (*History of Civilization*)....... 1822..1862
Buckminster, Joseph Stephens. American Divine..... 1784..1812
Bucquet, John Baptist Mary. Fr. Experimental Philos. 1746..1780
Budæus, or Budé, William. Critic. (*De Asse*)........ 1467..1540
Buddæus, John Francis, of Jena. Theol. (*Ger. Hist. Dict.*) 1667..1729
Budgell, Eustace. Writer. (*Lives of the Boyles*)....... 1685?.1736
Buffalmacco, Buonamico. Italian Historical Painter... 1262..1340
Buffler, Claude. French Writer..................... 1661..1737

BORN. DIED.

Buffon, Geo. Louis Le Clerc, Count de. Naturalist. Life by Joseph Aude, 1788; M. Humbert-Bazile, 1863.... 1707..1788
Bugeaud de la Piconnerie, Thomas Robert, Duke d'Isly. French Marshal.................................. 1784..1849
Bugenhagen, John. *Pomeranus.* Reformer. Life by Vincentius, 1558; Jaencke, 1730; Lange, 1731; Engelcken, 1817; Koch, 1817; Zietz, 1829; Biesner, 1837 1485..1558
Bugiardini, Julian. Painter of Florence............. 1481..1556
Buhle, John Theophilus. German Philosopher......... 1763..1821
Buister, Philip. Sculptor of Brussels................ 1595..1688
Bukentop, Henry van, of Antwerp. Controv. Divine... — ..1716
Bulgarin, Thaddeus. Russian Novelist and Essayist ... 1789.. —
Bulkley, Charles. Baptist Divine..................... 1719..1797
Bull, Geo. Bp. of St. David's. L. by Robert Nelson, 1717 1634..1710
Bull, John, MUS. DOCT. Composer.................... 1563?.1622?
Bullant, John. French Architect..................... 1520?.1578
Buller, Right Honorable Charles. Statesman.......... 1806..1848
Buller, Sir Francis. Judge. (*Introduction to Nisi Prius*) 1745..1800
Bullet, J. Bapt. Theologian and Antiquary at Besançon 1699..1775
Bulleyn, William. Medical Writer at Durham......... 1500?.1576
Bullialdus, or Boulliaud, Ismael. French Astronomer and Mathematician. (*Philolaus*).................... 1605..1694
Bulliard, Peter. French Botanist.................... 1742?.1793
Bullinger, Henry. Swiss Reformer. Life by Simler, 1575; Lavater, 1576; Fels, 1600; Ziegler, 1719; Hess, 1828; Franz, 1828 .... 1504..1575
Bulow, Frederick William. Prussian General.......... 1755..1816
Bulow, Baron Henry von. Diplomatist................ 1790..1846
Bulstrode, Sir Richard. Royalist and Jacobite........ — ..1715?
Bulteau, Louis. French Writer on Monastic History.... 1625..1693
Bulwer, John, M. D. (*Chirographia; Anthropometamorphosis*) .... fl. 1644
Bunbury, Henry. Caricaturist....................... — ..1811
Bunel, Jacob. French Historical Painter............. 1558..1620?
Bunel, Peter, of Toulouse. Latin Scholar. (*Letters*)... 1499..1546
Bunn, Alfred. Theatrical Manager and Author........ — ..1860
Bunnick, Jacob van. Battle Painter................. — ..1725
Bunnick, John van, brother. Hist. and Portr. Painter.. 1654..1727
Bunon, Robert, of Paris. Dentist.................... 1702..1748
Bunsen, Christian Chas. Josias, Baron. Pruss. Ambass. 1791..1860
Bunting, Jabez. Wesleyan Minister.................. 1779..1858
Bunyan, John. Life by Ivimey, 1809; Southey; Robert Philip, 1839; George Offor, 1853................... 1628..1688
Buonaccorsi, or Pierino del Vaga. Tuscan Painter..... 1501..1547
Buonaccorsi, Philip. *Callimaco.* Italian Latin Writer. 1437..1496
Buonafede, Appian. Italian Philosophical Writer...... 1716..1793
Buonamici, Castruccio. Italian Historical Writer...... 1710..1761
Buonamici, Lazarus, of Padua. Latin Poet and Writer. 1479..1552
Buonamico di Christofano. *Buffalmacco.* Flor. Painter 1262..1340
Buonaparte. *See* Bonaparte.
Buonarotti, Michael Angelo. Painter, Sculptor, Architect. Life by R. Duppa, 1806................... 1474..1564
Buonarotti, Michael Angelo, jun. Dramatist......... 1568..1646
Buonfiglio, Joseph Constant. (*Hist. of Sicily and Venice*) fl. 1604

BORN. DIED.

Buoninsegni, Duccio di. Painter of Siena............ — ..1340?
Buonmattei, Benedict. Florentine Grammarian .... 1581..1647
Buononcini, J. Baptist. Musical Composer............ — ..1750?
Buontalenti, Bernard. *Girandole.* Florentine Painter,
    Sculptor, Architect...................... 1536..1608
Buranello. *Balthasar Galuppi.* Composer........... 1703..1785
Burbage, Richard. Shakespearian Actor .... — ..1629
Burchard, John, of Wesel. Reformer................. — ..1482
Burchiello, Dominic, of Florence. Burlesque Poet..... — ..1448
Burckhardt, John Charles. German Astronomer ...... 1773..1825
Burckhardt, John Louis. Swiss Traveler............. 1784..1817
Burder, George. Dissenting Preacher. (*Village Sermons*) 1752..1832
Burdett, Sir Francis, M. P. Politician................. 1770..1844
Burdon, William. (*Materials for Thinking*)........... 1764..1818
Bure, Catherine. Swedish Scholar.................... 1602?.1679
Bure, William Francis de, of Paris. Bibliographer...... 1731..1782
Buren, Martin van. *See* Van Buren .... 1782..1862
Burette, Peter John. French Archæologist............ 1665..1747
Bürger, Godf. Aug. German Poet. (*Wild Huntsman*).. 1748..1794
Burgersdicius, Francis. Dutch Logician.............. 1590..1629
Burges, George. Greek Scholar and Dramatist........ 1786..1864
Burgess, Daniel. Dissenting Preacher................ 1645..1713
Burgess, John. Painter in Water Colors............. 1788?.1863
Burgess, Thos. Bp. of Salisb. L. by C. J. Harford, 1839 1756..1837
Burggrave, John Philip. German Medical Writer...... 1700..1775
Burgh, Hubert de. Statesman...................... — ..1243
Burgh, James. Writer. (*Dignity of Human Nature*)... 1714..1775
Burgh, Ulick de, Marquess of Clanricarde. (*Memoirs
    of Irish Rebellion*)............................. — ..1657
Burgkmair, John. German Painter and Wood Engraver 1474..1543
Burgoyne, John. General. Dramatic Writer.......... — ..1792
Burgundy, Louis, Duke of. Grandson of Louis XIV.;
    Dauphin....................................... 1682..1712
Buridan, John. Philosopher and Schoolman........... — ..1358?
Burigny, John Levesque de. Hist. and Biog. Writer... 1692..1785
Burke, Edmund. Statesman. L. by McCormick, 1797;
    Bisset, 1798; Jas. Prior, 1824; T. Macknight; Geo.
    Croly, 1840; Sergeant Burke; Joseph Napier, 1862... 1729..1797
Burke, Robert O'Hara. Australian Explorer........... — ..1861
Burkitt, Wm. (*Expos. of N. Test.*) L. by Parkhurst, 1704 1650..1703
Burlamaqui, John James. Civilian.................. 1694..1748
Burleigh, Wm. Cecil, Lord. Lord Treasurer. *See* Cecil 1520..1598
Burley, Walter. English Priest and Aristotelian Scholar 1275..1357
Burlington, Richard Boyle, Third Earl of. Architect... 1695..1753
Burman, Nicholas Lawrence. Botanist. (*Flora Indica*) 1734..1793
Burmann, Francis. Theologian at Utrecht. (*On the
    Pentateuch*)................................... 1628..1679
Burmann, Francis, son. Theologian at Utrecht. (*Per-
    secution of Diocletian*).......................... 1671..1719
Burmann, Gaspar. Historian. (*Trajectum Eruditum*).. — ..1755
Burmann, John. Dutch Botanist and Physician. (*The-
    saurus Zeylanicus*)............................ 1707..1780
Burmann, Peter. Dutch Philologist.................. 1668..1741
Burmann, Peter. *Secundus.* Professor at Francker.... 1714..1778

BORN. DIED.

Burn, Rev. Richard, LL. D. Law Writer. (*Justice*)..... 1720?.1785
Burnes, Sir Alexander. Diplomatist in India......... 1805..1841
Burnet, Gilbert. Bishop of Salisbury (1689–1715). Life
    by Le Clerc, 1715; Flexman...................... 1643..1715
Burnet, Rev. Thomas, LL. D. (*De Statu Mortuorum.*)
    Life by Ralph Heathcoat, 1759.................. 1635?.1715
Burnet, Rev. Thomas, D. D. Divine. (*Answer to Tindal*) — ..1750
Burnet, Sir Thos., son of Gilbert. Judge & Polit. Writ. — ..1753
Burnett, Gilbert Thos. Botanist. (*Outlines of Botany*). 1800..1835
Burnett, Jas., Ld. Monboddo. (*Orig. and Prog. of Lang.*) 1714..1799
Burnett, John. Scottish Judge and Writer on Law .... 1764..1810
Burney, Charles. Classical Critic.................... 1757..1817
Burney, Dr. Charles. (*History of Music.*) Life by Ma-
    dame D'Arblay, 1832.......................... 1726..1814
Burney, Frances. *See* Madame D'Arblay. Novelist... 1752..1840
Burney, Jas. Rear-Adm. (*Hist. of Voyages of Discov.*) 1759..1821
Burney, William, LL. D. (*Naval Heroes*).............. 1762..1832
Burnouf, Eugene. French Orientalist................. 1801..1852
Burns, John, M. D., of Glasgow. (*Evid. of Christianity*).. 1780..1850
Burns, Robert. Poet. Life by James Currie, 1825; J. G.
    Lockhart; Allan Cunningham; R. Chambers........ 1759..1796
Burr, Aaron. Third Vice-President of the United States 1756..1836
Burrhus, Afranius. Roman Commander............... — .. 62
Burrough, Edward. Quaker Preacher............... 1634..1663
Burroughs, Jer., of Tivetshall. Puritan Div. (*On Hosea*) 1599..1646
Burroughs, Sir John. Garter King. (*Sovereignty of Seas*) — ..1643
Burrow, Sir James. Law Writer..................... 1701..1782
Burrow, Reuben. Mathematician..................... — ..1791
Burton, Cassibelan. Translator of Martial........... 1609..1681
Burton, Edw., D. D. Reg. Professor. (*Greek Testament*) 1794..1836
Burton, Henry. Sufferer with Bastwick and Prynne.... 1579?.1648
Burton, Hezekiah. Prebendary of Norwich. Divine.... — ..1681
Burton, John, D. D. Fell. of Eton. (*Opuscula Miscellanea*) 1696..1771
Burton, John, M. D. Antiquary. (*Eccles. Hist. of York*) 1697..1771
Burton, Rev. Robert. (*Anatomy of Melancholy*)........ 1576..1640
Burton, Wm. Topog. and Antiq. (*Hist. Leicestershire*) 1575..1645
Burton, Wm., of Kingston. Schol. (*Græcæ Linguæ Hist.*) 1609..1657
Burton, William, M. D. (*History of Yorkshire*)........ 1697?.1759
Bury, Arthur, D. D. Rector of Exeter College. Socinian.
    (*Naked Gospel*).................................. fl. 1665
Bury, Mrs. Eliz. Hebraist and Scholar. L. by Sam. Bury 1644..1720
Bury, Richard de. *See* Angarville.................... 1287?.1345
Bus, Cæsar de. Founder of the *Fathers of Christ. Doctrine* 1544..1607
Busbec, Augher Ghislen. *Busbequius.* Trav. & Ambass. 1522..1592
Busby, Richard. Master of Westminster School....... 1606..1695
Busche, Hermann von dem. *Buschius.* Reviv. of Learn. 1468..1534
Buschetto da Dulichio. Greek Architect at Pisa....1025?aft.1080
Busching, Anthony Frederick. German Writer........ 1724..1793
Busching, John Gust. Theoph., son. Writ. on Literature 1783..1829
Busembaum, Hermann. (*Medulla Theologiæ*)......... 1600..1668
Bushe, Sir Charles Kendal. Chief Justice of Ireland... — ..1843
Bushell, Thomas. Master of the Royal Mines. Royalist 1594?.1674
Bushnell, David. American Inventor................. 1742?.1826
Busleyden, Jerome. Diplomat.; Frd. of Erasmus & More 1470..1517

BORN. DIED.

Bussières, John de. French Historian and Latin Poet.. 1607..1678
Bussy d'Amboise, Louis de Clermont de.............. — ..1579
Bussy, Roger Rabutin, Count of. French Writer .... 1618..1693
Bute, John Stuart, Third Earl of. Premier............ 1713..1792
Buteo, John. French Mathematician................. 1492..1572
Buti, Francesco di Bartolo da. Commentator on Dante . 1324..1406
Butler, Alban. (*Lives of Saints.*) L. by Chas. Butler, 1799 1710..1773
Butler, Charles. Writer on Bees. (*Feminine Monarchy*) 1560..1647
Butler, Charles. Roman Catholic Writer. (*Reminiscences*) 1750..1832
Butler, Jas., Duke of Ormond. Statesman. Life by Carte 1610..1688
Butler, John. Bishop of Hereford. Political Writer.... 1717..1802
Butler, Joseph. Bishop of Durham. (*Analogy.*) Life by
    Bartlett, 1839; Rev. F. Steere.................... 1692..1752
Butler, Samuel. Poet. (*Hudibras*).............. 1600..1680
Butler, Samuel. Mast. of Shrewsb. Bp. Lichf. (*Atlas*). 1774..1840
Butler, Thomas, Earl of Ossory. Commander........ 1634..1680
Butler, Weeden. Theologian....................... 1742..1823
Butler, William. Irish Alchemist.................. 1534..1617
Butler, William, M. D. Medical Writer.............. 1726..1805
Butler, Wm. Writer of School Books. (*On the Globes*). 1748..1822
Butler, Rev. Wm. Archer, of Dublin. Prof. of Moral Philos. —..1848
Butt, George, D. D. Divine and Poet.................. 1741..1795
Butter, Nathaniel. Journalist........................ — ..1664
Buttern, William, M. D. Medical Writer in London .... 1726..1805
Buttmann, Philip Chas. Ger. Philologist. (*Lexilogus*) 1764..1829
Buttner, Christian William. Ger. Naturalist and Philol. 1716..1801
Button, Sir Thomas. Arctic Navigator............... fl. 1612
Butts, Sir William. Physician to Henry VIII......... — ..1545
Buxbaum, John Christian. German Botanist & Traveler 1694..1730
Buxton, Jedediah. Calculator..................... 1704?..1775?
Buxton, Sir Thomas Fowell. Philanthr. L. by C. Buxton 1786..1845
Buxtorf, John. Professor at Basel. (*Thesaurus Linguæ*
    Hebraicæ.) Life by Tossanus, 1630................ 1564..1629
Buxtorf, John, son. Professor at Basel. (*Hebr. Concord.*) 1599..1664
Buxtorf, John. Orientalist at Basel.................. — ..1732
Buxtorf, John James. Hebraist .... 1645..1704
Buy de Mornas, Claude. French Geographer.......... — ..1783
Buzot, Francis Nicholas Leonard. French Politician.... 1760..1793
Byfield, or Bifield, Nicholas. Calvinistic Divine........ 1578?.1622
Byles, Mather, D. D. American Clergyman............ 1706..1788
Bynæus, Anthony. Classical and Historical Scholar.... 1654..1698
Byng, George, First Visct. Torrington. Naval Commander 1663..1733
Byng, John. Admiral. Shot .... 1704..1757
Bynkershoek, Cornelius van. Civilian............... 1673..1763
Byrge, or Bvrgius, Justus. Fr. Mathematical Mechanician 1549..1632
Byrne, William. Engraver.......................... 1742..1805
Byrom, John. Poetical Writer. (*Short-hand*)......... 1691..1763
Byron, George Gordon, Lord. Poet. Life by T. Moore;
    R. C. Dallas; J. Galt, 1825; Noel Byron, 1825; J. W.
    Lake, 1826; E. Brydges, 1828; J. L. Armstrong, 1846. 1788..1824
Byron, Hon. John. Circumnavigator................. 1723..1786
Bythner, Victorinus. Linguist. (*Lyra Prophetica*)..... —aft.1664
Bzovius, or Bzovski, Abraham. Polish Theologian..... 1567..1637

C.

BORN. DIED.

Caab, or Cab ben Zohair. Arabian Poet .... — .. 622
Caballus, Francis. Medical Writer at Padua .... — ..1540
Cabanis, Peter John George. Fr. Phys., Philos., Politician 1757..1808
Cabarrus, Francis. French Financier in Spain......... 1752..1810
Cabassole, Philip de. French Writer; Friend of Petrarch 1305..1371
Cabassut, John. French Canonist..................... 1604..1685
Cabel, or Kabel, Adrian van der. Dutch Painter .... 1631..1695
Cabestan, or Cabestaing, William de. Provençal Poet.. — ..1213?
Cabet, Stephen. French Communist.................... 1788..1856
Cabot, Sebastian. Navigator. Life by R. Biddle, 1831 .. 1477?.1557?
Cabral, or Cabrara, Peter Alvarez de. Port. Navigator .. — ..1526?
Cabrillo, John Rodriguez. Portuguese Navigator ...... — ..1543
Cabrol, Barth. Fr. Anatomist. (Alphabeton Anatomicon) 1535?. —
Caccia, William. Il Montcalvo. Italian Fresco Painter. 1568..1625
Caccini, Julius. Giulio Romano. Italian Musical Comp. 1560?.1640?
Cachet, Christopher. Medical Writer................. 1572..1624
Cadamosto, Louis da. Venetian Navig. L. by Zurla, 1815 1432?.1480?
Cade, John. Rebel .... — ..1450
Cadell, Thomas. Publisher.......................... 1742..1803
Cadet de Gassicourt, Chas. Louis. (Dict. of Chemistry) 1769..1821
Cadet de Vaux, Anthony Alexis Francis. French Writer 1743..1828
Cadogan, William, First Earl of. Military Commander .. — ..1726
Cadogan, William. Medical Writer................... — ..1797
Cadogan, Hon. and Rev. Wm. Bromley. L. by Cecil, 1798 1751..1797
Cadoudal, George. French Royalist .... 1769..1804
Cadwaladyr, Casail. Welsh Poet..................... 16th c.
Cæcilius Statius. Latin Comic Poet................. — B.C.168
Cædmon. Anglo-Saxon Poet .... — .. 680?
Cælius Rhodiginus. Italian Scholar................. 1450?.1525?
Cæsalpinus, Andrew. Italian Naturalist .... 1519..1603
Cæsar, Caius. Grandson of Augustus................ B.C.20 A.D.4
Cæsar, C. Julius. Dictator. Life by Nicholas de Damas,
   1850; Archd. J. Williams, 1854; Napoleon III., 1865.. 100.44B.C.
Cæsar, Sir Julius. Civilian. Life by E. Lodge, 1727... 1557..1636
Cæsar, Lucius. Grandson of Augustus............... B.C.17 A.D.2
Caffa, Melchior. Le Maltais. Roman Sculptor........ 1631..1687
Caffarelli, Gaetano Majorano. Italian Singer.......... 1703..1783
Cafflaux, Philip Joseph. (Genealogical Treasury)...... 1712..1777
Caffieri, James. Sculptor .... — ..1755
Caffieri, John James. Sculptor .... 1723..1792
Caffieri, Philip. Sculptor at Rome .... 1634..1716
Cagliari, Benedict. Painter......................... 1538..1598
Cagliari, Paul, brother. Paul Veronese. Painter....... 1530?.1588
Cagliostro, Alexander, Count. Joseph Balsamo. Impostor 1743..1795
Cagnatus, Marsilius. Medical Writer at Rome......... — ..1610
Cagnola, Louis, Marquis. Italian Architect .... 1762..1833
Cagnoli, Anthony. Italian Astronomer and Philosopher 1743..1816
Cahaignes, James. Medical Writer of Caen .... 1548..1612
Cahusac, Louis de. French Dramatist .... 1700..1759
Caiet, or Cayet, Peter Victor Palma. French Writer.... 1525..1610

BORN. DIED.

Caille, Nicholas Louis de la.   French Astronomer . . . . 1713 . . 1762
Caillié, René, or Auguste.   French Traveler . . . . 1799 . . 1838
Cairo, Francis.   *Cavaliere del Cairo.*   Historical and Portrait Painter . . . . 1598 . . 1674
Caius, or Gaius.   Roman Jurist . . . . ti. Antonines
Caius, or Gaius.   Ecclesiastical Historian . . . . fl. 210?
Caius.   Bishop of Rome (283–96) . . . . — . . 296
Caius, Bernard.   Italian Medical Writer . . . . fl. 1610
Caius, *Kaye,* John.   Founder of Caius College . . . . 1510 . . 1573
Caius, Thomas.   Master of University College, Oxford . . — . . 1572
Cajetan, Constantine.   Italian Benedictine; Writer . . . . . 1560 . . 1650
Cajetan, Thomas de Vio, Cardinal.   Theologian . . . . 1469 . . 1534
Calaber, Quintus.   Greek Poet.   (*Paralipomena*) . . . . fl. 491 ?
Calabrese, Matthias Preti.   Italian Painter . . . . 1613 . . 1699
Calamy, Benj., D. D.   Church Div. (*Scrupulous Conscience*) — . . 1686
Calamy, Edmund.   Nonconformist. (*Smectymnuus*) . . . . 1600 . . 1666
Calamy, Edm., D. D.   Dissent. Div. (*Lives of Nonconf.*) 1677 . . 1732
Calandrucci, Hyacinth.   Roman Painter . . . . 1646 . . 1707
Calas, John.   Protestant of Toulouse; judicially murdered 1698 . . 1762
Calasio, Marius de.   Orient. at Rome. (*Heb. Concordance*) 1550? . 1620
Calatrava, Joseph Mary.   Spanish Statesman . . . . 1781 . . 1846
Calcagnini, Cœlio.   Soldier, Poet, and Antiquary . . . . 1479 . . 1541
Calcar, or Keikar, John Stephen von.   Painter . . . . 1499 . . 1546
Calceolari.   Italian Botanist.   (*Iter Baldi Montis*) . . . . . fl. 1566–86
Caldara, Anthony.   Italian Musical Composer . . . . 1678 . . 1763
Caldara, or Polydore da Caravaggio.   Painter . . . . 1495 . . 1543
Caldas, Francis Joseph.   Spanish Naturalist . . . . 1773? . 1816
Calder, Sir Robert.   Admiral . . . . 1745 . . 1818
Calderari, Ottone.   Italian Architect . . . . 1730 . . 1803
Calderini, Domitio.   Italian Philologist and Gen. Scholar 1446 . . 1478
Calderon de la Barca, Pedro.   Spanish Dramatist . . . . . 1601 . . 1687
Calderwood, David.   Scot. Presbyt. (*Altare Damascenum*) 1575 . . 1651?
Caldwall, Richard.   Physician . . . . 1513 . . 1585
Caled, or Khaled.   Mohammedan Commander . . . . — . . 642?
Calendario, Philip.   Venetian Architect and Sculptor . . . fl. 1354
Calentius, Elisius.   Neapol. Poet. (*Battle of Frogs & Mice*) 1450? . 1503
Calepino, or Da Calepio, Ambrose.   Lexicographer . . . . . 1435 . . 1511
Caletti, Joseph.   *Il Cremonese.*   Painter . . . . 1600? . 1660
Calhoun, John Caldwell.   American Statesman . . . . 1782 . . 1850
Caliavari, Luke.   Italian Painter . . . . 1665 . . 1715
Caligny, John Anténor Hue de.   French Engineer . . . . . . 1657 . . 1731
Caligula.   Roman Emperor (37–41) . . . . 12 . . 41
Calixtus, George, of Helmstadt.   Lutheran Theologian. Life by Dowding, 1864 . . . . 1586 . . 1656
Calkoen van Beek, John Frederick.   Dutch Astronomer and Mathematician . . . . 1772 . . 1811
Callard, J. Baptist, of Caen.   (*Etymological Med. Lexicon*) 1630 . . 1718
Callcott, Sir Augustus Wall, R. A.   Painter . . . . 1779 . . 1844
Callcott, John Wall.   Musical Composer.   Life by Horsley 1766 . . 1821
Callcott, Maria (Graham, and Dundas), Lady.   Writer . . . 1788 . . 1842
Calle, John Francis.   French Mathematician . . . . 1744 . . 1798
Callenberg, John Henry.   Orient. and Promot. of Missions 1694 . . 1760
Callott, John Francis.   French Mathematician . . . . 1744 . . 1798
Calliach, Nicholas.   Writer at Padua. (*De Ludis Scenicis*) 1645 . . 1707

BORN. DIED.

Callicratidas. Spartan Admiral................... — B.C.406
Callières, Francis de. French Statesman and Writer ... 1645..1717
Callimachus. Alexandrian Grammarian and Poet..... — B.C.240?
Callisthenes, of Olynthus. Greek Historian........... fl. B.C.328?
Callistus, Johannes Andronicus, of Constantinople. Pro-
    moter of Greek Learning in Italy .... fl. 1453
Callixtus I. Pope (219–22)........................... — .. 222
Callixtus II. (1119–24.) *Guy de Bourgogne* .... — ..1124
Callixtus III. (1455–58.) *Alphonse Borgia*........... — ..1458
Callot, James. French Artist and Engraver........... 1593..1635
Cally, Peter. French Divine and Cartesian Philosopher. — ..1709
Calmet, Augustin. (*Dict. of Bible.*) Life by Dom Fangé 1672..1757
Calmo, Andrew. Venetian Actor and Comic Writer .... 1510?.1571
Calogiera, Angelo. Italian Scholar .... 1699..1768
Calomarde, Francis Tadeo. Spanish Statesman........ 1775..1842
Calonne, Charles Alexander de. French Minister...... 1734..1802
Calovius, Abraham. Lutheran Polemical Divine....... 1612..1686
Calprenède, Gautier de Costes, Seign. de. Romance Writ. 1612?.1663
Calpurnius, Titus Julius. Sicilian Latin Pastoral Poet.. fl. ab. 290
Calvart, or Calvaert, Denis. *Fiammingo.* Dutch Painter 1555..1619
Calvert, Geo., First Lord Baltimore. Founder of Maryland 1582..1632
Calvert, James. Nonconformist. (*Naphthali*) .... — ..1698
Calvidus Lætus. *See* Quillet. (*Callipœdia*).......... 1602..1661
Calvin, John. Life by Bungener; Jerome Bolsec, 1572;
    Beza; Papire Masson; Dr. Paul Henry, 1835–44, tr. by
    Stebbing, 1849; J. M. V. Audin, 1840; J. Dyer, 1849;
    Strähelin, 1863 .... 1509..1564
Calvisius, Seth. German Chronologer .... 1556..1615
Calvus, C. Licinius Macer. Roman Advocate and Poet.. 82.46? B.C.
Camargo, Mary Ann Cuppi. Dancer of Brussels .... 1710..1770
Camassei, or Camace, Andrew. Italian Painter........ 1602..1648
Cambacérès, John James Régis de. French Statesman. 1753..1824
Cambert, Robert. French Musician in England........ 1628..1677
Cambiaso, Luca. *Luchetto of Genoa.* Fresco Painter... 1527..1585
Cambini, Louis. Italian Composer.................... 1746..1832?
Cambis-Velleron, Joseph Louis Dominic, Marquis de.
    Book Collector and Historian .... 1706..1772
Cambon, Joseph. French Statesman.................. 1754..1820
Cambridge, Adolphus Fred., Duke of. Son of George III. 1774..1850
Cambridge, Richard, Earl of. Conspirator; beheaded .. — ..1415
Cambridge, Richard Owen. Writer. (*Scribleriad*)..... 1717..1802
Cambronne, Peter Jas. Stephen, Baron de. Fr. General 1770..1842
Cambyses. Second King of Persia (B.C. 528–521)...... — B.C.521
Camden, Charles Pratt, First Earl. Lord Chancellor.... 1713..1794
Camden, John Jeffries Pratt, First Marquess. Lord-Lieut. 1759..1840
Camden, Wm. Antiq. Life by Thos. Smith, 1691; Gough 1551..1623
Camerarius, Joachim. German Scholar and Writer .... 1500..1574
Camerarius, Joachim, son. Botanist.................. 1534..1593
Cameron, Sir Alan. Colonel of *Cameron Highlanders*... — ..1828
Cameron, Donald, grandson of Evan. *The Gentle Lochiel* — ..1748
Cameron, Sir Evan. Ld. of Lochiel. *Ulysses of the Highlds.* — ..1719
Cameron, John. Scot. Theologian; taught in France..1580?.1625 or 6
Cameron, Richard. Covenanter. Founder of *Cameronians* — ..1680
Camidge, John, MUS. DOC. Musical Composer .... 1790?.1859

6

BORN. DIED.

Camillus, Marcus Furius. Dictator................... —B.C.365
Camoens, Louis de. Portuguese Poet. (*Lusiad.*) Life by
    Adamson, 1820............................... 1524?.1579
Campailla, Thomas. Italian Philosopher and Naturalist. 1668..1740
Campan, Madame de. Educationist................... 1752..1822
Campanella, Thos. Ital. Philos. L. by Baldacchini, 1840 1568..1639
Campani, John Anthony. Italian Scholar .... 1427..1477
Campani, Joseph and Matthew. Italian Opticians...... fl. 17th c.
Campanus, John, of Navara. Italian Mathematician ... fl. 13th c.
Campbell, Sir Alexander. Lieutenant-General .... 1759..1824
Campbell, Archib., Marq. Argyle. Covenanter. Beheaded 1598..1661
Campbell, Archib. E. Argyle, son. Royalist. Beheaded — ..1685
Campbell, Archib., Bishop of Aberdeen. (*Middle State*) — ..1744?
Campbell, Colin. Architect. (*Vitruvius Britannicus*)... — ..1734
Campbell, Colin, Lord Clyde. Field Marshal .... 1792..1863
Campbell, George, D. D. Principal of Marischal College.
    (*Gospels; Miracles.*) Life by Dr. Skene Keith ...... 1719..1796
Campbell, Sir James, of Ardkinglas. Life by self, 1832.. 1745..1840?
Campbell, John, Second Duke of Argyle and Greenwich.
    See Argyle and Greenwich..................... 1678..1743
Campbell, John, LL. D. Historian, Biographer, and Po-
    litical Writer. (*Admirals; Voyages and Travels*).... 1708..1775
Campbell, John. Admiral .... — ..1790
Campbell, Rev. John. Missionary to Africa. L. by Philip 1766..1840
Campbell, John, Lord. Lord Chanc. (*Lives of the Chanc.*) 1781..1861
Campbell, Rev. John N., D. D. American Clergyman and
    Scholar..................................... 1798..1864
Campbell, Sir Neil. General; Governor of Sierra Leone. 1770?.1827
Campbell, Thos., LL. D. Poet. L. by Dr. W. Beattie, 1849 1777..1844
Campe, Joachim Henry. German Writer............... 1746..1818
Campeggio, Lorenzo. Cardinal .... 1474..1539
Campeggio, Thomas, brother. Ecclesiastical Writer.... 1500..1564
Campenon, Francis Nicholas Vincent. French Poet.... 1772..1843
Camper, Peter. Dutch Physician and Naturalist....... 1722..1789
Camphuysen, Dyrk Theodore Raphael. Dutch Painter. 1586..1627
Campi, Anthony. Paint. & Arch. (*Hist of Cremona*). bef. 1536 aft.1591
Campi, Bernardin. Italian Painter & Writer on Painting 1522..1590?
Campi, Galeas. Italian Painter...................... 1475..1536
Campi, Julius. Italian Painter .... 1500?.1572
Campi, Vincent. Painter............................ 1532?.1591
Campian, Edmund. English Jesuit and Author......... 1540..1581
Campidoglio, Michael Angelo. Painter at Rome....... 1610..1670
Campion, Alexander de. French Historical Writer..... 1610..1670
Campion, or Champion, Thomas. Poet .... fl. 1604
Campistron, John Galbert de. French Dramatic Poet .. 1656..1723
Campo, or Campi, *q.v.*, Anthony. Ital. Hist.Writer. .bef.1536 aft.1591
Campolongo, Emmanuel. Italian Poet............... 1732..1801
Campomanes, Peter Rodriguez. Spanish Statesman ... 1723..1802
Campra, Andrew. French Musical Composer.......... 1660..1744
Camps, Francis de. Abbé de Ligny. Historical Writer 1643..1723
Camuccini, Vincent. Roman Painter .... 1775?.1844
Camus, Anthony le. French Physician and Writer..... 1722..1772
Camus, Armand Gaston. French Politician............ 1740..1804
Camus, Charles Stephen Louis. French Mathematician . 1699..1768

BORN. DIED.

Camus, Francis Joseph de. French Mechanician........ 1672..1732?
Camus, John Peter. *Pont Carré.* French Prelate...... 1582..1652
Camus, Stephen le. French Cardinal; Writer.......... 1632..1707
Camusat, Nicholas. Fr. Historian. (*Mélanges Historiques*) 1575..1655
Canaletto, or Canale, Anthony. *Il Tonino.* Venet. Paint. 1697..1768
Canani, John Baptist, of Ferrara. *The Young.* Anatomist 1515..1579
Canaye, Philip de la, Sieur du Fresne. Statesman...... 1551..1610
Cancellieri, Francis Jerome. Ital. Scholar. L. by Beraldi 1751..1826
Canorin, George. Russian Statesman................ 1774..1845
Candiac, John Louis Eliz. de Montcalm de. Precocious Child 1719..1726
Candido, Peter. Dutch Historical Painter .... 1548?.1599
Candolle, Augustin Pyramus de. Botanist............ 1778..1841
Cane, John Vincent. English Franciscan. Author .... — ..1672
Canga-Arguelles, Joseph. Spanish Statesman & Writer 1770..1843
Cange, Charles du Fresne du. *See Du Cange*.......... 1610..1688
Cangiago, or Cambisi, Louis. Genoese Painter........ 1527..1585
Canini, Angelo. Greek Scholar and Orientalist .... 1521..1557
Canino, Prince of. See Bonaparte.
Canisius, Henry. Canonist and Antiquary............ — ..1610
Canisius, Peter. German Jesuit; Theologian .... 1520..1597
Canitz, Fred. Rodolphus Louis, Baron von. Poet & Statesm. 1654..1699
Canne, John. English Puritan Divine at Amsterdam ... fl. 1664
Canning, Charles John, Earl. Governor-General of India 1812..1862
Canning, George. Statesman. Life by A. G. Stapleton,
 1831; Robert Bell, 1846.......................... 1770..1827
Cano, Alonzo. Spanish Painter...................... 1601..1665
Cano, John Sebastian del. Spanish Circumnavigator.... — ..1526
Cano, Melchior, of Salamanca. (*Loci Theologici*)....... 1523..1560
Canonica, Louis. Italian Architect .... 1742..1834
Canoppi, Anthony. Italian Artist in Russia............ 1773?.1832
Canormus. German Mineralogist .... 1738.. —
Canova, Anthony. Sculptor. Life by Missirini; Quatre-
 mère de Quincy................................ 1757..1822
Canovaï, Stanislaus. Italian Ecclesiastic and Historian.. 1740..1811
Canstein, Charles Hildebrand, Baron. German Printer.. 1667..1719
Cantacuzenus, John. Emp. of Constantinople. Historian 1300?.1411?
Cantarini, Simon. *Il Pezarese.* Painter............. 1612..1648
Cantel, Peter Joseph. Jesuit, of Caux; Writer .... 1645..1684
Cantemir, Antiochus. Russian Ambassador and Poet... 1709..1744
Cantemir, Demetrius. Moldavian Prince. Historian... 1673..1723
Canter, Theodore. Critic. (*Variæ Lectiones*)......... 1545..1617
Canter, William, brother. Critic. (*Novæ Lectiones*).... 1542..1575
Canterbury, Charles Manners Sutton, Visct. Statesman 1780..1845
Canton, John. Experimental Philosopher.............. 1718..1772
Cantoni, Simon. Milanese Architect.................. — ..1818
Cantwell, Andrew. Medical Writer of Tipperary....... — ..1764
Canute. King of England and Denmark. *The Great.* 995?.1035
Canuti, Dominic. Italian Painter.................... 1620..1678
Capaccio, Julius Cæsar. Italian Historical Writer...... 1560..1631
Capasso, Nicholas. Italian Theologian, Jurist, and Poet 1671..1745
Capèce-Latro, Joseph. Italian Prelate and Statesman.. 1744..1836
Capecio, Scipio. Neapolitan Latin Poet............... — ..1562?
Capel, Arthur, Ld. Royalist; behead. (*Daily Meditations*) 1600?.1649
Capel, Arthur, Earl Essex. Lord-Lieutenant of Ireland.. 1635..1683

BORN. DIED.

Capell, Edward. Editor of Shakespeare................ 1713..1781
Capella, Galeas Flavius. Italian Historian............ 1487..1537
Capella, Guarino. Italian Macaronic Poet............. fl. 16th c.
Capella, Marcianus Mineus Felix. Roman Polygrapher.. fl. 5th c.
Capellen, G. A. G. P. van der. Dutch Gov. of E. Indies. 1778..1848
Capello, Bianca. Wife of Cosmo de' Medici........... 1542?.1587
Capellus, or Cappel, Louis. French Divine and Hebraist 1585..1658
Capilupus, Lælius. Latin Poet.....................· 1498..1560
Capistran, St. John de. Neapol. Preacher against Heresy 1385..1458
Capito, Wolfgang Fabricius. Reformer and Scholar .... 1478..1541
Capitolinus, Julius. Roman Historian................ fl. 3d c.
Capmany y Montpalau, Anthony de. Spanish Philolo-
    gist and Historian................................ 1742..1813
Capo d'Istria, John Anthony, Count of............... 1776..1831
Caporali, Cæsar. French Comic Poet................. 1531..1601
Capozzoli, Dominic, Patrick, and Donlo. Neapolitan
    Patriot Brothers.................................. — ..1829
Cappe, Newcome. Dissenting Divine. (On Providence) 1733..1800
Cappel, James. French Jurisconsult.................. — ..1542
Cappel, James. French Jurisconsult .... 1525..1586
Cappel, James. French Theologian................... 1570..1624
Cappel, Louis. French Protestant Theologian......... 1534..1586
Cappel, Louis. French Theol. (Arcanum Punctuationis) 1585..1658
Cappel, William. French Theologian................. fl.15th c.
Cappel, William. French Writer..................... 1530..1586
Cappello, Bernard. Italian Poet..................... 1500?.1565
Capperonier, Claude. French Scholar................ 1671..1744
Capponi, Seraphino Annibal. Theologian............. 1536..1614
Caprara, John Baptist. Cardinal......·.............. 1733..1810
Caracalla. Emperor of Rome (211-17)............... 188.. 217
Caracci, Annibal. Painter.......................... 1560..1609
Caracci, Anthony. Venetian Painter................. 1583..1618
Caracci, Augustine. Painter........................ 1558..1602
Caracci, Francis. Franceschini. Italian Designer...... 1595..1622
Caracci, Louis. Painter............................ 1555..1619
Caraccio, Anthony. Italian Poet. (Coradino)......... 1630..1702
Caraccioli, Francis. Neapolitan Admiral; hanged..... 1770..1799
Caraccioli, Louis Anth. Fr. Writ. (Letters of Ganganelli) 1721..1803
Caraccioli, Robert. French Divine and Politician...... 1425..1495
Caractacus. British Chief.......................... fl. 51
Caradog. Historian. (Chronicle of Wales)............ — ..1156?
Caraglio, John James. Italian Engraver.............. 1500?.1571
Caramuel de Lobkowitz, John. Controversialist...... 1606..1682
Carausius. Usurper of the Empire in Britain (287-93).. 250?. 293
Caravaggio, Michael Angelo da. Amerighi. Painter... 1569..1609
Caravaggio, Polidoro da. Caldara. Painter.......... 1495..1543
Carcavi, Peter de. Mathematician and Bibliographer... — ..1684
Cardan, Jerome. Phys. and Mathem. L. by Morley, 1852 1501..1576
Cardi, Louis. Civoli, or Cigoli. Tuscan Paint. & Engrav. 1559..1613
Cardon, Anthony. Belgian Engraver.......... .... 1772..1813
Cardonne, Denis Dominic de. Orientalist............. 1720..1783
Carduccio, or Carducho, Bartholomew. Italian Painter,
    Architect, Sculptor, in Spain...................... 1560..1610
Carduccio, Vincent, brother. Italian Painter in Spain.. 1568..1638

BORN. DIED.

Cardwell, Rev. Dr. Edward, of Oxford. (*Conferences*).. 1787..1861
Carême, Mary Anthony. French Cook............... 1784..1833
Carew, Sir Alexander. Republican Politician.......... — ..1644
Carew, Bampfylde Moore. *King of Beggars*. L. by Goadby 1693..1770?
Carew, Sir George. Ambassador. (*Negotiations*)...... — ..1613
Carew, George, Earl of Totness. (*Pacata Hibernia*)..... 1557..1629
Carew, Sir Peter. Life by J. Maclean................. — ..1575
Carew, Richard. (*Survey of Cornwall*)................ 1555..1620
Carew, Thomas. Poet................................ 1589?.1639?
Carey, Henry, 2d E. Monmouth. Writer and Translator 1596..1661
Carey, Henry. Musician and Poet.................... — ..1743
Carey, Matthew. American Publisher and Author...... 1760..1839
Carey, Robert. First Earl of Monmouth. (*Memoirs*)... — ..1639
Carey, Dr. William. Baptist Missionary in India. Life
  by J. C. Marshman, 1859; Eustace Carey........... 1761..1834
Carez, Joseph. French Printer...................... 1753..1801
Cargill, Donald. Scotch Presbyterian and Covenanter.. 1610?.1681
Carinus, Emperor of Rome (283-85).................. — .. 285
Carissimi, John James. Roman Musical Composer...1582.aft.1672
Carleton, Sir Dudley, Ld. Dorchester. Statesm. (*Letters*) 1573..1632
Carleton, George. Bishop of Chichester............ 1559..1628
Carleton, Sir Guy, Lord Dorchester. General.......... 1724..1808
Carli, John Rinaldo. Italian Antiquary............... 1720..1795
Carlingford, Theobald Taafe, Earl of................. — ..1677
Carlini, Augustine. Italian Painter in England .... — ..1790
Carlini, Francis. Italian Astronomer................ 1785?.1862
Carlino, Charles Anthony Bertinazzi. Italian Harlequin 1713..1783
Carlisle, Sir Anthony. Surgeon and Physiologist...... 1768..1840
Carlisle, Frederick Howard, 5th Earl of; uncle of Byron 1748..1825
Carlisle, George William Frederick Howard, Seventh Earl
  of, and Lord Morpeth. Statesman................. 1802..1864
Carlisle, Nicholas. Antiquary....................... 1771..1847
Carlone, John. Genoese Painter.................... 1590..1630
Carlos, Don. Infant of Spain and Pretender.......... 1788..1855
Carlstadt, Andrew Bodenstein. Prot. Oppon. of Luther. 1483?.1541
Carlyle, Rev. Alexander, D.D. (*Memoirs of his Own Time*) 1721..1805
Carlyle, Rev. Joseph Dacre. Orientalist and Poet......' 1759..1804
Carlyon, Clement, M.D. (*Early Years and Late Reflections*) — ..1864
Carmagnola, Francis. *Bussone*. Italian General...... 1390?.1432
Carmer, John Henry Casimir, Ct. Prussian Statesman.. 1721..1801
Carmichael, Frederick. Scotch Divine. (*Sermons*)..l. 1708..1751
Carmichael, Gerrhom. Scottish Writer............... 1682..1738
Carmichael, Richard. Surgeon and Medical Writer.... 1779..1849
Carmontelle. French Writer. (*Proverbs*)............. 1717..1806
Carnarvon, Henry John George Herbert, Third Earl of.
  Author, Traveler, and Politician..................... 1800..1849
Carne, John. Traveler. (*Lives of Missionaries*)........ 1789..1844
Carneades, of Cyrene. Philosopher................. 213?.129 B.C.
Carnegie, Sir Robert, of Kinnaird. Statesman & Lawyer — ..1566
Carnot, Lazare Nicholas Marguerite. Math. and Statesm. 1753..1823
Caro, Annibal. Italian Poet........................ 1507..1566
Carolan, Turlough O'. Irish Poet and Musical Composer 1670..1738
Caroline, of Anspach. Queen of George I........... 1682..1737
Caroline, of Brunswick. Queen of George IV........ 1768..1821

BORN. DIED.

Caroline Matilda, Queen of Denmark .... 1751..1775
Caroto, John Francis. Italian Painter.................. 1470..1546
Carové, Frederick William. German Critical Writer ... 1789..1852
Carpani, Joseph. Italian Dramatist and Writer on Music 1752..1825
Carpenter, Dr. Lant. Unitarian Divine................ 1780..1840
Carpenter, Rev. Nathaniel. Writer .... 1588..1628?
Carpentier, Peter. (*Supplement to Du Cange*) .... 1697..1767
Carpentier. French Arithmetician.................... 1739?.1778
Carpi, Hugo da. Paint. & Engrav.; Invent. of Chiaroscuro 1486?.1530
Carpi, Jerome da. Painter of Ferrara................. 1501..1556
Carpini, John de Plano. Italian Traveler in Tartary.... fl.1245-48
Carpocrates, or Carpocras. Alexandrian Theologian ... fl. 2d c.
Carpone, Julius. Painter........................... 1611..1674
Carpzov, Benedict. Professor of Law at Wittemberg... 1565..1624
Carpzov, John Bened., sen. Lutheran Divine at Leipsic 1607..1657
Carpzov, John Bened., jr. Biblical & Rabbinical Writer 1639..1699
Carpzov, John Gottlob. Lutheran Orientalist.......... 1679..1767
Carr, John, of York. Architect...................... 1721..1807
Carr, Sir John. Attorney & Writ. (*Stranger in France*) 1772..1832
Carr, or Ker, Robert, Viscount Rochester, Earl of Somer-
    set. Favorite of James I......................... — ..1645
Carr, Rev. William Holwell. Picture Collector........ 1759..1830
Carra, John Louis. French Revolutionist............. 1743..1793
Carracci. *See* Caracci.
Carranza, Bartholomew. Abp. of Toledo and Writer... 1503..1576
Carré, Louis. French Mathematician.................. 1663..1711
Carrel, J. Bapt. Nich. Armand. French Political Writer 1800..1836
Carrenno de Miranda, John de. Spanish Painter .... 1614..1685
Carrer, Louis. Italian Poet. .·...................... 1801..1850
Carrera, Peter. Sicilian Writ. on Chess. (*Hist. of Catana*) 1571..1647
Carreri, John Francis Gemelli. Neapolitan Traveler.
    (*Giro del Mondo*)............................... 1651..1725
Carrier, John Baptist. French Revolutionist.......... 1756..1794
Carriera, Rosalba. Female Painter................... 1675..1757
Carrières, Louis de. French Biblical Commentator..... 1662..1717
Carrington, Noel Thomas. Poet. (*Dartmoor*)........ 1777..1830
Carro, John de. Champion of Vaccination............ 1770..1857
Carroll, Chas., of Carrollton. Amer. Revolutionary Patriot 1737..1832
Carroll, John. First Rom. Cath. Abp. in United States 1735..1815
Carron, Guy Toussaint Julian. (*Réflexions Chrétiennes*). 1760..1821
Carstairs, Rev. William. (*State Papers.*) Life by
    M'Cormick, 1774................................ 1649..1715
Carstens, Asmus Jacob. Danish Painter............... 1754..1798
Carsughi, Rainer. Tuscan Jesuit; Latin Poet and Writer 1647..1709
Carte, Rev. Samuel. Chronologist................... 1652..1740
Carte, Thomas. Historian........................... 1686..1754
Carter, Mrs. Elizabeth. Writer. L. by Pennington, 1816 1717..1806
Carter, Francis. Writ. (*Journey from Malaga to Gibraltar*) — ..1783
Carter, James Gordon. American Educationist......... 1795..1849
Carter, John. Artist, Architect, and Antiquary. Life
    by J. W. Dampier, 1850......................... 1748..1818
Carter, Nathaniel Hazeltine. American Writer .... 1787..1830
Carter, Thomas. Musical Composer.................. 1768..1804
Carteret, Sir George. Loyalist...................... 1599..1679

BORN. DIED.

Carteret, John, Earl Granville. Orator and Statesman.. 1690..1763
Carteret, Philip. Navigator...................... fl. 1766–69
Carteromaco, Scipio. Greek Scholar at Venice........ 1467..1513
Cartes, René des. See Descartes .... 1596..1650
Cartier, or Quartier, James. Fr. Navig. & Explorer.. 1494.aft.1536
Cartouche, Louis Dominic. French Bandit............ 1693..1721
Cartwright, Christopher. Divine and Hebraist......... 1602?.1652
Cartwright, Rev. Dr. Edmund. Poet. Inventor of
    Power Loom. (Armine and Elvira)............... 1743..1823
Cartwright, Major John. Polit. Wr. L. by his niece, 1826 1740..1824
Cartwright, Thomas. Puritan Divine................ 1535?.1603
Cartwright, William. Divine and Poet .... 1611..1643
Carus. Emperor of Rome (282–83)................... 223?. 283
Caruso, Louis. Neapolitan Musical Composer........ 1754.aft.1800
Carvajal, Thos. Jos. Gonzalez. Span. Statesman & Author 1753..1834
Carvalho da Costa, Anthony. (Corographia Portuguese) 1650..1715
Carvalho da Silva, Joseph. Spanish Writer & Publicist 1782..1845
Carver, John. First Governor of Plymouth Colony..... — ..1621
Carver, Capt. Jona. Traveler. L. by Dr. Lettsom, 1781 1732..1780
Cary, Col. Archibald. American Patriot and Statesman 1730..1786
Cary, Felix, of Marseilles. Medallic Historian......... 1699..1754
Cary, Henry. 1st Visct. Falkland. Ld. Deputy of Ireland — ..1633
Cary, Henry, Earl of Monmouth. Translator.......... 1596?.1661
Cary, Rev. Henry Francis. Translator of Dante. Life by
    Rev. H. Cary .... 1772..1844
Cary, Lott. Co-founder of Liberia................... 1710..1828
Cary, Lucius. Viscount Falkland; fell at Newbury..... 1610?.1643
Cary, Robert, LL.D. Chronologist. (Palæologia Chronica)·1615?.1688
Caryl, Joseph. Nonconf. Divine. (Commentary on Job) 1602..1673
Caryll, John. Earl Caryll. Poet... .... — ..1717?
Casa, John de la. Italian Writer. (Galateo)........... 1503..1556
Casanova, Francis. Painter........................ 1727..1805
Casanova, James. Adventurer...................... 1725..1803
Casanova, John Baptist. Painter................... 1730..1798
Casanova, Mark Anthony. Latin Poet............... 1476..1527
Casas, Bartholomew de las. Spanish Missionary to South
    America. (History of Indies)...................... 1474..1566
Casati, Paul. Italian Jesuit. Mathematician.......... 1617..1707
Casaubon, Isaac. Critic and Commentator........... 1559..1614
Casaubon, Meric, D.D., son. Writer. (Enthusiasm)... 1599..1671
Casca, P. Servilius. Conspirator against Julius Cæsar... 1st c. B.C.
Case, John. Physician and Philosopher. (Summa Vete-
    rum Interpretum).................................. — ..1600
Case, Thomas. Nonconformist Divine................ 1598?.1682
Casel, John. German Writer....................... 1533..1613
Caseneuve, Peter de. French Antiquary............. 1591..1652
Cases, Count de. See Las Cases.................... 1766..1842
Cases, Peter James. French Painter .... 1676..1754
Casimir I. King of Poland (1040–58) .... — ..1058
Casimir II. The Just. King of Poland (1177–94) ..... 1117..1194
Casimir III. The Great. King of Poland (1333–70)... 1309..1370
Casimir IV. King of Poland (1447–92) .... 1428..1492
Casimir V. John. Cardinal. King of Poland (1648–68) 1609..1672
Casimir Sarbievius. Polish Lyric Poet.............. 1595..1640

BORN. DIED.

Casiri, Michael. Spanish Orientalist .... 1710..1791
Caslon, William. Letter Founder..................... 1692..1766
Cassagues, James. French Poet....................... 1636..1679
Cassana, John Augustine. Animal Painter .... 1664..1720
Cassana, Nicholas, brother. Italian Painter .... 1659..1713
Cassander. General of Alexander. King of Macedon..354.296 B.C.
Cassander, Francis. French Classical Translator ..... — ..1695
Cassander, George. German Theologian. (*Consultatio*) 1515..1566
Cassandra, Fidele. Venetian Scholar................. 1465?.1558
Cassentino, James di. Florentine Painter............. 1276..1356
Casserio, Julius, of Placentia. Anatomist .... 1545..1616
Cassiani, Julian. Italian Lyric Poet................. 1712..1778
Cassianus, Joannes. *Joannes Massiliensis*, or *Joannes
    Eremita*. Christian Teacher of the Early Church .... — aft. 433
Cassini, Alexander Henry Gabriel, Count de, son of James
    Dominic. Magistrate and Naturalist .... 1781..1832
Cassini de Thury, Cæsar Francis, son of James. Astron. 1714..1784
Cassini, James, son of John Dominic. Astronomer ..... 1677..1756
Cassini, James Dominic, Count de, son of Cæs. F. Astron. 1747..1845
Cassini, John Dominic. French Astronomer Royal ..... 1625..1712
Cassiodorus, Magnus Aurelius. Statesman and Writer.
    Life by Denis Sainte Marthe, 1694.....'............ 468?. 568?
Cassius, Longinus Caius. Murderer of Cæsar......... — B.C. 42
Cassivelaunus. British Chief....................... fl. B.C. 54
Castagno, Andreas del. Historic Painter .... 1409?.1480?
Castaldi, Cornelius. Italian Poet .... 1480?.1537
Castalio, Sebastian. *Martin Bellius*. Genevese Theologian 1515..1563
Castanheda, Ferdinand Lopez de. Portuguese Historian 1501?.1559
Castaños, Francis Xavier de, Duke of Baylen. Span. Gen. 1756..1852
Casteels, Peter. Painter of Antwerp .... 1684..1749
Castel, Louis Bertrand. Jesuit of Montpellier; Mathem. 1688..1757
Castell, Rev. Edmund. (*Lexicon Heptaglotton*) .... 1606..1685
Castellane, Esprit V. É. B. Count de. Marshal of France 1788..1862
Castelli, Benedict. Italian Mathematician .... 1577..1644
Castelli, Bernard. Italian Painter and Engraver .... 1557..1629
Castelli, Valerio, son. Painter..................... 1625..1659
Castellio, Sebastian. French Theologian .... 1515.. —
Castello, Gabriel Lancelot. Sicilian Antiquary......... 1727..1794
Castelnau, Henrietta Julia de, Ctss. de Murat. Fr. Writer 1670..1716
Castelnau, Michael de. Statesman. (*Memoirs*)........ 1520?.1592
Castelvetro, Louis. Italian Scholar .... 1505..1571
Casti, John Baptist. Italian Poet .... 1721..1803
Castiglione, Balthazar. Statesm. & Poet. (*Il Cortegiano*) 1478..1529
Castiglione, John Benedict. *Il Grechetto*. Genoese Paint. 1616..1670
Castiglione, or Castaglione, Joseph. Poet and Critic... — ..1616
Castillejo, Christoval de. Spanish Poet............... — ..1556?
Castillo y Saavedra, Antonio del. Spanish Painter.... 1603..1667
Castillo, Fred. de. Spanish Writer on Dominican Order. 1529?.1593
Castillo, John Baptist. *Il Bergamasco*. Painter .... 1500..1570
Castlemaine, Roger Palmer, Earl of.................... — ..1705
Castlereagh, Robert Stewart, Viscount, Second Marquess
    of Londonderry. Life by Alison .... 1769..1822
Castracani. *See* Castruccio .... 1284..1328
Castrén, Matthias Alexander. Finnish Philologist...... 1813..1852

BORN. DIED.

Castries, C. E. G. de la Croix, Count de. French General 1727..1801
Castro, Alphonso de. Span. Franciscan. (*Against Heresies*) 1495?.1558
Castro, Ines de. Wife of Pedro of Portugal; assassinated — ..1355
Castro, John de. Port. Viceroy. L. by Freire de Andrada 1500..1548
Castro, Paul de. Italian Jurist...................... — .1437
Castro, Peter di. Italian Painter..................... — ..1663
Castrucci, Peter. Italian Violinist..................... 1690?.1769
Castruccio Castracani. Italian Soldier and Poet. Life
  by Aldus Manutius, jr.; Macchiavelli, tr. by Guillet. 1284..1328
Caswell, Richard. American Revolutionary Soldier..... 1729..1789
Cat, Claude Nicholas le. French Surgeon and Anatomist 1700..1768
Catalani, Angelica. Italian Singer.................... 1782..1849
Cataldi, Peter Anthony. Italian Computer............. 1548?.1626
Catchpole, Margaret. Convict. Life by R. Cobbold.... 1773..1841
Catel, Charles Simon. French Musician .... 1773..1830
Catel, Francis. German Artist....................... 1778..1856
Catel, Wm., of Toulouse. Hist. (*Hist. of Counts of Toulouse*) 1560..1626
Catellan, Maria C. P. M. de. French Poetess .... 1662..1745
Catesby, Mark. Naturalist........................... 1680?.1749
Cathcart, Sir George. General; fell in the Crimea...... 1794..1854
Cathcart, William Schaw, First Earl of. General ...... 1755..1843
Cathelineau, James. Vendean General................ 1759..1793
Catherine, St., of Sienna. Nun of Dominican Order ... 1347..1380
Catherine, St., of Bologna. Nun of Order St. Clare .... 1413..1463
Catherine of France. Queen of Henry V. of England.
  Life by Baudot de Juilli, 1696.................•..... 1401..1438
Catherine of Aragon. Queen of Henry VIII........... 1483..1536
Catherine Howard. Queen of Henry VIII.........1521 or 2.1542
Catherine Parr. Queen of Henry VIII............... 1513..1548
Catherine Paulowna. Queen of Würtemberg .... 1788..1819
Catherine de' Medici. Queen of Henry II. of France.
  Life by Eugenio Alberi, 1838 .... 1519..1589
Catherine of Braganza. Queen of Charles II. of England 1638..1705
Catherine I. Empress of Russia; wife of Peter the Great 1682..1727
Catherine II. Empress of Russia. Life by W. Tooke;
  Ségur; J. Mottley, 1744; J. Castera, tr. by Hunter, 1800 1729..1796
Catiline, Lucius Sergius. Conspirator. Life by Sallust . — B.C.62
Catineau-Laroche, Peter Mary Sebastian. Fr. Lexicog. 1772..1828
Catinat de la Fauconnerie, Nicholas. French General 1637..1712
Cato, Dionysius. Latin Moralist. (*Disticha de Moribus*.)
  See Travers, *Dissertatio*, &c., 1839.................ti. Antonines?
Cato, M. Portius, the Elder. The Censor. (*Origines*) .234?.149 B.C.
Cato, M. Portius, the Younger. *Uticensis*.............. 95..46 B.C.
Cato, Valerius. Latin Poet and Grammarian. (*Diræ*)... — B.C.20
Catrou, Francis. French Jesuit. Historian............ 1659..1737
Cattenburg, Adrian van. Dutch Remonstrant Divine .. 1664..1737
Cattho, Angelo. Italian Astrologer .... — ..1497
Cattier, Isaac. French Medical Writer (M. D. 1638)..... fl. 1657
Catullus, Caius Valerius. Roman Poet............... 87.47? B.C.
Catulus, Q. Lutatius. Roman Statesman. *Parens Patriæ* — B.C.60
Catz, or Cats, James. Dutch Statesman and Poet ...... 1577..1660
Cauchy, Augustine Louis. French Mathematician & Poet 1789..1857
Caulaincourt, Armand Aug. Louis. Officer and Diplom. 1773..1827
Cauliac, Guy de. Restorer of Surgery................ fl. 1348

BORN. DIED.

Caurroy, Francis Eustace du. French Musical Composer 1549..1609
Caus, Solomon de. Fr. Engineer, Architect, and Author — ..1635?
Caussin de Perceval, John Jas. Anthony. Fr. Orientalist 1759..1835
Caussin, Nicholas. French Jesuit. (La Cour Sainte)... 1580..1651
Cavaignac, Éléonore Godefroy. Fr. Republican Journalist 1801..1845
Cavaignac, John Baptist. French Revolutionist........ 1762..1829
Cavaignac, Louis Eugene. French General............ 1802..1857
Cavalcanti, Bartholomew. Italian Scholar 1503:.1562
Cavalcanti, Guy. Florentine Philosopher and Poet..... — ..1300
Cavalier, John. Camisard Leader.................... 1679?.1740
Cavalieri, Bonaventura. Italian Mathematician........ 1598..1647
Cavallini, Peter. Italian Historical Painter............ 1279..1364
Cavallo, Tiberius. Natural Philosopher................ 1749..1809
Cavanilles, Anthony Joseph. Spanish Divine & Botanist 1745..1804
Cave, Edward. Printer............................. 1691..1754
Cave, Dr. William. (Lives of the Apostles).............. 1637..1713
Cavedone, James. Italian Historical Painter.......... 1580..1660
Cavendish, Lord Charles. Mathematician............ — ..1783
Cavendish, Henry. Natural Philosopher. Life by G.
  Wilson, 1851...................................... 1731..1810
Cavendish, Margaret. Duchess of Newcastle, second
  wife. Writer. Life edited by Sir E. Brydges, 1814 . 1624?.1673
Cavendish, or Candish, Thomas. Navigator........... 1564..1593
Cavendish, Sir William. Biographer of Cardinal Wolsey 1505?.1557
Cavendish, William, Duke of Newcastle. Royalist. Life
  by second wife .... 1592..1676
Cavendish, William. First Duke of Devonshire. Patriot 1640..1707
Cavour, Camillo B. Count di. Italian Statesman. Life
  by W. de la Rive, tr. by E. Romilly; Devey......... 1809..1861
Cawdrey, Daniel. Nonconformist Divine.............. — ..1664
Cawthorne, James. Poet............................ 1719..1761
Cawton, Thos. Div. & Orient. at Rotterdam. Life by son 1605..1659
Cawton., Thos., son. Divine and Orient. at Westminster 1637?.1677
Caxton, William. Printer. Life by J. Lewis; Blades 1412?.1491 or 2
Cayley, Sir George. English Scientist................ 1773..1857
Caylus, Anne Claude Philip, Count of. French Amateur 1692..1765
Cazalès, John Anthony Mary de. Fr. Politician & Writer 1758..1805
Cazes, Peter James. French Painter.................. 1676..1754
Cazotte, James. French Humorous Poet .... 1720..1792
Cazwyny. Arabian Naturalist .... 1212..1283
Cean-Bermudez, John Augustin. Spanish Writer on Art 1749..1829
Ceba, Ansaldo. Genoese Poet....................... 1565..1623
Cebes. Greek Philosopher .... — . —
Cecchini, Peter Mary. Harlequin and Writer......... fl. 17th c.
Cecco de Ascoli. Francis de Gli Stabili. Italian Physi-
  cian, Astrologer, Mechanician, and Poet............ 1257..1327
Cecil, Rev. Richard. Divine. Life by Mrs. Cecil ...... 1748..1810
Cecil, Robert, Earl of Salisbury. Lord Treas. of James I. 1550?.1612
Cecil, William, Lord Burleigh. Lord Treasurer of Eliza-
  beth. L. by Arthur Collins, 1732; Dr. Edw. Nares, 1828 1520..1598
Cecilia, St. Martyr and Patroness of Music............ fl. ab. 2d c.
Cedrenus, George. Greek Monk and Historical Writer. fl. 11th c.
Celakowsky, Frantisek Ladislaus. Bohem. Poet & Philol. 1799..1852
Celesti, Andrea. Venetian Painter.................. 1637..1706

BORN. DIED.

Celestine I. Pope (422–32). *Saint*.................... — .. 432
Celestine II. (1143–44.) *Guy di Castello*............. — ..1144
Celestine III. (1191–98.) *Hyacinth Orsini*. Life by Pope
   Honorius III.. 1107..1198
Celestine IV. (1241.) *Geoffrey Castiglione*........... — ..1241
Celestine V. (1294–96.) *Saint. Peter de Murrone*.... 1215..1296
Celio Magno. Italian Lyric Poet..................... — ..1612
Cellamare, Anthony Giudice, Prince of. Span. Diplomat. 1657..1733
Cellarius, Andrew. (*Descriptio Poloniæ*)............... fl. 1659
Cellarius, Christopher. Critic and Geographer......... 1638..1707
Cellarius, Solomon. Physician. (*Origines Medicæ*).... 1676..1700
Cellier, Remi. Fr. Bened. (*Sacred and Eccles. Authors*) 1688..1761
Cellini, Benvenuto. Artist, Musician, &c. Life by self;
   tr. by Nugent, 1771; tr. by Roscoe, 1822 .... 1500..1570
Celsius, Andrew. Swedish Astronomer................. 1701..1744
Celsius, Olaus. Swed. Bot. and Orient. (*Hierobotanicon*) 1670..1756
Celsus, Aurelius Cornelius. Medical Writer......... ti. Aug. & Tib.
Celsus. Epicurean Philosopher. Antichristian Writer.. ti. Antonines
Celtes, Conrad. German Latin Poet .... 1459..1508
Cenci, Beatrice. *La Belle Parricide*.................. — ..1599
Cennick, John. Divine................................ — ..1755
Censorinus. Latin Grammarian and Chronologist..... fl. 3d c.
Centlivre, Susanna Freeman. Eng. Actress & Dram. Writ. 1667?.1723
Centorio degli Ortensi, Ascanius. Military Writer.... fl. 1569
Ceolnoth. Archbishop of Canterbury (833–70)........ — .. 870
Ceracchi, Joseph. Roman Sculptor.................. 1760?.1802
Ceratinus, Jas. Dutch Schol. (*De Sono Græc. Literarum*) — ..1530
Cerceau, John Anthony du. French Poet .... 1670..1730
Cerda, Bernarda Ferreira de la. Portuguese Scholar.... 1595..1644
Cerda, John Louis de la. Span. Jesuit. Class. Comment. 1560..1643
Céré, John Nicholas. French Botanist .... 1737..1810
Cereta, Laura, of Padua. Female Scholar............ 1469..1498
Cerini, John Dominic. *Il Cavaliere Perugino*. Ital. Paint. 1606..1681
Cerini, Joseph. Italian Poet and Dramatist........... 1738..1779
Cerinthus. Heresiarch............................... fl. 1st c.
Cerisantes, Mark Duncan de. Politician & Latin Writer 1600?.1648
Cermenati, John de. (*History of Milan*)............. —aft.1336
Cerquozzi, Michael Ang. *Di Battaglia*. Battle Paint..1600 or 2.1660
Cerrato, Paul. Italian Latin Poet. (*De Virginitate*).... 1485..1538
Ceruti, Frederick. Italian Scholar................... 1541..1579
Cerutti, Joseph Anthony Joachim. Jesuit. (*Apology*) .. 1738..1792
Cervantes Saavedra, Miguel de. Spanish Novelist. (*Don
   Quixote.*) Life by Father Sarmiento; Mayans; Los
   Rios; Fernandez de Navarrete, 1819; J. Finlay. ...... 1547...1616
Cervetto. *James Bassevi*. Italian Musician........... 1682..1783
Cesalpinus, Andrew. Ital. Phys. (*Quæstiones Peripateticæ*) 1519..1603
Cesare, Joseph. *Arpino* and *Giuseppino*. Italian Painter 1560..1640
Cesarini, Julian. Cardinal........................... — ..1444
Cesarini, Virginio. Italian Poet..................... 1595..1624
Cesarotti, Melchior. Italian Poet.................... 1730..1808
Cesi, Frederick, Prince de. Founder of Lyncean Society 1585..1630
Cespedes, Paul de. Spanish Painter, Sculptor, Architect,
   Poet, Linguist...................................... 1538..1608
Cesti, Mark Anthony. Italian Musical Composer....... 1620?.1681

BORN. DIED.

Ceva, Thos. Ital. Jesuit. Poet and Math. (*Jesus Puer*) 1648..1736
Cevallos, Peter. Spanish Diplomatist............... 1764.ab.1838
Cezelli, Constance de. Spanish Heroine .... fl. 1590?
Chabanon, Michael Paul Guy de. French Writer ...... 1730..1792
Chabert, Jos. Bernard, Marquis of. Navig., Astron., Geog. 1724..1805
Chabot, Francis. French Revolutionist............... 1759..1794
Chabot, Philip de. French General .... — ..1543
Chabrias. Athenian General......................... — B.C.355
Chabrit, Peter. French Advocate. (*French Monarchy*) — ..1785
Chabry, Mark. French Painter and Sculptor.......... 1660..1727
Chad, or Ceadde, St. .... — .. 673
Chaderton, Rev. Laurence, D. D., of Emmanuel College . 1546..1640
Chais, Charles Peter. Commentator.................. 1701..1785
Chaise, Francis de la. Fr. Jesuit. Confessor to Louis XIV. 1624..1709
Chalcondyles, Demetrius. Greek Scholar in Italy ..... 1430?.1510
Chales, or Challes, Millet Claude Francis de. Fr. Math.. 1621..1678
Chalier, Mary Joseph. Revolutionist at Lyons .... 1747..1793
Chalkley, Thomas. Quaker Preacher .... — ..1741
Challe, Charles Michael Angelo. French Painter ...... 1718..1778
Challoner, Richard. Vicar Apostolic. Life by Barnard,
    1784; Milner .... 1691..1741
Chalmers, Alexander. (*Biographical Dictionary*)....... 1759..1834
Chalmers, David. Scottish Historian .... 1530?.1592
Chalmers, George. Historian and Biographer. (*Treaties*) 1742..1825
Chalmers, Thomas, LL. D. Scottish Divine. L. by Hanna 1780..1847
Chaloner, Edward, D. D. Chaplain to James I. Preacher 1590..1625
Chaloner, James, M. P. Antiquary. (*Hist. of Isle of Man*) — ..1661
Chaloner, Sir Thomas. Soldier, Statesman, and Writer. 1515?.1565
Chaloner, Sir Thomas, son. Chem. and Nat. Philosopher 1559..1615
Chalotais, Louis René Caradeuc de la. French Writer.. 1701..1785
Chamberlaine, Robert. Poet .... — ..1637
Chamberlayne, Edw., LL. D. Writer. (*Angliæ Notitia*) 1616..1703
Chamberlayne, John. Writer. (*Contin. Angliæ Notitia*) — ..1724
Chamberlen, Hugh, of London. Accoucheur .... 1664..1728
Chambers, or Chalmers, David. Scottish Historian..... 1530?.1592
Chambers, Ephraim. (*Cyclopædia*)................... — ..1740
Chambers, George. Marine Painter................... — ..1840
Chambers, Sir Robert. Ch. Just. of Bengal. Vinerian Prof. 1737..1803
Chambers, Sir William. Architect................... 1726..1796
Chambray, Geo., Marquis de. Fr. Gen. & Military Writ. 1783..1850
Chamfort, Sebastian Roch Nicholas. Fr. Bibliographer. 1741..1794
Chamier, Daniel. French Prot. (*De Œcumenico Pontifico*) 1570?.1621
Chamillard, Michael de. Fav. and Minister of Louis XIV. 1651..1721
Chamillard, Stephen. French Jesuit and Antiquary.... 1656..1730
Chamisso, Adelbert von. Poet, Traveler, Naturalist.
    (*Peter Schlemihl*)............................... 1781..1838
Chamorro, Fruto. Central Amer. Soldier and Statesman 1806..1855
Chamousset, Claude Humbert Piarron de. Philanthr... 1717..1773
Champagne, John Baptist. Painter............... 1643 or 5.1688
Champagne, Philip de. Flemish Painter at Paris ...... 1602..1674
Champe, John. American Revolutionary Officer....... 1752.. —
Champeaux, Wm. de. Bp. of Châlons. (*Origin of the Soul*) — ..1121
Champier, Symphorien. *Camperius*. French Physician.
    (*Chroniques des Ducs de Savoie*).................... 1472..1540?

BORN. DIED.

Champion, Joseph. Penman...................... 1709.. —
Champion, or Campion, Thomas. Poet............... fl. 1604
Championnet, John Stephen. French General .... 1762..1800
Champlain, Samuel de. French Governor of Canada... 1570..1635
Champmeslé, Mary Desmares de. Actress........... 1644..1698
Champollion, John Francis. Le Jeune. Antiquary.... 1790..1832
Champollion-Figeac, John James. French Writer.... 1778.. —
Chancellor, Richard. Navigator.................... — ..1556
Chandler, Edw. Bp. of Durham. (Defence of Christianity) 1671..1750
Chandler, Mary. Poetess......................... 1687..1745
Chandler, Richard, D. D. Scholar and Antiquary ...... 1738..1810
Chandler, Sam. Dissent. Min. & Writ. L. by Thos. Amory 1693..1766
Chandler, Thos. Bradbury, D. D. Amer. Clerg. & Writer 1726..1790
Chandos, Sir John. Military Commander.............. — ..1369
Changeux, Peter James. French Savant.............. 1740..1800
Channing, Edward Tyrrel. American Scholar......... 1790..1856
Channing, Wm. Ellery, D. D., brother. American Writer 1780..1842
Chantal, St. Jane Frances Fremiot de. Life by Marsollier 1572..1641
Chantereau Lefebvre, Louis. Fr. Jurisconsult & Hist. 1588..1658
Chantrey, Sir Francis. Sculptor. Life by Jones, 1850;
  Holland, 1851............................... 1782..1841
Chanut, Peter. French Ambassador. (Mémoires)...... 1600..1662
Chapelain, John. French Poet. (La Pucelle).......... 1595..1674
Chapelier, Isaac René Guy le. French Politician ...... 1754..1794
Chapelle, Claude Emanuel. L'Huillier. French Poet .. 1626..1686
Chapelle, John de la. (Life of the Prince of Conti)...... 1655..1723
Chapin, Stephen, D. D. Amer. Clergyman & Educationist 1778..1845
Chaplin, Jeremiah, D. D. Amer. Clergyman & Educator 1776..1841
Chapman, Fred. Henry. Swed. Adm. (Marine Architect.) — ..1808
Chapman, Dr. George. Poet and Translator. (Homer). 1557..1634
Chapman, John, D. D. Archd. (Defence of Christianity) 1704..1784
Chapone, Mrs. Hester. Life by her family, pref. to Works 1727..1801
Chappe, Claude. French Mechanician .... 1763..1805
Chappe d'Auteroche, John. French Abbé and Astron. 1722..1769
Chappel, William. Bishop of Cork. (Methodus Concio-
  nandi.) Life by self............................ 1582..1649
Chapple, William. Topographer.................... 1718..1781
Chaptal, John Anthony Claude, Ct. of Cantcloup. Chemist 1756..1832
Chapuzeau, Samuel. Genevese Writer................ — ..1701
Charas, Moses. French Chemist.................... 1618..1698
Chardin, Sir John. Traveler...................... 1643..1713
Charenton, Joseph Nicholas. Fr. Jesuit Miss. in Persia. 1659..1735
Charette de la Contrie. Vendean Royalist.......... 1763..1796
Charizi, Judah. Hebrew Scholar and Poet, in Spain ... — bef.1235
Charke, Mrs. Charlotte, née Cibber. Actress ...... — ..1760
Charlemagne. L. by Eginhard; Acciajuoli, d. 1478;
  Petruccio Ubaldini, 1599; G. H. Gaillard, 1782; G. P.
  R. James, 1847; Bourgoing....................... 742.. 814
Charlemont, J. Caulfield, Earl of. Statesm. L. by Hardy 1728..1799
Charles I., Emperor of Germany. Charlemagne, q. v..... 742.. 814
Charles II. (875–77.) The Bald. I. of France........ 823.. 877
Charles III. The Fat. II. of France .... 832?. 888
Charles IV. (1347–78) and King of Bohemia.......... 1316..1378
Charles V. (I. of Spain.) Life by self; Louis Dolce, 1568;

BORN. DIED.

A. Desbarres, 1559; James Masen, 1681; Leti; Sandoval; Robertson; W. Stirling, 1852; Pichot, 1854; Mignet, 1854; Antonio de Vera....................... 1500..1558
Charles VI.. 1685..1740
Charles VII.. 1697..1745
Charles I.   *The Bald.*   King of France (840–77.) II. Emperor (875–77)................................. 823.. 877
Charles II.   *The Fat.*   III. Emperor................ 832?. 888
Charles III.   *The Simple.*   (893–922)............... 879.. 929
Charles IV.   *The Fair.*   (1322–28)................. 1294..1328
Charles V.   *The Wise.*   Life by Christina de Pisan.... 1337..1380
Charles VI.   *The Well-beloved.*   Life by Juvénal des Ursins; Baudot de Juilli, 1753................... 1368..1422
Charles VII.   *The Victorious.*   L. by Baudot de Juilli, 1697 1403..1461
Charles VIII. (1483–98.) L. by A. de la Vigne; M. Guazzi 1470..1498
Charles IX.   (1560–74)............................. 1550..1574
Charles X.. 1757..1836
Charles I., Duke of Lorraine. Claimant of French Crown 953.. 994
Charles II. (or I.).................................. 1365..1431
Charles III. (or II.)   *The Great*.................. 1543..1608
Charles IV. (or III.)................................ 1604..1675
Charles V... 1643..1690
Charles I., King of Naples. Count of Anjou.......... 1220..1285
Charles II.   *Le Boiteux.*.......................... 1248..1309
Charles III. of Durazzo.   *De la Paix* and *Le Petit*..... 1345..1386
Charles X. Gustavus. King of Sweden. Life by Prade, tr. by Spence, 1689; Puffendorf.................... 1622..1660
Charles XI. (1660–97)................................ 1655..1697
Charles XII. (1697–1718). Life by Grimarest; Joran Nordberg, 1730; Voltaire........................... 1682..1718
Charles XIII... 1748..1818
Charles XIV. (Bernadotte.) Life by Touchard-Lafosse 1764..1844
Charles I. King of England. Life by Peter Heylin, 1658; L. Wood, 1659; Fulman and Perrinchief, 1662; Sir P. Warwick; Dr. William Harris, 1758; Guizot... 1600..1649
Charles II. Life by Dr. William Harris, 1765; Francis Eglesfield, 1822.................................... 1630..1685
Charles I. King of Spain. V. Emperor.............. 1500..1558
Charles II.. 1661..1700
Charles III... 1716..1788
Charles IV.. 1748..1819
Charles II.   *The Bad.* King of Navarre. L. by Secousse 1332..1387
Charles III.   *The Noble*.......................... 1361..1425
Charles IV.. 1421..1461
Charles, Archduke of Austria. Commander........... 1771..1847
Charles de Blois. Pretender to Brittany............ — ..1364
Charles de Valois. Count of Maine and Anjou, brother of Philip IV....................................... 1270..1325
Charles the Bold. Duke of Burgundy. Life by Barland; Kirk, 1863.................................... 1433..1477
Charles Albert. King of Sardinia (1831–49)......... 1798..1849
Charles Alexander, of Lorraine. Gov. of Netherlands. 1712..1780
Charles Edward Stuart. Young Pretender. Life by C. L. Klose, 1835.................................. 1720..1788

BORN. DIED.

Charles Emanuel I. *The Great.* Duke of Savoy..... 1562..1630
Charles Emanuel II. (1638–75) .... 1634..1675
Charles Emanuel III. Duke of Savoy. K. of Sardinia 1701..1773
Charles Emanuel IV. (1796–1802.) King of Sardinia — ..1819
Charles Martel. Duke of Austrasia & Mayor of Palace 694.. 741
Charlet, Nicholas Toussaint. Fr. Painter and Engraver. 1792..1845
Charleton, Louis de. Bp. of Hereford. Theol. & Math. — ..1369
Charleton, Robert M. American Lawyer and Author.. 1807..1854
Charleton, Walter, M. D. Naturalist and Theologian... 1619..1707
Charleval, Chas. Faucon de Ry, Ld. of. Scholar & Poet 1613..1693
Charlevoix, Peter Francis Xavier de. Jesuit Missionary
     in America. (*History of Paraguay*)................ 1682..1761
Charlier, John. *Gerson.* French Writer........... 1363..1429
Charlotte. Queen of George III. L. by Watkins, 1819. 1744..1818
Charlotte Augusta. Princess. Daughter of George IV. 1796..1817
Charlotte Elizabeth, *Mrs. Tonna.* Religious Writer.
     (*Personal Recollections*)........................ 1792..1846
Charnock, John. (*Biographia Navalis*). .... 1756..1807
Charnock, Stephen. (*Providence.*) Life by Parsons.... 1628..1680
Charnock, Thomas. Alchemist. (*Philosopher's Stone*). 1524..1581
Charnois, John Charles le Vacheur de. French Politician 1750?.1792
Charost, Armand Joseph de Béthune. Fr. Philanthropist 1738..1800
Charpentier, Francis. (*Excellence of French Language*) 1620..1702
Charras, J. Bapt. Adolph. Fr. Politician & Military Writ. 1808..1865
Charrier, Mark Anthony. French Royalist........... 1753..1793
Charrière, Joseph de la. French Surgical Writer....... fl. 1690
Charrière, Madame de St. Hyacinthe de. French Writer 1740?.1805
Charron, Peter. French Writer. (*Des Trois Vérités*).. 1541..1603
Chartier, Alain. French Writer..................... 1386..1449?
Chartier, John, of St. Denys. (*Chroniques de St. Denys*) — ..1462?
Chartier, René. Fr. Phys. Edit. of Hippocrates & Galen 1572..1654
Chase, Irah, D.D. American Clergyman and Theologian 1793..1864
Chase, Philander, D.D. Amer. Episc. Bp. (*Reminiscences*) 1775..1852
Chasles, or Challes, Gregory de. Fr. Officer and Humorist 1659..1720?
Chassé, David Henry, Baron. Defender of Antwerp.... 1765..1849
Chasseneuz, Bartholomew de. French Lawyer........ 1480..1541
Chastelain, Claude. (*Universal Martyrology*)......... 1639..1712
Chastelard, or Chastellet, Peter de Boscobel de. Fr. Poet 1540?.1563
Chastelet, Gabrielle Émilie de Breteuil, Marchioness of.
     Scientific Writer..............................·. 1706..1749
Chastellux, Francis John, Marquis de. French Officer,
     Poet, Musician ....·. 1734..1788
Châteaubriand, Francis Augustus, Vicomte de. (*Génie
     du Christianisme.*) Life by self; Villemain........ 1768..1848
Châteaubriant, Francis de Foix, Countess of. Favorite
     of Francis I.................................. 1475?.1537
Châteaubrun, John Baptist Vivian de. Dramatic Writer 1686..1775
Châteaurenard, Francis Louis Rousselet, Count de.
     Admiral and Marshal of France .... 1637..1716
Châtel, Ferd. Francis. Found. of so-called Fr. Cath. Ch. 1795..1857
Châtel, Francis du. Flemish Painter............... 1625..1679
Châtel, Peter du. *Castellanus.* Bp. of Orleans. Scholar — ..1552
Châtel, Tanneguy du. French General.............. 1360..1449
Châtelet, Paul du Hay, Lord of. (*Bertrand du Guesclin*) 1593..1636

BORN. DIED.

Chatham, William Pitt, First Earl of. Life by Almon;
    Thackeray; Macaulay.............................. 1708..1778
Chatterton, Thomas. Poet. Life by Dr. Gregory, ed.
    by Southey, 1803; D. Masson .... 1752..1770
Chaucer, Geoffrey. Poet. Life by Todd; W. Godwin,
    1804; Singer, 1822; Sir H. Nicholas, 1843 .... 1328..1400
Chaudet, Anthony Denis. French Painter and Sculptor. 1763..1810
Chaudon, Esprit Joseph. French Author.............. 1738..1800
Chaudon, Louis Mayeul. French Historical Writer..... 1737..1817
Chauffepié, James George de. (*Biographical Dictionary*) 1702..1786
Chauliac, Cauliac, or Chaulieu, Guy de. French Surgeon fl. 14th c.
Chaulieu, William Amfrye de. French Lyric Poet..... 1639..1720
Chaulnes, Albert, Duke de. French Chemical Philosopher 1714..1769
Chaumette, Anthony. Fr. Surg. (*Enchirid. Chirurgicum*) fl. 1560
Chaumette, Peter Gaspar. French Revolutionist....... 1763..1794
Chaumonot, or Chaumonnot, Peter Mary Joseph. French
    Jesuit...................................... 1611..1693
Chauncey, Sir Henry. Judge & Antiq. (*Hertfordshire*) 1632..1716
Chauncey, Ichabod. Ejected Nonconformist at Bristol.. — ..1691
Chauncey, Isaac. Dissenting Divine and Physician ... — ..1700?
Chauncy, Charles, D. D. American Divine............ 1705..1787
Chausse, Michael Angelo de la. Antiquary. (*Musœum
    Romanum*)...................................1660?.aft.1738
Chauveau Lagarde, Claude Francis. French Advocate 1767..1841
Chauveau, Francis. French Engraver................. 1613..1676
Chauveau, René, son. Engraver .... 1663..1722
Chauvin, Stephen. Prot. Refugee. (*Lexicon Philosoph.*) 1649..1725
Chaves, Emanuel de Silveyra Pinto de Fonseca, Marquis.
    Portuguese General and Statesman................. — ..1830
Chazelles, John Matthew. French Math. and Engineer 1657..1710
Chefontaines, Christopher de, of Brittany. Theologian . 1532?.1595
Cheke, Sir John. Statesman and Scholar. Life by Dr.
    Langbaine; Strype, 1705......................... 1514..1557
Chelsum, Rev. James, D. D. Critic of Gibbon......... 1740?.1801
Chemin, Catherine du. French Flower Painter........ 1630..1698
Cheminais, Timoleon. French Preacher.............. 1652..1689
Chemnitz, Bogeslaus Philip. (*Swed. Wars in Germany*) 1605..1678
Chemnitz, Martin. Protestant Divine............... 1522..1588
Chemnitzer, Ivan Ivanovitch. Russian Soldier and Poet 1744..1784
Chenevix, Richard. Bishop of Waterford .... — ..1779
Chenevix, Richard. Irish Writer.................... — ..1830
Chénier, Andrew Mary de. French Poet.............. 1762..1794
Chénier, Louis de. French Historian................. 1723..1796
Chénier, Mary Joseph de. French Dramatist. (*Death of
    Calas*)....................................... 1764..1811
Chenot, Claude Bernard Adrian. French Engineer..... 1803..1855
Chéron, Elizabeth Sophia. French Portrait Painter .... 1648..1711
Chéron, Louis, brother. Painter..................... 1660..1713
Cherry, Andrew. Comedian .... 1762..1812
Cherubini, Mary Louis Charles Zenobi Salvador. Italian
    Musical Composer .... 1760..1842
Chervin, Nicholas. French Physician .... 1783..1843
Chéry, Philip. French Painter .... 1759..1838
Cheselden, William. Surgeon and Writer............. 1688..1752

BORN. DIED.

Chesne, Andrew du.   French Historian............... 1584..1640
Chesne, or Quesne, Joseph du. *Quercetanus.* Med. Writer 1544?.1609
Chesneau, Nicholas, of Toulouse.   Medical Writer..... 1601.. —
Chesterfield, Philip Dormer Stanhope, Earl of. (*Letters.*)
  Life by Dr. Maty, 1777............................ 1694..1773
Chetham, Humphrey, of Manchester. Benefactor...... 1580..1653
Chettle, Henry. Dramatist fl.1592–1600
Chetwood, Knightly, D.D. Dean of Gloucester. Writer 1652..1720
Chetwood, Wm. Rufus. Dramatist. (*Hist. of the Stage*) — ..1766
Chevalier, Anthony Rodolph le. French Scholar....... 1507..1572
Chevalier, Louis. French Lawyer................... 1663?.1744
Chevert, Francis de. French General................ 1695..1760
Cheverus, John Louis Anne Madeleine Lefebvre de.
  French Cardinal................................... 1768..1836
Cheves, Langdon. American Statesman............... 1776..1857
Chevillier, Andrew. French Antiquary.............. 1636..1700
Chevreau, Urban. French Scholar................... 1613..1701
Cheyne, George. Physician and Mathematician........ 1671..1743
Cheynell, Francis, D. D. Ejected Nonconformist....... 1608..1665
Chézy, Anthony Leonard de. French Orientalist....... 1773..1832
Chiabrera, Gabriel. Italian Lyric Poet.............. 1552..1637
Chiaramonti, Scipio. Mathemat. & Natural Philosopher 1565..1652
Chiari, Fabricius. Italian Painter and Engraver........ 1621..1695
Chiari, Joseph. Italian Historical Painter............. 1654..1727
Chiari, Peter. Italian Poet......................... — ..1788
Chiavistelli, Jacob. Perspective Painter of Florence... 1621..1698
Chicheley, or Chichele, Henry. Abp. Cant. 1414–31.
  Life by Arthur Duck, 1617; O. L. Spencer, 1783..... 1362?.1443
Chicoyneau, Aimé Francis. Physician, Lawyer, Scholar 1699..1740
Chicoyneau, Francis. Fr. Physician. (*On the Plague*) 1672..1752
Chicoyneau, Michael. French Physician and Statesman 1626?.1701
Chifflet, John James. Fr. Medical and Political Writer. 1588..1660
Child, Sir Josiah. Writer. (*Discourse on Trade*)...... 1630..1699
Child, William, MUS. DOC. Musical Composer......... 1607..1697
Childebert I. King of France (511–58).............. 495?. 558
Childebert II. (575–96)............................ 570?. 596
Childebert III.................................. 683?. 711
Childéric I. King of France....................... 436?. 481
Childéric II................................... 649.. 673
Childéric III. (742–52).............................. — .. 755
Children, John George. Chemist..................... 1777..1852
Chillingworth, William. Theologian. Life by Birch.. 1602?.1644
Chilmead, Edmund. Mathematician & Mus. Composer 1611..1654
Chilo. One of the Seven Sages.....................fl. 6th c. B.C.
Chilpéric I. King of Soissons (561–84).............. •539.. 584
Chilpéric II. (715–20)............................ — .. 720
Chimay, Jane Mary Ignace Theresa, Princess of. Beauty 1775?.1835
Chiocco, Andrew. Italian Physician.................. — ..1624
Chipman, Daniel, LL. D. American Jurist............ 1762..1850
Chipman, Nathaniel, LL. D., brother. Jurist.......... 1752..1843
Chirac, Peter. French Medical Writer............... 1650..1732
Chishull, Rev. Edmund. Antiquary................. 1670..1733
Chitty, Joseph. English Jurist...................... 1776?.1841
Chladni, Ernest Florens Frederick. German Physicist.. 1756..1827

7

BORN. DIED.

Chlopicki, Joseph.   Polish General and Dictator .... 1772..1854
Chmielnicki, Bogdan.   Cossack Chief .... 1593..1657
Choate, Rufus.   American Advocate and Jurist......... 1799..1859
Chodowiecki, Daniel Nich.   Ger. Designer & Engraver 1726..1801
Choiseul - Gouffier, Mary Gabriel Florent Augustus,
     Count of.   French Classical Scholar............... 1752..1817
Choiseul-Amboise, Stephen Francis, Duke of. French
     Statesman .... 1719..1785
Choisy, Francis Timoléon de. Abbé. Writer.......... 1644..1724
Chomel, James Francis. Medical Writer.............. fl. 1708–38
Chomel, John Baptist Louis. Medical Writer.......... 1700?.1765
Chomel, Peter John Baptist.   French Medical Writer.. 1671..1740
Chopin, Frederick. Musical Composer and Pianist ..... 1810..1849
Chopin, René. French Law Writer................... 1537..1606
Chorier, Nicholas. (History of Dauphiny)............. 1609..1692
Choris, Louis. Russian Artist and Traveler........... 1795..1828
Choron, Alexander Stephen. French Writer on Music.. 1772..1834
Chosroes I., or Khosru. King of Persia (531–79)....... — .. 579
Chosroes II. (590–628), grandson .... — .. 628
Chouet, John Robert. Philos. and Magistrate of Geneva 1642..1731
Choul, William du. Caulius. French Antiquary....... fl. 1556
Choules, John Overton, D.D. Amer. Clerg. and Author. 1801..1856
Chrétien, Florence. French Poet and Writer.......... 1541..1596
Christian I. King of Denmark (1448–81)..........:... 1425?.1481
Christian II. (1513–23)............................. 1480..1559
Christian III. (1534–58).......................... 1502..1558
Christian IV. (1588–1648)........................ 1577..1648
Christian V. (1670–99)........................... 1645..1699
Christian VI. (1730–46) .... 1699..1746
Christian VII. (1766–1808) .... 1749..1808
Christian, Andrew.   Danish Medical Writer.......... 1551..1606
Christian, Edward.   Law Writer .... — ..1823
Christie, James.   Antiquary .... — ..1831
Christie, Samuel Hunter, of Woolwich. Magnetist..... 1784..1865
Christie, Thomas.   Writer. (Miscellanies)............ 1761..1796
Christie, William.   Scottish Grammarian............. 1730..1774
Christina.   Queen of Sweden. Life by H. Woodhead;
     C. G. Franckenstein; Catteau Calleville; J. Lacombe;
     Archenholz...................................... 1626..1689
Christine, of Pisa.   Scholar and Poetess in France....... 1363?.1431?
Christophe, Henry.   Negro King of Hayti............. 1767..1820
Christopherson, John.   Bp. of Chichester. Translator. — ..1558
Christopulos, Athanasius.   Modern Greek Poet....... 1772..1847
Chrysippus.   Stoic Philosopher ....280?.207 B.C.
Chrysologue, Noel Andrew.   Fr. Geogr. & Astronomer 1728..1808
Chrysoloras, Manuel.   Reviver of Greek in Italy....... 1355?.1415
Chrysostom, John.   Life by Palladius, tr. by Americ
     Bigot, 1680; Godfrey Hermant, alias Dr. Menard, 1683 347?. 407
Chubb, Thomas.   Deistical Writer................... 1679..1747
Chudleigh, Mary, Lady.   Poetess.................... 1656..1710
Church, Benjamin.   American Soldier in Indian Wars.. 1639..1718
Church, Sir Richard.   Commander in Greek War of In-
     dependence .... 1780..1850
Church, Thomas, D. D.   Controversialist.............. 1707..1756

BORN. DIED.

Churchill, Arabella. Mistress of James II............. 1648..1730
Churchill, Rev. Charles. Poet. Life by Tooke........ 1731..1746
Churchill, John, First Duke of Marlborough. Life by
    Coxe; Lediard; Alison............................. 1650..1722
Churchill, Sir Winston. (*Divi Britannici*)............ 1620..1688
Churchyard, Thomas. Poet. L. by Geo. Chalmers, 1817 1520?.1604
Churrucca y Elorza, Cosme Damian de. Span. Admiral 1761..1805
Chytræus, David. Divine at Rostock. (*Apocalypse*)... 1530..1600
Ciaconius, Alphonso. Span. Schol. (*Column of Trajan*) 1540..1599
Ciaconius, or Chacon, Peter. Spanish Scholar. (*De Tri-*
    clinio.) Life by A. Schott...................... 1525..1581
Ciamberlano, Luke. Italian Painter and Engraver .... 1586..1641
Ciampelli, Augustine, of Florence. Historical Painter .. 1578..1640
Ciampini, John Justin. Antiq. and Hist. (*Lives of Popes*) 1633..1698
Ciampoli, John Baptist. Italian Poet................. 1589..1643
Cibber, Caius Gabriel. German Sculptor .... 1630?.1700
Cibber, Colley. Actor. Poet Laureate. Life by self... 1671..1757
Cibber, Susannah Maria. Actress.................... 1714..1766
Cibber, Theophilus. Actor, Dramatist, Biographer ..... 1703..1758
Cibot, Peter Martial. French Jesuit Missionary in China 1727..1780
Ciccarelli, Alphonso. Italian Writer................ — ..1580
Cicero, Marcus Tullius. Life by Ramus; Facciolati; Mo-
    rabin; Leonard Aretino, 1804; Conyers Middleton;
    Abeken, tr. by Merivale; Wm. Forsyth, 1864 .... 106. 43 B.C.
Cicognara, Leopold, Count. (*Hist. of Modern Sculpture*) 1767..1834
Cid, The. *See* Bivar .... 1040?.1099
Cienfuegos, Nicasio Alvarez de. Span. Poet & Dramatist 1764..1809
Cignani, Charles. Italian Painter.................... 1628..1719
Cignaroli, Giambettino. Italian Painter.............. 1706..1770
Cigoli, or Civoli, Louis. *Cardi.* Florentine Painter..... 1559..1613
Cimabue, John. Italian Painter..................... 1240..1300
Cimarosa, Domenico. Neapolitan Musical Composer.... 1749..1801
Cimon. Athenian Commander....................... — B.C.449
Cincinato, Diego Romulo. Painter .... — ..1626
Cincinato, Romulo. Florentine Painter ..'............ 1525?.1600
Cincinnatus, Lucius Quintus. Dictator...........519?.aft.439 B.C.
Cinna, Lucius Cornelius. Roman Popular Leader....... — B. C. 84
Cinnamus, John. Greek Historian .... fl. 12th c.
Cino da Pistoia. Italian Jurist and Poet.............. 1270..1337
Cinq-Mars, Henry Coiffier de Ruzé, Marquis of. Favorite
    of Louis XIII.................................. 1620..1642
Cinthio, Giraldi. Italian Dramatist. (*Orbecche*)....... 1504..1573
Cintra, Gonçalo de. Portuguese Navigator .... fl. 15th c.
Cioli, Valerio. Italian Sculptor..................... 1530?.1600?
Cione, Andrea di. *Orcagna.* Painter, Sculptor, Architect 1329..1389
Ciprian Rore. Italian Musical Composer.............. 1516..1565
Cipriani, or Cypriani, John Baptist. Italian Painter .... 1727..1785
Circignano, Anthony. *Pomerancio.* Painter......... 1560..1620
Circignano, Nicholas. *Pomerancio.* Italian Painter.... 1516..1588
Cirillo, Dominic, of Naples. Botanist................ 1734..1799
Ciroferri. Painter and Architect of Rome............. 1634..1689
Cisner, Nicholas. German Writer .... 1529..1583
Cisneros, Francis Ximenes de. Span. Card. Statesman 1436..1517
Citois, or Citesius, Francis. Physician of Poictiers...... 1572..1652

BORN. DIED.

Cittadini, Peter Francis. *Il Milanese.* Painter .... 1613?.1681
Civilis, Claudius, or Julius. Leader of the Batavi....... fl. 69-70
Civitali, Matthew. Italian Sculptor and Architect...... 1435..1501
Claesson, Arnold. Dutch Painter...................... 1498..1564
Clagett, William, D. D. Controversial Writer........... 1646..1688
Clair, John Mary le. French Violinist................. 1697..1764
Clairault, Alexis Claude. Mathematician .... 1713..1765
Claire, Martin. French Jesuit, Preacher, and Hymnologist 1612..1690
Clairfait, or Clerfayt, F. S. C. J. de Croix de. Austr. Gen. 1733..1798
Clairon, Claire Josephine de la Tude. French Actress ... 1723..1803
Clap, Thomas. American Divine and Educator .... 1703..1767
Clapperton, Captain Hugh. African Traveler .... 1788..1827
Clarac, Charles Otho Frederick John Baptist, Count.
   French Antiquary and Artist...................... 1777..1847
Clare, John. Northamptonshire Poet.................. 1793..1864
Clare, or Clara, St. Founder of Order of Nuns .... 1193..1253
Clarendon, Edward Hyde, First Earl of. Lord Chancellor.
   (*History of the Rebellion.*) Life by self; T. II. Lister.. 1608..1674
Clarendon, Henry Hyde, Second Earl of. Lord Lieuten-
   ant. (*History of the Irish Rebellion*)............... 1638..1709
Claret, Joan. Flemish Painter...................... fl. 1600?
Claridge, Richard. Quaker Writer. Life by Jos. Besse 1649..1723
Clario, Isidore. Tridentine Divine; Annotator on Vulgate 1495..1555
Clark, John, of Hull. Critic and Classical Commentator. — ..1734
Clark, John, of Edinb. Book Illustrator. (*Myriorama*). 1772?.1863
Clark, William. American General .... 1770..1838
Clark, William Tierney. Civil Engineer............. 1783..1852
Clark, Willis Gaylord. American Author............. 1810..1841
Clarke, Adam, LL. D. Wesleyan Commentator. Life by
   J. B. B. Clarke, 1833; S. Dunn, 1863 .... 1760..1832
Clarke, Dr. Alured. Divine and Benefactor........... 1696..1742
Clarke, Sir Arthur. Irish Phys., Med. Writ., & Philanthr. 1773..1857
Clarke, Rev. Edward. Scholar .... 1730..1786
Clarke, Edward Daniel, LL. D. Traveler and Mineralogist.
   Life by Bishop Otter, 1825....................... 1769..1822
Clarke, George Roger. American General .... — ..1808
Clarke, Henry, LL. D. Mathematician................. 1745..1818
Clarke, Henry Jas.Wm., Duke of Feltre. Marsh. of France 1765..1818
Clarke, Rev. James Stanier. Naval and Historical Writer.
   (*Life of James II.*)............................. — ..1834
Clarke, Jeremiah. Musical Composer................. — ..1707
Clarke, John. One of the Founders of Rhode Island .... — ..1676
Clarke, John. Scottish Portrait Engraver. .... 1650?.1721
Clarke, John, D. D. Dean of Salisbury. (*Origin of Evil*) — ..1759
Clarke, John, M. D. Scottish Medical Writer........... 1744..1805
Clarke, M'Donald. American Poet................... 1798..1842
Clarke, Samuel, M. A. Orientalist.................. 1623..1669
Clarke, Rev. Sam. Biographer. Ejected Nonconformist 1599..1682
Clarke, Samuel, son. Dissenter. (*Annotations on Bible*) 1627?.1701
Clarke, Samuel, D.D. Class. Commentator. (*Doctrine of
   the Trinity.*) Life by Hoadly, 1738; W. Whiston, 1748 1675..1729
Clarke, or Clark, Dr. Samuel. Dissenting Minister of St.
   Albans. (*Scripture Promises*) .... — ..1769
Clarke, William. Divine and Antiquary............. 1696..1771

BORN. DIED.

Clarkson, David. Ejected Nonconformist .... 1622..1686
Clarkson, Thos. Slavery Abolitionist. L. by Thos. Taylor 1760..1846
Clason, Isaac S. American Author and Actor.......... 1789..1834
Clauberg, John. German Metaphysician .... 1622..1665
Claude, Le Jeune, or Claudin. Huguenot Composer .... —aft.1580
Claude Lorraine. Claude Gelée. Painter............. 1600..1682
Claude, John. Fr. Prot. (Ess. on Sermon.) L. by Robinson 1619..1687
Clauder, Gabriel. German Medical Writer............ 1633..1691
Claudian, Claudius. Latin Poet..................... — aft. 404?
Claudius I. Roman Emperor (41–54)................B.C.10 A.D.54
Claudius II. Gothicus. Emperor (268–70)............ 214.. 270
Claudius Crassus, Appius. Roman Decemvir........ — B.C.449
Claudius Nero. Roman General .... fl. 3d c. B.C.
Clausel, Bertrand, Count. French General .... 1772..1842
Claverhouse, John Graham of, Viscount Dundee ..... 1650?.1689
Clavière, Stephen. French Statesman and Financier ... 1735..1793
Clavigero, Francis Xavier. Mexican Historian........ 1720..1793
Clavijo, Ruy Gonzalez de. Span. Ambassador and Writer — ..1412
Clavijo y Faxardo, Joseph. Spanish Writer.......... 1726..1806
Clavius, Christopher. German Jesuit. Mathematician.. 1537..1612
Clay, Henry. American Statesman .... 1777..1852
Clay, John. Jail Chaplain........................... — ..1858
Clayton, Augustin Smith. American Jurist............ 1783..1839
Clayton, John. American Botanist .... 1686..1773
Clayton, John Middleton. American Statesman........ 1796..1856
Clayton, Robert. Bishop of Clogher .... 1695..1758
Cleanthes. Stoic Philosopher. (Hymn to Zeus)........ ab. B.C. 210
Clearchus. Lacedæmonian General.................. fl. B.C. 400
Cleaveland, Parker. American Mineralogist and Scientist 1780..1858
Cleaver, William. Bishop of St. Asaph .... — ..1815
Cleef, Henry van. Painter of Antwerp .... 1510?.1589
Cleef, John van. Flemish Painter.................... 1646..1716
Cleef, or Cleve, Joseph, Joas, or Joost, van. Paint. of Antw. fl. 1511
Cleef, Martin van. Painter.......................... 1501?.1551
Clegg, John. Violinist...............................1714.aft.1742
Cleghorn, George. Scottish Physician and Anatomist.. 1716..1789
Cleland, James, LL. D. Statistical Writer............. 1770..1840
Cleland, John. Writer. (Woman of Pleasure)......... 1707?.1789
Clemangis, or Claminges, Matthew Nicholas. Fr. Theol. 1360?.1440?
Clemencet, Charles. Fr. Benedictine. (L'Art de Vérif.) 1704..1778
Clemencin, Diego. Spanish Statesman and Writer .... 1765..1834
Clement I. Bishop of Rome .... 30?. 100
Clement II. Pope (1046–47). Life by P. F. Lafitau ... — ..1047
Clement III. (1187–91)............................. — ..1191
Clement IV. (1265–68.) Guy de Foulques. Life by Clau-
   dius Clemens...................................... — ..1268
Clement V. (1305–14.) Bertrand de Goth. (Clem. Code) 1264..1314
Clement VI. (1342–52.) Peter Roger................ 1292..1352
Clement VII. (1523–34.) Julius de' Medici .... — ..1534
Clement VIII. (1592–1605.) Hippolytus Aldobrandin .. 1536..1605
Clement IX. (1667–69.) Jul. Rospigliosi. L. by Lafitau 1600..1669
Clement X. (1670–76.) John Baptist Emilius Altieri... 1590..1676
Clement XI. (1700–21.) John Francis Albani. Life by
   Reboulet... 1649..1721

BORN. DIED.

Clement XII. (1730–40.) *Lawrence Corsini* .... 1652..1740
Clement XIII. (1758–69.) *Charles Rezzonico* .... 1693..1769
Clement XIV. (1769–74.) *John Vincent Ganganelli* .... 1705..1774
Clement, David. Hessian Bibliographer .... 1701..1760
Clément, Francis. French Benedictine. (*L'Art de Vérif.*) 1714..1793
Clément, James. Assassin of Henry III. of France..... 1567..1589
Clement, John. Greek Professor at Oxford .... — ..1572
Clément, John Mary Bernard. Fr. Critic and Dramatist 1742..1812
Clement, Joseph. Mechanic .... 1779..1844
Clément, Julian. French Accoucheur................ 1630..1729
Clément, Peter, of Geneva. Poetical Writer.......... 1707..1767
Clement, Titus Flavius, of Alexandria. Christian Writer — .. 220?
Clementi, Muzio. Musical Composer .... 1752..1832
Clenardus, or Cleynaerts, Nicholas. Flemish Philologist 1495..1542
Cleobulus. One of the Seven Sages of Greece........ 6th c. B.C.
Cleombrotus I. King of Sparta; fell at Leuctra .... — B.C.371
Cleomedes. Greek Astronomer. (*Circular Theory*).... fl. 2d. c.?
Cleomenes. Spartan King (B. c. 236–220) and Reformer — B.C.220
Cleon. Athenian Politician .... — B.C.422
Cleopatra. Queen of Egypt .... 69..30 B.C.
Clerc, John le. *Le Chevalier.* Fr. Painter and Engraver 1587..1633
Clerc, John le. Critic. *See* Leclerc................. 1657..1736
Clerc, Nicholas. French Medical Writer.............. —aft.1771
Clerc, Sebastian le. French Designer and Etcher....... 1637..1714
Clerc, Sebastian le, son. Historical Painter .... 1684?.1767
Clerc, Le. *See* Leclerc.
Clerck, Chas. Swed. Entomologist. (*Icones Insectorum*) fl. 1750
Clerfayt, Francis S. C. J., Count de. Austrian General .. 1733..1798
Clerk, John, of Eldin. Naval Tactician.............. — ..1812
Clerk, John, Lord Eldin, son. Scottish Judge......... 1757?.1832
Clerke, Charles. Navigator......................... 1741..1779
Clerke, Gilbert. Divine and Mathematician .... 1626?.1695?
Clermont Tonnerre, Stanislaus, Ct. of. Fr. Polit.Writer 1747..1792
Clerselier, Claude. French Metaphysician............. 1614?.1684
Cléry, John Baptist. Servant of Louis XVI. (*Journal*) 1759..1809
Clery, Michael. One of the "Four Masters".......... — ..1643
Cleveland, John. Loyalist and Poet.................. 1613..1659
Clevenger, Shobal Vail. American Sculptor........... 1812..1843
Cleyer, Andrew. German Medical Writer............. fl. 1680
Cleyn, or Clenn, Francis de. German Painter in England — ..1658
Clifford, Ann, Countess of Dorset. Author & Benefactor 1589..1676
Clifford, George, 3d E. Cumberland. Naval Commander 1558..1605
Clifford, Henry, Tenth Lord. *Shepherd Lord*......... — ..1523
Clifford, John, Ninth Lord. *The Black* and *The Butcher* — ..1461
Clifford, Martin. Writer. (*On Human Reason*)........ — ..1677
Clifford, Thos., 8th Lord. Lancastrian; fell at St. Albans — ..1455
Clift, William. Naturalist........................... 1775..1849
Clifton, Francis. Medical Writer.................... fl. 1732
Clifton, William. American Poet .... 1772..1799
Clinton, De Witt. American Statesman.............. 1769..1828
Clinton, George. American Statesman and General.... 1739..1812
Clinton, Sir Henry. English General in America ...... — ..1795
Clinton, Henry Fynes. Chronologist. (*Fasti.*) Life by
     self, edited by C. J. F. Clinton, 1854............... 1781..1852

BORN. DIED.

Clinton, James. American General..................... 1736..1812
Clisson, Oliver de. Constable of France............... 1332?.1407
Clisthenes. Athenian Demagogue.................... fl. B.C. 510
Clitus. Greek Gen. of Macedon; slain by Alex. the Great — B.C.328
Clive, Mrs. Catherine. Actress .... 1711..1785
Clive, Robert, First Lord. Life by Sir J. Malcolm, 1836;
    Macaulay; G. R. Gleig, 1848; C. Caraccioli......... 1725..1774
Clodius Pulcher, Publius. Roman Tribune (B. C. 58).. — B.C. 52
Cloncurry, Valentine Browne Lawless, Lord. Life by
    Fitzpatrick.. 1773..1853
Clootz, John Baptist. *Anacharsis Clootz.* Fr. Revolutionist 1755..1794
Clopinel, or John de Meung. French Poet............ 1250?.1318?
Closterman, John. German Portrait Painter.......... 1656..1713
Clotaire I. son of Clovis. King of France (511–61)..... 497.. 561
Clotaire II. son of Chilpéric. King of France.......... 584?. 628
Clotaire III. King of France....................... 652?. 670?
Clotilde. Wife of Clovis............................ 475.. 545
Cloud, or Clodoald, St., grandson of Clovis............ — .. 560
Clouet, Albert. Engraver........................... fl. 1641–75
Clouet, Peter, of Antwerp. Engraver................ 1606..1668
Clouet. French Chemist and Metallurgist............. 1751..1801
Clough, Arthur Hugh. Poet....................... 1819?.1861
Clovio, Julius. Missal Illuminator................... 1498..1578
Clovis I. King of the Franks........................ 465.. 511
Clovis II. King of France........................... 633.. 656
Clovis III.. 681.. 695
Clowes, John. Swedenborgian Divine................ 1743..1831
Clowes, William. Surgeon.......................... —aft.1596
Clowes, William. Printer........................... 1779..1847
Clubbe, Rev. John. Humorist...................... 1703..1773
Clubbe, William. Poet. Translator of Horace........ — ..1814
Cluentius Habitus, A. Defended by Cicero........103 aft.66 B.C.
Clusius, or De l'Ecluse, Chas. Dutch Phys. and Botanist 1526..1609
Clutterbuck, Robert. Antiquary.................... 1772..1831
Cluvier, Philip. *Cluverius.* Geographer............. 1580..1623
Clyde, Colin Campbell, Lord. Field Marshal.......... 1792..1863
Clymer, George. American Statesman................ 1739..1813
Cobb, James. Dramatic Writer...................... 1756..1818
Cobb, Lyman. American Lexicographer and Author.... — ..1863
Cobb, Samuel. Poet................................ — ..1713
Cobbett, William. Writer. L. by his sons; Huish, 1835 1762..1835
Cobden, Richard, M. P. Politician and Economist...... 1804..1865
Cobentzel, or Cobenzl, Charles, Count de. Statesman.. 1712..1770
Cobentzel, John Philip, Count de. Statesman......... 1741..1810
Cobentzel, Louis, Count de. Statesman.............. 1753..1808
Cobham, John, Lord. English Warrior in France...... — ..1407
Cobham, Sir John Oldcastle, Lord. Martyr........... 1360..1417
Coburg-Saxe, Josias, Prince of. Austrian Field Marshal 1737..1815
Coccapani, Sigismund, of Florence. Painter and Architect 1583..1642
Cocceius, Henry Freiherr von. Dutch Jurist.......... 1644..1719
Cocceius, John. Hebraist. Commentator............. 1603..1669
Cocceius, Samuel. Prussian Statesman.............. 1679..1755
Cocchi, Anthony. Italian Physician................. 1695..1758
Coccopani, John. Architect......................... 1582..1649

BORN. DIED.

Cochin, Charles Nicholas. French Engraver and Writer 1688..1754
Cochin, Henry. French Lawyer and Divine........... 1687..1747
Cochlæus, John. Roman Catholic Controversialist ..... 1479..1552
Cochran, William. Scottish Artist................... 1738..1785
Cochrane, Archibald, Earl Dundonald. Scientific Writer 1749..1831
Cochrane, John Dundas. Traveler on foot............ 1780?.1825
Cochrane, Thos., Earl of Dundonald. Nav. Commander 1775..1860
Cock, Jerome. Painter............................ 1510?.1570
Cock, Matthew, of Antwerp, brother. Painter......... 1500?.1554
Cockain, or Cokayne, Sir Aston. Poetical Writer...... 1608..1684
Cockburn, Mrs. Catherine. Miscel.Writer. L. by Birch 1679..1749
Cockburn, Sir George. Admiral..................... 1772..1853
Cockburn, Henry Dundas, Lord. Scottish Judge....... 1779..1854
Cockburne, William. Medical Writer................ 1650?.1736?
Cocker, Edward. Arithmetician..................... 1631..1677?
Cockerill, John. English Engineer .... 1790..1840
Cookson, Thomas. Engraver........................ fl. 1630
Coda, Benedict. Ferrarese Painter .... 1460?.1520?
Coddington, William. Founder of the Colony of Rhode
    Island... 1601..1678
Codinus, Georgius. *Curopalates.* Greek Compiler..... —aft.1453
Codratus. Greek Physician, Saint, and Martyr .... — .. 258?
Codrington, Christopher. Scholar and Benefactor..... 1668..1710
Codrington, Sir Edward. Vice-Admiral .... 1770..1851
Codrington, Robert. Miscel. Writer and Translator.... 1602..1665
Codrus. Last King of Athens.................... —ab.B.C.1068
Coeck, or Koeck, Peter, or Van Aelst. Flemish Painter. 1500..1550
Coeffeteau, Nicholas. Translator of Florus........... 1574..1623
Coehorn, or Cohorn, Menno, Baron von. Dutch Engineer 1641?.1704?
Cœlestius. Heresiarch; Partisan of Pelagius.......... —aft. 430
Coello, Alonzo Sanchez. *Portuguese Titian.* Painter... 1515..1590
Coello, Claudio. Spanish Painter................... 1621..1693
Coelmans, James. Engraver of Antwerp............. 1670?.1735
Coeln, William von. *Meister Wilhelm.* German Painter fl. 1370
Coen, John Peterson. Dutch Governor in East Indies... 1587..1629
Coëssin, F. G. French Mystic.....................1782.1842 or 3
Cœur, James. French Merchant..................... — ..1456
Coffey, Charles. Poet............................ — ..1745
Coffin, Sir Isaac. English Admiral.................. 1759..1839
Coffin, Richard, or Robert. South American Poet...... 1797..1827
Cogan, Thomas, M. D., of Manchester. Medical Writer.. — ..1607
Cogan, Thomas, M. D. Co-founder of the Royal Humane
    Society. (*On the Passions*)..................... 1736..1818
Coggeshalle, Ralph, Abbot of. Historian............. — ..1228
Cogswell, William. American Clergyman and Writer... 1789..1850
Cohausen, John Henry. German Physician. (*Hermip-
    pus Redivivus*)................................. 1665..1750
Cohorn, or Coehorn, Menno, Baron von. Dutch Engineer 1641?.1704?
Coictier, or Coitier, James. Physician to Louis XI...... — ..1505?
Coignet, Giles. *Giles of Antwerp.* Painter........... 1530..1600
Cointe, Charles le. French Ecclesiastical Historian..... 1611..1681
Coiter, Volcher. Anatomist at Groningen .... 1534..1576?
Cokayne, Sir Aston. Poet......................... 1608..1684
Coke, Sir Edward. Lord Chief Justice................ 1549..1634

BORN. DIED.

Coke, Dr. Thomas. Founder of Wesleyan Missions..... 1747..1814
Cola, Gennaro di. Neapolitan Painter................. 1320..1370?
Cola dell' Amatrice. Painter and Architect.......... fl.1525-42
Colantonio, Marzio di. Italian Painter............... 1662..1701
Colardeau, Charles Peter. French Poet.............. 1732..1766
Colbach, John. Medical Writer.....................fl.1695-1719
Colbert, John Baptist. Financier. L. by P. Clément, 1846 1619..1683
Colbert, John Baptist, Marquis de Torci, son. French
 Minister of Marine.............................. 1665..1746
Colburn, Warren. American Mathematician.......... 1793..1833
Colburn, Zerah. American Mathematical Prodigy...... 1804..1840
Colby, Thomas, Major-General. Ordnance Surveyor... 1784..1852
Colchester, Charles Abbot, Lord. Speaker........... 1757..1829
Colden, Cadwallader. Naturalist. (Five Nations)...... 1688..1776
Cole, Charles Nelson. Legal Antiquary............... 1722..1804
Cole, Henry, D. D. Dean of St. Paul's. Roman Catholic
 Controversialist .... — ..1579
Cole, Thomas. Dissenting Divine. (On Regeneration).. — ..1697
Cole, Thomas. Painter .... 1801..1848
Cole, William. Herbalist. (Adam in Eden)............ 1626..1662
Cole, William. Medical Writer (M. D. 1666)............ fl. 17th c.
Cole, Rev. William. Antiquary..................... 1714..1782
Colebrooke, Henry Thomas. Orientalist............. 1765..1837
Coleridge, Hartley. Writer & Poet. L. by brother, 1851 1796..1849
Coleridge, Henry Nelson. Writer................... 1800..1843
Coleridge, Samuel Taylor. Metaphysician & Poet. L. by
 self (Biographia Literaria); Gilman, 1840; Cottle, 1847 1772..1834
Coleridge, Sara, daughter. Writer.................. 1803..1852
Coles, Elisha. (Dictionary)......................... 1640?.1700?
Colet, John. Dean of St. Paul's. Life by Dr. Samuel
 Knight, 1726; Erasmus, in "Phœnix," Vol. II...... 1466..1519
Coley, Henry. Astrologer........................... 1633..1690
Colgan, John. Irish Franciscan. Hagiologist......... — ..1658
Coli, John. Italian Fresco Painter.................. 1634..1681
Coligni, Gaspard de. Admiral. Life by Courtiltz, 1686. 1517..1572
Coligni, Henrietta, Countess de la Suze, dau. Poetical Wr. 1618..1673
Colignon, Francis. French Engraver................. 1621?.1671
Colin, Alexander. Belgian Sculptor................. 1520..1612
Colinæus, or Colines, Simon. Printer at Paris......... — 1546 or 7
Collado, Diego. Spanish Missionary in the East....... — .. 1638
Collaert, Adrian. Engraver and Printseller of Antwerp. 1520?.1567
Collaert, Hans, or John, son. Designer and Engraver. fl.1555-1622
Collanges, Gabriel de. French Writer. (Polygraphy).. 1521..1572
Collé, Charles. French Poet and Song Writer .... 1709..1783
Colle, John. Italian Medical Writer.................. 1558..1630
Colle, Raffaellino del. Italian Painter.............. 1490..1530
Colleone, Bartholomew. Venetian Generalissimo....... 1400..1475
Colleoni, Jerome. Painter of Bergamo.............. fl. 1556
Colles, Christopher. Philosophic Adventurer.......... 1738?.1821
Collet, John. English Humorous Painter............. 1725..1780
Collet, Peter. French Controversial Divine........... 1693..1770
Collet, Philibert. French Writer.................... 1643..1718
Colletet, William. French Poet.................... 1598..1659
Colletta, Peter. Neapolitan Patriot .... 1775..1831

BORN. DIED.

Collier, Arthur.   English Philosopher .... 1680..1732
Collier, Jeremy.   Nonjuring Bishop. (*Eccles. History*).. 1650..1726
Collin, Henry Joseph.   German Medical Writer .... 1731..1784
Collin, Henry Joseph von.   German Poet............... 1772..1811
Collin, Matthew von, brother.   German Tragic Poet .... 1779..1826
Collin d'Harleville, John Francis.   Dramatist and Poet 1755..1806
Collings, John.   Ejected Nonconformist and Critic...... 1623..1690
Collingwood, Cuthbert, Admiral Lord. Life by G. L. N.
    Collingwood, 1829 .... 1748..1810
Collini, Cosmo Alexander.   Italian Scholar............ 1727..1806
Collins, Anthony.   Deist.............................. 1676..1729
Collins, Arthur.   (*Peerage*).......................... 1682..1760
Collins, David.   Governor of Van Diemen's Land. (*His-
    tory of Botany Bay*)................................. 1756..1810
Collins, John.   Mathematician........................ 1624..1683
Collins, Richard.   Engraver at Brussels fl.1664–85
Collins, Samuel.   Eng. Phys. and Naturalist in Russia.. fl.1650–85
Collins, William.   Poet. Life by W. Moy Thomas....... 1720..1756
Collins, Wm., R.A.   Painter. L. by W. W. Collins, 1848 1787..1847
Collinson, Rev. John.   Topographer. (*Somerset*)....... — ..1793
Collinson, Peter.   Botanist........................... 1694..1768
Collius, Francis, of Milan.   Writer. (*De Animabus Pag-
    anorum*) .... — ..1640
Collot, Germain.   French Surgeon. *See Colot*......... fl.1461–80
Collot d'Herbois, John Mary.   French Revolutionist... 1750..1796
Collyer, Joseph.   Engraver........................... 1748..1827
Colman, George.   Dramatic Poet. Translator of Terence 1733?.1794
Colman, George, son.   Dramatic Poet ....:............ 1762..1836
Colocci, Angelo.   Italian Bishop and Latin Poet .... 1467..1549
Colocotronis, Theodore .... 1770..1843
Cologne, Peter de.   Protestant Minister at Metz........ — ..1558
Colomb, Paul de Batines.   French Writer on Dante..... 1812..1855
Colombel, Nicholas.   French Painter .... 1646..1717
Colombière, Claude de la.   French Jesuit............. 1611..1682
Colomboni, Angiol Maria.   Painter................... 1608..1672
Colomiès, or Colomesius, Paul. (*Icon Theologorum Pres-
    byterianorum*)....................................... 1638..1692
Coloni, Adam.   *The Old.* Dutch Painter in London..... 1634..1685
Coloni, Henry Adrian.   *The Young,* son. Painter ...... 1668..1701
Colonna, Ascanius.   Cardinal. Collector of Books...... 1560?.1608
Colonna, Fabio.   Italian Philosopher.................. 1567?.1650
Colonna, Francis.   Venetian Writer. (*Hypnerotomachia*) 1443..1527
Colonna, Francis Maria Pompeo.   Botanist. (*Natural
    History of the Universe*)............................ 1649?.1726
Colonna, Giles.   Italian Theologian .... — ..1316
Colonna, John Paul.   Composer of Church Music....... fl. 1690?
Colonna, Mark Anthony, jr.   Italian General........... — ..1584
Colonna, Michael Angelo.   Italian Painter............ 1600..1687
Colonna, Pompeo.   Cardinal. (*De Laudibus Muliebrum*) — ..1532
Colonna, Prospero.   Italian General.................. 1452..1523
Colonna, Vittoria, Marchioness of Pescara.   Poetess 1490:.1547
Colot, Francis.   Lithotomist .... — ..1706
Colot, or Collot, Germain.   Fr. Surgeon and Lithotomist. fl. 1461–80
Colot, Lawrence.   Lithotomist....................... fl. 1550

BORN. DIED.

Colotes. Sculptor of Paros .... fl. B. C. 444
Colquhoun, Patrick, LL. D. Statistical Writer........ 1745..1820
Colrane, Henry Hare, Ld. Scot.Writ. and Book Collector 1693..1749
Colson, John. Lucasian Professor at Cambridge........ — ..1760
Colston, Edward. Benefactor .... 1636..1721
Colt, Samuel. Amer. Mechanician; Invent. of Colt's Rifle 1814..1862
Colton, Calvin. Amer. Clergyman and Political Writer. 1789..1857
Colton, Rev. Charles Caleb. (*Lacon*) .... 1780..1832
Colton, Walter. American Clergyman and Writer ..... 1797..1851
Columba, St. Life by Adamanus; J. Smith, 1798 ...... 521?. 597
Columbanus, St. Life by Jonas of Bobbio .... 543?. 615
Columbus, Bartholomew........................... 1437..1514
Columbus, Christopher, brother. Life by his son Ferdinand, 1530; Cotolendi; Spotorno, 1823; Washington Irving, 1825........................... 1436?.1506
Columbus, Rualdus. Anatomist..................... — ..1577
Columella. Roman Agricultural Writer............fl. ti. Seneca
Columna, Guy. Sicilian Chronicler.................. fl. 1287
Coluthus. Greek Epic Poet. (Ἑλένης ἁρπαγή)........ fl. 500?
Colville, John. Scottish Writer .... — ..1607
Colvius, Andrew. Dutch Poet and Book Collector ..... 1594..1671
Colvius, Nicholas, son. Divine.................... 1634..1717
Colwill, Alexander. Scottish Satirical Poet........... 1620..1676
Combe, Andrew, M.D. Physiologist. L. by G. Combe, 1850 1797..1847
Combe, Charles, M.D. Classical Scholar and Numismatist 1743..1817
Combe, George. Phrenologist. (*Constitution of Man*) .. 1788..1858
Combefis, Francis. French Writer.................. 1605..1679
Comber, Thos. Dean of Durham. L. by T. Comber, 1799 1644..1699
Comenius, John Amos. Moravian. (*Janua Linguarum*) 1592..1671
Comes, Natalis. *Natal Conti*. Greek and Latin Poet... — ..1582?
Comiers, Claude. French Mathematician .... — ..1693
Comines, Philip de. Historian .... 1445..1509
Comitolo, Paul. Jesuit Writer..................... 1545..1626
Commandine, Frederick. Italian Mathematician ...... 1509..1575
Commelin, Gaspar. Botanist .... 1667..1731
Commelin, Isaac. Dutch Historian.................. 1598..1676
Commelin, Jerome. French Printer.................. — ..1598
Commelin, John. Dutch Botanist.................... 1629..1692
Commendone, John Francis. Card. Latin Poet of Italy 1524..1584
Commerson, Philibert. French Physician and Botanist. 1727..1773
Commire, John. French Jesuit. Latin Poet .... 1625..1702
Commodianus, of Gaza. Christian Poet. (*Institutiones*) fl. 4th c.
Commodo, Andrew. Italian Historical Painter .... 1560..1638
Commodus. Roman Emperor (180–92) .... 161.. 192
Commonfort, Ygnacio. Mexican General and Statesman 1812..1863
Como, Fra Emanuel da. Historical Painter............ 1625?.1701
Comodi, or Commodo, Andrew. Florentine Hist. Painter 1560..1638
Compton, Henry. Bishop of London.................. 1632..1713
Compton, Spencer, Earl of Northampton. Royalist..... 1601..1643
Comstock, John Lee, M. D. Amer. Auth. of School Books 1789..1858
Comte, Auguste. French Philosopher .... 1798..1857
Comte, Louis le. Jesuit Missionary to China........... — ..1729
Comte, Nicholas de. French Monk and Writer .... — ..1689
Comyns, Sir John. Judge. (*Digest of English Law*)... — ..1740

	BORN.	DIED.

Conant, John. Divine............................ 1608..1693
Conca, Sebastian. Italian Historical Painter........... 1676..1764
Concanen, Matthew. Political Writer and Poet........ — ..1749
Concina, Daniel, of Venice. (*System of Theology*)...... 1686..1756
Concini, or Marshal D'Ancre. Marshal of France ..... — ..1617
Condamine, Charles Mary de la. Traveler........... 1701..1774
Condé, Henry I., Prince of........................... 1552..1588
Condé, Henry II., Prince of. Renounced Protestantism.
   Minister of State. Life by Renaudot, 1646.......... 1588..1646
Condé, Joseph Anthony. Spanish Orientalist .... 1765?.1820
Condé, Louis, First Prince of. Huguenot; killed at Jarnac 1530..1569
Condé, Louis II., Prince of. *The Great.* Duc d'Enghien;
   Commander. Life by Coste; Desormeaux, 1768; Lord
   Mahon, 1845 .... 1621..1686
Conder, John, D. D. Dissenting Divine................ 1714..1781
Conder, Josiah. Poet. Life by E. R. Conder, 1857..... 1789..1855
Condillac, Stephen-Bonnot de. Metaphysician......... 1715?.1780
Condivi, Ascanius. Painter and Sculptor. (*Life of Michael Angelo*)................................. 1520.. —
Condorcet, M. J. A. N. Caritat, Marquis of. Metaphys.. 1743?.1794
Condren, Charles de. French Oratorian. L. by Amelotte 1588..1641
Conecte, Thomas de. French Carmelite Preacher ..... — ..1434
Conegliano, Il. *John Baptist Cima.* Painter.......... 1460..1517?
Conei, or Cowne, George. Scottish Roman Catholic.
   (*Life of Mary Stuart*)............................ — ..1640
Coney, John. Engraver........................... 1787?.1833
Confucius. *Kung-fu-tse.* Chinese Philosopher ....551. 479 B. C.
Congleton, Henry Brooke Parnell, Lord. Politician .... 1776..1842
Congreve, Wm. Dramatic Poet. L. by Chas. Wilson, 1730 1670..1729
Congreve, Sir Wm. Lieut.-Colonel. Inventor of Rockets 1772..1828
Conington, Rev. F. T., of Oxford. Scholar and Writer. 1828?.1863
Conner, David. American Naval Officer .... 1792?.1856
Connor, Bernard. Irish Physician. (*History of Poland*). 1666..1698
Conolly, Colonel. Envoy to Bokhara; murdered ...... — ..1843
Conon. Athenian Commander....................... — aft.B.C.393
Conrad I. Count of Franconia. King of Germany..... — .. 918
Conrad II. Emperor of Germany. *The Salic*.......... — ..1039
Conrad III........................................ 1093..1152
Conrad IV........................................ 1228..1254
Conrad, or Conradin, son; beheaded by Charles of Anjou 1252..1268
Conrad, of Wurtzburg. German Minnesinger.......... — ..1287
Conrad, or Coenrads, Abraham. Dutch Engr. & Designer 1620?. —
Conrad, Robert T. American Judge and Poet .... 1810..1858
Conrart, Valentine. Founder of the French Academy... 1603..1675
Conri, Florence. Irish Friar and Theologian .... 1560..1629
Conringius, Hermann. Jurist, Antiquarian, & Philosopher 1606..1681
Consalvi, Ercole. Cardinal. Roman Statesman .... 1757..1824
Consentius. Grammarian of Constantinople........... fl. 450?
Consetti, Anthony. Italian Historical Painter......... 1686..1766
Constable, Archibald. Publisher. (*Miscellany*)........ 1775..1827
Constable, Henry. Poet........................... fl. 16th c.
Constable, John, R. A. Painter. L. by C. R. Leslie, 1815 1776..1837
Constans I. Emperor of Rome (337–50)............... 320.. 350
Constans II. (641–68.) Roman Emperor of the East... 630.. 668

BORN. DIED.

Constant de Rebecque, David. Swiss Prot. Theologian 1638..1733
Constant de Rebecque, Henry Benjamin. French Orator, Statesman, and Writer........................ 1767..1830
Constantin Faulcon. Greek Adventurer............ 1648..1688
Constantine I. *The Great.* Emperor of Rome (306–37).
    Life by Eusebius; J. Reuchlin...................... 272?. 337
Constantine II. (337–40)........................... 316?. 340
Constantine III. (641).............................. 612.. 641
Constantine IV. (668–85.) *Pogonatus, or Barbatus* ... 648.. 685
Constantine V. *Copronymus.* (741–75).............. 718.. 775
Constantine VI. (780–797).......................... 771.. 797
Constantine VII. *Porphyrogenitus.* (911–59)......... 905.. 959
Constantine VIII. (944–45)......................... — .. 947
Constantine IX. (976–1028)......................... 961..1028
Constantine X. *Monomachus.* (1042–54)............. 1000?.1054
Constantine XI. *Ducas.* (1059–67)................. 1007?.1067
Constantine XII. *Ducas.* (1067–78)................ —1078 or 82
Constantine XIII. *Palæologus.* (1448–53)........... 1394..1453
Constantine. Pope (708–15)......................... — .. 715
Constantine. *The African.* Orientalist and Physician. — ..1087
Constantine. Grand Prince of Russia, son of Paul ..... 1779..1831
Constantine, Anthony. Physician at Lyons........... — ..1616
Constantine, Robt. Fr. Schol. (*Lexicon Græco-Latinum*) — ..1605
Constantius I. *Chlorus.* Emperor of Rome (305–6) .... 250?. 306
Constantius II. (337–61)........................... 317.. 361
Constantius III. (421)............................. — .. 421
Constanzo, Angelo de. Hist. & Poet. (*History of Naples*) 1507..1591?
Contarini, Gaspar. Cardinal. Divine and Statesman.
    Life by John de la Casa......................... 1483..1542
Contarini, John. Historical and Portrait Painter....... 1549..1605
Contarini, Vincent. Ital. Classical Scholar & Antiquary 1577..1617
Conte, Guido del, or Fassi. Inventor of Scagliola....... 1584..1649
Conte, Jacopino del. Ital. Historical and Portrait Painter 1510..1598
Conte, Nicholas James. French Painter and Mechanician 1755..1805
Conti, Armand de Bourbon, Prince of.................. 1629..1666
Conti, Charles. Engraver at Vienna.................. 1742..1790
Conti, Francis. Florentine Historical Painter........... 1681..1760
Conti de Val Montone, Giusto de. Ital. Poet & Lawyer — ..1449
Conti, Luke. Engraver and Architect................. 1749..1790
Conti, Nicholas di. *De Comitibus.* Traveler........... fl. 1444
Contini, John Baptist. Architect..................... 1641..1723
Conto-Pertana, Joseph. Portuguese Poet............. — ..1735
Conway, Thos. Major-Gen. in Army of Amer. Revolution —aft.1778
Conybeare, John. Bishop of Bristol. (*Defence of Revealed Religion*)................................... 1692..1755
Conybeare, John Josias. Divine, Critic, Antiquary .... 1779..1824
Conybeare, Wm. Daniel. Dean of Llandaff. Geologist 1787..1857
Conybeare, Rev. Wm. John. (*L. of St. Paul; Ch. Parties*) — ..1857
Cooghen, Leonard van. Painter...................... 1610..1681
Cook, George, D. D. Scottish Divine and Historian...... 1795..1845
Cook, Henry. Painter............................... 1642..1700
Cook, Captain James. Navigator. Life by Kippis, 1788 1728..1779
Cooke, Sir Anthony. Preceptor to Edward VI.......... 1506?.1576
Cooke, Dr. Benjamin. Musical Composer............. 1739..1793

BORN. DIED.

Cooke, George. Engraver............................ 1781..1834
Cooke, George Frederick. Actor.................... 1755..1812
Cooke, John Rodgers. American Jurist.............. 1788..1854
Cooke, Philip Pendleton. American Poet .... 1816..1850
Cooke, Robert. Divine and Scholar................. — ..1614
Cooke, Thomas. Poet. Translator of Hesiod........... 1702?.1756
Cooke, Thomas. Musician........................... 1781..1848
Cooke, T. P. Actor................................ 1786?.1864
Cooke, Rev. Wm. Poet and Biographer. (*Conversation*) — ..1814
Cooke, William. Lawyer. (*Bankrupt Laws*).......... 1757..1832
Cooley, Thomas. Irish Architect.................... 1740..1784
Coombe, William. (*Dr. Syntax*) .... 1741..1823
Cooper, Anthony Ashley, 1st E. Shaftesbury. Statesman 1621..1683
Cooper, Anthony Ashley, 3d E. Shaft. (*Characteristics*) 1671..1713
Cooper, Sir Astley Paston. Surgeon. L. by B. B. Cooper 1768..1841
Cooper, James Fenimore. American Novelist......... 1789..1851
Cooper, John Gilbert. Poet and Miscellaneous Writer.. 1723..1769
Cooper, Dr. Miles. Divine and Poet .... — ..1785
Cooper, Richard. *British Poussin.* Painter and Engraver.
    (*Views of Windsor*)............................ —aft.1806
Cooper, Richard. Paint. & Engrav. (*View of St.Peter's*) 1730..1820?
Cooper, Samuel. Miniature Painter................. 1609..1672
Cooper, Rev. Samuel. American Patriot and Theologian 1725..1823
Cooper, Thomas. Bishop of Winchester (1584–94)...... 1517?.1594
Cooper, Thomas. Natural Philos., Lawyer, & Politician 1759..1840
Coote, Sir Charles, Viscount. Irish Politician.......... — ..1661
Coote, Sir Eyre. Commander in India................. 1726..1783
Cootwyck, or Kootwyck, Jurian. Dutch Goldsm. & Engr. 1714.. —
Cop, William. Swiss Physician (M. D. 1495)........... — ..1532
Cope, Sir John. Eng. General; defeated at Prestonpans. 1745.. —
Copernicus, Nicholas. Astronomer.................. 1473..1543
Cophsis, Samuel. Spanish Rabbi.................... — ..1034
Coplestone, Edward. Bishop of Llandaff (1827–49). Life
    by W. J. Coplestone, 1851........................ 1776..1849
Copley, John Singleton. Painter .... 1737..1815
Copley, John Singleton, Ld. Lyndhurst, son. Ld. Chanc. 1772..1863
Coppa, Il Cavalier. *Antony Giarola.* Historical Painter 1595..1665
Coppetta. *Francis Beccuti.* Italian Poet .... 1509..1553
Coppi, James. Florentine Painter.................. 1523..1591
Coq, Peter le. French Canonist.................... 1728..1777
Coquelin, Charles. French Political Economist........ 1803..1852
Coques, Gonzalo, of Antwerp. Painter.............. 1618..1684
Coradi, or Curadi, Octavius. Bolognese Painter....... — ..1643
Coram, Capt. Thomas. Founder of Foundling Hospital . 1668?.1751
Coras, James de. Fr. Poetical Writ. (*Jonah and Nineveh*) 1630..1677
Coras, John de. Fr. Civilian. Life by James de Coras. 1513..1572
Coray, Adamantios. Modern Greek Author............ 1748..1833
Corbet, John. Ejected Nonconformist. Writer........ 1620..1680
Corbet, Richard. Bishop. Poet. Life by Gilchrist, 1807 1582..1635
Corbulo, Cneius Domitius. Roman Commander....... — .. 67
Corcoran, Michael. American General............... 1827..1863
Cordara, Julius Cæsar. (*Historia Societatis Jesu*)....... 1704..1784
Corday d'Armans, Marianne Charlotte de. Assassinator
    of Marat... 1768..1793

BORN. DIED.

Corde, Maurice de la. Fr. Huguenot Scholar and Phys. fl. 1559–84
Cordemoy, Gerard de. French Historian.............. — ..1684
Cordemoy, Louis Gerard de, son. French Theologian .. 1651..1722
Corder, Balthasar. Dutch Jesuit; Greek Critic........ 1592..1650
Cordes, John de. French Writer.................... 1570..1642
Cordier, or Corderius, Mathurin. (*Colloquies*).......... 1478..1564
Cordieri, Nicholas. *Il Franciosino*. Sculptor......... 1561..1612
Cordiner, Charles. Topographer and Antiquary........ 1746..1794
Cordova, Adrian of. Spanish Carmelite; Hist. Painter.. — ..1630
Cordova, Francis Fernandez de. Spanish Navigator.... — ..1518
Cordova, Joseph M. South American General .... 1797?.1829
Cordova, Louis Fernandez de. Spanish General ...... 1799..1840
Corduba, Francis. Italian Painter and Engraver....... — .. —
Cordus, Euricius. German Medical and Poetical Writer. 1486..1538
Cordus, Valerius, son. Botanist .... 1515..1544
Corelli, Arcangelo. Italian Violinist ....:........... 1653..1713
Corenzio, Belisarius. Greek Painter at Naples........ 1558?.1643
Coriate, or Coryate, George. Latin Poet.............. — ..1606
Coriate, or Coryate, Thomas. Traveler and Writer..... 1577..1617
Corilla. *Mary Magdalen Fernandez*. Improvvisatrice.. 1740..1800
Corinna. Greek Poetess............................ fl. B.C. 490?
Corio, Bernardine. Historian of Milan............... 1459..1519
Coriolano, Bartholomew. Engraver .... 1590..1654
Coriolano, Christopher. Designer and Engraver on Wood 1560?.1600?
Coriolano, John Baptist. Engraver.................... 1595..1649
Coriolanus. Roman General .... —aft.B.C.489
Cormontaigne, Louis de. French Military Engineer.... 1696?.1752
Cornachini, Mark. Medical Writer.................... fl. 1607
Cornachini, Thomas. Italian Medical Writer.......... — ..1605
Cornarius, John. German Medical Writer............. 1500..1558
Cornaro, or Cornelio, Flaminius. Italian Historian..... 1693..1778
Cornaro, Francis. Cardinal Bishop of Brescia.......... 1479?.1543
Cornaro, George Basil. Cardinal Bishop of Padua..... 1658..1722
Cornaro, Louis, of Venice. (*Discorsi della Vita Sobria*). 1467..1566
Cornaro-Piscopia, Lucretia Helena. Venetian Scholar. 1646..1684
Cornazzani, Anthony. Italian Poet.................. fl. 15th c.
Corneille, John Baptist. Painter and Engraver........ 1646..1695
Corneille, Michael. French Painter and Engraver...... 1603..1664
Corneille, Michael, son. Painter and Engraver........ 1642..1708
Corneille, Peter. Dramatic Poet.................... 1606..1684
Corneille, Thomas, brother. Dramatist. (*Dict. of Art*) 1625..1709
Cornelia. Roman Matron; wife of Gracchus.......... 2d c. B.C.
Cornelis, or Cornely. *Cornelius van Haerlem*. Painter. 1562..1638
Cornelisz, or Cornelissen, Jacob, of Amsterdam. Painter 1471?.1567
Cornelisz, or Cornelius, Lucas. Dutch Painter........ 1493..1552
Cornelius, St. Bishop of Rome (250–52).............. — .. 252
Corner, George Richard. Antiquary and Legal Writer.. 1801?.1863
Cornetto, Adrian. *Castellesi*. Cardinal. Bishop of Bath
    and Wells....................................... —aft.1518
Cornhert, or Coornhert, Diederik. Dutch Writer....... 1522..1590
Corniani, John Baptist, Count de. Italian Writer...... 1742..1813
Cornwallis, Sir Charles. Ambassador to Spain........ — ..1630?
Cornwallis, Charles, 1st Marquess of. Gov.-Gen. of India 1738..1805
Corona, Leonard. Historical Painter.................. 1561..1605

BORN. DIED.

Coronado, Francis Vasquez de. Spanish Explorer..... — ..1542
Coronelli, Mark Vincent, of Venice. Math. & Geographer 1650?.1718
Corr, Erin. Belgian Engraver....................... 1803..1862
Corradi, Dominic. *Il Ghirlandajo.* Florentine Painter. 1449..1498
Corradini de Sezza, Peter Marcellinus. Cardinal...... 1658..1743
Corradus, Sebastian. Grammarian of Bologna........ — ..1556
Correa de Serra, Joseph Francis. Portuguese Scholar.. 1750..1823
Correggio, Antonio Allegri da. Italian Painter. Life by
    Mengs; Coxe, 1823 .... 1494..1534
Corri, Dominic. Musical Composer. (*The Traveler*)... 1744..1825
Corrie, Daniel. Bishop of Madras. Life by his brothers 1777..1837
Corrozet, Giles. Bookseller and Writer at Paris........ 1510..1568
Corsini, Edward, of Pisa. Philosopher & Mathematician 1702..1765
Cort, Cornelius. Dutch Artist and Engraver .... 1536..1578
Cort, Henry, of Gosport. Metallurgist................. 1740..1800
Corte, Cæsar. Genoese Painter....................... 1550..1613?
Corte, David, son. Painter........................ — ..1657
Cortereal, Gasper. Portuguese Navigator........... — ..1502?
Cortesi, Giovanna. Painter of Florence............... 1670?.1736
Cortés, Hernando. Conqueror of Mexico............. 1485..1554
Cortesi, or Courtois, Jas. *Il Borgognone.* Pa. of Battles. 1621..1676
Cortesi, Wm., brother. *Il Borgognone.* Historical Painter 1628..1679
Cortesius, Paul. Ital. Theologian. (*De Hominibus Doctis*) 1465..1510
Cortez, Gregory. Italian Classical Scholar............ 1483..1548
Cortez, Hernando. *See* Cortés....................... 1485..1554
Corti, Matthew. *Curtius.* Italian Medical Writer...... 1475..1544
Corticelli, Salvator. Italian Grammarian............. 1690..1758
Cortona, Pietro da. *Berettini.* Ital. Painter & Architect 1596..1669
Corvini, Matthew. King of Hungary and Bohemia..... — ..1490
Corvinus, John Augustus. German Engraver .... 1682..1738
Corvisart Desmarets, John Nicholas. Fr. Med. Writer 1755..1821
Coryate. *See* Coriate.
Cosimo, Peter da. Italian Painter................... 1441..1521
Cosin, John. Bishop of Durham..................... 1594..1672
Cosmas. *Indicopleustes.* Egyptian Merchant.......... fl. 522–47
Cosmas, of Jerusalem. Monk and Hymnologist .... fl. 743?
Cosme, John Baseilhac. French Lithotomist.......... 1703..1781
Cosmo I. De' Medici. Grand Duke of Tuscany. Life
    by Aldus Manutius, jr., 1585...................... 1519..1574
Cosmo II. De' Medici. Grand Duke of Tuscany....... 1590..1621
Cosmo III. De' Medici. Grand Duke of Tuscany. Life
    by R. Stewart, 1821............................... 1642..1723
Cospean, or Cospeau, Philip. Fr. Prelate and Preacher. 1568..1646
Cossali, Peter. Italian Mathematician. (*Hist. of Algebra*) 1748..1815
Cossart, Gabriel. French Jesuit; Writer .... 1615..1674
Cossé, Charles de, Count de Brissac. French Marshal... 1505..1563
Cossiers, John, of Antwerp. Historical Painter .... 1603..1652
Cossin, Coquin, or Cawquin, Louis. French Engraver.. 1633..1682
Costa, Emanuel Mendez da. Naturalist............ — .. —
Costa, George da. Portuguese Cardinal. Statesman.... 1406..1508
Costa, Isaac de. Dutch Poet....................... 1798..1860
Costa, Lorenzo. Ferrarese Painter.................. — ..1530?
Costa, Paul. Italian Author....................... 1771..1836
Costanzi, Placido. Italian Painter................... 1688..1759

BORN. DIED.

Costanzo, Angelo di. Neapolitan Poet. (*Hist. of Naples*) 1507..1591
Costard, Rev. George. Oriental Writer................. 1710?.1782
Coste, Peter. French Protestant Writer .... 1668..1747
Coster, Lawrence Jansen, of Haarlem. Printer........ 1370?.1440?
Cosway, Richard, R. A. Miniature Portrait Painter..... 1740..1821
Cota, Rodriguez de. *Elder.* Spanish Poet............ 15th c.
Cotelerius, J. Bapt. Gr. Scholar & Editor. L. by Baluze 1627..1686
Cotes, Francis. Painter................................ 1726..1770
Cotes, Roger. Mathematician and Astronomer......... 1682..1716
Cotin, Charles. French Poet............................ 1604..1682
Cotman, John Sell. Artist of Norman Antiquities....... 1780?.1843
Cotolendi, Charles. French Biographer.............. — ..1710?
Cotta, John. Italian Scholar and Poet................ 1483?.1510
Cotta, John Fred., Baron von Cottendorf. Ger. Publisher 1764..1832
Cotte, Robert de. French Architect.................... 1656..1735
Cotterell, Sir Charles. Linguist and Scholar.......... — ..1687
Cottin, Sophia de. French Novelist. (*Elizabeth, or Exiles
    of Siberia*).. 1773..1807
Cottington, Francis, Lord. Statesman .... 1574?.1651
Cottle, Amos. Verse Writer......................... — ..1800
Cottle, Joseph. Publisher. (*Recollections of Coleridge*).. 1770..1853
Cotton, Charles. Burlesque Poet and Angler.......... 1630..1687
Cotton, John. American Divine....................... 1585..1652
Cotton, Nathaniel, M. D. Poet. (*Visions in Verse*)..... 1707..1788
Cotton, or Coton, Peter. Confessor to Henry IV. Life
    by P. J. Orleans.................................... 1564..1626
Cotton, Sir Robert Bruce. Collector of Cottonian Library 1570..1631
Cotugno, or Cotunius, Dominic. Anatomist. (*De Aqua-
    ductibus Auris*).................................... 1736..1822
Couch, Richard Quillar. English Surgeon and Scientist. 1816..1863
Couché, John. French Designer and Engraver .... — ..1759
Coucy, Rénaud, or Raoul de. French Minstrel........ fl. 12th c.
Coudrette, Christopher. Anti-Jesuit Writer........... 1701..1774
Coulet, Ann Philibert. French Engraver.............. 1736.. —
Coulomb, Charles Augustus de. Experimental Philosopher 1736..1806
Coulon, Louis. French Historian .... 1605..1664
Couperin, Francis. *The Great.* Fr. Musical Composer. 1668..1733
Couplet, Philip. Flemish Missionary to China .... 1628..1692
Courayer, Peter Francis le. French Divine .... 1681..1776
Courbes, John de. French Engraver.................. 1592?.
Courcelles, Stephen de. Arminian Divine and Critic ... 1586..1658
Courcelles, Thomas de. French Theologian.......... 1400..1469
Courier de Méré, Paul Louis. French Political Writer. 1773..1825
Courtanvaux, Francis Cæsar de Tellier, Marquis of. Offi-
    cer. Natural Philosopher .... 1718..1781
Court de Gébelin, Anthony. Writ. (*Le Monde Primitif*) 1725..1784
Courten, Sir Wm. Merchant and Capitalist in London. 1572?.1636
Courten, William. English Naturalist and Collector.... 1642..1702
Courtiltz de Sandras, Gatien. French Writer .... 1644..1712
Courtivron, Gaspar, Marquis of. Fr. Soldier and Scholar 1715..1785
Courtnay, John, M. P. (*Poetical Review of Dr. Johnson*) 1741..1816
Courtney, William. Archbishop of Canterbury (1381-96) 1341..1396
Courtois, or Cortesi, James. *Bourguignon.* French Painter 1621..1676
Courtois, William, brother. *Bourguignon.* Painter .... 1628..1679

8

BORN. DIED.

Cousin, John. French Painter, Sculptor, Geometrician.
  (*Livre de Perspective*) .... 1500?.1590
Cousinet, Catherine Elizabeth. French Engraver ...... 1726.. —
Coustou, Nicholas. French Sculptor .... 1658..1733
Coustou, William, brother. Sculptor................. 1678..1746
Coustou, William. Sculptor and Architect .... 1716..1777
Coutelle, John Mary Joseph. French Engineer .... 1748..1835
Couthon, George. French Revolutionist .... 1756..1794
Coutts, Thomas. Banker .... 1731..1822
Couvay, John. French Designer and Engraver......... 1622.. —
Couvreur, Adrienne le. French Actress............... 1692..1730
Covarruvias, Diego. *Le Bartole Espagnole*. Canonist.. 1512..1577
Covell, John, D. D. Ambass. Vice-Chanc. of Cambridge 1638..1722
Coventry, Henry. (*Letters of Philemon*)............... — ..1752
Coventry, James. Mechanician .... 1812.. —
Coventry, Thos. Ld. Coventry of Aylesborough. Ld.Keeper 1578..1640
Coverdale, Miles. Bishop of Exeter (1551–53) .... 1485..1565
Coward, William, M.D. Medical and Metaphysical Writer 1656?.1725
Cowell, John, LL. D. Lawyer and Antiquary........... 1554..1611
Cowherd, Rev. William. Founder of the *Bible Christians* — ..1816
Cowley, Abraham. Poet. Life by Bishop Sprat........ 1618..1667
Cowley, Mrs. Hannah. Dramatic Poet................ 1743..1809
Cowley, Henry Wellesley, Lord. Diplomatist.......... 1773..1847
Cowper, Edward. Mechanician....................... 1790..1852
Cowper, William. Bishop of Galloway................ 1566..1619
Cowper, William. Anatomist of London. (*Myotomia*) .. 1666..1709
Cowper, William, First Earl Cowper. Lord Chancellor.. — ..1723
Cowper, Wm., D. D. Dean of Durham. Geom. and Writer 1714?.1772
Cowper, Wm. Poet. L. by Hayley; Southey; Grimshawe 1731..1800
Cox, David. Landscape Painter .... 1793..1859
Cox, Francis Aug., D. D. English Clergyman and Writer 1783..1853
Cox, Leonard. (*The Art or Craft of Rhetoryke*)......... — ..1549
Cox, Richard. Bishop of Ely (1559–81) .... 1499..1581
Cox, Sir Richard. Lord Chancellor of Ireland. Historian 1650..1733
Coxcie, or Coxis, Michael van. Flemish Painter........ 1497..1592
Coxe, Wm. Archdeacon. Historian. (*House of Austria*) 1747..1828
Coxeter, Thomas. Literary Collector .... 1689..1747
Coyer, Gabriel Francis. French Writer............... 1707..1782
Coypel, Anthony, son of Noel. French Painter........ 1661..1722
Coypel, Charles Anthony, son. French Painter .... 1694..1752
Coypel, Noel. French Painter........................ 1628..1707
Coypel, Noel Nicholas. *The Uncle*. French Painter.... 1688..1734
Coysevox, Anthony. Spanish Sculptor in France ...... 1640..1720
Cozza, Francis. Sicilian Historical Painter .... 1605..1682
Cozza, John Baptist. Italian Historical Painter .... 1676..1742
Craaneu, Theodore. Dutch Medical Writer............. — ..1688
Crabb, George. English Barrister and Philologist...... 1778..1854
Crabbe, Rev. George. Poet. Life by his son.......... 1754..1832
Crabeth, Dirk. Dutch Painter on Glass............... — ..1601
Crabeth, Wouter, brother. *The Elder*. Painter on Glass fl. 1560–68
Cradock, Luke. Painter of Birds..................... 1660?.1717
Cradock, Samuel. Ejected Nonconformist Writer ...... 1620..1706
Craesbeke, Joseph van, of Brussels. Painter .... 1608..1668
Crafts, William. American Lawyer and Author........ 1787..1826

BORN. DIED.

Craig, James. Scottish Divine and Poet.............. 1682..1744
Craig, Sir James Henry. General.................... 1748..1812
Craig, John. Scottish Reformer..................... 1511..1600
Craig, John. (*Theologiæ Christianæ Principia Mathematica*) fl. 1699
Craig, Nicholas. Danish Scholar and Historian........ 1549?.1602
Craig, Sir Thomas. Writer on Feudal Law. Life by P. F.
   Tytler, 1823.......................... 1548?.1608
Craig, William, D. D. Scottish Divine............... 1709..1784
Craig, William. Scottish Judge and Writer........... 1745..1813
Crakanthorpe, Richard. Preacher and Controv. Divine 1567..1624
Cramaud, Simon de. Cardinal .... —aft.1409
Cramer, Daniel. German Divine and Metaphysician ... 1568..1637
Cramer, Francis. Musical Composer.................. 1772..1848
Cramer, Gabriel. Swiss Mathematician .... 1704..1752
Cramer, John Andrew. German Chemist.............. 1710..1777
Cramer, John Andrew. German Theologian .... 1723..1788
Cramer, John Anthony, D. D. Classical Geographer.... 1793..1848
Cramer, John Baptist. Musical Artist and Composer... 1771..1858
Cramer, John Frederick. German Scholar and Historian — ..1715
Cramer, John Isaac, of Geneva. Medical Writer....... fl. 1700
Cramer, John James. Orientalist.................... 1673..1702
Cramer, John Rudolph. Hebraist at Zurich .... 1678..1737
Cramer, Nicholas. Flemish Painter................. 1670?.1710
Cranach, or Kranach, Lucas. German Painter........ 1472..1553
Cranch, William. American Jurist.................. 1769..1855
Crane, Thomas. Ejected Nonconformist. (*On Providence*) — ..1714
Crane, William M. American Naval Officer........... 1776..1846
Cranmer, Thomas, Archb. of Canterbury (1533–55). L.
   by Strype, 1694; Gilpin, 1784; Archd. H. J. Todd, 1831 1489..1556
Cranz, or Kranz, David. Moravian Missionary .... 1723..1777
Crapelet, Charles. French Printer.................. 1762..1809
Crapelet, George Adrian, son. Printer and Author..... 1789..1842
Crapone, Adam de. French Canal Engineer........... 1519..1559
Crashaw, Richard. Poet (B. A. 1633) .... — ..1650
Crasso, Lawrence. Italian Writer.................. fl. 1666
Crassus, Lucius Licinius. Orator .... 140–91 B.C.
Crassus, Marcus Licinius. Triumvir. *Dives*. Slain by
   Parthians.......................... 115?.53 B.C.
Craterus. General of Alexander the Great........... — B.C.321
Crates. Athenian Comic Poet .... fl. B.C. 450
Crates. Cynic Philosopher.......................... fl. B.C. 320
Crates. Athenian Philos.; Instructor of Arcesilaus.... fl. 3d c. B.C.
Cratinus. Athenian Comic Poet.................... 519–422 B.C.
Cratippus. Peripatetic Philosopher.
Craton, or Crafftheim, John .... 1519..1585
Craven, Eliz., Lady. Margravine of Anspach. *See* Anspach 1750..1828
Craveta, Aimon. Piedmontese Law Writer........... 1504..1569
Crawford, Adair. Physician and Naturalist .... 1749..1795
Crawford, Anne. Actress.......................... 1734..1801
Crawford, Geo. Historiographer. (*Lives of Officers of State*) fl. 1725
Crawford, Quintin. Writer .... 1743..1819
Crawford, Thomas. American Sculptor .... 1814..1857
Crawford, William. Scottish Divine. (*Dying Thoughts*) 1676..1742
Crawford, William Harris. American Statesman ...... 1772..1834

BORN. DIED.

Crawford, William Sharman, M. P. Politician .... — ..1861
Crawfurd, David. Historian and Antiquary. (*Memoirs*) 1665..1726
Crawfurd, John Lindsay, Earl of. Life by Richard Rolt. 1702..1749
Crawfurd, Thomas. Professor at Edinburgh .... — ..1662
Crayer, Gaspar. Flemish Painter................... 1582..1669
Creagh, Richard. Roman Catholic Archbishop of Armagh — ..1585
Crébillon, Claude Prosper Joliot de. French Novelist... 1707..1777
Crébillon, Prosper Joliot de. Classical Dramatical Writer 1674..1762
Credi, Lawrence Andrew di. Italian Painter........... 1454?.1536?
Creech, Thomas. Poet. Classical Translator......... 1659..1700
Creichton, John. Irish Soldier of Fortune............ 1648..1733
Creighton, Robert. Bp. of Bath and Wells. (*I will arise*) 1593..1672
Crell, Louis Christian. German Writer.............. 1671..1735
Crell, or Crellius, John. German Unitarian Divine ..... 1590..1633
Crell, Nicholas. Prime Minister of Christian I. of Saxony 1550?.1601
Cremonese. Painter. *See* Caletti .... 1600?.1660
Cremonini, Cæsar, of Padua. Aristotelian Philosopher.. 1550..1631
Cremonini, John Baptist. Painter at Bologna .... 1560?.1610
Crenius, Thomas. Dutch Philologist................. 1648..1728
Créqui de Blanchefort, Francis de. Marshal of France 1624?.1687
Crescentini, Jerome. Singer .... 1769..1846
Crescenzi. *Bartholomew Cavarazzi*. Painter......... 1590?.1625
Crescenzi, John Baptist, Marquis de la Torre. Painter . 1595..1660
Crescenzi, Peter de. *De Crescentiis*. Writer on Agriculture 1230..1320
Crescimbeni, John Maria. Italian Poet and Critic ..... 1663..1728
Crespi, Anthony, brother of Louis. Painter........... — ..1782?
Crespi, Daniel, of Milan. Painter.................. 1590..1630
Crespi, Giuseppe Maria. *Il Spagnuolo*. Bolognese Painter 1665..1747
Crespi, John Baptist. *Il Cerano*. Italian Painter...... 1557..1633
Crespi, Louis. Italian Painter and Writer .... — ..1779
Cresson, Elliott. American Philanthropist............ 1796..1854
Cresswell, Sir Cresswell. Judge of Divorce Court...... — ..1863
Cressy, Hugh Paulin. Rom. Cath. Eccles. Hist. & Div. . 1605..1674
Cresti, Dominic. *Passignano*. Italian Historical Painter 1558..1638
Creti, Donato. Italian Painter...................... 1671..1749
Crétin, William Dubois. French Poet................ — ..1525
Creutz, Gustavus Philip, Ct. of. Swed. Poet & Statesman 1726..1785
Creutzfelder, John George. German Portrait Painter.. — ..1633
Creuzer, George Fred. Ger. Antiq. (*Myth. of Antiquity*) 1771..1858
Crevalcore, Anthony da. Portrait Painter at Bologna.. fl. 1490
Crevier, John Baptist Louis. Historical Writer .... 1693..1765
Crew, Nathaniel, 3d Lord. Bishop of Durham (1674–1722) 1633..1722
Crichton, James. *The Admirable*. L. by Sir T. Urquhart;
    P. F. Tytler, 1823 .... 1560..1583
Crillon, Louis Athanasius B. B. de. Fr. Scholar & Divine 1726..1789
Crillon, Louis de Balbes de Berton de. French General.
    Besieged Rochelle. Life by Margaret de Lussan, 1757 1541..1615
Crillon Mahon, Louis de Berthon, Duke of. General.
    Besieged Gibraltar. (*Military Memoirs*) .... 1718..1796
Crillon Mahon, Louis Anthony Francis de Paule de,
    Duke of, son................................... 1775..1832
Crinesius, Christopher. Orientalist at Altorf........... 1584..1629
Crinitus, Peter. *Riccio*. Florentine Scholar........... 1465?.1505?
Crisp, Tobias, D. D. Puritan Divine. L. by Dr. John Gill 1600..1642

BORN. DIED.

Crispe, Sir Nicholas, of London. Royalist .... 1598..1666
Crispus, Anthony. Sicilian Physician................ 1600..1688
Cristofane. Painter of Bologna .... 1349..1387
Cristofori, or Cristofani, Fabio. Painter of Mosaic...... fl. 17th c.
Critias. Athenian Statesman; pupil of Socrates .... — B.C.404
Crittenden, John Jay. American Statesman .... 1786..1863
Crivellari, Bartholomew. Italian Sculptor and Engraver 1725..1777
Crivelli, Angelo Mary. Il Crivellone. Milanese Painter — ..1730
Crivelli, Charles. Venetian Painter .... —aft.1476
Crivelli, James. Painter of Birds and Fishes.......... — ..1760
Croce, Balthasar. Bolognese Painter.................. 1553..1628
Croce, St. Jerome di. Italian Painter ..:.............. fl.1520–49
Crockett, David. Am. Backwoodsman. L. by self, 1834. 1786..1836
Croese, Gerard. Dutch Protestant Divine and Historian 1642..1710
Crœsus, King of Lydia (B. C. 560–546)............... — B.C.546
Croft, Herbert. Bishop of Hereford (1662–91).......... 1603..1691
Croft, Rev. Sir Herbert. (Love and Madness) .... 1751..1816
Croft, William, MUS. DOC. Musical Composer.......... 1657?.1727
Crofton, Zachary. Nonconformist Divine .... — ..1672
Croius, or De Croi, John. French Divine. (Observationes
    in Novum Testamentum)......................... — ..1659
Croix, Alexander Louis Mary Petis de la. Orientalist... 1698..1751
Croix, Francis Petis de la. French Orientalist......... 1653..1713
Croix-du-Maine, Francis Grudé de la. Bibliographer.. 1552..1592
Croke, Sir Alexander, D. C. L. Civil and Miscel. Writer.. 1800..1842
Croke, or Crook, Sir George. Judge................. 1559..1641
Croke, Richard, D. D. Crocus. Reviver of Class. Learn. — ..1558
Croker, John Wilson. Writer....................... 1780..1857
Croker, Thomas Crofton, F. S. A. Antiquary.......... 1798..1854
Croll, Oswald. Ger. Medical Writer. (Basilica Chimica) — ..1609
Croly, Rev. George, LL. D. Writer.................. 1780..1860
Cromek, R. H. Editor of Scottish Ballads............. fl. 1811
Cromer, Julius. Il Croma. Italian Painter........... 1572?.1632
Cromer, Martin. Polish Historian.................. 1512..1589
Crompton, Samuel, of Bolton. Inventor of Spinning
    Mule. Life by G. J. French, 1859 .... 1753..1827
Crompton, William. Ejected Nonconformist Divine.... — ..1696
Cromwell, Henry, son of Oliver. Lord-Lieut. of Ireland 1628..1675
Cromwell, Oliver. Protector. Life by James Heath,
    1663; Raguenet, 1691; Leti, 1692; Isaac Kimber,
    1725; J. Banks, 1739; F. Peck, 1740; Dr. Wm. Har-
    ris, 1766; Mark Noble, 1791; Bishop Russell; Oli-
    ver Cromwell, 1822; Villemain; Southey; Philarète
    Chasles, 1847; F. P. G. Guizot, 1854; Hazlitt, 1857;
    Sawford; Wilson; Thomas Carlyle; Merle D'Aubigné 1599..1658
Cromwell, Richard, son. ....,... 1626..1712
Cromwell, Thomas, Earl of Essex.................... 1490?.1540
Cronegk, John Frederick, Baron de. German Poet..... 1731..1758
Cronstedt, Axel Frederick. Swedish Mineralogist..... 1722..1765
Crook, or Croke, Sir George. Judge................. 1559..1641
Croone, William, M. D. Medical Writer.............. — ..1684
Crosby, Brass. Lord Mayor. Popular Champion...... 1725..1793
Cross, John. Painter. (Richard I. pardoning the Archer) — ..1861
Cross, Louis. Painter .... — ..1724

BORN. DIED.

Cross, or De la Crux, Michael. Artist .... fl.ti.Ch.I.& II.
Crosse, Andrew. Experimenter on Electricity .... 1784..1855
Crosswell, Harry, D.D. Amer. Journalist and Clergyman 1778..1858
Crosswell, William, D.D., son. Clergyman .... 1804..1851
Crotch, Dr. William. Musical Composer............... 1775..1847
Crousaz, John Peter de. Swiss Divine and Philosopher. 1663..1748
Crowley, Robert. Divine and Poet .... — ..1588
Crowne, John. Dramatist .... — ..1703?
Croxall, Dr. Samuel. Political Writer and Poet........ — ..1752
Croze, Mathurin Veyssière de la. French Orientalist.... 1661..1739
Cruciger, Gaspar. Reformer........................ 1504..1548
Cruciger, George. Philologist. (*Harmonia Linguarum*) 1575..1636
Cruden, Alexander. (*Concordance*)................. 1701..1770
Cruickshank, Robert. Humorous Artist.............. 1791?.1856
Cruickshank, William. Anatomist................... 1746..1800
Cruquius, or De Crusques, of Ypres. Editor of Horace.. fl. 1578
Crusius, Christian Augustus. Ger. Philosophical Writer. 1715..1775
Crusius, or Kraus, Martin. German Greek Scholar ..... 1526..1607
Crux, Michael de la. *See* Cross .... fl.ti.Ch.I.& II.
Cruyl, Levinus. Flemish Engraver.................... 1640?. —
Cruys, Cornelius. Russian Naval Officer.............. 1657..1727
Cruz Cano y Olmeida, Anthony de la. Span. Geogr... 1735..1794?
Cruz, John Pantoja de la. Spanish Painter .... 1545..1610
Cruz, Juana Inez de la. Mexican Poetess and Scholar .. 1651..1695
Csángi, László. Hungarian Statesman .... 1790..1849
Csokonai, Mihaly Vitez. Hungarian Poet............. 1773..1805
Csoma de Körös, Alex. Hung. Scholar and Traveler . 1791..1842
Ctesias. Greek Physician and Historian.............. B.C.401–384
Ctesibius, of Alexandria. Mechanical Inventor........ 250 B. C.
Cubières, Amédée Louis Despons. French General .... 1786..1853
Cubitt, Thomas. Builder .... 1788..1855
Cubitt, Sir William. Civil Engineer................. 1785..1861
Cudworth, Ralph, D. D. (*Intellectual System.*) L. by Birch 1617..1688
Cuerenhert, Theodore van. Engraver................ 1522..1590
Cueva, Alonsus de la. *Bedmar.* Cardinal. Politician . 1572..1655
Cueva, John de la. Spanish Poet. (*Art of Poetry*)..... fl. 1582
Cuffe, Henry. Wit & Schol. Gr. Prof. at Oxf. Hanged 1560?.1601
Cujacius, or Cujas, James. French Jurist. L. by Berriot 1520..1590
Cullen, William. Scottish Medical Writer............. 1712..1790
Cullum, Rev. Sir John. Antiquary.................. 1733..1785
Culpeper, Sir Thomas. Writer on Usury............. 1636..1706?
Culpepper, Nicholas. Herbalist and Astrologer........ 1616..1654
Culvert, George. Choctaw Chief and Warrior .... 1744..1839
Culy, David, of Guyhirn. Sectary and Author......... — ..1718
Cumberland, Ernest Augustus, Duke of. Fifth son of
  George III. King of Hanover...................... 1771..1851
Cumberland, Richard. Bishop of Peterborough. Phi-
  losopher and Philologist. Opponent of Hobbes...... 1632..1718
Cumberland, Richard, great-grandson. Dramatic and
  Miscellaneous Writer. Life by self................ 1732..1811
Cumberland, William Augustus, Duke of. Son of
  George II. Commander. Life by Henderson, 1766.. 1721..1765
Cunæus, Peter. Lawyer and Antiquary. (*Jus Regium
  Hebræorum*).................................... 1586..1638

BORN. DIED.

Cunego, Domenico. Italian Engraver................ 1727..1794
Cunha, Barbosa, January da. Braz. Prel. and Statesman 1780..1846
Cunha, Mattos, Raymond Jos. da. Brazilian General... 1776..1840
Cunha, Tristan da. Portuguese Naval Commander .... fl. 15th c.
Cuningham, Edmund Francis. Scottish Painter .... 1742?.1793
Cuningham, William. Engraver and Phys. at Norwich 1520?.1577
Cunio, Daniel. Milanese Painter...................... fl. 16th c.
Cunio, Ridolfo. Milanese Painter..................... fl. 1650?
Cunitia, Maria. Silesian Scholar. (Urania Propitia).. — ..1664
Cunningham, Alexander. Scottish Historian......... 1654..1737
Cunningham, Allan. Poet, Novelist, and Misc. Writer. 1785..1842
Cunningham, John. Irish Poet and Actor .... 1729..1773
Cunningham, Rev. John Wm. Poet & Div. of Harrow. 1780?.1861
Cunningham, Rev. Wm., D.D., of Edinburgh. Principal 1805..1861
Cupani, Francis. Sicilian Botanist .... 1657..1711
Cuperus, Gisbert, of Deventer. Critic and Historian.... 1644..1716
Curæus, Joachim. Ger. Physician. (Annals of Silesia).. 1532..1573
Curcellæus, or Courcelles, Stephen. Arminian Divine.. 1586..1658
Cureton, Rev. William. Orientalist.................. 1808?.1864
Curio, Caius Scribonius. Roman General and Statesman — B.C. 53
Curio, C. Scribonius, son. Roman Orator and Statesman — B.C. 46
Curio, Cælius Secundus. Piedmontese Prot. Theologian. 1503..1569
Curita. See Zurita. Spanish Historian .... 1512..1581
Curl, Edmund. London Bookseller.................... — ..1748
Curling, Captain Henry. Novelist..................... — ..1864
Curradi, Cavalier Francis. Florentine Painter......... 1570..1661
Curran, John Philpot. Orator. Life by O'Regan, 1818;
    W. H. Curran, 1819; A. Barrister, 1844; T. Davis, 1846 1750..1817
Currie, James, M. D., of Liverpool. Physician and Writer.
    Life by W. W. Currie, 1831 .... 1756..1805
Curson, or Corceone, Robert. English Cardinal at Paris — ..1218
Curteis, Thomas. Divine and Poet................... 1690..1747
Curtis, William. Botanist........................... 1746..1770
Curtius, Marcus. Roman Hero .... fl.4th c. B.C.
Curtius, Rufus Quintus. (Hist. of Alexander the Great).fl.ti.Vespasian?
Curwen, John Christian, M. P. Agriculturist.......... 1756..1828
Cusa, Nicholas de. Cardinal. Theol. and Mathem. .... 1401..1464
Cushing, William. American Jurist .... 1733..1810
Cushman, Robert. One of the Founders of Plymouth
    Colony... 1580?.1625
Cuspinian, John. German Historian. Life by Gerbelius 1473..1529
Cusson, Peter. French Physician and Botanist........ 1727..1783
Custine, Adam Philip, Count de. French General...... 1740..1793
Custis, Geo. Washington Parke. Amer. Auth. & Painter 1781..1857
Custos, Dominic, son of Peter. Engraver at Augsburg.. 1560..1612
Custos, Peter. Peter Balthasar, or Balteus. Pa. at Antwerp fl. 1579
Cuthbert. Archbishop of Canterbury (741–58)........ — .. 758
Cuthbert, St. Bp. Durh. L. by Allan, 1777; Eyre, 1849 — .. 686
Cutler, Manasseh. Amer. Clergyman and Scientist..... 1744..1823
Cutler, Timothy, D.D. Am. Schol.; Pres. of Yale College 1685..1765
Cutts, John, Lord. Soldier and Poet................. — ..1707
Cuvier, Frederick. Naturalist....................... 1773..1838
Cuvier, George Christian Leopold Dagobert, Baron de., br.
    Naturalist. Life by Mrs. Lee, 1833 .... 1769..1832

BORN.   DIED.

Cuviller, Francis.   French Architect .... 1693.. —
Cuyp, or Kuyp, Albert.   Dutch Painter................ 1606..1667
Cuyp, or Kuyp, Jacob Gerritse, father.   *The Old.* ┆ Dutch
　　Portrait Painter .... 1575..1650
Cyaxares.   King of Media (B. C. 634–594).............. — B.C.594
Cygne, Martin du.   French Jesuit; Writer on Rhetoric.. 1619..1669
Cyprian, St.   Bishop of Carthage (248–58).   Life by
　　Pontius; A. S. Gervase........................... 200?. 258
Cypriani, or Cipriani, John Bapt.   Ital. Painter in Eng.. 1727..1785
Cypselus.   Tyrant of Corinth (B. C. 655–625) .... — B.C.625
Cyrano, Bergerac.   French Writer .... 1620..1655
Cyril, St.   Bishop of Jerusalem (348–86).............. 315?. 386
Cyril, St.   Bishop of Alexandria (412–44)..... .... 376?. 444
Cyrill Lucar.   Patriarch of Constantinople..............1572..1638?
Cyrus.   King of Persia (B. C. 559–529).   *The Elder.*   Life
　　by Xenophon .... — B.C.529
Cyrus.   *The Younger.*   Prince, in Xenophon's *Anabasis* — B.C.401
Czacki, Thaddeus.   Polish Statesman and Writer....... 1765..1813
Czarniecki, or Czarnecki, Stephen.   Polish General.... 1599..1665
Czartoryski, Prince Adam.   Polish Revolutionist....... 1770..1861
Czerny, Charles.   German Composer.................. 1791..1857
Czerny, George.   Leader of the Servians.............. 1770..1817

D.

BORN. DIED.

Dac, or Dach, John. German Painter................... 1566..1650
D'Achery, Luke. Benedictine. Life by Maugendre, 1776 1609..1685
Dacier, Andrew. Critic and Philologist................ 1651..1722
Dacier, Anne le Fevre, Madame, wife. Greek Scholar .. 1654..1720
Daddi, Bernard. Painter at Florence................... — ..1380
Daddi, Cosimo. Painter at Florence .... — ..1630
Daeliker, John Rudolph. Prussian Painter in Switzerland 1694..1769
Daendels, Herman William. Dutch General .... 1762..1818
Daffy, Rev. Thomas. Inventor of *Daffy's Elixir*........ — ..1680
D'Agar, James. French Painter...................... 1640..1715
Daggett, David, LL. D. American Jurist............... 1764..1851
Daggett, Naphtali, D. D. American Divine............ 1727..1780
D'Agincourt, John Baptist Louis Seroux. French Writer
(*L'Histoire de L'Art*) .... 1730..1814
Dagobert I. King of France (628-38)................. 602.. 638
Dagobert II. *The Young*........................... 652.. 679
Dagobert III..................................... 699.. 715
Dagoumer, William. French Philosopher............. — ..1745
Daguerre, Louis James Mandé. Photographer......... 1789..1851
D'Aguesseau, Henry Francis. Chancellor of France.
Life by his son, 1778; Charles Butler; Thomas, 1760;
Bourlot de Vauxcelles, 1760; Morlhon, 1760; Boinvilliers, 1848; Boullée, 1849 .... 1668..1751
Dahl, John Chr. Chausen. Norwegian Landscape Painter 1788..1857
Dahl, Michael. Swedish Portrait Painter.............. 1656..1743
Dahlberg, Eric. Swedish General. (*Succia Antiqua*) .. 1625..1703
Dahlgren, Charles John. Swedish Poet.............. 1791..1844
Daillé, John. Fr. Prot. Divine. (*De l'Usage des Pères*) 1594?..1670
Dakins, William. Translator of the Bible .... — ..1607
Dalayrac, Nich. Fr. Comp. (*Les deux petits Savoyards*) 1753..1809
Dalberg, Charles Theodore Anthony Maria. Grand-Duke
of Frankfort, Archbishop of Ratisbon. Writer. Life by
Zapf, 1810; Cramer .... 1744..1817
D'Albret, Charles. Constable of France; fell at Agincourt — ..1415
D'Albret, Charlotte, wife of Cæsar Borgia. Poetess..... — ..1514
D'Albret, Jane. Qu. of Navarre. L. by Vauvilliers, 1818 1528..1572
Dalby, Isaac. Mathematician. (*Course of Mathematics*) 1744..1824
Dale, or Dalen, Anthony van. Dutch Antiquary & Philos. 1638..1708
Dale, David, of New Lanark. Manufact. & Philanthropist 1738..1806
Dale, Richard. American Naval Officer .... 1756..1826
Dale, Samuel, M. D. Botanist and Antiquary........... 1659..1739
Dalechamp, James. French Physician and Botanist.... 1513..1588
D'Alembert, Jean le Rond. Math. L. by Condorcet, 1784 1717..1783
Dalen, Cornelius van, jr. Dutch Artist and Engraver ... 1640.. —
Dalens, Dirk van. Painter of Amsterdam .... 1659..1688
Dalgarno, George, of Aberdeen. (*Ars Signorum*)...... 1627?-1687
Dalhousie, Jas. Andrew Broun Ramsay, First Marquess
of. Governor-General of India.................... 1812..1860
D'Alibrai, Charles Vion. French Poet .... — ..1655
Dalin, Olof von. Swedish Historian and Poet......... 1708..1763

BORN. DIED.

Dallamano, Joseph. Italian Painter .... 1679..1758
Dallans, Ralph. Organ Builder........................ — ..1672
Dallas, Alexander James. American Statesman........ 1759..1817
Dallas, Sir George. Chief Justice. Political Writer .... 1758..1833
Dallas, George Mifflin. American Statesman.......... 1793?.1865
Dallas, Sir Robert. Judge .... — ..1824
Dallas, Robert Charles. Novelist. (*Recoll. of Lord Byron*) 1754..1824
Dallaway, Rev. James. Antiquary .... 1763..1834
Dallington, Sir Robert. Traveler. (*Method of Travel*). — ..1637
Dalmasio, Lippo. *Lippo del Madonne.* Italian Painter.. — ..1410
Dalrymple, Alex. Hydrographer. Writer on India, &c. 1737..1808
Dalrymple, Sir David, Lord Hailes, Scottish Judge.
   (*Annals of Scotland*)................................ 1726..1792
Dalrymple, Jas., 1st Visc. Stair, *q. v.* (*Inst. of Law of Scot.*) 1619..1695
Dalrymple, John, 2d E. Stair. Statesman and Diplom. 1673..1747
Dalrymple, Sir John Scottish Baron of Exchequer. (*Me-*
   moirs of Great Britain and Ireland) .... 1726..1810
Dalrymple, John. Surgeon and Oculist.............. 1804..1852
Dalton, John, D. D. Prebend. of Worcester. Writer, Poet 1709..1763
Dalton, John, D. C. L. Natural Philosopher........... 1766..1844
Dalton, Michael. Lawyer. (*Justice of the Peace*) ...... 1554..1620
Dalzell, Andrew, M. A. Greek Professor at Edinburgh .. 1750?.1806
Damascenus, John. Christian Father............... — .. 750?
Damascenus, Nicholas. Greek Historian............. fl. ab.13 B.C.
Damascius, Philosopher .... 480?.. —
Damasus I. Pope (366–84)........................... 304.. 384
Damasus II. Pope (1048) .... — ..1048
D'Amboise, Geo. Cardinal. Minister of Louis XII. L. by
   Sirmond, 1631; Michael Baudier, 1651; Le Gendre, 1721 1460..1510
Dambourney, Louis Augustus. Exper. Philos. of Rouen 1722..1795
Damer, Mrs. Anne Seymour. Sculptor.............. 1748..1828
Damiani, Peter. Cardinal Legate and Writer. Life by
   Le Grandi, 1702 .... 988?.1072
Damiens, Robert Francis. Attempted to assass. Louis XV. 1714..1757
Damini, George. Painter............................ — ..1631
Damini, Peter, brother. Italian Painter .... 1592..1631
Damjanics, János. Hungarian General............. 1804..1849
Damm, Christian Tobias. Prot. Divine. (*Gr. Etym. Lex.*) 1699?.1778
Damon, William. English Musical Composer.......... ti. Eliz.
Damours, Louis. French Jurist and Writer........... 1720?.1788
Dampe, Jacob Jacobson. Danish Philosopher.......... 1790..1850
Dampier, Captain William. Navigator .... 1652..1712?
Dampierre, John. *Dampetrus.* Fr. Jurist & Latin Poet — ..1550?
Dana, Francis. American Jurist..................... 1743..1811
Danby, Francis, R. A. Painter....................... 1793..1861
Danby, Henry Danvers, First Earl .... 1573..1644
Danby, Sir Thomas Osborn, Earl of. Lord Treasurer ... — ..1712
Danby, William. Writer on Moral Philosophy......... — ..1833
Dance, Charles. Comic Dramatist .... 1794?.1863
Dance, George. Architect. City Surveyor............ — ..1768
Dance, George, son. Architect. City Surveyor........ 1740..1825
Dancer, Daniel. Miser............................. 1716..1794
Danchet, Anthony. French Poet..................... 1671..1748
Danckerts, Cornelius. Dutch Artist and Engraver..... 1561..1620?

BORN. DIED.

Danckerts, Danckert, son. Dutch Artist and Engraver. 1600.. —
Danckerts, Henry. Dutch Artist and Engraver........ — ..1689?
Danckerts, John. Dutch Artist and Engraver .... fl. 1654
Dancourt, Florence Carton. French Dramatist........ 1661..1726
Dandini, Cæsar. Italian Painter .... 1595?.1658
Dandini, Hercules Francis. Italian Lawyer and Writer.. 1696?.1747
Dandini, Jerome. Ital. Jesuit. Commentator on Aristotle 1554..1634
Dandini, Peter... 1646..1712
Dandini, Vincent. Italian Painter.................... 1608..1675
Dandolo, Andrew. Doge of Venice (1344–54).......... 1310?.1354
Dandolo, Henry. Blind Doge of Venice (1192–1205).... 1108..1205
Dandolo, Vincent. Italian Chemist................... 1758..1819
D'Andrada, Anthony. Port. Jesuit Missionary. (*Thibet*) 1580?.1634
D'Andrada, Diego Payva. Apol. for Council of Trent.. 1528..1575
D'Andrada, Francis, br. (*Hist. of John III. of Portugal*) fl. 1600
D'Andrada, Thos. *Thomas of Jesus.* (*Sufferings of Jesus*) — ..1582
Dandre-Bardon, Michael Francis. Fr. Painter & Writer 1700..1783
Dane, Nathan. American Jurist and Statesman........ 1752..1834
Danedi, John Stephen. Painter .... 1608..1689
Danedi, Joseph, brother. Italian Painter............. 1618..1688
Danet, Peter. French Latinist....................... — ..1709
Dangeau, Louis de Courcillon, Abbé de............... 1643..1723
Dangeau, Philip de Courcillon, Marquis de. Hist. Writer 1638..1720
Danhewer, John Conrad. Lutheran Theol. at Strasburg. 1603..1666
Danican, Francis Andrew. *Philidor.* French Musician
    and Chess Player............................. 1727..1795
Daniel, Arnauld. Provençal Poet..................... — ..1198
Daniel, Gabriel. Fr. Jesuit Historian. (*History of France.*) 1649..1728
Daniel, George. Antiquary and Writer................ 1790?.1864 .
Daniel, Peter. French Scholar; friend of Buchanan .... 1530..1603
Daniel, Samuel. Eng. Poet and Hist. (*History of England*) 1562..1619
Daniel, Rev. William Barker. (*Rural Sports*) .... — .. 1833
Danieli, Francis. Italian Medalist and Antiquary ..... 1740..1812
Daniell, John Frederick, D. C. L. Professor of Chemistry 1790..1845
Daniell, Sam. Artist. (*African Scenery; Scenery of Ceylon*) — ..1811
Daniell, Thomas. Landscape Painter and Engraver .... 1749..1840
Daniell, Wm., R. A. Artist. (*Zoögraphy; Oriental Scenery*) 1769..1837
Dannecker, John Henry. Sculptor.................... 1758..1841
Dante degli Alighieri. Life by Boccaccio, 1544; Bruno
    Aretino, 1672; Chabanon, 1773; Fabroni, 1803; Balbo,
    1839; Artaud de Montor, 1841; Torri, 1843; Wegele,
    1852; Véricour, 1858............................ 1265..1321
Dante, Ignatius. Mathem. Writer on the Astrolabe.. 1537?.1586
Dante, John Baptist. Mathematician and Mechanician.. fl. 15th c.
Dante, Peter Vincent. Poet, Mathematician, & Architect — ..1512
Dante, Vincent, grandson. Painter, Sculptor, Mathemat. 1530..1576
D'Antine, Francis. French Benedictine. (*L'Art de Veri-
    fier les Dates*)................................. 1688..1746
Danton, George James. French Revolutionist.......... 1759..1794
Dantz, John Andrew. Lutheran Div. and Orient. at Jena 1654..1727
Danvers, Henry, Earl of Danby....................... 1573..1644
D'Anville, John Baptist. Bourguignon. Geographer.
    Life by Barbié du Bocage, 1802.................. 1697..1782
Danzi, Francis. Musical Composer................... 1763..1826

BORN. DIED.

Da Ponte, Lorenzo. Italian Poet. (*Don Juan*)......... 1749..1837
Dapper, Oliver. Dutch Geographer................... — ..1690
Daran, James. French Surgeon .... 1701..1784
D'Arblay, Madame Frances, *née* Burney. Novelist..... 1752..1840
Darby, Abraham. Iron Manufacturer .... — ..1717
Darc, or D'Arc, Jeanne. *Maid of Orleans.* L. by Lord Mahon 1412?.1431
Darcet, John. French Physician and Chemist.......... 1725..1801
D'Arcq, Philip Augustus. Chevalier. Historical Writer — ..1779
D'Arcy, Patrick, Count. Irish Soldier, Engineer, Writer 1725..1779
Darden, Miles. Fat Man. (Height, 7 feet 6 inches;
    weight, 1000 pounds) .... 1798..1857
Dare, Virginia. First child of English Parents in America 1587.. —
D'Argensola, Bartholomew. Poet and Historian....... 1566..1631
D'Argensola, Lupercio Leonardo, brother. Spanish Poet 1565..1613
D'Argenson, Mark René. Statesman................ 1652..1721
D'Argental, Charles Augustin Feriol, Count. Diplomatist 1700..1788
D'Argentre, Charles Duplessis. French Bishop. Scholar 1673..1740
D'Argenville, Anthony Joseph Desallier. Naturalist... 1680..1765
D'Argillate, Peter, of Bologna. Medical Writer........ — ..1423
D'Argonne, Noel Bonaventure. (*Mélanges d' Histoire*).. 1634..1704
D'Argota, Jerome Contador. Portuguese Antiquary.... 1676..1749
D'Argues, or Desargues, Gerard. French Mathematician 1593. 1662
Darius I. *Hystaspis.* King of Persia (B. C. 521–485)... — B.C.485
Darius II. *Nothus* (B. C. 423–404).................. — B.C.404
Darius III. *Codomannus.* (B. C. 336–330.) Defeated by
    Alexander .... 380.330 B.C.
Darley, George. British Author..................... 1785..1849
Darling, Grace, of Fern Islands. Heroine .... 1815..1842
D'Arnaud, George. French Critic .... 1711..1740
D'Arnex, or D'Arnay, Simon Augustus. Swiss Writer 1750.aft.1802
Darnley, Henry, Earl of. Husband of Mary Qu. of Scots 1541..1567
Darquier, Augustin. French Astronomer............. 1718..1802
Dart, John. (*Antiquities of Westminster Abbey*) .... fl. 1727
Daru, Peter Anthony Noel Bruno, Count. French Writer 1767..1829
Darwin, Charles. Medical Writer.................... 1758..1778
Darwin, Erasmus. Phys. & Po. L. by Anna Seward, 1804 1731..1802
Dashkoff, Ekaterina Romanova. Russian Princess...... 1744..1810
Dassier, Jacob Anthony, son of John. Medalist........ 1715..1759
Dassier, John. French Medalist..................... 1678..1763
Dassouci, Charles Coypeau. French Musician and Poet. 1604?.1679
Dati, Augustin, of Sienna. Writer.................. 1420. 1478
Dati, Charles, of Florence. Philologist................ 1619..1676
D'Attaignant, Gabriel Charles. French Poet.......... 1697..1779
Daub, Charles. German Theologian.................. 1765..1836
Daubenton, Louis John Mary. Fr. Anat. and Naturalist 1716..1800
Daubenton, William. Confessor to Philip V. of Spain.. 1648..1723
D'Aubigné, Theodore Agrippa. Historian............. 1550..1630
Daudin, Francis Mary. French Naturalist. (*Reptiles*).. 1774..1804
Daum, Christian. Classical Scholar at Zwickau....... 1612..1687
Daun, Leopold Jos. Maria, Ct. of. Austrian Field Marsh. 1705..1766
Daundelyon, Marcellus. Abbot...................... 1426.. —
Daunois, M. C. J. de Bernville, Ctss. Romancist & Trav. — ..1705
Daunou, Peter Claude Francis. French Political Writer.
    Life by Taillandier, 1841........................ 1761..1840

BORN. DIED.

Daurat, or Dorat, John. *Auralus.* French Poet........ 1507?.1588
Daval, Peter. Mathematician, of London.............. — ..1763
Davanzati, Bernard. Florentine Writer.............. 1529..1606
Davenant, Chas., LL. D. Political and Commercial Writer 1656..1714
Davenant, John. Bishop of Salisbury. Life by Allport 1576..1641
Davenant, Sir William. Poet..................... 1605..1668
Davenport, Christopher. English Franciscan Theologian 1598?.1680
Davenport, John. Puritan Divine .... 1597..1670
David, Second King of Israel...................... —B.C.1015
David, St. Archbishop. Patron Saint of Wales .... — .. 544?
David I. K. Scot. (1124–53). L. by Adam Scotus, 12th c. — ..1153
David II. King of Scotland, son of Robert Bruce...... 1324..1371
David, Francis Anne. French Engraver..............1741..1824
David, George. Fanatic of Ghent................... 1501..1556
David, James Louis. French Painter. .... 1748..1825
David, Peter John, of Angers. Sculptor.............. 1789..1856
David ap Gwilym. Welsh Bard..................... fl. 14th c.
David de Pomis. Jewish Physician and Lexicographer 1525..1600?
David de St. George, John Joseph Alexis. Philologist. 1759..1809
Davidis, Francis. Hungarian Theologian............. 1510?.1579
Davids, Arthur Lumley. Orientalist.................. — ..1832
Davidson, John. Traveler; murdered................ — ..1836
Davidson, Lucretia Maria. American Poetess. Life by
  Miss Sedgwick, 1843............................... 1808..1825
Davidson, Margaret Miller. Poetess. Life by Washing-
  ton Irving, 1842................................... 1823..1838
Davidson, William. American Revolutionary General.. 1746..1781
Daviel, James. French Oculist.....................; 1696..1762
Davies, Rev. Hugh. Botanist...................... 1739?.1821
Davies, Sir John. Poet and Statesman. (*Nosce teipsum.*)
  Life by G. Chalmers; Tom Davies.................. 1570..1626
Davies, John, D. D. Writer and Antiquary........... fl. ab. 1630
Davies, Dr. John. Welsh Div. and Gram. (*Brit. Dict.*) — ..1644
Davies, John. Translator........................... 1625..1693
Davies, John. Critic............................... 1679..1732
Davies, Miles. Welsh Clergyman. (*Athenæ Britannicæ*) fl. ti. Geo. I.
Davies, Robert. Welsh Poet. *Bard Nantglyn*........ 1770..1836
Davies, Robert, of Llanerch. Antiquary.............. 1684?.1728
Davies, Samuel, D. D. American Divine.............. 1724..1761
Davies, Rev. Sneyd. Archdeacon of Derby. Poet..... — ..1769
Davies, Thomas. Publisher, Actor, Writer............ 1712?.1785
Davies, Rev. Walter. Writer on Wales............... 1761..1849
Davila, Henry Catherine. (*Civil Wars in France*)...... 1576..1631
Davila, John. Apostle of Andalusia................. 1500..1569
Davila, Peter Francis. Spanish Naturalist............ — ..1785
Da Vinci, Leonardo. Painter. L. by J. W. Brown, 1828 1452..1519?
Davis, Rev. Henry Edwards. Historical Writer........ 1756..1784
Davis, John. Navigator and Discoverer............... — ..1605?
Davis, John. American Jurist...................... 1761..1847
Davis, John. American Statesman................... 1787..1854
Davis, or Davies, John, of Hereford. Poet & Schoolmast. — ..1618?
Davis, J. P. Historical Painter...................... 1783?.1862.
Davis, Matthew L. American Writer................ 1766..1850
Davis, Thomas. Irish Poet........................ 1814..1845

BORN. DIED

Davison, Jeremiah. Painter.......................... — ..1745
Davison, Wm. Statesman. Life by Sir H. Nicolas, 1823 fl. ti. Eliz.
Davoust, or Davout, Louis Nicholas. Duke of Auerstadt.
    Marshal of France............................... 1770..1823
D'Avrigny, Hyacinth Robillard. French Historian..... 1675..1719
Davy, Sir Humphry. Natural Philosopher. Life by Ayr-
    ton, 1830; Dr. J. Davy, 1839...................... 1778..1829
Davy, John. Musical Composer..................... 1765..1824
Davys, George. Bishop of Peterborough.............. — ..1864
Dawe, George, R. A. Painter and Biographer.......... 1775?.1829
Dawes, Manasseh. Writer on Law & Political Economy — ..1829
Dawes, Richard. Greek Critic. (Miscellanea Critica)... 1708..1766
Dawes, Sir Wm. Abp. of York (1713-24). Preach.& Writ. 1671..1724
Dawson, George. (Origo Legum)...................... — ..1700
Day, John. Printer................................. 1522..1584
Day, John. Poet................................... fl. ti. Jas. I.
Day, Stephen. American Printer..................... 1611..1668
Day, Thomas. Poet and Writer. (Sandford and Merton.)
    Life by J. Blackman, 1862......................... 1748..1789
Dayton, Elias. American Revolutionary Officer........ 1737..1807
Dayton, William L. American Statesman............. 1807..1865
Deageant de St. Marcellan, Guichard. French Writer — ..1639
Deane, James. American Physician and Scientist...... 1801..1858
Deane, Silas. American Diplomatist.................. — ..1789
Dearborn, Henry. American General................. 1751..1829
De Bergh, Augustus. Scientific Writer.............. — ..1864
De Bernard du Grail, Charles. French Novelist...... 1805..1850
Debrett, John. Bookseller. (Debrett's Peerage)....... 1752?.1822
Debrowsky, Joseph. Bohemian Writer................ 1753..1829
De Bure, Francis. Booksell. at Paris. (Bibliog. Instruct.) 1731..1782
De Bury, Richard. Bishop of Durham. See Angarville.
    Life by S. Gibson, 1850........................... 1287?.1345
De Candolle, Augustin Pyramus. Botanist............ 1778..1841
De Castro, Guillen. Spanish Dramatist.............. 1569..1631
De Castro, John. Portuguese General and Governor.
    Life by J. F. D'Andrada, 1786..................... 1500..1548
Decatur, Stephen. American Naval Officer........... 1779..1820
Decembrio, Pietro Candido. Milanese Statesm. & Writer 1399..1477
Dechales, Millet Claude Francis. French Mathematician. 1621..1678
Decio, Philip. Italian Lawyer....................... 1454..1535
Decius. Roman Emperor (249-51).................... 201.. 251
Decker, Francis. Dutch Medical Writer.............. fl. 1670?
Decker, or Dekker, Jeremias de. Dutch Poet.......... 1610..1666
Decker, or Dekker, John. Dutch Chronol. and Historian 1550?.1619
Decker, Sir Matthew. Political Economist............. — ..1749
Decker, or Dekker, Thomas. Dramatist.............. — ..1641?
Dedekind, Frederick. German Writer................ 1550..1598
De Dominis, Mark Anthony. Archbishop of Spoleto;
    Dean of Windsor. (De Republicâ Ecclesiasticâ)..... 1556..1624
Dee, John. Mathematician and Astrologer............ 1527..1608
Deering, J. P., M. P., R. A., (originally Gandy). Architect 1780..1850
Defesch, William. German Violinist............... 1680?.aft.1757
Deffand, Maria de Vichy Chamrond, Marchioness du.
    Life by Miss Berry, 1844.......................... 1697..1780

BORN.   DIED

De Foe, Daniel. (*Robinson Crusoe.*) L. by Geo. Chalmers;
  Walter Wilson, 1830; J. Forster; W. Chadwick, 1859.. 1663?.1731
De Gerando, Joseph Mary, Baron. French Statesman.. 1772..1842
De Grey, Thomas Philip, Earl. Architect............. 1781..1859
De Guignes, Joseph. Historian and Orient. (*The Huns*) 1721..1800
Deidier, Anthony. French Medical Writer....:........ — ..1746
Dejaure, John Elias Bedenc. French Poet............. 1761..1799
Dejoces. Founder of the Median Empire............. —B.C.657?
De Kalb, John, Baron. German General in America ... 1732?.1780
Dekker. *See* Decker.
De la Beche, Sir Henry Thomas. Geologist........... 1796..1855
Delaborde, John Benjamin. French Musical Composer.. 1734..1794
Delacepède, Bernard G. S. L. French Naturalist...... 1756..1825
Delacour, James. Irish Poetical Writer.............. 1709..1781?
Delacroix, Ferdinand Victor Eugene. French Painter.. 1798..1863
Delalande, Peter Anthony. Fr. Naturalist and Traveler. 1787..1823
Delambre, John Baptist Joseph. French Astronomer... 1749..1822
Delamet, Adrian Augustin de Bussy. Casuist........ 1621..1691
Delandine, Anthony Francis. French Writer.......... 1756..1820
Delane, William Aug. Fred. English Journalist........ 1793..1857
Delany, Mary. Life by self, and Lady Llanover, 1862... 1700..1788
Delany, Patrick. Dean of Down. Divine..........•.... 1686?.1768
Delaroche, Hippolyte, or Paul. French Painter...... 1797..1856
Delarue, Gervaise. Abbé. Antiquary................ 1751..1835
Delaune, Thomas. (*Plea for Nonconformists*)........ — ..1685?
Delauney, Count d'Antraigues. Political Agent....... 1756..1812
Delaval, Edward Hussey. Chemist and Nat. Philosopher 1729..1814
Delavigne, John Francis Casimir. French Poet........ 1793..1843
Delessert, Benjamin. French Financier.............. 1773..1847
Deleyre, Alexander. French Writer.................. 1726..1797
Delfau, Francis. French Monk and Writer............ 1637..1676
Delfico, Melchior. Neapolitan Writer................ 1744..1835
Delfino, John, of Aquileia. Italian Poet.............. 1617..1699
Delft, van, or Delphus, Wm. James. Painter & Engraver 1619..1661
Delille, James French Poet. Translator of Virgil..... 1738..1813
Deliniers, Jas. Anth. Mary. Viceroy of Buenos Ayres.. 1756..1810
Delisle, Claude. Historian......................... 1644..1720
Delisle, John Baptist Isoard. *De Sales.* French Writer 1743..1816
Delisle, Jos. Nicholas. Astronomer. (*Hist. of Astronomy*) 1688..1768
Delisle, Louis. Astronomer, Geographer, and Traveler.. — ..1741
Delisle, William. Geographer. (*Atlas*).............. 1675..1726
Delius, Christopher Traugott. Mineralogist........... 1728..1779
Della Maria, Dominic. Musical Composer............. 1768..1800
Delmont, Deodato. Historical Painter............... 1581..1634
Delolme, John Louis. Polit.Writ. L. by J. Macgregor, M. P. 1740..1806
Delorme, Marion ....:............ 1612?.1650
Delorme, Philibert. French Architect................ 1518..1577
Delpini, Charles Anthony. Clown and Dramatic Writer — ..1828
Delrio, John. Dean of Antwerp. (*Ps. CXIX.*)........ — ..1624
Delrio, Martin Anthony. Jesuit, Biblical Commentator.. 1551..1608
Del Sarto, Andrea Vanucchi. Italian Painter.......... 1488..1530
Deluc, John Andrew. Genevese Naturalist............ 1727..1817
Demades. Athenian Orator and Statesman............ —B.C.318
Demeste, John, M. D., of Liege...................... 1743..1783

BORN. DIED.

Demetrius. *Phalereus.* Attic Orator .... 345 282[?] B.C.
Demetrius. Czar of Russia. *The False*.............. 1581..1606
Demetrius Nicator. 12th K. Syria (B.C. 146–2, 128–5) 165[?].125 B.C.
Demetrius Poliorcetes. King Maced. (B.C. 294–287)..337.283 B. C.
Demetrius Soter. Tenth King of Syria (B.C. 162–150) 187[?].150[?] B.C.
De Missy, Cæsar. German Divine................... 1703..1775
Democedes. Greek Physician..................... 550 B.C.,—
Democritus. *Laughing Philosopher*................460.357 B.C.
Demoivre, Abraham. Mathematician............... 1667..1754
Demosthenes. Athenian Orator....................385[?].322 B.C.
Demours, Peter. French Oculist.................... 1702..1795
Demoustier, Charles Albert. French Dramatic Writer.. 1760..1801
Dempster, Geo. Agriculturist and Miscellaneous Writer 1736..1818
Dempster, Thomas. Scottish Writer............... 1579..1625
Dempster, Wm. Scottish Writ. (*Eccles. Hist. of Scot.*) 1490..1557
Denham, Dixon. Lieutenant-Colonel. African Traveler 1786..1828
Denham, Sir John. Poet .... 1615..1668
Denina, Mary James Charles. Italian Historian........ 1731..1813
Denison, Joseph, M. P. Historical Writer and Poet..... — ..1806
Denistoun, James. Historian and Biographer.......... — ..1855
Denman, Thomas, M. D. Medical Writer............. 1733..1815
Denman, Thomas, Lord. Chief Justice .... 1779 .1854
Denne, John. Divine and Antiquary.................. 1693..1767
Denne, Samuel. Writer on History and Antiquities .... 1730..1799
Denner, Balthazar. German Portrait Painter.......... 1685..1747[?]
Dennie, Joseph. American Journalist and Author...... 1768..1812
Dennie, William Henry. Colonel; Indian Officer...... — ..1842
Dennis, John. Poet, Critic, and Political Writer....... 1657..1734
Denny, Sir Anthony. Favorite of Henry VIII........... — ..1550
Denon, Dominique Vivant, Baron de. Egyptian Traveler 1747..1825
Dens, Peter. Roman Catholic Theologian .... — ..1690
Dentatus, Marcus Curius. Roman Consul............. fl.3d c. B.C.
Denton, John. Ejected Nonconformist Divine .... 1625..1708
Denton, William, M. D. Political Writer .... 1605..1691
Dentrecolles, Francis Xavier. Jesuit Missionary to China 1664..1741
Denys, James. French Lithotomist and Accoucheur.... fl. 1730
Denys, James. Historical & Portrait Painter, of Antwerp 1645.. —
Denys, John Baptist. Fr. Physician; Transfuser of Blood 1704
Denys, St. Apostle of France......................... fl. 3d c.
D'Éon, Chevalier. Equerry to Louis XV., &c., &c...... 1728..1810
Déparcieux, Anthony. French Mathematician........ 1703..1768
Depping, George Bernard. Writer at Paris .... 1784..1853
De Quincey, Thomas. Writer. Life by self, 1853 ..... 1785..1859
Derbishire, Stewart. Journalist and Writer........... — ..1863
Derby, George H. American Writer and Soldier....... — ..1861
Derby, James Stanley, Earl of. Royalist. Beheaded ... 1596..1651
Derfflinger, Geo. von. General .... 1606..1695
Derham, William, D.D. Divine....................... 1657..1735
Dering, Edward. Puritan Divine...................... — ..1576
Dering, Sir Edward. Politician...................... 1598..1644
Dermody, Thomas. Poet. Life by J. G. Raymond, 1806 1775..1802
Derrick, Samuel. Poet and Miscellaneous Writer ...... 1724..1769
Derschawin, or Derzhavin, Gabriel Romanovitch. Russian
    Poet and Statesman........................... 1743..1816

BORN. DIED.

Derwentwater, James Radcliffe, Third Earl of. Jacobite.
  Life by Sydney Gibson.............:............. 1689..1716
Deryck, Peter Cornelius. Dutch Landscape Painter .... 1568..1630
Deryke, William. Historical Painter of Antwerp....... 1635..1697
Desaguliers, Rev. Dr. John Theoph. Experim. Philos... 1683..1744
Desaix de Veygoux, Louis Chas. Anthony. Fr. General 1768..1800
Desargues, Gerard. Mathematician.................. 1593..1662
Désaugiers, Mark Anthony Madeleine. French Song-
  Writer and Dramatist .... 1772..1827
Desault, Peter. French Physician .... 1675..1737
Desault, Peter Joseph. Fr. Surgical Writ. L. by Caillau 1744..1795
Des Barreaux, James Vallée, Lord. French Poet; Writer 1602..1673
Des Barres, Jos. Fred. Wallet. Soldier and Hydrographer 1722..1824
Desbillons, Francis Joseph Terrasse. French Writer.... 1711..1789
Desbois, Francis Alexander. Compiler of Dictionaries .. 1699..1784
Descartes, René. Philosopher. Life by Baillet........ 1596..1650
Desericius, or Deseritz, Joseph Innocent. Hung. Writer 1702..1765
Desèze, Raymond. French Magistrate................ 1750..1828
Desfontaines, Peter Francis Guyot. French Critic ..... 1685..1745
Desfontaines, René Louiche. French Naturalist....... 1751?.1833
Desgodets, Anthony. French Architect.............. 1653..1728
Deshays, J. Baptist Henry. French Painter .... 1729..1765
Deshoulières, Antoinette du Ligier. French Poetess.... 1634?.1694
Deshoulières, Antoinette Theresa, daughter. Poetess .. 1662..1718
Desmahis, Jos. Francis Edw. de Corsembleu. Fr. Poet 1722..1761
Desmaizeaux, Peter. Biographer.................... 1666..1745
Desmares, Mary.· *La Champmesle.* French Actress ... 1644..1698
Desmares, Toussaint. Jansenist. *(Nécrologe de P. Royal)* 1599..1669
Desmarets, Francis Seraphin Regnier. Fr. Poet and Critic 1632..1713
Desmars, Nicholas. Physician and Naturalist of Boulogne — ..1767
Desmolets, Peter Nicholas. French Writer........... 1678..1760
Desmoulins, Benoît Camille. French Revolutionist .... 1762..1794
Desnoyers, Aug. Gaspar Louis Boucher, Baron. French
  Engraver....................................... 1779..1857
De Soto, Fernando. Discoverer of the Mississippi...... 1500..1542
D'Espagne, John. French Protestant Preacher in London 1591..1659
Despard, Edward Marcus. Irish Officer and Conspirator 1755? 1803
Despars, or De Partibus, James. French Medical Writer 1380?.1458
Despautere, or Van Pauteren, John. Flemish Grammarian 1460?.1520
Despencer, Hugh le. Favorite of Edward II........... — ..1326
Despencer, Hugh le, son. Favorite of Edward II...... — ..1326
Despièrres, John. Mathematician, Mechan., Commentator 1597..1664
Desplaces, Louis. French Engraver .... 1682..1733
Desportes, Claude Francis. Painter.................. 1696?.1774
Desportes, Francis. French Painter .... 1661..1743
Desportes, John Baptist. French Phys. at St. Domingo 1704..1748
Despretz, Cæsar Mansuète. French Savant and Author 1789..1863
Dessaix, Jos. Mary. French General................. 1764..1834
Dessalines, John Jas. Negro Emperor of Hayti (1804–6) 1760?.1806
Dessenius, Bernard. Dutch Medical Writer .... 1510..1574
Dessolles, John Jos. Paul Augustin, Marquis. French
  General and Statesman........................... 1767..1828
Destouches, Philip Héricault. French Dramatic Writer 1680..1754
D'Estrées, Gabrielle. Mistress of Henry IV........... 1571?.1599

9

BORN. DIED

Destutt de Tracy, Anth. Louis Claude. Fr. Philosopher 1754..1836
Detharding, George. German Medical Writer .... — aft.1696
De Tott, Francis, Baron. French Negotiator........... 1733..1793
Deusdedit. Archbishop of Canterbury (655–64)....... — .. 664
Deusdedit I. Pope (615–18)......................... — .. 618
Deusdedit II. (672–76)............................. — .. 676
Deusing, Anthony. Flemish Medical Writer........... 1612..1666
Deutsch, Nicholas Manuel. Swiss Painter............. 1484..1530
Devaux, John. French Surgical Writer .... 1610..1695
Devaux, John, son. Surgeon. Transl. of Medical Works 1649..1729
Deventer, Henry. Dutch Accoucheur.................. — ..1739
De Vere, Sir Aubrey. Dramatic Poet .... — ..1846
De Vere, Edward. Seventeenth Earl of Oxford. Poet .. 1540?.1604
Devereux, Robert, 2d Earl of Essex. Beheaded by Eliz. 1567..1601
Devereux, Robert, Third Earl of Essex. Parliam. General 1592..1646
Devereux, Walter, First Earl of Essex................. 1540?.1576
De Vigny, Alfred, Count. French Poet and Novelist ... 1799..1863
Devis, Arthur William. Painter .... 1762..1822
Devonshire, Georgiana Cavendish, Duchess of. Poetess
    and Beauty.................................... 1757..1806
D'Ewes, Sir Symonds. Hist. and Antiq. (*Parl. Journal*) 1602..1650
De Wette, Wm. Martin Leberecht. German Theologian
    and Biblical Critic.............................. 1780..1849
De Wint, Peter. English Artist..................... 1783..1849
De Winter, John William. Dutch Admiral .... 1750..1812
De Witt, James. Painter........................... 1695..1744
De Witt, John. Grand Pensionary. *See* Witt..:...... 1625..1672
Dexter, Samuel. American Statesman and Jurist....... 1761..1816
Deynum, John Baptist van. Dutch Painter .... 1620.. —
Deyster, Anna. Painter .... 1696?.1746
Deyster, Louis. Flemish Historical Painter.......... 1656..1711
Dezallier d'Argenville, Anthony Joseph. Conchologist 1680..1765
D'Herbelot, Bartholomew. Orientalist .... 1625..1695
D'Hilliers, Louis Baraguay. French General.......... 1764..1812
D'Hozier, Peter. French Genealogist .... 1592..1660
Diagoras. Greek Poet and Philosopher.......... fl. B.C. 430?
Diana of Poitiers. Mistress of Henry II. of France .... 1499..1566
Dias, Bartholomew. Navigator....................:... — ..1500
Diaz, Michael. Aragonese Explorer .... —ab.1514
Diaz del Castillo, Bernal. Span. Advent. & Chronicler fl. 15th c.
Dibdin, Charles. Naval Song-Writer. Life by T. Dibdin 1745..1814
Dibdin, Thomas, son. Dramatist and Song-Writer .... 1771..1841
Dibdin, Rev. Thomas Frognall, D.D. Miscellaneous Writer 1770..1847
Diceto, Ralph de. Historian......................... — ..1283
Dick, Dr. Thomas. Writer on Natural Philosophy...... 1772..1857
Dickenson, Edm. Physician, Chemist, and Orientalist.
    (*Delphi Phœnicizantes*.) Life by Blomberg, 1739 .... 1624..1707
Dickenson, Philemon. American Revolutionary Officer. — ..1809
Dickinson, Grace. Poet. (*Songs in the Night*)........ — ..1863
Dickinson, John. American Political Writer .... 1732..1808
Dickinson, Jonathan. American Divine and Educator.. 1688..1747
Dickons, Mrs. Vocalist ....1775?.1833
Dickson, David. Scottish Divine and Commentator .... 1583?.1662
Dickson, James. Scottish Botanist................... 1738..1822

BORN. DIED.

Dicquemare, Jos. Francis. Fr. Naturalist and Astron.. 1733..1789
Diderot, Denis. French Writer .... 1713..1784
Didius. Roman Emperor (193) .... 133?. 193
Didot, Firmin. Printer and Writer.................... 1764..1836
Didot, Francis Ambrose. French Printer............. 1730..1804
Diebitsch, John Chas. Fred. Anthony, Count. Russian
  Field Marshal...................................... 1785..1831
Diecman, John, of Stade. Theologian & Metaphysician 1647?.1720
Dieffenbach, John Frederick. Surgical Operator....... 1795..1847
Diemen, Anthony van. Dutch Governor in India...... 1593..1645
Diemerbroeck, Isbrand van. Dutch Medical Writer ... 1609..1674
Diepenbeck, Abraham van. Dutch Painter.......... 1607?.1675
Dies, Albert. German Painter and Engraver........... 1755..1822
Dieskau, Louis Aug. German General................ 1701..1767
Diest, Adrian van. Dutch Painter and Engraver....... 1655..1704
Dietrich, Christian William Ernest. German Painter... 1712..1774
Dietrich, John Conrad. German Scholar and Antiquary 1612..1669
Dietrich, Philip Frederick, Baron de. Fr. Mineralogist. 1748..1793
Dieu, Louis de. Dutch Protestant Divine............. 1590..1642
Diez, John Martin. Spanish Guerrilla. The Empecinado 1775..1825
Digby, Sir Everard, of the Gunpowder Plot............. 1581..1606
Digby, George, Second Earl of Bristol. Publicist........ 1612..1676
Digby, John. First Earl of Bristol.................... 1580..1653
Digby, Sir Kenelm. Writ. L. by self & Sir N. H. Nicolas. 1603..1665
Digges, Sir Dudley. Politician and Writer .... 1583..1639
Digges, Leonard.' Geometrician and Meteorologist...... — ..1573?
Digges, Thomas, son. Astronomer and Mathematician.. — ..1595
Dilke, Charles Wentworth. Editor of Athenæum........ 1810..1864
Dillenius, John James. Botanist .... 1687..1747
Dillon, Wentworth, Earl of Roscommon. Poet .... 1633?.1684
Dilworth, Thomas. Writer of School-Books........... — ..1780
Dimsdale, Thomas, Baron, M. D. Inoculator.......... 1712..1800
Dinarchus. Attic Orator ....361? B.C. aft.292
Dingley, Robert. Puritan Divine .... 1619..1659
Dinocrates. Macedonian Architect.................... fl. ti. Alex.
Dinoth, Richard, of Coutances. (De Bello Civili Gallico). — ..1590?
Dinouart, Anthony Joseph Toussaint. Writer at Paris.. 1715..1786
Dinwiddie, Robert. Lieutenant-Governor of Virginia.... 1690?.1770
Diocletian. Emperor (284–305) .... 245.. 313
Diodati, John. Divine; Translator of Bible .... 1576..1649
Diodorus Siculus. Historian ....fl.ti.Augustus.
Diogenes. Cynic Philosopher ....412? B.C. 323
Diogenes of Apollonia. Greek Philosopher.......... fl.5th c. B.C.
Diogenes Laertius. (Lives of the Philosophers)...........fl.2d c.? A.D.
Dion, of Syracuse. Patriot .... — B.C.353
Dion Cassius. Historian ....155? aft. 229
Dion Chrysostom. Rhetorician and Sophist .... — .. 117?
Dionis, Peter. French Surgeon and Anatomist........ —...1718
Dionysius. Bishop of Rome (259–269)................. — .. 269
Dionysius. Tyrant of Syracuse (405–367). The Elder. 430? B.C. 367
Dionysius, son. Tyrant of Syracuse (367–343). The
  Younger................................... 397?B.C.aft.343
Dionysius. Bishop of Alexandria (247–265) .... — ..265
Dionysius. Periegetes. Geographer .... fl.A.D. 300?

BORN. DIED.

Dionysius Exiguus. Roman Monk.................. — .. 540
Dionysius of Halicarnassus. Historian bef.A.D.18
Diophantus. Greek Algebraist of Alexandria .... fl.5th c.? A.D.
Dioscorides, Pedanius. Gr. Phys. & Botanist of Cilicia.. fl.2d c.? A.D.
Dippel, John Conrad. German Physician and Alchemist 1672..1734
Dirois, Francis. Doctor of Sorbonne. (*Preuves et Préjugés*) 1620..1690
Disney, Rev. John. Divine and Magistrate............ 1677..1730
Disraeli, Isaac. (*Curiosities of Literature*)............ 1767..1848
Dissen, George. Ludolph. German Scholar.......... 1784..1837
Dithmar, Justus Christopher. Writ. on German History 1677..1737
Ditmar, Bishop of Mersburgh. Historian .... 976..1028
Ditters, Charles. German Musician.................... 1739..1799
Ditton, Humphrey. Mathematician.................... 1675..1715
Divini, Eustachius. Italian Telescope Maker........... 1620?..1664?
Dixon, George. Navigator........................... — ..1800?
Dixwell, Col. John. Regicide Judge.................... 1608..1689
Dlugoss, John. Polish Archbishop. (*History of Poland*) 1415..1480
Dmitrieff, Ivan Ivanovitch. Russian Poet............. 1760..1837
Doane, Geo. Washington, D.D. Amer. Divine and Writer 1799..1859
Dobree, Peter Paul. Classical Scholar................ 1782..1825
Döbrentey, Gábor, or Gabriel. Hungarian Antiquary... 1786..1851
Dobrizhoffer, Martin. Jesuit Missionary in S. America 1717..1791
Dobrovsky, Joseph. Bohemian Writer .... 1753..1829
Dobson, William. Painter........................... 1610..1647
Doca, Frederick M. (*Triglott Grammar*).............. 1794?..1864
Dod, Albert Baldwin, D. D. American Scholar...:..... 1805..1845
Dod, Charles Roger. Peerage Compiler................ 1793..1855
Dod, John. *Decalogist.* Puritan Divine .... 1547..1645
Dodart, Denis. French Physician and Botanist........ 1634..1707
Dodd, Charles. Rom. Cath. Hist. (*Ch. Hist. of Eng.*).. — ..1745?
Dodd, Ralph. Civil Engineer......................... 1761..1822
Dodd, Thomas. (*Connoisseur's Repertory*) .... — ..1850
Dodd, Rev. William, D. D. Executed. L. by Reed, 1777 1729..1777
Doddridge, Sir John. Lawyer and Writer.............. 1555..1628
Doddridge, Philip. Dissenting Divine. Life by Orton.. 1702..1751
Doddridge, Philip. American Lawyer and Politician... 1772..1832
Döderlein, Louis. Professor at Tübingen.............. 1791?..1863
Dodington, George Bubb, Lord Melcombe. Politician.. 1691..1762
Dodoens, or Dodonæus, Rembert. Dutch Botanist ..... 1518..1585
Dodsley, Robert. Poet and Writer.................... 1703..1764
Dodson, Michael. Lawyer and Biblical Writer......... 1732..1799
Dodsworth, Roger. Antiquary and Topographer ...... 1585..1654
Dodvens, or Doudyns, William. Dutch Historical Painter 1630..1697
Dodwell, Edward. (*Classical Tour through Greece*).... 1767..1832
Dodwell, Henry. Theologian. Life by Brokesby, 1715 1641..1711
Dodwell, William. Divine........................... 1709..1785
Doederlein, John Christopher, of Jena. Theologian.... 1748..1792
Does, Jacob van der, *The Old.* Dutch Paint. and Engrav. 1623..1673
Does, Jacob van der, *The Young,* son. Dutch Painter... 1654..1693
Does, Simon van der, brother. Dutch Painter.......... 1653..1717
Doggett, Thomas. Author and Actor.................. — ..1721
Doissin, Louis. Latin Poet........................... 1721..1753
Dolabella, Publius Cornelius. Son-in-law of Cicero.... — B.C.43
Dolben, John. Archbishop of York.................... 1625..1686

BORN. DIED.

Dolce, or Dolci, Carlo. Tuscan Painter............... 1616..1686
Dolce, Louis. Italian Writer......................... 1508..1568
Dole, or Dolæus, John. German Medical Writer........ 1651..1712
Dolet, Stephen. French Jurist....................... 1509..1546
Döllinger, Ignatius. German Physiologist............. 1770..1841
Dollond, George. Optician............................ 1774..1852
Dollond, John. Optician. L. by Rev. John Kelly, LL. D. 1706..1761
Dolomieu, Déodat Guy Silvain Tancred Gratet de.
  French Geologist.................................. 1750..1801
Domat, or Daumat, John. French Jurist............... 1625..1696
Dombey, Joseph. French Botanist and Traveler....... 1742..1796
Dombrowski, John Henry. Polish General............. 1755..1818
Domenichi, Louis. Italian Writer and Translator...... 1500?.1564
Domenichino. *Dominic Zampieri.* Painter........... 1581..1641
Dominic de Guzman, St. Founder of Dominicans and
  Inquisitor. L. by John Anthony Flaminio; Malvenda 1170..1221
Dominis, Mark Anthony de. Abp. of Spalatro; Dean of
  Windsor. (*De Republ. Ecclesiast.; De Radiis Visûs*) .. 1566..1624
Domitian. Roman Emperor (81–96).................... 52.. 96
Domna, Julia. Empress; wife of Septimius Severus.... 158?. 217
Don, David. Scottish Botanist....................... 1800..1840
Donaldson, John William, D. D. Philologist.......... 1812..1861
Donatello. *Donato di Bello di Bardi.* Florentine Sculp. 1383..1466
Donati, Vitalian. (*Natural History of Adriatic Sea*).... 1713..1763
Donato. *See* Donatello. Architect and Sculptor....... 1383..1466
Donato, Alex. Jesuit at Sienna. (*Roma Vetus et Recens*) 1584..1640
Donato, Bernardino. Translator...................... — ..1550
Donato, Jerome. Statesman and Writer............... 1454?.1513
Donato, Marcellus. Italian Count. (*Scholia*)......... fl. 1607
Donatus. Bishop of Casa Nigra. Founder of *Donatists* fl. 212
Donatus, Ælius. Grammarian at Rome .... fl. 356
Doncker, or Donkers, Peter. Painter, of Gouda. 1612..1668
Dondis, James de. *Aggregator.* Med.Writ. & Mathemat. 1298..1359
Donducci, John Andrew. *Il Mastelleta.* Painter...... 1575..1655
Doneau, or Donellus, Hugh. (*De Jure Civili*)......... 1527..1591
Donelli, Sir Ross. Admiral........................... — ..1841
Doni, Anthony Francis. Italian Musician and Poet..... 1513?.1574
Doni, John Baptist. Florentine Musical Writer......... 1593..1647
Doni d'Attichi, Louis. Florentine Writer in France.... 1596..1664
Donizetti, Gaetano. Musical Composer............... 1798..1848
Donne, Benjamin. Mathematician.................... 1729..1798
Donne, John, D. D. Divine and Poet. Life by I. Walton,
  1640; H. Alford, 1839 .... 1573..1631
Donoso Cortes, John Francis Maria de la Salud. Span-
  ish Statesman .... 1809..1853
Donovan, Edward. Naturalist .... 1798..1837
Doolittle, Thomas. Nonconformist Divine............. 1630..1707
Doppelmaier, John Gabriel, of Nuremberg. Mathemat. 1671..1750
Doppet, Francis Amadeus. French Writer and General 1753..1800?
Dorat, Claude Joseph. French Poet.................. 1734..1780
Dorat, or Daurat, John. French Poet................. 1507?.1588
Dorbay, Francis. French Architect .... — ..1697
Dorchester, Carleton Dudley, Viscount. Statesman.... 1573..1632
Dorchester, Catherine Sedley, Countess of............ — ..1692

BORN. DIED.

Doré, Peter. French Theologian.................... 1500?.1559
Doria, Andrew. Genoese Admiral. Life by Richer..... 1468..1560
Dorigny, Louis. Historical Painter................. 1654..1742
Dorigny, Michael. French Painter and Engraver...... 1617..1665
Dorigny, Sir Nicholas. Engraver.................... 1657..1746
Dörink, or Döring, Matthias. German Theologian.
    (*Chronicles of Nuremberg?*).................... 1415? 1464?
Dorislaus, Isaac. Dutch Civil. and Repub. in England — ..1649
D'Orléans, Louis. French Poet and Jurist........... 1542..1629
D'Orleans, Peter Joseph. Jesuit Historian.......... 1644..1698
Dormans, John de. French Cardinal; Founder........ — ..1373
Dornavius, Gaspar. Physician and Humorous Writer.. 1577..1632
Dorr, Thomas Wilson. American Politician........... 1805..1854
D'Orsay, Count Alfred. Artist and Author........... 1798..1852
Dorsch, Everard. Engraver on Gems................. 1649..1712
Dorsch, John Christopher, son. Portrait Engrav. on Gems 1676..1732
Dorset, Ann Clifford, Countess of. Auth. and Benefactor 1589..1676
Dorset, Charles Sackville, Earl of. Wit and Poet...... 1637..1706
Dorset, Edward Sackville, 4th Earl of, K. G. Royalist .. 1590..1652
Dorset, Thos. Sackville, Earl of. Statesman and Author 1527..1608
Dorsey, John Syng. American Physician............. 1783..1818
D'Orville, James Philip. Critic and Classical Editor.... 1696..1751
D'Ossat, Arnaud. Cardinal. French Statesman....... 1536..1604
Dossi, Dosso. Historical Painter.................... — ..1560?
Dost-Mohammed. Emir of Cabul.................... 1785?.1863
Douaren, or Duaren, Francis. French Civilian........ 1509..1559
Doubleday, Edward. Naturalist..................... 1810..1849
Douce, Francis. Antiquary. Benefactor of Oxford Univ. 1762..1834
Doucin, Louis. French Jesuit. (*Hist. of Nestorianism*) 1652..1726
Doudyns, or Dodvens, William. Dutch Historical Paint. 1630..1697
Douffet, or Duffeit, Gerard. Painter, of Liege......... 1594..1660
Dougados, John Francis. *Father Venance.* Polit. & Poet 1763..1794
Doughty, Thos. American Landscape Painter......... 1793..1856
Douglas, Archib., 4th Earl of. *Tineman.* Fell at Verneuil — ..1424
Douglas, Archibald. *Great Earl of Angus.* *Bell-the-Cat* — ..1514
Douglas, David. Botanic Traveler.................... 1798..1834
Douglas, Gawin, or Gavin. Bishop of Dunkeld. Poet.
    Life by Sage .... 1474?.1522
Douglas, General Sir Howard. L. by S. W. Fullom,1863 1776..1861
Douglas, Sir Jas. *The Good Sir James.* Friend of Bruce — ..1330
Douglas, James, 2d Earl of. Slain at Otterburn........ — ..1388
Douglas, James, 9th and last Earl of. Died at Lindores — ..1488
Douglas, James, Earl of Morton. Regent. Beheaded.. 1530..1581
Douglas, James, M. D. Anatomist................... 1675..1742
Douglas, James, Earl of Morton and Aberdeen. Astron. 1707..1768
Douglas, John, Bishop of Salisbury. (*Criterion*)....... 1721..1807
Douglas, Stephen Arnold. American Statesman........ 1813..1861
Douglas, Sylvester, Lord Glenbervie. Politician........ 1743..1823
Douglas, Wm., Knt. of Liddesdale; taken at Nevil's Cross — ..1353
Douglas, William, 1st Earl of. Fought at Poictiers..... — ..1384
Douglas, William, Lord of Nithsdale. *Black Douglas*... — ..1390
Douglas, William. *The Hardy.* Defender of Berwick.. — ..1302
Douglas, William, 6th Earl of. Slain at royal banquet.. — ..1437
Douglas, William, 8th Earl of. Assassinated by James II. — ..1452

Douglass, David Bates, LL. D.   American Engineer .... 1790..1849
Dousa, Janus. Dutch Sch., Sold., & Poet. (*Ann. of Holland*) 1545..1604
Dousa, Janus, son.   Poet, Critic, Philosopher, and Math. 1571..1596
Douven, John Francis.   Dutch Painter............... 1656..1710
Douville, John Baptist.   French Traveler and Naturalist — ..1794
Douvre, Thomas de, of Bayeux.   Archbishop of York.. 1027..1100
Douvre, Thomas de, nephew.   Archbishop of York..... — ..1114
Douw, or Dow, Gerhard.   Dutch Painter.............. 1613..1674?
Dove, Nathaniel.   Penman. (*The Progress of Time*).... 1710?.1754
Dover, G. J. W. Agar Ellis, Lord.   Historical Writer... 1797..1833
Dow, Alex., Lieut.-Col.   Pers. Schol. (*Hist. of Indostan*) — ..1779
Dow, Lorenzo.   Eccentric American Methodist Preacher 1777..1834
Dowland, John.   Musician........................ 1562..1615?
Downes, John.   American Naval Officer .... 1786..1855
Downham, George. Bp. of Derry. (*Christian Warfare*) — ..1644
Downing, Andrew Jackson.   Amer. Landscape Gardener 1815..1852
Downing, Calybute.   Political Divine................. 1606..1644
Downman, Rev. Hugh.   Physician and Poet,.......... 1740..1809
Dowse, Thomas.   American Book-Collector........... 1772..1856
Doyen, Gabriel Francis.   French Painter.............. 1726..1806
Doyle, Sir Charles William.   Military Officer .... — ..1843
Doyle, Jas.   Irish R. C. Bishop. L. by W. J. Fitzpatrick 1786..1834
Doyle, Sir John.   Military Officer..................... 1756..1834
D'Oyly, George, D. D.   Biblical Commentator......... — ..1846
Drabicius, Nicholas.   Moravian Visionary............. 1587..1671
Draco.   Athenian Lawgiver......................... fl. B.C. 621?
Draconites, John.   Lutheran Divine and Commentator 1494..1566
Dragut.   Barbary Corsair .... — ..1565
Drake, Daniel.   American Physician .... 1785..1852
Drake, Sir Francis.   Adm. L. by John Barrow, jr., 1843 1545..1596
Drake, Francis.   Surg. and Antiq. at York. (*Eboracum*) — ..1770
Drake, James.   Phys. and Polit. Writ. Transl. Herodotus 1667..1707
Drake, Joseph Rodman.   American Physician and Poet 1795..1820
Drake, Dr. Nathan.   Physician and Writer .... 1766..1836
Drakenberg, Christian Jacobsen.   Norwegian Centenarian 1624..1770
Drakenborch, Arnold.   Classical Editor............... 1684..1747
Dran, Henry Francis le.   French Surgical Operator ..... 1685..1770
Drant, Rev. Thos.   Archd. of Lewes.   Divine and Poet — ..1578?
Draparnaud, Jas. Philip Raymond. Fr. Phys. and Natur. 1772..1805
Draper, Sir W., K. B., Lieut.-Gen.   Controversial Writer 1721..1787
Drayton, Michael.   Poet. (*Polyolbion*)............... 1563..1631
Drayton, William Henry.   American Political Writer ... 1742..1779
Drebbel, Cornelius van.   Dutch Chemist and Nat. Phil. 1572..1634
Drelincourt, Charles.   French Protestant Divine....... 1595..1669
Drelincourt, Charles, son.   French Medical Writer..... 1633..1697
Drelincourt, Lawrence.   Preacher and Poet........... 1626..1681
Dresser, Matthew.   German Scholar................. 1536..1607
Dreux de Radier, John Francis.   Historical Writer.... 1714..1780
Drevet, Peter.   Engraver at Paris.................... 1664..1739
Drevet, Peter, son.   Engraver .... 1697..1739
Drew, Samuel.   Methodist Divine & Metaphysical Writer.
    Life by his son, J. H. Drew, 1834............ 1765..1833
Drexelius, Jeremiah.   Jesuit, of Augsburg; Writer..... 1581..1638
Driedo, John.   Theologian, of Louvain .... — ..1535

BORN. DIED.

Drinker, Edward. American Centenarian .... 1680..1782
Drinkwater Bethune, John. Colonel. (*Siege of Gibraltar*) 1762?.1844
Drollinger, Charles Frederick. Ger. Poet and Scholar.. 1688..1742
Droste-Hülshoff, Annette Elizabeth. German Lyric Poet 1798..1848
Drouais, Hubert. French Painter..................:.... 1699..1767
Drouet, J. Baptist. French Revolutionist............. 1763..1824
Drouet, Stephen Francis. French Writer .... 1715..1779
Drouet d'Erlon, J. Baptist. Marshal of France. L. by self 1765..1844
Drouot, Anthony, Count. General; friend of Napoleon.. 1774..1847
Droz, Henry Louis Jacquet. Swiss Mechanician .... 1752..1791
Droz, Francis Xavier Joseph. French Writer .... 1773..1850
Druey, Charles. Swiss Statesman .... 1799..1855
Drummond, Geo., of Edinb. Magistrate and Benefactor. 1687..1766
Drummond, Robert Hay. Archbishop of York .... 1711..1776
Drummond, Captain Thomas. Statesman & Philosopher.
    Inventor of *Drummond Light*...................... 1797..1840
Drummond, William, of Hawthornden. Poet. Life by
    P. Cunningham, 1823 .... 1585..1649
Drummond, Sir Wm. Antiquary, Statesman, and Author 1760? 1828
Drury, Dru. Naturalist............................. — ..1804
Drury, Rev. Joseph. Master of Harrow School......... 1750..1834
Drury, Robert. Seaman. Writer on Madagascar ...... 1687..1735?
Drusius, John. French Protestant Theologian .... 1550..1616
Drusus, M. Livius. Trib. Plebis B.C. 91. Assassinated. — B.C. 91
Drusus, Nero Claudius. *Germanicus.* Br. of Emp. Tiberius 38 B.C. 9
Drusus, son of Germanicus Cæsar. Starved by Tiberius — A.D. 33
Drusus Cæsar, son of Tiberius. Poisoned B.C.13.A.D.23
Druthmar, Christian. Monk of Corby. Commentator fl.ab.860 A.D.
Dryander, John. German Mathematician and Anatomist — ..1560
Dryander, Jonas. Swedish Naturalist................. 1748..1810
Dryden, John. Poet. Life by Sir Walter Scott; Malone,
    1800; R. Hooper.............................. 1631..1701
Drysdale, Rev. John, D.D. Scottish Div. Life by Dalzel 1718..1788
Duane, William. American Politician................. 1760..1835
Duaren, or Douaren, Francis. *Durenius.* French Civilian 1509..1559
Dubarry, Marie Jeanne, Countess. Favorite of Louis XV. 1746..1793
Dubartas, William de Sallust. Poet, Warrior, Statesman 1544..1590
Dubellay, Joachim. French Poet.................... 1524?.1560
Dubellay, John. Cardinal Archbishop .... 1492..1560
Dubellay, Martin. Prince of Yvetot. General, Negotiator,
    and Writer. (*Memoirs*)............................ — ..1559
Dubellay, Wm. Ld. of Langey. Gen., Negot., and Writer 1491..1543
Dubelloy, Peter Lawrence Buyrette. Dramatic Writer.
    (*Siege of Calais.*) Life by Gaillard................. 1727..1775
Dubocage, Marie Anne le Page. French Poet .... 1710..1802
Dubofe, Claude Mary. French Painter................ 1790?.1864
Dubois, Anthony. French Surgeon .... 1756..1837
Dubois, Charles Francis. Ecclesiastical Writer........ 1661..1724
Dubois, Dorothea. Novelist....................... — ..1774
Dubois, Edward. English Satirical Writer............. 1775..1850
Dubois, Francis. Dutch Medical Writer .... 1614..1672
Dubois, James. *Sylvius.* French Medical Writer ...... 1478..1555
Dubois, John. Flemish Medical Writer ....,. — ..1576
Dubois, John Anthony. French Abbé and Missionary .. 1765..1848

BORN. DIED.

Dubois, Simon. Dutch Painter...................... — ..1708
Dubois, William. Cardinal and Prime Minister of France 1656..1723
Dubois de Crancé, Edm. Louis Alexis. Fr. Statesman 1747..1814
Dubos, Charles Francis. French Theologian.......... 1661..1724
Dubos, Jerome. Dutch Painter .... fl. 16th c.
Dubos, J. Bapt. Abbé. Statesman, Hist., and Art Writer 1670..1742
Duboucher, Matthew. French Law Writer and Poet.... — ..1801
Dubourg, Anne, or Annas. French Protestant Martyr .. 1521..1559
Dubourg, Matthew. English Violinist............... 1703..1767
Dubraw, John, or Dubravius Scala. German Prelate,
   Statesman, and Historian.......................... — ..1553
Dubreul, James. French Jesuit Writer on Perspective.. 1528..1614
Dubuisson, Francis René Andrew.................... 1763..1836
Dubuisson, Paul Ulrich. French Author............. 1746..1794
Duc, Fronton du. French Jesuit Writer.............. 1558..1624
Duc, John le. Dutch Painter of Animals............. 1636..1671
Ducange, Charles Dufresne, Sieur. French Antiquary .. 1610..1688
Ducarel, Andrew Coltee. English Antiquary .... 1713..1785
Ducart, Isaac. Dutch Flower-Painter .... 1630..1697
Ducas, Michael. Byzantine Historian................ fl. 15th c.
Ducasse, J. Baptist. French Admiral............... — ..1715
Duccio di Buoninsegna. Painter of Sienna.......... — ..1340?
Duchal, James. Irish Divine....................... 1697..1761
Duchange, Gaspar. French Engraver .... 1662..1756
Duchat, Jacob le. French Editor at Berlin.......... 1658..1735
Duchâtel, Gaspar. French Statesman................ 1766..1793
Duchâtel, Tanneguy. French Warrior............... 1360?.1449
Duchâtelet, Gabrielle, Émilie le Tonnelier de Breteuil,
   Marchioness. Translator of *Principia* .... 1706..1749
Duchatelet d'Haraucourt, Louis Mary Flo. Politician 1626?.1792
Duché, Jacob. American Clergyman.
Duché de Vancey, Joseph Francis. French Poet...... 1668..1704
Duchesne, Andrew. French Geographer and Historian. 1584..1640
Duchesne de Gisors, J. Bapt. Jos. French Painter.... 1770..1856
Ducis, John Francis. French Dramatist .... 1733..1816
Duck, Arthur. Civilian and Historical Writer......... 1580..1649
Duck, Rev. Steph. Poet. Life by Rev. Jos. Spence, 1764 1700..1756
Duckworth, Sir John Thomas. Admiral............. 1748..1817
Duclos, Charles Pineau. Historical Writer and Biographer 1704..1772
Duclos, John Francis. French Poet................. 1705..1752
Duclos, Mary Ann. French Actress................. 1664?.1748
Ducornet, Louis Cæsar Jos. French Artist........... 1806..1856
Ducrest de Villeneuve, Alex. Louis. French Admiral. 1777..1852
Ducreux, Joseph. French Portrait Painter.......... 1737..1802
Dudeffant. *See* Deffand. Literary Lady at Paris...... 1697..1780
Dudith, Andrew. Scholar and Statesman .... 1533..1589
Dudley, Ambrose, Baron L'Isle and Earl of Warwick.... 1530?.1589
Dudley, Charles Edw. American Statesman .... 1780..1841
Dudley, Dud. Ironmaster. (*Metallum Martis*)........ 1599..1684
Dudley, Edm. Statesm. (*Tree of the Commonwealth*.) Beh. 1462..1510
Dudley, Lord Guilford, husband of Jane Grey. Beheaded — ..1554
Dudley, Rev. Sir Henry Bate. Miscellaneous Writer ... 1745..1824
Dudley, John, Duke of Northumberland. Beheaded..... 1502..1553
Dudley, John William Ward, Earl of. Statesman ...... 1781..1833

BORN. DIED.
Dudley, Paul. Colonial Chief Justice of Massachusetts.. 1675. 1751
Dudley, Robert, Earl of Leicester; rival of Essex .... 1532? 1588
Dudley, Sir Robert, son. Philosopher and Engineer .... 1573..1639
Duer, John. American Jurist .... 1782..1858
Duer, William Alex., brother. Jurist .... 1780..1858
Du Fay, Chas. Francis de Cisternay. French Savant .. 1698..1739
Dufrénoy, Peter Armand. Fr. Geologist and Mineral... 1792..1857
Dufresne, Abraham Alexis Quinault. French Actor.... 1695..1767
Dufresne, Charles, Sieur Ducange. French Antiquary.. 1610..1688
Dufresne, Philip Canoy, Sieur. Statesman and Lawyer. 1551..1610
Dufresnoy, Charles Alfonso. French Painter and Poet.
  (De Arte Graphicâ)................................ 1611..1665
Dufresnoy. Historian. See Lenglet.................. 1674..1755
Dufresny, Charles Rivière. French Comic Writer .... 1648..1724
Dugard, William. English Scholar. (Lexic. Græci Test.) 1606..1662
Dugdale, Sir Wm. Antiq. and Hist. Life by Hamper, 1827 1605..1686
Dughet, Gaspar. Gaspar Poussin. French Painter ..... 1613..1675
Dugommier, John Francis Coquille. Fr. Repub. General 1736..1794
Duguay-Trouin, René. French Admiral.............. 1673..1736
Duguesclin, Bertrand. Constable of France. Life by
  Claude Menard; Guyard de Berville; Jamison, 1864.. 1314?.1380
Duguet, James Joseph. French Theologian........... 1649..1733
Du Halde, J. Baptist. French Jesuit. (History of China) 1674..1743
Duhamel, J. Baptist. Commentator and Naturalist .... 1624..1706
Duhamel, John Peter Francis Guillot. French Metallurgist 1730..1816
Duhamel du Monceau, Henry Louis. French Philos. 1700..1782
Duhan, Lawrence. (Philosophus in Utramque Partem)... 1656?.1726
Duigenan, Dr. Patrick. Irish Civilian and Politician.
  (Lacrymæ Academicæ)............................. 1735?.1816
Duilius, Caius. Consul and Admiral, B. C. 260.......fl.260-231 B.C.
Duisburg, Peter de. (Chronicle of Prussia)........... fl. 16th c.
Dujardin, Charles. Dutch Painter................... 1640..1678
Dujarry, Lawrence Juillard. French Theologian & Poet 1658..1730
Duke, Rev. Richard. Divine and Poet .... 1655?.1711
Duker, Charles Andrew. German Classical Editor ..... 1670..1752
Dulaure, James Anthony. French Historical Writer.... 1755..1835
Dulcinus. Leader of the Dulcinists................... — ..1308
Dullaert, Heyman, or Herman. Dutch Painter .... 1636..1684
Dulon, Frederick Louis. Prussian Flutist and Composer 1769..1826
Dulong, Peter Louis. French Chemist .... 1785..1838
Dumandre, Anthony. Sculptor .... — ..1761
Dumandre, Hubert, brother. Sculptor and Architect... 1701..1781
Dumaniant, Anthony John Bourlin. Fr. Actor and Dram. 1752..1828
Dumaresq, Henry. British Officer................... 1792..1838
Dumas, Alex. Davy. French General................ 1762..1806
Dumas, Louis. French Musician .... 1676..1744
Dumas, Matthew, Count. French Soldier and Historian . 1753..1837
Dumée, Joan. French Astronomer .... fl. 1680
Dumesnil, J. Bap. Gardin. Fr. Writ. (Synonymes Latines) 1720..1802
Dumesnil, Mary Frances. French Actress............ 1711..1803
Dummer, Jere. American Writer and Political Agent... 1680?.1739
Dumont, George. Statistical Writer................. 1725..1788
Dumont, John. Baron of Carlscroon. Hist. & Publicist — ..1726?
Dumont, John. Le Romain. French Painter .... 1700..1781

BORN. DIED.

Dumont, Peter Stephen Louis. Writer on Legislation.. 1759..1829
Dumont d'Urville, Jul. Sebast.Cæsar. French Navigator 1790..1842
Dumoulin, Charles. *Molinæus.* French Jurist .... 1500..1566
Dumoulin, Louis, br. Independent. (*Patronus Bonæ Fidei*) 1606..1683
Dumoulin, Peter. *Molinæus.* French Protestant Divine 1568..1658
Dumoulin, Pet., son. Engl. Div. (*Regii Sanguinis Clamor*) 1600..1684
Dumouriez, Anne Francis Dupérier. French Poetess .. 1707..1769
Dumouriez, Charles Francis Dupérier. French General 1739..1823
Dun, David Erskine, Lord. Scottish Judge .... 1670..1755
Dunbar, George. Prof. of Greek at Edinburgh. (*Lexicon*) 1774?.1851
Dunbar, William. Scottish Poet. Life by Laing .... 1465?.1530?
Duncan, Adam, Lord. Admiral .... 1731..1804
Duncan, Daniel. Physician....................... 1649...1735
Duncan, Mark. Scottish Phys. and Philosoph. Writer.. — ..1640
Duncan, Philip Bury, D. C. L. Naturalist, Antiq.,Philanth. — ..1863
Duncan, Thomas, R. S. A. Scottish Painter........... 1807..1845
Duncan,Wm. Prof. at Aberdeen. Writ. & Transl. (*Logic*) 1717..1760
Duncan, Rev. William Cecil, D. D. American Clergyman
    and Writer .... 1824..1864
Duncombe, Rev. John. Poet. (*Feminead*)............ 1730..1786
Duncombe, Wm. Poet & Misc. Writ. (*L. Jun. Brutus*) 1690..1769
Dundas, Sir David. General........................ 1736..1820
Dundas, Henry, First Viscount Melville. Statesman.... 1740..1811
Dundas, Sir Jas. Whitley Deans. Admiral in Black Sea 1785..1862
Dundas, Sir Richard Saunders. Admiral in the Baltic.. 1802..1861
Dundas, Thomas. British Officer.................... 1750..1795
Dundee, John Graham of Claverhouse, Viscount........ 1650? 1689
Dundonald, Thomas Cochrane, Tenth Earl of. Naval
    Officer. (*Autobiography of a Seaman*) .... 1775..1860
Duni, Egidio Romualdo. Italian Musical Composer .... 1709..1775
Dunlap, William. American Artist and Writer........ 1760..1839
Dunlop, Alex. Prof. at Glasgow. (*Greek Grammar*) 1684..1742
Dunlop, Wm., brother. Prof. and Preach. at Edinburgh 1692..1720
Dunn, Samuel. Mathematician at Chelsea............. — ..1792
Dunning, John, First Lord Ashburton. Lawyer........ 1731..1783
Dunod de Charnage, Francis Ign., of Besançon. Writer 1679..1752
Dunois, John d'Orleans, Count. French Commander.... 1402?.1468
Duns Scotus, John. Schoolman..................... 1265?.1308
Dunstable, John. Musical Composer and Mathematician 1400?.1458
Dunstan, St. Archbishop of Canterbury. Life by Ada-
    lard; Bridferth; Osbern; Eadmer; Wm. Malmesbury 925.. 988
Dunster, Rev. Charles. Divine and Scholar .... — ..1816
Dunster, Rev. Henry. 1st President of Harvard College — ..1659
Dunthorne, Richard. Astron., Engineer, & Antiq. Artist — ..1775
Dunton, John. Bookseller & Auth. L. by Nicholas, 1818 1659..1733
Dunz, or Duns, John. Swiss Painter................. 1645..1736
Du Pan, Mallet. Political Writer................... 1749..1800
Dupaty, Chas. Marg. J. Baptist Mercier. Fr. Publicist 1746..1788
Dupaty, Charles Mercier, son. Sculptor............. 1771..1825
Duperray, Michael. French Lawyer and Eccles. Writer 1640?.1730
Duperré, Victor Guy, Baron. French Admiral......... 1775..1846
Duperron, Anquetil. French Orientalist .... 1731..1805
Duperron, James Davy. Cardinal Archbishop of Sens.
    Life by Burigny .... 1556..1618

BORN. DIED.

Dupetit Thouars, Louis Mary Albert. French Botanist 1758..1831
Dupin, Louis Ellies. Ecclesiastical Historian......... 1657..1719
Dupino, Chas. Francis. Fr. Philos. (*La Relig. Universelle*) 1742..1809
Dupleix, Joseph Francis, Marquis. Fr. Governor in India 1700?.1763
Dupleix, Scipio. French Historian................... 1569..1661
Duplessis-Mornay, Philip de. Statesman and Writer 1549..1623
Duponceau, Peter Steph. Fr. Writer. (*Primitive World*) 1760..1844
Dupont, James Charles de l'Eure. French Statesman... 1767..1855
Dupont de l'Étang, Peter, Count. French General.... 1765..1838
Dupont de Nemours, Peter Samuel. Polit. Economist 1739..1817
Duport, Francis Mathurin. French Revolutionist....... 1748?.1794
Duport, James, D. D. Greek Scholar and Commentator 1606..1679
Duppa, Brian. Bishop of Salisbury and Winchester..... 1589..1662
Duppa, Richard. Biographer and Writer............ 1755?.1831
Duprat, Anthony. Cardinal. French Statesman....... 1463..1535?
Dupré d'Aulnay, Louis. French Physiologist......... 1670?.1758
Dupré de St. Maur, Nicholas Francis. French Writer.. 1696..1774
Dupuis, Charles. French Engraver.................. 1685..1742
Dupuis, Charles Francis. Writer and Philosopher...... 1742..1809
Dupuis, Nicholas Gabriel, brother. Engraver.......... 1695..1771
Dupuis, Dr. Thomas Saunders. Eng. Musical Composer 1733..1796
Dupuy, Peter. Fr. Antiquarian and Hist. L. by Rigault 1582..1651
Dupuytren, William le, Baron. French Anatomist..... 1777..1835
Duquesne, Abraham, Marquis. Fr. Naval Commander 1610..1688
Duquesnoy, Francis. Flemish Sculptor.............. 1594..1646
Durand, David. Fr. Protestant. Preacher and Historian 1679?.1763
Durand, John Nicholas Louis. French Architect....... 1760..1834
Durand, Wm. Fr. Lawyer and Prelate. (*Speculum Juris*) 1230?.1296
Durand de Maillane, Peter Toussaint. French Lawyer 1729..1814
Durand de St. Pourçain, William. Bishop. *Most Reso-*
    lute Doctor...................................... — ..1332
Durant, Giles. French Humorous Poet.............. 1550?.1615
Durante, Francis. Sacred Music Composer........... 1693..1755
Duranti, Durante. Italian Poet and Orator.......... 1718..1780
Duranti, John Stephen. (*De ritibus Ecclesiæ*)......... 1534..1589
Durão, or Duram, Joseph de Santa Rita. Brazilian Poet 1737..1783
Duras, Clara, Duchess de. Writer and Philanthropist... 1779..1828
Durbach, Ann Louisa. German Poetess.............. 1722..1791
Dureau de la Malle, Adolphus Julius Cæsar Augustus.
    French Author.................................. 1777..1857
Durell, David. Biblical Critic..................... 1728?.1775
Durell, John. Dean of Windsor. Apologist for Ch. of Eng. 1626..1683
Dürer, Albert. Engraver and Painter............... 1471..1528
Duret, Louis. French Medical Writer............... 1527..1586
Durfee, Job. American Writer and Jurist............ 1790..1847
D'Urfey, Thomas. Dramatic Author................. 1628?.1723
Durham, Simeon of. Historian.................... — ..1130?
Durham, James. Scottish Divine................... 1622?..1658
Durham, John Geo. Lambton, 1st Earl of. Gov. of Canada 1792..1840
Durham, Sir Philip Charles Calderwood. Admiral. Life
    by Captain A. Murray, 1846................... 1763..1845
Duringer, Melchior. Ecclesiastical Historian at Berne... 1647?.1723
Duroc, Gerard Christopher Michael, Duke of Friuli. Mar-
    shal of France................................ 1772..1813

BORN. DIED.

Dury, or Duræus, John. Scottish Divine.............. —aft.1674
Dusart, Cornelius. Dutch Painter.................... 1665..1704
Dusatoy, James. Poet............................... 1796?.1815
Du Sommerard, Alexander. French Archæologist..... 1779..1842
Dussault, John Joseph. Fr. Writ. (*Annales Littéraires*) 1769..1824
Dussaulx, John. Erench Politician and Writer......... 1728..1799
Dussek, John Louis. Musical Composer.............. 1762..1812
Dutens, Joseph Michael. French Engineer............ 1765..1848
Dutens, Louis. French Miscellaneous Writer.......... 1730..1812
Dutertre, John Baptist. (*Histoire des Antilles*)........ 1610..1687
Dutrochet, René Joachim Henry. French Naturalist... 1776..1847
Duval, Alexander Vincent Pineu. French Writer....... 1767..1842
Duval, Amaury Pineu. French Writer................ 1760..1838
Duval, Claude. Highwayman. Life by Dr. Walter Pope — ..1670
Duval, Nicholas. Dutch Painter..................... 1644..1732
Duval, Peter. French Geographer and Chronologist..... 1618..1683
Duval, Valentine Jamarai. Scholar.................. 1695..1775
Duvaucel, Alfred. French Naturalist................. 1581..1643
Duvenede, Mark van. Dutch Historical Painter....... 1674..1729
Du Verdier, Anthony. Biographer and Bibliographer.. 1544..1600
Duvergier de Hauranne, John. Abbot of St. Oyran.
   Theologian .... 1581..1643
Duverney, Joseph Guichard. French Anatomist....... 1648..1730
Duvernoy, George Louis. Fr. Anatomist and Zoölogist 1777..1855
Duvoisin, John Baptist. Bishop of Nantes. Theologian 1744..1813
Duyckinck, George Long. American Author. (*Cyclopæ-*
   dia of American Literature)........................ 1822..1863
Dwarris, Sir Fortunatus William Lilley. Antiquarian
   and Legal Writer................................. 1787?.1860
Dwight, Theo. American Author and Journalist....... 1765..1846
Dwight, Timothy. American Divine................... 1752..1817
Dwnn, Lewis. Welsh Herald....................... fl. 1614
Dyce, William, R. A. Painter, Composer, and Writer... 1806..1864
Dyche, Thomas. Schoolmaster and Schoolbook Writer.. — ..1750
Dyer, Sir Edward. Poet............................. 1540?.1610
Dyer, George. Classical Scholar and Writer........... 1755..1841
Dyer, Sir James, Chief Justice. (*Reports.*) L, by Vaillant 1512?.1582
Dyer, Rev. John. Poet. (*The Fleece; Ruins of Rome*).. 1700..1758
Dyer, Samuel. Writer.............................. 1725?.1772
Dyer, William. Ejected Nonconformist Divine......... — ..1696
Dymond, Jonathan. Quaker. (*Principles of Morality*) 1796..1828

E.

	BORN.	DIED.
Eachard, John, D. D. Divine. Life by Thomas Davies	1636..	1697
Eadmer, or Edmer. Historian and Biographer.ʼ........	— ..	1124?
Eadsige. Archbishop of Canterbury (1038–50).........	— ..	1050
Eardley, Sir Culling E. English Publicist............	1805..	1863
Earle, John. Bp. of Worc. & Salisb. (*Microcosmography*)	1601..	1665
Earle, Pliny. American Inventor....................	1762..	1832
Earle, Thomas, brother. Writer on Law.............	1791..	1849
Earlom, Richard. Mezzotint Engraver. (*Liber Veritatis*)	1740..	1822
Eastburn, James Wallis. American Author............	1797..	1819
Eaton, John. Antinomian Divine...................	1575..	1641
Eaton, William. American Soldier..................	1764..	1811
Ebedjesu. *Bar Bricha.* Nestorian Writer of Syria....	— ..	1318
Ebel, John Godfrey. Ger. Writ. on Statistics & Geology	1764..	1830
Ebeling, Christopher Daniel. Geographer............	1741..	1817
Ebelmen, James Joseph. French Chemist............	1814..	1852
Eberhard, Augustus Theophilus. German Author......	1769..	1845
Eberhard, Conrad. German Artist	1768..	1859
Eberhard, John Augustus. German Divine...........	1739..	1809
Eberhard im Bart. First Duke of Würtemberg.......	1445..	1496
Ebert, Theod. Ger. Hebraist. (*Eulogia Jurisconsultorum*)	— ..	1630
Eberus, Paul. Reformer...........................	1511..	1589
Ebroin. Mayor of the Palace of Neustria............	— ..	681
Eccard, or Eckhart, John George. Ger. Hist. and Antiq.	1674..	1730
Ecchellensis, or Echellensis, Abr. Maronite Orientalist.	— ..	1664
Eccles, John. Violinist............................	— ..	1735
Echard, Father James. Biographer of Dominican Order	1644..	1724
Echard, Lawrence. Archdeacon. (*History of England*)	1671?.	1730
Echinus, or Erizzo, Sebastian. Venetian Medalist.....	1525..	1585
Eck, or Eckius, John, of Ingoldstadt. Opponent of Luther	1486..	1543
Eckermann, John Peter. German Scholar and Author	1792..	1854
Eckhard, John Frederick. Philologist and Bibliographer	1723..	1794
Eckhard, or Eccard, John George. Ger. Hist. and Antiq.	1674..	1730
Eckhel, Joseph Hilary. Jesuit, Antiquary and Medalist	1737..	1798
Ecluse, Charles de lʼ. *Clusius.* Dutch Phys. & Botanist	1526..	1609
Edelinck, Gerard. Dutch Engraver in France........	1649..	1707
Edema, Gerard. Dutch Landscape Painter...........	1654?.	1700?
Eden, Sir Fred. Morton. Statist.Writ. (*Laboring Classes*)	1766?.	1809
Eden, Sir Morton, First Lord Henley. Ambassador.....	— ..	1802
Eder, George. German Lawyer. (*Œconomia Bibliorum*)	1524..	1586
Edgar. King of England (959–75)....................	943?.	975
Edgar. King of Scotland...........................	— ..	1107
Edgar, John George. Biographer, Novelist, &c........	1834?.	1864
Edgar Atheling. Heir of the Anglo-Saxon Line	— ..	1120?
Edgeworth, Miss Maria. Novelist...................	1767..	1849
Edgeworth, Richard Lovell. Agriculturist and Writer..	1744..	1817
Edgeworth de Firmont, Henry Allen. Confessor to Louis XVI......................................	1745..	1807
Edmer, or Eadmer. Historian and Biographer........	— ..	1124?
Edmondes, Clement. Scholar......................	1566..	1622
Edmondes, Sir Thomas. Statesman.................	1563?.	1639

BORN. DIED.

Edmondson, Joseph. Heraldic Writer................ — ..1786
Edmund, St. King of East Anglia (854–70) and Martyr 841.. 870
Edmund I. *The Elder.* King of England (940–46)...923..946 or 8
Edmund II. *Ironside.* (1016–17)................... 989..1017
Edmund D'Abingdon, St. Archbishop of Canterbury
(1234–40). Life by Robert Bacon................... — ..1240
Edred. King of England (946–55)................... — .. 955?
Edrisi. Arabian Geographer.......................'.......... 1099..1164?
Edward I. King of England........................ 1239..1307
Edward II. Life by Thomas de la More; Edward Fan-
nant, 1680; Henry Viscount Faulkland, 1680......... 1284..1327
Edward III. Life by Thomas May, 1635; Barnes, 1688 1312..1377
Edward IV. Life by J. Habington................... 1441..1483
Edward V. Life by Sir Thomas More................ 1470..1483
Edward VI. Life by Sir J. Hayward, 1630.......... 1537..1553
Edward. Pr. of Wales; son of Henry VI.; sl. at Tewkesb. 1543..1572
Edward the Black Prince. Life by Arthur Collins,
1740; G. P. R. James; A. P. Stanley, in *Memor. Cant.* 1330..1376
Edward the Confessor. King of England (1042–66). Life
by Ailred; Lives, edited by Luard.............. 1004?.1066
Edward the Elder. King of the West Saxons (901–24) 870?. 924
Edward the Martyr. King of England (975–8)........ 961?. 978
Edward Plantagenet, Earl of Warwick, nephew of
Edward IV. Beheaded........................... 1445..1499
Edwards, Bela Bates, D. D. American Author......... 1802..1852
Edwards, Bryan. Historian of West Indies. Life by self 1743..1800
Edwards, Edward. Artist and Writer. (*Perspective*).. 1738..1806
Edwards, George. Naturalist. (*History of Birds*)...... 1693..1773
Edwards, John, D. D. Divine...................... 1637..1716
Edwards, Jonathan, D. D. Anti-Socinian Writer....... 1629..1712
Edwards, Jonathan. President of New Jersey College.
Calvinistic Divine. (*Freedom of Will.*) L. by Hopkins 1703..1758
Edwards, Jona., D. D., son. Metaphysician and Theologian 1745..1801
Edwards, Justin, D. D. American Divine and Temperance
Reformer.. 1787..1853
Edwards, Richard. Poet.......................... 1523..1566?
Edwards, Thomas. Presbyterian Writer. (*Gangræna*). 1599?.1647
Edwards, Thomas. Poetical Writer. (*Canons of Criticism*) 1699..1757
Edwards, Thomas, D. D. Divine. (*Selecta Theocriti*)... 1729..1785
Edwards, William. Bridge Engineer................ 1719..1789
Edwin. King of Northumbria (617–33). Bretwalda.... 585?. 633
Edwin, John. Comic Actor........................ 1750..1790
Edwy. King of England (955–59)................... 939?. 959
Eeckhout, Anthony van den. Flemish Painter........ 1656..1695
Eeckhout, Gerbrandt van den. Dutch Painter........ 1621..1674
Effen, Justus van. Dutch Writer.................. 1684..1735
Egbert. King of England (802–839)................ — .. 839?
Egede, Hans, or John. Danish Missionary to Greenland 1686..1758
Egede, Paul, son. Miss. to Greenland, & Lexicographer. 1708..1789
Egerton, Daniel. Actor........................... 1772..1835
Egerton, Francis, Duke of Bridgew. Promoter of Canals 1729..1803
Egerton, Rev. Francis Henry. Earl of Bridgewater. Pro-
moter of *Essays*................................. 1758..1829
Egerton, Francis Leveson, E. of Ellesmere. *See* Ellesmere 1800..1857

BORN. DIED.

Egerton, John. Bishop of Durham.................... 1721..1787
Egerton, Thomas. First Lord Ellesmere, Viscount Brack-
  ley. Lord Chancellor............................. 1540?.1617
Egg, Augustus Leopold. Painter...................... 1817?.1863
Eggeling, John Henry, of Bremen. Medalist & Antiquary 1639..1713
Eginhard. Biographer of Charlemagne................ 771?. 840?
Eginton, Francis. Painter on Glass.................. 1737..1805
Eglantine. See Fabre. Fr. Writer and Revolutionist .. 1755..1794
Egmont, Justus van. Historical Painter.............. 1602..1674
Egmont, Lamoral, Ct. of. Flemish Statesman. Behead. 1522..1568
Egnazio, J. Bapt. Cipelli. Venetian Orator and Scholar.. 1473..1553
Egremont, George O'Brien Wyndham, Third Earl of ... 1751..1837
Ehret, George Dionysius. Botanical Painter.......... 1710..1770
Eichendorff, Jos. Chas. Benedict, Baron. Ger. Author. 1788..1857
Eichhorn, Charles Frederick. Jurisconsult............ 1781..1854
Eichhorn, John Godfrey. Biblical Critic .... 1752..1827
Eichman, John. Dryander. Physician and Astronomer — ..1560
Eichner, Ernest. German Musical Composer .... 1740..1778
Eisen, Charles. Artist at Brussels .... 1721..1778
Eisengrein, Martin, D. D. German Controversial Divine — ..1578
Eisenschmidt, John Gaspar. German Mathematician.. 1656..1712
Ekins, Jeffrey, D. D. Divine and Scholar............. — ..1791
Elagabalus. Rom. Emp. (218–222). L. by Æ. Lampridius 205?. 222
Elbée, Gigot d'. Royalist Leader of La Vendée........ 1752..1794
Elbene, Alphonsus d'. Bishop. (De Regno Burgundiæ) 1540?.1608
Elbert, Samuel. American Revolutionary Officer....... 1743..1788
Elbœuf, Charles de Lorraine, Marquis d'. Politician.... 1596..1657
Elbœuf, Eman. Maurice, Duc d'. Discov. of Herculaneum 1677..1763
Elbœuf, René de Lorraine, Marquis d'. Politician...... — ..1566
Elburcht, John van. Painter at Antwerp.............. 1500.. —
Eldon, John Scott, Earl of. Lord Chancellor. Life by
  H. Twiss; W. E. Surtees, 1846.................... 1751..1838
Eleanor of Aquit. Q. of Henry II. L. by Isaac de Larrey 1122..1204?
Eleanor of Castile. Queen of Edward I............... — ..1290
Eleanor of Este. Italian Princess beloved by Tasso.... 1537..1581
Eleanor of Provence. Queen of Henry III........... — ..1291
Eleanor of Toledo................................... 1526.. —
Eleanora Tellez. Portuguese Beauty; Q. of Ferd. I... 1330..1405
Eleutherius. Bishop of Rome (177–192) .... — .. 192
Elfric. Archbishop of Canterbury (995–1006) .... — ..1006
Elgin and Kincardine, James Bruce, Eighth Earl of.
  Governor-General of India.......................... 1811..1863
Elgin and Kincardine, Thos. Bruce, 7th E. of. (Marbles) 1766..1841
Elias, Matthew. Portrait and Historical Painter........ 1658..1741
Elias Levita. Jewish Rabbi .... 1472..1549
Elich, Louis Philip. Ger. Writer. (De Magiâ Diabolicâ) fl. 1607
Elichman, John. Physician and Orientalist at Leyden.. — ..1639
Élie de Beaumont, Ann Louisa. Writer............... 1729..1783
Élie de Beaumont, J. Baptist James. French Writer . 1732..1786
Eliot, Sir John. Statesman. Life by John Forster, 1864. 1590..1632
Eliot, John. Apostle of the Indians. Missionary. Life by
  Cotton Mather.................................... 1604..1689
Eliot, John, D. D. Amer. Writer. (New Eng. Biog. Dict.) 1754..1813
Eliot, or Elyot, Sir Thomas. Writer. (The Governor).. 1495?.1546

BORN. DIED.

Elliott, Geo. Aug., 1st Ld. Heathfield. Defender of Gibraltar 1718?.1790
Eliott, Sir John. Physician in London .... — ..1787
Eliott, Rev. Richard. Controversial Divine .... — ..1789
Elisha. Hebrew Prophet; successor of Elijah .... ab.840 B.C.
Elizabeth, or Isabella, of Austria. Queen of Charles IX.
   of France.. 1454..1592
Elizabeth. Queen of England. L. by Leti; Dr. T. Birch,
   1754; Camden; Thomas Heywood; Madame Robert .. 1533..1603
Elizabeth, Madame, sister of Louis XVI................. 1764..1794
Elizabeth Farnese. Queen of Spain................. 1692..1766
Elizabeth-Christina. Queen of Frederick the Great of
   Prussia. Life by Von Hahnke, 1848............... 1715..1797
Elizabeth-Petrovna. Empress of Russia .... 1709..1761
Elizabeth, St., of Hungary. Life by Simon; Count
   Montalembert...................................... 1207..1231
Elizabeth Stuart. Queen of Bohemia. Life by Miss
   Benger, 1825....................................... 1596..1662
Elizabeth Woodville. Q. of England. Wife of Edw. IV. — ..1488
Elizabeth of York. Q. of England. Wife of Henry VII. 1466..1502
Ellenborough, Edward Law, First Lord. Lord Chief
   Justice. Life by Lord Campbell .... 1748..1818
Eller de Brookhusen, John Theodore. Medical Writer 1689..1760
Ellery, William. American Statesman .... 1727..1820
Ellesmere, Francis Egerton, Earl of. (*Medit. Sketches*) 1800..1857
Ellesmere, Thomas Egerton, Baron. Lord Chancellor... 1540?.1617
Ellet, William Henry. American Chemist .... 1804?.1859
Ellicott, Andrew. Amer. Astron. and Civil Engineer... 1754..1820
Elliger, Ottomar. Painter of Fruits and Flowers.... 1632 or 3..1688
Elliger, Ottomar, son. Historical Painter............. 1666..1732
Elliott, Ebenezer. *Corn Law Rhymer.* L. by Searle, 1852 1781..1849
Elliott, Jesse Duncan. American Naval Officer......... 1782..1845
Elliott, Stephen. American Naturalist .... 1771..1830
Elliott, William. Engraver .... 1717..1766
Ellis, Clement. Divine. Life by Veneer................ 1630..1700
Ellis, George. (*Specimens of Early English Poets*) ...... 1745..1815
Ellis, G. J. W. Agar, Lord Dover. Historical Writer....1797..1833
Ellis, Henry. Voyager and Governor of Georgia........ 1721..1806
Ellis, John. Writer on Zoöphytes..................... 1710?.1776
Ellis, John. Poet................................... 1698..1791
Elliston, Robert William. Comedian.................. 1774..1831
Ellsworth, Oliver, LL. D. American Jurist............. 1745..1807
Ellwood, Thomas. Quaker Writer. Life by self....... 1639..1713
Ellys, Anthony. Bishop of St. David's. Theologian.... 1693..1761
Ellys, Sir Richard, Bart. Writer...................... — ..1742
Elmacinus, George. Saracen Historian .... 1223..1273
Elmenhorst, Geverhard, of Hamburg. Critic. (*Cebes*). — ..1621
Elmenhorst, Henry. Writer on Public Spectacles...... 1632..1704
Elmer, John. Bishop of London. *See Aylmer* .... 1521..1594
Elmes, Harvey Lonsdale. Architect................... 1814?.1847
Elmore, Franklin Harper. American Financier .... 1799..1850
Elmsley, Peter, D. D. Critic........................ 1773..1825
Elphege. Archbishop of Canterbury .... 954?.1012
Elphinston, Arthur, Lord Balmerino. Beheaded....... 1688..1746
Elphinston, James. Misc. Writer. (*English Orthography*) 1721..1809

10

BORN. DIED.

Elphinston, William. Bishop of Aberdeen. Statesman.
  Founder of King's College, Aberdeen .... 1431?.1514
Elphinstone, Geo. Keith, Visc. Keith. Naval Commander 1746..1823
Elphinstone, Hon. Mountstuart. (*History of India*)..... 1778..1859
Elrington, Thomas. Bp. of Ferns. Divine & Classical Ed. — ..1835
Elsheimer, Adam. Painter .... 1574..1620
Elsner, James. Prussian Divine .... 1692..1750
Elstob, Elizabeth. Saxonist...................... 1683..1756
Elstob, William, brother. Divine, Antiquary, & Saxonist 1673..1714
Elsynge, Henry. Historical Writer.................. 1598..1654
Elton, Sir Charles Abraham. Poet and Historical Writer 1778..1853
Elvius, Peter. Swedish Mechanician and Astronomer... 1710..1749
Elwall, Edward. Politician and Polemical Writer ...... — ..1745?
Elwes, John, M. P. Miser. Life by Maj. F. Topham, 1805 1714?.1789
Elyot, Sir Thomas. *See* Eliot..................... 1495?.1546
Elys, Rev. Edmund. *Eliseus.* Nonjuror, Divine, and Poet — aft.1693
Elzevirs, Family of. Printers....................fl.1595–1680
Emanuel. King of Portugal (1495–1521) .... 1469..1521
Embury, Emma Catharine. American Authoress...... 1806..1863
Emerson, Wm. Mathematician. Life by W. Bowe, 1793 1701..1782
Emery, John. Actor .... 1777..1822
Emilio, Paul. *Paulus Æmilius.* Italian Historian...... — ..1529
Emlyn, Thomas. Unitarian Divine. Life by his son... 1663..1743
Emma of Normandy. Queen of Ethelred .... — ..1052
Emmett, Robert. United Irishman. Executed........ 1780..1803
Emmett, Thomas Addis, brother. United Irishman and
  American Barrister .... 1763..1827
Emmius, Ubbo. Philologist and Hist. (*Vetus Græcia*). 1547..1626
Emmons, Ebenezer. American Geologist and Author... 1798..1863
Emmons, Nathaniel. American Theologian and Writer 1745..1840
Emory, John, D.D. Bp. of the Meth. Epis. Church; Writer 1789..1835
Emory, Robert, son. Clergyman and Writer......... 1814..1848
Empecinado, John Martin Diaz, el. Span. Revolutionist 1775..1825
Empedocles. Sicilian Philosopher.................. fl.444 B.C.?
Empereur, Constantine l'. Anti-Jewish Theologian.... 1570?.1648
Empoli, Jacopo Chimenti da. Florentine Painter....... 1554..1640
Empson, Sir Richard. Favorite of Henry VII......... — ..1510
Empson, Wm. Professor. Editor of *Edinburgh Review* 1790?.1852
Emser, Hieronymus. Opponent of Luther............ 1472..1527
Énambuc, Peter Vandrosque Diel d'. French Navigator — ..1636
Encke, John Francis. German Astronomer........... 1791..1865
Enclos, Ninon l'. French Beauty.................... 1616..1706
Encontre, Daniel, of Montauban. Theologian and Math. 1762..1818
Endicott, John. Colonial Governor of Massachusetts... 1589..1665
Endlicher, Steph. Ladislaus. Botanist and Linguist..... 1804..1849
Enfantin, Barthélemy Prosper. *Père Enfantin.* French
  Social Theorist................................. 1796..1864
Enfield, William. Dissenting Divine. (*Speaker*)...... 1741..1797
Engel, John James. German Philosophical Writer..... 1741..1802
Engelbrecht, John. Fanatic........................ 1599..1642
Engelbrechtsen, Cornelius. Dutch Painter........... 1468..1533
Enghelrams, Cornelius. Painter in Water Colors...... 1527..1583
Enghien, Louis Anthony Henry de Bourbon, Duke of.
  Executed by Bonaparte .... 1772..1804

BORN. DIED.

England, John, D. D. Roman Catholic Bishop; Writer. 1786..1842
Englefield, Sir Henry Charles. (*Isle of Wight*)........ 1752..1822
English, George Bethune. American Adventurer ...... 1789..1828
English, Hester. Caligraphist........................ — aft.1617
Enjedius, or Enyedin, George. Socinian Writer........ 1550?.1597
Ennemoser, Joseph. German Physiologist............ 1787 .1854
Ennius, Quintus. Roman Poet.......................239 B.C..169
Ennodius, Magnus Felix. Bishop of Pavia. Writer.. 473?. 521
Enriquez, Gomez Anthony (properly Enriquez de Paz).
    Spanish Poet.. fl. 17th c.
Ent, Sir George. Medical Writer..................... 1604..1689
Entick, or Entinck, Rev. John. (*History of London*).... 1713..1773
Entinopus. Architect of Candia. Founder of Venice.. — .. 420?
Entrecasteaux, Joseph Anthony Bruni d'. French Ad-
    miral and Explorer. ,.............................. 1739..1793
Enzinas, Francis. *Dryander.* Sp. Transl. of New Test. 1520?.1570?
Enzinas, John, brother. Protestant Martyr at Rome.... — ..1545
Enzio. Natural Son of Frederick II. of Germany.....1224 or5.1272
Eobanus, Helius. German Latin Poet................. 1488..1540
Éon de Beaumont, Chas. Geneviève Louis Augustus
    Andrew Timothy d'. *Chevalier d' Éon.* French Soldier 1728..1810
Epaminondas. Theban General. Life by Meissner, 1801 — B.C.362
Épée, Charles Michael de l'. Abbé. Philanthropist.... 1712..1789
Ephraem Syrus, St. Christian Writer .... — .. 378?
Epicharmus. Greek Dramatic Poet...................540 B.C.?.443
Epictetus. Greek Philosopher .... — aft. 118
Epicurus. Greek Philosopher 342 B.C.270
Epimenides. Cretan Poet and Hero.................. fl. B. C. 596
Épinay, Louisa Florence Pétronille de la Live d'. Friend of
    Rousseau.. 1725?.1783
Epiphanius. Bishop of Constantia (367–403). (*Contra
    Manichœos*)..................................... 310?. 403
Epiphanius. *The Scholastic.* Italian Scholar and Transl. fl. 510?
Episcopius, Simon. Arminian Divine. Life by Limborch 1583..1643
Érard, Sebastian. Fr. Manufacturer of Musical Instrum. 1752..1831
Erasistratus. Physician and Anatomist............fl.300–260B.C.
Erasmus, Desiderius. Scholar. L. by P. Merula; Jortin;
    Dr. Sam. Knight, 1724; Burigni; Charles Butler, 1825 1467..1536
Erastus, Thomas. Physician and Polemical Divine.
    Founder of Erastianism .... 1524..1583
Eratosthenes. Geographer, Astronomer, &c. ....274B.C.?.194
Erceldoune, Thomas of. *Thomas the Rhymer* .... fl. 1280?
Ercilla y Zuñiga, Alonzo de. Span. Poet. (*Araucana*) 1533..1595?
Erdl, Michael Pius. German Savant .... 1815..1848
Eremita, Daniel. (*De Aulicâ Vitâ ac Civili*) .... 1584..1613
Eric IX. King of Sweden (1155–60). *The Pious* or *Saint* — ..1160
Eric XIII. King of Sweden, Denmark (VII.). (*History
    of Denmark*)..................................... 1382..1459
Eric XIV. King of Sweden (1560–69)................. 1533..1577
Ericsson, John. Swedish Engineer in America .... 1803..1853
Erigena, John Scotus. Schoolman.................... — .. 875?
Erinna. Greek Poetess............................ fl. 352 B.C.
Erizzo, Sebastian. Venetian Medalist and Antiquary... 1525..1585
Erkivins. Architect of Steinbach..................... — ..1305

BORN. DIED.

Erlach, John Louis. French Commander.............. 1595..1650
Erman, Paul. German Physicist...................... 1764..1851
Ernest. Duke of Gotha............................. 1601..1674
Ernest. Elector of Saxony.......................... — ..1486
Ernest-Augustus, son of George III. Duke of Cumberland and King of Hanover .... 1771..1851
Ernesti, Augustus William. Professor of Eloquence and Classical Editor (*Livy, Quintilian, &c.*) .... 1733..1801
Ernesti, John Augustus. Philologist, Theologian, and Classical Editor (*Homer, Cicero, Tacitus, &c.*)........ 1707..1781
Ernesti, John Christian Theoph. (*Lexicon Technologiæ*) 1756..1802
Ernst, Henry William. Violinist.................... 1814..1865
Ernulph, or Arnulph. Bishop of Roch. (*Textus Roffensis*) 1040?.1124
Erostratus, or Herostratus. Ephesian Incendiary...... fl.4th c.B.C.
Erotianus. Author of a Glossary to Hippocrates....... fl. ti. Nero.
Erpen, Thomas van. *Erpenius.* Dutch Orientalist..... 1584..1624
Errard, Charles. French Painter and Architect .... 1606..1689
Errington, Edward. Railway Engineer .... 1806..1862
Ersch, John Samuel. German Cyclopædist .... 1766..1828
Erskine, David, Lord Dun. Judge .... 1670..1755
Erskine, Rev. Ebenezer, M. A. Scottish Seceder .... 1680..1754
Erskine, Henry. Scottish Divine.................... 1624..1696
Erskine, Henry. Lord Advocate. Orator and Wit..... 1746..1817
Erskine, John, Baron of Dun. Scottish Reformer ...... 1508?.1591
Erskine, John. (*Principles of the Law of Scotland*)..... 1695..1765
Erskine, John, D. D. Scottish Divine. Life by Rev. Sir H. Moncrieff Wellwood, 1818 .... 1721..1803
Erskine, Ralph, A. M. Divine. (*Gospel Sonnets*)....... 1685..1752
Erskine, Thomas, Lord. Lord Chancellor .... 1750..1823
Erwin, of Steinbach. Architect of Strasbourg Cathedral — ..1318
Erxleben, John Christian Polycarp. German Naturalist 1744..1777
Eryceira, Ferd. de Menezes, Count. (*Hist. of Portugal*) 1614..1699
Eryceira, Francis Xavier de Menezes, Count, great-grandson. Soldier and Author...................... 1673..1743
Eschenbach, Wolfram von. German Minnesinger ..... — aft.1227
Eschenmayer, Adolphus Chas. Aug. von. Ger. Philos.. 1768..1852
Eschscholtz, John Frederick. German Naturalist..... 1793..1831
Escobar, Bartholomew. Jesuit Missionary and Author.. 1562..1624
Escobar, Marine d'. Span. Foundress. Life by Dupont. 1554..1633
Escobar y Mendoza, Anthony. Sp. Jesuit and Casuist. 1589..1669
Escoiquiz, John de. Spanish Diplomatist and Author .. 1762..1820
Esmenard, Joseph Alphonse. Fr. Poet and Polit. Writer 1770..1811
Espagnac, John Baptist, Baron d'. Military Writer .... 1713..1783
Espagnandel, Matthew l'. French Sculptor........... 1610..1689
Espagnet, John d', of Bordeaux. (*Enchiridion Physicæ*). fl. 1623
Espagnolet, Joseph Ribera l'. Spanish Painter .... 1589..1656
Esparron, Chas. d'Arcussia Visct. d'. Writ. on Falconry 1547..1617
Espen, Zeger Bernard van. Dutch Canonist .... 1646..1728
Espence, Claude d'. Cardinal. Biblical Commentator.. 1511..1571
Esper, Eugene John Christopher. German Naturalist... 1742..1810
Esper, John Frederick. Naturalist and Astronomer..... 1732..1781
Esperiente, Philip Callimachus. Italian Writer........ — ..1496
Espinasse, Esprit Charles Mary. French General...... 1815..1859
Espinasse, Julia Jane Eleanor de l'. Fr. Beauty and Wit 1732..1776

BORN. DIED.

Espinel, Vincent de. Spanish Poet and Musician....... 1551..1634
Esprémesnil, James Duval d'. French Politician...... 1746..1794
Esprit, James. French Academician; Writer.......... 1611..1678
Espronceda, Joseph de. Spanish Poet................ 1808..1842
Espy, James P. American Meteorologist.............. 1785..1860
Esquirol, John Stephen Dominic. French Physician and
    Writer. (*Maladies Mentales*)..................... 1772..1840
Ess, Henry Leander van. Ger. Rom. Cath. Theologian.. 1772..1847
Esse, André de Montalembert d'. French General...... 1483..1558
Essen, John Henry. Swedish General................. 1755..1824
Essex, James, F. S. A. Architect.................... 1723..1784
Essex, Robert Devereux, 2d Earl. Beheaded by Elizabeth 1567..1601
Essex, Robert Devereux, 3d Earl. Parliamentary General 1592..1646
Essex, Thomas Cromwell, Earl of. Beheaded......... 1490?.1540
Essex, Walter Devereux, 1st Earl of................. 1540?.1576
Estaço, Achilles. Latin Poet of Portugal. *See* Statius 1524..1581
Estaing, Charles Hector, Count d'. French Commander 1729..1794
Estampes, Anne de Pisseleu, Duchesse d'. Mistress of
    Francis I...................................... 1508..1576?
Estcourt, Richard. Actor and Dramatic.Writer........ 1668..1713
Estienne. Printers. *See* Stephen.
Estius, William. Dutch Divine...................... 1542..1613
Estoile, Claude de l'. French Academician; Poet ...1597?.1651 or 2
Estoile, Peter de l'. French Jurist and Historical Writer 1540?.1611
Estrades, Godfrey, Count d'. Fr. General and Statesman 1607..1686
Estrées, Cæsar d'. Cardinal; Statesman.............. 1628..1714
Estrées, Francis Annibal d'. Fr. Gen. and Hist. Writer 1573..1670
Estrées, Gabrielle d'. Mistress of Henry IV.......... 1571?.1599
Estrées, Louis Cæsar, Duc d'. Marshal of France...... 1695..1771
Estrées, Victor Mary d'. Vice-Adm. and Marsh. of France 1660..1737
Ethelbald. King of Wessex (855-60).................. — .. 860?
Ethelbert. King of Kent (560?-616).................. 545?. 616
Ethelbert. King of Wessex (860-66)................. — .. 866?
Ethelgar. Archbishop of Canterbury (988-89)......... — .. 989?
Ethelhard. Archbishop of Canterbury (793-805)....... — .. 805
Ethelnoth. Archbishop of Canterbury (1020-38)....... — ..1038
Ethelred. Archbishop of Canterbury (870-889)........ — .. 889
Ethelred I. *Saint.* King of Wessex (866-71)........ — .. 871
Ethelred II. *The Unready.* King of England (978-1016) — ..1016
Ethelreda, St. *St. Audrey*........................ fl. 7th c.
Ethelwold, St. Bp. of Winch (963-84). L. by Wolstan 925?. 984
Ethelwolf. King of Wessex (836-58)................. — .. 858
Etherege, Sir George. Wit and Comic Writer........ 1636?.1689
Ethicus, or Æthicus. Lat.Writ. of Istria. (*Cosmographia*) fl. 4th c.
Etienne. Printers. *See* Stephen.
Étienne, Charles William. French Writer............ 1778..1845
Étoile, Peter de l'. French Historical Writer.......... 1540?.1611
Ettmüller, Ernest Michael. Medical Writer .... 1673..1732
Ettmüller, Michael, of Leipsic. Medical Writer........ 1644..1683
Etty, William, R. A. Painter. Life by A. Gilchrist, 1855. 1787..1849
Eubulides of Miletus. Greek Philosopher........... 4th c. B.C.
Euclid of Alexandria. Mathematician. (*Elements*) ti.Ptolemy Soter
Euclid of Megara. Philosopher..................... fl. 400 B.C.
Eudæmon, John Andrew. Jesuit Writer............. 1560? 1625

BORN. DIED.

Eudes. King of France (888–898)..................... — .. 899
Eudes, John. French Devotional Writer.............. 1601..1680
Eudocia. Roman Empress, wife of Theodosius II. Writer.
(*Homero-Centones*)................................394?.460 or 1
Eudocia. Empress (1059–71). Wife of Constantine XI.,
&c. (*Violarium*) .... — aft.1071
Eudoxia. Empress. Wife of Arcadius, Persecutor of
Chrysostom .... — .. 404
Eudoxus, of Cnidus. Greek Astronomer .... fl. B.C. 366?
Eudoxus, of Cyzicus. Greek Navigator............... 2d c. B. C.
Eugene, Francis, of Savoy, Prince. Life by self; Prince
de Ligne, 1790; Ducasse, 1858–9; Ritter von Arneth;
Maubillon .... 1663..1736
Eugenius. Bishop of Carthage (481–505).............. — .. 505
Eugenius I. Pope (654–57). *Saint*.................... — .. 658
Eugenius II. (824–27)................................ — .. 827
Eugenius III. (1145–53). *Bernard*.................... — ..1153
Eugenius IV. (1431–47). *Gabriel Condolmerio*........ — ..1447
Euler, Leonard. Mathematician. (*Elements of Algebra*) 1707..1783
Eunapius. Greek Sophist, Phys., and Biographer....... 347.. 420?
Eunomius. Founder of the Eunomians............... — .. 393
Eupolis. Greek Comic Poet....................446 B.C.?.411?
Euripides. Greek Tragedian...................... 480 B.C.406
Eusden, Rev. Lawrence. Poet-Laureate............... — ..1730
Eusebius. Pope (310)................................ — .. 310
Eusebius. Bishop of Nicomedia..................... 324?.. 342
Eusebius. *Pamphili*. Bp. of Cæsarea. Eccles. Historian 265?. 338?
Eustachius, Bartholomew. Anatomical Discoverer..... — ..1574
Eustathius. Abp. of Thessalonica. Classical Comment. — ..1198?
Eustis, William. American Physician and Politician... 1753..1825
Eutocius, of Ascalon. Mathematician................. fl. 560 A.D.
Eutropius, Flavius. Roman Historian.............fl.4th c.A.D.
Eutyches. Heresiarch................................. 378.. 454?
Eutychius. Patriarch of Alexandria; Arabic Annalist.. 876.. 940
Evagrius Scholasticus. Ecclesiastical Historian...... 536?. 600?
Evangelista. Italian Capuchin; Canonist............. 1511?.1595
Evans, Abel, D.D. Epigrammatist. (M. A. 1699)...... — aft.1711
Evans, Arise. Welsh Conjuror and Impostor.......... fl.17th c.
Evans, Caleb, D. D., of Bristol. Baptist Minister....... 1737..1791
Evans, Evan. Welsh Divine and Poet................. 1730?.1790
Evans, John, D. D. Welsh Dissenting Divine.......... 1680..1730
Evans, John. Publisher. (*Christian Denominations*) ... 1742..1827
Evans, Lewis. American Geographer.................. 1700?.1756
Evans, Oliver. Amer. Mechanical Engineer and Inventor 1755..1811
Evanson, Rev. Edward. Infidel Writer............... 1731..1805
Evaristus. Bishop of Rome (100–109)................. — .. 109?
Evarts, Jeremiah. American Editor and Writer........ 1781..1831
Evelyn, John. (*Sylva.*) Memoirs edited by Bray, 1818 1620..1706
Evelyn, John, son. Scholar and Poetical Writer .... 1654..1698
Everard, Johannes Secundus. Dutch Statesman. (*Basia*) 1511..1536
Everdingen, Albert van. Dutch Painter.............. 1621..1675
Everdingen, Cæsar van. Dutch Painter .... 1606..1679
Everett, Alexander Hill. Amer. Diplomatist & Scholar 1792..1847
Everett, Edward. American Statesman and Orator .... 1794..1865

BORN. DIED.

Evremond, St.   *See* St. Evremond.   Soldier and Writer 1613..1703
Ewald, John.   Danish Poet .... 1743..1781
Ewing, Greville.   Scottish Divine and Lexicographer.... 1767..1841
Ewing, John.   American Divine and Natural Philosopher 1732..1802
Ewliya Effendi.   Turkish Traveler................... 1611..1679?
Exelmans, Remi Joseph Isidore, Baron.   Marshal .. .... 1775..1852
Exmouth, Edw. Pellew, Visc.   Admiral.   L. by Osler, 1833 1757..1833
Expilly, Claude d', of Grenoble.   Lawyer and Writer.... 1561..1636
Expilly, John Joseph.   Geographer and Traveler....... 1719..1793
Eyck, Hubert van.   Flemish Painter................... 1366..1426
Eyck, John van, brother.   *John of Bruges.*   Painter..... 1370..1441
Eyck, Margaret van, sister.   Painter .... — ..1430?
Eykens, Peter.   *The Old.*   Painter of Antwerp......... 1599..1649
Eyre, Rev. Charles.   Biblical Scholar, Poet, Journalist.. 1784?.1864
Eyries, J. Baptist.   Benedict.   French Writer......... 1767..1846
Ezekiel.   Hebrew Prophet..........................6th & 7th c.b.c.
Ezra.   Jewish Lawgiver .... 5th c. b. c.

F.

BORN. DIED.

Faber, Anthony. Jurist.   *See* Favre................. 1557..1624
Faber, Basil.   German Protestant Divine.   (*Thesaurus*). 1520..1575
Faber, Dr. Fred. Wm., of the Brompton Oratory. Poet... 1815..1863
Faber, Rev. George Stanley. Divine.................... 1773..1854
Faber, John. *Malleus Hereticorum.* German Divine.... 1470?.1541
Faber, Nicholas.   *See* Fevre. French Philologist....... 1544..1612
Faber, Tanaquil.   *See* Fevre, Tannegui le....,....... 1615..1672
Faber Stapulensis.   *See* Lefèvre, James, of Étaples.... 1455?.1537
Fabert, Abraham. Marshal of France. Life by J. Barre 1599..1662
Fabian, or Fabyan, Robert. Historian................. 1450?.1512
Fabianus.   Bishop of Rome (236–50)................. — .. 250
Fabius Maximus, Q. Dictator and six times Consul... aft.296 B.C.
Fabius Maximus, Q. *Cunctator.* Opponent of Hannibal — B.C. 203
Fabius Pictor, Q. Roman Historian ....fl.225–216 B.C.
Fabre, or Faber, Anthony. Jurist................... 1557..1624
Fabre, John Claude. Ecclesiastical History Writer..... 1668..1753
Fabre d'Églantine, Philip Francis Nazaire.   French
    Revolutionist and Author.......................... 1755..1794
Fabretti, Raphael. Antiquary......................... 1619..1700
Fabri, Honoré. Jesuit Philosopher................... 1607?.1688
Fabriano, Francis di Gentile da. Italian Painter....... 1370?.1450
Fabricius, Caius. Consul. Opponent of Pyrrhus..... aft.275 B.C.
Fabricius, David. German Astronomer and Divine.... 1564..1617
Fabricius, George.   Latin Poet and Antiquary. (*Rome*) 1516..1571
Fabricius, James. Physician and Mathematician ...... 1577..1652
Fabricius, Jerome, of Aquapendente. Physician........ 1537..1619
Fabricius, John (son of David). Astronomer........ — ..1625
Fabricius, John Louis. Swiss Divine and Diplomatist... 1632..1697
Fabricius, John Albert. Scholar. (*Bibliotheca Græca.*)
    Life by H. S. Reimarus, 1737 .... 1668..1736
Fabricius, John Christian. Danish Entomologist ...... 1743..1807
Fabricius, Vincent. German Latin Poet .... 1612..1667
Fabricius, William. *Hildanus.* German Surgeon...... 1560..1634
Fabris, Nicholas. Italian Mechanician .... 1739..1801
Fabroni, Angelo. Biographer. Life by Pozzett........ 1732..1803
Fabroni, John Valentine Mathias. Italian Naturalist... 1752..1822
Fabrot, Charles Annibal. French Jurist.............. 1581..1659
Fabry, John Baptist Germain. French Writer.......... 1780..1821
Fabyan, or Fabian, Robert. Historian............... 1450?.1512
Facchetti, Peter. Painter of Mantua................. 1535..1613
Facciolato, or Facciolati, James. Grammarian........ 1682..1769
Facini, Peter. Historical Painter of Bologna.......... 1560..1602
Facio, or Fazio, Bartholomew. Italian Scholar and Hist. 1400?.1457
Faernus, Gabriel. Italian Critic and Latin Poet .... — ..1561
Fagan, Christopher Bartholomew. French Comic Author 1702..1755
Fage, Raymond de la. French Engraver and Designer.. 1656..1690
Fagel, Gaspar. Dutch Statesman..................... 1629..1688
Fagel, Francis Nicholas, nephew. Dutch General ...... — ..1718
Fagius, Paul. German Reformer..................... 1504..1550
Fagnani, Prosper. Italian Canonist................. 1598..1678

BORN. DIED.

Fagnano, Julius Charles, Count of. Italian Mathematician 1682..1766
Fagon, Guy Crescent. Physician and Botanist......... 1638..1718
Fagundy, Stephen. Portuguese Jesuit; Casuist........ 1577?.1645
Fahie, Sir William Charles. Admiral................. 1763..1833
Fahrenheit, Gabriel Daniel. Philosopher .... 1686..1736
Faidit, Anselm. Troubadour........................ — ..1220?
Faille, Germain de la. Fr. Hist. (*History of Toulouse*) 1616..1711
Fairfax, Edward. Poet. Translator of Tasso.......... — ..1632?
Fairfax, Robert. Musical Composer.............ti.Hen.VII. & VIII.
Fairfax, Thos., Lord. Parliamentary General. L. by self 1611..1671
Fairfax, Thomas. Sixth Baron Fairfax of Cameron.... 1690?.1782
Faistenberger, Anthony. Painter of Innspruck........ 1678..1722
Faithorne, William. Painter and Engraver........... 1616?.1691
Falcandus, Hugo. (*History of Sicily*)................. fl. 1190?
Falck, Anthony Renard. Dutch Statesman............ 1776..1843
Falconberg, Mary, Countess of. Daughter of Cromwell — .. 1712
Falcone, Ancillo. Italian Battle-Painter .... 1600..1663
Falcone, da Benevento. Italian Chronicler............ fl. 1150?
Falconer, Sir Alex., cr. Lord Halkertoun. Scot. Judge. — ..1671
Falconer, Sir David. Ld. Pres. Scotland. (*Decisions*).. 1639..1685
Falconer, Hugh, M. D. Botanist and Palæontologist.... 1809..1865
Falconer, Sir James. *Lord Phesdo.* Scottish Judge.... — ..1705
Falconer, Thos., of Bath. Edit. of Strabo. (*Voy. of Hanno*) 1772..1839
Falconer, Thomas. (*Voyage of Hanno; Chronol. Tables*) 1736..1792
Falconer, William. Poet. (*Shipwreck.*) Life by Mitford 1730?.1769
Falconer, Wm., M. D., of Bath. Med. & Chemical Writer 1743..1824
Falconet, Camille. French Physician & Book Collector 1671..1762
Falconet, Stephen Maurice. French Sculptor.......... 1716..1791
Falda, John Baptist. Italian Engraver................ 1640?.1700?
Faleti, Jerome, of Savona. Poet and Statesman........ 1518?.1564
Falieri, Marino. Doge of Venice .... 1278..1355
Falk, John Daniel. German Philanthropist and Author . 1768..1826
Falk, John Peter. Swedish Botanist................. 1727..1774
Falkenstein, John Henry. German Antiquary .... 1682..1760
Falkland, Henry Cary, 1st Visct. Ld. Dep. of Irel., & Writ. — ..1633
Falkland, Lucius Cary, Viscount, son; slain at Newbury 1610?.1643
Falkner, Thomas. Jesuit Missionary to Paraguay...... 1710..1784
Falle, Rev. Philip, of Jersey. (*History of Jersey*)...... 1655..1742
Fallopius, or Faloppio, Gabriel. Anatomical Discoverer 1523?.1562
Fallows, Fearon. Astronomer....................... — ..1832
Fals, or Falz, Raymond. Medal Engraver .... 1658..1703
Falster, Christian. Danish Critic.................... fl. 1717–31
Fancourt, Samuel. Dissenting Minister and Writer.... 1678..1768
Fane, Rob. Geo. Cecil. Commiss. of Bankruptcy. Leg. Wr. 1795?.1864
Faneuil, Peter. American Merchant .... 1700..1743
Fanning, David. American Freebooter................ 1756?.1825
Fanshawe, Ann, Lady. Life by Sir N. H. Nicolas, 1829 1625..1679
Fanshawe, Sir Richard. Statesman and Poet.......... 1608..1666
Fant, Eric Michael. Swedish Archæologist and Historian 1754..1817
Fardella, Mich. Angelo. Naturalist and Astron. at Padua 1650..1718
Fare, Chas. Aug., Marquis de la. French Poet and Writer 1644..1712
Farel, William. French Reformer. Life by D. Ancillon 1489..1565
Faret, Nicholas. French Academician................ 1600?.1646
Farey, John. Geologist............................. 1766..1826

BORN. DIED.

Farey, John. Civil Engineer........................ 1791..1851
Faria y Souza, Manuel de. Portuguese Historian & Poet 1590..1649
Farinaccio, Prosper. Italian Law Writer.............. 1554..1618
Farinato, Paul, of Verona. Painter................... 1525..1606
Farinelli. *Carlo Broschi.* Neapolitan Singer......... 1705..1782
Faringdon, Anthony. Divine. Life by T. Jackson, 1849 1596..1658
Farington, George. Historical Painter................ 1754..1788
Farington, Joseph, brother. Landscape Painter....... — ..1818
Farmer, Hugh. Dissenting Divine. Life by Dodson.. 1714..1787
Farmer, John. American Genealogist and Antiquary.... 1789..1838
Farmer, Richard, D. D. Critic and Scholar........... 1735..1797
Farnaby, Thomas. Schoolmaster and Classical Editor.. 1575..1647
Farnese, Alexander. Third Duke of Parma............ 1546..1592
Farnese, Alexander. Cardinal. Ambassador.......... 1520..1589
Farnese, Octavius. Second Duke of Parma........... 1520?.1585
Farnese, Peter Louis. First Duke of Parma (1545-47).. 1490?.1547
Farneworth, Ellis. Historical Translator............. — ..1763
Farnham, Thomas J. American Traveler and Writer.. 1804..1848
Farquhar, George. Comic Writer.................... 1678..1707
Farrant, Richard. Composer of Church Music......... — ..1585?
Farrar, John. American Mathematician.............. 1779..1853
Farren, Eliza. Actress, afterwards Countess of Derby .. 1759..1829
Farren, William. Comedian .... 1791?.1861
Fastolff, Sir John. Commander .... 1378?.1459
Fatio de Duillers, Nicholas. Swiss Geometrician and
    Religious Enthusiast............................. 1664..1753
Faucher, Léon. French Political Economist........... 1803..1854
Fauchet, Claude. French Historian.................. 1530..1601
Fauchet, Claude. French Bishop and Politician .... 1744..1793
Faucheur, Michael le. French Prot. Divine & Preacher. — ..1667
Faulkner, George. Irish Printer and Author......... 1700?.1775
Fauques, Marianne Agnes de. *Mme. de Vaucluse.* Romanc.1720 aft.1777
Faur, Guy de. Lord of Pibrach. Advocate. (*Quatrains*) 1529..1584
Fauriel, Claude. Fr. Hist. and Belles-lettres Writer... 1772..1844
Faust, or Fust, John. One of the Inventors of Printing .. — ..1470?
Faust, or Faustus, Dr. John. Occult Philosopher....... fl. 1550?
Fausta, Flavia Maximiniana. Wife of Constantine ..... — .. 327
Faustina, Annia Galeria. *The Elder.* W. of Antoninus Pius 105?. 141
Faustina, Annia, daughter. *The Younger.* Wife of
    Marcus Aurelius................................. — .. 175
Faustina, Bordone. Italian Singer .... 1702..1783
Favart, Charles Simon. French Poet................. 1710..1792
Favart, Mary Justine Benoîte. French Comic Actress.. 1727..1772
Faversham, Hamo de. Aristotelian Philosopher....... — ..1244
Favolius, Hugo. Dutch Physician and Poet........... 1523..1585
Favorinus. Platonic Philosopher...............fl.ti.Traj.& Hadr.
Favorinus, Narinus. (*Thesaurus Linguæ Græcæ*)...... 1450?.1537
Bavras, Thomas Mahi, Marquis of. French Conspirator
    against the Revolution............................ 1745..1790
Favre, or Faber, Anthony, of Savoy. Jurist. (*Codex Fa-
    brianus*)....................................... 1557..1624
Favre, Claude. Lord de Vaugelas. Writ. on Fr. Language. 1585?.1650
Fawcett, John. Actor.............................. 1768..1837
Fawcett, Sir Wm. General. Governor of Chelsea Hosp. 1728..1804

BORN. DIED.

Fawkes, Rev. Francis. Writer and Class. Poet; Transl. 1721..1777
Fawkes, Guy. Conspirator....................... — ..1606
Faxardo, Diego Saavedra. Span. Author and Statesman 1584..1648
Fay, Chas. Francis de Cisternai du. Natural Philosopher 1698..1739
Faydit, Anselm. Troubadour....................... — ..1220?
Faydit, Peter. French Theologian and Historian....... 1649..1709
Fayette, Louisa de la. French Maid of Honor........ 1616?.1665
Fayette, Mary Magd. de la Vergne, Countess of. Novelist 1632..1693
Fazio, Bartholomew. Italian Hist. (*De Viris Illustribus*) 1400?.1457
Fearn, John. Metaphysician....................... fl. 1812–15
Fearne, Charles. Law Writer. (*Contingent Remainders*) 1749..1794
Featley, or Fairclough, Rev. Daniel. Controv. Divine.. 1582..1645
Fecht, or Fechtius, John. Lutheran Divine........... 1636..1716
Feckenham, John de. Abbot of Westminster........ — ..1585
Federici, Camillo. Italian Dramatist.............. 1749..1802
Fëdor I. *Ivanovitch.* Czar of Russia (1584–98)....·... 1557..1598
Fëdor II. *Alexeyevitch.* (1676–82)................. 1657..1682
Feijoo, Francis Benedict Jerome. Spanish Moralist.
(*Teatro Critico*)........................... 1701..1764
Feith, Rhynvis. Dutch Writer and Poet............. 1753..1824
Fejer, György. Hungarian Writer................... 1766.. —
Félibien, Andrew. Historiographer................. 1619..1695
Félibien, James. (*Pentateuchus Historicus*)......... 1636..1716
Félibien, John Francis. (*Lives of Celebrated Architects*) 1658?.1733
Félibien, Michael, of St. Maur. (*History of Paris*)...... 1666..1719
Félice, Fortuné Barthélemy de. (*Encyclop. of Yverdun*) 1723..1789
Felix, Antonius or Claudius. Procurator of Judæa...... —aft.62A.D.
Felix, M. Minutius. Roman Lawyer. (*Octavius*)....... fl. A.D.230?
Felix I. Pope (269–274?). *Saint.*................... — .. 274?
Felix II. (355.) Antipope; expelled................. — .. 365
Felix III. (or II.) Pope (483–92)................... — .. 492
Felix IV. (or III.) (526–30)....................... — .. 530?
Fell, John, D.D. Dean of Christ Church & Bp. of Oxford 1625..1686
Fell, John. Dissenting Minister.................... 1735..1797
Fell, Samuel, D.D. Dean of Christ Church............ 1594..1649
Fellenburg, Emanuel de. Educationist.............. 1771..1844
Feller, Francis Xavier de. Ex-Jesuit. (*Hist. Dictionary*) 1735..1802
Feller, Joachim Frederick. (*House of Brunswick*)....... 1673..1726
Fellowes, Robert, LL.D. Religious and Political Writer 1770..1847
Fellows, Sir Charles. Classical Archæologist.......... 1799..1860
Feltham, Owen. (*Resolves.*) Life by Cumming, 1806 .. 1610?.1678?
Felton, Cornelius Conway. Amer. Author and Educator 1807..1862
Felton, Henry, D.D. Divine....................... 1679..1740
Feltre, Hen. Jas. Wm. Clarke, Duke de. Marshal of Fr. 1765..1818
Fénelon, Francis de Salignac de la Mothe. Archbishop.
L. by Card. Bausset, 1812; Chas. Butler; A. M. Ramsay 1651..1715
Fenin, Peter de. Chronicler....................... — ..1433
Fenn, Lady Eleanor. Writer of Books for the Young.. 1743?.1813
Fenn, Sir John. Antiquary....................... 1739..1794
Fenner, William. Puritan Divine................... 1560..1640?
Fenouillot de Falbaire, Charles Geo. Fr. Dramatist 1727..1800
Fenton, Edward. Naval Commander .... 1550?.1603
Fenton, Elijah. Poet............................. 1683..1730
Fenton, Sir Geoffrey. Writer and Statesman.......... — ..1608

BORN. DIED.

Fenwick, Rev. George. (*Hebrew Titles of the Psalms*).. — ..1760
Ferdinand I. King of Aragon. *The Just* .... 1373..1416
Ferdinand II. (V. of Castile and Leon). *The Catholic*.. 1452..1516
Ferdinand I. King of Castile and Leon. *The Great*.. — ..1065
Ferdinand II. Life by Pineda...................... — ..1188
Ferdinand III. *Saint* .... 1200..1252
Ferdinand IV.. 1285..1312
Ferdinand V. (II. of Aragon). *The Catholic.* Husband
   of Isabella. Life by Carvajal; Prescott............. 1452..1516
Ferdinand VI. King of Spain (1746–59) .... 1713..1759
Ferdinand VII. .... 1784..1833
Ferdinand I. Emperor (1558–64). Life by Jas. Masen 1503..1564
Ferdinand II., grandson. (1619–37)................. 1578..1637
Ferdinand III., son. (1637–57)...................... 1608..1657
Ferdinand I. King of Naples .... 1423..1494
Ferdinand II. .... — ..1496
Ferdinand III. (V. of Castile and Leon). *The Catholic* 1452..1516
Ferdinand I. King of the Two Sicilies............... 1751..1825
Ferdinand II. *Bomba* .... 1810..1859
Ferdinand, Charles, of Bruges. Poet and Philosopher.
   (*Tranquillitas Animi*) .... 1450?.1496
Ferdinand, John. Jesuit of Toledo. (*Script. Thesaurus*) 1536?.1595
Ferdinand de Cordova. Scholar............................ 1420?.1480?
Ferdinandi, Epiphanius. Medical Writer .... 1569..1638
Ferdusi. Persian Poet .... 940..1020?
Ferg, or Fergire, Francis Paul. German Painter .... 1689..1740
Ferguson, Adam, LL. D. (*History of the Roman Republic*) 1724..1816
Ferguson, James. Natural Philosopher and Astronomer 1710..1776
Ferguson, Robt. Ejected Nonconf.,Divine and Politician — ..1714
Ferguson, Robt. Poet. L. by Peterkin; D. Irving, 1799 1750?.1774
Ferguson, Robert, M. D. Med. Writ. (*Puerperal Fever*). 1799..1865
Ferguson, William. Scottish Artist................... — ..1690
Ferishtah, Mohammed Casim. Persian Historian...... 1570?.1626?
Fermat, Peter de. Mathematician, Poet, and Civilian .. 1601..1665
Fermor, William, Count von. Russian General .... 1704..1771
Fernandez, Alfonso. Spanish Ecclesiastical Historian.. — ..1640
Fernandez, Anthony. Port. Miss. in India and Abyssinia — ..1642
Fernandez, Juan. Spanish Navigator and Discoverer.. fl. 1572
Fernandez Ximenes de Navarette, John. Painter... 1524?.1577
Ferne, Sir John. Antiquary .... — ..1610?
Fernel, or Fernelius, John Francis. Fr. Medical Writer 1497..1558
Ferracino, Barthol. It. Mechanician. L. by Memo, 1764 1692..1777
Ferrajuoli, Nunzio. Italian Painter .... 1660..1735
Ferrand, Anthony. French Poet.................... : 1678..1719
Ferrand, Anthony Francis Claude, Ct. Fr. Polit. & Hist. 1751..1825
Ferrand, James. French Physician. (*Distemper of Love*) fl. 1622
Ferrand, James Philip. French Painter in Enamel..... 1653?.1732
Ferrand, Louis. French Theologian .... 1645..1699
Ferrar, Nicholas; friend of G. Herbert. Life by Ferrar;
   Jebb and Mayor, 1857 .... 1592..1637
Ferrar, Robert. Bishop of St. David's. Martyr....... — ..1555
Ferrara, Andrea de. Swordsmith in Scotland ......fl.ti.Jas.IV.or V.
Ferrara, Renée of France, Duchess of. *See* Renée ..... 1510..1575
Ferrari, Francis Bernardin. Book-Collector and Scholar 1577?.1669

BORN. DIED.

Ferrari, Gaudentio, of Milan. Painter................. 1484..1550
Ferrari, John Andrew. Italian Painter................. 1599..1669
Ferrari, John Baptist, of Sienna. Syriac Scholar...... 1584..1655
Ferrari, Louis, of Bologna. Mathematician............ 1522..1565
Ferrari, Octavian. Ital. Archæol. (*De Orig. Romanorum*) 1518..1586
Ferrari, Octavius, of Milan. Archæologist .... 1607..1684
Ferraris, Joseph, Count de. Austrian Field Marshal.... 1726..1814
Ferrars, Edward. Warwickshire Poet .... — ..1564
Ferrars, George. Historian, Poet, and Courtier........ 1512?.1579
Ferrars, Henry. Poet and Antiquary of Warwickshire.. 1549..1633
Ferrato, Sasso. *John Baptist Salvi.* Painter.......... 1605..1685
Ferreira, Antonio. Portuguese Poet. (*Ines de Castro*)... 1528..1569
Ferreras, John de. Span. Historian. (*History of Spain*) 1652..1735
Ferreti, Emilius. Italian Jurist. (*Opera Juridica*).... 1489..1552
Ferreti, John Baptist, of Vicenza. (*Musæ Lapidariæ*).. 1639..1682
Ferreto, of Vicenza. Historian and Poet.............. 1296?.1335?
Ferri, Ciro. Roman Fresco Painter................... 1634..1689
Ferri, Paul, of Metz. Protestant Divine and Preacher.. 1591..1669
Ferriar, John. Physician and Writer................. 1764..1815
Ferrier, Arnold du. French Lawyer and Diplomatist... 1506?.1585
Ferrier, Claude de. Civilian .... 1639..1715
Ferrier, John. French Jesuit and Anti-Jansenist....... — ..1674
Ferrier, J. F. Writer on Moral Philosophy .... 1806?.1864
Ferrier, Louis. French Poet......................... 1652..1721
Ferrier, Mary. Novelist. (*Marriage*)................ 1782..1854
Ferrière, Claude de, of Paris. Jurist................. 1639..1715
Ferron, Arnauld le. French Latin Writer.............. 1515..1563
Fersen, Axel, Ct..................................... 1755..1810
Ferté-Senneterre, Henry, Duke de. Marshal of France 1600..1681
Ferus, John, of Metz. *Wild.* Commentator........... — ..1554
Fesch, Joseph, Cardinal. Archbishop of Lyons........ 1763..1839
Fessenden, Thomas Green. American Author......... 1771..1837
Feti, Dominic. *Il Mantuano.* Painter .... 1589..1624
Feuchères, Sophia de, Baroness...................... 1795?.1841
Feuerbach, Paul Jos. Anselm. Ger. Writ. on Crim. Law 1775..1833
Feuillée, Louis. Fr. Naturalist, Geographer, and Math. 1660..1732
Feuquière, Anthony de Pas, Marquis de. Milit. Writer 1648..1711
Feurborn, Justus, of Westphalia. Protestant Theologian 1587?.1656
Feutsking, John Henry. German Writer............... 1672..1713
Fevardentius, or Fewardent, Francis. Controv. Divine 1541..1641
Fèvre, Anne le. *Madame Dacier*, which see........... 1654..1720
Fèvre, Anthony le. French Statesman and Ambassador 1555?.1615
Fèvre, Claude le. French Painter in England.......... 1633..1675
Fèvre, Guy le, Sieur de la Broderie. Fr. Oriental. and Poet 1541..1598
Fèvre, James le, of Étaples. *See* Faber Stapulensis .... 1455?.1537
Fèvre, Nicholas le. French Philologist............... 1544..1612
Fèvre, Nicholas le. French Jesuit; Divine and Critic... — ..1755
Fèvre, Roland le. French Painter .... 1605?.1677
Fèvre, Tannegui le. *Tanaquil Faber*................. 1615..1672
Fevret, Charles. French Civilian.................... 1583..1661
Fevret de Fontette, Charles Mary. Lawyer and Writer 1710..1772
Few, Col. William. American Revolutionary Officer... 1748..1828
Feydeau, Matthew. Jansenist Writer................. 1616..1694
Feyjoo, or Feijoo, Benedict Jerome. *The Spanish Addison* 1701..1764

BORN. DIED.

Fiammingo, Arrigo. Flemish Artist................ 1523?.1601?
Fiard, J. Bapt. French Demonologist................ 1736..1818
Fiasella, Dominic. *Sarezena.* Historical Painter...... 1589..1669
Fichard, John, of Frankfort. Lawyer and Biographer.. 1512..1581
Fichte, John Theoph. Metaphysician. L. by W. Smith 1762..1814
Ficinus, Marsilius. Italian Platonic Philosopher .... 1433..1499
Fiooroni, Francis. Roman Medalist and Antiquary... 1664..1747
Ficquelmont, Charles Louis, Count. Austrian States-
    man and General.................................. 1777..1859
Fidanza, John. *St. Bonaventure,* which see............ 1221..1274
Fiddes, Richard, D. D. Divine........................ 1671..1725
Field, John. Proto-Copernican of England. L. by Hunter — ..1587
Field, Nathaniel. Actor and Dramatist................ — ..1641
Field, Richard, D. D. (*The Church.*) Life by his son.... 1561..1616
Fielding, Copley Vandyke. Landscape Painter........ 1787..1855
Fielding, Henry. Novelist. L. by Murphy; Lawrence, 1855 1707..1754
Fielding, Sir John. Magistrate and Writer........... — ..1780
Fielding, Miss Sarah. Novelist...................... 1714..1768
Fiennes, Nathaniel. Republican Polit., and Commander 1608..1669
Fiennes, Wm., Ld. Say and Sele. Writer and Statesman 1582..1662
Fienus, or Fyens, Thomas. Medical Writer at Louvain . 1567..1631
Fieschi, John Louis d'. Genoese Conspirator........... 1523?.1547
Fiesole, Fra Giovanni da. *Beato Angelico.* Painter.... 1387..1455
Fiévée, Joseph. French Politician and Author......... 1767..1839
Figg, James. Prizefighter............................ — ..1734
Figino, Ambrose. Italian Painter................... 1550.aft.1595
Figrelius, Edmund. Swedish Scholar and Historian ... — ..1676
Filangieri, Gaetano. Ital. Publicist. (*On Legislation*).. 1752..1788
Filelfo, Francis. Ital. Schol. & Hist. L. by Rosmini, 1808 1398..1481
Filesac, John. Doctor of the Sorbonne .... 1550?.1638
Filicaja, Vincenzo da. Florentine Poet. (*Siege of Vienna*) 1642..1707
Filipepi, Sandro, or Alessandro. *Botticelli.* Ital. Painter 1437..1515
Fillans, James. Scottish Sculptor.................. 1808..1852
Filmer, Sir Robert. Political Writer. (*Patriarcha*).... — ..1688
Finæus, Orontius. *Finé.* French Mathematical Writer 1494..1555
Finch, Anne, Countess of Winchelsea. Poet .... 1660?.1720
Finch, Daniel, Second Earl of Nottingham. Statesman. 1647..1730
Finch, Francis Oliver. Painter in Water Colors........ — ..1862
Finch, Heneage, First E. of Nottingham. Ld. Chancellor 1621..1682
Finch, Rev. Robert. Antiquary .... 1783..1830
Finck, Thomas. Danish Physician and Mathematician.. 1561..1656
Finden, William. Engraver .... 1787..1852
Finé, Oronce. *Finæus.* French Mathematician........ 1494..1555
Fingal. Prince of Morven............................. 282?. —
Finiguerra, Thomas. Florentine Goldsmith and Sculptor 1410?.1475
Finlay, John. Scottish Poet.......................... 1782..1810
Finlayson, George. Surgeon, Naturalist, and Traveler.. 1790?.1823
Finley, James Bradley. Amer. Clergyman and Author. 1781..1857
Finley, Robert, D. D. Amer. Scholar and Philanthropist 1772..1817
Finley, Samuel, D. D. American Educator............. 1715..1766
Fiori, Mario de, Italian Flower Painter............... 1603..1673
Fiorillo, John Dominic. German Painter and Writer .. 1748..1821
Firenzuola, Angelo. Italian Poet. .... 1493..1545
Firmicus Maternus, Julius. Christian Writer fl.334-355

BORN. DIED.

Firmilian. Bishop of Cæsaræa (233–69) .... 200?. 269
Firmin, Giles. Eject. Nonconf. & Phys. (*Real Christian*) 1617..1697
Firmin, Thomas. Benefactor. Life by Cornish, 1780... 1632..1697
Fischer, Charles von, of Munich. Architect .... 1782..1820
Fischer von Erlach, John Bernard. Archt. of Vienna. 1650..1724
Fish, Simon. English Reformer. (*Supplication of Beggars*) — ..1531?
Fisher, John. Bishop of Roch. L. by Dr. Rd. Hall; J. Lewis 1459..1535
Fisher, John. Bishop of Salisbury .... 1748..1825
Fisher, Payne. *Paganus Piscator.* Poet-Laureate ..... 1616..1693
Fisher, Thomas. Antiquary .... 1772..1836
Fisk, Wilbur, D. D. American Clergyman and Educator. 1792..1839
Fitch, John. American Inventor..................... 1743..1798
Fitzgerald, Ld. Edward. Revolutionist. Life by T. Moore 1763..1798
Fitzgerald, Lady Edward. *Pamela*.................... — ..1831
Fitzgibbon, John, Earl of Clare. Lord. Chanc. of Ireland 1749..1802
Fitzherbert, Sir Anthony. Lawyer.................... — ..1538
Fitzherbert, Maria Anna, Mrs. Life by Langdale, 1856 1756..1837
Fitzherbert, Nicholas. (*Life of Cardinal Allen*)........ 1550?.1612
Fitzherbert, Thomas. Roman Catholic Controversialist 1552..1640
Fitzjames, James, Dk. Berwick. Military Commander. 1670..1734
Fitzjocelin, Reginald. Archbishop of Canterbury (1191) 1141..1191
Fitzpatrick, Richard. General and Statesman......... 1747..1813
Fitzroy, Jas., Duke of Monmouth. Life by Roberts, 1844 1649..1685
Fitzroy, Robert. Admiral. Meteorologist .... 1805..1865
Fitzstephen, William. Historian. (*London*) .... — ..1191?
Fitzwilliam, Richard. Viscount. (M. A. 1764.) Founder of Fitzwilliam Museum....................... — ..1816
Fitzwilliam, Wm., E. of Southampton. Naval Command. — ..1542
Fitzwilliam, William Wentworth, Second Earl of. Statesman. Founder of Fitzwilliam Museum .... 1748..1833
Fixmillner, Placidus. German Astronomer and Canonist 1721..1791
Fizes, Anthony. Medical Writer at Montpellier........ 1690..1765
Flaccus, C. Valerius. Poet. (*Argonautica*)........... — .. 88?
Flacius Illyricus. *Matthias Francowitz.* Divine ...... 1520..1575
Flambard, Ralph. Bp. of Dur. (1099–1128). Justiciary. — ..1128
Flameel, or Flamel, Bertholet. Historical Painter of Liege 1614..1675
Flamel, Nicholas, of Paris. Alchemist and Benefactor .. — ..1418
Flaminio, John Anthony, of Bologna. Orator, Poet, Hist. 1464?.1536
Flaminio, Mark Anthony. Latin Poet. (*Carmina Sacra*) 1498..1550
Flaminius, Caius. Censor. Constructor of *Via Flaminia* — 217 B.C.
Flaminius, Nobilius. Italian Divine and Critic.,...... 1532..1590
Flaminius, T. Quint. Consul. Victor at Cynoscephalæ..230?B.C.174
Flamsteed, John. Astronomer....................... 1646?.1719
Flandrin, John Hippolytus. French Painter .... 1809?.1864
Flandrin, Peter. French Veterinary Writer .... 1752..1796
Flatman, Thomas. Poet............................. 1633?.1688
Flaust, John Baptist, of Rouen. (*Usage of Normandy*).. 1711?.1783
Flavel, John. Ejected Nonconformist Divine........... 1627?.1691
Flaxman, John. Sculptor. Life by Teniswood, 1864... 1755..1826
Fléchier, Esprit. Bishop of Nismes. Preacher .... 1632..1710
Flecknoe, Richard. Poet............................ — ..1678
Fleetwood, Chas. Lord Deputy of Irel. and Parl. General — ..1692
Fleetwood, William. Lawyer and Historical Writer ... — ..1593
Fleetwood, Wm., Bishop of Ely. Scholar & Theologian 1656..1723

BORN. DIED.

Fleming, Abraham. Poetical Writer & Class. Translator.fl.1575–1589
Fleming, Caleb. Unitarian Writer.................. 1698..1779
Fleming, John. Scottish Naturalist.................. 1785..1857
Fleming, Marjorie. *Pet.* Life by J. Brown, M. D. ..... 1803..1811
Fleming, Patrick. Irish Roman Ecclesiastic........... 1599..1631
Fleming, Robert. Scottish Pastor in Holland. (*Fulfilling*
 of the Scriptures)................................. 1630..1694
Fleming, Robt. Scot. Past. in Lond. (*Rise & Fall of Papacy*) — ..1716
Flemyng, Richard. Bishop of Lincoln (1419–31). Oppo-
 nent of Lollards. Founder of Lincoln College........ — ..1431
Fletcher, Abraham. Mathem. (*Universal Measurer*) .. 1714..1793
Fletcher, Rev. Alexander, D. D. Presbyterian Divine... 1787?.1860
Fletcher, Andrew, of Saltoun. Scottish Politician. Life
 by D. S. Erskine, 1792............................... 1653..1716
Fletcher, Giles, LL. D. Envoy. (*Russian Commonwealth*) — ..1610
Fletcher, Giles, br. of Phineas. Poet. (*Christ's Victory*) 1588?.1623
Fletcher, James. Historian. (*History of Poland*)...... 1811..1832
Fletcher, John. Poet; Colleag. of Beaumont. L. by Dyce 1576..1625
Fletcher, Rev. John Wm. (*Checks to Antinomianism*).. 1729..1785
Fletcher, Phineas. Poet. (*Purple Island*)............ 1584?.1650?
Fletcher, Richard. Bishop of London .... — ..1596
Fleury, Andrew Hercules de. Cardinal & Prime Minister 1653..1743
Fleury, Claude. Abbé. (*Histoire Ecclesiastique*)....... 1640..1723
Bliedner, Theod. Prus. Clergyman and Philanthropist. 1798..1864
Flinders, Matthew. Navigator...................... 1780?.1814
Flinck, Govaërt, or Godfrey. Dutch Painter........... 1616..1660
Flint, Rev. Timothy. American Writer .... 1780..1840
Flipart, John James. French Engraver .... 1723..1782
Flodoard, or Frodoard. Historian .... 894.. 966
Flogel, Charles Frederick. German Writer............. 1729..1788
Flood, Henry, M. P. Irish Orator and Writer .... 1732..1791
Flood, Sir William, M. P. Statesman................ 1741..1824
Eloquet, Stephen Joseph. French Musical Composer ... 1750..1785
Florence of Worcester. Historian.................. — ..1118
Florentino, Stephen. Historical Painter of Florence.... 1301?.1350
Florez, Henry. Spanish Historian .... 1701..1773
Florian, John Peter Claris de. French Writer .... 1755..1794
Florimond de Remond, of Bordeaux. Lawyer & Writ. — ..1602
Florio, John. *The Resolute.* Tutor to Prince Henry. Writer 1545?.1625
Floris, Francis. Flemish Historical Painter........... 1520..1570
Florus, L. Annæus. (*Epitome de Gestis Romanorum*).. ti.Traj.&Adrian
Floyd, Gen. John. American Statesman and Soldier... 1769..1839
Floyd, Wm. American General...................... 1734..1821
Floyer, Sir John. Physician .... 1649..1734
Fludd, Robert. *De Fluctibus.* Rosicrucian Philosopher.. 1574..1637
Foes, or Foesius, Anutius. Phys. and Scholar in Lorraine 1528..1595
Fogliano, Louis. *Folianus.* Writer on Music .... — ..1540?
Foglieta, or Folieta, Uberto. Genoese Writer.......... 1518..1581
Fohr, Charles Philip. German Landscape Painter...... 1795..1818
Foinard, Fred. Maurice. Fr. Eccles. and Biblical Writer 1683?.1743
Foix, Gaston III., Count de, Viscount de Béarn. (*Phœbus*) 1331..1391
Foix, Gaston de. *Thunderbolt of Italy.* Commander.... 1489..1512
Foix, Mark Anthony. French Jesuit; Preacher .... 1627..1687
Foix, Odet de, Lord of Lautrec. French General .... — ..1528

BORN. DIED.

Foix, Paul de. Archbishop of Toulouse. Diplomatist .. 1528..1584
Folard, John Charles de. French Tactician............ 1669..1752
Folengo, John Bapt. Italian Benedictine; Biblical Writer 1490..1559
Folengo, Theophilus. *Merlin Coccaye.* Ital. Burlesque Poet 1491..1544
Foley, Sir Thomas. Naval Officer......,............ 1757..1833
Folianus, Ludovicus. Writer on Music .... — ..1540?
Folkes, Martin. Scholar and Antiquary.............. 1690..1754
Follen, August. German Poet................... 1794..1855
Follen, Charles. German Writer. L. by L. Follen, 1843 1795..1841
Follett, Sir William Webb. Lawyer................. 1798..1845
Fonblanque, John de la Grenier. English Lawyer.
  (*Treatise on Equity*)............................... 1759..1837
Fonblanque, John Samuel Martin. Commissioner of
  Bankruptcy. (*Medical Jurisprudence*) .... 1787..1865
Fonseca, Peter. Portug. Writer. (*System of Metaphysics*) 1528..1599
Font, Joseph de la. French Comic Writer .... 1686..1725
Font, Peter de la. Fr. Divine. (*Entretiens Ecclesiastiques*) — ..1699
Fontaine, Alexis. French Geometer................. 1705?.1771
Fontaine, John de la. French Poet and Fabulist....... 1621..1695
Fontaine, Nicholas. French Jansenist .... 1625..1709
Fontaine, Peter Francis Leonard. French Architect.... 1762..1853
Fontaines, Peter Francis Guyot des. French Critic .... 1685..1745
Fontana, Charles. Italian Architect .... 1634..1714
Fontana, Dominic. Italian Architect................ 1543..1607
Fontana, Felix. Philosopher and Naturalist........... 1730..1805
Fontana, Francis, of Naples. Astronomer .... 1580..1656
Fontana, Gaetano, of Modena. Astronomer........... 1645..1719
Fontana, Gregory. Mathematician .... 1735..1803
Fontana, John. Hydraulic Engineer.................. 1540..1614
Fontana, Lavinia. Italian Portrait Painter........... 1552..1614
Fontana, Prospero. Italian Historical Painter .... 1512..1597
Fontanelle, John Gaspar Dubois. French Writer...... 1737..1812
Fontanes, Louis de. Orator, Politician, Poet.......... 1757..1821
Fontanges, Marie Angélique, Dss. of. Fav. of Louis XIV. 1661..1681
Fontanini, Justus. Archbishop of Ancyra. Writer.... 1666..1736
Fonte-Moderata. *Modesta Pozzo.* Venetian Poetess .. 1555..1592
Fontenay, John Baptist Blain de. French Painter ..... 1654..1715
Fontenay, Peter Claude. French Jesuit; Writer....... 1663..1742
Fontenay, Theresa de Cabarrus, Marchss. de. Fr. Beauty 1773..1835
Fontenelle, Bernard le Bovier de. Poet & Misc. Writ. 1657..1757
Fontenu, Louis Francis de. French Writer........... 1667..1759
Fontius, or Fonti, Bartholomew. Historian of Florence.. 1445..1513
Foote, Andrew Hull. American Admiral.............. 1806..1863
Foote, Sir Edw. James. Admiral................... 1767..1833
Foote, Jesse. Surgeon and Miscellaneous Writer....... 1743..1826
Foote, Samuel. Comedian. Life by W. Cooke, 1805 ... 1720?.1777
Foppens, John Francis. Flemish Hist., Biog., and Divine 1689?.1761
Forabosco, Girolamo, of Venice. Portrait Painter...1600?.aft.1659
Forbes, Alexander, Lord, of Pitsligo. (*Moral and Philo-
  sophical Essays*).................................. — ..1762
Forbes, Duncan. Scottish Judge. Religious Writer.
  Life by J. H. Burton, 1847......................... 1685..1747
Forbes, Edward. Naturalist. Life by Wilson .... 1815..1854
Forbes, James. E. I. C. Civil Serv. (*Oriental Memoirs*) 1749..1819

11

BORN. DIED.

Forbes, John, of Corse. (*Historico-Theolog. Institutions*) 1593..1648
Forbes, John. Botanist and Trav. (*Climate of Penzance*) 1799..1824
Forbes, Sir John, M. D. Scottish Medical Writer...... 1787?.1861
Forbes, Patrick. Bishop of Aberdeen (1618–35)....... 1564..1635
Forbes, Robert. Bishop of Caithness. Historical Writer — ..1776
Forbes, Sir Wm., of Pitsligo. Banker. (*Life of Beattie*) 1739..1806
Forbes, William. Bishop of Edinburgh............... 1585..1634
Forbin, Claude, Chevalier de. Admiral. L. by Reboulet 1656..1733
Forbonnais, Francis Veron de. French Commercial and
    Financial Writer................................. 1722..1800
Force, Charlotte Rose de Caumont de la. Poetess...... 1654?.1724
Force, James N. de Caumont Duc de la. Marshal. *See*
    Laforce... 1558..1652
Forcellini, Giles. Lexicographer.................... 1688..1768
. **Ford**, John. Dramatic Writer. (*The Broken Heart*).... 1586..1639?
Ford, Sir John. Loyalist and Hydraulic Inventor...... 1605..1670
Ford, Richard. Trav. and Writer. (*Handbook of Spain*) 1796..1858
Ford, Rev. Simon. Latin Poet...................... 1679..1699
Fordun, John de. Scottish Historian. (*Scotichronicon*) — ..1386?
Fordyce, David. Philosopher. (*Theodorus*)........... 1711..1751
Fordyce, George. Scottish Medical Writer............ 1736..1802
Fordyce, James, D. D. (*Sermons to Young Women*)..... 1720?.1796
Fordyce, Sir William. Scottish Medical Writer........ 1724..1792
Foreest, or Forestus, Peter van. Dutch Medical Writer 1522..1597
Foreiro, Francis. Portuguese Biblical Commentator.... — ..1587
Forest, John. French Landscape Painter............. 1636..1712
Foresti, E. Felice. Italian Patriot.................. 1793?.1858
Foresti, James Philip. *Philip of Bergamo.* Chronicler. 1434..1520
Forkel, John Nich. Musical Writer. (*History of Music*) 1749..1818
Forli, Melozzo da. Painter of Forli................. 1436?. —
Forman, Simon. Astrologer........................ 1552..1611
Formey, John Henry Sam. Pruss. Philos. and Theolog. 1711..1797
Formosus. Pope (891–96)......................... — .. 896
Forqueray, Anthony. French Violinist............... 1671..1745?
Forrest, Thomas. Navigator and Discoverer........... — ..1802?
Forsell, Charles af. Swedish Philanth. and Statistician. 1783..1848
Forshal, Rev. Josiah. Biblical Critic................ 1794?.1863
Forskal, Peter. Swedish Naturalist................. 1736..1763
Forster, Frank. Civil Engineer.................... 1800..1852
Forster, Geo. Traveler. (*Journey from Bengal to Eng.*) 1754..1792
Forster, John. Protestant Hebraist, of Wittemberg .... 1495..1556
Forster, John George Adam. German Traveler........ 1754..1794
Forster, John Reinhold. Naturalist and Geographer.... 1729..1798
Forster, Nathaniel. Scholar and Divine............. 1717..1757
Forster, Thomas, of Northumberland. Jacobite....... 1675..1734?
Forster, Thos. Ignatius Maria. English Meteorologist.1789.ab.1850
Forstner, Christopher. Austrian Statesman and Writer 1598..1667
Forsyth, Alex. John. Discov. of the Percussion Principle 1769..1843
Forsyth, John. American Statesman .... 1781?.1841
Forsyth, William. Scottish Horticulturist............ 1737..1804
Fort, Francis le. Soldier & Statesm. under Peter the Great 1656..1699
Fortescue, Sir John. Judge. (*De Laudibus Legum Angliæ*) 1395..1485
Fortiguerra, Nicholas. Italian Bishop and Poet........ 1674..1735
Fortis, John Baptist. Naturalist. (*Viaggio in Dalmazia*) 1741..1803

BORN. DIED.

Fortius, or Fortis, Joachim. *Ringelbergius.* Scholar.... — ..1536
Fortoul, Hippolytus Nicholas Honoré. French Writer. 1811..1856
Forward, Walter. American Lawyer and Statesman... 1786..1842
Fosbrooke, Rev. Thomas Dudley. Antiquary......... 1770..1842
Foscari, Francesco. Doge of Venice (1423–57). Byron's
  Two Foscari.................................... 1373?.1457
Foscari, Giacopo, the son............................ — aft.1457
Foscarini, Mark. Venetian Statesman................ 1696..1763
Foscarini, Michael. Venetian Historian.............. 1632..1692
Foschini, Anthony. Italian Architect................. 1741..1803
Foscolo, Nicolo Ugo. Ital. Poet. L. by C. Gemelli, 1849 1777..1827
Fossati, Dominic. Italian Painter.................... 1743..1784
Fosse, Anthony de la. Fr. Traged. (*Manlius Capitolinus*) 1653..1708
Fosse, Charles de la. French Painter .... 1640..1716
Fossombroni, Victor. Italian Mathematician .... 1754..1844
Foster, Henry. Navigator............................ 1797..1831
Foster, Dr. James. Dissenting Preacher .... 1697..1753
Foster, John. Essayist. Life by Ryland and Shepherd 1770..1843
Foster, John, of Liverpool. Architect................ 1786..1846
Foster, Rev. John, of Eton. (*Accent and Quantity*)... 1731..1773
Foster, Sir Mich. Judge. Life by Michael Dodson, 1795 1689..1763
Foster, Samuel. Gresham Professor of Astronomy..... — ..1652
Foster, Stephen C. Musical Composer .... 1826..1864
Fothergill, Geo., D. D., of St. Edmund's Hall. (*Sermons*) 1705..1760
Fothergill, John. Physician and Writer. Life by Gil-
  bert Thompson, 1782; Lettsom, 1783 .... 1712..1780
Fothergill, Samuel. Quaker Controversialist....... 1705?.1772
Foucault, Nicholas Joseph. French Antiquary. Life by
  self, and F. Baudry, 1862........................ 1643..1721
Fouché, Joseph, Duke of Otranto. French Revolutionist 1763..1820
Foucher, Simon. French Writer .... 1644..1696
Fouchier, Bertram de. Dutch Painter .... 1609..1674
Fouchs, or Fux, John Joseph. German Musical Writer 1660?.1740?
Foucquet, Chas. Louis Aug., Duke of Belle-Isle. Marshal 1684..1761
Foucquet, Nicholas, Marquis of Belle-Isle. Superin-
  tendent of Finances.............................. 1615..1680
Fougeroux, Augustus Denis. French Writer.......... 1732..1789
Fouillou, James. French Jansenist Writer .... 1670..1736
Foulis, Andrew, of Glasgow. Printer................ — ..1774
Foulis, Robert, brother and colleague................ — ..1776
Foulon, John Erard. Flemish Theolog. and Hist. Writer 1609..1668
Foulon, William. *Gnaphœus.* Dutch Latin Writer .... 1493..1568
Foulston, John, of Plymouth. Architect............. 1773?.1842
Fountaine, Sir Andrew. Antiquary, Collector, and Writ. 1680?.1753
Fouqué, Fred. Henry Charles de la Motte, Baron. (*Sin-
  tram; Undine*)................................... 1777..1843
Fouqué, Henry Aug. de la Motte, Baron. Prussian Gen. 1698..1774
Fouquières, James. Flemish Landscape Painter ...... 1580..1659
Fouquier-Tinville, Anth. Quentin. Fr. Revolutionist. 1747..1795
Fourcroy, Anth. Francis de, Ct. Fr. Chem. & Nat. Philos. 1755..1809
Fourcroy, Charles René de. French Officer and Engineer 1715..1791
Fourier, Francis Mary Chas. French Socialist .... 1772..1837
Fourier, J. Bapt. Jos. Fr. Nat. Phil. (*Théo. de la Châleur*) 1768..1830
Fourmont, Claude Louis. (*Heliopolis and Memphis*) .... 1703..1780

BORN. DIED.

Fourmont, Michael. Collector of Inscriptions .... 1690..1746
Fourmont, Stephen. French Orientalist .... 1683..1745
Fournier, Peter Simon. Fr. Engraver and Typefounder 1712..1768
Fourquevaux, Raymond of Pavia, Bn. of. Gen. & Writ. 1509..1574
Fowler, Christopher. Ejected Nonconformist........... 1611..1676
Fowler, Edw. Bp. of Gloucester. (*Design of Christianity*) 1632..1714
Fowler, John. Printer and Writer................... 1530?.1579
Fowler, Richard. English Physician and Author....... 1765..1833
Fowler, Thomas. Medical Writer .... 1736..1801
Fowler, William. Scottish Poet................:... fl. 1603
Fox, Charles James. Statesman. Life by R. Fell, 1808;
  J. B. Trotter, 1811; Lord J. Russell .... 1749..1806
Fox, Edward. Bishop of Hereford. Statesman........ — ..1538
Fox, Rev. Francis, of Reading. (*New Test. Explained*) — ..1738
Fox, George. Quaker. Life by J. S. Watson; Josiah
  Marsh, 1847.. 1624..1690
Fox, Henry, First Lord Holland. Statesman........... 1705..1774
Fox, Henry Watson. Missionary. L. by Geo. T. Fox, 1850 1817..1848
Fox, John. Martyrologist. (*Book of Martyrs*)........ 1517..1587
Fox, Luke. Navigator. (*The North-West Fox*)......1585.aft.1635
Fox, Richard. Bishop of Winchester. Statesman ...... 1466?.1528
Fox, Sir Stephen. Statesman......................... 1627..1716
Fox, Wm. Johnson, M.P. Unitarian Preacher and Author 1786..1864
Foy, Maximilian Sebastian. French General........... 1775..1825
Fra Bartolomeo di St. Marco. *Baccio della Porta.*
  Italian Painter .... 1469..1517
Fracastorius, Hieronymus, of Verona. Poet, Philosopher,
  Astronomer, Physician. (*Syphilis*) .... 1483..1553
Frachetta, Jerome. Ital. Polit. Writer. (*Il Seminario*) 1560?.1620
Fra Diavolo. *Michael Pezza.* Neapolitan Bandit...... 1769?.1806
Fraguier, Claude Francis, Abbé. Critic & Writ. on Music 1666..1728
Framery, Nicholas Stephen. French Musician and Poet 1745..1810
Francesca, Peter Borghese della. Italian Painter ...... 1398?.1483
Franceschini, Baldassare. *Volterrano.* Painter .... 1621..1689
Franceschini, Mark Anthony. Historical Painter...... 1648..1728
Francescina, Signora. Italian Singer................ fl. 1740?
Franchi, Anthony. Painter of Lucca .... 1634..1709
Franchinus, Gaffurius, of Lodi. Writer on Music...... 1451..1522
Francia, Francesco. *Raibolini.* Painter. Life by Calvi 1450..1518
Francia, James, son. Painter .... — ..1557
Francia, Dr. Jos. Gaspar Rodriguez. Dictat. of Paraguay 1757?.1840
Franciabigio, Mark Anthony. Italian Historical Painter 1483..1524
Francis I. King of France (1515-47). Life by Varillas;
  Capefigue; Miss Pardoe; G. H. Gaillard, 1769....... 1494..1547
Francis II. (1559-60)............................. 1543..1560
Francis I. Emperor of Germany (1745-65). *Of Lorraine* 1708..1765
Francis II. of Germany (1792-1804); I. of Austria (1804-
  1835)... 1768..1835
Francis, *De Jesu Maria.* Spanish Carmelite. (*On the
  Apocalypse*).. — ..1677
Francis, *De Victoria.* Dominican. (*Theol. Prælectiones*) — ..1549
Francis, John Charles. French Engraver............. 1717..1769
Francis, John Wakefield. Amer. Physician and Author 1789..1861
Francis, Lawrence. Abbé. French Christian Apologist 1698..1782

BORN. DIED.

Francis, Luke, of Mechlin. Painter................... 1574..1643
Francis, Luke, son. *The Young.* Painter........... 1606?.1654
Francis, Rev. Philip, D. D. Poet, Transl. of Horace, &c. — ..1773
Francis, Sir Philip, son. Politician and Writer .... 1740..1818
Francis, Simon, of Tours. Portrait Painter........... 1606..1671
Francis Romain. Architect and Engineer of Ghent ... 1646?.1735
Francis, St. *De Borgia.* Spanish Jesuit............ 1510..1572
Francis, St. *D'Assisi.* Life by Ph. Arrighetti; Chavin
de Malan; St. Bonaventure; Peter d'Alva.......... 1182..1226
Francis, St. *De Paulo.* Founder of *Fratres Minimi*... 1416..1507
Francis, St. *De Sales.* Life by Marsollier........... 1567..1622
Francis Xavier, St. Missionary. *See* Xavier........ 1506..1552
Francius, Peter. Dutch Greek and Latin Poet........ 1645..1704
Franck von Franckenau, George de. German Scholar
and Physician................................ 1643..1704
Francke, August Hermann, of Halle. Lutheran Divine.
Founder of Orphan House...................... 1663..1727
Francken, Christian. Ger.Writ. (*Colloquium Jesuiticum*) 1549.aft.1595
Franckenstein, Christian Godfrey, of Leipsic. Writer.. 1661..1717
Franckenstein, James Augustus, son. Writer .... 1689..1733
Francklin, Thomas, D. D. Miscellaneous Writer ...... 1721..1784
Francks, or Francken, Francis. *Old.* Flemish Painter. 1544..1616
Francks, or Francken, Francis. *Young.* Flemish Painter 1580..1642
Francks, or Vranx, J. Baptist. Dutch Historical Painter 1600..1653
Franco. *Magister.* German Writer on Music .... — aft.1083
Franco, Baptist. Painter of Venice.................. 1498..1561
Franco, Nicholas. Italian Satirist .... 1505..1569
François. *See* Francis.
François de Neufchâteau, Nich., Ct. Writer & Polit. 1750..1828
Franconi, Anthony. Equestrian Artist............... 1738..1836
Francowitz, Matthias. *Flacius Illyricus.* Luth. Divine 1520..1575
Frank, John Pet. Ger. Phys. (*Système de Police Médicale*) 1745..1821
Frankland, Thomas. Physician and Historian........ 1633..1690
Franklin, Benjamin. Philosopher. Life by self and W.
T. Franklin, 1817; J. Sparks, 1840; self and H. H.
Weld, 1849 .... 1706..1790
Franklin, Mrs. Eleanor Anne(*née* Porden). Authoress .. 1795..1825
Franklin, Sir John, Rear-Admiral. Arctic Navigator... 1786..1847?
Franklin, William, son of Benjamin. Last Royal Gov-
ernor of New Jersey........................... 1731?.1813
Franks, John Baptist. Painter of Antwerp .... 1600..1653
Franks, Sebastian. Painter of Antwerp.............. 1573?.1636
Frantzius, Wolfgang. German Lutheran Divine....... 1564..1628
Franzen, Francis Michael. Swedish Poet............. 1772..1847
Fraser, Alexander. Painter......................... 1787?.1865
Fraser, James Baillie. Traveler and Novelist......... 1783..1856
Fraser, Simon, Ld. Lovat. Scottish Jacobite. Beheaded. 1667..1747
Frasi, Julia. Italian Singer .... fl. 18th c.
Frassen, Claude. Doctor of the Sorbonne .... 1620..1711
Fratellini, Giovanna. Florentine Painter?............ 1666..1731
Fratellini, Lawrence Mary, son. Painter............. 1690..1729
Fraunhofer, Joseph von. Bavarian Optician.......... 1787..1826
Frayssinous, Denis Luc, Count. French Prelate....... 1765..1841
Fredegarius. French Historian...................... fl. 658

BORN. DIED.

Frédégonde. Queen of Chilperic, of France .... 545?. 596
Frederic, Colonel, son of Theodore, K. of Corsica. Writer 1730?.1797
Frederick I. Emperor (1152–90). *Barbarossa.* Life by
   Cosmo Bartoli................................ 1121..1190
Frederick II. (1210–50.) Life by Knighton, 1862..... 1194..1250
Frederick (III.), elected 1314; conpet. of Louis of Bavaria — ..1330
Frederick III. (1440–1493.) *The Pacific* .... 1415..1493
Frederick I. King of Denmark (1523–33)............. 1471..1533
Frederick II. (1558–88)............................ 1534..1588
Frederick III. (1648–70) .... 1609..1670
Frederick IV. (1699–1730) .... 1671..1730
Frederick V. (1746–66)............................. 1723..1766
Frederick VI. (1808–39) .... 1768..1839
Frederick VII. (1848–63) .... 1808..1863
Frederick V. Elector Palatine. *Winter King.* Son-in-
   law of James I................................. 1596..1632
Frederick William. Elector of Brandenburg. *Great
   Elector.* Life by Puffendorf..................... 1620..1688
Frederick I. King of Prussia (1701–13) .... 1657..1713
Frederick William I. (1713–40)..................... 1688..1740
Frederick II. (1740–86.) *The Great.* Life by Dr. J.
   Towers, 1788; Lord Dover, 1832; Thomas Campbell,
   1841; T. B. Macaulay; Segur; Klopp; T. Carlyle .... 1712..1786
Frederick William II. (1786–97) ......:........... 1744..1797
Frederick William III. (1797–1840)................ 1770..1840
Frederick William IV. (1840–58) .... 1795..1861
Frederick. Elector of Saxony. *The Wise* .... 1463..1554
Frederick Augustus I. King of Poland and Elector
   of Saxony (1697–1733) .... 1670..1733
Frederick Augustus II. (1733–63) .... 1696..1733
Frederick. Pr. of Wales. Life by Dr. J. Campbell, 1751 1707..1751
Fredro, Maximilian. Polish Writer.................. — ..1676
Freeling, Sir Francis. Secretary to the Post-Office ..... 1764?.1836
Freeman, James, D. D. American Unitarian Minister .. 1759..1835
Freeman, John. Painter............................ ti. Chas. II.
Fregoso, Baptist. Doge of Genoa (1478). Writer ...... fl. 1478
Freher, Marquard. German Jurist.................... 1565..1614
Freigius, John Thomas. German Scholar............. — ..1583
Freind, John, M. D. English Medical Writer.......... 1675..1728
Freinsheim, or Freinshemius, John. German Critic.... 1608..1660
Freire de Andrada, Hyacinth. Portuguese Writer .... 1597..1657
Freitag, John. German Medical Writer............... 1581..1641
Freke, William. Socinian Writer.................... 1663..1746
Frelinghuysen, Theod. American Statesman & Scholar 1787..1862
Fréminet, Martin. French Painter .... 1567..1619
Frémont d'Ablancourt, Nicholas. French Historian .. 1625?.1693
Frend, William. Mathematician..................... 1757..1841
Freneau, Philip. American Poet and Journalist .... 1752..1832
Frenicle de Bessy, Bernard. French Mathematician .. 1605..1675
Frere, John, M. P., F. R. S., F. S. A. Antiquary........ — ..1807
Frere, John Hookham. Poet and Diplomatist......... 1769..1846
Freres, Theodore. Dutch Painter................... 1643..1693
Fréret, Nicholas. French Antiquary and Chronologist.. 1688..1749
Fréron, Elias Catherine. French Critic.............. 1719..1776

BORN. DIED.

Fréron, Louis Stanislaus, son. French Revolutionist.... 1757..1802
Frescobaldi, Jerome. Italian Musical Composer .... 1587?.1654?
Fresnaye, John Vauquelin de la. French Poet .... 1534..1606
Fresne, Charles du Cange du. French Antiquary ...... 1610..1688
Fresnel, Augustine John. French Experimental Philos.. 1788..1827
Fresnoy, Charles Alphonse du. French Painter and Poet.
    Life by Wills and Mason .... 1611..1665
Fresny, Charles Rivière du. French Poet .... 1648..1724
Fréteau de St. Just, Emanuel M. M. P. French Polit.. 1745..1794
Frey, John Cecil. German Physician and Greek Scholar. 1580?.1631
Frey, John James. Swiss Engraver.................. 1681..1752
Freycinet, Louis Claude Desaulses de. French Navigator 1779..1842
Freytag, Frederick Theophilus, of Nuremberg. Scholar. 1723..1776
Frezier, Amadæus Francis. French Mathematician .... 1682..1773
Friche, or Frische, James de. Fr. Benedictine. Writer 1640..1693
Fries, Jacob Fred. German Philosopher.............. 1773..1843
Frisbie, Levi. American Writer....................... 1784..1822
Frisch, John Leonard. German Naturalist and Divine.. 1666..1743
Frischlein, Nicodemus. German Critic and Poet ...... 1547..1590
Frischmuth, John. Theologian of Jena............... 1619..1687
Frisi, Paul, of Milan. Mathematician .... 1728..1784
Frisius, Henry. Scholar of Zurich. (De Sede Animæ).. — ..1718
Frisius, or Fries, John. Orientalist of Zurich .... 1505..1565
Frith, John. Protestant Martyr........................ — ..1533
Fritz, Samuel. German Roman Catholic Missionary.... 1650..1730
Frizon, Peter. French Historian and Theologian....... — ..1651?
Froben, John. German Printer .... 1460..1527
Frobisher, Sir Martin. Navigator .... — ..1594
Froebel, Fred. German Educator; Founder of Kinder-
    gärten Schools.................................... 1782..1852
Froelich, Erasmus. Mathematician and Medalist ...... 1700..1758
Froidmont, Libert. Dutch Biblical Commentator...... 1587..1653
Froissart, John. Historian. L. by St. Palaye, tr. by Johnes 1337..1410?
Fromage, Peter. French Jesuit Missionary in the Levant 1678..1740
Fronteau, John. French Writer.................... 1614..1662
Frontinus, Sext. Julius. (Strategemeta; De Aquæductibus) — A.D.106?
Fronto, M. Cornelius. Roman Rhetorician............. — aft. 166
Frost, John. American Revolutionary General........ 1738..1810
Froude, Rev. Richard Hurrell. Anglo-Catholic Divine.. 1803..1836
Frowde, Philip. Poet .... 1680?.1738
Frugoni, Charles Innocent. Italian Poet .... 1692..1768
Frumentius, St. Apostle of Ethiopia .... — .. 360?
Fry, Caroline (afterwardsWilson). (The Listener.) L.by self 1787.. —
Fry, Edmund, M. D. Type Founder .... — ..1835
Fry, Mrs. Elizabeth. Philanthropist. Life by Daughters,
    1847; Rev. T. Timpson, 1847..................... 1780..1845
Fry, John, M.P. Socinian Writer .... — ..1650
Fry, Wm. Henry. Amer. Musical Composer and Editor. 1815..1864
Frye, Thomas. Irish Designer and Mezzotint Engraver.. 1710..1762
Fryth, or Frith, John. Protestant Martyr............. — ..1533
Fuca, John de. Apostolos Valerianos. Spanish Navigator — ..1632
Fuchs, or Fuchsius, Leonard. Ger. Phys. and Botanist 1501..1566
Fuentes, Peter Henry d'Azevedo, Count of. Spanish
    General and Statesman........................... 1560..1643

BORN. DIED.

Fuessli, John Gaspar. *The Elder.* Swiss Paint. *See* Fuseli 1706..1781
Fuger, Frederick Henry. German Painter.............. 1751..1818
Fugger, Ulrich. German Scholar and Collector of MSS. 1526..1584
Fulbert. Bishop of Chartres. Theologian............ 950?.1028
Fulda, Charles Frederick. Ger. Hist., Antiq., Philologist 1724..1788
Fulgentius, St. African Bishop; Writer.............. 468?. 533
Fulke, William, D. D. Divine...................... 1540..1589
Fuller, Andrew. Baptist Divine. Life by Dr. Ryland.. 1754..1815
Fuller, Isaac. Painter .... — .1672
Fuller, Nicholas. (*Miscellanea Theologica*)............ 1557..1622
Fuller, Sarah Margaret, Marchioness of Ossoli. American
    Writer. Life by Clarke, Emerson, and Channing, 1852 1810..1850
Fuller, Thos. (*Church History.*) L. by A. T. Russell, 1844 1608..1661
Fulton, Robert. American Inventor and Civil Engineer.
    Life by C. D. Colden, 1817........................... 1765..1815
Funccius, or Funck, John Nicholas. German Philologist 1693..1777
Funck, John. German Divine and Biographer. Beheaded 1518..1566
Funes, Gregory, of La Plata. Patriot & Historical Writer — ..1820
Furetière, Anthony. Philologist. (*Diction. Universel*).. 1620..1688
Furini, Francis. Painter of Florence .... 1604..1646
Furius, Frederick. *Cœriolanus.* Spanish Historian..... 1510?.1592
Furneaux, Dr. Philip. Dissenting Divine .... 1726..1783
Furst, Walter. Swiss Patriot....................... fl. 1307
Fürstemberg, Ferdinand de. (*Monumen. Paderbornensia*) 1626..1683
Fursteneau, John Hermann. Medical Writer .... 1688..1756
Fuseli, or Fuessli, Henry. Painter. Life by Knowles .. 1742?.1825
Fuseli, John Gaspar. Swiss Artist. (*Helvetic Painters*) 1706..1781
Fusi, Anthony. Doct. of the Sorbonne; Protest. Convert 1565?.aft.1633
Fuss, Nicholas von. Mathemat. and Natural Philosopher 1755..1826
Fust, John. One of the Inventors of Printing .... — ..1470?
Fux, or Fouchs, John Joseph. German Musical Composer 1660?.1740?
Fuzelier, Louis. French Dramatist .... 1672..1752
Fyot de la Marche, Claude, Ct. of Bosjam. French Hist. 1630..1721
Fyt, John. Dutch Painter............................ 1625..1671

G.

BORN. DIED.

Gaal, Barent. Dutch Landscape Painter.............. 1650..1671
Gabbiani, Anthony Dominic. Florentine Painter....... 1652..1726
Gabinius, Aulus. Consul: defended by Cicero .... — B.C. 48?
Gabriel, James. French Architect and Engineer....... 1667..1742
Gabrielli, Cattarina. Italian Singer................. 1730..1796
Gabrini, Nicholas. *Rienzi.* Reformer at Rome........ 1313..1354
Gacon, Francis. French Poet and Satirist............. 1667..1725
Gadbury, John. Astrologer...................... 1627..1692?
Gaddesden, John of. Phys. and Philos. (*Rosa Anglica*) fl. 1320?
Gaddi, Angelo. Painter............................ 1324..1387
Gaddi, Gaddo. Italian Painter in Mosaic............. 1239..1312
Gaddi, Taddeo. Florentine Painter................. 1300..1352?
Gadebusch, Frederick Conrad. Ger. Writer on Livonia. 1719..1788
Gadsden, Christopher. Amer. Revolutionary Statesman. 1724..1805
Gadsden, Christopher Edwards, D. D., grandson .... 1785..1852
Gadsden, James. American Statesman............... 1788..1858
Gaelen, Alexander van. Dutch Painter.............. 1670..1728
Gaertner, or Gärtner, Frederick von. Architect........ 1792..1847
Gaertner, or Gärtner, John Andrew. German Architect 1743..1826
Gaertner, Joseph. German Botanist.................. 1732..1791
Gaetano. *Scipio Pulyeone.* Florentine Painter........ 1550..1588
Gaffarell, James. French Hebraist and Astrologer...... 1601..1681
Gaffurius, or Gaforio. *See* Franchinus.............. 1451..1522
Gage, Thomas. Missionary. (*Survey of the West Indies*) 1597?.1655
Gage, Thomas. British General in America............ — ..1787
Gagern, John Christopher Ernest, Baron von. States-
    man and Writer.............................. 1766..1852
Gagnier, John. Arabic Professor at Oxford............ 1670?.1740
Gaguin, Robert. Fr. Historian. (*De Gestis Francorum*). 1425?.1501
Gahn, John Theodore. Swedish Mineralogist......... 1745..1818
Gaigny, or Gagny, John. French Theologian.......... — ..1549
Gaillard, Gabriel Henry. French Historian and Publicist 1726..1806
Gaillard, John Ernest. Musical Composer............. 1687..1749
Gainas. Gothic General of Arcadius.,................ — .. 400
Gaines, Edm. Pendleton. American General......... 1777..1849
Gainsborough, Thomas. Painter. Life by Thicknesse,
    1788; Fulcher, 1856........................ 1727..1788
Gaisford, Thomas. Dean of Christ Church. Critic..... 1780..1855
Gaius. *See* Caius.
Galadin, Mahomet. Emperor of the Moguls........... — ..1605
Galanino. *Balthasar Aloisi.* Italian Painter........ 1578..1638
Galantini, Hippolytus. *Cappuccino & Prete Genovese.* Pa. 1627..1706
Galas, Matthew. Imperial Commander............... 1589..1647
Galateo, Anthony. Italian Physician............... 1444..1517
Galatin, Peter. Franciscan. (*De Arcanis Catholicæ
    Veritatis*)................................ fl. 1530?
Galba. Emperor of Rome (68–69) .... B.C.3..A.D.69
Gale, John. Baptist Writer. (*Reflections on Wall*). 1680..1721
Gale, Roger. Antiquary. (*Honor on Richmond*)....... 1672..1744
Gale, Samuel, brother. Antiquary.................. 1682..1754

BORN. DIED.

Gale, Theophilus. Nonconf. Div. (*Court of the Gentiles*) 1628..1678
Gale, Thomas, D. D. Editor of *Hist. Anglicanæ Scriptores* 1636..1702
Galeano, Joseph, of Palermo. Medical Writer......... 1605..1675
Galen, Christopher Bernard von. Bishop of Munster.
    German General and Statesman.................... 1605..1678
Galen, Claudius. Medical, Philolog., and Philos. Writer. 130.. 200
Galen, Matthew. Theologian at Douay................ — ..1573
Galeotti, Nicholas. Italian Jesuit; Writer........... 1692..1758
Galerius. Roman Emperor (305–11)................. — .. 311
Gales, Joseph. American Journalist .... 1760..1841
Galiani, Ferdinand. Abbé. (*Traité sur les Monnaies.*)
    Life by Louis Deodati, 1788...................... 1728..1787
Galilei, Galileo. Astronomer. Life by Viviari; Nelli,
    1793; Venturi, 1818; Libri, 1841; Marini; Drinkwater
    Bethune; Brewster; Chasles, 1862................. 1564..1642
Galilei, Vincent. Florentine Writ. (*Dialogo della Musica*) 1533?. —
Gall, Francis Joseph. German Phrenologist........... 1758..1828
Galland, Anthony. Orient. Transl. of *Arabian Nights*. 1646..1715
Galland, Augustus. French Genealogist and Archivist.. — ..1644?
Gallatin, Albert. American Statesman............... 1761..1849
Gallaudet, Rev. Thomas Hopkins. American Teacher of
    Deaf and Dumb........................... 1787..1851
Galle, or Gallæus, Servatius, of Haarlem. Scholar.:..... 1630?.1709
Gallienus. Roman Emperor (253–268) .... 218?. 268
Gallio, Junius. Proconsul of Achaia................. —.. 65
Gallitzin, Demetrius Augustine. Russian Noblem. & Miss. 1770..1840
Galloche, Louis. French Painter.................... 1670..1761
Gallois, Chas. Andrew Gustavus Léon. Fr. Publicist... 1789..1851
Gallois, John. French Critic...................... 1632..1707
Gallonius, Anthony. (*De Martyrum Cruciatibus*)...... — ..1605
Galloway, Joseph. American Loyalist................ 1730?.1803
Gallucci, Angelo. Italian Scholar. (*De Bello Belgico*). 1593..1674
Gallucci, John Paul. Italian Astronomer............. fl. 1593
Gallucci, Tarquinius. Italian Scholar. (*Virgilianæ In-
    dicationes*)................................... 1574..1649
Gallup, Jos. Adam. American Physician and Author ... 1769..1849
Gallus, C. Cornelius. Roman Poet.................66 or 9 B.C.26
Gally, Rev. Henry, D. D. Scholar.................. 1696..1769
Galt, John. Novelist. (*Autobiography*)............. 1779..1839
Galuppi, Balthasar. *Buranello*. Musical Composer.... 1703..1785
Galvani, Louis. Discoverer of Galvanism............ 1737..1798
Gama, Joseph Basil de. Brazilian Poet. (*L'Uraguay*).. 1740..1795
Gama, Vasco da. Navigator: doubled Cape of Good Hope 1469?.1525
Gamaches, Philip de. French Theologian............. 1568..1625
Gamaches, Stephen Simon. Philolog. and Nat. Philos. 1672..1756
Gambara, Lorenzo. Latin Poet. (*Columbus*)......... 1506..1596
Gambara, Veronica. Italian Poetess................. 1485..1550
Gambier, Jas., Lord. Admiral. L. by Lady Chatterton 1756..1833
Gambold, John. Moravian Bishop................... 1710..1771
Gandon, James. Architect. (*Vitruvius Britannicus*) ... 1741?.1824
Gandy. Architect. *See* Deering .... 1780..1850
Gandy, James. Painter............................ 1619..1689
Ganganelli, John Vincent Anthony. Pope Clement XIV. 1705..1774
Ganilh, Charles. French Economist................. 1758..1836

BORN. DIED.

Gannal, John Nicholas. French Chemist.............. 1791..1852
Gans, Edward. German Jurist. (*Das Erbrecht*) .... 1798..1839
Garamond, Claude. Fr. Engraver and Letter Founder.. — ..1561
Garasse, Francis. Jesuit Preacher and Controversialist.. 1585..1631
Garat, Dominic Joseph. Fr. Metaphysician and Publicist 1749..1833
Garay, John. Hungarian Poet....................... 1812..1853
Garbieri, Lorenzo. Painter of Bologna .... 1580..1654
Garbo, Raphael del. Florentine Painter .... 1476..1534
Garçam, Peter Anthony Correa. Portuguese Poet...... 1724..1772
Garcia, Manuel de Populo Vicente. Span. Mus. Composer 1775..1832
Garcilasso de la Vega, or Garcias Lasso. Spanish Poet 1503..1536
Garcilasso de la Vega. *Inca.* (*History of Peru*)..... 1530..1568
Garczynski, Stephen. Writer on Poland.............. — ..1755
Garden, Alexander, M. D. Botanist and Zoölogist...... 1730..1791
Garden, Peter. Scottish Centenarian................ 1644?.1775
Gardin Dumesnil, John Baptist. (*Synonymes Latines*).. 1720..1802
Gardiner, Allen Francis. Commander, R.N. Missionary
  to Patagonia. Life by J. W. Marsh .... 1794..1851
Gardiner, James. Colonel. Life by Doddridge........ 1688..1745
Gardiner, John. American Advocate .... 1731..1793
Gardiner, John Sylvester John, son. Clergyman & Writ. 1775..1830
Gardiner, Stephen. Bishop of Winchester .... 1483..1555
Gardiner, William. Musical Writer................... 1770..1853
Gardner, Alan, Lord. Admiral...................... 1742..1809
Garengeot, René James Croissant de. French Surgeon 1688..1759
Garet, John, of St. Maur. Editor of Cassiodorus....... 1627..1694
Garissoles, Anthony. French Divine .... 1587..1650
Garland, Hugh A. American Author and Politician.... 1805..1854
Garlande, John de. Norman Writer.................. — aft.1081
Garnerin, Andrew James. French Aëronaut .... 1769..1823
Garnet, Henry. Jesuit Conspirator................... 1555..1606
Garnet, Thomas, M. D. Writer on Chem. and Nat. Phil. 1766..1802
Garnett, Jas. Mercer. Amer. Polit., Agriculturist, & Writ. 1770..1843
Garnier, Charles George Thomas. French Author..... 1746..1795
Garnier, Germain. French Political Economist .... 1754..1821
Garnier, John. French Jesuit; Writer............... 1612..1681
Garnier, John James. French Historian.............. 1729..1805
Garnier, Robert. French Tragic Poet................. 1534..1590
Garnier, Stephen Bartholomew. French Painter....... 1759..1849
Garnier Pagès, Steph. Jos. Louis. Fr. Publicist & Orator 1801..1841
Garofalo, Il. *Benvenuto Tisio*, of Ferrara. Painter...... 1481..1559
Garrard, Mark. Flemish Painter in England .... 1561..1635
Garrick, David. Tragedian. Life by Tom Davies, 1780;
  A. Murphy, 1801 .... 1716..1779
Garriel, or Gariel, Peter, of Montpellier. Historian..... 1583?.1670?
Garsault, Francis Alexander. Fr. Writer on the Horse 1693?.1778
Garth, Sir Samuel. Physician and Poet. (*Dispensary*).. — ..1719
Gartner. *See* Gaertner.
Garve, Christian. German Philosophical Writer........ 1742..1798
Garzi, Louis. Italian Painter....................... 1638..1721
Garzoni, Thomas. Ital. Writer. (*La Piazza Universale*) 1549..1589
Gascoigne, George. Poet........................... 1536?.1577
Gascoigne, Sir William. Lord Chief Justice.......... 1350?.1413
Gascoygne, William. Inventor of Micrometer........ 1621?.1644

BORN. DIED.

Gaskell, Mrs. Mary Elizabeth Cleghorne. English Authoress. (*Mary Barton*) .... 1820?.1865
Gasparini, Francis. Italian Musical Composer......... 1665?.1727
Gasparino. *Barziza*. Italian Restorer of Learning .... 1370?.1431
Gasse, Louis. Architect.............................. 1778..1833
Gasse, Stephen, twin brother. Italian Architect........ 1778..1840
Gassendi, Peter. Math. and Philos. L. by Bourgerelle 1592..1655
Gassicourt, Charles Louis Cadet de. Fr. Natural Philos. 1769..1821
Gassion, John de. Marshal of Fr. Life by T. Renaudot 1609..1647
Gassman, Florian. German Musical Composer .... 1729..1774
Gast, John, D. D. Irish Writ. (*Rudiments of Grecian Hist.*) 1715..1788
Gastaldi, John Baptist. French Medical Writer .... 1674..1747
Gaston, William. American Jurist and Statesman .... 1778..1844
Gaston de Foix, Duke de Nemours. Governor of Milan. 1488..1512
Gaston, of France, John Baptist, Duke of Orleans; opponent of Richelieu .... 1608..1660
Gastrell, Francis. Bp. of Chester. Controversial Divine 1662..1725
Gataker, Charles. Controversial Divine.............. 1614? 1680
Gataker, Thomas. Divine and Critic .... 1574..1654
Gates, Horatio. American Commander................ 1728..1806
Gatterer, John Christopher. German Historian........ 1727..1799
Gatti, Bernardine. *Il Soiaro*. Italian Painter.......... 1495? 1575
Gattinara, Mercurino Arborio, Count di. Italian Jurist.. 1465..1530
Gattly, Alfred. Sculptor .... — ..1863
Gaubil, Anthony. French Missionary to China....... 1689..1759
Gaubius, Jerome David. Medical Writer at Leyden.... 1705..1780
Gaud, or Goud, Henry, Ct. van. Pa. & Engrav. of Utrecht 1585..1639
Gauden, John. Bp. of Worc. (1662). (*Eikon Basiliké?*) 1605..1662
Gaudentio, of Milan. *Ferrari*. Historical Painter .... 1484..1550
Gaudentius, St. Bishop of Brescia................... —410 or 27
Gaudenzio, Paganin. Italian Scholar............... 1596..1648
Gaudichaud Beaupré, Charles. French Botanist...... 1780..1854
Gaudin, Mart. Mich. Chas., Duke of Gaeta. Fr. Statesm. 1756..1844
Gauli, John Baptist. *Baciccio*. Painter of Genoa...... 1639..1709
Gaulmin, Gilbert. French Writer .... 1585..1665
Gaultier, Aloïsius Edw. Camillus. Fr. Educational Writ. 1746..1818
Gaupp, John. Mathematician of Lindau............. 1667..1738
Gaurico, Luke, Bishop of Civita Ducale. Astrologer.... 1746..1558
Gauss, Charles Frederick. Ger. Math. and Astronomer 1777..1855
Gaussem, Jane Catherine. *Gaussin*. French Actress... 1711..1767
Gauthey, Emiland Mary. French Engineer............ 1732..1806
Gauthier, John Baptist. Abbé. Religious Writer....... 1685..1755
Gavanti, Bartholomew. Italian Ecclesiastical Antiquary 1569..1638
Gavard, Hyacinth. French Anatomist .... 1753..1802
Gaveston, Piers, or Peter. Favorite of Edward II....... — ..1312
Gay, Claude. French Botanist and Traveler .... 1795..1864
Gay, John. Poet. (*Beggar's Opera*)................. 1688..1732
Gay, Maria Frances Sophia. French Novelist .... 1776..1852
Gay Lussac, Joseph Louis. Fr. Experimental Philosoph. 1778..1850
Gayot de Pitaval, Francis. Fr. Writer. (*Causes Célèbres*) 1673..1743
Gayton, Edmund. Humorous Writer .... 1609..1666
Gaza, Theodore. Reviver of Greek................... 1398..1478
Gazet, Wm., of Arras. *Gazæus*. Ecclesiastical Historian 1554..1611
Gazola, Joseph. Medical Writer of Verona .... 1661..1715

BORN. DIED.

Gazon-Dourxigné, S. M. M. Critic and Poet......... — ..1784
Gazzoli, Benozzo. Italian Painter.................... 1400..1478
Gebelin, Anthony Court de. (*Le Monde Primatif*)...... 1725..1784
Geber, or Yeber. Arab. Alchemist. (*Lapis Philosophorum*) fl. 800?
Gebhardi, John Louis Levin. German Historian....... 1699..1764
Ged, Wm. Inventor of Stereotype. Life by Nichols, 1819 — ..1749?
Geddes, Alexander, LL. D. Roman Catholic Divine.
   Translator of Bible. Life by J. M. Good, 1803...... 1737..1802
Geddes, James. Writer on Classics.................. 1710..1749?
Geddes, Mich., LL. D. Writer on Ecclesiastical History 1640..1714?
Gedike, Frederick. German Educationist............. 1754..1803
Gedoyn, Nicholas. French Critic and Translator....... 1667..1744
Geer, Charles de, Baron. Swedish Naturalist........ 1720..1778
Gehler, John Sam.,of Leipsic. (*Physikalisches Wörterbuch*) 1751..1795
Geijer, Eric Gustavus. Swedish Historian............. 1783..1847
Geiler von Kaiserberg, John. Pulpit Orator......... 1455..1510
Geinoz, Francis. Swiss Scholar .... 1696..1752
Gejer, or Geier, Martin. German Biblical Commentator 1614..1681
Gelasius I. Pope (492-96).......................... — .. 496
Gelasius II. (1118-19) *John Cajetan*............... 1050?.1119
Geldenhaur, Gerard. Dutch Theologian and Historian 1482..1542
Gelder, Arnold de. Dutch Painter................... 1645..1727
Geldorp, or Gualdorp, Gortzius. Painter of Louvain.... 1553..1618
Gelée, Claude. *Claude Lorraine.* Fr. Landscape Painter 1600..1682
Gelenius, or Ghelen, Sigismund. Bohemian Scholar 1477?.1554 or 5
Gell, Sir William. Antiquary and Classical Scholar.... 1777..1836
Gellert, Christian Fürchtegott. German Divine and Poet 1715..1769
Gellert, Christlieb Ehregott, brother. Metallurgist..... 1713..1795
Gelli, John Baptist. Italian Poet................... 1498..1563
Gellibrand, Henry. Gresham Professor of Astronomy...1597..1636
Gellius, Aulus. Latin Writer. (*Noctes Atticæ*)...fl.ab.117-180 A.D.
Gelon. Tyrant of Syracuse (B. C. 491-78)......... — ..B.C.478
Gemelli Carreri, John Francis. Italian Traveler..... 1651..1725
Gemignano, or Geminiani, Hyacinth. Italian Painter.. 1611..1681
Gemignano, Vincent di San. Italian Painter......... 1490..1530
Geminiani, Francis. Italian Musical Composer........ 1680?.1762
Gemistus Pletho, George. Greek Philosopher........ 1350?.1450
Gemma, Cornelius. Physician and Mathematician..... 1535..1577
Gemma, Reinier. *Frisius.* Dutch Phys. and Mathemat. 1508..1555
Gence, John Baptist Modeste. French Writer......... 1755..1840
Gendre, le. *See* Le Gendre.
Genebrard, Gilbert. French Theologian .... 1537..1597
Genesius, Josephus. Byzantine Historian............ fl. 940
Genest, Charles Claude. French Poet................ 1639..1719
Genest, or Genet, Edm. Chas. Fr. Minister to the U. S. 1765?.1832
Genet, Francis. Bp. of Vaison. (*Theology of Grenoble*) 1640..1707
Genevieve, St. .... 422.. 512
Genga, Bartholomew. Architect..................... 1518..1558
Genga, Jerome. Italian Painter .... 1476..1551
Genghis-Khan. Mogul Conqueror. Life by De la Croix 1163..1227
Genlis, Stephanie Félicité, Countess de. French Writer 1746..1830
Gennadius. Patriarch of Constantinople (1453-58).... — ..1460
Gennari, Benedict. *The Young.* Painter to James II... 1633..1715
Gennari, Cæsar, son. Painter of Bologna............. 1641..1688

BORN. DIED.

Gennaro, Joseph Aurelius, of Naples. Civilian .... 1701..1761
Genoels, Abraham. Painter of Antwerp .... 1640.. —
Genoude, Anthony Eugene de. French Journalist ..... 1792..1849
Genovesi, Anthony, of Naples. Metaphysician .... 1712..1769
Genseric. King of the Vandals (429–477).............. — .. 477
Gensonné, Armand. French Girondist................ 1758..1793
Gent, Thomas. Topographical Antiquary.............. 1691..1778
Gentile, Louis Primo. Painter of Brussels .... 1606..1670
Gentileschi, Artemisia. Historical Painter............ 1590..1642
Gentileschi, Horatio Louis. Italian Painter .... 1563..1647
Gentilis, Albericus. Ital. Civilian. Professor at Oxford 1550?.1611
Gentilis, John Valentine. Arian of Naples .... 1520?.1566
Gentilis, Scipio. Italian Civilian at Altorf.......... 1563..1616
Gentilis de Foligno. Medical Writer................ — ..1348
Gentillet, Innocent. Protestant Theologian of Geneva.. — ..1595?
Gentleman, Francis. Irish Actor and Dramatic Writer 1728..1784
Gentz, Frederick von. Publicist. Life by Haym ...... 1764..1832
Geoffrey, Duke of Brittany, son of Henry II........... 1158..1186
Geoffrey-Gaimar. Anglo-Norman Poet. (*L'Estorie des
    Engles*).. fl. 1150?
Geoffrey of Monmouth. Historian.................. 1110?.1154
Geoffrey of Vinsauf. English Latin Poet .... fl. 12th c.
Geoffrey Plantagenet, Ct. of Anjou, father of Henry II. 1113..1151
Geoffrin, Maria Theresa, Madame. Patron of Learning 1699..1777
Geoffroy, Julian Louis. French Critic .... 1743..1814
Geoffroy, Stephen Francis. French Physician. (*Le Code
    Médicamentaire*).................................. 1672..1731
Geoffroy, Stephen Louis, son. Physician and Naturalist 1725..1810
Geoffroy Saint-Hilaire, Isidore. Fr. Physiologist and
    Naturalist. (*Histoire des Règnes Organiques*)....... 1805..1861
Geoffroy Saint-Hilaire, Stephen. Naturalist........ 1772..1844
George, of Cappadocia. Patriarch of Constantinople... — .. 361?
George, of Cyprus, Jr. Patriarch of Const'ple. Writer — ..1290
George, of Trebizond. Restorer of Greek Learning...1396.1485 or 6
George, Duke of Saxony. *The Bearded* .... 1471..1530
George I. King of England (1714–27)................. 1660..1727
George II. (1727–60)................................ 1683..1760
George III. (1760–1820.) Life by Adolphus......... 1738..1820
George IV. (1820–30.) Life by Croly, 1840 .... 1762..1830
George of Denmark. Prince Consort of Queen Anne.. 1653..1708
Georgel, John Francis. Fr. Histor. Writer, and Diplom. 1731..1813
Geramb, Ferdinand de, Baron. Adventurer and Trappist 1770..1848
Gerando, Joseph Mary, Baron de. French Statesman
    and Philosophical Writer........................... 1772..1842
Gerard, Alexander, of Aberdeen. Divine............. 1728..1795
Gerard, Balthazar. Assassin of William of Orange .... 1558..1584
Gérard, Cécile Jules Basil. *Lion-Killer.* Fr. Traveler.. 1817..1864
Gérard, Francis Pascal Simon, Baron. French Painter.. 1770..1837
Gérard, John Ignatius Isidore. *Grandville.* French Cari-
    caturist... 1803..1847
Gérard, Louis. Fr. Physician. (*Flora Gallo-Provincialis*) 1733..1819
Gérard, Stephen Maurice, Count. Marshal of France... 1773..1852
Gerard, Thom or Tung. Gd. Master of Knts. of St. John 1040?.1121?
Gerard. *See* Gerhard.

BORN. DIED.

Gerard, of Cremona. Italian Translator and Orientalist 1114..1187
Gérard de Nerval. *Gérard Labrunie*. French Author. 1808..1855
Gérard de Rayneval, Joseph Matthias. Fr. Diplomatist 1736..1812
Gerarde, John. Botanist and Surgeon. (*Herbal*)...... 1545..1607
Gerardi, Christopher. Painter of Florence............ 1500..1556
Gerards, Mark, of Bruges. Painter.................. 1561..1635
Gerbais, John. Doctor of the Sorbonne. Eccles. Writer 1629..1699
Gerbel, Nicholas. German Jurist.................... — ..1560
Gerber, Ernest Louis. Ger. Organist & Writer on Music 1746..1819
Gerberon, Gabriel, of St. Maur. (*History of Jansenism*) 1628..1711
Gerbert, Martin. Prince-Abbot. Writ. on Sacred Music 1720..1793
Gerbert, Pope Silvester II. *The Musician*. Universal
   Scholar.. — ..1003
Gerbier d'Ouvilly, Sir Balthasar. Painter, Architect,
   Diplomatist...................................... 1592..1667
Gerbillon, John Francis. Jesuit Missionary to China... 1654..1707
Gerdes, Daniel, of Groningen. Theologian........... 1698..1765
Gerhard, Ephraim, of Altdorf. (*Delineatio Philosophiæ*) 1682..1718
Gerhard, John. German Protestant Divine. (*Aphorismi*) 1582..1637
Gerhard, John Ernest. Lutheran Divine and Orientalist 1621..1688
Gerhardt, Charles Frederick. German Chemist........ 1816..1856
Géricault, John Louis Theod. Andrew. French Painter. 1790..1824
Gering, Ulric. Introducer of Printing into France...... — ..1510
Gerlach, Stephen. Historical and Theological Writer... 1546..1612
Germain, Thomas. French Artist in Metals.......... 1675..1748
Germanicus Cæsar, married to Agrippina. Life by Louis
   de Beaufort.................................B.C.14.A.D.19
Germonio, Anastasius. Abp. of Tarantaise. Ital. Writ. 1551..1627
Germyn, Simon. Dutch Painter..................... 1650?.1719
Gerry, Elbridge. 5th Vice-President of the United States 1744..1814
Gerson, John Charlier de. (*Doctor Christianissimus*).... 1363..1429
Gerstein, Christian Louis. Mathematician .... 1701..1762
Gervaise, Francis Armand. Fr. Biographer and Theolog. 1660..1751
Gervaise, Nicholas. French Missionary to Siam .... 1662?.1729
Gervase, of Canterbury. Chronicler................. fl. 12th c.
Gervase, of Tilbury. Chronicler. (*Otia Imperialia*) ... fl. 12th c.
Gesenius, Frederick Henry William. German Orientalist 1786..1842
Gesner, Conrad von. Swiss Naturalist and Universal
   Scholar.. 1516..1565
Gesner, John, of Zurich. (*Phytographia Sacra*) .... 1709..1790
Gesner, John James, of Zurich. Numismatist........ 1707..1787
Gesner, John Matthias. Classical Critic and Editor .... 1691..1761
Gessler, Albert, or Gesseler von Bruneck. Killed by Tell — ..1307
Gessner, Solomon. Swiss Poet and Painter........... 1730..1788
Gessner, Solomon. Biblical Writer at Wittemberg...... 1559..1605
Geta. Emperor of Rome. Life by Ælius Spartianus.... 189.. 212
Gethin, Grace, Lady. (*Reliquiæ Gethinianæ*)........... 1676..1697
Gething, Richard. Penman in London................ fl. 1616–45
Geuss, John Michael. Mathematician at Copenhagen .. 1745..1786
Gevartius, or Gevaerts, John Gaspar. Critic of Antwerp 1593..1666
Geyer, Henry Sheffie. American Jurist.............. 1790..1859
Geyler, John, of Kaiserberg. German Preacher........ 1445..1510
Gezelius, George. Swedish Biographer .... 1736..1789
Gezelius, John. Bishop of Abo. (*Pentaglott Dictionary*) 1615..1690

BORN. DIED.

Gezelius, John, son. Bp. of Abo. (*Nomenclator Adami*) 1647..1718
Ghazzali, Abu Hámid Mohammad Ibn Ahmad. Moham-
    medan Philosopher and Divine........................ 1058..1111
Ghetaldi, Marino, of Ragusa. Mathematician .... — bef. 1630
Ghezzi, Peter Leone. Italian Painter .... 1674..1755
Ghiberti, Lorenzo. Florentine Sculptor and Architect.. 1378..1455?
Ghika, Gregory X. Hospodar of Moldavia............. 1807..1857
Ghilini, Jerome. Italian Writer..................... 1589..1670?
Ghirlandajo, Il. *Dominic Currado*. Florentine Painter.. 1449..1498
Ghirlandajo, Ridolpho, son. Painter.................. 1482..1560
Ghisolfi, John. Painter of Milan .... 1624..1683
Giamberti, Julian. *San Gallo*. Ital. Architect & Sculptor 1443..1517
Gianibelli, or Giambelli, Fred. Italian Military Engineer 1530?. —
Gianni, Francis. Italian Poet .... 1759..1822
Giannone, Peter. (*History of Naples*)................. 1676..1748
Giardini, Felix. Italian Violinist .... 1716..1796
Gibbon, Edward. (*Decline and Fall*.)   Life by Lord
    Sheffield, 1799; H. A. Milman, 1839; W. Youngman. 1737..1794
Gibbons, Dr. Christopher. Organist and Composer..... — ..1676
Gibbons, Grinling. Carver in Wood.................. 1648..1721
Gibbons, Orlando. Musical Composer................. 1583..1625
Gibbs, George. American Mineralogist................ 1782..1833
Gibbs, James. Architect .... 1674?.1754
Gibbs, Josiah Willard. American Philologist .... 1790..1861
Gibbs, Sir Vicary. Judge............................ 1752..1820
Gibert, Balthasar. French Writer. (*Jugement des Savants*) 1662..1741
Gibert, John Peter.   French Canonist .... 1660..1736
Giberti, John Matthew. Bp. of Verona. Patron of Learn. 1495..1543
Gibieuf, Wm. Priest of the Oratory. (*Liberty of God*).. — ..1650
Gibson, Edm. Bp. of London. Saxonist. (*Preservative*) 1669..1748
Gibson, John Bannister, LL. D.   American Jurist....... 1780..1853
Gibson, Richard. *The Dwarf*. Painter.............. 1615..1690
Gibson, Thomas. Phys., Naturalist, and Protestant Divine — ..1562
Gibson, Thomas. Painter............................ 1680?.1751
Gibson, William. Painter .... 1644?.1702
Giddings, Joshua Reed. Amer. Anti-slavery Statesman. 1795..1864
Giddings, Salmon. Missionary....................... 1782..1828
Gideon. Judge of Israel............................. B. C. 1236
Gieseler, John Charles Louis. German Church Historian 1792..1854
Gifanius, or Hubert van Giffen. Dutch Critic and Civilian 1534..1604
Gifford, Andrew, D. D. Baptist Minister and Antiquary. 1700..1784
Gifford, John. *John Rd. Green*. Polit. & Historical Writer 1758..1818
Gifford, Rev. Richard. Divine and Poet.............. 1725?.1807
Gifford, Robert, Lord. Judge .... 1779..1826
Gifford, William. Critic and Satirist. Editor of *Quarterly
    Review*. (*Baviad*)............................... 1757..1826
Giggeo, Anthony. Italian Divine and Arabic Scholar... — ..1632
Gilbart, James William. Writer on Banking .... 1794..1863
Gilbert, Davis (*née* Giddy). Antiquary.............. 1767..1839
Gilbert, Sir Humphrey. Navigator................... 1539..1584
Gilbert, Sir Jeffrey. Judge and Law Writer .... 1674..1726
Gilbert, Nicholas Joseph Lawrence. French Satiric Poet 1751..1780
Gilbert, Nicholas Peter. French Army Physician ...... 1751..1814
Gilbert, Thomas. Ejected Nonconformist Divine....... 1611?.1694

BORN. DIED.
Gilbert, Wm. Physician & Exper. Philos. (*De Magnate*) 1540..1603
Gilbert, of La Porrée. *Gislebertus Porretanus*........... 1070?..1154
Gilbert, of Sempringham. Founder of *Gilbertines*...... 1083..1189
Gilbertus Anglicus. Medical Writer .... fl. 1200?
Gilchrist, Alex. Writer on Art; Biogr. of Etty & Blake 1827..1861
Gilchrist, John Borthwick. Orientalist .... 1759..1841
Gilchrist, Octavius. Writer on the Drama .... 1779..1823
Gildas. *The Wise.* British Hist. (*De Excidio Britanniæ*) 6th c. A. D.
Gildon, Charles. Dramatic and Miscellaneous Writer... 1665..1724
Giles, William Branch. American Statesman .... 1762..1830
Giles, of Viterbo. Italian Cardinal. Biblical Writer ... — ..1532
Gilfillan, Robert. Scotch Poet .... 1798?.1850
Gilimer. Last King of African Vandals .... — aft. 534
Gill, Alex. Mast. of St. Paul's School. (*Logonomia Anglica*) 1564..1635
Gill, Alex., son. Friend of Milton. (*Poetici Conatus*).... 1597..1642
Gill, John, D. D. Baptist Divine and Biblical Expositor.. 1697..1771
Gilles, Peter. French Naturalist...................... 1490..1555
Gillespie, George. Scottish Divine. (*Aaron's Rod*) .... — ..1648
Gillies, John, LL. D. Historical Writer .... 1747..1836
Gillis, James. Roman Catholic Bishop in Scotland ..... — ..1864
Gillot, Claude. French Painter and Engraver ...... 1673..1722
Gilly, Rev. Dr. Wm. Stephen. Writer on the Vaudois .. 1789?.1855
Gilman, John Taylor. Governor of New Hampshire.... 1759..1828
Gilman, Samuel, D. D. American Clergyman and Author 1791..1858
Gilpin, Bernard. (*Apostle of the North.*) Life by Bishop
   Carleton, 1636; W. Gilpin, 1753 .... 1517..1583
Gilpin, Rd. Ejected Nonconf. Div. (*Satan's Temptations*) — ..1657
Gilpin, Sawrey. Animal Painter...................... 1733..1807
Gilpin, Rev. William, brother. Writer. (*Forest Scenery*) 1724..1804
Gil Polo, Gaspar. Spanish Poet .... 1516..1572
Gilray, James. Caricaturist.......................... 1785..1815
Gil Vicente. Portuguese Dramatist................... 1485?.1557
Ginguené, Peter Louis. (*Histoire Littéraire d'Italie*) ... 1748..1816
Ginkell, Godart van, First Earl of Athlone. Commander.. 1630?.1703
Ginnani, Francis. Italian Naturalist .... 1716..1766
Gioberti, John Anthony. Italian Chemist .... 1761..1834
Gioberti, Vincent. Italian Writer and Statesman ...... 1801..1852
Giocondo, John. *Fra Giovanni.* Ital. Schol. & Antiquary 1450?.1521?
Gioffredo, Mario. Gaetano. Neapolitan Architect ... 1718..1785
Gioja, Flavio, of Amalfi. Reputed Inventor of Compass. 1300?. —
Gioja, Melchior. Italian Writer. (*Nuovo Prospetto*) .... 1767..1829
Giolito de' Ferrari, Gabriel. Italian Printer .... — ..1581
Giordani, Vital. Neapolitan Mathematician .... 1633..1711
Giordano, Luke. *Luca fa Presto.* Neapolitan Painter 1632.1704 or 5
Giorgi, Anthony Augustine. (*Alphabetum Thibetanum*).. 1711..1797
Giorgione. *Giorgio Barbarelli.* Venetian Painter...... 1477..1511
Gioseppino. Neapolitan Painter...................... 1560?.1540
Giottino, Il. *Thomas di Stefano.* Florentine Painter ... 1324..1356
Giotto, or Ambrogiotto. Florentine Pa., Sculptor, Architect 1276..1336
Giovanni. *Mannozzi.* Italian Fresco Painter.......... 1590..1636
Giovanni da Fiesole. *Fra Angelico.* Florentine Painter 1387..1455
Giovio, Paul. Italian Historical Writer............... 1483..1552
Giraldi, Julius Gregory. Ital. Scholar. (*De Diis Gentium*) 1479..1552
Giraldi-Cintio, J. Bapt. Ital. Poet & Phys. (*Hecatommiti*) 1504..1573

BORN. DIED.

Giraldus Cambrensis, or Gerald de Barri. Historian.. 1147..1222?
Girard, Gabriel. French Philologist. (*Synonymes François*) 1677?.1748
Girard, Gregory. Swiss Educator .... 1765..1850
Girard, Philip Henry de. French Engineer........... 1775..1845
Girard, Stephen. Amer. Banker; Found. of Girard College 1746..1831
Girardin, Madame Émile de. *Delphine Gay.* Fr. Writer. 1804..1855
Girardin, Louis Stanislaus de, Count. French Publicist.. 1762..1827
Girardon, Francis. Sculptor and Architect........... 1628..1715
Giraud, John, Count. Italian Comic Dramatist......... 1776..1834
Girodet-Trioson, Anne Louis. French Painter........ 1767..1824
Giroust, James. French Preacher.................... 1624..1689
Girtin, Thomas. Landscape Painter .... 1773..1802
Giry, Louis. French Academician .... 1595..1665
Gisbert, Blaise. Fr. Theol. & Philos. (*Educat. of a Prince*) 1657..1731
Gisbert, John. French Canonist. (*Anti-Probalasimus*) . 1639..1711
Gisborne, Rev. Thos. Philos., Theol., and Misc. Writer 1758..1846
Giulano, Majano di. Florentine Sculptor and Architect.. 1377?.1447
Giulini, George. Historian and Antiquary. (*Memoirs
   Concerning the Government of Milan*)............... 1714..1780
Giulio Romano. *Julius Caccini.* Ital. Music. Composer 1560?.1640?
Giulio Romano. *Pippi.* Italian Painter............. 1492..1546
Giusti, Anthony. Florentine Painter................. 1624?.1705
Giusti, Joseph. Italian Poet and Satirist............. 1809..1850
Glaber, Ralph. Benedictine Monk. (*Chronique de France*) 990?.1050?
Glandorp, Matthias. German Medical Writer......... 1595..1652?
Glanvil, Sir John. Lawyer and Statesman .... 1590?.1661
Glanvil, Ranulph de. Lawyer & Warrior. (*De Leg. Angliæ*) — ..1190
Glanvill, Rev. Joseph. (*Vanity of Dogmatizing*)........ 1636..1680
Glareanus, or Henry Lorit. Scholar and Writer .... 1488..1563
Glaser, Christopher. Swiss Chemist................. — ..1679?
Glass, John. Scotch Sectary .... 1698..1773
Glass, John, son. Navigator and Writer.............. 1725..1764
Glassius, Solomon, of Gotha. (*Philologia Sacra*),...... 1593..1656
Glauber, Diana. Painter .... 1650..1720?
Glauber, John. *Polydore.* Painter of Utrecht .... 1646..1726
Glauber, John Rudolph. Chemist. Discoverer of *Glauber's
   Salt*.. 1604..1668
Glauber, John Theophilus, brother. Painter.......... 1656..1703
Gleditsch, John Theophilus. German Phys. and Botanist 1714..1786
Gleichen, Frederick William von. German Naturalist.. 1717..1783
Gleig, George. Bishop of Brechin. Theol. and Metaphys. 1753..1839
Gleim, John William Louis. German Lyric Poet....... 1719..1803
Glen, John. Painter and Engraver of Liege .... fl. 16th c.
Glendower, Owen. Welsh Chieftain .... 1349?.1415
Glenie, James. Scottish Mathematician .... 1750..1817
Glentworth, George. American Physician and Surgeon 1735..1792
Gliddon, George Robins. English Egyptologist .... 1809..1857
Glinka, Gregory Andrievitch. Russian Writer......... 1774..1818
Glinka, Sergy Nikolaevitch. Russian Writer......... 1771..1845?
Glisson, Francis. Anatomist and Physician........... 1597..1677
Gloucester, Robert of. English Historian and Poet..... fl. 1280
Gloucester, Wm. Fred., Duke of, nephew of George III. 1776..1834
Glover, Charles. Song Composer.................... — ..1863
Glover, Richard. Poet. Life by R. Duppa, 1814....... 1712..1785

BORN. DIED.

Glover, Mrs. Actress............................... 1781..1850
Gluck, Christopher Willibald von: Composer. Life by
Schmid, 1855 .... 1714..1787
Glynn, Robert, M. D., of Cambridge. (*Day of Judgment*) 1718?.1800
Gmelin, John Fred. Phys. and Chemist. Ed. of Linnæus 1748..1804
Gmelin, John Geo. Botanist and Phys. (*Flora Sibirica*) 1709..1755
Gmelin, Leopold. German Chemist.................... 1788..1853
Gmelin, Samuel Theoph. Traveler. (*Historia Fucorum*) 1743..1774
Gneisenau, Aug. Neidhardt, Count of. Marsh. of Prussia 1760..1831
Gnieditch, Nicholas. Russian Poet................... 1784..1833
Goad, John. Schoolmaster and Astrologer........... 1615..1689
Goadby, Robert. Printer and Writer of Sherborne...... 1721..1778
Gobbo, Andrew. Italian Historical Painter .... 1470?.1527
Gobbo, Il. *Peter Paul Bonzi*, of Cortona. Painter ..... 1580?.1640?
Gobel, J. Bap. Jos. Abp. of Paris. Atheist; guillotined 1727..1794 ⸱
Göbel, Traugott Friedemann. Ger. Trav. & Writ. on Chem. 1794..1851
Gobelin, John, *alias* Giles. French Dyer and Inventor.. — ..1476?
Gobien, Charles le. French Jesuit; Historian .... 1653..1708
Goclenius, Conrad. German Critic................... 1485..1539
Goclenius, Rodolph. Magnetist and Math. at Marpurg 1572..1621
Goclenius, Rodolph. Philosophical Writer at Marpurg.. 1547..1628
Goddard, Jonathan. Chemist and Physician .... 1617..1674
Goddard, Rev. Wm. Stanley D. D. Mast. of Winch. Coll. 1757..1845
Godden, Thomas, D. D. Rom. Catholic Controversialist. — ..1688
Godeau, Anthony. Bishop of Venice. Church Historian 1605..1672
Godefroi, Denys. (*Corpus Juris Civilis*).............. 1549..1622
Godefroi, Denys. (*Les Droits du Roi*).............. 1615..1681
Godefroi, James. (*Codex Theodosianus*)............... 1587..1652
Godefroi, John. Editor of *Memoirs of Philip de Comines* 1656..1732
Godefroi, Theodore. (*Le Cérémonial François*)......... 1580..1649
Godewyck, Margarita. Paintress of Dort............. 1627..1677
Godfrey, Charles. Musician...................... 1790?.1863
Godfrey, Sir Edmundbury. Magistrate. L. by R. Tuke,
1682..•— ..1678
Godfrey, Thomas. American Mathematician .... — ..1749
Godfrey of Bouillon. Crusader, and King of Jerusalem 1058?.1100
Godfrey of Viterbo. Historian .... — ..1191
Godley, John Robert. Politician. Life by J. E. Fitzgerald — ..1862
Godman, John D. American Anatomist and Naturalist.. 1794..1830
Godolphin, John. Civilian .... 1617..1678
Godolphin, Sidney. Poet........................ 1610.·.1643
Godolphin, Sidney, Earl of. Lord High Treasurer ..... 1630?.1712
Godoonoff, or Godunov, Boris. Czar of Moscow....... 1552..1605
Godoy, Manuel de. *Prince of the Peace.* Span. Minister 1767..1851
Godric, St. Hermit of Finchale. Life by Reginald..... — ..1170
Godwin, Earl of Kent.............................. — ..1053
Godwin, Francis. Bishop of Hereford. Antiquary and
Historical Writer. (*Man in the Moon*) .... 1561..1633
Godwin, Mary, *née* Wollstonecraft. Life by Godwin, 1798 1759..1797
Godwin, Thomas, D. D. Hebrew Antiquary.......... 1587..1643
Godwin, Wm. Novelist & Hist. Writ. (*Caleb Williams*) 1756..1836
Goeckingk, Leop. Frederick Gunther von. German Poet 1748..1828
Goeree, Wm. Scholar of Middleburg. (*Jewish Antiq.*) 1635..1711
Goerres, Jacob Joseph von. German Publicist and Writer 1776..1848

BORN. DIED.

Goertz, George Henry de.   Baron de Schlitz.   Swedish
  Statesman ....   — ..1719
Goes, Hugh van der.   Dutch Painter ....   — ..1480?
Goesius, (William van der Goes.)   Dutch Critic........   1611..1686
Goethe, John Wolfgang von.   Poet.   Life by self, 1811–
  1812, Engl. by Oxenford, 1848; Doering, 1828; Falk,
  1832, Engl. by Mrs. Austin, 1835; Sendtner, 1832;
  Vogel, 1834; Voss, 1834; Marmier, 1835; Riemer,
  1841; Browning, 1844; Viehoff, 1847; Schaefer,
  1850–51; Bowring, 1853; Lewes, 1855, enlarged, 1863.   1749..1832
Goetze, Geo. Henry.   Theologian and Critic at Lubec 1667.1728 or 9
Goetze, John Augustus Ephraim.   German Naturalist...   1731..1793
Goez, Damian de.   Portuguese Historian ....   1501..1560
Goff, Rev. Thomas.   Divine and Dramatist.............   1592..1627
Goffe, William.   Regicide.............................   1605?.1679
Gogol, Nicholas.   Russian Writer ....   1810..1852
Goguet, Anthony Yves.   French Jurist.................   1716..1758
Goldast von Hemingsfeld, Melchior.   Historical Writ.   1576..1635
Goldhagen, John Eustace, of Magdeburg.   Translator of
  Greek Classics.....................................   1701..1772
Golding, Arthur.   Poet, Translator of Ovid, Cæsar, &c...   — ..1590?
Goldman, Nicholas.   Mathematician ....   1623..1665
Goldoni, Charles.   Dramatic Poet....................   1707..1793
Goldsmith, Oliver.   Poet.   Life by J. Prior, 1836; John
  Forster, 1848; W. Irving, 1850; Dr. Kalisch, 1860...   1728..1774
Golius, James.   Orientalist and Mathematician.........   1596..1667
Golius, Peter, br.   Roman Cath. Missionary to East Indies   — ..1673?
Golovnin, Basil.   Russian Navigator..................   1776..1831
Goltzius, Henry.   Painter and Engraver..............   1558..1617
Goltzius, Hubert.   Dutch Painter and Antiquary ....   1526..1583
Gomar, Francis.   Flemish Calvinistic Theologian.......   1563..1641
Gombauld, John Ogier de.   French Poet..............   1567?.1666
Gomberville, Marin le Roy, Sieur de.   French Writer ..   1600..1674
Gomersal, Rev. Robert.   Poet.   (*Levite's Revenge*) .....   1600..1646
Gomes, Francis Dias.   Portuguese Poet................   — ..1795
Gomez, Magdalen Angelica Poisson de.   Fr. Romancist   1684..1770
Gomez, Sebastian.   Spanish Painter ....   — ..1685?
Gomez de Castro, Alvarez.   (*Life of Ximenes*) ......,   1515..1580
Gomez de Ciudad Real, Alvarez.   Latin Poet.........   1488..1538
Gompertz, Benjamin.   Mathematician and Actuary.....   1778?.1865
Gonçalvez, Joachim Alfonso.   Portuguese Missionary to
  China.   (*Diccionario China Portuguez*) ....   1780..1841
Gondebaud.   Fourth King of Burgundy (491–516)......   — .. 516
Gondi, Albert de.   *Marshal de Retz.*   French Courtier ..   1533..1602
Gondi, John Francis Paul de.   Cardinal de Retz II.   French
  Statesman ....   1614..1679
Gondi, Peter de.   Cardinal de Retz I.   French Statesman   1533..1616
Gonet, John Baptist, of Bordeaux.   (*System of Theology*)   1616..1681
Gongora y Argote, Louis de.   Spanish Poet ....   1561..1627
Gonsalvo de Cordova, Fernandez.   *Great Captain.*   See
  Gonzalo..   1443..1515
Gonthier, John.   German Physician and Scholar.......   1487..1574
Gonzaga, Lucretia.   Italian Scholar...................   — ..1576
Gonzaga, Scipio.   Spanish Cardinal and Scholar ....   1542..1593

BORN. DIED.

Gonzaga, Thomas Anthony Costa de, of Brazil. *Dirceo.*
   Portuguese Poet. (*Marilia de Dirceo*)............. 1747..1793
Gonzaga, Vespasian, Duke of Sabionetta. Patron of Arts 1531..1591
Gonzales, Bartholomew. Spanish Painter............. 1564..1627
Gonzales, Thyrsus. Sp. Jesuit. (*Doctrine of Probability*) — ..1705
Gonzalo, Fernandez de Cordova y Aguilar. *Great Capt.* 1443..1515
Gonzalo de Berceo, John. Earliest Spanish Poet...... 1196..1266?
Good, John Mason, M. D. Writer. L. by O. Gregory, 1828 1764..1827
Goodall, Walter. Scottish Antiquary & Historical Writer 1706?.1766
Goode, Rev. Francis. Divine. (*The Better Covenant*)... 1797?.1842
Goodman, Godfrey. English Bishop; conformed to Rome 1583..1655
Goodrich, Chauncey. American Statesman........... 1759..1815
Goodrich, Chauncey Allen, D. D. American Divine and
   Scholar; Editor of Webster's Dictionaries.......... 1790..1860 .
Goodrich, Elizur, D. D. American Clergyman & Scholar 1734..1797
Goodrich, Sam. Griswold. *Peter Parley.* Amer. Author 1793.. —
Goodrich, Thomas. Bishop of Ely (1534–54). Reformer 1480?.1554
Goodwin, John. Independent Divine and Politician.... 1593..1665
Goodwin, Thomas. Calvinistic Independent Divine.... 1600..1679
Gookin, Gen. Daniel. American Writer............. 1612?.1687
Gool, John van. Dutch Painter..................... 1685..1763
Gordian I. M. Antonius. Rom. Emp. (238). *Africanus* 157.. 238
Gordian II. Son; colleague of his father (238)........ 192.. 238
Gordian III. (238–44)............................. 226.. 244
Gordon, Alexander. Historical Writer and Egyptologist — ..1750?
Gordon, Andrew. Scottish Benedictine; Electrician.... 1712..1751
Gordon, Bernard. *Gordonus.* Medical Reformer....... —aft.1310?
Gordon, Eliz. Brodie, last Duchess of. L. by A. M. Stuart 1774..1864
Gordon, Lord George. Anti-Papist Politician.......... 1750..1793
Gordon, James. Scot. Jesuit. (*Controversiarum Epitome*) 1543..1620
Gordon, Sir John Watson, R. A. Portrait Painter....... 1790?.1864
Gordon, Robt., of Stralogh. Geog. (*Theatrum Scotiæ*) — ..1650?
Gordon, Thos. Controversialist. (*Pillars of Priestcraft*) 1684?.1750
Gordon, William. Anglo-American Divine & Historian 1730..1807
Gordon, William, M. D. *People's Friend.* Philanthropist 1801..1849
Gore, Catherine Grace Francis, Mrs. Novelist......... 1799..1861
Gore, Christopher. American Statesman; Governor of
   Massachusetts.................................... 1758..1827
Gorges, Sir Ferdinando. Proprietor of Province of Maine
   and Governor of Plymouth........................ — ..1647
Gorgias, of Leontini. Sophist.................485?.380? B.C.
Gori, Anthony Francis. Florentine Antiquary......... 1691..1757
Gorlæus, Abraham. Dutch Antiquary. (*Dactyliotheca*) 1549..1609
Goropius, John. *Van Gorp.* (*Origines Antverpianæ*)... 1518..1572
Gorran, Nicholas de. French Preacher and Divine..... 1230..1295
Görres, Jacob Joseph von. *See* Goerres .... 1776..1848
Gorsas, Anthony Joseph. French Politician........... 1751..1793
Gortchakoff, Demetrius. Russian Poet................ 1756..1824
Gortchakoff, Michael, Prince. Russian Commander.... 1795..1861
Gorter, John de. Dutch Medical Writer.............. 1688..1762
Gorton, Samuel. New England Enthusiast............. 1600?.1677
Goselini, Julian. Italian Writer.................... 1525..1587
Goslicki, Lawrence. Polish Writ. (*De Optimo Senatore*) 1535..1607
Gosnold, Bartholomew. Navigator.................. — ..1607

BORN. DIED.

Gosseo, Francis Joseph. Belgian Musical Composer .... 1733..1829
Gosselin, Pascal Francis Joseph. French Geographer... 1751..1830
Gosselini, Julian. Italian Writer.................. 1525..1587
Gosson, Stephen. Divine and Poet.................. 1554..1623
Göthe. *See* Goethe........................... 1749..1832
Gother, John. Roman Cath. Divine and Controversialist — ..1704
Gothescalcus, or Gottschalk. German Heresiarch...... 808?. 867
Gothofred, or Godefroi, *which see.*
Gotti, Vincent Louis. Italian Cardinal and Theologian.. 1664..1742
Gottignies, Giles Francis. Belgian Mathematician..... 1630..1689
Gottleber, John Christopher. German Critic .... 1733..1785
Gottsched, John Christopher. Ger. Poet and Philosopher 1700..1766
Gottsched, Madame, wife. Dramatic Writer........... 1713..1762
Goudelin, or Goudouli, Peter. Gascon Poet........... 1579..1649
Goudimel, Claude. French Musical Composer .... 1510?.1572
Gouffler, Mary Gabriel Augustus Laurent, Count de
    Choiseul. (*Voyage Pittoresque*).................... 1752..1817
Gouge, Thomas. Ejected Nonconformist Divine........ 1605..1681
Gouge, William. Puritan Divine. (*Whole Armor of God*) 1575..1653
Gougeon, or Goujon, John. Fr. Sculptor and Medalist 1515?.1572
Gouges, Mary Olympe de. French Revolutionary Writer 1755..1793
Gough, Richard. Antiquary....................... 1735..1809
Goujet, Claude Peter. French Scholar and Writer...... 1697..1767
Goulart, Simon. Fr. Protestant Divine and Hist. Writer 1543..1628
Goulburn, Rt. Hon. Henry, M.P. Statesman.......... — ..1856
Gould, Hannah Flagg. American Poetess .... — ..1865
Gould, James. American Jurist .... 1770?.1838
Gould, Robert. Poet............................ — ..1708
Goulin, John. French Writer .... 1728..1799
Goulston, Theodore, M.D. Founder of Goulstonian Lect. 1576?.1632
Goulu, John. French Translator from the Greek........ 1576..1629
Goupy, Joseph. French Artist...................... — ..1763
Gourdan, Simon. French Casuist................... 1646..1729
Gourgaud, Gaspar, Baron. Fr. Gen. (*Napoleon Mem.*) 1783..1852
Gournay, Mary de Jars de. *Tenth Muse.* French Writer 1566..1645
Gourville, John Hérault de. (*Mémoires,* 1642–98)...... 1625..1704
Gousset, James. French Protestant Divine and Hebraist 1635..1704
Gouthière, James. *Gutherius.* Fr. Advocate and Writer 1568..1638
Gouvea, Anthony de. *Goveanus.* Portuguese Jurist.... 1505..1566
Gouvea, Anthony de. Portuguese Historian .... 1570?.1628
Gouvion St. Cyr, Lawrence. Marshal of France ...... 1764..1830
Gouye, Thomas. French Mathematician .... 1650..1725
Gouye de Longuemarre. French Historical Writer... 1715..1763
Gouz de la Boulaye, Francis le. French Traveler ..... 1610?.1669?
Govona, Rosa. Italian Philanthropist.................. 1716..1776
Gower, John. Poet............................... 1320..1402
Goya y Lucientes, Francis. Spanish Painter.......... 1746..1828
Goyen, John Joseph van. Dutch Painter.............. 1596..1656
Gozzi, Charles, Count. Italian Dramatist.............. 1772..1806
Gozzi, Gaspar, Count. Italian Writer................ 1713..1786
Gozzoli, Benozzo. Florentine Painter................. 1408..1478
Graaf, Reinier de. Dutch Medical Writer.............. 1641..1673
Graat, or Graet, Bernard. Dutch Historical Painter..... 1628..1709
Graaw, or Grauw, Henry. Dutch Painter.............. 1627..1682

BORN. DIED.

Grabbe, Christian Dietrich. German Dramatist........ 1801..1836
Grabe, John Ernest, D. D. Divine and Critic.......... 1666..1711
Gracchus, Caius. Tribune..........................154.121 B.C.
Gracchus, Tiberius, brother. Roman Tribune.........163.133 B.C.
Gracian, Balthasar. Span. Jesuit, Preacher, and Writer 1584..1658
Gradenigo, Peter. Doge of Venice................... 1249..1311
Graefe, Charles Ferdinand von. German Surgeon...... 1787..1840
Græme, John. Scottish Poet......................... 1748..1772
Grævius, John George. Classical Antiquary.......... 1632..1703
Graff, Anthony. German Portrait Painter............. 1736..1813
Graffigny, Frances. (*Lettres d'une Péruvienne*) .... 1694..1758
Grafton, Aug. Hen. Fitzroy, Duke of. Polit. and Writer 1736..1811
Grafton, Charles Fitzroy, Duke of. Politician.......... 1683..1757
Grafton, Richard. Chronicler and Printer .... —aft.1572
Graggini, Anthony Francis. Italian Poet.............. 1503..1583
Graham, Catherine Macaulay, Mrs.................... 1733..1791
Graham, George. Mechanician....................... 1675..1751
Graham, Isabella. Philanthropist.................... 1742..1814
Graham, Sir James. Companion of Wallace........... — ..1298
Graham, James, Marquis of Montrose. Scottish Royalist,
   executed. Life by Wishart, 1819; M. Napier, 1840 .. 1612..1650
Graham, Sir James Robert George. Statesman. Life by
   Torrens, 1863 .... 1792..1861
Graham, John, of Claverhouse, Viscount Dundee .... 1650?.1689
Graham, John Andrew, LL. D. Amer. Advocate & Author 1764..1841
Graham, Joseph. American Revolutionary Soldier ..... 1759..1836
Graham, Mrs. Maria. *See* Callcott................... 1788..1842
Graham, Sir Richard, Visct. Preston. Statesm. & Writer 1648..1695
Graham, Robert, M. D. Professor of Botany, Glasgow... 1786..1845
Graham, Sylvester. Vegetarian...................... 1794..1851
Grahame, Rev. James. Poet. (*The Sabbath*).......... 1765..1811
Grahame, James. Scottish Historian................. 1790..1842
Grain, John Baptiste le. French Historical Writer ...... 1565..1642
Graindorge, Andrew. Fr. Physician and Natural Philos. 1616..1676
Grainger, James. Physician and Poet. (*Sugar-Cane*).. 1723?.1767
Grainger, Richard, of Newcastle. Architect and Builder 1798..1861
Gramaye, John Baptist. Flemish Traveler, Poet, Hist. 1580?.1635
Grammont, Anthony Louis Mary, Duke of. General ... 1775..1836
Grammont, Gabriel de Barthélemi, Seigneur de. Hist. 1590?.1654
Grammont, Philibert, Count of. Wit and Courtier..... 1621..1707
Gramont, Anthony, Duke of. Marshal of Fr. (*Memoirs*) 1604..1678
Granby, John Manners, Marquis of. General.......... 1721..1770
Grand, Anthony le. Fr. Cartesian Philosopher and Hist. 17th c.
Grand, Joachim le. French Political Writer .... 1653..1733
Grand, Louis le. Doctor of the Sorbonne; Theologian... 1711..1780
Grand, Mark Anthony le. French Actor .... 1673..1728
Grand. *See* Legrand.
Grandet, Joseph, of Angers. Biographer .... 1646..1724
Grandi, Ercole. *Ercole da Ferrara.* Italian Painter ... 1491..1531
Grandi, Guy le. Italian Math. (*De Infinitis Infinitorum*) 1671..1742
Grandin, Martin. Doctor of the Sorbonne. (*Popular
   Course of Theology*)............................. 1604..1691
Grandmaison, Michael. French Revolutionist......... 1771..1794
Grandpré, Louis Mary Jos. Ohier, Ct. de. Navig. & Trav. 1761..1846

BORN. DIED.

Grandville, John Ign. Isid. Gérard. French Caricaturist 1803..1847
Granet, Francis. French Critic..................... 1692..1741
Granet, Francis Marius. French Painter............. 1775..1849
Grange, Joseph de Chancel de la. Fr. Poet. (*Philippics*) 1677..1758
Granger, Gideon. American Statesman............. 1767..1822
Granger, Rev. James. (*Biographical History of England*) 1716?.1776
Grant, Mrs. Anne, of Laggan. Writer. Life by her son 1755..1838
Grant, Charles, M. P. East India Director and Writer... 1746..1823
Grant, Edward. Classical Poet and Writer............. — ..1601
Grant, Francis, Lord Cullen. Scottish Judge........... 1660?.1726
Grant, James. Scottish Barrister and Archæologist..... 1743..1835
Grant, Patrick, Lord Preston-Grange. Scottish Judge.. 1698..1762
Grant, Sir William. Master of the Rolls............. 1754..1832
Granvelle, Anthony Perrenot, Lord of. Cardinal....... 1516..1586
Granville, George, Viscount Lansdowne. Poet and Polit. 1667..1735
Granville, Granville Leveson-Gower, Earl of. Statesman 1773..1846
Granville, John Carteret, Earl of. Statesman......... 1690..1763
Granville, or Greenville, Sir Richard. Admiral........ 1540..1591
Gras, Anthony le. French Writer. (*Apostolic Fathers*) . 1680?.1751
Graswinkel, Theodore. Dutch Publicist.............. 1600..1666
Gratarolus, William. Ital. Physician & Writer at Basle 1516..1568
Gratian. Roman Emperor (367–83)................... 359.. 383
Gratiani, Jerome. Italian Poetical and Prose Writer.... fl. 17th c.
Gratiolet, Louis Peter. Physiologist. (*Anatomie Compa-
    rée du Système Nerveux*)........................... 1815..1865
Gratius, Ortwinus. *Graes.* German Writer. (*Lamenta-
    tiones Obscurorum Virorum*)....................... — ..1541
Grattan, Henry. Orator and Statesman. Life by sons,
    1841; D. O. Madden, 1846........................ 1750..1820
Grattan, Thomas Colley. Novelist.................. 1796?.1864
Graun, Charles Henry. German Musical Composer..... 1701..1759
Graunt, Edward. Master of Westminster School. (*Græcæ
    Linguæ Specilegium*)......................... 1550?.1601
Graunt, John. Citizen of London. (*Bills of Mortality*) 1620..1674
Gravelot, Hubert Francis Bourguignon. Fr. Engraver.. 1699..1773
Graverol, Francis. French Advocate. (*Soberiana*).... 1636..1694
Graves, Rev. John. Antiquary...................... — ..1729
Graves, Rev. Richard. Novelist and Poet............. 1715..1804
Graves, Richard. Dean of Ardagh. (*Pentateuch*)...... 1763..1829
Gravesande, Wm. Jas. van 's. Dutch Geomet. & Philos. 1688..1742
Gravina, Dominic da. Italian Hist. (*Lo Storico di Napoli*) fl. 1330–50
Gravina, John Vincent. Italian Jurist .... 1664..1718
Gravina, Peter. Italian Poet....................... 1453..1527
Gray, Thomas. Poet. Life by Mitford; Mason, 1778 ... 1716..1771
Graydon, Alexander. American Writer.............. 1752..1818
Graziani, Anthony Mary. Italian Bishop and Writer... 1537..1611
Grazzini, Anthony Francis. *Il Lasca.* Italian Writer .. 1503..1583
Grazzini, John Paul, of Ferrara. Painter..'........... — ..1632
Greatorex, Thomas. Musical Composer.............. 1758..1831
Greatrakes, Valentine. Irish Medical Empiric....... 1628.aft.1680
Greaves, John. Orientalist & Math. (*Pyramidographia*) 1602..1652
Grechetto. *Benedict Castiglione.* Genoese Painter..... 1616..1670
Grécourt, J. Bapt. Jos. Villart de. French Poet and Wit 1683..1743
Green, Ashbel, D. D. American Clergyman and Writer 1762..1848

BORN. DIED.

Green, Edward Burnaby. Poetical Writer and Translator 1740?.1788
Green, Jacob. American Writer on Science............ 1790..1841
Green, John. Bishop of Lincoln. (*Religious Enthusiasm*) 1706..1779
Green, John Richard. *See* Gifford.................... 1758..1818
Green, Joseph Henry. Anatomist. (*Vital Dynamics*)... 1791?.1863
Green, Matthew. Poet. *The Spleen*................. 1696..1737
Green, Richard. Ship Owner of London.............. 1804?.1863
Green, Thomas. Writer. (*Micthodian*).............. 1770..1825
Green, Valentine. Engraver. (*History of Worcester*)... 1739..1813
Greene, Dr. Maurice. Musical Composer............. 1696..1755
Greene, Nathaniel. American Revolutionary General... 1742..1786
Greene, Robert. Humorous Poet. Life by Dyce....... 1560?.1592
Greene, Thomas. Bishop. (*Four Last Things*)........ 1658..1738
Greenfield, William. Orientalist. (*Comprehensive Bible*) — ..1832
Greenhill, John. Painter.................... 1649..1676
Greenhill, Rev. William, of Stepney. (*On Ezekiel*)..... — ..1671
Greenhow, Robert. American Author .... 1800..1854
Greenleaf, Simon. American Jurist .... 1783..1853
Greenough, Horatio. American Sculptor .... 1805..1852
Greenville, Sir Bevil. Royalist, fell at Landsdowne.... 1596..1643
Greenville, or Grenville, Sir Richard. Admiral........ 1540..1591
Greenwood, Francis William Pitt, D. D. Amer. Divine 1797..1843
Gregan, John Edgar. Architect of Manchester........ 1813..1855
Grégoire, Henry. "Constitutional" Bishop of France .. 1750..1831
Gregor, Rev. William. Chemist .... 1762..1817
Gregorio, Rosario. Sicilian Historian and Archæologist 1753..1809
Gregory. *Thaumaturgus.* Bishop of Cæsarea.......... 212?. 270?
Gregory Nazianzen. Bishop of Constantinople (380–81).
  Life by Godfrey Hermant; Ullmann, 1825........... 314?. 390?
Gregory, St. Bishop of Nyssa....................... 332?. 396?
Gregory, St. Bishop of Tours (573–95). Historian..... 544.. 595
Gregory I. Pope (590–604). *The Great.* (*Gregorian
  Chant.*) Life by Denis de Sainte-Marthe, 1697 ...... 544?. 604
Gregory II. (715–731) .... — .. 731
Gregory III. (731–41) .... — .. 741
Gregory IV. (827–44) .... — .. 844
Gregory V. (996–99.) *Bruno*....................... 972.. 999
Gregory VI. (1044–46.) *John Gratian* .... — ..1047?
Gregory VII. (1073–85.) *Hildebrand.* Life by J. C.
  Dithmar; Voigt; Sonstral; J. W. Bowden, 1841 ..... — ..1085
Gregory VIII. (1187.) *Albert di Mora* .... — ..1187
Gregory IX. (1227–41.) *Ugolino de' Conti di Segni*.... — ..1241
Gregory X. (1271–76.) *Theobald Visconti*.......... — ..1276
Gregory XI. (1370–78.) *Peter Roger de Montroux* .... 1329..1378
Gregory XII. (1406–9.) *Angelo Conrario*............ 1325..1417
Gregory XIII. (1572–85.) *Hugh Buoncompagno* ...... 1502..1585
Gregory XIV. (1590–91.) *Nicholas Sfondrati* .... 1534..1591
Gregory XV. (1621–23.) *Alexander Ludovisio*........ 1554..1623
Gregory XVI. (1831–46.) *Mauro Capellari*.......... 1765..1846
Gregory, David. Savilian Professor. (*Catenary*).... 1661..1708
Gregory, Edmund. (*Anatomy of Christian Melancholy*).. — ..1650
Gregory, Geo., D. D. Divine and Misc. Writer. (*Essays*) 1754..1808
Gregory, Jas. Math. Inventor of Reflecting Telescope. 1638..1675
Gregory, John. Divine and Historical Writer.......... 1607..1646

BORN. DIED.

Gregory, John, M. D.   Professor.   (*Human and Animal Faculties.*) Life by Lord Woodhouselee; Smellie .... 1724..1773
Gregory, Olynthus Gilbert, LL. D.   Mathematician and Religious Writer. Life by Robert Hall, 1849........ 1774..1841
Gregory, Peter, of Toulouse.   Writer.................. 1540..1597
Greig, Samuel Carlowitz.   Russian Naval Officer....... — ..1788
Grellet, Stephen.   Quaker Missionary .... 1773..1855
Grenada, Louis de.   Dominican Writer and Preacher ... 1505..1588
Grenan, Benignus.   French Latin Poet.............. 1681?.1723
Grenfell, Pascoe, M. P.   Slavery Abolitionist .... 1762..1838
Grenier, James Raymond.   French Hydrographer...... 1736..1803
Grenville, George.   Statesman .... 1712..1770
Grenville, George, Lord Nugent.   Statesman .... 1788..1851
Grenville, Thos.   Statesman. Collector of Grenville Lib. 1755..1846
Grenville, William Wyndham, Lord.   Statesman ...... 1759..1834
Greppi, John.   Italian Dramatist...................... 1751..1811
Gresham, Sir Thomas. Life by Seth Ward; Burgon, 1839 1519..1579
Gresset, J. Bapt. Louis. Fr. Poet and Dram. (*Vert Vert*) 1709..1777
Gressly, Amand.   Swiss Geologist.................... 1814?.1865
Grétry, Andrew Ernest Modeste.   Fr. Musical Composer. 1741..1813
Gretser, James. Ger. Jesuit, Theologian, and Antiquary 1561..1625
Greuze, John Baptist.   French Painter .... 1726..1805
Grevenbroeck.   Flemish Painter..................... fl. 17th c.
Greville, Charles.   Politician .... 1794..1865
Greville, Sir Fulke, Lord Brooke.   Poet and Philosopher 1554..1628
Grévin, James. French Poet, Painter, and Medical Writer 1539..1570
Grevius, or Grævius, John George.   Classical Antiquary. 1632..1703
Grew, Nehemiah.   Vegetable Physiologist .... 1628..1711
Grew, Obadiah. Ejected Nonconf. Div. (*The Prodigal Son*) 1607..1698
Grey, Charles, Second Earl.   Prime Minister (1830–34) . 1764..1845
Grey, Lady Jane. L. by G. Howard, 1822; Sir H. Nicolas, 1825 1537..1554
Grey, Richard, D. D.   Divine. (*Memoria Technica*) .... 1694..1771
Grey, Zachary, LL. D.   Divine, and Miscellaneous Writer 1687..1766
Gribaldi, Matthew. *Mofa.* Italian Writer on Civil Law — ..1564
Griboyédov, Alex. Sergievich. Russian Poet and Diplom. 1795..1829
Gridley, Philo.   American Jurist...................... 1796..1864
Gridley, Jeremiah.   American Lawyer................. 1705?.1767
Griebner, Michael Henry.   Jurist at Wittemberg....... 1682..1734
Grierson, Constantia.   Irish Scholar .... 1706..1733
Griesbach, John James.   Editor of Greek Testament ... 1745..1812
Griffat, Henry.   French Jesuit Writer .... 1698..1771
Griffier, John.   *The Elder.*   Landscape Painter ...... 1645..1718
Griffier, Robert, son. *The Younger.* Painter in England 1688. aft.1713
Griffin, Edmund Dorr.   American Divine and Writer ... 1804..1830
Griffin, Edward Dorr.   American Divine and Educator 1770..1837
Griffin, Gerald.   Irish Novelist...................... 1803..1840
Griffith, Mrs. Elizabeth.   Novelist.................. 1730?.1793
Griffith, Michael. Jesuit. (*Annales Ecclesiæ Britannicæ*) 1587..1652
Griffith, William.   Naturalist....................... 1810..1845
Griffiths, Ralph.   Editor of the *Monthly Review*........ 1720..1803
Grignan, Frances Margaret de Sévigné, Countess of. Epistolographer .... 1646..1705
Grignon, James.   French Engraver................... fl. 1680
Grijalva, John de.   Spanish Navigator .... — ..1527

BORN. DIED.

Grimaldi, Francis Mary. Jesuit Mathematician........ 1618..1663
Grimaldi, Jerome. Cardinal and Nuncio............. 1597..1685
Grimaldi, John Francis. *Il Bolognese.* Painter........ 1606..1680
Grimaldi, Joseph. Clown............................ 1779..1837
Grimaldi, Stacey, F. S. A. Antiquary and Genealogist .. — ..1863
Grimani, Dominic. Cardinal. Patron of Art.......... 1460..1523
Grimani, Hubert. Portrait Painter of Delft............ 1599..1629
Grimarest, John Léonor le Gallois, Sieur de. Fr. Writer — ..1720
Grimaud, John Chas. M. W. de. Med. Writ at Montpellier 1750..1789
Grimké, Thomas Smith. American Lawyer and Scholar 1778..1834
Grimm, Frederick Melchior, Baron. Diplomatist. (*Correspondance Littéraire*)............................ 1723..1807
Grimm, Jacob Louis Chas. Philol. (*Deutsches Wörterbuch*) 1785..1863
Grimm, William Charles. Philologist.................. 1786..1859
Grimmer, James. Landscape Painter of Antwerp...... 1510..1546
Grimoard, Philip Henry, Count de. French Diplomatist,
    General, Writer .... 1750..1815
Grimoux, Alexis, or John. Swiss Painter............. 1688..1740
Grimston, Sir Harbottle. Lawyer, Speaker........... 1594..1683
Grindal, Edm. Abp. of Cant. (1576–83). L. by Strype, 1710 1519..1583
Grinfield, Rev. E. W. Biblical Critic .... 1784?.1864
Gringoire, or Gringore, Peter. French Poet .... 1478?.1544?
Grisaunt, William. English Astrologer and Physician.. —aft.1360
Griscom, John, LL. D. American Educator............ 1774..1852
Griswold, Alexander Viets, D. D. American Divine.... 1766..1843
Griswold, Roger. Governor of Connecticut........... 1762..1812
Griswold, Rufus Wilmot. American Author.......... 1815..1854
Gritti, Andrew. Doge of Venice..................... 1454..1538
Grive, John de la. French Geographer............... 1689..1757
Grocyn, William, of Oxford. Scholar................ 1442..1519
Grohmann, John Godfrey. Compiler and Translator... — ..1805
Grolier, John. Fr. Statesm., Patr. of Learn., & Collector 1479..1565
Grolmann, Charles Louis William. German Jurist..... 1775..1829
Gronovius, James. (*Thesaurus Antiquitatum Græcarum*) 1645..1716
Gronovius, John Fred., of Leyden. Critic. (*Observations*) 1611..1671
Gronovius, John Frederick. Botanist. (*Flora Orientalis*) 1690..1762
Gronovius, Laur. Theod. Nat. (*Museum Icthyologicum*) 1730..1777
Gronow, Rees Howell. Captain. Writer. (*Recollections*) 1794..1865
Groot, Gerhard. Founder of the "Brethren and Clerks
    of the Common Life " .... 1340..1384
Groot, or Grotius, Hugo de, *which see*.................. 1583..1645
Gros, Anthony John, Baron. French Painter.......... 1771..1835
Gros, Nicholas le. French Theologian................ 1675..1751
Gros, Peter le. French Sculptor .... 1666..1719
Grose, Francis. Antiquary and Miscellaneous Writer... 1731..1791
Grosley, Peter John. French Law Writer. (*Londres*).. 1718..1785
Grosseteste, or Greathead, Robert. Bishop of Lincoln.
    Life by Bardney; Pegge.......................... 1175?.1253
Grossmann, Gustavus Fred. Wm. Ger. Actor and Dram. 1746..1796
Grotefend, Dr. George Frederick. Cuneiform Decipherer 1775..1853
Grotius, Hugo. *De Groot.* Life by Cattenberg; Barksdale,
    1652; J. L. de Burigny, 1754; Luden, 1806; Chas. Butler, 1826.. 1583..1645
Grotius, Wm., br. Lawyer. (*Enchiridion de Principiis*) 1597..1662

BORN. DIED.

Groto, Louis. *Il Cieco.* Italian Poet.................. 1541..1585
Grouchy, Emanuel, Marquis of. Marshal of France .... 1766..1847
Grove, Henry. Nonconformist Divine. L. by T. Amory 1683..1738
Grove, Joseph. (*Life of Cardinal Wolsey*)............. — ..1764
Gruber, John Godfrey. German Writer................ 1774..1851
Gruchius, or Grouchy, Nich. Fr. Scholar. (*De Comitiis*) 1520?..1572
Grudius, Nicholas Everard, of Brabant. Latin Poet.... 1515?..1571
Grundy, Felix. American Statesman.................. 1777..1840
Gruner, John Frederick. German Theologian & Scholar 1723..1778
Gruter, John. (*Inscriptiones; Thesaurus; Deliciæ Poet.*) 1560..1627
Gruter, Peter. Flemish Phys. (*Century of Latin Letters*) 1555?..1634
Grynæus, John James. Swiss Protestant Divine....... 1540..1617
Grynæus, Simon. Swiss Classical Scholar and Reformer 1493..1541
Gryphius, Andrew. German Dramatist................ 1616..1664
Gryphius, Christian. Scholar. (*Poems in German*).... 1649..1706
Gryphius, Sebastian, of Lyons. Printer............. 1493..1556
Guadagno, Gaetano. Singer....................... 1725?..1797
Guadagnoli, Philip. Orientalist................... 1596?..1656
Gua de Malves, John Paul de. French Writer. (*L'Analyse de Descartes*).............................. 1713..1786
Guadet, Margaret Eli. French (Girondist) Statesman... 1758..1794
Guagnino, Alexander. (*Rerum Polonicarum Scriptores*) 1538?..1614
Gualdo-Priorato, Galeas. Italian Soldier and Historian 1606..1678
Gualterus, Rodolphus. *Walther.* Swiss Prot. Theologian 1519..1586
Guarin, Peter. Benedictine of Rouen. Hebraist....... 1678..1729
Guarini, Camillo Guarino. Italian Architect.......... 1624..1683
Guarini, John Baptist. Italian Poet. (*Il Pastor Fido*).. 1537..1612
Guarino, of Verona. Reviver of Learning. Life by Rosmini, 1805............................... 1370..1460
Guasco, Octavian. Italian Writer.................. 1712..1781
Guatimozin. Last King of Mexico; murdered by Cortés — ..1522
Guay-Trouin, René du. French Naval Officer......... 1673..1736
Guazzo, Mark. Italian Historical Writer.............. 1496?..1556
Guazzo, Stephen. Italian Poet and Writer............ 1530..1593
Gubbio, Oderigi da. Italian Painter................ — ..1300?
Gude, or Gudius, Marquard. German Antiquary....... 1635..1689
Gudin de la Brenellerie, Paul Philip. French Writer 1738..1812
Gudius, Gottlob Fred. Lutheran Minister and Writer .. 1701..1756
Guedier de St. Aubin, Hen. Mich. (*Des deux Alliances*) 1695..1742
Guérard, Benjamin Edme Charles. French Archæologist 1797..1854
Guérard, Robt. Fr. Benedict. (*Abridgment of the Bible*) 1641..1715
Guerchi, Claude Louis Francis Regnier, Count de. General and Ambassador........................ 1715..1767
Guercino da Cento. *See* Barbieri. Painter......... 1590..1666
Guéret, Gabriel. (*Le Parnasse Réformé*).............. 1641..1688
Guericke, Otto von. Experimental Philosopher........ 1602..1686
Guérin, Eugénie de. (*Journal*)..................... — ..1848
Guérin, John Baptist Paulin. French Painter......... 1783..1855
Guérin, Maurice de. French Writer................. — ..1839
Guérin, Peter Narcissus. French Painter............. 1774..1833
Guerinière, Frs. Robichion de la. (*L'École de Cavalerie*) — ..1751
Gueroult, Peter Claude Bernard? French Writer....... 1744..1821
Guerrero, Vincent. Mexican Dictator.............. — ..1831
Guesclin, Bertrand du. *See* Duguesclin............. 1314?..1380

BORN. DIED.

Guess, Geo. *Sequoyah.* Inventor of Cherokee Alphabet 1770?..1843
Guettard, John Stephen. Fr. Botanist and Mineralogist 1715..1786
Gueulette, Thomas Simon. Fr. Novelist and Dramatist 1683?.1766
Guevara, Anthony de. Span. Writer. (*Dial of Princes*) 1490..1544
Guevara, John Ninno de. Spanish Painter............ 1632..1698
Guevara, Louis Velez de. Spanish Poet. (*El Diab. Coju.*) 1574..1646
Guglielmi, Peter. Italian Musician and Composer...... 1727..1804
Guglielmini, Dominic. Italian Phys. and Mathematician 1655..1710
Guibert, Abbot, of Nogent. (*Gesta Dei per Francos*)... 1053..1124
Guibert, James Anthony Hippolytus, Count de. French
  Soldier and Writer. (*Essai Général de Tactique*)..... 1743..1790
Guicciardini, Francis, of Florence. (*History of Italy*).. 1482..1540
Guicciardini, Louis, neph. (*Descript. of the Low Countries*) 1523..1589
Guichard, Claude de. (*Funerals of the Ancients*)...... — ..1607
Guichenon, Samuel. French Historian. (*House of Savoy*) 1607..1664
Guidi, Charles Alexander. Italian Poet.............. 1650..1712
Guidi, Thomas. *Il Masaccio.* Florentine Painter...... 1402..1443
Guidiccioni, John. Italian Statesman and Writer ..... 1500..1541
Guido Aretino, or d'Arezzo. Restorer of Music....... 990?. —
Guido Canlassi. *Cagnacci.* Italian Historical Painter 1601..1681
Guido Reni. Italian Painter.................... 1574?.1642
Guido Ubaldo, Mary. Italian Mathematician......... 1540?.1601?
Guidott, Thos. (*On Natural Baths and Mineral Waters*) 1638..aft.1695
Guidotti Borghese, Paul. Italian Painter, Sculptor, and
  Architect...................................... 1569..1629
Guignard, John. *Briquarel.* French Jesuit; executed — ..1595
Guignes, Christopher Louis Joseph. French Orientalist 1759..1845
Guignes, Joseph de. Orientalist. (*Hist. of the Huns, &c.*) 1721..1800
Guignon, John Peter. Violinist.................... 1702..1774
Guilandinus, Melchior. Phys. and Bot. of Königsberg — ..1589
Guilbert de Pixérécourt, René Charles. Fr. Dramatist 1773..1844
Guild, William. Scottish Divine. Life by Dr. Shirreffs 1586..1657
Guilford, Francis North, Lord. Lord Keeper........ 1637..1685
Guilhem de Clermont-Lodeve, William Emanuel Jo-
  seph, Baron de St. Croix. French Historian and Pub-
  licist. (*Examen des Historiens d'Alexandre*)......... 1746..1809
Guillain, Simon. Sculptor of Paris................. 1581..1658
Guillelmus Gemmeticensis. *William of Jumieges.*... fl. 1070-87
Guillelmus Pictavensis. *William of Poitiers*...... 1020?.aft.1088?
Guillemain, Gabriel. Violinist.................... 1705..1770
Guillemeau, James. French Surgeon............... 1550?.1613
Guilleminot, Armand Charles, Count. French General
  and Diplomatist.................................. 1774..1840
Guillet de St. Georges, George. French Historian..... 1625?.1705
Guilliaud, Claude. French Biblical Writer........... fl. 16th c.
Guillim, John. Heraldic Writer. (*Display of Heraldry*) 1565..1621
Guillon, Mary Nich. Silvester. Bp. of Beauvais. Writer 1760..1847
Guillotin, Joseph Ignatius. French Physician .... 1738..1814
Guinand, M. Swiss Optician...................... 1745?.1825
Guinicelli, Guido. Italian Judge and Poet........... — ..1276
Guinther, John. German Medical Writer............ 1487..1574
Guiscard, Robert, Duke of Apulia. Norman Conqueror 1015?.1085
Guischard, or Guischardt, Charles Theophilus. *Quintus
  Icilius.* Tactician............................. 1742..1775

BORN. DIED.

Guise, Antoinette de Bourbon, Duchess of............. 1493..1583
Guise, Charles of. Cardinal of Lorraine. Minister of
    Francis II. and Charles IX......................... 1525..1574
Guise, Charles de Lorraine, Fourth Duke of.......... 1571..1640
Guise, Claude de Lorraine, First Duke of............. 1496..1550
Guise, Francis of Lorraine, Duke of. Commander; as-
    sassinated...................................... 1519..1563
Guise, Francis Joseph de Lorraine, 7th and last Duke of 1670..1675
Guise, Henry of Lorraine, Duke of. *Balafré.* Persecu-
    tor; assassinated. Life by Valincourt............. 1550..1558
Guise, Henry II. de Lorraine, Fifth Duke of. Warrior.. 1614..1664
Guise, John de Lorraine de. Cardinal............... 1498..1550
Guise, Louis II. de Lorraine, Cardinal de............. 1555..1588
Guise, Louis III. de Lorraine, Cardinal de.........1575 or 85.1621
Guise, Louis Joseph de Lorraine, Sixth Duke of........ 1650..1671
Guise, William. English Divine and Orientalist.......; 1653..1684
Guittone d'Arezzo, Fra. Italian Poet................ 1230?.1294
Guizot, Madame Elizabeth Charlotte Pauline. Writer... 1773..1827
Guldenstaedt, John Anthony. Russian Naturalist..... 1745..1781
Guldinus, Habakkuk. Mathemat. (*De Centro Gravitatis*) 1577..1643
Günderode, Caroline von. German Poetess........... 1780..1806
Gundling, Nicholas Jerome. German Philosopher...... 1671..1729
Gundulitsch, Ivan. Serbian Poet.................... 1588..1638
Gundulph. Bishop of Rochester. Architect.........: —..1108
Gunner, John Ernest. Norwegian Naturalist.......... 1718..1773
Gunning, Peter. Bishop of Ely (1675–84)............ 1613..1684
Gunst, Peter van. Dutch Portrait Engraver........... 1667?. —
Gunter, Rev. Edmund. Inventor of *Gunter's Scale*..... 1581..1626
Gurnal, William, of Lavenham. Divine. (*Christian in
    Complete Armor*) .... 1617..1679
Gurney, Hudson, M.P. Antiquarian and Poet. (*Cupid
    and Psyche*) .... 1774?.1864
Gurney, Jos. John, of Earlham. L. by Braithwaite, 1851 1788..1847
Gurney, Thomas. Short-hand Writer. (*Brachygraphy*) 1705?.1770
Gurwood, John. Colonel. Ed. of *Wellington Dispatches* 1790..1845
Gusman, Bartholomew Lawrence de. Brazilian Engi-
    neer.......................................1685?.aft.1724
Gusman, Louis. Spanish Jesuit; Writer............. —..1605
Gustavus I. King of Sweden (1523–60). *Vasa.* Life by
    Archenholz; Count Selly, 1807.................... 1490..1560
Gustavus II. (1611–32.) *Adolphus.* Life by Chapman;
    De Prade, tr. by Spence, 1689; E. D. Mauvillon, 1764;
    W. Harte and Stockdale, 1807; A. F. Gfroerer, 1831;
    J. F. Holling, 1839; Oxenstierna................. 1594..1632
Gustavus III. (1771–92.) Life by Possett; Geisler;
    Oxenstierna.................................... 1746..1792
Gustavus IV. (1792–1809) .... 1778..1837
Gutch, John. Antiquary. (*Collectanea Curiosa*)....... 1745..1831
Gutch, John Mathew, F. S. A., son. Author........... 1777..1861
Gutenberg, John, of Mentz. Printer .... 1400?.1468?
Guthières, James. French Advocate and Antiquary ... —..1638
Guthrie, William. Historical and Miscellaneous Writer 1708..1770
Guthry, Henry. Bishop of Dunkeld. Historian. Life by
    George Crawford................................. —..1676

BORN. DIED.

Guts-Muths, John Christopher Frederick. German Instructor of Youth................................. 1759..1839
Gützlaff, Dr. Charles. Chinese Scholar and Missionary.. 1803..1851
Guy of Lusignan. King of Jerusalem and of Cyprus.. 1140?.1194
Guy, Thomas. Founder of Guy's Hospital............. 1644..1724
Guyard de Berville. French Historical Writer........ 1697..1770
Guyet, Francis. French Critic...................... 1575..1655
Guyon, Claude Mary. French Historical Writer........ 1699..1771
Guyon, Madame Jane Mary Bouvier de la Mothe. Mystic.
    Life by self, translated by Cowper; T. C. Upham, 1851 1648..1717
Guyon, Richard Debaufré. Hungarian General during
    1848–49.. 1813..1856
Guys, Peter Augustine. (*Voyage Littéraire de la Grèce*) 1720..1799
Guyse, John. Independent Div. (*Paraphrase on N. Test.*) 1680..1761
Guyton de Morveau, Louis Bernard. French Chemist 1737..1816
Gwilt, George. Architect and Antiquary............. 1775..1856
Gwilt, Joseph. Saxonist and Writer on Architecture.... 1784..1863
Gwilym, David ap. *David of Glamorgan.* Welsh Bard 1340..1400?
Gwinne, Matthew, M.D. Gresham Profess. Med. Writer 1554?.1627
Gwynn, Eleanor. Actress. Favorite of Charles II...... — ..1687
Gyges. Lydian Prince.............................. fl.8th c. B.C.
Gyllenborg-Ehrensverd, Thomasina Christina Buntzen,
    Madame. Danish Romancist....................... 1773..1856
Gyrowetz, Adalbert. Bohemian Composer............ 1763..1850
Gyzen, Peter. Flemish Painter...................... 1636..1700?

H.

BORN. DIED.

Haansbergen, John van. Painter of Utrecht......... 1642..1705
Haas, John Matthew. Ger. Geogr. and Hist. (*Hist. Atlas*) 1684..1742
Haas, John Philip de. American General............. 1735?.1794?
Haas, William. Swiss Type Founder and Printer....... 1741..1800
Habakkuk. Prophet of Judah...................... fl. B.C. 600?
Haberlin, Charles Frederick. Jurist................ — ..1808
Haberlin, Francis Dominic. Ger. Historian and Antiq. 1720..1787
Habert, Francis. French Poet...................... 1520?.1562?
Habert, Isaac. French Bishop and Anti-Jansenist.... — ..1668
Habert, Philip. French Academician. Poetical Writer.. 1605?.1637
Habert de Cérisy, Germain. French Writer and Poet.. 1615?.1655
Habicot, Nicholas. French Surgeon and Medical Writer 1550..1624
Habington, Thomas. Conspirator................... 1560..1647
Habington, William, son. Poet and Historian........ 1605..1645
Hachette, John Nicholas Peter. French Mathematician 1769..1834
Hackaert, or Hakkert, John. Dutch Landscape Painter 1636..1699
Hackert, Philip. German Landscape Painter.......... 1737..1807
Hacket, John. Bp. of Lichfield and Cov. L. by Plume 1592..1670
Hacket, William. Fanatic........................ — ..1592
Hackley, Rev. Charles W. Mathematical Writer....... 1809..1861
Hackspan, Theodore. Ger. Orientalist and Theologian 1607..1659
Hacquet, Balthasar. French Naturalist............. 1740..1815
Haddik, Andrew, Count von. German Field Marshal... 1710..1790
Haddon, Walter. (*Reformatio Legum Ecclesiasticarum*) 1516..1572
Hadji Khalifah. *Mustafa-ben-Abdallah.* Turkish Hist. — ..1658
Hadley, John. Inventor of the Quadrant............. — ..1744
Hadrian. Roman Emperor (117–138). L. by Spartianus 76.. 138
Haen, Anthony van. Dutch Medical Writer.......... 1704..1776
Haerlem, Theodore, or Dirk van. Dutch Painter...... 1410?.1470
Hafenreffer, Samuel. German Medical Writer......... 1587..1660
Hafiz, Mohammed. Persian Poet; tr. by Sir W. Jones.. — ..1389
Hagedorn, Christian Louis von. (*Remarks on Painting*) 1713..1780?
Hagedorn, Frederick von. German Poet............. 1708..1754
Hagen, Fred. Henry von der. Ger. Literary Hist. & Critic 1780..1856
Hagen, John van. Landscape Painter............... fl.1650–62
Hager, Joseph von. Italian Orientalist.............. 1757..1819
Haggai. Prophet of Judah......................... fl. B.C. 530?
Hague, Dr. Charles. Musical Composer .... 1769..1821
Haguenier, John. French Poet..................... — ..1738
Haguenot, Henry. Medical Writer of Montpellier ..... 1687..1775
Hahn, Dr. Charles Augustus. Philologist............ 1807..1857 '
Hahn, Philip Matthew. Mechanical Inventor......... 1739..1790
Hahn, Simon Frederick. Historian .... 1692..1729
Hahnemann, Samuel Christian Frederick. Founder of
    Homœopathy .... 1755..1843
Hailes, Dav. Dalrymple, Ld. Judge. (*Annals of Scotland*) 1726..1792
Haillan, Bernard de Girard, Sieur d'. (*Hist. of France*) 1535..1610
Haines, Joseph. Comedian........................ — ..1701
Hakem-Bamrillah. Caliph of Egypt (996–1020)...... 985..1021
Hakewill, Rev. George. (*Power and Providence of God*) 1579..1649

BORN. DIED.

Hakewill, James. (*History of Windsor*)................ — ..1843
Hakim Ben Allah, or Ben Hashem. Arabian Moham-
medan Sectary.................................... 8th c.
Hakluyt, Richard. (*Voyages and Discoveries*).......... 1553?.1616
Haldane, James Alexander. Preacher. (*Atonement.*)
Life by Alexander Haldane...................... 1768..1857
Haldane, Robert. Writer. (*Evidences; Romans.*) Life
by Alexander Haldane.......................... 1764..1842
Halde, John Baptist du. Jesuit. Writer on China..... 1674..1743
Hale, David. American Journalist................... 1791..1849
Hale, Sir Matthew. Judge. Life by Bishop Burnet,1682;
Dr. Williams; Roscoe............................ 1609..1676
Hale, Nathan. American Revolutionary Officer........ 1755..1776
Hale, Nathan, LL. D. American Journalist........... 1784..1863
Hales, Alexander. *Irrefragable Doctor.* Theologian... — ..1245
Hales, John, of Eton. *Ever Memorable.* L. by Des Maizeaux 1584..1656
Hales, Stephen, D. D. Philosopher. (*Vegetable Statics*) 1677..1761
Hales, Rev. Dr. Wm.,of Kildare. (*Analysis of Chronology*) — ..1821?
Halévy, Jas. Francis Fromenthal Élie. Fr. Mus. Comp. 1799..1862
Halford, Sir Henry, M. D. Physician................. 1766..1844
Halhed, Nathaniel Brassy. Orientalist.............. 1751..1830
Haliburton,Thomas Chandler, M. P. Nova Scotian Judge,
Author, and Politician. (*Sam Slick*) .... 1796..1865
Halifax, Charles Montague, Earl of. Statesman and Poet 1661..1715
Halifax, Geo. Saville, 1st V. C. & 1st Marquess of. Statesm. 1630..1695
Halifax, Samuel. Bishop of St. Asaph. Editor of Butler 1733..1790
Halket, Lady Anne. Medical and Theological Writer... 1622..1699
Hall, Basil. Capt. R. N. Writer of Voyages and Travels 1788..1844
Hall, Edward. Historian. (*Chronicles*).............. 1499?.1547
Hall, Gordon. American Missionary .... 1784..1826
Hall, Sir James, of Edinburgh. Scientific Writer....... 1760..1832
Hall, John, of Durham. Poet...................... 1627..1656
Hall, John E. American Author.................... 1783..1829
Hall, Joseph. Bishop of Norwich. (*Contemplations.*) Life
by Pratt, 1808................................. 1574..1656
Hall, Dr. Marshall. Physician. Life by Mrs. Hall...... 1790..1857
Hall, Rd. Rom. Cath. Div. (*Hist. of the Troubles of his Time*) — ..1604
Hall, Robert. Baptist Preacher. Life by O. Gregory; J.
W. Morris, 1846 .... 1764..1831
Hall, Robert Pleasants. American Lawyer and Poet.... 1825..1854
Hallam, Arthur Henry. Life by J. Brown, M. D. .... 1811..1833
Hallam, Henry. Historian. (*Europe in the Middle Ages*) 1778..1859
Hallé, Anthony. French Latin Poet................. 1593..1675
Hallé, Claude Guy. French Painter................. 1652..1736
Hallé, or Halley, Peter. French Civilian and Poet...... 1611..1689
Haller, Albert von. Physician, Philosopher, Poet. Life
by J. G. Zimmermann, 1755; Thomas Henry, 1783... 1708..1777
Haller, Amadeus Emanuel, son. Hist. and Numismatist 1735..1786
Haller, John. German Sculptor .... 1782..1826
Hallet, Joseph. Controv. Div. (*Study of Holy Scripture*) 1692..1744
Halley, Edmund. Astronomer...................... 1656..1742
Halliday, Sir Andrew. Physician and Historical Writer — ..1840
Hallier, Francis. French Theologian................ 1595..1659
Hallifax, or Halifax, Samuel. Bishop. Editor of Butler 1733..1790

13

BORN. DIED.

Hallock, Jeremiah. American Divine................ 1758..1826
Hallock, Moses, brother. Clergyman................. 1760..1837
Hals, Dirk van. Painter..................... 1589..1656
Hals, Francis van, brother. Dutch Portrait Painter..... 1584..1656
Halton, Immanuel. Astronomer and Mathematician.... 1627?.1699
Halyburton, Thomas. Scottish Divine. Life by self... 1674..1712
Hamann, John Geo. Ger. Philos. (*Magus of the North*) 1730..1788
Hamberger, George Albert. Mathematician of Franconia 1662..1716
Hamberger, George Christopher. Scholar of Göttingen 1729..1773
Hamberger, George Edward. Medical Writer......... 1697..1755
Hamel, John Baptist du. French Divine.............. 1624 :1706
Hamel, Dr. Joseph. Writer on Physical Science....... 1788?.1862
Hamel du Monceau, Henry Louis du. French Botanist 1700..1782
Hamilcar Barca. Punic General; father of Hannibal .. —B.C.229
Hamilton, Alexander. American Statesman. Life by J.
  C. Hamilton, 1842.................................. 1757..1804
Hamilton, Anthony, Count. (*Memoirs of Grammont*) .. 1646..1720
Hamilton, David. Scottish Architect................ 1768..1843
Hamilton, Mrs. Eliz. Writer. Life by Miss Benger, 1818 1758..1816
Hamilton, Emma, Lady. Friend of Nelson........... 1761..1815
Hamilton, Gavin. Historical Painter................ 1730?.1797
Hamilton, Hugh. Bp. Ossory. Math. (*Conic Sections*) 1729..1805
Hamilton, James, First Duke of. Defeated at Preston;
  beheaded. L. by Nedham, 1649; Bishop Burnet, 1676 1606..1649
Hamilton, James. Author of *Hamiltonian System*...... 1775..1829
Hamilton, James. American Statesman.............. 1786..1857
Hamilton, John. Secular Priest. Life by Lord Hailes fl. 1600?
Hamilton, Patrick. Scottish Reformer............... 1503..1527
Hamilton, Robert. Scottish Math. and Polit. Economist 1743..1829
Hamilton, Captain Thomas. Writer. (*Cyril Thornton*) 1789..1842
Hamilton, Wm., Duke of. Taken at Worc. L. by Burnet 1616..1652
Hamilton, Wm., of Bangour. Poet. (*Braes of Yarrow*) 1704..1754
Hamilton, William, R. A. Historical Painter.......... 1750..1801
Hamilton, Sir William. Ambassador at Naples........ 1730..1803
Hamilton, Sir William. Professor of Metaphysics at
  Edinburgh. · Editor of Reid...................... 1788..1856
Hamilton, William Gerard, M. P. *Single-Speech*....... 1729..1796
Hamilton, William Richard. English Archæologist.... 1777..1859
Hamilton, Sir Wm. Rowan. Math. Astron. Royal of Irel. 1805..1865
Hammarskoeld, Lars. Swedish Author and Critic..... 1787..1827
Hammer-Purgstall, Joseph von. German Orientalist.. 1774..1856
Hammond, Anthony. *Silver-Tongue*. Poet........... 1668..1738
Hammond, Henry, D. D. Commentator. Life by Bishop
  Fell, 1661; R. Fulman, 1684...................... 1605..1660
Hammond, James. Poet. (*Love Elegies*)............. 1710..1742
Hammond, James Hamilton. American Statesman.... 1807..1861
Hammond, Le Roy. American Revolutionary Officer... 1740?.1800?
Hammond, Samuel. American Revolutionary Officer... 1757..1842
Hamon, John. Phys. of Cherbourg. Religious Writer 1618..1687
Hampden, John. Patriot. Life by Lord Nugent, 1832.. 1594..1643
Hamper, William. Antiquary and Miscellaneous Writer 1776..1831
Hampton, Wade. American General.................. 1755..1835
Hanbal, Ahmed Ebn. Mohammedan Sectary.......... 789.. 855
Hanckius, Martin. (*De Romanarum Rerum Scriptoribus*) 1633..1709

BORN. DIED.

Hancock, John. American Patriot and Statesman...... 1737..1793
Handel, George Fred. Mus. Comp. Life by Schoelcher;
  Mainwaring, 1760; Mattheson, 1764; Burney, 1784 к684..1759
Hangest, Jerome de. French Writer against Luther.... — ..1538
Hankinson, Rev. Thomas Edwards. Poet............ — ..1843
Hanmer, Jonathan, of Barnstaple. Ejected Nonconformist — ..1687
Hanmer, Rev. Meredith, D. D. Translator............ 1543..1604
Hanmer, Sir Thos. Statesman. L. by Sir H. Bunbury, 1838 1676?..1746
Hannecken, Memnon. Historian and Divine.......... 1595..1671
Hannecken, Philip Louis. Theologian.............. 1637..1706
Hanneman, Adrian. Dutch Painter.................. 1611..1680?
Hannibal. Carthaginian General...................247.183?B.C.
Hanno. Carthaginian Navigator. (Periplus).......... fl. 570?B.C.
Hanriot, or Henriot, Francis. French Revolutionist..... 1761..1794
Hansard, Luke. Parliamentary Printer.............. 1752..1828
Hansen, Maurice Christopher. Danish Writer......... 1794..1842
Hans Grün. German Painter & Engraver. See Baldung 1470..1545?
Hans Sachs. German Shoemaker and Poet........... 1494..1578
Hanway, Jonas. Philanthropist and Tourist. (Farmer
  Trueman.) Life by Pugh, 1787.................. 1712..1786
Harcourt, Sir Geoff. Norman Baron with Edward III. — ..1356
Harcourt, Harriet Eusebia, of Yorks. Found. of Nunneries 1706..1745
Harcourt, Henry, Duc d'. Fr. Ambassador at Madrid.. 1654..1718
Harcourt, Sir Simon, cr. Baron Harcourt. Lord Keeper — ..1727
Harcourt, William, Earl of. English Officer in America 1743..1830
Hardeby, Geoffrey. Augustine Monk and Writer...... — ..1360
Hardenberg, Chas. Aug. von. Prince of Pruss. Statesm. 1750..1822
Hardenberg, Frederick von. Novalis................ 1772..1801
Harder, John James, of Basle. Physician............ 1656..1711
Hardi, or Hardy, Alexander. French Dramatist........ 1560?.1630?
Hardicanute. King of England (1040–42)............. — ..1042
Hardime, Peter. Painter of Antwerp.............. 1678..1748
Hardime, Simon, brother. Painter................ 1672..1737
Harding, G. P. Landscape Painter.................. — ..1853
Harding, James Duffield. Landscape Painter.......... 1798?.1863
Harding, or Hardyng, John. Metrical Chronicler..... 1378..1465?
Harding, Stephen. Abbot of Citeaux; Religious Reformer fl.12th c.
Harding, Thomas. Jesuit; opponent of Jewell........ 1512..1572
Hardinge, Henry, Viscount, F. M. Gov.-General of India 1785..1856
Hardinge, Nicholas. Scholar.................... 1700..1758
Hardion, James. French Writer.................... 1686..1766
Hardouin, John. Père Hardouin. Jesuit Writer........ 1646..1729
Hardt, Hermann von der. (Hist. Literaria Reformationis) 1660..1746
Harduin, Alexander Xavier. Fr. Poet and Grammarian 1718..1785
Hardwick, Charles. English Theologian............. 1821..1859
Hardwicke, Elizabeth, Lady Cavendish, Lady St. Loe,
  Countess of Shrewsbury......................... 1519..1608
Hardwicke, Philip Yorke, First Earl of. Lord Chan-
  cellor. Life by G. Harris, 1847.................. 1690..1764
Hardwicke, Philip Yorke, Second Earl of. Writer. (State
  Papers.) Life by R. Cooksey, 1791.............. 1720..1790
Hardwicke, Philip Yorke, 3d E. of. Lord Lieut. of Irel. 1757..1834
Hardy, Alexander. French Dramatist................ 1560?.1630?
Hardy, Sir Thos. Masterman. Admiral. Nelson's friend 1769..1839

BORN.   DIED.

Hardyng, or Harding, John.   Metrical Chronicler ...... 1378 .1465[?]
Hare, Rev. Augustus Wm. (*Sermons to a Country Congreg.*) 1792..1834
Hare, Francis.   Bishop of Chichester (1731–40) .... 1665[?].1740
Hare, James.   M. P. for Knaresborough.   Wit........... — ..1804
Hare, Julius Charles.   Archdeacon.   (*Victory of Faith*).. 1795..1855
Hare, Robert.   American Chemist and Physicist .... 1781..1858
Hargrave, Francis.   Law Writer..................... 1741..1821
Hargreaves, James.   Mechanician .... — ..1770[?]
Harington, Sir John.   *See* Harrington.   Poet......... 1561..1612
Hariot, or Harriott, Thomas.   Mathematician.......... 1560..1621
Hariri, Abu Mohammed Kasem ben Ali.   Arabian Writer 1054[?].1122
Harles, Theophilus Christopher.   German Philologist ... 1738..1852
Harley, Edw., 2d E. Oxford.   Found. of Harleian Library — ..1741
Harley, Robt., 1st E. Oxford.   Statesman.; MSS. Collector 1661..1724
Harlow, George Henry.   Portrait and Historical Painter. 1787..1819
Harmer, Thomas.   Dissenting Divine.   (*Observations*).. 1715..1788
Harms, Claus.   German Theologian................... 1778..1855
Harnett, Cornelius.   American Revolutionary Statesman 1723..1781
Haro, Louis de.   Spanish Statesman .... 1598..1661
Harold I.   King of England (1035–40).   *Harefoot* ...... — ..1040
Harold II.   King of England (1066); fell at Hastings ... — ..1066
Haroun-al-Rashid.   Caliph (786–809) ....765 or 6.809
Harpe, John Francis de la.   Dramatic Poet and Critic ... 1739..1803
Harper, Robert Goodloe.   Amer. Lawyer and Statesman 1765..1825
Harper, William.   American Lawyer and Statesman.... 1790..1847
Harpocration, Valerius.   Greek Philologist .... fl. 4th c.
Harpsfield, Nicholas.   Roman Catholic Divine .... — ..1583
Harrington, Chas Stanhope, Third Earl of.   Commander 1753..1829
Harrington, James.   Political Writer.   (*Oceana.*)   Life
    by Toland, 1771 .... 1611..1677
Harrington, Sir John.   Poet.   Translator of Ariosto.... 1561..1612
Harriott, Thos. Mathematician. (*Artis Analyticæ Praxis*) 1560..1621
Harris, George, Lord.   General; distinguished in India.. 1746..1829
Harris, James, of Salisbury.   Scholar.   (*Hermes.*)   Life
    by son, Earl of Malmesbury, 1801 .... 1709..1780
Harris, James.   First Earl of Malmesbury.   Diplomatist.
    (*Diaries and Correspondence*) .... 1746..1820
Harris, John.   (*Lexicon Technicum; History of Kent*)... 1667[?].1719
Harris, John, D. D.   Divine and Author............... 1804..1856
Harris, Robert.   Divine .... 1578..1658
Harris, Thaddeus William.   American Naturalist....... 1795..1856
Harris, Walter, M. D.   (*De Morbis Acutis Infantum*)..... 1647..1725
Harris, William, D. D.   Biographer.................... 1720..1770
Harris, William, D. D.   American Educator............ 1765..1829
Harrison, Benjamin.   American Statesman .... 1740[?].1791
Harrison, Colonel John.   Regicide .... — ..1660
Harrison, John.   Inventor of Chronometer............. 1693..1776
Harrison, Thomas, of Chester.   Architect.............. 1744..1829
Harrison, William.   Poet.............................. — ..1713
Harrison, Wm. Henry.   General.   Ninth President U. S. 1775..1841
Harrowby, Dudley Ryder, Earl of.   Statesman......... 1762..1847
Harry, Blind, or Henry the Minstrel .... fl. 1470–80
Harsnett, Samuel.   Archbishop of York (1628–31)....... 1561..1631
Hart, John.   American Patriot .... — ..1780

BORN. DIED.

Harte, Rev. Walter. Poet and Hist. (*Gustavus Adolphus*) 1700?.1774
Hartley, David, M. D. (*Observations on Man.*) L. by his son 1705..1757
Hartley, David, M. P. Politician and Inventor .... 1730..1813
Hartman, George, of Nuremberg. Mathematician ..... 1489..1564
Hartman, John Adolphus. (*Vitæ Pontificum*)........... 1680..1744
Hartmann, John, M. D. Medical Writer.............. 1568..1631
Hartmann von der Aue, or Von Aue. Old German Poet —aft.1207
Hartshorne, Rev. Charles Henry. Antiquary .... 1803?.1865
Hartsoeker, Nicholas. Dutch Metaphys. and Nat. Philos. 1656..1725
Hartzheim, Jos., of Cologne. Scholar. (*Summa Historiæ*) 1694..1763
Harvard, John. Founder of Harvard College .... — .;1688
Harvey, Daniel Whittle. Politician................... 1784?.1863
Harvey, Gabriel. Writer; friend of Spenser........... 1545..1630?
Harvey, Gideon, M. D. Medical Writer.............. 1625?.1700
Harvey, William, M. D. Discoverer of Circulation of the
    Blood. Life by Laurence .... 1578..1657
Harwood, Sir Busick, M. D. Anatomist.............. 1745?.1814
Harwood, Edward, of Bristol. Socinian Writer .... 1729..1794
Hasdrubal. Carthaginian General; brother of Hannibal —B.C.207
Hase, Theodore von. German Divine .... 1682..1731
Hasenclever, John Peter. German Painter .... 1810..1853
Hasenclever, Peter. German Manufacturer and Writer 1716..1792
Hasenmueller, Daniel. Ger. Greek and Oriental Scholar 1651..1691
Haslam, John, M. D. Writer on Insanity .... 1763..1844
Haslewood, Thomas. Schoolmaster and Historian...... ti. Rd. II.
Hassan. Son of Ali and Fatima. Caliph (660-69)..... 625.. 669
Hasse, Frederick Christian Augustus. German Author.. 1773..1848
Hasse, John Adolphus. *Il Sassone.* German Composer 1699..1783
Hassel, John George Henry. German Statistician...... 1770..1829
Hasselquist, Frederick. Swedish Naturalist and Traveler 1722..1752
Hasted, Edward. Antiquary. (*History of Kent*) .... 1732..1812
Hastings, Lady Eliz. Benefactor. L. by Barnard, 1742 1682..1739
Hastings, Lady Flora. Maid of Honor................ 1803..1839
Hastings, Francis Rawdon. Cr. Marquess of Hastings 1754..1823
Hastings, Warren. Gov. of India. L. by Gleig; Macaulay 1733..1818
Hatfield, Thomas. Bishop of Durham (1345-81) .... — ..1381
Hatsell, John. Clerk to House of Commons. Writer... 1742?.1820
Hatton, Sir Christoph. Ld. Chanc. L. by Sir N. H. Nicolas — ..1591
Hatzfeld, Francis Louis, Prince of. German Diplomatist 1756..1827
Haubold, Christian Theophilus. German Jurist........ 1766..1824
Hauff, William. German Prose Writer................ 1802..1827
Haughton, Sir Graves Chamney. Orientalist .... 1789..1849
Haughton, William. Dramatist................... fl. 1600?
Haugwitz, Christian Henry Chas., Ct. of. Pruss. Statesman 1752..1832
Haukal, Abul Kasem Mohammed Ibn. Arab.Trav.& Geog. fl. 942-76
Hauksbee, or Hawksbee, Francis. Electrician. F.R.S. 1705 —aft.1731
Hauser, Caspar. Foundling of Nuremberg .... — ..1833
Hautefeuille, John de. French Mechanician........... 1647..1724
Hauteroche, Noel le Breton de. French Dramatist ..... 1617?.1707
Hauteserre, Anth. Dadin de. Hist. and Jurist at Toulouse 1602?.1682
Haüy, René Just. Abbé. Mineralogist .... 1743..1822
Havelock, Sir Henry. General. Life by J. T. Headley,
    1859; W. Brock; J. C. Marshman, 1860............. 1795..1857
Haven, Nath. Appleton. Amer. Lawyer and *Littérateur* 1790..1826

BORN. DIED.

Havercamp, Sigebert. Philologist and Medalist .... 1683..1742
Havers, Clopton. Physician and Anatomist........... fl. 1691
Haviland, John. American Architect and Engineer .... 1792..1852
Hawes, Stephen. (*Passetyme of Pleasure*)............ ti. Hen. VII.
Hawes, William, M. D. Founder of R. Humane Society 1736..1808
Hawke, Edward, Lord. Admiral .... 1715..1781
Hawker, Peter. Colonel. (*Instruct. to Young Sportsmen*) 1786?.1853
Hawker, Rev. Robert, D. D. Divine and Commentator.. 1753..1827
Hawkesworth, John, LL. D. Writer. (*The Adventurer*) 1715?.1773
Hawkins, Sir John. Naval Commander.............. 1520?.1595
Hawkins, Sir John. Writer........................ 1719..1789
Hawkins, Sir Thomas. Translator of Horace .... ti. Chas. I.
Hawksmoor, Nicholas. Architect .... 1666..1736
Hawkwood, Sir John.. English Soldier of Fortune ..... — ..1393
Hawley, Gideon. American Missionary to the Indians.. 1727..1807
Hawley, Joseph. American Patriot and Statesman ..... 1724..1788
Hawthorne, Nathaniel. American Romancist .... 1804..1864
Hawtrey, Edward Craven, D. D. Provost of Eton ...... 1789..1862
Hay, James, Earl of Carlisle. Statesman .... — ..1636
Hay, William, M. P. Writer. (*Essay on Deformity*)..... 1695..1755
Haydn, Francis Joseph. Musical Composer. (*Creation.*)
    Life by Bombet (*i. e.* Beyle), 1817; W. Gardiner ..... 1732..1809
Haydn, John Michael, brother. Musical Composer...... 1737..1808
Haydn, Joseph. (*Dictionary of Dates*) .... — ..1856
Haydock, Rev. Geo. Leo. Rom. Cath. Div. Ed. of Bible — ..1848
Haydon, Benj. Robt. Paint. L. by self; Tom Taylor, 1853 1786..1846
Haye, John de la. Jesuit. (*Harmony of the Evangelists*) 1540..1614
Haye, John de la. Franciscan. (*Biblia Maxima*)...... 1593..1661
Hayer, John Nicholas Hubert. French Theologian ..... 1708..1780
Hayer du Perron, Peter le. French Poet............ 1603.aft.1678
Hayes, Catherine. Irish Vocalist .... — ..1861
Hayes, Charles. Mathematician and Chronologist ...... 1678..1760
Hayes, William. Musical Composer.................. 1708..1777
Hayley, William. Poet. (*L. of Cowper.*) L. by self, 1823 1745..1820
Hayman, Francis, R. A. Historical Painter............ 1708..1776
Haynau, Julius Jacob, Baron von. Austrian General.... 1786..1853
Hayne, Isaac. American Patriot.................... 1745..1781
Hayne, Robert Young. American Lawyer and Statesman 1791..1839
Hayne, Thomas. Schoolmaster and Benefactor......... 1581..1645
Haynes, Hopton. Writ. on the Trinity. (*Scripture Account*) 1672..1749
Haynes, John. Gov. of Massachusetts and of Connecticut — ..1654
Haynes, Lemuel. American Colored Minister.......... 1753..1834
Hayward, Sir John. Historian .... — ..1627
Haywood, Elizabeth. Writer .... 1693..1756
Hazlitt, William. Critic and Essayist. Life by his son.. 1778..1830
Head, Sir George. Writer .... 1782..1855
Head, Richard. Dramatist........................ — ..1678
Headley, Henry. Poet and Critic. Life by Kett, 1810.. 1766..1788
Heapy, Thomas. Painter in Water Colors............ 1775..1835
Hearne, Samuel. Explorer .... 1745..1792
Hearne, Thomas. Antiquary. Life by Huddesford, 1772;
    Kett, 1810; Henry Headley..................... 1678..1735
Hearne, Thomas. Artist.......................... 1744..1817
Heath, Benjamin, D. C. L., of Exeter. Lawyer and Writer — ..1766

BORN. DIED.

Heath, Charles. Engraver. (*Book of Beauty*)......... 1784..1848
Heath, James. Historical Writer .... 1629..1664
Heath, William. American Revolutionary General..... 1737..1814
Heathcote, Rev. Ralph, D. D. Writer................ 1721..1795
Heathfield, Geo. A. Elliot, Lord. Defender of Gibraltar 1718?.1790
Hebbel, Frederick. German Poet.................... 1813..1863
Hebel, John Peter. German Poet.................... 1760..1826
Hebenstreit, John Ernest, of Leipsic. Medical Writer.. 1703..1757
Heber, Reginald. Bishop of Calcutta. Life by Potter;
  his Widow, 1830; Thomas Taylor .... 1783..1826
Heber, Richard. Bibliomaniac .... 1773..1833
Heberden, William, M. D. Medical Writer........... 1710..1801
Hebert, James René. (*Père Duchêne*.) Fr. Revolutionist 1755?.1794
Hecatæus, of Miletus. Greek Historian.............550?.476?B.C.
Hecht, Christian. German Philologist................ 1696..1748
Heck, John van. Painter of Oudenard............... 1625?.1669
Heck, Nicholas van der. Dutch Painter .... 1580..1638
Heckewelder, John. Moravian Missionary in America 1743..1823
Hecquet, Philip. French Medical Writer............. 1661..1737
Hedding, Elijah, D. D. American Divine............. 1780..1852
Hédelin, Francis, Abbé d'Aubignac. French Poet...... 1604..1676
Hederic, Benjamin. Lexicographer.................. 1675..1748
Hedio, Gaspar. Protestant Reformer................ 1495..1552
Hedlinger, John Charles. Swiss Die Cutter........... 1691..1771
Hedwig, John. Botanist.......................... 1730..1799
Heede, Vigor van. Historical Painter............... 1659..1718
Heede, William van, brother. Historical Painter....... 1660..1728
Heem, John David van. Dutch Painter .... 1600..1674
Heemskerk, or Hemskerk, James van. Dutch Admiral — ..1607
Heemskerk, or Hemskerk, Martin van. Dutch Painter 1498..1574
Heere, Luke van. Dutch Painter................... 1534..1584
Heeren, Arnold Hermann Louis. German Historian.... 1760..1842
Heers, Henry van, of Liege. Medical Writer .... 1570?.1636?
Hegel, George William Frederick. Philosopher. Life by
  Goeschel, 1832; Rosencranz, 1844; Haym......... 1770..1831
Heiberg, Peter Andrew. Danish Dramatist and Writer 1758..1841
Heidegger, John Henry. Swiss Protestant Divine ..... 1633..1698
Heidegger, John James. *Swiss Count*. Adventurer.... 1660..1749
Heil, Daniel van. Painter of Brussels .... 1604..1662
Heil, John Baptist van, brother. Painter............ 1609.aft.1661
Heil, Leonard van, brother. Painter of Flowers & Insects 1603.. —
Hein, or Heyn, Peter. Dutch Admiral.............. 1570..1629
Heine, Henry. German Poet, Essayist, and Satirist..... 1799?.1856
Heineccius, John Theophilus. German Civilian .... 1681..1741
Heinecken, Christian Henry. *Infant of Lubeck* .... 1721..1725
Heinefetter, Clara. German Vocalist................ — ..1857
Heinefetter, Kathinka, sister. Vocalist.............. — ..1858
Heinicke, John David. Musical Composer .... 1683..1729
Heinrich, Charles Frederick. German Scholar......... 1774..1838
Heinroth, John Christian Frederick Augustus. German
  Physician and Writer on Psychology .... 1773..1843
Heinse, John James William. German Writer on Art .. 1746..1803
Heinsius, Anthony. Grand Pensionary of Holland..... 1641?.1720
Heinsius, Daniel, of Leyden. Latin Poet and Philologist 1580?.1655

BORN. DIED.

Heinsius, Nich., son. Poet & Critic. L. by Burmann, 1742 1620..1681
Heinsius, Otto Frederick Theodore. German Philologist 1770..1849
Heister, Lawrence. Physician, Surgeon, and Anatomist 1683..1758
Hele, Thomas. English Dramatist at Paris............. 1740?.1780
Helena, St. Mother of Constantine.................. 248?. 328?
Heliodorus, of Larissa. Greek Writer on Optics....... fl. 1st c.
Heliodorus. Bishop of Tricca. Romancist. (*Æthiopica*) fl. 400?
Heliogabalus, or Elagabalus. Roman Emperor (218-222) 205?. 222
Hell, Maximilian. Astronomer....................... 1720..1792
Heller, Joseph. German Art Historian............... 1798..1849
Hellot, John. French Chemist....................... 1685..1766
Helmbreker, Theodore. Dutch Painter............... 1624..1694
Helmers, John Frederick. Dutch Poet............... 1767..1813
Helmont, Francis Mercury van. Chemist............. 1618..1699
Helmont, John Baptist van. Flemish Chemist........ 1577..1644
Helmont, Matthew van. Painter of Antwerp......... 1653..1726
Helmont, Segres James van. Flemish Historical Painter 1683..1726
Héloïse, or Éloïse. Friend of Abelard. L. by Gervase, 1720 1101..1164
Helst, Bartholomew van der. Dutch Painter......... 1613..1670?
Helvetius, Claude Adrian. French Philos. (*L'Esprit*) 1715..1771
Helvetius, John Adrian. Dutch Physician at Paris..... 1661?.1727.
Helvetius, John Claude Adrian, son. Medical Writer .. 1685..1755
Helvicus, Christopher. German Philol. and Chronologist 1581..1617
Helwig, Amelia von. German Poetess................. 1776..1832
Helwig, George Andrew. Pruss. Botanist & Mineralogist 1666..1748
Helwig, Sir John Otto. Physician and Collector........ 1654..1698
Helyot, Peter. Franciscan Friar. (*Hist. of Monast. Orders*) 1660..1716
Hemans, Mrs. Felicia Dorothea. Poetess. Life by H. F.
    Chorley, 1837; Mrs. Hughes, 1839.................. 1794..1835
Hemelar, John. Flemish Medalist.................... — ..1640
Hemingburgh, or Hemingford, Walter de. Historian... — ..1347
Hemling, or Memling, Hans. Flemish Painter........ 1425?.1500?
Hemskerck, Egbert. *The Old*....................... 1610?.1680?
Hemskerck, Egbert. *The Younger*. Dutch Painter.... 1645..1704
Hemskerck, Martin van. Dutch Painter............. 1498..1574
Hemsterhusius, Francis. (*Œuvres Philosophiques*).... 1720..1790
Hemsterhuys, Tiberius. Dutch Philologist........... 1685..1766
Henao, Gabriel de. Spanish Theol. (*Biscaya Illustrata*) 1611..1704
Hénault, Charles John Francis. (*Abrégé Chronologique*) 1685..1770
Hénault, or Hesnault, John. French Poet........... — ..1682
Henckel, John Fred. Saxon Chemist and Mineralogist 1679..1744
Henderson, Alexander. Principal, of Edinburgh...... — ..1646
Henderson, Rev. Dr. Ebenezer. Missionary and Traveler.
    Life by T. S. Henderson, 1859.................. 1784..1858
Henderson, John. Actor. L. by T. Davies; J. Ireland, 1786 1747..1785
Henderson, John. Genius, born in Ireland........... 1757..1788
Henderson, or Henryson, Robert. Scottish Poet....... — ..1508?
Henderson, Thomas. Scottish Astronomer............ 1798..1844
Hengist. King of Kent.............................. — .. 488
Henke, Henry Philip Conrad. Theol. (*Eccles. History*) 1752..1809
Henkel, John Frederick. *See* Henckel.............. 1679..1744
Henley, Anthony, M. P. Writer..................... 1660?.1711
Henley, Rev. John. *Orator*. Preacher and Polit. Lecturer 1692..1756
Henley, Sir Morton Eden, First Lord. Ambassador..... — ..1802

BORN. DIED.

Henley, Robert, Lord Northington. Lord Chancellor... 1708..1772
Hennepin, Louis. Missionary, and Explorer of the River
  Mississippi.......................................1640?.aft.1699
Henninges, Jerome. German Genealogist............. 1550?.1597
Henrietta Anna, of England. Duchess of Orleans.
  Life by Lafayette, 1720............................ 1644..1670
Henrietta Maria, of France. Queen of Chas. I. of Eng. 1609..1669
Henrion, Nicholas. French Archæologist.............. 1663..1720
Henriot, Francis. French Revolutionist............... 1761..1794
Henrique, Duke of Viseo. Portuguese Prince; Promoter
  of Navigation. Life by Candido Lusitano.......... 1394..1460
Henry I. Emperor of Germany (919–36). *The Fowler*.. 876.. 936
Henry II. (1002–24.) Life by Adelbold, d. 1027....... 972..1024
Henry III. (1039–56.)............................... 1017..1056
Henry IV. (1058–1106.) Life by Aventinus, 1518; Stumpf,
  1556; Soeltl, 1823................................. 1050..1106
Henry V. (1106–25.)................................. 1081..1125
Henry VI. (1190–97.) Life by Jaeger, 1790........... 1165..1197
Henry VII. (1308–13.) L. by Veccrius, 1531; Mussati,
  1636; Gundling, 1719; Barthold, 1830; Doenniges, 1839 1263..1313
Henry I. King of France (1031–60)................... 1011?.1060
Henry II. (1547–59.) Life by Lambert, 1755......... 1519..1559
Henry III. (1574–89.) Life by Sossius, 1628; Varillas,
  1694; Garden, 1783; Billardon de Sauvigny, 1788;
  Miss Freer, 1858 .... 1551..1589
Henry IV. (1589–1610.) *The Great.* Life by Péréfixe,
  1661; Scip. Dupleix, 1632; Richard de Bury, 1795;
  Miss Freer; Gurney................................. 1553..1610
Henry I. King of England (1100–35). *Beauclerc.* Life
  by Sir J. Hayward, 1613 .... 1068..1135
Henry II. (1154–89.) Life by Benedict of Peterborough;
  Edm. Bolton; Lord Lyttelton, 1767; Berington, 1790 1133..1189
Henry III. (1216–72.) *Of Winchester.* Life by R. Cot-
  ton, 1627; Prynne, 1670 .... 1206..1272
Henry IV. (1399–1413.) *Bolingbroke.* Life by Sir J.
  Hayward, 1599; G. P. R. James, 1847............... 1366?.1413
Henry V. (1413–22.) *Of Monmouth.* Life by Tit. Livius;
  Robert Redman; T. Elmham; Goodwin, 1604; P. F.
  Tytler, 1830....................................... 1388..1422
Henry VI. (1422–71.)............................... 1421..1471
Henry VII. (1485–1509.) Life by Aleyn, 1638; Lord
  Bacon, 1642; Marsollier, 1697..................... 1457..1509
Henry VIII. (1509–47.) Life by Godwin, 1616; Lord
  Herbert of Cherbury, 1649; P. F. Tytler, 1837....... 1491..1547
Henry, Prince of Wales: son of James I. Life by Sir
  Charles Cornwallis; T. Birch, 1760................. 1594..1612
Henry de Blois. Cardinal. Bishop of Winchester .... — ..1171
Henry of Huntingdon. Historian .... —aft.1154
Henry the Lion. Duke of Bavaria and Saxony. L. by
  Reineccius, 1557; Stederburgensis, 1614; Meyer, 1694 1129..1195
Henry the Minstrel, or Blind Harry. Scottish Poet... fl. 1470–80
Henry the Navigator. *See* Henrique .... 1394..1460
Henry, Alexander. American Traveler and Writer..... 1739.. —
Henry, David. Printer; conductor of *Gentleman's Mag.* 1710..1792

BORN. DIED.

Henry, Matt. Commentator. L. by Tong, 1716; Williams 1662..1714
Henry, Patrick. American Statesman. L. by Wirt, 1817 1736..1799
Henry, Philip. Nonconformist Divine. Life by son, Matthew Henry, 1696; William Bates, 1699. . . . . 1631..1696
Henry, Robert. Scottish Divine. (*Hist. of Great Britain*) 1718..1790
Henry, Robert, LL. D. American Educator and Writer. . 1792..1856
Henry, William, M. D. Chemist. . . . . 1775..1836
Henryson, or Henderson, Robert. Scottish Poet . . . . . . — ..1508?
Henshaw, John Prentiss Kewley, D. D. Amer. Divine. . 1792..1852
Henslow, J. S. Professor of Botany. L. by Jenyns, 1862 — ..1861
Hensman, Rev. John, of Clifton. Divine. . . . . 1781?.1864
Hentz, Caroline Lee. American Authoress. . . . . — ..1856
Hepburn, James Bonaventura. Scottish Linguist and Orientalist in Italy. . . . . 1573..1620
Hepburn, John. Prior of St. Andrew's; Founder of St. Leonard's College (1512). fl.1480–1520
Hepburn, Robert. Miscellaneous Writer . . . . 1619..1712
Hephæstion. General of Alexander . . . . — B.C.325
Heraclitus, of Ephesus. *Weeping Philosopher* . . . . fl. 513? B.C.
Heraclius. Emperor of the East (610–41) . . . . 575?. 641
Heraldus, Desiderius. *Didier Hérault.* French Writer. . 1575?.1649
Hérault de Séchelles, Mary John. French Revolutionist 1760..1794
Herbart, John Frederick. German Metaphysician. . . . . . 1776..1841
Herbelot, Barthol. d'. Fr. Orient. (*Biblioth. Orientale*) 1625..1695
Herbert, Edward, Lord, of Cherbury. Historical and Deist. Writer. (*Hist. of Henry VIII.*) L. by self, 1764 1581..1648
Herbert, Rev. George. (*Country Parson.*) Life by Izaak Walton, 1670; Duyckinck, 1858. . . . . 1593..1633
Herbert, Henry William. English Writer in America. . . 1707..1858
Herbert, Mary (*née* Sidney), Countess Pembroke. Poet and Writer. " Sidney's sister, Pembroke's mother " — ..1621
Herbert, Sidney, Lord of Lea. Statesman. . . . . 1810?.1861
Herbert, Sir Thomas. Royalist. (*Threnodia Carolina*) 1610..1682
Herbert, William. Earl of Pembroke. Poet. . . . . 1580..1630
Herbert, William, of Cheshunt. Typographical Antiquary 1718..1795
Herbert, Rev. William. Author. (*Attila*) . . . . 1778..1847
Herbin, Augustus Francis Julian. French Orientalist . . . 1783..1806
Herbinius, John. Polish Divine and Natural Philosopher 1633..1676
Herbst, John Andrew. German Musical Writer. . . . . 1588..1660?
Herder, John Godfrey von. (*Philosophy of History*). . . . . 1744..1803
Hereward. English Partisan Captain at the Conquest. . . — ..1072
Héricourt, Louis de. French Jurist. . . . . 1687..1752
Heriot, Geo. Goldsmith. Founder of Hospital in Edinb. 1563?.1624
Hérissant, Louis Anthony Prosper. Fr. Phys. and Nat. 1745..1769
Héritier de Brutelle, Charles Louis l'. French Botanist 1746..1800
Héritier de Villandon, Mary Jane l'. Writer. . . . . 1664..1734
Héritier de Villandon, Nicholas l'. French Poet. . . . . . 1630?.1680
Herlicius, David. German Astrologer. . . . . 1558..1636
Hermann, James. Swiss Mathem. and Nat. Philosopher 1678..1733
Hermann, John. Physician and Naturalist. . . . . 1738..1800
Hermann, John Godfrey Jacob. Editor of Greek Plays . 1772..1848
Hermann, Paul. German Botanist. . . . . 1646..1695
Hermannus, *Contractus*, of Suabia. Musical Writer. . . . 1013..1054
Hermant, Godfrey. Dr. of the Sorbonne. Theol. & Biog. 1617..1690

BORN. DIED.

Hermas. Christian Writer. (*The Shepherd*)........... fl. 1st c.
Hermelin, Samuel Gustavus, Baron. Swedish Mineral. 1744..1820
Hermes, George. German Roman Catholic Theologian . 1775..1831
Hermilly, Vaquette d'. French Historian............. 1710..1778
Hermolaus Barbarus. Venetian Scholar. *See* Barbaro 1454..1495
Hernandez, Francis. Spanish Physician and Naturalist fl. 16th c.
Herndon, William Lewis. American Naval Officer..... 1813..1857
Herod Agrippa I. *Great.* Tetrarch of Abilene; be-
  headed James. (Acts xii.) .... — .. 44
Herod Agrippa II., son. King of Chalcis. (Acts xxv.) 31.. 100
Herod Antipas. Tetrarch of Galilee; deposed A. D. 39 — aft. 39
Herod the Great. King of the Jews (B. C. 47–4)....... 73..4 B.C.
Herod Philip, son. Tetrarch..................... — A.D. 34
Herodes Atticus. Embellisher of Athens .... 104?. 180?
Herodian. Greek Historian of the Roman Empire...... fl. ab. 238
Herodotus. Greek Historian. Life by Wheeler; Dahl-
  mann, translated by Cox ....484.408? B.C.
Herold, Louis Joseph Ferdinand. French Composer .... 1791..1833
Heron, or Hero. Philos. and Mathem. of Alexandria.... fl. 3d c. B.C.
Herrera, Ferdinand de. *The Divine.* Spanish Poet .... 1516?.1595
Herrera, Francis de. *El Viego, the Elder.* Span. Paint. 1576.1650 or 6
Herrera, Francis de, son. *El Mozo, the Younger.* Painter 1622..1685
Herrera, Joseph Joachim de. President of Mexico..... — ..1851
Herrera y Tordesillas, Anthony. Spanish Historian .. 1565..1625
Herrgott, John James. *Marquard.* Ger. Diplom. and Hist. 1694..1762
Herrick, Rev. Robert. Poet. (*Hesperides*) .... 1591..1674
Herring, John Frederick. Horse Painter.............. 1795..1865
Herring, Thomas. Archbishop of Canterbury (1747–57). 1693..1757
Herschel, Miss Caroline Lucretia. Astronomer........ 1750..1848
Herschel, Sir F. William. Discoverer of Uranus....... 1738..1822
Hersent, or Hersan, Charles. Opponent of Richelieu.... —aft.1660
Hertius, John Nicholas. German Historical Writer..... 1651..1710
Hertzberg, Ewald Frederick von. Prussian Statesman. 1725..1795
Hervey, Rev. James. (*Meditations.*) Life by John Brown,
  1822; John Cole, 1822–26 .... 1714..1758
Hervey, John, Lord. Political and Poetical Writer ..... 1696..1743
Hervey, Thomas Kibble. Author...................... 1799..1859
Herwart, John George. German Critic................ 1554..1622
Héry, Thierry de. *Theodoricus.* French Medical Writer 1505..1599
Herz, Henrietta. German Beauty and Wit .... 1764..1847
Heshusius, Tilemannus. Anti-Calvinist Theologian.... 1526..1588
Hesiod. Greek Epic Poet. (*Works and Days*) ..... fl. 859-824? B.C.
Hess, Charles Ernest Christopher. German Engraver... 1755..1828
Hesse, William, Prince of. Astronomer............... 1545..1597
Hessels, or Hesselius, John, of Louvain. Theologian.... 1522..1566
Hesychius. Alexandrian Grammarian................ fl. 380?
Hetzer, Louis. German Socinian .... — ..1540
Heugh, Hugh, D. D. Scottish Div. L. by Hamilton McGill 1782..1846
Heurnius, John. Medical Writer at Leyden........... 1543..1601
Heusch, Abraham van. Painter..................... 1650..1712
Heusch, Jacob van. Painter........................ 1657..1701
Heusch, William van. Landscape Painter of Utrecht... 1630?.1700?
Heusde, Philip William. Dutch Philosopher .... 1778..1839
Heusinger, James Frederick. Philologist............. 1719..1778

BORN. DIED.

Heusinger, John Michael. Saxon Divine .... 1690..1751
Hevelius, or Hevelke, John, of Dantzic. Astronomer.... 1611..1687
Hevin, Prudént. French Surgical Writer............. 1715..1789
Hewes, Joseph. American Patriot.................... 1730..1779
Hewson, William. Anatomist........................ 1739..1774
Hexham, John, Prior of. (*Chronicle*).............. fl. 1170
Hexham, Rd., Prior of. (*Bps. of Hexham; B. of Standard*) fl. 1138
Hey, John, D. D. Norrisian Prof. of Divinity, Cambridge 1734..1815
Hey, William, F. R. S., of Leeds. Surgeon; Friend of
    Wilberforce. Life by John Pearson............... 1736..1819
Heyden, Fred. August von. German Novelist and Poet 1789..1851
Heyden, John van der. Flemish Painter .... 1637..1712
Heylin, Rev. Peter, D. D. Historical Writer. Life by
    Vernon, 1681; Bernard, 1682....................... 1600..1662
Heyne, Christian Gottlob. Classical Editor. Life by A.
    H. L. Heeren, 1812................................ 1729..1812
Heyward, Thomas. American Patriot................. 1746..1809
Heywood, Mrs. Eliza. Romancist .... 1693..1756
Heywood, Gaspar. Poet. (*Paradise of Dainty Devices*). 1535..1598
Heywood, John. Dram. Poet. (*The Spider and the Fly*) — ..1565?
Heywood, Oliver. Nonconformist Divine. Life by Faw-
    cett, 1798; Rev. Joseph Hunter, 1842.............. 1629..1702
Heywood, Thomas. Actor and Writer. Life by J. P.
    Collier, 1850....................................Eliz.–Chas. I.
Hezekiah. King of Judah (B. C. 726–698)............751?.698 B.C.
Hickes, George. Nonjuror and Saxonist. (*Thesaurus*). 1642..1715
Hickes, John, brother. Ejected Nonconformist; executed — ..1685
Hickman, Henry. Ejected Nonconformist Divine ...... — ..1692
Hicks, Elias. American Quaker Preacher............. 1748..1830
Hidalgo y Costilla, Michael. Mexican Revolutionist... — ..1811
Hiero I. Tyrant of Syracuse (B. C. 478–467) .... —B.C.467
Hiero II. King of Syracuse (B. C. 270–216) ....308.216 B.C.
Hierocles. Neoplatonist. Life by Andrew Dacier, 1706 fl. 450?
Hieronymus, or Jerome, St. Christian Writer .... 345?..420
Hifferman, Paul. Irish Dramatic Poet .... 1719..1777
Higden, Ralph. Historian. (*Polychronicon*) .... — ..1367?
Higgins, or Higins, John. Divine and Schoolmaster.... 1544?.1605?
Higginson, Francis. Anglo-American Clergymań...... 1587..1630
Higgons, Bevil. Historical Writer and Poet.......... 1670..1735
Higgons, Sir Thomas. Politician and Writer.......... 1624..1691
Highmore, Joseph. Portrait and Historical Painter..... 1692..1780
Highmore, Nathaniel. Anatomist .... 1613..1684
Hilaire, Geoffrey St. *See* St. Hilaire............. 1772..1844
Hilarion. Promoter of Monachism. Life by Jerome .... 291..371
Hilariuse, Joseph. German Antiquary and Medalist .... 1737..1798
Hilary, St. Bp. Poictiers (350–67). *Malleus Arianorum* — .. 367
Hilary, St. Bishop of Arles (429–49) .... 401.. 449
Hilary. Bishop of Rome (461–67)..................... — .. 467
Hilda, St. Abbess of Whitby .... — .. 680
Hildebrand. *See* Pope Gregory VII................. — ..1085
Hildegarde, St. Abbess of St. Rupert's Mount....... . 1098..1180
Hildesley, Mark. Bishop of Man. L. by W. Butler, 1799 1698..1772
Hildreth, Richard. Amer. Journalist, Hist., and Novelist 1807..1863
Hildreth, Samuel P., M. D. Amer. Historian & Physicist 1783..1863

BORN. DIED.

Hill, Aaron. Poet and Dramatic Writer............... 1685..1750
Hill, Geo., D.D. Principal, St. Andr. Lead. in Gen. Assemb. 1750..1819
Hill, Isaac. American Journalist and Politician .... 1788..1851
Hill, Sir John. Physician and Writer................. 1716..1775
Hill, Joseph. Divine and Lexicographer.............. 1625..1707
Hill, Sir Richard, M. P. Controversial Writer.......... 1733..1808
Hill, Robert. Self-taught Genius.................... 1699..1777
Hill, Rev. Rowland. Life by Sidney, 1834; Sherman, 1851 1744..1833
Hill, Rowland, Viscount. Commander-in-Chief......... 1772..1842
Hill, Thomas Ford. Antiquary and Philologist......... — ..1795
Hill, William, D. D. American Divine................. 1769..1852
Hillel. *Elder. Ha Zaken* and *Pollio*. Jewish Rabbi ...B.C.112?A.D.8?
Hillel. *Younger. Nasi.* Jewish Rabbi .... fl 300?
Hillhouse, James Abraham. Amer. Poet & Miscell.Writer 1789..1841
Hilliard, Nicholas. Goldsmith and Portrait Painter..... 1547..1619
Hilton, John. Musical Composer.................... — ..1655?
Hilton, Walter. Monk of Sheen. (*Ladder of Perfection*) fl. 15th c.
Hilton, William, R. A. Painter...................... 1786..1839
Himilco. Carthaginian General................;..... fl. B.C.408
Himilco. Carthaginian Navigator...................fl. 5th c. B.C.
Himmel, Frederick Henry. German Composer......... 1765..1814
Hinchcliffe, John. Bishop of Peterborough .... 1731..1794
Hinckeldey, Charles Louis Frederick von. Prussian
    Minister of Police............................... 1803..1856
Hinckley, John, D. D. Divine...................... 1617..1695
Hincks, Rev. T. D. Orientalist.................... — ..1857
Hincmar. Archbishop of Rheims. Life by S. C. Prichard 806?. 882
Hipparchus, son of Pisistratus, of Athens .... — B.C.514
Hipparchus. Greek Astronomer ....fl. (160–145) B.C.
Hippesley, Sir John Coxe, M. P. Political Writer ...... — ..1825
Hippocrates. Greek Physician. *Father of Medicine*...460.357 B.C.
Hippolytus, St. Ecclesiastical Writer................. — .. 230
Hipponax. Greek Lyric Poet........................ fl. 6th c. B.C.
Hire, Gabriel Philip de la. Painter................... 1677..1719
Hire, Lawrence de la. French Painter................ 1606..1656
Hire, Philip de la. Mathematician .... 1640..1718
Hitchcock, Edw., D. D., LL. D. Amer. Geologist & Writer 1793..1864
Hitchcock, Peter. American Jurist.................. 1781..1853
Hoadly, Benjamin. Bishop of Winchester (1734–61).... 1676..1761
Hoadly, Benj., M. D., son. Medical and Dramatic Writer 1706..1757
Hoadly, Rev. John, LL. D., brother. Dramatist........ 1711..1776
Hoare, Prince, F. S. A. Dramatic Writer............. 1755..1834
Hoare, Sir Richard Colt. Topographer. (*Classical Tour*) 1758..1838
Hoare, William, R. A. Historical and Portrait Painter .. 1707..1792
Hobart, John Henry, D. D. American Divine........... 1776..1830
Hobbema, or Hobbima, Minderhout. Painter.......... 1611?. —
Hobbes, Thomas, of Malmesbury. Philosopher. (*Levi-
    athan.*) Life by self; Richard Blackburne, 1681 ..... 1588..1679
Hobhouse, Sir Benjamin. Statesman .... 1757..1831
Hoblyn, Robert, M. P. Book Collector.............. 1710?.1756
Hobson, Thomas. Cambr. Carrier; celebrated by Milton 1544?.1631
Hoccleve, or Occleve, Thomas. Poet ....1370?.1454?
Hoche, Lazarus. French General. Life by Rousselin, 1798 1768..1797
Hochstetter, Andrew.Adam. Prot. Divine of Tübingen 1688..1717

BORN. DIED.

Hodges, Nathaniel, M. D.   Writer on the London Plague 1630?.1684
Hodges, William, R. A.   Painter...................... 1744..1797
Hodgson, Francis.   Provost of Eton.   Scholar and Poet. 1780..1752
Hodgson, Rev. John.   (*History of Northumberland*)...... — ..1845
Hodgson, Robt., D. D.   Dean of Carlisle. (*Life of Porteus*) — ..1844
Hodson, William Stephens Raikes.   English Soldier.... 1821..1858
Hody, Humphrey. (*History of English Convocations*).... 1659..1706
Hoe, Matthias de Hoenegg.   German Controversial Divine 1580..1645
Hoeck, or Houk, John van, of Antwerp.   Painter....... 1600..1650
Hoeck, or Houk, Robert van, of Antwerp.   Painter..... 1609..1668
Höelty, Louis Henry Christopher.   German Poet........ 1748..1776
Hoeltzlinus, Jeremiah.   German Philologist at Leyden.. — ..1641
Hoerberg, Peter.   Swedish Painter.   Life by self, 1817.. 1746..1819
Hoeschelius, David.   German Scholar and Coll. of MSS. 1556..1617
Hoet, Gerard.   Dutch Painter........................ 1648..1733
Hofer, Andrew.   Tyrolese Patriot.   L. by C. H. Hall, 1826 1767..1810
Hoffman, David.   Amer. Lawyer & Miscellaneous Writer 1784..1854
Hoffman, Francis Benedict.   Fr. Dramatic Poet, Critic.. 1760 .1828
Hoffman, John James, of Basle. (*Lexicon Universale*) . 1635..1706
Hoffmann, Christian Godfrey.   German Jurist......... 1692..1735
Hoffmann, Christopher Louis.   German Medical Writer. 1721..1807
Hoffmann, Ernest Theod. Wm.   Writer. (*Devil's Elixir*) 1776..1822
Hoffmann, Frederick, of Halle. (*Medicina Consultatoria*) 1660..1742
Hoffmann, Gaspar.   Medical Writer................... 1572..1648
Hoffmann, John Maurice.   Medical Writer............. 1653..1727
Hoffmann, Maurice.   Anatomist and Botanist; discoverer
    of Pancreatic Duct. (*Floræ Altdorffinæ*)............ 1622..1698
Hoffmannsegg, John Centurius, Count.   Ger. Botanist 1766..1849
Hoffmanowa, Clementina.   Polish Authoress.......... 1798..1845
Hofland, Mrs. Barbara.   Writer.   Life by Ramsay, 1849 1770..1844
Hofland, Thomas Christopher.   Landscape Painter..... 1777..1843
Hofmann, Daniel.   German Divine.................... 1538..1621
Hogan, John.   Irish Sculptor....................... 1800?.1858
Hogarth, William.   Painter.   Life by Nichols.......... 1697..1764
Hogg, James. *The Ettrick Shepherd.* Poet............ 1772..1835
Hohenlohe, Alex. Leopold, Prince of.   Medical Empiric. 1794..1849
Hohenlohe - Ingelfingen, Frederick Louis, Prince of.
    Prussian General.............................. 1746..1817
Hohenlohe-Waldenburg-Schillingsfurst, Alex. Leo-
    pold Francis Emmerich, Prince of.   Hungarian Prelate 1793..1849
Hoijer, Benjamin Charles Henry.   Swedish Philosopher 1767..1812
Holbach, Paul Thierry, Baron von.   Natural Philosopher 1723..1789
Holbein, Hans, or John.   Painter.   Life by C. Patinus.. 1498?.1543
Holbein, Sigismond.   Painter........................ —aft.1540
Holberg, Louis, Baron.   Danish Historian. (*Peder-Paars*) 1684..1754
Holcroft, Fanny.   Novelist.......................... — ..1844
Holcroft, Thomas.   Dramatic and Miscellaneous Writer
    and Translator.   Life by self and Hazlitt, 1816...... 1745..1809
Holden, Henry.   Roman Cath. Divine. (*Notes on N. T.*) 1596..1665?
Holder, William, D. D.   Mathematician and Philosopher. 1614..1697
Holdsworth, Edward.   Writer. (*Muscipula*).......... 1688..1746
Hole, Matthew, D. D.   Rector of Exeter College, Oxford.
    (*On the Liturgy*)................................... 1640?.1730
Hole, Rev. Richard, of Farringdon.   Poet. Writer. (*Arthur*) 1750?.1803

BORN. DIED.

Hole, William. Engraver.......................... fl. 1613
Holinshed, or Holingshed, Raphael. Historian........ — ..1580?
Holkar, Jeswunt Rao. Mahratta Chief................. — ..1811
Holkar, Mulhar Rao. Mahratta Chief................. — ..1766
Holl, Elias. German Architect....................... 1573..1636
Holl, Francis X. Ger. Jes. (*Statistica Ecclesiæ Germaniæ*) 1720..1784
Holland, Edwin Clifford. American Poet and Essayist.. 1793..1824
Holland, Elizabeth Vassall, Lady. Life by Sydney Smith 1770..1845
Holland, Henry. Architect.......................... 1746?.1806
Holland, Henry Fox, First Lord. Statesman.......... 1705..1774
Holland, Henry Richard Vassall Fox, Lord. (*Memoirs of Whig Party*)..................................... 1773..1840
Holland, Hugh. Poet............................... fl. 1604
Holland, Sir Nathaniel Dance. Painter.............. 1734..1811
Holland, Philemon. Translator...................... 1551..1636
Hollar, Wenzel. Engraver. Life by Geo. Vertue, 1745. 1607..1677
Hollerius, or Houllier, James. French Medical Writer.. — ..1562
Holles, Denzil, Lord. Statesman.................... 1597..1680
Holley, Horace, LL. D. American Divine and Educator. Life by his widow.................................. 1781..1827
Hollis, Thomas. Benefactor of Harvard College....... 1659..1731
Hollis, Thos. Philanthropist. Memoirs, 2 vols. 4to, 1780 1720..1774
Hollis, Thos. Brand. L. by Blackburne, 1780; Disney, 1808 — ..1804
Hollman, Samuel Christian, of Göttingen. Philosopher 1696..1787
Holman, Lieutenant James. *The Blind Traveler*....... 1787..1857
Holman, Joseph George. Dramatic Writer............ 1764..1817
Holmes, Abiel, D. D., LL. D. Amer. Divine and Historian 1768..1837
Holmes, George. Antiquary......................... 1662..1749
Holmes, Dr. Nathaniel. Ejected Nonconformist; Hebraist — ..1678
Holmes, Robert. Dean of Winchester. Divine and Poet 1749..1805
Holroyd, John Baker, Lord Sheffield. Political Writer, Soldier, Statesman............................... 1741..1821
Holstein, Luke. Scholar & Writer. L. by Wilkins, 1723 1596..1661
Holt, Francis Ludlow, Q. C. Law Writer and Journalist — ..1844
Holt, Sir John. Ld. Chief Justice. Life, Lond. 1764, 8vo 1642..1709
Holwell, John Zephaniah. Governor of Bengal........ 1711..1798
Holyday, Rev. Barten. Divine. Translator of Juvenal 1593..1661
Holyoake, Francis. (*Etymological Dict. of Latin Words*) 1567?.1653
Holyoke, Edward Augustus. American Physician, Meteorologist, and Natural Philosopher.................. 1728..1829
Holywood, John. *De Sacrobosco*. Mathematician..... — ..1256
Holzer, John Evangelist. German Fresco Painter...... 1709..1740
Homberg, William. Physician and Chemist........... 1652..1715
Home, David. Scottish Divine. (*Apologia Basilica*)... ti. James I.
Home, Sir Everard. Surgeon........................ 1756..1832
Home, Henry, Lord Kames. Scottish Judge. (*Elements of Criticism.*) Life by Lord Woodhouselee, 1807 .... 1696..1782
Home, Rev. John. (*Douglas.*) Life by Mackenzie, 1822 1724..1808
Homer. Greek Epic Poet............................ fl. B.C. 962–927
Homer, Rev. Henry. Classical Scholar and Editor..... 1752..1791
Homilius, Godfrey Aug., of Dresden. Organist and Comp. 1714..1785
Hommel, Charles Ferdinand. Civilian, of Leipsic...... 1722..1781
Homond, Charles Francis l'. French Instructor........ 1727..1794
Hompesch, Ferd. de. Last Grand Master of Kts. of Malta 1744..1803

BORN. DIED.

Hondekoeter, Giles, of Utrecht. Landscape Painter... 1583..1626?
Hondekoeter, Gysbrecht, son. Bird Painter .... 1613..1653
Hondekoeter, Melchior, son. Painter.................. 1636..1695
Hondius, or Hondt, Abraham. Dutch Painter .... 1638..1691
Hondius, Josse. Flemish Engraver and Letter Founder 1546..1611
Hone, George Paul. Lawyer and Writer at Coburg .... 1662..1747
Hone, Nathaniel. Painter in Enamel .... — ..1784
Hone, William. Writer. (*Every-Day Book*)............ 1779..1842
Honestis, Petrus de. *Peter Damiani.* Cardinal........ 988?.1072
Honorius, Flavius. Roman Emperor (395–423) .... 384.. 423
Honorius. Archbishop of Canterbury (627–53)........· — .. 653
Honorius I. Pope (626–38)............................ — .. 638
Honorius II. (1124–30.) *Lambert.*.....:............ — ..1130
Honorius III. (1216–27.) *Cencius Sabelli* .... — ..1227
Honorius IV. (1285–87.) *James Sabelli*.............. — ..1287
Hontheim, John Nich. de, of Trèves. (*History of Trèves*) 1701..1790
Honthorst, Gerard. *Dalle Notti.* Dutch Painter....... 1592..1660
Honthorst, William, brother. Painter .... 1604..1683
Hood, Alex., Adm., Lord Bridport, br. of Viscount Hood — ..1814
Hood, Robin. Outlaw......................... Rd. I. or Hen. III.?
Hood, Sir Samuel. Vice-Admiral. Cousin of Visct. Hood — ..1814
Hood, Samuel, Viscount. Admiral..................... 1724..1816
Hood, Thomas. Mathematician. Inventor of *Hood's Staff* fl. 1690
Hood, Thomas. Poet, Humorist, and Miscellaneous Writer 1798..1845
Hooft, Peter Corneliszoon. Dutch Poet and Historian... 1581..1647
Hooge, Peter van. Dutch Painter..................... 1643?.1708
Hoogeveen, Henry. Dutch Philologist................. 1712..1791
Hoogstraten, David van. Dutch Poet and Critic ...... 1658..1724
Hoogstraten, James van. Inquisitor; Opponent of Luther — ..1527
Hoogstraten, Samuel van. Painter...................... 1627..1678
Hoogstraten, Theodore, or Dirk van. Paint. of Antwerp 1596..1640
Hoogue, Romain de. Dutch Engraver and Designer..... 1638?.1725
Hoogvliet, Arnold. Dutch Poet. (*Abraham the Patriarch*) 1687..1763
Hook, James. Musical Composer .... 1746..1827
Hook, Dr. James, son. Dean of Worc. Polemical Writ. 1771..1828
Hook, Theodore Edward. Journalist, Novelist, and Dramatic Writer. Life by Barham, 1848 .... 1788..1841
Hooke, Nathaniel. (*Roman History*) .... 1690?.1763
Hooke, Robt., M.D. Math. (*Micrographia.*) L. by Waller 1635..1702
Hooker, John, of Exeter. Antiquary .... 1524?.1601
Hooker, Richard, son. (*Eccles. Polity.*) L. by Walton, 1665 1553?.1600
Hooker, Rev. Thos. One of the Founders of Conn. Colony — ..1647
Hooker, Sir William Jackson. Botanist............... 1785..1865
Hoole, Charles, of Rotheram. Translator of Terence... 1610..1666
Hoole, John. Dram. Poet, Transl. of Tasso and Ariosto 1727..1803
Hooper, Edmund. Composer of Anthems.............. — ..1621
Hooper, George. Bishop of Bath and Wells........... 1640..1727
Hooper, John. Bishop of Gloucester, Martyr.......... 1495..1555
Hooper, William. American Patriot .... 1742..1790
Hoornbeck, John. Dutch Writer..................... 1617..1666
Hoorne, John van. Anatomist and Physician.......... 1621..1670
Hoost, Peter Cornelius van. (*Hist. of the Low Countries*) 1581..1647
Hope, Rev. Frederick William. Naturalist............. 1797?.1862
Hope, Admiral Sir Henry, K. C. B....................... 1787..1863

BORN. DIED.

Hope, John, M. D. Naturalist. L. by Andr. Duncan, 1786 1725..1786
Hope, Sir Thomas. Scottish Lawyer................. — ..1646
Hope, Thomas. Writer on Art. (*Anastasius*)......... 1770?.1831
Hope, Thomas Charles. Scottish Chemist............ 1766..1844
Hope, Wm. Williams. Eccentric Millionnaire.......... — ..1854
Hôpital, Michael de l'. Chancellor of France. Life by
 Bernardi; Villemain............................... 1505..1573
Hôpital, Wm. Francis Anthony de l'. Fr. Mathematician 1661..1704
Hopkins, Charles. Dramatic Poet, Translator of Ovid.. 1664..1699
Hopkins, Edward. Governor of Connecticut.......... — ..1657
Hopkins, Esek. American Naval Officer.............. 1718..1802
Hopkins, Ezekiel. Bishop of Londonderry............ 1633..1690
Hopkins, John. Poet. (*Amasia*)................... 1675.aft.1700
Hopkins, Lemuel. Amer. Physician and Political Writer 1750..1801
Hopkins, Samuel, D. D. American Divine. Author of
 Hopkinsianism................................... 1721..1803
Hopkins, Stephen. American Statesman............. 1707..1785
Hopkins, Wm., D. D. Antiquary. L. by Dr. Hickes, 1708 1647..1700
Hopkins, Rev. Wm. Arian. (*Appeal to Common Sense*) 1706..1786
Hopkinson, Francis. American Political Writer....... 1738..1791
Hopkinson, Joseph. American Jurist and Poet........ 1770..1842
Hopper, Thomas. Architect......................... 1775?.1856
Hoppner, John, R. A. Painter and Writer .... 1759..1810
Hopton, Arthur. Mathematician..................... 1589?.1614
Hopton, Susanna. Religious Writer. (*Hexameron*).... 1627..1709
Horace. Latin Poet................................ 65..8 B.C.
Horman, William, of Eton College. Divine and Botanist 1470?.1535
Hormayr, Joseph von, Baron. Tyrolese Hist. and Patriot 1781..1848
Hormisdas. Pope (514–23) .... — .. 523
Horn, Philip Montmorency, Ct. of. Dutch Statesm.; beh. 1522..1568
Hornblower, Joseph C., LL. D. American Jurist....... 1777..1864
Horne, Charles Edward. Musical Composer.......... 1786..1849
Horne, George. *Hornius*. Hist. and Geog. at Leyden 1620..1670
Horne, George. Bishop of Norwich. (*On the Psalms*.)
 Life by Jones of Nayland, 1795.....:.............. 1730..1792
Horne, Rev.Thos. Hartwell. (*Introduction.*) L. by Cheyne 1780..1862
Horne Tooke, John. *See* Tooke .... 1736..1812
Horneck, Dr. Anth. Eng. Divine. L. by Bp. Kidder, 1698 1641..1696
Hornemann, Frederick Conrad. African Traveler ... 1772.aft.1800
Horner, Francis. Writer. L. by Leonard Horner, 1843 1778..1817
Horner, Leonard. Geological Writer.................. 1785?.1864
Horrebow, Christian. Writer on Parallax....:........ — ..1776
Horrebow, Peter. Danish Astronomer............... 1679..1764
Horrocks, or Horrox, Jeremiah. Astronomer. (*Venus in
 Sole Visa*)...................................... 1619?.1641
Horsfield, Rev. Thos. Walker, F. S. A. (*History of Sussex*) — ..1837
Horsley, John. Antiquary. (*Britannia Romana*)...... 1685..1732
Horsley, Samuel. Bishop of St. Asaph..:............ 1733..1806
Horstius, Gregory. Physician...................... 1578..1636
Horstius, James. German Physician and Botanist ..... 1537..1600
Horte, Josiah. Archbishop of Tuam. (*Sermons*).... — ..1751
Hortense. Queen of Holland. Life by Lascelles Wraxall 1783..1837
Hortensius, Lambert. Dutch Philol., Poet, Historian.. 1501..1575?
Hortensius, Martin. Dutch Astronomer.............. 1605..1639

14

BORN. DIED.

Hortensius, Quintus. Roman Advocate and Orator.... 114.50 B.C.
Horvát, Stephen. Hungarian Writer.................. 1784..1846
Hosack, David. American Physician and Author...... 1769..1835
Hosea. Hebrew Prophet............................. 8th c. B.C.
Hoshea. Last King of Israel (B. C. 730–721)........ — aft. B.C. 721
Hosius, Stanislaus. Polish Cardinal .... 1504..1579
Hoskins, John. Lawyer and Poet .... 1566..1638
Hoskins, John. Portrait Painter................... — ..1664
Hospinian, Rodolph. Swiss Protestant Divine....... 1547..1626
Hospital. See Hôpital.
Hossch, Sidronius. Flemish Jesuit; Latin Poet .... 1596..1653
Host, Jens Kragh. Danish Historian................ 1772..1844
Hoste, John l'. Fr. Mathem. (De la Sphère Artificielle) — ..1631
Hoste, Paul l'. Fr. Mathem. (L'Art des Armées Navales) 1652..1700
Hostus, Matthew. German Antiquary................. 1509..1587
Hothom, Walter. Poet. (Biblia Versificata)........... fl. 15th c.
Hotman, or Hotomanus, Francis. See Hottoman....... 1524..1590
Hotspur. See Henry Percy.......................... — ..1403
Hottinger, or Hottinguer, John Conrad. Banker....... 1764..1841
Hottinger, or Hottinguer, John Henry. Swiss Protestant
    Divine and Orientalist. Life by Heidegger, 1667.... 1620..1667
Hottinger, or Hottinguer, John James, son. (Ecclesiasti-
    cal History of Switzerland)....................... 1652..1735
Hottoman, Francis. French Lawyer. (Anti-Tribonianus) 1524..1590
Houard de la Mothe, Anthony. Legal Antiquary..... 1725..1803
Houbigant, Charles Francis. French Theologian. Trans-
    lator of the Bible. Life by Adry, 1806............. 1686..1783
Houbraken, Arnold. Dutch Pa. (Lives of Dutch Painters) 1660..1719
Houbraken, Jacob, son. Engraver.................... 1698..1780
Houchard, John Nicholas. French Republican General. 1740..1793
Houdon, John Anthony. French Sculptor............. 1741..1828
Houdry, Vincent. French Jesuit, Preacher, and Writer.. 1631..1729
Houel, John Peter Louis Lawrence. Fr. Paint. & Engrav. 1735..1813
Hough, John. President of Magdalen College and Bishop
    of Worcester. Life by J. E. Wilmot, 1812; Wm. Russell 1651..1743
Houghton, Major. African Explorer................ 1750?.aft.1793
Houlières, Antoinette du Ligier de la Garde des. French
    Poetess .... 1634?.1694
Houllier, James. Hollerius. French Medical Writer.... — ..1562
Houseman, Cornelius, of Mechlin. Painter............ 1643..1727
Houseman, James. Painter in England.............. 1656..1696
Houston, Sam. Amer. General; Gov. and Pres. of Texas 1793..1862
Houston, William. Physician and Botanist........... 1695?.1733
Houteville, Claude Francis. (Truth of the Christ. Religion) 1686..1742
Hoveden, Roger de. Historian .... —aft.1201
How, William. Physician and Botanist.............. 1619..1656
Howard, Catherine. Queen of Henry VIII. .... 1520?.1542
Howard, Charles, created Earl of Nottingham. Command-
    er against the Armada........................... 1536..1624
Howard, Charles, Earl of Carlisle. Diplomatist........ 1629..1686
Howard, Sir Edward. Lord High Admiral .... — ..1513
Howard, Edward. Lieutenant R. N. Naval Novelist ... — ..1841
Howard, Frances, Countess of Essex, afterwards Countess
    of Somerset...................................... 1594..1632

BORN. DIED.

Howard, George Edmund. Polit. Writer and Dramatist 1725?.1786
Howard, Henry, Earl of Surrey. Poet; beh. Life by Nott 1515?.1547
Howard, Henry, Earl of Northampton. Scholar & Writer 1539?.1614
Howard, Henry, R. A. Painter .... 1769..1847
Howard, John. Philanthropist. Life by John Aikin,
  1792; J. B. Brown, 1818; Thomas Taylor, 1836; W. H.
  Dixon, 1848; J. Field, 1850........................ 1726?.1790
Howard, Luke. Meteorologist........................ 1771?.1864
Howard, Philip, Earl of Arundel. Life by Duke of Nor-
  folk, 1857.. 1557..1595
Howard, Philip, Thomas. Cardinal.................... — ..1694
Howard, Sir Robert. Writer. (Reigns of Edward II. and
  Richard II.; History of Religion)................. 1626..1698
Howard, Samuel. Musical Composer................... — ..1783?
Howard, Thomas, Earl of Surrey and Third Duke of Nor-
  folk. Naval and Military Commander............... 1473..1554
Howard, Thos., E. Arund. Coll. of the Arundelian Marbles — ..1646
Howe, Charles. Religious Writer. (Devout Meditations) 1661..1745
Howe, John. Chaplain to Cromwell. Life by Calamy;
  J. Hunt, 1823; H. Rogers, 1836 .... 1630..1705
Howe, Richard, Fourth Viscount. First Earl. Admiral.
  Life by George Mason, 1803; Sir J. Barrow, 1838 .... 1725..1799
Howe, Sir William, brother. General in America...... — ..1814
Howell, James. Miscel. Writer. (Epistolæ Howellianæ). 1594?.1666
Howell, Dr. William. Hist. Writer. (History of the World) 1630?.1683
Howells, Rev. William, of Long Acre Chapel. Life by
  Bowdler, 1836 .... 1778..1832
Howley, William. Archbishop of Canterbury (1828–48). 1765..1848
Hoyle, Edmund. English Writer on Games........... 1672..1769
Hoyt, Gen. Epaphras. Amer. Historical & Antiq. Writer 1765..1850
Hozier, Peter d'. Historian and Genealogist........... 1592..1660
Huarte, John. Spanish Writer. (Trial of Wits) .... 1530?.1600?
Huarte, Vincent Garcia de la. See Huerta............. 1729..1797
Hubald, of St. Amand. Poet and Musical Writer....... 840.. 930.
Hubbard, William. American Divine and Historian ... 1621..1704
Huber, Francis. Naturalist. (Observations on Bees).... 1750..1830
Huber, John. Genevese Painter and Profile Cutter...... 1722..1790
Huber, John James. Anat. & Bot. (De Medullâ Spinali) 1707..1778
Huber, John Rudolph, of Basle. Painter.............. 1668..1748
Huber, Mary. Deistical Writer...................... 1695..1753
Huber, Michael. French Writer and Translator........ 1727..1804
Huber, Peter. Swiss Naturalist...................... 1777..1840
Huber, Theresa. German Novelist.................... 1764..1829
Huber, Ulric, of Friesland. (De Jure Civitatis)........ 1636..1694
Hubert, Matthew. French Preacher.................. 1640..1717
Huc, Évariste Régis. French Missionary and Traveler .. 1813..1860
Huchtenburg, John van. Dutch Battle Painter........ 1646..1733
Hudde, John, of Amsterdam. Statesman and Mathem... 1633..1704
Huddleston, Robert. Antiquary..................... 1776..1826
Hudson, Captain Henry. Discoverer of Hudson's Bay .. — ..1611
Hudson, Jeffrey. Dwarf at the Court of Charles I...... —aft.1682
Hudson, John, D. D., of St. Mary Hall. Classical Editor 1662..1719
Hudson, Thomas. Portrait Painter .... 1701..1779
Hudson, William. Botanist. (Flora Anglica) .... 1730..1793

BORN. DIED.

Huebner, John, of Hamburg. Historical Writer........ 1668..1731
Huerta, Vincent Garcia de la. Spanish Poet and Critic.. 1729..1797
Huet, Peter Daniel. Bishop of Avranches. Editor of
　Delphin Classics.· (*Demonstratio Evangelica.*) Life by
　self, translated by Aikin, 1810 .... 1630..1721
Huett, Thomas. Translator of Welsh Bible .... — ..1591
Hufeland, Christopher William. German Physician.
　(*The Art of Prolonging Life*) .... 1762..1836
Hüfnagel, or Hüfnäghel, George. Flemish Painter ..... 1545..1600
Hug, John Leonard. German Biblical Scholar and Writer 1765..1846
Huger, Francis Kinlock. American Military Officer .... 1764..1855
Huger, Isaac. American Revolutionary General........ 1725?.1782
Hugh the Great, Duke of France .... — .. 956
Hugh Capet, King of France (987–96), son .... 939?. 996
Hugh de Cluni. Abbot of Cluni........................ 1024..1109
Hugh de Flavigny. Abbot. (*Chronicon Verdunense*) 1065.aft.1115
Hugh de Fleury. Chronicler. (*De la Puissance Royale*) — ..1130?
Hugh de St. Cher. Cardinal. Biblical Commentator .. — ..1263
Hugh de St. Victor. Divine.......................... 1098..1141?
Hughes, Jabez. Scholar and Classical Translator .... 1685..1731
Hughes, John. Poet and Essayist. (*Siege of Damascus*) 1677..1720
Hughes, John, D. D. American Roman Catholic Prelate 1797..1864
Hugo, Chas. Louis. Fr. Writ. (*Annales Premonstratensium*) 1667..1739
Hugo, Gustavus. Writer on Jurisprudence............. 1764..1844
Hugo, Herman. Jesuit. Latin Poet................... 1588..1629
Hugtenburgh, John van. Dutch Painter.............. 1646..1733
Huldric, John James. Theologian of Zurich............ 1683..1731
Hulin, or Hullin, Peter Augustine, Count. Fr. General.. 1758..1841
Hull, Isaac. American Naval Officer .... 1775..1843
Hull, Thos. Dram. Writer, Actor. (*Richard Plantagenet*) 1728..1808
Hull, William. American Revolutionary Officer........ 1753..1825
Hulse, Rev. John, B. A. (1728). Founder of Hulsean Lect. — ..1777?
Hulse, Rev. John. Founder of Hulsean Prize........... — ..1800
Hulsemann, John. Lutheran Theologian at Leipsic..... 1602..1661
Hulsius, Anthony. Theol. at Leyden. (*Theol. Judaica*) 1615..1685
Hulsius, Henry. Theol. at Donisburg. (*Summa Theologiæ*) 1624..1723
Hulst, Peter van der. Dutch Painter .... 1652..1708
Humayun. Mogul Emperor. Life trans. by Stewart, 1832 1508..1556
Humbert, Cardinal. Theologian...................... — ..1063?
Humbert, Joseph Amable. French Revolutionary General 1767..1823
Humboldt, Charles William von. Statesman and Philolo-
　gist. Life by Klencke and Schlesier................ 1767..1835
Humboldt, Frederick Henry Alexander von. Naturalist
　and Traveler. (*Kosmos*) .... 1769..1859
Hume, David. Philosopher and Hist. Life by self, 1777,
　ed. by Adam Smith, 1789; Robert Pratt, 1777; David
　Dalrymple, 1787; T. E. Ritchie, 1807; J. H. Burton, 1846 1711..1776
Hume, James Deacon. Financier. L by C. Badham, 1859 1774..1842
Hume, Joseph, M. P. Politician .... 1777..1855
Hume, Sir Patrick. Scottish Commentator on Milton... fl. 1695
Hummel, John Nepomuk. Musical Composer.......... 1778..1837
Humphrey, Heman, D. D. American Divine and Writer 1779..1859
Humphrey, Dr. Lawrence. Divine and Biographer..... 1527?.1590
Humphrey, Pelham. Musical Composer............... 1647..1674

BORN. DIED.

Humphreys, David.   American Statesman............ 1753..1818
Humphreys, Jas. Lawyer. (*Eng. Law of Real Property*) — ..1830
Humphries, John. Musical Composer................ — ..1730?
Humphry, Ozias, R. A. Miniature Painter........... 1743..1810
Hunauld, Francis Joseph. Anatomist and Physician.... 1701..1742
Hunneric. King of the Vandals in Africa (477–84)..... — .. 484
Hunniades, John Corvinus. Hungarian General....... 1400?.1456
Hunnis, William. Poetical Writer................... fl. ti. Eliz.
Hunnius, Giles. Lutheran Writer against Calvinists ... 1550..1603
Hunt, Mrs. Arabella. Singer........................ — ..1705
Hunt, Freeman. American Journalist and Author...... 1804..1858
Hunt, Henry, M. P. Politician...................... 1773..1835
Hunt, Jas. Henry Leigh. Poet & Essayist. (*Autobiog.* 1850) 1784..1859
Hunt, Jeremiah, D. D. Dissenting Divine............. 1678..1744
Hunt, Thomas. Hebrew Prof. at Oxford. (*On Proverbs*) 1696..1774
Hunt, William Henry. Painter in Water Colors........ 1790..1864
Hunter, Mrs. Anne Home. Poetess .... 1741..1821
Hunter, Christopher, of Durham. Phys. and Antiquary. 1675..1757
Hunter, Henry. Scottish Preacher and Biographer..... 1741..1802
Hunter, Rev. Humphrey. American Patriot........... 1755..1827
Hunter, John. Surgeon & Comparative Anatomist. L. by
   Everard Home; Jesse Foot, 1794; Joseph Adams, 1816 1728..1793
Hunter, John. Admiral.............................. 1738..1821
Hunter, John, LL. D., of St. Andrew's. Classical Editor. 1747..1837
Hunter, Rev. Joseph, F. S. A.   Topographer and Literary
   Antiquary. (*Hallamshire; Illustrations of Shakespeare*) 1783..1861
Hunter, Robert. Gov. of Jamaica. (*Letter on Enthusiasm*) — ..1734
Hunter, William, M.D. Physician & Anatomist. Founder
   of Hunterian Museum. Life by S. F. Simmons, 1783. 1718..1783
Hunter, William. Scottish Surgeon and Orientalist .... — ..1815
Huntingdon, Henry of. Historian. Life by Smith..... —aft.1154
Huntingdon, Selina, Countess of. Life by a member of
   · the Houses of Shirley and Hastings, 1839........... 1707..1791
Huntingdon, William. *S. S.* (*i. e.*, Sinner Saved). Meth-
   odist Preacher.................................. 1744..1813
Huntingford, Geo. Isaac. Bp. of Hereford. Class. Scholar 1748..1832
Huntington, Robt. Bp. Raphoe. L. by Dr. T. Smith, 1704 1636..1701
Huntington, Samuel. American Jurist and Patriot.... 1732..1796
Huntsman, Benjamin, of Sheffield. Inventor of Cast Steel 1704..1776
Hunyady. *See* Hunniades......................... 1400?.1456
Huppazoli, Francis. Italian Centenarian .... 1587..1702
Hurd, Richard. Bishop of Worcester. Life by self; Kilvert 1720..1808
Hurdis, James, D.D. Poet .... 1763..1801
Huré, Charles. French Jansenist. (*Dict. of the Bible*).. 1639..1717
Husbands, Herman. American Patriot .... — ..1794?
Huskisson, William. Statesman. Life by Wright..... 1770..1830
Huss, John. Bohemian Reformer. Life by Cochlæus,
   1547; Herzovinus, 1618; Theobald, 1626: Werner, 1671;
   Esberg, 1699; Seyfried, 1711; Gilpin, 1765; Zitte, 1786;
   Tischer, 1798; Wendt, 1845; Lommel, 1847; A. Nean-
   der, 1849... 1376?.1415
Hussey, Giles. Painter .... 1710..1788
Husson, Aristides. French Sculptor................. 1803?.1864
Hutcheson, Francis, LL. D. Metaphysician........... 1694..1747

BORN. DIED.

Hutchins, John. Topog. Historian. (*History of Dorset*) 1698..1773
Hutchins, Thomas. American Geographer .... 1730?.1789
Hutchinson, Anne. Religious Enthusiast in America... — ..1643
Hutchinson, John, Colonel. Life by Lucy Hutchinson.. 1617..1664
Hutchinson, John. Philos. Author of Hutchinsonianism 1674..1737
Hutchinson, John Hely. Irish Lawyer and Statesman.. 1715..1794
Hutchinson, John Hely, Earl of Donoughmore. General 1757..1832
Hutchinson, Mrs. Lucy Apsley, w. of Col. John. L. by self 1620.. —
Hutchinson, Roger, of Eton .... 16th c.
Hutchinson, Thomas. Chief Just. Gov. of Massachusetts 1711..1730
Hutten, Ulric von. Soldier, Poet, Writer. L. by Meiners 1488..1523
Hutter, Elias, of Nuremberg. Polyglottist........... 1553.aft.1602
Hutter, Leonard, brother. Protestant Controversialist... 1563..1616
Hutton, Charles, LL. D. (*Mathematical Course*) .... 1737..1823
Hutton, James. Geologist. (*Plutonian Theory*)........ 1726..1797
Hutton, Matthew. Bishop of Durham (1489–95), Arch-
    bishop of York (1595–1606)...................... 1529..1606
Hutton, Matthew. Bishop of Bangor (1743–47), Arch-
    bishop of York (1747–57), Archbishop of Canterbury — ..1758
Hutton, Wm., of Birmingham. Topog. Hist. L. by self 1723..1815
Huxham, John, M. D., of Plymouth. Medical Writer... — ..1768
Huyghens, Christian. Mathematician and Astronomer.. 1629..1695
Huyghens, Constantine. Dutch Statesman and Latin
    Poet. (*Momenta Desultoria*)................... 1596..1687
Huyghens, Gomarus. Dutch Theologian............. 1631..1702
Huysum, Jacob van. Painter...................... 1680..1740
Huysum, John van. Painter of Flowers and Fruit ..... 1682..1749
Huysum, Justus van. *The Old.* Dutch Painter........ 1659..1716
Huysum, Justus van. *The Young.* Dutch Painter..... 1684..1706
Hyatt, John. Wesleyan Preacher. Life by Dr. Morison 1767..1826
Hyde, Edward, First Earl of Clarendon. Lord Chancellor.
    (*History of Rebellion.*) Life by self; H. T. Lister, 1838 1608..1674
Hyde, Henry, Second Earl of Clarendon, son. Lord Lieu-
    tenant of Ireland. (*History of the Irish Rebellion*) ... 1638..1709
Hyde, Lawrence, K. G., First Earl of Rochester, younger
    brother. Statesman. Lord Lieutenant............. — ..1711
Hyde, Sir Nicholas. Lord Chief Justice .... 1572?.1631
Hyde, Thos., D. D. Orient. (*Religionis Persarum Historia*) 1636..1703
Hyde de Neuville, John William, Baron. Fr. Politician 1776..1857
Hyder Ali. Sultan of Mysore. Life by Meer Hussein
    Ali Khan, translated by Colonel Miles, 1842 .... 1717..1782
Hyginus, Caius Julius. Roman Writer. (*Poeticon Astro-
    nomicon*).................................fl. ti. Augustus
Hyginus. Bishop of Rome (138–42)................. — .. 142
Hyndford, John Carmichael, Third Earl of. Scot. Diplom. 1701..1767
Hypatia, of Alexandria. Philosopher............... — .. 415
Hyperides. Athenian Orator...................... 396?.322 B.C.
Hyperius, Gerard Andrew, of Ypres. Theologian...... 1511..1564
Hyrcanus I., John. High Priest and Prince of the Jews — B.C.106
Hyrcanus II. High Priest and King of the Jews...... 110?.30 B.C.
Hywell ap Morgan Mawr. Prince of Glamorgan..... 983..1043
Hywell ap Owain Gwynedd. Pr. of N. Wales. Poet — ..1171

I.

BORN. DIED.

Ibarra, Joachim. Spanish Printer .... 1725..1785
Ibbetson, Mrs. Agnes. Philosophical Writer........... 1757..1823
Ibbetson, Julius Cæsar. Landscape Painter .... — ..1817
Ibbot, Benjamin, D. D. Boylean Lecturer .... 1680..1725
Iberville, Lemorne d'. Canadian Navigator........... 1642..1706
Ibn Tofail, Jaafer. Arabian Philosopher .... — ..1188
Ibrahim Pasha. Viceroy of Egypt................... 1789..1848
Ibycus. Greek Lyric Poet.......................... fl. B.C. 540
Ideler, Christian Louis. German Savant .... 1766..1846
Ietzeler, Christopher. Swiss Architect & Mathematician 1734..1791
Iffland, Augustus Wm. Ger. Actor and Dramatic Writer 1759..1814
Ignarra, Nicholas. Antiquary. (*De Palæstrâ Neapolitanâ*) 1728..1808
Ignatius, St. Bishop of Antioch, and Martyr.......... — .. 115
Ignatius, St. Patriarch of Constantinople............. 799.. 877
Ignatius Loyola. *See* Loyola....................... 1491..1556
Ihre, John. Swedish Scholar and Antiquary........... 1707..1780
Ildefonse, St. Bp. of Toledo. (*Account of Eccles. Writers*) 607.. 669
Ilive, Jacob. English Printer and Writer.............. 1710..1763
Illescas, Gonsalvo. Sp. Eccles. (*Hist. of Cath. Pontifical*) — ..1580
Illyrius, Matthias Flacius, or Francowitz. Lutheran Div. 1520..1575
Ilmoni, Immanuel. Finnish Physician .... 1797..1856
Imbert, Bartholomew. Poet, of Nismes .... 1747..1790
Imbert, John. French Advocate and Law Writer ...... 1522?.1599?
Imbert, Joseph Gabriel. French Painter .... 1654..1740
Imhoff, John (or James) William. Genealogist........ 1651..1728
Immermann, Charles Lebrecht. Ger. Poet and Novelist 1796..1840
Imola, Innocent da. *Francucci.* Italian Painter....... 1480?.1550?
Imperiali, John. Physician. (*Museum Historicum*) .... 1602..1664?
Imperiali, John Baptist. Italian Physician and Poet.
    (*Exercitationum Exoticarum*)...................... 1568..1623
Imperiali, Joseph René. Cardinal.................... 1651..1737
Ina. King of Wessex (689–728)...................... —aft. 728
Inchbald, Mrs. Elizabeth. Novelist and Dramatist. Life
    by Boaden, 1833............................... 1753..1821
Inchoffer, Melchior. German Jesuit................. 1584..1648
Incledon, Benjamin Charles. Singer................ 1764..1826
Inez de Castro. Queen of Portugal .... — ..1355
Ingegno, L'. *See* L'Ingegno. Painter .... 1450?.1520
Ingenhousz, John. Dutch Physician and Chemist..... 1730..1799
Ingersoll, Charles Jared. American Statesman ...., 1782..1862
Ingersoll, Jared. American Lawyer.................. 1749..1822
Inghen, William van. Dutch Historical Painter........ 1651..1709
Inghirami, Cavaliere Francesco. Italian Archæologist.
    (*Monumenti Etruschi*).............................. 1772..1846
Inglis, Henry David. Tourist and Writer............. 1795..1835
Inglis, James. Poet. Murdered. (*Complaynt of Scotland*) — ..1530
Inglis, John, D. D. Scot. Div. (*Evidences of Christianity*) 1763..1834
Inglis, Sir John Eardley Wilmot, K. C. B. Defender of
    Lucknow .... 1814..1862
Inglis, Sir Robert Harry, M. P. Politician............. 1786..1855

BORN. DIED

Ingram, Rev. Dr. James. Saxonist.................. 1774..1850
Ingram, Rev. Robert. Biblical Writer. (*The Ten Tribes*) 1727..1804
Ingrassias, John Philip, of Palermo. Physician....... 1510..1580
Inguimberti, Dominic Joseph Mary de. Bishop of Charpentras. Writer................................ 1683..1757
Ingulph. Abbot of Croyland. Historian.............. 1030?.1109
Inman, Henry. American Artist.................... 1801..1846
Inman, Rev. James. Mathematician and Naval Architect 1776..1859
Inman, John. Amer. Journalist & Miscellaneous Writer — ..1850
Innes, Father. Historical Writer.................. 1662..1744
Innocent I. Pope (402–17)...................... — .. 417
Innocent II. (1130–43.) *Gregorio Papi*.......... — ..1143
Innocent III. (1198–1216.) *Lothario Conti.* Life by Lessinan, 1830; Rottengatter, 1831; Hurter, 1836; Waibel, 1845........................... 1161..1216
Innocent IV. (1243–54.) *Sinibaldo de' Fieschi* .... — ..1254
Innocent V. (1276.) *Peter de' Champagniaco* .... 1225..1276
Innocent VI. (1352–62.) *Stephen Albert*.......... — ..1362
Innocent VII. (1404–6.) *Cosmo de' Migliorati*...... 1336..1406
Innocent VIII. (1484–92.) *John Baptist Cibo*....... 1432..1492
Innocent IX. (1591.) *John Anthony Facchinetti* ..... 1519..1591
Innocent X. (1644–55.) *John Baptist Panfili*....... 1572..1655
Innocent XI. (1676–89.) *Benedict Odescalchi* ...... 1611..1689
Innocent XII. (1691–1700.) *Anthony Pignatelli* ..... 1615..1700
Innocent XIII. (1721–24.) *Michael Angelo Conti.*.... 1655..1724
Interian de Ayala, John. Spanish Ecclesiastic. (*Pictor Christianus Eruditus*)....................... 1656..1730
Inveges, Augustine. Sicilian Historian and Antiquary. (*History of Palermo*)...................... 1595..1677
Inwood, Charles Frederick. Architect .... 1798..1840
Inwood, Henry Wm. Architect. (*Athenian Architecture*) 1794?..1843
Inwood, William. Architect and Surveyor.* (*Tables*).. 1771?..1843
Iolo Gotch. Welsh Bard with Owen Glendower .... fl. 1400?
Iphicrates. Athenian General....................419?.348?B.C.
Irailh, Augustin Simon. French Writer .... 1719..1794
Iredell, James. American Jurist.................. 1751..1799
Iredell, James, son. Writer on Law .... 1788..1853
Ireland, John. Writer. (*Hogarth Illustrated*)........ — ..1808
Ireland, John. Dean of Westm. Founder of Professorship 1762..1842
Ireland, Sam. Writer and Publisher. (*Picturesque Tours*) 1750?.1800
Ireland, Samuel William Henry. Novelist. (*Vortigern*) 1777..1835
Irenæus. Bishop of Lyons. Life by Deyling, 1721; A. F. Gervaise, 1723; Beaven, 1841; Prat, 1843 ..... 130?. 200?
Irene. Empress of Constantinople (797–802). Life by Mignot, 1762.......................... 752?. 803?
Ireton, Henry. Republican Officer and Statesman...... 1610..1651
Irnerius, or Wernerius. Italian Jurist.............. —aft.1118
Iron Mask. History of, by Lord Dover; J. Delort, 1825 — ..1703
Irvine, William. American Revolutionary General...... 1742?.1804
Irving, Rev. Edward. Scottish Divine. Life by Washington Wilks, 1854; Mrs. Oliphant............... 1792..1834
Irving, Peter. American Writer................... 1771..1838
Irving, Washington, brother. American Writer. Life by P. M. Irving, 1862 .... 1783..1859

BORN. DIED.

Irving, William, brother. Writer .... 1766..1821
Irwin, Eyles. Writer on Eastern subjects............. 1748..1817
Isaac. Patriarch.................................1896.1716 B.C.
Isaac I. Emperor of the East (1057–59). *Comnenus.*... — ..1061
Isaac II. (1185–1204.) *Angelus* .... 1154..1204
Isaacson, Henry. Chronologist .... 1581..1654
Isabella, of Angoulême. Queen of England, wife of John — ..1245
Isabella, of Bavaria. Qu. of France, wife of Charles VI. 1371..1435
Isabella, of France. Queen of Eng., wife of Edward II. 1292..1358
Isabella, of France. Queen of Eng., wife of Richard II. 1389..1409
Isabella. Queen of Castile. *The Catholic.* Wife of Ferdi-
  nand of Aragon. Life by Pulgar, 1545; Bravo, 1564;
  Zurita, 1580; Molina, 1587; Marineus, 1587; Gracian,
  1641; Mignot, 1766; Prescott, 1839................ 1451..1504
Isabella. Queen of Hungary, wife of John Zapolita.... 1518..1558
Isabey, John Baptist. French Miniature Painter....... 1767..1855
Isæus. Athenian Orator...........................fl. 420–348 B.C.
Isaiah. Hebrew Prophet ....fl. 760–710 B.C.
Isambert, Francis Andrew. French Politician and Jurist 1792..1857
Iscanus, Josephus, or Joseph, of Exeter. Poet. (*Anti-
  ocheis*)....................................fl. ti. Rd. I. & John
Iselin, Isaac. German Philosopher. (*Hist. of Mankind*) 1728..1782
Iselin, James Christopher. Historical Writer at Basle... 1681..1737
Ishmael, son of Abraham and Hagar................1910.1773 B.C.
Isidore, St., of Pelusium. Monk and Scholar. (*Epistles*) 370?. 450?
Isidore, St., of Seville. *Hispalensis.* L. by Lucas Tudensis 570?. 636
Isidore. *Mercator,* or *Peccator.* Author of the *Decretals* fl. 800?
Isla, Jos. Francis de. Sp. Satirist. (*L. of Friar Gerund*) 1714..1783
Isnard, Maximin. French Political Orator............. 1751..1830
Isocrates. Athenian Orator ....436.338 B.C.
Itard, John Mary Gaspar. Fr. Surgeon and Philosopher 1775..1838
Ittigius, Thomas. Lutheran Theologian and Scholar ... 1643..1710
Iturbide, Augustin. Emperor of Mexico............. 1784..1824
Ivan I., or III. Czar of Russia (1462–1505). *Vasilivitch*.. 1438..1505
Ivan II., or IV. (1533–84.) *Vasilivitch; The Terrible*.. 1529..1584
Ivan III., or V. (1682–89.) *Alexiovitch*.............. 1666..1696
Ivan IV., or VI. (1740–41.) Of Brunswick Bevern.... 1740..1764
Ivanof, Feodor Feodorovitch. Russian Dramatist....... 1777..1816
Ives, Ivo, or Yves, St. Bishop of Chartres (1093–1115).. 1035..1115
Ives, John. Antiquary and Herald .... 1751..1776
Iveteaux, Nicholas Vauquelin, Seigneur de. French Poet 1559..1649
Ivory, James. Scottish Mathematician................ 1765..1842
Ixtilxochitl, Fernando de Alva. Indian Historian...... fl. 16th c.
Izaacke, Richard. (*Antiquities of Exeter*)............· 1624..1700
Izard, Ralph. American Statesman .... 1742..1804
Iziocalt II. (1433–45.) Founder of Mexican Empire .. — ..1445

J.

BORN. DIED.

Jaaphar-ebn-Tophail. Arabian Philosopher......... — ..1188
Jablonowsky, Jos. Alex. von. Polish Prince & Scholar 1711..1777
Jablonsky, Charles Gustavus. Prussian Entomologist .. 1756..1787
Jablonsky, Daniel Ernest. (*Jura Dissidentium*)........ 1660..1741
Jablonsky, John Theod. Pruss. Scholar. (*Dict. of Arts*) 1654..1731
Jablonsky, Paul Ernest. Theologian and Egyptologist.. 1693..1757
Jacaia-ben-Joseph. Port. Rabbi; Biblical Commentator — ..1539
Jacetius, Francis de Cataneis. Ital. Platonic Philosopher 1466..1522
Jackson, Andrew. General. Seventh President of the
  United States (1829–37). Life by Eaton, 1831; Down-
  ing, 1834; Bouis, 1841; Parton................... 1767..1845
Jackson, Arthur. Ejected Nonconformist. Commentator 1593..1666
Jackson, Charles. American Jurist.................. 1775..1855
Jackson, Cyril, D. D. Dean of Christ Church. Scholar 1742..1819
Jackson, James. American Soldier and Statesman.... 1757..1806
Jackson, Rev. John. Arian Div. (*Chronolog. Antiquities*) 1686..1763
Jackson, John, R. A. Portrait Painter............... 1778..1831
Jackson, Joseph. Letter Founder .... 1733..1792
Jackson, Patrick Tracy. Amer. Merch. L. by J. A. Lowell 1780..1847
Jackson, Robert, M. D. Writer on Fever............ 1751..1827
Jackson, Thos. Dean of Peterborough. (*On the Creed*) 1579..1640
Jackson, Thomas Jonathan. *Stonewall.* American "Con-
  federate" General. Life by Dr. Dabney; J. M. Daniels 1826..1863
Jackson, Wm., of Exeter. Musical Composer and Writer 1730..1803
Jackson, William. Greek Professor and Bishop of Ox-
  ford. Translator of Eratosthenes .... 1750..1815
Jacob. Patriarch ....1836.1689 B.C.
Jacob, of Edessa. *Zanzalus.* Found. of Jacobite Churches — .. 578
Jacob, of Nisibis.................................. — 350 or 338
Jacob, Giles. Law Writer and Biographer............ 1686..1744
Jacob, Henry. Independent Divine .... 1561..1626
Jacob, Hen., son. Philol. & Orient. (*Gr. et Lat. Poemata*) 1607?.1652
Jacob, John. Commander of the Scinde Horse........ 1813..1858
Jacob, John. Mechanical Inventor and Printer in Persia fl. 1650?
Jacobæus, Oliger. Danish Physician and Latin Poet... 1650..1701
Jacobazzi, Dominic. Cardinal. (*A Treatise on Councils*) 1443..1527
Jacobi, Charles Gustavus Jacob. German Mathematician 1804..1851
Jacobi, Fred. Henry. Metaphysician. L. by Kuhn, 1834 1743..1819
Jacobi, John George, brother. German Poet.......... 1740..1814
Jacobi, Maximilian. German Physician.............. 1775..1858
Jacobs, Christian Fred. Wm. Ger. Philol. and Tale Writer 1764..1847
Jacobs, Jurien. Swiss Painter....................... 1610..1664
Jacobs, Lucas. *Lucas van Leyden.* Painter.......... 1494..1533
Jacobson, John Charles Godfrey. Prussian Technologist 1726..1789
Jacomb, Thomas. Ejected Nonconformist Divine .... 1622..1687
Jacopone da Todi. Italian Poet. (*Spiritual Canticles*) — ..1306
Jacotot, John Joseph. French Educationist........... 1770..1840
Jacquard, Joseph Mary. Mechanician. L. by De Fortis 1752..1834
Jacquelot, Isaac. Fr. Prot. Theologian. (*Existence of God*) 1647..1708
Jacquemont, Victor. French Traveler and Naturalist.. 1801..1832

BORN.   DIED.

Jacques, Frère. *Baulot.* French Lithotomist.......... 1651..1720
Jacquet, Louis. French Essayist...................... 1732..1793
Jacquier, Francis. Jesuit. Editor of Newton .... 1711..1788
Jacquin, Nicholas Joseph. Botanist. (*Floræ Austriacæ*) 1727..1817
Jadelot, Nicholas. French Medical Writer............. 1736..1793
Jaeger, John Wolfgang. Lutheran Divine............. 1647..1720
Jaenbert. Archbishop of Canterbury (766–90) .... — .. 790
Jago, Richard. English Poet. (*Edgehill*)............. 1715..1781
Jahn, Frederick Louis. Ger. *Littérateur* and Politician 1778..1852
Jahn, John. Orientalist............................. 1750..1817
Jaillot, Hubert Alexis. French Geographer............ 1640?.1712
Jaillot, *né* Renou, John Baptist Michael, son-in-law. (*Re-*
  cherches sur Paris)................................ 1710?.1780
Jakob, Louis Henry von. Ger. Philos. & Polit. Economist 1759..1827
Jamblichus. Neoplatonist............................ — bef.330
James, St. *The Elder.* Apostle...................... — .. 44?
James, St. *The Less.* Apostle....................... — .. 62?
James I. King of Aragon. *The Conqueror*............. 1206..1276
James II. *The Just* .... 1261..1327
James I. King of Scotland (1406–37). Life by Arthur
  Wilson; Robert Chalmers, 1830.................... 1394..1437
James II. (1437–60)................................ 1430..1460
James III. (1460–88)............................... 1453..1488
James IV. (1488–1513.) Fell at Flodden............. 1473..1513
James V. (1513–42.) Life by Paterson................ 1512..1542
James I. King of England (1603–25). Life by Arthur
  Wilson, 1653; W. Sanderson, 1656; Wm. Harris, 1753;
  Laing, 1804; Thomas Thomson, 1825............... 1566..1625
James II. (1685–88.) L. by Bishop Burnet; J. S. Clarke,
  1816; Lord Lonsdale; Richard Burton, 1693; David
  Jones, 1702; Bretonneau; M. T. C. Duplessis, 1740.. 1633..1701
James, Geo. Payne Rainsford. Novelist, Hist., and Poet 1801..1860
James, John Angell. Dissenting Divine of Birmingham 1785..1859
James, John Thomas. Bishop of Calcutta. Life by son 1786..1829
James, Richard. Scholar, Antiquary, and Divine....... 1592..1638
James, Robert, M. D. Inventor of *James's Powder*...... 1703..1776
James, Thomas. Arctic Navigator....................   17th c.
James, Thos., D. D. Coll. of MSS. (*Corruption of Script.*) 1571..1629
James, Thos., D. D. Mast. of Rugby. (*Compend. of Geog.*) — ..1804
James, Rev. Thomas. Antiquary & Miscellaneous Writer — ..1863
James, William. (*Naval History of Great Britain*)..... — ..1827
James, William. Railway Projector................... 1770..1837
James Francis Edward. The Elder Pretender. *Cheva-*
  lier de St. George .... 1688..1765
James de Vitry. Cardinal. (*Eastern & Western History*) — ..1244
James de Voragine. Abp. of Genoa. (*Golden Legend*) 1230?.1298
Jameson, Mrs. Anna. Writer on Art................... 1797..1860
Jameson, Robert. Scottish Naturalist................. 1774..1854
Jamesone, George. Scottish Portrait Painter.......... 1586..1644
Jamet, Peter Charles. Fr. Writer. (*Metaphysical Essays*) 1701..1770?
Jami, or Djami. Persian Poet........................ 1414..1492
Jamieson, John, D. D. Theologian and Philologist..... 1758..1838
Jamyn, Amadis. French Poet......................... 1530?.1585?
Jane I. Queen of Naples (1343–82) .... 1327..1382

BORN. DIED.

Jane II. Queen of Naples (1414–35)................. 1370..1435
Jane d'Albret. Queen of Navarre. L. by M. W. Freer 1528..1572
Janeway, Jas. Ejected Nonconf. (*Token for Children*) 1636..1674
Janicon, Francis Michael. Fr. Polit. Writer in Holland 1674?.1730
Janozki, John Daniel Andrew. Polish Writer......... 1720..1786
Jansenius, Cornelius. Bishop of Ghent. (*Harmony of*
    the Gospels) .... 1510..1576
Jansenius, Cornelius. Bp. of Ypres. Auth. of Jansenism.
    (*Augustinus.*) Life by Leydecker, 1695; Frick, 1717.. 1585..1638
Jansenius, James, of Louvain. Commentator......... 1547..1625
Janson, Jansonius, or Jenson, Nicholas. French Printer
    and Type Founder...................................... — ..1481?
Janssens, Abraham. Dutch Historical Painter......... 1569..1631
Janssens, or Johnson, Cornelius. Dutch Portrait Painter
    in England .... 1590..1665
Janssens, Victor Honorius. Dutch Historical Painter .. 1664..1739
Januarius, St. Bishop of Benevento. Martyr........ fl. ti. Dioclet.
Japix, or Japicks, Gysbert. Frisian Poet.............. 1603..1666
Jarchi, Solomon Benj. Isaac. Rabbi and Commentator.. 1104..1180
Jardine, George, of Glasgow. Professor of Logic....... 1743..1827
Jardins, Mary Hortense des. French Novelist......... 1632..1683
Jardyn, Karel, or Charles, du. Dutch Painter......... 1640..1678
Jarnowich, or Giornovichi, Giovanna Mane. Violinist.. 1745..1804
Jarrige, Peter. French Jesuit. (*Jesuits on a Scaffold*) .. 1605..1660
Jarry, Lawrence Juillard du. French Poet and Divine.. 1658..1730
Jarry, Nicholas. French Caligraphist.................. 1620?   —
Jars, Gabriel. French Metallurgist..................... 1732..1769
Jarvis, Abraham, D. D. American Divine.............. 1739..1813
Jarvis, John. Painter on Glass....................... 1749..1804
Jarvis, Samuel Farmar. American Divine and Author.. 1786..1851
Jasmin, James, of Agen. *Barber Poet*................. 1798..1864
Jason. Tyrant of Pheræ.............................. — B.C.370
Jasper, William. American Revolutionary Soldier .....1750?.1779
Jaubert, Peter Amédée Émilien Probe, Chevalier. French
    Orientalist .... 1779..1847
Jaucourt, Louis de, Chevalier. French Medical Writer.. 1704..1779
Jault, Augustus Francis. Fr. Med. Writer and Translator 1700..1757
Jaureguy y Aguilar. Spanish Poet and Painter....... 1566..1650
Jay, Anthony. French Publicist...................... 1770..1854
Jay, Guy Michael le. French Orientalist. (*Polyglot Bible*) 1588..1674
Jay, John. Amer. Jurist & Statesm. L. by Wm. Jay, 1832 1745..1829
Jay, Rev. Wm., of Bath. Life by Redford and James, 1854 1769..1853
Jay, William. American Jurist and Philanthropist...... 1779..1858
Jayadeva. Hindoo Poet. (*Gita Govinda*) .... fl. 1150?
Jazikoff, Nicholas. Russian Poet .... 1805?.1847
Jeacock, Caleb. Writer and Orator. (*Vind. of St. Paul*) — ..1786?
Jeanes, Rev. Henry. Divine..........................: 1611..1662
Jean Jacques. *See* Rousseau......................... 1712..1778
Jeanne d'Arc. *Maid of Orleans. See* Darc........... 1412?.1431
Jeannin, Peter. Fr. Statesm. (*Memoirs & Negotiations*) 1540..1622
Jean Paul. *See* Richter .... 1763..1825
Jeaurat, Edme Sebastian. French Mathematician...... 1724..1803
Jebb, John, M. D. Theological, Political, & Med. Writer 1736..1786
Jebb, John. Bishop of Limerick. L. by C. Forster, 1836 1775..1833

BORN. DIED.

Jebb, Sir Joshua, K. C. B. General. Surveyor-General
of Prisons.. 1793?..1863
Jebb, Samuel, M. D. Classical Writer .... — ..1772
Jefferson, Thomas. Third President of the United States.
Life by T. J. Randolph, 1829; George Tucker, 1836.. 1743..1826
Jeffery, John. Archdeacon of Norwich. Divine....... 1647..1720
Jeffrey, Francis, Lord. Scotch Judge. Editor of *Edin-*
burgh Review. Life by Lord Cockburn, 1852........ 1773..1850
Jeffreys, George. Judge. Life by Woolrych, 1827 ..... 1640?.1689
Jeffreys, George. Poet............................. 1678..1755
Jeffries, John. American Physician................... 1744..1819
Jehanghir. Mogul Emperor of India (1605–27)........ — ..1627
Jehoahaz, son of Jehu, King of Israel (B. C. 856–840).. — B.C.840
Jehoahaz, son of Josiah, King of Judah (B. C. 610).
Shallum.... — aft.B.C.610
Jehoiachin, Jecqniah, or Coniah (B. C. 599)... 607 or 617.aft.599 B.C.
Jehoiakim, King of Judah (B. C. 610–599). *Eliakim.*....635.599 B.C.
Jehoram, or Joram, son of Ahab, K. of Israel (B.C. 896–884) —B.C.884
Jehoram, or Joram, son of Jehoshaphat, King of Judah
(B. C. 893?–885?) ....924?.885?B.C.
Jehoshaphat, King of Judah (B. C. 914–889?)........949?.889?B.C.
Jehu, King of Israel (B. C. 884–856).................. — B.C.856
Jejeebhoy, Sir Jamsetjee. Benefactor of Bombay...... 1783..1859
Jekyll, Sir Joseph. Lawyer and Statesman........... 1664..1738
Jellachich de Buzim, Joseph, Baron. Ban of Croatia,
&c.; General.................................... 1801..1859
Jenischius, Paul. Dutch Writ. (*Theatrum Animarum*) 1558..1647
Jenkin, Robt. Nonjuror. (*Reasonableness of Christ. Rel.*) 1656..1727
Jenkins, David. Judge .... 1586?.1667
Jenkins, Henry, of Yorkshire. Centenarian.......... 1501..1670
Jenkins, John. Musical Composer..................... 1592..1678
Jenkins, Sir Leoline. Statesman. Life by Wynne, 1724 1623?.1685
Jenkinson, Anthony. English Traveler in Asia .... — ..1584
Jenkinson, Charles, First Earl Liverpool. Statesman .. 1727..1808
Jenkinson, Robert Banks, Second Earl Liverpool. Pre-
mier (1812–27) .... 1770..1828
Jenks, Benjamin. Religious Writer. (*Prayers*)....... 1646..1724
Jenkyns, William. Nonconformist Divine. (*On Jude*) 1612..1685
Jennens, Charles. Composer of words for Handel...... — ..1773
Jenner, Edward, M. D. Inventor of Vaccination. Life by
Dr. Baron, 1827; J. C. Lettsom.................... 1749..1823
Jenner, William. English Miser....................... 1701..1797
Jennings, David, D. D. Dissent. Div. (*Jewish Antiquities*) 1691..1762
Jennings, Henry Constantine. Antiquary and Virtuoso. 1731..1819
Jenson, or Janson, Nich. Fr. Printer and Type Founder — ..1481?
Jenyns, Soame. Poet and Writer. L. by C. Nalson Cole 1704..1787
Jephson, Robert. Dramatic Poet .... 1736..1803
Jeremiah. Hebrew Prophet.....................fl. 678–570 B. C.
Jeremie, Sir John. Colonial Judge .... 1795..1841
Jerningham, Edward. Poet........................... 1727..1812
Jeroboam, son of Nebat, First K. of Israel (B. C. 975–953) — B.C.953
Jeroboam, son of Joash, King of Israel (B. C. 825–784).. — B.C.784
Jerome, St. Life by Erasmus, 1519; Stigelius, 1546; Si-
guenza, 1600; Martianay, 1706; F. Z. Collombet, 1845 345?..420

BORN. DIED.

Jerome, of Prague. Reformer. Life by G. H. A. Wagner,
  1803; Heller, 1835.................................... 1378?.1416
Jerram, Rev. Chas. (*Inf. Baptism.*) L. by J. Jerram, 1855 1770..1853
Jerrold, Douglas Wm. Humorist. L. by B. Jerrold, 1859 1803..1857
Jervas, Charles. Portrait Painter...................... 1675?.1739 ,
Jervis, Sir John, First Earl of St. Vincent. Admiral. Life
  by Captain Edward P. Brenton, 1838; Tucker, 1844.. 1734..1823
Jesi, Samuel. Italian Engraver........................ 1789..1853
Jessey, Henry. Ejected Nonconf. Divine and Orientalist — ..1663
Jeuffroy, R. V. French Gem and Medal Engraver...... 1749..1826
Jeune, John le. French Oratorian Divine. (*Sermons*).. 1592..1672
Jewel, or **Jewell,** John. Bishop of Salisbury. Life by
  Dr. Humfrey, 1573; Featley, 1645; E. Bohun, 1685;
  C. W. Le Bas; Isaacson, 1823...................... 1522..1571
Jewsbury, Miss Maria Jane (Mrs. Fletcher). Essayist.. — ..1833
Jezed I. Fifth Caliph (680–83)...................... — .. 683
Joachim. *Prophet.* Abbot of Fiore. L. by Gervaise, 1745 1130..1202
Joachim, George. Swiss Mathematician and Astronomer 1514..1576
Joachim, John Frederick. Ger. Historian and Medalist 1713..1767
Joan of Arc. *Maid of Orleans.* See Darc .... 1412?.1431
Joan. Queen of Naples. *See Jane.*
Joanes, or **Juanes,** J. Bapt. Spanish Painter.......... 1523..1579
Joanna. Queen of Naples. *See Jane.*
Joanna, or **Juana.** Q. of Spain, wife of Archduke Philip 1479..1555
Joash, or **Jehoash,** son of Ahaziah, King of Judah (B. C.
  878–838)... —B.C. 838
Joash, or **Jehoash,** son of Jehoahaz, King of Israel (B. C.
  839–823)... —B.C. 823
Jobert, Louis. French Jesuit. (*La Science des Médailles*) 1637..1719
Jöcher, Christian Theophilus, of Leipsic. (*Dictionary of
  Learned Men*)..................................... 1694..1758
Jocundus, Francis John. *See Giocondo*............. 1450?.1521?
Joddrell, Richard Paul. English Writer............... 1745..1831
Jode, Arnold de. Engraver. (*Mercury instructing Cupid*) 1636?. —
Jode, Peter de, of Antwerp. Engraver. (*Last Judgment*) 1570..1634
Jode, Peter de, son. Engraver..................... 1602.. —
Jodelle, Stephen. Father of the French Theater........ 1532..1573
Joecher, or **Jöcher,** Christian Theophilus. *See Jöcher*... 1694..1758
Joel. Hebrew Prophet............................. fl. B.C. 800?
Joffredy, Geoffroi, or Jouffroy. Cardinal.............. 1412..1473
Joffrid. Abbot of Croyland. Promoter of Learn. at Camb. fl. 12th c.
Jogues, Isaac. Fr. Miss. among the North Amer. Indians 1607..1646
Johannæus, Finnur. Icelandic Writer. *See Jonsson*... 1704..1789
Johannes Secundus. *See Everard.* (*Basia*)......... 1511..1536
Johannot, Chas. Hen. Alfred. Fr. Paint. & Book Illustrat. 1800..1837
Johannot, Tony, brother. Painter and Book Illustrator. 1803..1852
John I. Emperor of the East (969–76). *Zimisces* ...... — .. 976
John II. (1118–43.) *Comnenus*...................... — ..1143
John III. (1222–55.) *Ducas* .... 1193..1255
John IV. (1259.) *Lascaris*......................... 1253?.1284
John V. *Cantacuzenus.* Regent (1341–47); usurper
  (1347–55)... 1311?.1411?
John VI. *Palæologus.* Under Regent (1341–47); alone
  (1353–91)... — ..1391

	BORN.	DIED.
John VII. Emperor of the East (1425–48)	—	1448
John I. Pope (523–26)	—	526
John II. (532–35)	—	535
John III. (560–73)	—	573
John IV. (640–42)	—	642
John V. (685–87)	—	687
John VI. (701–5)	—	705
John VII. (705–7)	—	707
John VIII. (872–82)	—	882
John IX. (898–900)	—	900
John X. (914–28)	—	928
John XI. (931–36.)	906?	936
John XII. (956–63.) *Octavian.* Deposed	938?	964
John XIII. (965–72)	—	972
John XIV. (983–84.) Deposed	—	995
John XV. (985) by some not reckoned	—	985
John XV., or XVI. (985–96)	—	996
John XVI., or XVII. (997–98.) *Philagathus.* Antipope	—	998
John XVII., or XVIII. (1003)	—	1003
John XVIII., or XIX. (1003–9)	—	1009
John XIX., or XX. (1024–33)	—	1033
John XX., or XXI. (1276–77)	—	1277
John XXI., or XXII. (1316–34.) *James de Ossa*	1244?	1334
John XXII., or XXIII. (1410–15.) *Balthasar Cossa.* Deposed	—	1419
John. King of England. Life by William Prynne, 1670; Berington, 1790	1166	1216
John I. King of France (1316)	1316	1316
John II. (1350–64.) *Le Bon.* Life by F. T. De Choisy, 1388; De Monmerque, 1944	1319?	1364
John I. K. of Portugal (1385–1433). L. by Eryceira, sen.	1357	1433
John II. (1481–95.) *The Great*	1455	1495
John III. (1521–57.) Life by Francis d'Andrada, 1533	1502	1557
John IV. (1640–56.) Duke of Braganza. *The Fortunate*	1604	1656
John V. (1707–50)	1689	1750
John VI. (1821–26)	1769	1826
John I. King of Castile and Leon (1379–90)	1358	1390
John II. (1406–54)	1405	1454
John I. King of Aragon (1387–95)	1350	1395
John II. (1458–79.) King of Navarre (1425–79)	1397	1479
John I. King of Navarre = John II. of France	1319?	1364
John II. (1425–79) = John II. of Aragon (1458–79)	1397	1479
John III. (1494–1516)	—	1516
John. King of Bohemia (1310–46). Fell at Crecy	1295?	1346
John I. King of Poland (1492–1501)	1459	1501
John II. (1648–68.) *Casimir* (or Casimir V.)	1609	1672
John III. (1674–96.) *Sobieski*	1629	1696
John I. King of Sweden (1216–22)	— 1222 or 3	
John II. (1497–1513) and I. of Denmark (1481–1513)	1455	1513
John III. (1568–92)	1537	1592
John. Emperor of Russia. *See* Ivan.		
John I. King of Denmark (1481–1513). King of Sweden (1497–1513)	1455	1513
John I. Duke of Brittany (1237–86)	1217	1286

BORN. DIED.

John II. Duke of Britany (1286–1304)................ 1239..1304
John III. (1312–41.) *The Good* .... 1286..1341
John, Ct. of Montfort, reckoned by some IV. of Brittany. — ..1345
John IV., or V. (1364–99.) *The Valiant.* .... 1338..1399
John V., or VI. (1399–1442.) *The Good* and *the Wise* . 1389..1442
John, Duke of Burgundy. *Sans Peur* .... 1371..1419
John of Austria, Don. Governor of the Netherlands ... 1545..1578
John of Beverly. Bishop of Hexham and of York .... — .. 722
John of Bologna. French Sculptor .... 1524..1608
John of Bruges, or John Van Eyck. Painter 1370. 1441
John of Cappadocia. Patriarch of Constantinople. Writ. — .. 596?
John of the Cross, St. Spanish Ascetic Divine .... 1542..1591
John of Damascus, St. Ecclesiastical Writer .... — .. 756?
John of Gaunt, or Ghent. Duke of Lancaster, son of
     Edward III....................................... 1340..1399
John of Hexham. *Johannes Hagustaldensis.* Chronicler fl. 1170
John of Leyden, or John Boccold. Fanatic........... 1510?.1536
John of Paris. Theol. (*De Regiâ Potestate et Papali*) — ..1304
John of Ragusa. Orientalist and Theologian .... fl. 15th c.
John of Salisbury. Bishop of Chartres .... 1110..1180
John of Udino. Italian Painter...................... 1494..1564
John the Baptist, St. Forerunner of Christ......... B.C. 5.A.D. 28?
John the Evangelist, St. Apostle................... — ab. 100
John the Scholastic. (Συναγωνὴ κανόνων). .... — .. 578
Johnes, Thomas. Translator of Froissart.............. 1748..1816
Johnson, Charles. Dramatic Writer .... 1679..1748
Johnson, Edward. Historian of New England .... 1600?.1672
Johnson, Miss Hester. *Stella.* Friend of Swift........ 1684..1727
Johnson, Rev. John. Nonjuring Divine. (*The Unbloody
     Sacrifice.*) Life by Dr. Brett..................... 1662..1725
Johnson, Martin. Landscape Painter ....:.... — ..1685?
Johnson, Maurice. Antiquary .... 1687..1755
Johnson, Rd., of Nottingham. (*Grammat. Commentaries*) — ..1721
Johnson, Richard Mentor. Vice-President of the U. S.. 1780..1850
Johnson, Rev. Samuel. Prot. Controv. and Polit. Writer 1649..1703
Johnson, Samuel, D. D. American Educator and Writer 1696..1772
Johnson, Sam. Dramatist & Humorist. (*Hurlothrumbo*) 1705?.1773
Johnson, Samuel, LL. D. Essayist, Poet, and Lexicogra-
     pher. Life by Boswell; Thos. Tyers; Sir J. H. Haw-
     kins, 1787; Dr. Robert Anderson, 1795; J. F. Russell,
     1847; Thomas Carlyle, 1853....................... 1709..1784
Johnson, Thomas. Botanist. Editor of *Gerard's Herbal* 1561..1644
Johnson, Thomas, of Eton and Brentford. Class. Editor 1675?.1750?
Johnson, W. A. B. African Missionary .... 1787..1823
Johnson, Walter Rogers. American Physicist........ 1794..1852
Johnson, Sir William. Superintendent-General of Indian
     Affairs in North America .... 1715..1774
Johnson, William. American Jurist .... 1771..1834
Johnston, Albert Sydney. Amer. " Confederate " General 1803..1862
Johnston, or Jonston, Arthur. Physician and Latin Poet.
     Translator of the Psalms..................;...... 1587..1641
Johnston, Charles. Writer. (*Chrysal*)............... — ..1800?
Johnston, Gabriel. Colonial Governor of South Carolina — ..1752
Johnston, George. Naturalist....................... 1789..1855

BORN. DIED.

Johnston, James F. W. Scottish Chemist and Agricult.
  Writer. Prof. at Durham. (*Chemistry of Common Life*) 1796..1853
Johnston, John. Naturalist............................ 1603..1675
Johnstone, Archibald, of Warriston. Presbyt. Leader.. — ..1663
Johnstone, Dr. Bryce. Scot. Div. (*On the Revelation*) 1747..1805
Johnstone, Chevalier de. Jacobite. (*Memoirs of the Re-*
  bellion of 1745–46)............................. 1720..1800?
Johnstone, George, M. P. Captain R. N. (*Our Acquisi-*
  tions in the East Indies)......................... — ..1787
Johnstone, James, M. D., of Worcester. Medical and
  Physiological Writer. L. by Hen. Jas. Johnstone, 1846 1730..1802
Johnstone, John, M. D., of Birmingham. Medical Writ-
  er. Biographer of Parr......................... 1768..1836
Johnstone, John Henry. Comic Actor and Vocalist.... 1750..1828
Joinville, John, Sieur de. Statesm. (*Hist. of Louis IX.*) 1223 or 4.1319?
Jolivet, John Baptist Moyse, Count de. Statistical Writer 1754..1818
Jolliet, or Joliet, Louis. One of the Discoverers of the
  Mississippi River................................. —ab.1730
Joly, Claude. French Political Writer. (*Maxims for*
  Education of a Prince)........................... 1607..1700
Joly, Francis Anthony. French Comic Writer.......... 1672..1753
Joly, Guy. (*Historical Memoirs*)..................... fl. 1665?
Joly, Mary Elizabeth. French Actress................. 1761..1798
Jomard, M. French Geographer...................... 1776?.1862
Jomelli, Nicholas. Italian Musical Composer.......... 1714..1774
Jonah. Hebrew Prophet............................. fl. B.C. 862
Jonas, Arngrim. Historian and Antiquary of Iceland... 1568..1648
Jonas, Justus. German Protestant Reformer.......... 1493..1555
Jones, Anson. Last President of Texas............... 1798..1858
Jones, David. Welsh Poet and Collector of Welsh MSS. — ..1785?.
Jones, Edward. Welsh Musician...................... 1751?.1821
Jones, Rev. Griffith. Welsh Philanthropist........... 1684..1761
Jones, Griffith. Writer of Juvenile Books and Journalist 1721..1786
Jones, Henry. Dramatic Poet. (*Earl of Essex*)....... 1720?.1770
Jones, Inigo. Architect. Life by Peter Cunningham... 1572?.1652
Jones, Jacob. American Naval Officer................ 1770..1850
Jones, James Chamberlain. American Statesman...... 1809..1859
Jones, Jeremiah. Dissent. Div. (*Canon. Authority of N. T.*) 1693..1724
Jones, John. Medical Writer........................ —aft.1579
Jones, John. Eng. Benedictine in Spain. Biblical Writer 1575..1636
Jones, John, LL. D. Unitarian Minister and Philologist 1765?.1827
Jones, John Edward. Sculptor...................... 1806?.1862
Jones, John Gale. Political Orator.................. 1771..1838
Jones, John Paul. Naval Adventurer. Life by A. S. Mac-
  kenzie, 1841; W. G. Simms, 1845.................. 1747..1792
Jones, Leslie Grove, Colonel. Political Writer......... 1779..1839
Jones, Noble Wimberly. American Physician and Patriot 1725..1805
Jones, Owen. Welsh Antiquary...................... 1740..1814
Jones, Rice. Welsh Poet. (*Welsh Anthology*)......... 1716..1801
Jones, Richard. Welsh Divine. (*Gemma Cambricum*)... — ..1652?
Jones, William, father of Sir William. Mathematician.. 1680..1749
Jones, Sir Wm. Orient. Life by Lord Teignmouth, 1804 1746..1794
Jones, Rev. William, of Nayland. Hutchinsonian Divine.
  (*Catholic Doctrine of the Trinity.*) Life by Wm. Stevens 1726..1800

15

BORN. DIED.

Jong, Ludolph de. Dutch Painter...................... 1616..1697
Jonin, Gilbert. French Jesuit and Poet.............. 1596..1638
Jonsius, John. ' (*De Scriptoribus Historiæ Philosophiæ*)... 1624..1659
Jonson, Ben. Poet. L. by Gifford; Barry Cornwall, 1838 1574..1637
Jonsson, Finnur. (*Historia Ecclesiastica Islandiæ*)..... 1704..1789
Jonston, Arthur. Scottish Latin Poet................ 1587..1641
Jonston, John. Polish Writer. (*Nat. Hist. of Animals*).. 1603..1675
Jordaens, Jacob. Flemish Hist. and Portrait Painter ... 1594..1678
Jordan, Camille. French Religious and Political Writer 1771..1821
Jordan, Chas. Stephen. Prus. Writer. (*Literary Travels*) 1700..1745
Jordan, Mrs. Dorothea. *Dorothy Bland.* Actress....... 1762?.1816
Jordan, John Christopher. Chronologist and Antiquary — ..1740
Jordano, Luca. Neapolitan Painter.................. 1632..1705
Jordano Bruno. *See* Bruno........................ 1550..1600
Jorden, Edward, M. D. Medical Writer...'........... 1569..1632
Jorgenson, Jorgen. Danish Adventurer. Eng. Writer.1779.aft.1825
Jornandes, or Jordanes. Gothic Historian............ 6th c.
Jortin, John, D. D. Life by Dr. J. Disney, 1792......... 1698..1770
Joseph. Jewish Patriarch.......................1745.1635 B.C.
Joseph I. Emperor of Germany (1705–11)............. 1678..1711
Joseph II. (1765–90.) Life by L. A. de Caraccioli, 1790;
    C. Paganel, 1843................................... 1741..1790
Joseph Emanuel. King of Portugal (1750–77) .... 1714..1777
Joseph Meir. French Rabbi. Historical Writer....... 1496..1554
Joseph of Exeter. Latin Poet. (*Antiocheis*)......ti. Rd. I. & John
Joseph of Paris. *Francis Leclerc du Tremblay*........ 1577..1638
Josephine. Empress of France, first wife of Napoleon.
    Life by Bornschein, 1803; Regnault-Warin, 1819; M.
    A. Le Normand, 1820; Ducrest, 1830; Avrillon, 1831;
    Garriga y Baucis, 1836; Dibelius, 1845.............. 1763..1814
Josephus, Flavius. Jewish Historian. Life by Tilmann,
    1548; J. F. Eckhard, 1785 .... 38?, 100?
Joshua. Leader of Israelites; Successor of Moses..ab.1537–1427 B.C.
Josiah. King of Judah (B. C. 641–610.)............. 648.610 B.C.
Jósika. Micklós, Baron. Hung. Politician and Novelist 1796..1865
Josquin Desprez. *Jodocus Pratensis.* Mus. Composer.. 1450?. —
Jost, Isaac Mark. Jewish Scholar of Germany......... 1793..1862
Jotham. King of Judah (B. C. 758–742).......,783.742 B.C.
Joubert, Bartholomew Catherine. Fr. Republican Gen... 1769..1799
Joubert, Francis, of Montpellier. Jansenist Divine..... 1689..1763
Joubert, Lawrence. French Medical Writer........... 1529..1583
Jouffroy, Claude Francis Dorothea, Marquis de. Steam
    Mechanician..................................... 1751?.1832
Jouffroy, John de. *Joffredus.* Cardinal............. 1412..1473
Jouffroy, Theodore Simon. French Philosophical Writer 1796..1842
Jourdain, Amable Louis Mary Michael Bréchillet.
    French Orientalist............................... 1788..1818
Jourdan, John Baptist, Count. Marshal of France ..... 1762..1833
Journet, Frances. French Actress.................. — ..1722
Jousse, Daniel. French Lawyer .... 1704..1781
Jouvenci, Joseph' de. Jesuit. French Writer .... 1643..1719
Jouvenet, John. French Painter.................... 1644..1717
Jouy, Victor Joseph Stephen de. French Writer....... 1674?.1846
Jovellanos, Gaspar Melchior de. Span. Writer and Polit. 1749..1811

BORN. DIED.

Jovian. Emperor (363–64). Life by Schenkel, 1617; La
  Bletterie, 1748.. 332.. 364
Jovinian, of Milan. Monk and Writer................ — aft. 412
Jovius, or Giovio, Paul. Italian Historian............ 1483..1552
Jowett, Rev. Wm. Missionary. (*Christian Researches*) 1787?.1855
Joy, Henry. Irish Judge............................... 1767..1838
Joy, Joye, or Gee, John. Reformer.................... 1492?.1553
Joyce, Jeremiah. Compiler. (*Scientific Dialogues*)..... 1764..1816
Joyeuse, Anne, Duke de. Admiral of France........... 1561..1587
Joyeuse, Francis de. Cardinal, Statesman. Life by Au-
  bery, 1654.. 1562..1615
Joyner, William, or Lyde. Writer.................... 1622..1706
Juan. King of Aragon. *See* John.
Juan y Santicilia, George. Sp. Math. and Naval Officer 1712..1774
Juana. Queen of Spain, wife of Archduke Philip...... 1479..1555
Juanes, John Baptist. Spanish Painter .... 1523..1579
Juba I. King of Numidia; defeated at Thapsus........ — B.C. 46
Juba II., son. King of Mauritania & Numidia. Writer — A.D. 19?
Juda, Leo. German Protestant Reformer .... 1482..1542
Judah Chiug. Jewish Rabbi. Phys. and Grammarian fl. 1040
Judah Hakkadosh. Compiler of the Mishna.......... 123.. 190
Judas Levita, or Ha-Levi. Rabbi. Poet, Gram., Philos. 1080?.1140
Judas Maccabæus. Jewish Patriot (B. C. 166–160)..... — B.C. 160
Judd, Sylvester. American Clergyman and Author..... 1813..1853
Jude, St. *Thaddeus* or *Lebbeus*. Apostle .... 1st c.
Judson, Adoniram, D. D. American Missionary to Bur-
  mah. Life by Mrs. H. C. Conant, 1856; Clements;
  Gillette; Wayland....................................... 1788..1850
Judson, Mrs. Anne Hasseltine, wife. (*Hist. Burm. Miss.*) 1789..1826
Judson, Sarah Hall, (Mrs. Boardman,) second wife. Life
  by Mrs. E. C. Judson, 1850 .... 1803..1845
Judson, Mrs. Emily Chubbuck, third wife. *Fanny For-
  ester.* (*Life of Mrs. Sarah B. Judson*, 1850; *Alder-
  brook*)... 1817..1854
Juel, Nicholas. Danish Admiral...................... 1629..1697
Juglaris, Louis. Italian Jesuit and Panegyrist......... 1607..1653
Jugurtha. King of Numidia .... — B.C. 104
Juigné Broissinière, Seig. de Molière. (*Dictionnaire*) fl. 1647
Julia. Daughter of Cæsar, wife of Pompey .... 83?.54 B.C.
Julia. Daughter of Augustus, wife of Marcellus, Agrippa,
  Tiberius..B.C.39?.A.D. 14
Julia, daughter. Wife of Æmilius Paulus.............. — .. 28
Julia. Daughter of Germanicus and Agrippina........ 18.aft.41
Julia. Daughter of Drusus & Livia, niece of Germanicus — .. 59
Julia Domna. Wife of Septimius Severus............ 158?. 217
Julian. Emp. (361–63). *Apostate.* L. by Neander; Thos.
  Long; La Bletterie, 1735, translated by Anna Williams,
  1746; Desvoeux, 1746; Joudot, 1817; Koerner, 1830.. 331.. 363
Julian, St. Archbp. of Toledo. Writer against the Jews — .. 690
Julien, Peter. French Sculptor. (*Dying Gladiator*).... 1731..1804
Julien, Simon. Swiss Painter......................... 1736..1799
Julius I. Pope (337–52). *Saint* .... — .. 352
Julius II. (1503–13.) *Julian della Rovere*............ 1441..1513
Julius III. (1550–55.) *John Maria del Monte*......... 1487..1555

BORN. DIED.

Jullien, Camille. Musician .... 1812..1860
Jullien, Louis George. Fr. Comp. and Director of Music 1812..1860
Juncker, Christian. German Medalist and Writer...... 1663..1714
Juncker, Theodore John. German Medical Writer ..... 1680..1759
Junctin, or Giuntini, Francis, of Florence. Mathem.... 1522..1590
Jung-Stilling. (John Henry Jung.) Ger. Mystic Author 1740..1817
Junge, or Jungius, Joachim, of Hamburg. Philosopher.
  (*Isagoge Phytoscopica*) .... 1587..1657
Jungermann, Louis. German Botanist and Naturalist.. 1572..1653
Jungmann, Jos. Jacob. Bohemian Lexicog. and Bibliog. 1773..1847
Junius, Adrian. Dutch Physician and Scholar......... 1512..1575
Junius, or Du Jon, Francis. French Protestant. Trans-
  lator of the Bible into Latin .... 1545..1602
Junius, Francis, son. Saxonist in Eng. L. by Grævius 1589..1677
Junot, Andoche, Duke of Abrantes. Marshal of France 1771..1813
Junta, Philip. Printer at Geneva.................... 1450..1519
Junta, Thomas. Venetian Phys. (*Battles of the Ancients*) fl. 1554
Juret, Francis. French Critic and Poet.............. 1553..1626
Jurieu, Peter. French Protestant Polemical Divine..... 1637..1713
Jurin, James. Physician and Mathematician .... 1684..1750
Jussieu, Adrian de. Botanist .... 1797..1853
Jussieu, Anthony de. Botanist and Physician.......... 1686..1758
Jussieu, Anthony Lawrence de. (*Genera Plantarum*)... 1748..1836
Jussieu, Bernard de. Botanist and Physician. (*Plants in
  Environs of Paris*).............................. 1699..1777
Jussieu, Joseph de. Naturalist, Phys., Engin., Traveler 1704..1779
Just, John. Philologist and Natural Philosopher....... 1797?.1852
Justel, Christopher. Eccles. Antiquary and Canonist.... 1580..1649
Justel, Henry, LL. D., son. Royal Librarian in England 1620..1693
Justi, John Henry Theophilus. German Mineralogist... 1705?.1771
Justin. Latin Historian ....not aft.5th c.
Justin I. Emperor of East (518–27).................   450.. 527
Justin II. (565–74).............................   — .. 578
Justin Martyr. Christian Writer .... 103?. 167?
Justinian I. (527–65.) *Great.* Life by Gilles Perrin,
  1576; Corvinus de Beldern, 1618; Guinet, 1628; Rango,
  1661; Ludewig, 1731; Invernizzi, 1743.............   483.. 565
Justinian II. (685–711).........................   689.. 711
Justiniani, Augustin. Orientalist. (*Annals of Genoa*).. 1470..1536
Justiniani, Bernard. (*History of Venice*)............. 1408..1489
Justiniani, Fabian. (*Index Materiarum Biblicarum*)... 1578..1627
Justiniani, Lawrence. *Saint.* Patriarch of Venice. De-
  votional Writer. Life by B. Justiniani .... 1380..1465
Justus. Archbishop of Canterbury (624–27) .... — ..627
Justus, of Padua. Painter........................ fl. 1367
Juvara, or Ivara, Philip. Sicilian Architect............ 1685..1735
Juvenal. Roman Satirist .... fl. 83–100
Juvenal des Ursins. Archbishop of Rheims. Historian 1388..1473
Juvencus, Caius Vettius Aquilinus. Christian Latin
  Poet. (*Historia Evangelica*) .... fl. 332? ·
Juxon, William. Archbishop of Canterbury (1660–63).. 1582..1663

K.

	BORN.	DIED.

Kaab. Arabian Poet.................................. — .. 662
Kaas, Nicholas. Danish Statesman .... 1535..1594
Kabbete, John. Dutch Painter........................ — ..1660
Kaempfer, or Kämpfer, Engelbrecht. Ger. Bot. and Trav. 1651..1716
Kaestner, or Kästner, Abraham Gotthelf. Mathematician
   and Poet. (*History of Mathematics*) .... 1719..1800
Kahler, John. German Theologian and Philosopher .... 1649..1727
Kain, Henry Louis le. French Actor.................. 1728..1778
Kalb, John, Baron de. German General in America..... 1732?.1780
Kaldi, George. Hung. Jesuit. Preacher & Transl. of Bible 1572..1634
Kale, or Kalf, William. Dutch Painter .... 1630..1693
Kalgreen, or Kellgren, John Henry. Swedish Poet .... 1751..1795
Kalidasa. Indian Poet. (*Sakontala*)..............fl. ab. 1st c. B.C.
Kalide. German Sculptor. (*Boy with Swan*) .... — ..1863
Kalkbrenner, Christian F. Prussian Pianist and Comp. 1755..1806
Kalm, Peter. Swedish Traveler and Natural Philosopher 1715..1779
Kalraat, Bernard van, of Dort. Painter .... 1650..1721
Kalubko, Vincent. Polish Historian .... — ..1223
Kamehameha III. King of the Sandwich Islands..... 1817..1854
Kames, Henry Home, Lord. Scottish Judge and Writer.
   Life by Lord Woodhouselee, 1807 .... 1696..1782
Kampen, Jacob van. Dutch Painter.................. 1658.. —
Kampen, Nicholas Godfrey van. Dutch Historian...... 1776..1839
Kämpfer, Engelbrecht. *See* Kaempfer .... 1651..1716
Kandler, John Joachim. Modeler in Porcelain .... 1706..1776
Kane, Dr. Elisha Kent. American Arctic Explorer. Life
   by Smucker; Dr. Elder, 1857 .... 1820..1857
Kanold, John. German Writer...................... 1679?.1729
Kant, Immanuel. Philosopher. Life by Borowski, 1804;
   Jachmann, 1804; Wasianski, 1804; Wald, 1804; Bou-
   terwek, 1804; Rinck, 1805; Schubert, 1842; Saintes, 1844 1724..1804
Kantemir, A. D., Prince. Russ. Diplomatist and Writer 1708..1774
Karamsin, Nicholas Michaelovitch. Russian Writer.... 1765..1826
Karnkowsky, Stanislaus. Polish Writer and Statesman 1525..1603
Karpinsky, Francis. Polish Poet.................... 1760?.1823
Kästner, Abraham Gotthelf. *See* Kaestner .... 1719..1800
Kastner, Charles William Gottlob. German Naturalist 1783..1857
Kater, Captain Henry. Mathematician .... 1777..1835
Katona, Stephen. (*History of Hungary*) .... 1732..1811
Kauffmann, Maria Anna Angelica. Swiss Painter...... 1741..1807
Kaunitz, Wenzel Anthony, Prince of. Austrian Statesman 1711..1794
Kay, William. Poet and Historical Painter .... 1520..1568
Kaye, or Caius, John. Founder of Caius College........ 1510..1573
Kaye, John. Bishop of Lincoln .... 1783..1853
Kazinczy, Francis. Hungarian Writer................. 1759..1831
Keach, Benj. Bapt. Writer. (*Trav. of True Godliness*) 1640..1704
Kean, Edmund. Tragedian. Life by Procter, 1835..... 1787?.1833
Keane, John, Lord. General; Capturer of Ghuznee..... 1781..1844
Kearny, Philip. American General .... 1815..1862
Kearny, Stephen Watts. American General .... 1794..1848

BORN. DIED.

Keate, George. Poet and Miscellaneous Writer......... 1729?.1797
Keating, Geoffrey. Irish Historical Writer .... — ..1625?
Keats, John. Poet. (*Endymion.*) Life by M. Milnes, 1845 1796..1821
Keble, Joseph. Writer on Law..................... 1632..1710
Keckerman, Bartholomew, of Dantzic. Teacher & Writer 1573..1609
Keilhau, Baltbazar Mathias. Norwegian Geologist ..... 1797..1858
Keill, James, M. D. Physician .... 1673..1719?
Keill, John, M. D., brother. Mathematician & Nat. Philos. 1671..1721
Keim, Francis Xavier. German Architect.............. 1769..1864
Keiser, Reinhard. Mus. Comp., Poet. Writ., Hist. Writer 1673..1739
Keith, Geo., 5th E. Marischal. Founder of Marischal Coll. — ..1623
Keith, George, Tenth Earl Marischal. Scottish Jacobite,
    Prussian Diplomatist............................. 1693..1778
Keith, George Keith Elpbinstone, Viscount. Admiral... 1746..1823
Keith, James. Scottish Jacobite and Prussian General.. 1696..1758
Keith, Sir Robert Murray. Life by Mrs. G. Smyth, 1849 — ..1795
Keith, Thomas. Mathematician. (*Use of the Globes*)*.*... 1759..1824
Keller, James. German Statesman. (*Mysteria Politica*) 1568..1631
Keller, John Balthasar. Swiss Founder in Brass........ 1638..1702
Kellermann, Francis Christopher, Duke of Valmy. Mar-
    shal of France. Life by Botidoux, 1817............. 1735..1820
Kellermann, Francis Stephen, son. General. (*Mémoires*) 1770..1835
Kelley, or Talbot, Edward. Necromancer and Alchemist;
    Friend of Dee.................................. 1555..1595
Kellgren, John Henry. Swedish Poet.................. 1751..1795
Kellison, Matthew. Rom. Catholic Controversial Divine 1560?.1641
Kelly, Hugh. Irish Dramatic Poet.................... 1739..1777
Kelly, Rev. John, LL. D. Celtic Scholar............... 1750..1809
Kelly, Michael. Musical Composer................... 1762..1825
Kelly, Thomas. Roman Catholic Primate of all Ireland — ..1835
Kelway, Joseph. Organist in London .... — ..1782
Kemble, Charles, brother of John Philip. Actor........ 1775..1854
Kemble, George Stephen, brother. Actor............. 1758..1822
Kemble, John Mitchell, son of Charles. Saxonist...... 1807..1857
Kemble, John Philip. Actor. Life by J. Boaden, 1825. 1757..1823
Kemble, Mrs. Priscilla, wife. Actress................ 1755?.1845
Kemp, George Mickle. Scottish Architect............. 1794..1844
Kemp, James, D. D. Bp. of Prot. Episc. Ch. in Maryland 1764..1827
Kemp, John, Cardinal Archbp. of Canterbury. Ld. Chanc. 1380..1454
Kemp, Joseph. Musical Composer .... 1778..1824
Kempelen, Wolfgang, Baron. Hung. Mechan. and Writer 1734..1804
Kemper, Reuben. American Soldier .... — ..1826
Kempis, Thomas à. Life by Brewer, 1676; Zuniga, 1762;
    Cesarini, 1835; Chas. Butler; Baehring, 1849 .... 1380?.1471
Ken, Thomas. Bp. of Bath & Wells. L. by W. Hawkins,
    1713; Canon W. L. Bowles, 1830; A Layman, 1854.. 1637..1711
Kendal, George. Ejected Nonconformist Divine........ — ..1663
Kendrick, Nath., D. D. Amer. Divine. L. by S. W. Adams 1777..1848
Kenmure, Wm. Gordon, Visct. Scottish Jacobite; beh.. 1643..1716
Kennaway, Sir John. Officer and Diplomatist......... 1758..1836
Kennedy, Miss Grace. Writer. (*Father Clement*)..... 1782..1825
Kennedy, James. Bishop of St. Andrew's. Statesman. 1405..1466
Kennedy, John, M. D. Scottish Medalist and Collector.. — ..1760
Kennedy, Rev. John. Mathem. (*Scripture Chronology*) 1700?.1770?

BORN. DIED.

Kennedy, William. Antiquary. (*Annals of Aberdeen*). 1759..1836
Kennet, Basil, D.D. Class. & Theol. Writ. (*Roman Antiq.*) 1674..1715
Kennet, White. Bp. of Peterb. Hist. Life by Newton 1660..1728
Kenneth I. King of Scotland (604–5)................ — .. 605
Kenneth II. (823–54) .... — .. 854
Kenneth III. (969–94)............................. — .. 994
Kenney, James. Dramatist. ....1770? 1849
Kennicott, Benjamin, D.D. Biblical Critic .... 1718..1783
Kenrick, Francis Patrick, D.D. Amer. Rom. Cath. Abp. 1797..1863
Kenrick, William. Miscellaneous Writer............. 1720?.1779
Kent, Edw. Aug., Dk. of; son of Geo. III. L. by Neale, 1850 1767..1820
Kent, James. Musical Composer..................... 1700..1776
Kent, James. Amer. Jurist. (*Comment. on Amer. Law*) 1763..1847
Kent, John de. Schoolman......................... fl. 1248
Kent, Marie Louise Victoria, Duchess of.............. 1786..1861
Kent, Wm. Paint., Architect, Sculpt., Landsc. Gardener 1684..1748
Kenton, Simon. American Pioneer .... 1755..1836
Kenyon, John. English Poet........................ 1783?.1856
Kenyon, Lloyd, Lord. Judge. Life by Lord Campbell 1733..1802
Kepler, John. Astronomer. Life by Breitschwert, 1831;
   Sir David Brewster, 1841; Reuschle, 1841 ...... 1571..1630
Keppel, Augustus, Visct. Admiral. L. by T. Keppel, 1842 1725..1786
Ker, John, of Kersland. Scottish Philologist .... fl. 1726
Keratry, Auguste Hilarion de. Fr. Author & Statesman 1769..1859
Kerckchove, Joseph van den, of Bruges. Painter...... 1669..1724
Kerckherdere, John Gerard. Dutch Historian & Theol. 1678?.1738
Kerckring, Theodore. Dutch Physician.............. — .1693
Kerguélen Trémarec, Yves Joseph de. Fr. Navigator 1745..1797
Kerhallet, Chas. Philip de. Fr. Hydrograph. & Meteorol. 1809..1863
Keri, Francis Borgia. Hung. Historian and Astronomer — ..1769
Keroual, Louisa Penhoet, Duchess of Portsmouth .... 1652? 1734
Kerr, Robt. Historian. (*Collection of Voyayes and Trav.*) 1750?.1814
Kersaint, Armand Guy Simon, Ct. of. French Politician 1741?.1793
Kersey, John. Math. and Philol. (*Elements of Algebra*) 1616?.1690?
Kervillars, John Mary de. Fr. Jesuit. Transl. of Ovid 1668..1745
Kessel, John van. Dutch Painter..................... 1626..1708
Ketel, Cornelius. Dutch Painter...................... 1548..1602
Kett, Rev. Henry. Divine.......................... 1761..1825
Kett, William, of Norfolk. Rebel Leader .... — ..1549
Kettlewell, John. Nonj. L. by Hickes and Nelson, 1718 1653..1695
Keulen, Janssen van. Dutch Portrait Painter......... — ..1665
Keulen, Ludolph van. Dutch Geometer.............. — ..1610
Key, Francis Scott. American Lawyer and Song Writer.
   (*Star-Spangled Banner*) .... 1779..1843
Keysler, John George, F. R. S. Ger. Traveler and Antiq. 1683..1743
Khaled. Moslem General.......................... 582.. 642?
Khalekan. Arabian Biographer. (*Deaths of Illust. Men*) 1230?.1303?
Khemnitzer, Ivan Ivanovitch. Russian Fabulist....... 1744..1784
Kheraskoff, Michael. Russian Poet. (*Rossiad*)........ 1733..1807
Khilkof, Andrew Jacob. Prince. Russ. Statesm. and Hist. — ..1718
Khosru I., or Chosroes. King of Persia (531–79) .... — .. 579
Khosru II. (590–628)............................. — .. 628
Kick, Cornelius, of Amsterdam. Painter.............. 1635..1675
Kidd, Dr. John. Prof. of Chem. (*Bridgewater Treatise*) 1775..1851

BORN. DIED.

Kidd, William. American Pirate .... — ..1701
Kidder, Richard. Bishop of Bath and Wells .... 1635?.1703
Kien Long, or Khihan Loung. Emp. of China (1735–96) 1711..1799
Kierings, Alexander, of Utrecht. Landscape Painter ... 1590..1646
Kiesewetter, Christopher Godfrey. Violinist .... 1777..1827
Kiffin, William. Life by Orme, 1822................. 1616..1701
Kilbourne, James. American Pioneer .... 1770..1850
Kilburne, Richard. (*Topographie of Kent*)............ 1606?.1678
Kilbye, Rd., of Derby. (*Burthen of a Loaden Conscience*) — ..1617
Kilbye, Rd. Rector of Lincoln Coll. Translator of Bible — ..1620
Kilham, Alex. Founder of New Methodist Connection — ..1798
Kilian, Bartholomew. Engraver...................... 1630..1696
Kilian, Luke, of Augsburg. Engraver................. 1579..1637
Kilian, Philip Andrew. Engraver .... 1714..1759
Kilian, Wolffgang. Engraver .... 1581..1662
Killigrew, Ann. Maid of Honor. Painter and Poet ... 1660..1685
Killigrew, Catherine. Scholar and Poet............. 1530?.1600?
Killigrew, Henry. Prebendary. Royalist, Dramatist .. 1612..1690?
Killigrew, Margaret, Duchess of Newcastle. Writer .... 1624?.1674
Killigrew, Thomas. *King Charles's Jester*. Dramatist.. 1611..1682
Killigrew, Sir William. Royalist and Writer .... 1605?.1693
Kilmarnock, Wm. Boyd, 4th E. of. Scot. Jacobite; beh. 1702..1746
Kilvert, Rev. Francis. English Scholar and Author.... 1793..1863
Kilwarden, Arthur Wolfe, Lord. Irish Chief Justice.... — ..1803
Kimber, Edw. Peerage Compiler. (*Hist. Eng.* 10 vols.) — ..1769
Kimber, Isaac. Dissent. Minister. (*Hist. Eng.* 4 vols.) 1692..1758
Kimchi, or Kimhi, David. Rabbi. Biblical Commentator — ..1240
Kinaston, Sir Francis. Scholar .... 1587..1642?
King, Charles. Composer of Church Services .... — ..1745
King, Daniel. (*The Vale Royal of England*)........... fl. 1660
King, Edward. Poet; Subject of Milton's *Lycidas*...... 1610..1637
King, Edward. Antiquary. (*Munimenta Antiqua*)...... 1736..1807
King, Gregory. Heraldic and Commercial Writer ...... 1648..1712
King, Henry. Bishop of Chichester. Poet and Writer.. 1591..1669
King, John. Bishop of London. Preacher............. 1559?.1621
King, John. Public Orator of Oxford................. — ..1639
King, John, D. D., of Chelsea. Controversial Divine. (*To-
     lando Pseudologo-Mastix*)........................ 1652..1732
King, John Glen, D. D. Writer and Antiquary....... 1735..1787
King, Peter, First Lord. Lord Chancellor and Theologian 1669..1734
King, Peter, Seventh Lord. Biographer of Locke ...... 1775..1833
King, Philip Barker. Admiral...................... 1793..1855
King, Rufus. American Statesman and Diplomatist .... 1755..1827
King, Thomas. Actor and Dramatic Writer........... 1730..1805
King, Thomas Starr. American Clergyman and Writer 1824..1864
King, William, LL. D. Mythol., Poet., and Polit. Writer. 1663..1712
King, Wm. Abp. of Dublin. Metaphys. (*De Orig. Mali*) 1650..1729
King, William, LL. D., of Oxford. (*Anecdotes of his own
     Times.*) Life by Nichols, 1770.................... 1685..1763
King, Wm. Rufus. Statesman. Vice-President of U. S. 1786..1853
Kingsborough, Edward King, Visct. (*Antiq. of Mexico*) 1795..1837
Kingsley, James Luce, LL. D. American Scholar....... 1778..1852
Kingsmill, Andrew. Puritan Divine................. 1538..1569
Kingston, Eliz. Chudleigh, Duchess of. Life, Lond. 1789 1720..1788

BORN.   DIED.
Kippingius, Henry. German Scholar .... 1623?.1678
Kippis, Andrew. Editor of *Biographia Britannica*...... 1725..1795
Kirby, John Joshua. Artist......................... 1716..1774
Kirby, Rev. Wm. Entomologist. Life by Freeman, 1852 1759..1850
Kirch, Christian Frederick, son of Godfrey. Astronomer. 1694..1740
Kirch, Godfrey. German Astronomer .... 1639..1710
Kirch, Mary Margaret, wife. Astronomer .... 1670..1720
Kircher, Athanasius. Mathem. (*Mundus Subterraneus*) 1602..1680
Kircher, Conrad. (*Concordantia Veteris Testamenti*).... —aft.1622?
Kirchmann, John. Antiq. (*De Funeribus Romanorum*) 1575..1643
Kirchmann. Russian Electrician...................... — ..1753
Kirchmayer, Geo. Gaspar. Ger. Classical Commentator 1635..1700
Kirckman, John. Harpsichord Maker................. — ..1778
Kirkaldy, Sir William, of Grange. Soldier. Life by J.
  Grant, 1841................................... — ..1573
Kirke, Percy. Colonel of *Kirke's Lambs*.....ti. Jas. II. & Wm. III.
Kirke White, Henry. *See* White .... 1785..1806
Kirkland, Caroline Matilda, *née* Stanbury. American
  Authoress.................................... 1801..1864
Kirkland, John Thornton, D. D. American Clergyman
  and Scholar; President of Harvard College .... 1770..1840
Kirkland, Thos., M.D., of Ashby-de-la-Zouch. Med. Writ. 1721..1798
Kirkpatrick, William James. Orientalist .... 1760..1812
Kirkton, Rev. James. (*Church History of Scotland*).... — .. 1699
Kirnberger, John Philip. German Musical Composer .. 1721..1783
Kirstenius, George, of Stettin. Medical Writer........ 1613..1660
Kirstenius, Peter. Swedish Orientalist .... 1577..1640
Kirwan, Richard, LL. D. Scientific Writer............ 1750?.1812
Kirwan, Walter Blake. Dean. Irish Divine & Preacher 1754?.1805
Kisfaludy, Alexander. Hungarian Poet............... 1772..1844
Kisfaludy, Charles, brother. Hungarian Dramatic Poet. 1788..1830
Kiss, Augustus. German Sculptor .... 1802..1865
Kissel, John van. Dutch Painter................... 1626..1708
Kitchiner, William, M. D. Miscellaneous Writer........ 1775?.1827
Kitto, John, D. D. Biblical Writer. Life by Ryland, 1856 1804..1854
Klaproth, Henry Jules. Orientalist................. 1783..1835
Klaproth, Martin Henry. Chemist and Mineralogist.... 1743..1817
Kléber, John Baptist. French General. Life by Héri-
  court, 1800; Cousin d'Avallon, 1801 .... 1754?.1800
Klein, James Theodore. German Naturalist........... 1685..1759
Kleist, Ewald Christian von. Prussian Officer and Poet.
  (*Spring*)..................................... 1715..1759
Kleist, Henry von. German Dramatic Writer......... 1776..1811
Kleist von Nollendorf, Emilius Frederick, Count. Prus-
  sian General .... 1762..1823
Klenze, Leo von, of Munich. Architect .... 1784..1864
Klicpera, Wenceslaus. Bohemian Dramatist.......... 1792?.1859
Klingemann, Ern. Aug. Fred., of Brunswick. Dramatist 1777..1831
Klingenstierna, Samuel. Swedish Mathematician..... 1689..1785
Klinger, Fred. Maximilian von. Russ. Officer and Writer 1753?.1831
Klingstadt, Chas. Gustavus. Russian Miniature Painter 1657..1734
Klocker, David. Historical Painter at Stockholm ...... 1629..1698
Klopstock, Frederick Theophilus. German Poet. Life
  by Elizabeth Smith, 1811; Doering, 1825; Gruber, 1832 1724..1803

BORN. DIED.

Klose, F. J., of London. Musical Composer............ — ..1830
Klotz, Christian Adolphus. Critic, Lat. Poet, Numismatist 1738..1771
Kluit, Adrian. Dutch Historian .... 1735..1807
Kmety, Geo. *Ismail Pacha.* Hung. General in Turkey 1813..1865
Knapp, George Christian. German Theologian......... 1753..1825
Knapp, Samuel Lorenzo. American Author............ 1784..1838
Knapton, George. Portrait Painter in Crayons......... 1698..1788
Kneller, Sir Godfrey. Painter....................... 1648?.1723
Kniaziewicz, Charles. Polish General................ 1762..1842
Kniaznin, Francis Dionysius. Polish Poet............. 1750..1807
Knibb, William. Baptist Missionary in Jamaica........ 1800?.1845
Knight, Edward. Comic Actor .... 1774..1826
Knight, Gowin, M. D. Natural Philosopher............ — ..1772
Knight, Henry Gally, M. P. Traveler and Antiquary.... 1786..1846
Knight, Richard Payne. Writer on Art .... 1750..1824
Knight, Samuel, D. D. Divine and Biographer......... 1674..1746
Knight, Thomas Andrew. Vegetable Physiologist...... 1758..1838
Knight, William H. Artist........................ 1823?.1863
Knighton, Henry, of Leicester. (*Chron. of English Hist.*) fl. ti. Rd. II.
Knighton, Sir William, Bart., M. D. Phys. and Courtier 1775?.1836
Knipperdolling, Bernard. Anabaptist................. — ..1536
Knoller, Martin von. German Painter................ 1725..1804
Knolles, Richard. Grammarian. (*History of Turks*) ... 1540?.1610
Knolles, Sir Robert. English Commander in France.... 1317..1407
Knollis, or Knowles, Sir Francis. Statesman and Writer 1530?.1596
Knorr, George Wolfgang. Ger. Engraver and Naturalist 1705..1761
Knorr von Rosenroth, Christian. German Orientalist.
   (*Kabbala Denudata*)............................... 1636..1689
Knott, Edward. *Matthias Wilson.* Jesuit Writer....... 1580..1656
Knowler, William. Divine; Translator of Chrysostom.. 1699?.1767
Knowles, James Davis. Amer. Clergyman and Author.. 1798..1838
Knowles, James Sheridan. Dramatist and Writer ..... 1784..1862
Knowles, Rev. Thomas. Divine and Classical Scholar.. 1723..1802
Knowlton, Thomas. English Botanist................ 1692..1782
Knox, Henry. American General and Statesman....... 1750..1806
Knox, John. Scottish Reformer. Life by McCrie, 1812;
   T. Brandes, 1863 .... 1505..1572
Knox, John. Bookseller and Projector. (*Systematic View
   of Scotland*) .... 1720..1791
Knox, Vicesimus, D. D. Theological Writer............ 1752..1821
Knox, William. Poet.............................. — ..1825
Knupfer, Nicholas. German Painter................. 1603..1660
Knutzen, Martin. Prussian Philosopher. (*Defense of
   the Christian Religion*) .... 1713..1751
Knutzen, Matthias. German Atheist................. fl. 1674
Knyghton, Henry, of Leicester. (*Chron. of English Hist.*) fl. ti. Rd. II.
Knyphausen, Baron. Lieutenant-General in British Ser-
   vice in American Revolutionary War............... 1730?.1789
Kobell, Ferdinand. German Painter and Etcher ...... 1740..1799
Kobell, Francis, brother. Artist .... 1749..1822
Koch, Christopher Wm. Genealogist, Canonist, Hist... 1737..1813
Koch, Joseph Anthony. German Landscape Painter.... 1768..1839
Kochanowski, John. Polish Poet.................... 1532..1584
Koeberger, Wenceslaus, of Antwerp. Painter .... 1554..1634

BORN. DIED.

Koehler, John David. German Writer .... 1684..1755
Koekkoek, Bernard Cornelius. Dutch Landscape Painter 1803..1858
Koelcsey, Francis. Hungarian Poet, Critic, Orator .... 1790..1838
Koenig, Emanuel. Swiss Medical Writer.............. 1658..1731
Koenig, Frederick. German Inventor .... 1775..1833
Koenig, George Matthias. (*Bibliotheca Vetus et Nova*)... 1616..1699
Koenig, John Gerard, of Courland. Phys., Bot., Traveler 1728..1785
Koenig, Samuel. Mathematician and Philosopher...... 1712..1757
Koenigsmarck. *See* Königsmarck.
Koerner, Charles Theodore. *See* Körner............. 1791..1813
Koerten-Block, Joanna. Dutch Painter, Modeler, and
    Profile Cutter...................................... 1650..1715
Koets, Roelof, of Zwoll. Portrait Painter............. 1655..1725
Kolbe, or Kolben, Peter. Traveler. (*Cape of Good Hope*) 1675..1726
Kölcsey, Francis. Hungarian Poet, Critic, Orator...... 1790..1838
Kollar, John. Hungarian Poet and Preacher........... 1793..1852
Koller, Francis, Baron von. Austrian General......... 1767..1826
Kollmann, Aug. Fred. Chas. Ger. Composer in London 1756..1824
Kollontaj, Hugh. Polish Statesman and Author....... 1750..1812
Kolzow, Alexèi Vassilievitch. Russian Poet........... 1809..1842
König. *See* Koenig.
Königsmarck, Mary Aurora, Countess of. Mother of
    Marshal Saxe .... 1668?.1728
Königsmarck, Philip Christopher, Count, brother. Swed-
    ish Adventurer .... 1640?.1694
Koninck, or Koning, David van. Dutch Painter....... — ..1687
Koninck, or Koning, Philip van. Dutch Painter....... 1619..1689
Koornhert, Theodore. Dutch Advocate for Toleration.. 1522..1590
Kopp, John Adam. German Publicist................. 1698..1748
Koray, Adamantius. Greek Patriot and Writer .... 1748..1833
Körner, or Koerner, Charles Theodore. Poet. Life by
    his father, translated by G. F. Richardson; Lehmann,
    1819; Erhard, 1821................................ 1791..1813
Kortholt, Christian. German Scholar................ 1633..1694
Kosciuszko, Thaddeus. Polish General. Life by Jullien,
    1818; Low, 1820; Fayot, 1820; Falkenstein, 1827;
    Chodzko, 1837..................... .... 1745? 1817
Kosegarten, Louis Theobul. German Poet and Divine. 1758..1818
Koster, Lawrence Janszoon, of Haarlem. Printer...... 1370?.—
Kostrow, Ermilius Ivanovitch. Russian Poet......... — ..1796
Kotter, Christopher, of Sprottow. Enthusiast......... 1585..1647
Kotzebue, Augustus Frederick Ferd. von. Ger. Writer.. 1761..1819
Kotzebue, Otto von, brother. Circumnavigator........ 1757..1846
Kotzebue, Otto von, son of Augustus. Traveler........ 1787..1846
Kouck, Peter. Painter at Antwerp................... 1500?.1550
Kouli Khan. *Nadir Shah.* Persian Warrior .... 1687..1747
Koumas, Constantine Michael. Greek Scholar & Author 1775?.1836
Kozak, John Sophronius. Bohemian Medical Writer.... 1603..1685
Kozeluch, Leopold. Composer for the Harpsichord..... 1753..1814
Kozloff, Ivan Ivanovitch. Russian Poet.............. 1774..1838
Kozmian, Cajetan. Polish Poet...................... — ..1856
Kracheninnikow, Stephen. Russian Nat. and Traveler 1713..1755
Krafft, Adam, of Nuremberg. Sculptor and Architect .. 1435?.1507
Krafft, George Wolfgang. Ger. Mathem. and Philosopher 1701..1754

BORN. DIED.

Kraitsir, Charles. Hung. Phys. and Philol. in America.. 1804..1860
Kranach, or Cranach, Luke. *Sunder.* German Painter 1472..1553
Kranach, or Cranach, Luke, son. Painter .... 1515?.1586
Krantz, Albert. Historian. Life by Wilkens, 1722..... 1450?.1517
Kranz, or Cranz, David. Moravian Missionary......... 1723..1777
Krasicki, Ignatius. Polish Bishop, Poet, and Writer... 1735..1801
Krasinski, Valerian, Count. Polish Protestant Writer .. 1780?.1855
Kraus, Martin. *Crusius.* Ger. Scholar. (*Turco-Græcia*) 1526..1607
Krause, Charles Christian Frederick. Ger. Philosopher 1781..1832
Krause, Francis, of Augsburg. Historical Painter...... 1706..1754
Krauss, John Baptist. Ger. Theol., Historian, and Critic 1700..1762
Kray de Krajof, Paul, Baron von. Austrian General... 1735..1804
Kresa, Father. Moravian Scholar.................... 1648..1715
Kreutzer, Rodolph. Violinist and Musical Composer... 1766..1831
Kromayer, Jerome. German Theologian and Historian. 1610..1670
Krüdener, or Kruedener, Juliana Wietinghoff, Baroness
    von. Russian Mystic and Novelist................ 1764..1824
Krug, William Traugott. German Philosopher......... 1770..1842
Krummacher, Fred. Adolph. Theol. & Poet. (*Parables*) 1768..1845
Krummacher, Godfrey Dan., br. (*Wanderings of Israel*) 1774..1837
Krunitz, John Geo. Ger. Phys. & Nat. Philos. (*Encyclop.*) 1728..1796
Krusemark, Baron von. Prussian General and Diplom. — ..1821
Krusenstern, Adam John, Chev. de. Russian Navigator 1770..1846
Kryloff, or Kriloff, Ivan Andreevitch. Russian Fabulist. 1768..1844
Kublai-Khan. Founder of the Mogul Dynasty of China — ..1294
Kügelgen, or Kuegelgen, Charles Ferdinand von. Ger-
    man Painter................................... 1772..1832
Kügelgen, or Kuegelgen, Gerard von, twin-brother.
    Painter. Life by Hasse, 1824.................... 1772..1820
Kugler, Francis Theodore. German Art Critic .... 1808..1858
Kuh, Ephraim Moses. German Poet.................. 1731..1790
Kuhlman, Quirinus. Fanatic; burnt in Russia......... 1651..1689
Kuhnau, John. German Organist and Musical Composer 1667..1722
Kuhnius, or Kuhn, Joachim. Philologist............. 1647..1697
Kuhnoel, Christian Theophilus. German Critic .... 1768..1841
Kuick, or Kuyk, John van, of Dort. Painter.......... 1530..1572
Kunckel, John. German Chemist................... 1630..1703
Kunzen, Charles Adolphus. Mus. Performer and Comp. 1720..1781
Kupetzky, John. Hungarian Portrait Painter....... 1666 or 7.1740
Kuster, Ludolph. German Scholar and Critic .... 1670..1716
Kuttner, Charles Gottlob. German Traveler .... 1755..1805
Kutusoff, Michael, Prince of. *Smolenskoi.* Russ. General 1745..1813
Kuyk Wouterszoon, John van. Painter............. 1530..1572
Kuyp, or Cuyp, Albert. Landscape Painter.......... 1606..1667
Kuyp, or Cuyp, Jacob Gerritse, of Dort. *The Old.*
    Dutch Portrait Painter......................... 1575..1650
Kyd, Thomas. Dramatic Writer.................... fl. ti. Eliz.
Kydermynster, Richard. Abbot of Winchcombe. Hist. — ..1531
Kynaston, Sir Francis. Poet....................... 1587..1642?
Kynaston, John, of Brazenose College. Divine........ 1728..1783
Kyper, Albert. Medical Writer.................... 1605?.1655
Kypke, Geo. David. Orientalist. (*Observationes Sacræ*) 1724..1779
Kyrle, John. *Man of Ross.* Philanthropist............ 1664..1754

L.

BORN. DIED.

Laar, Peter van. *Bamboccio.* Dutch Painter....... 1613..1673 or 5
Labadie, John de. French Mystic .... 1610..1674
Labat, John Baptist. French Missionary and Traveler.. 1663..1738
Labbe, Philip. French Jesuit. (*Collection of Councils*).. 1607..1667
Labé, Louise, of Lyons. *La Belle Cordière.* Poetess.... 1526..1566
La Beaumelle, Lawrence de. (*Letters to Voltaire*)...... 1727..1773
La Bédoyère, Charles Angelica Francis Huchet, Count
  de. French General; shot........................ 1786..1815
Laberius, Decimus. Roman Dramatic Writer.......... — B.C. 44
La Billardière, Jas. Julian Houton de. Fr. Trav. & Nat. 1755..1834
Lablache, Louis. Italian Singer..................... 1794..1858
La Boetie, Stephen de. Fr. Republican. (*Le Contr' Un*) 1530..1563
Laborde, Alex. Louis Joseph, Count. (*Pictorial Travels*) 1774..1842
Laborde, John Benjamin de. French Musician & Writer 1734..1794
Laborde, John Joseph, Marquis de. French Financier.. 1724..1794
Labourdonnais, Bertrand Francis Mahé de. French Na-
  val Officer. Governor of Mauritius .... 1699..1753
Laboureur, John le. Historian and Antiquary......... 1623..1675
Labrosse, Guy de. Fr. Bot. and Phys. (*On the Plague*) — ..1641
Labrouse, Clotilde Susan Courcelles de. Fr. Enthusiast 1741..1821
La Bruyère, John de. French Writer. (*Caractères*)... 1644?.1696
La Butte, Réné. French Scholar and Mathematician... — ..1790
La Caille, Nicholas Louis de. French Astronomer...... 1713..1762
La Calprenède, Walter de Costes de. French Dramatic
  Writer and Romancist...................... 1612?.1663
Lacarry, Giles. Historian and Antiquary .... 1605..1684
Lacépède, Bernard Germain Stephen de la Ville, Count
  de. French Naturalist .... 1756..1825
La Cerda, Bernarda Ferreira de. Portuguese Poetess.... 1595..1644
Lacerda, Francis Joseph de. Portuguese Traveler...... — ..1800?
Lachaise d'Aix, Francis de. Jesuit. Confess. to Louis XIV. 1624..1709
Lachmann, Charles, of Berlin. Critic and Philologist... 1793..1851
Lackington, James. Life by self, 1792 .... 1746?.1816
Laclos, Peter Ambrose Francis Chonderlos de. French
  Writer and Soldier .... 1741..1803
La Colonie, John Martin de. (*History of Bordeaux*).... 1674..1759
Lacombe, James. Hist. Writ. (*Letters of Qu. Christina*) 1724..1811
Lacombe de Prezel, Honoré, brother. (*Dict. de Citoyen*) 1725.. —
La Condamine, Charles Mary de. Mathem. and Traveler 1701..1774
Lacordaire, John Baptist Henry. Dominican Preacher.
  Life by Count Montalembert...................... 1802..1861
Lacretelle, John Charles Dominic de. French Historian 1766..1855
Lacretelle, Peter Louis, brother. French Writer .... 1751..1824
Lacroix, Anthony Nicholas. (*Géographie Moderne*) .... 1704..1760
Lacroix, Silvester Francis. French Mathematician .... 1765..1843
Lacruz y Cano, Ramonde. Spanish Dramatic Poet...... 1728..1795
Lactantius, Lucius Cœlius Firmianus. Christian Writer — aft. 317
Lacuna, or Laguna, Andrew. Spanish Medical Writer.. 1499..1560
Lacy, Edmund. Bishop of Exeter.................... — ..1455
Lacy, John. Actor and Dramatist.................... — ..1681

BORN. DIED.

Ladd, William. American Philanthropist.............. 1778..1841
Ladislaus I. King of Hungary (1077–95). *Saint*...... 1041..1095
Ladislaus II. reckoned by some...................... 1134?.1162
Ladislaus II., or III. (1204–5)..................... 1185?.1205
Ladislaus III., or IV. (1272–90.) *Le Chuman* .... 1250?.1290
Ladislaus IV., or V. (1440–44.) VI. of Poland (1435–44) 1400?.1444
Ladislaus V., or VI. (1444–57.) *Le Posthume* .... 1439..1457
Ladislaus VI., or VII. (1490–1516.) King of Bohemia
    (1470–1516)............................. 1450?.1516
Ladislaus I. King of Poland (1081–1102). *Hermann*.. 1044?.1102
Ladislaus II. (1139–46)........................... 1104?.1163
Ladislaus III. (1296–1333)........................ — ..1333
Ladislaus IV. .... — —
Ladislaus V. (1386–1434.) *Jagellon*................ 1354..1434
Ladislaus VI. (1435–44.) IV. of Hungary (1440–44)... 1400?.1444
Ladislaus VII., Sigismund (1632–48)................ 1596?.1648
Ladislaus, or Launcelot, Ct. of Provence. King of Naples 1376..1414
Ladvocat, John Baptist. Fr. Writer. (*Historical Dict.*) 1709..1765
Ladvocat, Louis Francis. (*Entretiens sur un nouveau*
    Système)............................... 1645?.1735
Lælius, Caius. *Sapiens.* Roman Publicist........... 186.115 B.C.
Laennec, René Theodore Hyacinth. (*De l'Auscultation.*)
    Life by Forbes............................ 1781..1826
Laer, or Laar, Peter van. *Bamboccio.* Dutch Painter 1613.1673 or 5
Laet, John de. Dutch Historical and Geographical Writer — ..1649
Lævinus, Torrentius. *Van der Beken.* Dutch Poet.... 1525..1595
La Fayette, Louisa Motier, Mdlle. de. Beauty and Wit.. 1616?.1665
La Fayette, Ctss. de. Novelist. (*Zayde.*) *See* La Vergne 1632..1693
Lafayette, Mary Jane Paul Roch Yves Gilbert Motier,
    Marquis de. Life by his family............. 1757..1834
La Ferté Imbault, Maria Theresa Geoffrin, Marchss. de 1715..1791
Laffitte, James. French Banker and Financier....... 1767..1844
Laffon de Ladébat, Andrew Daniel. Statesm., Financier 1746..1829
Lafitau, Joseph Francis. Jesuit Missionary in America.. 1670..1740
Lafitau, Peter Francis, br. Jesuit. Preacher & Hist. Writer 1685..1764
Lafitte, John. Corsair .... 1780?.1817 or 26
Lafont, Joseph de. French Dramatist .... 1686..1725
Lafontaine, Augustus Henry Julius. German Romancist 1756..1831
Lafontaine, John de. Fabulist. L. by Walckenaer, 1820 1621..1695
Laforce, Jas. Nompar de Caumont, Duc de. Marsh. of Fr. 1558..1652
Lafosse, Anthony de. Tragedian. (*Manlius Capitolinus*) 1653..1708
La Fuente, Alcantara Michael. Spanish Historian ..... 1817..1850
Lagalla, Julius Cæsar. Italian Phys. (*De Cœlo Animato*) 1576..1624
Lagaraye, Claude Toussaint Marot de. Philanthropist.. 1675..1755
Lagerbring, Suen. Swedish Historian................ 1707..1788
Lagerloef, Peter. Swedish Historiographer........... 1648..1699
Lagerstroem, Magnus von. Swedish Philosopher...... 1696..1759
Lagny, Thomas Fantet, Sieur de. Mathematician ...... 1660..1734
Lagomarsini, Jerome. Italian Jesuit. Philologist ..... 1698..1773
Lagrange, Joseph Louis. Mathematician............. 1736..1813
Laguerre, Louis. Painter......................... 1663..1721
Laguna, Andrew. Spanish Physician and Writer ...... 1499..1560
La Harpe, Frederick Cæsar. Swiss Patriot .... 1754..1838
La Harpe, John Francis de. Writer. Life by Mely-Janin 1739..1803

BORN. DIED.

Lahaye, William Nicholas de. French Engraver....... 1725..1802
La Hire, Philip de. French Mathematician............ 1640..1718
Laidlaw, William. Poetical Writer................... 1780..1845
Lainez, Alexander. French Poet .... 1650..1710
Lainez, James. General of the Jesuits. L. by Ribadeneira 1512..1565
Laing, Alexander. ⸱Antiquary....................... 1778..1838
Laing, Alexander. The Brechin Poet. (*Wayside Flowers*) 1787?.1857
Laing, Alexander Gordon. African Traveler........... 1794..1826
Laing, Malcolm. Historian. (*History of Scotland*)...... 1762..1818
Laire, Francis Xavier. French Bibliographer .... 1739..1801
Lairesse, Gerard. Flemish Portr. and Historical Painter 1640..1711
Lais. Grecian Courtesan .... 5th c. B.C.
Lais. Grecian Courtesan .... 4th c. B.C.
Lake, Arthur. Bishop of Bath and Wells.............. 1550?.1626
Lake, Gerard, Viscount. General .... 1744..1808
Lake, John. Bishop of Chichester .... — ..1689
Lalande, James de, of Orleans. Legal Antiquary ...... 1622..1703
Lalande, Joseph Jerome Francis de. Astronomer ...... 1732..1807
Lalande, Michael Richard de. French Musical Composer 1657..1726
Lallemand, Claude Francis. French Physician .... 1790..1854
Lalli, John Baptist. Italian Poet and Lawyer .... 1572..1637
Lally, Thomas Arthur, Ct. de. French General; beheaded 1702..1766
Lally Tollendal, Trophime Gérard, Marquis de. Statesm. 1751..1830
Lalor, John. Journalist and Essayist.................. — ..1856
Laluzerne, Cæsar Wm. de. Cardinal. Theol. & Polit. Writ. 1738..1821
Lamanon, Robert de Paul, Chev. de. French Nat. Philos. 1752..1787
Lamar, Mirabeau B. Second President of Texas....... 1798..1859
Lamarck, John Baptist Peter Anthony de Monnet, Cheva-
    lier de. Naturalist................................ 1744..1829
Lamarque, Maximilian, Ct. de. Fr. Officer and Politician 1770..1832
Lamb, Caroline, Lady. Novelist...................... 1785..1828
Lamb, Charles. Essayist. Life by Talfourd, 1850...... 1775..1834
Lamb, Hon. George. Under-Sec. Translator of Catullus — ..1834
Lamb, Sir Jas. Bland Burges, D. C. L. Under-Sec. Writ. 1752..1824
Lamb, John, D. D. Antiquary .... 1790?.1850
Lamballe, Maria Theresa Louise de Savoie - Carignan,
    Princess de. Friend of Marie Antoinette............ 1749..1792
Lambarde, Wm. Antiquary. (*Perambulation of Kent*). 1536..1601
Lambecius,, or Lambeck, Peter. German Writer .... 1628..1680
Lambert, St. Bishop of Maestricht. Life by De Tello,
    1622; Roberti, 1633; Dubosc Montandré, 1637........ 640?. 708
Lambert d'Aschaffenbourg. Historical Writer. (*Annals*) 1020?.1080?
Lambert, Anne Theresa de Marguenat de Courcelles,
    Marchioness of. Writer and Patron of Learning..... 1647..1733
.Lambert, Aylmer Bourke. Botanist.................. 1762..1842
Lambert, Claude Francis. French Historical Writer.... 1705?.1765
Lambert, Daniel. Fat man.......................... 1769..1809
Lambert, Francis. *John Serranus*. French Reformer .. 1487..1530
Lambert, George. English Landscape Painter*........ 1710..1765
Lambert, John. *Nichols*. Protestant Martyr.......... — ..1538
Lambert, John. Parliamentarian General............. 1620?.1694
Lambert, John Henry. Mathematician .... 1728..1777
Lamberti, Louis. Italian Greek Scholar .... 1758..1813
Lambin, Dennis. Fr. Protestant. Critic and Grammarian 1516..1572

BORN. DIED.

Lambinet, Peter. Fr. Bibliog. (*Recherches Historiques*) 1742..1813
Lambruschini, Louis. Italian Prelate .... 1776..1854
Lambton, John Geo. First E. of Durham. Gov. of Canada 1792..1840
Lambton, Wm. Colonel. Trigonomet. Surveyor of India — ..1823
Lamennais, Hugh Félicité Robert, Abbé de. Writer... 1782..1854
Lamennais, John Mary, Abbé de, brother............. 1780..1860
Lamettrie, Julian Offray de. Fr. Physician and Philos. 1709..1751
Lamey, Andrew. German Historian and Diplomatist ... 1726..1802
Lami, or Lamy, Bernard. Fr. Writ. (*Apparatus Biblicus*) 1645..1715
Lami, or Lamy, Francis. Fr. Theol. Opponent of Spinoza 1636..1711
Lami, John Baptist. Ital. Theologian. Ed. of Meursius 1697..1770
Lammetrie, Julian Offray de. Fr. Physician and Philos. 1709..1751
Lamoignon, William de. French Judge .... 1617..1677
Lamont, David, D. D. Scottish Divine .... — ..1837
Lamoricière, Christopher Louis Leon Juchault de. French
  General... 1806..1865
La Mothe le Vayer, Francis de. French Skeptical Philos. 1588..1672
Lamotte, Anth. Houdart de. Dram. Poet. (*Inez de Castro*) 1672..1731
Lamotte, Jane de Valois, Countess de. Intriguer....... 1756..1791
Lamotte, William. French Surgeon and Accoucheur ... fl. 1720
La Motte Fouqué, Caroline, Baroness de. Novelist .... 1773..1831
La Motte Fouqué, Frederick, Baron de. (*Undine*).... 1777..1843
Lamourette, Adrian. French Ecclesiastic and Politician 1742..1794
Lamouroux, John Vincent Felix. French Naturalist... 1779..1825
Lampe, Frederick Adolphus. Theol. & Antiq. (*St. John*) 1683..1729
Lampe, John Frederick. German Composer in England 1692?.1756
Lampillas, Francis Xavier. Spanish Jesuit Writer.... 1739..1798
Lamplugh, Thomas. Bp. of Exeter and Abp. of York.. 1615..1691
Lampridio, Benedict. Latin Poet .... — ..1540
Lampridius, Ælius. Historian and Biographer... ti. Diocl. & Const.
Lamy, Bernard. (*De Tabernaculo Fœderis*)........... 1645..1715
Lamy, Francis. French Benedictine. (*On Self-Knowledge*) 1636..1711
Lana-Terzi, Francis de. Ital. Math. (*Magisterium Naturæ*) 1631..1687
Lancaster, Sir James. Navigator................... — ..1620
Lancaster, or Lankester, Joseph. Educationist .... 1771..1838
Lancaster, Nathaniel, D. D. Divine and Poetical Writer 1700..1775
Lance, George. Painter............................. 1802?.1864
Lance, William. American Author and Politician...... 1791..1840
Lancelot, Anthony. French Writer.................. 1675..1740
Lancelot, Claude, of Port Royal. Grammarian .... 1615?.1695
Lancelotti, John Paul. Italian Canonist .... 1511..1591
Lancisi, John Mary. Italian Physician............... 1654..1720
Lancjean, Remi. Flemish Painter.................... — ..1671
Lancre, Peter de, of Bordeaux. Writer on Demonology — ..1630
Lancret, Nicholas. French Painter................... 1690..1743 .
Lancrinck, Prosper Henry. Flemish Painter in England 1628..1692
Landais, or Landois, Peter. French Politician .... — ..1485
Landen, John. Mathematician. (*Mathematical Memoirs*) 1719..1790
Lander, Frederick William. American Military Officer. 1822..1862
Lander, John. African Traveler .... 1807..1839
Lander, Richard, brother. African Traveler .... 1804..1834
Landi, Hortensius. Italian Writer .... — ..1560?
Landino, Christopher. Italian Scholar and Latin Poet.. 1424..1504
Lando. Pope (913 or 914) .... — .. 914

BORN. DIED.

Lando, Conrad. *Count.* German Adventurer.......... — ..1363
Lando, Peter. Doge of Venice (1539–45)............. — ..1545
Landon, Letitia Elizabeth (Mrs. Maclean). *L. E. L.* Poetess. Life by Blanchard, 1841..................... 1802..1838
Landor, Walter Savage. Writer and Poet............. 1775..1864
Landseer, John. Engraver .... 1769..1852
Lane, Ralph. Discoverer of Virginia under Raleigh..... fl. 1583
Lane, Sir Richard. Lord Keeper..................... —aft.1645
Lane, Samuel. Painter.............................. 1780?.1859
Lane, Timothy. Scientific Writer and Inventor........ — ..1807
Lane, William. Painter............................. — ..1819
Lanfranc, Archbishop of Canterbury................... 1005?.1089
Lanfranc, of Milan. (*Chirurgia Magna et Parva*)...... — ..1300?
Lanfranc, John. Italian Painter.................... 1581..1647
Lang, Charles Nicholas. Swiss Naturalist .... 1670..1741
Lang, John Michael. German Prot. Divine and Orient. 1664..1737
Lang, Oliver. Shipbuilder and Inventor.............. — ..1853
Langbaine, Gerard, D. D. Provost. Collector of MSS. 1608?.1658
Langbaine, Gerard, son. (*Account of Dramatic Poets*).. 1656..1692
Langbein, Augustus Frederick Ernest. German Author 1757..1835
Langdale, Alban, D. D. Roman Catholic Controversialist —aft.1584
Langdale, Henry Bickersteth, Lord. Master of Rolls ... 1783..1851
Langdale, Sir Marmaduke, Lord. Royalist Officer..... — ..1661
Langdon, John. American Statesman .... 1739..1819
Lange, or Langius, John. German Medical Writer ..... 1485..1565
Lange, Lawrence. Swedish Traveler.................. —aft.1737
Lange, or Langius, Rodolph, of Munster. (*De Excidio Hierosolymæ*)..................................... 1438?.1519
Langebeck, James. (*Scriptores Rerum Danicarum*).... 1710..1774
Langeland, or Longland, Robert. Poet. (*Piers Plowman*) fl. 1370?
Langeron, Andrault, Count. Russian General .... 1763..1831
Langham, Simon de. Cardinal. Archbp. of Canterbury 1310?.1376
Langhans, Charles Gothard. German Architect........ 1733..1808
Langhorne, Rev. Daniel. Historian and Antiquary .... — ..1681
Langhorne, Rev. John, D. D. Poet................... 1735..1779
Langius. *See* Lange.
Langland, or Longland, John. Bp. of Lincoln. Writer 1473..1547
Langlande, or Longland, Robert. (*Piers Plowman*) .... fl. 14th c.
Langle, John Maximilian de. Protestant Divine of Rouen 1590..1674
Langlès, Louis Matthew. French Orientalist.......... 1763..1824
Langley, Batty. Architect........................... — ..1751
Langley, Rev. Thos. Topographer. (*Hist. of Desborough*) — ..1801
Langtoft, Peter. English Chronicler .... fl. 1300?
Langton, Christopher, M. D. Medical Writer......... — ..1578
Langton, Stephen. Cardinal. Archbp. of Canterbury — ..1228
Languet, Hubert. French Protestant. (*Vindiciæ*) ..... 1518..1581
Languet de Gergy, J. Bapt. Joseph. Fr. Philanthropist 1675..1750
Languet de Gergy, John Joseph, br. Controversial Div. 1677..1753
Langwith, Benjamin, D. D. Natural Philosopher....... — ..1743
Laniere, Nicholas. Painter, Engraver, and Musician ... 1568..1646
Lanigan, John, D. D. Irish Clergyman and Author..... 1758..1828
Lanjuinais, John Denis, Count de. French Politician... 1753..1827
Lanjuinais, Joseph de. French Ecclesiastic; Writer.... — ..1808
Lankester, or Lancaster, Joseph. Educationist......... 1771..1838

BORN. DIED.

Lannes, John, Duke of Montebello. Marshal of France 1769..1809
Lannoy, Charles de. General of Charles V............ 1470?.1527
La Noue, Francis de. *Bras de Fer.* Huguenot. (*Discourses*) 1531..1591
Lansberghe, Philip van. Dutch Mathematician & Divine 1561..1632
Lansdowne, George Grandville, Visct. Politician & Poet 1667..1735
Lansdowne, Henry Petty Fitzmaurice, Marquess of..... 1780..1863
Lansdowne, William Petty, First Marquess of. Premier
    as Earl Shelburne.................................... 1737..1805
Lantier, Stephen Francis de. Poet, Dramatist, and Writer 1734..1826
Lanzani, Andrew. Italian Painter.................... 1645?.1712
Lanzi, Louis. Antiquary. (*History of Painting*) .... 1732..1810
Lanzoni, Joseph. Physician and Writer.............. 1663..1730
Lao-Tsee. Chinese Philosopher..................600.aft.517 B.C.
Laparelli, Francis. Italian Architect and Mechanician.. 1521..1570
La Pérouse, John Francis Gallaup, Ct. of. Fr. Navigator 1741..1788?
Lapide, Cornelius à. Biblical Commentator............ — ..1657
Laplace, or Plateanus, Peter de. Fr. Magistrate & Writer 1526..1572
Laplace, Peter Simon, Marquis de. (*Mechanique Céleste*) 1749..1827
Lapo, Arnulph. Architect and Sculptor...........?...... 1232?.1300
Lapo, James. Italian Architect..................... — ..1262
Larcher, Peter Henry. Classical Scholar and Translator 1726..1812
Lardner, Dionysius, LL. D. Scientific Writer. (*Cyclop.*) 1793..1859
Lardner, Nathaniel, D. D. (*Credibility.*) Life by Kippis 1684..1768
Larfarge, Mary Cappelle. French Poisoner........... 1816..1852
Largillière, Nicholas de. Portrait and Historical Painter 1656..1746
Larive, John Mauduit de. French Tragedian .... 1747..1827
Larivey, Peter de. French Dramatic Writer.......... 1550?.1612?
Larned, Sylvester. American Clergyman............. 1796..1820
La Rochefoucauld, Francis VI., Duc de. French States-
    man and Moralist. (*Maximes*).................... 1613..1680
La Rochefoucauld Liancourt, Francis Alexander Fred-
    erick, Duc de. Politician and Philanthropist. (*Trav-
    els in United States*)............................. 1747..1827
La Rochejaquelein, Henry du Verger, Count de. Ven-
    dean Royalist .... 1772..1794
Laromiguière, Peter. French Philosopher .... 1756..1837
Laroon, Marcellus. Flemish Painter .... 1653..1705
Larra, Mariano Joseph de. Spanish Writer .... 1809..1837
Larrey, Dominic John, Baron. French Army Surgeon.. 1766..1841
Larrey, Isaac de. Historian........................ 1638..1719
Larrivée, Henry. French Actor and Vocalist.......... 1733..1802
Larroque, Daniel de. Satirist. Roman Cath. Convert 1660?.1731
Larroque, Matthew de. Fr. Prot. (*Hist. of the Eucharist*) 1619..1684
La Salle, Anthony Charles Louis, Count de. Fr. General 1775..1809
La Salle, Robert Cavelier, Sieur de. French Navigator.. 1635?.1687
Lascaris, Andrew John. *Rhyndacenus.* Gr. Schol. in Italy 1445?.1535
Lascaris, Constantine. Greek Grammarian in Italy .... — ..1500?
Las Casas, Bartholomew de. Spanish Missionary to
    South America. (*History of the Indies*)........... 1474..1566
Las Cases, Emmanuel Augustine Dieudonné Marin Jo-
    seph, Count de. *Le Sage.* (*Historical Atlas*)........ 1766..1842
Lascelles, Rowley. Antiquary. (*Liber Hiberniæ*)...... 1770?.1841
Lascy, Jos. Francis Maurice, Ct. de. Austr. Field Marsh. 1725..1801
Lasena, or Lascena, Peter. Ital. Schol. (*Nepenthes Homeri*) 1590..1636

BORN. DIED.

Laski, or Lasco, John à. Polish Scholar and Reformer.. 1499..1560
Lassels, Richard. Rom. Cath. Writer. (*Travels in Italy*) 1603..1668
Lasso, Orlando di, or Orlandus Lassus. Musical Composer 1520..1594
Lassone, Joseph Mary Francis de. Fr. Phys. and Chemist 1717..1788
Latham, John, M. D. Ornithologist and Antiquary ..... 1740..1837
Lathrop, Joseph, D. D. American Clergyman and Writer 1731..1820
Latimer, Hugh. Bishop of Worcester. Protestant Martyr.
    Life by W. Gilpin, 1780 .... 1472?.1555
Latimer, Wm. Gr. Schol. Teacher of Erasmus and Pole — ..1545
Latini, Brunetto. Grammarian of Florence. (*Tesoro*) .. 1230..1294
Latinus, Latinius. Ital. Schol. (*Latin Letters and Poems*) 1513..1593
Latour d'Auvergne, Theophilus Malo Corret de. Sol-
    dier and Philologist............................. 1743..1800
Latreille, Peter Andrew. French Naturalist........... 1762..1833
Lattaignant, Gabriel Charles, Abbé de. French Poet... 1697..1779
Lattanzio, Gambara. Ital. Historical and Portrait Painter 1538?.1570?
Latude, Henry Masers de. Prisoner in Bastile. (*Memoirs*) 1725..1805
Laud, William. Archbishop of Canterbury. Life by
    Prynne, 1644; Heylin, 1671; C. W. Le Bas; Lawson,
    1829; Baines, 1855................................ 1573..1645
Lauder, Sir Thomas Dick, Bart. Scottish Writer ...... 1784..1848
Lauder, William. Literary Impostor................. 1710?.1771
Lauderdale, James Maitland, Earl of. Statesman...... 1759..1839
Lauderdale, John Maitland, Duke of. *Cabal* Minister.. 1616..1682
Laudon, or Laudohn, Gideon Ernest.' Austrian General 1716..1790
Laugier, Mark Anthony. French Historical Writer..... 1713..1769
Launay, Francis de. (*Roman and French Jurisprudence*) 1612..1693
Launay, Peter. French Protestant Theologian......... 1573..1661
Launey, Bernard René Jourdan de. Gov. of the Bastile 1740..1789
Launoi, John de. French Divine .... 1603..1678
Laura, of Vaucluse. Friend of Petrarch............... 1310?.1348
Laura, or Lauri, Philip. Flemish Painter .... 1623..1694
Laurati, Peter. Italian Fresco Painter................ 1282..1340
Laurenberg, Peter. German Physician................ 1575?.1639
Laurence, French, D. C. L. Poet and Writer .... — ..1809
Laurence, Richard. Abp. Cashel. Theologian. (*Baptism*) 1761..1838
Laurence, Roger. Nonjuring Bishop.................. — ..1736
Laurens, Andrew du. French Physician and Anatomist — ..1609
Laurens, Henry. American Statesman................ 1724..1792
Laurens, John, Lieutenant-Colonel. American Patriot.. 1756..1782
Laurent, Peter Joseph. Flemish Engineer............ 1715..1773
Laurentius. Archbishop of Canterbury (604–19)....... — .. 619
Lauri, or Laura, Philip. Flemish Painter............. 1623..1694
Lauriston, Alexander James Bernard Law, Marquis de.
    French General and Diplomatist.................. 1768..1828
Lauzun, Anthony Nompar de Caumont, Duc de. Favor-
    ite of Louis XIV.............................. 1633..1723
La Valette, Anthony Mary Chamans, Ct. de. Fr. General 1769..1830
La Valette, John Parisot de. Gd. Master; founded Valetta 1494..1568
La Vallière, Frances Louisa de la Baume le Blanc, Duch-
    ess de. Favorite of Louis XIV.................. 1644..1710
Lavater, John Gaspar Christian. Swiss Physiognomist 1741..1801
Lavater, Louis. Canon of Zurich. Protestant Controv. 1536..1586
La Vergne, Mary Magd. de, Ctss. de la Fayette. *Laverna* 1632..1693

BORN. DIED.

Lavington, George. Bishop of Exeter................. 1683..1762
Lavirotte, Louis Anne. French Medical Writer........ 1725..1759
Lavoisier, Anthony Lawrence. Chemical Philosopher.. 1743..1794
Law, Edmund. Bishop of Carlisle. Metaphysical Writer 1703..1787
Law, Edward, First Lord Ellenborough. Judge .... 1750..1818
Law, George Henry. Bishop of Bath and Wells........ 1761?.1845
Law, John, of Lauriston. Projector. L. by P.Wood, 1826 1671..1729
Law, John. Bishop of Elphin .... — ..1810
Law, William. Mystic Divine. (*Serious Call*)......... 1686..1761
Lawes, Henry. Musical Composer..................... 1600..1662
Lawes, William. Musical Composer; killed at Chester.. — ..1645
Lawless, John. Irish Agitator....................... 1772..1837
Lawless, Matthew James. Artist.................... — ..1864
Lawless, Valentine Browne, Ld. Cloncurry. (*Recollect.*) 1773..1853
Lawrance, John. American Statesman and Judge ..... 1750..1810
Lawrence, Abbott. American Merchant and Statesman 1792..1855
Lawrence, Amos, brother. Merchant and Philanthropist 1786..1852
Lawrence, Sir Henry Montgomery. Statesman. De-
    fender of Lucknow .... 1806..1857
Lawrence, James. American Naval Officer. " Don't
    give up the ship " .... 1781..1813
Lawrence, Rev. John. Agricultural Writer .... — ..1732
Lawrence, or Laurent, Peter Joseph. Flemish Engineer 1715..1773
Lawrence, Stringer. General in India.............. 1697..1775
Lawrence, Thomas, M. D. Medical Writer. (*De Hydrope*) 1711..1783
Lawrence, Sir Thos. Paint. L. by D. E. Williams, 1831 1769..1830
Lawson, Henry. English Savant..................... 1774..1858
Lawson, Sir John. Admiral .... — ..1665
Lawson, John, B. D. Mathematician................. — ..1779
Lawson, Rev. John Parker, of Scotch Episcopal Church.
    (*Life of Laud*)................................. — ..1852
Lax, Rev. William. Math. & Astron. Prof. at Cambridge 1751..1836
Layfield, John, D. D. One of the Translators of the Bible — ..1617
Laynez, or Lainez, James. Jesuit................... 1512..1565
Lazarelli, John Francis. Italian Poet .... 1621..1694
Lea, Isaac. American Naturalist.................... — ..1792
Leach, William Elford. English Naturalist .... 1790..1836
Leadbetter, Charles. Mathematician............... — ..1744
Leake, Sir John. Admiral. Life by S. M. Leake, 1750.. 1656..1720
Leake, John, M. D. Medical Writer .... 1720?.1792
Leake, Richard. Master Gunner of England.......... 1629..1686
Leake, Stephen Martin. (*Nummi Britannici Historia*)... 1702..1773
Leake, William Martin. Colonel. Topographer ...... 1777..1860
Leander. Fr. Capuchin. Writer. (*Truths of the Gospel*) — ..1667
Leapor, Mrs. Mary. Poetess .... 1722..1746
Lear, Tobias. American Diplomatist .... 1760?.1826
Learchus. Greek Sculptor.......................... 7th c. B.C.
Lebeuf, John. French Antiquary. (*History of Paris*) .. 1687..1760
Le Blanc, John Bernard. (*Letters on the English Nation*) 1707..1781
Le Blanc, Marcel. Jesuit Missionary to Siam.......... 1653..1693
Le Blanc, Nicholas. French Chemist .... 1753..1806
Le Blanc. *See* Blanc.
Lebrun, Charles. French Painter.................... 1619..1690
Lebrun, Chas. Francis, Duke of Placentia. Fr. Statesm. 1739..1824

BORN. DIED.

Lebrun, Peter. Divine. (*Hist. of Superstitious Practices*) 1661..1729
Lebrun, Pigault. French Novelist.................... 1742..1835
Lebrun, Ponce Denis Écouchard. *French Pindar.* Poet 1729..1807
Lecchi, John Anthony. Italian Mathem. and Philosopher 1702..1776
Leclair, John. Musical Composer .... 1697..1764
Leclerc, Daniel. French Medical Writer .... 1652..1728
Leclerc, John. Biblical Critic....................... 1657..1736
Leclerc, Nicholas Gabriel. Medical and Historical Writer.
    (*History of Russia*).............................. 1726..1798
Leclerc, Sebastian. French Designer and Engraver .... 1637..1714
Leclerc, Sebastian. Historical Painter .... 1684?.1767
Leclerc, Victor Emanuel. French General .... 1772..1802
L'Écluse, Charles de. *Clusius.* Dutch Phys. & Botanist 1526..1609
Lecomte, Felix. French Sculptor. (*Fénelon*)......... 1737..1817
Lecomte, Louis. Traveler and Missionary in China..... 1650?.1729
Le Conteur, John. English General.................. 1761..1835
Le Coq, Anthony. French Physician................. — ..1550
Le Courayer, Peter Francis. French Roman Catholic
    Refugee in England .... 1681..1776
Lectius, or Lect, James, of Geneva. Critic and Poet ... 1560..1611
Ledebour, Chas. Fred. von. Ger. Botanist and Traveler 1785..1851
Ledesma, Alphonso. Spanish Poet.................. 1552..1623
Ledoux, Claude Nicholas. French Architect.......... 1736..1806
Le Dran, Henry Francis. French Surgical Operator .... 1685..1770
Le Duc, John. Dutch Painter of Animals............. 1636..1671
Ledwich, Edward, LL. D. Antiquary and Topographer.. 1739..1823
Ledyard, John. Amer. Traveler. Life by J. Sparks, 1828 1751..1788
Ledyard, Thomas. Naval Historian .... 1482..1544
Lee, Ann. Founder of Shakers in America .... 1736..1784
Lee, Arthur. Amer. Statesman. Life by R. H. Lee, 1829 1740..1792
Lee, Charles. General. Life by Langworthy, 1792 ..... 1730?.1782
Lee, Edward. Archbishop of York. Writer .... 1482?.1544
Lee, Francis Lightfoot. American Patriot and Statesman 1734..1797
Lee, Miss Harriet, sister of Sophia. Novelist .... 1756..1851
Lee, Henry. American Soldier and Statesman .... 1756..1816
Lee, Henry. Dramatist. (*Caleb Quotem*)............. — ..1836?
Lee, Rev. Jesse. (*Notes*) .... 1758..1816
Lee, John, D. D. Principal, of Edinburgh............. — ..1859
Lee, Mary E. American Authoress.................... 1813..1849
Lee, Nathaniel. Dramatic Poet...................... 1655..1692
Lee, Mrs. R. Bowdich. English Authoress............ 1800?.1856
Lee, Mrs. Rachel Fanny Antonina. Writer............ — ..1829
Lee, Richard Henry. American Statesman. Life by R.
    H. Lee, 1825.................................... 1732..1794
Lee, Rowland. Bishop of Lichfield and Coventry; Lord
    President of Wales .... — ..1543
Lee, Samuel. Ejected Nonconformist Divine and Antiq. 1625..1691
Lee, Samuel, D. D. Orientalist; Professor at Cambridge.. 1783..1852
Lee, Miss Sophia. Novelist. (*Chapt. of Accidents; Recess*) 1750..1824
Lee, Thomas. American Judge and Politician .... 1769..1839
Lee Boo, Prince of Goo-roo-raa .... — ..1784
Leech, John. Humorous Artist....................... 1817?.1864
Leechman, William. Scottish Controversial Divine.... 1706..1785
Leepe, John Anthony van der. Painter of Bruges...... 1664..1720

BORN. DIED.

Leet, James, of Geneva. Politician and Lawyer........ 1560..1611
Leeuw, Gabriel van der. Animal Painter of Bruges.... 1643..1688
Leeuwenhoeck, Anthony van. Nat. Philos. and Anat. 1632..1723
Leeves, Rev. William. Composer. (*Auld Robin Gray*).. 1749..1828
Lefebvre, Francis Joseph, Duke of Dantzic. Marsh. of Fr. 1755..1820
Lefebvre, Tanneguy. *Tanaquil Faber.* Philologist.... 1615..1672
Lefebvre de St. Remy, John. Historian .... 1394?.1468
Lefebvre-Desnouettes, Charles, Count. French General 1773..1822
Lefèvre, James, of Étaples. Scholar and Theologian.... 1455?.1537
Lefèvre, Robert. French Historical and Portrait Painter 1756..1831
Le Fort, Francis. Commander and Statesman of Russia 1656..1699
Legallois, Julian John Cæsar. French Physiologist.... 1770..1814
Legaré, Hugh Swinton. Amer. Statesm. & Man of Letters 1797..1843
Legate, Bartholomew. Martyr .... — ..1612
Legendre, Adrian Mary. Mathematician.............. 1752..1833
Legendre, Louis. Historian .... 1659..1733
Legendre, Louis. French Revolutionist .... 1755..1797
Leger, Anthony. Piedmontese Prot. Editor of N. Test. 1594..1661
Leger, Anthony, son. Preacher...................: 1652..1719
Leger, John, cousin. Hist. of the Piedmont. Protestants 1615..1670?
Leger, St. *See* Saint Leger.
Legge, George, Baron Dartmouth. Admiral .... 1648..1691
Legge, Thomas, LL. D. Master of Caius Coll. Dramatist 1536?.1607
Leggett, William. American Journalist and Author.... 1802..1839
Legouvé, Gabriel Mary John Baptist. Fr. Dram. and Poet 1764..1812
Legrain, John Baptist. French Historian.............. 1565..1642
Legrand, James William. French Writer on Architecture 1743..1807
Legrand d'Aussy, Peter J. B. Jesuit Writer.......... 1737..1800
Legrenzi, John. Italian Musical Composer .... fl. 1664–84
Leguano, Stephen Mary. Italian Historical Painter..... 1660..1715
Leibnitz, Godfrey William, Baron. Mathematician. Life
  by Dr. G. G. Guhrauer, 1842 .... 1646..1716
Leicester, Robert Dudley, Earl of. Favorite of Elizabeth.
  Life by Dr. S. Jebb, 1727; James Drake .... 1532?.1588
Leicester of Holkham, Thomas William, Earl of, Vis-
  count Coke. Agriculturist .... 1752..1842
Leifchild, Dr. Independent Divine. L. by J. R. Leifchild 1780..1862
Leigh, Benjamin Watkins. Amer. Lawyer and Statesm. 1781..1849
Leigh, Charles. Physician and Naturalist........... 1660?.aft.1705
Leigh, Sir Edward. Bibl. Critic and Hist. (*Crit. Sacra*) 1602..1671
Leighton, Alexander. Scottish Puritan. (*Zion's Plea*) 1587..1644
Leighton, Robert, son. Archbishop of Glasgow. (*St.
  Peter.*) Life by Pearson; Burnet............... 1613..1684
Leiningen, Charles, Prince of. Half-brother of Queen
  Victoria. Philanthropist...................... 1804..1856
Leisler, Jacob. Amer. Polit. Adventurer. L. by Hoffman — ..1691
Leismann, John Anthony. German Landscape Painter 1604..1698
Le Jay, Guy Michael. • Fr. Orientalist. (*Polyglot Bible*) 1588..1674
Lekain, Henry Louis Cain. French Actor.......... 1728..1778
Le Keux, John. English Architectural Engraver....... 1784..1846
Leland, John. Antiquary. Life by Huddesford, 1772... 1506?.1552
Leland, John, D.D. Dissent. Divine. (*Deistical Writers*) 1691..1766
Leland, Rev. John. Writer. Life by self and L. F. Green 1754..1841
Leland, Rev. Thomas. Irish Divine; Transl. of Demosth. 1722..1785

BORN. DIED.

Lelli, Hercules. Italian Painter and Modeler......... 1700..1766
Le Long, James. French Historian. (*Bibliotheca Sacra*) 1665..1721
Lely, Sir Peter. Painter .... 1617..1680
Lemaire, James. Dutch Navigator.................... — ..1616
Lemaire, Nicholas Éloi. French Classical Scholar...... 1767..1832
Le Maistre, Anthony, of Port Royal. (*Pleadings*) ..... 1608..1658
Le Maistre, Louis Isaac. *Sacy.* Jansenist Writer ..... 1613..1684
Leman, Rev. Thomas. Antiquary.................... 1751..1827
Le Marchant, John Gaspar. Eng. Gen. (*Sword Exercise*) 1767..1812
Lemens, Balthasar van. Dutch Hist. Painter in London 1637?.1704
Le Mercier, John. Biblical Commentator & Orientalist — ..1570
Lémery, Louis. Chemist and Physician............. 1677..1743
Lémery, Nicholas. French Chemist. (*Cours de Chymie*) 1645..1715
Lemierre, Anthony Marin. French Dramatist........ 1733..1793
Lemnius, or Lemmens, Liéven. Dutch Phys. and Theol. 1505..1568
Lemoine, Abraham. French Prot. Div. (*On Miracles*) — ..1760
Lemoine, Francis. French Historical Painter.......... 1688..1737
Lemoine, John. French Cardinal. Canonist.......... — ..1313
Lemoine, Peter. French Poet. (*St. Louis*)......... 1602..1672
Lemoine, Stephen. French Prot. Divine. (*Varia Sacra*) 1624..1689
Lemon, Geo. William. (*Etymological English Dictionary*) 1726..1797
Lemonnier, Louis William. Fr. Physician and Botanist 1717..1799
Lemonnier, Peter Charles. French Astronomer........ 1715..1799
Lemontey, Peter Edward. French Poet and Jurist..... 1762..1826
Lemot, Francis Frederick. French Statuary .... 1773..1827
Lemoyne, John Baptist. French Musical Composer .... 1751..1796
Lempriere, John, D. D. Scholar. (*Classical Dictionary*) 1765..1824
Lenau, Nicholas. German Poet .... 1802..1850
L'Enclos, Ninon, or Anne de. French Beauty. Life by
    Bret; Damours....................... 1616..1706
Le Neve, John. Antiquary. (*Fasti Ecclesiæ Anglicanæ*) 1679..1741?
Le Neve, Peter. Norroy King-at-Arms .... 1662..1729
Lenfant, David. Fr. Dominican. (*Gen. Hist. of all Ages*) 1603..1688
Lenfant, James. French Protestant Divine........... 1661..1728
Lenglet du Fresnoy, Nicholas. Historical Writer..... 1674..1755
Lennard, Sampson. Antiquary and Writer........... — ..1633
Lennep, John Daniel van. (*Etymologicum Linguæ Græcæ*) 1724..1771
Lennox, Mrs. Charlotte. Writer. (*Shakespeare Illust.*) 1720..1804
Lenormand, Mary Anne Adelaide. French Fortune-teller 1772..1843
Lenotre, Andrew. Fr. Architect & Ornamental Gardener 1613..1700
Lens, Bernard. Miniature Painter.................... — ..1741
Lenthall, William. Speaker .... 1591..1682
Lentino, Jacopo Notaro da. Italian Poet............. fl.1250
Leo I. Emperor of the East (457-74). *Thracian*....... 400?. 474
Leo II. (474, Jan. 26–Nov.) *Young*.................. 470?. 474
Leo III. (717–41.) *Isaurian* .... 680?. 741
Leo IV. (775–80) .... 750.. 780
Leo V. (813–20.) *Armenian* .... — .. 820
Leo VI. (886–911.) *Philosopher*.................... 866.. 911
Leo I. Pope (440–61.) *The Great* .... 390?. 461
Leo II. (682–84.)................................. — .. 684
Leo III. (795–816.)................................ — .. 816
Leo IV. (847–55.)................................. — .. 855
Leo V. (903)..................................... — .. 903

	BORN. DIED.
Leo VI. (928–29)	— .. 929
Leo VII. (936–39)	— .. 939
Leo VIII. (963–65)	— .. 965
Leo IX. (1049–54.) *Brunon. Saint*	1002..1054
Leo X. (1513–21.) *John de' Medici.* Life by Roscoe; J. M. V. Audin, 1844; A. Fabroni	1475..1521
Leo XI. (Elected April 1, 1605.) *Alexander de' Medici*	1535..1605
Leo XII. (1823–29.) *Annibal della Genga*	1760..1829
Leo, of Modena. Jewish Antiquary	1571..1654
Leo Allatius. Greek Scholar in Italy. (*Apes Urbanæ*)	1586..1669
Leo de St. John. (*Studium Sapientiæ Universalis*)	1600..1671
Leo Juda. German Protestant Reformer	1482..1542
Leo, John. *Africanus.* Traveler and Geographer	1483?.1552
Leo, Leonard. Neapolitan Musical Composer	1694..1745
Leon, Fra Louis Ponce de. Spanish Poet	1528..1591
Leonardo Bonacci, of Pisa. Mathematician	fl. 1200?
Leonardo da Vinci. Painter. Life by Amaretti; J. W. Brown, 1828	1452..1520
Leoni, Jacomo. Venetian Architect	— ..1746?
Leonicenus, Nicholas. Italian Physician	1428..1524
Leonico, Thomas Nicholas. Italian Scholar	1456..1531
Leonidas. King of Sparta (B. C. 491–480)	— B.C.480
Leopardi, James, Count. Italian Poet and Class. Scholar	1798..1837
Leopold I. Emperor of Germany (1657–1705)	1640..1705
Leopold II. (1790–92.) I. Grand Duke of Tuscany (1765–90)	1747..1792
Leopold I. King of Belgium	1790..1865
Leopold. Duke of Lorraine	1679..1729
Leosthenes. Athenian General	fl. B.C.323
Leotaud, Vincent. (*Examen Circuli Quadraturæ*)	1595..1672
Leowitz, or Leovitius, Cyprian. German Astronomer	1524..1574
Lepaute, John Andrew. French Horologist	1709..1789
Lepautre, or Lepotre, Anthony. French Architect	1614..1691
Lepautre, Peter, son. Sculptor	1660..1744
Lepicier, Bernard. French Engraver	1698..1755
Lepicier, Nicholas Bernard, son. Painter	1735..1784
Lepidus, Marcus Æmilius. Triumvir	— B.C.13
Lepois, Charles. *Charles Piso.* Medical Writer	1563..1633
Lepois, Nicholas. Medical Writer	1527.. —
Leprince, John. French Musician and Painter	1733..1781
Le Quien, Michael. Theologian	1661..1733
Lerebours, Noel John. French Optician	1762..1840
Leri, John de. French Protestant. (*Siege of Sancerre*)	1534..1611
Lermontoff, Michael Ivanovitch. Russ. Poet & Novelist	1811..1841
Lernutius, John. Dutch Latin Poet. (*Basia, Ocelli*, &c.)	1545..1619
Leroy, Julian David. (*Ruines des Monuments de la Grèce*)	1724..1803
Leroy de St. Arnaud, Arnaud James. Marshal of France	1801..1854
Le Sage, Alain René. Novelist. (*Gil Blas*)	1668..1747
Le Sage, David. French Poet. (*Les Folies du Sage*)	— ..1650?
Le Sage. (*Historical Atlas.*) See Las Cases	1766..1842
Lesage, George Louis. Swiss Philosopher. (*Final Causes*)	1724..1803
Lescaille, Catherine. *Dutch Sappho*	1649..1711
Lescaille, James. Dutch Printer and Poet	1610..1677
Lescot, Peter. French Architect	1510..1571

BORN. DIED.

Lescure, Louis Mary, Marquis de. Fr. Royalist General 1766..1793
Lesdiguières, Francis de Bonne, Dk. of. French General 1543..1626
Lesley, John. Bishop of Ross; Friend of Mary Stuart .. 1527..1596
Leslie, Charles. Irish Divine. (*Short and Easy Method*) 1650?..1722
Leslie, Charles Robert, R. A. Painter and Writer....... 1794..1859
Leslie, Eliza. American Authoress .... 1787..1857
Leslie, John. Bishop of Clogher. Scholar and Politician 1570?..1671
Leslie, Sir John. Math. and Nat. L. by Macvey Napier 1766..1832
Lespinasse, Julia Jane Eleanore, of Paris............. 1732..1776
Lessing, Gotthold Ephraim. Writer. L. by K. G. Lessing 1729..1781
Lessius, Leonard. Dutch Jesuit. (*Immortality of the Soul*) 1554..1623
Lestocq, John Hermann, Count. Physician. Favorite of
    Elizabeth of Russia............................... 1692..1767
L'Estrange, Sir Roger. Prot. Controv. and Translator 1616..1704
Lesueur, Eustace. French Painter.................... 1617..1655
Lesueur, John Francis. French Musical Composer..... 1760..1837
Lesueur, Thomas. French Mathematician............. 1703..1770
Lethieullier, Smart. English Antiquary and Virtuoso.. 1701..1760
Leti, Gregory. Italian Historian..................... 1630..1701
Letourneur, Peter. French Writer................... 1736..1788
Letronne, John Anthony. Fr. Archæologist and Critic.. 1787..1848
Lettice, John. Poet and Divine..................... 1737..1832
Lettsom, John Coakley, M.D. Life by Pettigrew, 1817.. 1744..1814
Leucippus. Greek Philosopher....................fl. 5th c. B.C.
Leunclavius, John. Ger. Traveler. (*Ottoman Empire*) 1533..1593
Leupold, James. Mechanician. (*Theatrum Machinarum*) 1674..1727
Leuret, Francis. French Anatomist.................. 1797..1851
Leusden, John. Orientalist.......................... 1624..1699
Leutholf, or Ludolph, Job. German Orientalist........ 1624..1704
Leutzelburger, or Lützelburger, Hans. Engraver ..... fl. 16th c.
Leuwenhoek, Anthony van. Dutch Natural Philosopher 1632..1723
Le Vaillant, Francis. Naturalist and Traveler........ 1753..1824
Lever, Sir Ashton. Naturalist and Collector .... — ..1788
Lever, Ralph, D.D. Divine and Author.............. — ..1585
Lever, Thomas. Master of St. John's Coll., Camb. Writer — ..1577
Leverett, Frederick Percival. American Classical Scholar.
    (*Latin Lexicon*)................................. 1803..1836
Leverett, Sir John. Gov. of the Colony of Massachusetts 1616..1679
Leveridge, Richard. Singer and Musical Composer .... 1670..1758
Lévesque, Peter Charles. Historian .... 1736..1812
Lévesque de Pouilli, Louis John. (*Sentiments Agréables*) 1691..1750
Levi, David. Jewish Controversialist................. 1740..1799
Levi-ben-Gershom. Rabbi. Biblical Commentator... 1290?.1370
Levingston, James, Earl of Callendar. Scottish Royalist — ..1672
Levis, Peter Mark Gaston, Duc de. Fr. Royalist; Writer 1764..1830
Levita, Elijah. Jewish Grammarian and Exegete ...... 1470..1549
Lévizac, John Pons Victor Lecoutz de. French Póet and
    Philologist...................................... — ..1813
Levret, Andrew. French Surgeon and Accoucheur..... 1703..1780
Lewis, Andrew. American Revolutionary General...... 1730?.1780
Lewis, Enoch. American Mathematician.............. 1776..1856
Lewis, Francis. American Revolutionary Statesman.... 1713..1803
Lewis, Sir George Cornewall. Statesman and Writer... 1806..1863
Lewis, Rev. John. Antiquary and Divine .... 1675..1746

BORN. DIED.

Lewis, Maria Therese, Lady. Novelist and Biographer.. 1803..1865
Lewis, Matthew Gregory. *Monk Lewis.* Romancist.... 1775..1818
Lewis, Meriwether. American Soldier and Explorer.... 1774..1809
Lewis, Morgan. American Soldier, Jurist, and Politician 1754..1844
Lewis, Samuel. American Educationist .... 1799..1854
Ley, Sir James. Judge .... 1552?.1628
Leybourn, William. Mathematical Writer .... — ..1690?
Leydecker, Melchior. Dutch Theologian .... 1642..1722
Leyden, John, M. D. Poet & Orient. L. by Moreton, 1819 1775..1811
Leyden, Luke van. *Lucas Jacobze.* Dutch Painter .... 1494..1533
Leyland, Joseph Bentley, of Halifax. Sculptor .... — ..1851 ᵥ
Leyssens. Painter of Antwerp...................... 1661..1720
Lezay-Marnezia, Adrian, Count de. Diplom. and Polit. 1770..1814
Lezay-Marnezia, Claude Francis Adrian, Mqs. de. Polit. 1735..1800
L'Hôpital, Michael de. Chancellor of France .... 1505..1573
Lhuyd, Edw. Antiq. and Nat. (*Archæologia Britannica*) 1670?.1709
Lhuyd, Humphrey. Antiquary...................... — ..1570
Libanius. Greek Sophist and Rhetorician............. 314.aft.390
Libavius, Andreco. German Physician and Chemist.... — ..1616
Liberi, Peter. Italian Painter .... 1605..1687
Liberius. Bishop of Rome (352–66)................... — .. 366
Liceti, Fortunio. Italian Physician and Philosopher.... 1577..1657
Lichnowsky, Felix, Prince. Prussian General......... 1814..1848
Lichtenberg, George Christopher. Writer. (*On Hogarth*) 1742..1799
Lichtenstein, Jos. Wenceslaus, Prince of. Austrian Gen. 1696..1772
Lichtenstein, Martin Henry Charles. German Naturalist 1780..1857
Lichtwer, Magnus Godfrey. German Poet and Fabulist 1719..1783
Licinius. Roman Emperor (307–24) .... — .. 324
Liddel, Duncan. Scottish Mathematician and Physician.
    Life by James Stuart............................ 1561..1613
Lieutaud, Joseph. French Medical Writer............ 1703..1780
Lieven, Dorothea, Princess of. Russian Diplomatist .... 1784..1857
Lievens, or Livineius, John, of Antwerp. Greek Scholar 1546?.1599
Lievens, John. Dutch Portrait Painter for Charles I.... 1607..1663
Lightfoot, John, D. D. Divine...................... 1602..1675
Lightfoot, John. Botanist. (*Flora Scotica*) .... 1735..1788
Lignac, Joseph Adrian le Large de. Abbé. Philoso-
    pher, Naturalist, Theologian .... 1710?.1762
Ligne, Chas. Joseph, Prince de. Austrian Field Marshal 1735..1814
Ligonier, John, Earl of. Field Marshal............... 1678..1770
Ligorio, Peter, of Naples. (*Designs after the Antique*) .. 1530?.1580
Liguori, St. Alphonsus Maria di. Italian Theologian ... 1696..1787
Lilburne, John. Republican Writer and Sectary....... 1618..1657
Lillo, George. Dramatic Writer. Life by Thos. Davies 1693..1739
Lilly, or Lylye, John. Dramatic Writer. (*Euphues*).... 1553? 1601?
Lilly, William. Astrologer. Life by self .... 1602..1681
Lily, or Lilye, William. Schoolmaster and Grammarian.. 1468?.1523
Limborch, Philip van. Dutch Theologian............. 1633..1712
Limbourg, John Philip de, of Spain. Medical Writer... fl. 1736–65
Limnæus, John. German Jurist..................... 1592..1663
Linacre, Thomas, M. D. Physician and Scholar .... 1460?.1524
Linant, Michael. French Poet; Friend of Voltaire...... 1708..1749
Lincoln, Abraham. Sixteenth President of the United
    States; assassinated by Booth..................... 1809..1865

BORN. DIED.

Lincoln, Benjamin. American Revolutionary General.. 1733..1810
Lincoln, Levi. American Statesman.................. 1749..1820
Lind, James, M. D. Medical Writer. (*On the Scurvy*)... — ..1794
Lindanus, William. Dutch Divine .... 1525..1588
Lindblad, Otto. German Song Composer.............. — ..1864
Lindblom, Axel. Archbishop of Upsal. Lexicographer 1746..1819
Linde, Samuel Theophilus. Polish Philologist........ 1771..1847
Lindenau, Bernard Augustus von. German Astronomer 1780..1854
Lindenbruch, Frederick. (*Codex Legum Antiquarum*).. 1573..1648
Lindley, John, M. D. Prof. of Botany. (*Botanical Dict.*) 1799..1865
Lindpaintner, Peter Joseph von. German Composer.
    (*Sicilian Vespers*) ...., 1791..1856
Lindsay, Sir David. Poet. Life by Chalmers .... 1490..1557?
Lindsay, John, E. of Crawford. General. L. by Rolt, 1753 1702..1749
Lindsay, John. Nonj. Divine. (*Hist. of Regal Succession*) — ..1768
Lindsey, Theoph. Socin. Writer. L. by T. Belsham, 1812 1723..1808
Lindsley, Philip, D. D. Amer. Clergyman and Educator 1786..1855
Ling, Peter Henry. Swedish Physiologist and Poet..... 1766..1839
Lingard, John, D. D., LL. D. Roman Catholic Historian 1771..1851
L'Ingegno, or Andrea di Luigi. Painter..:........... 1450?.1520
Lingendes, Claude de. French Jesuit; Preacher....... 1591..1660
Linglebach, John. German Painter of the Grotesque .. 1625..1687
Linguet, Simon Nicholas Henry. Polit. and Misc.Writer 1736..1794
Linière, Francis Payot de. French Poet.............. 1628..1704
Linley, George. Song Writer and Composer.......... 1798?.1865
Linley, Thomas. Musical Composer. (*Twelve Ballads*) 1725?.1795
Linley, Thomas, son. Musician; drowned .... 1756..1788
Linley, William, br. Mus. Comp. (*Songs of Shakespeare*) 1771..1835
Linn, John Blair. American Poet. (*Powers of Genius*).. 1777..1804
Linnæus, Charles von. The great Botanist. Life by Miss
    Brightwell; Trap of Stoever; Pulteney .... 1707..1778
Linnæus, Charles, son. Botanist.................... 1741..1783
Linschoten, John Hugh van. Dutch Voyager......... 1536..1633
Linsenbahrt. *Rosinus Lentilius*. Medical Writer...... 1657..1733
Lint, Peter van. Dutch Historical and Portrait Painter.. 1609..1668
Lin-tseh-su. Chinese Imperial Commissioner & Author 1785..1850
Linwood, Wm. Bishop of St. David's. Eccles. Lawyer — ..1446
Lionel, Duke of Clarence, son of Edward III........... — ..1368
Liotard, John Stephen. Swiss Painter in Crayons..... 1702.aft.1776
Liotard, Peter. French Botanist..................... 1729..1796
Lipenius, Martin. Ger. Lutheran. (*Bibliotheca Realis*) 1630..1692
Lippi, Lawrence. Pa. & Poet. (*Il Malmantile Racquistato*) 1606..1664
Lippi, Philip. Painter of Florence. (*Adoration of Virgin*) 1412..1469
Lippi, Philip, or Philippin, son. Painter.............. 1460..1505
Lippoman, Louis. Italian Bishop, Persecutor, and Writer 1500..1559
Lipsius, Justus. Critic. Life by Miræus............. 1547..1606
Liron, John. Benedictine of St. Maur. (*Auteurs Chartrains*) 1665..1749
Lis, John van der. Dutch Painter................... 1570..1629
Liscoff, Christian Louis. German Satirist............ 1701..1760
Lisle, de. *See* Delisle.
Lisle, Mrs., or Lady Alice. Victim of Judge Jeffreys.... — ..1685
Lisle, Sir Geo. Royalist; Defender of Colchester; shot .. — ..1648
Lisola, Francis Paul, Baron von. Diplomatist. (*Bou-*
    clier d'Etat)...................................... 1613..1675

BORN. DIED.
List, Frederick. German Political Economist.......... 1789..1846
Lista y Aragon, Albert. Spanish Mathem., Poet, Critic 1775..1848
Lister, Martin. Phys. and Nat. (*Historia Conchyliorum*) 1638?.1712
Lister, Sir Matthew, M. D. Physician................. 1565?.1657
Lister, Thomas Henry. Novelist and Historian........ 1801..1842
Liston, John. Comedian............................. 1776..1846
Liston, Robert. Surgeon............................. 1794..1848
Lithgow, William. Scottish Pedestrian Traveler....... — ..1640
Litta, Pompey, Count. Italian Historian :........... 1781..1852
Little, William. *William of Newburgh.* Historian......1136..1208
Littleton, Rev. Adam. Divine and Philol. (*Lat. Dict.*) 1627..1694
Littleton, or Lyttelton, which see.
Littrow, Joseph John von. German Astronomer .... 1781..1840
Liutprand, or Luitprand. Lombard Historian.......... 920?. 972
Lively, Edward. Hebrew Professor at Cambridge. One
   of the Translators of the Bible.................... — ..1605
Liverpool, Charles Jenkinson, First Earl of. Statesman 1727..1808
Liverpool, Robert Banks Jenkinson, Second Earl of.
   Premier (1812-27)................................. 1770..1828
Livia Drusilla, the wife of Augustus............. B.C.55?.A.D.29
Livineius, or Lievens, John, of Antwerp. Greek Scholar 1546?.1599
Living, or Elfstan. Archbishop of Canterbury (1013-20) — ..1020
Livingston, Brockholst, LL. D. Amer. Soldier and Jurist 1757..1823
Livingston, Edward. American Legislator and Jurist.
   Life by Hunt...................................... 1764..1836
Livingston, John. Scotch Presbyterian Divine .... 1603..1672
Livingston, Philip. American Patriot .... 1716..1778
Livingston, Robt. R. Amer. Polit.; Ambass. to France 1746..1813
Livingston, William. American Writer and Statesman.
   Life by Theodore Sedgwick, 1835 .... 1723..1790
Livius Andronicus. Roman Poet.................... fl. B.C. 240
Livy. Roman Historian.............................B.C.59.A.D.17
Llewellyn. Prince of Wales; defeated by Edward I..... 1224?.1282
Llorente, Bernard German y. Spanish Painter........ 1685..1757
Llorente, John Anthony. Spanish Historian........... 1756..1823
Lloyd, Charles, of Birmingham. Translator of Horace.. — ..1827
Lloyd, Charles. Bishop of Oxford................... 1784..1829
Lloyd, Charles. Poet; Friend of Wordsworth, Lamb, and
   Southey .... — ..1839
Lloyd, Rev. David. Biographer and Historian .... 1625..1691
Lloyd, Henry Humphrey Evans. Military Historian.... 1729..1783
Lloyd, Rev. Nicholas. Philologist .... 1634..1680
Lloyd, Robert. Poet. Life by Dr. Kenrick............ 1733..1764
Lloyd, William. Bishop of Worcester. Scholar........ 1627..1717
Llywelyn, Sion, of Glamorgan. Poet .... — ..1616
Lobau, George Mouton, Count de. Marshal of France... 1770..1838
Lobb, Theophilus, of London. Medical Writer......... 1676?.1763
Lobeira, Vasco de. Portuguese Writer. (*Amadis of Gaul*) — ..1403
Lobel, or L'Obel, Matthias de. Bot. (*Stirpium Adversaria*) 1538..1616
Lobineau, Guy Alexis. Fr. Writ. (*History of Brittany*) 1666..1727
Lobkowitz, Boleslaus de Hassenstein, Baron de. Diplo-
   matist and Latin Poet............................. — ..1510
Lobo, Jerome. Portuguese Jesuit Missionary.......... 1593?.1678
Locatelli, Peter. Italian Violinist................... 1693..1764

BORN. DIED.

Loch, David. Writer on Trade........................ — ..1780
Loch, James, M. P. Scot. Writer. (*County of Sutherland*) 1780..1855
Lochner, Stephen, of Cologne. Painter .... — ..1451
Lock, Matthew. Musical Composer ....1630?.1677
Lockart, Alex. Scot. Politician. (*Memoirs of Scotland*) 1675?.1732
Locke, John. Philosopher. Life by Lord King; Le Clerc 1632..1704
Locke, Joseph. Engineer. Life by J. Devey, 1862......1805..1860
Locker, Edw. Hawke, of Greenw. Hosp. Popular Writer 1777..1849
Locker, John. English Greek Scholar and Writer. ....— ..1760
Lockhart, John Gibson. Writer. (*Life of Scott*)...... 1794..1854
Lockman, John. Musical Writer .... 1698..1771
Lodge, Edmund. Herald and Antiquary. (*Portraits*) .. 1756..1839
Lodge, Thomas, M. D. Dramatic Poet .... 1555?.1625
Lodge, William. Engraver .... 1649..1689
Loewendal, Ulric Frederick Waldemar, Ct. of. General 1700..1755
Loewenthal, Rev. Isidore. Missionary at Peshawer .... 1827..1864
Lofft, Capel. Writer............................... 1751..1824
Loftus, Adam. Archbishop of Dublin .... 1534?.1605
Loftus, Dudley. Orientalist........................ 1618..1695
Loftus, William Kennett. English Archæologist........ 1820?.1858
Logan. *Tah-gah-jute.* Indian Chief.................. — ..1781
Logan, George, M. D. Amer. Statesman and Philanthr. 1753..1821
Logan, James. American Colonial Statesman and Author 1674..1751
Logan, Rev. John. Scottish Divine, Poet, and Writer .. 1748..1788
Logau, Frederick, Baron von. German Poet........... 1604..1655
Loggan, David. Engraver. (*Oxonia Illustrata*)........ 1635?.1693
Lohenstein, Daniel Gaspar. German Poet .... 1635..1683
Loir, Nicholas. French Painter...................... 1624..1679
Lola Montez, (Maria Dolores Porris y Montez,) Countess
   of Landsfeld. Adventuress........................ 1824..1861
Lollard, Walter. Protestant; burnt at Cologne .... — ..1322
Lolli, or Lolly, Anthony. Italian Violinist........... 1728..1802
Lom, Josse van, or Lommius. Dutch Medical Writer.. 1500.aft.1562
Lombard, John Louis. French Artillerist.............. 1723..1794
Lombard, Lambert, of Liège. Painter................ 1506..1565
Lombard, Peter. *Master of Sentences.* Schoolman .... — ..1164
Loménie, Henry Augustus, Count de Brienne. French
   Ambassador in England.......................... 1595..1666
Loménie, Henry Louis, Count de Brienne, son. States-
   man. (*Memoirs of Own Life*) .... 1635..1698
Loménie de Brienne, Stephen Charles de. Cardinal .. 1727..1798
Lommius, Jodocus, or Josse van Lom. Dutch Med.Writ. 1500.aft.1562
Lomonosoff, Michael Vasilovitch. Russ. Poet and Hist. 1711..1765
Londe, Francis Richard de la. French Poet........... 1685?.1765
Londonderry, Charles William Vane Stewart, Third Mar-
   quess of. General under Wellington.............. 1778..1854
Londonderry, Robert Stewart, brother, Lord Castlereagh
   and Second Marquess of. Statesman.............. 1769..1822
Long, Edward, of Jamaica. Judge. (*Hist. of Jamaica*) 1734..1813
Long, James le. Fr. Hist. & Bibliog. (*Bibliotheca Sacra*) 1665..1721
Long, John St. John. Medical Empiric.............. 1798..1834
Long, Roger, D. D., of Cambridge. Professor of Astronomy 1680..1770
Long, Thomas. Nonjuring Divine .... 1621..1700
Longbeard, William, of London. Popular Champion... — ..1196

BORN. DIED.

Longepierre, Hilary Bernard de. Critic and Class. Dram. 1659..1721
Longhi, Joseph. Italian Painter and Engraver......... 1766..1831
Longinus, Dionysius Cassius. Greek Philosopher ...... 213?. 273
Longland, or Langland, John. Bishop of Lincoln ...... 1473..1547
Longland, or Langeland, Robt. Poet. (*Piers Plowman*) fl. 1370?
Longman, Thomas Norton. London Publisher........ 1770?.1842
Longolius, or Longueil, *which see.*
Longomontanus, Christian. Danish Astronomer ...... 1562..1647
Longstreet, William. American Inventor............. — ..1814
Longueil, Christopher de. Ciceronian Scholar......... 1490..1522
Longueil, Gilbert de. Dutch Phys. and Class. Scholar 1507..1543
Longuerue, Louis Dufour de. Fr. Abbé and Hist. Writer 1652..1733
Longueval, James. Jesuit; Ecclesiastical Historian .... 1680..1735
Longueville, Anne Genevieve de Bourbon, Duchess de,
     daughter of Henry II.; Prince of Condé. L. by Villefore 1619..1679
Longus. Greek Romance Writer. (*Pastorals*) .... 4th or 5th c.
Loni, Alexander, of Florence. Painter.............. 1655..1702
Lonicerus, Adam. Physician and Naturalist .... 1528..1586
Lonicerus, John. Ger. Philologist. (*Greek and Lat. Lex.*) 1499..1569
Loon, Theodore van. Dutch Painter.............. 1630..1678
Loos, Cornelius. Dutch Divine. (*De Verâ et Falsâ Magiâ*) 1546?.1595
Loosjes, Adrian. Dutch Novelist and Poet............. 1761..1818
Lope de Rueda. Spanish Dramatist and Actor .... 1500?.1564
Lope de Vega. Spanish Poet................. 1562..1635
Lopes, Fernando. Portuguese Historian.............. 1380?.1449
Lopez, Narcisso. Cuban Revolutionist .... 1799..1851
Loredano, John Francis. (*History of the Kings of Cyprus*) 1606..1661
Lorenze, John Michael. French Historian............. 1723..1801
Lorenzetti, Ambrose. Painter of Sienna .... 1257..1340
Lorenzini, or Laurentini, Francis Mary. Poet .... 1680..1743
Lorenzini, Lawrence. Mathematician................. 1652..1721
Lorenzo. *The Magnificent.* See Medici .... 1448..1492
Lorgna, Anthony Mary. Italian Mathematician........ 1730?.1796
Loriot, Anthony Joseph. French Mechanician .... 1716..1782
Lorit, Henry. *Glareanus.* German Scholar .... 1488..1563
Lorkin, Thomas, M. D. Medical Writer.......... 1528?.1591
Lorme, Charles de. Physician to Louis XIII. Writer. 1584..1678
Lorme, Marion de, or Delorme. French Courtesan .... 1612?.1650
Lorme, Philibert de. French Architect .... 1518..1577
Lorraine, Charles de Guise, Cardinal de .... 1525..1574
Lorraine, Claude. *Gelée.* French Landscape Painter .. 1600..1682
Lorraine, Robert le. French Sculptor................ 1666..1743
Lorris, William de. French Poet. (*Roman de la Rose*) — ..1260?
Lorry, Anne Charles. French Medical Writer.......... 1726..1783
Lortzing, Albert Gustavus. German Composer .... 1803..1851
Losa, Isabella, D. D., of Cordova. Scholar............. 1473?.1546
Loten, John. Dutch Landscape Painter in England .... — ..1681
Lothaire I. Emperor of Germany .... 795?. 855
Lothaire II. (1125-37.) Duke of Saxony and Emperor 1075..1137
Lothaire. King of Lorraine................ 825.. 869
Lothaire. King of France (954-86)................ 941.. 986
Lotich, John Peter. Physician and Latin Poet......... 1598..1669
Lotich, Peter. *Secundus.* Latin Poet................. 1528..1560
Lotto, Lorenzo. Venetian Painter .... fl. 1513-54

BORN. DIED.

Loubère, Simon de la. French Jesuit Envoy to Siam .. 1642..1729
Loudon, or Laudon, Gideon Ernest, Baron. Austrian
  Field Marshal .... 1716..1790
Loudon, Mrs. Jane Webb. Horticult. & Botanical Writer 1800..1858
Loudon, John Claudius. Horticultural Writer.......... 1783..1843
Louis I. Emp. of Ger. (814–40), and I. of Fr., *which see* 778.. 840
Louis II. (855–75.) *The Young*..................... 822?. 875
Louis III. (890–903.) *The Blind* .... 880?. 928?
Louis IV. (900–11.) *The Infant*. (Not reckoned by some) 893?. 912?
Louis V., or IV., (1314–47) *of Bavaria*................ 1287?.1347
Louis I. King of France (814–40) and Emperor. *Le
  Débonnaire*. Life by Astronome.................... 778.. 840
Louis II. (877–79.) *Le Bègue, or Stammerer* .... 846.. 879
Louis III. (879–82.) .... — .. 882
Louis IV. (936–54.) *L' Outre-Mer*.................. 921.. 954
Louis V. (986–87.) *Le Fainéant* .... 966.. 987
Louis VI. (1108–37.) *Le Gros*. Life by Suger....... 1078..1137
Louis VII. (1137–80.) *Le Jeune*.................... 1120..1180
Louis VIII. (1223–26.) *Le Lion* .... 1187..1226
Louis IX. (1226–70.) *Saint*. Life by Nangis; Joinville;
  J. H. Gurney, 1855................................ 1215..1270
Louis X. (1314–16.) *Hutin*........................ 1289..1316
Louis XI. (1461–83.) Life by C. P. Duclos, 1745; Jean
  de Troyes; Baudot de Juilli, 1756 .... 1423..1483
Louis XII. (1498–1515.) Life by Tailhé; Claude Scyssel 1462..1515
Louis XIII. (1610–43.) Life by Gabriel, Lord of Gram-
  mont; James Howell; Le Vassor, 1710–21 .... 1601..1643
Louis XIV. (1643–1715.) L. by P. Pellisson-Fontanier;
  Isaac de Larrey; Leti; Reboulet; G. P. R. James..... 1638..1715
Louis XV. (1715–74.) Life by Voltaire.............. 1710..1774
Louis XVI. (1774–93) .... 1754..1793
Louis XVII. Life by A. de Beauchesne, 1853 .... 1785..1795
Louis XVIII. (1814–24).............................. 1755..1824
Louis I. King of Hungary (1342–82) and of Poland .... 1326..1382
Louis II. (1516–26)................................. 1506..1526
Louis le Germanique. King of Germany .... 806.. 876
Louis of France. Duke of Anjou, son of John III...... — ..1384
Louis Philippe. King of the French. Life by M. A.
  Boullée, 1849; L. G. Michaud, 1849; Nouvion, 1859.. 1773..1850
Louis, Anthony. French Surgeon..................... 1723..1792
Louisa of Orleans. Q. of Belgians, dau. of Louis Philippe 1812..1850
Louisa of Savoy. Regent of France................. 1476..1531
Louisa, Augusta Wilhelmina Amelia. Queen of Prussia.
  Life by Mrs. Richardson........................... 1776..1810
Louptière, John Charles de Relongue de la. French Poet 1727..1784
Loureiro, John de. Portuguese Botanist and Missionary 1715?.1796
Loutherbourg, or Lutherburg, Philip James. French
  Landscape Painter................................. 1740..1812
Louvel, Louis Peter. French Assassin .... 1783..1820
Louvet, Peter. Antiquary of Beauvais................ 1569?.1646
Louvet de Couvray, John Baptist. French Politician.. 1764..1797
Louville, Eugene d'Alonville. French Astronomer..... 1671..1732
Louvois, Francis Michael Le Tellier, Marquis de. Minister
  of Louis XIV..................................... 1641..1691

BORN. DIED.

Lovat, Simon Fraser, Lord. L. by self; J. H. Burton, 1847 1667..1747
Love, Christopher. Presbyterian Divine.............. 1618..1651
Love, James. Dramatic Writer and Actor............ — ..1774
Lovejoy, Rev. Elijah P. American Abolitionist........ 1802..1837
Lovejoy, Owen. American Abolitionist and Statesman.. 1811..1864
Lovelace, Richard. Poet....................... 1618..1658
Lovett, Richard. Lay Clerk of Worcester. Philos. Writer — ..1780
Lovibond, Edward. Poet...................... — ..1775
Lowe, Sir Hudson. General. Governor of St. Helena.. 1767..1844
Lowe, Peter. Scottish Surgeon. (*Discourse on Chirugery*) — ..1612
Lowell, Francis Cabot. American Merchant.......... 1775..1817
Lowell, John, LL. D. American Statesman and Jurist... 1743..1802
Lowell, John, LL. D., son. Lawyer and Political Writer 1769..1840
Lowell, John. Founder of Lowell Institute at Boston... 1799..1836
Lowen, John Frederick. German Poet and Romancist .. 1729?.1773
Löwendal, Ulric Frederick Waldemar, Count of. General 1700..1755
Löwenthal, Rev. Isidore. Philologist and Missionary .. 1827..1864
Lower, Richard. Physician and Anatomist............ 1631?.1691
Lowman, Moses, of Clapham. Biblical Commentator... 1680..1752
Lowndes, Rawlin. American Lawyer and Statesman... 1722..1800
Lowndes, Thomas. Founder of Astronom. Professorship — ..1748
Lowndes, William Jones. American Statesman........ 1782..1822
Lowndes, William Thomas. Bibliographer. (*Bibliographer's Manual*)................................ — ..1843
Lowry, Wilson. Engraver........................ 1762..1824
Lowth, Robert. Bp. Lond. (*Isaiah*.) L. by P. Hall, 1834 1710..1787
Lowth, William. Prebend of Winchester. Scholar and Commentator .... 1661..1732
Loyd, Lewis. London Banker...................... 1768..1858
Loyer, Peter le, Sieur de la Brosse. (*Apparitions*)...... 1550..1634
Loyola, Ignatius. Founder of the Jesuits. Life by Riba-
deneira, 1570; John Peter Maffei, 1584; Stein, 1598;
Gretser, 1599–1604; Bombino, 1615; Mayr, 1616; Mich.
.Walpole, 1617; Ferus, or Plachy, 1617; Diez, 1619;
Binct, 1622; Bidermann, 1625; Nigroni, 1630; La Mis-
ma, 1633; Arcones, 1633; Halkett, 1648; Bartoli, 1650;
Kastel, 1667; Bussières, 1670; Bonhours, 1679; Coret,
1679; Nolarci, 1680; Garcia, 1685; Nossius, 1690; Nie-
berlein, 1721; Hane, 1721; Rasiel de Selva, or Ques-
nel de Dieppe, 1736; Mariani, 1741; Wolffer, 1788;
Frank, 1802; Geiss, 1804; Dewora, 1816; Charra, 1840;
Du Thairel, 1844; Bruehl, 1845; Genelli, 1848; Rau, 1851 1491..1556
Lubbert, Sibrand. Dutch Controversial Divine........ 1556?.1625
Lubbock, Sir John William, F. R. S. Math. and Philos. 1803..1865
Lubienetski, Theodore, of Cracow. Hist. and Portr. Pa. 1653?.1716
Lubieniczki, Stanisl. Unitarian. (*Theatrum Cometicum*) 1623..1675
Lubin, Augustin. Geographical Writer.............. 1624..1695
Lubin, Eilhard. (*De Causâ et Naturâ Mali*).......... 1556..1621
Luca, John Baptist. Cardinal. (*Analysis of Civil Law*) 1614..1683
Lucan, Marcus Annæus. Roman Poet.............. 39.. 65
Lucaris, Cyril. Greek Theologian.................. 1572.. —
Lucas, Charles. Irish Physician and Patriot............ 1713..1771
Lucas, Frederick, M. P. Rom. Cath. Polit. Ed. of *Tablet* 1812..1855
Lucas, Paul. French Traveler .... 1664..1737

BORN. DIED.

Lucas, Rev. Richard. Divine .... 1648..1715
Lucas, Samuel. Journalist and Writer. (Secularia) ... 1818..1865
Lucas Brugensis, Francis. Dutch Orient. and Bib. Writ. 1552?.1619
Lucas van Leyden. Dutch Painter and Engraver..... 1494..1533
Lucchesini, Jerome, Marquis of. Prussian Statesman .. 1752:..1825
Lucchesini, John Vincent. Italian Historian.......... 1660..1744
Luchetto, of Genoa. See Cambiaso.................... 1527..1585
Lucian. Greek Writer............................... 120?. 200
Lucian, St. Presbyter of Antioch. Martyr .... — .. 312
Lucifer. Bishop of Cagliari. Writer................. — ab. 370
Lucilius, Caius. Roman Satirist..................... 148.103 B.C.
Lucius I. Pope (252–53) .... — .. 253
Lucius II. (1144–45.) Gerard de Caccianamici .... — ..1145
Lucius III. (1181–85.) Ubaldo Allucingoli .... — ..1185
Lücke, Godfrey Christian Frederick. German Theologian 1792..1855
Lucretius. Roman Philosopher and Poet............. 95.55 B.C.
Lucullus, Lucius Licinius. Conqueror of Mithridates...110?.57 B.C.
Luden, Henry. German Historian.................... 1780..1847
Ludlow, Edmund. Parliamentarian General......... 1620?.1693
Ludolph, Henry William. (Gram. of Russian Language) 1655..1710
Ludolph, Job. Orientalist. (History of Ethopia)....... 1624..1704
Ludwig, Christian Theophilus. Botanist .... 1709..1773
Ludwig, John Peter, of Magdeburg. (Manuscripta Omnis
    Ævi).. 1668..1743
Luecke. See Lücke................................. 1792..1855
Luetzow. See Lützow.
Lugo, Francis de. Sp. Jesuit Miss. (On Thomas Aquinas) 1580..1652
Lugo, John de, br. Sp. Jesuit and Cardinal. Theologian 1583..1660
Luigi, Andrea di. L'Ingegno. Painter. See L'Ingegno 1450?.1520
Luini, Bernardin. Italian Painter.................... —aft.1530
Luini, Francis. Italian Mathematician .... 1740..1792
Luisino, Francis. Italian Greek and Latin Scholar..... 1523..1568
Luitprand. King of Lombards (712–44).............. — .. 744
Luitprand. Lombard Historian .... 920?. 972
Luke, St. Evangelist............................... 1st c.
Lukin, Lionel. Inventor of Life-boat................. 1742?.1834
Lully, or Lulli, John Baptist. French Musical Composer 1633..1687
Lully, or Lulle, Raymd. Doctor Illuminatus. (Ars Magna) 1234..1315
Lumsden, Matthew, LL. D., of Calcutta. Orientalist.... 1777..1835
Lundin, Sir Alan. Earl of Athol. Justiciar of Scotland — ..1275
Lundy, Benjamin. American Abolitionist .... 1789..1839
Luneau de Boisjermain, Peter Jos. Francis. Fr. Writer 1732..1801
Lunn, Joseph. Dramatist .... 1784?.1863
Lupset, Thos. Div. & Writer; Friend of Pole & Erasmus 1498?.1530
Lupton, Donald. Biographer .... fl. 1674
Lupus, or Wolf, Christian. Flemish Writer on Councils 1612..1681
Lupus Servatus. French Abbot. Theologian ....805?.aft.861
Lusignan, Guy de. King of Jerusalem and Cyprus..... — ..1194
Lussan, Margaret de. Romance and Historical Writer.. 1682..1758
Luthbert, or Lubbert, Sibrand. Dutch Controv. Divine 1556?.1625
Luther, Martin. German Reformer. Life by Melanchthon,
    1546 (also in English, German, French, and Swedish);
    Cochlæus, 1549 (also in German); Mathesius, 1565;
    Selnecker, 1575; Taillepied, 1577; Seidel, 1581; Glo-

17

BORN. DIED.

cerus, 1586; Dresser, 1598; Brerely, 1624; Hayne, 1641, Juncker, 1699 (also in German and Dutch); Forstmann, 1717; Grinsius, 1721; Herrenschmidt, 1742 (also in German and Danish); Walter, 1749–54; Kiel, 1753; Schroekh, 1773 (also in Danish and Swedish); Wagenseil, 1782; Tischer, 1783 (also in English, Danish, and Dutch); Zimmermann, 1812; Bower, 1813; H. Mueller, 1817; Ukert, 1817; Stange, 1835; Pfizer, 1836; Riddle, 1837; J. Scott, 1838; Audin, 1839 (also in German and Italian); H. Lee, 1839; Jürgens, 1840; Genth, 1842 (also in Dutch); Michelet, 1845 (also in English and German); Meurer, 1843–46 (also in English); R. Ferguson, 1848; Neudecker, 1850; Ratzeberger, 1850; König, 1853 (in English, 1854); Jander, 1853; Thoden van Velzen, 1853; Worsley, 1856 .... 1483..1546
Lutherburg, or Loutherbourg, Philip James. Fr. Painter 1740..1812
Luti, Benedict. Italian Painter .... 1666..1724
Luttrell, Henry. Poet. (*Memoirs of Thomas Moore*)... — ..1851
Lützelburger, Hans. *Hans Frank.* Swiss Wood Engrav. fl. 16th c.
Lützow, Louis Adolphus William, Baron. Prussian Gen. 1782..1834
Lützow, Theresa von. German Authoress .... 1804..1852
Luxembourg, Francis Henry de Montmorenci Bouteville, Duke of .... 1628..1695
Luyken, John. Dutch Engraver...................... 1649..1712
Luyts, John. Philosopher and Astronomer............. 1665..1721
Luzac, John. Dutch Philologist and Publicist.......... 1746..1807
Lycon. Greek Peripatetic Philosopher .... 300?.226 B.C.
Lycophron. Greek Poet and Gram. (*Cassandra*).. fl. B.C.(285–47)
Lycurgus. Spartan Lawgiver. Life by Dean Chetwood fl. B.C. 825?
Lydgate, John. Poet................................ 1375?.1460?
Lydiat, Thos. Chronol. & Math. (*Emendatio Temporum*) 1572..1646
Lydus, Johannes Laurentius. Byzantine Writer .... 490?. 560?
Lye, Edward. Antiquary and Saxonist................ 1704..1767
Lylye, or Lilly, John. Dramatist. (*Euphues*).......... 1553?.1601?
Lynch, Thomas. American Revolutionary Statesman... 1749..1779
Lynde, Sir Humphrey, M. P. Writer against Popery. (*Via Tuta*).. 1579..1636
Lyndhurst, John Singleton Copley, Baron. Ld. Chanc. 1772..1863
Lyndsay, or Lindsay, Sir David. Poet. L. by Chalmers 1490..1557?
Lyndwode, or Lindwood. Ecclesiastical Lawyer. Bishop of St. David's.................................... — ..1446
Lynedoch, Thomas Graham, Lord. General.......... 1750..1843
Lyon, George Francis, Captain R. N. Trav. and Explorer 1795..1832
Lyon, Mary. Amer. Educat. L. by Edw. Hitchcock, 1860 1797..1849
Lyon, Matthew. American Politician................. 1746..1822
Lyon, Nathaniel. American General................. 1819..1861
Lyonnet, Peter. Dutch Naturalist.................... 1707..1789
Lyons, Edmund, Lord. Admiral...................... 1790..1858
Lyons, Israel. Hebrew Scholar...................... — ..1770
Lyons, Israel, son. Botanist. Mathem. of Cambridge 1739..1775
Lyra, or Lyranus, Nicholas de. Biblical Commentator .. 1270?.1340
Lysander. Spartan General.......................... —B.C.395
Lyserus, John. Lutheran Div. (*Polygamia Triumphatrix*) — ..1684
Lyserus, Polycarp. Lutheran Divine. Commentator... 1552..1601

BORN. DIED.

Lysias. Greek Orator ....458.378 B.C.
Lysimachus. General of Alexander; King of Thrace 360?.281 B.C.
Lysippus. Greek Sculptor .... fl. ti. Alex. Gt.
Lysons, Daniel, M. D., of Bath. Medical Writer........ — ..1800
Lysons, Rev. Daniel. Topographer. (*Environs of London*) 1760..1834
Lysons, Samuel. Antiquary and Topographer......... 1763..1819
Lyte, Henry. Botanist .... 1529..1607
Lyte, Rev. Henry Francis. Poet. (*Spirit of the Psalms*) — ..1847
Lyttelton, Charles. Bishop of Carlisle. Antiquary.... 1714..1768
Lyttelton, Edward, Baron Lyttelton of Mounslow. Lord
    Keeper... 1589..1645
Lyttelton, George, of Frankley, First Lord. (*Henry II.;
    Conversion of St. Paul.*) Life by Phillimore, 1845... 1709..1773
Lyttelton, Sir Thomas, of Frankley. Judge. (*Tenures*) 1421?.1481
Lyttelton, Thomas, 2d Lord; Subject of the Ghost Story — ..1779
Lyttolton, William Henry, Baron Westcote. Governor of
    Jamaica .... — ..1808

M.

BORN. DIED.

Maan, John. Fr. Hist. and Theol. (*Ecclesia Turonensis*) fl. 1667
Maas, Dirk. Dutch Painter............................. 1656..1715
Maas, or Macs, Nicholas. Dutch Painter.............. 1632..1693
Maat, Jan. Flemish Painter. *See* Blankoff........... 1628..1670
Mabillon, John. Fr. Benedictine. L. by Ruinart, 1709 1632..1707
Mably, Gabriel Bonnot, Abbé de. Political Writer .... 1709..1785
Maboul, James. Fr. Bp. & Preach. (*Oraisons funèbres*) 1650?.1723
Mabuse, or Maubeuge, John. *Gossaert.* Flem. Painter 1499..1562?
Macadam, John Loudon. Improver of Roads......... 1756..1836
Mac Ardell, James. English Mezzotint Engraver ..... 1710?.1765
Macarius, St., of Alexandria. Anchorite and Writer..301?.390 or 1
Macarius, St., *the Younger*, of Alexandria. Monk ....304?. 404?
Macarthur, Duncan. American Pioneer and Statesman 1772..1840
Macartney, Geo., E. of. Envoy. L. by Sir John Barrow 1737..1806
Macaulay, Mrs. Catherine (Sawbridge). Historian .. 1733..1791
Macaulay, Thomas Babington, Lord. Historian. Life
    by Rev. F. Arnold, 1862 .... 1800..1859
Macaulay, Zachary. Slavery Abolitionist............. 1768..1838
Macauley, Elizabeth Wright. Actress and Preacher... 1785..1837
Macbeth. King of Scotland (1040–56)............ — ..1056
Macbride, David, M. D. Irish Phys. (*Theory & Practice*) 1726..1778
Maccabæus, Judas. Jewish Patriot (B. C. 166–160) .... — B.C.160
Maccabæus, Simon, brother. Jewish Patriot.......... — B.C.135
Mac Caul, Alexander, D. D. Divine and Hebraist. Life
    by J. B. M'Caul................................... 1799..1863
Mac Cheyne, Rev. Robert Murray. Scottish Divine... 1813..1843
Macchiavelli, Nicholas. Florentine Writ. (*Del Principe*) 1469..1527
Macclesfield, Thomas Parker, First Earl of. Ld. Chanc. 1666..1732
Maccord, David J. American Lawyer and Author .... 1797..1855
Mac Cormic, Charles. Historical Writer .... 1744..1807
Maccovius, or Makouski, John. Polish Protestant Div. 1588..1644
Maccrea, Jane. Killed by Indians................... — ..1777
Mac Crie, Thomas, D. D. Historical Writer. Life by
    Thomas M'Crie, 1840............................. 1772..1835
Mac Culloch, Benjamin. " Confederate " General..... 1814..1862
Mac Culloch, John, M. D. Geological Writer .... 1773..1835
Mac Culloch, John Ramsay. Statistican and Political
    Economist. (*Dictionary of Commerce*)........... 1789..1864
Macdiarmid, John. (*Lives of British Statesmen*)...... 1779..1808
Macdiarmid, John. Ed. of *Dumfries Courier* and Writer 1789?.1852
Macdonald, Andrew. Scottish Dramatic Writer....... 1755?.1790
Macdonald, Flora. Heroic Scottish Jacobite.......... 1720..1790
Macdonald, James, M. D. Amer. Phys. and Med. Writer 1803..1849
Macdonald, John, Colonel. Military Writer .... 1759..1831
Macdonald, Stephen James Joseph Alexander. Duke of
    Taranto. Marshal of France...................... 1765..1840
Macdonough, Thomas. American Naval Officer ...... 1784..1825
Macdougal, Alexander. Amer. Revolutionary Officer. 1750?.1786
Macduffie, George. American Statesman .... 1788?.1851
Macé, Francis. Biblical Writer .... 1640?.1721

BORN. DIED.

Mace, Thomas. Musician. (*Musik's Monument*) ...... 1613..1709
Macedo, Francis de. Portuguese Scholar .... 1596..1681
Macedo, Joseph Augustine de. Portuguese Poet....... 1770?.1831
Macfarlane, Charles. Writer....................... — ..1858
Macfarlane, Duncan, D. D. Principal of Glasgow Univ. 1771?.1858
Macfarlane, Robert. Political Writer. (*Reign of George
 III.*) Life by G. Lawson, 1862 .... 1734..1804
Macgillivray, Alexander. Chief of Creek Indians ..... 1740?.1793
Macgillivray, William, LL. D. Naturalist .... 1796..1852
Macgregor, John. British Statistician and Politician .. 1797..1857
Macgregor Campbell, Robert. *Rob Roy, q. v.* .... 1660?.1735?
Machault, James de. Writer on Jesuit Missions & Travels 1599..1680
Machault, John de. Fr. Jesuit. Annotator of Thuanus 1561..1619
Machault, John Baptist. French Jesuit. Writer...... 1591..1640
Machault d'Arnouville, John Baptist. Financier .... 1701..1794
Machiavelli, Nicholas. *See* Macchiavelli .... 1469..1527
Machin, John. Gresham Professor of Astronomy....... — ..1751
Mac Intosh, John. American Revolutionary Soldier... — ..1826
Mac Intosh, Lachlan. American Revolutionary Soldier 1727..1806
Mack von Leiberich, Charles, Baron. Austrian General 1752..1828
Mackay, Andrew, LL. D. Mathematician............. — ..1809
Mackean, Thomas. American Jurist and Statesman... 1734..1817
Mackeever, Isaac. American Naval Officer .... 1793..1856
Mackendree, Rev. William. Bishop .... 1757..1835
Mackenzie, Sir Alexander. Explorer in North America 1760..1820
Mackenzie, Alex. Slidell. Amer. Naval Officer & Writer 1803..1848
Mackenzie, Charles Frazer. Missionary Bishop in Af-
 rica. Life by Dean Goodwin..................... 1825..1862
Mackenzie, Sir George. Legal and Historical Writer.. 1636..1691
Mackenzie, Geo., 1st. E. of Cromarty. Statesman & Hist. 1631?.1714
Mackenzie, George, M. D. (*Lives of Scottish Writers*).. 18th c.
Mackenzie, Henry. Essayist & Nov. (*Man of Feeling*) 1745..1831
Mackenzie, William Lyon. Canadian Journalist & Polit. 1794..1861
Mackey, John. Writer & Polit. (*Court of St. Germains*) — ..1726
Mackinnon, Daniel, Col. (*History of Coldstream Guards*) 1791..1836
Mackintosh, Sir James. Historian. Life by Mackintosh 1765..1832
Macklin, Charles. Actor and Dramatist. Life by Kirk-
 man, 1799; William Cooke...............'......... 1690..1797
Macknight, James, D. D. Scottish Commentator....... 1721..1800
Maclaine, Archibald. (*Letters to Soame Jenyns*) .. 1722..1804
Maclane, Louis. American Statesman..............: 1786..1857
Maclaurin, Colin. Mathem. and Philosopher. L. by self 1698..1746
Maclaurin, John, son. Ld. Dreghorn. Scot. Judge & Writ. 1734..1796
Maclean, John, LL. D. American Jurist and Statesman 1785..1861
Maclean, Mrs. Letitia Elizabeth, *née* Landon, *which see*.. 1802..1838
Macleay, William Sharp. Botanist and Zoölogist...... 1793?.1865
Macleod, Alexander, D. D. American Writer.......... 1774..1833
Macleod, John, M. D. Naval Surg. (*Voyage of the Alceste*) 1782..1820
Maclure, William. American Geologist .... 1763..1840
Macnab, Sir Alan Napier. Canadian Statesman...... 1798..1862
Macnaghten, Sir William. Envoy; assassinated at Cabul — ..1841
Macnally, Leonard. Lawyer and Dramatist .... 1752..1820
Macneil, John. American General .... 1784..1850
Macneill, Hector. Scottish Poet................... 1746..1818

BORN. DIED.

Macnevin, William James. American Writer & Scientist 1763..1841
Macnichol, Rev. Dr. Donald. Celtic Antiquary ...... 1735..1802
Macnish, Robert, M. D. and LL. D. (*Philosophy of Sleep*) 1802..1837
Macomb, Alexander. American Military Commander.. 1782..1841
Macon, Nathaniel. American Politician and Legislator 1757..1837
Macpherson, David. Commercial Writer. (*Annals of
    Commerce*) .... — .. —
Macpherson, Jas. Poet and Hist.Writ. (*Ossian's Poems*) 1738..1796
Mac Pherson, James Birdseye. American General.... 1828..1864
Macquer, Peter Joseph. French Chemist .... 1718..1784
Macquer, Philip, brother. Historical Writer.......... 1720..1770
Macret, Charles Francis Adrian. French Engraver .... 1750..1783
Macrianus. Pretender to the Roman Empire (260–62).. — .. 262
M'Crie, Dr. Thomas. Scottish Divine and Historian.. 1772..1835
Macrinus. Roman Emperor (217, April—June, 218)... — .. 218
Macrinus, Charles. Poet............................ — ..1572
Macrinus, or Salmon, John. *French Horace.* Latin Poet 1490..1557
Macrobius. Grammarian....................... ti. Theodosius
Madach, Emerich. Hungarian Poet.................. — ..1864
Madan, Rev. Martin. Preacher & Writer. (*Thelyphthora*) 1726..1790
Madan, Spencer. Bishop of Peterborough .... — ..1813
Madden, Samuel, D. D., of Dublin. Writer and Benefac-
    tor. (*Memoirs of the Twentieth Century*) .... 1687..1765
Maddersteg, Michael. Dutch Painter................1659?.1709
Maddox, Isaac. Bishop of Worcester. Writer .... 1697..1759
Maderno, Charles. Italian Architect .... 1556..1629
Maderno, Stephen. Italian Sculptor................. 1576..1636
Madison, James. Fourth President of the United States 1751..1836
Madox, Thomas. Legal Antiquary. (*Hist. of Exchequer*) — ..1735?
Madrazo, Joseph y Aguda. Spanish Painter.......... 1781..1859
Mæcenas, C. Cilnius. Rom. Statesman. Patron of Letters 73?.8 B.C.
Maerlant, Jacob. Dutch Poet. .... 1235?.1300
Maes, or Maas, Nicholas. Dutch Painter............. 1632..1693
Maestlin, Michael. German Astronomer............. 1550..1631
Maffei, Bernardin. Card. Writ. on Cicero, Medals, Inscrip. 1513..1553
Maffei, Francis Scipio, Marquis. Antiq. (*Verona Illustrata*) 1675..1755
Maffei, John Peter. Jesuit. (*L. of Loyola; Hist. of Indies*) 1536..1603
Maffei, or Maffæus, Vegio. Latin Poet. (*Epigrams.*)
    Life by J. H. Meibomius, 1653..................... 1406..1458
Maffitt, Rev. John Newland. Writer. Life by self.... 1794..1850
Magalhaens, or Magellan, Ferd. de. Port. Navigator 1470?.1521
Magalhaens, John Hyacinth de. Port. Nat. Philosopher 1723..1790
Magalotti, Lawrence, Count. Philosopher and Mathem. 1637..1712
Maganza, John Baptist, of Vicenza. Historical Painter 1577..1617
Magati, or Magatus, Cæsar. Italian Surgeon .... 1579..1647
Magee, William. Archbp. of Dublin. (*The Atonement*) 1765..1831
Magellan, or Magalhaens, Ferd. de. Port. Navigator.. 1470?.1521
Magendie, Francis. French Physician and Physiologist 1783..1855
Mageoghegan, James. (*History of Ireland*)........... 1702..1764
Maggi, Charles Mary. Italian Poet................... 1630..1699
Maggi, or Magius, Jerome. Venetian Engineer .... — ..1572
Magini, or Maginus, John Anthony. Math. and Astron. 1555..1617
Maginn, William, LL. D. Writer..................... 1793..1842
Magistris, Hyacinth de. Italian Missionary to India... 1605..1666

BORN. DIED.

Magistris, Simon de. Italian Orientalist.............. 1728..1802
Magliabecchi, Anthony, of Florence. Librarian....... 1633..1714
Magnan, Dominic. Numismatist. (*Ville de Rome*)..... 1731..1796
Magnentius. Roman Emperor (350–53)............. — .. 353
Magni, Valerian. Italian Missionary in North Europe... 1586?.1661
Magnol, Peter. French Botanist .... 1638..1715
Magnon, John. French Poet .... — ..1662
Magnus, Albertus. Schoolman. Life by Flaminio ..... 1193?.1280
Magnus, John. Archbp. of Upsal. (*Historia Gothorum*) 1488..1554
Magnus, Olaus, brother. (*De Gentibus Septentrionalibus*) — ..1568
Magnusson, Finnur. Icelandic Archæologist.......... 1781..1847
Mahmoud. Sultan of Ghizni (997–1030)............. 967..1030
Mahmoud I. Sultan of Turkey (1730–54) .... 1696..1754
Mahmoud II. (1808–39) .... 1785..1839
Mahomet. Arabian Prophet. Life by Abulfeda; Maracci;
    Savary; Sale; Dean Prideaux; Boulainvilliers; D'Her-
    belot; John Gagnier, 1748; Godfrey Higgins, 1829;
    Bush, 1832; Hammer-Purgstall, 1837; Weil, 1843; A.
    Sprenger, 1851; W. Irving, 1852; W. Muir, 1858; Ar-
    nold, 1859; Daniel Larroque; Michael Baudier; F. H.
    Turpin .... 570 or 1.632
Mahomet I. Sultan of the Turks (1413–21).......... 1374?.1421
Mahomet II. (1451–81.) *The Great.* Conqueror of
    Constantinople. Life by Guillet................... 1430..1481
Mahomet III. (1595–1603) .... 1564..1603
Mahomet IV. (1649–87); defeated by Sobieski .... 1642..1691
Mahomet V., or Mahmoud I. (1730–54)............. 1696..1754
Mahomet VI., or Mahmoud II. (1808–39)............ 1785..1839
Mahudel, Nich. Fr. Antiq. (*Monnaies antiq. d'Espagne*) 1673..1747
Mai, Angelo. Cardinal. Papal Librarian and Scholar.. 1782..1854
Maiano, Benedict da. Sculptor and Architect......... 1424..1498
Maiano, Julian da. Italian Sculptor and Architect.....1387.aft.1470
Maier, Michael. German Alchemist and Rosicrusian.. 1568..1662
Maignan, Emanuel. Mathem. (*De Perspectivâ Horariâ*) 1601..1676
Maigrot, Charles. Fr. Miss. to China. (*De Sinicâ Relig.*) 1652..1730
Maikoff, Basil Ivanovitch. Russian Poet.............. 1725..1778
Mailáth, John Nepomuk Joseph. Hung. Poet & Historian 1786..1855
Mailla, or Maillac, Joseph Anne Mary de Moyrac de. Jes-
    uit Missionary to China............................ 1670..1748
Maillard, Oliver. French Cordelier. Preacher .... — ..1502
Maillé, Urban de, Marquis de Brezé. Marshal of France 1597?.1650
Maillé de Brezé, Simon de. Tridentine Divine .... 1515..1597
Maillebois, J. Bapt. Desmarets, Mqs. of. Marshal of Fr. 1682..1762
Maillet, Benedict de. Fr. Traveler & Diplom. (*Telliamed*) 1656..1738
Mailly, John Baptist. Historian..................... 1744..1794
Maimbourg, Louis. Historian....................... 1610..1686
Maimonides, Moses. Rabbi........................ 1131?.1204
Maine de Biran, Francis Peter Gouthier. Fr. Metaphys. 1766..1824
Mainfroy, or Manfred, son of Emperor Frederick II.
    Prince of Tarentum, King of Naples and Sicily...... 1233..1266
Maino, Jason del. Italian Jurist.................... 1435..1519
Maintenon, Frances d'Aubigné, Madame de. Life by
    La Beaumelle:................................... 1635..1719
Mainville, Peter. French Politician .... 1765..1792

BORN. DIED.

Mainzer, Dr. Joseph.   Musical Composer .... 1801..1851
Mair, or Major, John.   Scottish Divine & Hist. in France 1469..1550?
Mairan, John James d'Ortous de.   Natural Philosopher 1678..1771
Maire, James le.   Dutch Navigator.................. — ..1616
Maire, John le.   French Poet.................... 1473.1524 or 48
Maire, — le, of Lyons.   Medical Writer.............. — ..1787
Mairet, John.   French Dramatic Writer. (*Sophonisbe*) 1604..1686
Maistre, Anthony le.   Lawyer and Divine of Port Royal 1608..1658
Maistre, Joseph, Count de.   Ital. Statesman and Author 1753..1821
Maistre, Louis Isaac le.   *Sacy.*   Jansenist............. 1613..1684
Maistre, Xavier de.   French Novelist................. 1763..1852
Maitland, Sir Frederick Lewis.   Rear Admiral .... 1799..1839
Maitland, John, Lord.   Chancellor of Scot.   Latin Poet 1537?.1595
Maitland, John, Duke of Lauderdale.   Statesman...... 1616..1682
Maitland, Sir Richard, Lord Lethington.   Poet and Col-
    lector of Poems .... 1496..1586
Maitland, Wm.   Topographical Hist.   (*Hist. of London*) 1693?.1757
Maittaire, Mich.   Philol. & Bibliog.   (*Annales Typograph.*) 1668..1747
Maius, or May, John Henry.   Lutheran Divine .... 1653..1719
Maizeroi, Paul Gideon Joly de.   Fr. Officer & Tactician 1719..1780
Majo, Francis, or Ciccio di.   Musical Composer........ 1745..1774
Major, or Mair, John.   Scotch Divine and Hist. in France 1469..1550?
Major, John Daniel.   Physician and Naturalist .... 1634..1693
Majoragius, Mark Anthony, of Milan.   Class. Comment. 1514..1555
Majorianus.   Roman Emperor (457–61).............. — .. 461
Mako, Paul.   Hungarian Jesuit.   Promoter of Learning 1723..1793
Makouski, or Maccovius, John.   Polish Protestant Divine 1588 .1644
Makrizi, Ahmed al.   Arabic Historical Writer at Cairo 1360?.1442
Malachi.   Hebrew Prophet.........................fl. 5th c. B.C.
Malagrida, Gabriel.   Ital. Jesuit Miss. to Portugal; burnt 1689..1761
Malan, Abraham Henry Cæsar, D. D.   Swiss Theologian
    and Author...................................... 1787..1864
Malapert, Charles.   Poet and Mathematician.......... 1581..1630
Malatesti, Anthony.   Florentine Poet................ — ..1672
Malaval, Francis, of Marseilles. Mystic. (*Lives of Saints*) 1627?.1719
Malbone, Edward G.   American Portrait Painter ...... 1777..1807
Malcolm I.   King of Scotland (944–52).............. — .. 952
Malcolm II.   (1003–33) .... 953?.1033
Malcolm III.   *Canmore.*   (1057–93), son of Duncan.. — ..1093
Malcolm IV.   (1153–65)......................... — ..1165
Malcolm, James Peller.   Artist and Antiquary.   (*Lon-
    dinium Redivivum*)............................. 1760?.1815
Malcolm, Sir John.   Diplomatist and Writer on India.
    Life by Kaye, 1856............................. 1769..1833
Malczewski, or Malczeski, Anthony.   Polish Poet..... 1792?.1826
Maldonatus, John.   Spanish Jesuit.   Commentator.... 1534. 1583
Malebranche, Nicholas.   Philosopher.   Life by Adry.. 1638..1715
Malek-Shah.   Sultan of Seljukian Turks (1072–92).... 1054..1092
Malesherbes, Christian William de Lamoignon de.
    French Lawyer.   Life by G. H. Gaillard, 1805 ... 1721..1794
Malezieu, Nicholas de.   French Mathematician and Poet 1650..1727
Malfillastre, James Charles Louis.   French Poet....... 1732..1767
Malherbe, Francis de.   French Poet................. 1555?.1628
Malibran de Beriot, Maria Felicitas.   Vocalist........ 1808..1836

BORN. DIED.

Malingre, Claude. French Historian. (*Dignités Hono-raires de France*)................................... 1580?.1653?
Mallary, Rollin Carlos. Amer. Lawyer and Statesman. 1784..1831
Mallemans, Claude. Fr. Writ. (*L' Ouvrage de la Création*) 1653..1723
Mallemans, John, brother. (*Histoire de l'Église*) ...... 1649..1740
Mallet, or Malloch, David. Poet & Miscellaneous Writer 1700?.1765
Mallet, Paul Henry. Swiss Historian and Antiquary .. 1730..1807
Mallet du Pan, Jas. Swiss Publicist. (*Mercure Britann.*) 1749..1800
Mallet Favre, James Andrew, of Geneva. Mathem... 1740..1790
Mallett, Edmund, Abbé. French Encyclopædist....... 1713..1755
Mallinkrott, Bernard, of Munster. Scholar.......... — ..1664
Malmesbury, James Harris, First Earl of. Diplomatist 1746..1820
Malmesbury, William H. Historian .... 1095?.1143?
Malone, Edmond. Shakespearian Critic .... 1741..1812
Malouin, Paul Jas. Fr. Phys. (*Solid and Fluid Bodies*) 1701..1778
Malpighi, Marcellus. Naturalist, Phys., and Anatomist 1628..1694
Maltby, Edward. Bishop of Durham............... 1770..1859
Malte-brun, Conrad. Poet, Geogr. and Political Writer 1775..1826
Malthus, Rev. Thomas Robert. Writer on Population.
    Life by Bishop Otter .... 1766..1834
Malus, Stephen Louis. Fr. Physicist and Mil. Engineer 1775..1812
Malvasia, Chas. Cæsar. (*Hist. of the Painters of Bologna*) 1616..1693
Malvezzi, Virgilio, Marquis of. Spanish Statesman.
    Writer on Tacitus............................. 1599..1654
Malvoisine, or Mawmoisine, Wm. de. Bp. of St. Andrew's — ..1238
Mambrun, Peter. French Jesuit. Latin Poet. (*Ec-logues; Georgics*)............................. 1581..1661
Mammæa, Julia. Mother of Alexander Severus....... — .. 235
Mamun, Abul Abbas Abdallah. Seventh Abbaside Caliph 786.. 833
Man, Cornelius de. Dutch Historical & Portrait Painter 1621..1706
Manara, Prosper, Marquis of. Italian Poet........... 1714..1800
Manardi, John, of Ferrara. Physician .... 1462..1536
Manasseh. King of Judah (B. C. 698–643).........710?.643 B.C.
Manby, Capt. Geo. Wm. Invent. of Shipwreck Apparatus 1765..1854
Manchester, Chas. Montagu, 1st Duke of. Ambassador — ..1722
Manchester, Sir Henry Montagu, 1st Earl of. Ld. Treas. — ..1642
Mancinelli, Anthony. Italian Poet and Orator. (*Silva Vitæ Suæ*)................................... 1452..1506?
Manco Capac. Inca of Peru...................... — ..1544
Mandar, Theoph. Fr. Revolutionist. Poet & Polit. Writ. 1759..1823
Mandeville, Bernard de. Writer. (*Fable of the Bees*).. 1670?.1733
Mandeville, Sir John. Traveler .... 1300?.1372
Manes. Philosopher .... 240.. 274?
Manetho. Egyptian Historian.................. fl. B.C.323–285
Manetti, Gianozzo. Florentine Orator and Scholar .... 1396..1459
Manetti, Rutilio. Italian Painter................. 1571..1639
Manetti, Xavier. Physician and Botanist of Florence.. 1723..1785
Manfred, or Mainfroy, son of Emperor Frederick II.
    Prince of Tarentum, King of Naples and Sicily..... 1233..1266
Manfredi, Bartholomew. Italian Painter .... 1574..1617
Manfredi, Eustace. Ital. Astron. Life by J. P. Zanotti 1674..1739
Manfredi, Gabriel. Algebraist.................... 1681..1761
Mangeart, Thos. (*Introduction to the Science of Medals*) 1695..1762
Manget, John James, of Geneva. Medical Writer..... 1652..1742

BORN. DIED.

Mangey, Rev. Thomas, D. D.   Theological Writer...... 1684..1755
Manigault, Gabriel.   American Merchant and Revolu-
    tionary Patriot... 1704..1781
Manilius, Marcus.   Latin Poet. (*Astronomica*)........ti. Augustus
Manin, Daniel.   Italian Patriot....................... 1804..1857
Manley, John.   American Naval Commander......... 1734..1793
Manley, Mary.   Dramatic and Political Writer..... 1672?.1724
Manlius Capitolinus, Marcus.   Deliverer of the Capitol —B.C.384
Mann, A. T.   Flemish Antiquary and Physicist..... 1740?.aft.1802
Mann, Horace, LL. D.   Amer. Educationist & Statesman 1796..1859
Manna, John.   Italian Scholar........................ — ..1865
Manners, John, Marquis of Granby.   Soldier.......... 1721..1770
Mannert, Conrad.   Historian and Geographer......... 1756..1834
Manni, Dominic Mary.   Italian Historian............. 1690..1788
Manning, James, D. D.   Amer. Clergyman and Educator 1738..1791
Manning, Rev. Owen.   Antiquary and Topographer ... 1721..1801
Mannori, Louis.   Fr. Advocate. (*Memoirs and Pleadings*) 1696..1777
Mannozzi, John.   Painter of Florence.   *See* Giovanni.. 1590..1636
Manny, Sir Walter.   Warrior of Edward III........... — ..1372
Mannyng, Robt. *De Brune.* Eng. Metrical Chronicler ti.Edw.I.&II.
Manrique, George.   Spanish Poet..................... 1420?.1485?
Mansard, or Mansart, Francis.   French Architect...... 1598..1666
Mansard, Jules Hardouin, nephew.   Architect......... 1645..1708
Mansell, William Lort.   Bishop of Bristol. Wit...... 1750?.1820
Mansfeld, Ernest, Count of.   Anti-Austrian General.... 1585..1626
Mansfeld, Peter Ernest, Ct. of.   Ger. Statesman and Gen. 1517..1604
Mansfield, William Murray, Earl of.   Ld. Chief Justice 1705..1793
Mansi, John Dominic.   Italian Bishop and Antiquary .. 1692..1769
Manso, John Baptist.   Ital. Poet and Patron of Learning 1561..1645
Manstein, Christopher Herman de.   Russian General.
    (*Memoirs of Russia*)................................... 1711..1757
Mant, Richard.   Bishop of Down. Commentator...... 1776..1848
Mantegna, Andrew.   Painter.......................... 1431..1506
Mantell, Gideon Algernon, LL. D.   Geologist.......... 1799..1852
Mantica, Francis.   Italian Writer.................... 1534..1614
Manton, Dr. Thomas.   Ejected Nonconformist Divine.. 1620..1677
Mantuan, Baptist.   Italian Latin Poet................ 1448..1516
Mantuan, George. *Ghisi.* Ital. Painter and Engraver. 1520?.aft.1577
Manuel I. *Comnenus.* Emperor of the East (1143–80).. 1120?.1180
Manuel II. *Palæologus.* Emperor of the East........ 1349?.1425
Manuel, Francis.   Portuguese Poet................... 1734..1819
Manuel, James Anthony.   French Politician........... 1775..1827
Manuel, Nicholas. *Deutsch.* Swiss Reform., Paint. & Poet 1484..1530
Manuel, Peter Louis.   French Politician; guillotined .. 1751..1793
Manutius, or Manuzio, Aldus, the elder.   Printer..... 1449..1515
Manutius, Aldus, junior.   Printer and Writer......... 1547..1597
Manutius, Paul.   Printer and Latin Scholar........... 1511..1574
Manwood, Sir Roger.   Chief Baron. Writ. on Forest Laws 1525..1593
Manzo, or Manso (*q. v.*), J. Bapt., of Naples. (*L. of Tasso*) 1561..1645
Manzoli, John.   Italian Singer....................... — ..1791
Manzolli. *Palingenius Stellatus.* Latin Poet. (*Zodia-
    cus Vitæ*).. fl. 1500?
Manzuoli, Thomas. *Da San Friano.* Italian Painter.. 1536..1575
Mapes, James W.   American Agricultural Writer...... — ..1865

BORN. DIED.

Mapes, or Map, Walter. Eng. Poet and Prose Writ. 1150?.aft.1196
Maphæus, Vegius. Latin Poet. *See* Maffei .... 1406..1458
Mapletoft, Dr. John. Medical and Theological Writer.. 1631..1721
Mar, John Erskine, Eleventh Earl of. Scottish Jacobite 1671..1732
Mara, Madame Elizabeth. German Singer........... 1749..1833
Maracci, John. Italian Historical Painter............ 1637..1704
Maracci, Louis. Italian Orientalist; Editor of Koran .. 1612..1700
Marais, Marin. Musical Composer................... 1656..1728
Maraldi, James Philip. Mathematician and Astronomer 1665..1729
Marana, John Paul. Italian Writer. (*Turkish Spy*)... 1642?.1693
Maranta, Bartholomew. Italian Botanist............ — ..1554
Marat, John Paul. French Revolutionist............. 1744..1793
Maratti, Charles. Italian Painter.................... 1625..1713
Marbach, John. Prot. Div. (*Fides Jesus et Jesuitarum*) — ..1581
Marbeck, John. Sacred Composer. (*Lives of Saints*).. — ..1585
Marc Anthony. Engraver. *See* Raimondi.......... 1475?.1534
Marca, Peter de. French Bishop. (*De Concordiâ*)..... 1594..1662
Marceau, Francis Severin Desgraviers. French General 1769..1796
Marcel. Painter of Frankfort....................... 1628..1683
Marcel, John Joseph. French Orientalist............ 1776..1854
Marcel, William. French Writer.................... 1612?.1702
Marcel, William. Fr. Chronol. (*Origin of Fr. Monarchy*) 1647..1708
Marcellinus. Bishop of Rome (296–304) .... — .. 304
Marcellinus. Count of Illyria. Chronicler .... — .. 468
Marcellinus, Ammianus. Soldier and Historian ...... — .. 390?
Marcello, Benedict. Italian Musical Composer........ 1686..1739
Marcellus I. Bishop of Rome (308–10).............. — .. 310
Marcellus II. (1555)............................. 1501..1555
Marcellus, Donatus. Italian Physician.............. fl. 16th c.
Marcellus, *Empiricus*, of Bordeaux. Medical Writer .. —aft. 408
Marcellus, Marcus Claudius. Conqueror of Syracuse.270?.208 B.C.
Marcellus, M. Claudius, nephew of Augustus (*Æn.* VI.) 43.23 B.C.
Marcet, Alexander. Physician and Natural Philosopher 1770..1822
Marcet, Mrs. Jane. Scientific Writer................ 1769..1858
Marchand, John Louis. French Organist............ 1669..1732
Marchand, Prosper. Bibliographer .... 1675..1756
Marchant, James, of Couvin. Divine .... — ..1648
Marche, Oliver de la. Burgundian Writer .... 1426?.1502
Marchetti, Alexander. Poet and Mathematician ...... 1633..1714
Marchettis, Peter de. Italian Physician and Anatomist 1593..1673
Marchi, Francis. Italian Military Engineer .... 1506?.1599
Marchmont, Hugh Hume-Campbell, 3d Earl of. Polit. 1708..1794
Marcianus. Roman Emperor of the East (450–57)..... 388?. 457
Marcilius, Theodore. German Critic................. 1548..1617
Marcion. Heresiarch.............................. fl. 2d c.
Marco Polo. Venetian Traveler .... 1256?.1323
Marcus Aurelius Antoninus. Emperor (161–80).... 121.. 180
Marcy, William Learned. American Statesman......: 1786..1857
Mardonius. Persian General in Greece.............. — B.C.479
Mare, Nicholas de la. Magistrate. (*Traité de la Police*) 1639..1723
Mare, Philibert de la. Latin Historical Writer........ 1615..1687
Mare, William de la. French Latin Poet............. fl. 1514
Maréchal, or Mareschal, Peter Silvan. (*Dict. of Atheists*) 1750..1803
Marenzio, Luke. Italian Musical Composer .... 1550..1599

BORN. DIED.

Marets, Roland des. *Maresius.* Fr. Advoc. (*Latin Letters*) 1594..1653
Marets, Samuel de. *Little Preacher.* Prot. Controv... 1599..1663
Marets de Sorlin, John des. Anti-Jansenist .... 1595..1676
Margaret. Queen of Scotland, sister of Edgar Atheling 1046?.1093
Margaret. Queen of Denmark, Sweden, and Norway.
 Semiramis of the North.......................... 1353..1412
Margaret, of Anjou. Queen of Eng., wife of Henry VI. 1429..1482
Margaret, of Austria. Governess of the Netherlands... 1480?.1530
Margaret, of France. Queen of England, wife of Ed-
 ward I. (1299–1307)............................. — ..1317
Margaret, of France, daughter of Hen. II. Qu. of Navarre 1552..1615
Margaret, of Parma. Regent of Netherlands under
 Philip II. of Spain............................. 1522..1586
Margaret, of Provence. Queen of France, wife of Louis
 IX. (1234–70)................................. 1221..1295
Margaret, of Valois - Angoulême. Sister of Francis I.
 Queen of Navarre............................. 1492..1549
Margaret Beaufort, Countess of Richmond, mother of
 Henry VII.................................... 1441..1509
Margarita de l'Erpine, Frances. Singer .... — ..1740
Margaritone d'Arezzo. Italian Painter............. 1212..1289?
Marggraf, Andrew Sigismond. German Chemist...... 1709..1782
Margon, Wm. Plantavit de la Pause, Abbé de. Hist.Writ. 1685?.1760
Margunio, Massineo. Greek Poet and Printer......... 1522?.1602
Marheineke, Philip Conrad. German Theologian..... 1780..1846
Maria Louisa. Empress of France................. 1791..1847
Maria Theresa, of Austria, wife of Louis XIV. of France 1638..1683
Maria Theresa. Queen of Hungary and Empress of Ger. 1717..1780
Mariamne, wife of Herod the Great .... — B.C. 28
Mariana, John de. Spanish Historian. (*De Rege*) .... 1536..1623
Marianus Scotus. Scottish Monk and Chronicler..... 1028..1086
Marie Antoinette. Queen of France. Life by Madame
 Guénard; E. and J. de Goncourt, 1859 .... 1755..1793
Marie Louise, d'Orleans. Queen of Spain. Life by
 Madame S. Gay, 1722–23 .... 1662..1689
Mariette, Peter John. French Amateur in Art....... 1694..1774
Marignan, John James Medichino, Marquis de. Ital. Gen. 1497..1555
Marigny, Francis Augier de. Fr. Orient. (*Hist. des Arabes*) — ..1762
Marigny, James Carpentier de. French Wit and Writer — ..1670
Marin, Michael Angelo. French Novelist .... 1697..1767
Marinella, Lucretia. Venetian Poet. (*Life of the Virgin*) 1571..1653
Marini, John Baptist. *Il Cavaliere.* Ital. Poet. (*Adone*) 1569..1625
Marino Falieri. Doge of Venice................... 1278..1355
Marinoni, John James. Mathematician and Astronomer 1676..1755
Marinus I. Pope (882–84). See Martin II............ — .. 884
Marinus II. (942–46.) See Martin III. .... — .. 946
Mario Nuzzi, or de' Fiori. Painter of Flowers & Landsc. 1603..1673
Marion, Francis. American Revolutionary Officer ..... 1732..1795
Mariotte, Edmund. Mathematician and Experim. Philos. — ..1684
Marischal, George Keith, Earl. Scottish Jacobite...... 1668?.1751
Marius, Caius. Roman Dictator.................... 157.86 B.C.
Marius, Leonard. Dutch Theologian. (*Pentateuch*) ... — ..1628
Marivaux, Peter Carlet de Chamblain de. French Dram-
 atist and Novelist .... 1688..1763

BORN. DIED.

Marjorie, *Pet.* Infant Genius. *See* Fleming.......... 1803..1811
Mark, St. Evangelist.............................. 1st c.
Mark. Bishop of Rome (336, Jan. 18–Oct. 7).......... — .. 336
Markham, Gervase. Poet and Georgic Writer........ 1570?.1655?
Markland, Abraham. Divine and Poet...........:.. 1645..1720
Markland, James Henry. Antiquary................ 1787?.1864
Markland, Jeremiah. Critic...................... 1693..1776
Marlborough, John Churchill, Duke of. Life by Lediard,
    1736; Life by order of Napoleon I., 1808; Coxe, 1818;
    Bucke, 1839; C. G. Simon, 1841; Alison, 1852 ...... 1650..1722
Marlborough, Sarah Jennings, Duchess of. Life by C.
    G. Simon, 1841.................................... 1660..1744
Marlorat, Augustine. Protestant Convert & Theologian 1506..1562
Marlowe, Christopher. Poet...................... 1564..1593
Marmion, Shakerley. Poet and Dramatist........... 1602..1639
Marmont, Augustus Frederick Louis Viesse de, Duke of
    Ragusa. Marshal of France...................... 1774..1852
Marmontel, John Francis. French Writer........... 1723..1799
Marnix, Philip van. Calvinist Writer and Diplomatist.
    Defender of Antwerp............................ 1538..1598
Maro. Founder of the Maronites .... — .. 707
Marolles, Michael de. Classical Scholar & Print Collector 1600..1681
Marot, Clément. French Poet..................... 1495..1544
Marot, Francis. French Painter.................. 1667..1719
Marot, John. French Poet .... 1463..1523
Marozia. Roman Beauty and Intriguer............. — .. 938
Marpurg, Frederick William. German Musical Writer 1718..1795
Marquard Freher. German Historian............... 1565..1614
Marquet, Francis Nicholas. Fr. Physician and Botanist 1687..1759
Marquette, James. Explorer of the Mississippi River... 1637..1675
Marracci, Louis. Italian Orientalist. Editor of Koran 1612..1700
Marrast, Armand. French Political Writer .... 1802..1852
Marrier, Martin, of Cluni. (*Bibliotheca Cluniacensis*)... 1572..1644
Marryat, Frederick. Captain R. N. Naval Novelist.... 1792..1848
Mars, Anne Frances Hyppolyte Boutet. French Actress 1778..1847
Marsais, Cæsar Chesneau du. French Grammarian .... 1676..1756
Marsden, Samuel. Apostle of New Zealand .... 1764..1838
Marsden, William, D. C. L. Orientalist and Antiquary. 1754..1836
Marsh, Herbert, D. D. Bishop of Peterborough .... 1758..1839
Marsh, James. American Scholar.................... 1794..1847
Marsh, Narcissus. Archbishop of Armagh............ 1638..1713
Marsh, William, D. D. Divine .... 1775..1864
Marshal, Walter. Nonconformist Divine. (*Sanctification*) — ..1690?
Marshall, John. American Chief Justice and Writer.
    (*Life of Washington*)............................ 1755..1835
Marshall, Nathaniel, D. D. Dean of Windsor. Divine — ..1730?
Marshall, Thomas. Saxonist and Orientalist......... 1621..1685
Marshall, William Humphrey. Agricultural Writer ... 1745..1818
Marsham, Sir John. Historian and Chronologist...... 1602..1685
Marshman, James. American Missionary and Orientalist 1799..1837
Marshman, Joshua, D. D. Baptist Missionary in India.
    Life by John C. Marshman....................... 1767?.1837
Marsigli, Louis Ferdinand, Count. Italian Naturalist .. 1658..1730
Marsilius, of Padua. *See* Menandrino............. — ..1328

BORN. DIED.

Marsollier, James. French Historical Writer .... 1647..1724
Marston, John. Dramatist .... —aft.1633
Marsy, Balthasar, of Cambray. Sculptor............. 1624..1674
Marsy, Francis Maria de. Historical Writer........... 1714..1763
Marsy, Gaspar. Sculptor .... 1628..1681
Martel, Charles. Mayor of the Palace. Duke of Austrasia 694.. 741
Martelière, Peter de la. French Advocate .... — ..1631
Martelli, Louis. Italian Poet. (*Tullia*) .... 1499..1527
Martelli, Peter James. Italian Poet and Writer........ 1665..1727
Martene, Edmund. Benedictine of St. Maur. Histori-
     cal Collector.................................... 1654..1739
Martens, George Frederick von. German Diplomatist.. 1756..1821
Martens, Thierry. Flemish Printer.................. 1453?.1534
Martial. Roman Epigrammatist .... 43.. 104?
Martial d'Auvergne. Fr. Poet. (*Vigiles de Chas. VII.*) 1440?.1508
Martianay, John. French Benedictine. Biblical Writer 1647..1717
Martignac, John Baptist Silvère Algay, Viscount de.
     French Statesman.............................:.. 1776..1832
Martignac, Stephen Algai, Sieur de. Class. Translator 1620 or 8.1698
Martilière, Count de la. French Artillerist............ — ..1819
Martin, St. Bp. of Tours (371–97). Life by N. Gervaise 316.. 397
Martin. Missionary & Bishop in Sp. (*Collectio Canonum*) — .. 583
Martin I. Pope (649–55). Saint and Martyr .... — .. 655
Martin II. (882–84), sometimes called *Marinus I.*..... — .. 884
Martin III. (942–46), or *Marinus II.* .... — .. 946
Martin IV. (1281–85.) *Simon de Brie*............... — ..1285
Martin V. (1417–31.) *Otho Colonna*................. 1368..1431
Martin, of Poland. Chronicler. (*Chronicle of the Popes*) — ..1278
Martin, Benjamin. Mathematician and Optician ...... 1704..1782
Martin, Bernard. French Advocate and Critic .... 1574..1639
Martin, Claude. Colonel. Founder of La Martinière Coll. 1732..1800
Martin, David. French Protestant Divine .... 1639..1721
Martin, Francis Xavier. American Jurist and Author.. 1764..1846
Martin, Gregory. Roman Catholic Writer .... — ..1582
Martin, James, of St. Maur. Hist., Theol., Antiquary.. 1684..1751
Martin, John. Painter. (*The Last Judgment*) .... 1789..1854
Martin, Louis Aimé. French Writer and Critic........ 1782..1847
Martin, Sarah. English Philanthropist................ 1791..1843
Martin, Thomas. Antiquary. (*Monumenta Anglicana*). 1697..1771
Martin, William. Naturalist. (*Petrificata Derbiensia*) 1767..1810
Martin, W. C. L. Writer on Natural History .... 1798?.1864
Martindale, Adam. Nonconformist Divine and Mathem. — ..1700
Martine, George. Medical and Philosophical Writer... 1702..1743
Martineau, Isaac. Jesuit, of Angers. Devotional Writer 1640..1720
Martini, John Bapt. *Padre.* Comp. (*Stor. della Musica*) 1706..1784
Martini, Joseph San. Italian Musical Composer....... — ..1750
Martini, Martin. Jesuit Missionary to China.......... 1614..1661
Martini, Vincent, of Madrid. Musical Composer....... 1754..1810
Martinière, Anthony Augustus Bruzen de la. Historical
     and Geographical Writer........................ 1684..1749
Martinius, Matthias. German Prot. Divine and Philol. 1572..1630
Martino, Simon di. *Memmi.* Italian Painter .... 1284..1344
Martirelli. Italian Landscape Painter................. 1670..1720
Martos, Ivan Petrovitch. Russian Sculptor .... 1755?.1835

BORN. DIED.

Martyn, Henry. Lawyer. Writer in the *Spectator* .... — ..1721
Martyn, Rev. Henry. Missionary. L. by Sargent, 1819 1781..1812
Martyn, John. Botanist. Translator of the *Georgics* ... 1699..1768
Martyn, Thos. Antiq. and Nat. (*Plantæ Cantabrigienses*) 1735..1825
Martyr, Justin. Christian Apologist................. 103?. 167?
Martyr, Peter. Ital. Diplomatist. (*De Rebus Hispanicis*) 1455..1526
Martyr, Peter. Protestant Reformer................. 1500..1562
Marucelli, John Stephen. Italian Painter........... 1586..1646
Marullus, Michael Tarchaniotes. Greek Scholar in Italy — ..1500
Marvell, Andrew. Political Writer................. 1620..1678
Marville, Vigneul de. *See* Argonne .... 1640?.1704
Mary I. Queen of England.................... 1516..1558
Mary II. Queen of England. Life by Dr. Jebb....... 1662..1694
Mary. Queen of Hungary, sister of Emperor Charles V.,
   Governess of the Low Countries (1531–55).......... — ..1558
Mary, of Anjou, wife of Charles VII. of France .... 1404..1463
Mary, Heiress of Burgundy. Wife of Maximilian...... 1457..1482
Mary, of Cleves, Princess of Condé.................. 1556..1574
Mary, of England, daughter of Henry VII............. 1497..1534
Mary, de' Medici. Queen of Henry IV. of France. Life
   by Miss Pardoe............................. 1573..1642
Mary Beatrix, d'Este, wife of James II. of England.... 1658..1718
Mary Stuart. Queen of Scots. Life by Dr. Samuel Jebb,
   1725; F. M. de Marsy; Miss Benger, 1823; G. Conei,
   or Cowne; Bell, 1831; Buckingham, 1844; Mignet,
   1854; Ryan, 1857......................... 1542..1587
Masaccio. *Tommaso Guidi.* Painter................. 1402?.1443
Masaniello. *Tommaso Anniello.* Neapol. Revolutionist 1623..1646
Mascagni, Paul. Italian Anatomist................. 1752..1815
Mascardi, Augustin. Italian Writer. (*Dell' Arte Istorica*) 1591..1640
Mascaron, Julius. French Preacher. (*Funeral Orations*) 1634..1703
Mascheroni, Lawrence. Math. (*Geometria del Compasso*) 1750..1800
Masclef, Francis. French Theologian and Orientalist ... 1662..1728
Mascov, or Mascou, John James. German Publicist ... 1689..1762
Mascrier, John Baptist de. Abbé. Writer.......... 1697..1760
Masdeu, John Francis. Spanish Jesuit. (*Historia Critica
   de España*)................................. 1740..1817
Masenius, or Masen, James. German Jesuit .... 1606..1681
Masères, Francis. Baron of Exch. Writer and Mathem. 1731..1824
Masham, Mrs. Abigail. Favorite of Queen Anne ...... 1670?.1734
Masham, Damaris, Lady. Scholar .... 1658..1708
Masi, Simon, or del Pollajuolo, *which see*........... 1454..1509
Masinissa. King of Numidia .... 239.149 B.C.
Masius, Andrew. Dutch Philologist and Theologian ... 1526..1573
Maskeleyne, Nevil. Astronomer................. 1732..1811
Masolino da Panicale. Italian Painter........... 1378?.1415?
Mason, Francis. Divine. (*Vindiciæ Ecclesiæ Anglicanæ*) 1566..1621
Mason, George. American Statesman .... 1726..1792
Mason, George. Miscellaneous Writer............. 1735..1806
Mason, Jeremiah. American Jurist and Statesman..... 1768..1848
Mason, Sir John. Statesman.................. 1500..1566
Mason, John. Military Officer of Connecticut Colony .. 1600..1672
Mason, John. Nonconformist Divine. (*Self-Knowledge*) 1706..1763
Mason, John Mitchell, D. D. American Divine .... 1770..1829

BORN. DIED.

Mason, Rev. William. Poet and Divine .... 1725..1797
Masoudi, Aboul Hassan Ali. Arab. Geogr. & Historian — .. 956?
Masque de Fer, or Iron Mask. Unknown Prisoner.... — ..1703
Massao, John Baptist. French Painter................ 1687..1767
Massari, Lucio. Historical Painter .... 1569?.1633
Massaria, Alexander. Italian Phys. (*Practica Medica*) 1528?.1598
Massasoit. Indian Sachem............................. — ..1661
Masséna, André, Duke of Rivoli. French Marshal..... 1758..1817
Masseville, Louis de Vavasseur de. (*History and Geog-
    raphy of Normandy*)................................ 1667..1733
Massieu, John. Deaf Mute and Educator .... 1772..1846
Massieu, Wm. Fr. Jesuit. (*Hist. de la Poésie Françoise*) 1665..1722
Massillon, John Baptist. French Preacher............ 1663..1742
Massinger, Philip. Dramatic Poet.................... 1584..1640
Massolino. Italian Painter. *See Masolino* .... 1378?.1415?
Masson, Anthony. French Engraver.................. 1636..1700
Masson, Francis. Scottish Botanist .... 1741..1805
Masson, John. Fr. Prot. in Holland. Biogr. and Critic — ..1750?
Masson, John Papirius. French Historical Writer..... 1544..1611
Massuet, René. Benedictine of St. Maur............. 1665..1716
Mastelleta, Il. *John Andrew Donducci*. Painter....... 1575..1655
Master, or Masters, Thomas. Poet and Historian...... 1600..1643
Masters, Joseph. London Publisher.................. 1795?.1863
Mästlin, or Maestlin, Michael. German Astronomer ... 1550..1631
Masudi. Arabian Scholar and Author .... — .. 956
Matani, Anthony Mary. Italian Medical Writer....... 1730..1799
Maternus de Cilano, George Christian. Natural Phi-
    losopher and Archæologist .... — ..1773
Matham, Jacob. Dutch Engraver and Painter .... 1571..1631
Mather, Dr. Cotton. Divine. (*Magnalia*) .... 1663..1728
Mather, Increase, D.D. American Divine and Historian 1639..1723
Mathew, Theobald. Apostle of Temperance. Life by
    J. F. Maguire, 1863................................ 1790..1856
Mathews, Charles. Comedian .... 1776..1835
Mathews, George. American Jurist.................. 1774..1836
Mathias. Emperor of Germany (1612–19)............ 1557..1619
Mathias, Christian. Ger. Philos. & Div. (*Hist. Patriarch.*) 1584?.1655
Mathias, Thomas James. Satirist. (*Pursuits of Lit.*).. 1757..1835
Mathon de la Cour, Charles Joseph. French Writer .. 1738..1793
Mathon de la Cour, James, of Lyons. Natural Philos. 1712..1770
Matilda, of Flanders. Wife of William the Conqueror — ..1083
Matilda, Countess of Tuscany .... 1046..1115
Matilda, or Maude, of Scot. Wife of Henry I. of Eng. — ..1118
Matilda, or Maud, daughter of Henry I. Empress..... 1102?.1167
Matsys, Metsys, or Messys, Quintin. Dutch Painter... 1460..1529
Mattathias. Jewish Priest and Patriot .... — B.C.166
Mattei, Paul da. *Paoluccio*. Neapolitan Painter ...... 1662..1728
Mattheson, John. German Musical Composer .... 1681..1764
Matthew, St. One of the Twelve Apostles .... 1st c.
Matthew of Westminster. English Historian....... fl. 14th c.
Matthew Paris. English Historian................... — ..1259
Matthew, Tobias. Archbishop of York.............. 1546..1628
Matthew, Sir Tobias, son. Writer; conformed to Rome 1578..1655
Matthews, George. American Soldier and Statesman.. 1739..1812

BORN. DIED.

Matthews, Thomas. Admiral .... 1681..1751
Matthiæ, Augustus Henry. Philologist. (*Greek Gram.*) 1769..1835
Matthias. Emperor of Germany (1612–19). *See* Mathias 1557..1619
Matthias. *Robert Matthews.* Amer. Religious Impostor 1790?.18
Matthias Corvinus. King of Hungary (1458–90)..... 1443..1490!
Matthieu, Peter. French Historian and Poet.......... 1563..1621
Matthiolus, Peter Andrew. Ital. Bot. (*On Dioscorides*) 1590..1577
Matthisson, Frederick von. German Poet. (*Adelaide*) 1761..1831
Matti, Emanuel. Spanish Poet...................... 1663..1737
Mattocks, Isabella. Actress....................... 1746..1826
Maturin, Rev. Chas. Robt. Irish Dram., Poet, and Nov. 1782..1824
Maturino. Florentine Painter .... 1490?.1527?
Maty, Matthew. Dutch Physician and Writer in English 1718..1776
Maty, Paul Henry, son. Writer in England........... 1745..1787
Maucroix, Francis de. French Translator .... 1619..1708
Maudslay, Henry. Mechanist....................... 1771..1831
Maudslay, Thomas Henry. Mechanical Engineer...... 1792?.1864
Mauduit, Israel. English Political Writer .... 1708..1787
Mauduit, Michael. French Divine .... 1644..1709
Maunder, Samuel. Compiler. (*Biographical Treasury*) 1790?.1849
Maundrell, Rev. Henry. Traveler.................. 1650?.1710?
Maupertuis, Peter Louis Moreau de. French Geometri-
    cian and Astronomer........................... 1698..1759
Maupin, Madame la. French Singer and Adventuress.. 1673..1707
Maur, St. Disciple of Benedict.................... — .. 584?
Maur, Charles de. Spanish Mathematician and Engineer — ..1785
Maure, Mademoiselle Catherine Nicole le. Singer....1704.aft.1762
Maurepas, John Fred. Phelypeaux, Ct. de. Statesman 1701..1781
Maurice. Emperor of the East (582–602)............ 539.. 602
Maurice. Elector of Saxony. Protestant Prince...... 1521..1553
Maurice of Nassau, Prince of Orange, son of William
    the Silent. Life by Isaac Commelin, 1651.......... 1567..1625
Maurice, Thomas. Orientalist. (*History of Hindostan;
    Memoirs; Poems*)............................... 1754..1824
Mauriceau, Francis. Surgeon and Accoucheur........ — ..1709
Maurolico, Francis, of Messina. Mathematician....... 1494..1575
Maurus Terentianus. Latin Poet and Grammarian... fl. 100?
Maury, John Siffrein. Cardinal.................... 1746..1817
Maussac, Philip James. French Critic.............. 1590?.1650
Mauvillon, James. German Writer.................. 1743..1794
Mavor, Rev. William, LL. D. Writer and Compiler .... 1758..1837
Mawe, John. Conchologist. (*Travels in Brazil*)....... 1764..1829
Mawmoisine, or Malvoisine,Wm. de. Bp. of St. Andrew's — ..1238
Maxcy, Jonathan, D. D. American Divine............ 1768..1820
Maxentius. Roman Emperor (306–12) .... — .. 312
Maximian I. Roman Emperor (286–305).............. 250.. 310
Maximian II., or Galerius. Roman Emperor (305–11).. — .. 311
Maximilian I. Emperor of Germany (1493–1519)..... 1459..1519
Maximilian II. (1564–76).......................... 1527..1576
Maximilian II. King of Bavaria (1848–64).......... 1811..1864
Maximilian, Duke of Bavaria. *Great.* Victor of Prague 1573..1651
Maximilian Emanuel, Elector of Bavaria............ 1662..1726
Maximilian Joseph, Elector of Bavaria (1746–77)..... — ..1777
Maximilian Joseph, First King of Bavaria.......... 1756..1825

BORN. DIED.

Maximin I. Roman Emperor (235–38) .... — .. 238
Maximin II. Roman Emperor (308–13) .... — .. 313
Maximus Magnus Clemens. Rom. Emperor (383–88) — .. 388?
Maximus Petronius. Roman Emperor (455)........ 395?. 455
Maximus Tyrius. Greek Rhetorician and Philosopher fl. 2d c.
Maximus Verrucosus, Quintus Fabius. *Cunctator.* Roman General against Hannibal .... — B.C.203
Maxwell, Sir Murray, Captain, R. N. Navigator....... 1766..1831
Maxwell, Robert, Lord. Scottish Statesman .... — ..1546
Maxwell, Wm. Hamilton. Writer. (*Life of Wellington*) 1795..1851
May, John. Bishop of Carlisle .... — ..1598
May, Louis du. French Protestant Historian.......... — ..1681
May, Thomas. Poet and Historian. (*Supplement to Lucan; History of Parliament*)...................... 1594?.1650
May, William. Archbishop elect of York.............. — ..1560
Mayenne, Chas. of Lorraine, Duke of. Head of League 1554..1611
Mayer, John Fred. Lutheran Divine and Commentator 1650..1712
Mayer, or Mayr, John Simon. Musical Composer...... 1763?.1845
Mayer, John Tobias. German Astronomer............ 1723..1762
Mayerne, Sir Theodore Turquet de. Swiss Physician and Chemist........................... 1573..1655
Mayhew, Jonathan, D. D. Amer. Clergyman and Writer 1720..1766
Maynard, Francis. French Poet .... 1582..1646
Maynard, Sir John. Lawyer and Patriot............. 1602..1690
Mayne, Jaspar. Poet and Divine .... 1604..1672
Maynwaring, Authur. Polit. and Miscellaneous Writer 1668..1712
Mayo, Herbert, M. D. Hydropathic Physician. (*Cold Water Cure*)....................................... — ..1852
Mayo, Richard. Nonconformist Divine .... — ..1695
Mayow, John. Physician and Physiologist .... 1645..1679
Mayr, John Simon. German Musical Composer .... 1763?.1845
Mazarin, Julius. Cardinal. Life by T. Renaudot; A. Aubery, 1751....................................... 1602..1661
Mazeline, Peter. French Sculptor .... 1633..1708
Mazeppa, John. Cossack Hetman, celebrated by Byron 1644..1709
Mazois, Francis. French Architect and Archæologist. (*Ruines de Pompeii*)........................... 1783..1826
Mazza, Angelo. Italian Poet .... 1741..1817
Mazzinghi, Joseph, Count. English Musical Composer 1768..1844
Mazzochi, Alexius Symmachus. Italian Antiquary.... 1684..1771
Mazzolini, Louis. *Il Ferrarese.* Painter .... 1481?.1530
Mazzucchelli, John Mary, Count. Italian Jurist, Antiquary, and Biographer. (*Notizie Historiche*) ..... 1707..1765
Mazzucchelli, Peter Francis. *Morazzone.* Ital. Painter 1571..1626
Mazzuoli, Francis. *Il Parmigiano.* Painter.......... 1503..1540
Mead, Matthew. Nonconf. Divine. (*Ezekiel's Wheels*) 1629..1699
Mead, Richard, M. D. Phys. Life by Matth. Matv, 1755 1673..1754
Meade, William, D. D. Amer. Episc. Bishop and Writer 1789..1862
Meadowbank, Alexander Maconochie Welwood, Lord. Scottish Judge .... 1777..1861
Meadowcourt, Richard. Divine. Annotator of Milton 1697..1769
Méchain, Peter Francis Andrew. French Mathematician and Astronomer.................................. 1774..1805
Mechitar, or Mekhitar. Reviver of Learning in Armenia 1676..1749

BORN. DIED.

Meckenen, Mekenen, or Mecheln, Israel von. Gold-
smith, Engraver, and Painter...................... — ..1503
Mede, Joseph. Divine. (*Clavis Apocalyptica*)........ 1586..1638
Medhurst, Walter Henry. Eng. Orient. and Missionary 1796..1857
Medici, Alexander de', First Duke of Florence (1530–37) 1510..1537
Medici, Catherine de'. Wife of Henry II. of France... 1519..1589
Medici, Cosmo de'. *Father of his Country.* Statesman 1389..1464
Medici, Cosmo de'. *The Great.* First Grand-Duke of
Tuscany. Life by Baldini...................... 1519..1574
Medici, Hippolytus de'. Cardinal.................... 1511..1535
Medici, John de'. Merchant of Florence: found. of family — ..1428
Medici, John James, Marquis of Marignano. General 1495..1555
Medici, Lorenzo de'. *Magnificent.* Life by Roscoe.... 1448..1492
Medina, Sir John Baptist. Portrait Painter......... 1659..1711
Medina, Peter de. Spanish Historian and Mathematician 1510?. —
Meer, Meeren, or Meire, John van der. *The Young.*
Painter... 1627..1691
Meerman, Gerard. Dutch Writer. (*Novus Thesaurus*
Juris Civilis)................................ 1722..1771
Meerman, John, son. Historical Writer............. 1753..1815
Mehegan, William Alexander. French Historian...... 1721..1766
Mehemet Ali. Pasha of Egypt. .... 1769..1849
Méhul, Stephen Henry. Musical Composer........... 1763..1817
Meibom, or Meibomius, Henry. Writer.............. 1638..1700
Meibom, or Meibomius, John Henry. Physician...... 1590..1655
Meibom, or Meibomius, Marcus. Writer on Music and
Philologist.................................... 1630?.1711
Meier, George Frederick. German Philosophical Writer 1718..1777
Meigs, Return Jonathan. Amer. Revolutionary Officer 1740..1823
Meiners, Christopher. Ger. Historian and Miscell. Writer 1747..1810
Meire, Meer, or Meeren, John van der. *See* Meer...... 1627..1691
Meisner, Balthasar. German Lutheran Divine........ 1587..1626
Meissner, Augustus Theophilus. Novelist & Dramatist 1753..1807
Meissonier, Justus Aurelius. Painter, Sculptor, Gold-
smith, Architect .... 1695..1750
Mekenen, Israel von. *See* Meckenen.................. — ..1503
Mela, Pomponius. Latin Geographer. (*De Situ Orbis*).. fl. 50?
Melanchthon, Philip. German Reformer. Life by Joa-
chim Camerarius................................ 1497..1560
Melbourne, William Lamb, Viscount. Premier....... 1779..1848
Melchthal, Arnold of. Swiss Patriot................ — ..1317
Melcombe, Lord. *See* Dodington................... 1691..1762
Meldola, Dr. Raphael. High Rabbi, in England. (*Hu-*
pat Hatanim)................................. — ..1828
Meleager. Greek Writer and Collector of Epigrams... fl. B.C. 60?
Melendez Valdez, John. Spanish Poet.............. 1754..1817
Meletius. Bishop of Antioch.......................... — .. 381
Meletius. Bishop of Lycopolis .... fl. 4th c.
Meletius. Modern Greek Geographer .... 1661..1714
Meli, John. Poet. *Sicilian Anacreon*.............. 1740..1815
Melito. Bishop of Sardis............................ fl. 170?
Mellan, Claude. French Engraver and Designer ...... 1598..1688
Mellen, Grenville. American Poet................... 1799..1841
Mellitus. Archbishop of Canterbury (619–24)......... — .. 624

BORN. DIED.

Mellon, Harriet.   Actress; married Duke of St. Albans. 1775..1837
Melloni, Macedonio.   Italian Physicist.............. 1800..1854
Melmoth,William.   Lawyer and Religious Writer. (*Great
   Importance.*)   Life by son...................... 1666..1743
Melmoth, William, son.   Writer & Classical Translator 1710..1799
Melo, or Mello, Francis Manuel de. Sp. and Port. Author 1611..1666
Melon, John Francis, of Bordeaux. Writer........... — ..1738
Melot, Anicet.   French Writer .... 1697..1759
Melozzo da Forli, Francis.   Painter............... 1438..1494?
Melvil, Sir James.   Scot. Statesm. and Hist. (*Memoirs*) 1535?.1607
Melville, Andrew.   Orientalist ,and Scottish Reformer.
   Life by McCrie .... 1545..1622
Melville, Henry Dundas, Viscount. Statesman........ 1740..1811
Melvin, James, of Aberdeen. Latinist............... 1794..1851
Memling, Hans, or John.   Painter. *See Hemling* ..... 1425?.1500?
Memmi, or di Martino, Simon, of Sienna. Portrait Painter 1284..1344
Mena, John de.   Castilian Poet .... 1412..1456
Ménage, Giles.   Fr. Scholar. (*Dictionnaire Etymologique*) 1613..1692
Menahem.   King of Israel (B. C. 772–761)........... —B.C. 761
Menander.   Athenian Comic Poet ....342.291 B.C.
Menandrino, Marsilio, of Padua. Jurist. (*Defensor Pacis*) — ..1328
Ménard, Claude, of Angers. Magistrate and Antiquary 1574..1652
Ménard, Leon.   Historical Writer .... 1706..1767
Ménard, Nicholas Hugh, of St. Maur. (*Benedictine Mar-
   tyrology*)....................................... 1587..1644
Menasseh ben Israel. Dutch Rabbi. Writer & Scholar 1604?.1659?
Mencke, John Burchard. (*Scriptores Rerum Germanic.*) 1674..1732
Mencke, Otho.   German Writer. (*Acta Eruditorum*).. 1644..1707
Mendelssohn, Moses.   Jewish Philosopher........... 1729..1786
Mendelssohn-Bartholdy, Felix. Musical Composer .. 1809..1847
Mendez, Moses.   English Poet..................... — ..1758
Mendez-Pinto, Ferdinand. Portuguese Traveler...... 1509?.1583
Mendip, Welbore Ellis, created Earl of. Politician... 1714..1802
Mendizabal, John Alvarez y. Spanish Financier...... 1790..1853
Mendoza, Diego Hurtado de. Spanish Statesman and
   Scholar. (*History of the War of Granada*)......... 1503..1575
Mendoza, Iñigo Lopez de, Marquis de Santillana. Span-
   ish Poet and Writer .... 1398..1458
Mendoza, John Gonzales. Ambassador to China. (*His-
   tory of China*).................................. 1540?.1617
Mendoza, Peter Gonzales de. *Great Cardinal of Spain.*
   Statesman...................................... 1428..1495
Meneses, Alexis de. Port. Augustinian Monk & Writer 1559..1617
Menestrier, Claude le. Antiq. (*Symbolicæ Dianæ Statua*) — ..1639
Menestrier, Claude Francis. Fr. Jesuit. Writ. on Heraldry 1631..1705
Menestrier, John Baptist le. Fr. Medalist & Antiquary 1564..1634
Mengoli, Peter.   Italian Mathematician............ 1625..1686
Mengs, Anthony Raphael. Painter. L. by J. N. D'Azara 1728..1779
Meninski, or Menin, Francis. (*Thesaurus Linguarum
   Orientalium*).................................. 1623..1698
Menippus.   Cynic Philosopher..................... 3d c. B.C.
Mennes, Sir John.   Seaman, Traveler, and Poet .... 1591..1671
Menno, Simon.   Dutch Sectary .... 1505..1561
Menochio, James.   Italian Jurist.................. 1532..1607

BORN. DIED.

Menochio, John Stephen. Italian Jesuit. Biblical Writer 1576..1655
Mentchikoff, Alex. Danilovitch. Russ. Statesm. and Gen. 1672.°1729
Mentel, John, of Strasburg. Printer.................. 1410?.1478
Mentzel, Christian. Physician and Botanist........... 1622..1701
Menzel, Charles Adolphus. German Historian........ 1784..1855
Menzini, Benedict. Italian Poet..................... 1646..1704
Mercarti, or Mercado, Michael. Tuscan Phys. and Nat. 1541..1593
Mercator, Gerard. Flemish Geogr. and Math. (*Charts*) 1512..1594
Mercator, Marius. Pupil of Augustine. Writer....... — .. 451?
Mercator, Nicholas. Danish Astronomer............. 1640..1687
Mercer, Hugh. American Revolutionary General...... 1720?.1777
Mercer, Major James. Lyric Poet.................... 1734..1804
Mercier, Bartholomew. *Abbé de St. Leger.* Bibliographer 1734..1799
Mercier, John le. Orientalist and Biblical Commentator — ..1570
Mercier, Louis Sebast. Poet & Critic. (*Tableau de Paris*) 1740..1814
Merck, John Henry. German Scholar................. 1741..1791
Mercklein, George Abraham. German Physician..... 1644..1702
Mercuriali, Jerome. Italian Physician .... 1530..1606
Mercy, Florimond de. Marsh. of the Empire; fell at Parma — ..1734
Mercy, Francis de. Bavarian General; fell at Nordlingen — ..1645
Merewether, Rev. Francis. Author................. 1784..1864
Meriam, Eben. American Statistician and Meteorologist 1794..1864
Merian, John Bernard, of Berlin. Scholar .... 1723..1807
Merian, Maria Sibylla. Naturalist .... 1647..1717
Merian, Matthew. Swiss Engraver................... 1593..1650
Merian, Matthew, son. Swiss Painter............... 1621..1687
Merino, Jerome. *Priest Merino.* Span. Guerrilla Leader 1770?.1847
Merivale, John Herman. Poet...................... 1779..1844
Merovæus. Founder of the Merovingian Dynasty ..... 411?. 457
Merret, Christopher. Physician and Naturalist........ 1614..1695
Merrick, Rev. James. Div. & Poet. (*Version of the Psalms*) 1720..1769
Merry, Robert. Dramatic Writer.................. 1755..1798
Mersch, John Andrew van der. *Brave Fleming.* Patriot 1734..1792
Mersenne, Marin. French Mathematician .... 1588..1648
Merton, Walter de. Bishop of Rochester. Founder of
  College. Life by Bishop Hobhouse................. —. ..1277
Merula, George. Historian and Classical Editor.·....... 1424?.1494
Merula, Paul. Dutch Scholar...................... 1558..1607
Merville, Michael Guyot de. French Writer.......... 1696..1755
Méry, John. French Anatomist and Surgeon..:...... 1654..1722
Merzliakov, Alexius Feodorovitch. Russian Writer ... 1778..1830
Mesa, Christopher de. Spanish Poet................. 1550?.1620?
Mesengui, Francis Philip. French Ecclesiastical Writer 1677..1763
Mesmer, Fred. Anthony, M. D. Promoter of Mesmerism 1734..1815
Mesmes, Claude de, Count d'Avaux. Negotiator...... 1595..1650
Mesmes, John Anthony de, Count d'Avaux, nephew.
  Negotiator....................................... 1640..1709
Mesnager, Nicholas. French Negotiator............. 1658..1714
Mesnardière, Hippolytus J. P. de la. French Poet .... 1610..1663
Messala Corvinus, M. Valerius. Statesman & Writer B.C.70?.A.D.1?
Messalina Statilius. Third wife of Nero. ....·... fl. 1st c.
Messalina Valeria. Third wife of Claudius........... — .. 48
Messenius, Arnold. Historian and Satirist; beheaded.. — ..1651
Messenius, John. Swedish Lawyer. (*Scandia Illustrata*) 1584..1637

BORN. DIED.

Messina, Antonello da. Italian Painter........... 1414?.1493 or 6
Meston, William. Burlesque Poet...................... 1688..1745
Mestrezat, John. French Protestant Theologian....... 1592..1657
Mészáros, Lazarus. Hungarian General.............. 1796..1858
Metastasio, Peter Anthony Dominic Bonaventura. Poet.
    Life by Fabroni; Dr. Burney...................... 1698..1782
Metcalfe, Chas. Theophilus, Lord. Gov.-Gen. L. by Kaye 1785..1864
Metcalfe, Thomas. American Statesman............,..... 1780..1855
Metelli, Augustin. Italian Painter .... 1609..1660
Metellus, Quintus Cæcilius. *Numidicus.* Commander .
    against Jugurtha................................. fl. B.C. 100
Meteren, Emanuel van. (*History of the Low Countries*) 1535..1612
Methodius. Missionary to the Sclavonians .... — .. 900
Methuen, John. Diplomatist .... — ..1706
Metius, Adrian, brother of James. Mathematician..... 1571..1635
Metius, James, of Alkmaër. Invent. Refract. Telescope fl. 1609?
Metkerke, Sir Adolphus van. Envoy and Classical Writer 1528..1591
Metochita, Theodore. Greek Historian of Constantinople — ..1332
Meton. Athenian Astronomer. Inventor of Lunar Cycle fl. B.C. 432
Metternich, Clement Wenzel Nepomuk Lothar, Prince
    de. Austrian Statesman........................... 1773..1859
Mettrie, Julian Offray de la. Physician. Materialist .. 1709..1751
Metz, Conrad Martin. German Engraver............. 1755..1827
Metzu, Gabriel. Dutch Painter.................... 1615.aft.1661
Meulen, Anthony Francis van der. Flemish Painter ... 1634..1690
Meulen, Peter van der. Paint. to William III. in England fl. 1670
Meun, or Meung, John de. French Poet .... 1250?.1318?
Meursius, or De Meur, John. Greek Antiquary .... 1579..1639
Meusel, John George. Ger. Historian and Bibliographer 1743..1820
Meusnier, Philip. French Painter.................... 1655..1734
Mexia, Peter. Spanish Writer .... 1496..1552?
Meyer, Felix. German Painter .... 1653..1713
Meyer, James. Flemish Historian.................,..... 1491..1552
Meyer, John Henry. German Antiquary and Artist.... 1759..1832
Meyerbeer, James. German Musical Composer .... 1791..1864
Meyers, Jeremiah. Miniature Painter .... 1728..1789
Meyrick, Sir Samuel Rush. Antiquary............... 1783..1848
Mézeray, Francis Eudes de. Hist. L. by Dan. Larroque 1610..1683
Meziriac, Claude Gaspar Bachet. Fr. Jesuit. Scholar. 1581..1638
Mezzofanti, Joseph Gaspar. Cardinal. Linguist. Life
    by Dr. C. W. Russell, 1858...................... 1774..1849
Miaulis, Andrew. Grecian Admiral.............. 1772..1835
Miazzi, John. Italian Architect .... 1699..1780
Micah. Prophet of Judah .... fl. B.C.750?
Mical, Abbé. French Mechanician .... 1730?.1789
Michael I. Emperor of the East (811-13). *Rhangabe*.. — .. 845?
Michael II. (820-29.) *Le Bègue*..................... — .. 829
Michael III. (842-67.) .... 839?. 867
Michael IV. (1034-41.) *The Paphlagonian* ....·.. — ..1041
Michael V. (1041-42.) *Calaphates* .... —aft.1042
Michael VI. (1056-57.) *Stratioticus* .... —aft.1057
Michael VII. (1071-78.) *Parapinaces*................ —aft.1078
Michael VIII. (1259-82.) *Palæologus*................ 1224..1282
Michael. Czar of Russia (1613-45). *Feodorovitch*..... 1596..1645

BORN. DIED.

Michael Angelo. Italian Painter. *See* Angelo. Life by Condivi, 1553; Vasari, 1568; Gori, 1746; Vignali, 1753; Hauchecorne, 1783; Richard Duppa, 1806; Piacenza, 1813; Reumont, 1834; Guidici, 1834; Quatremère de Quincy, 1835; Nagler, 1836; Grimm, translated by F. E. Bunnet, 1864 .... 1474..1564
Michael Angelo. *Delle Battaglie.* Roman Battle Painter 1602?.1660
Michaelis, John Benjamin. German Poet............ 1746..1772
Michaelis, John David. Orientalist and Biblical Critic. (*Introduction to the New Testament*) .... 1717..1791
Michaelis, John Henry. German Divine and Orientalist 1668..1738
Michaud, Joseph. Fr. Hist. & Poet. (*Hist. of Crusades*) 1767..1839
Michaux, Andrew. French Botanist and Traveler. (*Flora Boreali Americana*)................................ 1746..1802
Micheli, Peter Anthony. Italian Botanist............. 1679..1737
Micheli du Crest, James Bartholomew. Astron. & Math. 1690..1766
Michelozzi, Michelozzo. Florentine Sculptor & Architect 1402?.1470?
Mickiewicz, Adam. Polish Poet.................... 1798..1855
Mickle, William Julius. Poet. Translator of the *Lusiad* 1734..1788
Micrelius, John. Ger. Lutheran Divine and Philologist 1597..1658
Middleton, Arthur. American Patriot and Statesman.. 1743..1787
Middleton, Conyers, D.D. Scholar. (*Life of Cicero*).. 1683..1750
Middleton, Rev. Erasmus, of Turvey. (*Biograph. Evang.*) — ..1805
Middleton, Sir Hugh. Projector of the New River..... 1565?.1631
Middleton, John Izard. Amer. Schol. (*Cyclopean Walls*) 1785..1849
Middleton, Richard. *The Profound.* Theologian .... — ..1304
Middleton, Thomas. Dramatic Poet. Life by Dyce, 1840 — ..1626?
Middleton, Thos. Fanshaw. Bp. of Calcutta. (*Gr. Article*) 1769..1822
Middleton, William. Welsh Poet.................... — ..1602
Miel, John. *Giovanni della Vite.* Flemish Painter .... 1599..1664
Mierevelt, Michael Jansen. Dutch Portrait Painter .... 1568..1641
Mieris, Francis. *The Elder.* Flemish Painter & Modeler 1635..1681
Mieris, Francis. *Young Francis.* Flemish Painter .... 1689..1763
Mieris, William. *The Younger.* Flem. Painter & Modeler 1662..1747
Mifflin, Thomas. American Revolutionary Patriot..... 1744..1800
Migliara, John. Italian Architectural Painter .... 1785..1837
Mignard, Nicholas. French Painter .... 1608..1668
Mignard, Peter. *The Roman.* Painter .... 1610..1695
Mignon, Abraham. Painter of Frankfort............. 1639..1679
Mignot, Stephen. Fr. Hist., Commerc., & Theol. Writer 1698..1771
Mignot, Vincent. Fr. Writer. (*Hist. de l'Empire Ottoman*) 1730..1790
Milbourne, Rev. Luke. Poetical Writer.............. 1667..1720
Mildmay, Sir Walter. Statesman.................... 1522..1589
Milfort, Le Clerc. French Adventurer................. —aft.1814
Milhouse, Robert. Weaver and Poet................. — ..1839
Milizia, Francis. Architect. (*Vite degli Architetti*).... 1725..1798
Mill, Henry. Engineer of Water Works.............. 1680..1770
Mill, James. Metaphysician and Political Economist. (*History of British India*)......................... 1773..1836
Mill, John, D.D. Editor of Greek Testament.......... 1645?.1707
Mill, W. H., D.D. Divine and Orientalist............ — ..1853
Millar, John, of Glasgow. Professor. L. by Craig, 1806 1735..1801
Milledge, John. American Soldier and Statesman..... 1757..1818
Miller, Lady, of Bath. (*Letters from Italy*) .... 1741?.1781

BORN. DIED.

Miller, Edward, MUS. DOC. Antiquary............... 1756..1807
Miller, Edward. American Physician and Author..... 1760..1812
Miller, Hugh. Scottish Geologist .... 1802..1856
Miller, James. Political and Dramatic Writer......... 1703..1744
Miller, James. Surgical Writer .... 1812?.1864
Miller, John Martin. Ger. Novelist & Poet. (*Siegwart*) 1750..1814
Miller, Joseph. Comic Actor..................... 1684..1738
Miller, Philip. Botanical Writ. (*Gardener's Dictionary*) 1691..1771
Miller, Samuel. American Divine................... 1769..1850
Miller, William. Founder of the Millerites........... 1781..1849
Milles, Jeremiah, D. D. Divine and Antiquary .... 1714..1784
Milles, Thomas. Genealogist and Antiquary .... fl. 16th c.
Millevoye, Charles Hubert. French Poet............. 1782..1816
Millin, Aubin Louis. Fr. Archæologist and Naturalist 1759..1818
Millingen, James. English Archæologist .... 1774..1845
Millot, Claude Francis Xavier. French Historian...... 1726..1785
Mills, Charles. Historical Writer. (*History of Crusades*) 1788..1825
Mills, Samuel John. American Clergyman and Promoter
    of Missions................................. 1783..1818
Milman, Sir Francis, M. D. Medical Writer........... 1746..1821
Milne, Rev. Colin. Botanist .... — ..1815
Milne, Joshua. Actuary .... 1773..1851
Milne, William. English Missionary .... — ..1822
Milner, Isaac, D. D. President of Queen's College; Dean
    of Carlisle. Life by Mrs. Mary Milner, 1843 ..... 1751..1820
Milner, John, D. D. Rom. Cath. Divine & Eccles. Antiq. 1752..1826
Milner, Rev. Joseph, of Hull. (*History of the Church of
    Christ.*) Life by Isaac Milner.................. 1744..1797
Milo. Grecian Athlete .... fl. 6th c. B.C.
Milo, Titus Annius Papinianus. Roman Tribune, de-
    fended by Cicero............................ — .. 48
Milonov, Michael. Russian Poet................... 1792..1821
Milosh. *See* Obrenovitch......................... 1780?.1860
Miltiades. Athenian General at Marathon........... fl. B.C. 490
Milton, John. Poet. Life by E. Philips, 1694; Toland,
    1698; J. Richardson, 1734; Peck, 1740; Newton, 1749;
    Birch, 1753; Hayley, 1794; Mosneron, 1803; Morti-
    mer (Pseudonym), 1805; Symmons, 1806; Byerley,
    1822; Todd, 1826; Mitford, 1832; Ivimey, 1833;
    Brydges, 1835; Stebbing, 1840; Montgomery, 1843;
    Keightley, 1849; Hunter, 1850; Edmonds, 1851; Hood,
    1851; Illustr. Papers, Marsh, *Chetham Society*, 1851;
    Cleveland, 1853; Masson, 1858; Original Papers, Ham-
    ilton, *Camden Society*, 1859; J. W. Morris, 1862. Ac-
    count of Disinterment of body, Neve, 1790 .... 1608..1674
Mimnermus. Greek Elegiac Poet............... fl. B.C. 634?–600
Mina, Francis Espoz y. Spanish General .... 1781..1836
Mind, Godfrey. Swiss Artist .... 1768..1814
Minellius, John, of Rotterdam. Editor of School Classics 1625?.1683
Miner, Thomas. Amer. Physician and Medical Writer 1777..1841
Minot, George Richards. American Historian and Jurist 1758..1802
Minot, Lawrence. English Poet .... — ..1352?
Minto, Sir Gilbert Elliott, 1st Earl of. Gov.-Gen. of Bengal 1751..1814
Minucius Felix, Marcus. Christian Rhetorician ...... fl. 270?

BORN. DIED.

Minutoli, Henry Menu von, Baron. German Traveler
and Archæologist .... 1772..1846
Minuziano, or Minutianus, Alexander. Italian Printer 1450?.1522
Minzoni, Onofrio. Italian Poet .... 1734..1817
Mirabaud, John Baptist de. French Writer........... 1675..1760
Mirabeau, Gabriel Honoré de Riquetti, Comte de. Revo-
lutionist. Life by Gassicourt..................... 1749..1791
Mirabeau, Victor Riquetti, Mqs. de. (Ami des Hommes) 1715..1789
Mirabella, Vincent. (Ancient History of Syracuse)..... 1570..1624
Miræus, or Lemire, Aubert. German Writer.......... 1573..1640
Miranda, Francis. Spanish American General .... 1750?.1816
Miranda, Sa de. Portuguese Poet................... 1495..1558
Mirandola, John Picus, Count of. Universal Scholar.. 1463..1494
Mirandola, John Francis Picus, Prince of, nephew. Writ. 1469..1533
Mirbel, Charles Francis Brisseau de. French Naturalist 1776..1854
Mirevelt, or Mierevelt, Michael Jansen. Dutch Painter 1568..1641
Misson, Maximilian. French Writer. (Voyage d'Italie) — ..1721
Mita, James. Historical Engraver.................... 1776..1822
Mitchel, Ormsby McKnight. Amer. Astron. and Gen. 1810..1862
Mitchell, Sir Andrew. Ambassador. Life by A. Bisset 1695?.1771
Mitchell, Andrew. Admiral .... 1757?.1806
Mitchell, Sir David. Admiral .... — ..1719
Mitchell, Elisha, D. D. American Chemist .... 1793..1857
Mitchell, John Kearsley. Amer. Physician and Author 1796..1858
Mitchell, Joseph. Dramatic Writer.................. 1684?.1738
Mitchell, Thos. Philologist. Ed. of Greek Dramatists 1783..1845
Mitchell, Sir Thomas Livingstone. Voyager and Geogr. 1792..1855
Mitchill, Samuel Latham. Amer. Physician and Writer 1764..1831
Mitford, John. Miscellaneous Writer. (Johnny Newcome) — ..1831
Mitford, Rev. John. Writer. Editor of Gray......... 1781..1859
Mitford, John Freeman, Baron Redesdale. Statesman.. 1748..1830
Mitford, Miss Mary Russell. Writer. (Our Village)... 1786..1855
Mitford, William. (Hist. of Greece.) L. by Ld. Redesdale 1744..1827
Mithridates. King of Pontus (B. C. 120–63). The Great 131?.63 B.C.
Mitscherlich, Eilhard, of Berlin. Chemical Philosopher 1794..1863
Mittarelli, John Benedict. History of the Calmudenses 1707..1777
Mitzler, Lawrence Christopher, of Kolof. Musical Writer 1711..1778
Mochnachi, Maurycy. Polish Critic and Historian .... 1804..1834
Mocquard, John Francis Constant. French Littérateur ;
Private Secretary to Napoleon III.................. 1791..1864
Modena, or Mutina, Thomas da. Italian Painter ...... fl. 14th c.
Moebius, George. Ger. Theologian. (Pagan Oracles) 1616?.1697
Moebius, Godfrey. German Medical Writer........... 1611?.1664
Moehler, John Adam. Rom. Catholic Polemical Divine 1796..1838
Moehsen, John Charles William. Ger. Medical Writer 1722..1795
Moellendorf, Richard Joachim Henry, Ct. of. Pruss. Gen. 1725..1816
Moeller, John. Danish Theologian and Author........ 1779..1833
Moeser, Justus. German Advocate and Writer........ 1720..1794
Mohammed. Arabian Prophet. See Mahomet........570 or 1.632
Mohs, Frederick. German Mineralogist.............. 1774..1839
Moine, Le. See Lemoine.
Moir, David Macbeth. Poet and Novelist. L. by T. Aird 1798..1851
Moitte, John William, Chevalier. French Sculptor..... 1747..1810
Moivre, Abraham de. Mathematician .... 1667..1754

BORN. DIED.

Mola, John Baptist. Landscape Painter............... 1620..1661
Mola, Peter Francis. Painter........................ 1612..1668
Molai, James de. Last Grand Master of the Templars.. — ..1314
Molanus, Gerard Walter. Ger. Writer (*Lipsanographia*) 1633..1722
Molanus, or Vermeulen, John. Dutch Writer .... 1533..1585
Molbech, Christian. Danish Scholar and Author ...... 1783..1857
Molé, Francis René. French Comedian................ 1734..1802
Molé, John. English Calculator...................... — ..1827
Molé, Louis Matthew, Count de. French Statesman.... 1780..1855
Molé, Matthew. French Magistrate and Statesman..... 1584..1656
Molé, Thomas. Dissenting Divine..................... — ..1780
Molesworth, Robert, Viscount. Irish Statesman ...... 1656..1725
Molesworth, Sir William. English Statesman........ 1810..1855
Molière, John Baptist Poquelin de. French Dramatist 1622..1673
Molières, Joseph Privat de. French Mathematician.... 1677..1742
Molina, Louis de. Spanish Jesuit, Theologian......... 1535..1601
Molinæus, Charles. *See* Dumoulin................... 1500..1566
Molinæus, Peter. *See* Dumoulin.................... 1568..1658
Molinari, or Mulinari, John Anthony. Italian Painter.. 1577..1640?
Molinet, Claude du. Ecclesiastical Antiq. and Historian 1620..1687
Molinet, John. French Poet .... — ..1507
Molinier, John Baptist. Preacher and Devotional Writer 1675..1745
Molinos, Michael de. Spanish Quietist .... 1627..1696
Moll, Herman. English Geographer.................. — ..1732
Moller, Daniel William. Ger. Trav., Metaph., and Hist. 1642..1712
Moller, Henry. German Protestant, Biblical Commentator 1530?.1589
Moller, John. (*History of Sleswick and Holstein.*) Life
    by his són, 1734................................. 1661..1725
Molloy, Charles. Polish Writer and Dramatist .... 1706..1767
Molyneux, William. Mathematician and Astronomer.. 1656..1698
Molza, Francis Mary. Italian Poet .... 1489..1544
Molza, Tarquinia, granddaughter. Ital. Transl. and Poet 1542..1617
Monaldeschi, Louis Bonconte de. Italian Chronicler .. 1327..1442
Monamy, Peter. Painter of Sea Pieces............... — ..1749
Monantheuil, Henry de. *Monantholius.* French Mathem. 1536?.1606
Monardes, Nicholas. Spanish Physician.............. — ..1578
Monboddo, James Burnet, Lord. Metaphysician ...... 1714..1799
Monbron, Fougeret de. French Writer................ — ..1761
Monceaux, Francis de. Statesm. & Wr. (*Bucolica Sacra*) fl. 1589
Moncey, Adrien. Marshal of France................. 1754..1842
Monconys, Balthasar de. Trav. in the East, and Astrol. — ..1665
Moncrieff Wellwood, Rev. Sir Henry. Moderator.... 1750..1827
Moncrif, Francis Augustin Paradis de. Fr. Poet & Writer 1687..1770
Mondino, or Mundinus. Physician and Anatomist..... 1250?.1326
Mondonville, John Joseph Cassanea de. Mus. Composer 1715..1772
Mongault, Nicholas Hubert de. French Writer .... 1674..1746
Monge, Gaspar. French Mathematician and Nat. Philos. 1746..1818
Moniglia, John Andrew, of Florence. Dramatic Poet.. 1640?.1700
Monin, John Edward du. French Poet .... 1557..1586
Monk, George, Duke of Albemarle. Life by T. Skinner,
    1724; Dr. Thomas Gumble, 1761; Guizot, translated
    by Stuart Wortley, 1838........................... 1608..1670
Monk, James Henry. English Prelate and Author..... 1784..1856
Monk, Hon. Mary. Poetess .... — ..1715

BORN. DIED.

Monmouth, Geoffrey of. Archd. of Monmouth. Hist. 1100..1154
Monmouth, James Scott, Duke of. Rebel. Life by
George Roberts, 1844 .... 1649..1685
Monnet, Anthony Grimoald. French Chemist........ 1734..1817
Monnier, Peter le. French Philosopher............ 1675..1757
Monnier, Peter Charles le. French Astronomer....... 1715..1799
Monnoye, Bernard de la. Poetical and Prose Writer .. 1641..1728
Monnoyer, John Baptist. Fr. Fruit and Flower Painter 1635..1699
Monod, Adolphe. French Protestant Pastor at Paris... 1802..1856
Monod, Dr. Frederick. Protestant Pastor at Paris ..... 1794..1863
Monod, John. French Protestant Clergyman.......... 1760?.1836
Monro, Alexander, M. D., primus. Physician and Anato-
mist. (Medical Essays) .... 1697..1767
Monro, Alexander, secundus, son. Phys. and Med. Prof. 1733..1817
Monro, Alexander, tertius, son. Anatomist............ 1773..1859
Monro, Donald. Army Physician..................... 1729..1802
Monro, John, brother. Physician for Insanity......... 1715..1791
Monroe, James. Fifth President of the United States.. 1758..1831
Monsignori, Francis. Portrait and Historical Painter.. 1455..1519
Monson, Sir William. Admiral. (Naval Tracts)..... 1569..1643
Monson, William John, Lord. Traveler and Antiquary 1796..1862
Monstrelet, Enguerrand de. Historian.............. 1390?.1453
Mont, Deodate del. Painter .... 1581..1634
Montagu, Basil, Q. C. Editor of Bacon.............. 1770..1851
Montagu, Charles, 1st Duke of Manchester. Ambassador — ..1722
Montagu, Sir Edward. Judge...................... — ..1557
Montagu, Edward, First Earl of Sandwich. Commander
and Statesman.................................. 1625..1672
Montagu, Edward Wortley. Writer.................. 1713..1776
Montagu, George. Naturalist .... — ..1815
Montagu, Sir Henry, 1st Earl of Manchester. Ld. Treas. — ..1642
Montagu, John, Fourth Earl of Sandwich. Life by J.
Cooke, 1799 .... 1718..1792
Montagu, Lady Mary Wortley. Writer. (Letters.) Life
by Dallaway, 1803; Moy Thomas .... 1690..1762
Montagu, Walter. Abbot of Pontoise. Poet, Courtier — ..1669
Montague, Chas., First E. of Halifax. Statesm. and Poet 1661..1715
Montague, Edward Wortley........................ 1713..1776
Montague, Mrs. Eliz. (Writings and Genius of Shakesp.) 1720..1800
Montague, Lady Mary Wortley. See Montagu .... 1690..1762
Montague, or Mountagu, Richard. Bishop of Chichester
and Norwich .... 1578..1641
Montaigne, Michael de. Essayist .... 1533..1592
Montalbani, Ovid. Italian Physician and Botanist..... 1602?.1671
Montalembert, Mark René, Mqs. of. Military Engineer 1714..1800
Montalembert, Mark René Anne Mary, Count de.
French Diplomatist............................. 1777..1831
Montalvan, John Perez de. Spanish Dramatist........ 1602..1638
Montanari, Geminiano. Nat. Philos. and Mathematician 1632..1687
Montanelli, Joseph. Italian Poet................... 1813?.1862
Montanus. Heresiarch. .... 140?. 200?
Montanus, Benedict Arias. Spanish Writer. (Polyglot) 1527..1598
Montanus, or Da Monte, John Baptist. Italian Physi-
cian and Classical Writer .... 1488?.1551

BORN. DIED.

Montarroyo, Joseph Freyre de. Portuguese Writer .... 1670..1730
Montault, Philip de, Duke of Noailles. Commander... 1619..1684
Montausier, Charles de St. Maure, Duke of. (*Garland
    of Julia*).. 1610..1690
Montbéliard, Philibert Gueneau. Naturalist .... 1720..1785
Montbrun, Charles Du Puy. Life by Guy Allard, 1675;
    Martin, 1816 .... 1530..1575
Montcalm, Louis Joseph de St.Véran, Marquis de. French
    General in Canada .... 1712;..1759
Montcalvo. Italian Fresco Painter. *See* Caccia....... 1568..1625
Montchal, Charles de. Archbishop of Toulouse; Scholar 1589..1651
Montchrestien, Anthony. Poet and Economist.......1570?.1621
Monte, Guidubalde, Marquis del. Italian Mathematician 1540?.1601?
Montecatinus, Anthony. Italian Philos. (*On Aristotle*) 1536..1599
Montecuculi, or Montecuccoli, Raymond, Ct. Austr. Gen. 1608..1681
Monteith, or Monteth, Robert. Scottish Historian ..... — bef.1660
Montemayor, George de. Castilian Poet. (*Diana*).... 1520..1562
Monten, Dietrich. German Battle Painter .... 1799..1843
Montenault, or Monthenault, Charles Philip. French
    Historical Writer .... 1696..1749
Montespan, Frances Athénaïs de Rochechouart de Morte-
    mart, Marchioness de. Favorite of Louis XIV. ...... 1641..1707
Montesquieu, Charles de Secondat, Baron de. (*L'Esprit
    des Lois*) .... 1689..1755
Monteth, or Monteith, Robert. Scottish Historian..... — bef.1660
Monteverde, Claudio. Italian Musical Composer.......1565?.1649
Montez, Lola. Life by self. *See* Lola Montez......... 1824..1861
Montezuma I. Emperor of Mexico (1436 or 8–1471) ... — ..1471
Montezuma II., nephew.............................. 1480?.1520
Montfaucon, Bernard de. Critic and Antiquary....... 1655..1741
Montfort, John (IV.) de, Duke of Brittany............ 1293..1345
Montfort, Simon de. Crusader..................... 1150?.1218
Montfort, Simon de, Earl of Leicester; fell at Evesham 1206?.1265
Montgolfier, James Stephen. Inventor of Air Balloons 1745..1799
Montgomery, Alexander. Poet. L. by Dr. Irving, 1821 — ..1607?
Montgomery, Gabriel, Count of. Fr. Protestant General 1530?.1574
Montgomery, James. Poet. L. by Holland and Everett 1771..1854
Montgomery, Richard. American Revolutionary General 1736..1775
Montgomery, Rev. Robert. Preacher and Poet .... 1807..1855
Montgon, Charles Alexander. Confessor to Philip V. of
    Spain. (*Memoirs*)................................ 1690..1770
Monthenault d'Egly, Charles Philip. French Writer.. 1696..1749
Montholon, Chas. Tristan de, Count of Lee. Fr. General 1782..1853
Monthyon, or Montyon, Anthony John Baptist Robert
    Auget, Baron de. French Philanthropist........... 1733..1820
Monti, Joseph. Italian Botanist .... 1682..1760
Monti, Vincent. Italian Poet....................... 1754..1828
Monticelli, Andrew, of Bologna. Painter .... 1640..1716
Monticelli, Angelo Mary. Singer.................. — ..1750
Montigni, Stephen Mignol de. Math. and Mechanician 1714..1782
Montjosieu, Louis de. (*Gallus Romæ Hospes*) .... fl. 1585
Montluc, Blaise de. Marshal of France .... 1509?.1577
Montmaur, Peter de. Satirical Poet .... 1576?.1648
Montmorency, Anne de. Constable of France........ 1493..1567

BORN. DIED.

Montmorency, Charles de. Marshal of France .... — ..1381
Montmorency, Henry I. de. Constable of France .... 1534..1614
Montmorency, Henry II., Duc de. Admiral of France 1595..1632
Montmorency, Matthew de. *The Great.* Constable of Fr. 1174?.1230
Montmorency, Matthew John Félicité, Duke of. French
  Statesman.. 1767..1826
Montmort, Peter Raymond de. French Mathematician 1678..1719
Montorsoli, Fra Giovann' Angelo. Italian Sculptor ... 1507..1563
Montpensier, Anne Maria Louisa d'Orleans, Duchess de.
  Grande Mademoiselle. (*Memoirs*) .... 1627..1693
Montpetit, Armand Vincent. Fr. Painter and Mechanic 1713..1800
Montreuil, Bernardin. French Jesuit................ 1569..1646
Montrose, James Graham, First Marquess of. Scottish
  Royalist. Life by Bishop Wishart; M. Napier, 1840;
  Grant, 1859..................................... 1612..1650
Mont Ste-Aldegonde, Philip van Marnix, Lord du.
  Statesman and Writer............................. 1538..1598
Montucci, Anthony. Philologist and Chinese Scholar.. 1762..1829
Montucla, John Stephen. French Mathematician. (*History of Mathematics*)............................... 1725..1799
Moody, Christopher Lake, LL. D. (*Sketch of Modern France*)... — ..1816
Moon, Joseph. Mathematician....................... — ..1817
Mooney, Daniel, D. D. Writer on Logic and Mathematics — ..1818
Moor, Karel de. Portrait Painter .... 1656..1738
Moorcroft, William. English Traveler .... 1780?.1825
Moore, Benjamin, D. D. American Divine .... 1748..1816
Moore, Clement C., LL. D. American Scholar .... 1779..1863
Moore, Edward. Poet and Writer.................... 1712..1757
Moore, Elizabeth. Devotional Writer .... — ..1657
Moore, Francis. Mechanic .... — ..1787
Moore, Jacob Bailey. American Journalist and Author 1797..1853
Moore, John. Bishop of Ely .... 1644..1714
Moore, John. Phys. and Writer. L. by Dr. R. Anderson 1730..1802
Moore, John. Archbishop of Canterbury (1783-1804).. 1733..1805
Moore, Sir John. General; fell at Corunna .... 1761..1809
Moore, John, LL. B. Biblical Scholar and Antiquary ... — ..1821
Moore, Maurice. American Patriot and Jurist......... — ..1777
Moore, Rev. Philip, of the Isle of Man. Writer ...... 1706..1783
Moore, Richard Channing, D. D. American Divine..... 1762..1841
Moore, Robert. Penman .... — ..1727?
Moore, Thomas. Poet. Life by Earl Russell.......... 1779..1852
Moore, Zephaniah Swift, D. D. Amer. Divine and Scholar 1770..1823
Moorsom, William Scarth. Captain. Writer.......... — ..1863
Morabin, James. Fr. Writer & Transl. (*Life of Cicero*) 1687..1762
Morales, Ambrose de. Spanish Historian and Antiquary 1513..1591
Morales, Louis. *El Divino.* Spanish Painter .... 1509..1586
Morand, John Anthony. Architect of Lyons........... 1727..1794
Morand, John Francis Clement. Parisian Physician ... 1726..1784
Morand, Peter de. Poet and Dramatic Writer .... 1701..1757
Morand, Sauveur François. Parisian Surgeon .... 1697..1773
Morandi, John Mary. Italian Painter................ 1625..1715?
Morandi Manzolini, Anna. Female Anatomist....... 1716..1774
Morant, Philip. Antiquary and Biographer .... 1700..1770

BORN. DIED.

Morata, Olympia Fulvia. Protestant Writer. Life by
Jules Bonnet, 1851 .... 1526..1555
Moratin, Leander Fernandez de. Span. Dramatic Poet 1760..1828
Moratin, Nicholas Fernandez de. Span. Dramatic Poet 1737..1780
Morazan, Francis. Central Amer. Statesm. and General 1799..1842
Morcelli, Stephen Anthony. Ital. Writ. on Inscriptions 1737..1821
Mordaunt, Charles, Third Earl of Peterborough. Com-
mander in Spain. Life by C. Warburton, 1853...... 1658..1735
More, Alexander. French Protestant Preacher & Writer 1616..1670
More, Sir Anthony. *Antoni Moro.* Dutch Portr. Painter 1519..1581
More, Hannah. Writer. Life by Rev. H. Thompson,
1838; A. Roberts, 1859 .... 1745..1833
More, Dr. Henry. Cambr. Platonist. L. by R. Ward, 1710 1614..1687
More, Henry, of Liskeard. Dissenting Minister; Poet.. — ..1802
More, or Moore, James. Writer. (*Rival Modes*) ...... — ..1734
More, John, of Norwich. Puritan Divine .... — ..1592
More, Sir Thomas. Chancellor. (*Utopia.*) Life by J.
Hoddesdon, 1652; W. Roper, 1716; Warner, 1758; C.
More, 1828; Stapleton; Cayley; T. More (great-grand-
son); William Rastall .... 1480..1535
Moreau, Hegesippus. French Poet. (*Myosotis*) .... 1810..1838
Moreau, Jacob Nicholas. Historiographer .... 1717..1803
Moreau, James. French Medical Writer .... 1647..1729
Moreau, John Michael. French Designer and Engraver 1741..1814
Moreau, John Victor. French General .... 1763..1813
Moreau, René. French Physician .... 1587..1656
Moreau de la Sarthe, James Louis. Fr. Medical Writer 1771..1826
Moreelze, Paul. Dutch Painter .... 1571..1638
Morel, Christopher Edward. Fr. Teacher of Deaf Mutes 1805..1857
Morel, Claude. Printer; Editor of Greek Authors.... 1574..1626
Morel, Frederick. *The Old.* French Printer and Writer 1523..1583
Morel, Frederick, son. Printer and Scholar.......... 1558..1630
Morel, William. Fr. Classical Editor and Lexicographer 1505..1564
Morell, Andrew. Swiss Medalist and Antiquary....... 1646..1703
Morell, Thomas. Lexicographer and Classical Writer.. 1703..1784
Morell, Thomas. Dissenting Minister and Author...... 1782?.1840
Morellet, Andrew. Abbé. Writer on Political Economy 1727..1819
Morelli, Cosimo. Italian Architect.................. 1732..1812
Morelli, James. Librarian and Scholar............... 1745..1819
Morelos, Joseph Maria. Mexican Revolutionist .... — ..1815
Moréri, Louis. (*Historical Dictionary*)............... 1643..1680
Mores, Edward Rowe. Antiquary.................... 1730..1778
Moreto y Cabana, Augustin. Spanish Comic Poet.... 1600?.1669
Moreton, or Morton, John. Cardinal. Abp. of Canter-
bury; Statesman. Life by Rev. W. Cole; Budden.. 1410..1500
Morgagni, John Baptist. Ital. Physician and Anatomist 1682..1771
Morgan, Daniel. American Revolutionary General .... 1736..1802
Morgan, George Cadogan. Writer on Nat. Philosophy 1754..1798
Morgan, Sir Henry John. Buccaneer. Life by Edward
Howard .... 1637?.1690
Morgan, (Miss Sydney Owenson) Lady, Irish Novelist 1783..1859
Morgan, Sylvanus. Heraldic Writer. (*Sphere of Gentry*) — ..1693
Morgan, Thomas. Deistical Writer .... — ..1741
Morgan, Sir Thomas Charles, M. D. .... 1783?.1843

BORN. DIED.

Morgan, William. Bishop of St. Asaph. Translator of the Bible into Welsh .... — ..1604
Morgan, William. Mathematician and Actuary .... — ..1833
Morghen, Raphael Sanzio. Italian Engraver .... 1758..1833
Morgues, Matthew de. Court Preacher and Writer.... 1582..1670
Morhof, Daniel George. German Writer. (*Polyhistor*) 1639..1691
Morice, Sir William. Statesman. (*Common Right of Lord's Supper*)................................... — ..1676
Morier, James. Oriental Traveler and Novelist .... 1780..1849
Morillo, Pablo. Spanish General................... 1777..1838
Morin, Henry. Writer in *Mémoires de l'Acad. des Inscrip.* 1655..1728
Morin, John. French Ecclesiastic and Orientalist...... 1591..1659
Morin, John. French Experimental Philosopher. (*Méchanisme Universel*) .... 1705..1764
Morin, John Baptist. French Physician and Mathematician. (*Astrologia Gallica*) .... 1583..1656
Morin, Louis. *De St. Victor.* Fr. Physician and Botanist 1635..1715
Morin, Peter. French Biblical Scholar and Critic...... 1531..1608
Morin, Simon. French Visionary .... 1623?.1663
Morin, Stephen. French Protestant Divine .... 1625..1700
Morinière, Adrian Claude Lefort de la. French Writer 1698..1768
Morison, or Moryson, Fynes. Traveler .... 1566..1614?
Morison, John, D. D., LL. D. Life by John Kennedy... 1791..1859
Morison, Robert, M. D. Physician and Botanist. (*Historia Plantarum*)................................. 1620..1683
Morisot, Claude Bartholomew. Fr. Writer. (*Peruviana*) 1592..1661
Moritz, Charles Philip. German Writer .... 1757..1793
Morland, George. Painter. Life by W. Collins; George Dawe; Hassell, 1806 .... 1763..1804
Morland, Sir Samuel. Statesman and Mechanician. Life by J. O. Halliwell .... 1625?.1695
Morley, George. Bishop of Winchester .... 1597..1684
Morley, Thomas. Musical Composer................. — ..1604?
Morlière, Charles James Louis Augustus de la Rochette, Chevalier de. Romance Writer .... 1701..1785
Mornac, Anthony. Fr. Jurist and Poet. (*Feriæ Forenses*) 1554..1619
Mornay, Philip de, Sieur du Plessis Morlay. Protestant Statesman. Life by Crusius; De Liques........... 1549..1623
Mornington, Garret Wellesley, Earl of. Composer .... 1720..1781
Morny, Chas. Augustus Louis Joseph de, Ct. Fr. Statesm. 1811..1865
Moro, Antoni, or Sir Anthony More, *which see* .... 1519..1581
Morone, John. Cardinal and Statesman.............. 1509..1580
Moroni, John Baptist. Ital. Historical and Portr. Painter 1510..1578
Morosini, Andrew. Senator of Venice and Historian.. 1558..1618
Morosini, Francis. Doge of Venice and Commander .. 1618..1694
Morres, Harvey Redmond, Visct. Mountmorres. Writer — ..1797
Morris, Capt. Charles. Song Composer............... 1739..1832
Morris, Charles. American Naval Officer............. 1784..1856
Morris, George P. American Journalist and Poet ..... 1802..1864
Morris, Gouverneur. American Patriot and Statesman 1752..1816
Morris, Lewis. Welsh Antiquary and Poet .... 1702..1765
Morris, Richard, brother. Welsh Poet and Critic...... — ..1779
Morris, Robert. American Financier .... 1734..1806
Morris, Robert, M.P. Legal Writer .... — ..1818

BORN. DIED.

Morris, Thomas. American Statesman................ 1766..1844
Morrison, Sir Richard. Architect.................... 1767..1849
Morrison, Rev. Robert, D. D. Missionary to China. Life
    by Mrs. Morrison, 1839........................... 1782..1834
Morse, Rev. Jedediah. American Geographer......... 1761..1826
Mortier, Edward Adolphus Casimir Joseph, Duke of
    Treviso. Marshal of France..................... 1768..1835
Mortimer, Edmund, Third Earl of March; married to
    Philippa.........................:................ 1352?.1381
Mortimer, Edmund. Fifth Earl of March............ 1392?.1424
Mortimer, John Hamilton. Artist .... 1741..1779
Mortimer, Roger, Baron, of Wigmore, First Earl of
    March. Favorite of Queen Isabella............... 1286?.1330
Mortimer, Roger, Fourth Earl of March. Lieut. of Ireland 1377?.1398
Mortimer, Thomas. Miscell. Writer. (British Plutarch) 1730..1809
Morton, Charles, of Harvard College. Writer on Phi-
    losophy and Divinity .... — ..1697
Morton, James Douglas, Earl of. Regent of Scotland;
    beheaded... 1530..1581
Morton, James Douglas, Earl of. Philosopher & Astron. 1707..1768
Morton, John. Cardinal. See Moreton .... 1410..1500
Morton, John. Agriculturist. (The Soil)............ 1781?.1864
Morton, Marcus. American Jurist and Statesman ..... 1784..1864
Morton, Nathaniel. Secretary of Plymouth Colony. (New
    England's Memorial).............................. 1612..1685
Morton, Richard, M. D. Medical Writer.............. 1635?.1698
Morton, Samuel Geo., M. D. Amer. Nat. and Ethnologist 1799..1851
Morton, Thomas. Bishop of Durham (1632–59). Life
    by Dean Barwick, 1660; Baddily and Naylor, 1669.. 1564..1659
Morton, Thomas. Dramatic Poet .... 1764..1838
Morveau, Guyton de. See Guyton.................... 1737..1816
Moryson, or Morison, Fynes. Traveler.............. 1566..1614?
Moryson, Sir Richard. Politician, Diplom., and Author — ..1556
Moscherosch, John Michael. (Philander von Sittewald.)
    German Writer................................... 1600..1669
Moschus. Syracusan Bucolic Poet.................... fl. B.C. 250
Moseley, Benjamin, D. D. Medical Writer .... 1739?.1819
Moser, Frederick Charles von. Ger. Statesm. & Publicist 1723..1798
Moser, George Michael. Gold Chaser and Enamel Painter
    in London....................................... 1705..1783
Moser, John Jacob. German Jurist .... 1701..1785
Möser, Justus. German Statesman and Author........ 1720..1794
Moser, Miss Mary, R. A. Flower Painter.............. — ..1819
Moses. Lawgiver of the Jews.................... 1571.1451 B.C.
Moses Chorenensis. Armen. Abp. (Hist. of Armenia) fl. 462?
Mosheim, John Lawrence von. (Ecclesiastical History) 1694..1755
Moss, Robert, Dean of Ely. Divine and Poet. (Sermons) 1666..1729
Mossom, Robert. Bishop of Derry. Writer .... — ..1679
Mossop, Henry. Tragedian .... 1729..1773
Mostert, or Mostaert, John. Dutch Painter .... 1499..1555
Mothe, Jane Mary de la, Madame Guyon, q. v. Mystic 1648..1717
Mothe le Vayer, Francis de la. Fr. Skeptic. (Dialogues) 1588..1672
Motherby, George, M. D. (Medical Dictionary)........ 1731..1793
Motherwell, Wm. Journalist & Poet. L. by M'Conochy 1798..1835

BORN. DIED.

Motte, Anthony Houdart de la. French Writer........ 1672..1731
Motte Cadillac, Anthony de la. Founder of Detroit 1660?.aft.1717
Motteux, Peter Anthony. Fr. Dram. Writer in English 1660..1718
Motteville, Frances Bertaut de. (*Mem. of Anne of Austr.*) 1621..1689
Mottley, John. Historical and Humorous Writer...... 1692..1750
Moucheron, Frederick. *The Old.* Dutch Landsc. Paint. 1633..1686
Moucheron, Isaac, son. Painter.................... 1670..1744
Moufet, or Muffet, Thomas, M. D. (*Theatrum Insectorum*) — ..1605
Mouhy, Charles de Fieux. Romance Writer.......... 1702..1784
Moulin, Du. *See* Dumoulin.
Moultrie, William. American Revolutionary Officer... 1731..1805
Mounier, John Joseph. French Politician .... 1758..1806
Mountagu, or Montague, Richard. Bishop of Chichester 1578..1641
Mountain, Geo. Jehoshaphat. Ld. Bp. of Quebec; Writer 1789..1863
Mountfort, William. Actor and Dramatic Writer ..... 1659..1692
Mountnorris, George Annesley, Earl of, and Lord Va-
    lentia, *q. v.* .... 1770..1844
Mourad Bey. Mameluke Chief.................... 1750..1801
Mouradja d'Ohsson, Ignatius. (*The Ottoman Empire*) 1740..1807
Mouret, John Joseph. French Musical Composer ...... 1682..1738
Mourgues, Matthew de. Controversial Writer .... 1582..1670
Mourgues, Michael. French Mathematician.......... 1642?.1713
Moustier, Charles Albert de. French Dramatic Writer 1760..1801
Movers, Francis Charles. German Orientalist......... 1806..1856
Moxon, Joseph. Hydrographer and Mathematical Writer 1627..1700
Moyle, Robert. Legal Writer...................... — ..1638
Moyle, Walter. Political Writer .... 1672..1721
Moyses, David. Scottish Diarist. (*Affairs of Scotland*) 1573..1630
Mozart, John Chrysostom Wolfgang Amadeus. Musical
    Composer. Life by Edward Holmes; Herr Jahn.... 1756..1791
Mozart, John George Leopold. German Musician...... 1719..1787
Mozeen, Thomas. Dramatist and Song Writer....... — ..1768
Mudge, John, M. D. Physician and Mechanic. Improver
    of Telescope..................................... — ..1793
Mudge, Thomas. Mechanic. Improver of Chronometer 1715..1794
Mudge, William. General. Trigonometrical Surveyor 1762..1821
Mudge, Rev. Zachary. Divine. Friend of Dr. Johnson — ..1769
Mudie, Robert. Naturalist .... 1777..1842
Mudo, Fernandez el. *John Fernandez Navarrete.* Paint. 1524?.1577
Muehlenbruch, Christian Frederick. German Jurist .. 1785..1843
Mueller. *See* Müller.
Muellner, Amadeus Godfrey Adolphus. Ger. Dramatist 1774..1829
Muencer, or Muenzer. *See* Müncer .... — ..1525
Muench, Ernest Hermann Joseph von. Ger. Historian 1798..1841
Muenchhausen. *See* Münchhausen.
Muennich, Burchard Christopher, Count. *See* Münnich 1683..1767
Muenster. *See* Münster.
Muenter, Balthasar. German Divine and Poet........ 1735..1793
Muet, Peter le. French Architect.................... 1591..1669
Muggleton, Lodowicke. English Sectary .... 1609..1697
Muhlenberg, Henry Ernest, D. D. American Clergyman
    and Divine....................................... 1753..1815
Muhlenberg, Peter. American Revolutionary General 1746..1807
Mühlenbruch, Christian Frederick. German Jurist ... 1785..1843

19

BORN. DIED.

Muilman, Peter. Historian of Essex................. — ..1790
Muis, Simon Marotte de. French Hebraist........... 1587..1644
Mulcaster, Richard. Schoolmaster and Writer........ 1535?.1611
Mulgrave, Constantine John Phipps, Earl of. Navigator 1744..1792
Mulgrave, John Sheffield, Earl of, and Duke of Bucks.
  Poet. (*Essay on Poetry*)........................ 1649..1721
Mulinari, or Molinari, John Anthony. Italian Painter.. 1577..1640?
Müller, Andrew. German Orientalist................ 1630..1694
Müller, Charles Ottfried. Classical Scholar. (*Dorians*) 1797..1840
Müller, Christian Frederick von. Engraver........⌐.... 1783..1816
Müller, Frederick. German Painter and Poet.......... 1750..1825
Müller, Gerard Frederick. Traveler and Historian. (*Col-
  lection of Russian Histories*)..................... 1705..1783
Müller, Henry. Lutheran Div. (*Harmonia N. et V. Test.*) 1631..1675
Müller, John. *Regiomontanus.* Archbishop of Ratisbon.
  Astronomer and Mechanician .... 1436..1476
Müller, John. Engraver of Amsterdam.............fl. 1589–1625
Muller, John. Mathematician and Writer on Artillery.. — ..1784
Müller, John von. Swiss Historian. (*Universal History*) 1752..1809
Müller, John. German Physiologist................. 1801..1858
Müller, John Gotthard von. Engraver.............. 1747..1830
Müller, Louis Christian. Prussian Engineer. (*Wars of
  Frederick the Great*) .... 1735..1804
Müller, Otho Frederick. Danish Naturalist .... 1730..1784
Müller, Peter Erasmus. Dan. Theologian and Antiquary 1776..1834
Müller, William. German Writer and Lyric Poet ..... 1794..1827
Muller, William John. English Artist .... 1812..1845
Müllner, Amadeus Godfrey Adolphus. Ger. Dramatist 1774..1829
Mulready, William, R. A. Painter .... 1786..1863
Müncer, or Münzer, Thomas. German Anabaptist. Life
  by Strobel...................................... — ..1525
Münch, Ernest Herrmann Joseph von. Ger. Historian 1798..1841
Münchhausen, Gerlach Adolphus, Baron. Hanoverian
  Statesman...................................... 1688..1770
Münchhausen, Jerome Charles Frederick von. (*Mar-
  velous Travels.*) Life by Bürgen.................. 1720..1797
Munck, John. Danish Navigator................... 1589..1628
Muncker, Thomas. (*Mythographi Latini*)........... — ..1680
Munday, Anthony. Dramatic Poet. (*City Pageants*).. 1554..1633
Munden, Joseph Shepherd. Comedian. Life by J. S.
  Munden, 1843.................................. 1758..1832
Mundinus, or Mondino. Ital. Physician and Anatomist 1250?.1326
Münnich, Burchard Christopher, Count. Russian Mar-
  shal and Exile.................................. 1683..1767
Muñoz, or Mugnoz, John Baptist. Spanish Historian.. 1745..1799
Munro, Sir Thomas. Gov. of Madras. L. by Gleig, 1850 1760..1827
Münster, Ernest Frederick Herbert, Count von. Hano-
  verian Statesman .... 1766..1839
Munster, George Fitzclarence, Earl of .... 1794..1842
Münster, Sebastian. Mathematician and Philologist.
  (*Universal Cosmography*) .... 1489..1552
Münter, Balthasar. German Divine and Poet......... 1735..1793
Munting, Abraham. German Botanist.............. 1626..1683
Münzer. *See* Müncer................................ — ..1525

BORN. DIED.

Murad I., Morad, or Amurath. Ottoman Sultan (1360–89) 1319..1389
Murad II. (1422–51) .... 1404..1451
Murad III. (1574–95). .... 1544..1595
Murad IV. (1623–40) .... 1610?.1640
Muralt, Béat Louis de. Swiss Traveler in Europe ..... — ..1760
Muralt, John. Swiss Physician and Anatomist.. .... 1645..1733
Murat, Joachim. Marshal of France. King of Naples 1771?.1815
Muratori, Louis Anthony. Italian Historian .... 1672..1750
Muravieff, Michael Nikititch. Russian Writer........ 1757..1807
Murdock, James, D. D. American Divine and Writer .. 1776..1856
Mure, Sir William. Scottish Poet................... 1594..1657
Mure, William, of Caldwell. Classical Writer........ 1799..1860
Muret, or Muretus, Mark Anthony. Classical Scholar.
   (*Variæ Lectiones*) .... 1526..1585
Murger, Henry. Fr. Writer. (*Scenes of Bohemian Life*) 1822..1860
Murillo, Bartholomew Stephen. Spanish Painter...... 1618..1682
Murimuth, A'dam. Chronicler...................... fl. 1350?
Muris, John de. Doctor of the Sorbonne............. —aft.1345
Murner, Thomas. Ger. Satirist and Opponent of the Ref. 1475..1536?
Murphy, Arthur. Writer. Transl. of Tacitus. L. by Foote 1727..1805
Murphy, James Cavanagh. Architect, Antiquary, and
   Traveler. (*Antiquities of the Arabians in Spain*) .... 1760?.1816
Murphy, Robert. Mathematician .... 1806..1843
Murr, Christopher Theophilus von. Bibliogr. and Antiq. 1733..1811
Murray, Alexander, D. D. Philologist. (*History of Euro-
   pean Languages*)................................. 1775..1813
Murray, Alexander. American Naval Officer......... 1755..1821
Murray, Lord Charles. Scottish Jacobite .... 1687..1729
Murray, Lord George. Scottish Jacobite Commander.. 1705..1760
Murray, Sir George. General and Statesman .... 1772..1846
Murray, Hugh. Geographical Writer. (*Encyc. of Geog.*) 1779..1846
Murray, James. Scot. Dissent. Div. in Lond. (*Aletheia*) 1702..1758
Murray, James. Scot. Dissenting Minister. Hist. Writer — ..1782
Murray, or Moray, James Stuart, Earl of. *Good Regent.*
   Assassinated...................................... 1531..1570
Murray, John. American Clergyman .... 1741..1815
Murray, John. Physician and Natural Philosopher.... — ..1820
Murray, Dr. John. Musical Composer................ — ..1833
Murray, John. Publisher.......................... 1778..1843
Murray, John Andrew. Physician and Naturalist ..... 1740..1791
Murray, Lindley. Grammarian. L. by self & Frank, 1826 1745..1826
Murray, Matthew, of Leeds. Mechanist............. 1763..1826
Murray, Nicholas, D. D. Amer. Clergyman and Author 1803..1861
Murray, Patrick, Fifth Lord Elibank. Scottish Writer.. 1703..1778
Murray, Sir Robert. Scottish Statesman .... — ..1673
Murray, Thomas. Scottish Portrait Painter......:.... 1666?.1724
Murray, William. Earl of Mansfield. Lord Chief Jus-
   tice. Life by Halliday .... 1705..1793
Murray, William. Actor........................... 1791..1852
Murray, William Vans. American Diplomatist .... 1762?.1803
Musa Ibn-Nosseyr. Arab Conqueror................ 640.. 717
Musaeus, John Charles Augustus. German Writer.... 1735..1787
Musculus, Andrew. Lutheran Div. Writer on Prophecy — ..1580
Musculus, Wolfgang. Protestant Reformer.......... 1497..1563

BORN. DIED.

Musgrave, Sir Richard, M. P. (*Mem. of Irish Rebellions*) 1758?..1818
Musgrave, Samuel, M. D. Physician and Greek Scholar — ..1782
Musgrave, William, M. D. Physician and Antiquary... 1657..1721
Mushet, David. Inventor in Iron.................... 1772..1847
Mushet, Robert. Writer on the Currency............. — ..1828
Musitau, Charles. Italian Medical Writer .... 1635..1714
Musius, or Muys, Cornelius. Dutch Schol. & Lat. Poet 1503..1572
Musonius, Caius Rufus. Roman Stoic Philosopher.... fl. 1st c.
Muss, Charles. Painter in Enamel. (*Holy Family*).... — ..1824
Mussato, Albertin. Italian Historian and Poet .... 1261..1330
Musschenbroek, Peter van. Dutch Natural Philoso-
pher and Mathematician........................... 1692..1761
Musset, Louis Charles Alfred de. French Poet........ 1810..1857
Musso, Cornelius. Italian Bishop and Preacher........ 1511..1574
Mustapha I. Sultan of Turkey (1617–23) .... — ..1639
Mustapha II. (1695–1703)....................... — ..1703
Mustapha III. (1757–74)........................... — ..1774
Mustapha IV. (1807–8)............................. — ..1808
Musurus, Marcus. Greek Scholar at Venice. (*Etymo-
logicum Magnum Græcum*).......................... 1470?.1517
Mutiano, or Muziano, Jerome. Italian Painter......1528.1590 or 2
Mutis, Joseph Celestine. Spanish Naturalist.......... 1734..1808
Muy, Louis Nicholas Victor, Ct. de. Marshal of France 1711..1775
Muys, Wyer William. Dutch Physician and Mathem. 1682..1744
Muziano, Jerome. Italian Painter and Architect.... 1528.1590 or 2
Muzio, Jerome. Italian Writer .... 1496..1576
Myconius, Frederick. German Reformer............. 1491..1546
Myconius, Oswald. Swiss Reformer. (*Life of Zwingli*) 1488..1552
Myddelton, Sir Hugh. Civil Engineer. *See* Middleton 1565?.1631
Mydorge, Claude. French Mathematician............. 1585..1647
Myers, Thomas, LL. D. Writer on Geography......... — ..1834
Mylne, Robert. Architect......................... 1734..1811
Myn, Hubert van der. Dutch Painter .... 1684..1741
Mynsicht, Adrian von. Physician and Chemist....... fl. 1631
Mynster, Jacob Peter. Danish Theologian .... 1775..1854
Myrepsus, Nicholas. Greek Physician of Alexandria.
(*Antidotarium*)................................... fl. 13th c.
Myron. Greek Sculptor............................. fl. B.C. 480
Mytens, Arnold. Flemish Painter in Italy............ 1541..1602
Mytens, Daniel. *The Elder.* Flemish Painter in Eng. 1590..1660?
Mytens, Daniel. Flemish Painter.................... 1636..1688
Mytens, Martin. Swedish Painter at Vienna .... 1695..1755
Mytton, Thomas. Parliamentarian General.......... — ..1656

N.

BORN. DIED.

Nabis. Tyrant of Sparta (B. C. 207–192)............. — B.C.192
Nabunal, Elias de. Cardinal. Divine .... — ..1367
Nachman, Moses Ben. Spanish Rabbi............. 1194.. —
Naclantus, or Nacchiante, James. Italian Theologian.. — ..1569
Nadab. King of Israel (B. C. 954–953)............... — B.C.953
Nadeshdin, Nicolai Ivanovitch. Russian Author...... 1804..1856
Nadir Shah, or Kouli Khan. King of Persia. Life by
　　Fraser, 1742; Sir Wm. Jones, tr. from Persian....... 1687..1747
Nævius, Cneius. Roman Poet.................... 274?.202? B.C.
Nagy Sándor, Joseph. Hungarian General........... 1804..1849
Nahl, John Augustus. Prussian Sculptor .... 1710..1781
Nahum. Hebrew Prophet....................... fl. 7th c. B.C.
Nairn, Caroline. Poetess........................ 1766..1845
Nairn, William Murray, Lord. Scottish Jacobite ..... 1657..1725
Nakhimoff, Nicolavitch. Russian Poet .... 1782..1814
Naldi, Sebastian. Italian Singer .... — ..1819
Nalson, John. Divine and Historian.................. 1638?.1686
Nanek, or Nanuk. Founder of the Sikh Sect.......... 1469..1539
Nangis, William de. Historian. (*Life of St. Louis*) ... — ..1302?
Nani, John Baptist. Venetian Statesm. (*Hist. of Venice*) 1616..1678
Nanni, John. *Giovanni da Udino.* Ornamental Artist.. 1494..1564
Nanni, or Nannius, Peter. Dutch Critic and Philologist 1500..1557
Nannini, Agnolo. Italian Writer .... 1493.. —
Nanteuil, Robert. Fr. Miniature Painter and Engraver 1630..1678
Nantigni, Louis Chazot de. Genealogical Writer...... 1692..1755
Napier, Sir Chas. Admiral. L. by Maj.-Gen. Elers Napier 1786..1860
Napier, Sir Charles James. General; Conqueror of
　　Scinde. Life by Sir W. F. P. Napier .... 1782..1853
Napier, Henry Edward. Naval Officer and Author .... 1789..1853
Napier, John, Lord, of Merchiston. Inventor of Loga-
　　rithms. Life by Earl Buchan and Walter Minto .... 1550..1617
Napier, Macvey. Editor of *Edinburgh Review* .... 1776..1847
Napier, Sir William Francis Patrick. General. (*History
　　of the Peninsular War.*) Life by H. A. Bruce, 1863. . 1785..1860
Napoleon I. Emperor of France. *See* Bonaparte..... 1769..1821
Napoleon II. *King of Rome. See* Bonaparte......... 1811..1832
Narbonne-Lara, Louis, Count of. French Statesman.. 1755..1813
Narborough, Sir John. Admiral .... — ..1688
Nardi, James. Italian Historian .... 1476..1556?
Nardini, Peter. Violinist........................ 1722..1793
Nares, Rev. Edmund, D. C. L. Professor at Oxford.
　　(*Thinks I to Myself*)............................ 1762..1841
Nares, James, MUS. DOC. Musical Composer .... 1715..1783
Nares, Rev. Robert. (*Glossary; Chron. View of Prophecy*) 1753..1829
Narses. Byzantine General and Statesman........... 473?. 568
Naruszewicz, Adam Stanislaus. Polish Hist. and Poet 1733..1796
Narvaez, Pamphila de. Spanish Commander......... —aft.1528
Nash, Abner. American Lawyer and Politician........ — ..1786
Nash, Francis, brother. Soldier .... — ..1777
Nash, Frederick. American Jurist .... 1781..1858

BORN. DIED.

Nash, John.   Architect .... 1752..1835
Nash, Richard, of Bath.   *Beau.*   Life by Goldsmith.... 1674..1761
Nash, Samuel, LL. B.   Poetical Writer .... — ..1829
Nash, Thomas.   Dramatist and Satiric Writer .... 1567..1600?
Nash, Thomas.   Miscellaneous Writer................. — ..1648
Nash, Dr. Treadway Russell.   (*History of Worcester*)... 1726..1811
Nasini, Joseph Nicholas.   Italian Historical Painter .... 1660?.1736
Nasmith, David.   Scot. Philanthr.   L. by Dr. Campbell 1799..1839
Nasmith, James, D. D.   Divine and Antiquary......... 1740..1808
Nasmyth, Alexander.   Scottish Landscape Painter .... 1758..1840
Nasmyth, Peter, or Patrick, son.   Landscape Painter... 1786..1831
Nassir-eddin.   Mahometan Philosopher and Astronomer 1201..1274
Natalis, Michael, of Liège.   Engraver .... 1609?.1670
Nathan, Isaac, or Mordecai.   Rabbi.   (*Heb. Concordance*) fl. 1450?
Nattier, John Mark le.   French Artist; Professor at Paris 1685..1766
Nattier, Lawrence.   Engraver of Intaglios at Petersburg — ..1763
Naudé, or Naudæus, Gabriel.   Fr. Writer.   (*Naudæana*) 1600..1653
Naudé, Philip.   French Mathematician at Berlin....... 1654..1729
Naudet, Thomas Charles.   French Landscape Painter.. 1774..1810
Naumann, John Frederick.   German Ornithologist .... 1780..1857
Naumann, John Theophilus.   German Composer ...... 1741..1801
Naunton, Sir Robert.   Statesman.   (*Fragmenta Regalia*) 1563..1635
Navagero, or Naugerius, Andrew.   Ital. Orator and Poet 1483..1529
Navagero, Bernard.   Cardinal; Venetian Statesman and
    Scholar .... 1507..1565
Navarette, or Navarrete, John Fernandez Ximenes de.
    El Mudo.   Spanish Painter .... 1524?.1577
Navarre, Peter de.   Spanish Warrior................. — ..1528
Navarrete, Domingo Fernandez.   Span. Miss. to China — ..1689
Navarrete, Martin Fernandez de.   (*Coleccion de los Via-
    jes; Coleccion de Documentos*) .... 1765..1844
Navier, Peter Toussaint.   French Physician and Chemist 1712..1779
Naylor, James.   Enthusiast .... 1616?.1660
Neal, Daniel.   Divine and Hist.   (*Hist. of the Puritans*) 1678..1743
Neal, Joseph C.   American Miscellaneous Writer.   (*Char-
    coal Sketches*)................................... 1807..1848
Neander, Christopher Frederick.   German Poet.   (*Geist-
    liche Lieder*)..................................... 1724..1802
Neander, John Augustus William.   Ecclesiastical Hist. 1789..1850
Neander, Michael.   Ger. Physician and Mathematician 1529..1581
Neander, Michael, of Ilfeldt.   (*Erotemata Græcæ Ling.*) 1525..1595
Nearchus.   Greek Admiral......................... 4th c. B.C.
Nebuchadnezzar.   King of Babylon................. — B.C.562
Neck, John van.   Dutch Painter .... 1635..1714
Neckar, Professor.   Swiss Naturalist in Skye .... — ..1862
Necker, James.   Statesman and Financier.   Life by Mme.
    de Staël....................................... 1732..1804
Necker, Noel Joseph.   Dutch Bot.   (*Elementa Botanica*) 1729..1793
Necker, Susanne Curchod de Nasse, wife of James.   (*Ré-
    flexions sur le Divorce*)........................... 1739..1794
Neckham, Alexander.   English Abbot; Scholar & Poet — ..1227
Needham, John Turberville.   Roman Catholic Divine
    and Naturalist.................................. 1713..1781
Needham, or Nedham, Marchamont.   Political Writer 1620..1678

BORN. DIED.

Neef, or Neefs, Peter. *The Elder.* Dutch Painter of Architecture .... 1570..1651
Neele, Henry. Poet and Miscellaneous Writer......... 1798..1828
Neer, Arnold van der. Dutch Landscape Painter...... 1619..1683
Neer, Eglon Hendrick van der, son. Historical and Portrait Painter..................................... 1643..1703
Neercassel, John de. Dutch Bishop. (*Amor Pœnitens*) 1626..1686
Nees von Esenbeck, Christian Godfrey Daniel. German Botanist and Naturalist..................... 1776..1858
Neff, Felix. *Apostle of the Alps.* L. by W. S. Gilly; Bost 1798..1829
Nehemiah. Governor of Judæa .... fl. B.C. 444
Neledinski-Meletzki, Yourgi, or George. Russian Ballad Writer .... 1752..1829
Neller, George Christopher. German Archæologist .... 1709..1783
Nelson, David. American Physician and Clergyman .. 1793..1844
Nelson, Horatio, Viscount. Admiral. Life by Harrison, 1806; Clarke & McArthur, 1809; Southey; Pettigrew 1758..1805
Nelson, Robert. (*Fasts and Festivals.*) Life by Secretan 1656..1715
Nelson, Thomas. American Revolutionary Officer and Statesman.. 1738..1789
Nelson, William. American General................. 1825..1862
Nelson, Wolfred, M. D. Canadian Physician, Politician, and Philanthropist............................... 1802..1863
Nemesianus, Marcus Aurelius Olympius. Latin Poet. (*Cynegetica*)....................................... fl. 283
Nemesius. Bp. of Emesa. Philos. (*De Naturâ Hominis*) fl. 400?
Nemours, Mary de Longueville, Duchess de. (*Memoirs of the Court of France*)........................... 1625..1707
Nennius. Abbot of Bangor. Historian............. fl. 620?
Neper, or Napier. Inventor of Logarithms. *See* Napier 1550..1617
Nepomucen, John, St., or John of Nepomuck......... 1320..1383
Nepos, Cornelius. Rom. Historian. (*Vitæ Imperatorum*) fl. ti. Aug.
Nepos, Flavius Julius. Emperor of the West (473-80).. — .. 480
Neri, Philip de, St. Founder of the Oratory .... 1515..1595
Neri, Pompeio. Italian Political Economist .... 1707..1776
Nerli, Philip. Italian Historian .... 1485..1556
Nero. Roman Emperor (54-68)..................... 37.. 68
Nerva. Roman Emperor (96-98)..................... 32.. 98
Nesbit, Anthony. Writer on Land Surveying & Agricul. 1777?.1859
Nesbit, Alexander. Scott. Antiquary and Heraldic Writer 1672..1725
Nesle, — de. French Poetical and Prose Writer...... — ..1767
Nesse, Christopher. Nonconformist Divine. L. by Silver 1621..1705
Nesselrode, Charles Robert, Count von. Russ. Diplom. 1780..1862
Nestor. Earliest Russian Chronicler.................. 1056?.1116?
Nestorius. Patriarch of Constantinople; Heresiarch .. — .. 450?
Netscher, Constantine. Painter..................... 1670..1722
Netscher, Gaspar. Flemish Painter.................. 1639..1684
Netscher, Theodore, son. Painter.................. 1661..1732
Netter, Thomas. English Carmelite; Theologian...... 1367?.1430
Nettlebladt, Christian, Baron de. Swedish Writer .... 1696..1776
Nettlebladt, Daniel. German Jurist .... 1719..1791
Nettleton, Dr. Asahel. American Revival Preacher. Life by Bennet Tyler.............................. 1783..1844
Neubauer, Ernest Frederick. Ger. Theol. and Antiq. 1641?.1684

BORN. DIED.

Neuhof, Theodore Stephen, Baron von. German Adventurer. King of Corsica .... 1690..1756
Neukirch, Benjamin. German Poet .... 1665..1729
Neukomm, Sigismund, Chevalier. German Composer 1778..1857
Neumann, Gaspar. German Chemist .... 1682..1737
Neumann, John George. German Lutheran Divine ... 1661..1709
Neuville, Charles Frey de. Jesuit Preacher.......... 1693..1774
Neuville, Didier Peter Chicaneau de. (*Dictionnaire Philosophique*) .... 1720..1781
Nevile, or Nevyle, Alex. Poet & Writer; tr. of *Œdipus* 1544..1614
Nevile, Henry. Republican Writer. (*Plato Redivivus*) 1620..1694
Nevile, Thomas. Dean of Canterbury; Benefactor to Trinity College .... — ..1615
Neville, Rev. Robert, B. D. Divine and Dramatist ..... — ..1694
Newburgh, William of. Historian................... 1136..1208
Newcastle, Henry Clinton, Duke of. Statesman ...... 1811..1864
Newcastle, Henry Pelham Fiennes Pelham Clinton, Duke of. Statesman .... 1785..1851
Newcastle, Margaret Cavendish, Duchess of. Life by self and Brydges .... — ..1673
Newcastle, Thomas Holles Pelham, Duke of. Statesm. 1694..1768
Newcastle, Wm. Cavendish, Duke of. Royalist & Writer 1592..1676
Newcome, Rev. Henry. Divine and Author .... — ..1713
Newcome, Rev. Peter. Divine and Author .... 1656..1738
Newcome, William. Archbishop of Armagh .... 1729..1800
Newcomen, Matthew. Nonconformist Divine... — ..1766
Newdigate, Sir Roger. Founder of Prize at Oxford... 1719..1806
Newell, Mrs. Harriet (Atwood). American Missionary.. 1793..1812
Newell, Robert Hassell, B. D. Editor of Goldsmith .... 1780..1852
Newell, Samuel. American Missionary............... 1784..1821
Newland, John. Abbot. Diplomatist................. — ..1515
Newland, Peter. Dutch Mathematician .... 1764..1794
Newman, Rev. John. Translator of Xenophon........ — ..1719
Newman, Wm., D. D. Bapt. Minister. L. by G. Prichard 1772..1835
Newman, William Lewis. Miscellaneous Writer ...... 1760..1834
Newport, George. Naturalist and Physiologist........ 1803..1854
Newton, Gilbert Stuart, R. A. Painter............... 1794..1835
Newton, Henry, LL. D. Diplomatist and Latin Poet.... — ..1715
Newton, Sir Isaac. Life by Fontenelle, 1728 (in English same year); Frisi, 1778; Biot, 1822; Brewster, 1831 (also in German and French); De Morgan, 1833; Whewell (*Newton and Flamsteed*), 1836; Correspondence with Cotes, 1850; Brewster, 1855. .... 1642..1727
Newton, John, D. D. Mathematician and Divine ..... 1622..1678
Newton, Rev. John. (*Cardiphonia*.) Life by Rd. Cecil 1725..1807
Newton, Richard. Canon of Christ Church, Oxford; Benefactor .... 1676?.1753
Newton, Robert, D. D. Scottish Clergyman .... 1780..1854
Newton, Thomas. Latin Poet and Divine, Historical and Medical Writer .... — ..1607
Newton, Thomas. Bishop of Bristol. (*On the Prophecies.*) Life by self .... 1704..1782
Newton, William. (*History of Maidstone*) .... — ..1744
Newton, William. *The Peak Minstrel.*............... — ..1830

BORN. DIED.

Ney, Joseph Napoleon, Prince of the Moskva .... 1803..1857
Ney, Michael. Marshal of France.................... 1769..1815
Nibby, Anthony. Roman Archæologist.............. 1792..1839
Nicaise, Claude. French Scholar .... 1623..1701
Nicander. Greek Poet and Grammarian .... fl. 2d c. B.C.
Nicander, Charles Augustus. Swedish Poet .... 1799..1839
Niccola di Pisa. *Il Pisano.* Sculptor and Architect 1200?.aft.1273
Niccoli, Nicholas. Restorer of Learning.............. 1363..1437
Niccolini, John Baptist. Italian Poet .... 1785..1861
Nicephorus I. Emp. of the East (802–11). *Logotheta* — .. 811
Nicephorus II. (963–69.) *Phocas* .... 912?. 969
Nicephorus III. (1078–81.) *Botoniates* .... —aft.1081
Nicephorus. Patriarch of Constantinople. (*Breviarium*) 758.. 828
Nicephorus Callistus. Monk of Constantinople. (*Ecclesiastical History*) .... fl. 1450?
Nicephorus Gregoras. Byzantine Historian......... 1295?.1359?
Niceron, John Francis. Optical Writer.............. 1613..1646
Nicéron, John Peter. French Biographer........... 1685..1738
Nicetas, Acominatus. Byzantine Historian .... — ..1216?
Nichol, John Pringle, LL. D. Prof. of Astron. at Glasgow 1804..1859
Nicholas I. Pope (858–67). *The Great* .... — .. 867
Nicholas II. (1058–61.) *Gerard*.................... — ..1061
Nicholas III. (1277–80.) *John Cajetan* .... — ..1280
Nicholas IV. (1288–92.) *Jerome of Ascoli.* .... — ..1292
Nicholas V. (1447–55.) *Thomas Parentucelli, or of Sarzana.* Life by Manetti; Georgi, 1742 .... 1398..1455
Nicholas I. Emperor of Russia (1825–55). Life by Miss Mayne; E. H. Michelsen .... 1796..1855
Nicholas, Abraham. Penman .... 1692?.1744?
Nicholls, Frank, M. D. Medical Writer............... 1699..1778
Nicholls, Sir Geo. Publicist. (*History of the Poor Laws*) 1780..1865
Nicholls, William. Divine. (*Conference with a Theist*) 1664..1712?
Nichols, Ichabod, D. D. American Divine............. 1784..1859
Nichols, James. Printer and Writer. (*Arminianism and Calvinism*) .... — ..1861
Nichols, John. Printer, with Bowyer. (*Anec. of Bowyer*) 1745..1826
Nichols, John Bowyer. Printer and Archæologist ..... 1807?.1863
Nicholson, Alfred. Painter in Water Colors .... — ..1836
Nicholson, James. American Naval Officer .... 1737..1804
Nicholson, John. Dramatic Writer .... — ..1822
Nicholson, John. Brigadier-General; fell at Delhi .... 1821..1857
Nicholson, William. Chemist and Natural Philosopher 1758..1815
Nicias. Athenian General in Sicily .... — B.C. 413
Nicias. Athenian Painter........................... fl. B.C. 320
Nicolai, Christopher Frederick. Ger. Bookseller & Writ. 1733..1811
Nicolai, John, of Paris. Theologian; Editor of Aquinas 1594?.1673
Nicolas, of Cusa. Bishop of Brixen. Theologian..... 1401..1454
Nicolas, of Lyra. Biblical Commentator .... — ..1340
Nicolas, Sir Nicholas Harris. Antiquary .... 1799..1848
Nicolaus Myrepsus. Greek Medical Writer .... fl. 1240–80?
Nicolay, Louis Henry, Baron. German Poet.......... 1737..1820
Nicole, Claude. French Poet........................ 1611..1685
Nicole, Francis. French Mathematician .... 1683..1758
Nicole, Peter. Jansenist of Port Royal. (*Essais de Morale*) 1625..1695

BORN. DIED.

Nicoll, Robert. Scottish Poet; Editor of *Leeds Times* .. 1814..1837
Nicollet, J. N. Fr. Astronomer and Geological Explorer 1795?.1843
Nicolo del Abbate. Italian Painter .... 1512..1572
Nicolo Isouard. French Dramatic Writer............ 1777..1818
Nicolosio, John Baptist. Sicilian Geographer......... 1610..1670
Nicolson, William. Archbishop of Cashel. Antiqnary 1655..1727
Nicomedes I. King of Bithynia; Founder of Nicomedia — B.C.250?
Nicomedes II. (B. C. 149–91.) *Epiphanes* .... — B.C. 91
Nicomedes III. (B. C. 91–74.) *Philopator* .... — B.C. 74
Nicon, or Nikon. Patriarch of Russia. Historian ..... 1605..1681
Nicot, John. French Statesman; introduced Tobacco.. 1530..1600
Nidhard, John Everard. Cardinal. Spanish Statesman 1608..1681
Niebuhr, Barthold George. German Historian. (*History of Rome.*) L. by Bunsen; Brandis & Loebell, 1851 1776..1831
Niebuhr, Carsten. Traveler and Biographer.......... 1733..1815
Nield, James. Philanthropist....................... 1744..1814
Niemcewicz, Julian Ursin. Polish Author & Statesman 1757..1841
Niemeyer, Augustus Hermann. German Theologian and Miscellaneous Writer...................... 1754..1828
Niepce, Joseph Nicéphore. French Chemist; one of the Inventors of Photography .... 1769..1833
Nieremberg, John Eusebius. Spanish Jesuit .... 1590..1658
Nieuhoff, John. Dutch Voyager.................... —aft.1671
Nieulandt, William van der. Dutch Painter and Writer 1584..1635
Nieuport, Charles Francis Ferdinand Anthony de Preud'-homme d'Hailly, Viscount de. Dutch Mathematician 1746..1827
Nieuwentyt, Bernard. Dutch Philosopher and Mathem. 1654..1718
Nieuwland, Peter. Dutch Poet and Natural Philosopher 1764..1794
Nifo, or Niphus, Augustinus. Italian Philosopher...... 1473?.1538
Niger, Pescennius. Pretender to the Rom. Emp. (193–94) — .. 194
Nightingale, Joseph. Unitarian Minister; Writer..... 1775..1824
Nikon. Russian Patriarch. Theologian............. 1605..1681
Niles, Hezekiah. American Journalist. (*Niles's Register*) 1777..1839
Niles, John Milton. American Author and Statesman.. 1787..1856
Niles, Nathaniel. Amer. Clergyman, Inventor, and Polit. 1741..1828
Nisbet, or Nesbit, Alexander. Antiq. & Heraldic Writer 1672..1725
Nithard, Count of Ponthieu. Historian............. 790?. 859?
Nithisdale, Wm. Maxwell, Fifth E. of. Scottish Jacobite 1702..1744
Nivelle de la Chaussée, Peter Claude. Dramatist.... 1692..1754
Nivernais, Louis Julius Barbon Mancini-Marini, Duke de. Diplomatist and Writer...................... 1716..1798
Nixon, John. Divine, Poet, and Natural Philosopher... — ..1777
Nizam al Mulk. Persian General and Statesman ..... 1648?.1748
Nizami, or Nidhami. Persian Poet.................. — ..1180
Nizzoli, or Nizolius, Marius. (*Thesaurus Ciceronianus*) 1498..1566
Noah. Patriarch.......................... 2948?.1998? B.C.
Noah, Mordecai Manuel. Amer. Journalist and Politician 1785..1851
Noailles, Adrian Maurice, Duke of. Marshal of France and Statesman .... 1678..1766
Noailles, Anthony de. Admiral of France. Ambassador to Mary of England .... 1504..1582
Noailles, Francis de, brother. Ambassador in Eng., 1556 1519..1585
Noailles, Louis Anthony de. Cardinal Archbp. of Paris 1651..1729
Noailles, Louis Mary, Viscount. General............ 1756..1804

BORN. DIED.

Noble, Edward. Hydrographer & Writer on Perspective — ..1784
Noble, Eustace le. Historian, Poet, and Romancist .... 1643..1711
Noble, Rev. Mark. Historian and Antiquary .... — ..1827
Noble, Samuel. Clergyman and Author............. 1779..1853
Noble, Thomas. Journalist, Novelist, Poet............ — ..1837
Nobrega, Manuel da. Port. Jesuit; Missionary to Brazil — ..1570
Nodier, Charles. French Writer.................... 1783?.1844
Noehden, or Nöhden, George Henry. Grammarian and
    Medalist in England .... 1770..1826
Nogarola, Isotta, of Verona. Scholar .... 1430?.1466
Nogarola, Louis. Italian Scholar and Tridentine Divine 1509?.1559
Noinville, James Bernard Durey de. (Hist. of the Opera) 1682..1768
Noire, John le. French Jansenist Writer .... 1622..1692
Nolan, Michael. Writer of Law Books .... — ..1827
Noldius, Christian. Danish Divine and Biblical Writer 1626..1683
Nolin, Denis. French Biblical Critic .... 1648..1710
Nollekens, Francis Joseph. Antwerp Painter in London 1688..1748
Nollekens, Joseph, son. Sculptor. Life by J. T. Smith 1737..1823
Nollet, John Anthony. Abbé. Natural Philosopher... 1700..1770
Nomsz, John. Dutch Poet........................ 1738..1803
Nonnius, or Nuñez, Peter. Port. Mathem. & Physician 1492?.1577
Nonnius Pincianus. Spanish Scholar. See Nuñez .. 1470?.1553
Nonnus. Greek Poet. (Dionysiaca; Paraphr. of St. John) fl. 410?
Nonnus, or Nonus. Greek Phys. ('Επιτομὴ τῆς ἰατρικῆς) fl. 950?
Noodt, Gerard. Dutch Jurist. Life by Barbeyrac..... 1647..1725
Noradin, or Noureddin. Sultan of Syria and Egypt ... 1116..1174
Norbert, St. Founder of Prémontré Order .... 1092?.1134
Norbert, Peter Parisot. (Sur les Missions des Indes).... 1697..1769
Nordberg, Joran, or George. Swedish Divine and Hist. 1677..1744
Norden, Frederick Louis. Danish Traveler .... 1708..1742
Norden, John. Topographer. (Survey of Middlesex).. 1548?.1626?
Nordenfleicht, Chederig Charlotte de. Swedish Poetess 1749..1793
Nores, Jason de. Ital. Philosopher and Political Writer — ..1590
Norfolk, Charles Howard, Duke of. Politician .... 1746..1815
Norfolk, Thomas Howard, Earl of Surrey, and Third
    Duke of. Commander.......................... 1473..1554
Norgate, Edward. Windsor Herald; Illuminator .... — ..1650
Noris, Henry. Ital. Cardinal. (History of Pelagianism) 1631..1704
Normanby, Constantine Henry Phipps, Marquess of.
    Statesman.................................. 1797..1863
Normandy, Dr. Alphonse. Chemist and Writer .... 1811?.1864
Norris, James, of Devizes. Miser................... — ..1835
Norris, John. English Platonist. (Essay on Ideal World) 1657..1711
Norris, Sir John. Admiral. Foul-weather Jack .... — ..1749
Norris, John. Founder of Professorship and Prize... 1734..1777
North, Dudley, Third Lord. Courtier and Writer...... 1581..1666
North, Dudley, Lord, son. (Life of Edward Lord North) 1604..1677
North, Sir Dudley. Lord of the Treasury. Writer on
    the Turks. Life by Roger North .... 1641..1691
North, Edward, Lord. Lawyer...................... 1496?.1564
North, Francis. First Baron Guilford. Lord Keeper.
    Life by Roger North............................ 1637..1685
North, Fred., Second Earl Guilford. Premier; Ld. North 1732..1792
North, Rev. George. Antiquary..................... 1710..1772

BORN. DIED.

North, John, D. D. Master of Trinity College. Life by
  Roger North.................................... 1645..1683
North, Roger, Lord. Statesman and Soldier.......... 1531?.1600
North, Roger. Att.-Gen. (*Examen; Lives of the Norths*) 1650?.1734
North, Sir Thomas. Translator and Author........ 1535?.aft.1579
Northampton, Spencer J. A. Compton, Marquess of.... 1790..1851
Northcote, James. Painter and Writer on Art........ 1746..1831
Northouck, John. (*History of London*)............ 1746..1816
Northumberland, Algernon Percy, Duke of .... 1792..1865
Northumberland, Henry Percy, E. of; father of Hotspur — ..1408
Northumberland, Henry Percy, Ninth Earl of. *Wizard* 1564..1632
Northumberland, John Dudley, Duke of; beheaded... 1502..1553
Norton, Andrews. American Scholar and Theologian.
  (*Genuineness of the Gospels*)...................... 1786..1853
Norton, Fletcher, Lord Grantley.................... — ..1789
Norton, Frances, Lady. Moral Writer. (*Memento Mori*) 1650..1720
Norton, Rev. John. Writer ....·.... 1606..1663
Norton, Samuel. Writer on Alchemy .... 1548..1599?
Norton, Thomas. *Archicarnifex.* Persecutor and Writer 1532..1584
Norwood, Richard. Mathematician .... fl. 1635
Nostradamus, Michael de. Physician and Astrologer.. 1503..1566
Nothelm. Archbishop of Canterbury (735–41)........ — .. 741
Notker, or Notger, *The Stammerer,* of St. Gall. Writer.. 830?. 912
Notker, or Notger. Bishop of Liège. (*History of the
  Bishops of Liège*)................................ — ..1008
Nott, Abraham. American Judge and Politician....... 1767..1830
Nott, Eliphalet, D. D. American Educator............ 1773..1866
Nott, Henry Junius. American Scholar and Author.... 1797..1837
Nott, John, M. D. Poet and Orientalist .... 1751..1826
Nott, Sir Thomas, F. R. S.......................... — ..1681
Nott, Sir William, K. C. B. General in the Afghan War 1782..1845
Nottingham, Daniel Finch, Earl of. Statesm. and Theol. 1647..1730
Nottingham, Heneage Finch, cr. Earl of. Lord. Chanc. 1621..1682
Noue, Denis de la, of Paris. Printer.................. — ..1650
Noue, Francis de la. *Bras de Fer.* Huguenot Soldier.
  (*Discourses*) .... 1531..1591
Noureddin Mahmoud. Sultan of Syria and Egypt... 1116..1174
Nour-jehan. Sultana of Hindostan.................. 1585..1645
Nourse, Sir Charles. Surgeon .... 1714..1789
Novalis, or Frederick von Hardenberg. German Writer 1772..1801
Novarini, Louis. Biblical Commentator, of Verona ... 1594..1650
Novatian. Antipope (251)........................... fl. 251
Novello, Edward Petre. Painter...................... — ..1836
Novello, Vincent. Musician. L. by Mrs. Cowden Clarke 1781..1861
Noverre, John George. French Writer on Dancing.... 1727..1810
Noves, Laura de; loved by Petrarch.................. 1307..1348
Novikoff, Nich. Ivanovitch. Editor of Russian Authors 1744..1818
Nowell, Alexander. Dean of St. Paul's. (*Catechism.*)
  Life by Churton, 1809........................ 1507 or 8.1602
Nowell, Lawrence, brother. Dean of Lichfield; Saxonist
  and Antiquary.................................... 1516?.1576
Noy, William. Attorney-General .... 1577..1634
Noyes, William Curtis. American Jurist .... 1805..1864
Nuck, Anthony. Dutch Physician and Anatomist ..... 1660?.1692?

BORN. DIED.

Nugent, Christopher, Lord Delvin.................... 1544..1602
Nugent, Eugene. Journalist........................ — ..1835
Nugent, George Grenville, Lord. Poet and Misc. Writer 1788..1851
Nugent, Maria, Lady............................... — ..1834
Nugent, Robert Craggs, Earl. Poet .... 1709?.1788
Nugent, Thomas. Miscellaneous Writer and Translator — ..1772
Numerian. Roman Emperor (283).................... — .. 283
Nuñez, Alvar Cabeça de Vaca. Explorer............ — ..1564
Nuñez, Ferdinand de Guzman. *Nonnius Pincianus.* Pro-
    moter of Greek learning in Spain. Life by A. Schott 1470?.1553
Nuñez, or Nonnius, Peter. Portuguese Mathematician.. 1492?.1577
Nutt, Robert. Pirate; hanged at the Groyne .... — ..1632
Nuttall, Thomas. American Naturalist .... 1786..1859
Nuwayri. Arabian Historian....................... 1281?.1331?
Nuzzi, Mario. *De' Fiori.* Italian Flower Painter ...... 1603..1673
Nye, Philip. Nonconformist Divine .... 1596?.1672
Nyerup, Nasmus. Danish Antiquary................ 1759..1829
Nysten, Peter Hubert. Phys. and Physiologist at Paris 1771..1818

O.

BORN. DIED.

Oakes, Urian. President of Harvard College......... 1631..1681
Oastler, Richard. Political Writer .... — ..1861
Oates, Titus. Contriver of the "Popish Plot" .... 1619?.1705
Obadiah. Hebrew Prophet .... fl. 6th c. B.C.
Obeidah, or Abu-Obeidah. Saracen Conqueror....... 581.. 639
O'Beirne, Thomas Lewis. Bishop of Meath........... 1748..1823
Oberkampf, Christopher Philip. Promoter of Cotton
    Manufacture in France .... 1738..1815
Oberlin, Jeremiah James. Philologist and Antiquary.
    Life by Winckler .... 1735..1806
Oberlin, John Frederick. French Philanthropist ...... 1740..1826
Obrecht, Ulric, of Strasburg. Philologist............. 1646..1701
Obrenovitch, Milosh. Servian Soldier .... 1780?.1860
O'Brien, Henry. (Round Towers of Ireland) .... — ..1835
O'Brien, John. Rom. Catholic Bishop of Cloyne and Ross — ..1775
O'Brien, Sir Lucius. Writer on Trade................ — ..1795
O'Brien, William Smith. Irish Politician............. 1803?.1864
Ocaritz, Joseph, Chevalier d'. Spanish Diplomatist.... 1750..1805
Occam, or Ockham, Wm. Invincible Doctor. Schoolman — ..1347
Occleve, Thomas. Poet............................... 1370?.1454?
Ocellus Lucanus. Pythagorean Philosopher......... fl. 5th c. B.C.
Ochinus, Bernardin. Protestant Reformer........... 1487..1564
Ochs, Peter, of Basle. Politician. (History of Basle).. 1749..1821
Ochterlony, Sir David. British General.............. 1758..1825
Ockley, Rev. Simon. Orientalist..................... 1678..1720
O'Connell, Daniel. Irish Agitator. Life by Daunt, 1848;
    W. Fagan; John O'Connell...................... 1775..1847
O'Connor, Arthur. Leader in Irish Rebellion of 1798.. 1763..1852
O'Connor, Charles. Historical Writer................ — ..1828
O'Connor, Feargus Edward. Chartist.............1795 or 6.1855
Octavia. Sister of Augustus......................... — B.C. 11
Octavianus, or Augustus. Roman Emperor... B.C.63.A.D.14
O'Curry, Eugene. Irish Professor and Archæologist ... — ..1862
Odazzi, John. Painter and Engraver .... 1663?.1731
Odenatus. King of Palmyra, husband of Zenobia..... — .. 267
Oderico, Gaspar Louis. Antiquary and Medalist....... 1725..1803
Odescalchi, Mark Anthony. Philanthropist, of Rome.. — ..1670
Odescalchi, Thomas. Philanthropist, of St. Gale ..... — ..1692
Odespung de la Meschinière, Louis. Document Coll. 1597.. —
Odevaere, Josephus Dionysius. Historical Painter..... 1778..1830
Odington, Walter. Walter of Evesham. Writer on Mu-
    sic and Astronomy .... ti. Hen. III.
Odo, St. Abbot of Cluny .... 879.. 943
Odo, St. Archbishop of Canterbury (942–58).......... 875?. 961
Odo, Bishop of Bayeux, brother of William the Con-
    queror .... — ..1097
Odo of Kent. Abbot of Battle; Friend of Becket..... — ..1200
Odoacer. Gothic King of Italy (476–93).............. — .. 493
O'Donovan, Dr. John. Irish Archæologist............ 1808?.1861
Odoran, of Sens. Chronica Rerum in Orbe Gestarum) 985.aft.1045

BORN. DIED.

Œcolampadius, John. German Reformer. L. by Wolf-
gang Capito, tr. by Callesian, 1561; Simon Prynæus 1482..1531
Oeder, Geo. Christian. Phys. and Bot. (*Flora Danica*) 1728..1791
Oehlenschlaeger, Adam Gottlob. Dramatic Poet..... 1779..1850
Oelrichs, John Charles Conrad. Ger. Hist. and Bibliog. 1722..1798
Oelschlaeger, or Olearius, Adam. Traveler and Orient. 1599?.1671
Oernhielm, Claudius. *Arrhenius.* Swedish Historian.. 1627..1695
Oersted, Andrew Sandöe. Danish Statesman........ 1778..1860
Oersted, Hans Christian, br. Danish Electro-magnetist 1777..1851
Oetinger, Frederick Christopher. German Theologian.. 1702..1782
Offor, George. Biographer of Bunyan................ 1786?.1864
Ogden, James, of Manchester. Poetical Writer........ — ..1802
Ogden, Dr. Samuel. Divine......................... 1716..1778
Oggione, or Uggione, Mark da. Milanese Painter ..... 1480?.1530
Ogier, Charles. French Scholar..................... 1595..1654
Ogilby, or Ogilvy, John. Poet and Classical Translator 1600..1676
Ogilvie, John. Scottish Poet and Divine............. 1733..1814
Oginski, Michael Casimir. Polish Patriot............ 1731..1803
Oginski, Michael Cleofas, nephew. Composer .... 1765..1831
Ogle, Right Hon. George, M. P. Ballad Writer .... — ..1814
Oglethorpe, James. General .... 1688?.1785
O'Halloran, Sylvester. Antiquary and Historian...... 1728..1807
O'Hara, Kane. Irish Dramatist...................... — ..1782
Ohlmüller, or Ohlmueller, Daniel Joseph. Ger. Architect 1791..1839
Ohmacht, Landelin. German Sculptor............... 1760..1834
Oisel, James. Critic and Medalist .... 1631..1686
O'Keeffe, John. Dramatist. Life by self, 1826........ 1747..1833
Oken, Lawrence. Swiss Naturalist.................. 1779..1851
Okolski, Simon. Polish Historian. (*Orbis Polonus*) ... fl. 1650
Oktai-Khan. Tartar Conqueror ..../............... — ..1241
Olaf. *See* Olaus.
Olafsen, Eggert. Icelandic Scholar .... 1721..1768
Olahus, Nicholas. Hungarian Prelate and Historian ... 1493..1568
Olaus I. King of Norway. *Trygvason* .... 956..1000
Olaus II. *The Fat* and *The Saint*.................. 992?.1030
Olaus III. *The Pacific* .... — ..1093
Olaus IV.. 1098..1116
Olaus V.. 1371..1387
Olaus Magnus. Antiquary. (*De Gentibus Septentrion.*) 1500?.1568
Olavide, Paul Anthony Joseph. Spanish Statesman.
(*Triumph of the Gospel*)........................ 1725..1803
Olbers, Henry William Matthias. German Astronomer 1758..1840
Oldcastle, Sir John, Lord Cobham. Protestant Martyr 1360?.1417
Oldenburg, Henry. German Writer .... 1626..1678
Oldenburger, Philip Andrew. Jurist of Geneva ...... — ..1678
Oldermann, John, of Helmstadt. Scholar .... 1686?.1723
Oldfield, Anne. Actress .... 1683..1730
Oldfield, Thomas. Parliamentary Historian.......... — ..1822
Oldham, John. Poet. Life by E. Thompson.......... 1653..1683
Oldisworth, Wm. Polit. and Poet. Transl. of Horace — ..1734
Oldmixon, John. Historian......................... 1673..1742
Oldys, William. Norroy King-at-Arms. Biographer .. 1687..1761
Olearius, or Oelschlaeger, Adam. Traveler and Orient. 1599?.1671
Olearius, Godfrey. Lutheran Divine................ 1604..1685

BORN. DIED.

Olearius, Godfrey, of Leipsic. Philosopher and Theol. 1639..1713
Olearius, Godfrey, son. Theologian and Philosopher... 1672..1715
O'Leary, Arthur. Irish Roman Catholic Preacher and
    Political Writer.................................... 1729..1802
Oleaster, Jerome. Portuguese Biblical Commentator .. — ..1563
Ölenschläger. See Oehlenschlaeger .... 1779..1850
Olin, Stephen. American Clergyman and Writer ...... 1797..1851
Oliva, Alexander. Cardinal. Preacher and Theologian 1408..1463
Oliva, John. Italian Antiquary .... 1689..1757
Olivarez, Gaspar de Guzman, Duke of. Spanish Statesm. 1587..1645
Olive, Peter John de. Writer on Papal Corruptions.... 1247..1298
Olivecrantz, John Paulin. Swed. Statesm. & Latin Poet 1633..1707
Oliver, Andrew. Lieutenant-Governor of Massachusetts 1707..1774
Oliver, George, D. D. Rom. Cath. Antiq.; Writ. on Devon 1781..1861
Oliver, Isaac. English Portrait Painter.............. 1556..1617
Oliver, Peter, son. Portrait Painter.................. 1601..1654?
Oliver, Peter. Chief Justice and Antiquary........... 1712..1791
Oliver, William, M. D., of Bath. Writ. on the Bath Waters — ..1764
Olivet, Joseph Thoulier d'. Fr. Writer; Editor of Cicero 1682..1768
Olivetan, Robert. Fr. Reformer and Translator of Bible — ..1538
Oliveyra, Francis Xavier de. Port. Prot. (Oliveyriana) 1702..1783
Olivier, Claude Matt. Fr. Scholar. (Philip of Macedon) 1701..1736
Olivier, William Anthony. Fr. Traveler and Naturalist 1756..1814
Olivieri degli Abbati, Annibal. Antiquary, of Pesaro 1708..1789
Olmos, Francis Andrew de. Spanish Poet and Philolo-
    gist in Mexico.................................... — ..1571
Olmsted, Denison. American Savant .... 1791..1859
Olmutz, Augustinus von, of Moravia. Reviver of Learn. 1470?.1513
Olshausen, Hermann. German Protestant Theologian 1796..1839
Olybrius, Flavius Anicius. Roman Emperor (472)..... — .. 472
Olympias, wife of Philip of Macedon .... — B.C.316
Olympiodorus. Platonic Philosopher of Alexandria... fl. 520?
Omar I. Caliph (634-44). Captor of Jerusalem....... 581.. 644
Omar II. Caliph (717-20) .... — .. 720
Omar-ibn-Hafssun. Spanish Rebel................... — .. 883
O'Meara, Barry Edwards. Writ. (Voice from St. Helena) 1778..1836
Omri. King of Israel (B. C. 929-918) .... — B.C.918
Onatas, of Ægina. Sculptor and Painter .... fl. B.C. 460?
Onderdonk, Benjamin Treadwell. Amer. Episc. Bishop 1791..1861
Onkelos. Rabbi. (Targum)......................... 2d or 3d c.
Onslow, Arthur, M. P. Speaker...................... 1691..1768
Onslow, George. French Musical Composer .... 1784..1852
Onuphrius, Panvinius. Hist. Continuator of Platina 1529..1568
Oort, Adam van. Painter of Perspective & Architecture 1557..1641
Oost, Jacob van. Flemish Painter................... 1600?.1671
Oost, Jacob van, son. Younger. Portrait Painter...... 1637..1713
Opie, Mrs. Amelia. Novelist. Life by Brightwell, 1854 1769..1853
Opie, John. Historical Painter. Life by Amelia Opie.. 1761..1807
Opitz, or Opitius, Henry. German Orientalist .... 1642..1712
Opitz, or Opitius, Martin. German Poet.............. 1597..1639
Oporinus, John. Printer and Scholar .... 1507..1568
Oppede, John de Maynier, Baron d'. Persec. of Vaudois 1495..1558
Oppian. Greek Poet .... fl. ab. 180
Opsopæus, John. Ger. Phys.; Ed. of Sibylline Oracles 1556..1596

BORN. DIED.

Orange, Frederick Henry, Prince of. Stadtholder...... 1584..1647
Orange, Morris, Prince of. Stadtholder............... 1567..1625
Orange, William I., Prince of. *The Silent.* Assassinated 1533..1584
Orange, William II., Prince of. Stadtholder .... 1626..1650
Orange, William III., Prince of. Stadtholder and King
   of England...................................... 1650..1702
Orbigny, Alcide d'. French Naturalist .... 1802..1857
Orcagna, Orgagna, or L'Arcagnuolo. *Andrea di Cione.*
   Painter, Sculptor, Architect .... 1329..1389
Ord, John Walker. Topographer, Poet, Medical Writer 1811..1853
Ordericus Vitalis. Historian...................... 1075.aft.1143
Oregius, Augustine. Italian Cardinal and Philosopher. 1577..1635
Orellana, Francis. Companion of Pizarro; Discoverer.. — ..1549
Orelli, John Gaspar. German Philologist and Critic.... 1787..1849
Oresme, Nicholas. French Writer .... — ..1382
Orfanel, Hyacinth. Spanish Missionary to Japan...... 1578..1623
Orffyreus, John Ernest Elias. German Mechanician... 1680..1745
Orfila, Matthew Joseph Bonaventura. French Physician
   and Toxicologist................................ 1787..1853
Orford, Edward Russell, Earl of. Admiral .... 1651..1727
Orford, Horace Walpole, Earl of................... 1717..1797
Orford, Sir Robert Walpole (*q. v.*), Earl of. Premier..... 1676..1745
Orgagna, or Orcagna, Andrew. Paint., Sculpt., Architect 1329..1389
Oriani, Barnaby. Italian Astronomer................ 1753..1832
Oribasius. Medical Writer; Friend of Julian.......... 325?. 400?
Origen. Greek Father........................... 185?.253or4
Origny, Peter Adam. French Egyptologist .... 1697..1774
Orizzonte, or John Francis van Bloemen. Painter..... 1656..1740
Orlandi, Perègrine Anthony. Italian Bibliographer and
   Writer on Art .... 1660..1727
Orlandin, Nicholas. Italian Jesuit Historian.......... 1554..1606
Orlando di Lasso. Italian Musical Composer........ 1520..1594
Orlay, Bernard van, of Brussels. Painter............. 1490?.1560
Orlay, Richard van. Flemish Painter................ 1652..1732
Orleans, Adelaide Eugénie L., Princess of, sister of Louis
   Philippe.. 1777..1847
Orleans, Charles, Duke of; taken at Agincourt........ 1391..1465
Orleans, Ferdinand Philip Louis, Duke of. Prince Royal.
   Heir of Louis Philippe........................... 1810..1842
Orleans, Gaston John Baptist, Duke of, son of Henry IV. 1608..1660
Orleans, Hélène Louise Elizabeth, Duchess d', mother of
   the Count de Paris .... 1814..1858
Orleans, Louis d'. French Advocate and Political Writer 1542..1629
Orleans, Louis, Duke of. Philanthropist and Scholar... 1703..1752
Orleans, Louis Philip, Duke of, son................ 1725..1785
Orleans, Louis Philip Joseph, Duke of, son. *Égalité* ... 1747..1793
Orleans, Louis de Valois, Duke of; assassinated in Paris 1372..1407
Orleans, Mary, Princess of. Sculptor. (*Joan of Arc*).. 1813..1839
Orleans, Peter Joseph d'. French Historian.......... 1644..1698
Orleans, Philip I., Duke of, brother of Louis XIV....... 1640..1701
Orleans, Philip II., Duke of, son. Regent........... 1674..1723
Orleans de la Motte, Louis Francis Gabriel d'. Bishop
   of Amiens. (*Spiritual Letters.*) Life by Proyart, 1788 1683..1774
Orloff, Alexis Feodorovitch. Russian General .... 1786..1861

20

BORN. DIED.

Ossuña, Peter Tellez y Giron, Duke of. Span. Statesman 1579..1624
Ostade, Adrian van. Painter .... 1610..1685
Ostade, Isaac van, brother. Dutch Painter........... 1617..1671
Ostermann, Henry John Frederick, Count d'. Russian
  Statesman.. 1686..1747
Osterwald, John Frederick. Swiss Divine..........,... 1663..1747
Osterwick, Maria van. Dutch Flower Painter......... 1630..1693
Oswald, St. King of Northumbria.................. 605.. 642
Oswald, St. Bishop of Worcester. Archbishop of York.
  Life by Eadmer................................... — .. 992
Oswald, Erasmus. German Math. and Biblical Writer 1511..1579
Otfride, or Ottfride. German Monk. Metrical Writer fl. bef. 876
Othman, Third Saracen Caliph (634–55) .... 574?. 656
Othman. Founder of the Ottoman Dynasty. See Osman 1259..1326
Otho I. Emperor of Germany (936–73). Great .... 912.. 973
Otho II. (973–83.) The Bloody .... 955.. 983
Otho III. (996–1002)............................. 980..1002
Otho IV. (1209–15.) The Proud................... 1175..1218
Otho, or Otto. Bishop of Freysinger. Chronicler...... — ..1158
Otho, Marcus Salvius. Roman Emperor (A. D. 69, Janu-
  ary 15–April 15)................................ 32.. 69
Otho, Venius. Dutch Painter...................... 1556..1634
Otis, Harrison Gray. American Orator and Statesman.. 1765..1848
Otis, James. American Orator and Statesman........ 1725..1783
Otrokotskiforis, Francis. (Origines Hungaricæ)...... — ..1718
Ott, John Baptist. Orientalist and Antiquary.......... 1661.. —
Ott, John Henry. Swiss Divine and Orientalist ...... 1617..1682
Otter, John. Swedish Orientalist and Eastern Traveler 1707..1748
Otterbein, Philip William. Founder of United Brethren
  in Christ .... 1726..1813
Otterburn, Sir Adam. Ld. of Session, Diplomatist, Poet — ..1548
Ottley, William Young. Writer on Fine Arts .... 1771..1836
Ottmer, Charles Theodore, of Brunswick. Architect ... 1800..1843
Otto, Louis William, Count de Mosloy. Fr. Diplomatist 1754..1817
Ottocar II. King of Bohemia (1253–78). Opponent of
  Rodolph of Hapsburg............................. — ..1278
Otway, Thomas. Dramatist. (Venice Preserved.) Life
  by Thornton..................................... 1651..1685
Oudenarde, Robert van, of Ghent. Painter........... 1663..1743
Oudet, James Joseph. French Republican Officer:..... 1773..1809
Oudin, Casimir. Historical Writer.................. 1638..1717
Oudin, Francis. French Jesuit. Antiquary and Medalist 1673..1752
Oudinet, Mark Anthony. French Medalist............ 1643..1712
Oudinot, Nicholas Charles, Duke of Reggio. Marshal of
  France .... 1767..1847
Oudry, John Baptist. Fr. Historical and Portrait Painter 1686..1755
Oughtred, William. Mathem. (Clavis Mathematica).. 1574..1660
Oulough Beyg. Astronomer of Samarcand........... 1394..1449'
Ousel, Oisel, or Loisel, Philip. German Hebraist...... 1671..1724
Ouseley, Gideon. Irish Clergyman and Writer........ 1762..1839
Ousely, Sir Gore, Viscount Claramont. Diplomatist.... 1769..1844
Ousely, Sir William, Viscount Claramont, br. Orientalist 1771..1839
Outram, Benjamin. Civil Engineer .... — ..1805
Outram, Sir James. General in India................ 1802..1863

BORN. DIED.

Outram, William. Divine and Hebraist. (*De Sacrificiis*) 1625..1679
Ouvrard, Gabriel Julien. French Financier .... 1770..1846
Ouvrard, René. French Divine, Poet, Musician, Math. 1624..1694
Ouwater, Albert van. Historical Painter of Haarlem... 1444..1515
Overall, John. Bishop of Norwich. (*Convocation Book*) 1559..1619
Overbeek, Bonaventure van. Artist and Antiquary.... 1660..1706
Overbury, Sir Thomas. Poet. (*The Wife*) .... 1581..1613
Overton, William. Bishop of Lichfield and Coventry.. 1525..1609
Overweg, Dr. Adolphus. German Traveler in Africa... 1822..1852
Ovid. Latin Poet. Life by Rosimini B.C.43.A.D.18
Oviedo, Andrew de. Span. Jesuit Missionary to Abyssinia — ..1577
Oviedo y Valdes, Gonzalo Fernandez de. (*W. Indies*) 1478..1557
Owen, Rev. Edward Pryce. (*Book of Etchings*) .... 1787?.1863
Owen, Rev. Henry, M.D. Biblical Critic. .... 1716..1795
Owen, John. *Audoenus.* Latin Poet and Epigrammatist 1560?.1622?
Owen, John, D.D. Independent. (*Holy Spirit.*) Life by
 W. Orme.. 1616..1683
Owen, Rev. John, of the Bible Society............... 1765..1822
Owen, Robert. Socialist & Philanthropist. L. by Sargent 1771..1858
Owen, William. English Painter..................... 1769..1825
Owen Glendower. Welsh Chieftain .... 1349?.1415
Owenson, Sydney, Lady Morgan. Writer .... 1783..1859
Owtram, or Outram, William. Hebraist. (*De Sacrificiis*) 1625..1679
Oxenden, Sir Henry. Poet........................... — ..1670
Oxenstiern, or Oxenstjerna, Axel, Ct. Swedish Statesm. 1583..1654
Oxford, Edward Harley, Second Earl of. Founder of Har-
 leian Library .... — ..1741
Oxford, Edward de Vere, Seventeenth Earl of. Politi-
 cian and Poet.................................. 1540?.1604
Oxford, Robert Harley, First Earl of. Statesman; Col-
 lector of MSS................................... 1661..1724
Oxlee, Rev. John. Orientalist and Biblical Critic ...... 1779..1854
Ozanam, James. French Mathematician .... 1640..1717
Ozell, John. Translator and Miscellaneous Writer ..... — ..1743
Ozeretzkoffsky, Nicholas Yakovlevitch. Russian Writer 1751..1827
Ozeroff, Vladislas Alexandrovitch. Russian Tragic Poet 1770..1816

P.

BORN. DIED.

Paas, Pas, or Passe, Crispin. German Engraver .... — ..1643?
Paaw, or Pauw, Peter. *Pavius*. Dutch Phys. and Anat. 1564..1617
Pacatianus, Titus Julius Marinus. Roman Usurper.... — .. 249
Pacca, Cardinal. Nuncio. (*Memoirs*)................ 1756..1844
Pacchiarotto, James, of Sienna. Painter............ fl. 1497-1535
Pacchioni, Anthony. Physician and Anatomist....... 1665..1726
Pace, Richard. Divine and Statesman .... 1482?.1532
Pacheco, Francis. Spanish Painter and Writer .... 1571..1654
Pacheco, John de, Marquis de Villena. Castilian Statesm. — ..1473
Pachomius. Egyptian Monk........................ 292.. 348
Pachymeres, George. Greek Historian............... 1242?.1315?
Paciaudi, Paul Maria. Antiquary and Historian ...... 1710..1785
Pacificus, Maximus. Italian Latin Poet. (*Hecatalegium*) 1400..1500?
Pacio, Julius. Jurist and Philosopher................ 1550..1635
Pacioli, Luke. *Luca di Borgo*. Italian Geometrician.. —aft.1509
Pack, Richardson, Major. Poet and Miscellaneous Writer 1680?.1728
Pacuvius, Marcus. Roman Tragedian.............. 220?.130? B.C.
Paderna, Paul Anthony. Italian Painter .... 1649..1708
Padilla, John Lopez de. Spanish Patriot............. — ..1522
Padilla, Lorenzo de. Span. Antiq. and Historiographer 1485?.1540?
Paduanino, Dario. *Varotari*. Painter............... 1539..1596
Paduanino, Francis. Historical Painter .... 1552..1617
Paer, Ferdinand. Italian Musical Composer.......... 1771..1839
Paez, Francis Alvarez. Port. Div. (*De Planctu Ecclesiæ*) — ..1532
Paez, Peter. Spanish Jesuit. Missionary to Abyssinia 1564..1622
Pagan, Blaise Francis, Count de. Military Engineer ... 1604..1665
Pagan, Peter. German Poet and Historian........... — ..1576
Paganel, Peter. Fr. Politician. (*La Révolution Française*) 1745..1826
Pagani, Gregory. Italian Painter .... 1558..1605
Pagani, Paul, of Milan. Painter................... 1661..1716
Paganini, Nicholas. Violinist. L. by G. C. Conestable 1784..1840
Paganucci, John. Commercial Writer. (*Manuel des Né-
gocians*).. 1729..1797
Page, John. American Statesman................... 1743..1808
Page, William, D. D. Divine. Royalist............. 1590..1663
Pagès, Francis Xavier. French Romance Writer ...... 1745..1802
Pagès, Peter Mary Francis, Viscount de. Fr. Navigator 1748..1793
Paget, Sir William, First Lord. Statesman.......... 1506..1563
Pagi, Anthony. French Chronologist and Historian.... 1624..1699
Pagi, Francis, nephew. (*Breviarium Historico-Chronolog-
ico-Criticum*) .... 1654..1721
Pagi, or Paggi, John Baptist. Ital. Paint., Engrav., Writ. 1554..1627
Pagninus, Sanctes. Ital. Orientalist and Biblical Scholar 1470?.1536
Pahlen, Peter. Soldier............................ 1746..1826
Paine, Elijah, LL. D. American Jurist .... 1757..1842
Paine, Elijah, son. Jurist......................... 1796..1853
Paine, Robert Treat. American Lawyer and Patriot... 1731..1814
Paine, Robert Treat, son. Author.................. 1773..1811
Paine, Thomas. American Political and Deistical Writer.
(*Age of Reason.*) Life by J. Cheetham .... 1737..1809

BORN. DIED.

Paisiello, John. Singer and Composer .... 1741..1816
Paixhans, Henry Joseph. French General of Artillery 1783..1854
Pajol, Claude Peter. French General................. 1772..1844
Pajon, Claude. French Calvinistic Divine............ 1626..1685
Pajot, Louis Leo, Ct. d'Ons-en-Bray. Scientific Collector 1678..1753
Pajou, Augustine. French Sculptor .... 1730..1809
Pakington, Dorothy, Lady. Scholar .... — ..1679
Paladini, Archangela. Portrait Painter. .... 1599..1622
Palæmon, Quintus Remmius. Roman Grammarian.... fl. 48
Palafox y Melzi, Joseph. Spanish General........... 1780..1847
Palafox y Mendoza, John de. Span. Bishop and Hist. 1600..1659
Palaprat, John. French Dramatist and Poet .... 1650..1721
Palaye. See Sainte-Palaye. (Ancient Chivalry)....... 1697..1781
Paleario, Aonio. Italian Theologian and Poet......... — ..1570
Palencia, Alfonso de. Span. Hist. (Chron. of Henry IV.) 1423..1495?
Paleotti, Gabriel. Italian Cardinal and Writer........ 1524..1597
Palestrina, John Peter Louis. Musical Composer...... 1529?.1594
Paley, William, D.D. (Evidences.) L. by Meadley; Paley 1743..1805
Palfyn, John. French Surgeon and Anatomist .... 1650..1730
Palgrave, Sir Francis. Antiquary. (Hist. of Normandy) 1788..1861
Palingenius Stellatus, or Manzolli. Latin Poet ...... fl. 1500?
Palisot de Beauvois, Ambrose Mary Francis Joseph.
    French Naturalist................................. 1752..1820
Palissot de Montenoy, Charles. French Dramatist... 1730..1814
Palissy, Bernard. French Potter. Life by H. Morley,
    1852; Brightwell, 1858............................ 1510?.1590
Palladino, James. De Teramo. (Consolatio Peccatorum) 1349..1417
Palladio, Andrew. Italian Architect .... 1518..1580
Palladius. Eastern Bishop and Writ. (Lausiac History) 368?.431?
Palladius, Rutilius Taurus Æmilianus. Roman Agricult-
    ural Writer...................................... fl. 4th c.
Pallajuolo, or Pollajuolo, Anthony. Florentine Painter. 1426..1498
Pallajuolo, or Pollajuolo, Peter, brother. Painter...... 1428..1498
Pallas. Freedman and Favorite of Claudius........... — .. 63
Pallas, Peter Simon. German Naturalist and Traveler 1741..1811
Pallavicino, Ferrante. Satirist. (The Courier Robbed) 1615..1644
Pallavicino, Sforza. Cardinal. (Hist. Council of Trent) 1607..1667
Palliot, Peter, of Dijon. Genealogist and Heraldic Writer 1608..1698
Palliser, Sir Hugh. English Admiral................. 1721..1796
Palluel, Francis Cretté de. French Agriculturist....... 1741..1798
Palm, John Philip, of Nuremberg; shot by Bonaparte.. 1766..1806
Palma, Jacob. The Old. Italian Painter.............. 1480?.1548?
Palma, Jacob. The Young, of Venice. Painter........ 1544..1628
Palmaroli, Peter. Painter and Picture Restorer ...... — ..1828
Palmblad, William Frederick. Swedish Writer .... 1788..1852
Palmegiani, Mark. Italian Painter .... —aft.1537
Palmella, Peter de Souza-Holstein, Duke of. Portuguese
    Statesman.. 1786..1850
Palmer, Rev. John. Dissenting Divine and Author.... 1729..1790
Palmer, John. Actor .... 1741..1798
Palmer, John. Postal Reformer...................... 1742..1818
Palmer, Samuel. Printer. (History of Printing) ...... — ..1732
Palmerston, Henry John Temple, 3d Vsct. Statesman 1784..1865
Palmieri, Matthew. Ital. Hist. (Chronicle; Vita Civile) 1405..1475

BORN. DIED.

Palomino y Velasco, Acislo Antonio. Spanish Painter
and Writer.................................... 1653..1726
Palsgrave, John. English Writer. (*French Grammar*) 1480?.1554
Paludanus, Bernard. Dutch Philosopher and Traveler 1550..1633
Paludanus, John. Dutch Theologian................ 1565..1630
Pamelius,.James. Flemish Theologian .... 1536..1587
Pamphilus. Bp. of Cæsarea; Friend of Eusebius; Martyr 240?. 309
Pamphilus of Amphipolis. Painter.............fl. B.C.388–348?
Panænus, of Athens. Painter. (*Battle of Marathon*).. fl. B.C. 450?
Panætius. Greek Philosopher...................... fl. B.C. 140
Panard, Charles Francis. French Poet and Dramatist.. 1689..1769
Panciroli, Guido. Jurist and Antiquary............ 1523..1599
Panckoucke, Andrew Joseph. French Writer........ 1700..1753
Panckoucke, Charles Joseph, son. Typographer, Pub-
lisher, Writer.................................... 1736..1798
Pancoucke, Charles Louis Fleury, grandson. Writer .. 1780..1844
Panel, Alexander Xavier. French Jesuit. Medalist ... 1699..1777
Panicale, Masolino da. Italian Painter.............. 1378?.1415?
Panigarola, Francis. Italian Bishop and Preacher. (*Il
Predicatore*).................................... 1548..1594
Panin, Nakita Ivanovitch. Russian Statesman .... 1718..1783
Panini, or Pannini, John Paul. Italian Painter........ 1695..1768
Pannonius, Janus. Hungarian Bishop and Latin Poet 1434..1472
Panormita. *See* Beccadelli..................... 1394..1471
Pantænus. Christian Teacher of Alexandria .... 155?. 216
Pantin, Peter. Scholar .... 1555?.1611
Pantin, William, of Bruges. Medical Writer.......... — ..1583
Panvinius, Onuphrius. Historian and Antiquary...... 1529..1568
Panzacchia, Maria Helena, of Bologna. Painter ...... 1668..1709
Panzer, Geo. Wolfgang. Bibliog. (*Annales Typographici*) 1729..1804
Paoli, Pascal de. Corsican Patriot. Life by Pommereul 1726..1807
Paoli, Sebastian. Scholar and Biographer .... 1684..1751
Paolo Sarpi. *See* Sarpi........................... 1552..1623
Paolo Veronese. *See* Cagliari .... 1530?.1588
Papebroch, Daniel. Dutch Jesuit; Theologian........ 1628..1714
Papias. Bishop of Herapolis. Millennarian .... — .. 169?
Papias. Grammarian. (*Vocabularium Latinum*)....... fl. 1053?
Papillon, Philibert, of Dijon. Abbé. (*Auteurs de Bour-
gogne*).. 1666..1738
Papillon, Ralph. Abbot of Westminster.............. — ..1223
Papillon, Thomas, of Dijon. Jurist .... 1514..1596
Papin, Denys. French Nat. Philos. Inventor of Digester 1647..1710
Papin, Isaac. French Theologian..................... 1657..1709
Papinianus, Æmilius. Roman Lawyer............... — .. 212
Papire-Masson, John. Fr. Historian. Life by De Thou 1544..1611
Papirius, Justus. Roman Jurist .... ti. Antonines
Papirius Cursor. Dictator in Second Samnite War fl. 333–309 B.C.
Papirius Cursor, son. Consul in Third Samnite War fl. 293–272 B.C.
Papon, John Peter. Fr. Writer. (*Histoire de Provence*) 1734..1803
Pappenheim, Godfrey Henry, Count von. Imperial Gen-
eral in Thirty Years' War .... 1594..1632
Pappus, of Alexandria. (*Mathematical Collections*) .... fl. 385?
Paracelsus, Philip Aureolus Theophrastus. Swiss Phys. 1493..1541
Paradin, William. Fr. Hist. Writer. (*Chronicle of Savoy*) 1501?.1590

BORN. DIED.

Paradisi, Augustine, Count. Italian Poet . . . . 1736. .1783
Paradisi, John, Count. Ital. Politician and Nat. Philos. 1760. .1826
Paræus, or Paré, David. German Protestant Theologian 1548. .1622
Paramo, Louis de. Span. Inquisitor. (*The Holy Office*) 1545?.1619?
Parcelles, John. Dutch Painter of Sea Pieces . . . . 1597. .1641
Parcieux, Anthony de. French Mathematician . . . . 1753. .1799
Pardies, Ignatius Gaston. Fr. Mathem. and Philosopher 1636. .1673
Pardoe, Miss Julia. Novelist and Historical Writer. . . . 1806. .1862
Paré, Ambrose. French Surgeon . . . . 1517. .1590
Paré, or Paræus, David. German Protestant Theologian 1548. .1622
Paré, John Philip, son. Class. Schol. (*Lexicon Criticum*) 1576. .1648
Paredes, Diego Garcia y. General. *Spanish Bayard* . . 1466. .1530
Pareja, John de. Spanish Painter. . . . . 1610. .1670
Parennin, Dominic. French Jesuit Missionary to China 1665. .1741
Parent, Anthony. French Mathematician . . . . 1666. .1716
Parent-du-Châtelet, Alex. John Bapt. Sanitary Writer 1790. .1836
Parfait, Francis. Historian of the French Drama . . . . . . 1698. .1753
Parini, Joseph. Italian Poet. (*Il Giorno*). . . . . 1729. .1799
Paris, Francis. French Ecclesiastic. (*Lives of the Saints*) — . .1718
Paris, Francis, Abbé. French Ascetic. . . . . 1690. .1727
Paris, John Ayrton, M. D. English Physician. (*Philosophy in Sport*). . . . . 1785. .1856
Paris, Matthew. Historian . . . . — . .1259
Parish, Elijah. American Clergyman and Author. . . . . . 1762. .1825
Parisot, Peter. *Father Norbert.* French Missionary. . . 1697. .1769
Park, Sir James Allan. Lawyer and Religious Writer. . — . .1839
Park, Thomas. Antiquary and Poet . . . . 1759?.1834
Parke, John. Musician. . . . . 1745. .1829
Parke, Mungo. Traveler. Life by Rennell, 1815 . . . . . . 1771. .1805
Parker, Henry, Lord Morley. Favorite of Henry VII. . . 1476?.1556
Parker, Isaac. American Jurist. 1768. .1830
Parker, John. Dissenting Minister and Poet . . . . — . .1793
Parker, Matthew. Abp. of Canterbury. L. by Strype, 1711 1504. .1575
Parker, Nathan. American Clergyman . . . . 1782. .1833
Parker, Richard. Seaman; Mutineer at the Nore. . . . . . — . .1797
Parker, Sam. Bp. of Oxford. (*De Rebus sui Temporis*) 1640. .1688
Parker, Theodore. Amer. Unitarian. L. by Weiss, 1863 1810. .1860
Parkes, Joseph, M. P. Politician . . . . 1796. .1865
Parkes, Samuel. Chemical Philosopher. . . . . 1759. .1825
Parkhurst, John, Bp. of Norwich. Protestant Reformer 1511. .1574
Parkhurst, John. (*Lexicon of the Greek Testament*). . . . 1728. .1797
Parkinson, John. Herbalist. (*Paradisus*). . . . . 1567. .1640?
Parkinson, Thomas. Mathematician . . . . 1745. .1830
Parma, Alex. Farnese, 3d. Duke of. Regent of Netherlands 1546. .1592
Parmenides. Eleatic Philosopher. . . . . 5th c. B.C.
Parmenio. Macedonian General. . . . . 490?.330 B.C.
Parmentier, James. French Painter in England . . . . . . 1658. .1730
Parmentier, John. French Navigator and Geographer 1494. .1530
Parmigiano, or Parmigianino, Il. *Francis Mazzuoli.*
    Italian Painter. Life by Coxe, 1823 . . . . 1503. .1540
Parnell, Sir Henry Brooke, First Lord Congleton. Polit. 1776. .1842
Parnell, Rev. Dr. Thomas. Poet. Life by O. Goldsmith 1679. .1717
Parny, Évariste Désiré Desforges. French Poet. . . . . . . 1753. .1814
Parodi, Dominic, of Genoa. Painter and Sculptor. . . . . . 1668. .1740

BORN. DIED.

Parr, Catherine. Queen of Henry VIII. .... 1509..1548
Parr, Richard, D. D. Divine. (*Life of Usher*)......... 1617..1691
Parr, Dr. Samuel. Divine and Scholar. Life by John
    Johnstone, 1828................................... 1747..1825
Parr, Thomas. *Old Parr.* Centenarian............... 1483..1635
Parrenin, or Parennin, Dominic. Fr. Jesuit Missionary 1665..1741
Parrhasius. Greek Painter. Life by Carlo Dati...... fl. B.C. 400?
Parrhasius, Aulus Janus. *Gianpaolo Parisio.* Ital. Critic 1470..1534
Parrocel, Charles. Painter .... 1688..1753
Parrocel, Joseph. French Painter and Engraver ...... 1648..1704
Parrocel, Peter. Painter of Battles.................. 1665?.1739
Parrot, John James Frederick William. German Natural
    Philosopher....................................... 1792..1841
Parry, Caleb Hillier. Physician and Naturalist........ 1756..1822
Parry, John. *The Blind Harper*.................... — ..1782
Parry, Richard, D. D. Theologian .... 1722..1780
Parry, Sir Wm. Edward. Arctic Navig. L. by E. Parry 1790..1855
Parsons, Mrs. Novelist and Dramatist................ — ..1811
Parsons, James. Physician and Antiquary........... 1705..1770
Parsons, Robert. Jesuit. Life by Thomas James, 1612 1546..1610
Parsons, Theophilus. American Jurist .... 1750..1813
Parsons, William. Comic Actor and Painter......... 1736..1795
Parthenay, Catherine de. French Writer............. 1554..1631
Partridge, Alden. American Soldier .... 1785?.1854
Paruta, Paul. Venetian Historian. (*Discorsi Politici*).. 1540..1598
Paruta, Philip. Sicilian Antiquary.................. — ..1629
Pas, Anthony de, Marquis de Feuquière. Field Marshal 1648..1711
Pas, Passe, or Paas, Crispin. German Engraver........ — ..1643?
Pas, Manasses de, Mqs. de Feuquière. Gen. & Negotiator 1590..1640
Pascal, Blaise. French Mathematician and Philosopher.
    (*Pensées*.) Life by Bossut; Madame Périer .... 1623..1662
Pascal, Jacqueline, sister. Misc. Writ. L. by Cousin, 1849 1625..1661
Paschal I. Pope (817–24).......................... — .. 824
Paschal II. (1099–1118.) *Rainerius,* or *Raginerus*.... — ..1118
Paschal III. (1164–68.) *Guy de Crema.* Antipope... — ..1168
Paschal, or Pasquali, Charles. French Writer......... 1547..1625
Paschasius-Radbert. French Monk. (*Sacrament*) ... fl. 840?
Paschius, George. German Lutheran Divine and Scholar 1661..1707
Paskevitch, Ivan Feodorovitch. Russian General ..... 1782..1856
Pasley, General Sir Charles William. Engineer .... 1781..1861
Pasquali, Signor, of Edinburgh. Violinist........... — ..1757
Pasqualino. *Pasquale Rossi.* Italian Painter........ 1641..1700
Pasquier, Stephen. Fr. Civilian and Poet. (*Recherches*) 1529..1615
Pasquier, Stephen Denis. French Statesman.......... 1767..1862
Passe, Pas, or Paas, Crispin. German Engraver....... — ..1643?
Passemant, Claude Simeon. French Mechanician..... 1702..1769
Passerat, John. French Critic and Poet.............. 1534..1602
Passeri, John Baptist. Painter & Poet. (*Lives of Painters*) 1610?.1679
Passeri, John Baptist. Italian Antiquary............. 1694..1780
Passeri, Joseph. Portrait Painter .... 1654..1714
Passeroni, John Charles. Italian Poet .... 1713..1803
Passerotti, Bartholomew, of Bologna. Portrait Painter 1540?.1595
Passignano, Dominic Cresti, Il. Painter.............. 1558..1638
Passinelli, Lorenzo. Bolognese Painter.............. 1629?.1700

BORN. DIED.

Passionei, Dominic, Cardinal. Nuncio. (*Acta Legatio-
nis Helveticæ.*) Life by Galetti, 1762.............. 1682..1761
Passow, Francis Louis Charles Frederick. Ger. Philol. 1786..1833
Pasta, Judith. Italian Singer....................... 1798..1865
Patel, Peter. French Painter .... 1654..1703
Patenier, Joachim de. Painter................... 1490..1545?
Pater, John Baptist. French Painter .... 1695..1736
Pater, Paul. Hungarian Protestant Exile. Mathematician 1656..1724
Paterculus, Caius Velleius. Roman Historian...... B.C.19?.A.D.31?
Paterson, Sam. Bibliographer. (*Bibliotheca Universalis*) 1728..1802
Paterson, William. Projector. Life by Bannister, 1858 1660.. —
Patin, Charles. Physician and Antiquary............ 1633..1693
Patin, Guy. French Physician...................... 1601..1672
Patkul, John Reginald. Livonian Patriot............ 1660..1707
Patrick, St. Apostle of Ireland. Life by Probus; Joce-
lin, tr. by E. L. Swift, 1809; J. H. Todd, 1863 ...... 372.. 493?
Patrick, Samuel. Critic. (*Clavis Homerica*)......... — ..1748
Patrick, Simon. Bishop of Chichester. Commentator.
Life by self.................................... 1626..1707
Patrin, Eugene Louis Melchior. Fr. Geol. & Mineralogist 1742..1815
Patrix, Peter. French Poet....................... 1583..1671
Patrizi, Francis. Ital. Philos. (*Discussiones Peripateticæ*) 1529..1597
Patru, Oliver. Fr. Lawyer, Critic, & Orator. (*Plaidoyers*) 1604..1681
Patten, Thomas, D. D. Theologian.... .... — ..1762
Patterson, Daniel T. American Naval Officer......... — ..1839
Pattison, William. Poet........................ 1706..1727
Patu, Claude Peter. French Poet and Dramatist....... 1729..1757
Paucton, Alexis John Peter. French Mathematician... 1732..1798
Paul, St. Apostle of the Gentiles .... — .. 65?
Paul, of Samosata. Bishop of Antioch .... — .. 273?
Paul, the Deacon, of Aquileia. (*History of the Lombards*) 740?. 799?
Paul I. Pope (757–67). Life by Cardinal Querini .... — .. 767
Paul II. (1464–71.) *Peter Barbo.* Life by Querini.. 1418..1471
Paul III. (1534–49.) *Alexander Farnese.* L. by Querini 1468..1549
Paul IV. (1555–59.) *John Peter Caraffa.* Life by Car-
dinal Navagero..................................... 1476..1559
Paul V. (1605–21.) *Camillus Borghese*.............. 1552..1621
Paul I. Emperor of Russia (1796–1801).............. 1754..1801
Paul, Duke of Würtemberg. Ger. Trav. and Naturalist 1797..1860
Paul of Burgos, or de Santa Maria. (*Scrutinium*) ..... 1350?.1435
Paul Veronese. Painter. *See* Cagliari .... 1530?.1588
Paul, Father. *See* Sarpi .... 1552..1623
Paul, Vincent de. Philanthropist. Life by Collet, 1818 1576..1660
Paula, St. Roman Ascetic; Disciple of St. Jerome..... 347.. 404
Paulding, James Kirke. American Author............ 1779..1860
Paulett, Lord William. M. P. for Lymington .... 1666..1729
Pauli, Gregory. Polish Protestant Divine............. — ..1591?
Paulian, Aimé Henry. French Jesuit. Writer........ 1722..1802
Paulin de St. Barthélemi. Missionary in India....... 1748..1806
Paulinus. Bishop of York and of Rochester. *Apostle
of Yorkshire*...................................... 597?. 644
Paulinus. Patriarch of Aquileia. Trinitarian Writer .. 726?. 804
Paulinus, Pontius Meropius, St. Bishop of Nola. (*Let-
ters; Poems*)...................................... 353.. 431

BORN. DIED.

Paulli, Simon. Physician and Naturalist. (*Flora Danica*) 1603..1680
Paullini, Christian Francis. Physician and Naturalist.. 1643..1712
Paulmier de Grentemesnil, James. Phys., Critic, Poet 1587..1670
Paulmier de Grentemesnil, Julian de. Physician.... 1520..1598
Paulmy, Mark Anthony René de Voyer, Marquis of.
  Statesman. (*Mélanges*)........................ 1722..1787
Paulus, Dr. Henry Eberhard Gottlob. Ger. Theologian 1761..1851
Paulus, Julius. Roman Lawyer .... ti. Alex. Severus
Paulus, Peter. Grand Pensionary. (*Treaty of Utrecht*) 1754..1796
Paulus Ægineta. Greek Medical Writer .... fl. 7th c.
Paulus Æmilius. Italian Historian.................. — ..1529
Paulus Æmilius, Lucius. Rom. General; fell at Cannæ — B.C.216
Paulus Æmilius, L. *Macedonicus.* Conq. of Perseus 230?.160 B.C.
Pausanias. Spartan Commander .... — B.C.470?
Pausanias. Greek Topographer..................... fl. 174
Pausias. Painter of Sicyon.......................... fl. B.C. 350?
Pautre, Anthony le. French Architect................ 1614..1691
Pautre, John le. Engraver........................ 1617..1682
Pautre, Peter le. Sculptor. (*Æneas and Anchises*).... 1660..1744
Pauw, Cornelius, or Nicholas de. Dutch Writ. in Germany 1739..1799
Pauw, or Paaw, Peter. *Pavius.* Dutch Phys. and Anat. 1564..1617
Pavillon, Nicholas. French Bishop and Divine........ 1597..1677
Pavillon, Stephen. French Scholar and Poet.......... 1632..1705
Pawlett, William, First Marquess of Winchester. Life by
  Rowland Broughton, ed. by Sir E. Brydges, 1818.... 1475..1572
Paxton, Sir Joseph, M.P. Horticulturist and Architect.. 1803..1865
Payne, John Howard. American Actor and Dramatist 1792..1852
Payne, Roger. Bookbinder......................... 1739..1797
Pays, René le. Fr. Writ. (*Amitiés, Amours, et Amourettes*) 1636..1690
Payson, Edward, D.D. Amer. Div. L. by Asa Cummings 1783..1827
Pazmani, Peter. Hungarian Cardinal. Theologian.... 1570..1637
Peabody, Oliver Wm. Bourn. Amer. Clergym. & Writer 1799..1848
Peabody, William Bourn Oliver, brother. Clergyman. 1799..1847
Peacham, Henry. Writer. (*Complete Gentleman*)..... — ..1640?
Peacock, George. Dean of Ely. Mathem. and Astron. — ..1858
Peacock, Reginald. Bp. of Chichester. L. by J. Lewis 1390?.1460?
Peale, Charles Wilson. American Painter............. 1741..1827
Peale, Rembrandt, son. Painter..................... 1778..1860
Pearce, Nathaniel. Adventurer in Abyssinia. L. by Hall 1780..1820
Pearce, Zachary. Bishop of Rochester. Commentator.
  Life by Derby .... 1690..1774
Pearne, Thomas. *Gregory Blunt.* Unitarian Writer... — ..1827
Pearson, Edward, D.D., of Cambridge. Controversialist 1760?.1811
Pearson, George, M.D. Physician and Experim. Chemist 1751..1828
Pearson, John, Bishop of Chester. (*Expos. of the Creed*) 1613..1686
Pearson, John, F.R.S. Surgeon. Biographer of Hey.. 1758..1826
Pearson, Mrs. Margaret Eglinton. Painter on Glass.... — ..1823
Pearson, Richard, M.D. Phys. (*Thesaur. Medicaminum*) 1765..1836
Pease, Calvin, D.D. American Writer and Educator ... 1813..1863
Pecchio, Joseph. Italian Writer .... 1785..1835
Pechantre, Nicholas de. French Poet and Dramatist .. 1638..1708
Pechlin, John Nicholas. Dutch Medical Writer .... 1646..1706
Pechmeja, John. French Writer. (*Télèphe*).......... 1741..1785
Peck, Rev. Francis. Antiq. (*Desiderata.*) L. by Evans 1692..1743

BORN. DIED.

Peck, John Mason, D. D.   American Divine............ 1789..1858
Peckham, John. Archbishop of Canterbury (1279–92) .. — ..1292
Pecorone, John Florentino. Florentine Writer. (*Novellï*) — ..1380?
Pecquet, Anthony. French Writer................... 1704..1762
Pecquet, John. Fr. Physician & Anatomical Discoverer 1622..1674
Pedro, of Portugal and Brazil. *See* Peter .... 1798..1834
Pedrusi, or Pedruzzi, Paul. Historian and Antiquary.. 1644..1720
Peel, Sir Robert, First Baronet. Cotton Manufacturer .. 1750..1830
Peel, Sir Robert. Prime Minister. Life by Dr. W. C.
    Taylor and C. Mackay, 1847–51; Doubleday, 1856;
    Lawrence Peel, 1860; Guizot...................... 1788..1850
Peel, Sir William. Captain of Naval Brigade in India.. 1824..1858
Peele, George. Poet. Life by Dyce.............. 1552?.1598?
Pegge, Rev. Samuel, LL. D. Antiq. L. by Samuel Pegge 1704..1796
Pegge, Samuel, son. (*Curialia*)................ 1731..1800
Peignot, Stephen Gabriel. French Bibliographer ...... 1767..1849
Peins, Gregory. *See* Pens...................... 1500..1550?
Peirce, Cyrus. American Educator................. 1790..1859
Peirce, James. Dissenting Divine................. 1673..1726
Peiresc, Nicholas Claude Fabri de. Scholar and Promoter
    of Learning. Life by Gassendi, 1641, tr. by Rand, 1657 1580..1637
Pekah. King of Israel (B. C. 759–739).............. —B.C. 739
Pekahiah. King of Israel (B.C. 761–759)............ — B.C. 759
Pelagius. British Heresiarch .... fl. 410
Pelagius I. Pope (555–60)..................... 495?. 560
Pelagius II. (578–90)....................... 520.. 590
Pelayo, First King of Asturias (718–37)............... — .. 737
Pelham, Henry. Statesman .... 1695..1764
Pelham-Hollez, Thomas, Duke of Newcastle. Statesm. 1694..1768
Pelhestre, Peter. French Writer................... 1635?.1710
Pélissier, Aimable John James, Duke of Malakoff. Mar-
    shal of France............................. 1794..1864
Pell, John. Mathematician and Divine............... 1610..1685
Pellegrin, Simon Joseph. French Ecclesiastic and Poet 1663..1745
Pellegrini, Anthony. Historical Painter............. 1674..1741
Pellegrini, Camillo. Italian Antiquary and Poet ...... 1598..1663
Pellegrino, Tibaldi, of Bologna. Architect and Painter 1527..1600
Pellerin, Joseph. French Medalist................. 1684..1782
Pelletier, Bertrand. French Chemist............... 1761..1797
Pelletier, Claude le. French Financier .... 1630..1711
Pelletier, Gaspar. Physician & Botanist of Middleburg — ..1659
Pelletier, James, of Mans. Physician and Scholar ..... 1517..1582
Pelletier, John le. French Writer .... 1633..1711
Pelletier, Peter Joseph. Chemist.................. 1788..1842
Pellican, Conrad. Reformer and Scholar............. 1478..1556
Pellicer, Joseph de Ossau. Spanish Writer .... 1602..1679
Pellico, Silvio. Ital. Writer & Patriot. L. by Chiala, 1852 1789..1854
Pellison-Fontanier, Paul. French Writer .... 1624..1693
Pelloutier, Simon. (*Histoire des Celtes*)............ 1694..1757
Pelopidas. Theban General...................... —B.C. 364
Peltanus, Theo. Anthony. Jesuit. (*Theologia Naturalis*) — ..1584
Pemberton, Henry. Physician and Mathematician.... 1694..1771
Pembroke, Mary Sidney, Countess of. *See* Sidney .... — ..1621
Pembroke, Thomas. Painter...................... 1702..1730

BORN. DIED.

Pendleton, Edmund. American Statesman and Jurist 1721..1803
Pendleton, Henry. American Jurist .... — ..1788
Pene, or Pesne, John. French Painter and Engraver.... 1623..1700
Penington, Isaac. Persecuted Quaker Divine......... 1617..1679
Penn, Granville. Author......................... 1761..1844
Penn, Sir William. Admiral...................... 1621..1670
Penn, William, son. Quaker. Life by Janney; Thomas
 Clarkson, 1836; W. H. Dixon, 1851............... 1644..1718
Pennant, Thomas. Nat. and Antiq. (*London*.) L. by self 1726..1798
Penni, John Francis. *Il Fattore*. Italian Painter ..... 1488..1528
Pennicuick, Alexander. Scot. Physician, Poet, Writer. 1652..1722
Penrose, Thomas. Poet.......................... 1743..1779
Penruddock, John, Col. Royalist; beh. by Col. Croke — ..1655
Penry, John. Puritan Libeler. (*Martin Mar-Prelate?*).. 1559..1593
Pens, Peins, Pentz, or Pencz, Gregory. Paint. and Engrav. 1500..1550?
Pepagomenus. Greek Medical Writer. (*De Podagrá*) fl. 1270?
Pepe, William. Italian General. (*Personal Memoirs*).. 1783..1855
Pepin, son of Louis Débonnaire, King of Aquitaine
 (817–38?).. 802?.838 or 9
Pepin d'Héristal. Mayor of Palace; Duke of Austrasia — .. 714
Pepin the Short. Mayor of the Palace (741–52); King
 of France (752–68)............................... 714.. 768
Pepperell, Sir William. Amer. Gen. L. by Parsons, 1855 1697..1759
Pepusch, John Christopher. Musical Composer........ 1667..1752
Pepys, Samuel. (*Diary*.) Life by Smith, 1840........ 1632..1703
Pepys, William Haseldine, F. R. S. Experimental Philos. 1775..1856
Peranda, Santo. Historical Painter .... 1566..1638
Perau, Gabriel Louis Calabre. French Biographer..... 1700..1767
Perceval, Spencer. Prime Minister .... 1762..1812
Percier, Charles. French Architect................. 1764..1838
Percival, James Gates. American Poet............... 1795..1857
Percival, Thomas, M. D. Scottish Physician and Miscel-
 laneous Writer. (*Medical Ethics*.) Life by his son.. 1740..1804
Percy, Sir Henry. *Hotspur*. Slain at Shrewsbury..... — ..1403
Percy, Henry, Ninth Earl of Northumberland. *Wizard* 1564..1632
Percy, Thomas, D. D. Bishop of Dromore. (*Reliques*).. 1728..1811
Perdiccas. Macedonian General .... — B.C.321
Péréfixe, Hardouin de Beaumont de. (*Hist. Henry IV.*) 1605..1676
Pereira, Bartholomew. Portuguese Epic Poet. (*Paciecis*) fl. 1640
Pereira, James Roger. Spanish Instructor of Deaf Mutes 1716..1780
Pereira, Jonathan, M. D. Eng. Phys. (*Materia Medica*) 1804..1853
Pereira, Nuñez Alvarez. *Portuguese Cid.* General and
 Diplomatist .... 1360..1431
Pereira de Figueiredo, Anthony. Divine & Grammarian 1725..1797
Pereira-Gomez, Geo. Sp. Phys. (*Margarita Antoniana*) fl. 1554
Peretto. Philosopher of Padua. *See* Pomponatius.. 1462.1524 or 6
Perez, Anthony. Span. Statesman. (*Memoirs and Letters*) 1539..1611
Perez, David. Musical Composer.................... 1711..1778
Pergolesi, John Baptist. Musical Composer.......... 1710..1736
Periander. Tyrant of Corinth (B. C. 625–585)........ 665.585 B.C.
Pericles. Athenian Statesman...................... — B.C. 429
Périer, Casimir. French Financier and Statesman ..... 1777..1832
Périer, James Constantine. Fr. Mechanic. (*Steam Engines*) 1742..1818
Periers, Bonaventure des. Fr. Writer. (*Cymbalum Mundi*) — ..1544?

BORN. DIED.

Perignon, Dominic Catherine de. Peer & Marsh. of France 1754..1818
Peringskiold, John. Swed. Historian and Chronologist 1654..1720
Perit, Pelatiah. American Philanthropist .... 1785..1864
Perizonius, James Voorbroek. Dutch Philologist ..... 1651..1715
Perkin Warbeck. Pretender and Impostor .... — ..1499
Perkins, Elisha. American Physician. Inventor of Me-
    tallic Tractors................................... 1740..1799
Perkins, Jacob. American Inventor.................. 1766..1849
Perkins, Thos. Handasyd. Amer. Merchant & Philanthr. 1764..1854
Perkins, William. Calvinistic Divine .... 1558..1602
Pernety, Anthony Joseph. French Writer............ 1716..1801
Pernety, James, of Lyons. Historiographer........... 1696..1777
Péron, Francis. French Voyager and Naturalist....... 1775..1810
Perotti, Nicholas. Italian Scholar. (Cornucopia)...... 1430..1480
Pérouse, John Francis de Galaup de la. Circumnavigator 1741..1788?
Perrault, Charles. Writ. and Biog. (Parallèle des Anciens
    et Modernes; Contes de ma Mère L'Oye.) Life by self 1628..1703
Perrault, Claude. Architect......................... 1613..1688
Perrenot, Anthony. Minister of Philip II. See Granvelle 1516..1586
Perrier, Charles du. French Poet .... — ..1692
Perrier, Francis. French Painter and Engraver .... 1590?.1650
Perron, Anquetil du. French Orientalist.............. 1731..1805
Perron, James Davy du. Cardinal. (Perroniana)..... 1556..1618
Perronet, John Rodolph. French Civil Engineer ...... 1708..1794
Perrot, Sir John. Statesman .... 1527..1592
Perrot d'Ablancourt, Nicholas. French Writer ...... 1606..1664
Perry, James. Polit. Writer. Ed. of Morning Chronicle 1756..1821
Perry, John, Captain R. N. Engineer .... 1670?.1733
Perry, Matthew Calbraith. United States Naval Officer 1795..1858
Perry, Oliver Hazard. American Naval Officer........ 1785..1820
Perseus. Last King of Macedon (B. C. 178–168) .... aft. 167 B.C.
Persius Flaccus, Aulus. Roman Satirist............. 34.. 62
Perth, James Drummond, Sixth Earl of, and Third
    (titular) Duke of. Jacobite .... 1706..1746
Perthes, Christopher Frederick. German Bookseller.
    Life by his son................................... 1772..1843
Pertinax. Roman Emperor (193, Jan. 1–Mar. 28)...... 126.. 193
Perugino. Pietro Vanucci. Painter .... 1446..1524
Peruzzi, Balthasar da Siena. Ital. Painter and Architect 1481..1536
Pesce, Cola, or Nicholas. Sicilian Swimmer and Diver.. fl. 14th c.
Pescennius Niger. Pretender to Roman Empire...... — .. 194
Peselli, Pesello, of Florence. Painter .... 1404..1481
Pesellier, Charles Stephen. French Financier and Poet 1712..1763
Pesellino, or Francis Pesello Peselli. Painter........ 1426..1457
Pesne, or Pene, John. French Painter and Engraver... 1623..1700
Pestalozzi, John Henry. Educationist. Life by Biber,
    1841; Von Raumer, 1855........................ 1746..1827
Petavius, or Petau, Dionysius. French Jesuit. Chronol-
    ogist, Theologian, and Divine .... 1583..1652
Peter, St. One of the Twelve Apostles .... — ab. 65
Peter, St. Bishop of Alexandria (300–11)............ — .. 311
Peter, St. Chrysologus. Bishop of Ravenna (433–50).. — .. 450
Peter. The Hermit. Preacher of the First Crusade .... 1050?.1115
Peter. The Venerable. Abbot of Clugny .... 1093?.1156

BORN. DIED.

Peter I. King of Aragon (1094–1104) .... — ..1104
Peter II. (1196–1213) .... 1174..1213
Peter III. (1276–1285.) *The Great* .... 1239..1285
Peter IV. (1336–87.) *The Ceremonious*............. 1317..1387
Peter. King of Castile. *The Cruel*. L. by Dillon, 1788 1319..1369
Peter I. Emperor of Russia (1689–1725). *The Great.*
    Life by Mottley, 1739; Prince Sherebatoff, 1774; Von
    Halem, 1804... 1672..1725
Peter II. (1727–30.) *Alexievitch*..................... 1715..1730
Peter III. (1762.) *Feodorovitch*...................... 1728..1762
Peter I. King of Portugal (1357–67). *The Severe* .... 1320..1367
Peter II. Regent (1667–83), King (1683–1706)........ 1648..1706
Peter III.. — ..1786
Peter IV. (1826, Feb. 18–May 2), I. Emperor of Brazil
    (1822–31).. 1798..1834
Peter V. (1853–61)................................... 1837..1861
Peter I. Emp. of Brazil (1822–31), IV. King of Portugal 1798..1834
Peter. *The Wild Boy*. Found 1725 .... 1713..1785
Peter, Duke of Coimbra. *Dom Pedro*. Regent of Portugal 1392..1449
Peter of Blois. *Petrus Blesensis*. Archd. of Lond. Writ. 1120?..1200?.
Peter of Calabria. *Pomponius Lætus*. Hist. and Antiq. 1425..1497
Peter Comestor. Fr. Ecclesiastic. (*Hist. Ecclesiastica*) — ..1198
Peter Nolasque, St. Founder of the Order of Mercy .. 1189?.1256
Peterborough, Chas. Mordaunt, 3d Earl of. Commander 1658..1735
Peterkin. Scottish Miscellaneous Writer .... 1781..1846
Peters, Bonaventure, of Antwerp. Marine Painter..... 1614..1652
Peters, Francis Lucas, of Mechlin. Painter.......... 1606..1654
Peters, or Peter, Hugh. Fanatic. L. by Wm. Harris, 1751 1599..1660
Peters, John. Marine Painter....................... 1625..1677
Peters, Richard. American Jurist.................... 1744..1828
Peters, Rev. Samuel. American Historian .... 1735..1826
Péthion de Villeneuve, Jerome. French Revolutionist 1753..1794
Petigru, James Louis. American Lawyer and Statesman 1789..1863
Pétion. *Anne Alex. Sabès*. President of St. Domingo.. 1770..1818
Pétis de la Croix, Francis. French Orientalist........ 1653..1713
Petit, Anthony, of Orleans. Physician and Anatomist.. 1722..1794
Petit, Francis. *Pourfour du Petit*. Fr. Phys. & Anatomist 1664..1741
Petit, John Louis. French Surgeon.................. 1674..1750
Petit, Lewis Hayes, F. R. S., M. P. Patron of Literature.. 1774..1849
Petit, Peter. Fr. Mathematician and Natural Philosopher 1598?.1677
Petit, Peter. French Physician, Historian, and Poet.... 1617..1687
Petit, Samuel. French Protestant Divine. (*Leges Atticæ*) 1594..1643
Petit-Thouars, Louis Mary Albert du. French Botanist 1758..1831
Petitot, Claude Bernard. Historical Collector .... 1772..1825
Petitot, John. Painter in Enamel................... 1607..1691
Petiver, James. Naturalist......................... — ..1718
Petoefi, Sandor, or Alexander. Hungarian Song Writer 1823..1849
Petrarch, Francis. Italian Poet. L. by Leonard Aretino,
    1672; Manetti; Tommasini; Abbé de Sade, 1764; Fa-
    broni, 1799; Mrs. Dobson, 1805; Thomas Campbell, 1841 1304..1374
Petre, Edward. Jesuit. Confessor to James II........ 1631..1699
Petre, Sir William. Statesman and Scholar....:...... — ..1572
Petrie, Henry. Record Antiquary................... 1768..1842
Petronius, Titus. *Arbiter*. Friend of Nero. (*Satyricon*) — .. 66

BORN. DIED.

Petroff, Basil Petrovitch. Russian Poet............... 1736..1799
Petrus Aponis, or Peter di Abano. Phys. and Astrologer 1250..1315
Petrus Hispanus. Medical Writer, afterwards Pope
    John XX. or XXI. .... — ..1277
Pett, Sir Peter. Political Writer .... 1630.. —
Pettigrew, Thomas James, F. R. S. Antiquary .... 1790..1865
Pettus, Sir John, M. P. Writer on Mines and Metals ... — ..1690
Petty, Sir William. (*Political Arithmetic*)............ 1623..1687
Petty, William, Earl of Shelburne, Marquess of Lans-
    downe. Premier................................. 1737..1805
Petty-Fitzmaurice, Henry, Marquess of Lansdowne... 1780..1863
Petyt, William. Legal Antiquary.................... 1636..1707
Peucer, Gaspard. German Physician and Mathematician 1525..1602
Peurbach, or Purbach, George. German Astronomer .. 1423..1461
Peuteman, Peter. Dutch Painter .... 1650..1692
Peutinger, Conrad. German Scholar and Antiquary... 1465..1547
Peyer, John Conrad. Swiss Anatomist. Discoverer ... 1653..1712
Peyre, Anthony Francis. French Painter and Architect 1739..1823
Peyrère, Isaac de la. French Writer. (*Præ-Adamitæ*) 1594..1676
·**Peyron,** John Francis Peter. French Historical Painter 1744..1814
Peyronnet, Charles Ignatius, Count de. Fr. Statesman 1775..1854
Peysonnel, Charles de, of Marseilles. Antiq. and Trav. 1700..1757
Peysonnel, Charles de, son. Historical and Polit. Writer 1727..1790
Pezarese, Il. Painter. *See* Cantarini .... 1612:..1648
Pezay, Alex. Fred. James Masson, Mqs. de. Fr. Writer 1741..1777
Pezenas, Esprit. French Mathematician .... 1692..1776
Pezron, Paul. Abbé. Biblical Writer................ 1639..1706
Pfanner, Tobias. German Historian and Political Writer 1641..1717
Pfeffel, Christian Frederick. Jurisconsult & Diplomatist 1726..1807
Pfeffel, Theophilus Conrad, of Colmar. Poet........ 1736..1809
Pfeffercorn, John. Converted Jew. (*De Abolendis*).... — ..1520?
Pfeiffer, Augustus. German Orientalist............... 1640..1698
Pfeiffer, Francis Louis. Swiss General in France ...... 1716..1802
Pfeiffer, Ida. Traveler........................... 1795..1858
Pfeiffer, Louis, of Lucerne. General of Charles IX..... 1530..1594
Pfister, Albert. Printer .... 1420?.1470?
Phædrus. Latin Fabulist........................... fl. 8
Phaer, Thomas. Welsh Physician and Poet........... — ..1560
Phalaris. Tyrant of Agrigentum .... —B.C.554?
Phavorinus. *Guarino.* (*Etymologicum Magnum*) ..... — ..1537
Phelps, Elizabeth Stuart. American Writer........... 1815..1852
Pherecydes. Greek Philosopher .... fl. ab. B.C.544
Pherecydes. Greek Logographer.................... fl. ab. B.C.480
Phidias. Greek Sculptor .... 490?.432 B.C.
Philander, William. French Writer on Vitruvius, &c... 1505..1565
Philelphus, Francis. Italian Scholar .... 1398..1481
Philemon. Athenian Comic Poet.................... 360?.262 B.C.
Philidor, Francis Andrew Danican. Musician and Chess
    Player .... 1726..1795
Philip II. King of Macedon (B. C. 359–336). Father of
    Alexander. Life by Olivier; Leland, 1758 .... 382.336 B.C.
Philip Arrhidæus, son................................ —B.C. 317?
Philip V. (B. C. 220–179.) Defeated at Cynoscephalæ. 237.179 B.C.
Philip. Emperor of Rome. (244–249)................ — .. 249?

BORN. DIED.

Philip I. King of France. (1060–1108)............... 1052..1108
Philip II. (1130–1223.) *Augustus.* Life by Gulielmus
  Brito; Baudot de Juilli, 1702..................... 1165..1223
Philip III. (1270–85.) *The Hardy.* L. by Wm. de Nangis 1245..1285
Philip IV. (1285–1314.) *The Fair*................. 1268..1314
Philip V. (1317–22.) *The Long*.................... 1294..1322
Philip VI. (1328–50.) *De Valois*.................. 1293..1350
Philip I. King of Spain (1504–6).................. 1478..1506
Philip II. (1555–98.) Life by Cabrera; Leti; Prescott 1527..1598
Philip III. (1598–1621)............................ 1578..1621
Philip IV. (1621–65).............................. 1605..1665
Philip V. (1700–46.) *Duke of Anjou.* L. by Baccal. Sanna 1683..1746
Philip II. Duke of Burgundy. (House of Valois.)
  (1363–82.) *The Hardy*........................... 1342..1404
Philip III. (1419–67.) *The Good*................. 1396..1467
Philip. Duke of Swabia. Elected Emperor, 1198 ..... 1178..1208
Philip. Duke of Orleans. Regent of France.......... 1674..1723
Philip. *King.* Sachem of Pokanoket................ — ..1676
Philip, St., of Neri. Founder of the Oratory........ 1515..1595
Philip, of the Holy Trinity. Fr. Miss. (*Itin. Orientale*) 1603..1671
Philipot, John. (*Villare Cantianum*)............... — ..1645
Philippa, of Hainault, Queen of Edward III. .... — ..1369
Philippi, Henry. German Jesuit. Chronological Writer 1575..1636
Philippon, Armand, Baron. French General.......... 1761..1836
Philips, Ambrose. Poet .... 1671..1749
Philips, Mrs. Catherine. Poetess .... 1631..1664
Philips, Charles. Captain R. N. Navigator .... 1780..1840
Philips, Fabian. Royalist. Political Writer .... 1601..1690
Philips, John. Poet. (*Splendid Shilling ; Blenheim.*) Life
  by Sewel... 1676..1708
Philistus. Greek Historian of Syracuse............. 435?.356 B.C.
Phillimore, John Geo., Q. C., M. P. Law Writer & Hist. 1809..1865
Phillip, Arthur. Navigator......................... 1738..1814
Phillips, Charles. Irish Barrister.................. 1789..1859
Phillips, Edw.; nephew of Milton. (*Theatrum Poetarum*) 1630..1680
Phillips, George. German Jurist.................... 1804..1860
Phillips, John. American Merchant and Scholar ...... 1719..1795
Phillips, Sir Richard. Writer...................... 1768..1840?
Phillips, Richard, F. R. S. Pharmaceutical Chemist .... 1778..1851
Phillips, Samuel. Amer. Merchant and Philanthropist 1751..1802
Phillips, Samuel, LL. D. Essayist and Novelist .... 1815..1854
Phillips, Thomas. Rom. Cath. Div. (*Life of Card. Pole*) 1708..1774
Phillips, Thomas. (*History of Shrewsbury*)............ — ..1815
Phillips, Thomas, R. A. Portrait Painter............ 1770..1845
Phillips, Wm., F. R. S., F. G. S. Mineralog. & Crystallog. 1773..1828
Philo Judæus. Jewish Philos., of Alexandria... B.C.20?.aft.A.D.40
Philopœmen. Greek Commander .... 252.183 B.C.
Philostorgius. Ecclesiastical Historian............... 367?. 430?
Philostratus. (*De Vitâ Apollonii*)................... 172?. —
Philotheus. Patriarch of Constantinople............. — ..1371?
Philpot, Rev. Charles. Poetical Writer............. — ..1823
Philpot, John. Archdeacon. Protestant Martyr....... — ..1555
Phipps, Constantine, Lord Mulgrave. Navig. and Polit. 1744..1792
Phipps, Constantine Henry. Mqs. of Normanby. Statesm. 1797..1863

21

BORN. DIED.

Phips, or **Phipps**, Sir William. Colonial Governor of Massachusetts .... 1651..1695
Phocas. Emperor of the East (602-10) .... — .. 610
Phocion. Athenian General. Life by Hugh Todd... 402?.317 B.C.
Phocylides, of Miletus. Philosopher and Poet .... fl. B.C. 535?
Photius. Patriarch of Constantinople. (*Myriobiblon*).. 815?. 891?
Phranza, George. Greek Historian.................. 1401..1478?
Phryne. Athenian Courtesan...................... fl. 4th c. B.C.
Physick, Philip Syng. Amer. Physician and Surgeon.. 1768..1837
Pia, Philip Nicholas. French Chemist; Restorer of the drowned .... 1721..1799?
Piazza, Jerome Bartholomew. Writer on the Inquisition — ..1745?
Piazzetta, John Baptist, of Venice. Painter........ 1682 or 3.1754
Piazzi, Joseph. Italian Astronomer.................. 1746..1826
Pibrac, Guy de Faur, Lord of. Lawyer and Poet. (*Quatrains*).................................... 1529..1584
Picard, John. French Astronomer and Mathematician.. 1620..1682
Picard, Louis Benedict. French Dramatic Writer...... 1769..1828
Picart, Bernard. French Engraver .... 1673..1733
Picart, Stephen. *Le Romain.* French Engraver....... 1631..1721
Piccart, Michael. German Philosopher and Critic ..... 1574..1620
Piccini, Nicholas. Neapolitan Musical Composer ...... 1728..1800
Piccolomini, Alexander. Abp. Dramatist and Philos. 1508..1578
Piccolomini, Francis. Italian Philosopher........... 1520..1604
Piccolomini, James. Cardinal. *Ammanati.* Historian 1422..1479
Piccolomini, Octavius. Austrian Gen. in 30 Years' War 1599..1656
Pichegru, Charles. French General .... 1761..1804
Pichler, Caroline. German Novelist................. 1769..1843
Pichon, John. French Jesuit. (*The Spirit of Jesus Christ*) 1683..1751
Picken, Andrew. Miscellaneous Writer.............. 1788..1833
Pickens, Andrew. American Revolutionary General.... 1739..1817
Pickering, John. Amer. Scholar, Philologist, and Jurist 1777..1846
Pickering, Timothy. Amer. Revolutionary Statesman 1746..1829
Pickersgill, Henry William. Artist .... 1782..1861
Pickett, Albert James. American Historian........... 1810..1858
Pico, John, della Mirandola. Ital. Philos. and Theologian 1463..1494
Pictet, Benedict, of Geneva. Divine and Historian .... 1655..1724
Pictet, Mark Augustus, of Geneva. Natural Philosopher 1752..1825
Pictet de Richemont, Charles. Swiss Agriculturist... 1755..1824
Picton, Sir Thomas. General. Life by H. B. Robinson — ..1815
Picus, John, of Mirandola. Scholar. L. by J. F. Picus 1463..1494
Picus, John Francis, nephew. Theologian and Poet.... 1469..1533
Pidding, H. J. Artist............................... 1797?.1864
Pidou de St. Olon, Francis. Fr. Ambassador and Writ. 1640..1720
Pierce, Edward. Painter............................ — ..1680?
Pierce, James, of Exeter. Presbyterian Divine........ — ..1730
Pierer, Henry Augustus. German Publisher........... 1794..1850
Pierino, or Pierino del Vaga. *Buonaccorsi.* Ital. Painter 1501..1547
Piermarini, Joseph. Italian Architect............... 1734..1808
Pierquin, John. French Divine..................... 1672..1742
Pierre, Corneille de la, or Cornelius à Lapide. Comment. — ..1657
Pierson, Christopher. Historical and Portrait Painter.. 1631..1714
Pietro da Pietri. Historical Painter of Rome......... 1671..1716
Pietro della Francesca. Florentine Painter.......... 1398?.1483?

BORN. DIED.

Pigafetta, Francis Anthony. Voyager .... 1491?.aft.1534
Pigalle, John Baptist. French Sculptor .... 1714..1785
Piganiol de la Force, John Aymar. (*History of Paris*) 1673..1753
Pighius, Albert. Ger. Roman Catholic Controversialist 1490?.1542
Pighius, Stephen Wynants, nephew. Antiquary....... 1520..1604
Pignone, Simon, of Florence. Painter.............. 1614..1698
Pignoria, Lawrence. Ital. Antiquary. (*The Isiac Tablet*) 1571..1631
Pignotti, Lawrence. Ital. Poet & Hist. (*Fables; Tuscany*) 1739..1812
Pigray, Peter. French Surgeon .... — ..1613
Pike, Zebulon Montgomery. American General........ 1779..1813
Pilate, Pontius. Roman Governor of Judæa........... — .. 38?
Pilatre du Rosiér, Francis. Aëronaut .... 1756..1785
Piles, Roger de. French Writer and Painter......... 1635..1709
Pilkington, James. Bishop of Durham. Prot. Reformer 1520..1575
Pilkington, Jas. Dissenting Div. (*View of Derbyshire*) 1752..1804
Pilkington, Mrs. Lætitia. Poetess.................. 1712..1750
Pilkington, Mrs. Mary. Writer..................... 1766..1840?
Pilkington, Rev. Matthew, LL. B. Biblical Scholar.... — ..1765
Pillans, James, LL. D. Prof. at Edinburgh. Educationist 1778..1864
Pilon, Frederick. Irish Dramatic Writer............. 1750..1788
Pilon, Germain. French Sculptor and Architect ...... 1515?.1590?
Pinæus, or Pineau, Severinus. French Surgeon .... 1550..1619
Pinchbeck, Thomas. Mechanician................... — ..1783
Pinciano, Alonzo Lopez. Span. Phys. (*Art of Poetry*) 1250?. —
Pinckney, Charles Cotesworth. American Revolution-
  ary Officer and Diplomatist .... — ..1825
Pinckney, Thomas, brother. Officer and Statesman ... — ..1828
Pindar. Theban Lyric Poet........................ 518.442? B.C.
Pindar, Sir Paul. Diplomatist...................... — ..1650
Pindemonte, Hippolytus, Count. Italian Poet........ 1753..1828
Pindemonte, John, brother. Dramatic Writer .... 1751..1812
Pine, John. Engraver and Printer. (*Virgil; Mag. Charta*) 1690..1756
Pineau, Gabriel du. Fr. Lawyer. *Father of the People* 1573..1644
Pineda, John de. Span. Orientalist and Biblical Writer 1557..1637
Pinel, Philip. French Medical Writer .... 1745..1826
Pinelli, Bartholomew. Painter and Etcher at Rome.... 1781..1835
Pinelli, John Vincent. Italian Patron of Letters....... 1535..1601
Pinet, Anthony du, Lord of Norroy. French Writer ... — ..1584?
Pingeron, John Claude, of Lyons. Political Writer.... 1730?.1795
Pingré, Alexander Guy. Fr. Astron. (*Cométographie*) 1711..1796
Pinkerton, John. Miscellaneous Writer............. 1758..1826
Pinkney, Edward Coate. American Poet............. 1802..1828
Pinkney, William. American Lawyer. L. by Wheaton 1764..1822
Pinon, James. Fr. Lawyer and Poet. (*De Anno Romano*) — ..1641
Pinson, Richard. Printer.......................... — ..1530?
Pintelli, Baccio. Italian Architect .... — ..1494?
Pinto. Portuguese Traveler. *See* Mendez .... 1509?.1583
Pintor, Peter. Spanish Physician .... 1423..1503
Pinturicchio, Bernardin. *Bernardino Betti.* Painter.. 1454..1513
Pinzon, Martin Alonzo. Navigator.................. —aft.1492
Pinzon, Vincent Yañez. Navigator .... fl. 16th c.
Pio, Albert, Prince of Carpi. Opponent of the Reformation 1475?.1531
Piombino, Maria Anne Eliza Bonapart, Princess....... 1777..1820
Piombo, Sebastiano del. Painter................... 1485..1547

BORN. DIED.

Piozzi, Mrs. Hester Lynch. L. by self, and Hayward, 1861 1739..1821
Piper, Charles, Count. Minister of Chas. XII. of Sweden — ..1716
Piper, Francis le. English Comic Painter . . . . — ..1740
Pippi, Julius. *Giulio Romano* . . . . 1492..1546
Piranesi, Francis. Artist. . . . . 1748..1810
Piranesi, John Baptist. Engraver, Architect, Antiquary 1720..1778
Piranesi, Laura. Engraver. . . . . — ..1785
Piroli, Thomas. Italian Designer and Engraver. . . . . . . 1750..1824
Piromalli, Paul. Italian Orientalist and Missionary. . . . 1591?.1667
Piron, Alexis. French Poet and Dramatist. . . . . 1689..1773
Pisa, Leonard of, or Leonardo Fibonacci. Arithmetician. fl. 1220?
Pisan, Christina de. Historical and Poetical Writer. . . . 1363?.1431?
Pisan, Thomas. Astrologer, of Bologna. . . . . — ..1380
Pisani, Victor. Venetian General. . . . . — ..1380
Pisano, Il. *Nicholas di Pisa*. Sculptor and Architect 1200?.aft.1273
Pisano, Andrew. Architect, Sculptor, Metal Founder . . 1270..1345
Pisano, Giunta. *Giunta di Pisa*. Tuscan Painter . . . 1180?.aft.1236
Pisano, John. Architect and Sculptor. . . . . 1235?.1320
Piscator, John Fischer. German Calvinistic Divine. . . . 1546..1626
Pisistratus. Tyrant of Athens (B. C. 560–527). . . . . . . 612?.527 B.C.
Pisseleu, Anne de, Duchess d'Étampes. Favorite of
   Francis I. . . . . 1508..1576?
Pistorius, John. German Historian and Controversialist 1546..1608
Pitau, Nicholas, of Antwerp. Painter and Engraver. . . . 1633?.1676?
Pitcairn, Archibald, M.D. (*Elementa Physico-Mathemat.*) 1652..1713
Pithou, Francis. Jurist. . . . . 1544..1621
Pithou, Peter, brother. French Jurist and Philologist. . 1539..1596
Pitiscus, Bartholomew. Divine and Mathematician. . . . 1561..1613
Pitiscus, Samuel. Philologist. . . . . 1637..1717
Pitkin, Timothy. American Historian . . . . 1765..1847
Pitot, Henry. Mathematician and Engineer. . . . . 1695..1771
Pits, or Pitsius, John. Roman Catholic Biographer. . . . . 1560..1616
Pitt, Rev. Christopher. Poet and Translator. . . . . 1699..1748
Pitt, Thomas. Governor of Fort St. George. . . . . 1653..1726
Pitt, William, First Earl of Chatham. *See* Chatham. . . . 1708..1778
Pitt, Wm., son. Premier. L. by Gifford; Earl Stanhope 1759..1806
Pittacus, of Mitylene. Warrior and Sage. . . . . 652?.569 B.C.
Pitts, William. Artist . . . . 1790..1840
Pius I. Pope (142–157) . . . . — ..157
Pius II. (1458–64.) *Æneas Sylvius Piccolomini*. Life
   by J. Gobelin, 1584. . . . . 1405..1464
Pius III. (1503.) *Francis Todeschini Piccolomini*. . . . . 1439..1503
Pius IV. (1559–65.) *John Angelo de' Medici* . . . . 1499..1565
Pius V. (1566–72.) *Michael Ghislieri*. . . . . 1504..1572
Pius VI. (1775–99.) *John Ang. Braschi*. L. by Bourgoing 1717..1799
Pius VII. (1800–23.) *Barnabas Louis Chiaramonti* . . . 1742..1823
Pius VIII. (1829–30.) *Castiglione* . . . . 1761..1830
Pizarro, Francis. Conqueror of Peru . . . . 1475?.1541
Pizarro, Gonzalo, brother. Spanish Adventurer. . . . . 1506..1548
Pizzi, Joachim. Italian Poet. . . . . 1716..1790
Placcius, Vincent. German Jurist. . . . . 1642..1699
Place, Francis. Painter and Engraver. . . . . — ..1728
Place, Peter de la. French Magistrate and Writer. . . . . . 1526..1572
Placentius, Peter, or John Leo. (*Pugna Porcorum*). . . . 1500?.1550?

BORN. DIED.

Placette, John de la. Fr. Protestant. (*Essais de Morale*) 1639..1718
Placidia. Roman Empress, mother of Valentinian III... 390?. 450
Placitus Papyriensis, Sextus. (*De Medicamentis*).... fl. 4th c.
Planche, John Baptist Gustavus. French Critic .... 1808..1857
Planck, Theophilus James. German Theologian .... 1751..1833
Plantin, Christopher. French Printer at Antwerp...... 1514..1589
Planudes Maximus. Greek Monk. (*Life of Æsop*) .. —aft.1340
Plater, Felix, of Basle. French Medical Writer....... 1536..1614
Platina, Bartholomew de' Sacchi. (*History of the Popes*) 1421..1481
Plato. Greek Philosopher........................ 428?.347 B.C.
Platoff, Matvei Ivanovitch. Russian General......... 1757..1818
Platon. Archbishop of Moscow.................... 1737..1802
Plautus, Titus Maccius. Latin Comic Poet.......... 254?.184 B.C.
Playfair, John. Mathem. and Nat. Philos. of Edinburgh 1749..1819
Playfair, William. Political Writer .... 1759..1823
Playford, Henry. (*Orpheus Britannicus*)............. — ..1710?
Playford, John. Writer on Music.................... 1613..1693
Plegmund. Archbishop of Canterbury (890–914)...... — .. 914
Plempius, Vopiscus Fortunatus. Dutch Medical Writer 1601..1671
Pleyel, Ignatius. German Musical Composer.......... 1757..1831
Pleyel, Joseph Stephen Camille, son. Comp. and Pianist 1788..1855
Pliny, the Elder. (*Historia Naturalis*) .... 23.. 79
Pliny, the Younger. Proprætor; Author............. 61.aft.105
Ploos van Amstel, Cornelius. Dutch Engraver....... 1726..1798
Plot, Robert, LL. D. Natural Philosopher and Antiquary 1641..1696
Plotinus. Neoplatonic Philosopher................... 205.. 270
Plowden, Edmund. Rom. Cath. Politician & Law Writer 1518..1585
Plowden, Francis. Historical and Miscellaneous Writer — ..1829
Pluche, Noel Anthony. French Writer............... 1688..1761
Plukenet, Leonard. Botanist .... 1642..1710?
Plume, Thomas. Founder of Plumian Professorship.... 1630.. —
Plumer, William. Amer. Politician. L. by his son, 1856 1759..1850
Plumier, Charles. French Botanist .... 1646..1704
Plumptre, Rev. James. Miscellaneous Writer........ 1771..1832
Plunket, Oliver. Archbishop of Armagh; executed.... 1629..1681
Plunket, Wm. Conyngham, Lord. Ld. Chanc. of Ireland 1764..1854
Pluquet, Francis Andrew Adrian. French Writer...... 1716..1790
Plutarch. Greek Biographer and Philosopher......... 46?. 120?
Pocahontas. Daughter of Powhatan.................. 1595?.1617
Poccetti. Italian Painter. *See* Barbatelli............. 1542..1612
Pocock, Edward, D. D. Orientalist and Biblical Com-
   mentator. Life by Twells, 1740.................... 1604..1691
Pocock, Isaac. Artist and Dramatist .... 1782..1835
Pococke, Richard. Bp. of Meath. Traveler in the East 1704..1765
Podiebrad, George. King of Bohemia; Hussite....... 1420..1471
Poe, Edgar Allan. American Poet and Tale Writer .... 1811..1849
Poelemburg, Cornelius. Dutch Painter .... 1586..1660
Poellnitz, Chas. Louis, Baron von. Ger.Writer of Memoirs 1692..1775
Poerson, Charles Francis. Fr. Hist. and Portr. Painter 1653?.1725
Poggio Bracciolini, John Francis. Reviver of Learn-
   ing. Life by Dr. W. Shepherd, 1802 .... 1380..1459
Poilly, Francis. French Engraver................... 1622..1693
Poindexter, George. American Politician............ — ..1853
Poinsett, Joel Roberts. American Statesman........ 1779..1851

BORN. DIED.

Poiret, Peter. Mystical Enthusiast. (*Divine Economy*) 1646..1719
Poirier, Germain. French Chronologist and Antiquary. 1724..1803
Poirson, John Baptist. French Geographer .... 1760..1831
Pois, Anthony le. French Physician and Numismatist. 1525..1578
Poisson, Nicholas Joseph. Abbé. Philosopher....... 1637..1710
Poisson, Raymond. French Actor and Dramatist...... 1633..1690
Poisson, Simeon Denis. French Mathematician ...... 1781..1840
Poissonnier, Peter Isaac. Fr. Physician and Chemist.. 1720..1798
Poitiers, Diana de, Duchess de Valentinois............ 1500..1556
Poivre, Peter. French Naturalist and Traveler........ 1719..1786
Polan, Amand. Protestant Theologian of Basle ...... 1561..1610
Pole, Reginald. Cardinal. Abp. of Canterbury (1556–58).
  Life by T. Phillips; Beccadelli, translated by Pye.... 1500..1558
Polemo. Grecian Philosopher................. 340?.272? B.C.
Polemo. Grecian Geographer .... fl. 2d c.
Poleni, John, Marquis. Italian Mathematician........ 1683..1761
Polevoy, Nicholas Alexievitch. Siberian Writer....... 1796..1846
Polhem, Christopher. Swedish Engineer .... 1661..1751
Poli, Joseph Xavier. Italian Naturalist .... 1746..1825
Poli, Martin. Italian Chemist................... 1662..1714
Polidoro. *Da Caravaggio.* Painter................. 1495..1543
Polignac, Jules Augustus Armand Mary, Prince de.
  French Statesman; Minister of Charles X. .... 1780..1847
Polignac, Melchior de. Cardinal. Statesm. and Writer.
  (*Anti-Lucretius.*) L. by F. Chrysostom Faucher, 1777 1661..1741
Polinière, Peter. French Mathematician............. 1671..1734
Politi, Alexander. Italian Scholar.................... 1679..1752
Politian, or Poliziano, Angelo. Scholar. L. by Gresswell 1454..1494
Polk, James Knox. Eleventh President of United States 1795..1849
Polk, Leonidas. "Confederate" Bishop and General... 1806..1864
Pollajuolo, Anthony. Florentine Painter and Sculptor. 1426..1498
Pollajuolo, Peter, brother. Painter and Sculptor ...... 1428..1498
Pollajuolo, Simon del. *Il Cronaca.* Architect........ 1454..1509
Pollexfen, Sir Henry. Judge .... — ..1682
Pollio, Caius Asinius. Roman Orator, Poet, and Hist.. B.C.76.A.D.4
Pollio, Trebellius. One of the Writers of the *Historia*
  Augusta .... ti. Constantine
Pöllnitz, Chas. Louis, Baron von. Ger. Writer of Memoirs 1692..1775
Pollok, Robert. Poet. (*Course of Time.*) Life by Pol-
  lok, 1842 .... 1799..1827
Pollux, Julius. Greek Grammarian. (*Onomasticon*)... 180.. 238
Polo, Gaspar Gil. Spanish Poet and Romancist .... 1516..1572
Polo, Marco. Traveler......................... 1256?.1323
Polus, Matthæus. (*Synopsis Criticorum.*) *See* Poole... 1624..1679
Polwhele, Rev. Richard. Antiquary, Historian, Poet.
  (*Cornwall*) .... 1760..1838
Polyænus, Julius. *The Macedonian.* Writer. (*Strata-*
  gemata)... fl. 150
Polybius. Greek Historian .... 204?.122? B.C.
Polycarp. Bishop of Smyrna. Martyr.............. 80?. 160?
Polycletus. Greek Sculptor.................. fl. 452–412 B.C.
Polycrates. Tyrant of Samos.................... — B.C.522
Polydore Vergil. Historian .... 1470?.1555
Polygnotus. Greek Painter................... fl. 463–435 B.C.

BORN. DIED.

Pombal, Sebastian Joseph de Carvalho, Marquis of. Portuguese Statesman. Life, Paris, 4 vols. 12mo, 1783; J. Smith, 1843.................................... 1699..1782
Pomeranus, or John Bugenhagen. Protestant Reformer 1485..1558
Pomet, Peter, of Paris. (*General History of Drugs*).... 1658..1699
Pomey, Francis. French Jesuit. (*Pantheum Mysticum*) 1618..1673
Pomfret, John. Poet............................... 1667?.1703
Pommeraye, John Francis, of St. Maur. Eccles. Hist. 1617..1687
Pompadour, Jane Antoinette Poisson, Marchioness of... 1722..1764
Pompei, Jerome. Italian Poet. Life by Pindemonte; Cardinal Fontana.................................. 1731..1788
Pompeius, Sextus. Roman Commander .... 75.35 B.C.
Pompey the Great. Roman General .... 106.48 B.C.
Pompignan, John George le Franc de. Archbp.; Writer 1715..1790
Pompignan, John James le Franc, Marquis de, brother. Poet and Writer .... 1709..1784
Pomponatius, or Pomponazzi, Peter. *Peretto.* Aristotelian Philosopher. (*De Immortalitate Animæ*).. 1462.1524 or 6
Pomponius Lætus, Julius. *Peter of Calabria.* Historian 1425..1497
Pomponius Mela. Roman Geographer.............. fl. 50?
Pona, Francis, of Verona. Physician................. 1594..1652?
Pona, John Baptist, of Verona. Philosopher and Poet. — ..1588
Ponce, Peter de. Spanish Teacher of the Dumb........ 1530?.1584
Ponce de Leon, John. Spanish Discoverer in America 1460?.1521
Ponce de Leon, Louis. Spanish Lyric Poet .... 1528..1591
Ponce de Leon, Roderick. Spanish Commander...... 1443..1492
Pond, John. Astronomer Royal...................... 1767?.1836
Ponet, or Poynet, John. Bp. of Winchester. Reformer 1514?.1556
Poniatowski, Joseph Anthony, Prince. Polish General; Marshal of France .... 1762..1813
Poniatowski, Stanislaus. Ambassador .... 1677..1762
Poniatowski, Stanislaus Augustus, last King of Poland (1764-92)... 1732..1798
Pons, John Francis de. French Writer............... 1683..1732
Pons, Louis. French Astronomer.................... 1761..1831
Ponsonby, Sir Fred. Cavendish, K. C. B. Major-General 1783..1837
Pontanus, James. Bohemian Jesuit ; Philologist and Classical Scholar................................. 1542..1626
Pontanus, John Isaac. Danish Historian and Antiquary 1571..1639
Pontanus, Jovianus. Italian Latin Poet .... 1426..1503
Pontas, John. French Religious Writer .... 1638..1728
Ponte, Lorenzo da. Italian Poet. (*Don Juan*)........ 1749..1837
Pontedera, Julius. Italian Botanist .... 1688..1757
Pontiac. North American Indian Chief.............. 1712?.1769
Pontianus. Bishop of Rome (230-35)................ — .. 235
Pontius. Ecclesiastical Writer. (*Life of Cyprian*).... — .. 258?
Pontius, or De Fuente, Constantine. Spanish Divine... — ..1559
Pontius, Paul. Engraver .... 1596?.aft.1653
Pontoppidan, Eric. Danish Divine and Grammarian .. 1621..1678
Pontoppidan, Eric, nephew. (*Annals of Danish Church*) 1698..1764
Pontormo, James da. *Jacopo Carrucci.* Italian Painter 1493..1558
Ponz, Anthony. Span. Topographer and Writer on Art 1725..1792
Pool, Jurian van. Dutch Portrait Painter .... 1666..1745
Pool, Rachel van, wife. Flower Painter............. 1664..1750

BORN. DIED.

Poole, Matthew. (*Annotations; Synopsis Criticorum*)... 1624..1679
Poor, Daniel. American Missionary .... 1789..1855
Pope, Alexander. Poet. Life by W. Ayre, 1745; Owen
    Ruffhead, 1767; Bowles; Roscoe, 1824; R. Carruthers 1688..1744
Pope, Sir Thomas. Treasurer. L. by Rev. T. Warton, 1772 1508?.1559
Pope, Walter, M. D. Gresham Professor; Humorist..... — ..1714
Popham, Sir Home Riggs. Naval Commander........... 1762..1820
Popham, Sir John. Judge .... 1531..1607
Poppæa Sabina. Wife of Nero..................:...... — .. 65
Popple, William. Governor of Bermuda. Dramatist... 1701?.1764
Porbus, Francis. *The Elder.* Dutch Painter.......... 1540..1580?
Porbus, Francis, son. *The Younger.* Painter......... 1570..1622
Porcacchi, Thomas. Venetian Collector and Writer... 1530..1585
Porcheron, David Placide. French Benedictine; Scholar 1652..1694
Porcia, daughter of Cato, wife of Brutus............ — .. 42
Pordage, John. Astrologer and Alchemist............ 1625..1698
Porden, Miss Eleanor Anne. Writer. See Franklin ... 1795..1825
Pordenone, Il. *John Anthony Licinio Regillo.* Ital. Paint. 1484..1540
Porée, Charles. French Rhetorician and Writer. (*Collec-
    tion of Harangues*)................................ 1675..1741
Porée, Charles Gabriel, br. (*Nouvelles Littéraires de Caen*) 1685..1770
Porphyry, of Tyre. Greek Philos.; Antichristian Writer 233.. 305
Porpora, Nicholas. Italian Musical Composer .... 1685..1767
Porporati, Charles Anthony. Italian Engraver........ 1741..1816
Porson, Richard. Critic. Life by J. S. Watson, 1861 .. 1759..1808
Porta, Baccio della. *Fra Bartolomeo di San Marco, or
    Il Frate.* Painter................................ 1469..1517
Porta, Costanzo. Italian Musical Composer .... — ..1641
Porta, James della. Italian Architect................ 1530?.1595?
Porta, J. Baptist della. Neapol. Phys. (*Magia Naturalis*) 1550?.1615
Porta, Simon. Italian Aristotelian Philosopher...... 1496..1554
Portal, Anthony. Ital. Phys. (*Hist. of Anat. and Surgery*) 1742..1832
Portalis, John Stephen Mary. Fr. Lawyer & Statesman 1746..1807
Porte, Peter de la. French Courtier. (*Memoirs*)....... 1603..1680
Porter, Alexander. American Jurist .... 1786..1844
Porter, Miss Anna Maria. Novelist. (*Hungarian Brothers*) 1781..1832
Porter, David. American Naval Officer ....·........ 1780..1843
Porter, Ebenezer. American Divine................. 1772..1834
Porter, Francis. Irish Theologian at Rome........... — ..1702
Porter, George Richardson. (*Progress of the Nation*)... 1792..1855
Porter, Miss Jane. Novelist. (*Thaddeus of Warsaw;
    Scottish Chiefs*) .... 1776..1850
Porter, Peter Buel. American Soldier............... 1773..1844
Porter, Sir Robert Ker. Diplom., Paint., Writ. (*Travels*) 1780..1842
Porter, William David. American Naval Officer ...... — ..1864
Portes, Philip des. French Poet .... 1546..1606
Porteus, Beilby. Bishop of London (1787–1808). Life
    by Hodgson .... 1731..1808
Portlock, J. E. Major-General. Engineer and Geologist 1795?.1864
Portsmouth, Duchess of. See Querouaille .... 1652?.1734
Portus, Æmilius. Greek Lexicographer............. 1550.aft.1612
Portus, Francis. Greek Scholar..................... 1511..1581
Posidonius. Greek Philosopher.................... 135?.50?B.C.
Possevin, Anthony. Italian Jesuit. Politician and Writer 1534..1611

BORN. DIED.

Post, Francis, of Haarlem. Painter and Engraver ...... 1614..1680
Postel, William. French Visionary................... 1510..1581
Postlethwayte, Malachi. Commercial Writer......... 1707?.1767
Pote, Joseph, of Eton. (*History of Windsor Castle*)..... — ..1787
Potemkin, Gregory Alexandrovitch. Russ. Field Marshal 1736..1791
Potenger, or Pottinger, John. Poet. (*On Death*)..... 1647..1733
Poter, or Potter, Paul. Dutch Painter of Animals...... 1625..1654
Pothier, Robert Joseph. French Lawyer............. 1699..1772
Potocki, Claudia, Countess. Benefactress............. 1802..1836
Potocki, Ignatius, Count. Polish Patriot............. 1751..1809
Potocki, John, Count. Polish Historian............... 1761..1815
Potocki, Stanislaus Kostka, Ct. Polish Statesm. and Writ. 1757..1821
Pott, John Henry. Professor of Chemistry at Berlin.... 1692..1777
Pott, Joseph Holden. Archdeacon of London. Poet & Div. 1779..1847
Pott, Percival. Surgical Writer. Life by Earle........ 1713..1788
Potter, Alonzo, D.D. American Divine and Writer .... 1800..1863
Potter, Christopher. Dean of Worcester. Anti-Calvinist
   Divine .... 1591?.1646
Potter, Francis. Divine and Mechanician. (*Explication
   of No. 666*)..................................... 1594..1678
Potter, John. Archbishop of Canterbury (1737–47). (*An-
   tiquities of Greece.*) Life by Anderson and Dunbar.. 1674?.1747
Potter, Louis Joseph Anthony de. Belgian Revolutionist 1786..1859
Potter, Paul. Dutch Painter of Animals.............. 1625..1654
Potter, Robert. Poet and Translator of Greek Plays ... 1721..1804
Pottier, Francis. French Missionary.................. 1718..1792
Pottinger, Sir Henry. Commander and Envoy........ 1789..1856
Potts, Rev. George, D.D. American Divine........... 1801..1864
Pouget, Francis Aimé. French Theologian............ 1666..1723
Poulle, Nicholas Louis. Abbé. Preacher............. 1703..1781
Pounds, John. English Philanthropist................. 1766..1839
Poupart, Francis. French Physician and Anatomist ... 1661..1709
Pourbus, or Porbus, Francis. *The Elder*. Dutch Painter 1540..1580?
Pourbus, or Porbus, Francis, son. *The Younger*. Portrait
   Painter... 1570..1622
Pourchot, Edmund. French Orientalist and Philosopher 1651..1734
Pourfour du Petit, Francis, of Paris. Phys. & Herbalist 1664..1741
Pouschkin, Alexander. Russian Poet................. 1799..1837
Poussin, Gaspar. Painter .... 1613..1675
Poussin, Nicholas. Painter .... 1594..1665
Powell, Rev. Baden. Professor .... 1796..1860
Powell, David. Welsh Divine .... 1552?.1598
Powell, Edward. Roman Catholic Divine; hanged.
   (*Propugnaculum*)................................ — ..1540
Powell, Foster. Pedestrian .... 1734?.1793
Powell, Gabriel. Writer. (*Unlawfulness of Toleration*). 1575..1611
Powell, George. Actor and Dramatist .... — ..1714
Powell, Griffith, of Jesus Coll., Oxf. (*De Demonstratione*) 1561..1620
Powell, Sir John. Judge............................ — ..1713
Powell, John Joseph. Jurist........................ — ..1801
Powell, William. Actor............................ — ..1769
Powell, William Samuel. Archdeacon of Colchester.
   Life by T. Balguy................................ 1717..1775
Power, Henry, M.D. Natural Philosopher .... — ..1668

BORN. DIED.

Power, Tyrone. Irish Actor and Author............. 1795..1841
Powhatan. Indian Sachem .... — ..1618
Powis, Percy Herbert, Lord. Royalist and Writer .... — ..1667
Powlett, First Marquess of Winchester. *See* Pawlett... 1475..1572
Pownall, Thomas, M. P. Political & Antiquarian Writer 1722..1805
Poynet, or Ponet, John. Bp. of Winchester. Reformer 1514?.1556
Poynings, Sir Edward. Author of "Poynings's Law"
  in Ireland .... — ..1512
Poyntel, Daniel. Nonconformist Divine .... — ..1674
Pozzetti, Pompilius. Florentine Writer............... 1769..1816
Pozzo, Andrew. Painter and Architect................ 1642..1709
Pozzo, Modesta. *Fonte-Moderata.* Venetian Poetess... 1555..1592
Pozzo di Borgo, Charles Andrew. Diplomatist....... 1764..1842
Pradier, John James. Sculptor at Paris .... 1792..1852
Pradon, John Nicholas. French Poet .... 1632..1698
Pradt, Dominique Dufour. Abbé. Political Writer ... 1759..1837
Praed, Winthrop Mackworth. Poet .... 1802..1839
Pram, Christian Henriksen. Danish Writer .... 1756..1821
Pratt, Charles, First Earl Camden. Lord Chancellor ... 1713..1794
Pratt, Sir Charles. Lieutenant-General .... 1771..1839
Pratt, Rev. Josiah. Divine .... — ..1844
Pratt, Samuel Jackson. Poet, Novelist, and Misc. Writer 1749..1814
Praxiteles. Greek Statuary......................... fl. B.C. 364
Preble, Edward. American Naval Officer............. 1761..1807
Preis, Joachim Frederick. Swedish Ambassador....... 1660..1759
Premontval, Andrew Peter le Guay de. (*Monogamia*).. 1716..1764
Prentiss, Seargent Smith. American Orator .... 1808..1850
Prescott, Oliver. American Patriot .... 1731..1804
Prescott, William, LL. D. American Lawyer .... 1762..1844
Prescott, William Hickling, son. Hist. Life by Ticknor 1796..1859
Preston, John, D. D. Puritan Writer. (*New Covenant*) 1587..1628
Preston, Thomas, D. C. L. Dramatic Writer .... 1537..1598
Preston, William Campbell. Amer. Statesman & Orator 1794..1860
Preti, Jerome. Tuscan Poet .... 1582..1626
Préville, Peter Louis Dubus de. French Actor .... 1721..1799
Prevost, Isaac Benedict. Swiss Naturalist............ 1755..1819
Prevost, Peter. French Painter of Panoramas........ 1764..1823
Prévost-d'Exiles, Anthony Francis. French Writer .. 1697..1763
Price, David. Major. Historian and Orientalist....... 1762..1835
Price, James, M. D., F. R. S. Last of the Alchemists .... 1758..1783
Price, Sir John. Antiquary. (*Defence of British History*) — ..1553?
Price, or Pricæus, John. English Critic and Biblical
  Writer, settled at Florence .... 1600..1676
Price, Peter Charles. Surgeon and Medical Writer .... 1832?.1864
Price, Richard, D. D. Political Writer. Life by W. Mor-
  gan, 1815.. 1723..1791
Price, Rev. Thomas. Welsh Scholar. Life by Jane Wil-
  liams, 1854 .... 1787..1848
Price, Sir Uvedale. Writer on Art. (*Essay on the Pictur-
  esque*)... 1747..1829
Prichard, James Cowles, M. D. Ethnologist.......... 1785..1848
Prichard, Rev. Rees. Welsh Poet................... 1574?.1644
Prideaux, Humphrey. Dean of Norwich. (*Connection*) 1648..1724
Prideaux, John. Prof. at Oxford. Bishop of Worcester 1578..1650

BORN. DIED.

Priessnitz, Vincent. Hydropathic Physician.......... 1799..1851
Priestley, Dr. Joseph. Unitarian Writer and Natural Phi-
losoper. Life by self and son, 1806–7; Rutt, 1831.... 1733..1804
Primaticcio, Francis. Italian Artist.................. 1490..1570
Prime, John. Puritan Divine...................... — ..1596
Primrose, Gilbert, D. D. Scottish Divine. (*Jacob's Vow*) — ..1642
Primrose, James, M. D., son. Medical Writer; Oppo-
nent of Harvey................................... — ..1660?
Prince, Rev. John. Antiquary. (*Worthies of Devon*).. 1643..1720?
Prince, Rev. Thomas. American Historian .... 1687..1758
Prince de Beaumont, Mme. le. Writer for the Young — ..1780
Pringle, Sir John, M. D. President of the Royal Society.
Natural Philosopher. Life by Dr. Kippis.......... 1707..1782
Pringle, Thomas. Poetical and Miscellaneous Writer.
(*African Sketches.*) Life by Ritchie .... 1789..1834
Prinsep, Charles Robert, LL. D. Political Economist ... 1788?.1864
Prinsep, James. Orientalist. (*Sketches of Benares*) ... 1800..1840
Prinsep, John. Alderman of London. Writer on Trade
and Finance .... 1747?.1831
Printz, Wolfgang Gaspar. German Musical Writer.... 1641.. —
Priolo, or Prioli, Benjamin. French Historical Writer.. 1602..1667
Prior, Matthew. Poet............................ 1664..1721
Priscian. Latin Grammarian. (*De Arte Grammaticâ*) fl. 525?
Priscillian. Spanish Heretic...................... — .. 385
Pritz, or Pritius, John George. Lutheran Divine....... 1662..1732
Probus, Marcus Aurelius. Roman Emperor (276–82)... 232.. 282
Procaccini, Camillus. Italian Painter.............. 1546..1626
Procaccini, Charles Anthony, brother. Landsc. Painter fl. 1605
Procaccini, Hercules. *The Elder.* Painter 1520.aft.1590
Procaccini, Hercules, grandson. *The Younger.* Flower
Painter... 1596..1676
Procaccini, Julius Cæsar. Painter.................. 1548..1626
Procida, John of. Sicilian Patriot................. 1225?.1303
Proclus. Neoplatonic Philosopher.................. 412.. 485
Procope Couteau. French Physician and Comic Writer 1684..1753
Procopius. Byzantine Historian.................... 500?. 565
Procopius, of Gaza. Biblical Commentator........... fl. 560?
Procopius, Anthemius. Roman Emperor .... — .. 472
Procopius Rasa. Hussite Leader .... — ..1434
Procter, Miss Adelaide Anne. Poetess............. — ..1864
Prodicus. Grecian Sophist....................... fl. 5th c. B.C.
Prokophiev, Ivan Prokophievitch. Russian Artist..... 1758..1828
Prony, Gaspar Clair Francis Mary Riche de. French
Mathematician................................. 1755..1839
Propertius. Roman Poet .... 51?.aft.16 B.C.
Prosper, of Aquitaine. Christian Writer 403.aft.463
Protagoras. Greek Sophist....................... 480?.411? B.C.
Protogenes. Painter of Rhodes. Life by Carlo Dati.. — B.C.300?
Proudhon, John Baptist Victor. French Jurist........ 1758..1838
Proudhon, Peter Joseph. French Socialist Writer..... 1809..1865
Prout, Samuel. Painter in Water Colors............ 1783..1852
Prout, William, M. D. Medical Writer.............. 1786..1850
Prouvençale de Saint-Hilaire, Auguste. French Bot-
anist. (*Flora Brasiliæ*)........................... 1779..1853

BORN. DIED.

Provenzale, Marcello da Cento.   Painter in Mosaic .... 1575..1639
Provoost, Samuel, D. D.   American Divine............ 1742..1815
Proyart, Lievain Bonaventure.   French Historical Writer 1743?.1808
Prudentius, Aurelius Clemens.   Christian Latin Poet .. 348.aft.404
Prudhomme, Louis Mary.   Writer on Fr. Revolutions 1752..1830
Prud'hon, Peter Paul.   French Painter .... 1758..1823
Prynne, William.   Lawyer and Writer.   (*Histriomastix*) 1600..1699
Przipcovius, Samuel.   Polish Knight.   Socinian Writer 1592?.1670
Psalmanazer, George.   Literary Impostor.   (*History of*
   Formosa.)   Life by self......................... 1679?.1763?
Psammetichus.   Egyptian King................. — B.C. 609 or 10
Psellus, Michael.   Greek Writer........._......... — ..1078
Ptolemy I. *Soter.*   King of Egypt (B. C. 323 or 306–285) 367.282 B.C.
Ptolemy II. *Philadelphus.*   (B. C. 285–247.)   Founder
   of Museum and Library of Alexandria .... 309.247 B.C.
Ptolemy III. *Euergetes.*   (B. C. 247–222) .... — B.C.222
Ptolemy IV. *Philopator.*   (B. C. 222–205)...........:. — B.C.205
Ptolemy V. *Epiphanes.*   (B. C. 205–181) .... 210.181 B.C.
Ptolemy VI. *Philometer.*   (B. C. 181–146, with interrup-
   tions).. — B.C.146
Ptolemy VII. *Euergetes II.,* or *Physcon.*   (B. C. 146–117,
   with interruptions)............................ — B.C.117
Ptolemy VIII. *Soter II.,* or *Lathyrus.*   (B. C. 117–81,
   with interruptions)............................ — B.C. 81
Ptolemy IX. *Neos, Dionysus,* or *Auletes.*   (B. C. 80–51) — B.C. 51
Ptolemy, Claudius.   Mathem., Astronomer, Geographer fl.139–161
Publicola, Publius Valerius.   Consul (B. C. 509)....... — B.C.503
Publius Syrus.   Latin Comic Poet.................. fl. B.C. 42
Puchta, Wolfgang Henry.   German Jurist .... 1769..1845
Pudsey, Hugh.   Bishop of Durham (1153–95) .... 1125?.1195
Pufendorf, Isaiah.   (*Anecdotes of Sweden*) .... 1628..1689
Pufendorf, Samuel, Baron von, br.   Civilian and Hist. 1632..1694
Pugatcheff, Yemelyan.   Cossack Chieftain and Pretender
   to Russian Throne............................... 1726..1775
Puget, Peter.   French Sculptor, Painter, Architect ..... 1622..1694
Pughe, Dr. William Owen.   Welsh Lexicog. and Writer 1759..1835
Pugin, Augustus.   French Architectural Draughtsman.. 1769..1832
Pugin, Augustus Welby Northmore, son.   Architect.
   Life by Ferrey................................. 1811..1852
Puisaye, Joseph, Count.   French Royalist............. 1754?.1827
Pujol.   Abel de..   French Painter................... 1785..1861
Pulaski, Casimir, Count.   Polish Patriot.   General in
   American Revolutionary War .... 1747..1779
Pulcheria, sister of Theodosius II., daughter of Arcadius 399.. 453
Pulci, Louis.   Italian Poet.   (*Morgante Maggiore*)..... 1432..1487?
Pulgar, Ferdinand del.   Spanish Historian .... 1436..1486?
Puligo, or Puglio, Dominic, of Florence.   Painter ...... 1475..1527
Pullus, or Pullen, Robert.   Cardinal; Promoter of Learn. — ..1150
Pulmann, or Poelmann, Theodore.   Philologist ...... 1510?.1580?
Pulteney, Richard.   Phys. and Botanist.   Life by Maton 1730..1801
Pulteney, William, Earl of Bath.   Statesman .... 1682..1764
Pultock, Robert.   Author.   (*Peter Wilkins*)........... fl. 18th c.
Purbach, or Peurbach, George.   Ger. Mathem. & Astron. 1423..1461
Purcell, Henry.   Musical Composer.................. 1658..1695

BORN. DIED.

Purcell, Thomas. Musical Composer .... — ..1682
Purchas, Rev. Samuel. Collector of Voyages. (*Pilgrim-
age; Pilgrims*)........ .... 1577..1628?
Pursh, Frederick. American Botanist .... 1774..1820
Purver, Anthony. Scholar and Biblical Translator..... 1702?.1777
Pusey, Philip, M. P. Agriculturist .... 1799..1855
Pushkin, Alexander Sergeivitch. Russian Poet and Prose
Writer... 1799..1837
Putnam, Israel. American Revolutionary General ..... 1718..1790
Putnam, Rufus. Pioneer Settler of Ohio.............. 1738..1824
Putschius, Elias. Dutch Grammarian................ 1580..1606
Putten, Henry van der. *Puteanus* or *Dupuy*. Scholar.. 1574..1646
Puttenham, George. Poet and Critic................. fl. 1589
Puy, Mademoiselle du. Harpist .... — ..1777
Puy, Louis du. French Scholar .... 1709..1795
Puy, Peter du. Hist. and Antiq. L. by Nicholas Rigault 1582..1651
Puysegur, James de Chastenet, Lord of. General. (*Me-
moirs*)... 1600..1682
Puysegur, James Francis, son. Marshal of France.
(*Military Art*)................................. 1655..1743
Pye, Henry James. Poet Laureate................... 1745..1813
Pyle, Rev. Thomas. Biblical Commentator........... 1674..1756
Pym, John. Republican Politician .... 1584..1643
Pynaker, Adam. Dutch Landscape Painter........... 1621..1673
Pynchon, William. Founder of Springfield, New Eng-
land. Theological Writer....................... 1591?.1662
Pyne, William Henry. Artist and Writer............. 1770..1843
Pynson, or Pinson, Richard. Printer................. — ..1530?
Pyrrho. Greek Skeptic Philosopher................ 375?.285? B.C.
Pyrrhus. King of Epirus.........................318.272 B.C.
Pythagoras. Greek Philosopher. Life by Jamblicus;
Dacier, 1706................................ fl. 540–510 B.C.
Pytheas. Greek Navigator and Discoverer, of Mar-
seilles.....................................ti. Alex. Great

Q.

BORN. DIED.

Quade, Michael Frederick. German Scholar.......... 1682..1757
Quadratus. Christian Apologist..................... ti. Hadrian
Quadrio, Francis Xavier. Ital. Critic. (*History of Poetry*) 1695..1756
Quaglio, Angelo. Scene Painter .... 1778?.1815
Quaglio, Dominic. Architectural Painter .... 1786..1837
Quaglio, Joseph. Scene Painter and Decorator .... 1747..1828
Quaglio, Julius. Scene Painter at Munich............. — ..1800
Quaglio, Lorenzo. Italian Architect in Germany ...... 1730..1804
Quain, Jones, M. D. Anatomist .... — ..1865
Quaini, Francis. Italian Architectural Painter........ 1611..1680
Quaini, Louis, son. Historical Painter............... 1643..1717
Quanz, John Joachim. Musical Composer and Flutist.. 1697..1773
Quarenghi, James. *Cavaliere.* Italian Architect...... 1744..1817
Quarles, Francis. Poet. (*Emblems*)................. 1592..1644
Quarles, John, son. Poet. Loyalist................. 1624..1665
Quatremère, Stephen Mark. French Orientalist ...... 1782..1857
Quatremère de Quincy, Anthony Chrysostom. Ar-
    chæologist................................... 1755..1849
Quattromani, Sertorius. Italian Writer .... 1541..1611
Queensberry, William Douglas, Fourth Duke of....... 1724?.1810
Quekett, John. Microscopist...................... 1815..1861
Quellinus, or Quellyn, Erasmus. Dutch Painter....... 1607..1678
Quellinus, John Erasmus, son. Painter .... 1629..1715
Quenstedt, John Andrew. Lutheran Divine. (*Sculptura
    Veterum*).................................... 1611..1688
Quental, Bartholomew du. Portuguese Religious Writer 1626..1698
Quer y Martinez, Joseph. Spanish Botanist .... 1695..1764
Quérard, Joseph Mary. French Bibliographer .... 1795..1865
Querenghi, Anthony. Italian Poet.................. 1546..1633
Querini, Angelo Mary. Italian Cardinal. Historian... 1680..1755
Querlon, Anne Gabriel Meusnier de. Journalist & Writer 1702..1780
Querno, Camillus. Italian Poet. (*Alexiadu*)......... 1470..1528
Querouaille, Louisa de, Duchess of Portsmouth........ 1652?.1734
Quesnay, Francis. French Physician.............. 1694..1774
Quesne, Abraham du. French Admiral.............. 1610..1688
Quesne, Henry du, son. Naval Officer and Writer at
    Geneva...................................... 1652..1722
Quesnel, Pasquier. French Jansenist Divine. (*Moral
    Reflections*) .... 1634..1719
Quesnel, Peter. (*History of the Jesuits*)............. 1699..1774
Quesnoy, Francis du. Flemish Sculptor............. 1594..1646
Quesnoy, Jerome, brother. Sculptor. Burnt .... 1612..1654
Quetif, James. French Dominican. Writer........... 1618..1698
Quevedo y Villegas, Francis Gomez de. Span. Writer 1580..1645
Quick, John. Comic Actor .... 1748..1831
Quien, Michael le. French Scholar and Orientalist..... 1661..1733
Quien de la Neufville, James le. Historian .... 1647..1728
Quignonez, Francis de. Spanish Cardinal .... — ..1539
Quillett, Claude, of Chinon. *Calvidus Lætus.* Latin Poet.
    (*Callipædia*) .... 1602..1661

BORN. DIED.

Quin, Edward. Actor and Dramatist .... — ..1823
Quin, James. Actor. Life, 8vo, 1766 .... 1693..1766
Quinault, Jane Frances. *La Cadette.* Fr. Comic Actress 1700?.1783
Quinault, Philip. French Dramatic Poet. .... 1635..1688
Quinault Dufresne, Abraham Alexis. Fr. Comedian 1693..1741
Quincey, Thomas de. *See* De Quincey............... 1785..1859
Quincy, John, M. D. Medical Writer. (*Lexicon Physico-
    Medicum*)..................................... — ..1723
Quincy, Josiah, Jr. American Lawyer, Orator, and Po-
    litical Writer .... 1744..1775
Quincy, Josiah, son. American Statesman........... 1772..1864
Quincy, Quatremère de. *See* Quatremère de Quincy... 1755..1849
Quinette, Nicholas Mary. French Politician .... 1762..1821
Quintana, Manuel Joseph. Spanish Poet and Patriot .. 1772..1857
Quintilian. Roman Rhetorician. Life by Burmann... 42.. 118?
Quintinie, John de la. French Horticulturist .... 1626..1688
Quintus Curtius. Historian..................... fl. ti.Vespasian?
Quirini, or Querini, Angelo Mary. Cardinal. Historian 1680..1755
Quiroga, Joseph. Spanish Jesuit. Missionary in America 1707..1784
Quiros, or Queiros, Peter Fernandez de. Span. Navigator 1560..1614
Quistorp, John. Lutheran Divine. Biblical Commentator 1584..1648
Quita, Domingos dos Reis. Portuguese Poet.......... 1728..1770
Quitman, John Anthony. Amer. Politician and Soldier 1799..1858

R.

BORN. DIED.

Raban Maur. *Magnentius.* Archbp. of Mentz. Writer 786?. 856
Rabaut de St. Étienne, John Paul. Politician........ 1743..1793
Rabel, John. French Portrait Painter.............. 1545?.1603
Rabelais, Francis. French Satirist. (*Gargantua*)...... 1495..1553?
Rabener, Theophilus William. German Writer........ 1714..1771
Rabuel, Claude. French Jesuit. Mathematician...... 1669..1728
Rabutin, Francis de. French Historical Writer........ —aft.1582
Rabutin, Roger de, Ct. de Bussy. Fr. Wit and Satirist 1618..1693
Racan, Honórat de Bueil, Marquis de. French Poet.... 1589..1670
Racchetti, Bernard. Italian Painter.................. 1639..1702
Rachel, or Eliza Rachel Félix. French Actress........ 1820..1858
Racine, Bonaventure. Ecclesiastical Historian......... 1708..1755
Racine, John. Fr. Dramatic Poet. Life by Louis Racine 1639..1699
Racine, Louis. Poetical Writer. (*Life of John Racine*) 1692..1763
Rack, Edmund. Poet...................... 1735..1787
Racle, Leonard. French Architect.................. 1736..1791
Raczynski, Edward. Polish Nobleman. Writer...... 1786..1845
Radcliffe, Alexander. Burlesque Poet.............. — ..1700?
Radcliffe, Ann, Mrs. Novelist. (*Mysteries of Udolpho*) 1764..1823
Radcliffe, Charles. Adherent of Pretender. Beheaded.
　　Life by Sydney Gibson...................... 1693..1746
Radcliffe, James, brother, Third Earl of Derwentwater.
　　Adherent of Pretender. Beheaded. Life by Sydney
　　Gibson........................ 1689..1716
Radcliffe, John, M. D. Founder of Library at Oxford .. 1650..1714
Radegonde, St. Consort of Clotaire I.............. 519?. 587
Rademaker, Abraham. Dutch Landscape Painter..... 1675..1735
Rademaker, Gerard. Dutch Architectural Painter..... 1673..1711
Radetzky, Joseph Wenzel. Austrian General .... 1766..1858
Radowitz, Joseph von. Statesman .... 1797..1853
Radziwill, Nicholas. Palatine of Wilna. Polish Protestant 1500?.1567
Raeburn, Sir Henry. Portrait Painter.............. 1756..1823
Raffaelle da Urbino. *See* Raphael da Urbino .... 1483..1520
Raffenel, Claude Denis. French Writer.............. 1797..1827
Raffles, Thomas, D. D., LL. D., of Liverpool. Dissenting
　　Divine. Life by Baldwin Brown, 1863............ 1788..1863
Raffles, Sir Thomas Stamford. Statesman and Naturalist 1781..1826
Rafin, Catharine Josephine. *Duchesnois.* French Actress 1777..1835
Rafinesque, S. C. S. American Botanist .... 1784..1842
Raghib Pasha, Mohammed. Turkish Vizier.......... 1702..1768
Raglan, Fitzroy Somerset, Lord. General in the Crimea 1788..1855
Ragland, Thos. Cajetan. Missionary. L. by T. Perowne 1815..1858
Ragotski, Francis. Prince of Transylvania. Patriot... 1676..1735
Raguenet, Francis. French Writer.................. 1660?.1722
Raguet, Condy. Amer. Merchant and Polit. Economist. 1784..1842
Ragusa, Augustus Frederick de Marmot, Duke of. Mar-
　　shal of France...................... 1774..1852
Rahbek, Knud Lyne. Danish Writer.............. 1760..1830
Raikes, Robt., of Gloucester. Founder of Sunday Schools 1735..1811
Raimbach, Abraham. Engraver. Life by self and son 1776..1843

	BORN.	DIED.
Raimondi, John Baptist. Orientalist	1540?	1610?
Raimondi, Mark Anthony. Engraver	1475?	1534?
Rainaldi, or Rinaldi, Oderic. Continuator of Baronius	1595	1671
Rainaud, Theophilus. Jesuit. Scholar and Writer	1583	1663
Raine, James, D. C. L. (History of North Durham)	1791	1858
Rainolds, John. Puritan Divine	1549	1607
Rainolds, William, brother. Roman Catholic Writer	—	1594
Rainsford, or Raynsford, Sir Richard. Ld. Chief Justice	1604?	1679
Rákóczy. See Ragotski	1676	1735
Rale, or Rasles, Sebastian. French Missionary to North American Indians	1658	1724
Raleigh, or Ralegh, Sir Walter. Life by Whitehead; Oldys; Birch; A. Cayley, 1805; Mrs. A. T. Thomson, 1830; P. F. Tytler, 1833; Macvey Napier, 1857	1552	1618
Ralph, James. Polit. and Poet. Writer. (Hist. of Eng.)	—	1762
Ralph de Turbine. Archbp. of Canterbury (1114–22)	—	1122
Ramazzini, Bernardin. Italian Physician	1633	1714
Ramberg, John Henry. Draughtsman and Engraver	1763	1840
Rameau, John Philip. Musical Composer	1683	1764
Ramelli, Augustin. Italian Mechanician and Engineer	1531?	1590
Ramelli, Felix. Italian Painter	1666	1740
Ramenghi, Bartholomew. Il Bagnacavallo. Painter	1484	1542
Ramiro I. King of Asturias	—	850
Ramiro II. King of Asturias	—	950
Ramler, Charles Wm. German Poet and Misc. Writer	1725	1798
Rammohun Roy. Hindoo Writer and Reformer	1774	1833
Ramond de Carbonnières, Louis Francis Elizabeth, Baron. Geologist	1755	1827
Ramorino, Jerome. Military Adventurer	1792	1849
Ramsay, Sir Alexander. Scottish Knight	—	1342
Ramsay, Allan. Poet. (Gentle Shepherd; Evergreen)	1685	1758
Ramsay, Allan, son. Portrait Painter	1713	1784
Ramsay, Andrew Michael. Chevalier. Writer	1686	1743
Ramsay, David. American Physician and Historian	1749	1815
Ramsay, Rev. James. Philanthropist	1733	1789
Ramsay, William. Professor. Classical Scholar	1806?	1865
Ramsden, Jesse. Optician	1735	1800
Ramus, or La Ramée, Peter. Fr. Philosopher & Scholar	1515	1572
Ramusio, or Rannusio, John Bapt. Collector of Voyages	1485	1557
Ranc, John. French Painter in Spain	1674	1735
Rancé, Armand John le Bouthillier de. Monk of La Trappe. Life by Maupeau, Marsollier, and Lenain de Tillemont; Châteaubriand, 1844; C. Butler, 1814	1626	1700
Randal, Dr. John. Musical Composer	1715	1799
Randolph, John. Bishop of London	1749	1813
Randolph, John, of Roanoke. American Statesman	1773	1833
Randolph, Peyton. American Patriot	1723	1775
Randolph, Sir Thomas. Diplomatist	1523	1590
Randolph, Thomas. Poet	1605	1634
Randolph, Thomas, Archdeacon	1701	1783
Rannequin, of Liège. Hydraulic Engineer	1644	1708
Ransom, Thomas Edward Greenfield. American General	1834	1864
Ransome, James. Agricultural Machinist	1783	1849
Rantoul, Robert. American Statesman	1805	1852

BORN. DIED.

Rantzau, John. Danish General and Military Writer .. 1492..1565
Rantzau, Josiah, Count de. Marshal of France and
    Protestant Reformer in Denmark.................... 1609..1650
Ranzani, Camillo. Italian Naturalist................. 1775..1841
Raoul-Rochette, Désiré. French Archæologist .... 1789..1854
Raoux, John. French Historical Painter.............. 1677..1734
Raphael, of Volterra. *Maffei.* Antiquary .... 1451..1522
Raphael da Rhegio. *Raffaelino.* Hist. and Portr. Paint. 1552..1580
Raphael da Urbino. Painter. Life by Duppa; Quatre-
    mère de Quincy, tr. by Hazlitt; J. S. Harford .... 1483..1520
Raphelengius, or Rapheling, Francis. Critic and Orient. 1539..1597
Raphelius, George. (*Annotationes in Sacr. Script.* 1747) . — .. —
Rapicio, Grovita. Italian Writer. (*De Numero Oratorio*) 1480?.1553
Rapin, Nicholas. French Poet .....;.............. 1540?.1609
Rapin, René. French Jesuit. Latin Poet. (*Hortorum*) 1621..1687
Rapin-Thoyras, Paul de. (*History of England*)....... 1661..1725
Rapp, George. Founder of the Sect of the Harmonists.. 1770..1847
Rapp, John, Count de. French General............... 1772..1821
Rasario, John Baptist. Italian Medical Writer .... 1517..1578
Rasis, or Arrazi. Arabian Historian of Spain......... 870?.bef.961
Rask, Rasmus Christian. Danish Philol. and Orientalist 1787..1832
Rasles, or Rale, Sebastian. *See* Rale .... 1658..1724
Rasori, John. Italian Physician .... 1767..1837
Rastall, John. Printer and Author .... — ..1536
Rastall, William, son. Printer and Judge............. 1508..1565
Ratcliffe, James and Charles. Jacobites. *See* Radcliffe.
Ratcliffe, Thomas. Earl of Sussex................... — ..1583
Rater, Anthony, of Lyons. Architect................ 1729..1794
Ratherius. Bishop of Verona. Writer .... — .. 974
Ratramnus, Bertramus, or Bertram. *Presbyter.* (*De
    Corpore et Sanguine Domini*) .... — aft.868
Ratte, Stephen Hyacinth de. French Astronomer...... 1722..1805
Rau, or Ravius, Christian. German Orientalist........ 1613..1677
Rauch, Christian Daniel. German Sculptor .... 1777..1857
Rauch, Fred. Augustus, D. D. Ger. Philos. and Divine 1806..1841
Raulin, John. French Preacher..................... 1443..1514
Raulin, Joseph. French Physician .... 1708..1784
Raupach, Ernest Benjamin Solomon. Ger. Dramatist.. 1784..1852
Rauwolf, Leonard. Botanical Traveler .... — ..1596
Ravaillac, Francis. Murderer of Henry IV. of France,
    May 14, 1610 .... 1579..1610
Ravenet, Simon Francis. French Engraver........... 1706..1774
Ravenscroft, John Stark. American Divine.......... 1772..1830
Ravenscroft, Thomas. Musician 1592.aft.1635
Ravesteyn, Hubert van. Dutch Pa. of Fairs, Markets, &c. 1647.. —
Ravesteyn, John van. Dutch Portrait Painter........ 1572..1657
Ravesteyn, Nich. van. Dutch Hist. and Portr. Painter 1661..1750
Ravignan, Gustavus Francis Xavier Delacroix de. French
    Jesuit Preacher .... 1795..1858
Ravius, Rave, or Rau, Christian. German Orientalist .. 1613..1677
Rawdon, Marmaduke. Mercht. L. ed. by R. Davies, 1863 1610..1669
Rawle, William. American Jurist.................... 1759..1836
Rawlet, John, of Newcastle. Divine. (*Christian Monitor*) 1642..1686
Rawley, William, D. D. Editor and Biographer of Bacon 1588..1667

BORN. DIED.

Rawlinson, Christopher. Saxonist................... 1677..1733
Rawlinson, Richard, LL. D. (*English Topographer*).... — ..1755
Rawlinson, Sir Thomas. Lord Mayor of London...... 1647..1705
Rawlinson, Thomas. *Tom Folio.* Bibliomaniac ...... 1681..1725
Rawson, Sir William Adams. Oculist.................. — ..1829
Rawwolf, or Rauwolf, Leonard. Botanical Traveler.... — ..1596
Ray, or Wray, Rev. John. Naturalist. Life by Derham 1628..1705
Raymond VI. Count of Toulouse................... 1156..1222
Raymond VII., son. Last Count of Toulouse .... 1197..1249
Raymond, Robert, Lord. Lord Chief Justice. (*Reports*) — ..1732
Raymond de Lully. Chemist and Trav. (*Ars Magna*) 1234..1315
Raymond de Pegnafort, St. Spanish Dominican.
    (*Decretals*)..................................... 1175..1275
Raynal, Wm. Thomas Francis. Abbé. Hist. and Philos. 1711..1796
Raynard, Theophilus, of Lyons. Jesuit. (*Historical Tables*) 1583..1663
Raynerius, of Pisa. Theologian. (*Pantheologia*) ..... — ..1649
Raynolds, or Rainolds, John. Puritan Divine........ 1549..1607
Raynouard, Francis Juste Mary. Miscellaneous Writer 1761..1836
Raynsford, Sir Richard. Lord Chief Justice .... 1604?.1679
Razzi, John Anthony. *Il Sodoma.* Painter........... 1479..1554
Re, Philip. Italian Agriculturist .... 1763..1817
Reach, Angus Bethune. Journalist and Author........ 1821..1856
Read, Alexander, M. D. Scottish Med. and Anat. Writer — ..1680
Read, George. American Patriot..................... 1734..1798
Read, Nathan. American Inventor.................... 1759..1849
Réal, Cæsar Vichard de Saint. *See* Saint-Réal......... 1639..1692
Réal, Gaspard de. Fr. Publicist. (*Science of Government*) 1682..1752
Réaumur, René Anthony Ferchault de. French Natural
    Philosopher. Life by Cuvier..................... 1683..1757
Rebolledo, Bernardin, Count de. Spanish Soldier, Di-
    plomatist, and Author .... 1597..1677
Reboul, of Nîmes. Baker and Poet .... 1796?.1864
Reboulet, Simon. French Historical Writer .... 1687..1752
Récamier, Mme. Jane Frances Julia Adelaide, of Paris. 1777..1849
Recke, Eliz. Charlotte Constantia von der. Ger. Authoress 1754..1833
Recorde, Robert. Mathematician. (*Whetstone of Witte*) 1500?.1558
Reden, Fred. Wm. Otto Louis, Baron. Ger. Statistician 1804..1857
Redesdale, John Freeman Mitford, Baron. Lord Chanc. 1748..1830
Redfield, William C. Amer. Meteorologist and Geologist 1789..1857
Redi, Francis. Ital. Nat. Philosopher, Poet, and Scholar 1626..1698
Redi, Thomas. Florentine Painter .... 1665..1726
Reding, Aloys, Baron von. Swiss General .... 1755..1818
Red Jacket. North American Indian Chief........... 1759?.1830
Redmayne, John. Divine .... 1499..1551
Redouté, Peter Joseph. French Flower Painter .... 1759..1840
Reed, Andrew, D. D. Philanthropist. L. by A. and C. Reed 1787..1862
Reed, Henry. American Author..................... 1808..1854
Reed, Isaac. Critic and Miscellaneous Writer......... 1742..1807
Reed, Joseph. American Officer .... 1741..1785
Reed, Joseph. Dramatic Writer .... 1723..1787
Reenberg, Theocarus. Danish Poet.................. 1656..1742
Rees, Abraham, D. D. Dissent. Divine; Ed. of *Cyclopædia* 1743..1825
Reeve, Clara. Novelist. (*Old English Baron*) .... 1725?.1803
Reeve, John. Comic Actor.......................... 1799..1838

BORN. DIED.

Reeve, Lovell A., F. L. S. Conchologist and Publisher .. 1814..1865
Reeve, Tapping. American Jurist..................... 1744..1823
Reeves, John. Political Writer..................... 1752..1829
Reeves, Rev. William. Patristic Writer .... 1668..1726
Rega, Henry Joseph, of Louvain. Phys. & Philanthropist 1690..1754
Regino. Abbot of Prum. Eccles. Writer and Chronicler — .. 915
Regiomontanus. See John Müller .... 1436..1476
Regis, John Baptist. Jesuit Missionary in China....... 1665..1737
Regis, Peter Sylvain. French Cartesian Philosopher ... 1632..1707
Regius, or Le Roy, Urban. Poet and Protestant Controv. — ..1541
Regnard, John Francis. French Poet and Comic Writer
    (*Le Joueur*)......................... 1647?.1710
Regnault, Michael Louis Stephen. French Statesman.. 1760..1819
Regnault, Noel. French Mathematician and Philosopher 1683..1762
Régnier, Claude Ambrose. French Politician......... 1736..1814
Régnier, Mathurin. French Poet. (*Satires*) .... 1573..1613
Régnier-Desmarais, Francis Seraphin. French Poet.. 1632..1713
Regulus, Marcus Atilius. Consul................... — —B.C.250
Rehoboam, son of Solomon. K. of Israel (B. C. 990–973) 1031.973 B.C.
Reicha, Anthony Joseph. Musical Writer and Composer 1770..1836
Reichard, Henry Augustus Ottocar. (*Traveler's Guide
    in Europe*).................................. 1751..1828
Reichardt, John Frederick. Musical Composer & Writer 1752..1814
Reichenbach, George of. Mechanician.............. 1772..1826
Reichstadt, Duc de. *Napoleon II.* See Bonaparte .... 1811..1832
Reid, David Boswell, M. D. Scot. Phys. & Writ. on Chem. 1805..1864
Reid, Samuel Chester. American Naval Officer........ 1783..1861
Reid, Thomas. Metaphysician. Life by Dugald Stewart;
    Sir W. Hamilton................................. 1710..1796
Reid, Sir William. Major-General. (*Law of Storms*)... 1791..1858
Reigny, Louis Abel Beffroi. *Cousin Jacques.* Fr. Writer 1757..1810
Reihing, James. Lutheran Controversial Divine .... 1580?.1628
Reimarus, Herman Samuel. Class. and Hebrew Scholar 1694..1768
Reimarus, John Albert Henry, son. Phys. and Philos. 1729..1814
Reinbeck, John Gustavus. Pruss. Divine and Metaphys. 1683..1741
Reineccius, Reinier. German Historian and Genealogist 1541..1595
Reiner, Wenceslaus Lawrence, of Prague. Painter .... 1686?.1743
Reinesius, Thomas. German Physician and Philologist.
    (*Variæ Lectiones*)............................. 1587..1667
Reinhard, Francis Volkmar. German Theologian ..... 1753..1812
Reinhold, Charles Leonard. German Metaphysician... 1758..1823
Reinhold, Erasmus. Ger. Astronomer. (*Prussian Tables*) 1511..1553
Reiske, Mrs. Ernestine Christine, *née* Müller. Writer... 1735..1798
Reiske, John. German Biblical Writer............... 1641..1701
Reiske, John Jas. Philologist. L. by self and Mrs. Reiske 1716..1774
Reiz, or Reitz, Frederick Wolfgang. German Philologist 1733..1790
Reland, Adrian. Orientalist and Writer on Jewish Antiq. 1676..1718
Rembertus. Abp. of Hamburg. Missionary in Denmark — .. 888
Rembrandt van Ryn, Paul Gerritz. Dutch Painter.
    Life by J. Burnet, 1848 .... 1606..1669
Remi, Joseph Honoré. Burlesque Poet and *Éloge* Writer 1738..1782
Remigio, Florentine, of Florence. Writer........... 1518?.1580
Remigius, or Remi, St. Archbishop of Rheims........ — .. 533
Remigius, or Remi, St. Archbishop of Lyons......... — .. 875

BORN. DIED.

Remigius, of Auxerre. Benedictine. Biblical Writer .. — .. 908?
Rémond de St. Mard, Toussaint. Fr. Writer and Poet 1682..1757
.Rémusat, John Peter Abel. Orientalist. Life by Syl-
    vester de Sacy.................................... 1788..1832
Renau d'Elisagaray, Bernard. Naval Architect...... 1652..1719
Renaudot, Eusebius. French Orientalist.............. 1646..1720
Renaudot, Theophrastus. French Physician and Writer 1584..1653
René, Duke of Anjou, titular King of Sicily............ 1409..1480
Renée, of France, Duchess of Ferrara. Patron of Letters
  . and Religion. Life by I. M, B., London, 1859 ...... 1510..1575
Renehan, Laurence F., D. D. President of Maynooth
    College. (Collection of Records for Irish History).... 1797?.1857
Reni, Guido. See Guido Reni .... 1574?.1642
Rennel, Major James. Geographer.................. 1742..1830
Rennell, Thomas, of Devonshire. Painter and Poet.... 1718..1788
Rennell, Rev. Thomas. Divine...................... 1787..1824
Rennell, Thos., D. D. Dean of Winch. Div. and Preacher 1753..1840
Rennie, John. Architect and Constructive Engineer ... 1761..1821
Reno, Jesse L. American General.................... 1825..1862
Renti, Gaston John Baptist, Baron de. Ascetic. Life
    by St. Jure, abridged by John Wesley .... 1611..1649
Renwick, Rev. James. Scottish Minister and Martyr .. — ..1688
Repnine, Nicholas Vassilievitch. Russ. Gen. and Diplom. 1734..1801
Repton, Humphry. Landscape Gardener.............. 1752..1818
Repton, John Adey, F. S. A. Architect................ 1775..1860
Reresby, Sir John. Governor of York. (Memoirs).... — ..1689
Resende, Garcia de. Portuguese Historian and Poet... 1478..1554
Resende, Lucius. Portuguese Restorer of Letters...... 1498..1573
Resenius, John Paul. Danish Bishop; Biblical Translator 1561..1638
Resenius, Peter. Danish Statesman and Scholar...... 1625..1688
Reshid Pasha, Mustapha. Ottoman Statesman .... 1799..1858
Ressius, Rutgar, of Louvain. Critic.................. — ..1545
Restaut, Peter. (Principes de la Grammaire Françoise) 1694..1764
Restout, John. French Painter .... 1692..1768
Restout, John Bernard, son. Painter .... 1732..1795
Retz, Gilles de Laval, Baron. Marshal of France...... 1396?.1440
Retz, John Francis Paul de Gondi, Cardinal. (Memoirs). 1614..1679
Retzsch, Frederick Augustus Maurice. German Painter
    and Designer...................................... 1779..1859
Reuchlin, John. Kapnio. German Scholar. Life by
    Meiners; Maius; Barham.......................... 1455..1522
Reuven, Peter. Dutch Painter...................... 1650..1718
Reuvens, John Everard. Dutch Lawyer.............. 1763..1816
Reveley, Willey. Architect and Antiquary .... — ..1799
Revellière-Lepaux, Louis Mary. French Politician... 1753..1824
Revere, Paul. American Engraver and Patriot........ 1735..1818
Reves, or Revius, James de. Prot. Theologian at Leyden 1586..1658
Rewbell, John Baptist. French Republican .... 1746..1810
Rey, John. French Physician and Chemist............ — ..1645?
Rey, John Baptist. French Musical Composer .... 1734..1810
Rey, William. French Physician..................... 1687..1756
Reyher, Samuel. German Mathematician............. 1635..1714
Reylof, Oliver. Dutch Latin Poet.................... 1670..1742
Reyn, John de. Rheni or Lang Jan. Dutch Painter ... 1610..1678

BORN. DIED.

Reyneau, Charles René. French Mathematician...... 1656..1728
Reyner, Edward. Nonconformist. (*Precepts for Christian Practice*)................................ — ..1670?
Reynier, John Louis Anthony. (*Egypt under the Romans*) 1762..1824
Reynier, John Louis Ebenezer. Fr. General and Writer 1771..1814
Reynolds, Edward. Bishop of Norwich .... 1599..1676
Reynolds, or Rainolds, John. Puritan Divine......... 1549..1607
Reynolds, John Fulton. American General .... 1820..1863
Reynolds, Sir Joshua. Painter. Life by Malone; J. Northcote; Farrington, 1819; Cotton and Burnet; C. R. Leslie, edited by Tom Taylor, 1863.............. 1723..1792
Reynolds, Richard, M. D. Historical Writer........... — ..1606
Reynolds, Richard, of Bristol. Ironmaster............ 1735..1816
Reyrac, Francis Philip Laurence de. French Poet ..... 1734..1782
Reys, Anthony dos. Portuguese Divine, Hist., and Poet 1690..1738
Rezzonico, Anthony Joseph, Ct. Ital. Soldier and Poet 1709..1785
Rham, Rev. William Lewis. Agricultural Writer...... 1778..1843
Rhaw, George, of Wittemberg. Musical Publisher..... 1488..1548
Rhazes. Arabian Physician .... 852?. 923?
Rheed, Henry van. Gov. of Malabar. (*Hortus Malabaricus*) —aft.1696
Rhegas, Constantine. Greek Patriot.................. 1753?.1798
Rheinek, Christopher. German Musical Composer..... 1748..1796
Rhenanus, Beatus. German Historian................ 1485..1547
Rhenferd, James. German Orientalist............... 1654..1712
Rhese, John David, M. D. Welsh Philologist......... 1534..1609
Rheticus, George Joachim. Ger. Astron. (*Ephemerides*) 1514..1576
Rhode, John George, of Breslau. Orientalist.......... — ..1827
Rhodes, Alexander de. Jesuit Missionary in India..... 1591..1660
Rhodiginus, Ludovicus Coelius. Italian Scholar....... 1450?.1525
Rhodius, Ambrose. Phys. and Math. (*Transmigration*) 1577?.1633
Rhodius, or Rhode, John. Danish Medical Writer..... 1587?.1659
Rhodomann, Lawrence. German Greek Poet. (*Life of Luther*)................................... 1546..1606
Rhunken, David. Critic. Life by Whyttenbach ...... 1723..1798
Rhyndacenus. *Andrew John Lascaris.* Gr. Schol. in Italy 1445?.1535
Rhyne, William Ten. Dutch Physician and Naturalist.. 1640?. —
Rhyzelius, Andrew. Swedish Historian and Antiquary 1677..1761
Ribadeneira, Peter, of Toledo. Jesuit; Biographer.... 1527..1611
Ribalta, Francis. Spanish Painter.................... 1551..1628
Ribas, Joseph de. Russian Admiral and Diplomatist ... 1735..1797?
Ribault, John. French Navigator and Adventurer in Florida. Life by Sparks......................... 1520?.1565
Ribera, Anastasius Pantaleon de. Span. Burlesque Poet 1580..1629
Ribera, Joseph. *Spagnoletto.* Spanish Painter .... 1588..1656
Ribes, Anne Arnaud de. French Officer of Engineers .. 1731..1811
Ribeyro, Bernardin. Portuguese Pastoral Poet .... fl. 16th c.
Ricard, Dominic. Fr. Scholar & Poet; Transl. of Plutarch 1741..1803
Ricardo, David. Merchant and Political Economist. Life by J. R. McCulloch, 1846 .... 1772..1823
Ricardo, Joseph Lewis. Writer on International Law... 1812?.1862
Ricaut, or Rycaut, Sir Paul. Traveler and Biographer.. — ..1700
Riccati, Vincent. Italian Math. and Hydraulic Engineer 1707..1775
Ricci, Bartholomew. Italian Latinist. (*Apparatus*).... 1490..1569
Ricci, Lorenzo. General of the Jesuits............... 1703..1775

BORN. DIED.

Ricci, Mark. Landscape and Historical Painter........ — ..1730
Ricci, Matthew. Jesuit Missionary in China. Life by
  D'Orleans, 1693................................... 1552..1610
Ricci, Michael Angelo. Cardinal. Mathematician..... 1619..1682
Ricci, Scipio de. Bishop of Pistoia; Tuscan Reformer.
  Life by M. de Potter, translated by Thos. Roscoe, 1825 1741..1810
Ricci, or Rizzi, Sebastian. Italian Painter .... 1662..1734
Ricciarelli, Daniel. *Daniele di Volterra.* Painter...... 1509..1566
Riccio, Dominic, of Verona. *Il Brusasorchi.* Painter.. 1494..1567
Riccioli, John Baptist. Ital. Astronomer and Geographer 1598..1671
Riccoboni, Anthony, of Padua. Philologist............ 1541..1599
Riccoboni, Anthony Francis. Actor and Alchemist.... 1707..1772
Riccoboni, Louis. Comic Actor. (*Hist. of Ital. Theater*) 1674..1753
Riccoboni, Mary Jane Laboras de Mézières. Actress
  and Novelist..................................... 1714..1792
Rice, Rev. Luther. American Missionary .... 1783..1836
Rich, Claudius James, of East India Company. Orientalist 1787..1821
Richard I. Duke of Normandy (942–96). *Sans Peur*.. 932.. 996
Richard II. (996–1026.) *Le Bon* .... — ..1026
Richard III. (1026–28.) .... — ..1028
Richard I. King of England (1189–99). Life by Bene-
  dict of Peterborough; G. P. R. James, 1841–43 ..... 1157..1199
Richard II. (1377–99.) Life by Jacob Abbott, 1858... 1366..1400
Richard III. (1483–85.) L. by Halsted, 1844; Jesse, 1861 1452..1485
Richard, Archbishop of Canterbury (1174–84)......... — ..1184
Richard, Earl of Cornwall, brother of Henry III....... 1209..1272
Richard, of Cirencester. Historian. Life by Hatchard —1401 or 2
Richard, of Devizes. Historian..................... fl. 1191
Richard, of Hexham. Historian. (*Battle of the Standard*) fl. 1138
Richard, Achilles. French Botanist................. 1794..1852
Richard, Charles Louis. French Benedictine. (*Diction-
  ary of Ecclesiastical Knowledge*)................... 1711..1784
Richard, Francis. *Richard Lenoir.* French Manufacturer 1765..1839
Richard, John. French Theologian. (*Moral Dictionary*) 1639..1719
Richard, Louis Claude Mary. French Botanist........ 1754..1821
Richard, Martin. Dutch Painter..................... 1591..1636
Richard, René. French Oratorian. Writer........... 1654..1727
Richard de Bury. Prelate and Statesman............ 1287..1345
Richards, William. American Missionary .... 1792..1847
Richardson, Charles, LL. D. Philologist. (*English Dict.*) 1775..1865
Richardson, Israel B. American General............. 1819..1862
Richardson, John. Bishop of Ardagh. (*On Ezekiel*).. — ..1654
Richardson, Sir John, F. R. S. Naturalist............. 1787..1865
Richardson, Jonathan. Painter and Writer on Painting 1665?.1745
Richardson, Joseph. Poet. (*Criticisms on the Rolliad*) — ..1803
Richardson, Richard. American Revolutionary Soldier 1704..1780
Richardson, Samuel. Novelist. Life by Mrs. Barbauld,
  1804... 1689..1761
Richardson, Thomas Mills. Artist................... — ..1848
Richardson, William, D. D. Divine.................. 1698..1775
Richardson, William. Poet and Miscellaneous Writer.. 1743..1814
Richelet, Cæsar Peter. (*Dictionnaire François*)........ 1631..1698
Richelieu, Armand Emanuel Duplessis, Duke of. Min-
  ister of Louis XVIII. .... 1776..1822

BORN. DIED.

Richelieu, Armand John Duplessis. Cardinal. Prime
Minister. Life by Aubery, 1660; John Le Clerc, 1718;
Joy, 1816...................................... 1585..1642
Richelieu, Louis Francis Armand Duplessis, Duke of.
Marshal. Life by Faur, 1790.................... 1696..1788
Richer. French Chronicler. (*Historiarum Libri IV.*).. 950?.1010?
Richer, Edmund. Fr. Theol. (*De Auctoritate Ecclesiæ*) 1559..1631
Richer, Edward. French Author. L. by Émile Souvestre 1792..1834
Richer, Henry. French Poet......................... 1685..1748
Richer, John. Fr. Astronomer and Natural Philosopher — ..1696
Richer d'Aube, Francis. Fr. Writ. (*Principles of Right*) 1686..1752
Richer du Bouchet, Claude. French Mathematician
and Egyptologist. .:.......................... 1680..1756
Richmond, Rev. Legh. (*Annals of the Poor.*) Life by
Grimshawe; Wickens; Bedell.................... 1772..1827
Richter, John Paul Frederick. *Jean Paul.* Novelist. Life
by Eliza B. Lee, 1842; E. Forster, 1863............ 1763..1825
Richter, Otto Frederick von. Russian Traveler........ 1792..1816
Ricimer, Count and Patrician of the West............ — .. 472
Rickman, George William. Russian Electrician; killed
by lightning................................. 1711..1753
Rickman, John, F. R. S. Statistical Writer............ 1771..1840
Rickman, Thomas. Writer on Gothic Architecture .... 1776..1841
Rider, William. Hist. and Divine. (*History of England*) — ..1785
Ridgely, Thomas, D. D. Dissent. Div. (*Assembly's Catech.*) 1667?.1734
Ridinger, John Elias. German Painter of Animals..... 1695..1767
Ridley, Gloster, D. D. Divine...................... 1702..1774
Ridley, James. (*Tales of the Genii*) .... — ..1765
Ridley, Nicholas. Bishop & Martyr. L. by Gloster Ridley 1500?.1555
Ridley, Sir Thomas. Civilian. (*Civil and Eccles. Law*) — ..1629
Ridolfi, Charles. Venetian Hist.and Portrait Painter 1600 or 2..1660?
Ridolfi, Claudio, of Verona. Historical and Portr. Paint. 1560..1644
Ridpath, Rev. George, of Stitchill. (*Border History*) ... 1663?.1717
Riedesel, Frederica Charlotte Louise, Baroness. (*Voyage
de Mission*) .... 1744..1808
Riedesel, Frederick Adolphus, Baron. German Officer.. 1738..1800
Riedesel, Jos. Hermann, Baron de. (*Travels in Greece*) 1740..1785 ·
Riedinger, or Ridinger, John Elias, of Ulm. Painter... 1695..1767
Riedlin, Vitus. German Physician.................. 1656..1724
Riegels. Danish Historian......................... 1728?.1802
Riego y Nuñez, Rafael del. Spanish Revolutionist .... 1785..1823
Rienzi, Nich. Gabrini (*q. v.*) di. L. by Brumoy; Cerceau 1313..1354
Ries, Ferdinand. Musical Composer.................. 1784..1838
Rigaud, Hyacinth. Portrait Painter................. 1659..1743
Rigaud, Stephen Peter. Professor of Astronomy at Oxford 1775..1839
Rigault, Nicholas. French Critic................... 1577..1654
Righini, Vincent. Italian Musical Composer .... 1756..1812
Riley, John. Portrait Painter...................... 1646..1691
Riminaldi, Horace. Italian Historical Painter........ 1598..1630
Rinaldi, Oderic. Continuator of Baronius .... 1595..1671
Rinaldo, of Capua. Musical Composer............... fl. 16th c.
Rincon, Anthony del. Spanish Painter .... 1446?.1500
Ring, John. Surgeon. Medical and Poetical Writer ... 1751..1821
Ringelbergius, Joachim Fortius. Flemish Philosopher. — ..1536?

BORN. DIED.

Ringgli, Gothard. Swiss Artist .... 1575..1635
Ringgold, Samuel. American Military Officer......... 1800..1846
Rintoul, Robert Stephen. Journalist. Founder of the
    Spectator .... 1787..1858
Rinuccini, Octavius. Florentine Poet .... — ..1621
Rioja, Francis de. Spanish Poet.................... 1600..1659
Riolan, John. French Physician .... 1539..1605
Riolan, John, son. Anatomist and Botanist........... 1577..1657
Ripley, Eleazer Wheelock. American General........ 1782..1839
Ripley, George, or Gregory. Alchemist and Poet ...... — ..1490
Ripon, Fred. John Robinson, First Earl of. Statesman.. 1782..1859
Ripperda, John William, Baron and Duke of. Dutch
    Adventurer. Life by G. Moore; Dr. John Campbell. 1680..1737
Riquet, Peter Paul de. French Civil Engineer......... 1604..1680
Risard, Francis. French Mathematician .... — ..1778
Risbeck, Gaspar. German Writer. (*History of Germany*) 1750..1786
Risdon, Tristram. Topographer .... 1580..1640
Risley, Thomas. Puritan Divine. (*Family Religion*)... 1630..1716
Ritchie, Joseph. African Traveler .... — ..1819
Ritchie, Leitch. Journalist and Author.............. 1800?.1865
Ritchie, Thomas. American Journalist .... 1778..1854
Ritson, Isaac. Poet and Miscellaneous Writer......... 1761..1789
Ritson, Joseph. Antiquary and Poetical Critic. (*Robin
    Hood*.) Life by Haslewood, 1824; Sir Harris Nicolas,
    1833 .... 1752..1803
Rittangel, John Stephen. German Orientalist........ —aft.1652
Rittenhouse, David. American Mathematician and As-
    tronomer. Life by Barton, 1813; Renwick .... 1732..1796
Ritter, Charles. Geographer....................... 1779..1859
Ritter, John William. Philosopher.................. 1776..1810
Rittershuys, Conrad. Jurist and Philologist.......... 1560..1613
Rittershuys, Nich., son. Historical & Genealogical Writ. 1597..1670
Rivalz, Anthony. French Portrait and Historical Painter 1667..1735
Rivard, Denis. Surgeon at Neufchâteau. Lithotomist.. — ..1746
Rivard, Francis. Mathematician.................... 1697..1778
Rivarol, Anthony, Count de. French Writer.......... 1757..1801
Rivault, David. French Mathematician.............. 1571?.1616
Rivaz, Peter Joseph de. Fr. Mechanist and Chronologist 1711..1772
Rive, John Joseph. French Bibliographer............ 1730..1792
Riverius, or Rivière, Lazarus. French Medical Writer.. 1589..1655
Rivers, Anthony Woodville, Earl; beheaded at Pomfret 1442..1483
Rives, John C. American Editor.................... 1796?.1864
Rivet, Andrew. French Protestant Divine........... 1572..1651
Rivet de la Grange, Anthony. (*Literary Hist. of France*) 1683..1749
Rivière, Henry Francis de la, of Paris. (*Letters*)....... 1649..1738
Rivière, Mercier de la. French Political Economist. 1720?.1793 or 4
Rivière, Roch le Baillif, Sieur de la. Phys. and Astrol. — ..1605
Rivington, James. Royalist Printer of New York ..... 1724?.1802
Rivinus, Andrew. German Medical and Poetical Writer 1600..1656
Rivinus, Augustus Quirinus. Ger. Phys. and Botanist 1652..1723
Rizi, Francis. Spanish Painter..................... 1608..1685
Rizi, Fray John, brother. Painter .... 1595..1675
Rizzio, or Ricci, David. Favorite of Mary Queen of Scots 1540..1566
Robbins, Ashur. American Statesman .... 1757..1845

BORN. DIED.

Robert, the Strong, Duke or Marquis of France......... — .. 866
Robert I., son. King of France (922–23).............. — .. 923
Robert II. (996–1031)........................... 971..1031
Robert I. Duke of Normandy (1028–35). *Le Diable*.. — ..1035
Robert II. (1087–1134.) *Curt-hose*................. — ..1134
Robert I. *Bruce*. King of Scotland (1306–29)........ 1276?.1329
Robert II. *Stuart*. (1371–90)..................... 1316..1390
Robert III. *Stuart*. (1390–1406)................... 1340?.1406
Robert. King of Naples (1309–43) .... 1279..1343
Robert. Emperor of Germany (1400–10). *Short*...... 1352..1410
Robert, of Artois. Counselor of Edward III. .... 1287..1343
Robert, of Avesbury. Historian...................... — ..1356?
Robert, of France, Count of Clermont; br. of Louis IX. 1216..1250
Robert, of Geneva. Antipope (1378–94). *Clement VII.* — ..1394
Robert, of Gloucester. Chronicler in Verse........... ti. Hen. III.
Robert, of Jumièges. Archbp. of Canterbury (1051–52) — ..1052
Robert, Claude. Fr. Chronologist. (*Gallia Christiana*) 1564..1637
Robert, Francis. Geogr. Royal of France, and Traveler 1737..1819
Robert, Hubert. French Architectural Painter .... 1733..1808
Robert, Louis Leopold. French Painter............... 1794..1835
Robert, Louise Félicité de Keralio. Writer........... 1758..1821
Robert, Nicholas. French Miniature Painter .... 1610?.1684
Robert, Peter Francis Joseph. Fr. Revolutionary Statesm. 1763..1826
Robert de Vaugondy, Didier. (*Tablettes Parisiennes*). 1723..1786
Robert de Vaugondy, Giles. (*Atlas Universel*) .... 1688..1766
Roberti, John Baptist, Count. Italian Writer......... 1719..1786
Roberts, David, R. A. Painter. (*Sketches in Holy Land*) 1796..1864
Roberts, Miss Emma. (*Houses of York and Lancaster*) . — ..1840
Roberts, Richard. Civil Engineer .... 1789?.1864
Roberts, William. Writer. (*Life of Hannah More*.)
  Life by A. Roberts, 1850 .... 1768..1849
Robertson, Rev. Frederick William, of Brighton. Divine.
  (*Sermons*.) Life by Stopford A. Brooke............ 1816..1853
Robertson, George. Landscape Painter .... — ..1788
Robertson, James, D. D. Prof. of Eccles. History, Edinb. 1803..1860
Robertson, John, D.D., of Glasgow. Divine. (*Sermons*) 1824..1865
Robertson, Rev. Joseph. Writer. (*On Punctuation*) .. 1726..1802
Robertson, Patrick. Scottish Judge. Poet........... 1794..1855
Robertson, Stephen Gaspar. French Natural Philosopher
  and Aëronaut.................................. 1763..1837
Robertson, Thomas. Grammarian.................... — ..1560?
Robertson, William, D.D. Unitarian Writer......... 1705..1783
Robertson, William, D. D. (*Chas. V.*) L. by Stewart, 1801 1721..1793
Roberval, Gilles Persone, or Personier, de. Fr. Geometer 1602..1675
Robespierre, Francis Joseph Maximilian Isidore. French
  Revolutionist. Life by Lewes, 1849.............. 1759?.1794
Robin, John. French Botanist..................... 1550..1597
Robin Hood. Outlaw................ti. Rd. I. or Hen. III.?
Robins, Benjamin. (*Gunnery*.) Life by Dr. Wilson.... 1707..1751
Robins, or Robyns, John. Astronomer & Mathematician 1500?.1558
Robinson, Anastasia, Countess of Peterborough. Singer — ..1750
Robinson, Rev. Edward, D. D. American Philologist
  and Biblical Scholar........................... 1794..1864
Robinson, John. English Dissenting Clergyman ...... 1575..1625

BORN. DIED.

Robinson, Mrs. Mary. Poetess...................... 1758..1800
Robinson, Richard, Lord Rokeby. Archbishop of Armagh. Benefactor............................... 1709..1794
Robinson, Robert. Dissenting Divine. L. by Dyer, 1796 1735..1790
Robinson, Tancred. Writer on Medicine and Nat. Philos. — ..1748
Robinson, Rev. Thomas, of Cumberland. Naturalist ... — ..1719
Robinson, Rev. Thomas, of Leicester. Life by Rev. E.
     T. Vaughan, 1815.............................. 1749..1813
Robison, John. Scottish Mathematician and Nat. Philos. 1739..1805
Robortello, Francis. Italian Scholar and Antiquary ... 1516..1567
Rob Roy Macgregor. Highland Freebooter.......... 1660?.1743
Robson, Frederick. Actor........................... — ..1864
Robson, George Fennel. Painter.................... — ..1833
Robusti, Dominick. Painter........................ 1562..1637
Robusti, James. *Il Tintoretto* .... 1512..1594
Robusti, Marietta, daughter. Portrait Painter........ 1560..1590
Roby, John, of Rochdale. (*Traditions of Lancashire*)... — ..1850
Rocaberti, John Thomas de. Spanish Writer on Papacy 1624..1699
Rocca, Angelus. Italian Scholar and Theologian...... 1545..1620
Rochambeau, Donatien Mary Joseph, son of John Baptist 1750..1813
Rochambeau, John Baptist Donatien de Vimeur, Count
     de. Marshal .... 1725..1807
Roche, Regina Maria. Novelist .... 1766..1845
Rochefort, Wm. de. (*Réfutation du Système de la Nature*) 1731..1788
Rochefoucauld, Francis, Duc de la. (*Maxims*)........ 1613..1680
Rochejacquelein, Madame de la. L. tr. by Sir W. Scott 1772..1857
Rochejacquelein, Henry la. Vendean Royalist....... 1772..1794
Rochester, John Wilmot, Second Earl of. Courtier and
     Satirical Poet. L. by Bp. Burnet, 1680; Dr. Johnson 1647..1680
Rochester, Lawrence Hyde, First Earl of. Lord Lieut. — ..1711
Rochon, Alexis Mary de. Fr. Astronomer and Navigator 1741..1817
Rochon de Chabannes, Mark Anthony Jas. Dramatist 1730..1800
Rockingham, Charles Watson Wentworth, Marquess of.
     Premier. Life by Lord Albemarle, 1852 .... 1730..1782
Rodger, Alexander. Scottish Poet.................... 1784..1846
Rodgers, John. United States Naval Officer.......... 1771..1838
Rodman, Isaac Peace. American General............. 1822..1862
Rodney, Cæsar. American Patriot.................... 1730?.1783
Rodney, George Brydges, Lord. Admiral............. 1718..1792
Rodolph I., of Hapsburg. Emperor of Germany (1272–91) 1218..1291
Rodolph II. (1576–1612)............................. 1552..1612
Rodriguez, Ventura. Spanish Architect.............. 1717..1785
Roe, Sir Thomas. Statesman and Ambassador .... 1580?.1644
Roebuck, John, M. D., of Carron. Ironmaster. Life by
     Smiles .... 1718..1794
Roehr, John Frederick. German Theologian.......... 1777..1848
Roelas, John de las. Spanish Painter................ 1560..1625
Roemer, Olaus. Danish Astronomer .... 1644..1710
Roepel, Conrad. Dutch Painter...................... 1679..1748
Roestraeten, Peter. Dutch Portrait Painter.......... 1627..1698
Roger I. Count of Sicily .... 1031..1101
Roger II., son. First King of Sicily................. 1093..1154
Roger, Joseph Louis, of Strasburg. Medical Writer.... — ..1761
Rogers, Benjamin. Musical Composer................ —aft.1685

BORN. DIED.

Rogers, Rev. George, of Sproughton. Theological Writer 1741..1835
Rogers, James Blythe. American Physician and Chemist 1803..1852
Rogers, John. Protestant Martyr. Life by Chester, 1861 1500?.1555
Rogers, Dr. John. Controversial Divine .... 1679..1729
Rogers, Samuel. Poet. (*Recollections*.) Life by self... 1763..1855
Rogers, William, D. D. American Divine .... 1751..1824
Rogers, Woods. Captain, R. N. Circumnavigator...... — ..1732
Roghman, Roland. Dutch Landscape Painter......... 1597..1686
Rohan, Anne de. Reformer...................... 1584?.1646
Rohan, Henry, Duke of, br. Huguenot General. Writer 1579..1638
Rohan, Louis René Edward, Prince of. French Cardinal 1734..1803
Rohault, James. French Philosopher and Mathematician 1620..1675
Röhr, John Frederick. German Theologian .... 1777..1848
Rokewode, John Gage. Director of Society of Antiqua-
    ries. (*History of Suffolk*)...................... 1786..1842
Roland, Madame Manon Jane Philipon. Republican
    Politician....................................... 1754..1793
Roland, Philip Lawrence. French Sculptor .... 1746..1816
Roland d'Erceville, B. G. French Scholar and Politician 1730..1794
Roland de la Platière, John Mary. French Statesman 1732..1793
Rolandino. Italian Historian..................... 1200..1276
Rolle, Dennis, M. P., of Devonshire. Colonizer of Florida 1725..1797
Rolle, Henry. Judge.............................. 1589..1656
Rolle, John, M. P., afterwards Lord. Colonel. Arbori-
    culturist; occasioned the *Rolliad*................. 1751..1842
Rolle, Michael. French Mathematician .... 1652..1719
Rolli, Paul Anthony. Italian Poet.................:. 1687..1767
Rollin, Charles. Historian......................... 1661..1741
Rollo, Rou, or Raoul. First Duke of Normandy (911-27) — .. 931?
Rollock, Robert. First Principal of Edinburgh University 1555..1598
Rolt, Richard. Historical and Miscellaneous Writer..... 1724?.1770
Romagnosi, John Dominic. Italian Jurist............ 1761..1835
Romaine, Rev. William. Life by Rev. W. B. Cadogan.. 1714..1795
Romana, Peter Caro y Sureda, Mqs. de la. Span. General 1761..1811
Romanelli, John Francis. Italian Painter .... 1617..1662
Romanelli, Urban, son. Painter..................... 1638..1682
Romano, Julius. Italian Painter and Architect........ 1492..1546
Romanoff, Mich. Fedorovitch. Emp. of Russia (1613-45). 1598..1645
Romanus. Pope (897-98) .... — .. 898
Romanus I. Emperor of the East (919-44). *Lecapenus* — .. 948
Romanus II. (959-963.) *The Young*............... 939.. 963
Romanus III. (1028-34.) *Argyrus*.................. — ..1034
Romanus IV. (1067-71.) *Diogenes* .... — ..1071
Romanzoff, Michael Paul, Count. Diplomatist....... 1753..1826
Romanzoff, Peter Alexandrovitch, Count. Russian Gen. 1730?.1796
Romberg, Andrew. German Musical Composer .... 1767..1821
Romberg, Bernard Henry, cousin. Musical Composer.. 1767?.1841
Rombouts, Theodore. Dutch Painter .... 1597.1637 or 40
Rome de l'Isle, John Bapt. Louis. French Mineralogist 1736..1790
Romer, Olaus. Danish Astronomer .... 1644..1702
Romilly, John, of Geneva. Mechanic and Horologist .. 1714..1796
Romilly, Sir Samuel. Lawyer...................... 1757..1818
Romney, George. Painter. Life by Hayley .... 1734..1802
Romulus Augustulus. Last Roman Emperor of West. — aft. 476

BORN. DIED.

Roncalli, Christopher. *Pomerancio.* Historical Painter 1552..1626
Rondelet, Wm. Phys. and Nat. (*De Piscibus Marinis*) 1507..1566
Ronsard, Peter de. French Poet...................... 1524..1585
Ronsin, Charles Philip. French Politician .... 1752..1794
Roodtseus, John Albert.´ Dutch Portrait Painter...... 1617..1674
Rooke, Sir George. Admiral .... 1650..1709
Rooke, Lawrence. Geometrician and Astronomer...... 1623..1662
Rooker, Michael Angelo. English Artist.............. 1743..1801
Roome, Edward. Lawyer. Satirist. (*Pasquin*)...... — ..1729
Roomen, Adrian van. *Adrianus Romanus.* Mathem... 1561..1615
Roore, James. Dutch Historical Painter.............. 1686..1747
Roos, John Henry, of Ottenburg. Painter .... 1631..1685
Roos, Philip Peter. *Rosa di Tivoli.* Flemish Painter... 1655..1705
Roque, John de la. Writer of Voyages and Travels ... 1661..1745
Roquefort, John Baptist Bonaventura. (*État de la Poé-
    sie Française*)..................................... 1777..1834
Roques, Peter. French Protestant Divine............. 1685..1748
Rosa, Francis Martinez de la. Span. Statesman and Poet 1786..1862
Rosa, Salvator. Painter, Poet, Architect, Actor........ 1615..1673
Rosa di Tivoli. *Philip Peter Roos.* Flemish Painter.. 1655..1705
Rosalba, Carriera. Italian Miniature Painter......... 1675..1757
Rosamond. *Fair Rosamond.* Daughter of Walter Lord
    Clifford; Favorite of Henry II. of England......... — ..1177
Rosapina, Francis. Italian Engraver................. 1762..1841
Roscelin, of Compiègne. Fr. Schoolman. Nominalist., — ..1106?
Roscius, Quintus. Roman Actor .... — B.C. 62
Roscoe, Henry. (*British Lawyers*) .... 1800..1836
Roscoe, James. Poet and Periodical Writer........... 1791?.1864
Roscoe, Robert. Poet. (*Alfred*) .... 1790..1850
Roscoe, William. Writer. (*Life of Leo X.*).......... 1753..1831
Roscoe, W. S. Poet................................ 1781..1843
Roscommon, Wentworth Dillon, Earl of. Poet........ 1633?.1684
Rose, George. Statesman and Political Writer .... 1744..1818
Rose, Hugh James, B. D. Ed. of Parkhurst. (*Biog. Dict.*) 1795..1838
Rose, William. Bishop of Senlis. *See Rossæus* ...... 1542?.1602
Rose, William Stuart. Translator of Ariosto .... 1775?.1843
Roseingrave, Thomas. Musician .... — ..1750
Rosellini, Hippolytus. Archæologist .... 1800..1843
Rosen, Frederick Augustus. German Orientalist....... 1805..1837
Rosenmüller, or Rosenmueller, Ernest Frederick Charles.
    (*Scholia in Vetus Testamentum*) .... 1768..1835
Rosenmüller, or Rosenmueller, John George. (*Historia
    Interpretationis*)................................. 1736..1815
Rosetti, Donato. Italian Mathematician.............. —aft.1678
Rosetti, Gabriel. Poet and Commentator on Dante .... 1783..1854
Rosewell, Thomas. Nonconformist Divine............ 1630?.1691
Rosin, or Rosinus, John. German Antiquary.......... 1551..1626
Rosmini, Charles de. Italian Biographer .... 1758..1827
Rosmini Serbati, Anthony. Ital. Eccles. & Philosopher 1797..1855
Ross, Alexander. Divine. (*Virgilius Evangelizans*).... 1590..1654
Ross, Alexander. Scottish Poet...................... 1699..1784
Ross, David. Actor .... — ..1790
Ross, George. American Patriot..................... 1730..1779
Ross, Admiral Sir James Clark. Arctic Navigator ..... 1800..1862

BORN. DIED.

Ross, or Rouse, John. Antiquary of Warwick .... — ..1491
Ross, John. Bishop of Exeter. Writer.............. — ..1792
Ross, Admiral Sir John. Arctic Navigator........... 1777..1856
Ross, Sir John Lockhart. Admiral................ 1721..1790
Rossæus, or Rose, Bishop of Senlis. (*De Justâ Potestate*) 1542?.1602
Rosselli, Cosimo. Florentine Painter................ 1416..1484
Rossi, Bernard Mary de. *Rubeis*. (*Church of Aquileia*) 1687?.1775
Rossi, Jerome, of Ravenna. (*History of Ravenna*) ..... 1539..1607
Rossi, John Charles Felix, R. A. Sculptor............ 1762..1839
Rossi, John Victor. *Erythræus*. (*Pinacotheca Illustrium*) 1577..1647
Rossi, Pellegrino, Count. Statesman and Writer....... 1787..1848
Rossi, Rosso de', or Il Rosso. *Maître Roux*. Painter .. 1496..1541
Rosslyn, Alexander Wedderburn, Earl of. Lord Chanc. 1733..1805
Rosslyn, James St. Clair Erskine, Earl of. Statesman.. 1762?.1837
Rosso, Il, of Florence. *Maître Roux*. Painter. *See* Rossi 1496..1541
Rostgaard, Frederick. Danish Writer............... 1671..1745
Rostoptchin, Feodor, Ct. Russian Officer and Statesman 1765..1826
Rosweide, Heribert. Dutch Jesuit. Eccles. Antiquary 1569..1629
Rota, Bernardin. Italian Poet...................... 1509..1575
Rotari, Peter. Italian Portrait and Historical Painter.. 1707..1764
Rotgans, Luke. Dutch Poet. (*Life of William III.*)... 1645..1710
Roth, John Rudolph. German Naturalist and Traveler.. 1815..1858
Rothenhamer, John, of Munich. Painter............ 1564..1604
Rotheram, John, M. D. (*Nature and Properties of Water*) — ..1787
Rotheram, Rev. John, of Houghton le Spring. Theol. — ..1788
Rothman, Christopher. Ger. Astronomer. (*On Comets*) — ..1592
Rothschild, Mayer Anselm, of Frankfort. Banker..... 1743..1812
Rothschild, Nathan Mayer, son. Capitalist.......... 1777..1836
Rotrou, John de. French Dramatic Writer........... 1609..1650
Rotteck, Charles Wenceslaus Rodecker von. Historian. 1775..1840
Rottenhamer, or Rothenhamer, John. German Painter 1564..1604
Roubiliac, Louis Francis. Sculptor .... 1695..1762
Roucher, John Anthony. Fr. Poet & Writer. (*Les Mois*) 1745..1794
Rouelle, Hilary Marinus. Experimental Philosopher .. 1718..1779
Rouelle, William Francis, brother. French Chemist.... 1703..1770
Rouille, Peter Julian. French Jesuit. Writer......... 1681..1740
Rous, Francis. English Republican .... 1579..1659
Rouse, or Ross, John. Antiquary, of Warwick .... — ..1491
Rousseau, James. French Painter................... 1630..1693
Rousseau, John Baptist. French Lyric Poet.......... 1670..1741
Rousseau, John James. *Jean Jacques*. French Writer.
   (*Confessions.*) Life by V. D. Musset; Pathay; Bar-
   ruel de Beauvert .... 1712..1778
Roussel, Peter. French Medical Writer .... 1742..1802
Roussel, William. French Benedictine. Writer....... 1658..1717
Rousselin de Corbeau, Alexander Charles, Count de
   St. Albin. French Publicist. (*Vie de Hoche*) ...... 1773..1847
Routh, Martin Joseph, D. D. (*Reliquiæ Sacræ*) .... 1755..1854
Roux, Augustin. Fr. Physician. (*Typographical Annals*) 1726..1776
Rowe, Mrs. Elizabeth. Poetical and Prose Writer.... 1674..1737
Rowe, John, of Tiverton. Nonconf. Div. (*Love of Christ*) — ..1677
Rowe, Nicholas. Poet Laureate. Translator of Lucan.. 1673..1718
Rowe, Thomas. Nonconf. Div. (*The Christian's Works*) — ..1698?
Rowe, Thomas. Poetical and Historical Writer........ 1687..1715

BORN. DIED.

Rowlands, Henry. Welsh Antiquary. (*Mona Restaurata*) — ..1722
Rowlandson, Thomas. Caricaturist................. 1756..1827
Rowley, William. Dramatic Writer................. ti. Jas. I.
Rowley, Wm., M. D. (*Schola Medicinæ Universalis Nova*) 1743..1806
Rowning, John. Mathematician and Divine .... 1699..1771
Roxana. Bactrian Princess; wife of Alexander the Great — B.C.311
Roxburgh, Wm., M.D. Scottish Botanist. (*Flora Indica*) 1759..1815
Roy, Anthony, Count. French Statesman............. 1764..1847
Roy, Julian le. French Horologist................... 1686..1759
Roy, Julian David le, son. Architect and Antiquary.... 1724..1803
Roy, Louis le. French Scholar. (*Life of Budæus*) ..... — ..1577
Roy, Peter le. Horologist. (*Étrennes Chronométriques*) 1717..1785
Roy, Peter Charles. French Satirist and Dramatic Poet 1683..1764
Roy, Wm. Maj.-Gen. (*Antiquities of Romans in Britain*) — ..1790
Royer-Collard, Peter Paul. Fr. Statesman and Philos. 1763..1845
Royse, John. Popular Preacher. (*Spirit's Touchstone*).. — ..1663
Rozée, Mademoiselle, of Leyden. Artist in Silk....... 1632..1682
Rozier, Francis. French Botanist and Agriculturist.... 1734..1793
Rualt, or Rualdus, John. French Scholar............. 1580?.1636
Ruarus, Martin. Socinian Writer.................... 1587?.1657
Rubens, Albert. Antiquary......................... 1614..1657
Rubens, Peter Paul. Painter. Life by Van Hassell.... 1577..1640
Rubini, John Baptist. Vocalist .... 1795..1854
Rubruquis, or De Ruysbroeck, William. Traveler .. 1230?.aft.1293
Rucellai, Bernard. Italian Statesman, Historian, Poet.. 1449..1514
Rucellai, John, son. Scholar and Poet. (*The Bees*) ... 1475..1525
Rudbeck, John. Swedish Bishop and Theologian...... 1581..1646
Rudbeck, Olaus. Swed. Anatomist, Botanist, Antiquary 1630..1702
Rudbeck, Olaus, son. Botanist and Orientalist........ 1660..1740
Rudborne, Thomas. Bishop of St. David's........... — ..1442?
Rudborne, Thos. Monk. (*Historia Major Wintoniensis*) — ..1450?
Ruddiman, Thomas. Critic. L. by Geo. Chalmers, 1794 1674..1757
Rüdiger, Feodor Vasilievitch, Count. Russian General.. 1780..1856
Ruding, Rev. Rogers. Antiquary. (*Annals of Coinage*) 1751..1820
Rudolph I., or Rodolph, of Hapsburg. Emp. (1272–91) 1218..1291
Rudolph II., or Rodolph. (1576–1612)............... 1552..1612
Rue, Charles de la. Fr. Poet, Preacher, Classical Editor 1643..1725
Rue, Charles de la. Fr. Benedictine. Editor of Origen 1684..1739
Rueda, Lope de. Spanish Dramatist.................. 1500?.1564
Ruediger, Feodor Vasilievitch, Count. Russian General 1780..1856
Ruel, John, of Soissons. Botanist. (*De Naturâ Stirpium*) 1479..1539
Ruffhead, Owen. Miscellaneous Writer .... 1723?.1769
Ruffi, Anthony de. French Lawyer and Historian...... 1607..1689
Ruffinus, Peter John Mary. French Diplomatist....... 1742..1824
Ruffo, Fabricius. Cardinal. Neapolitan Politician ..... 1750?.1827
Rufilius Numantianus, Claudius. Roman Poet. (*Itinerarium*) .... fl. 414
Rufinus. Chief Minister of Theodosius the Great...... — .. 395
Rufinus. *Toranus*. Ecclesiastical Writer............. 345?. 410
Rufus Ephesius. Greek Physician .... ti. Trajan
Rugendas, George Philip. German Battle Painter..... 1666..1742
Ruggle, George. Dramatic Satirist. (*Ignoramus*)... 1575.1621 or 2
Rugman, Jonas John. Icelandic Scholar............. 1636..1669
Ruhnken, David. Philologist........................ 1723..1798

BORN DIED.

Ruhs, Frederick. German Historian . . . . 1780. .1820
Ruinart, Thierry. Fr. Writ. (*Acta Primorum Martyrum*) 1657. .1709
Ruisch, or Ruysch, Rachel, of Amsterdam. Flower Paint. 1664. .1750
Rule, Gilbert, M. D. Nonconformist Divine . . . . 1623?.1705
Rulhière, Claudius Carloman de. French Historian. . . . 1735. .1791
Rulland, Martin. German Medical Writer . . . . 1532?.1602
Rumford, Benjamin Thompson, Count. American Natu-
ral Philosopher and Philanthropist. . . . . 1752. .1814
Rumiantzoff. *See* Romanzoff.
Rumohr, Charles Fred. Louis Felix von. Writer on Art 1785. .1843
Rumph, George Everard. Botanist. (*Herbarium Am-
boinense*) . . . . 1637. .1706
Rumsey, James. American Inventor . . . . 1743?.1792
Runciman, Alexander. Scottish Painter. . . . . 1736. .1785
Runius, John. Swedish Poet. . . . . 1679. .1713
Runjeet Singh. Chief of Lahore and Cashmere. . . . . . . 1780. .1839
Runnington, Charles. Law Writer . . . . 1751. .1821
Rupert, Prince, of Bavaria, nephew of Charles I. . . . . . . 1619. .1682
Ruscelli, Jerome. Italian Scholar. . . . . — . .1566
Rush, Benjamin, M. D. American Physician. . . . . 1745. .1813
Rush, Richard, son. Statesman and Diplomatist. . . . . . . 1780. .1859
Rushworth, John. (*Historical Collections*). . . . . .1607?.1690
Russell, Alexander, M. D. Scottish Physician at Aleppo.
(*Natural History of Aleppo*). . . . . — . .1770
Russell, Benjamin. American Journalist . . . . 1761. .1845
Russell, Edward, Earl of Orford. Admiral. . . . . 1651. .1727
Russell, Francis, Duke of Bedford. Statesman and Agri-
culturist. . . . . 1765. .1802
Russell, Michael, LL. D. Bishop of Glasgow. Writer.
(*Connection of Sacred and Profane History*). . . . . 1781. .1848
Russell, Patrick, M. D. Phys. at Aleppo. (*On Plague*) 1726. .1805
Russell, Rachel Wriothesley, Lady, wife of Lord William 1636?.1723
Russell, Richard, M. D. Writer on Sea Water . . . . — . .1768
Russell, Lord William. Beheaded. Life by Earl Russell 1639. .1683
Russell, William, Fifth Earl, First Duke of Bedford.
Royalist. . . . . 1614. .1700
Russell, Wm., LL. D. (*Mod. Europe.*) L. by Irvine, 1801 1746. .1794
Rust, George. Bishop of Dromore. . . . . — . .1670
Rutgers, John. Dutch Critic. (*Variæ Lectiones*) . . . . . . 1589. .1625
Rutherford, Daniel, M. D. Natural Philosopher. . . . . . . 1749. .1819
Rutherford, Samuel. Prof. at St. Andrew's. (*Letters*) 1600?.1661
Rutherforth, Thomas, D. D. Archdeacon . . . . 1712. .1771
Rutledge, Edward. American Statesman. . . . . 1749. .1800
Rutledge, John, brother. Statesman and Jurist. . . . . 1739. .1800
Ruxton, George Frederick. Traveler . . . . 1820. .1848
Ruysbroek, John. *Divine,* or *Ecstatic, Doctor.* Mystic. . 1293?.1381
Ruysch, Frederick. Dutch Anatomist . . . . 1638. .1731
Ruysch, Henry, son. Anatomist. (*Theatrum Universale*) — . .1727
Ruysch, Rachel, of Amsterdam. Flower Painter . . . . . . 1664. .1750
Ruysdaal, or Ruysdael, Jacob. Dutch Painter. . . . . 1636. .1681
Ruyter, Michael Adriaenzoon de. Admiral . . . . 1607. .1676
Ryan, Lacy. Dramatic Writer . . . . 1694?.1760
Rycaut, or Ricaut, Sir Paul. Traveler and Biographer.
(B. A. 1650) . . . . — . .1700

BORN. DIED.

Ryckaert, David. Dutch Painter ....1615..1677
Ryckaert, Martin. Dutch Landscape Painter.........1591..1636
Rycke, Theodore van. Dutch Critic.................1640..1690
Rycquius, Justus. Dutch Antiq. and Poet. (*De Capitolio*) 1587..1627
Ryder, Sir Dudley. Lord Chief Justice..............1691..1756
Ryder, Hon. Henry. Bishop of Lichfield and Coventry 1778..1836
Ryer, Peter du. Dramatist and Miscellaneous Writer... 1605..1658
Ryland, John, D. D. Dissenting Minister. Writer..... — ..1792
Ryland, Wm. Wynne. Engraver; executed for Forgery 1732..1783
Rymer, Thomas. Critic and Antiquary. (*Fœdera*).... 1638?.1713
Rysbraeck, John Michael. Dutch Sculptor .... 1694..1770
Rysbraeck, Peter. Dutch Landscape Painter.........1657..1716
Ryves, Bruno. Chaplain to Charles I. Preacher ...... — ..1677
Ryves, Eliza. Irish Novelist. (*Hermit of Snowdon*).... — ..1797
Ryves, Sir Thomas. Civilian. (*Historia Navalis Antiqua*) — ..1651
Rzewusky, or Rzewiesky, Wenceslaus. Polish States-
    man and Writer.................................. 1705..1779

23

S.

BORN. DIED.

Sa, or Saa, Emanuel. Portuguese Jesuit and Divine.... 1530..1596
Sa de Miranda, Francis. Portuguese Satirist and Poet 1495..1558
Saad ed-deen, Mohammed Effendi. Turkish Historian — ..1599
Saadi, or Sadi. Persian Poet..................... 1175 or 6.1291
Saadia, or Saadiah (ben Joseph). Jewish Philosopher,
    Poet, and Scholar........................... 892?.941 or 2
Saas, John, of Rouen. (*Abridgment of Hist. Dictionary*) 1703..1774
Saavedra, Michael de Cervantes. *See* Cervantes....... 1547..1616
Saavedra Faxardo, Diego de. Span. Writer & Diplom. 1584..1648
Sabatai-Sevi. Jewish Impostor...'................... 1625..1676
Sabatier, Anthony, of Castres. Writer.............. 1742..1817
Sabatier, Peter. French Benedictine. (*Latinæ Versiones*) 1682..1742
Sabatini, Francis. Spanish Architect................ 1722..1798
Sabbatini, Andrew. *Andrea da Salerno.* Neapolitan
    Painter.. 1480?.1545?
Sabbatini, Lorenzo. *Lorenzin di Bologna.* Painter.... — ..1577
Sabbatini, Louis Anthony, of Padua. Comp. and Writer 1739..1809
Sabellicus, Mark Anthony Cocceius. Italian Historian
    and Philologist ...."..................... 1436..1508
Sabellius. African Bishop or Presbyter; Heretic....... fl. 256-70
Sabeo, Faustus. Venetian Poet .... 1478?.1558?
Sabina, wife of Hadrian (100?-138?)................. — .. 138?
Sabine, Joseph, F. R. S. Savant..................... 1770..1837
Sabinianus, of Volterra. Bishop of Rome (604-6)..... — .. 606
Sabinus, Francis Floridus. Italian Writer. (*Interpreta-
    tion of Civil Law*)............................. — ..1547
Sabinus, George. *Schaller.* German Latin Poet ...... 1508..1560
Sablier, Charles. French Writer .... 1693..1785
Sablière, Anthony de Rambouillet de la. French Poet.. 1615?.1680
Sacchetti, Francis. Italian Novelist and Poet....... 1335?.aft.1400
Sacchetti, John Baptist. Italian Architect........... 1736..1764
Sacchi, Andrew. Italian Painter.................... 1598..1661
Sacchini, Anthony Mary Gaspar. Ital. Musical Composer 1735..1786
Sacchini, Juvenal, of Milan. Writer on Music .... 1726..1789
Sacheverell, Henry, D. D. Tory Divine.............. 1672?.1724
Sachs, Hans. Shoemaker of Nuremberg. Dramatic Poet 1494..1578
Sachtleevin, or Zachtleevin, Cornelius. Dutch Painter. 1612.. —
Sachtleevin, Herman. Dutch Landscape Painter....... 1609..1685
Sack, Frederick Samuel Godfrey. German Theologian.. 1738..1817
Sackville, Charles, Sixth Earl of Dorset and Middlesex.
    Wit and Poet.................................. 1637..1706
Sackville, Edward, Fourth Earl of Dorset, K. G. Royalist 1590..1652
Sackville, George, First Viscount. Soldier & Statesman 1716..1785
Sackville, Thomas, Lord Buckhurst and Earl of Dorset.
    Statesman and Poet............................ 1527..1608
Sacrobosco. (*De Sphærâ Mundi.*) *See* Holywood..... — ..1256
Sacy, Anthony Isaac Sylvestre de, Baron. Orientalist.. 1758..1838
Sacy, Louis de. French Advocate and Writer......... 1654..1727
Sacy, Louis Isaac. *Le Maistre.* Jansenist; Transl. of Bible 1613..1684
Sade, Donatian Alfonso Francis, Count. Novelist ...... 1740..1814

BORN. DIED.

Sade, James Francis Paul Aldonce de. Abbé. (*Life of Petrarch*) .... 1705..1767
Sadeel, Anthony. French Huguenot; Theologian...... 1534..1591
· Sadeler, Giles. Engraver. (*Vestiges of Antiq. of Rome*) 1570..1629
Sadeler, John. Dutch Engraver..................... 1550..1600
Sadeler, Raphael, brother. Engraver................ 1555..1616
Sadi, or Saadi. Persian Poet .... 1175 or 6.1291
Sadler, John. Political Writer. (*Rights of the Kingdom*) 1615..1674
Sadler, Michael Thomas. Philanthropist. (*Ireland*)... 1780..1835
Sadler, Sir Ralph. Statesman. Life by Sir W. Scott... 1507..1587
Sadler, William Windham. Aëronaut and Chemist.... 1796..1824
Sadolet, James. Italian Cardinal; Writer .... 1477..1547
Sadoleto, Paul. Italian Poet and Epistolographer ..... 1508..1572
Saemund, Sigfusson. Icelandic Writer .... 1054?.1133
Safarik, or Schafarik, Paul Joseph. Antiq. & Philologist 1795..1861
Sage, Alain René le. Novelist. (*Gil Blas*)........... 1668..1747
Sage, Balthasar George. French Chemist .... 1740..1824
Sage, David le. French Poet. (*Les Folies du Sage*).... — ..1650?
Sage, John. Bp. of Edinburgh. L. by John Gillan, 1714 1652..1711
Sagittarius, Gaspar. German Historian and Antiquary 1643..1694
Sagredo, John. Venetian Historian. (*Ottoman Empire*) 1616?.aft.1691
Sahuguet Amazit, F. French General and Tactician.. 1713..1783
Said ibn Batric. *Eutychius*. Arab. Phys. and Historian 876.. 940
Said Pasha, Mohammed. Viceroy of Egypt........... 1822..1863
Sailer, John Michael. Roman Catholic Theologian..... 1751..1832
Sainct Paule, Sir George. Benefactor............... 1562?.1613
Sainctes, Claude de. Bp. of Évreux. (*On the Eucharist*) 1525..1591
Saint Albans, Harriet Mellon, Duchess of. Actress.... 1775..1837
Saint-Amant, Mark Anthony Gerard, Sieur de. Fr. Poet 1594..1661
Saint-Amour, William de. Oppon. of Mendicant Orders .— ..1272
Saint-André, John Bon, Baron. French Revolutionist and Administrator under Napoleon .... 1749..1813
Saint-Ange, Angelo Francis Farian de. Transl. of Ovid 1747..1810
Saint-Arnaud, James Achille Leroy de. Marsh. of France 1798..1854
Saint-Aubin, Gabriel James de. Fr. Painter & Engraver 1724..1770
Saint-Aulaire, Francis Joseph de Beaupoil, Marquis de. Poet .... 1643..1742
Saint Clair, Arthur. American General .... 1735..1813
Saint-Cosme, John de. French Monk. Lithotomist. 1703.aft.1763
Saint-Cyr, Lawrence Gouvion de. Marshal of France; Military Writer.................................. 1764..1830
Saint-Cyran, Jean du Verger de Hauranne, Abbé de... 1581..1643
Saint-Évremond, Charles de Marguetel de St. Denis, Lord of. Writer.............................. 1613..1703
Saint-Foix, Germain Francis Poullain de. Dram. & Writ. 1698..1776
Saint-Gelais, Mellin de. French Poet............... 1491..1559
Saint-Gelais, Octavian de. French Archbishop and Poet 1466..1502
Saint-Geniès, John de. French Poet............... 1607..1663
Saint-George, Chevalier de. Violinist and Composer.. 1745..1799
Saint-Germain, Christopher. *Seintgermun*. English Law Writer. (*Doctor and Student*).................. — ..1540
Saint-Germain, Claude Louis, Count de. Adventurer. (*Memoirs*)...................................... 1707..1778
Saint-Hilaire, Auguste de. Botanist. (*Flora Brasilica*) 1799..1861

BORN. DIED.

Saint-Hilaire, Geoffrey Stephen.   Naturalist and Anatomist.   Life by son.. . . . . 1772..1844
Saint-Hyacinthe, Hyacinth Cordonnier de.   *Themiseuil* 1684..1746
Saint-John, Bayle.   Writer . . . . 1822..1859
Saint-John, Henry, Viscount Bolingbroke.   Statesman and Writer.   Life by Goldsmith. . . . . 1678..1751
Saint-Just, Anthony Louis Leo de.   Revolutionist . . . . . 1768..1794
Saint-Lambert, Charles Francis, Marquis de.   French Soldier, Poet, and Writer . . . . 1717..1803
Saint-Leger, Bartholomew Mercier, Abbé de.   Bibliographer . . . . , ... 1734..1799
Saint-Leger, Francis Barry Boyle.   Writer . . . . 1799..1829
Saint-Leonard, Robert Gifford, Baron.   Lord Chancellor 1779..1826
Saint-Marc, Chas. Hugh Lefebvre de.   Historical Writer 1698..1769
Saint-Marc, John Paul Andrew des Rasins, Marquis de.   French Lyric Poet . . . . : . . . . 1728..1818
Saint-Martin, John Anthony.   Fr. Orientalist and Hist. 1791..1832
Saint-Martin, Louis Claude de.   *Le Philosophe Inconnu.*   French Writer.   (*Error and Truth*) . . . . 1743..1803
Saint-Maure, Charles de, Duke of Montausier (*q. v.*) . . . 1610..1690
Saint-Non, John Claude Richard de.   (*Voyage Pittoresque*). . . . . 1727..1791
Saint-Pavin, Denis Sanguin de. . French Poet . . . . — ..1670
Saint-Pierre, Charles Irénée Castel de.   Abbé; Philanthropist.   (*Projet de Paix Perpétuelle*). . . . . 1658..1743
Saint-Pierre, Eust. de, of Calais.   Pensionary of Edw. III. — ..1371
Saint-Pierre, James Henry Bernardin de.   French Author.   (*Paul and Virginia*) . . . . 1737..1814
Saint-Priest, Alexis de Guignard, Count.   French Writer.   (*Histoire de la Chute des Jesuites*). . . . . 1815..1851
Saint-Priest, Francis Emanuel Guignard, Count de.   French Statesman . . . . 1735..1821
Saint-Réal, Cæsar Vichard de.   Writer. . . . . 1639..1692
Saint-Simon, Claudius Henry, Count de.   Philosopher; Founder of St. Simonianism. 1760..1825
Saint-Simon, Louis de Rouvroy, Duke de.   (*Memoirs of Louis XIV.*). . . . . 1675..1755
Saint-Urban, Ferdinand de.   Artist, Architect, Medalist 1654..1738
Saint-Vincent, John Francis Fauris de. Medalist & Antiq. 1718..1798
Saint-Vincent, John Jervis, First Earl of.   Admiral.   Life by E. P. Brenton, 1830; J. S. Tucker, 1844. . . . . 1734..1823
Saint-Yves, Charles.   French Oculist. . . . . 1667..1733
Sainte-Aulaire, Louis de, Ct.   Fr. Statesm. and Diplom. 1778..1849
Sainte-Beuve, James de.   French Theologian. . . . . 1613..1677
Sainte-Croix, William Emanuel Joseph, Baron de.   Writ. 1746..1809
Sainte-Félix, Armand Philip Germain de, Marquis.   French Admiral and Administrator . . . . 1737..1819
Sainte-Marthe, Abel de.   Poet . . . . 1566..1652
Sainte-Marthe, Abel Louis de, nephew.   General of the Oratory.   Fr. Theol. and Hist.   (*Orbis Christianus*) 1621..1697
Sainte-Marthe, Denis de.   French Theologian and Historian.   (*Gallia Christiana*). 1650..1725
Sainte-Marthe, Gaucher de, or Scævola.   (*Geneal. Hist.*) 1571..1650
Sainte-Marthe, Louis de, twin-brother and Colleague .. 1571..1656

BORN. DIED.

Sainte-Marthe, *Sammarthanus*, Scævola, or Gaucher de.
   Writer and Latin Poet.......................... 1536..1623
Sainte-Palaye, John Baptist de la Curne de. (*Chivalry*) 1697..1781
Saladin. Sultan. Life by Abulfeda; Bohadini, 1732... 1137..1193
Salario, Andrew, of Milan. Painter................. 1487..1559
Saldanha Oliveira, John Charles. Portuguese Statesm. 1791..1861
Salden, William. Dutch Divine. (*Otia Theologica*).... — ..1694
Sale, George. Orientalist. (*Koran*)................. 1680..1736
Sale, Sir Robt. Henry. Maj.-Gen.; Defender of Jellalabad 1782..1845
Salerne, Francis, of Orleans. Physician and Naturalist — ..1760
Sales, Francis de, St. Titular Bishop of Geneva. Devo-
   tional Writer. Life by Marsollier; Cotolendi .... 1567..1622
Sales, Louis de. Commander. Life by Bouffier, 1708... 1577..1654
Salfi, Francis. Ital. Writer. Ed. of *Literary Hist. of Italy* 1759..1832
Salian, or Sallian, James. French Jesuit. (*Ecclesiastical
   Annals of Old Testament*) .... 1557..1640
Saliceti, Christopher, of Corsica. Fr. Administrat. in Italy 1757..1809
Salieri, Anthony. Italian Musical Composer .... 1750..1825
Salih ben Bahleh. Indian Physician at Bagdad ......, fl. 800?
Salimbeni, Ventura. *Bevilaqua*. Italian Painter...... 1557..1613
Salinas, Francis de. Spanish Writer on Music......... 1512?.1690
Salisbury, Ela, Countess of .... — ..1263
Salisbury, John of. Bishop of Chartres. Writer ...... 1110..1180
Salisbury, Margaret Pole, Countess of; beheaded....... — ..1541
Salisbury, Robert Cecil, First Earl of. Statesman...... 1550?.1612
Salisbury, Thomas de Montacute, Fourth Earl of; slain
   at Orleans...................................... — ..1428
Salisbury, Wm. Welsh Lawyer; Transl. of the Liturgy —aft.1567
Salisbury, William Longespée, Earl of. Warrior ...... — ..1226
Salle, John Baptist de la. French Ecclesiastic .... 1651..1719
Sallengre, Albert Henry de. Dutch Scholar........... 1694..1723
Sallet, Frederick von. German Poet................. 1812..1843
Sallo, Denis de. Originator of Literary Journals....... 1626..1669
Sallust. Roman Historian. L. by Dr. Steuart; Dr. Rose 86.34 B.C.
Salmasius, or Saumaise, Claudius. Universal Scholar.
   Life by Clement.................................. 1588..1653
Salmeron, Alphonso. Commentator. Life by Ribadeneira 1516..1585
Salmon, Nathaniel. Antiquary. (*Lives of Bishops*).... — ..1742
Salmon, Thomas, brother. Historical Writer.......... — ..1743
Salmon, William. Empiric and Writer............... — .1700?
Salomon, Haym. American Financier................ 1740?.1785
Salomon, John Peter. German Violinist and Composer 1745..1815
Salonina. Roman Empress, wife of Gallienus .... — .. 268
Salt, Henry. Consul-General in Egypt. L. by Halls, 1834 — ..1827
Salt, W. Antiquary................................ — ..1863
Salter, Rev. Samuel. Master of Charter-House School.. — ..1778
Salutatio, Lino Coluccio Pierio. Scholar & Poet Laureate 1330..1406
Salvandy, Narcisse Achille, Count de. Political Writer 1796..1856
Salvator Rosa. Painter, Poet, Architect, Actor........ 1615..1673
Salverte, Anne Jos. Eusebius Baconnière de. Fr. Writ. 1771..1839
Salvi, John Baptist. *Sassoferrato*. Italian Painter ..... 1605..1685
Salvi, Nicholas. Italian Architect................... 1699?.1752
Salviani, Hippolytus. Italian Physician and Naturalist.
   (*History of Fishes*) .... 1514..1572

BORN. DIED.

Salvianus. Presbyter of Marseilles. (*De Providentiâ*) — .. 495?
Salviati, Il. *Francis Rossi.* Florentine Painter .... 1510..1563
Salviati, Joseph. *Porta.* Venetian Painter.......... 1535..1585
Salviati, Leonard. Italian Dramatist and Critic .... 1540..1589
Salvini, Anthony Mary. Greek Scholar and Translator
    of Florence .... 1653..1729
Salvini, Salvino. (*Fasti Consolari delle' Acad. Fiorentina*) 1667..1751
Salzmann, Christian Gottbilf. German Protestant Cler-
    gyman and Teacher............................. 1744..1811
Sambucus, John. Hungarian Scholar and Historian... 1531..1584
Samerius, Henry, of Luxembourg. Jesuit. (*Chron. Sacra*) 1540..1610
Sammarthanus. *See* Sainte-Marthe .... 1536..1623
Sampson, Thomas. Dean of Christ Ch. Puritan Divine 1517..1589
Samsoe, Olaus John. Danish Writer .... 1759..1796
Samson. Judge of Israel .... fl. 12th c. B.C.
Samuel. Last of the Judges of Israel............. — bef.1060 B.C.
Samwell, David. Surgeon with Captain Cook......... — ..1799
Sanadon, Noel Stephen. Translator of Horace .... 1676..1733
Sanchez, Anthony Nuñes Ribeiro. Port. Phys. & Philos. 1699..1783
Sanchez, Francis. *El Brocense.* Grammarian. (*Minerva*) 1523..1601
Sanchez, Francis. Physician. Commentator on Aristotle — 1632
Sanchez, or Sanctius, Gaspar. Jesuit. Commentator.. 1553?.1628
Sanchez, Thomas, of Cordova. Jesuit. (*Monastic Vows*) 1550..1610
Sanchez de Arevalo, or Sanctius, Roderick. Spanish
    Bishop and Writer .... 1404..1470
Sancho, Ignatius. Literary Negro. Life by Jekyll .... 1729..1780
Sanchoniathon. Phœnician Writer.............. fl. 14th c.? B.C.
Sancroft, William. Archbishop of Canterbury (1677–89).
    Nonjurer. Life by Dr. G. D'Oyly .... 1616..1693
Sanctius. *See* Sanchez.
Sanctorius, Sanctorius, of Venice. (*De Staticâ Medicinâ*) 1561..1636
Sand, Charles Louis. Murderer of Kotzebue .... 1795..1820
Sandby, Paul, R. A. Artist .... 1732..1809
Sandby, Thomas, R. A., brother. Artist and Architect.. 1721..1798
Sandeman, Robert. Scottish Sectary .... 1723..1771
Sanders, Nich. Rom. Cath. Div. (*Schismatis Anglicani*) 1527?.1580
Sanders, Robert. Scottish Novelist and Compiler...... 1729?.1783
Sanderson, John. American Author .... 1783..1844
Sanderson, Robert. Bp. of Lincoln. L. by Walton, 1678 1587..1663
Sanderson, Robert. Antiquary. Continuator of Rymer 1660..1741
Sanderus, or Sander, Anthony. Flem. Topog. and Biog. 1586..1664
Sandford, Sir Daniel Keyte, D. C. L. Greek Professor .. — ..1838
Sandford, Francis. Herald. (*Genealogical Hist. England*) 1630..1693
Sandini, Anthony. Italian Ecclesiastical Historian...... 1692..1751
Sandius, Christopher. *Van den Sand.* Prussian Unitarian 1644..1680
Sandoval, Fray Prudencio de. Spanish Historian...... 1560?.1621
Sandrart, Joachim von. Ger. Paint. (*Acad. Artis Pictoriæ*) 1606..1688
Sands, Robert Charles. American Author............. 1799..1832
Sandwich, Edward Montagu, First Earl of. Naval Com-
    mander. Life by Cooke, 1799.................... 1625..1672
Sandwich, John Montagu, Fourth Earl of. L. by Cooke 1718..1792
Sandys, Edwin. Archbp. of York. L. by Dr. Whitaker 1519..1588
Sandys, Sir Edwin. Envoy & Writer. (*Europæ Speculum*) 1561?.1629
Sandys, George, brother. Traveler and Poet .... 1577..1644

BORN. DIED.

Sanford, Nathan. American Statesman and Jurist..... 1779..1838
Sangallo, Anthony. Sculptor, Architect, Agriculturist.. — ..1534
Sangallo, Anthony de. Italian Architect.............. 1482?.1546
Sangallo, Julian. Italian Architect .... 1443..1517
Sankaracharya. Sanskrit Theologian and Philosopher fl. 1000
Sanmicheli, Michael. Ital. Civil and Military Architect 1484..1559
Sannazarius, or Sannazaro, James. Italian Poet. (De
    Partu Virginis).................................... 1458..1530
Sansevero, Raymond di Sangro, of Naples. Inventor
    and Discoverer.................................... 1710..1771
Sanson, Adrian. Geographer........................ — ..1718
Sanson, Nicholas. Geographer. Life by H. Sanson, 1863 1600..1667
Sanson, Nicholas, son. Geographer. (Europe)........ — ..1648
Sanson, William, brother. Geographer .... — ..1705
Sansovino, Francis. Scholar and Printer. (Venice).... 1521..1586
Sansovino, James. Tatti. Sculptor and Architect .... 1479..1570
Santa Cruz de Marzenado, Alvar de Navia Osorio,
    Marquis of. Spanish Soldier and Diplomatist....... 1687?.1732
Santana, Peter. Ex-President and Gen. of San Domingo — ..1864
Santander, Francis de Paula. President of New Granada 1792..1840
Santerre, Anthony Joseph. French Revolutionist...... 1752..1809
Santerre, John Baptist. French Historical Painter..... 1651..1717
Santeul, Claude. French Ecclesiastic. Latin Poet..... 1627?.1684
Santeul, or Santolius, John Baptist. Latin Poet....... 1630..1697
Santi di Titi. Florentine Historical and Portrait Painter 1538..1603
Santillana, Iñigo Lopez de Mendoza, Marquis of. Span-
    ish Poet and Statesman........................... 1398..1458
Santorio, or Sanctorius (q. v.). Italian Physician..... 1561..1636
Sanuto, Marino. Torsello. Venetian Traveler .... —aft.1329
Sanz, Augustine. Spanish Architect.................. 1724..1801
Sanzio, Raphael. Raphael. Italian Painter........... 1483..1520
Sapor I., or Shahpor. King of Persia (240–73) .... — .. 273
Sapor II. (310–81.) Postumus .... 310.. 381
Sapor III. (385–90).............................. — .. 390
Sappho. Greek Poetess .... fl. 611–592 B.C.
Sarah, wife of Abraham.......................... 1986.1859 B.C.
Sarasin, or Sarrasin, John Francis. Fr. Poet and Writer 1603?.1654
Saravia, Hadrian. English Divine; Friend of Hooker.. 1531..1613
Sarazin, James. French Sculptor .... 1590..1660
Sarazin, John. French Marshal; served under England 1770..1840?
Sarbievius, or Sarbiewski, Matthias Casimir. Polish Poet 1595..1642
Sardanapalus. King of Nineveh .... — .. 876?
Sarjeant, John. Smith. Secular Priest. Controversialist 1621?.1707
Sarnelli, Pompey. Italian Prelate and Writer .... 1649..1724
Sarpi, Paul. Father Paul. Theologian, &c. (Council of
    Trent.) Life by Fulgentio, 1651; Sir H. Wotton; Abp.
    G. Fontanini, 1803; A. Blanchi; Giovanni, 1836 .... 1552..1623
Sarrasin, John Francis. French Poet and Prose Writer 1603?.1654
Sarti, Joseph. Italian Musical Composer .... 1730..1802
Sarto, Andrea Vanucci del. Painter................. 1488..1530
Sartorius, Ernest William Christian. German Theologian 1797..1859
Sartorius, George Frederick Christopher, Baron von
    Waltershausen. German Historian................ 1765..1828
Sassoferrato. John Baptist Salvi. Italian Painter..... 1605..1685

BORN. DIED.

Saul. First King of Israel (B. c. 1095–1055) .... —B.C.1055
Saumaise, or Salmasius, *which see*.................. 1588..1653
Saumarez, or Sausmarez, James, Lord de. Admiral.
　Life by Sir John Ross, 1808 .... 1757..1836
Saunders, Sir Edmund. Lord Chief Justice. (*Reports*) 1600?.1683
Saunders, Prince. Attorney-General of Hayti........ 1775?.1840
Saunders, Richard. Astrological Writer.............. — ..1680
Saunderson, Nicholas, LL. D., of Cambridge. Mathema-
　tician. (*Algebra*) .... 1682..1739
Saurin, Bernard Joseph. French Dramatic Writer..... 1706..1781
Saurin, Elias. Piedmontese Protestant Divine......... 1639..1703
Saurin, James. French Prot. Preacher. L. by Robinson 1677..1730
Saurin, Joseph. French Mathematician. Life by self .. 1659..1737
Saurin, William. Irish Lawyer...................... 1767..1839
Saussure, Albertine Adrienne Necker de. Writer...... 1766..1841
Saussure, Horace Benedict de. Naturalist and Alpine
　Traveler. Life by Senebier...................... 1740..1799
Saussure, Nicholas de, of Geneva. Agricultural Writer 1709..1790
Saussure, Nich. Theo. de. Chemist, Mineralogist, & Geol. 1767..1845
Sauvages, Francis Boissier de. Physician and Botanist 1706..1767
Sauval, Henry, of Paris. (*Hist. and Antiquities of Paris*) 1620?.1670
Sauveur, Joseph. French Mathematician .... 1653..1716
Savage, Richard. Poet. Life by Dr. Johnson......... 1698..1743
Savage, William. ` (*Dictionary of Printing*)............ 1771..1844
Savaron, John. French Critic and Political Writer..... 1550?.1622
Savary, Anne John Mary René, Dk. of Rovigo. Fr. Gen. 1774..1833
Savary, James. French Negotiator. (*Code Savary*).... 1622..1690
Savary, Nicholas. French Traveler. (*Life of Mahomet;
　Letters on Egypt*)............................... 1750..1788
Savary des Brulons, James. (*Dictionnaire de Commerce*) 1657..1716
Saverein, Alexander. Fr. Mathematician & Philosopher 1720..1805
Savery, Roland. Flemish Painter .... 1576..1639
Savigny, Frederick Charles von. German Jurist. (*Rö-
　mischen Rechts*) .... 1779..1861
Savile, Sir George, Marquess of Halifax. Statesman.... 1630?.1695
Savile, Sir George, Bart., M. P. Politician............. 1725..1784
Savile, Sir Henry. Found. of Professorships. (*Scriptores*) 1549..1622
Savonarola, Jerome. Italian Reformer. Life by J. F.
　Picus of Mirandola; J. S. Harford, 1837; J. A. Héraud,
　1843; F. T. Perrens, 1854; Dr. R. R. Madden, 1855;
　Pasquale Villari, translated by L. Horner, 1863...... 1452..1498
Savot, Louis. French Physician and Antiquary........ 1579?.1640
Saxe, Maurice, Count of. Marshal of France. Life, 3
　vols. 12mo, 1752; Espagnac .... 1696..1750
Saxe-Weimar, Bernard, Duke of. General in Thirty
　Years' War..................................... 1600..1639
Saxo Grammaticus. Danish Historian............... 1134?.1204?
Saxonia, Hercules. Italian Medical Writer............ 1551..1607
Say, John Baptist. Writer on Political Economy....... 1767..1832
Say, Samuel. Dissenting Minister. Poetical Writer.... 1675..1743
Say, Thomas. American Naturalist. L. by G. Ord, 1859 1787..1834
Scævola, Quintus Mucius. Augur.................... — B.C. 88?
Scævola, Quintus Mucius. Pontifex Maximus......... — B.C. 82
Scala, Alexandra. Scholar .... — ..1506

BORN. DIED.

Scala, Bartholomew. Statesman. (*History of Florence*) 1424?.1497
Scaliger, Joseph Justus. (*De Emendatione.*) Life by
    Bernays, 1855.................................... 1540..1609
Scaliger, Julius Cæsar. *The Elder.* (*De Arte Poeticâ*) 1484..1558
Scamozzi, Vincent. Italian Architect................ 1552..1616
Scanderbeg. *George Castriota.* Prince of Albania.
    Soldier. Life by Marinus Barletius, 1537; Du Poncet;
    C. Paganel, 1856; C. C. Moore, 1850.............. 1404..1467?
Scapula, John. (*Greek Lexicon*)..................... 1540?.1600
Scarborough, Sir Charles. Physician & Mathematician 1616?.1693
Scarcellino, Lo. *Hippolytus Scarsella.* Italian Painter 1560..1621
Scarella, John Bapt., of Brescia. Newtonian Philosopher 1709..1779
Scargill, W. P. Writer............................ — ..1836
Scarlatti, Alexander. *Il Cavaliere.* Italian Composer.. 1659?.1725
Scarlatti, Dominic, son. Musical Composer............ 1683..1757
Scarlatti, Joseph. Musical Composer................. 1718..1776
Scarlett, James, First Lord Abinger. Judge .... 1769..1844
Scarpa, Anthony. Italian Medical Writer............. 1748..1832
Scarron, Paul. Comic Poet. (*Roman Comique*) .... 1610?.1660
Scaurus, Marcus Æmilius. Consul and Censor........ 163.89? B.C.
Schaaf, Charles. German Orientalist .... 1646..1719
Schadow, John Geoffrey. Sculptor.................. 1764..1850
Schadow, John Ridolfo, son. Sculptor.............. 1786..1822
Schaefer, or·Schäfer, Geoffrey Henry. Philologist..... 1764..1840
Schaeffor, or Schäffer, Jacob Christian. German Philos-
    opher and Naturalist.............................. 1718..1790
Schaeffer, or Schäffer, Peter. Printer .... — ..1502?
Schafarik, or Safarik (*q. v.*), Paul Joseph. Slavic Writer 1795..1861
Schafei, Mohammed Ben Edris. Mohammedan Jurist.. 767.. 819
Schagen, Giles van. Historical and Portrait Painter ... 1616..1668
Schalcken, Godfrey. Dutch Painter................. 1643..1706
Schall, John Adam. Jesuit Missionary in China ...... 1591..1669?
Schank, John. Scottish Admiral and Naval Architect.. 1746?.1823
Scharnhorst, Gebhard David von. German Soldier.... 1756..1813
Schatten, Nicholas. Ger. Jesuit. (*Historia Westphaliæ*) 1608..1676
Schatz, George. German Critic .... 1763..1795
Schauffelein, or Scheuffelin, Hans Leonard. Engraver 1487?.1550
Schedius, Paul. *Melissus.* German Latin Poet...... 1539..1602
Schedone, or Schidoni, Bartholomew. Italian Painter.. 1560..1616
Scheele, Charles William. Swedish Chemist.......... 1742..1786
Scheemakers, Peter. Flemish Sculptor .... 1691..1773?
Scheffer, Arnold. French Historical and Political Writer 1796..1853
Scheffer, Ary. Fr. Hist. Painter. L. by Mrs. Grote, 1860 1795..1858
Scheffer, Henry. French Historical Painter .... 1799?.1862
Scheffer, Henry Theophilus. Swedish Chemist....... 1710..1759
Scheffer, John. German Philologist and Antiquary.... 1621..1679
Schegkins, James. German Theologian .... — ..1587
Scheid, Everard. German Orientalist .... 1742..1795
Scheidt, Balthasar. Ger. Talmudist and Biblical Writer 1614..1670
Scheidt, Christian Louis. Jurist. (*Origines Guelphicæ*) 1709..1761
Scheiner, Christopher. Ger. Mathem. and Astronomer 1575..1650
Schelhammer, Gonthier Christopher. Medical Writer.. 1649..1716
Scheller, Immanuel John Gerhard. German Philologist.
    (*Latin-German Dictionary*) .... 1735..1803

BORN. DIED.

Schelling, Frederick Augustus. German Novelist ..... 1766..1839
Schelling, Frederick William Joseph. Ger. Metaphysician 1775..1854
Schellinks, Daniel. Dutch Landscape Painter......... 1633..1701
Schellinks, William, brother. Dutch Painter......... 1631..1678
Schelstraate, Emanuel, of Antwerp. (*Antiq. Ecclesiæ*) 1649..1692
Schenck, John, of Gräfenburg. Medical Writer....... 1531..1598
Schenck, John George, son. Medical Writer at the Hague — ..1620?
Schenckius, John Theodore, of Jena. Medical Writer.. 1619?..1671
Schérer, Bartholomew Louis Joseph. Fr. Republican Gen. 1747..1804
Scheuchzer, John James, of Zurich. Mathem. and Phys. 1672..1733
Scheuffelin, Hans Leonard. German Engraver .... 1487?.1550
Schiavone, Andrew. *Medula.* Venetian Painter..... 1522..1582
Schiavonetti, Louis. Italian Engraver in England ... 1765..1810
Schickard, William. Astronomer and Orientalist. (*Series Regum Persiæ*)................................ 1592..1635
Schidoni, or Schedone, Bartholomew. Italian Painter.. 1560..1616
Schill, Ferdinand von. Prussian Partisan Officer. Life by J. C. L. Haken, 1824; H. Döring, 1838.......... 1776..1809
Schiller, John Christopher Frederick von. Historian and Dramatic Writer. (*Thirty Years' War.*) Life by Döring; Mme. von Wolzogen; Hoffmeister; Palleske, translated into English by Lady Wallace, 1859; Carlyle; Sir Bulwer Lytton........................ 1759..1805
Schilling, Diebold, of Soleure. (*Wars against Charles the Bold*).. fl. 15th c.
Schiltberger, John, of Munich. Traveler............ — ..1405
Schimmelpenninck, Mary Anne. (*Port Royal; Autobiography*).................................... 1778..1856
Schimmelpenninck, Rutger John. Dutch Statesman.. 1761..1825
Schinkel, Charles Frederick. Ger. Architectural Artist 1781..1841
Schlagintweit, Adolphus. German Savant and Traveler 1829..1857
Schlatter, Michael. Missionary.................... 1716..1790
Schlegel, Augustus William von. (*Greek Drama*)..... 1767..1845
Schlegel, Frederick Charles William von, brother. (*Philosophy of History*)............................ 1772..1829
Schlegel, John Adolphus. Ger. Theologian and Preacher 1721..1793
Schlegel, John Elias, br. Dramatic and Poetical Writer 1718..1749
Schlegel, John Henry, br. Danish Historiographer Royal 1724..1780
Schleiermacher, Frederick Daniel Ernest, D. D. Ger. Divine, Philos. and Philol. L. by self (till 1794), 1851 1768..1834
Schleusner, John Frederick. Lexicographer......... 1759..1831
Schlictingius, Jonas. Polish Socinian. Bib. Comment. 1596..1664
Schlosser, Frederick Christopher. German Historian... 1776..1861
Schlözer, or Schloezer, Augustus Louis von. German Political and Historical Writer. (*History of Lithuania.*) Life by C. von Schlözer, 1828 .... 1737..1809
Schmauss, John James. German Historian and Publicist 1690..1747
Schmeitzel, Martin. German Historical Writer........ 1679..1747
Schmeller, John Andrew. German Philologist .... 1785..1852
Schmidt, Erasmus. Editor of Pindar. (*Concordance of Greek Testament*) .... 1560..1637
Schmidt, George Frederick. Engraver .... 1712..1775
Schmidt, John Andrew. German Lutheran Divine .... 1652..1726
Schmith, Nicholas. Hungarian Jesuit. Hist. Writer.. — ..1767

BORN. DIED.
Schmucker, Samuel Mosheim, LL. D. American Author 1823..1863
Schneider, Conrad Victor. Ger. Physician & Anatomist 1610..1680
Schneider, John Christian Frederick. Musical Composer 1785..1853
Schneider, John Gottlob. Philologist and Naturalist .. 1750..1822
Schneider, Dr. John Gottlob. German Organist....... 1789..1864
Schnorr von Karolsfeld, Julius. German Painter .... 1794..1853
Schnurrer, Christian Frederick. (*Bibliotheca Arabica*).. 1742..1822
Schoeffer, or Schöffer, Peter. Printer; Partner of Fust.. 1430?.1502?
Schoemann, George Frederick. (*Athenian Assemblies*).. 1793.. —
Schoepflin, John Daniel. Historical Writer........... 1694..1771
Schoettgen, Christian. Ger. Philol. (*Horæ Hebraicæ*). 1687..1751
Scholefield, Rev. James, of Cambridge. Professor. Life
     by Mrs. Scholefield, 1855......................... 1789..1853
Scholz, John Matthias Augustus. Philologist.......... 1794..1852
Schömann, George Frederick. (*Athenian Assemblies*).. 1793.. —
Schomberg, Frederick Herman, Ct. Gen.; fell at Boyne 1615?.1690
Schomberg, Henry, Count de. Marshal of France..... 1583..1632
Schomberg, Isaac. Naval Officer. (*Naval Chronology*) — ..1813
Schomburgk, Otto. Writer........................ 1810..1857
Schomburgk, Sir Robt. Herman, br. Traveler and Nat. 1804..1865
Schon, or Schongauer, Martin. Painter and Engraver.. 1420?.1486
Schoner, John. German Mathematician and Astrologer 1477..1547
Schoning, or Schonning, Gerard. Norwegian Writer .. 1722..1780
Schoockius, Martin. Dutch Critic and Miscel. Writer.. 1614..1669
Schoolcraft, Henry Rowe, LL. D. Amer. Ethnol. & Auth. 1793..1864
Schoonfield, John Henry. German Painter .... 1619?.1689
Schoonjans, Anthony. Dutch Painter at Vienna ...... 1655..1726
Schoorel, or Schorel, John. Flemish Painter.......... 1495..1562
Schooten, Francis. Dutch Mathematician .... — ..1659
Schopenhauer, Adele. German Writer............... — ..1849
Schopenhauer, Arthur. German Philosopher....:.... 1788..1860
Schopenhauer, Johanna, wife. Authoress. Life by self 1770..1838
Schöpflin, John Daniel. Historical Writer........... 1694..1771
Schorel, or Schoorel, John. Flemish Painter.......... 1495..1562
Schotanus, Christian. Frisian Historical Writer....... 1603..1671
Schott, Andrew. Dutch Jesuit. Philol. and Biographer 1552..1629
Schott, Gaspar. Jesuit. Experimental Philosopher.... 1608..1666
Schöttgen, Christian. Ger. Philologist. (*Horæ Hebraicæ*) 1687..1751
Schouw, Joachim Frederick. Danish Botanist......... 1789..1852
Schrevelius, Cornelius. (*Lexicon*) .... 1614?.1664 or 7
Schroeckh, or Schröckh, John Matthew. Ger. Ch. Hist. 1733..1808
Schroeder, or Schröder, Fred. Louis. Ger. Actor & Dram. 1744..1813
Schroeder, or Schröder, John Joachim. Orientalist.... 1680..1756
Schroeter, or Schröter, John Samuel. German Musician 1750..1788
Schryver, or Scriverius, Peter. (*Batavia Illustrata*) .... 1576..1660
Schubart, Christian Fred. Daniel. Ger. Poet & Musician 1739..1791
Schubert, Francis. Ger. Musical Composer. (*Lieder*) . 1797..1828
Schubert, Gotthilf Henry von. German Mystic .... 1780..1860
Schultens, Albert. Hebraist and Biblical Commentator 1686..1750
Schultens, Henry Albert. Hebraist .... 1749..1793
Schultens, John Jacob. Orientalist .... 1716..1778
Schultet, Abraham. *Scultetus*. Ger. Protestant Divine. 1556..1625
Schulting, Anthony. German Jurist .... 1659..1734
Schultze, Benjamin. Philologist..................... 1761..1833

BORN. DIED.

Schulze, Ernest Conrad Frederick.   German Poet...... 1789..1817
Schulze, John Henry.   Anatomist and Scholar......... 1687..1744
Schumacher, Henry Christian.   Dutch Astronomer .... 1780..1850
Schumann, Robert.   German Musical Composer....... 1815?.1856
Schurmann, Anna Maria.   German Scholar and Mystic 1607..1678
Schurtzfleisch, Conrad Samuel.   German Writer...... 1641..1708
Schuster, Ignatius, of Vienna.   Comedian .... 1779..1835
Schut, Cornelius, of Antwerp.   Painter............... 1600..1660
Schuur, Theodore van der.   Dutch Painter........... 1628..1705
Schuyler, Philip.   Amer. General.   Life by Lossing, 1860 1733..1804
Schwab, Gustavus.   German Author................. 1792..1850
Schwab, Lamprecht.   See Suavius................. 1506..1565
Schwanhard, Geo.   Lapidary at Prague and Nuremberg 1601..1667
Schwanhard, George, son.   Lapidary at Nuremberg ... — ..1676
Schwanthaler, Louis Michael von.   German Sculptor.. 1802..1848
Schwartz, Berthold.   German Monk and Alchemist.... fl. 1340?
Schwartz, Christopher.   Painter .... 1550..1594
Schwartzenberg, Chas. Philip, Prince.   Austr. General 1771..1820
Schwartzenberg, Felix.   Prince.   Austrian Statesman 1800..1852
Schwarz, Christian Fred. Missionary.   L. by Pearson, 1834 1726..1798
Schwegler, Albert.   German Theologian and Historian. 1819..1857
Schweighaeuser, John.   (Lexicon Herodotum) .... 1742..1830
Schweinitz, Lewis David von.   Amer. Divine & Botanist 1780..1834
Schwenkfeld, Gaspar von.   Religious Enthusiast...... 1490..1561?
Schwerin, Kurt Christopher, Count.   Prussian General;
    fell at Prague..................................... 1684..1757
Schyndal, or Schendal, Bernard.   Dutch Painter....... 1659..1716
Scina, Dominic, of Palermo.   Mathematician .... 1765..1837
Scioppius, Gaspar.   German Philologist and Latinist... 1576..1649
Scipio Africanus, Major.   General in 2d Punic War .. B.C. 234.183?
Scipio Africanus, Minor.   General in 3d Punic War.. 185.129 B.C.
Sclater, William.   Poet and Historian .... — ..1647
Scopas.   Greek Architect and Sculptor .... fl. 395–350 B.C.
Scopoli, John Anthony.   Ital. Naturalist and Physician 1725..1788
Scoresby, William.   Arctic Navigator................. 1760..1829?
Scoresby, Rev. William, D. D., son.   Arctic Navigator.
    Naval Writer.   (Arctic Voyages; Discourses to Sea-
    men.)   Life by R. E. Scoresby Jackson, 1861.. .. .... 1790..1857
Scorza, Sinibaldo, of Voltaggio.   Painter and Engraver.. 1589..1631
Scot, Reginald.   (Discoverie of Witchcraft) .... 1545..1599
Scott, Alexander.   Scottish Poet.................... fl. 1562
Scott, Daniel, LL. D.   Biblical Writer.   (On the Trinity) — ..1759
Scott, David.   (History of Scotland.)................. 1675..1742
Scott, David.   Scottish Painter and Writer.   Life by W.
    B. Scott, 1850.................................. 1806..1849
Scott, Sir Francis Edward.   Writer on Art .... — ..1863
Scott, Helenus, M.D.   Scot. Phys. (Adventures of a Rupee) — ..1821
Scott, Rev. James.   English Pulpit Orator and Politician 1733..1814
Scott, Rev. John, D. D.   English Divine. (Christian Life) 1638..1694
Scott, John.   Quaker, of Amwell.   Poet .... 1739..1783
Scott, John.   Writer.   (View of Paris)............... — ..1821
Scott, John, Lord Eldon (q. v.).   Lord Chancellor ...... 1751..1838
Scott, Sir Michael.   Occult Philosopher............... — ..1291?
Scott, Michael.   (Tom Cringle's Log) .... 1789..1835
Scott, Samuel.   Landscape Painter .... — ..1772

BORN. DIED.

Scott, Rev. Thomas. Commentator. Life by son...... 1747..1821
Scott, Sir Walter. Novelist and Poet. Life by Lockhart 1771..1832
Scott, William, Lord Stowell (*q. v.*). Admiralty Judge. 1745..1836
Scotti, Marcellus Eusebius. Neapolitan Writer........ 1742..1800
Scotus, John. *Erigena.* Schoolman................ — .. 875?
Scotus, John Duns. Schoolman..................... 1265?.1308
Scougal, Henry. Scot. Divine. (*Life of God in the Soul*) 1650..1678
Scribe, Augustine Eugene. French Dramatic Writer... 1791..1861
Scriverius, or Schryver, Peter. Dutch Historical Writer 1576..1660
Scroggs, Sir William. Lord Chief Justice............. — ..1683
Scrope, of Masham, Henry, Ld.; beheaded for Conspiracy — ..1415
Scrope, Richard. Abp. of York (1398–1405). Beheaded — ..1405
Scudder, John, M. D. American Missionary........... 1793..1855
Scudéry, or Scudéri, George de. Fr. Poet and Dramatist 1601..1667
Scudéry, Mdlle. Magdalen de, sister. French Romancist 1607..1701
Scultetus, Abraham. German Protestant Divine...... 1556..1625
Scultetus, or Schultz, John. Dutch Surgeon......... 1595..1645
Scylitzes. Byzantine Historian..................... fl. 1080
Seabury, Samuel, D. D. American Divine; Bishop..... 1729..1796
Sealsfield, Charles. American Novelist............... 1797?.1864
Seaton, Sir John Colborne, Lord. Field Marshal. Governor-General of Canada........................ 1779..1863
Seaton, Rev. Thomas. Founder of Prize............. — ..1741
Seba, Albert. Dutch Naturalist...................... 1665..1736
Sebastian, St. Roman Martyr................ 255?. 288
Sebastian. King of Portugal (1557–78). Warrior..... 1554..1578
Sébastiani, Horace Francis, Count. Fr. Gen. and Diplom. 1776..1851
Sebastiano del Piombo. Italian Painter............. 1485..1547
Seber, Wolfgang. Ger. Philosopher and Divine. (*Index*) 1573..1634
Sebizus, John Albert. Medical Writer.............. 1615..1685
Sebizus, or Sebisch, Melchior, of Strasburg. Med. Writer 1578..1674
Sebonde, Raymond de. Philos., Physician, Theologian — ..1432
Seckendorf, Frederick Henry, Ct. Gen. and Diplomatist 1673..1763
Seckendorf, Vitus Louis von. Ger. Statesman and Hist. 1626..1692
Secker, Thomas. Archbishop of Canterbury (1758–68).
Life by Bishop Porteus .... 1693..1768
Secousse, Denis Francis. French Historical Writer.... 1691..1754
Secundus, Johannes. *John Everard.* Dutch Statesman;
Latin Poet.. 1511..1536
Securis, John. English Physician and Writer......... fl. 1580
Sédaine, Michael John. French Dramatic Writer...... 1719..1797
Sedano, John Joseph Lopez de. Spanish Antiquary.
(*Parnaso Español*)............................... 1729..1801
Sedgwick, John. American General................. 1815?.1864
Sedgwick, Theodore. American Statesman and Jurist. 1746..1813
Sedgwick, Theodore, son. Lawyer and Writer........ 1780..1839
Sedgwick, Theodore, son. Lawyer and Writer........ 1811..1859
Sedley, Catherine, Countess of Dorchester............ — ..1692
Sedley, Sir Charles. Wit, Courtier, and Poet........ 1639?.1701
Sedulius, Caius Cœlius, of Rome. (*Carmen Paschale*).. fl. 5th c.
Seed, Rev. Jeremiah. Divine. (*Sermons*)........... — ..1747
Seetzen, Ulric Jasper. German Traveler and Naturalist 1767..1811
Sefstroem, or Sefström, Nils Gabriel. Swedish Chemist 1787..1854
Segar, Sir Wm. Herald. (*Honor, Civil and Military*).. — ..1633
Segers, Daniel. Dutch Painter...................... 1590..1660

BORN. DIED.

Segers, or Seghers, Gerard, brother. Painter. . . . . 1589..1651
Segneri, Paul. Italian Preacher. Life by Maffei. . . . . . 1624..1694
Segni, Bernard. Italian Historian. . . . . — ..1558
Segrais, John Regnault de. French Poet and Novelist . 1624..1701
Séguier, Anthony Louis. French Judge and Statesman 1726..1792
Séguier, John Francis. French Botanist and Medalist.. 1703..1784
Séguier, Peter. President of the Parliament of Paris... 1504..1580
Séguier, Peter. President of the French Academy..... 1588..1672
Séguier, Wm. Virtuoso. Keeper, British Institution.. 1772..1844
Ségur, Joseph Alexander, Viscount de. French Writer 1756..1805
Ségur, Louis Philip, Count de. Diplom. and Hist. Writer 1753..1830
Ségur, Philip Henry, Marquis de. Marshal of France... 1724..1801
Ségur, Philip Paul, Count de. General of Bonaparte ... 1780.. —
Seignette, Peter. Apothecary at Rochelle. Inventor of
    Seignette's Salt . . . . — ..1719
Sejanus, Ælius. Roman Statesman . . . . — .. 31
Selden, John. Lawyer and Statesman. Life by Wilkins,
    1726; Dr. J. Aikin, 1773; G. W. Johnson, 1835. . . . . 1584..1654
Seleucus. *Nicator*. 1st King of Syria (B. C. 312–280) 358?.280 B.C.
Seleucus. *Callinicus*. Fourth King (B. C. 246–226) .... — B.C.226
Seleucus. *Ceraunus*. Fifth King (B. C. 226–223) . . . . . . — B.C.223
Seleucus. *Philopator*. Seventh King(B. C. 187–175) 222?.175 B.C.
Selim I. Sultan of Turkey (1512–20). Conq. of Egypt 1467..1520
Selim II. (1566–74). . . . . 1552?.1574
Selim III. (1789–1808). . . . . 1761..1808
Selis, Nicholas Joseph. French Poet. . . . . 1737..1802
Selkirk, Alexander. Scottish Seaman and Adventurer.. 1676?.1723
Selle, Christian Theophilus. German Medical Writer... 1748..1800
Seller, Abednego. Nonjuring Divine. . . . . 1647?.1720?
Sellius, Godfrey. Dutch Historian and Geogr. Writer.. — ..1767
Sellon, Baker John. Lawyer. (*Analysis of Practice*) .. 1762..1835
Selva, John Anthony. Italian Architect . . . . 1753..1819
Selwyn, George Augustus. Life by J. H. Jesse, 1843 .. 1719..1791
Selwyn, William, Q. C. (*Nisi Prius*) . . . . 1775..1855
Semiramis. Queen of Assyria. . . . . fl. B.C.1250
Semler, John Solomon. Lutheran Divine . . . . 1725..1791
Semple, Robert Baylor. Amer. Clergyman and Writer.. 1769..1831
Sénac, John Baptist. French Medical Writer . . . . 1693..1770
Senancour, Stephen Pivert de. French Writer. . . . . 1770..1846
Senault, John Francis. Preacher and Moral Writer.... 1599..1672
Senebier, John. Natural Philosopher and Historian.... 1742..1809
Seneca, L. Annæus. Philosopher. L. by Rosmini, 1793 .. — 65
Seneca, Marcus Annæus. Roman Pleader and Orator B.C.58?.A.D.32?
Senecai, or Senecé, Anthony Bauderon de. French Poet 1643..1737
Senefelder, Aloys, of Munich. Inventor of Lithography 1771..1834
Senior, Nassau William. Political Economist . . . . 1790..1864
Sennamont, H. Harran de. Mineralogist . . . . 1808?.1862
Sennertus, Daniel. German Medical Writer . . . . 1572..1637
Seppings, Sir Robert. Naval Architect . . . . 1768..1840
Sepulveda, John Genesius de. Spanish Historian . . . . . 1491..1573
Serarius, Nicholas. French Jesuit; Commentator . . . . . 1545..1610
Serassi, Peter Anthony. Italian Biographer. . . . . 1721..1791
Sergardi, Louis, of Sienna. *Quintus Sectanus*. Lat. Poet 1660..1726
Sergeant, John. American Jurist . . . . 1779..1852
Sergel, John Tobias. Swedish Sculptor. . . . . 1740..1814

BORN. DIED.

Sergius. Patriarch of Constantinople (610–39). Monothelite .... — .. 639
Sergius I. Pope. (687–701)......................... 630?. 701
Sergius II. (844–47) .... — .. 847
Sergius III. (905–12)............................. — .. 912
Sergius IV. (1009–12.) *Peter Buccaporci*........... — ..1012
Serle, Ambrose. Devotional Writer................. 1741?.1812
Serlio, Sebastian. Italian Architect .... 1475..1552
Serres, John de. *Serranus*. Protestant Divine and Hist. 1540?.1598
Serres, Olive. *Princess of Cumberland* .... 1772..1834
Serres, Oliver de. French Agriculturist.............. 1539..1619
Sertorius, Quintus. Roman Naval Commander....... 121?.72 B.C.
Servandoni, John Jerome. Italian Architect and Painter 1695..1766
Servetus, Michael. Spanish Scientific and Theological Writer. Life by Mosheim; Allwoerden, 1728; Chaufepie, translated by James Yair, 1771; Trechsel, 1839; Drummond, 1848................................... 1509..1553
Servius, Maurus Honoratus. Commentator on Virgil... end of 4th c.
Sesostris. King of Egypt .... fl. B.C. 1500?
Sestini, Dominic. Italian Numismatist .... 1750?.1832
Seton, Eliza Ann. Founder of Sisters of Charity in U. S. 1774..1821
Settle, Elkanah. Poet............................. 1648..1724
Sevajee. *Bosla.* Founder of the Mahratta Empire..... 1627..1680
Severino, Marcus Aurelius. Neapolitan Physician..... 1580..1656
Severinus. Pope (640)............................. — .. 640
Severus, Alexander. Roman Emperor (222–35)........ 205.. 235
Severus, Cornelius. Roman Poet. (*Ætna*)........ fl. ti. Augustus
Severus, Lucius Septimius. Roman Emperor (193–211). 146.. 211
Severus, Sulpicius. Ecclesiastical Historian......... 363?.aft.410
Sévigné, Mary de Rabutin - Chantal, Marchioness de. (*Letters.*) Life by Baron Walckenaer, 1820; J. A. Aubenas, 1842................................... 1626..1696
Sevin, Francis. French Scholar and Collector of MSS... 1682..1741
Seward, Anna. Poetess. (*Letters.*) Life by Walter Scott 1747..1809
Seward, Rev. Thomas. Divine and Poet.............. 1708..1790
Seward, William. Biographer. (*Biographiana*)....... 1747..1799
Seward, William Wenman. (*Topographia Hibernica*).. fl. 1795
Sewell, George. Physician and Poet................. — ..1726
Sewell, Dr. Richard Clare. Writer on Law........... 1804?.1864
Sewell, William. (*History of the Quakers*) .... 1650?.1725?
Sextus Empiricus. Greek Physician .... fl. 3d c.?
Seydlitz, Frederick William, Baron de. Prussian General 1722..1773
Seymour, Lady Arabella (Stuart).................... 1575?.1615
Seymour, Edward, Duke of Somerset. Protector...... — ..1552
Seymour, Jane. Queen of Henry VIII. .... — ..1538
Seymour, Robert. Caricaturist .... — ..1836
Seymour, Thomas, Lord. Lord High Admiral .... — ..1549
Seyssel, Claude de. Fr. Historical and Political Writer 1450?.1520
Sfondrati, Francis. Italian Cardinal; Poet and Writer. 1493..1550
Sforza, Francis Alex., Duke of Milan. L. by Decembrio 1401..1466
Sforza, Galeas Mary, son, Duke of Milan. Assassinated 1444..1476
Sforza, Giacomuzzo Attendolo. *The Great.* Ital. General 1339..1424
Sforza, Louis. *Il Moro*.............................. — ..1510
'SGravesande, or **Gravesande,** William James van. Dutch Mathematician .... 1688..1742

BORN. DIED.

Shadwell, Sir Lancelot. Vice-Chancellor .... 1779..1850
Shadwell, Thomas. Dramatist and Poet Laureate ..... 1640..1692
Shafei. Mohammedan Doctor .... 767.. 819
Shaftesbury, Anthony Ashley Cooper, 1st Earl of. States-
   man. Life by G. H. Cooke, ed. by Kippis and Martin 1621..1683
Shaftesbury, Anthony Ashley Cooper, grandson, Third
   Earl of. Writer. (*Characteristics*) .... 1671..1713
Shah-Alum I. Mogul Emperor of India (1707–12) .... 1642?.1712
Shah-Alum II. (1759–1806) .... 1719?.1806
Shah-Jehan. Mogul Emperor of India (1627–66) ...... 1593?.1666
Shakespear, John. Orientalist .... 1774..1858
Shakespeare, Shakspeare, or Shakspere, William. Life
   by Rowe, 1709; F. Gentleman, 1774; Moratin (in
   Spanish), 1795; A. Chalmers, 1805; Wheler, 1806; J.
   Britton, 1814; Drake, 1817; Malone, 1821; Guizot,
   1821, and enlarged, 1851; Skottowe, 1824 (also in
   German same year); Buchon (in Dutch), 1824; C. H.
   Wheeler, 1824; Moncrieff, 1824; Meyer (in German,
   also in French), 1825; Harvey, 1825; Symmons, 1826;
   Havard, 1834; Harness, 1836; T. Campbell, 1838;
   Villemain, 1840; Collier, 1841, enlarged 1858; Pichot,
   1841; Knight, 1842, enlarged 1850, &c., re-edited
   1865; Procter, 1843; Verplanck, 1847; Halliwell,
   1848; P. Chasles, 1851; Hudson, 1852; Sillig, 1854;
   Huelsmann, 1856; Lloyd, 1856; Dyce, 1857; Staun-
   ton, 1858; Neil, 1861; Fullom, 1862; Kenny, 1864;
   R. G. White, 1865 .... 1564..1616
Shakhovsky, Alex. Alexandrovitch, Pr. Russian Dram. 1777..1846
Shallum. King of Israel (B. C. 770) .... — B.C.770
Shamoul, or Samoul. Jewish Mathematician and Phys. —1201 or 2
Sharp, Abraham. Mathematician and Astronomer..... 1651..1742
Sharp, Daniel, D. D. American Divine .... 1783..1853
Sharp, Granville. Abolitionist. L. by Prince Hoare, 1820 1735..1813
Sharp, James. Archbishop of St. Andrew's. Assassinated 1618..1679
Sharp, John. Abp. of York. L. by Dr. Thos. Sharp, 1829 1644..1714
Sharp, Richard. *Conversation Sharp.* Critic .... 1759..1835
Sharp, Samuel. Surgical Writer .... — ..1776
Sharp, Thomas, D. D. Divine and Hebraist. .... 1693?.1758
Sharp, Thomas. Antiquary. (*Coventry Mysteries*) ..... 1770..1841
Sharp, William. Engraver .... 1749..1824
Sharpe, Daniel. Geologist...................... 1806..1856
Sharpe, Gregory, D. D. Divine and Orientalist. (*Hebrew
   Lexicon*) .... 1713..1771
Sharroch, Robert, LL. D. (*On Vegetables; De Officiis*).. — ..1684
Shaw, Cuthbert. Poet........................... 1738?.1771
Shaw, Emanuel. Ejected Nonconformist. (*Immanuel*). 1635..1696
Shaw, George, M. D. Naturalist. (*General Zoölogy*) ... 1751..1813
Shaw, Lemuel, LL. D. American Jurist .... 1781..1861
Shaw, Sir James, M. P. Lord Mayor of London .... 1764..1843
Shaw, Peter, M. D. Medical Writ. (*Lessons on Chemistry*) 1695..1763
Shaw, Stebbing. (*History of Staffordshire*) .... 1762..1802
Shaw, Rev. Thomas. Traveler in the East .... 1692?.1751
Shaw, Thomas Budd. English Writer at Petersburg... 1813..1862
Shays, Daniel. Leader in *Shay's Rebellion* .... 1740..1825
Shea, Daniel. Orientalist .... 1772..1836

BORN. DIED.

Shea, John Augustus. Novelist .... — ..1845
Shebbeare, John. Physician and Political Writer ..... 1709..1788
Shee, Sir Martin Archer. President of the Royal Acad-
emy. Painter and Poet. Life by his son, 1860 ..... 1770..1850
Sheepshanks, John. Founder of Sheepshanks Gallery . 1787?.1863
Sheepshanks, Rev. Richard. Astronomer............. 1794..1855
Sheepshanks, Rev. William. Scholar............... 1740..1810
Sheffield, John, Earl of Mulgrave, Duke of Bucks. Poet 1649..1721
Sheil, Richard Lalor. Statesman, Author, and Orator.
Life by McNevin, 1845; Torrens W. McCulloch, 1855 1794..1851
Shelburne, Wm. Petty, E. of. Premier. Mqs. Lansdowne 1737..1805
Shelby, Isaac. American Revolutionary Officer .... 1750..1826
Sheldon, Gilbert. Archbishop of Canterbury (1663–77) 1598..1677
Sheldon, Ralph, of Besley. Antiquary .... — ..1864
Shelley, George. Penman........................... 1666?.1736
Shelley, Mrs. (Mary Wollstonecraft). Writer .... 1797..1851
Shelley, Percy Bysshe. Poet. Life by C. S. Middleton;
Hogg, 1838; Capt. T. Medwin, 1847 .... 1792..1822
Shenstone, William. Poet. Life by Greaves......... 1714..1763
Shepard, Rev. Samuel. American Controversialist .... 1739..1815
Shepard, Rev. Thomas. American Theological Writer. 1605..1649
Sheppard, Jack. Burglar; executed .... — ..1724
Shepreve, or Shepery, John. Latin Poet and Scholar.. 1509?.1542
Sherard, or Sherwood, William. Botanist .... 1659..1728
Sherburne, Sir Edward. Poet. (Manilius)........... 1618..1702
Sheridan, Frances. Novelist and Dramatist........... 1724..1766
Sheridan, Richard Brinsley Butler, son, M. P. Wit, Dram-
atist, and Politician. L. by T. Moore; Watkins, 1817 1751..1816
Sheridan, Thos., D. D. Friend of Swift. Transl. of Persius 1684..1738
Sheridan, Thos., son. Actor and Writ. (Life of Swift) 1721..1788
Sherif-ed-deen. Persian Historian .... fl. 1424
Sherley, Sir Thomas. Traveler and Knight-errant..... 1564.. —
Sherlock, Richard, D. D. Divine. (Practical Christian) 1613..1689
Sherlock, Thomas. Bishop of London (1748–61)...... 1678..1761
Sherlock, Wm., D. D. Dean of St. Paul's. (On Death) 1641?.1707
Sherman, Roger. American Statesman............... 1721..1793
Sherwin, John Keyse. Engraver..................... 1751?.1790
Sherwood, Mrs. Mary Martha. Writer. Life by self..: 1775..1851
Shew, Joel, M. D. Hydropathist and Writer......... 1816..1855
Shield, William. Dramatic and Musical Composer..... 1754..1829
Shipley, Jonathan. Bp. of St. Asaph. Divine and Poet 1714..1778
Shipley, Wm. Davies. Dean of St. Asaph. (Dialogue) 1745..1826
Shirley, Sir Anthony. Traveler................... 1565.1630 or 1
Shirley, James. Dramatic Poet..................... 1596..1666
Shirley, Robert. English Traveler settled in Persia.... 1564..1627
Shirley, Thomas. Medical Writer. (Cochlearia Curiosa) 1638..1678
Shirley, Walter Augustus. Bishop of Sodor and Man
(1846–47). Life by Archdeacon Hill, 1849.......... 1797..1847
Shishkoff, Alex. Semenovitch. Russ. Adm. and Statesm. 1754..1841
Shokhnah, Ibn. Mohammedan Writer .... — ..1478
Shore, Jane. Mistress of Edward IV............fl. ti. Edward IV.
Shore, John, Ld. Teignmouth. Gov.-Gen. L. by son, 1843 1751..1834
Short, James. Natural Philosopher and Optician ...... 1710..1768
Short, Thomas, M.D. Medical and Meteorological Writer — ..1772
Shovel, Sir Cloudesley. Admiral..................... 1650?.1707

BORN. DIED.

Shower, Sir Barthol. Lawyer. (*Cases in Parliament*).. — ..1701
Shower, John, brother. Puritan Divine............. 1657..1715
Shrapnel, Henry. Lieut.-General. Inventor of Shell.. — ..1843
Shrewsbury, Charles Talbot, Duke of. Statesman..... 1660..1717
Shrewsbury, Elizabeth Hardwicke, Countess of .... 1519..1608
Shrewsbury, John Talbot. First Earl of............. 1373..1453
Shubrick, John Templar. American Naval Officer..... 1778..1815
Shuckburgh Evelyn, Sir Geo. Class. and Math. Scholar 1750..1804
Shuckford, Rev. Samuel. Historian .... — ..1754
Shute, Josias. Archdeacon. (*Sermons on Gen. XVI.*).. — ..1643
Shuter, Edward. Comic Actor...................... — ..1776
Shuttleworth, Philip Nich. Bp. of Chichester (1840–42) 1782..1842
Sibbald, Sir Robert. Physician, Naturalist, Antiquary.. 1643?.1712?
Sibbs, or Sibbes, Richard. Puritan Div. (*Bruised Reed*) 1577..1635
Sibly, Manoah. Pastor of New Jerusalem Society .... 1757..1840
Sibour, Mary Dominic Augustus. French Prelate...... 1792..1857
Sibrechts, John. Dutch Painter.................. 1625..1703
Sibthorp, John, M. D. Botanist and Traveler......... 1758..1796
Sicard, Claude. Jesuit Missionary to the East .... 1677..1726
Sicard, Roch Ambrose Cucurron, Abbé. Teacher of the
    Deaf and Dumb................................ 1742..1822
Siciolante, or Da Sermoneta, Jerome. Italian Painter.. 1504..1550
Sickingen, Francis von. German General. Lutheran.. 1484..1523
Siddons, Mrs Sarah (Kemble). Actress. Life by Camp-
    bell, 1834................................... 1755..1831
Sidmouth, Henry Addington, First Viscount. States-
    man. Life by Dean of Norwich, 1847............. 1755..1844
Sidney, Algernon. Republican; beh. L. by Meadley, 1813 1622..1683
Sidney, Henry, K. G. Statesman.................... — ..1586
Sidney, Mary, Countess of Pembroke, "Sidney's sister,
    Pembroke's mother,"........................... — ..1621
Sidney, Sir Philip. Statesman, Poet, Soldier. (*Arcadia.*)
    Life by Sir F. Grevile, Lord Brook, 1652; Dr. Zouch,
    1808; W. Gray, 1829; Julius Lloyd, 1862; H. R. F.
    Bourne, 1862 .... 1554..1586
Sidonius, Caius Sollius Apollinaris Modestus. Latin Poet 431?. 484?
Siebenkees, John Philip. German Philos. and Orient.. 1759..1796
Siegen, Louis von. Inventor of Mezzotint Engraving.. 1609..1676
Siegfrid, Dr. Rudolph Thos. Sanskrit and Celtic Schol. — ..1863
Sieveking, Amalie. Philanthropist. L. tr. by Winkworth 1794..1859
Sieyès, Count Emanuel Joseph. Abbé. Revolutionist.. 1748..1836
Sigaud de Lafond, John René. Surg. and Nat. Philos. 1740..1810
Sigebert I. King of Austrasia (561–75).............. 535?. 575
Sigebert II. *The Younger*...................... 630.. 654
Sigebert. King of East Anglia .... — .. 642
Sigismund. King of Hungary and Emperor of Germany
    (1411–37)................................... 1366..1437
Sigismund I. King of Poland (1506–48). *The Great*.. 1466..1548
Sigismund II. *Augustus*. (1548–72)............. 1520..1572
Sigismund III. (1587–1632.) *De Vasa*........... 1566..1632
Signorelli, Luke. Italian Painter .... 1439..1521
Signorelli, Peter Napoli. Critical and Historical Writer 1731..1815
Sigonio, Charles. Antiq. and Hist. (*Fasti Consulares*) 1520?.1584
Sigourney, Mrs. Lydia Huntley. Amer. Writ. L. by self. 1791..1865
Sike, or Siecke, Henry. Orientalist.................. — ..1712

BORN. DIED.

Silanion. Greek Sculptor .... fl. B.C. 324?
Silbermann, John Andrew. German Organ Builder ... 1712..1783
Silberschlag, John Isaiah. Ger. Mathem. and Mechan. 1721..1791
Silhouette, Stephen de. Fr. Statesman and Polit. Writer 1709..1767
Silius Italicus, Caius. Roman Poet..:................ 25?. 99?
Silliman, Benjamin, LL. D. American Scientist. (Ameri-
    can Journal of Science) .... 1779..1864
Silva, John Baptist. French Physician. Life by Bruhier 1683..1744
Silva y Figueroa, Garcia de. Spanish Diplomatist .... 1574?.1628?
Silverius. Bishop of Rome (536–38)................. — .. 538
Silvester I. Pope (314–35)......................... — .. 335
Silvester II. (999–1003.) Gerbert. .... — ..1003
Silvester, Israel. French Engraver.................. 1621..1691
Silvester, Louis. French Painter.................... 1675..1760
Simeon, of Durham. Historian...................... — ..1130?
Simeon, Rev. Charles, of Cambridge. L. by Carus, 1847 1759..1836
Simeon Metaphrastes. Greek Ecclesiastical Historian — .. 976?
Simeon Sethus. Greek Writer at Constantinople...... fl. 11th c.
Simeon Stylites. Syrian Ascetic .... 392?. 461?
Simler, John. Swiss Portrait Painter............... 1693?.1748
Simler, Josias. Prot. Divine at Zurich and Hist. Writer 1530..1576
Simmias, of Rhodes. Grammarian and Poet......... fl. B.C. 300?
Simnel, Lambert. Impostor .... 1472?.aft.1487
Simon, Richard. French Hebraist. (Critical History of
    the Old Testament)............................. 1638..1712
Simon Maccabæus. High Priest of the Jews .... — B.C.135
Simonet, Edmund. Fr. Jesuit. (Institutiones Theologicæ) 1662..1733
Simonetta, John. Italian Historian................. — ..1491?
Simonides, of Amorgus. Greek Iambic Poet .... fl. B.C. 660?
Simonides, of Ceos. Greek Lyric Poet............. 557.467 B.C.
Simonneau, Charles. French Engraver.............. 1639?.1728
Simonneau, Louis. French Engraver. (History of Paint-
    ing and Engraving)............................. 1660..1728
Simplicius. Neoplatonic Philosopher................ ti. Justinian
Simpson, Edward, D. D. (Universal Chronology)....... 1578..1651
Simpson, John. Dissenting Minister. Biblical Critic.. 1746..1813
Simpson, Thomas. Mathematician .... 1710..1761
Sims, James, M. D. Physician and Botanist .... — ..1831
Simson, Dr. Robert, of Glasgow. Mathematician; Editor
    of Euclid. Life by W. Traill...................... 1687..1768
Sinclair, Miss Catharine. Writer of Fiction........... 1800..1864
Sinclair, Charles Gideon, Baron. Swedish Tactician.. — ..1803
Sinclair, George, of Glasgow. Professor............. — ..1696
Sinclair, John. Master of Sinclair. Scottish Jacobite.. 1685?.1755?
Sinclair, Sir John, M. P. Life by his son, 1837 .... 1754..1835
Sindiah, Dowlut Row; defeated at Assaye............. 1781..1827
Sindiah, Madhajee. Mahratta Prince................. 1743?.1794
Singh, Runjeet. Chief of Lahore and Cashmere .... 1780..1839
Singleton, Henry. Historical Painter .... 1766..1839
Singlin, Anthony. Abbé of Port Royal. (Christian In-
    structions)....................................... — ..1664
Sionita, Gabriel. Hebraist; Editor of Parisian Polyglot 1577?.1648
Sirani, Elizabeth. Historical Painter .... 1638..1665
Sirani, John Andrew, of Bologna. Painter............ 1610..1670
Siri, Victor. Italian Political and Historical Writer..... 1608..1685

BORN. DIED.

Siric. Archbishop of Canterbury (990–94) .... — .. 994
Siricius. Bishop of Rome (385–99). .... — .. 399
Siries, Violante Beatrice. Italian Portrait Painter ..... 1710..1770[t]
Sirlet, Flavius. Jewel Engraver..................... — ..1737
Sirmond, James. French Jesuit Writer............... 1559..1651
Sirmond, John, neph. Latin Poet. (*Life of D'Amboise*) 1589?.1649
Sisicus. Bishop of Rome (384–98) .... — .. 398
Sisinnius. Bishop of Rome (708) .... — .. 708
Sismondi, John Charles Leonard Simonde de. French
  Historian and Political Economist .... 1773..1842
Sivers, Henry Jacob. Ger. Prot. Div., Naturalist, Antiq. 1709..1758
Siward, Earl of Northumberland.................... — ..1055
Six, John. Dutch Dramatic Poet .... 1618..1700
Sixtus I. Bishop of Rome (119?–28)................... — .. 128
Sixtus II. (257–53)................................. — .. 259
Sixtus III. (432–40)................................. — .. 440
Sixtus IV. (1471–84.) *Francis Albescola della Rovere.*. 1414..1484
Sixtus V. (1585–90.) *Felix Peretti.* Life by Gregory
  Leti, translated by Farneworth, 1754; Archenholz... 1521..1590
Sixtus. Cordelier of Sienna; Theologian .... 1520..1569
Sjöberg, or Sjoeberg, Eric. Swedish Lyric Poet........ 1794..1828
Skardsa, Biorna á. Icelandic Writer .... 1574..1655
Skarga Poweski, Peter. Polish Preacher............. 1536.. —
Skelton, John. Poet Laureate. Life by Dyce, 1843.... 1460?.1529
Skelton, Rev. Philip. Irish Divine. Life by Bardy.... 1707..1787
Skinner, Ezekiel, M. D. Amer. Clergyman and Physician 1777..1855
Skinner, James. Lieut.-Col., of Delhi. L. by J. B. Fraser — ..1841
Skinner, John. Scottish Clergyman and Poet......... 1721..1807
Skinner, John Stuart. Amer. Editor & Agricult. Writer 1788..1851
Skinner, Richard. American Statesman and Jurist .... 1778..1833
Skinner, Stephen, M. D. Philologist and Antiquary.... 1622?.1667
Skinner, William. Bishop of Aberdeen............... 1779?.1857
Skovoroda. *Gregory Savitch.* Divine of Ukraine..... 1730?.1778[t]
Skrzynecki, Jan, or John. Polish General............ 1786..1860
Skytte, Benedict. Swedish Statesman and Writer ..... 1614..1683
Skytte, John. Swedish Statesman and Writer......... 1577..1645
Slange, Nicholas. Dutch Historian................... 1657..1737
Slater, Samuel. American Manufacturer............... 1768..1835
Sleeman, Sir William Henry. Resident at Lucknow... 1788..1856
Sleidan, or Sleidanus, John. *Philipson.* Ger. Historian 1506..1556
Slingelandt, John Peter van. Dutch Painter.......... 1640..1691
Sloane, Sir Hans, M. D. Collector of Natural History .. 1660..1752
Slodtz, René Michael. *Michael Angelo.* Sculptor ..... 1705..1764
Slowacki, Julius. Polish Poet .... 1809..1849
Sluse, René Francis Walter, of Liège. Mathem. & Orient. 1622..1685
Sluter, Matthew, of Hamburg. Jurist and Meteorologist 1648..1719
Sluys, James van der. Dutch Painter................. 1660..1736
Smalbroke, Richard. Bishop of St. David's. Theologian 1673..1749
Smalcius, Valentine. German Unitarian Writer....... — ..1622
Smalridge, George. Bishop of Bristol............... 1663..1719
Smart, Christopher. Poet. Life prefixed to Works.... 1722..1771
Smart, Peter. Puritan Divine and Poet.............. —aft.1654
Smeaton, John. Civil Engineer...................... 1724..1792
Smedley, Rev. Edward. Poet and Historical Writer ... 1789?.1836
Smedley, Frank E. Novelist .... 1814?.1864

BORN. DIED.

Smellie, William, M. D. Scottish Writer on Midwifery.. — ..1763
Smellie, William. Naturalist. Life by Kerr, 1811..... 1740..1795
Smetius. *John Smith van der Ketten.* Antiquary...... — ..1651
Smibert, or Smybert, John. Scottish Painter......... 1684?.1751
Smigletius, Martin. Polish Jesuit, Theol., and Logician 1562..1618
Smirke, Robert, R. A. Painter .... 1752..1845
Smith, Adam, LL. D. (*Wealth of Nations.*) Life by
 Dugald Stewart................................. 1723..1790
Smith, Albert. Novelist and Humorist .... 1816..1860
Smith, Anker. Engraver........................... 1759..1819
Smith, Colonel Baird. Civil Engineer in India........ — ..1861
Smith, Caleb Blood. American Statesman .... 1808..1864
Smith, Charles. Writer on the Corn Trade........... 1713..1777
Smith, Charles Ferguson. American General .... 1806?.1862
Smith, Mrs. Charlotte. Poetess and Novelist .... 1749..1806
Smith, Christian. Botanist and Traveler............. 1785..1816
Smith, Edmund Neale. Poet .... 1668..1710
Smith, Miss Eliz. (*L. of Klopstock.*) L. by Miss Bowdler 1776..1806
Smith, Gabriel. Engraver.......................... 1724?.1783?
Smith, George, of Chichester. Landscape Painter ..... 1714..1776
Smith, Henry. *Silver-tongued.* Preacher. L. by Fuller 1550..1600?
Smith, Sir Henry George Wakelyn. General. Governor
 of Cape of Good Hope.......................... 1788.. —
Smith, Horace. Writer. (*Rejected Addresses*):........ 1779..1849
Smith, James, brother. Writer. (*Rejected Addresses*).. 1775..1839
Smith, James. American Patriot.................... 1719?.1806
Smith, James, of Deanstone. Manufacturer and Agri-
 culturist... 1789..1850
Smith, Sir James Edw., M. D. Botanist. (*English Botany*) 1759..1828
Smith, Sir John. Traveler & Ambassador. L. by Strype —aft.1595
Smith, Rev. John. Divine. (*Essex Dove; The Creed*).. 1563..1616
Smith, John. Capt. (*Hist. of Virginia.*) L. by Hill, 1858 1579..1631
Smith, John, of Queen's College, Cambridge. Divine.
 (*Ten Select Discourses*) .... 1618..1652
Smith, John, M. D. (*Portrait of Old Age — Eccles. xii.*). 1630..1679
Smith, John. Writer on Northern Literature and Antiq. 1659..1715
Smith, John. Engraver............................ 1654..1720?
Smith, John, of Chichester. Landscape Painter........ 1717..1764
Smith, Rev. Dr. John. Antiquary, Celtic Scholar, Trans-
 lator of Bible................................... 1747..1807
Smith, John. Missionary to Demerara................ 1790..1824
Smith, John Pye, D. D. Nonconformist Divine........ 1775..1851
Smith, John Raphael. Mezzotint Engraver........... 1752..1812
Smith, John Spencer. Archæologist................. 1769..1845
Smith, John Stafford. Musical Composer .... 1750?.1826
Smith, John Thos. Artist & Antiq. (*Antiquities of Lond.*) 1766..1833
Smith, Joseph. Mormon Prophet. Life by J. B. Turner 1805..1844
Smith, Miles. Bishop of Gloucester. Translator of Bible 1568..1624
Smith, Richard. Roman Catholic Divine............. 1500..1563
Smith, Richard. Book Collector .... 1590..1675
Smith, Robert, D. D. Master of Trinity College. Prize
 Founder....................................... 1689..1768
Smith, Samuel. Ejected Nonconformist. Tract Writer.
 (*Great Assize*)................................. 1588..1663?
Smith, Samuel, of New Jersey. Historian .... — ..1778

BORN. DIED.

Smith, Samuel Stanhope, D. D. Amer. Divine and Writer 1750..1819
Smith, Rev. Sydney. Writer. Life by Lady Holland.. 1769..1845
Smith, Sir Thomas. Statesman. (*Commonwealth.*) Life
    by Strype .... 1514?.1577
Smith, Thomas, D. D. Divine, Hist., Biographer, Critic 1638..1710
Smith, Thomas Assheton. Sportsman. Reminiscences
    by Sir J. E. Wilmot............................... 1776..1858
Smith, Thomas Southwood, M. D. ....:.... 1790?.1861
Smith, William. Herald and Antiquary .... — ..1618
Smith, William, of Chichester. Portrait Painter....... 1707..1764
Smith, William. Dean of Chester; Transl. of Thucydides 1711..1787
Smith, Wm., LL. D. Geologist. L. by John Phillips, 1844 1769..1839
Smith, Sir William Cusack. Irish Judge............. 1766..1836
Smith, Sir William Sidney. Admiral. Life by E. How-
    ard, 1830; Sir John Barrow, 1848................ 1764..1840
Smithson, James. English Physicist. Founder of Smith-
    sonian Institution at Washington .... — ..1829
Smitz, Gaspar. *Magdalen Smith.* Dutch Portrait Painter — ..1689
Smitz, Louis. Dutch Fruit Painter .... 1635..1675
Smollett, Tobias. Life by Dr. R. Anderson; Dr. Moore 1721..1771
Smybert, or Smibert, John. Scottish Painter .... 1684?.1751
Smyth, James Carmichael, M. D., F. R. S. Medical Writer 1741..1821
Smyth, William. Bishop of Lincoln. Co-founder of Bra-
    zenose College. Life by Churton .... 1450?.1514
Smyth, William. Professor of History at Cambridge... 1764..1849
Smyth, William Henry. Admiral. Naval Surveyor... 1788..1865
Snape, Andrew, D. D. Controversialist; Oppon. of Hoadly 1670..1742
Snayers, Peter. Dutch Painter .... 1593..1670
Snell, Louis. Swiss Author and Politician............. 1785..1854
Snell, Rodolph. Dutch Mathematician and Philologist.. 1547..1613
Snell, Willebrord, son. Dutch Mathem. (*Cyclometricus*) 1591..1626
Snellincks, John. Dutch Painter .... 1544..1638
Snethen, Rev. Nicholas. American Writer........... 1769..1845
Sneyders, or Snyders, Francis. Dutch Painter........ 1579..1657
Sniadecki, Andrew. Polish Medical & Chemical Writer 1768..1838
Sniadecki, John, brother. Mathematician............. 1756..1830
Snorro Sturleson, or Sturlason. Icelandic Poet, Histo-
    rian, and Statesman................................ 1178..1241
Snoy, Lambert. Dutch Genealogist................... 1574?.1638
Snoy, Renier. Dutch Diplomatist. (*History of Holland*) 1477..1537
Snyders, or Sneyders, Francis. Dutch Painter .... 1579..1657
Soane, Sir John. Architect.......................... 1753..1837
Soanen, John. French Bishop; Pulpit Orator......... 1647..1740
Sobieski, John III., King of Poland. L. by G. F. Coyer 1629..1696
Socinus, Faustus. Promoter of Socinianism. Life by J.
    Toulmin, 1777 .... 1539..1604
Socinus, Lælius. Originator of Socinianism. Life by
    C. F. Illgen .... 1525..1562
Socrates. Athenian Philosopher. Life by Wiggers... 468.399 B.C.
Socrates. Ecclesiastical Historian to 439.............. — aft. 439
Sodoma, Il. *John Anthony Razzi.* Italian Painter ..... 1479..1554
Soemmering, Samuel Thomas von. German Anatomist
    and Physiologist .... 1755..1830
Soest, or Zoest, Gerard. German Painter............. 1637..1681
Sœur, Hubert le. French Sculptor in England......... — ..1670?

BORN. DIED.

Solander, Daniel Charles, M. D. Swedish Naturalist ... 1736..1782
Solari, Andrew. *Del Gobbo.* Italian Painter.......... 1470?.1527
Solario, Anthony de. *Il Zingaro.* Painter & Illuminator 1382..1455
Sole, Anthony Mary dal. Italian Landscape Painter.... 1597..1677
Sole, John Joseph dal. Historical and Landscape Painter 1654..1719
Solger, Chas. Wm. Ferdinand. Ger. Writer on Æsthetics 1780..1819
Solignac, Peter Jos. de la Pimpie, Chevalier de. Fr. Hist. 1687..1773
Soliman. *Ebn Abd-al-Malek.* Seventh Ommiyade Caliph
   (715-17).. — .. 717
Soliman. *Ebn-al-Hakem.* King of Cordova (1009-16).. — ..1016
Soliman. *Ebn-Cutulmish.* Seljuk Turk. Conqueror of
   Asia Minor.. — ..1084
Soliman. *Tchelibi, The Noble.* Turkish Pr. at Adrianople — ..1410
Soliman I. *Magnificent.* Ottoman Sultan (1520-66).. 1494..1566
Soliman II. (1687-91.) Life by Charles Ancillon..... — ..1691
Solimene, Francis. *L'Abate Ciccio.* Italian Painter... 1657..1747
Solinus, Caius Julius. Hist. & Geographer. (*Polyhistor*) fl. 230
Solis, Anthony de. Span. Hist. and Poet. (*Conq. Mexico*) 1610..1686
Solis, John Diaz de. Spanish Navigator .... — ..1515?
Solomon. King of Israel (B. C. 1015-975)...........1033?.975 B.C.
Solomon. *Ben Virga.* Historian .... fl. 16th c.
Solomon, Abraham. Historical Painter.............. 1823?.1862
Solomon Ben Isaac. *Rashi.* Jewish Rabbi......... 1040?.1105
Solon. Athenian Lawgiver......................638?.558? B.C.
Soltikoff, Nicholas Ivanovitch. Russian Statesman .... 1736..1816
Solvyns, Francis Balthasar. Dutch Artist. (*Les Hindous*) 1760..1824
Solyman. *See* Soliman.
Somer, John van. Dutch Mezzotint Engraver......... — ..1694
Somers, John, Ld. Ld. Chanc. L. by Cooksey; Maddock 1650?.1716
Somerset, Edmund de Beaufort, Duke of; Regent of Fr. — ..1455
Somerset, Henry de Beaufort, son; taken at Hexham;
   beheaded....................................... — ..1463
Somerset, John de Beaufort, Earl of, K. G., son of John
   of Gaunt. Lord High Admiral.................... — ..1410
Somerset, John de Beaufort, son, First Duke of........ 1392?.1444
Somerset, Robert Carr, Viscount Rochester, Earl of..... — ..1645
Somerset, William Seymour, Duke of. Husband of
   Arabella Stuart................................ — ..1660
Somerville, Thomas, D. D. Historian .... 1741..1813
Somerville, William. Poet. (*The Chase*)........... 1692..1742
Sommariva, John Bapt. de. Ital. Polit. and Art Collector 1760?.1826
Sömmering, Samuel Thomas von. German Anatomist
   and Physiologist .... 1755..1830
Sommery, Fontette de. French Writer.............. — ..1792?
Sommier, John Claude. French Writer .... 1661..1737
Somner, William. Antiquary. Life by Bp. Kennett, 1693 1606..1669
Sonnerat, Peter. Naturalist and Traveler............ 1748?.1814
Sonnini de Manoncourt, Charles Nicholas Sigisbert.
   French Naturalist and Traveler................... 1751..1812
Sontag, Madame Henrietta, Countess Rossi. Ger. Singer 1805..1854
Sophia, Princess. Regent of Russia................ 1667..1704
Sophia. Electress of Hanover, mother of George I..... — ..1714
Sophia Dorothea. Daughter of George I. Queen of
   Prussia. Life, 2 vols. 8vo, 1845................. 1687..1757
Sophocles. Attic Tragedian .... 495?.405? B.C.

BORN. DIED.

Sophonisba. Queen of Numidia .... — B.C.203
Sorbait, Paul de. Dutch Medical Writer.............. — ..1691
Sorbière, Samuel. French Writer. (*Sorberiana*)...... 1615..1670
Sorbonne, Robert de. Founder of College............ 1201..1274
Sordello. Provençal Poet .... 1189..1281?
Sorel, Agnes. Mistress of Charles VII. of France....... 1409?.1450
Sorgh, Henry, of Rotterdam. Paint. of Fairs, Markets, &c. 1621..1684
Sorri, Peter. Italian Painter .... 1556..1622
Sortain, Rev. Joseph, of Brighton. Life by Mrs. Sortain 1809..1860
Söst, or Zöst, Gerard. German Painter .... 1637..1681
Sostratus, of Cnidos. Architect of the Pharos .... fl. B.C. 273
Soter. Bishop of Rome (168–76)...................... — .. 176
Sotheby, Samuel Leigh. Antiquary and Bibliographer — ..1861
Sotheby, William. Poet and Translator .... 1757..1833
Soto, Barahona de. Spanish Poet.................... fl. 1586
Soto, Dominic. Spanish Tridentine Divine .... 1494?.1560
Soto, Peter. Confessor to Charles V.; Tridentine Divine — ..1563
Soubise, Benj. de Rohan, Sieur de. Huguenot Soldier... 1589?.1641
Soubise, Chas. de Rohan, Prince de. Marshal of France 1715..1787
Soubise, John de Parthenai, Lord of. Huguenot Leader.. 1512?.1566
Souchai, John Baptist. French Writer .... 1688..1746
Souchiet, Stephen. French Divine.................. 1671..1744
Souchiet, Stephen Augustine, brother. (*Poems on Comets*) — ..1744
Soufflot, James Germain. French Architect .... 1714..1781
Soulié, Melchior Frederick. Fr. Novelist and Dramatist 1800..1847
Soulouque, Faustin. *Faustin I.* Emperor of Hayti.... 1789.. —
Soult, Nicholas John de Dieu. Marshal of France; States-
    man. (*Memoirs*).............................. 1769?.1852
South, Robert, D.D. Divine .... 1633..1716
Southard, Samuel L. American Statesman .... 1787..1842
Southcott, Joanna. Religious Enthusiast .... 1750..1814
Southern, Thomas. Dramatic Writer. (*Fatal Discovery*) 1660..1746
Southey, Mrs. (Caroline Bowles). Poetess............ 1787..1854
Southey, Robert. Poet Laureate. Life by C. C. Southey 1774..1843
Southey, Thomas, M.D. Medical Writer. (*Pulmonary
    Consumption*) .... 1777..1865
Southwell, Nath. Jesuit. Continuator of *Jesuits' Library* — ..1676
Southwell, Robert. Jesuit Seminary Priest; Poet...... 1560..1595
Soutman, Peter. Painter and Engraver of Haarlem .... 1580?. —
Souvestre, Émile. French Writer.................... 1806..1854
Souza, John de. Portuguese Historian and Philologist.. 1730?.1812
Souza, Manuel Faria y. Portuguese Poet and Historian 1590..1649
Souza Botelho, Joseph Mary. Portuguese Diplomatist 1758..1825
Sowerby, Charles Edward. Naturalist............... 1795..1842
Sowerby, George Bettingham, brother. Naturalist .... 1788..1854
Sowerby, James, brother. Naturalist and Artist .... 1767..1822
Soxini, or Soccini, Bartholomew. Civilian .... 1436..1507
Soxini, Lælius. Orientalist and Arian................ 1525..1562
Soxini, or Soccini, Mariano. *The Elder.* Italian Canonist 1401..1467
Soxini, Mariano. *The Younger.* Civilian and Canonist 1482..1556
Soyer, Alexis. French Cook in England; Writer ...... 1800?.1858
Soyuti. Arabic Scholar and Philosopher.............. 1445..1505
Sozomen. Ecclesiastical Historian (324–415).......... — aft. 443
Spada, Lionel. Italian Painter .... 1576..1622
Spaendonck, Gerard van. Flower and Miniature Painter 1752..1822

BORN. DIED.
Spagnoletto, Il. *Joseph Ribera.* Painter............. 1588..1656
Spagnoli, Baptist. General of the Carmelites. Writer.. 1444..1516
Spalatin, George. German Writer................... 1482..1545
Spalding, George Louis. German Philologist......... 1762..1811
Spalding, John, of Aberdeen. Hist. (*Troubles of Scotland*) 1609?.1670
Spalding, John Joachim. German Divine and Preacher 1714..1804
Spalding, Lyman. American Physician and Surgeon... 1775..1821
Spalding, Samuel. Philosophical Writer............. 1807..1834
Spalding, William. Professor of Logic, St. Andrew's... — ..1859
Spallanzani, Lazarus. Italian Naturalist .... 1729..1799
Spangenberg, Augustus Theophilus. German Divine.. 1704..1792
Spanheim, Ezekiel. Statesman and Classical Scholar.. 1629..1710
Spanheim, Frederick. Professor of Divinity at Leyden 1600..1649
Spanheim, Frederick, son. Rector of Leyden University 1632..1701
Sparre, Eric. Swedish Statesman and Writer......... 1550..1600
Sparrmann, Andrew. Swedish Naturalist and Traveler 1747?.1820
Sparrow, Anthony. Bishop of Exeter. (*Prayer Book*).. 1620?.1685
Spartacus. Roman Gladiator; Leader of Servile Rebel-
      lion (B. C. 73–71)............................ — B.C. 71
Speckter, Erwin. German Painter .... 1806..1835
Speed, John. Historian .... 1555?.1629
Spegel, Haquin. Swedish Archbishop; Historical Writer 1645..1714
Speke, Captain John Hanning. African Explorer; Dis-
      coverer of the Source of the Nile................. 1827..1864
Spelman, Edward. Classical Translator & Archæologist — ..1767
Spelman, Sir Henry. Hist. and Antiq. Life by Gibson 1562..1641
Spelman, Sir John, son. (*Life of Alfred the Great*).... — ..1643
Spence, Joseph. Divine and Critic. L. by Singer, 1820 1698..1768
Spence, William. Entomologist...................... 1783..1860
Spencer, Ambrose, LL. D. American Jurist .... 1765..1848
Spencer, Charles, Third Earl of Sunderland. Lord Lieut. 1674..1722
Spencer, Hon. & Rev. Geo. Passionist. *Brother Ignatius* — ..1864
Spencer, or Despencer, Hugh, Lord. Favorite of Edw. II. — ..1326
Spencer, or Despencer, Hugh, son. Favorite of Edw. II. — ..1326
Spencer, John, D. D. Divine. (*De Legibus Hebræorum*) 1630..1695
Spencer, John Canfield. American Jurist and Statesman 1788..1855
Spencer, John Charles, Earl, Viscount Althorp. Chan-
      cellor of Exchequer; Agricultural Reformer .... 1782..1845
Spencer, Robt., 2d E. of Sunderland. Minister of Jas. II. 1641?.1702
Spencer, William Robert. Translator of *Lenore* .... 1770..1834
Spener, Philip James. Lutheran Divine. Founder of
      the Pietists .... 1635..1705
Spenser, Edmund. Poet. (*Faëry Queen.*) Life by Todd;
      Dr. Aikin; J. Mitford; J. P. Collier .... 1553?.1599
Speranski, Michael. Russian Statesman and Reformer. 1771..1840
Sperling, John, of Wittemberg. Medical Writer .... 1603?.1658
Sperling, Otto. German Physician and Botanist....... 1602..1681
Sperling, Otto. (*Monumentum Hamburgense*)........... 1634..1715
Speroni, Sperone. Italian Writer .... 1500..1588
Speusippus, nephew of Plato. Academic Philosopher..380?.339 B.C.
Spiegel, Henry. Poet. *Dutch Ennius* .... 1549..1615
Spielman, Sir John. Paper Maker and Royal Jeweler.. — ..1626
Spielmann, James Reinhold. Ger. Chemist and Botanist 1722..1783
Spierings, Henry. Dutch Landscape Painter.......... 1633..1715
Spiers, Albert van. Dutch Historical Painter.......... 1666..1718

BORN. DIED.

Spigelius, or Vanden Spieghel, Adrian. Phys. and Anat. 1578..1625
Spilberg, John. Portrait and Historical Painter .... 1619..1690
Spiller, John. English Sculptor...................... 1763..1794
Spindler, Charles. German Novelist .... 1796..1855
Spinello, Aretino. Italian Historical and Portrait Painter 1308?.1400?
Spinello, Matthew. Italian Chronicler .... 1230..1268
Spinello, Paris, or Gaspar. Painter.................. 1366..1426?
Spinkes, Nathaniel. Nonjuring Bishop; Writer........ 1653?.1727
Spinola, Ambrose, Marquis of. Spanish General....... 1569..1630
Spinoza, Baruch, or Benedict. Dutch Philosopher. Life
   by Colerus, 1706; Boulainvilliers, 1731; Lucas; Len-
   glet du Fresnoy; Jaegar; Conrad von Orelli ; A.
   Saintes, 1842; Saisset, 1842; Berth. Auerbach, 1855.. 1632..1677
Spix, John Baptist von. Bavarian Medical Writer .... 1781..1826
Spizelius, Theophilus. Ger. Writer. (*Chinese Literature*) 1639..1691
Spofforth, Reginald. English Musical Composer....... 1768..1827
Spohn, Fred. Augustus William. Ger. Philos. and Philol. 1792..1824
Spohr, Louis. German Musical Composer............. 1784..1859
Spon, Charles. French Physician, Scholar, and Latin Poet 1609..1684
Spon, James. French Antiquary and Traveler......... 1647..1685
Spondanus, or De Sponde, Henry. (*Annales Sacri*).... 1568..1643
Spondanus, or De Sponde, John. Homeric Scholar.... 1557..1595
Spontini, Gaspar. Italian Musical Composer .... 1778..1851
Spooner, Richard, M. P. Politician .... 1783..1864
Spotswood, or Spottiswood, John. Archbishop of St.
   Andrew's. (*History of the Church of Scotland*)...... 1565..1639
Spragg, or Spragge, Sir Edward. Admiral............ — ..1673
Spranger, Bartholomew. Dutch Painter.............. 1546..1623
Sprat, Thomas. Bishop of Rochester. Historian and Poet 1636..1713
Sprengel, Kurt. German Physician and Botanist...... 1766..1833
Sprengel, Matthew Christian. German Historian...... 1746..1803
Spring, Samuel, D. D. American Divine .... 1746..1819
Spurstow, William, D. D. Nonconformist Divine ..... — ..1666
Spurzheim, John Gaspar. Ger. Philos. and Phrenologist 1776..1832
Squarcione, Francis. Italian Painter................. 1394..1474
Squire, Samuel. Bishop of St. David's. Writer....... 1714..1766
Staal, Margaret Jane Cordier de Launay, Baroness de.
   (*Memoirs of her Life*) .... 1693..1750
Staben, Henry. Flemish Historical and Portrait Painter 1578..1658
Stackhouse, John. Botanist......................... — ..1819
Stackhouse, Rev. Thomas. (*History of the Bible*)...... 1680..1752
Stadius, John. Dutch Historian and Astrologer....... 1527..1579
Staël-Holstein, Anne Mary Louisa Germaine, Baroness
   de, *née* Necker. Writer. Life by Maria Norris; Mme.
   Necker de Saussure .... 1766..1817
Staeudlin, Charles Frederick. German Theologian .... 1761..1826
Stafford, Anthony. Writer. (*Female Glory*).......... — ..1641
Stafford, William Howard, Viscount. Statesman. Vic-
   tim of Popish Plot............................... 1612..1680
Stagnelius, Eric John. Swedish Poet................. 1793..1823
Stahl, George Ernest. German Chemist and Physiologist 1660..1734
Stahl, Julius Frederick. German Statesman and Author 1802..1861
Stahremberg, Conrad Balthasar, Count de. Defender
   of Vienna....................................... — ..1687
Stahremberg, Guido Balde, Count de. Austrian General 1657..1737

BORN. DIED.

Stair, James Dalrymple (*q. v.*), First Viscount.......... 1619..1695
Stair, John Dalrymple, 2d Earl of. Life by Anderson, 1747 1673..1747
Stalbent, Adrian. Dutch Painter..................... 1580..1660
Stampa, Gaspara. *Anasilla.* Italian Poetess .... 1523?.1554
Stampart, Francis. Dutch Painter at Vienna.......... 1675..1750
Standish, Frank Hall. Writer...................... 1798..1840
Standish, Miles. Military Leader of Plymouth Pilgrims 1584?.1656
Stanford, Rev. John, D. D. American Philanthropist... 1754..1834
Stanhope, Charles, Third Earl. Polit. & Scientific Writ. 1753..1816
Stanhope, George, D. D. Dean of Canterbury. Divine. 1660..1728
Stanhope, Lady Hester Lucy. Life by Dr. Meryon, 1843 1766..1839
Stanhope, James, First Earl. General and Statesman .. 1673..1721
Stanhope, Philip, Earl. Scholar and Patron of Learning 1714..1786
Stanhope, Philip Dormer, Fourth Earl of Chesterfield.
    (*Letters.*) Life by Maty.......................... 1694..1773
Stanislaus I. *Leszczynski.* King of Poland........... 1677..1766
Stanislaus II. *Augustus Poniatowski.* King of Poland 1732..1798
Stanley, Edward. Bp. of Norwich. Life by A. P. Stanley 1779..1849
Stanley, John. Musical Composer.................... 1713..1786
Stanley, Thomas. Editor of Æschylus. (*History of Phi-
    losophy.*) Life by Sir E. Brydges .... 1625..1678
Stannina, Gerard. Historical Painter .... 1344?.1403
Stanyhurst, Richard. Historian, Poet, and Divine..... 1545?.1618
Stanzione, Cavaliere Masimus. Neapolitan Painter.... 1585..1656
Stapel, John Bodæus de. Dutch Physician and Botanist — ..1636
Stapledon, Walter. Bp. of Exeter. Found. of Exeter Coll. — ..1326
Stapleton, or Stapylton, Sir Robert. Royalist. Poet... — ..1669
Stapleton, Thomas. Roman Catholic Controversialist.. 1535..1598
Starck, John Augustus von. Theologian............. 1741..1816
Stark, John. American Revolutionary Officer. Life by
    Edward Everett................................ 1728..1822
Stark, William, M. D. Medical Writer .... 1740..1769
Starovloski, Simon. Polish Geog. and Biog. Writer ... — ..1656
Stassart, Goswin Joseph Augustine, Baron. Belgian
    Statesman and Writer .... 1780..1854
Staszic, Stanislaus. Polish Patriot and Philanthropist.. 1755..1806
Statius, or Estaço, Achilles. Portuguese Scholar....... 1524..1581
Statius, Publius Papinius. Lat. Poet. (*Thebaid; Achilles*) 61?. 96?
Staudenmaier, Francis Anthony. Ger. Theol. & Philos. 1800..1856
Stäudlin, Charles Frederick. German Theologian ..... 1761..1826
Staughton, Rev. Wm., D. D. Amer. Divine and Educator 1770..1829
Staunton, Sir George Leonard. (*History of Embassy to
    China.*) Life by Sir G. T. Staunton .... 1737..1801
Staunton, Sir George Thomas, son. Writer on China .. 1781..1859
Staupitz, John von. Vicar-Gen.; Friend & Patron of Luther — ..1524
Staveley, Thomas. Historian and Antiquary.......... — ..1683
Stay, Benedict. Philosopher and Latin Poet........... 1714..1801
Stayner, or Stainer, Sir Richard. Admiral .... — ..1662
Stebbing, Henry. Theologian. Opponent of Hoadly .. — ..1763
Stedman, John Gabriel. Captain. Historical Writer .. 1745..1797
Steele, Sir Richard. Essayist. Life by H. R. Mont-
    gomery, 1864 .... 1671..1729
Steen, John. Dutch Painter .... 1636..1689
Steenwyck, Henry. Flemish Painter................. 1550..1603
Steenwyck, Henry, son. Painter .... 1589.. —

BORN. DIED.

Steevens, George.   Commentator on Shakespeare...... 1736..1800
Stefaneschi, John Baptist.   Historical Painter of Florence 1582..1659
Stefano.   *Il Fiorentino.*   Italian Painter.............. 1301..1350
Stefano, Thomas di, son.   *Il Giottino.*   Painter .... 1324..1356
Steffani, Augustine.   Ital. Diplomatist and Mus. Composer 1655..1730
Steffens, Henry.   German Nat. and Novelist. (*Autobiog.*) 1773..1845
Steibelt, Daniel.   German Musical Composer .... 1765?.1823
Stein, Christian Godfrey Daniel.   German Geographer.. 1771..1830
Stein, Henry F. Charles, Baron von.   Prussian Statesman 1757..1831
Stella, Claudine Bousonnet.   Engraver .... 1634..1697
Stella, Francis.   Painter .... 1563..1605
Stella, Francis.   French Painter .... 1601..1661
Stella, James, brother.   Painter .... 1596..1647
Stellini, James.   Italian Ethical Writer .... 1699..1770
Stenbock, Magnus.   Swedish General............... 1664..1717
Steno, Nicholas.   Danish Prelate and Anatomist .... 1638..1687
Stephanus of Byzantium.   Grammarian............   fl. 500?
Stephen, St.   Protomartyr ....   — 36 or 7
Stephen I.   Pope (253–57)......................   — .. 257
Stephen II.   Elected 752, March 27; not consecrated;
        omitted by some ....   — .. 752
Stephen III., or II.   (752–57)....................   — .. 757
Stephen IV., or III.   (768–72)....................   — .. 772
Stephen V., or IV.   (816–17)....................   — .. 817
Stephen VI., or V.   (885–91.) *Basil.* ....   — .. 891
Stephen VII., or VI.   (896–97) ....   — .. 897
Stephen VIII., or VII.   (929–31) ....   — .. 931
Stephen IX., or VIII.   (939–42) ....   — .. 942
Stephen X., or IX.   (1057–58.) *Frederick*...........   — ..1058
Stephen I.   King of Hungary (997–1038).   *Saint* ...... 979..1038
Stephen II.   (1114–31)........................... 1100..1131
Stephen III.   (1161–73).......................   — ..1173
Stephen IV., or V.   (1270–72) ....   — ..1272
Stephen.   King of England........................ 1105..1154
Stephen, of Muret, St.   Founder of Monastery .... 1046?.1124
Stephen, of Tournay.   French Theologian .... 1135..1203
Stephen, Henry John.   Sergeant-at-Law.   Legal Writer 1786..1864
Stephen, James.   Master in Chancery.   Emancipationist 1759..1832
Stephen, Sir James.   Professor of History; Statesman and
        Author. (*Ecclesiastical Biography*)................ 1789..1859
Stephen, John.   Danish Historian and Antiquary...... 1599..1650
Stephen-Bathori.   King of Poland (1576–86)......... 1533..1586
Stephens, Alexander.   Miscellaneous Writer .... 1757?.1821
Stephens, Anthony.   Printer....................... 1592..1674
Stephens, Charles.   Printer....................... 1504?.1564
Stephens, Henry.   French Printer................... 1460?.1520
Stephens, Henry.   Printer. (*Greek Thesaurus*)........ 1528..1598
Stephens, James Francis.   Entomologist .... 1792..1852
Stephens, Rev. Jeremy.   Divine .... 1592..1665
Stephens, John.   Jacobite Officer.   Continuat. of Dugdale — ..1726
Stephens, John Lloyd.   American Traveler and Author.
        (*Incidents of Travel in Egypt,* etc.; *Yucatan*) .... 1805..1852
Stephens, Paul.   Printer .... 1566..1627?
Stephens, Robert.   Printer.   Editor of Greek Testament.
        (*Latin Thesaurus.*)   Life by W. P. Gresswell, 1833 .. 1503..1559

BORN. DIED.

Stephens, Robert, son. Printer...................... 1530..1570
Stephens, Robert. Antiquary...................... — ..1732
Stephenson, George. Engineer. Inventor of Locomotive
 Steam Engine and Railways. Life by Smiles, 1859.. 1781..1848
Stephenson, Robert, M. P., son. Engineer. Inventor of
 Tubular Bridge. Life by Jeaffreson and Pole....... 1803..1859
Stepney, George. Poet, Statesman, and Political Writer 1663..1707
Sterling John. Critic and Essayist. Life by Archdeacon
 Hare, 1848; Thomas Carlyle, 1851 .... 1806..1844
Sterne, Rev. Lawrence. (*Tristram Shandy.*) Life by Fitz-
 gerald, 1863 .... 1713..1768
Sterne, Richard. Archbishop of York................. 1596..1683
Sternhold, Thomas. Versifier of the Psalms........... — ..1549
Stesichorus. Greek Lyric Poet....................632?.552? B.C.
Steuart, Sir James. Writer on Political Economy...... 1713..1780
Steuben, Frederick William Augustus, Baron. German
 Officer in the American Army of the Revolutionary
 War. Life by Bowen; Kapp, 1860................. 1730..1794
Stevens, Alexander. Architect...................... — ..1796
Stevens, George Alexander. Novelist and Humorist.
 (*Lecturer on Heads*)............................. 1720?.1784
Stevens, Isaac Ingalls. American General .... 1817..1862
Stevens, John. American Inventor.................... 1749..1838
Stevens, Richard James Samuel. Glee Composer ...... 1756?.1837
Stevens, Robert Livingston. American Inventor ...... 1788..1856
Stevens, William. Citizen of London. Religious Writer 1732..1807
Stevens, Dr. Wm. Barshaw. Div. and Poet. (*Retirement*) 1755?.1800
Stevenson, Andrew. American Statesman............. 1784..1857
Stevenson, Sir John Andrew. Musical Composer...... 1761..1833
Stevenson, John Hall. Humorous Poet and Satirist.... 1718..1785
Stevenson, Robert. Engineer of Lighthouses.......... 1772..1850
Stevenson, Seth William. Journalist and Miscel. Writer 1784..1853
Stevenson, William. Antiquary...................... — ..1821
Stevenson, William. Writer. (*Progress of Discovery*) 1772..1829
Stevin, Simon. Dutch Mathematician and Mechanician — ..1633
Stewart, Rev. Alexander, D. D., of Dingwall. Gaelic Schol. — ..1821
Stewart, Sir Charles William Vane, Third Marquess of
 Londonderry. General. Life by Alison .... 1778..1854
Stewart, Dugald. Scottish Metaphysician. L. by Veitch 1753..1828
Stewart, Rev. James Haldane. Divine................. 1775..1854
Stewart, John. *Walking Stewart.* Traveler.......... — ..1822
Stewart, Matthew, D. D. Scottish Mathematician ...... 1717..1785
Stewart, Robert. Lord Castlereagh, Second Marquess of
 Londonderry. Statesman. Life by Alison.......... 1769..1822
Stewart Denham, Sir James. Political Economist .... 1713..1780
Stieglitz, Christian Louis. Ger. Writer on Architecture 1756..1836
Stieglitz, Henry. German Poet...................... 1803..1849
Stiernhielm, George. Swedish Scholar and Poet...... 1598..1672
Stiernhoek, John. Swedish Jurist and Antiquary...... 1576..1675
Stifelius, Michael. German Algebraist and Prot. Divine 1509?.1567
Stigand. Archbishop of Canterbury (1052-70)......... — ..1070
Stiglmayer, John Baptist. Bavarian Sculptor......... 1791..1844
Stiles, Ezra. Amer. Divine and Hist. Life by Kingsley 1727..1795
Stilicho, Flavius. Roman General under Theodosius;
 assassinated .... — .. 408

BORN. DIED.

Still, John. Bishop of Bath and Wells. (*Gammer Gurton's Needle*)................................. 1543..1607
Stilling, John Henry. *Jung.* Pietist. Life by self .... 1740..1817
Stillingfleet, Benjamin. Nat. and Poet. Life by Coxe 1702..1771
Stillingfleet, Edward. Bishop of Worcester. Life by
    Timothy Goodwin, 1710.............................. 1635..1699
Stillman, Rev. Samuel, D. D. American Clergyman.... 1737..1807
Stilpo. Greek Philosopher of Megara .... fl. B.C. 294
Stirling, James. Mathematician...................... —aft.1764
Stirling, Sir William Alexander, E. of. Poet. (*Domesday*) 1580?.1640
Stjernstolpe, Jonas Magnus. Swedish Writer......... 1777..1831
Stobæus, John. Classical Compiler .... fl. 5th c.?
Stock, Christian. German Orientalist. (*Clavis*) .... 1672..1733
Stock, Richard. Puritan Divine...................... — ..1626
Stock, Simon. General of the Carmelites.............. — ..1265
Stockdale, Rev. Perceval. Miscel. Writer. Life by self 1736..1811
Stocks, John Ellerton, M. D. Botanist .... 1822..1854
Stockton, Richard. American Statesman .... 1730..1781
Stodart, James, F. R. S. Cutler...................... 1760..1823
Stoddard, Solomon. American Clergyman and Writer 1643..1729
Stoddart, Captain. Envoy to Bokhara with Conolly.... — ..1843
Stoddart, Sir John. Lawyer and Political Writer...... 1773..1856
Stoffler, John. German Mathematician and Astrologer. 1452..1531
Stofflet, Nicholas. French Vendean Royalist.......... 1751..1796
Stolberg, Christian, Count von. Ger. Dramatist and Poet 1748..1821
Stolberg, Fred. Leopold, Count von, br. Poet and Trav. 1750..1819
Stone, Edmund. Mathematician .... — ..1768?
Stone, Frank. Painter............................... 1800..1859
Stone, Henry. *Old Stone.* Statuary and Painter ...... — ..1653
Stone, John, brother. Statuary .... — ..1660?
Stone, Nicholas. Sculptor; Master Mason to Charles I. 1586?.1647
Stone, Nicholas, son. Statuary .... — ..1647
Stone, Thomas. American Patriot..................... 1743..1787
Stone, William Leete. American Journalist and Author 1792..1844
Stonehouse, Rev. Sir James. Physician and Divine... 1716..1795
Storace, Anna Selina. Singer and Actress .... 1761..1814
Storace, Stephen, brother. English Musical Composer.. 1763..1796
Storch, Henry Frederick von. Political Economist..... 1766..1835
Storck, Anthony, Baron von, of Vienna. Medical Writer 1731..1803
Storer, James Sargent. (*Cathedrals*)................ 1771?.1853
Storer, Thomas. Poet. (*Wolsey*).................... — ..1604
Stork, Abraham. Dutch Marine Painter .... 1650..1708
Storm, Edward. Danish Poet.......................... 1749..1794
Storr, Gottlob Christian. German Theologian .... 1746..1805
Storrs, William Lucius, LL. D. American Jurist........ 1795..1861
Story, Joseph. Amer. Jurist & Judge. L. by W. W. Story 1779..1845
Story, Rev. Robert, of Rosneath. L. by R. H. Story, 1862 1790..1859
Stothard, Charles Alfred. Artist. (*Monumental Effigies.*)
    Life by Mrs. C. A. Stothard (Mrs. Bray), 1823 ...... 1786..1821
Stothard, Thomas, R. A. Painter. L. by Mrs. Bray, 1852 1755..1834
Stow, John. Antiq. (*Survey of London.*) Life by Strype 1525..1605
Stowell, Rev. Hugh, of Manchester. Theologian ...... 1799..1865
Stowell, William Scott, Lord. Admiralty Judge. Life by
    W. Falconer and H. C. Hamilton; W. E. Surtees, 1846 1745..1836
Strabo. Greek Geographer........................... B.C.54?.A.D.24?

BORN. DIED.

Strada, Famiano. Historian. (*Wars in the Low Countries*) 1572..1649
Strada, or Stradanus, John. Florentine Painter........ 1536..1604?
Stradella, Alexander. Italian Musical Composer ...... 1645?.1678
Stradivarius, Anthony. Ital. Stringed-instrument Maker 1670?.1728?
Straeten, or Streten, Henry van der. Dutch Landsc. Pa. 1680.. —
Strafford, Thomas Wentworth, Earl of. Statesman; exe-
cuted. Life by Sir G. Radcliffe.................... 1593..1641
Strahan, William. Scottish Printer.................. 1715..1785
Stralenburg, Philip John. Swedish Officer and Writer.. 1676..1747
Strange, Sir Robert. Engraver. Life by self and Den-
nistoun, 1855 .... 1721..1792
Strangford, Percy Clinton Sydney Smythe, Sixth Vis-
count. Diplomatist and Poet .... 1780..1855
Strathallan, William Drummond, Fourth Viscount. Jac-
obite; fell at Culloden .... 1690..1746
Stratico, Simon, Count. Italian Writer.............. 1733..1824
Strauch, Ægidius, or Giles. Mathem. and Controversialist 1632..1682
Strauss, John. German Composer.................... 1804..1849
Streater, Robert. English Painter.................... 1624..1680
Streek, Henry van. Flemish Historical Painter........ 1659..1713
Streek, Jurian van. Flemish Painter .... 1632..1678
Strein, or Strinius, Richard, Baron von Schwartzenau.
Antiquary.. 1538..1600
Strickland, Hugh Edwin. Naturalist................. 1811..1853
Strigelius, Victorinus. Reformer.................... 1524..1569
Strigul. *See* Strongbow.......................... — ..1176
Stroemer, or Strömer, Martin, of Upsal. Astronomer and
Natural Philosopher.............................. 1707..1770
Strong, Caleb. American Statesman .... 1745..1819
Strongbow, Gilbert de Clare, First Earl of Pembroke... — ..1149
Strongbow, Richard de Clare, Lord of Strigul. Justice
of Ireland.. — ..1176
Stroth, Frederick Andrew. German Scholar........... 1750..1795
Strozzi, Ciriaco. Italian Philosopher................. 1504..1565
Strozzi, Hercules. Latin Poet....................... 1471..1508
Strozzi, John Baptist. Writer and Patron of Learning.. 1551..1634
Strozzi, Julius. Latin Poet. (*Venetia Ædificata*)...... 1583..1660
Strozzi, Nicholas. Dramatic Poet .... 1590?.1654
Strozzi, Pallas. Statesman and Reviver of Learning ... 1372..1462
Strozzi, Philip. Republican of Florence. Life by Lorenzo
Strozzi; T. A. Trollope........................... 1488..1538
Strozzi, Titus Vespasianus. Italian Latin Poet........ 1422?.1505
Strudell, Peter, of Vienna. Painter................. 1660?.1717
Struensee, Chas. Augustus von. Ger. Statesm. & Auth. 1735..1804
Struensee, John Frederick, Count, br. Court Favorite 1737..1772
Strutt, Joseph. Antiquary.......................... 1749..1802
Struve, Burkhard Gotthelf. Jurist................... 1671..1738
Struve, Frederick George William von. Russian Astron-
omer. (*Observationes Dorpatenses*) .... 1793..1864
Struve, George Adam. German Jurist............... 1619..1692
Struve, Henry, of Lausanne. Chemist and Mineralogist 1751..1826
Struys, John. Dutch Traveler .... — ..1694
Strype, Rev. John. Historian and Biographer .... 1643..1737
Stuart, Arabella. Cousin of James I. .... 1575?.1615
Stuart, Sir Charles. General........................ 1753..1801

BORN. DIED.

Stuart, Charles Edward. *Young Pretender* .... 1720..1788
Stuart, Daniel. Political Writer; Editor of *Morning Post* 1766..1846
Stuart, Lord Dudley Coutts, M. P. Friend of Poland ... 1803..1854
Stuart, Gilbert, LL. D. Scottish Historian .... 1742?.1786
Stuart, Gilbert Charles. American Portrait Painter..... 1756..1828
Stuart, Henry Benedict Maria Clement. Cardinal York.
    Henry IX................................. 1725..1807
Stuart, James. Antiquary and Architect. *Athenian.*
    (*Antiquities of Athens*)............................. 1713..1788
Stuart, James, of Dunearn. Politician................. 1776..1849
Stuart, James E. B. "Confederate" General .... 1832?.1864
Stuart, James Francis Edward. *Elder Pretender.* Son
    of James II................................... 1688..1765
Stuart, John, Fourth Earl and First Marquess of Bute... 1744..1814
Stuart, John. Professor at Aberdeen. Antiquary...... 1751..1827
Stuart, Moses. American Divine and Author.......... 1780..1852
Stuart-Wortley, Lady Emmeline. Tourist and Writer 1806..1855
Stubbe, Henry. Writer .... 1631..1676
Stubbe, or Stubbs, John. Polit. Writer, and Sufferer 1541?.aft.1582
Stubbs, George. Anatomist and Painter of Animals ... 1724..1806
Stuckius, John William. Divine, Philologist, and Antiq. 1542..1607
Studly, John. English Poet .... — ..1587
Stuerbout, Dirk. *Dirk van Haarlem.* Dutch Painter... 1410?.1470
Stukeley, Rev. William, M. D. Antiquary............ 1687..1765
Stunica, James Lopez. Spanish Divine and Philologist — ..1530
Sturge, Joseph. Philanthropist. Life by Henry Richard — ..1859
Sturgeon, William. Electrician...................... 1783..1850
Sturleson. Icelandic Historian. *See* Snorro .... 1178..1241
Sturm. Abbot of Fulda. Life by Anscarius .... — .. 779
Sturm, Christopher Christian. Ger. Divine. (*Reflections*) 1740..1786
Sturm, or Sturmius, James, of Strasburg. Reformer ... 1489..1553
Sturm, Jas. Chas. Francis. Mathem. (*Sturm's Theorem*) 1803..1855
Sturm, John. *German Cicero.* Printer and Scholar.... 1507..1589
Sturm, John Christopher. Mathematician............. 1635..1703
Sturm, Leonard Christopher. German Architect....... 1669..1719
Sturt, John. Engraver............................... 1658..1730
Sturtevant, Simon. Metallurgist. (*Metallica*)........ fl. 1624
Sturz, Helfrich Peter. German Writer................ 1736..1776
Stuven, Ernest. German Painter.................... 1657..1712
Stuyvesant, Peter. Last Dutch Director-General of New
    Netherlands .... 1602..1682
Style, William. Law Writer. (*Reports*).............. 1603..1679
Stylites, Simeon. Syrian Ascetic .... fl. 5th c.
Suard, John Baptist Anthony. French Writer......... 1734..1817
Suarez, Francis, of Granada. Jesuit. Theologian. Life
    by Deschamps, 1671............................... 1548..1617
Suavius, or Schwab, Lambert. Engraver............. 1506..1565
Subleyras, Peter. French Painter................... 1699..1794
Subtermans, or Sustermans, Justus, of Antwerp. Paint. 1597..1681
Suchet, Louis Gabriel. French Marshal.............. 1772..1826
Suckling, Sir John. Poet and Courtier. Life by the Rev.
    A. Suckling, 1836................................ 1609..1642?
Sucre, Anthony Joseph de. South American General .. 1793..1830
Sue, Eugene. French Novelist .... 1804..1857
Sue, John. French Medical Writer .... 1699..1762

BORN. DIED.

Sue, John Joseph, brother. Anatomical Writer .... 1710..1792
Suetonius Paulinus. Roman Commander in Britain.. fl. ti. Nero
Suetonius Tranquillus, Caius. Roman Historian .... 70?. —
Suett, Richard. Comic Actor .... — ..1805
Sueur, Eustace Le. French Painter................. 1617..1655
Sueur, John Francis le. French Musical Composer..... 1760..1837
Sueur, Nich. le. *Sudorius.* Fr. Lawyer; Transl. of Pindar 1545?.1594
Sueur, Thomas le. French Mathematician .... 1703..1770
Suffolk, Henrietta, Countess of. Court Beauty .... — ..1767
Suffolk, Michael de la Pole, First Earl of. Lord Chanc. — ..1389
Suffolk, Michael de la Pole, son, Second Earl of; died at
    Harfleur .... — ..1415
Suffolk, Michael de la Pole, son, Third Earl of; fell at
    Agincourt.. — ..1415
Suffolk, William de la Pole, brother, First Duke of. Lord
    Chancellor, and Lord High Admiral. Beheaded .... — ..1450
Suffren, John. French Jesuit. (*Année Chrétienne*)..... 1565..1641
Suffren St.-Tropez, Peter Andrew de. French Admiral 1726..1788
Suger. Abbot of St. Denys. Minister of Louis VII. of
    France. Life by A. F. Gervaise; M. Baudier....... 1087..1152
Suhm, Peter Frederick von. Danish Historian .... 1728..1798
Suicer, John Gaspar. Patristic Scholar. (*Thesaurus*).. 1620..1684
Suicer, John Henry, son. Scholar. L. by J. R. Wolff, 1745 1644..1705
Suidas. Greek Lexicographer...................... fl. 10th c.?
Suleiman. *See* Soliman.
Sulivan, Sir Richard Joseph, M. P. Writer and Tourist — ..1806
Sulla, Lucius Cornelius. Roman Dictator .... 138.78 B.C.
Sullivan, George. American Lawyer and Statesman... 1774..1838
Sullivan, James. Gov. of Massachusetts; Polit. Writer 1744..1808
Sullivan, John. American Revolutionary General. Life
    by O. W. B. Peabody .... 1740..1795
Sullivan, William, LL. D. American Writer........... 1774..1839
Sully, Maximilian de Béthune, Duke of. French Soldier
    and Statesman. (*Memoirs*)...................... 1559..1641
Sulpicia. Latin Poetess........................:...... fl. 100?
Sulpicius Rufus, Publius. Roman Orator............. 124.87 B.C.
Sulpicius Severus. Roman Ecclesiastical Writer .... 363?.aft.410
Sulzer, John George. Swiss Writer .... 1720..1779
Sumarokoff, Alexander Petrovitch. Russian Poet and
    Dramatist....................................... 1727..1790
Summerfield, John. American Clergyman. Life by J.
    Holland, 1829...................................... 1798..1825
Sumner, Edwin Vose. American General .... 1796..1863
Sumner, Increase. American Judge and Statesman.... 1746..1799
Sumner, John Bird. Archbishop of Canterbury (1848–62) 1780..1862
Sumter, Thomas. American Revolutionary General.... 1734?.1832
Sunderland, Charles Spencer, Third Earl of. Statesman 1674..1722
Sunderland, Henry Spencer, First E. of; fell at Newbury 1620..1643
Sunderland, Robert Spencer, Second Earl of. Statesman 1641?.1702
Sundon, Charlotte, Viscountess. L. by Mrs. Thomson, 1847 — ..1742
Surenhusius, William. Orient.; Editor of the Mishna fl. 1698–1715
Surowiecki, Wawrzyniec. Polish Author .... 1796..1827
Surrey, Henry Howard, Earl of. Poet. L. by Dr. Nott 1515?.1547
Surtees, Robert. Antiquary and Poet. (*History of Dur-*
    ham.) Life by G. Taylor, in *Hist. of Durham*, 1839.. 1779..1834

BORN. DIED.

Suso, Henry. *Amandus.* German Mystic . . . . 1300?.1365
Sussex, Prince Augustus Frederick, Duke of . . . . 1773..1843
Süssmilch, John Peter. German Divine and Political
    Economist . . . . 1708..1767
Sustermans, or Sutermans, Justus. Flemish Painter. . . 1597..1681
Sutcliffe, Dr. Matthew. Controversialist Divine . . . . . . — ..1629
Sutton, Amos, D. D. Missionary . . . . 1798..1854
Sutton, Charles Manners. Abp. of Canterbury (1805–28) 1755..1828
Sutton, Christopher, D. D. (*Learn to Die*) . . . . fl. 1600
Sutton, Richard. Co-founder of Brazenose College . . . . . — ..1524
Sutton, Thomas. Merchant. Founder of Charter House 1532..1611
Suwarroff, Alexander Vasilievitch, Count. Russian Field
    Marshal and Generalissimo. Life by self; Anthing. . 1729..1800
Swammerdam, John. Naturalist and Anatomist . . . . . . 1637..1681
Swan, Rev. Charles. Author of Travels and Poems.
    (*Gesta Romanorum*) . . . . — ..1838
Swanevelt, or Swanefeld, Herman van. Painter . . . . . . 1620..1680
Swartz, Olof. Swedish Botanist . . . . 1760..1817
Swedberg, Jesper. Swedish Theologian . . . . 1653..1735
Swedenborg, Emanuel, son. Life by J. G. G. Wilkin-
    son, 1849; Hobart, 1831 and 1862. . . . . 1689..1772
Swett, John Appleton, M. D. American Physician . . . . . 1808..1854
Swieten, Gerard van. Dutch Phys. and Medical Writer 1700..1772
Swift, Deane. Biographer of Dean Swift . . . . — ..1783
Swift, Jonathan. Dean of St. Patrick's; Writer. Life by
    Hawkesworth; Sheridan; Johnson; Sir W. Scott; D.
    Swift, 1753 . . . . 1667..1745
Swift, Theophilus. Political Writer. . . . . — ..1815
Swift, Zephaniah. American Judge . . . . 1759..1823
Swinburne, Henry. Jurist. . . . . — 1620 or 4
Swinburne, Henry. Traveler . . . . 1752..1803
Swinden, John Henry van. Mathem. and Astronomer 1746..1823
Swinden, Tobias. English Divine. (*Nature of Hell*) . . . — ..1720
Swinnock, George. Ejected Nonconformist Divine . . . . — ..1673
Swinton, Rev. John. Antiquary . . . . 1703..1777
Swithun, St. Bishop of Winchester. Life by Wolstan — .. 862
Sybrecht, John. Landscape Painter. . . . . 1625..1703
Sydenham, Charles Edward Powlett Thompson, Lord.
    Governor-General of Canada. Life by Scrope, 1843 1799..1841
Sydenham, Floyer. Scholar; Translator of Plato . . . . . 1710..1787
Sydenham, Thos., M. D. Physician. L. by Dr. Johnson 1624..1689
Sykes, Authur Ashley, D. D. Divine. Life by Disney. . 1684?.1756
Sylburgius, Frederick. German Philologist. . . . . 1536..1596
Sylla, or Sulla, Lucius Cornelius. Roman Statesman and
    Soldier; Dictator. . . . . 138.78 B.C.
Sylverius, or Silverius. Bishop of Rome (536–38) . . . . . — .. 538
Sylvester. Pope. *See* Silvester.
Sylvester, Joshua. *Silver-tongued.* Poet . . . . 1563..1618
Sylvester, Matthew. Nonconf. Divine. Editor of Baxter — ..1708
Sylvius, Æneas. Pope Pius II. . . . . 1405..1464
Sylvius, Francis. *Du Bois.* French Classical Scholar. . — ..1530
Sylvius, Francis. *Dubois de le Boë.* Dutch Chemist and
    Physician . . . . 1614..1672
Sylvius, James. *Du Bois.* French Physician . . . . 1478..1555
Sylvius, Lambert. *Van den Bosch.* Dutch Writer . . . . . . 1610?.1688

BORN. DIED.

Symes, Michael. Colonel. Envoy. (*Embassy to Ava*).. — ..1809
Symmachus. Bishop of Rome (498–514)............ — .. 514
Symmachus, Quintus Aurelius. Roman Statesman and
    Author .... fl. 4th c.
Symmachus the Samaritan .... fl. ab. 200
Symmes, John Cleves. American Soldier and Projector 1780?.1829
Symmons, Caroline. Poet.......................... 1788..1812
Symmons, Rev. Charles, D. D. Poet and Writer....... 1749..1826
Symonds, Sir William. Admiral. L. by J. A. Sharp, 1857 1782..1856
Syncellus, George. Greek Historian. (*Chronography*) — .. 800?
Synesius, of Cyrene. Bp. of Ptolemais. Philos. and Poet 379?. 431?
Synge, Edward. Archbishop of Tuam .... 1659..1741
Syphax. Numidian Prince .... 249?.201 B.C.
Szalkai, Anthony von. Hungarian Poet .... — ..1804
Széchényi, Stephen, Count von. Hungarian Statesman 1791..1860
Szegedi, John Baptist. Jesuit. Writer on Hungary ... 1699..1760
Sze-ma-Kwang. Chinese Historian and Poet .... 1018?.1086
Sze-ma-tseen. Chinese Historian .... 145?.80? B.C.

T.

BORN. DIED.

Tabari, Abu Jaafar Mahomet. Arabian Historian...... 839.. 922
Tabernæmontanus, James Theodore. German Physician and Botanist................................ 1520?.1590
Tabor, John Otho. German Jurist .... 1604..1674
Tabourot, Stephen. French Writer .... 1547..1590
Tacca, Peter James. Italian Sculptor.............. — ..1640
Tachard, Guy. Jesuit Missionary to Siam .... — ..1694
Tacitus, Caius Cornelius. Historian. Life by Murphy.. 50?.aft.117?
Tacitus, Marcus Claudius. Roman Emperor (275–76) .. 200?. 276
Taconnet, Toussaint Gaspar. French Actor and Poet.. 1730..1774
Tacquet, Andrew. Dutch Jesuit; Mathematician...... 1611..1660
Taffi, Andrew. Italian Painter ..... 1213..1294
Tagliacozzi, or Taliacotius, Gaspar. Italian Surgeon... 1489..1553
Talbert, Francis Xavier. French *Eloge* Writer......... 1728..1803
Talbot, Miss Catherine. Writer. Life by Pennington.. 1720..1770
Talbot, Charles, Duke of Shrewsbury. Statesman ..... 1660..1717
Talbot, Charles, Lord. Lord Chancellor.............. 1684..1737
Talbot, John, 1st Earl of Shrewsbury. Warrior in France 1373..1453
Talbot, Peter. Roman Catholic Archbishop of Dublin.
   (*De Naturâ Fidei*)................................ 1620..1680
Talbot, Richard, Duke of Tyrconnel, brother. Lord Lieutenant of Ireland.................................. — ..1691
Talbot, Robert. Antiquary and Divine .... — ..1558
Talbot, Silas. American Military and Naval Officer.
   Life by H. T. Tuckerman, 1850.................... 1750?.1813
Talbot, William. Bishop of Durham .... 1659..1730
Talfourd, Francis. Comic Dramatist .... 1827?.1862
Talfourd, Sir Thomas Noon. Judge. Writer......... 1795..1854
Taliacotius. *See* Tagliacozzi........................ 1489..1553
Taliesin. Welsh Bard .... fl. 520–70
Tallart, or Tallard, Camille de la Baume, Count of. Marshal of France.................................. 1652..1728
Talleyrand, Henry de, Ct. de Chalais. Fav. of Louis XIII. 1599..1626
Talleyrand-Périgord, Alex. Angelique de. Card.-Abp. 1736..1821
Talleyrand-Périgord, Charles Maurice, Prince of. Fr.
   Diplomatist. (*Memoirs*).......................... 1754..1838
Talleyrand-Périgord, Elias de. Fr. Cardinal; Negotiator 1301..1364
Tallien, John Lambert. French Revolutionist........ 1769..1820
Tallis, Thomas. Musician...................... 1529..1585
Tallmadge, Benjamin. American Revolutionary Officer 1754..1835
Tallmadge, James, LL. D. Statesman .... 1778..1853
Talma, Francis Joseph. Fr. Tragedian. Life by Moreau 1763..1826
Talmont de la Trimoille, Prince de. Vendean Royalist — ..1793
Tambroni, Clotilda. Greek Professor at Bologna ...... 1758..1817
Tambroni, Joseph, brother. Italian Poet and Historian 1773..1824
Tamburini, Peter, of Brescia. Theologian. (*Idea della
   Santa Sede*)..................................... 1737..1827
Tamerlane, or Timour. Tartar Conqueror. Life by Arabschah; James Golius; Samuel Clarke, 1676; Pétis de
   la Croix, 1723.................................. 1336?.1405
Tancred. King of Sicily (1189–94).................... — ..1194

BORN. DIED.

Tandy, James Napper. Irish Rebel Politician .... 1757..1803
Taney, Roger Brooke. Chief Justice of the United States 1777..1864
Tannahill, Robert. Scottish Poet .... 1774..1810
Tanner, Thos. Bp. St. Asaph. Antiq. (*Notilia Monast.*) 1674..1735
Tannevot, Alexander. French Dramatist and Writer .. 1692..1773
Tansillo, Louis. Italian Poet........................ 1510?.1568
Tanucci, Bernard, Marquis de. Neapolitan Statesman
   and Patron of Letters .... 1698..1783
Tappan, Rev. David, D. D. Amer. Clergyman and Writer 1753..1803
Tardieu, Nicholas Henry. French Engraver .... 1674..1749
Targe, John Baptist. Italian Historian............... 1720?.1788
Targioni-Tozetti, John. Italian Physician .... 1712..1783
Tarin, Peter. French Medical Writer.................. — ..1761
Tarleton, Bannastre. English Officer in America...... 1754..1833
Tarleton, Richard. Jester............................ — ..1588
Tarquinius Superbus. Last King of Rome........ —aft.496 B.C.
Tarrakanoff, Anna Petrowna. Russian Princess....... 1755..1777
Tartaglia, Nicholas. Italian Mathematician.......... 1490?.1557
Tartini, Joseph. Italian Musical Composer........... 1692..1770
Taruffi, Emilius. Italian Landscape Painter.......... 1632..1694
Taruffi, Joseph Anthony. Italian Poet................ 1722..1786
Tarver, John Charles. French Philologist............. 1790..1851
Tasker, Rev. William. Translator of Horace and Pindar — ..1800
Tasman, Abel Janssen. Dutch Navigator.......... 1600?.aft.1644
Tassie, James. Scottish Modeler and Numismatist..... 1735..1799
Tassin, René Prosper, of St. Maur. Historian .... 1677..1777
Tasso, Bernardo. Italian Poet. (*Amadis*) .... 1493..1569
Tasso, Torquato, son. Poet. (*Jerusalem Delivered.*) Life
   by Battista Manso, 1634, abridged by Abbé de Charles,
   1690; Hoole, 1762; A. Fabroni, 1800; John Black, 1810;
   P. A. Serassi; J. B. A. Suard; Rev. R. Milman, 1850 1544..1595
Tassoni, Alexander. Italian Critic and Poet. (*La Sec-*
   chia Rapita.) Life by Gironi; Muratori............. 1565..1635
Tate, Francis. Lawyer and Antiquary .... 1560..1616
Tate, Nahum. Poet. Versifier of the Psalms .... 1652..1715
Tatian. Christian Apologist. (Λόγος πρὸς ῾Ελληνας).... fl. 172
Tatischef, Vassili. Russian Historian .... 1686..1750
Tatius, Achilles. Alexandrian Rhetorician and Bishop.. fl. 500?
Tatwine. Archbishop of Canterbury (731-34)......... — .. 734
Taube, Frederick William von, LL. D. Ger. Hist. Writer 1728..1778
Taubmann, Frederick. German Writer and Poet ..... 1565..1613
Tauler, John, of Strasbourg. Mystic Divine.......... 1290?.1361
Taurellius, or Torelli, Lælius. Italian Jurist; Editor of
   Pandects .... 1489..1576
Tausen, or Tagesen, John. Danish Protestant Reformer 1494..1561
Tavannes, Gaspar de Saulx, Lord of. Marshal of France.
   Life by his son John............................... 1509..1573
Tavannes, John de Saulx, Vsct. de, son. Marshal of Fr. 1555..1630?
Tavannes, William de Saulx, Ld. of, br. (*Hist. Memoirs*) 1553..1633
Tavarone, Lazarus. Genoese Painter................. 1556..1641
Taverner, John. Organist and Musical Composer ..... fl. 1533?
Taverner, Richard. Religious Writer................. 1505..1575
Tavernier, John Baptist, Baron d'Aubonne. French
   Traveler and Merchant.............................. 1605..1689
Taylor, Ann (Mrs. Gilbert). Writ. (*Maternal Solicitude*) — ..1830

BORN. DIED.

Taylor, Brook, LL. D. Mathematician .... 1685..1731
Taylor, Charles. Biblical Writer; Editor of Calmet.... — ..1821
Taylor, Chevalier John. Oculist .... —aft.1767
Taylor, George. American Patriot .... 1716..1781
Taylor, George W. American General............... 1808..1862
Taylor, Rev. Henry. Divine........................ 1711..1785
Taylor, Sir Herbert. General .... 1775..1839
Taylor, Isaac. Indep. Minister of Ongar; Writ. for Young 1759..1829
Taylor, Isaac. Author. (*Natural History of Enthusiasm*) 1787..1865
Taylor, James. Mechanician........................ 1757..1825
Taylor, Jane. (*Hymns for Infant Minds*) .... 1783..1824
Taylor, Jeremy. Bishop. Life by Bishop Heber; Rev.
    Kaye Bonney, 1815; Rev. R. A. Willmott, 1846..... 1613..1667
Taylor, John. *Water Poet* .... 1580?.1654
Taylor, John, D. D. Unitarian, of Norwich........... 1674..1761
Taylor, John, LL. D. Critic and Philosopher........... 1703..1766
Taylor, John. Poetical and Miscellaneous Writer...... — ..1832
Taylor, John. Mining Engineer and Mineralogist...... — ..1863
Taylor, John. Currency Reformer. (*Junius Identified*) 1781..1864
Taylor, Nathaniel William, D. D. American Theologian 1786..1858
Taylor, Richard. Printer and Naturalist.............. 1781..1858
Taylor, Richard Cowling. Geologist.................. 1789..1851
Taylor, Sir Robert. Sculptor and Architect. Founder
    of Taylor Institute ....: 1714..1788
Taylor, Rowland, LL. D. Marian Martyr.............. — ..1555
Taylor, Silas. *Domville* or *D' Omville*. Antiquary...... 1624..1678
Taylor, Stephen William, LL. D. American Educator... 1791..1856
Taylor, Thomas. Puritan Divine..................... 1576..1632
Taylor, Thomas. *Platonist*. Scholar and Translator... 1758..1835
Taylor, William, of Norwich. Critic and Translator from
    the German. Life by J. W. Robberds, 1843......... 1765..1836
Taylor, William Cooke, LL. D. Miscellaneous Writer... 1800..1849
Taylor, Gen. Zachary. 12th President of U. S. (1849–50) 1784..1850
Tching Tching Kong. *Koxinga*. Chinese Admiral... — ..1670
Tebaldeo, or Tibaldeo, Anthony. Italian Poet......... 1456..1538
Tecumseh. Indian Chief............................ 1770?.1813
Tedeschi, or Tudeschi, Nich. *Panormitanus*. Cardinal 1386..1445
Tegel, Eric. Swedish Historian .... — ..1638
Tegnér, Esaias. Swedish Poet and Divine .... 1782..1846
Teignmouth, John Shore, Lord. Gov.-Gen. L. by son 1751..1834
Teissier, Anthony. French Writer in Prussia. (*Éloges*) 1632..1715
Tekeli, Emeric. Hungarian Patriot.................. 1658..1705
Teleclides. Athenian Comic Poet.................... fl. B.C. 444?
Teleky, or Teleki, László, Count. Hungarian Patriot... 1811..1861
Telemann, George Philip. German Musical Composer.. 1681..1767
Telesio, Bernardin. Ital. Philos. (*De Natura Rerum*) 1508 or 9.1588
Telesphorus. Bishop of Rome, elected April 5, 127?... — .. 138
Telford, Thomas. Civil Engineer. Life by self, 1838... 1757..1834
Tell, William. Swiss Patriot........................ — ..1354?
Teller, William Abraham. German Protestant Theologian 1734..1804
Tellez, Balthasar. Portuguese Historian.............. 1595..1675
Tellez, Gabriel. *Tirso de Molina*. Spanish Dramatist.. 1585?.1648
Tellier, Michael. French Jesuit Theologian........... 1643..1719
Tellier, Michael le. French Lawyer and Statesman .... 1603..1685
Tellier, Michael Francis le, Mqs. of Louvois, son. Minister 1641..1691

BORN. DIED.

Temanza, Thomas. Italian Architect .... 1705..1789
Tempelhof, Geo. Fred. Ger. Officer and Military Writer 1737..1807
Tempesta, Anthony. Painter .... 1555..1630
Tempesta, or Molyn, Peter. *Pietro Mulier*. Storm Paint. 1637..1701
Temple, Sir John. (*History of the Irish Rebellion*) ..... — ..1677
Temple, Richard Grenville, Earl. Statesman.......... 1711..1777
Temple, Sir William. Statesman and Writer. Life by
    J. P. Courtenay, 1836 .... 1628..1699
Templeman, Peter, M. D. Physician and Writer; Trans-
    lator of *Norden's Travels*........................ 1711..1769
Tencin, Claudine Alexandrine Guérin de. Romancist.. 1681..1749
Tencin, Peter Guérin de, br. Cardinal; Prime Minister 1680..1758
Teniers, David. *Elder*. Flemish Painter .... 1582..1649
Teniers, David, son. *Younger*. Painter.............. 1610..1694?
Tenison, Thomas. Archbishop of Canterbury .... 1636..1715
Tennant, Smithson. Professor of Chemistry at Cambridge 1761..1815
Tennant, Prof. William. Poet and Philol. (*Anster Fair*) 1785..1848
Tennemann, Wm. Theoph. (*Geschichte der Philosophie*) 1761..1819
Tennent, Gilbert. American Clergyman and Writer... 1703..1764
Tennent, Rev. William, brother. Famous for Trance.
    Life by E. Boudinot ....:...... 1705..1777
Tenon, James René. French Medical Writer.......... 1724..1816
Tenterden, Charles Abbott, Lord. Lord Chief Justice.. 1762..1832
Tentori, Christopher. (*History of the Republic of Venice*) 1745..1810
Tentzel, William Ernest. Ger. Antiquary and Historian 1659..1707
Teploff, Gregory Nicolaievitch. Russian Writer .... — ..1779
Teramo, James de. *Palladino*. Archbishop of Tarentum.
    (*Trial of Belial*) .... 1349..1417
Terburg, Gerard. Dutch Painter..................... 1608..1681
Terceira, Duke of. Portuguese General and Statesman 1792..1860
Terence. Latin Comedian...................... 194?.159? B.C.
Terentianus, Maurus. Latin Poet and Grammarian... fl. 100?
Ternaux, William Louis, Baron. French Manufacturer 1763..1833
Terpander. Father of Greek Music................. fl. 7th c. B.C.
Terrasson, Anthony. Fr. Lawyer. (*Roman Jurisprudence*) 1705..1782
Terrasson, John. French Philosopher and Critic ...... 1670..1750
Terrasson, Matthew. French Lawyer .... 1669..1734
Terray, Joseph Mary. French Statesman............. 1715..1778
Terry, Daniel. Comedian .... 1780?.1828
Terry, Rev. Edward. Traveler to Mogul Court. (*Voyage
    to East Indies*)................................... 1590?.1660
Tersteegen, Gerhard. German Hymn Writer......... 1697..1769
Tertre, Francis Joachim Duport du. French Hist. Writer 1715..1759
Tertre, John Baptist du. Missionary to America. (*His-
    tory of Antilles*).............................. 1610..1687
Tertre, Rodolph. Fr. Jesuit; Divine and Metaphysician 1667?.1762
Tertullian, Quintus Septimius Florens. Latin Father.
    Life by Jerome; Neander, 1825; Hesselberg, 1848... 160?. 240?
Terwesten, Augustin. Dutch Painter ....:... 1649..1711
Terwesten, Elias, brother. Fruit and Flower Painter .. 1651..1724
Terwesten, Matthew, brother. Historical Painter...... 1670..1735
Tesi, Mauro Antonio. *Il Maurino*. Italian Painter .... 1730..1766
Tessier, Alexander Henry. French Agricultural Writer 1742..1837
Tessin, Charles Gustavus, Count. Swedish Statesman.. 1695..1770
Tessin, Nicodemus, Count. Swedish Architect .... 1654..1728

BORN. DIED.

Testa, Peter. *Il Lucchesino*. Painter and Engraver.... 1611..1650
Testelin, Henry. French Painter...................... 1616..1695
Testelin, or Tettelin, Louis, brother. Historical Painter 1615..1655
Testi, Fulvius, Count. Italian Poet................... 1593..1646
Tetzel, or Tezel, John. Vendor of Indulgences. Life by
    Hoffmann, 1844; Gröne, 1858................... 1450?.1519
Texeira, or Texera, Joseph. Portuguese Genealogist... 1543..1604
Texeira, or Texera, Peter. Portuguese Persian Scholar 1570.aft.1610
Textor, Ravisius. *John Tixier*. French Writer........ 1480?.1524
Thaarup, Thomas. Danish Poet and Dramatist........ 1749..1821
Thabet ben Korrah. Physician and Philos. at Bagdad 835 or 6.901
Thabet ben Senan, grandson. Phys. & Philos. at Bagdad — 973 or 4
Thacher, James, M. D. American Physician and Author 1754..1844
Thacher, Peter, D. D. American Clergyman .... 1752..1802
Thacher, Samuel Cooper, son. Clergyman. Life by F.
    W. P. Greenwood.................................. 1785..1815
Thackeray, William Makepeace. L. by Theoph. Taylor 1811..1863
Thaer, Albert. German Agricultural Writer.......... 1752..1828
Thais. Athenian Courtesan...................... ti. Alex. Great
Thales, of Miletus. Philosopher............ 636?.546? B.C.
Thatcher, Benjamin Bussey. American Author....... 1809..1848
Theden, John Christian Anthony. Ger. Surgical Writer 1714..1797
Theiner, John Anthony. German Theologian .... 1799..1860
Thellusson, Peter Isaac. London Merchant .... — ..1797
Thelwall, Rev. Algernon Sydney. Divine .... 1795..1863
Thelwall, John. Writer and Elocutionist............. 1764..1834
Themistius. Greek Orator........................... — .. 386
Themistocles. Athenian General and Statesman.... 514?.449 B.C.
Thénard, Louis James, Baron. French Chemist....... 1777..1857
Theobald. Archbishop of Canterbury (1139–61).....·.. — ..1161
Theobald. *See* Thibaud .... 1201..1253
Theobald, Lewis. Commentator on Shakespeare ...... — ..1744
Theocritus. Greek Pastoral Poet.............. fl. 283?–263? B.C.
Theodatus. King of the Italian Goths (534–36) ...... — .. 536
Theoderic. *The Great*. King of Ostrogoths (475–526) 455.. 526
Theodora. Eastern Empress; wife of Justinian I....... — .. 548
Theodore. Bishop of Heraclea. Arian Leader........ — .. 358?
Theodore. Bishop of Mopsuætia (394–429)............ — .. 429
Theodore I. Pope (642–49)......................... — .. 649
Theodore II. Elected February 12, 898 .... — .. 898
Theodore, of Tarsus. Archbishop of Canterbury (668–90) — .. 690
Theodore-Anthony I. King of Corsica.............. 1696?.1756
Theodore Lascaris. Greek Emperor (1206–22) .... 1177..1222
Theodore Studita. Abbot of Studium. Writer .... 759.. 826
Theodoret. Bishop of Cyrus. Ecclesiastical Historian. 393?. 457?
Theodoric I. K. of Visigoths (418–51); defeated by Attila — .. 451
Theodoric. *The Great*, or Theoderic, *which see*........ 455.. 526
Theodoric. Italian Bishop and Surgeon............. — ..1298
Theodoric, or Thierry, of Niem. (*Hist. of Schism of Popes*) — ..1417
Theodosius. Roman General; beheaded.............. — .. 376
Theodosius I. *The Great*. Emperor (378–95) .... 346?. 395
Theodosius II. (402–50)........................... 401.. 450
Theodosius III. *Adramytenus*. (715–16)............. —aft. 716
Theognis, of Megara. Elegiac Poet .... 570?.490? B.C.
Theon, Ælius, of Alexandria. Rhetorician and Gram..... fl. 315?

BORN. DIED.

Theophanes, George. Greek Monk and Chronicler .... 751?. 818
Theophanes, Procopovitch. Russian Historian & Writer 1681..1736
Theophilus. Patriarch of Alexandria (385–412)....... — .. 412
Theophilus. Jurist of Constantinople .... — .. 536
Theophilus. Emperor of the East (829–42) .... — .. 842
Theophrastus. Greek Philosopher and Author...... 370?.285 B.C.
Theophylact. Byzantine Historian .... — .. 630?
Theophylact. Archbishop of Bulgaria; Commentator.. — ..1112?
Theopompus. Greek Historian .... 380?.304? B.C.
Theotocopuli, Dominic. *El Greco.* Sculptor, Painter,
  and Architect................................... — ..1625
Theotocopuli, Geo. Manuel, son. Sculptor and Architect — ..1631
Theramenes. Athenian Commander .... —B.C.404
Theresa of Jesus, St. Spanish Carmelite Nun and Mys-
  tic Writer .... 1515..1582
Théroigne de Méricourt, Anne Joseph, or Lambertine.
  French Female Revolutionist .... 1759..1817
Theron. Tyrant of Agrigentum (B. C. 488–472)........ —B.C.472
Thévenot, John de. French Traveler................ 1633..1667
Thévenot, Nicholas Melchizedec, uncle. Traveler. (*Voy-
  ages and Travels*)................................. 1621..1692
Thevet, Andrew. Traveler and Writer .... 1502..1590
Thew, Robert. Engraver............................ 1758..1802
Thibaud, or Theobald, IV., or VI. Count of Champagne.
  King of Navarre. Trouvère...................... 1201..1253
Thibaut, Anthony Frederick Justus. German Jurist ... 1774..1840
Thicknesse, Anne. Biographer...................... 1737..1824
Thicknesse, Philip. Traveler .... 1719..1792
Thielen, John Philip van. Flemish Painter .... 1618?..1667
Thierry I., son of Clovis I. King of Austrasia........ 483?. 534
Thierry II., son of Childebert.· King of Burgundy and
  Austrasia.. 587.. 613
Thierry I., or III. King of France, son of Clovis II.... 652?. 691
Thierry II., or IV. King of France, son of Dagobert III. 712?. 737
Thierry, of Niem. Papal Secretary. (*Schism of the Popes*) — ..1417
Thierry, Henry. Printer at Paris .... — .. 712
Thierry, James Nicholas Augustine. French Historian.
  (*Norman Conquest*)............................./................. 1795..1856
Thierry, Madame Julia, wife. Writer................ — ..1844
Thiers, John Baptist. French Divine and Satirist...... 1636..1703
Thiersch, Frederick William. German Scholar........ 1784..1860
Thilo, John Charles. German Theologian............. 1794..1853
Thion de la Chaume, Claude Esprit. French Physician 1750..1786
Thirlby, Styan, LL. D. Critic .... 1692?.1753
Thistlewood, Arthur. Cato Street Conspirator........ 1772..1820
Thom, James. Scottish Sculptor .... 1799..1850
Thom, Walter. Historical and Miscellaneous Writer.
  (*History of Aberdeen*) .... 1770..1824
Thom, William. Scottish Weaver and Poet .... 1799..1850
Thomas, St. *Didymus.* Apostle .... fl. 1st c.
Thomas, Anthony Leonard. French Writer........... 1732..1785
Thomas, Catimpratensis. French Biog. and Moral Writer 1201..1270?
Thomas, Christian. German Philosopher .... 1655..1728
Thomas, David. Welsh Poet........................ 1760?.1822
Thomas, Elizabeth. *Corinna.* Poetess .... 1675..1730

BORN. DIED.

Thomas, Isaiah, LL. D.   American Printer . . . . 1749. .1831
Thomas, James Ernest.   German Landscape Painter. . . . 1588?.1653
Thomas, John.   Bishop of Salisbury. . . . . 1695. .1766
Thomas, John.   Bishop of Rochester. . . . . 1712. .1793
Thomas, John.   Sculptor . . . . 1813?.1862
Thomas, Robert, M. D.   Medical Writer . . . . 1743. .1835
Thomas, William.   (*History of Italy.*) Executed. . . . . . — . .1553
Thomas, William.   Bishop of Worcester. (*Roman Ora-*
    cles Silenced). . . . . 1613. .1689
Thomas, Rev. William.   Historian. (*Worcester Cathedral*) 1670. .1738
Thomas of Erceldoune.   *The Rhymer.* Scottish Poet fl. 1280?
Thomasin.   German Poet. *Zercläre.* (*The Italian Guest*) 1186?. —
Thomasius, Christian.   German Philosopher and Critic.
    Life by Luden, 1805 . . . . 1655. .1728
Thomasius, James.   German Philologist. . . . . 1622. .1684
Thomason, Thomas.   Missionary. Life by Sargent. . . . 1774. .1829
Thomassin, Louis.   French Theologian. . . . . 1619. .1695
Thomond, Thomas.   French Architect in Russia. . . . . . . 1759. .1813
Thompson, Sir Benjamin.   *Count Rumford.* Philosopher.
    Life by Pictet. . . . . 1752. .1814
Thompson, Edward.   Poet . . . . 1738?.1786
Thompson, William.   Dean of Raphoe. Poet . . . . — . .1766?
Thompson, William.   Naturalist. (*Natural History of*
    Ireland.) Life by Professor Dickie, 1856 . . . . 1805. .1852
Thompson, Zadoc.   American Naturalist. . . . . 1796. .1856
Thomson, Alexander.   Poet and Miscellaneous Writer 1762. .1803
Thomson, Dr. Andrew.   Scot. Div. (*Christian Instructor*) 1779. .1831
Thomson, Anthony Todd, M. D.   Medical and General
    Writer. (*Conspectus*) . . . . 1778. .1849
Thomson, Charles.   American Patriot. . . . . 1729. .1824
Thomson, James.   Poet. (*Seasons.*) Life by Murdock,
    1773; David E. Buchan, 1792; Sir H. Nicolas, 1847. 1700. .1748
Thomson, Rev. John.   Scottish Landscape Painter. . . . . 1778. .1840
Thomson, John Cockburn.   *Philip Wharton.* Writer. . — . .1860
Thomson, Mrs. Katherine, wife of Dr. Anthony T. *Grace*
    Wharton. Biographer and Novelist. . . . . — . .1862
Thomson, Richard.   (*Chronicles of London Bridge*) . . . . 1794?.1865
Thomson, Dr. Robt. Dundas.   Medical & Physical Writer 1805?.1864
Thomson, Thomas.   Professor of Chemistry at Glasgow 1773. .1852
Thomson, Dr. Wm.   Writer and Compiler. (*War in Asia*) 1746. .1818
Thordo.   *Diaconus,* or *Legifer.* Danish Jurist. . . . . fl. 1350
Thordsen, Sturla.   Icelandic Lawyer, Historian, Poet. . . 1218. .1288
Thoreau, Henry David.   American Author. . . . . 1817. .1862
Thoresby, Ralph.   Antiquarian Collector . . . . 1658. .1725
Thorild, Thomas.   Swedish Poet . . . . 1759. .1819
Thorius, Raphael.   French Physician of James I. . . . . . — . .1625
Thorkelin, Grim Jonsson.   Icelandic Scholar. . . . . 1752. .1829
Thorlaksen, Gudbrand.   Icelandic Prelate and Writer . 1542. .1629
Thorlaksson, John.   Icelandic Poet; Transl. of Milton. . 1744. .1819
Thorndike, Rev. Herbert.   Divine. (*Epilogus*). . . . . — . .1672
Thornhill, Sir James.   Painter. 1676. .1734
Thornton, Bonnel.   Humorous Poet. . . . . 1724. .1768
Thornton, Henry, M. P.   (*Paper Credit ; Family Prayers*) — . .1815
Thornton, John, of Clapham.   Merchant and Benefactor 1720. .1790
Thornton, Robert John.   Botanist. (*Temple of Flora*). 1758?.1837

BORN. DIED.

Thornton, Samuel, M. P., of Clapham Park and Bank of
England .... 1775..1838
Thornton, Rev. Spencer. L. by W. R. Freemantle, 1850 1813..1850
Thornton, Thomas, Lieut.-Col. Writer on Field Sports — ..1823
Thorpe, John, M. D. Antiquary, of Rochester......... 1682.'.1750
Thorpe, John, son. Antiq. of Roch. (*Registrum Roffensi*) 1714..1792
Thorwaldsen, Albert Bertel. Danish Sculptor .... 1770..1844
Thou, James Augustus de. *Thuanus*. President. His-
torian. Life by J. Collinson, 1807................. 1553..1617
Thouars, Louis Mary Albert du Petit. French Botanist 1758..1831
Thouret, Michael Augustin. French Medical Writer... 1748..1810
Thoynard, Nicholas. French Medalist and Biblical Critic 1629..1706
Thrasea Pætus. Roman Senator, condemned by Nero. 14?. 66
Thrasybulus. Athenian General; Friend of Alcibiades.. —B.C. 389
Throcmorton, Sir Nicholas. Statesman .... 1513?.1571
Throsby, John. Topographer of Leicester .... 1740..1803
Thuanus. *See* Thou .... 1553..1617
Thucydides. Greek Historian .... 471? 400? B.C.
Thuillier, Vincent. Benedictine of St. Maur.......... 1685..1736
Thulden, Theodore van. Dutch Painter............. 1607..1676
Thümmel, or Thuemmel, Moritz Augustus von. Ger-
man Writer. Life by Gruner, 1819 .... 1738..1817
Thunberg, Charles Peter. Swedish Physician and Trav. 1743..1828
Thurloe, John. Secretary. Life by Birch .... 1616..1668
Thurlow, Edward, Lord. Lord Chancellor............ 1732..1806
Thurmer, Joseph. German Architect................. 1789..1833
Thurneysser, Leonard. Alchemist and Astrologer .... 1531..1596
Thurot, Francis. Fr. Naval Officer. Invader of Ireland 1727..1760
Thwaites, Edward. Saxonist........................ 1667..1711
Thynne, Francis. Herald and Antiquary .... 1545..1608
Thysius, or Thys, Anthony. Dutch Philologist and Clas-
sical Editor....................................... 1603?.1665
Tiarini, Alexander. Italian Historical Painter........ 1577..1668
Tiarks, John Louis. German Astronomer............. 1789..1837
Tibaldi, Dominic. Italian Architect .... 1541..1582
Tibaldi, Peregrine, brother. Painter and Architect..... 1527..1598?
Tiberius. Roman Emperor (14–37)............... B.C.42.A.D.37
Tiberius. *Constantine*. Emperor of East (578–82)..... — .. 582
Tiberius. *Absimarius*. Emp. of East (698–704); Usurper — .. 705
Tibullus, Albius. Roman Poet...................... 54?.18? B.C.
Tickell, Richard. Poet and Polit. Writer. (*Anticipations*) — ..1793
Tickell, Thomas. Poet and Essayist.................. 1686..1740
Ticozzi, Stephen. Italian Historian .... 1762..1836
Tideman, or Tiédeman, Philip. Dutch Painter........ 1657..1705
Tieck, Christian Frederick. German Sculptor .... 1776..1851
Tieck, Louis, brother. Writer .... 1773..1853
Tiedemann, Dietrich. German Philosophical Writer... 1748..1803
Tiedge, Christopher Augustus. German Elegiac Poet.. 1752..1841
Tiepolo, John Baptist. Venetian Painter .... 1692..1769
Tierney, George, M. P. Statesman and Political Writer. 1761..1830
Tierney, Rev. Mark A., F. S. A. (*History of Arundel*)... 1785..1862
Tighe, Mrs. Mary (Blackford). Poetess. (*Psyche*) ..... 1774..1810
Tigny, Marin Grostête de. French Entomologist....... 1736..1799
Tigranes I. King of Armenia (B. C. 96?–55?); Ally of
Mithridates .... —B.C. 55?

BORN. DIED.

Tilbury, Gervase of. Chronicler...................... fl. 1210
Tilenius, Daniel. French Theologian .... 1563..1633
Tilghman, William. American Jurist................. 1756..1827
Tilingius, Matthias. German Medical Writer .... — ..1615
Tilletmans, Peter. Dutch Painter .... 1684?.1734
Tillemont, Louis Sebastian le Nain de. French Histo-
    rian and Critic. Life by Trouchay, 1711 .... 1637..1698
Tillet. French Agricultural Writer .... — ..1791
Tilli, Michael Angelo. Florentine Physician and Botanist 1655?.1740
Tilloch, Alexander, LL. D. Scottish Writer and Mechan-
    ical Inventor .... 1759..1825
Tillotson, John. Archbp. of Canterbury. L. by T. Birch 1630..1694
Tilly, Alexander de, Count. Royalist & Political Writer 1754..1822
Tilly, John Tzerklas, Ct. de. Ger. Soldier. L. by Klopp 1559..1632
Timæus. Greek Historian in Sicily............... 352?.256? B.C.
Timæus. Greek Sophist. (Lexicon to Plato) .... fl. ab. 3d c.
Timanthes. Greek Painter...................... fl. ab. 400 B.C.
Timoleon, of Corinth. Liberator of Syracuse........ 394?.337 B.C.
Timon. Greek Misanthrope .... fl. B.C. 433?
Timon. Greek Skeptic, Philosopher, and Poet. (Silli) . fl. B.C. 279?
Timon, Samuel. Hungarian Historian............... 1675..1736
Timoteo da Urbino. Della Vite. Painter .... 1470?.1524?
Timotheus. Athenian Commander................... — B.C.354?
Timothy. Disciple and Companion of St. Paul........ fl. 1st. c.
Timour Beg, or Tamerlane, which see................ 1336?.1405
Tindal, Matthew, LL. D. Theological and Political Writer 1657?.1733
Tindal, Rev. Nicholas. Historian; Translator and Con-
    tinuator of Rapin .... 1687..1774
Tindal, Sir Nicholas Conyngham. Judge............. 1777..1846
Tindal, or Tyndale,Wm. Translator of Bible and Martyr 1484?.1536
Tindall, Rev. William. Writer. (History of Evesham). 1754..1804
Tinelli, Tiberius. Italian Historical and Portrait Painter 1586..1638
Tintoretto, Il. James Robusti. Italian Painter .... 1512..1594
Tippoo Sahib. Last Independent Sultan of Mysore ... 1749..1799
Tiptoft, John, Earl Worcester; Lord Deputy. Writer .. — ..1470
Tiraboschi, Jerome. (Ital. Literature.) L. by Matthias 1731..1794
Tiraqueau, Andrew. French Lawyer................. 1480?.1558
Tischbein, John Henry. Ger. Painter. L. by Engelschall 1722..1789
Tischbein, John Henry Wm., neph. Historical Painter 1751..1829
Tisio, Benvenuto. Il Garofalo. Painter .... 1481..1559
Tissaphernes. Persian Satrap .... — B.C. 395
Tissot, Simon Andrew. Swiss Medical Writer......... 1728..1797
Titi, Santi di. Italian Painter....................... 1538..1603
Titi, Tiberius di, son. Painter...................... 1578..1637
Titian. Tiziano Vecelli. Italian Painter. Life by North-
    cote, 1830 .... 1477..1576
Titley, Walter. Envoy and Scholar .... 1706..1768
Titon du Tillet, Everard. (Le Parnasse Française) ... 1676..1762
Titsingh, Isaac. Eastern Traveler .... 1740..1812
Tittmann, John Augustus Henry. German Theologian 1773..1831
Titus. Companion and Fellow Laborer of St. Paul ..... fl. 1st c.
Titus. Roman Emperor (79–81)...................... 40.. 81
Tixier, John. Ravisius Textor. French Writer........ 1480?.1524
Toaldo, Joseph. Italian Physician and Meteorologist... 1719..1798
Tobin, John. Dramatist. Life by Miss Benger, 1820 .. 1770..1804

BORN. DIED.

Tocqueville, Alexis Charles Henry Clérel de. French
Publicist and Statesman. (*American Democracy*)... 1805..1859
Tod, James. Lieutenant-Colonel. Traveler and Writer 1782..1835
Todd, Henry John. Archdeacon; Biographer, and Editor
of Poets. (*Johnson's Dictionary; Deans of Canterbury*) 1763..1845
Todd, Hugh, D. D., of Carlisle. Eccles. Antiq. (*Carlisle*) 1658..1728
Todd, Robert Bentley, M. D. Medical Writer .... 1810?.1860
Toepffer, Rodolph. Swiss Author and Caricaturist .... 1779..1846
Tofino de San Miguel, Vincent. Spanish Astronomer 1740..1806
Tofts, Mrs. Katharine. Singer .... — ..1770
Toghrul Beg. First Sultan of the Seljuk Turks ...... 988?.1063
Tograi. Arabian Poet and Alchemist .... —aft.1120
Toiras, John du Caylar de St. Bonnet, Marquis de. Mar-
shal of France. Life by Michael Baudier .... 1585..1636
Tökölyi, or Toekoelyi. See Tekeli .... 1658..1705
Toland, John. Writer. Life by Des Maizeaux; Mosheim 1669?.1722
Toledo, Francis de. *Toletus.* Cardinal. Jesuit; Theol. 1532..1596
Toledo, Peter de. Spanish General. Viceroy of Naples 1484..1553
Toledo, Roderick de. *Toletanus.* Spanish Historian ... 1170?.1247
Toler, John, Earl of Norbury. Judge .... 1745..1831
Tollens, Henry Corneliszoon. Dutch Poet .... 1780..1856
Tollet, Miss Elizabeth. Poet and Scholar .... 1694..1754
Tollet, Thomas. Musical Composer.................... fl. 1694
Tollius, Cornelius. Dutch Philologist.............. 1620?.aft.1652
Tollius, James, M. D. Scholar....................... 1630?.1696
Tolommei, Claude. Italian Scholar and Poet .... 1492..1555
Tombes, John. Baptist Writer .... 1603..1676
Tomline, George. *Pretyman.* Bishop of Winchester .. 1750..1827
Tomlins, Miss Elizabeth Sophia. Novelist and Poet ... 1763..1828
Tommasi, Joseph Mary. Cardinal; Ecclesiastical Writer 1649..1713
Tommasini, James Philip. Ital. Antiq. and Biographer 1597..1654
Tompkins, Daniel D. American Statesman; Vice-Pres-
ident of United States........................... 1774..1825
Tone, Theobald Wolfe. Irish Polit. L. by W. T. W. Tone 1763..1798
Tonna, Mrs. Charlotte Elizabeth. Writer. (*Personal
Recollections*) .... 1792..1846
Tonstall, or Tunstall, Cuthbert. Bishop of Durham.... 1474?.1559
Tonti, Lawrence. Italian Banker; Originator of *Tontines* fl. 1653
Took, William. Writer on Science .... 1777?.1863
Tooke, Andrew. Gresham Professor of Geology....... 1673..1731
Tooke, John Horne. Politician and Philologist. (*Diver-
sions of Purley.*) Life by William Hamilton, 1812;
A. Stephens, 1813; W. H. Reid.................... 1736..1812
Tooke, Thomas. Financial Writer. (*History of Prices*) 1774..1858
Tooke, Rev. William, F. R. S. Writer on Russia .... 1744..1820
Töpffer, Rodolph. Swiss Author and Caricaturist ..... 1779..1846
Topham, John. Antiquary........................... — ..1803
Toplady, Augustus Montague. Divine. Life, 1778, 8vo 1740..1778
Torbido, or Turbido, Francis. *Il Moro.* Italian Painter 1500?.1581?
Torchilli, Jonas. Icelandic Scholar and Divine........ 1697..1759
Tordenskiold, Peter. Danish Admiral .... 1691..1720
Torelli, Joseph. Italian Mathem.; Editor of Archimedes 1721..1781
Torelli, or Taurellius, Lœlius. Jurist; Editor of *Pandects* 1489..1576
Torelli, Pomponius, Count of Montechiarugola. Poet and
Writer .... 1539..1608

BORN. DIED.

Toreño, Joseph Maria Queypo de Llano Ruiz de Savavia, Count de. Spanish Statesman and Historian ...... 1786..1843
Torfæus, or Tormodus. *Thormond Thorvesen.* Icelandic Historian... 1640..1719
Torinus, Albanus. *Alban Thorer.* Swiss Physician ... 1489..1550
Tornielli, Augustin. Italian Ecclesiastical Historian ... 1543..1622
Torporley, Nathaniel. Mathematician.................. 1573?.1632
Torquatus, T. Manlius Imperiosus. Roman Dictator. fl. 4th c. B.C.
Torquemada, John de. *Turrecremata.* Cardinal..... 1388..1468
Torquemada, Thomas de. Spanish Inquisitor-General. 1420?.1498
Torre, John Mary della. Italian Natural Philosopher .. 1710..1782
Torre, Philip del. Italian Antiquary.................. 1657..1717
Torrens, Sir Henry. Adjutant-General............... 1779..1828
Torrens, Robert, F. R. S. Lieut.-Colonel; Economist... 1780..1864
Torrentius. Dutch Scholar and Poet. *See* Lævinus.. 1525..1595
Torrentius, John. Dutch Painter.................... 1589..1640
Torres, Louis da' Motta. Port. Navigator and Statesman 1769..1822
Torricelli, Evangelista. Mathem. Inventor of Barometer 1608..1647
Torrigiano, Peter. Italian Sculptor .... 1472?.1522
Torrijos, Joseph Mary. Spanish Patriot .... 1791..1831
Torrington, George Byng, Sixth Viscount. Admiral .. 1768..1831
Torry, —. Bp. of St. Andrew's. L. by J. M. Neale, 1856 1763..1852
Torstenson, Leonard, Count. Swedish General .... 1603..1651
Torti, Francis. Italian Physician.................... 1658..1741
Tory, Geoffrey. French Bookseller and Engraver...... 1480?.1536?
Toscanelli, Paul. Italian Astronomer .... 1397..1482
Tostatus, Alphonso. Span. Theologian & Biblical Writ. 1400..1454
Tosti, Earl of Northumberland, son of Earl Godwin .... — ..1066
Totila. King of Ostrogoths (541–52). Captor of Rome — .. 552
Tott, Francis, Baron de. French Adventurer. (*Mémoires sur les Turcs*)... 1733..1793
Tottel, Richard. Publisher. (*Miscellanies*) .... — ..1593?
Totten, Joseph Gilbert. Amer. Gen. & Military Engineer 1788..1864
Tottenham, Edward. Controv. Div. L. by W. C. Magee 1810..1853
Tottie, John, Archdeacon. Preacher.................. —aft.1775
Touche, Claude Guymond de la. French Poet .... 1723..1760
Toulmin, Joshua, D. D. Unitarian Writer............ 1740..1815
Toulongeon, Francis Emanuel, Visct. de. Fr. Historian 1748..1812
Toup, Rev. Jonathan. Critic....................... 1713..1785
Tour, Maurice Quentin de la. French Portrait Painter.. 1704..1788
Tournefort, Joseph Pitton de. French Botanist. (*Voyage in Levant*)....................................... 1656..1708
Tournély, Honoré. Fr. Theologian. (*Course of Theology*) 1658..1729
Tournemine, René Joseph. Fr. Jesuit; Theologian, Hist. 1661..1739
Tourneur, Peter le. French Translator from English... 1736..1788
Touro, Judah. American Philanthropist .... 1776..1854
Tourrette, Mark Anthony Louis Claret de la, of Lyons. Naturalist... 1729..1793
Tourville, Anne Hilarion de Cotentin, Count de. French Admiral. Life by Margon....................... 1642..1701
Toussaint l'Ouverture, Francis Dominic. Negro Conqueror in St. Domingo. Life by St. Rémy, 1850; Dr. Beard, 1853.. 1743..1803
Towers, Joseph, LL. D. Polit. and Miscellaneous Writer 1737..1799
Towgood, Micajah. Dissenting Divine .... 1700..1792

BORN. DIED.

Townley, Charles. Scholar. Collector of *Townley Marbles* 1737..1805
Townley, Rev. Jas. Farce Writ. (*High Life below Stairs*) 1715..1778
Townley, Colonel John. Translator of Hudibras ...... — ..1782
Townsend, George. Prebendary of Durham. (*Bible*).. — ..1857
Townsend, John. Founder of Deaf and Dumb Asylum 1757..1826
Townsend, Rev. Joseph, of Pewsey. Physician, Divine,
     Naturalist. Chaplain to Lady Huntingdon. (*Travels*) 1740..1816
Townshend, Charles, Second Viscount. Statesman.... 1676..1738
Townshend, Chas., grandson. *Weather-Cock.* Statesm. 1725..1767
Townson, Thomas, D. D. Life by Churton .... 1715..1792
Towson, Nathan. American Soldier.................. 1784..1854
Tozer, Henry. Puritan Divine...................... 1602..1650
Tozetti, John Targioni, of Florence. Botanist......... 1712..1783
Tradescant, John. Horticulturist to Charles I....... — ..1652?
Tradescant, John, son. Horticult. (*Museum Tradescant.*) 1608..1662
Traetta, Thomas. Neapolitan Musical Composer....... 1727..1779
Tragus, Jerome. *Bock.* German Botanist .... 1498..1553
Traill, Robert. Scottish Divine .... 1642..1716
Traill, Thomas Stewart, M. D. Editor of *Encyclopædia
     Britannica*.. 1781..1862
Trajan. Roman Emperor (98–117). Life by Tillemont.. 52.. 117
Tralles, Balthasar Louis. German Physician .... 1708..1797
Trallianus, Alexander, of Tralles. Medical Writer .... fl. 550?
Trapp, John. Puritan Commentator.................. 1601..1669
Trapp, Joseph, D. D. Divine and Poet .... 1679..1747
Travers, John. Musical Composer.................... — ..1758
Traversari, Ambrose. Ital. Greek Scholar. L. by Mehus 1378..1439
Travis, George. Archdeacon. Writer against Gibbon.. — ..1797
Trebonius, Caius. Conspirator against Cæsar........ — B.C. 43
Treby, Sir George. Judge............................ 1644..1702
Tredgold, Thomas. Civil Engineer; Writer on Mechanics 1788..1829
Trediakovsky, Vassili Kirilovitch. Russian Poet...... 1703..1769
Trelauney, Sir Jonathan. Bp. of Exeter and Winchester 1648?.1721
Trembecki, Stanislaus. Polish Poet.................. 1724?.1812
Trembley, Abraham. Swiss Naturalist............... 1700..1784
Tremellius, Emanuel. Italian Hebraist.............. 1510?.1580
Tremoille, or Tremouille, Louis de la, Viscount de
     Thouars. Fr. General; fell at Pavia. L. by Bouchet 1460..1525
Tremollière, Peter Charles. French Painter .... 1703?.1739
Trenchard, Sir John. Statesman.................... 1650..1695
Trenchard, John. Political Writer................... 1669..1723
Trenck, Francis von der, Baron. Austrian Commander.
     Life by self, 1807; Huebner, 1788 .... 1711..1749
Trenck, Frederick von der, Baron, cousin. Adventurer;
     guillotined. Life by self......................... 1726..1794
Trento, Anthony da. Engraver.....................: fl. 1550?
Treschow, Niels. Danish Philosopher and Theologian . 1751..1833
Tresham, Henry. Painter and Poet.................. — ..1814
Tressan, Louis Elizabeth de la Vergne, Count de. Offi-
     cer and Writer................................... 1705..1782
Trevenen, James. Captain. Life by J. Penrose, 1849.. — ..1790
Treviranus, Godfrey Reynold. German Naturalist .... 1776..1837
Trevisani, Angelo, of Venice. Painter .... fl. 1750?
Trevisani, Francis. Italian Painter .... 1656..1746
Trevisi, Jerome. Painter and Engineer to Henry VIII. 1508..1544

BORN. DIED.

Treviso, Edward Adolphus Casimir Joseph Mortier, Duke
 of. Marshal of France .... 1768..1835
Trevor, Sir John. Secretary of State................ 1626..1672
Trevor, Sir John. Lawyer. Speak. of House of Commons 1633..1717
Trevor, Richard. Bp. of Durham. L. by Geo. Allan, 1776 — ..1771
Trew, Christopher James, of Nuremberg. Phys. and Bot. 1695..1769
Tribolo, Nicholas di. Italian Sculptor .... 1500..1550
Tribonian. Roman Jurist and Publicist.............. — .. 545
Triewald, Martin. Swedish Engineer and Mathematician 1691..1747
Trigault, Nicholas. French Jesuit Missionary to China 1577..1628
Triller, Daniel William. German Medical Writer...... 1695..1782
Trimble, Isaac R. "Confederate" General .... 1801?.1862
Trimmer, Mrs. Sarah. Writer. Life, 2 vols. 1814..... 1741..1810
Trincavelli, Victor. Ital. Physician and Greek Scholar 1496..1568
Trippel, Alexander. Swiss Sculptor.................. 1747..1793
Trissino, John George. Italian Poet. (*Italia Liberata*) 1478..1550
Tristan da Cunha. Portuguese Naval Commander.... fl. 15th c.
Tristan l'Hermite, Francis. French Dramatic Poet ... 1601..1655
Trithemius, John. Universal Scholar and Writer ..... 1462..1516
Trithen, Frederick Henry. Sanskrit & Sclavonic Schol. 1820..1854
Trivet, Nicholas. Historian......................... 1258?.1328
Trivulce, John Jas. Marshal of Fr. L. by Rosmini, 1815 1441..1518
Trogus Pompeius. Roman Historian. (*Univers. Hist.*) fl. B.C. 20?
Trollope, Mrs. Frances, *née* Milton. Novelist.......... 1778..1863
Trommius, Abraham. (*Greek Concord. of the Old Test.*) 1633..1719
Tromp, Sir Cornelius van. Dutch Admiral............ 1629..1691
Tromp, Martin Harpertzoon van. Dutch Admiral; Op-
 ponent of Blake.................................... 1597..1653
Tronchin, John Robert. Jurist; Writer against Rousseau 1711..1793
Tronchin, Theodore. Swiss Medical Writer........... 1709..1781
Tronson de Coudray, William Alexander. Fr. Advocate 1750..1798
Troost, Cornelius. Dutch Historian and Painter .... 1697..1750
Troost, Gerard. American Chemist and Geologist ..... 1776..1850
Trotter, Thomas, M. D., of Newcastle. Med. Writ. & Poet — ..1832
Troughton, Edward. Astronomical Instrument Maker . 1753..1835
Troup, George M. American Statesman .... 1780..1856
Trowbridge, Edmund. American Jurist.............. 1709..1793
Trowbridge, Sir Thomas. Admiral.................. 1750?.1807
Troy, Francis de. French Historical and Portrait Painter 1645..1730
Troy, John Francis de, son. Painter.................. 1676..1752
Troyen, Rombout van. Flem. Painter of Ruins and Caves 1600..1650
Troyon, Constantine. French Painter .... 1813..1865
Trublet, Nicholas Charles Joseph. French Essayist.... 1697..1770
Truchet, John. Fr. Mathem. and Hydraulic Engineer 1657..1729
Trueba y Cosio, Telesforo de. Span. Dramatist and Nov. 1805..1835
Truman, Rev. Joseph, B. D. Theologian............. 1631..1671
Trumbull, Benjamin, D. D. Amer. Clergyman and Hist. 1735..1820
Trumbull, John LL. D. American Poet. (*McFingal*).. 1750..1831
Trumbull, John. American Painter.................. 1756..1843
Trumbull, Jonathan. American Colonial Governor. Life
 by I. Stuart .... 1710..1785
Trumbull, Jonathan, son. Patriot; Gov. of Connecticut 1740..1809
Trumbull, Sir William. Statesman .... 1638..1716
Truro, Thomas Wilde, Baron. Statesman and Jurist.
 Lord Chancellor (1850–52)........................ 1782..1855

BORN. DIED.

Trusler, Rev. John, LL. D. Bookseller and Compiler... 1735..1820
Truxton, Thomas. American Naval Officer.......... 1755..1822
Tryphiodorus. Greek Poet and Grammarian .... fl. 5th c.?
Tschirner, Henry Theophilus. Ger. Theol. and Preacher 1778..1828
Tschirnhausen, Ehreufried Walter von, Ct. Ger. Math. 1651..1708
Tschudi, Giles. Father of Swiss History .... 1505..1572
Tucker, Abraham. *Search.* Writer. (*Light of Nature*) 1705..1774
Tucker, Beverly. American Lawyer and Novelist..... 1784..1851
Tucker, George. American Jurist.................... 1775..1861
Tucker, Henry St. George. Chairman East India Company. Life by Kaye, 1854........................ — ..1828
Tucker, Henry St. George. American Jurist........ 1779..1848
Tucker, Josiah, D. D. Dean of Gloucester. Polit. Writer 1711..1799
Tucker, St. George. American Poet and Jurist....... 1752..1827
Tuckerman, Joseph, D. D. Amer. Clergyman & Writer 1778..1840
Tuckey, Jas. Hingston. Explorer. (*Maritime Geography*) 1778..1816
Tuckney, Anthony. Puritan Divine.................. 1599..1670
Tude, Clairon de la. French Actress .... 1723..1803
Tudela, Benjamin of. Rabbi. Traveler .... — ..1173
Tudor, Owen; second husband of Catherine of France, Queen of England............................, — ..1461
Tudor, William. American Author.................. 1779..1830
Tudway, Dr. Thomas. Musical Composer .... fl. 1705
Tuerk. *See* Türk................................. 1774..1846
Tulden, or Thulden, Theodore van. Dutch Painter .... 1607..1676
Tull, Jethro. Agricultural Writer .... 1680?.1740
Tullia. Daughter of Cicero........................ 79?.45 B.C.
Tullibardine, Wm. Murray, Marquess of. Scot. Jacobite — ..1747
Tullus Hostilius. Third King of Rome........... fl. B.C. 673–641
Tully, Rev. George. Divine .... 1653..1697
Tully, Rev. Thomas. Controversial Divine.......... 1620..1676
Tully, William. American Physician and Botanist..... 1785..1859
Tulp, Nicholas. Dutch Medical Writer.............. 1594..1674
Tunstall, or Tonstall, Cuthbert. Roman Catholic Prelate 1474?.1559
Tunstall, James, D. D. (*Natural and Revealed Religion*) 1710? 1772
Turamini, Alexander. Italian Jurist .... 1558?. —
Turberville, George. Poet...................... 1530?.aft.1594
Turbido, or Torbido, Francis. Italian Painter .... 1500?.1581?
Turenne, Henry de la Tour d'Auvergne, Viscount de. Fr. Marshal. L. by Sandras; Raguenet; Gatien de Courtiltz; Chevalier Ramsay, 1749; T. O. Cockayne, 1853 1611..1675
Turgeneff, Alexander Ivanovitch. Russian Historian.. 1784..1845
Turgot, Anne Robert James, Baron de l'Aulne. French Statesman. Life by Condorcet, 1796 ....1727..1781
Türk, Charles Christian William von. German Educator and Philanthropist .... 1774..1846
Turnbull, Robert James. American Political Writer... 1775..1833
Turnebus, Adrian. Critic and Translator............. 1512..1565
Turner, Daniel. Baptist Divine.................... 1710..1798
Turner, Dawson. Bot. and Antiq. (*Tour in Normandy*) — ..1858
Turner, Edward, M. D. Professor of Chemistry. (*Elements of Chemistry*) .... 1798..1839
Turner, Francis. Bishop of Ely. Nonjurer. (*Life of Nicholas Ferrar*)................................ — ..1700
Turner, Sir James. Life by self, edited by Thompson.. fl. 1682
26

BORN. DIED.

Turner, Joseph Mallord Wm. Painter. L. by Thornbury 1775..1851
Turner, Robert. Eng. Rom. Cath. Divine & Commentator — ..1599
Turner, Samuel. Envoy to Mysore, and Traveler...... 1749?.1802
Turner, Rev. Sam. Hurlbeart, D. D. Amer. Theol. Writer 1790..1861
Turner, Sharon. Historian......................... 1768..1847
Turner, Thomas. Dean of Canterbury. Divine ...... 1591..1672
Turner, Thomas Hudson. Archæologist............. 1815..1852
Turner, Wm., M. D. Dean of Wells; Naturalist. (Herbal) 1520?.1568
Turner, William Wadden. American Philologist...... 1810..1859
Turpin, Francis Henry. Historian. (French Plutarch) 1709..1799
Turpin, or Tilpin, John. Archbishop of Rheims....... — .. 800?
Turpin, Richard. Highwayman...................... 1711?.1739
Turpin de Crisse, Lancelot. Fr. Gen. Military Writ. 1715?.aft.1789
Turrecremata. See Torquemada.................... 1388..1468
Turretin, Benedict. Theological Professor at Geneva .. 1588..1631
Turretin, Francis, son. Theological Professor at Geneva 1623..1687
Turretin, John Alfonso, son. Theological Professor.... 1671..1737
Tursellinus, Horatius. Jesuit. Latin Scholar........ 1545..1599
Turton, Thomas. Bishop of Ely (1845–64)........... 1780..1864
Tussaud, Madame. Artiste and Exhibit. of Wax-works 1760..1850
Tusser, Thomas. Georgical Poet. British Varro. Life
  by Dr. Mavor. (Five Hundred Points)............. 1515?.1580?
Tutchin, John. Political Writer .... — ..1707
Tuthill, Sir George, M. D. Physician............... — ..1835
Tutilo. Monk of St. Gall. Artist, Poet, &c.......... — .. 896?
Tweddell, John. Scholar and Traveler............... 1769..1799
Twells, Leonard. Divine............................ — ..1742
Twiggs, David Emanuel. American General .... 1790..1862
Twine. See Twyne.
Twining, Rev. Thomas. Translator of Aristotle .... 1734..1804
Twining, William. Army Physician and Medical Writer — ..1835
Twiss, Horace. Writer and Politician. (Life of Eldon) 1786..1849
Twiss, Richard. Traveler .... 1747..1821
Twiss, Dr. William. Nonconf. Divine. (Vindiciæ Gratiæ) 1575?.1646
Twyne, Bryan. Oxford Antiquary. (Apologia) .... 1579..1644
Twyne, John. Oxford Antiquary.................... — ..1581
Twysden, Sir Roger. Historian..................... 1597..1672
Tycho Brahé. See Brahé.......................... 1546..1601
Tychsen, Olaus Gerard. Danish Scholar............. 1734..1815
Tychsen, Thomas Christian. Oriental & Classical Schol. 1758..1834
Tye, Christopher. Musical Composer.......... ti. Hen. VIII.–Eliz.
Tyers, Thomas. Miscellaneous Writer............... 1726..1787
Tyler, Bennet, D. D. Amer. Controversialist. L. by Gale 1783..1858
Tyler, John. Tenth President of United States (1841–45) 1790..1862
Tyler, Royall. American Author and Judge........... 1756..1826
Tyler, Wat. Rebel .... — ..1381
Tyndale, or Tindal, William. Translat. of Bible; Martyr 1484?.1536
Tyrconnel, Richard Talbot, Duke of. Lord Lieutenant — ..1691
Tyrrell, James. Political Writer and Historian........ 1642..1718
Tyrtæus. Greek Poet............................. fl. B.C. 668
Tyrwhitt, Robert. Founder of Hebrew Prize.......... — ..1817
Tyrwhitt, Thomas, of Oxford. Clerk to House of Com-
  mons. Shakespearian Commentator. Classical Writer 1730..1786
Tyson, Edward, M. D. Writer and Anatomist.......... 1649..1708
Tyson, Rev. Michael. Divine and Artist .... 1740..1780

BORN. DIED.

Tyssens, Augustine. Flemish Painter .... 1662..1722
Tyssens, Nicholas, brother. Painter................. 1660..1719
Tyssens, Peter. Flemish Painter.................... 1625..1692
Tyssilio. Welsh Chronicler......................... fl. 7th c.
Tytler, Alexander Fraser, Lord Woodhouselee. Scottish Jurist and Author. (*Outlines of General History; Life of Kames*)................................... 1747..1813
Tytler, James. Scottish Writer. (*History of Edinburgh*) 1747..1805
Tytler, Patrick Fraser. Historian. (*History of Scotland.*) Life by J. W. Burgon, 1859 .... 1791..1849
Tytler, William. Historical and Miscellaneous Writer. (*Mary Queen of Scots*)........................... 1711..1792
Tzetzes, John. Greek Poet and Grammarian......... fl. ab. 1150
Tzschirner, Henry Theophilus. German Theologian.. 1778..1828

U.

BORN. DIED.

Ubaldini, Petrucchio. Illuminator on Vellum and Writer — aft.1588
Ubaldo, Guido. Italian Mathematician .... 1540?.1601?
Uberti, Fazio, or Boniface degli. Italian Poet. (*Il Ditta Mondo*) .... — ..1370?
Uccello, Paul. Florentine Painter.................... 1349?.1432
Udal, Ephraim. Episcopalian Div. (*Treat. on Sacrilege*) — ..1647
Udal, John. Puritan Divine and Sufferer.............. — ..1592
Udal, or Udall, Nicholas. Master of Eton and Westminster Schools. (*Ralph Royster Doyster*)............. 1506..1564
Udina, Martin da. *Pelegrino di San Daniello.* Painter 1480?.1545?
Udino, John da. Italian Painter .... 1494..1564
Uffenbach, Zacharias Conrad von. German Writer .... 1683..1734
Uggione, or Oggione, Mark da. Milanese Painter ...... 1480?:1530
Ughelli, Ferdinand. Italian Eccles. Hist. (*Italia Sacra*) 1595..1670
Ugone, Matthias. Italian Writer on Councils.......... — ..1616
Uhland, John Louis. German Lyric Poet............. 1787..1862
Uilkens, James Albert. Dutch Naturalist............. 1772..1825
Ulloa, Anthony de. Span. Mathematician & Naval Officer 1716..1795
Ulloa y Pereira, Louis de. Spanish Poet............. — ..1660
Ulphilas, or Ulfilas. Gothic Bishop and Writer (348-81) 311?. 381
Ulpian, Domitius. Roman Jurist..................... — .. 228
Ulug-Beg. Tartar Prince. Astronomer .... 1394..1449
Umbreit, Frederick William Charles. German Protestant Theologian .... 1795..1860
Uncas. North Amer. Indian Chief; Sachem of Mohegans — ..1680?
Underwood, T. R. Artist and Geologist.............. — ..1835
Unger, Frederica Helen. Novelist and Translator...... — ..1813
Unger, John Frederick Theophilus. German Printer and Wood Engraver.................................... 1750..1804
Unzer, John Augustus. German Medical and Physiological Writer .... 1727..1799
Upcott, William. Autograph Collector................ 1779..1845
Upshur, Abel Parker. American Jurist and Statesman. — ..1844
Upton, James. Divine and Scholar; Editor of Aristotle and Ascham .... 1670..1749
Upton, John. Prebendary of Rochester; Editor of Spenser 1707..1760
Urban I. Pope (222-30)............................... — .. 230
Urban II. (1088-99.) *Otho or Eudes* .... — ..1099
Urban III. (1185-87.) *Hubert Crivelli* .... — ..1187
Urban IV. (1261-64.) *James Pantaleon* .... — ..1264
Urban V. (1362-70.) *William de Grimoard* .... — ..1370
Urban VI. (1378-89.) *Bartholomew di Prignano* ...... 1318?.1389
Urban VII. Elected Sept. 15, 1590. *John Bapt. Castagna* — ..1590
Urban VIII. (1623-44.) *Maffeo Barberini.* Life by Dr. Brown .... 1568..1644
Urbino, Timotheus di. *See* Vite. .... 1470?.1524?
Urceo, Anthony. *Codrus Urceus.* Italian Scholar.... 1446..1500
Ure, Andrew, M. D. Scottish Chemist.................. 1778..1857
Urfé, Anne d'. French Poet......................... 1555..1621
Urfé, Honoré d', brother. Poet. (*L'Astrée*) .... 1567..1625
Urquhart, Sir Thomas, of Cromarty. Philol. and Math. — ..1642

BORN. DIED.

Urraca. Queen of Leon, Castile, and Asturias......... 1080..1126
Ursins, Anne Maria de la Tremoille, Princess des. Politician. (*Memoirs and Correspondence*)............. 1642?.1722
Ursins, John Juvenal des. Archbishop of Rheims. (*Reign of Charles VI.*).................................. 1388..1473
Ursinus, Benjamin. *Behr*. German Mathematician ... 1587..1633
Ursinus, Benjamin. Lutheran Bishop and Court Preacher fl. 1700
Ursinus, Fulvius. Scholar and Classical Editor........ 1529..1600
Ursinus, George Henry. Philologist.................. 1647..1707
Ursinus, John Henry. German Lutheran Divine. (*Rise of the Churches of Germany*)...................... — ..1667
Ursinus, Zachary. German Protestant Theologian..... 1534..1583
Ursticius, Christian. *See* Wursticius................ 1544..1588
Ursula, St. Virgin and Martyr.'..................... — .. 453?
Ursus, Nicholas Raymarus. Danish Mathematician .... 1550?.1600
Urville, Julius Sebastian Cæsar Dumont d'. French Navigator. (*Voyage to South Pole*) .... 1790..1842
Usez, Robert d'..................................... — ..1291
Usher, James. Archbishop. Life by Dr. Nicholas Bernard; Dr. Richard Parr and Thomas Marshall; Dr. John Aikin, 1773; Dr. Ebrington .... 1580..1656
Ustariz, Jerome. Spanish Political Economist .... — ..1750?
Usteri, Leonard. Swiss Educationist.................. 1741..1789
Utenhovius, Charles. Polemical and Political Divine .. 1536?.1600
Utrecht, Adrian van. Dutch Painter................. 1599..1651
Uvaroff, or Ouvaroff, Sergy Semenovitch. Russian Statesman and Writer.................................. 1785..1855
Uvedale, Robert, D. D. Botanist..................... 1642..1722
Uwins, David, M. D. Medical Writer .... 1780..1837
Uwins, Thomas, R. A. Life by Mrs. Uwins, 1858....... 1783..1857
Uz, John Peter. German Lyric Poet.................. 1720..1796
Uzziah. King of Judah (B. C. 808–756)............. 824?.756 B.C.

V.

Vaart, John van der. Flemish Painter and Engraver.. 1647..1721
Vacarius. Civilian at Oxford........................ fl. 1149
Vacca, Flaminius. Italian Sculptor.................. fl. 1594
Vacca-Berlinghieri, Francis. Italian Physician ...... 1732..1812
Vaccaro, Andrew. Italian Painter .... 1598..1670
Vaccaro, Francis. Italian Engraver and Painter....... 1636..1687
Vachet, John Anthony le. French Religious Writer and
  Benefactor .... 1603..1681
Vachet, Peter Joseph du. French Latin Poet.......... — ..1655?
Vacquette, John, Sieur de Cardonñoy. Jurist and Writer 1658..1739
Vadder, Louis de. Dutch Landscape Painter.......... 1560..1623
Vadé, John Joseph. French Humorous Poet .... 1720..1757
Vadianus, Joachim. Swiss Scholar .... 1484..1551
Vaga, Pierino del. *Peter Buonaccorsi.* Italian Painter.. 1501..1547
Vahl, Martin. Norwegian Botanist.................. 1749..1804
Vaillant, Francis le. French Naturalist.............. 1753..1824
Vaillant, John Foy. French Numismatist and Traveler 1632..1706
Vaillant, John Francis Foy, son. Medalist............ 1665..1708
Vaillant, Sebastian. French Botanist....:.......... 1669..1722
Vaillant, Wallerant. Flemish Portrait Painter .... 1623..1677
Vaillant de Guelle, Germain. Commentator on Virgil — ..1587
Vaissette, Joseph. Fr. Benedictine. (*Hist. of Languedoc*) 1685..1756
Valadé, James Francis. French Bibliographer........ — ..1784
Valazo, Charles Eleonore Dufriche. French Girondist .. 1751..1793
Valcarcel, Antonius, Count de Lumiares. Spanish Antiq. 1740?.1808
Valckenaër, John. Dutch Scholar, Statesman, & Jurist 1759..1821
Valckenaër, Louis Gaspar. Dutch Philologist and Critic 1715..1785
Valdes, or Valdesso, John. Spanish Reformer in Italy.. — ..1540
Valdez, John Melendez. Spanish Poet............... 1754..1817
Valdo, or Waldo, Peter, of Lyons. Religious Reformer. — ..1179
Valée, Sylvain Charles, Count. French General .... 1773..1846
Valence, or Lesignan, Aymer de. Bishop of Winchester — ..1260
Valens, Fabius. Roman General .... — .. 69
Valens, Flavius. Emperor of the East (364–78)........ 328?. 378
Valentia, George Annesley, Ninth Viscount. (*Voyages
  and Travels*)...................................... 1770..1844
Valentine, St. Bishop or Presbyter; beheaded........ — .. 270
Valentine. Elected September 1, 827.............. — .. 827
Valentine, of Milan, wife of Louis Duke of Orleans..... 1370?.1408
Valentine, Basil. Alchemist. (*Currus Triumphalis Anti-
  monii*)... fl. 16th c.
Valentine, Moses, or Peter. French Painter .... 1600..1632
Valentini, Michael Bernard. German Medical Writer.. 1657..1729
Valentini, Peter Francis, of Rome. Musical Composer — ..1654
Valentinian I. Roman Emperor (364–75)............. 321.. 375
Valentinian II. (375–92)......................... 371?. 392
Valentinian III. (425–55)......................... 419?. 455
Valentinus. Gnostic Heresiarch.................... fl. 140–160
Valerian. Roman Emperor (253–60) .... — aft. 260
Valerianus, Johannes Pierius. Italian Latin Poet..... 1477..1558
Valerius Corvus, Marcus. Roman General .... 371?.271? B.C.

BORN. DIED.

Valerius Flaccus, Caius. Latin Poet. (*Argonautica*) — .. 88?
Valerius Maximus. Roman Historian............. fl. ti. Tiberius
Valesio, Francis. Spanish Medical Writer............. ti. Phil. II.
Valesius, Adrian. *De Valois.* French Historian and Critic 1607..1692
Valesius, Henricus, brother. *De Valois.* French Critic 1603..1676
Valette, John Louis de Nogaret, Duc d'Épernon. French
  General .... 1554..1642
Valette, John Parisot de la. Founder of Valetta in Malta 1494..1568
Valiero, Augustin. Cardinal; Writer................ 1531..1606
Valin, René Joshua. (*Coutume de la Rochelle*) .... 1695..1765
Valincourt, John Bapt. du Trousset de. Critic & Writer 1653..1730
Valkenburgh, Theodore. Dutch Painter.............. 1675..1721
Valla, Lawrence. Italian Philologist................ 1406?.1457
Vallancey, Colonel Charles. Irish Antiquary .... 1721..1812
Valle, Peter della. *Il Pellegrino.* Italian Traveler..... 1586..1652
Vallemont, Peter le Lorrain de. Historian & Naturalist 1649..1721
Vallet, or Valet, William. Engraver................ 1634..1704
Valli, Eusebius. Italian Medical Writer.............. 1762..1816
Vallière, Frances Louisa, Duchess de la. Favorite of
  Louis XIV...................................... 1644..1710
Vallisnieri, Anthony. Italian Naturalist .... 1661..1730
Valmont de Bomare, James Christopher. Fr. Naturalist 1731..1807
Valois, Adrian de. French Historian .... 1607..1692
Valois, Henry de, brother. *Valesius.* French Critic.... 1603..1676
Valois de la Mare, Charles. Writer. (*Valesianæ*) .... 1671..1747
Valperga di Caluso, Thomas. Piedmontese Mathem... 1737..1815
Valpy, Rev. Edward. Master at Norwich. (*Elegantiæ
  Latinæ*) .... 1764?.1832
Valpy, Rev. Richard, D.D., br. Master of Reading School 1754..1836
Valsalva, Anthony Mary. Ital. Physician and Anatomist 1666..1723
Van Achen, or Aken, John. German Painter .... 1552..1615
Van Amburgh, Isaac. *Lion-King*.................... — ..1865
Van Buren, Martin. Eighth President of United States 1782..1862
Van Butchell, Martin. Empiric.................... 1734?.1814
Van Ceulen, or Keulen, Ludolph. Mathem. of Leyden. — ..1610
Van-Cleve, Joseph. French Sculptor .... 1644..1733
Van Diemen, Anthony. Dutch Governor in India..... 1593..1645
Van Dyck, or Vandyke, Sir Anthony. Flemish Painter.
  Life by Carpenter, 1844......................... 1599..1641
Van Effen, Justus. Dutch Writer................... 1684..1735
Van Helmont, Segres James. Flemish Historical Painter 1683..1726
Van Hoeck, John. Flemish Painter.................. 1600..1650
Van Mildert, William. Bishop of Durham............ 1765..1836
Van Néss, Cornelius P., LL. D. American Jurist and
  Diplomatist..................................... 1781..1852
Van Obstal, Gerard. Dutch Sculptor................ 1597..1663
Van Oort, Adam. Dutch Painter .... 1557..1641
Van Oost, Jacob. *Elder.* Flemish Historical Painter.. 1600?.1671
Van Oost, Jacob, son. *Younger.* Portrait Painter..... 1637..1713
Van Orlay, Bernard. *Bernard of Brussels.* Painter ... 1490?.1560
Van Orlay, Richard. Flemish Painter............... 1652..1732
Van Os, John. Flower and Marine Painter, and Poet... 1744..1818
Van Os, Peter Gerard, son. Animal Painter.......... 1776..1839
Van Ostade, Adrian. Dutch Painter .... 1610..1685
Van Rensselaer, Cortland, D. D. American Writer.... 1808..1860

BORN. DIED.

Van Rensselaer, Stephen, LL. D. *Patroon.* American Statesman and Patron of Learning . . . . 1764..1839
Van Spaendonck, Gerard. Flemish Painter of Flowers 1752..1822
Van Thulden, Theodore. Dutch Painter and Engraver 1607..1676
Van Utrecht, Adrian. Dutch Painter . . . . 1599..1651
Van Veen, or Venius, Otho. Dutch Painter . . . . 1556..1634
Van der Cabel, or Kabel, Adrian. Dutch Painter . . . . . 1631..1695
Van der Does, Jacob. *The Old.* Dutch Paint. & Engrav. 1623..1673
Van der Does, Jacob. *The Younger,* son. Painter. . . . 1654..1693
Van der Does, Simon, brother. Painter . . . . 1653..1717
Van der Helst, Bartholomew. Portrait Painter . . . . 1613..1670?
Van der Heyden, John. Flemish Architectural Painter 1637..1712
Van der Meer. Dutch Painter. *See* Meer. . . . . 1627..1691
Van der Monde, Charles Augustus. Medical Writer. . . 1727..1762
Van der Werf, Adrian. Dutch Painter . . . . 1659..1722
Van der Werf, Peter, brother. Painter . . . . 1665..1718
Van der Weyde, Roger. *Roger of Bruges.* Flemish Historical and Portrait Painter. 1455?.1529
Vanaken, Joseph. Dutch Painter. . . . . 1699..1749
Vanbrugh, Sir John. Architect and Dramatist . . . . 1666?.1726
Vancouver, George. Navigator and Discoverer . . . . . . 1758?.1798
Vandale, Anthony. Dutch Physician and Theologian. . 1638..1708
Vandamme, Dominic Joseph. French General . . . . 1771..1830
Vandelli, Dominic. Italian Physician and Naturalist. . . — ..1815?
Vanden-Eckout, Gerbrandt. Dutch Historian and Portrait Painter. . . . . 1621..1674
Vandenhoff, John. English Tragedian. . . . . 1790..1861
Vanderburch, Emile. French Dramatist. . . . . 1794?.1862
Vanderlyn, John. American Painter. . . . . 1776..1852
Vandermeulen, Anthony Francis. Flemish Painter . . . 1634..1690
Vandermeulen, Peter. Battle Painter in England . . . . fl. 1670
Vandermonde, —. Fr. Mathematician and Philosopher 1735..1796
Vandervelde, Adrian. Dutch Painter. . . . . 1639..1672
Vandervelde, Isaiah. Flemish Painter . . . . 1590?.1648
Vandervelde, John. Flemish Painter in England . . . 1598.aft.1677
Vandervelde, William. *The Elder.* Marine Painter . . 1610..1693
Vandervelde, William, son. *The Younger.* Marine Paint. 1633..1707
Vandyck, Philip. *Little.* Dutch Painter . . . . 1680..1752
Vandyk, Harry Stoe. English Poet and Miscel. Writer 1798?.1828
Vane, Sir Henry. Statesman . . . . 1589..1654
Vane, Sir Henry, son. Republican Statesman; beheaded.
Life by C. W. Upham. . . . . 1612..1662
Vanetti, Clementino. Italian Writer . . . . 1755..1794
Vaneyck, Hubert. Painter. . . . . 1366..1426
Vaneyck, John, brother. *John of Bruges.* Painter. . . . 1370..1441
Vanière, James. French Jesuit; Poet . . . . 1664..1739
Vanini, Lucilius. Italian Philosopher; burnt for Atheism.
Life by Schram, 1709; Durand, 1717; Fuhrmann, 1800 1585..1619
Vanloo, Charles Andrew. French Historical Painter.
Life by Dandre-Bardon . . . . 1705..1765
Vanloo, John Baptist, brother. Portrait Painter . . . . . . 1684..1746
Vanmander, Charles. Flemish Painter and Author. . . . 1548..1606
Vanni, Francis. Italian Historical Painter. . . . . 1565?.1610?
Vanni, John Baptist. Florentine Painter. . . . . 1599..1660
Vannucci, Andrew. *Del Sarto.* Painter . . . . 1488..1530

BORN. DIED.

Vannucci, Peter. *Perugino.* Painter:............... 1446..1524
Vanpraet. Bibliopolist. (*Cat. of Works printed on Vellum*) 1754..1837
Vansomer, Paul. Flemish Portrait Painter .... 1576?.1621
Vanswieten, Gerard. Dutch Medical Writer......... 1700..1772
Vanucci. *See* Vannucci.
Vanuden, Lucas. Landscape Painter................. 1595..1662
Vanvitelli, Louis. Italian Architect................. 1700..1773
Varchi, Benedict. Florentine Writer. (*Ercolano*)..... 1502..1565
Varenius, Augustus. Lutheran Divine and Hebraist... 1620..1684
Varenius, Bernard. Dutch Phys. (*Universal Geography*) — ..1660
Vargas, Louis de. Spanish Painter.................. 1502..1568
Vargas-Mexia, Francis de. Span. Lawyer and Statesm. — ..1560?
Varignon, Peter. Fr. Mathem. (*Nouvelle Méchanique*) 1654..1722
Varillas, Anthony. French Historian................. 1624..1696
Varius, Lucius. Latin Poet.......................... — B.C. 11?
Varley, John. English Water Color Painter........... 1777?.1842
Varnhagen von Ense, Charles Augustus Louis Philip.
  German Author .... 1785..1858
Varnhagen von Ense, Rachel Antonia Frederica, wife.. 1771..1833
Varnum, James Mitchell. American General......... 1749..1789
Varoli, Constant. Ital. Anatomist. Discov. of *Pons Varoli* 1542..1575
Varotari, Alexander. *Paduanino.* Painter......... 1590..1650
Varotari, Chiara, sister. Portrait Painter............ 1582..1639
Varro, Caius Terentius. Roman Consul (B. C. 216)... — aft. 202 B.C.
Varro, Marcus Terentius. Roman Writer. *Most Learned*
  of the Romans................................. 116.28 B.C.
Varro, Publius Terentius. *Atacinus.* Latin Author.
  (*Argonautica*) .... 82..37 B.C.
Varus, Quintilius. Poet; Friend of Virgil and Horace .. — B. C. 24
Vasa, Gustavus. *See* Gustavus..................... 1490..1560
Vasari, George. Ital. Painter, Biographer, and Architect 1512..1574
Vasconcellos, Michael. Portuguese Statesman .... — ..1640
Vascosan, Michael. French Printer.................. 1500?.1576
Vasques, Alphonso. Spanish Painter and Sculptor..... 1575?.1645?
Vasques, Gabriel. Spanish Theologian .... 1551..1604
Vasselier, Joseph. French Poet...................... 1735..1798
Vassor, Michael le. French Protestant Convert. (*His-*
  tory of Louis XIII.)............................. 1647?.1718
Vatable, Vateblé, or Gastebled, Francis. Fr. Orientalist — ..1547
Vater, John Severin. German Philologist and Theologian 1771..1826
Vattel, Emmerich de. Swiss Publicist and Jurist ...... 1714..1767
Vattier, Peter. French Arabic Scholar and Translator.. 1623..1667
Vauban, Sebastian Leprestre, Seigneur de. French Mili-
  tary Engineer .... 1633..1707
Vaucanson, James de. French Mechanician.......... 1709..1782
Vaucher, John Peter. Theologian & Botanist at Geneva — ..1841
Vaugelas, Claude Favre de. (*Sur la Langue Françoise*). 1585?.1650
Vaughan, Alfred. Poet & Reviewer. (*Hours with Mystics*) 1823..1857
Vaughan, Henry. Poet. *Silurist.* Life by H. F. Lyte 1621..1695
Vaughan, Sir John. Judge. (*Reports*).............. 1608..1674
Vaughan, Sir John, D. C. L. Judge .... 1772..1839
Vaughan, Thomas. *Eugenius Philalethes.* Alchemist.. — ..1666
Vaughan, William. Welsh Poet. (*Golden Grove*) ..... 1577..1640?
Vaumorière, Peter Dortigue, Sieur de. French Writer. 1610?.1693
Vauquelin, Louis Nicholas. French Analytical Chemist 1763..1829

BORN. DIED.

Vauvenargues, Luke de Clapiers, Mqs. of. Fr. Writer. 1715..1747
Vauvilliers, John Francis. French Classical Scholar; died in Russia........................ 1737..1801
Vaux, Sir Nicholas, Lord. Favorite of Henry VIII..... — ..1522
Vaux, Noel Jourdan de. Marshal of France........... 1705..1788
Vaux, Thomas, Lord. Poet..................... 1510..1557
Vavasseur, Francis. Fr. Jesuit; Latin Scholar and Poet 1605..1681
Vecchi, Horatio. Italian Musical Composer and Poet .. — ..1605
Vecchi, John de. Italian Painter.................. 1536..1614
Vecchia, Peter. Painter .... 1605..1678
Vecelli, Francis. Painter.................... 1483..1560
Vecelli, Horatio, son of Titian. Painter .... 1515..1576
Vecelli, Marcus. *Marco da Tiziano.* Painter .... 1545..1611
Vecelli, Tiziano, or Titian. *See* Titian............... 1477..1576
Veeninx, John Baptist. Dutch Painter........... 1621?.1660
Vega, Garcilasso de la. Spanish Poet. *See* Garcilasso. 1503..1536
Vega, Garcilasso de la. *Inca. See* Garcilasso .... 1530..1568
Vega, George von, Baron. Colonel. Ger. Mathematician 1754..1802
Vega, Lope de. Span. Poet. Life by Lord Holland, 1817 1562..1635
Vegetius, Flavius Renatus. Latin Military Writer..... fl. 385?
Veil, or Viel, Charles Mary de. Converted Jew. Commentator............................. — ..1680?
Veil, or Viel, Louis Compiègne de, brother. Converted Jew. Hebraist...................... — ..1700?
Veit, Philip. German Painter................... 1793..1854
Velasco, Antonio Palomino de Castro. Spanish Painter and Historian of Spanish Painters .... 1653..1726
Velasquez, James Rodriguez de Silva y. Spanish Painter. Life by Stirling, 1855..................... 1599..1660
Velde, Francis Charles van der. German Novelist..... 1779..1824
Veldeke, Henry von. German Minnesinger........... fl. 1170?
Velly, Paul Francis. Historian .... 1709?.1759
Velser, or Welser, Mark. German Civilian .... 1558..1614
Veltheim, Augustus Francis, Count von. Mineralogist 1741..1801
Velthuysen, Lambert. Dutch Physician, Theol., Philos. 1622..1685
Venables, Robert. Colonel. (*Experienced Angler*).... — ..1687
Vence, Henry Francis de. French Biblical Writer ..... 1676?.1749
Vendôme, Cæsar, Duke of, son of Gabrielle d'Estrées... 1594..1665
Vendôme, Louis, Duke of, son............. 1612..1699
Vendôme, Louis Joseph, Duke of. French General .... 1654..1712
Vendôme, Philip, Duke of. Commander.............. 1655..1727
Veneroni. *John Vigneron.* French Grammarian...... fl. 1708
Veneziano, Anthony. Italian Painter............. 1310?.1384
Veneziano, Augustine. Venetian Engraver........... 1490?.1540?
Veneziano, Dominic. Italian Painter .... 1406..1462
Venezianu, Anthony. Sicilian Poet.............. 1543..1593
Veniero, Dominic. Italian Poet..................... 1517?.1582
Venius, or Van Veen, Otho. Dutch Painter.......... 1556..1634
Venn, Rev. Henry. Rector of Yelling. (*Complete Duty*) 1725..1797
Venn, Rev. John, son. Rector of Clapham. (*Sermons*) 1759..1813
Venner, Thomas. Fanatic................... — ..1661
Venner, Tobias. English Medical Writer............. 1577..1660
Venning, Ralph. Ejected Nonconf. Div. (*Helps to Piety*) 1620?.1673
Ventenat, Stephen Peter. French Botanist .... 1757..1808
Ventimiglia, Joseph. Sicilian Prince and Statesman... 1761..1814

BORN. DIED.

Ventura, G. D. Joachim. Italian Jesuit; Orator and Theologian ...... 1792..1861
Venusti, Marcello. *Il Mantuano*. Italian Painter ..... 1515..1576
Veratti, Laura. Female Scholar .... 1711.. —
Verbiest, Ferdinand. Flemish Math. and Miss. to China 1630?.1688
Verdier, Anthony du. (*Bibliothèque des Auteurs François*) 1544..1600
Verdier, Cæsar. French Anatomist. .... 1685..1759
Vere, Sir Aubrey de. Dramatic Poet .... — ..1846
Vere, Edward de. Seventeenth Earl of Oxford. Poet .. 1540?.1604
Vere, Sir Francis. General. Defender of Ostend ...... 1554..1608
Vere, Sir Horace, Baron of Tilbury, brother. General .. 1565..1635
Verelius, Olaus. *Olaf Werl.* Swedish Antiquary..... 1618..1682
Verelst, Simon. Dutch Fruit and Flower Painter...... 1604..1651
Vergennes, Charles Gravier, Count de. Fr. Statesman. 1717..1787
Vergerio, Peter Paul. *The Elder.* Ital. Reviver of Learning 1349..1431?
Vergerio, Peter Paul. *The Younger.* Roman Catholic Bishop and Protestant Convert .... — ..1565
Vergier, James. French Poet..................... 1657..1720
Vergier de Hauranne, John du. Abbot of St. Çyran. Jansenist........................... 1581..1643
Vergil, Polydore. English Historian................. 1470?.1555
Vergne, Louis Elizabeth de la, Count de Tressan. French Writer .... 1705..1782
Vorgniaud, Peter Victurnien. French Girondist....... 1759..1793
Verheyen, Philip. Dutch Physician and Anatomist.... 1648..1710
Vermeulen, John. *See Molanus.* .... 1533..1585
Vermeyen, John Cornelius. Dutch Painter........... 1500..1559
Vermigli. *Peter Martyr.* Italian Protestant Reformer 1500..1562
Vermuyden, Sir Cornelius. Engineer............... — ..1665
Vernes, Jacob. Genevese Divine.................. 1728..1791
Vernet, Anthony Charles Horace. *Carle.* French Painter 1758..1836
Vernet, Claude Joseph. French Marine Painter........ 1714..1789
Vernet, Emile John Horace. Painter............... 1789..1863
Vernet, Jacob. Genevese Divine................. 1698..1789
Verney, Joseph Guichard du. French Anatomist...... 1648..1730
Vernier, Peter, of Franche Comté. Inventor of Scale... 1580?.1637
Vernon, Edward. Admiral........................ 1684..1757
Vernon, Robert. Founder of Vernon Gallery. ...... 1774..1849
Veronese, Alexander. *Turchi* and *L' Orbetto*. Ital. Painter 1582..1648
Veronese, Paul. Painter. *See Cagliari*.............. 1530?.1588
Verres, Caius. Roman Governor of Sicily............ — B. C. 43
Verri, Alexander. Italian Writer. (*Le Notti Romane*) . 1741..1816
Verri, Peter, brother. Economist.................. 1728..1797
Verrio, Anthony. Italian Painter .... 1639..1707
Verrocchio, Andrew del. Italian Painter............ 1432..1488
Verstegan, Richard. Antiquary .... — ..1635?
Vert, Claude de. French Benedictine. Liturgist ...... 1645..1708
Vertot D'Auboeuf, René Aubert de. French Historian 1655..1735
Vertue, George. Engraver and Antiquary .... 1684..1756
Verus, Lucius Aurelius. Colleague of M. Aurelius. Emp. 130.. 169
Vesalius, Andrew. Dutch Anatomist............... 1514..1564
Vesling, John. Physician, Anatomist, and Botanist ... 1598..1649
Vespasian, Titus Flavius. Roman Emperor (70–79).... 9.. 79
Vesputius, or Vespucci, Americus. Italian Navigator. L. by Lester, 1846; Santarem, tr. by E. V. Childe, 1850 1451..1516

BORN. DIED.

Vestris, Madame, *née* Bartolozzi. (Mrs. Matthews.)
Comic Actress .... 1797..1858
Vestris, Angiolo Mary Gaspar. Italian Dancer........ 1730..1809
Vestris, Gaetano Apolline Balthasar, brother. Dancer.. 1729..1808
Vestris, Mme. Mary Rose Gourgaud Dugazon. Actress 1746..1804
Vestris, Vestris Allard. *Vestris II.* Italian Dancer ... 1760..1862
Vettori, or Victorius, Peter. Italian Scholar and Poet.. 1499..1585
Viaud, Theophilus de. French Poet .... 1590..1626
Vicars, Hedley S. J. Captain. Life by Miss Marsh.... 1826..1855
Vicars, John. Presbyterian Enthusiast .... 1582..1652
Vicary, Thomas. Anat. (*A Treasure for Englishmen*). fl. 1548
Vicat, Louis Joseph. French Engineer.............. 1786..1861
Vicente, Gil. Portuguese Comic Poet and Dramatist... 1485?..1557
Vici, Andrew. Italian Architect.................... 1744..1817
Vico, Eneas, of Venice. Medalist..................... — ..1560?
Vico, Francis de. Italian Astronomer................ 1805..1848
Vico, John Baptist. Italian Critic, Historian, and Jurist.
  (*Scienza Nuova*) .... 1668..1744 .
Vicq-d'Azyr, Felix. French Physician and Naturalist.
(*Éloges Historiques*). .... 1714..1794
Victoire, Madame, aunt of Louis XVI................ 1733..1799
Victor, St., of Marseilles. Martyr................... — .. 303
Victor I. Pope (185–97) .... — .. 197
Victor II. (1055–57.) *Gebehard*.................. — ..1057
Victor III. Elected May 24, 1086. *Didier or Desiderius* 1027..1087
Victor IV. Antipope............................. — ..1164
Victor, Claude Perrin, Duke of Belluno. Marshal of
France. (*Memoirs*) .... 1764..1841
Victor, Sextus Aurelius. Latin Historian .... fl. 350?
Victor-Amadeus I. Duke of Savoy (1630–37)........ 1587..1637
Victor-Amadeus II. Duke of Savoy, and First King
of Sardinia (1713–32)............................ 1666..1732
Victor-Amadeus III. King of Sardinia (1773–96).... 1726..1796
Victor-Emmanuel I. King of Sardinia (1802–21) .... 1759..1824
Victorin, of Feltre. Instructor of Youth .... 1379?.1447
Victorinus, Caius, or Fabius Marius. African Philoso-
pher and Christian Convert .... — .. 386?
Victorius, Benedict. Medical Writer at Bologna ...... 1480?.1552?
Victorius, or Vettori, Peter. Classical Scholar and Editor 1499..1585
Vida, Mark Jerome, of Cremona. Italian Poet. (*Christiad*) 1480?.1566
Vidius, Vidus. *Guido Guidi.* Italian Anatomist at Paris — ..1569
Vidocq, Eugene Francis. French Adventurer; Chief of
Detective Police. (*Autobiography*) .... 1775..1850
Vien, Madame. French Painter of Flowers, Birds, &c... 1728?.1805
Vien, Joseph Mary, husband. Historical Painter....... 1716..1809
Vien, Joseph Mary. *The Younger*, son. Portrait Painter 1761..1809
Vieta, or Viète, Francis. French Mathematician....... 1540..1600
Vieussens, Raymond de, F. R. S., of Montpellier. Anat-
omist. (*Neurologia Universalis*).................. 1641..1716
Vieyra, or Vieira, Anthony. Port. Writer and Preacher 1608..1697
Vigand, or Wigand, John. Lutheran Divine .... 1523..1587
Vigee, Louis John Baptist Stephen. Fr. Poetical Writer 1758..1820
Vigenère, Blaise de. French Translator and Scholar... 1523..1596
Viger, Francis. Jesuit of Rouen. Philol. (*De Idiotismis*) — ..1647
Vigilantius. Christian Writer .... fl. 406

BORN. DIED.

Vigilius. African Prelate and Polemical Writer........ fl. 484?
Vigilius. Pope (537–55)............................... — .. 555
Vigne, Andrew de la. French Historical Writer .... — ..1527?
Vigne, Anne de la. French Poetess................... 1634..1684
Vigne, Peter delle. Italian Jurist and Politician. Chan-
  cellor of Frederick II.; Writer...... .... — ..1249
Vigneul de Marville. See Argonne................. 1640?.1704
Vignier, Jerome. Fr. Orientalist, Antiquary, Medalist.. 1606..1661
Vignier, Nicholas. French Historian and Chronologist 1530..1596
Vignola, James Barozzi da. Italian Architect........ 1507..1573
Vignoles, Alphonso des. Chronologist, Historian, and
  Antiquary.. 1649..1744
Vignoles, Stephen de. La Hire. French Commander 1390?.1443
Vigny, Alfred, Count de. French Poet and Novelist ... 1799..1863
Vigo, John da. Italian Surgeon...................... fl. 1514
Vigors, Nicholas Aylward. Irish Zoölogist........... 1787..1840
Villalpandi, John Bapt. Span. Jesuit Div. (On Ezekiel) 1552..1608
Villani, John. Florentine Historian .... — ..1348
Villani, Matthew, brother. Florentine Historian .... — ..1363
Villani, Philip, son. Florentine Historian .... — ..1404?
Villanueva, James. Spanish Writer. (Viage Literaria) 1765..1824
Villanueva, Joachim Lorenzo de, brother. Author and
  Patriot. (Poesias)............................... 1757..1837
Villaret, Claude. French Historian; Continuator of Velly 1715?.1766
Villars, Charles Louis Hector, Duke of. Marshal of
  France. Life by Margon; self and Anquetil, 1784... 1653..1734
Villars, Dominic. French Botanist................... 1745..1814
Villars, Montfaucon de. Fr. Preacher. (Comte de Gabalis) 1640?.1675
Villedieu, Mary Hortense Desjardins, Madame de. French
  Novelist... 1632..1683
Villefore, Joseph Francis Bourgoin de. Biographer.... 1652..1737
Villegas, Stephen Manuel de. Span. Poet. (Amatorias) 1596..1669
Villehardouin, Geoffrey de. French Historian .... 1167?.1213?
Villèle, Joseph, Count de. French Statesman.......... 1773..1854
Villena, Henry d'Aragon, Marquis de. Spanish Poet.
  (Gaya Sciencia)................................... 1384..1434
Villena, John de Pacheco, Mqs. de. Castilian Statesman — ..1473
Villeneuve, Christopher de. Soldier................. 1541..1615
Villeneuve, Gabrielle Susanna Barbot de. Fr. Novelist 1695?.1755
Villeneuve, Huon de. French Poet. (Les Quatre Fils
  d'Aymon) .... ti. Phil. Aug.
Villeneuve, Peter Charles John Baptist Sylvestre de.
  French Admiral................................. 1763..1806
Villeneuve, Romée de. Grand Seneschal of Provence 1170?.1250?
Villeneuve, Rosaline de. Saint. Ascetic............ 1263?.1329
Villeneuve, William de. Soldier and Writer. (Conquête
  de Naples)..................................... fl. 1497
Villers, Charles Francis Dominic de. French Writer.... 1767..1815
Villette, Charles, Marquis de. French Politician, Poet,
  and Writer...................................... 1736..1793
Villiers, George, First Duke of Buckingham. Favorite;
  assassinated .... 1592..1628
Villiers, George, Second Duke of Buckingham, son. Prof-
  ligate and Wit.................................. 1627..1688
Villiers, Montague. Bishop of Durham.............. 1813..1861

BORN. DIED.

Villiers de l'Isle Adam, Philip de.   Grand Master ....   1464..1534
Villoisin, John Baptist Gaspar d'Ansse de.   French Schol-
  ar and Collector of MSS............................ 1750..1805
Villotte, James.   Jesuit Divine and Traveler in Armenia 1656..1743
Vince, Rev. Samuel.   Mathematician; Plumian Professor
  of Astronomy & Experimental Philosophy, Cambridge   — ..1821
Vincent, of Beauvais.   French Writer. (*Speculum Majus*)   — ..1264
Vincent, Augustine.   Herald.   Life by Sir N. H. Nico-
  las, 1827..   — ..1626
Vincent, Nathaniel.   Nonconformist Divine...........   — ..1697
Vincent, Thomas.   Nonconf. Divine; Writer on the Plague 1634..1678
Vincent, William.   Dean of Westminster.   Divine, Clas-
  sic, Historian. (*Voyage of Nearchus*) .... 1739..1815
Vincent Ferrier.   Spanish Dominican; Missionary.... 1357..1410
Vincent de Paul, St.   Founder of Sisters of Charity.
  Life by Capefigue, 1827; Abelly, 1839; Collet, tr. 1846 1576..1660
Vincentius Lirinensis.   French Priest. (*Commonitorium*) fl. 5th c.
Vinci, Leonardo da.   Italian Painter.   Life by Amaretti;
  J. W. Brown, 1828 .... 1452..1519?
Vinci, Leonardo da.   Italian Musical Composer .... 1690..1732?
Vineis, Petrus de.   *See* Vigne, Peter delle ....   — ..1249
Viner, Charles.   Founder of Vinerian Professorship .... 1680..1756
Vines, Rev. Richard.   Presbyterian Divine and Preacher   — ..1655
Vinet, Alexander Rodolphe, of Lausanne.   Divine. (*Vi-
  tal Christianity.*)   Life by E. Scherer, 1853......... 1797..1847
Vinet, Elias.   French Mathematician and Antiquary.... 1519?.1587
Vinkenbooms, or Vinkoboon, David.   Dutch Painter.. 1578..1629
Vinnen, or Vinnius, Arnold.   Dutch Jurist............ 1588..1657
Vinton, Mrs. Calesta Holman.   American Missionary... 1809..1864
Vinton, Justus Hatch.   American Missionary.......... 1806..1858
Viot, Mary Anne Henrietta Payan de l'Estang.   Fr. Writ. 1746..1802
Viotti, John Baptist.   Italian Violinist .... 1755..1824
Viret, Peter.   Swiss Protestant Divine .... 1511..1571
Virey, Julian Joseph.   French Writer on Medicine and
  Natural History.................................... 1775..1846
Virgil. (Publius Virgilius Maro.)   Roman Poet.   Life
  by Dean Chetwood; Warton, 1753 .... 70.19 B.C.
Virgilius.   Bishop of Saltzburg.......................   — .. 784
Viriathus.   Lusitanian Chief ....   — B.C.140
Visconti, Azzo.   Lord of Milan .... 1302..1339
Visconti, Ennius Quirinus.   Antiquary.............. 1751..1818
Visconti, Galeas.   Lord of Milan (1322-28) .... 1277..1328
Visconti, John, brother.   Archbishop.   Lord of Milan..   — ..1354
Visconti, John Baptist Anthony.   Italian Antiquary ... 1722..1784
Visconti, Louis Joachim Tullius.   Architect.......... 1791..1853
Visconti, Luchino.   Lord of Milan .... 1287?.1349
Visconti, Matthew.   *The Great.*   Lord of Milan .... 1250..1322
Visconti, Philip Aurelius.   Antiquary ....   — ..1831
Visin, or Von Visin, Denis Ivanovitch.   Russian Writer 1745..1792
Vitalianus.   Pope (657-72)............................   — .. 672?
Vitalis.   *Eric Sjöberg.*   Swedish Poet................ 1794..1828
Vitalis, Ordericus.   Historian 1075.aft.1143
Vite, John della.   *Miel.*   Flemish Painter .... 1599..1664
Vite, Timothy della, of Urbino.   Painter .... 1470?.1524?
Vitellius.   Roman Emperor (69, Jan. 2-Dec. 22)....... 15.. 69

	BORN.	DIED.

Vitellius, Cornelius. Italian Teacher of Greek at Oxford   fl. 1488
Vitello, or Vitellio. Polish Mathematician . . . .   fl. 1254?
Viton de Saint-Allais, Nicholas. French Genealogist.
   (*Dictionnaire de la Noblesse de France*) . . . . 1773. .1842
Vitringa, Campegius. Dutch Protestant Theologian.
   (*On Isaiah*). . . . . 1659. .1722
Vitringa, Campegius, son. (*Summary of Nat. Theology*) 1693. .1723
Vitruvius Pollio, Marcus. Roman Architectural Writer   fl. B.C. 27
Vitry, James de. Historian. . . . .   — . .1244
Vittoria Colonna. Scholar. Life by J. S. Harford, 1827 1490. .1547
Vittorino da Feltre. Italian Preceptor . . . . 1379. . —
Vivaldi, Anthony. Italian Violinist and Composer. . . . .   — . .1743
Vivares, Francis. French Engraver . . . . 1709. .1780
Vives, John Louis. Spanish Scholar and Writer . . . . . . 1492. .1540
Vivian, Richard Hussey, Lord. Gen. under Wellington 1775. .1842
Viviani, Vincent. Italian Mathematician . . . . 1622. .1703
Vivien, Joseph. French Painter . . . . 1657. .1734
Vlacq, Adrian. Dutch Mathematician and Printer . . . . .   fl. 1630
Vladimir. *The Great.* Grand Duke of Russia. . . . .   — . .1015
Vladimir Monomachos. Grand Duke of Kiev. . . . . . . 1053. .1126
Vladislas, or Wladislas. *See* Ladislaus.
Voeroesmarty, Michael. Hungarian Poet and Writer. . 1800. .1856
Voet, Daniel. Philosopher. (*Meletemata*) . . . . 1629. .1660
Voet, or Voetius, Gisbert. Dutch Theol. (*Dissert.Theol.*) 1589. .1677
Voet, John. Jurist at Leyden. (*On the Pandects*) . . . . . 1647. .1714
Voet, Paul. Jurist at Utrecht. (*Theologia Naturalis*). . 1619. .1667
Voet, Paul Eusebius. Physician and Poet at the Hague   — . .1778
Vogel, Dr. Edward. German Traveler in Africa; murdered 1829. .1856
Vogel, Theodore. Botanist of the Niger Expedition. . . .   — . .1841
Vogler, George Joseph. Abbé. Mus. Comp. and Writer 1749. .1814
Vogler, Valentine Henry, of Helmstadt. Medical Writer 1622. .1677
Voigt, Godfrey. Lutheran Divine. (*Altars of Primitive
   Christians*) . . . . 1644. .1682
Voisenon, Claude Henry de Fusée du. Dram. and Poet 1708. .1775
Voisin, Daniel Francis. Chancellor of France. . . . . 1656. .1718
Voisin, Joseph de. French Theologian and Hebraist. . . 1610?.1685
Voiture, Vincent. French Poet and Writer. (*Letters*). . 1598. .1648
Volanus, Andreas. Polish Protestant Writer. . . . . 1530. .1610
Volder, Burchel de. Dutch Philos. and Mathematician. 1643. .1709
Volkelius, John. Socinian. (*De Verá Religione*) . . . . . .   fl. 17th c.
Volkoff, Theodore Gregorievitch. Russian Dramatist . . 1729. .1763
Volmar, Isaac. German Statesman and Writer. . . . .   — . .1662
Volney, Constantine Francis Chassebœuf, Count de.
   French Traveler and Writer. . . . . 1757. .1820
Volpato, John. Italian Engraver. . . . . 1733. .1802
Volpi, John Anthony. Italian Latin Poet . . . . 1514. .1588
Volta, Alexander. Italian Physicist . . . . 1745. .1826
Voltaire (anagram of *Arouet, l. j.,* i. e., *Arouet, jun.*),
   Francis Mary Arouet de. Life by Condorcet, 1789; O.
   Goldsmith; F. H. Standish, 1804; Mazure, 1821; Long-
   champ and Wagnière, 1826; Francis Espinasse 1864 1694. .1778
Volterra, Daniel di. *Ricciarelli.* Italian Painter. . . . . . 1509. .1566
Volterrano. *See* Franceschini. Painter. . . . . 1621. .1689
Volusenus, Florentius. *Florence Wilson.* Scottish Poet
   and Scholar in France . . . . 1500?.1547

W.

BORN. DIED.

Waal, or Wael, Luke van. Painter .... 1591..1676
Wace, Robert. Anglo-Norman Poet. (*Le Brut; Roman de Rou*) .... 1112?.1184?
Wachler, John Frederick Louis. Ger. Literary Historian 1767..1838
Wächter, John George. Ger. Scholar and Archæologist 1673..1757
Waddell, James, D. D. American Clergyman .... 1739..1805
Wadham, Nicholas. Founder of College at Oxford.... — ..1610?
Wading, or Wadding, Luke. Irish Cordelier at Rome.
   (*Annales Ordinis Minorum*)........................ 1588..1657
Wading, Peter. Irish Jesuit; Latin Poet and Writer... 1580..1644
Wadington, Wm. of. Eng. Writer in French. (*Manuel*) fl. 1300?
Wadström, or Wadstroem, Charles Bernard. Swedish
   Traveler and Philanthropist..................... 1746..1799
Wadsworth, James. American Philanthropist .... 1768..1844
Wadsworth, James Samuel. American General....... 1807..1864
Wadsworth, Thos. Nonconf. (*Immortality of the Soul*) 1630..1676
Waechter, John George. Ger. Scholar and Archæologist 1673..1757
Wael, or Waal, Cornelius van. Battle Painter .... 1594..1662
Wael, or Waal, Luke van, brother. Painter........... 1591..1676
Wafer, Lionel. English Voyager and Adventurer...... fl. 1690
Waga, Theodore. Polish Historian................... 1739..1801
Wageman, Thomas Charles. Portrait Painter........ 1787?.1863
Wagenaar, John. Dutch Historian................... 1709..1773
Wagenseil, George Christopher. Harpsichord Composer 1688..1779
Wagenseil, John Christopher. Ger. Scholar and Polemic 1633..1705
Wager, Sir Charles. Admiral....................... 1666..1743
Waghorn, Thos., Lt. R. N. Originator of Overland Route 1800..1850
Wagner, John Jas., of Zurich. (*Hist. Naturalis Helvetiæ*) 1641..1695
Wagner, Rudolph. Writer on Natural History .... 1814?.1864
Wagstaff, Thomas. Nonjuring Bishop................ 1645..1712
Wagstaff, William. Physician and Humorous Writer.. 1685..1725
Wahlenberg, George. German Botanist............. 1784..1814
Wailly, Charles de. French Architect .... 1729..1798
Wailly, Noel Francis de. French Grammarian .... 1724..1801
Wailly, Stephen Augustin de, son .... 1770..1821
Wainwright, Jonathan Mayhew, D. D. Protestant Epis-
   copal Bishop of New York; Writer................ 1792..1854
Waithman, Robert, M. P. Alderman; Popular Champion 1765..1833
Wake, Sir Isaac. Political Writer. (*Rex Platonicus*)... 1575?.1632
Wake, William. Archbishop of Canterbury (1716-37).. 1657..1737
Wakefield, Edward. Polit. Econ. (*Account of Ireland*) 1768?.1854
Wakefield, Edward Gibbon. Political Economist...... 1796?.1862
Wakefield, Rev. Gilbert. Scholar. (*Memoirs*)........ 1756..1801
Wakefield, Mrs. Priscilla. Writer of Juvenile Works.. 1750..1832
Wakefield, Robt. Heb. Prof. at Oxford. (*On Ecclesiastes*) — ..1537
Wakley, Thomas. Coroner; Editor of the *Lancet* ..... 1795?.1862
Walæus, Anthony. Dutch Protestant Divine.......... 1573..1639
Walæus, John. Dutch Anatomist.................... 1604..1649
Walafridus. *Strabo*. Ger. Monk; Div. & Poet. (*Hortulus*) 807.. 849?
Walbaum, John Julius. German Physician & Naturalist 1724..1799
Walch, Christian William Francis. Divine........... 1726..1784
27

BORN. DIED.

Walch, John Ernest Emanuel. Divine and Naturalist... 1725..1778
Walch, John George. German Divine and Scholar .... 1693..1775
Walckenaër, Charles Athanasius, Baron. French Savant
   and Author.. 1771..1852
Walckenaër, Louis Gaspar, and John. See Valckenaër.
Waldeck, Christian Augustus, Prince of. Austrian Gen. 1744..1798
Waldegrave, James, 2d Earl of. Statesman. (*Memoirs*) 1715..1763
Waldemar I. King of Denmark (1157–81?). *The Great* 1131..1181
Waldemar II. (1202–41.) *The Victorious* .... 1170..1241
Waldemar III., or IV. (1326–73) .... — ..1375
Waldensis, Thomas. *Netter.* Eng. Carmelite; Statesman 1367?.1430
Waldis, Burchard. German Fabulist .... — ..1554
Waldo, Daniel. American Clergyman .... 1762..1864
Waldo, or Valdo, Peter, of Lyons. Reformer .... — ..1179
Waldstein. *See* Wallenstein .... 1583..1634
Wale, Samuel. Painter and Designer.................. — ..1786
Wales, William. Mathematician and Astronomer...... 1734?.1798
Walker, Adam. Astronomical Lecturer and Writer.... 1731..1821
Walker, Clement. (*History of Independency*) .... 1599?.1651
Walker, Sir Edward. Garter King-at-Arms. (*Iter
   Carolinum*) .... 1610?.1677
Walker, George. Puritan Divine .... 1581..1651
Walker, George. Defender and Bishop of Derry....... — ..1690
Walker, George, F. R. S. Dissenting Divine and Mathem. 1734?.1807
Walker, George Washington, of Hobart Town. Quaker
   Minister. Life by Backhouse and Taylor, 1862 ..... 1800..1859
Walker, Rev. John, of Exeter. (*Sufferings of the Clergy*) — ..1730?
Walker, John. (*Critical Pronouncing Dictionary*)...... 1732..1807
Walker, John, M. D. (*Gazetteer*)..................... 1759..1830
Walker, Joseph Cooper. Irish Writer. (*Irish Bards*) .. 1766?.1810
Walker, Rev. Obadiah. Roman Catholic Master of Uni-
   versity College, Oxford .... 1616..1699
Walker, Robert. Portrait Painter..................... — ..1660?
Walker, Rev. Samuel, of Truro. Divine. Life by Sidney 1714..1761
Walker, Sears Cook. Amer. Mathematician and Astron. 1805..1853
Walker, Thomas. Actor and Dramatist .... 1698..1743
Walker, Thos. Magistrate & Humorist. (*The Original*) 1784..1836
Walker, Rev. William. Writer on Grammar & Rhetoric 1623..1684
Walker, William. American Adventurer .... 1824..1860
Walker, William Sydney. Poet. L. by J. Moultrie, 1852 1795.. —
Wall, John, M. D., of Worcester. Physician .... 1708..1776
Wall, Martin, M. D. Professor at Oxford .... 1744..1824
Wall, William, D. D. (*Infant Baptism*)................ 1646..1728
Wallace, Horace Binney. American Author .... 1817..1852
Wallace, Sir William. Scottish Patriot and Soldier. Life
   by Carrick; J. S. Watson, 1862.................... 1270?.1305
Wallace, William. Prof. of Mathematics at Edinburgh 1768..1843
Wallace, William Harvey Lamb. American General .. 1810..1862
Wallace, William Vincent. Musical Composer .... 1815?.1865
Wallack, James William. English Actor in America... 1795..1864
Wallenstein, Albert Wenzel Eusebius von, Count. Im-
   perial General against Gustavus Adolphus. Life by
   F. Förster, 1834; Colonel Mitchel, 1839 .... 1583..1634
Waller, Edmund. Poet .... 1605..1687
Waller, Rev. John Lightfoot, LL. D. American Editor .. 1809..1854

BORN. DIED.

Waller, Sir William. Parliamentarian General........ 1597.·.1668
Wallerius, John Gottschalk. Swedish Chem. & Mineral. 1709..1785
Wallerius, Nicholas. Swedish Philosopher and Divine 1706..1764
Wallich, Nathaniel, M. D. Botanist................. 1786..1854
Wallin, John Olof. Swedish Poet and Preacher....... 1779..1839
Wallis, John. Divine, Mathematician, and Decipherer 1616..1703
Wallis, Joshua. Landscape Painter .... 1789?.1862
Wallis, Samuel. Navigator .... — ..1795
Wallius, James, of Courtrai. Jesuit; Latin Poet....... 1599..1680?
Walmesley, Charles, D. D. Rom. Cath. Div. & Mathem. 1721..1797
Walpole, Horace, 4th Earl of Orford, youngest son of Sir
    Robert. (*Noble Authors.*) Life by Coxe; Macaulay 1717..1797
Walpole, Horatio, Lord. Diplom.; Hist. and Polit. Writer 1678..1757
Walpole, Sir Robert, brother. Premier. Life by Coxe 1676..1745
Walsh, Edward, M. D. Army Physician & Poetical Writer — ..1832
Walsh, John, of Cork. Writer on Mathematics .... 1786..1847
Walsh, Peter. Irish Roman Catholic Controversialist .. 1610..1687
Walsh, Robert. American Author and Journalist...... 1784..1858
Walsh, William. Critic and Poet .... 1663?.1708
Walsingham, Sir Francis. Secretary of State......... 1536..1590
Walsingham, Thomas. Historian .... fl. ab. 1440
Walstein. *See* Wallenstein .... 1583..1634
Walter, Hubert. Archbishop of Canterbury (1193-1205) — ..1205
Walter, Rev. Henry. (*History of England*)............ 1785..1859
Walter, John. Logographic Printer. Originator of *Times* 1739..1812
Walter, John, son. Proprietor and Manager of the *Times* 1784..1847
Walter, John Theophilus. German Anatomist .... 1739..1818
Walters, John. Welsh Divine and Lexicographer..... — ..1797
Waltham, John of. Bishop of Salisbury; Treasurer to
    Richard II.. — ..1395
Waltham, Roger of. Schoolman .... fl. ti. Hen. III.
Waltheof. Son of Siward, Earl of Northumberland.... — ..1075
Walther, Augustine Frederick. Anat. & Bot. at Leyden 1688..1746
Walther, Balthasar. *Waltherus*, or *Gualterus*. Orientalist — ..1640
Walther, Bernard, of Nuremberg. Astronomer .... 1430..1504
Walther, Christian. German Divine & Corrector of Press — ..1572?
Walther, Christian. German Divine at Königsberg.... 1655..1717
Walther, Christopher Theodosius. Miss. to Tranquebar 1699..1741
Walther, George Christopher. German Jurist......... 1601..1656
Walther, Henry Andrew. German Protestant Theologian 1696..1748
Walther, John Godfrey. (*Musical Lexicon*).......... 1684..1748
Walther, John Ludolph. (*Lexicon Diplomaticum*)...... fl. 18th c.
Walther, Michael. Professor at Helmstädt. (*Harmonia
    Biblica*)... 1593..1662
Walther, Rodolphus. *Gualterus*. Swiss Protestant Theol. 1519..1586
Walther von der Vogelweide. German Minnesinger 1170?.1228?
Walton, Brian. Bp. Chester. (*Polyglot.*) L. by Todd, 1821 1600..1661
Walton, George. American Patriot.................. 1740?.1804
Walton, Izaak. (*Complete Angler.*) Life by Sir J. Haw-
    kins, 1760; Dr. Zouch, 1816; Sir H. Nicolas, 1836;
    W. Dowling....................................... 1593..1683
Wanley, Humphrey. Antiquary.................... 1672..1726
Wanley, Rev. Nathaniel. (*Wonders of the Little World*) 1633..1680
Wansleben, John Michael. Orientalist .... 1635..1679
Warbeck, Perkin. Pretender to the Crown of England — ·.1499

BORN. DIED.

Warburton, Eliot Bartholomew George. Author. (*Crescent and Cross*)................................. 1810..1852

Warburton, John. Heraldic Writer and Antiquary. (*Vallum Romanum*).............................. 1682..1759

Warburton, William. Bishop of Gloucester. (*Divine Legation.*) Life by Hurd, 1795; J. S. Watson ...... 1698..1779

Ward, Artemas. American Revolutionary General..... 1727..1800

Ward, Edward. Burlesque Poet. (*London Spy*)....... 1667..1731

Ward, Sir Henry George. Minister to Mexico. Governor of the Ionian Islands and Ceylon.................. 1798?.1860

Ward, James, R. A. Painter.......................... 1770..1859

Ward, James Harman. American Naval Officer....... 1806..1861

Ward, John, LL. D. Writer. (*Lives of Gresham Professors.*) Life by Thomas Birch, 1766 .... 1679..1758

Ward, Rev. Nathaniel. (*Simple Cobbler of Agawam*)... 1570?.1653

Ward, Robert Plumer. Novelist, Hist. Writer, and Publicist. (*Tremaine; Diary.*) L. by Edmund Phipps, 1850 1765..1846

Ward, Samuel, D. D. Margaret Professor. Theologian — ..1643

Ward, Seth. Bishop of Salisbury. Mathematician and Astronomer. Life by Dr. Walter Pope, 1697........ 1617..1689

Ward, Thomas. Roman Catholic Poet. (*England's Reformation*)................................. — ..1689?

Ward, William. Missionary in India; Author. Life by Marshman, 1863................................. 1769..1823

Wardlaw, Elizabeth, Lady. Poet. (*Hardyknute*) ..... 1677..1727

Wardlaw, Henry. Bishop of St. Andrew's............ — ,1440

Wardlaw, Ralph, D. D. Div. L. by Dr. W. L. Alexander 1779..1853

Ware, Henry, D. D. American Divine .... 1764..1845

Ware, Henry, Jr., D. D., son. Divine and Author. Life by Dr. John Ware, 1846 .... 1794..1843

Ware, Sir James. Irish Antiquary .... 1594..1666

Ware, James. Oculist .... 1755..1815

Ware, Robert. Controversial Writer .... — ..1696

Ware, Rev. William. Author. (*Zenobia*) .... 1797..1852

Wargentin, Peter William. Swedish Mathematician .. 1717..1783

Warham, William. Archbishop of Canterbury (1504–32) — ..1532

Warin, John. Flemish Sculptor and Engraver .... 1604..1672

Waring, Edward, M. D. Mathematician.............. 1736..1798

Warneford, Rev. Samuel Wilson. Founder & Benefactor 1758..1855

Warner, Rev. Ferdinando, LL. D. Compiler and Writer 1703..1768

Warner, John. Bishop of Rochester. Founder........ 1585?.1666

Warner, Rev. John. Divine and Writer. (*Metronariston*) 1736..1800

Warner, Joseph. Surgeon .... 1717..1801

Warner, Richard. Botanist. (*Plantæ Woodfordienses*) 1711..1775

Warner, William. Poet. (*Albion's England*)......... 1558?.1609

Warren, Charles. Engraver......................... — ..1823

Warren, James. American Revolutionary Patriot ..... 1726..1808

Warren, John, M. D. American Physician .... 1753..1815

Warren, Sir John Borlase. Admiral and Plenipotentiary 1754..1822

Warren, John Collins, M. D. Physician and Writer. Life by Dr. Edward Warren, 1859..................... 1778..1856

Warren, Joseph. American Revolutionary Patriot. Life by A. H. Everett................................. 1741..1775

Warren, Mrs. Mercy. American Authoress. (*History of the American Revolution*) .... 1728..1814

BORN. DIED.

Warren, Sir Peter. Admiral........................ 1703..1752
Warrington, Lewis. American Naval Officer......... 1782..1851
Warton, Ann. Poetess............................. — ..1685
Warton, Sir George. Astrologer and Loyalist........ 1617..1681
Warton, Joseph, D. D. Master of Winchester. Poet and
  Critic. Editor of Pope. Life by Rev. John Wooll, 1806 1722..1800
Warton, Thomas. Prof. of Poetry at Oxford (1718–28).. 1687..1745
Warton, Thomas, son. Poet & Critic. Professor of Poetry
  (1756–66). (*Hist. of English Poetry.*) L. by Mant, 1802 1728..1790
Warwick, Edward Plantagenet, Earl of. (*Last of the
  Plantagenets.*) Beheaded by Henry VII............. — ..1499
Warwick, Henry de Beauchamp, 13th Earl and 1st Duke
  of, K. G. King of Isle of Wight, Jersey, and Guernsey — ..1444
Warwick, John Dudley, Earl of, Duke of Northumber-
  land. Beheaded.................................. 1502..1553
Warwick, Sir Philip. Political Writer and Historian .. 1608..1683
Warwick, Richard de Beauchamp, Twelfth Earl of, K. G.
  The Good. Regent of France; died at Rouen........ — ..1439
Warwick, Richard Neville, Earl of. *King Maker.* Fell·
  at Barnet....................................... 1420?.1471
Waser, Anna. Swiss Miniature Painter.............. 1679..1713
Washington, Bushrod. American Jurist.............. 1759..1829
Washington, George. First President of the United
  States. Life by Marshall, 1805 (revised and abridged,
  1832); D. Ramsay, 1807; Jared Sparks, 1839; Wash-
  ington Irving; 1859; C. W. Upham, 1851; Dr. Aaron
  Bancroft; James K. Paulding; J. T. Headley; Mrs.
  C. M. Kirkland; Edward Everett................... 1732..1799
Washington, William Augustine. American Revolu-
  tionary Officer................................... 1752..1810
Wasse, Christopher. English Greek Scholar and Transl. — ..1690
Watelet, Claude Henry. French Writer.............. 1718..1786
Waterhouse, Benjamin, M. D. Amer. Phys. and Author 1754..1846
Waterhouse, Edward. Heraldic & Miscellaneous Writer 1619..1670
Waterland, Daniel, D. D. Theologian. L. by Van Mildert 1683..1740
Waterloo, Anthony. Dutch Landscape Painter........ 1618?.1682
Waterton, Charles. Naturalist & Traveler. (*Wanderings*) 1782..1865
Watkinson, David. Amer. Merchant and Philanthropist 1778..1857
Wats, Gilbert. Divine and Translator.............. 1600..1657
Watson, Caroline. Engraver....................... 1760?.1814
Watson, Charles. Vice-Admiral. Coadjutor of Clive .. 1714..1757
Watson, David. Translator of Horace. (*Heathen Gods*) 1710..1756
Watson, Elkanah. American Merchant and Agricul-
  turist. Life by self.............................. 1758..1842
Watson, Henry. Colonel. Mathematician and Engineer 1735..1786
Watson, Henry. Anatomist......................... 1702?.1793
Watson, John. Bishop of Winchester .... 1520?.1584
Watson, Rev. John. (*History of Halifax*)............ 1724..1783
Watson, John Fanning. Amer. Antiquary and Annalist 1780..1860
Watson, Richard. Bishop of Llandaff. Natural Philos-
  opher and Theologian. (*Apology for Bible.*) Life by
  self and son, 1817............................... 1737..1816
Watson, Richard. Clergyman and Author. Life by T.
  Jackson .... 1781..1833
Watson, Dr. Robert. Historian. (*Philip II. and III.*) 1730?.1781?

BORN. DIED.

Watson, Thomas. Ejected Nonconformist Divine. (*Body of Divinity*).................................... — ..1690[?]
Watson, William. Secular Priest; hanged. (*Decacordon*) — ..1603
Watson, Sir William. Botanist and Electrician....... 1715..1787
Watson, William R. American Politician and Writer.. 1799..1864
Watt, Gregory. Geologist......................... 1777..1804
Watt, James. Scottish Mechanician, Engineer, and Inventor; Improver of the Steam Engine. Life by G. Williamson, 1856; J. P. Muirhead, 1858............ 1736..1819
Watt, James, son. Mechanical Engineer............. 1769..1848
Watt, Robert, M. D. Bibliog. (*Bibliotheca Britannica*) 1774..1819
Watteau, Anthony. French Painter.................. 1684..1721
Wattier-Ziesenis, Madame. Dutch Tragic Actress ... 1762..1827
Watts, Alaric Alexander. Writer.................... 1799..1864
Watts, Isaac, D. D. Divine and Poet. (*Hymns.*) Life by Samuel Palmer, 1785; Thomas Gibbons; Dr. Johnson; Robert Southey............................. 1674..1748
Wayland, Rev. Francis, D. D. Amer. Educator & Author 1796..1865
Wayne, Anthony. American Revolutionary General. Life by Armstrong.............................. 1745..1796
Wayneflete, William of. Bishop of Winchester and Lord Chancellor. Life by R. Chandler, 1811............. — ..1486
Weale, John. London Publisher and Editor.......... 1792..1862
Weaver, or Weever, John. Antiq. (*Funeral Monuments*) 1576..1632
Weaver, Thomas. Geologist........................ — ..1855
Webb, Daniel. (*Beauties of Poetry*)............... — ..1798
Webb, Philip Barker. Scholar and Botanist.......... — ..1854
Webb, Philip Carteret. Antiquary.................. 1700..1770
Webbe, Samuel. Musical Composer. (*Glorious Apollo*) 1740..1817
Webber, Charles Wilkins. American Author......... 1819..1856
Webber, John. Draughtsman. Companion of Cook.. 1751..1793
Webber, Samuel. Amer. Educator; Pres. of Harv. Coll. 1759..1810
Weber, Charles Maria Frederick Ernest, Baron von. German Composer. Life by Herr von Weber, 1864.. 1786..1826
Weber, Henry William, of Edinburgh. Archæological & Miscel. Writer. (*Flodden Field; Metrical Romances*) 1783..1813
Webster, Daniel. American Statesman and Jurist..... 1782..1852
Webster, Ebenezer. American Patriot .... 1739..1806
Webster, Ezekiel, son. American Lawyer............ 1780..1829
Webster, John. Dramatic Poet. (*Duchess of Malfy*).. 17th c.
Webster, Noah, LL. D. American Philologist and Writer. (*Dictionary.*) Life by C. A. Goodrich.............. 1758..1843
Webster, William. Mathematician. (*Arithmetic*)..... 1684[?].1744
Webster, William. Polemical Writer .... 1689..1758
Wechel, Andrew. French Printer at Basle........... 1510[?].1581
Wechel, Christian. French Printer.................. —aft.1552
Wedderburn, Alexander, Earl of Rosslyn. Jurist and Statesman; Lord Chancellor .... 1733..1805
Wedel, Ernest Henry. Phys. (*De Morbis Concionatorum*) 1671..1709
Wedel, George Wolfgang. Ger. Med. Writer and Astrol. 1645..1721
Wedel, John Adolphus, brother. Medical Writer.... 1675.aft.1746
Wedel, Dr. John Wolfgang, of Jena. Botanist........ 1708..1757
Wedgwood, Josiah. Potter. Life by Moteyard; Jewitt 1730..1795
Weems, Rev. Mason L. American Writer............ — ..1825
Weeninx, John. Dutch Painter. *The Young*........ 1644..1719

BORN. DIED.

Weeninx, or Weenix, John Bapt. Dutch Paint. *The Old* 1621..1660
Weever, or Weaver, John. Antiq. (*Funeral Monuments*) 1576..1632
Wegscheider, Julius Augustus Louis. Ger. Theologian 1771..1849
Weidler, John Frederick. Ger. Mathem. and Astronomer 1691..1755
Weigel, Christian Ehrenfried. Ger. Phys., Chem., Bot. fl. 1772
Weigel, Ehrard. German Mathematician and Astronomer 1625..1699
Weigel, Valentine. German Mystic .... 1533..1588
Weimar, Anne Amelia, Duchess of .... 1739..1807
Weinbrenner, Frederick. German Architect .... 1766..1826
Weishaupt, Adam. Founder of the Illuminati........ 1748..1830
Weisse, Christian Ernest. German Jurist............. 1766..1832
Weisse, Christian Felix. German Poet and Dramatist.
    (*Children's Friend*) .... 1726..1804
Welby, Amelia B. American Poetess .... 1821..1852
Welby, Henry. Recluse........................... — ..1636
Welchman, Edward. Archdeacon. (*Thirty-nine Articles*) 1665..1739
Weld, Thomas. Cardinal .... 1773..1837
Weldon, John. Composer of Cathedral Music........ 1670?.1736
Wellbeloved, Rev. Charles. Antiquary. (*Eburacum*).. 1769..1858
Wellens, James Thomas Joseph. Bishop of Antwerp.
    Scholar and Divine.............................. 1726..1784
Weller, James. Theol. and Orientalist at Wittemberg 1602..1664
Weller, Jerome. Biblical Commentator; Friend of Luther 1499..1572
Wellesley, Richard Cowley, Marquess of. Statesman;
    Commander in India and Governor-General. Life by
    R. R. Pearce, 1846 .... 1760..1842
Wellington, Arthur Wellesley, brother, Duke of. Sol-
    dier and Statesman. Life by W. H. Maxwell, 1839;
    Macfarlane, 1851; Yonge; Brialmont, translated by
    · Gleig; Lieutenant-Colonel Williams .... 1769..1852
Wells, Rev. Edward. (*Bible Geography*).............. — ..1727
Wells, Horace. American Dentist; Claimant of the Dis-
    covery of Anæsthesia.............................. 1815..1848
Wells, William Charles. American Physician. (*Experi-
    mental Philosophy*)................................ 1757..1817
Wellwood, Sir Henry Moncrieff, D. D. Scottish Divine 1750..1827
Wellwood, Thomas, M. D. (*Memoirs of Eng.*, 1588–1688) 1652..1716
Welsh, David, D. D. Professor at Edinburgh. Founder
    of *North British Review* .... 1794?.1845
Welsted, Leonard. Poet and Miscellaneous Writer.... 1689..1747
Wenceslaus, or Wenzel, St. Duke of Bohemia....... 908.. 936
Wenceslaus, or Wenzel. Emperor of Germany and
    King of Bohemia................................. 1361..1419
Wendover, Roger de. Historian .... — ..1237
Wentworth, Benning. Governor of New Hampshire.. 1696..1770
Wentworth, John. American Patriot................ 1719..1781
Wentworth, John. Eng. Lawyer. (*System of Pleading*) 1768..1816
Wentworth, Sir John. Governor of New Hampshire,
    and afterwards of Nova Scotia .... 1736..1820
Wentworth, Sir Thomas, Earl of Strafford. *Thorough* 1593..1641
Wepfer, John James. German Medical Writer........ 1620..1695
Werden, The Meister von. Painter .... fl. 1643–90
Werder, Thierry von. Translator of Ariosto.......... 1584..1657
Werdin, John Philip, or Paulin de St. Barthélemi, *q. v.*... 1748..1806
Werdmuller, John Rodolph. Swiss Painter.......... 1639..1668

BORN. DIED.

Werenfels, Peter. Theologian at Basle .... 1627..1703
Werenfels, Samuel, son, of Basle. Theologian and
   Scholar. (*De Logomachiis Eruditorum*) .... 1657..1740
Werf, Adrian van der, of Rotterdam. Painter......... 1659..1722
Werf, Peter van der, brother. Historical Painter ...... 1665..1718
Wergeland, Henry Arnold. Norweg. Poet & Polit.Writ. 1808..1845
Werkmeister, Andrew. Ger. Mus. Comp. and Writer 1645..1706
Werl, Olaf. *Verelius.* Swedish Antiquary........... 1618..1682
Werner, Abraham Gottlob. Ger. Geol. and Mineralogist 1750..1817
Werner, Frederick Louis Zacharias. German Dramatist 1768..1823
Werner, John. Ger. Mathem. (*Annotations on Ptolemy*) 1468..1528
Werner, Joseph. Swiss Painter .... 1637..1710
Werner, Paul de. Prussian General................. 1707..1785
Wesenbeck, Matthew. Flemish Jurist in Germany.... 1531..1586
Wesley, Rev. Charles. (*Hymns.*) Life by Whitehead, 1793 1708..1788
Wesley, Charles, son. Musical Performer............. 1757..1815
Wesley, Rev. John. Founder of Methodism. Life by
   Hampson, 1791; J. A. Colet, 1791; Dr. Coke and H.
   Moore, 1792; Richard Watson; Whitehead, 1796; R.
   Southey, 1820; G. Smith. .... 1703..1791
Wesley, Rev. Samuel, of Epworth. Poetical Writer ... 1662?.1735
Wesley, Rev. Sam., son. Mast. of Tiverton School. Poet 1692?.1739
Wesley, Samuel. Sacred Music Composer............ 1766..1837
Wesselényi, Miklós, Baron. Hungarian Statesman.... 1797..1850
Wesseling, Peter. German Philologist .... 1692..1764
Wesselus, John, of Groningen. Divine and Philosopher 1419?.1489
Wessenberg, Ignatius Henry Charles, Baron von. Ger-
   man Roman Catholic Theologian .... 1774..1860
West, Benjamin. Historical Painter. Life by John Galt 1738..1820
West, Elizabeth. Scottish Mystic. Life by self........ 1672?.1735
West, Gilbert. Poet & Transl.; Friend of Lord Lyttelton 1705?.1756
West, James, M. P., of Alscot. Antiquary .... — ..1772
West, Mrs. Jane. Novelist, Poet, Miscellaneous Writer 1759?.1852
West, Nathaniel, D. D. American Presbyterian Divine 1794..1864
West, Stephen, D. D. American Clergyman and Writer 1735..1819
West, Thomas. Topographical Writer. (*Hist. of Furness*) 1716..1779
Westall, Richard, R. A. Historical Painter and Illus-
   trator of Books.................................... 1765..1836
Westall, William, R. A., br. Designer for Engravings .. 1781..1850
Westfield, Thomas. Bp. of Bristol. Divine & Preacher — ..1644
Westmacott, Sir Richard, R. A. *The Elder.* Sculptor 1775..1856
Westmoreland, John Fane, Eleventh Earl of. General
   and Diplomatist. Musician...................... 1784..1859
Westmoreland, Mildmay Fane, Second Earl of. Poet.
   (*Otia Sacra*)................................... 1600?.1665
Weston, Elizabeth Jane. Scholar and Writer.... 1586 or 7 .aft.1605
Weston, Richard. Horticulturist .... 1732..1806
Weston, Stephen. Classical Scholar and Orientalist.... 1747..1830
Weston, Thomas. Comic Actor .... — ..1776
Weston, William. Rector of Camden. Divine........ — ..1760
Wetherell, Sir Charles. Chancery Lawyer; Recorder
   of Bristol... 1770..1846
Wetherell, Sir Charles .... — ..1864
Wetstein, John Henry. Scholar and Printer.......... 1649..1726
Wetstein, John James. Writer on Greek Testament... 1693..1754

BORN. DIED.

Wetstein, John Rodolph, of Basle. Greek Scholar and
Theologian .... 1647..1711
Wette, William Martin Leberecht de. *See* De Wette... 1780..1849
Wewitzer, Ralph. Comic Actor .... 1748..1824
Weyde, Roger van der. *Roger of Bruges.* Painter.... 1455?.1529
Weyermans, Jacob Kampo. Dutch Fruit & Flower Paint. 1679..1747
Weyse, Christopher Ernest Frederick. Musical Composer 1774..1842
Whalley, Edward. Regicide Judge .... — ..1674?
Whalley, Rev. Peter. Divine and Critic .... 1722..1791
Wharton, Sir George. Loyalist and Astrologer........ 1617..1681
Wharton, Rev. Henry. Writer. (*Anglia Sacra*) ...... 1664..1695
Wharton, Philip, Duke of. Poet; described by Pope... 1698..1731
Wharton, Thomas, M. D. Anatomist .... 1610..1673
Wharton, Thos., Marquess of. Statesman. (*Lillibulero*) 1640?.1715
Whately, Richard. Archbishop of Dublin. (*Logic*) ... 1787..1863
Whately, Rev. William. Divine. (*Sermons*) .... 1583..1639
Wheare, Degory. Historical Writer.................. 1573..1647
Wheatley, Rev. Chas. (*On the Book of Common Prayer*) 1686..1742
Wheatley, Francis, R. A. Painter.................... 1747..1801
Wheatley, Phillis. Negro Poetess .... 1753?.1794
Wheaton, Henry. American Jurist and Diplomatist.
(*International Law; History of the Northmen*) .... 1785..1848
Wheelock, Eleazar, D. D. Founder and First President
of Dartmouth College............................. 1711..1779
Wheelock, John, LL. D., son. Second President of Dart-
mouth College................................... 1754..1817
Wheelwright, John. Amer. Clergyman. (*Vindication*) 1594..1679
Wheler, or Wheeler, Rev. Sir George. Learned Traveler 1650..1724
Whethamstede, John. Abbot of St. Alban's. Chronicler — ..1464
Whetstone, George. Writer in Prose and Verse ...... ti. Eliz.
Whichcote, Benjamin, D. D. Divine .... 1610..1683
Whipple, Abraham. American Naval Officer .... 1733..1819
Whipple, William. American General................ 1730..1785
Whistler, George Washington. American Engineer... 1800..1849
Whiston, William. Divine and Philosopher. (*Josephus.*)
Life by self, 1749 .... 1667..1752
Whitaker, Edward W. Div. & Hist. (*The Prophecies*) 1750..1818
Whitaker, Rev. John. Divine and Antiquary. (*History
of Manchester*).................................. 1735?.1808
Whitaker, Rev. Thos. Dunham, LL. D. Topog. Historian 1759..1821
Whitaker, William. Master of St. John's, Cambridge.. 1547..1595
Whitbread, Samuel, M. P. Brewer................... 1720?.1796
Whitbread, Samuel, M. P., son. Brewer. Politician. 1758..1815
Whitby, Daniel, D. D. Divine. (*Paraphrase on New
Testament.*) Life by Dr. Sykes.................... 1638..1726
White, Francis. Bishop of Ely. Writer against Popery 1577..1638
White, George. Engraver........................... — ..1734?
White, Rev. Gilbert, of Selborne. (*Nat. Hist. of Selborne*) 1720..1793
White, Rev. Henry, of Lichfield; Friend of Dr. Johnson — ..1836
White, Henry Kirke. Poet. Life by Southey; Sir H.
Nicolas .... 1785..1806
White, Hugh Lawson. American Statesman.......... 1773..1840
White, James. Poet................................ — ..1790
White, Rev. James. Dramatist and Historian. (*Eighteen
Christian Centuries*)............................. 1785..1862

BORN. DIED.

White, Jeremy. Nonconformist Divine. (*Restoration of all Things*)...................................... 1629..1707
White, or Whyte, John. Bishop of Winchester. Anti-Reformer.. 1511..1560
White, John. *Century White*. Nonconformist Lawyer 1590..1645
White, Rev. John. *Patriarch of Dorchester*.......... 1574..1648
White, Rev. Joseph, D. D. Prof. of Hebrew. Orientalist 1746..1814
White, Rev. Joseph Blanco. Spanish Priest and English Author. Life by self and J. H. Thom, 1845......... 1775..1841
White, Peregrine. First Child born in New England of English Parents................................. 1620..1704
White, or Vitus, Richard. Historian and Roman Catholic Divine. (*Historia Britanniæ*).................... — ..1612
White, Robert. Engraver........................... 1645..1704
White, Sir Thomas. Founder of St. John's Coll., Oxford 1492..1566
White, Thomas. Founder of Sion College, London..... 1550?.1624
White, Thomas. *Anglus*, or *Albius*. Philosopher and Roman Catholic Priest........................... 1582..1676
White, Thomas. Philosopher; Friend of Hobbes...... — ..1696
White, William, D. D. Protestant Episcopal Bishop of Pennsylvania. Life by Dr. Bird Wilson, 1839...... 1748..1836
Whitefield, Rev. George. Methodist Preacher. Life by R. Philip; Gillies, 1772............................ 1714..1770
Whitehead, David. Divine. Chaplain to Anne Boleyn — ..1571
Whitehead, George. Quaker........................ 1636..1723
Whitehead, John. Physician and Wesleyan Preacher. (*History of Methodism*)........................... — ..1804
Whitehead, Paul. Poet and Satirist. Life by Captain Edward Thomson............................... 1709..1774
Whitehead, William. Poet. Life by Mason, 1788..... 1715..1785
Whitehurst, John. Philosopher. Life by Dr. Hutton.. 1713..1788
Whitelock, Bulstrode. Lawyer and Statesman. (*Memorials of English Affairs*)..................... 1605..1676
Whitelock, Sir James. Judge...................... 1570..1632
Whitfield, Dr. John Clarke. Prof. of Music at Cambridge — ..1836
Whitgift, John. Archbishop of Canterbury. Life by Sir George Paule, 1699; Strype, 1718; W. D. Garrow, 1818 (in *History of Croydon*)................... 1530..1604
Whiting, Henry. American General................. — ..1851
Whitlock, Mrs. Elizabeth. Actress................. 1761..1836
Whitney, Eli. American Inventor................... 1765..1825
Whittemore, Amos. American Inventor............. 1759..1828
Whittemore, Rev. Thos., D. D. Amer. Journalist & Writ. 1800..1861
Whittingham, Sir Samuel Ford. General............. — ..1841
Whittingham, William. Puritan Dean of Durham.... 1524..1589
Whittington, Sir Richard. Lord Mayor of London... fl. 1393–1419
Whittington, Robert. Grammarian.............. 1480?.aft.1530
Whittlesey, Frederick. American Jurist............. 1799..1851
Whitworth, Chas., Ld. Diplomatist. (*Account of Russia*) 1688?.1725
Whitworth, Charles, Earl, grandson. Diplomatist..... 1754..1825
Whyte, Robert. Composer of Church Services........ — ..1581?
Whytt, Robert, F. R. S., M. D. Scottish Medical Writer 1714..1766
Wiboldus. Abbot of Corvey. Statesman and Writer.. — ..1158
Wichmann, John Ernest. German Medical Writer. (*Ideen zur Diagnostik*)........................... 1740..1804

BORN. DIED.

Wiclif. See Wycliffe............................... 1324?.1384
Wicquefort, Abraham de. Dutch Statesman and Diplo-
  matist. (*L'Ambassadeur et ses Fonctions*)........... 1598..1682
Wida, Herman de. Abp. of Cologne (1515–47). Reformer — ..1552
Widdrington, William, Fourth Lord. Scottish Jacobite 1701..1743?
Widekindi, John. Swedish Historian............... 1620?.1678
Widmanstadt, John Albert. Editor of Syriac New Test. — ..1559?
Wiebeking, Charles Frederick. Pomeranian Engineer.. 1762..1842
Wieland, Christopher Martin. German Poet. (*Oberon.*)
  Life by Gruber, 1816; Doering, 1840 .... 1733..1813
Wier, John. Ger. Med. Writ. (*De Dæmonûm Præstigiis*) 1515..1588
Wiertz, Anthony. Belgian Painter.................. 1806..1865
Wiffen, Jeremiah Holme. Translator and Author. (*Rus-*
  sell Family).................................... 1792..1856
Wigand, John. German Protestant Divine .... 1523..1587
Wightman, Sir William. Judge.................... — ..1863
Wilberforce, Rev. Robert Isaac. Author............ 1802..1857
Wilberforce, William, M. P. Philanthropist and States-
  man. (*Practical View.*) Life by sons .... 1759..1833
Wilbrord, or Willibrod, St. Apostle of the Frisians.... 657?. 738?
Wilbye, John. Musical Composer. (*Madrigals*)...... fl. 1600
Wilcocks, Joseph. Philanthropist and Writer......... 1723..1791
Wilcox, Carlos. American Clergyman and Poet....... 1794..1827
Wild, Henry. Tailor and Orientalist .... 1684?.1734?
Wild, Robert. Nonconf. Div., Poet, Wit. (*Iter Boreale*) 1609..1679
Wildbore, Charles. Mathematician.................. — ..1802
Wilde, James. Swedish Historian .... 1679..1755
Wilde, or Wyld, John. Sergeant-at-Law .... — ..1669?
Wilde, Richard Henry. American Author and Statesman 1789..1847
Wilde, Sir William. Recorder of London; Judge ..... — ..1679
Wildens, John. Flemish Painter .... 1584..1644
Wilford, Francis. Lieutenant-Colonel. Orientalist.... — ..1822
Wilfrid, St. Bishop of York. Life by Eddius; Eadmer 634?. 709
Wilkes, John. Political Writer. Life by Almon, 1805.. 1727..1797
Wilkie, Sir David. Paint. L. by Allan Cunningham, 1843 1785..1841
Wilkie, Wm., D. D. Poet. *Scottish Homer.* (*Epigoniad*) 1721..1772
Wilkins, Sir Charles. Orientalist................... 1749..1836
Wilkins, Rev. David. (*Leges Saxonicæ; Concilia*)..... 1685..1745
Wilkins, George, D. D. Archd. of Nottingham. Divine 1784?.1865
Wilkins, John. Bishop of Chester. Mathem. and Theol. 1614..1672
Wilkins, William. Architect .... 1778..1839
Wilkinson, James. American General............... 1757..1825
Wilkinson, Jemima. Religious Impostor .... 1753..1819
Wilkinson, Jesse. U. S. Naval Officer............. 1784..1861
Willaert, Adrian. Flemish Musical Composer in Italy.. 1490?.1563
Willan, Robert, M. D. Medical Writer.............. 1757..1812
Willard, Rev. Joseph, D. D., LL. D. Pres. of Harvard Coll. 1738..1804
Willard, Sidney, son. Hebraist and Writer .... 1780..1856
Willdenow, Charles Louis. German Botanist......... 1765..1812
Wille, John George. German Engraver.............. 1715..1806
Willehad. Missionary. Bishop of Bremen.......... — .. 789
Willemet, Peter Remi Francis. French Physician in In-
  dia. (*Herbarium Mauritianum*).................... 1762..1790
Willems, John Francis. Flemish Philologist, Historian,
  and Poet; Reviver of Dutch Literature............. 1793..1846

BORN. DIED.

Willet, Andrew. Divine. (*Synopsis Papismi*)........ 1562..1621
William I. King of England (1066–87). *Conqueror*... 1027..1087
William II. (1087–1100.) · *Rufus*.................... 1056..1100
William III. (1669–1702.) *Of Orange*............. 1650..1702
William IV. (1830–37)......................... 1765..1837
William I. Stadtholder. *The Silent.* Great Prince of
　Orange; assassinated. Life by Isaac Commelin, 1651 1533..1584
William II. Stadtholder....................... 1626..1650
William III. Stadtholder, and King of England...... 1650..1702
William I. King of Netherlands (1815–40)........... 1772..1843
William II., son. (1840–48)................... 1792..1849
William. *Longue Epée.* 2d Dk. of Normandy, son of Rollo — .. 943
William, Prince, son of Henry I.; drowned........ 1103..1120
William. *Clito.* Son of Robert II.; Duke of Normandy 1102..1128
William. *The Lion.* King of Scotland (1165–1214).... — ..1214
William. King of Würtemberg (1816–64)........... 1781..1864
William, of Corbeuil. Archbp. of Canterbury (1123–36) — ..1136
William, of Jumièges. *Calculus.* Historian......... fl. 1070–87
William, of Malmesbury. Historian .... 1095?..1143?
William, of Newbury. Historian.................... 1136..1208
William, of Poictiers. Historian .... 1020?.aft.1088?
William, of Tyre. Bishop and Historian............. 1130?. —
William le Breton. (*De Gestis Philippi; Philippis*) 1170?.aft.1226
William of Champeaux. Fr. Scholastic Philosopher.. — ..1121
William de Nangis. Historian .... — ..1302?
William of Wykeham. Architect, Ecclesiastic, and
　Statesman.................................. 1324..1404
Williams, Miss Anna. Poetess and Writer; Guest of Dr.
　Johnson..................................... 1706..1783
Williams, Sir Chas. Hanbury. Statesm. and Poet. (*Odes*) 1709..1759
Williams, Charles Kilborn. American Jurist....... 1782..1853
Williams, Daniel, D.D. Nonconf. Div.; Found. of Library 1644?.1716
Williams, David. Founder of Literary Fund......... 1738..1816
Williams, Edward. *Iolo Morganwg.* Welsh & Eng. Poet 1747..1826
Williams, Edwin. Statist and Geographer........... — ..1854
Williams, Eleazar. American Clergyman; pretended
　son of Louis XVI............................. 1787?.1858
Williams, Col. Ephraim. Founder of Williams College 1715..1755
Williams, Frederick Sims. Barrister and Writer...... 1812..1863
Williams, Griffith. Bishop of Ossory. (*Seven Golden
　Candlesticks*)................................. 1589..1672
Williams, Miss Helen Maria. Poetess, Novelist, and Po-
　litical Writer .... 1762..1827
Williams, Rev. Isaac. Divine. (*Baptistery*)......... — ..1865
. Williams, John. Archbishop of York; Lord Keeper.
　Life by Bishop Hacket, 1693; Ambrose Phillips, 1700 1582..1650
, Williams, John. Bishop of Chichester............... 1634..1709
Williams, Rev. John. *Redeemed Captive*............. 1644..1729
Williams, Rev. John, LL. D. (*Concord. to Gr. Testament*) — ..1798
Williams, John. Missionary. Life by Prout......... 1796..1839
Williams, Rev. John. Welsh Scholar and Archæologist 1811..1862
Williams, Joseph, of Kidderminster .... — ..1775
Williams, Otho Holland. American General......... 1748..1794
Williams, Roger. Colonizer of Rhode Island. Life by
　Knowles, 1833; Gammell, 1846; Romeo Elton, 1852 1606..1683

BORN. DIED.

Williams, Rev. Samuel, LL. D. American Scholar ..... 1743..1817
Williams, Samuel. Wood Engraver .... 1788..1853
Williams, Thomas. American General .... 1818..1862
Williams, Thomas Scott, LL. D. American Jurist...... 1777..1861
Williams, William. American Patriot............... 1731..1811
Williamson, Hugh, M. D. American Physician. (*History of North Carolina*)............................... 1735..1819
Williamson, Sir Joseph. Statesman .... 1630?.1701
Willibrod, St. *See* Wilbrord...................... 657?. 738?
Willis, Browne. Antiquary. (*Cathedrals*)........... 1682..1760
Willis, Rev. Francis, M. D. Doctor for Insanity........ 1718?.1807
Willis, Thomas, M. D. Anatomical & Philosophical Writer 1621..1675
Willmore, James Tibbits. Engraver................. 1800..1863
Willmott, Rev. Robert Aris, of Bearwood. Writer..... — ..1863
Willock, or Willox, John. Scottish Reformer .... —aft.1568
Willoughby, Sir Hugh. Voyager.................... — ..1554?
Willshire, Sir Thomas, Bart. General.............. 1790..1862
Willughby, Francis. Naturalist; Companion of Ray... 1635..1672
Wilmot, John, Earl of Rochester. Converted Infidel. Life by Bishop Burnet............................ 1647..1680
Wilmot, Sir John Eardley. Judge. L. by J. W. E. Wilmot 1709..1792
Wilmot, John Wilmot Eardley, son. Lawyer. (*Laws and Customs of England*)......................... 1748..1815
Wilson, Alexander. Scottish Ornithologist .... 1766..1813
Wilson, Arthur. Historian. (*Life and Reign of James I.*) Life by self..................................... 1596..1652
Wilson, Mrs. Cornwall Barron. Writer.............. — ..1846
Wilson, Daniel. Author; Bishop of Calcutta. Life by Bateman, 1860.................................. 1778..1858
Wilson, Florence. *Florentius Volusenus.* Scottish Writer 1500?.1547
Wilson, George, M. D., of Edinburgh. Professor of Technology. (*Five Gateways of Knowledge.*) Life by sister 1818..1859
Wilson, Professor Horace Hayman. Orientalist .... 1786..1860
Wilson, James. American Patriot................... 1742..1798
Wilson, James. Scottish Naturalist and Author. Life by Dr. Hamilton, 1859.......................... 1795..1856
Wilson, James. Political Economist. Financier in India 1805..1860
Wilson, Dr. John. Composer to Charles I. (*Psalterium Carolinum*)................................... 1594..1673
Wilson, John, of Kendal. Botanist. (*Synopsis of British Plants*)...................................... — ..1750?
Wilson, John. Professor at Edinburgh. *Christopher North.* Poet and Essayist. (*Noctes Ambrosianæ.*) Life by Mrs. Gordon, 1862 .... 1785..1854
Wilson, Richard, R. A. Painter. L. by T. Wright, 1824 1713..1782
Wilson, General Sir Robert Thomas. Military Writer. Life by self and Rev. Herbert Randolph .... 1777..1849
Wilson, Sir Thomas. Statesman and Div. (*Art of Logic*) 1520?.1581
Wilson, Thomas. Puritan Divine. (*Christian Dictionary*) — ..1621
Wilson, Thomas. Bishop of Sodor and Man (1698–1755). (*Sacra Privata.*) Life by Cruttwell; Keble; Hugh Stowell, 1810 .... 1663..1755
Wilson, William Rae, LL. D. (*Travels in the Holy Land*) 1774..1849
Wilton, Rev. Edward. Divine. (*Negeb, or South Country*) 1820?.1864
Wilton, Joseph, R. A. Sculptor .... 1722..1803

BORN. DIED.

Wimpfeling, James, of Strasburg. Reviver of Learning 1450..1528
Wimpffen-Berneburg, Felix, Baron de. French General 1745..1814
Wimpina, Conrad, of Frankfort. Theologian; Anti-
  Reformer...................................... 1460..1531
Winchell, James Manning. American Clergyman..... 1791..1820
Winchelsea, Anne, Countess of. Poetess............ 1660?.1720
Winchester, Elhanan. American Clergyman and Writer.
  Life by Vidler; E. M. Stone, 1836 .... 1751..1797
Winchester, Thomas, D. D. Divine................ — ..1780
Winckelmann, John Joachim. Antiquary. L. by Heyne 1717..1768
Winckelmann, John Justus. German Historian ...... 1620..1697
Winckler, John Henry. German Philosopher......... 1703..1770
Winder, William H. American General.............. 1775..1824
Windham, Joseph. Artist and Antiquary .... 1739..1810
Windham, William. Statesman. L. by Thomas Amyot 1750..1810
Windischgratz, Alfred zu, Prince. Austrian General.. 1787..1862
Windischmann, Charles Joseph Jerome. Ger. Philos. 1775..1839
Winer, George Benedict. German Protestant Theologian 1789..1858
Wing, Vincent. Astrologer. (Astronomia Britannica).. — ..1661
Wingate, Edmund. Arithmetician.................. 1593..1656
Winkelried, Arnold Struth von. Swiss Patriot .... — ..1386
Winram, John. Scottish Ecclesiastic................ — ..1582
Winsemius, Menelaus. Medical Writer at Franeker... 1591?.1639
Winsemius, Peter, br. Flemish Historian at Franeker 1585?.1644
Winslow, Edward. Governor of Plymouth Colony.... 1595..1655
Winslow, Hubbard, D. D. American Author and Editor 1800..1864
Winslow, James Benignus. Danish Anatomist .... 1669..1760
Winslow, Miron, D. D., LL. D. American Missionary and
  Orientalist.................................... 1789..1864
Winsor, Frederick Albert. Introducer of Gas Lights... 1762?.1830
Winstanley, Henry. Architect of Eddystone Lighthouse — ..1703
Winstanley, William. Biographer. (Lives of Poets) .. — ..1684?
Winston, Charles. Painter on Glass .... 1814..1864
Winston, Thomas. Gresham Professor. (Anatomic Lec-
  turer)... 1575..1655
Wint, Peter de. English Water Color Painter......... 1783..1849
Winter, John William van. Dutch Admiral .... 1750..1812
Winter, Peter von. German Musical Composer........ 1754..1825
Winterton, Ralph. Editor of Poetæ Græci Minores .... — ..1636
Winthrop, John. Gov. of the Colony of Massachusetts 1588..1649
Winthrop, John, son. Governor of Connecticut .... 1606..1676
Winthrop, John, LL. D. American Scholar .... 1715..1779
Winthrop, Major Theodore. American Author........ 1828..1861
Winton, or Wyntoun, Andrew. Poet and Chronicler
  of Scotland .... —aft.1420
Wintoun, George Seton, Earl of. Scottish Jacobite.... 1690..1749
Wintringham, Clifton. Physician and Physiologist ... — ..1748
Wintringham, Sir Clifton, M. D., son. Medical Writer 1710..1794
Wintzingerode, Ferdinand, Baron. Russian General.. 1770..1818
Winwood, Sir Ralph. Statesman .... 1564?.1617
Winzet, or Winget, Ninian. Scottish Anti-Reformer ... 1518?.1592
Wirley, William. Heraldic Writer. (True Use of Armory) — ..1618
Wirsungus, John George. Discoverer of Pancreatic Duct — ..1643
Wirt, William. American Jurist and Author. Life by
  J. P. Kennedy, 1849 .... 1772..1834

BORN. DIED.

Wischart, William, D. D. Scottish Divine. (*Theologia*) 1657..1727
Wischeart, George, D. D. Bishop of Edinburgh. Biographer. (*Wars in Scotland*) .... 1609..1671
Wise, Rev. Francis. Antiquary and Divine. .... 1695..1767
Wise, Michael. Composer of Church Music .... — ..1687
Wiselius, Samuel Iperuszoon. Dutch Poet .... 1769..1845
Wiseman, Nicholas Patrick Stephen. Cardinal .... 1802..1865
Wiseman, Richard. Surgical Writer. .... — aft.1766
Wishart, George. The *Martyr*. Scottish Reformer and Martyr. .... — ..1546
Wishart, George. Bishop of Edinburgh. Biographer. (*Wars in Scotland*) .... 1609..1671
Wishaw, Francis. Engineer. .... 1805..1854
Wissing, William. Dutch Portrait Painter in England 1656..1687
Wissowatius, Andrew. Socinian Writer .... 1608..1678
Wistar, Caspar. American Anatomist .... 1761..1818
Witasse, Charles. French Theologian .... 1660..1716
Witchell, George. Astronomer and Mathematician .... 1728..1785
Wither, George. Poet. (*Abuses Stript and Whipt*) .... 1588..1667
Withering, William. Physician and Botanist........ 1741..1799
Witherington, W. F. Landscape Painter .... 1786..1865
Witherspoon, Dr. John. American Patriot; Writer; President of Princeton College. (*Characteristics; The Stage*) .... 1722..1794
Withof, John Philip Lawrence. Ger. Physician and Poet 1725..1789
Witikind, Wittekind, or Wittichind. Saxon Patriot; defeated by Charlemagne .... — .. 807?
Witikind. Saxon Historian. (*Annals of the Saxons*) .. — aft. 973
Witsius, Herman. Dutch Divine .... 1636..1708
Witt, Cornelius de. Life by Madame Zouteland, 1709 .. 1623..1671
Witt, Emanuel de, of Alkmaer. Painter .... 1607..1692
Witt, John de. Grand Pensionary. Life by Madame Zouteland, 1709 .... 1625..1672
Witte, or Witten, Henning. Ger. Divine and Biographer 1634..1696
Witte, Peter de. *Peter Candido*. Dutch Painter in Italy 1548?.1599
Wittgenstein, Louis Adolphus, Ct. of. Prussian General 1769..1843
Wittichius, Christopher. Protestant Theologian....... 1625..1687
Witzleben, Charles Augustus Frederick von. *Von Tromlitz*. Soldier and Writer. .... 1772..1839
Wodderspoon, John. Antiquary .... 1706?.1862
Wodhull, Michael. Poet; Translator of Euripides ..... 1740..1816
Wodrow, Robert. Scottish Ecclesiastical Historian .... 1679..1734
Woeiriot, Peter. Engraver of Lorraine .... fl. 1555–76
Woelffl, or Wölffl, Joseph. German Pianist & Composer 1772..1814
Woffington, Margaret. Irish Actress................ 1719..1760
Wogan, Nicholas. Jacobite. .... 1667?.1734
Wohlgemuth, Michael. German Painter and Engraver 1434..1519
Woide, Charles Godfrey, D. D. Orientalist. (*Novum Testamentum e Codice MS. Alexandrino*) .... 1725..1790
Wolcott, John. *Peter Pindar*. Satirical Poet .... 1738..1819
Wolcott, Oliver. American Statesman and General.... 1726..1797
Wolcott, Roger. Colonial Governor of Connecticut .... 1679..1767
Wolf, Fred. Augustus. Ger. Classical Scholar and Critic. (*Prolegomena ad Homerum.*) Life by W. Körte, 1833 1759..1824
Wolf, Jerome. Scholar and Philosopher at Augsburg.. 1516.;1580

BORN. DIED.

Wolf, John. German Jurisconsult and Compiler....... — ..1600
Wolf, John. German Medical Writer................. 1537..1616
Wolf, John Christian von. German Mathematician and
   Philosopher. (*Philosophia Rationalis*).............. 1679..1754
Wolf, John Christopher. Lutheran Divine, Orientalist,
   and Biblical Writer, at Hamburg ....:.. 1683..1739
Wolfe, Rev. Charles. Poet. (*Burial of Sir John Moore.*)
   Life by Archdeacon Russell, 1825................. 1791..1823
Wolfe, James. General; fell at Quebec. L. by Wright, 1863 1726..1759
Wolff, Dr. Joseph. Missionary and Traveler .... 1795..1862
Wolff, Oscar Louis Bernard. German Author......... 1799..1851
Wolff, Pius Alexander. German Actor............... 1782..1828
Wölffl, Joseph. German Pianist and Composer .... 1772..1814
Wolfram von Eschenbach. German Minnesinger ... — aft.1227
Wollaston, Rev. William. Philosophical Writer. (*Re-
   ligion of Nature.*) Life by Dr. Clarke .... 1659..1724
Wollaston, William Hyde, M. D. Natural Philosopher 1766..1828
Wollebius, John. Div. of Basle. (*Compendium Theologia*) 1536..1626
Wollstonecraft, Mary (Mrs. Godwin). Writer........ 1759..1797
Wolmar, or Volkmar, Melchior. Swiss Jurisconsult and
   Scholar .... 1497?.1561
Wolsey, Thomas. Cardinal and Statesman. Life by
   Fiddes, 1724; Grove; Sir William Cavendish; J. Galt,
   1818; Charles Howard, 1824; T. Storer............. 1471..1530
Wolters, Henrietta. Dutch Miniature Painter......... 1692..1741
Wolzogen, Caroline von. German Authoress .... 1763..1847
Wolzogen, John Louis. Socinian Writer .... 1596..1658
Wolzogen, Louis van. Socinian Writer at Amsterdam 1642..1690
Womack, Lawrence. Bishop of St. David's. Anti-Puri-
   tan Writer ....:.... 1612..1686
Wood, Sir Andrew. Scottish Admiral............... 1455?.1539?
Wood, Anthony à. Antiquary and Biographer. (*Athenæ
   Oxonienses.*) Life by self; Huddesford, 1772 .... 1632..1695
Wood, Isaac. Painter and Humorist .... 1689..1752
Wood, James, of Gloucester. Banker................. 1756..1836
Wood, James, D. D. Dean of Ely. Master of St. John's.
   (*Algebra*)................................ 1760?.1839
Wood, John, of Bath. Architect .... — ..1754
Wood, Sir Matthew, M. P. Lord Mayor.............. 1768..1843
Wood, Robert. *Palmyra Wood.* Secretary of State;
   Archæologist. (*Essay on Homer ; Ruins of Palmyra*) 1716..1771
Wood, William. Dissenting Minister, Scholar, and Writer 1745..1808
Woodall, John. Surgeon.......................... 1556?.1646?
Woodbridge, Wm. Channing. Amer. Educational Writ. 1794..1845
Woodbury, Levi. American Jurist and Statesman.... 1789..1851
Woodcock, Robert. Musical Composer and Painter ... 1692..1728
Woodd, Rev. Basil. Divine .... 1760..1831
Wooddeson, Dr. Richard. Vinerian Prof.; Law Writer 1745..1822
Woodfall, William. Newspaper Writer and Parliamen-
   tary Reporter .... 1745 or 6.1803
Woodford, Samuel, D. D. Divine and Poetical Writer 1636..1700
Woodhead, Abraham. Roman Catholic Writer .... — ..1678
Woodhouse, Robert. Mathematician and Astronomer 1773..1827
Woodhouselee, Alexander Fraser Tytler, Lord .... 1747..1813
Woods, Joseph. Architect and Botanist.............. 1776?.1864

BORN. DIED.

Woods, Leonard, D. D. American Divine............ 1774..1854
Woodville, Anthony, Earl Rivers; beheaded.......... 1442..1483
Woodville, or Wydville, Elizabeth, sister. Queen of
  Edward IV....................................... — ..1486?
Woodville, William, M. D. Medical Writer.......... 1752..1805
Woodward, Henry. Comedian...................... 1717..1777
Woodward, John. Geologist. Founder of Professorship
  at Cambridge. (Natural History of the Earth)...... 1665..1728
Woodward, Samuel Bayard, M. D. American Physician 1787..1850
Woodward, Dr. Samuel P. Geologist................ 1821..1865
Woodworth, Samuel. American Editor and Author.
  (The Old Oaken Bucket)......................... 1785..1842
Woolhouse, John Thomas. Surgeon and Oculist ..... — ..1730
Woollett, William. Engraver .... 1735..1785
Woolman, John. American Quaker. Abolitionist..... 1720..1773
Woolsey, Melancthon Taylor. United States Naval Officer 1782..1838
Woolston, Rev. Thomas. Theological Writer......... 1669..1733
Wooster, David. American Revolutionary General..... 1710..1777
Wootton, John. Painter........................... 1720..1765
Worcester, Edward Somerset, Marquess of. (Century of
  Inventions.) Life by Dircks, 1865................. — ..1667
Worcester, Joseph Emerson, LL. D. American Geogra-
  pher and Lexicographer .... 1784..1865
Worcester, Noah, D. D. American Divine........... 1758..1837
Worcester, Samuel, br. Clergyman. L. by his son, 1852 1770..1821
Worde, Wynkin de. Printer .... — ..1534?
Wordsworth, Rev. Christopher, D. D. Master of Trin-
  ity College. (Ecclesiastical Biography)............ 1774..1846
Wordsworth, William. Poet. Life by his nephew,
  Canon Wordsworth, 1851; Rev. E. Paxton Hood, 1856 1770..1850
Worlidge, Thomas. Portrait Painter and Engraver.... 1700..1766
Wormius, Olaus. Danish Physician, Antiquary, Historian 1588..1654
Wormius, Olaus. Medical Writer .... — ..1708
Wormius, William. Medical Writer. (Musæum Worm.) 1633..1704
Woronicz, John Paul. Polish Prelate and Poet....... 1757..1829
Woronzoff, Michael Ilarionovitch, Ct. Russian Diplom. 1714..1767
Woronzoff, Michael Semenovitch, Prince. Russ. General 1782..1856
Worsdale, James. Painter and Dramatic Writer...... — ..1767
Worsley, Sir Richard. Gov. of Isle of Wight. (I. Wight) 1751..1805
Worth, William Jenkins. American General.......... 1794..1849
Worthington, Thomas. Governor of Ohio........... 1773..1827
Worthington, Rev. William. Divine .... 1703..1778
Wortley, Emmeline Charlotte Elizabeth, Lady. Writer 1806..1855
Wotton, Edward, M. D. Naturalist. (De Differentiis
  Animalium)..................................... 1492..1555
Wotton, Sir Henry. Diplomatist and Author. Life by
  Izaak Walton................................... 1568..1639
Wotton, Nicholas. Dean of Canterbury and Statesman 1497..1566
Wotton, Rev. William, D. D. Divine, Critic, and His-
  torian. (Ancient and Modern Learning)............ 1666..1726
Woulfe, Peter. Chemist in London .... — ..1806
Wouters, Francis. Flemish Painter .... 1614..1659
Wouverman, Peter................................ 1625..1683
Wouverman, Philip, brother. Dutch Painter......... 1620..1668
Wower, John, of Hamburg. Politician and Writer .... 1574..1612

BORN. DIED.

Wrangel, Chas. Gustavus von, Ct. Swedish Commander 1613..1675
Wraxall, Sir Frederick Charles Lascelles. Writer ..... 1828..1865
Wraxall, Sir Nathaniel William. Traveler and Historian 1751..1831
Wray, Daniel. Archæologist .... 1701..1783
Wray, Robert Bateman. Engraver of Gems........... 1715..1770
Wrede, Charles Philip, Prince. Field Marshal......... 1767..1838
Wren, Sir Christopher. Architect. Life by son and
    grandson................................... 1632..1723
Wren, Christopher, son. Antiquary. (*Parentalia*) .... 1675..1747
Wren, Matthew. Bishop of Ely..................... 1585..1667
Wren, Matthew, M. P., son. Writer .... 1629..1672
Wright, Abraham. Divine and Poet. Writer. (*Par-*
    nassus Biceps)................................ 1611..1690
Wright, Edward. Mathematician .... — ..1615
Wright, Edward, M. D. Traveler with Lord Macclesfield.
    (*Observer*) .... — ..1761
Wright, Fanny. *Madame Darusmont*. Social Reformer
    and Philanthropist............................ 1796?.1853
Wright, John Wesley. Captain R. N................. 1769..1805
Wright, Joseph, of Derby. Painter .... 1734..1797
Wright, Sir Nathan. Lord Keeper.... .... — ..1721
Wright, Samuel. Dissenting Divine. (*The New Birth*) 1683..1746
Wright, Silas. American Statesman .... 1795..1847
Wright, Thomas, of Durham. Antiquary and Natural
    Philosopher.................................. 1711?.1785
Wright, Walter Rodwell. (*Horæ Ionicæ*) .... — ..1826
Wriothesley, Thomas, Fourth Earl of Southampton.... — ..1667
Wrisberg, Henry Augustus. German Anatomist...... 1739..1808
Wulf, Christian. Danish Writer.................... 1810..1856
Wulfen, Francis Xavier von. Natural Philosopher and
    Mathematician .... 1728..1806
Wulfhelm. Archbishop of Canterbury (923–42)....... — .. 942
Wulfred. Archbishop of Canterbury (805–32)......... — .. 832
Wulstan, or Wolstan. Monk of Winchester. (*Life of*
    Ethelwold) .... fl. 10th c.
Wulstan. Bishop of Worcester .... 1007 or 8.1096
Wurmser, Dagobert Sigismund, Ct. of. Austrian General 1724..1797
Wursticius, or Ursticius, Christian. Ital. Mathematician 1544..1588
Wurzelbau, John Philip. German Astronomer .... 1651..1725
Wyatt, James. Architect .... 1746..1813
Wyatt, Matthew Cotes. Sculptor................... 1778..1862
Wyatt, Richard James. Sculptor................... 1795..1850
Wyatt, Sir Thomas. *The Elder*. Statesman, Courtier,
    and Poet. Life by Dr. Nott.................... 1503..1542
Wyatt, Sir Thomas. *The Younger*. Insurgent; beheaded 1520?.1554
Wyatville, Sir Jeffrey. Architect.................. 1766..1840
Wycherly, William. Dramatic Writer. L. by Major Pack 1640? 1715
Wyck, John. Painter in England .... 1640?.1702
Wyck, Thomas. Dutch Painter .... 1616..1686
Wycliffe, John de. Reformer. Life by Rev. John Lewis,
    1719; Dr. Robert Vaughan, 1828 (revised, 1853); Rev.
    Webb Le Bas, 1832......................... 1324?.1384
Wykeham, William of. Life by Martin, 1597; Bishop
    Louth, 1754 .... 1324..1404
Wylie, Andrew, D. D. American Educator........... 1789..1851

BORN. DIED.

Wynants, John. Dutch Landscape Painter .... 1600?.1673?

Wyndham, Sir Charles, Earl of Egremont. Secretary of State.. — ..1763

Wyndham, Sir William. Statesman.................. 1687..1740

Wynn, Charles Watkin Williams, M. P. Politician..... 1775?.1850

Wynne, John Huddleston. (*History of Ireland*) .... 1743..1788

Wyntoun. Annalist in Verse. *See* Winton .... — aft.1420

Wyon, William, R. A. Engraver of Medals............ 1795..1851

Wyse, Sir John. Writer............................: 1792..1862

Wysocki, Joseph. Polish General................... 1809.. —

Wythe, George. American Jurist and Patriot......... 1726..1806

Wytman, Matthew. Painter .... 1650..1682

Wyttenbach, Daniel. Dutch Philologist .... 1746..1820

X.

BORN. DIED.

Xaupi, Joseph, of Perpignan. Antiquarian Writer ..... 1688..1778

Xavier, Francis, St.. *Apostle of the Indies.* Jesuit Missionary to the East. Life by Tursellini, 1594; Orlandino; Bartoli, 1666; Maffei; Bouhours, translated by. Dryden, 1688; Venn, 1863 .... 1506..1552

Xavier, Jerome. Jesuit Missionary to the East Indies .. — ..1617

Xenocrates. Greek Philosopher .... 396.314 B.C.

Xenophanes. Greek Philosopher and Poet......... fl. B.C. 540–500

Xenophon. Greek Soldier and Writer. (*Anabasis*).. 444?.355? B.C.

Xerxes I. King of Persia (B. C. 485–465)............ — B.C. 465

Xerxes II. (B. C. 425).......................... — B.C. 425

Ximenes, Augustine Mary, Marquis de. French Poet.. 1726..1817

Ximenes, Francis. Spanish Friar; Missionary to Mexico — ..1620?

Ximenes, Francis. Spanish Painter .... 1598..1666

Ximenes, Leonard. Sicilian Geometer and Astronomer 1716..1786

Ximenes, Peter. Theologian. (*Demonstratio Catholicæ Veritatis*)....................................... 1514..1595

Ximenes, Roderick. Archbishop of Toledo. (*History of Spain*)... — ..1247

Ximenes de Carmona, Francis. Spanish Physician and Naturalist .... fl. 1616

Ximenes de Cisneros, Francis. Spanish Cardinal and Statesman. Life by Flechier; Gomez de Castro; Marsollier.. 1436..1517

Ximenes de Quesada, Gonzalo. Spanish Explorer and Conqueror...................................... — ..1579

Ximeno, Vincent, of Valencia. Biographer .... — ..1703 .

Xiphilinus, John, of Trebizond. Patriarch of Constantinople .... 1005?.1075

Xiphilinus, John, nephew. Epitomizer of Dion Cassius fl. 1100?.

Xuares, Gaspar. Jesuit. Botanist .... 1731..1804

Xylander, William. *Holzmann.* German Philologer ... 1532..1576

Y.

BORN. DIED.

Yakoob-ibn-Lais. *Suffar.* Founder of the Dynasty of Suffarides in Persia............................. — .. 877
Yalden, Rev. Thomas. Poetical Writer. (*Hymn to Darkness*)............................ 1671..1736
Yale, Elihu. Early Patron of Yale College............ 1648..1721
Yancey, William Lowndes. American Politician...... 1815..1863
Yarrell, William. Naturalist........................ 1784..1856
Yarrenton, Andrew. Ironmaster and Soldier. (*England's Improvement.*) Life by Smiles............. 1616.aft.1681
Yart, Anthony. French Writer. (*Idea of English Poetry*) 1710..1791
Yates, Mrs. Anna Maria. Tragic Actress.............. — ..1787
Yates, Frederick Henry. Actor .... 1797?.1842
Yates, John Ashton. Political Economist. .... 1781?.1863
Yates, Richard. Comic Actor...................... — ..1796
Yates, Robert. American Statesman and Jurist........ 1738..1801
Yates, William, D. D. Missionary and Orientalist...... 1792..1845
Yearsley, Anne. Poetical and Dramatic Writer .... 1756?.1806
Yeates, Thomas. Orientalist .... 1768..1839
Yeates, Thomas Pattinson. Entomologist............. — ..1782
Yelverton, Sir Henry. Judge. (*Reports of Special Cases*) 1566..1630
Yepez, Anthony. Spanish Benedictine. (*Chronology of Benedictine Order*)............................. — ..1621
Yepez, Diego d'. Spanish Historical Writer.......... 1559..1613
Yorck von Wartenburg, John David Louis, Count. Prussian Field Marshal .... 1759..1830
York, Edmund of Langley, First Duke of. Son of Edward III. .... 1341..1402
York, Edward, son, Second Duke of; fell at Agincourt.. — ..1415
York, Richard, nephew. Claimant of Crown ; fell at Wakefield............................... — ..1460
York, Richard, Duke of. Son of Edward IV. Murdered in Tower.. — ..1483
York and Albany, Edward Augustus, Duke of. Brother of George III....................................... — ..1767
York and Albany, Ernest Augustus, Duke of. Brother of George I. .... — ..1728
York and Albany, Frederick, Duke of. Son of Geo. III. 1763..1827
Yorke, Charles. Lawyer and Statesman .... 1722..1770
Yorke, Sir Joseph Sidney, M. P. Admiral; Politician... 1768..1831
Yorke, Philip, Earl of Hardwicke, *which see.*
Youatt, William. Veterinary Surgeon and Writer..... 1777..1847
Young, Alexander, D. D. Amer. Clergyman and Writer 1800..1854
Young, Sir Aretas William. Colonel................. 1778? 1835
Young, Arthur. Agricultural Writer.................. 1741..1820
Young, Augustus. American Geologist and Naturalist . 1785..1857
Young, Charles. Actor............................. 1777?.1856
Young, Edward, D. C. L. Poet. (*Night Thoughts*)...... 1684..1765
Young, Matthew. Bishop of Clonfert. Mathematician.. 1750..1800
Young, Rev. Patrick. *Patricius Junius.* Scholar...... 1584..1652
Young, Sir Peter. Scottish Diplomatist and Writer .... 1544..1628
Young, Thomas. Puritan Divine; Milton's first tutor .. 1587?.1655

BORN. DIED.

Young, Thomas, M. D.   Physician and Natural Philoso-
pher.   Life by Dean Peacock, 1855................ 1773..1829
Young, Sir William, M. P.   Political and Miscellaneous
Writer .... 1750..1815
Yousouf-ben-Taschfin.   King of Morocco........... — ..1106
Ypres, Charles de.   Flemish Painter .... 1510..1563
Ypsilanti, Alexander, Prince.   Greek   Revolutionary
Statesman...................................... 1792..1828
Ypsilanti, Demetrius, brother.   Military Commander... 1793..1832
Yriarte, Bernard.   Spanish Statesman................ 1734?.1814
Yriarte, Domingo, brother.   Spanish Diplomatist ...... 1746..1795
Yriarte, Ignatius.   Spanish Landscape Painter .... 1635..1685
Yriarte, John de.   Spanish Linguist and Archæologist.. 1702..1771
Yriarte, Thomas de.   Spanish Poet.................. 1750..1791
Ysabeau, or Isabeau, Alexander Clement.   Fr. Statesman 1750?.1823
Yves, or Ivo.   Bishop of Chartres.   Ecclesiastical and His-
torical Writer................................... 1035..1115
Yveteaux, Nicholas Vauquelin.   Poetical Writer ...... 1559..1649

Z.

BORN. DIED.

Zabaglia, Nicholas. Italian Architect................. 1674..1750
Zabarella, Francis. *Cardinal de Florence.* Archbishop.
    Theologian....................................... 1339..1417
Zabarella, James. Astrol. (*Commentaries on Aristotle*) 1533..1589
Zacagni, Lawrence Alex. (*Collectanea Monumentorum*) — ..1712
Zaccaria, Francis Anthony. Jesuit. (*Lit. Hist. of Italy*) 1714+..1795
Zacchias, Paul. Italian Medical Writer............... 1584..1659
Zach, Anthony, Baron von. Austrian General .... 1744..1826
Zach, Francis Xavier, Baron von, brother. Astronomer. 1754..1832
Zachariae, or Zachariä, Justus Frederick William. Ger-
    man Comic Poet.................................. 1723..1777
Zachariae, or Zachariä, von Lingenthal, Charles Solo-
    mon. German Jurist and Political Writer.......... 1769..1843
Zachariah, son of Jeroboam II. King of Israel (B. C.
    793–771)...................................... 808.771 B.C.
Zacharias. Pope (741–52)........................... — .. 752
Zachaw, Frederick William. German Musical Composer 1663..1721
Zachtleevin, or Sachtleevin, Cornelius. Dutch Painter.. 1612.. —
Zachtleevin, Herman, brother. Painter .... 1609..1685
Zacutus Lusitanus. Portuguese Medical Writer...... 1575..1642
Zagoskin, or Sagoskin, Michael Nicolaevitch. Russian
    Dramatist and Novelist.......................... 1789..1852
Zahrtmann, Christian Christopher. Danish Admiral and
    Hydrographer................................... 1794?.1853
Zajonczek, Joseph. Polish Prince and General .... 1752..1826
Zaleucus. Locrian Legislator....................... fl. B.C. 500?
Zaluski, Andrew Chrysostom. Polish Statesm. & Writer 1650?.1711
Zaluski, Joseph Andrew. Polish Book Collector....... 1701..1774
Zambeccari, Francis, Count. Italian Aëronaut........ 1756..1812
Zamoyski, Andrew. Polish Statesman .... 1716..1792
Zamoyski, John. Polish Commander................. 1626..1665
Zamoyski, or Zamoscius, John Sarius. Grand Chancel-
    lor of Poland. Life by Bursius; Moslowski........ 1541..1605
Zampieri, Dominic. *Domenichino.* Italian Painter .... 1581..1641
Zanchi, Basil. Italian Latin Poet.................... 1501?.1558
Zanchi, Jerome. Italian Reformer. Life by Gallizoli... 1516..1590
Zanchi, John Chrysostom. Hist. (*De Orobiorum Origine*) 1490?.1566
Zanichelli, John Jerome. Italian Physician and Natural
    Philosopher..................................... 1662..1729
Zanoni, James. Physician and Botanist of Bologna.... 1615..1682
Zanotti, Francis Mary Cavazzoni. Italian Mathemati-
    cian and Philosopher............................ 1692..1777
Zanotti, John Peter Cavazzoni, br. Painter and Poet .. 1674..1765
Zanzalus, Jacob. *Baradæus.* Syrian Monk........... — .. 578
Zápolya. Hungarian Soldier.......................... —..1499
Zappi, John Baptist Felix. Italian Lawyer and Poet ... 1667..1719
Zarate, Augustine de. Span. Historian. (*Conq. of Peru*) 1500?.1558
Zarco, John Gonzales. Portuguese Navigator .... fl. 1420
Zarlino, Joseph. Italian Composer .... 1520..1599
Zazius, or Zasius, Ulric. Professor at Friburg. Jurist . 1461..1535
Zea, Francis Anthony. Statesman of Colombia .... 1770..1822

BORN. DIED.

Zechariah. Prophet of Judah .... fl. B.C. 520[?]
Zedekiah, son of Josiah. K. of Judah (B. C. 597–586) 618. aft. 586 B.C.
Zedlitz, Joseph Christian, Baron. German Poet........ 1786[?]. 1862
Zeeman, Remigius. Dutch Marine Painter........... 1612.. —
Zegedin, Stephen. Protestant Reformer in Hungary... 1505..1572
Zegers, or Segers, Hercules. Dutch Landscape Painter
    and Etcher .... 1629..1675
Zeiller, Martin. German Topographer................ 1589..1661
Zeisberger, David. Moravian Missionary............ 1721..1808
Zelotti, John Baptist. Italian Painter................. 1532..1592
Zelter, Charles Frederick. German Composer .... 1758..1832
Zendrini, Bernard. Italian Mathematician........... 1679..1747
Zeno, of Elea. Greek Philosopher .... 5th c. B.C.
Zeno. Founder of the Stoic School of Philosophy.... 362[?].264 B.C.
Zeno. *Isaurian.* Roman Emperor of the East (474–91).. 426[?]. 491
Zeno, Anthony, brother and companion of Nicholas..... — ..1405[?]
Zeno, Apostolo. Italian Poet and Historical Writer .... 1668..1750
Zeno, Caterino. Venetian Ambassador to Persia....... fl. 1472
Zeno, Charles. Admiral of Venice. Life by James Zeno 1334[?].1418
Zeno, James. Italian Orator...................... 1417..1481
Zeno, Nicholas. Venetian Traveler.................. — ..1395[?]
Zeno, Nicholas. Biographer of the Zeni .... 1515..1565
Zeno, Peter Caterino. Venetian Writer .... 1666..1732
Zenobia, Septimia. Queen of Palmyra (266–73) .... — aft.274
Zephaniah. Hebrew Prophet..................... fl. 630–624 B.C.
Zephyrinus. Bishop of Rome (197–217)............. — .. 217
Zerbi, Gabriel, of Verona. Anatomist .... fl. 1505
Zeunius, John Charles. Grammarian.................. 1736..1788
Zeuxis. Greek Painter. Life by Carlo Dati .... 450[?].400[?] B.C.
Zhukoffsky, Vasili Andreevitch. Russian Poet........ 1783..1852
Ziani, Sebastian. Doge; Embellisher of Venice....... — ..1179
Ziegenbalg, Bartholomew. Ger. Protestant Missionary. 1683..1719
Ziegler, Bernard. German Theologian of the Reformation 1496..1552
Ziegler, Frederick William. German Actor and Dramatist 1760..1827
Ziegler, Gaspar. German Jurist...................... 1621..1690
Ziegler, James. German Mathematician and Divine.... 1480[?].1549
Ziethen, John Ernest Charles, Ct. Prussian Field Marshal 1770..1848
Ziethen, John Joachim von. Prussian General......... 1699..1786
Zimmermann, Eberhard Augustus William. German
    Naturalist .... 1743..1815
Zimmermann, Ernest. Ger. Theologian. L. by his brother 1786..1832
Zimmermann, John George von. Swiss Physician and
    Philosopher. Life by Tissot .... 1728..1795
Zimmermann, Matthias. Protestant Divine at Meissen 1625..1689
Zimri. King of Israel (929)........................ — B.C. 929
Zincke, Christian Frederick. German Painter in Enamel 1684[?].1767
Zingarelli, Nicholas Anthony. Italian Musical Composer 1752..1837
Zingg, Adrian. Swiss Draughtsman and Engraver ..... 1734..1816
Zinn, John Godfrey. German Anatomist and Botanist.. 1727..1759
Zinzendorf, Nicholas Louis, Count von. Moravian. Life
    by Spangenberg, 1778, tr. by Samuel Jackson, 1838 .. 1700..1760
Ziska, or Zizka, of Trocznow, John. Hussite Leader ... 1360[?].1424
Zizim, or Djem. Turkish Prince..................... 1459..1495
Zobell, Benjamin. German Artist.... .... 1762..1831
Zoe. *Carbinopsina.* Empress of the East, wife of Leo VI. — .. 919

BORN. DIED.

Zoe. Empress of the East, wife of Romanus III........ 982?.1050
Zoëga, George. Danish Archæologist................. 1755..1809
Zoest, Gerard. See Zoust............................ 1637..1681
Zoffany, John, R. A. German Portrait Painter in England 1735..1810
Zoilus. Greek Critic .... fl. 366?–336? B.C.
Zollicoffer, Felix K. " Confederate " General . ... 1812..1862
Zollikofer, George Joachim. Swiss Divine............ 1730..1788
Zonaras, John. Byzantine Historian and Theologian .. fl. 1120?
Zonca, Victor. Ital. Mathem. (*Novo Teatro di Machini*) 1580?. —
Zoppo, Mark. Italian Historical and Portrait Painter .. 1451..1517
Zosimus. Greek Historian .... fl. 400?
Zosimus. Pope (417–18)............................ — .. 418
Zouch, Richard, LL. D. Jurist at Oxford............. 1590?.1660
Zouch, Thomas, D. D. Divine and Biographer........ 1737..1815
Zoust, or Zoest, Gerard. Ger. Portrait Painter in London 1637..1681
Zrinyi, Miklós, Count. Hungarian General...........1518..1566
Zrinyi, Nicholas. Hungarian Poet................... fl. 17th c.
Zschokke, John Henry Daniel. German Writer. (*Stun-*
    den der Andacht.) Life by self .... 1771..1848
Zuccarelli, Francis, R. A. Italian Landscape Painter ... 1702..1788
Zuccaro, or Zucchero, Frederick. Italian Painter...... 1543..1609
Zuccaro, or Zucchero, Thaddeus, brother. Painter..... 1529..1566
Zucchi, Anthony. Italian Painter................... 1726..1795
Zuinglius. Swiss Reformer. *See* Zwingli .... 1484..1531
Zumala-Carreguy, Thomas. Spanish Carlist General.. 1789..1835
Zumbo, Gaetano Julius. Sicilian Modeler in Wax...... 1656..1701
Zumpt, Chas. Gottlob. Ger. Philologist. (*Latin Gram.*) 1792..1858
Zurbaran, Francis. Spanish Painter................. 1598..1662
Zurita, Jerome. Spanish Historian .... 1512..1581
Zurlauben, Béat-Fidèle Anthony John Dominic, Baron
    de La Tour-Chatillon de. Swiss Officer and Writer.. 1720..1795
Zurlo, Joseph, Count. Italian Statesman............. 1759..1828
Zwicker, Daniel. Socinian. (*Irenicon Irenicorum*).... 1612..1678
Zwinger, Theodore, sen. (*Theatrum Vitæ Humanæ*).... 1533..1588
Zwinger, Theodore, jun. (*Theatrum Botanicum*)....... 1658..1724
Zwingli, or Zuinglius, Ulric. Swiss Reformer and Pa-
    triot. Life by J. G. Hess, tr. by Lucy Aikin; J. J.
    Hottinger, tr. by T. C. Porter; N. Christoffel, 1847... 1484..1531
Zwirner, Ernest Frederick. German Architect........ 1802..1861
Zylius, Otho. Dutch Jesuit. (*Lives of the Saints*)...... 1568..1655
Zypæus, or Van den Zype, Francis. Dutch Jurist...... 1578..1650
Zypæus, Henry, brother. Abbot. (*Gregorius Magnus*) 1577..1659

ADDENDA.

A.

DORN. DIED.

Aaron. First High Priest of the Jews .... 1574.1451 B.C.
Abercromby, David, M. D. Medical and Miscel. Writer — ..1701
Abert, John J. American Engineer .... 1790..1863
Abijah. King of Judah (B. C. 958–955) .... — B.C.955
Abner. Captain of Saul, King of Israel .... — B.C.1048
Abraham. Patriarch. .... 1996.1821 B.C.
Absalom, son of David, King of Israel .... — B.C.1021
Acton, Charles Januarius Edward. English Cardinal... 1803..1847
Acworth, George, LL. D. Civilian and Controversialist — ..1577?
Adams, Clement. Author of Travels .... 1519..1587
Adams, Daniel, M. D. Author of School Text-books.... — ..1863
Adams, Richard. Poet .... — ..1661
Adamson, John. Author............................. 1787..1855
Addison, John, D.D. Roman Catholic Writer .... fl. 1538
Ade, Charles. Antiquary and Artist .... — ..1858
Ahab. King of Israel (B. C. 918–897) .... — B.C.897
Ahaz. King of Judah (B. C. 742–726)........... ..... — B.C.726
Ahaziah, son of Ahab. King of Israel (B. C. 897–896).. — B.C.896
Ahaziah, son of Jehoram. King of Judah (B. C. 885–884) 926.884 B.C.
Aikins, Arthur. Scientist and Writer............... 1773..1854
Aldini, John. Italian Experimental Philosopher .... 1762..1834
Alexander, James Waddell, D. D. American Scholar
　　and Writer .... 1804..1859
Alexander, Joseph Addison, D. D., br. Div. and Linguist 1809..1860
Alkmar, Henry van. German Writer. (*Reineke de Voss*) fl. 1475?
Allen, David Oliver. American Missionary and Writer.. 1800..1863
Allen, or Alen, Edmund. Bp. elect of Rochester. Theol. — ..1559
Allen, John. Bibliographer............................ — ..1831
Allot, Wm. Rom. Cath. Divine. (*Thesaurus Bibliorum*) — ..1590?
Amaziah. King of Judah (B. C. 839–810) .... 863.810 B.C.
Ammen, Frederick Augustus von. Ger. Medical Writer 1799..1861
Amon. King of Judah (B. C. 643–641)............... 665.641 B.C.
Amos. Prophet of Israel .... fl. B.C. 787
Amyot, Thomas. Treas. Soc. Antiq. (*Life of Windham*) 1775..1850
Ancelot, James Arsène Francis Polycarp. Fr. Dramatist 1794..1854
Anderson, George B. "Confederate" General .... 1834?.1862
Andral, Gabriel. French Physician.................. 1797..1853
Angell, Joseph Kinnicutt. American Law Writer...... 1794..1857
Angoulême, Louis Anthony de Bourbon, Duc d', son of
　　Charles X............................... 1775..1844
Angus, Caleb. Agriculturist and Writer on Free Trade 1782..1860
Anlaby, William. Roman Catholic Missionary; martyred — ..1597
Annesley, Alexander. Legal and Political Writer ..... — ..1813
Antinori, Vincent, of Florence. Scholar.............. — ..1865
Appleton, Nathan. American Merchant .... 1779..1861

BORN. DIED.

Arago, James Stephen Victor. Fr. Journalist and Author 1790..1855
Arcano, Mauro d'. *Il Mauro.* Italian Burlesque Poet.. 1490?.1536
Argentine, Richard, M. D. *Sexten.* Rom. Cath. Writer — ..1568
Arjona, Manuel de. Spanish Ecclesiastic and Poet..... 1761..1820
Arlincourt, Victor, Viscount d'. Fr. Poet and Novelist 1789..1856
Armansperg, Joseph Louis, Count von. Ger. Statesman 1787..1853
Armellini, Charles. Italian Patriot .... 1776..1863
Armistead, Lewis A. " Confederate " General .... — ..1863
Arnott, Dr. Archibald. Scotch Physician............ 1771..1855
Arrowsmith, Edmund. Jesuit; executed............. — ..1628
Ashby, Turner. "Confederate" General............. 1824?.1862
Ashe, Thomas. *Captain Ashe.* Author of Travels..... — ..1835
Asplin, Rev. William. Theologian. *(Alkibla)*........ — ..1758
Assarotti, Octavius John Bapt. Teacher of Deaf & Dumb 1735..1829
Aster, Ernest Louis. German General................ 1778..1855
Aston, William. Jesuit. Writer .... — ..1800
Athaliah. Usurping Queen of Judah................. — B.C.878
Athanagildus. Gothic King in Spain .... — .. 567
Atherton, Charles Gordon. American Politician....... 1804..1853
Atherton, John. Bishop of Waterford; executed...... — ..1640
Attalus I. King of Pergamus (B. C. 241–197)........ 268?.197 B.C.
Attalus II. (B. C. 159–138.)' *Philadelphus* .... 220.138 B.C.
Attalus III. (B. C. 138–133.) *Philometor*............. — B.C.133
Atterbom, Peter Daniel Amadeus. Swedish Poet...... 1790..1855
Audley, Mervyn, Lord, and Earl of Castlehaven; executed — ..1631
Auenbrugger von Auenburg, Leopold. Physician at
    Vienna. Inventor of Percussion .... 1722..1809
Auffenberg, Joseph von, Baron. German Dramatist... 1798..1857
Aufrere, Anthony. Miscellaneous Writer and Translator 1756?.1833
Augur, Hezekiah. American Sculptor................ 1791..1858
Augusti, Christian John William. German Theologian 1771..1841
Aust, Mrs. Sarah (formerly Murray). *(Guide to the Lakes)* — ..1811
Austin, John. Jurist. *(Province of Jurisprudence)* .... 1797..1860
Avempace, or Ibn-Bäjja. Spanish Arabian Philosopher — ..1138?
Avenbrugger, or Auenbrugger, *which see*............. 1722..1809
Avenzohar, Abumeron. Arabian Physician in Spain... 1072?.1162
Avenzohar, Alhafid, son. Arabian Physician in Spain.. 1114..1199
Avicebron, or Solomon ben Gebirol. Jewish Philosopher fl. 11th c.
Ayrton, William. Writer on Music .... 1777..1858
Azaïs, Peter Hyacinth. French Philosopher .... 1766..1845
Azeglio, Massimo Taparella d', Marquis. Italian States-
    man, Author, and Artist .... 1798..1866

B.

Baasha. King of Israel (B. C. 953–930)................ — B.C.930
Bache, Franklin, M. D. American Physician, Savant,
    and Author................................ 1792..1864
Bacon, Francis, Viscount St. Alban's. Life by Anon. 1626
    (reprinted in Harl. Misc.); Rawley, 1657; R. Stephens,
    1736; Mallet, 1740 (also in German and French);
    . Pouillot, 1755; Anon. 1787; Bertin, 1788; Courtier,
    1803; Montagu, 1834; Ozanam, 1835; Macaulay, 1837;
    Wilhelmy, 1843; Craik, 1846; Sortain, 1851; M. Na-

BORN. DIED.

pier, 1853; Campbell, 1853; Rémusat, 1857; Spedding, 1861; Dixon, 1861, enlarged, 1862 .... 1561..1626
Bacon, Nathaniel. Insurrectionary Leader in Virginia (1675–77) .... 1630..1677
Bagby, Arthur P. American Statesman .... 1794..1858
Bagot, Richard. Bishop of Oxford .... 1782..1854
Bailey, Gamaliel. American Journalist .... 1807..1859
Bailey, Jacob Whitman. American Microscopist and Algologist .... 1806..1857
Balfour, Rev. Walter. Universalist Writer........... 1776..1852
Ballou, Hosea, 2d, D. D. Divine and Writer.......... — ..1861
Bangs, Nathan, D. D. Methodist Writer .... 1788..1862
Barker, James N. American Writer................. — ..1858
Barksdale, William. " Confederate " General......... 1821..1863
Barron, James. American Naval Officer.............. — ..1851
Bascom, Henry Bidleman, D. D. Amer. Divine & Writer 1796..1850
Batthyanyi, Casimir, Count. Hungarian Statesman ... 1807..1854
Bauer, Bruno. German Theologian and Metaphysician — ..1809
Baur, Ferdinand Christian. German Church Historian.. — ..1791
Baur, George Lawrence. German Theologian. (*Hermeneutica Sacra*)...................................... 1755..1806
Bayard, George D. American General.............. — ..1862
Beaufort, Henry Somerset, Duke of. Soldier in Peninsular War...................................... 1792..1854
Beck, Charles. American Scholar and Writer .... 1798..1866
Beck, John Brodhead. American Physician........... 1794..1851
Beck, Lewis C. American Naturalist .... 1800..1853
Beck, Theodore Romeyn, M. D. Amer. Medical Writer 1791..1855
Beckwith, John Charles. Major-General .... 1790..1862
Bee, Barnard E. " Confederate " General .... — ..1861
Benavides. Chilian General .... — ..1823
Benjamin, Park. American Editor and Poet.......... 1809..1864
Bennett, William. Bp. of Cloyne. Scholar and Archæol. 1745..1820
Benton, Thomas Hart. American Statesman.......... 1782..1858
Berrien, John Macpherson. Amer. Lawyer and Statesm. 1781..1856
Berry, Miss Mary. Friend of Horace Walpole......... 1763?..1852
Berthold, Arnold Adolphus. German Naturalist ...... 1803..1861
Bibb, George M. American Jurist and Statesman...... 1772..1859
Biel, Gabriel. German Theologian and Philosopher .... — ..1495
Bienville, John Baptist Lemoine, Sieur de. Second Colonial Governor of Louisiana .... 1680..1768
Bird, Rev. Charles Smith. Controversialist............ 1795..1862
Bird, Robert M., M. D. American Writer.............. 1803..1854
Birney, David Bell. American General .... 1825..1864
Birt, John Baptist. French Savant.................... 1774..1862
Bixby, Thomas. Classical Scholar and Book Collector.. 1799..1863
Blackford, Isaac. American Jurist and Law Writer.... — ..1859
Blake, Rev. John Lauris, D. D. Writer. (*Biogr. Dict.*) 1788..1857
Blanchard, Thomas. American Mechanic and Inventor 1788..1864
Blenker, Louis. American General .... 1812..1863
Bodisco, Alexander. Russian Diplomatist .... 1779..1854
Bohlen, Henry. American General.................... — ..1862
Boole, George. Professor. Mathem. and Metaphysician 1819?..1864
Borland, Solon. " Confederate " General .... — ..1864
Bourdon, Peter Louis Mary. French Mathematician... 1799..1854

BORN. DIED.

Bowen, John S. " Confederate " General............. — ..1863
Bowes, Andrew Robinson Stoney, M. P. Husband of
   Countess of Strathmore. Life by Jesse Foot....... 1745..1810
Boyd, James. Classical and General Editor........... 1795..1856
Brady, Hugh. American Military Officer............. 1768..1851
Brancaleone, Dandolo. Senator of Rome............ — ..1258
Branch, Lawrence O'Brien. " Confederate " General .. 1820..1862
Brande, William Thomas. Chemist................. 1780..1866
Bravo, Nicholas. Mexican General and Statesman .... 1792..1854
Braybrooke, Richard Neville Griffin, Third Lord. An-
   tiquary. (History of Audley End; Evelyn's Memoirs).. 1783..1858
Bremer, Miss Frederika. Swedish Novelist........... 1802..1865
Bright, Edmund, of Malden. Noted for weight, 616 lbs. 1721..1750
Briot, Peter Francis, of Besançon. Phys. Medical Writer 1773?.1826
Brockedon, William. Author, Artist, and Inventor.... 1787..1854
Brockett, John Trotter. Antiquary .... 1788..1842
Broderick, David Colbreth. American Politician...... 1819..1859
Bromme, Traugott. German Geographer............. 1771?.1865
Brooke, George M. American General .... — ..1851
Brooks, Preston S. American Politician .... 1819..1857
Brown, Sir George. General; distinguished in Crimea.. 1790..1865
Brown, Goold. American Grammarian .... 1791..1857
Brown, Dr. Samuel, of Edinb. Chemical Theorist; Poet 1817..1856
Brown, Sir William. Merchant and Philanthropist .... 1784..1864
Brownell, Rt. Rev. Thomas Church. American Theolo-
   gian and Educator .... 1779..1865
Bruat, Armand Joseph. French Admiral............. 1796..1855
Bruce, Archibald, M. D. Amer. Physician & Mineralogist 1777..1818
Bruck, Baron de. Austrian Financier .... 1799..1860
Buchan, Peter. Scottish Antiquary .... — ..1854
Buckingham, Joseph Tinker. American Journalist.... 1799..1861
Buford, John. American Cavalry Officer .... 1825..1863
Bullions, Rev. Peter, D. D. Amer. Educator and Author 1791..1864
Burgeoise, Sir Francis, R. A. Painter. Founder of Dul-
   wich Gallery...................................... — ..1811
Burges, Tristam. American Statesman............... 1770..1853
Burnap, Rev. George Washington. Amer. Theol. Writer 1802..1859
Burton, William Evans. Comedian. (Cyclopædia of
   Wit and Humor).................................... 1804..1860
Bury, Lady Charlotte. Novelist..................... 1775..1861
Bush, George. American Theologian .... 1796..1859
Bustamente, Anastasius. Mexican Soldier and Statesm. 1782..1851
Bute, John Stuart, Fourth Earl and First Marquess of... 1744..1814
Butler, Andrew Pickens. Amer. Lawyer and Politician 1796..1857
Butler, Benjamin F. American Lawyer and Statesman — ..1858
Byron, Lady Noel. Wife of Lord Byron............. 1793..1860

C.

Caldwell, Charles, M. D. Medical and Miscel. Writer 1772..1853
Calvin, John. Life by Beza, 1564 (also in Latin and
   German); Bolsec, 1572 (also in German); J. P. Masson,
   1598; Ziegenbein, 1789–90; Tischer, 1794; Mackenzie,
   1809; Henry, 1835, enlarged and rewritten, 1846 (also

BORN. DIED.

in English and Dutch); Audin, 1840 (also in German
and Italian); Haag, 1840; Guizot, 1844; Dyer, 1849;
Strähelin, 1863; Bungener ....: .... 1509..1564
Cameron, Dr. Archibald. Scottish Jacobite; executed.. 1698..1753
Cameron, James, of Lochiel, brother. Scottish Jacobite 1696..1758
Carbuccia, Gen. French Archæologist................ — ..1854
Carey, John L. American Political Economist......... — ..1852
Carnwath, Robert Dalziel, Sixth Earl of. Scot. Jacobite 1673..1726
Caroll, Sir William Farebrother. Naval Officer....... 1785..1862
Cartwright, Rev. Edmund, F.S.A. Topographer. (Sussex) 1777..1833
Caulfield, James, Earl of Charlemont. Life by Francis
Hardy, 1810 .... 1728..1799
Cavendish, Elizabeth Hardwicke, Lady.............. 1519..1608
Cavendish, George. Usher and Biographer of. Wolsey 1500?.1562?
Cervantes. Spanish Novelist. (Don Quixote.) Life by
Mayans y Siscar, 1737, Englished by Ozell, 1738; Sar-
miento; J. de Iriarte; Montiano y Luyando; J. M. de
Flores; V. de Los Rios, 1780; Claris de Florian, 1785?;
Pellicer, 1778, enlarged 1798; Jarvis, 1801; Merimée,
1806; Fernandez de Navarrete, 1819; Auger, 1825;
Filleau Saint-Martin, 1825; Roscoe, 1839; Aribau,
1849; Finlay.. 1547..1616
Cesare, Joseph. Italian Historian................... 1783..1856
Chandos, John Brydges, created Duke of............. 1673..1744
Charles, Thomas, of Bala. Methodist Minister. Life by
Morgan... 1755..1814
Charlon, John James. Painter .... — ..1854
Chetham-Strode, Sir Edward. Admiral .... 1775..1862
Chickering, Jesse. American Statistician............ 1798..1855
Christopher I. King of Denmark.................... — ..1259
Christopher II. .... 1276..1333
Christopher III. Of Bavaria .... — ..1448
Christy, Henry. Antiquary .... 1810..1865
Chrzanowski, Adalbert. Polish General .... 1789..1861
Clare. See Strongbow.
Clayton, John, of London. Dissenting Minister........ 1780?.1865
Cleburne, Patrick R. " Confederate " General .... 1828..1864
Cocke, Philip St. George. " Confederate " General..... — ..1861
Cockerell, Charles Robert, R. A. Architect .... 1788..1863
Cockton, Henry. Writer. (Valentine Vox) .... 1808..1853
Colborne, Sir John, Lord Seaton. Field Marshal. Gov-
ernor-General of Canada .... 1779..1863
Colburn, Henry. Publisher......................... — ..1855
Combe, Harvey Christian, M. P. Politician and Founder
of Brewery....................................... 1752..1818
Combermere, Sir Stapleton Stapleton Cotton, Viscount.
Field Marshal................................... 1773..1865
Comer, Thomas. Actor and Musician .... 1790..1862
Conant, H. C. American Authoress .... 1810..1865
Coningsby, Thomas, First Lord. Politician .... 1650?.1729
Connel, Sir John. Advocate. (Law of Scotland on Tithes) — ..1831
Connor, Charles. Comedian......................... — ..1826
Cook, Henry F. " Confederate " General............... — ..1863
Cook, John, D. D. Scottish Professor of Divinity....... 1771..1824
Cook, Rev. Russell S. American Clergyman .... 1811..1864

BORN. DIED.

Cooke, George Wingrove. Biographer and Historian... 1814..1865
Cooper, Bransby. Surgeon........................... 1792..1853
Cooper, Thomas Abthrope. Actor.................... 1776..1849
Costello, Dudley. Author and Journalist............. 1803?.1865
Coster, Francis. *Malleus Hæreticorum.* Belgian Theol. 1531..1691
Cottenham, Charles Christopher Pepys, Earl of. Lord
   High Chancellor................................. 1781..1851
Cotton, Sir Stapleton Stapleton, G. C. B., Viscount Com-
   bermere. Field Marshal......................... 1773..1865
Coxe, Richard Charles, Archdeacon of Lindisfarne. Di-
   vine and Poet.................................. 1799..1865
Cradock, Joseph, F. S. A. (*Literary Memoirs*)....... 1741 or 2.1826
Craggs, James. Politician.......................... — ..1720
Craven, Tunis Augustus Macdonough. American Naval
   Commander .... — ..1864
Crockford, William. Originator of Crockford's Club... 1775?.1844
Cromartie, George Mackenzie, Earl of. Scottish Jacobite 1710..1759
Crosby, Sir John. Alderman. Builder of Crosby Place — ..1475
Crowe, Rev. Frederick. Writer..................... — ..1858
Cuming, Hugh. Conchologist........................ 1791?.1865
Cunningham, Rev. Francis, of Harrow. Divine .... 1785?.1863
Curtis, Dr. Thomas. Editor of *Encyclopædia Metropoli-
   tana* and *London Encyclopædia*.................... 1788..1859

D.

Dahlgren, Colonel Ulric. American Military Officer... 1842..1864
Danby, John. Musical Composer .... — ..1798
Dandolo, Ct. Emilio. Ital. Patriot, Soldier, and *Littérateur* — ..1859
Daniel. Hebrew Prophet............................ fl. B.C. 607-534
Daniel, William Francis. Naturalist................. 1818?.1865
Daniels, John M. American Editor .... — ..1865
Dante degli Alighieri. Life by Filelfo, MS. until 1828;
   Villani, MS. until 1826; Boccaccio, 1544; Panchiatichi,
   1576; Bruno Aretino, 1672; Manetti, 1747; Pelli, 1759;
   Chabanon, 1773; Fabroni, 1803; Cesare, 1811; Petroni,
   1816; Orelli, 1822; Gamba, 1825; Blanc, 1834; Fauriel,
   1834; Balbo, 1839, and Engl. 1852; Missirini, 1840;
   Savelli, 1841; Artaud de Montor, 1841; Torri, 1843;
   Wegele, 1852; Véricour, 1858 .... 1265..1321
Darley, William. American Geographer and Statistician 1775..1854
Darling, James. London Publisher and Bibliographer.
   (*Cyclopædia Bibliographica*)...................... 1797..1862
Dartmouth, George Legge, First Baron. Admiral...... 1648..1691
Dartmouth, George Legge, Earl. Statesman.......... 1755..1810
Daubeny, Charles. Archdeacon of Sarum. (*Guide to
   the Church*)..................................... 1744..1827
Davies, Thomas Stephens. Mathematician .... 1794?.1851
Davison, John, B. D. Theol. (*Discourses on Prophecy*) 1777..1834
Dearborn, Henry Alexander Scammell. Amer. Writer 1783..1851
De Haven, Edwin J. American Arctic Voyager....... 1819..1865
Dembinski, Henry. Polish General .... 1791..1864
Devrient, Wilhelmina Schroeder. Ger. Singer and Actor 1805..1860
Dieudonné, Dr., of Brussels. Medical Writer......... 1811?.1865

BORN. DIED.

Dillwyn, Lewis W. Welsh Naturalist................ 1778..1855
Djelal-eddyn Roumi. Persian Mystic Poet....... 1195.1262 or 71
Dod, Captain Robert Phipps. Peerage Compiler........ — ..1864
Donoughmore, John Hely Hutchinson, Earl of. General 1757..1832
Donoughmore, Richard Hely Hutchinson, Earl of. Soldier and Statesman .... 1756..1825
Dubellay du Resnel, John Francis. French Writer ... 1692..1761
Duggan, Peter Paul. American Artist............... — ..1861
Dupin, Andrew Mary John James. French Jurist and Statesman...................................... 1783..1865
Dupont, Samuel Francis. Rear-Admiral U. S. Navy... 1803..1865
Dwight, Rev. Harrison Gray Otis. American Missionary and Writer...................................... 1803..1862
Dwight, Mary Anne. (*Mythology*)................... 1806..1858

E.

Eaton, Amos. American Botanist................ 1776?.1842
Edwin. English Earl; brother of Morcar............. — ..1071
Eglinton, Archibald William, Earl of. Lord Lieutenant of Ireland .... 1812..1861
Elah. King of Israel (B. C. 930–929)................ — B.C.929
Eli. High Priest and Judge of Israel .... fl. B.C. 1171
Eligius, or Eloy, St. Bishop of Tournay and Noyon ... 588.. 659
Elijah. Prophet of Israel .... fl B.C. 910–896
Elizabeth. Princess; daughter of Charles I........... 1635..1650
Ellet, Charles. American Engineer.................. 1810..1862
Ellice, Edward, M. P. Politician...................... 1789..1863
Elliott, Sir Gilbert, cr. Earl Minto. Gov.-Gen. of Bengal 1751..1814
Ellis, John Willis. Governor of North Carolina; Prominent Secessionist................................. 1820..1861
Ellis, Rev. Robert Leslie, of Cambridge. Mathematician and Philosopher .... 1817..1859
Ellis, Welbore, created Lord Mendip. Politician....... 1714..1802
Ellsworth, Ephraim Elmer. American Military Officer 1837..1861
Elmes, James. Architect and Author................ 1783..1862
Eloy, or Eligius, St. Bishop of Tournay and Noyon.... 588.. 659
Evans, Arthur Benoni. Classical Scholar; Writer..... 1781..1855
Eyre, Sir William. Major-General.................. — ..1859

F.

Fairbanks, Erastus. Amer. Manufacturer and Statesm. 1792..1864
Farnham, Mrs. Eliza W. Amer. Philanthr. and Writer 1815..1864
Field, George. Chemist and Writer.................. — ..1854
Fisher, Redwood. American Journalist, Political Economist, and Statistician............................. 1783..1856
Floyd, John Buchanan. American Politician and Secessionist; "Confederate" General.................... 1805..1863
Flusser, Charles W. American Naval Officer......... 1832?.1864
Forrest, Robert. Scottish Sculptor................... — ..1853
Fourdrinier, Henry. Inventor..................... 1766..1855
Francis, Rev. Convers, D. D. Amer. Theol. and Writer 1796..1863

BORN. DIED.

Frost, John. Compiler of School Books .... 1800..1859
Fry, Joseph Reese. Scholar and Musical Writer .... — ..1865

G.

Gardner, William. Writer on Music and Art.......... 1764..1854
Garnett, Richard B. "Confederate" General.......... — ..1863
Garnett, Robert Selden. "Confederate" General...... 1822..1861
Gibson, John. Sculptor............................. 1791..1866
Goodrich, Rev. Charles A. American Writer .... 1790..1862
Goodyear, Charles. American Inventor .... 1800..1860
Graul, Charles. German Scholar and Writer .... — ..1864
Gray, Francis Calley. American Scholar and Writer ... 1790..1856
Grayson, John Breckinridge. "Confederate" General. 1807..1862
Green, Thomas J. "Confederate" General .... 1801..1863
Greenough, George Bellas. Geol. and Physical Geog. 1777..1854
Gregg, John. "Confederate" General................ 1828..1864
Gregory, Dr. William. Chem. and Writer on Chemistry — ..1858
Griffin, George. American Theological Writer .... 1778..1860
Grimm, Louis Emilius. German Engraver............ 1790..1863
Grund, Francis J. American Writer.................. 1803?.1863
Gunnison, J. W. American Topographical Engineer ... — ..1853
Gurney, Rev. John Hampden. Writer................ 1802..1862
Gwinn, William. American Naval Officer .... 1831..1863

H.

Hackleman, Pleasant A. American General.......... — ..1862
Halbertsma, Hilde J. Anatomist and Physiologist .... 1820..1865
Hale, Benjamin, D. D. American Writer............. 1797..1863
Hall, Baynard, D. D. American Writer and Educator... 1798..1863
Hallett, Benjamin F. American Politician .... 1798..1862
Hammond, Jabez D. Amer. Lawyer, Legislator, & Auth. — ..1855
Hart, Joseph C. American Writer.................. — ..1855
Hays, Alexander. American General................ 1823..1864
Helm, Benjamin Hardin. "Confederate" General..... — ..1863
Henderson, J. Pinckney. Amer. Statesm. and Diplom. 1808..1858
Henshaw, David. American Politician.............. — ..1852
Henshaw, Joshua Sidney. *Belcher.* American Lawyer,
  Mathematician, and Writer....................... 1811..1859
Herrick, Edward Claudius. Amer. Scientist and Bibliog. 1811..1862
Hill, Ambrose Powell. "Confederate" General........ 1826..1865
Hoar, Samuel, LL. D. American Jurist.............. 1778..1856
Hulsemann, John George, Chevalier de. Austrian Min-
  ister to United States............................. — ..1864
Hunt, Edward B. American Military Officer; Inventor 1822..1863
Hunt, Frederick Knight. Journalist................. 1814..1854

I.

Ingham, Charles C. American Portrait Painter .... 1797..1863
Ives, Eli, M. D....................................... 1779..1861

29

J.

BORN. DIED.

Jackson, Claiborne F. American Secessionist; "Con-
federate" General................................. 1807..1862
Jackson, Conrad Feger. American General........... — ..1862
Jackson, James S. American General .... 1822..1862
James, Charles T. Inventor of Rifle-cannon and Shell.. 1806..1862
Jameson, Charles Davis. American General.......... 1827..1862
Jessup, Thomas S. American Military Officer........ 1790..1860
Jones, John N. "Confederate" General.............. 1820..1864
Jones, Roger. American General .... — ..1852

K.

Keim, William H. American General ..:............. 1813..1862
Keiser, Dr. German Writer........................ 1779..1862
Keitt, Lawrence M. Amer. Politician and Secessionist.. 1824..1864
Kemeny, Baron. Hungarian Patriot .... — ..1852
Kent, William. American Jurist .... 1802..1861
Kettell, Samuel. Amer. Journalist and Miscel. Writer 1800..1855
King, T. Butler. American Politician and Secessionist.. 1804..1864
Kirk, Edward N. American General.................. — ..1863
Knight, Dr. Jonathan. Professor of Surgery..........1789..1864

L.

Langsdorff, George Frederick, Baron von. Bot. & Trav. — ..1852
Laroche, Benj. Fr. Transl. of Shakespeare and Byron 1798..1852
Lindsay, James B. Scottish Linguist .... 1800..1862
Little, Henry. "Confederate" General.............. 1818..1862
Locke, John, M. D. American Geologist .... 1792..1856
Longworth, Nicholas. American Vintner............. 1782..1863
Lovelace, Ada Augusta, Countess of. Only child of
Lord Byron. "Sole daughter of my house and heart" 1815..1852
Lytle, William Haines. American General........... 1826..1863

M.

Mc Cluney, William J. American Naval Officer ...... — ..1864
Mc Cook, Robert L. American General.............. 1837..1862
Mc Grigor, Sir James. Surgeon and Writer .... 1772..1858
Mackay, Charles. Scotch Actor..................... 1787..1857
Mc Kean, William W. United States Naval Officer ... 1801..1865
Mackenzie, Charles Kenneth. Writer............... 1788..1860
Mc Leod, Rev. Xavier Donald. American Writer ..... 1821..1865
Maitland, Samuel Roffey, D. D. Writer.............. 1792?.1866
Malmstroem, or Malmström, B. Elis. Swedish Poet and
Writer .... 1816..1865
Mangum, Willie P. American Statesman .... 1792..1861
Mansfield, Joseph King Fenno. American General.... 1803..1862

BORN. DIED.

Marchi, Father. Italian Archæologist ....   — ..1860
Maria da Gloria. Queen of Portugal .... 1819..1853
Mason, J. L. American Military Engineer ....   — ..1853
Mason, John Y. American Statesman and Diplomatist 1795..1859
May, William. United States Naval Officer .... 1815..1861
Messaros, Lazarus. Hungarian General and Patriot... 1796..1858
Miles, Dixon H. Amercian Military Officer .... 1803..1862
Miller, James. American Soldier....................   — ..1851
Morehead, James T. American Statesman .... 1796..1854
Morgan, Charles W. American Naval Officer......... 1790..1853
Morgan, John H. "Confederate" Soldier .... 1826..1864
Morgan, John Minter. Philanthropist and Writer ..... 1783..1854
Morlot, Francis Nicholas Madeleine. Archbishop of
    Paris. Theological Writer....................... 1795..1862
Morris, Henry W. United States Naval Officer....... 1805..1863
Mott, Valentine. American Surgeon and Writer....... 1785..1865
Mügge, or Muegge, Theodore. Ger. Novelist and Editor 1806..1861
Müller, or Mueller, Jerome. German Scholar and Educa-
    tional Writer .... 1785..1861
Mundt, Theodore. German Writer................... 1808..1861

N.

Newcomb, Harvey, D. D. American Editor and Author 1803..1863
Nicol, Wm. Natural Philos.; Inventor of *Nicol's Prism*   — ..1851
Nicollini, John Baptist. Italian Sculptor .... 1782..1861
Nitzch, Gregory William. German Philologist .... 1790..1861

O.

Ormond, John Butler, Marquess of. Writer........... 1808..1854
Orton, Reginald. Surgeon and Writer on Med. Subjects 1810..1862
Otey, Rev. James Hervey. *Good Bishop*.............. 1799..1863
Owen, David Dale. Geologist...................... 1807..1860

P.

Pangalos, M. Varnavas. Modern Greek Patriot ....   — ..1855
Passavant, John David. Artist and Writer on Art ....   — ..1861
Patmore, Peter George. Writer .... 1787..1855
Patterson, Francis E. American General............. 1827..1862
Paxton, Edward F. "Confederate" General ....   — ..1863
Pearce, James A. American Legislator .... 1805..1862
Pegram, William Johnson. "Confederate" General ... 1841..1865
Pender, William D. "Confederate" General ....   — ..1863
Pennington, William. American Statesman.......... 1797..1862
Pinckney, Richard Shubrick. U. S. Naval Officer..... 1797..1854
Plummer, Joseph B. American General............. 1822..1862
Preller, Louis. Ger. Archæologist and Classical Scholar 1809..1861
Prossi, Thomas. Italian Poet and Author.......... 1789..1854
Protet, Augustus Leopold. French Admiral; African
    Explorer....................................... 1809..1862

R.

BORN. DIED.

Ray, Joseph.   American Mathematician . . . . 1807 . . 1855
Read, Abner.   United States Naval Officer . . . .   — . . 1863
Read, George Campbell.   American Admiral . . . .   — . . 1862
Renouard, Anthony Augustin.   French Bibliographer . . 1765 . . 1853
Renshaw, William B.   United States Naval Officer . . . .   — . . 1863
Rolph, John A.   Artist; Landscape Engraver . . . . 1798 . . 1862
Ross, William Charles.   Miniature Painter . . . . 1794 . . 1860
Rothschild, Anselm, Baron.   Financier . . . . 1773 . . 1855
Rude, Francis.   French Sculptor . . . . 1784 . . 1855
Rusk, Thomas J.   American General and Statesman . . . 1803 . . 1857

S.

Saltoun, Alexander George Fraser, Lord.   Defender of
   Hougoumont . . . . 1785 . . 1853
Sanders, William P.   American General . . . .   — . . 1863
San Miguel, Evaristo.   Spanish Journalist, Statesman,
   and Soldier . . . . 1780 . . 1862
Savage, John.   American Jurist . . . . 1779 . . 1863
Scroop, William.   Writer . . . . 1771 . . 1852
Seymour, Hezekiah C.   American Civil Engineer . . . . . 1812 . . 1853
Shakespear, Sir Richmond Campbell.   Military Officer   — . . 1861
Sheaffe, Sir Roger H.   Military Officer . . . . 1763 . . 1851
Sibley, Henry H.   " Confederate " General . . . . 1815 . . 1862
Sill, Joshua Woodrow.   American General . . . . 1831 . . 1862
Smith, Rev. Eli.   American Missionary and Orientalist 1801 . . 1857
Smith, Persifer F.   American General . . . .   — . . 1858
Smyth, Thomas A.   American General . . . .   — . . 1865
Somerset, Sir Henry.   Lieutenant-General . . . . 1794 . . 1862
Sparks, Jared.   Amer. Writer; Pres. of Harvard College 1789 . . 1866
Stanger, William.   Physician and Naturalist . . . .   — . . 1854
Stanley, Anthony Dumond.   American Mathematician 1812 . . 1853
Steele, William.   American Revolutionary Soldier . . . . . 1762 . . 1851
Steers, George.   American Naval Constructer . . . . 1821 . . 1856
Stephen, A. J.   Lawyer and Writer . . . . 1788 . . 1864
Stephens, Mrs. Harriet Marion.   Writer . . . . 1823 . . 1858
Susini, Mrs. Isabella Hinckley.   American Vocalist . . . .   — . . 1862
Symington, W.   Scottish Theological Writer . . . . 1795 . . 1862
Symons, Jelinger Cookson.   Writer . . . . 1810 . . 1860

T.

Terrill, William R.   American General . . . .   — . . 1862
Tildemann, Frederick.   Ger. Physiologist and Anatomist 1781 . . 1861
Tilghman, Lloyd.   " Confederate " General . . . .   — . . 1863

V.

	BORN.	DIED.
Valpy, Abraham John. Classical Editor	— ..	1854
Van Brunt, Gershom J. American Naval Officer......	1800..	1863
Van Dorn, Earl. "Confederate" General	1823..	1863
Van Eycken, John. Dutch Painter...................	— ..	1854
Villepigue, John B. "Confederate" General........	1834..	1862

W.

	BORN.	DIED.
Washington, John A. Proprietor of Mount Vernon...	— ..	1861
Watson, Walker. Scottish Song Writer..............	— ..	1854
Webb, Alexander Stuart. American General	1834?.	1864
Weed, Stephen H. American General................	— ..	1863
Whewell, Rev. William, F. R. S. Master of Trinity College	1795..	1866

THE END.

www.ingramcontent.com/pod-product-compliance
Lightning Source LLC
Chambersburg PA
CBHW052349110726
47901CB00005B/1419